WELCOME TO MANY ARROWS

. . . Toogwik Tuk said with a respectful bow. "The presence of Clan Karuck and its worthy leader makes us greater."

Grguch let his gaze drift slowly across the three visitors then around the gathering to Hakuun. "You will learn the truth of your hopeful claim," he said, his eyes turning back to Toogwik Tuk, "when I have the bones of dwarves and elves and ugly humans to crush beneath my boot."

Dnark couldn't suppress a grin as he looked to Ung-thol, who seemed similarly pleased. Despite their squeamishness at being so badly outnumbered among the fierce and unpredictable tribe, things were going quite well.

A KINGDOM OF ORCS THAT WILL CHANGE

THE MAP OF FAERÛN FOREVER!

"R.A. Salvatore is the best descriptive writer ever for fantasy battle scenes. No one writes them better than he."
—Conan Tigard, *Reading Review*

"By the end of *The Orc King*, the possibilities are almost endless, and Salvatore's message is clear—(change) can be terrifying, painful, glorious, and heartrending, but it is also inevitable, and it is coming to Drizzt's corner of the FORGOTTEN REALMS® (world)."
—David Craddock, Fantasy Book Critic
(fantasybookcritic.blogspot.com)

R.A. SALVATORE

R.A. SALVATORE

FORGOTTEN REALMS

THE ORC KING

TRANSITIONS I

Wizards
OF THE COAST®

THE ORC KING
Transitions, Book I

©2007 Wizards of the Coast, Inc.

Cover art by Todd Lockwood
Map by Todd Gamble
Original Hardcover Edition First Printing: October 2007
First Mass Market Paperback Printing: July 2008
This Edition First Printing: November 2008

9 8 7 6 5 4 3 2 1

ISBN: 978-0-7869-4912-0
620-21812740-001-EN

U.S., CANADA,   EUROPEAN HEADQUARTERS
ASIA, PACIFIC, & LATIN AMERICA   Hasbro UK Ltd
Wizards of the Coast, Inc.   Caswell Way
P.O. Box 707   Newport, Gwent NP9 0YH
Renton, WA 98057-0707   GREAT BRITAIN
+1-800-324-6496   Save this address for your records.

Visit our web site at www.wizards.com

PRELUDE

Drizzt Do'Urden crouched in a crevice between a pair of boulders on the side of a mountain, looking down at a curious gathering. A human, an elf, and a trio of dwarves—at least a trio—stood and sat around three flat-bedded wagons that were parked in a triangle around a small campfire. Sacks and kegs dotted the perimeter of the camp, along with a cluster of tents, reminding Drizzt that there was more to the company than the five in his view. He looked past the wagons to a small, grassy meadow, where several draft horses grazed. Just to the side of them, he saw again that which had brought him to the edge of the camp: a pair of stakes capped with the severed heads of orcs.

The band and their missing fellows, then, were indeed members of *Casin Cu Calas*, the "Triple C," an organization of vigilantes who took their name from the Elvish saying that meant "honor in battle."

Given the reputation of *Casin Cu Calas*, whose favorite tactic was to storm orc homesteads in the dark of night and decapitate any males found inside, Drizzt found the name more than a little ironic, and more than a little distasteful.

"Cowards, one and all," he whispered as he watched one man hold up a full-length black and red robe. The man flapped it clean of the night's dirt and reverently folded it, bringing it to his lips to kiss it before he replaced it in the back of one wagon. He reached down and picked up the second tell-tale garment, a black hood. He moved to put that, too, in the wagon but hesitated, then slipped the hood over his head, adjusting it

1

so that he could see through the two eye-holes. That drew the attention of the other four.

The other *five*, Drizzt noted as the fourth dwarf walked back around a corner of the wagon to regard the hooded man.

"Casin Cu Calas!" the man proclaimed, and held up both his arms, fists clenched, in an exaggerated victory pose. "Suffer no orc to live!"

"Death to the orcs!" the others cried in reply.

The hooded fool issued a barrage of insults and threats against the porcine-featured humanoids. Up on the side of the hill, Drizzt Do'Urden shook his head and deliberately slid his bow, Taulmaril, off his shoulder. He put it up, notched an arrow, and drew back in one fluid motion.

"Suffer no orc to live," the hooded man said again—or started to, until a flash of lightning shot through the camp and drove into a keg of warm ale beside him. As the keg exploded, liquid flying, a sheet of dissipating electricity momentarily stole the darkness from the growing twilight.

All six of the companions fell back, shielding their eyes. When they regained their sight, one and all saw the lone figure of a lean dark elf standing atop one of their wagons.

"Drizzt Do'Urden," gasped one of the dwarves, a fat fellow with an orange beard and an enormous temple-to-temple eyebrow.

A couple of the others nodded and mouthed their agreement, for there was no mistaking the dark elf standing before them, with his two scimitars belted at his hips and Taulmaril, the Heartseeker, again slung over one shoulder. The drow's long, thick white hair blew in the late afternoon breeze, his cloak flapped out behind him, and even the dull light remaining could do little to diminish the shine of his silvery-white mithral-lined shirt.

Slowly pulling off his hood, the human glanced at the elf then back at Drizzt. "Your reputation precedes you, Master Do'Urden," he said. "To what do we owe the honor of your presence?"

" 'Honor' is a strange word," Drizzt replied. "Stranger still coming from the lips of one who would wear the black hood."

A dwarf to the side of the wagon bristled and even stepped forward, but was blocked by the arm of the orange-bearded fellow.

The human cleared his throat uncomfortably and tossed the hood into the wagon behind him. "That thing?" he asked. "Found along the road, of course. Do you assign it any significance?"

"No more so than the significance I assign the robe you so reverently folded and kissed."

That brought another glance at the elf, who, Drizzt noticed, was sliding a bit more to the side—notably behind a line etched in the dirt, one glittering with shiny dust. When Drizzt brought his attention more fully back to the human, he noted the change in the man's demeanor, a clear scowl replacing the feigned innocence.

"A robe you yourself should wear," the man said boldly. "To honor King Bruenor Battlehammer, whose deeds—"

"Speak not his name," Drizzt interrupted. "You know nothing of Bruenor, of his exploits and his judgments."

"I know that he was no friend of—"

"You know nothing," Drizzt said again, more forcefully.

"The tale of Shallows!" one of the dwarves roared.

"I was there," Drizzt reminded him, silencing the fool.

The human spat upon the ground. "Once a hero, now gone soft," he muttered. "On orcs, no less."

"Perhaps," Drizzt replied, and in the blink of an astonished eye, he brought his scimitars out in his black-skinned hands. "But I've not gone soft on highwaymen and murderers."

"Murderers?" the human retorted incredulously. "Murderers of orcs?"

Even as he finished speaking, the dwarf at the side of the wagon pushed through his orange-bearded companion's arm and thrust his hand forward, sending a hand-axe spinning at the drow.

Drizzt easily side-stepped the unsurprising move, but not content to let the missile harmlessly fly past, and seeing a second dwarf charging from over to the left, he snapped out his scimitar Icingdeath into the path of the axe. He drew the blade back as it contacted the missile, absorbing the impact. A twist of his wrist had the scimitar's blade firmly up under the axe's head. In a single fluid movement, Drizzt pivoted back the other way and whipped Icingdeath around, launching the axe at the charging dwarf.

The rumbling warrior brought his shield up high to block the awkwardly spinning axe, which clunked against the wooden buckler and bounced aside. But so too fell away that dwarf's determined growl when he again lowered the shield, to find his intended target nowhere in sight.

For Drizzt, his speed enhanced by a pair of magical anklets, had timed his break perfectly with the rise of the dwarf's shield. He had taken only a few steps, but enough, he knew, to confuse the determined dwarf. At the last moment, the dwarf noticed him and skidded to a stop, throwing out a weak, backhanded swipe with his warhammer.

But Drizzt was inside the arch of the hammer, and he smacked its handle with one blade, stealing the minimal momentum of the swing. He struck harder with his second blade, finding the crease between the dwarf's heavy gauntlet and his metal-banded bracer. The hammer went flying, and the dwarf howled and grabbed at his bleeding, broken wrist.

Drizzt leaped atop his shoulder, kicked him in the face for good measure, and sprang away, charging at the orange-bearded dwarf and the axe thrower, both of whom were coming on fast.

Behind them, the human urged them in their charge, but did not follow, reaffirming Drizzt's suspicions regarding his courage, or lack thereof.

Drizzt's sudden reversal and rush had the two dwarves on their heels, and the drow came in furiously, his scimitars rolling over each other and striking from many different angles. The axe-thrower, a second small axe in hand, also held a shield, and so fared better in blocking the blades, but the poor orange-bearded fellow could only bring his great mace out diagonally before him, altering its angle furiously to keep up with the stream of strikes. He got nicked and clipped half a dozen times, drawing howls and grunts, and only the presence of his companion, and those others all around demanding the attention of the drow, prevented him from being seriously wounded, or even slain on the spot. For Drizzt could not finish his attacks without opening himself up to counters from the dwarf's companions.

After the initial momentum played out, the drow fell back. With typical stubbornness, the two dwarves advanced. The one with the orange beard, his hands bleeding and one finger hanging by a thread of skin, attempted a straightforward overhead chop. His companion half turned to lead with his shield then pivoted to launch a horizontal swing meant to come within a hair's breadth of his companion and swipe across from Drizzt's left to right.

The impressive coordination of the attack demanded either a

straight and swift retreat or a complex two-angled parry, and normally, Drizzt would have just used his superior speed to skip back out of range.

But he recognized the orange-bearded dwarf's tenuous grip, and he was a drow, after all, whose entire youth was spent in learning how to execute exactly those sorts of multi-angled defenses. He thrust his left scimitar out before him, rode his hand up high and turned the blade down to intercept the sidelong swing, and brought his right hand across up high over his left, blade horizontal, to block the downward strike.

As the hammer coming across connected with his blade, Drizzt punched his hand forward and turned his scimitar to divert the dwarf's weapon low, and in doing so, the drow was able to take half a step to his left, lining himself up more fully with the other's overhead strike. When he made contact with that weapon, he had his full balance, his feet squarely set beneath his shoulders.

He dropped into a crouch as the weapon came down, then pushed up hard with all his strength. The dwarf's badly-injured top hand could not hold, and the drow's move forced the diminutive warrior to go right up to his tip-toes to keep any grasp on his weapon at all.

Drizzt turned back to the right as he rose, and with a sudden and powerful move, he angled and drove the dwarf's weapon across to his right, putting it in the path of the other dwarf's returning backhand. As the pair tangled, Drizzt disengaged and executed a reverse spin on the ball of his left foot, coming all the way around to launch a circle kick into the back of the orange-bearded dwarf that shoved him into his companion. The great mace went flying, and so did the dwarf with the orange beard, as the other dwarf ducked a shoulder and angled his shield to guide him aside.

"Clear for a shot!" came a cry from the side, demanding Drizzt's attention, and the drow abruptly halted and turned to see the elf, who held a heavy crossbow leveled Drizzt's way.

Drizzt yelled and charged at the elf, diving into a forward roll and turning as he went so that he came up into a sidelong step. He closed rapidly.

Then he rammed into an invisible wall, as expected, for he understood that the crossbow had been only a ruse, and no missile could have crossed through to strike at him through the unseen magical barrier.

Drizzt rebounded back and fell to one knee, moving shakily. He started up, but seemed to stumble again, apparently dazed.

He heard the dwarves charging in at his back, and they believed beyond any doubt that there was no way he could recover in time to prevent their killing blows.

"And all for the sake of orcs, Drizzt Do'Urden," he heard the elf, a wizard by trade, remark, and he saw the lithe creature shaking his head in dismay as he dropped the crossbow aside. "Not so honorable an end for one of your reputation."

* * * * *

Taugmaelle lowered her gaze, stunned and fearful. Never could she have anticipated a visit from King Obould VI, Lord of Many-Arrows, particularly on this, the eve of her departure for the Glimmerwood, where she was to be wed.

"You are a beautiful bride," the young orc king remarked, and Taugmaelle dared glance up to see Obould nodding appreciatively. "This human—what is his name?"

"Handel Aviv," she said.

"Does he understand the good fortune that has shone upon him?"

As that question digested, Taugmaelle found courage. She looked up again at her king and did not avert her eyes, but rather met his gaze.

"I am the fortunate one," she said, but her smile went away almost immediately as Obould responded with a scowl.

"Because he is human?" Obould blustered, and the other orcs in the small house all stepped away from him fearfully. "A higher being? Because you, a mere orc, are being accepted by this Handel Aviv and his kin? Have you elevated yourself above your race with this joining, Taugmaelle of Clan Bignance?"

"No, my king!" Taugmaelle blurted, tears rushing from her eyes. "No. Of course, nothing of the sort . . ."

"Handel Aviv is the fortunate one!" Obould declared.

"I . . . I only meant that I love him, my king," Taugmaelle said, her voice barely above a whisper.

The sincerity of that statement was obvious, though, and had Taugmaelle not averted her gaze to the floor again, she would have seen the young orc king shift uncomfortably, his bluster melting away.

"Of course," he replied after a while. "You are both fortunate, then."

"Yes, my king."

"But do not ever view yourself as his lesser," Obould warned. "You are proud. You are orc. You are Many-Arrows orc. It is Handel Aviv who is marrying above his heritage. Do not ever forget that."

"Yes, my king."

Obould looked around the small room to the faces of his constituents, a couple standing slack-jawed as if they had no idea how to react to his unexpected appearance, and several others nodding dully.

"You are a beautiful bride," the king said again. "A sturdy representative of all that is good in the Kingdom of Many-Arrows. Go forth with my blessing."

"Thank you, my king," Taugmaelle replied, but Obould hardly heard her, for he had already turned on his heel and moved out the door. He felt a bit foolish for his overreaction, to be sure, but he reminded himself pointedly that his sentiments had not been without merit.

"This is good for our people," said Taska Toill, Obould's court advisor. "Each of these extra-racial joinings reinforces the message that is Obould. And that this union is to be sanctified in the former Moonwood is no small thing."

"The steps are slow," the king lamented.

"Not so many years ago, we were hunted and killed," Taska reminded. "Unending war. Conquest and defeat. It has been a century of progress."

Obould nodded, though he did remark, "We are still hunted," under his breath. Worse, he thought but did not say, were the quiet barbs, where even those who befriended the people of Many-Arrows did so with a sense of superiority, a deep-set inner voice that told them of their magnanimity in befriending, even championing the cause of such lesser creatures. The surrounding folk of the Silver Marches would often forgive an orc for behavior they would not accept among their own, and that wounded Obould as greatly as those elves, dwarves, and humans who outwardly and openly sneered at his people.

* * * * *

Drizzt looked up at the elf wizard's superior smile, but when the drow, too, grinned, and even offered a wink, the elf's face went blank.

A split second later, the elf shrieked and flew away, as Guenhwyvar, six hundred pounds of feline power, leaped against him, taking him far, and taking him down.

One of the dwarves charging at Drizzt let out a little cry in surprise, but despite the revelation of a panther companion, neither of the charging dwarves were remotely prepared when the supposedly stunned Drizzt spun up and around at them, fully aware and fully balanced. As he came around, a backhand from Twinkle, the scimitar in his left hand, took half the orange beard from one dwarf, who was charging with abandon, his heavy weapon up over his head. He still tried to strike at Drizzt, but swirled and staggered, lost within the burning pain and shock. He came forward with his strike, but the scimitar was already coming back the other way, catching him across the wrists.

His great mace went flying. The tough dwarf lowered his shoulder in an attempt to run over his enemy, but Drizzt was too agile, and he merely shifted to the side and trailed his left foot, over which the wounded dwarf tumbled, cracking his skull against the magical wall.

His companion fared no better. As Twinkle slashed across in the initial backhand, the dwarf shifted back on his heels, turning to bring his shield in line, and brought his weapon arm back to begin a heavy strike. Drizzt's second blade thrust in behind the backhand, however, the drow cleverly turning his wrist over so that the curving blade of the scimitar rolled over the edge of the shield and dived down to strike that retracted weapon arm right where the bicep met the shoulder. As the dwarf, too far into his move to halt it completely, came around and forward with the strike, his own momentum drove the scimitar deeper into his flesh.

He halted, he howled, he dropped his axe. He watched his companion go tumbling away. Then came a barrage as the deadly drow squared up against him. Left and right slashed the scimitars, always just ahead of the dwarf's pathetic attempts to get his shield in their way. He got nicked, he got slashed, he got shaved, as edges, points and flats of two blades made their way through his defenses. Every hit stung, but none of them were mortal.

But he couldn't regain his balance and any semblance of defense, nor did he hold anything with which to counter, except his shield. In desperation, the dwarf turned and lunged, butting his shield arm forward. The drow easily rolled around it, though, and as he pivoted to the dwarf's right he punched out behind him, driving the pommel of his right blade against the dwarf's temple. He followed with a heavy left hook as he completed his turn, and the dazed dwarf offered no defense at all as fist and hilt smashed him across the face.

He staggered two steps to the side, and crumbled into the dirt.

Drizzt didn't pause to confirm the effect, for back the other way, the first dwarf he had cut was back to his feet and staggering away. A few quick strides brought Drizzt up behind him, and the drow's scimitar slashed across the back of the dwarf's legs, drawing a howl and sending the battered creature whimpering to the ground.

Again, Drizzt looked past him even as he fell, for the remaining two members of the outlaw band were fast retreating. The drow put up Taulmaril and set an arrow retrieved from the enchanted quiver he wore on his back. He aimed center mass on the dwarf, but perhaps in deference to King Bruenor—or Thibbledorf, or Dagnabbit, or any of the other noble and fierce dwarves he had known those decades before, he lowered his angle and let fly. Like a bolt of lightning, the magical arrow slashed the air and drove through the fleshy part of the dwarf's thigh. The poor dwarf screamed and veered then fell down.

Drizzt notched another arrow and turned the bow until he had the human, whose longer legs had taken him even farther away, in his sight. He took aim and drew back steadily, but held his shot as he saw the man jerk suddenly then stagger.

He stood there for just a moment before falling over, and Drizzt knew by the way he tumbled that he was dead before he ever hit the ground.

The drow glanced back over his shoulder, to see the three wounded dwarves struggling, but defeated, and the elf wizard still pinned by the ferocious Guenhwyvar. Every time the poor elf moved, Guenhwyvar smothered his face under a huge paw.

By the time Drizzt looked back, the killers of the human were in view. A pair of elves moved to gather the arrow-shot dwarf, while another went to the dead man, and another pair approached Drizzt, one riding on a white-winged steed, the pegasus named Sunrise. Bells adorned the mount's harness, bridle, and saddle, tinkling sweetly—ironically so—as the riders trotted up to the drow.

"Lord Hralien," Drizzt greeted with a bow.

"Well met and well done, my friend," said the elf who ruled the ancient expanse of the Glimmerwood that the elves still called the Moonwood. He looked around, nodding with approval. "The Night Riders have been dealt yet one more serious blow," he said, using another of the names for the orc-killing vigilantes, as did all the elves, refusing to assign a title as honorable as *Casin Cu Calas* to a band they so abhorred.

"One of many we'll need, I fear, for their numbers do not seem diminished," said Drizzt.

"They are more visible of late," Hralien agreed, and dismounted to stand before his old friend. "The Night Riders are trying to take advantage of the unrest in Many-Arrows. They know that King Obould VI is in a tenuous position." The elf gave a sigh. "As he always seems to be, as his predecessors always seemed to be."

"He has allies as well as enemies," said Drizzt. "More allies than did the first of his line, surely."

"And more enemies, perhaps," Hralien replied.

Drizzt could not disagree. Many times over the last century, the Kingdom of Many-Arrows had known inner turmoil, most often, as was still the case, brewing from a rival group of orcs. The old cults of Gruumsh One-eye had not flourished under the rule of the Oboulds, but neither had they been fully eradicated. The rumors said that yet another group of shamans, following the old warlike ways of goblinkind, were creating unrest and plotting against the king who dared diplomacy and trade with the surrounding kingdoms of humans, elves, and even dwarves, the most ancient and hated enemy of the orcs.

"You killed not one of them," Hralien remarked, glancing around at his warriors who gathered up the five wounded Night Riders. "Is this not in your heart, Drizzt Do'Urden? Do you not strike with surety when you strike to defend the orcs?"

"They are caught, to be justly tried."

"By others."

"That is not my province."

"You would not allow it to be," Hralien said with a wry grin that was not accusatory. "A drow's memories are long, perhaps."

"No longer than a moon elf's."

"My arrow struck the human first, and mortally, I assure you."

"Because you fiercely battle those memories, while I try to mitigate them," Drizzt replied without hesitation, setting Hralien back on his heels. If the elf, startled though he was, took any real offense, he didn't show it.

"Some wounds are not so healed by the passage of a hundred years," Drizzt went on, looking from Hralien to the captured Night Riders. "Wounds felt keenly by some of our captives here, perhaps, or by the grandfather's grandfather of the man who lies dead in the field beyond."

"What of the wounds felt by Drizzt Do'Urden, who did battle with King Obould in the orc's initial sweep of the Spine of the World?" Hralien asked. "Before the settlement of his kingdom and the treaty of Garumn's Gorge? Or who fought again against Obould II in the great war in the Year of the Solitary Cloister?"

Drizzt nodded with every word, unable to deny the truth of it all. He had made his peace with the orcs of Many-Arrows, to a great extent. But still, he would be a liar to himself if he failed to admit a twinge of guilt in battling those who had refused to end the ancient wars and ancient ways, and had continued the fight against the orcs—a war that Drizzt, too, had once waged, and waged viciously.

"A Mithral Hall trade caravan was turned back from Five Tusks," Hralien said, changing his tone as he shifted the subject. "A similar report comes to us from Silverymoon, where one of their caravans was refused entry to Many-Arrows at Ungoor's Gate north of Nesmé. It is a clear violation of the treaty."

"King Obould's response?"

"We are not certain that he even knows of the incidents. But whether he does or not, it is apparent that his shaman rivals have spread their message of the old ways far beyond Dark Arrows Keep."

Drizzt nodded.

"King Obould is in need of your help, Drizzt," Hralien said. "We have walked this road before."

Drizzt nodded in resignation at the unavoidable truth of that statement. There were times when he felt as if the road he walked was not a straight line toward progress, but a circling track, a futile loop. He let that negative notion pass, and reminded himself of how far the region had come—and that in a world gone mad from the Spellplague. Few places in all of Faerûn could claim to be *more* civilized than they had been those hundred years before, but the region known as the Silver Marches, in no small part because of the courage of a succession of orc kings named Obould, had much to be proud of.

His perspective and memories of that time a hundred years gone, before the rise of the Empire of Netheril, the coming of the aboleths, and the discordant and disastrous joining of two worlds, brought to Drizzt thoughts of another predicament so much like the one playing out before him. He remembered the look on Bruenor's face, as incredulous as any expression he had ever seen before or since, when he had presented the dwarf with his surprising assessment and astounding recommendations.

He could almost hear the roar of protest: "Ye lost yer wits, ye durned orc-brained, pointy-eared elf!"

On the other side of the magical barrier, the elf shrieked and Guenhwyvar growled, and Drizzt looked up to see the wizard stubbornly trying to crawl away. Guenhwyvar's great paw thumped against his back, and the panther flexed, causing the elf to drop back to the ground, squirming to avoid the extending claws.

Hralien started to call to his comrades, but Drizzt held his hand up to halt them. He could have walked around the invisible wall, but instead he sprang into the air beside it, reaching his hand as high as he could. His fingers slid over the top and caught a hold, and the drow rolled his back against the invisible surface and reached up with his other hand. A tuck and roll vaulted him feet-over-head over the wall, and he landed nimbly on the far side.

He bade Guenhwyvar to move aside then reached down and pulled the elf wizard to his feet. He was young, as Drizzt had expected—while some older elves and dwarves were inciting the *Casin Cu Calas*, the younger members, full of fire and hatred, were the ones executing the unrest in brutal fashion.

The elf, uncompromising, stared at him hatefully. "You would betray your own kind," he spat.

Drizzt cocked his eyebrows curiously, and tightened his grip on the elf's shirt, holding him firmly. "My own kind?"

"Worse then," the elf spat. "You would betray those who gave shelter and friendship to the rogue Drizzt Do'Urden."

"No," he said.

"You would strike at elves and dwarves for the sake of orcs!"

"I would uphold the law and the peace."

The elf mocked him with a laugh. "To see the once-great ranger siding with orcs," he muttered, shaking his head.

Drizzt yanked him around, stealing his mirth, and tripped him, shoving him backward into the magical wall.

"Are you so eager for war?" the drow asked, his face barely an inch from the elf's. "Do you long to hear the screams of the dying, lying helplessly in fields amidst rows and rows of corpses? Have you ever borne witness to that?"

"Orcs!" the elf protested.

Drizzt grabbed him in both hands, pulled him forward, and slammed him back against the wall. Hralien called to Drizzt, but the dark elf hardly heard it.

"I have ventured outside of the Silver Marches," Drizzt said, "have you? I have witnessed the death of once-proud Luskan, and with it, the death of a dear, dear friend, whose dreams lay shattered and broken beside the bodies of five thousand victims. I have watched the greatest cathedral in the world burn and collapse. I witnessed the hope of the goodly drow, the rise of the followers of Eilistraee. But where are they now?"

"You speak in ridd—" the elf started, but Drizzt slammed him again.

"Gone!" Drizzt shouted. "Gone, and gone with them the hopes of a tamed and gentle world. I have watched once safe trails revert to wilderness, and have walked a dozen-dozen communities that you will never know. They are gone now, lost to the Spellplague or worse! Where are the benevolent gods? Where is the refuge from the tumult of a world gone mad? Where are the candles to chase away the darkness?"

Hralien had quietly moved around the wall and walked up beside Drizzt. He put a hand on the drow's shoulder, but that brought no more than a brief pause in the tirade. Drizzt glanced at him before turning back to the captured elf.

"They are here, those lights of hope," Drizzt said, to both elves. "In the Silver Marches. Or they are nowhere. Do we choose peace or do we choose war? If it is battle you seek, fool elf, then get you gone from this land. You will find death aplenty, I assure you. You will find ruins where once proud cities stood. You will find fields of wind-washed bones, or perhaps the remains of a single hearth, where once an entire village thrived.

"And in that hundred years of chaos, amidst the coming of darkness, few have escaped the swirl of destruction, but we have flourished. Can you say the same for Thay? Mulhorand? Sembia? You say I betray those who befriended me, yet it was the vision of one exceptional dwarf and one exceptional orc that built this island against the roiling sea."

The elf, his expression more cowed, nonetheless began to speak out again, but Drizzt pulled him forward from the wall and slammed him back even harder.

"You fall to your hatred and you seek excitement and glory," the drow said. "Because you do not know. Or is it because you do not care that your pursuits will bring utter misery to thousands in your wake?"

Drizzt shook his head, and threw the elf aside, where he was caught by two of Hralien's warriors and escorted away.

"I hate this," Drizzt admitted to Hralien, quietly so that no one else could hear. "All of it. It is a noble experiment a hundred years long, and still we have no answers."

"And no options," Hralien replied. "Save those you yourself just described. The chaos encroaches, Drizzt Do'Urden, from within and without."

Drizzt turned his lavender eyes to watch the departure of the elf and the captured dwarves.

"We must stand strong, my friend," Hralien offered, and he patted Drizzt on the shoulder and walked away.

"I'm not sure that I know what that means anymore," Drizzt admitted under his breath, too softly for anyone else to hear.

PART
1

THE PURSUIT OF
HIGHER TRUTH

THE PURSUIT OF
HIGHER TRUTH

One of the consequences of living an existence that spans centuries instead of decades is the inescapable curse of continually viewing the world through the focusing prism employed by an historian.

I say "curse"—when in truth I believe it to be a blessing—because any hope of prescience requires a constant questioning of what is, and a deep-seated belief in the possibility of what can be. Viewing events as might the historian requires an acceptance that my own initial, visceral reactions to seemingly momentous events may be errant, that my "gut instinct" and own emotional needs may not stand the light of reason in the wider view, or even that these events, so momentous in my personal experience, might not be so in the wider world and the long, slow passage of time.

How often have I seen that my first reaction is based on half-truths and biased perceptions! How often have I found expectations completely inverted or tossed aside as events played out to their fullest!

Because emotion clouds the rational, and many perspectives guide the full reality. To view current events as an historian is to account for all perspectives, even those of your enemy. It is to know the past and to use such relevant history as a template for expectations. It is, most of all, to force reason ahead of instinct, to refuse to demonize that which you hate, and to, most of all, accept your own fallibility.

And so I live on shifting sands, where absolutes melt away with the passage of decades. It is a natural extension, I expect, of an existence in which I have shattered the preconceptions of so many people. With every stranger who comes to accept me for who I am instead of who he or she expected me to be, I roil the sands beneath that person's feet. It is a growth experience for them, no doubt, but we are all creatures of ritual and habit and accepted notions of what is and what is not. When true reality cuts against that internalized expectation—when you meet a goodly drow!—there is created an internal dissonance, as uncomfortable as a springtime rash.

There is freedom in seeing the world as a painting in progress, instead of a place already painted, but there are times, my friend ...

There are times.

And such is one before me now, with Obould and his thousands camped upon the very door of Mithral Hall. In my heart I want nothing more than another try at the orc king, another opportunity to put my scimitar through his yellow-gray skin. I long to wipe the superior grin from his ugly face, to bury it beneath a spray of his own blood. I want him to hurt—to hurt for Shallows and all the other towns flattened beneath the stamp of orc feet. I want him to feel the pain he brought to Shoudra Stargleam, to Dagna and Dagnabbit, and to all the dwarves and others who lay dead on the battlefield that he created.

Will Catti-brie ever walk well again? That, too, is the fault of Obould.

And so I curse his name, and remember with joy those moments of retribution that Innovindil, Tarathiel, and I exacted upon the minions of the foul orc king. To strike back against an invading foe is indeed cathartic.

That, I cannot deny.

And yet, in moments of reason, in times when I sit back against a stony mountainside and overlook that which Obould has facilitated, I am simply not certain.

Of anything, I fear.

He came at the front of an army, one that brought pain and suffering to many people across this land I name as my home. But his army has stopped its march, for now at least, and the signs are visible that Obould seeks something more than plunder and victory.

Does he seek civilization?

Is it possible that we bear witness now to a monumental change in the nature of orc culture? Is it possible that Obould has established a situation, whether he intended this at first or not, where the interests of the orcs and the interests of all the other races of the region coalesce into a relationship of mutual benefit?

Is that possible? Is that even thinkable?

Do I betray the dead by considering such a thing?

Or does it serve the dead if I, if we all, rise above a cycle of revenge and war and find within us—orc and dwarf, human and elf alike—a common ground upon which to build an era of greater peace?

For time beyond the memory of the oldest elves, the orcs have warred with the "goodly" races. For all the victories—and they are countless!— and for all the sacrifices, are the orcs any less populous now than they were millennia ago?

I think not, and that raises the specter of unwinnable conflict. Are we doomed to repeat these wars, generation after generation, unendingly? Are we—elf and dwarf, human and orc alike—condemning our descendants to this same misery, to the pain of steel invading flesh?

I do not know.

And yet I want nothing more than to slide my blade between the ribs of King Obould Many-Arrows, to relish in the grimace of agony on his tusk-torn lips, to see the light dim in his yellow, bloodshot eyes.

But what will the historians say of Obould? Will he be the orc who breaks, at long, long last, this cycle of perpetual war? Will he, inadvertently or not, present the orcs with a path to a better life, a road they will walk—reluctantly at first, no doubt—in pursuit of bounties greater than those they might find at the end of a crude spear?

I do not know.

And therein lies my anguish.

I hope that we are on the threshold of a great era, and that within the orc character, there is the same spark, the same hopes and dreams, that guide the elves, dwarves, humans, halflings, and all the rest. I have heard it said that the universal hope of the world is that our children will find a better life than we.

Is that guiding principle of civilization itself within the emotional make-up of goblinkind? Or was Nojheim, that most unusual goblin slave I once knew, simply an anomaly?

Is Obould a visionary or an opportunist?

Is this the beginning of true progress for the orc race, or a fool's errand for any, myself included, who would suffer the beasts to live?

Because I admit that I do not know, it must give me pause. If I am to give in to the wants of my vengeful heart, then how might the historians view Drizzt Do'Urden?

Will I be seen in the company of those heroes before me who helped vanquish the charge of the orcs, whose names are held in noble esteem? If Obould is to lead the orcs forward, not in conquest, but in civilization, and I am the hand who lays him low, then misguided indeed will be those historians, who might never see the possibilities that I view coalescing before me.

Perhaps it is an experiment. Perhaps it is a grand step along a road worth walking.

Or perhaps I am wrong, and Obould seeks dominion and blood, and the orcs have no sense of commonality, have no aspirations for a better way, unless that way tramples the lands of their mortal, eternal enemies.

But I am given pause.

And so I wait, and so I watch, but my hands are near to my blades.

—Drizzt Do'Urden

CHAPTER

PRIDE AND PRACTICALITY

On the same day that Drizzt and Innovindil had set off for the east to find the body of Ellifain, Catti-brie and Wulfgar had crossed the Surbrin in search of Wulfgar's missing daughter. Their journey had lasted only a couple of days, however, before they had been turned back by the cold winds and darkening skies of a tremendous winter storm. With Catti-brie's injured leg, the pair simply could not hope to move fast enough to out-distance the coming front, and so Wulfgar had refused to continue. Colson was safe, by all accounts, and Wulfgar was confident that the trail would not grow cold during the delay, as all travel in the Silver Marches would come to a near stop through the frozen months. Over Catti-brie's objections, the pair had re-crossed the Surbrin and returned to Mithral Hall.

That same weather front destroyed the ferry soon after, and it remained out of commission though tendays passed. The winter was deep about them, closer to spring than to fall. The Year of Wild Magic had arrived.

For Catti-brie, the permeating cold seemed to forever settle on her injured hip and leg, and she hadn't seen much improvement in her mobility. She could walk with a crutch, but even then every stride made her wince. Still she wouldn't accept a chair with wheels, such as the one the dwarves had fashioned for the crippled Banak Brawnanvil, and she certainly wanted nothing to do with the contraption Nanfoodle had designed for her: a comfortable palanquin meant to be borne by four willing dwarves. Stubbornness aside, her injured hip would not support her weight very well, or for any length of time, and so Catti-brie had settled on the crutch.

For the last few days, she had loitered around the eastern edges of Mithral Hall, across Garumn's Gorge from the main chambers, always asking for word of the orcs who had dug in just outside of Keeper's Dale, or of Drizzt, who had at last been seen over the eastern fortifications, flying on a pegasus across the Surbrin beside Innovindil of the Moonwood.

Drizzt had left Mithral Hall with Catti-brie's blessing those tendays before, but she missed him dearly on the long, dark nights of winter. It had surprised her when he hadn't come directly back into the halls upon his return from the west, but she trusted his judgment. If something had compelled him to go on to the Moonwood, then it must have been a good reason.

"I got a hunnerd boys beggin' me to let 'em carry ye," Bruenor scolded her one day, when the pain in her hip was obviously flaring. She was back in the western chambers, in Bruenor's private den, but had already informed her father that she would go back to the east, across the gorge. "Take the gnome's chair, ye stubborn girl!"

"I have my own legs," she insisted.

"Legs that ain't healing, from what me eyes're telling me." He glanced across the hearth to Wulfgar, who reclined in a comfortable chair, staring into the orange flames. "What say ye, boy?"

Wulfgar looked at him blankly, obviously having no comprehension of the conversation between the dwarf and the woman.

"Ye heading out soon to find yer little one?" Bruenor asked. "With the melt?"

"Before the melt," Wulfgar corrected. "Before the river swells."

"A month, perhaps," said Bruenor, and Wulfgar nodded.

"Before Tarsakh," he said, referring to the fourth month of the year.

Catti-brie chewed her lip, understanding that Bruenor had initiated the discussion with Wulfgar for her benefit.

"Ye ain't going with him with that leg, girl," Bruenor stated. "Ye're limpin' about here and never giving the durned thing a chance at mending. Now take the gnome's chair and let me boys carry ye about, and it might be—it just might be—that ye'll be able to go with Wulfgar to find

Colson, as ye planned and as ye started afore."

Catti-brie looked from Bruenor to Wulfgar, and saw only the twisting orange flames reflected in the big man's eyes. He seemed lost to them all, she noted, wound up too tightly in inner turmoil. His shoulders were bowed by the weight of guilt, to be sure, and the burden of grief, for he had lost his wife, Delly Curtie, who still lay dead under a blanket of snow on a northern field, as far as they knew.

Catti-brie was no less consumed by guilt over that loss, for it had been her sword, the evil and sentient Khazid'hea, that had overwhelmed Delly Curtie and sent her running out from the safety of Mithral Hall. Thankfully—they all believed—Delly hadn't taken her and Wulfgar's adopted child, the toddler girl, Colson, with her, but had instead deposited Colson with one of the other refugees from the northland, who had crossed the River Surbrin on one of the last ferries to leave before the onslaught of winter. Colson might be in the enchanted city of Silverymoon, or in Sundabar, or in any of a host of other communities, but they had no reason to believe that she had been harmed, or would be.

And Wulfgar meant to find her—it was one of the few declarations that held any fire of conviction that Catti-brie had heard the barbarian make in tendays. He would go to find Colson, and Catti-brie felt it was her duty as his friend to go with him. After they had been turned back by the storm, in no small part because of her infirmity, Catti-brie was even more determined to see the journey through.

Truly Catti-brie hoped that Drizzt would return before that departure day arrived, however. For the spring would surely bring tumult across the land, with a vast orc army entrenched all over the lands surrounding Mithral Hall, from the Spine of the World mountains to the north, to the banks of the Surbrin to the east, and to the passes just north of the Trollmoors in the south. The clouds of war roiled, and only winter had held back the swarms.

When that storm finally broke, Drizzt Do'Urden would be in the middle of it, and Catti-brie did not intend to be riding through the streets of some distant city on that dark day.

"Take the chair," Bruenor said—or said again, it seemed, from his impatient tone.

Catti-brie blinked and looked back at him.

"I'll be needin' both o' ye at me side, and soon enough," Bruenor said.

"If ye're to be slowing Wulfgar down in this trip he's needing to make, then ye're not to be going."

"The indignity. . . ." Catti-brie said with a shake of her head.

But as she did that, she overbalanced just a bit on her crutch and lurched to the side. Her face twisted in a pained grimace as shooting pains like little fires rolled through her from her hip.

"Ye catched a giant-thrown boulder on yer leg," Bruenor retorted. "Ain't no indignity in that! Ye helped us hold the hall, and not a one o' Clan Battlehammer's thinking ye anything but a hero. Take the durned chair!"

"You really should," came a voice from the door, and Catti-brie and Bruenor turned to see Regis the halfling enter the room.

His belly was round once again, his cheeks full and rosy. He wore suspenders, as he had of late, and hooked his thumbs under them as he walked, eliciting an air of importance. And truly, as absurd as Regis sometimes seemed, no one in the hall would deny that pride to the halfling who had served so well as Steward of Mithral Hall in the days of constant battle, when Bruenor had lain near death.

"A conspiracy, then?" Catti-brie remarked with a grin, trying to lighten the mood.

They needed to smile more, all of them, and particularly the man seated across from where she stood. She watched Wulfgar as she spoke, and knew that her words had not even registered with him. He just stared into the flames, truly looking inward. The expression on Wulfgar's face, so utterly hopeless and lost, spoke truth to Catti-brie. She began to nod, and accepted her father's offer. Friendship demanded of her that she do whatever she could to ensure that she would be well enough to accompany Wulfgar on his most important journey.

So it was a few days later, that when Drizzt Do'Urden entered Mithral Hall through the eastern door, open to the Surbrin, that Catti-brie spotted him and called to him from on high. "Your step is lighter," she observed, and when Drizzt finally recognized her in her palanquin, carried on the shoulders of four strong dwarves, he offered her a laugh and a wide, wide smile.

"The Princess of Clan Battlehammer," the drow said with a polite and mocking bow.

On Catti-brie's orders, the dwarves placed her down and moved aside, and she had just managed to pull herself out of her chair and collect her crutch, when Drizzt crushed her in a tight and warm embrace.

"Tell me that you're home for a long while," she said after a lingering kiss. "The winter has been cold and lonely."

"I have duties in the field," Drizzt replied. He added, "Of course I do," when Catti-brie smirked helplessly at him. "But yes, I am returned, to Bruenor's side as I promised, before the snows retreat and the gathered armies move. We will know the designs of Obould before long."

"Obould?" Catti-brie asked, for she thought the orc king long dead.

"He lives," Drizzt replied. "Somehow he escaped the catastrophe of the landslide, and the gathered orcs are bound still by the will of that most powerful orc."

"Curse his name."

Drizzt smiled at her, but didn't quite agree.

"I am surprised that you and Wulfgar have already returned," Drizzt said. "What news of Colson?"

Catti-brie shook her head. "We do not know. We did cross the Sur-brin on the same morning you flew off with Innovindil for the Sword Coast, but winter was too close on our heels, and brought us back. We did learn that the refugee groups had marched for Silverymoon, at least, and so Wulfgar intends to be off for Lady Alustriel's fair city as soon as the ferry is prepared to run once more."

Drizzt pulled her back to arms' length and looked down at her wounded hip. She wore a dress, as she had been every day, for the tight fit of breeches was too uncomfortable. The drow looked at the crutch the dwarves had fashioned for her, but she caught his gaze with her own and held it.

"I am not healed," she admitted, "but I have rested enough to make the journey with Wulfgar." She paused and reached up with her free hand to gently stroke Drizzt's chin and cheek. "I have to."

"I am no less compelled," Drizzt assured her. "Only my responsibility to Bruenor keeps me here instead."

"Wulfgar will not be alone on this road," she assured him.

Drizzt nodded, and his smile showed that he did indeed take comfort in that. "We should go to Bruenor," he said and started away.

Catti-brie grabbed him by the shoulder. "With good news?"

Drizzt looked at her curiously.

"Your stride is lighter," she remarked. "You walk as if unburdened. What did you see out there? Are the orc armies set to collapse? Are the folk of the Silver Marches ready to rise as one to repel—"

"Nothing like that," Drizzt said. "All is as it was when I departed, except that Obould's forces dig in deeper, as if they mean to stay."

"Your smile does not deceive me," Catti-brie said.

"Because you know me too well," said Drizzt.

"The grim tides of war do not diminish your smile?"

"I have spoken with Ellifain."

Catti-brie gasped. "She lives?" Drizzt's expression showed her the absurdity of that conclusion. Hadn't Catti-brie been there when Ellifain had died, to Drizzt's own blade? "Resurrection?" the woman breathed. "Did the elves employ a powerful cleric to wrest the soul—"

"Nothing like that," Drizzt assured her. "But they did provide Ellifain a conduit to relate to me . . . an apology. And she accepted my own apology."

"You had no reason to apologize," Catti-brie insisted. "You did nothing wrong, nor could you have known."

"I know," Drizzt replied, and the serenity in his voice warmed Catti-brie. "Much has been put right. Ellifain is at peace."

"Drizzt Do'Urden is at peace, you mean."

Drizzt only smiled. "I cannot be," he said. "We approach an uncertain future, with tens of thousands of orcs on our doorstep. So many have died, friends included, and it seems likely that many more will fall."

Catti-brie hardly seemed convinced that his mood was dour.

"Drizzt Do'Urden is at peace," the drow agreed against her unrelenting grin.

He moved as if to lead the woman back to the carriage, but Catti-brie shook her head and motioned instead for him to lead her, crutching, along the corridor that would take them to the bridge across Garumn's Gorge, and to the western reaches of Mithral Hall where Bruenor sat in audience.

"It is a long walk," Drizzt warned her, eyeing her wounded leg.

"I have you to support me," Catti-brie replied, and Drizzt could hardly disagree.

With a grateful nod and a wave to the four dwarf bearers, the couple started away.

* * * * *

So real was his dream that he could feel the warm sun and the cold wind upon his cheeks. So vivid was the sensation that he could smell the cold saltiness of the air blowing down from the Sea of Moving Ice.

So real was it all that Wulfgar was truly surprised when he awoke from his nap to find himself in his small room in Mithral Hall. He closed his eyes again and tried to recapture the dream, tried to step again into the freedom of Icewind Dale.

But it was not possible, and the big man opened his eyes and pulled himself out of his chair. He looked across the room to the bed. He hardly slept there of late, for that had been the bed he'd shared with Delly, his dead wife. On the few occasions he had dared to recline upon it, he had found himself reaching for her, rolling to where she should have been.

The feeling of emptiness as reality invaded his slumber had left Wulfgar cold every time.

At the foot of the bed sat Colson's crib, and looking at it proved even more distressing.

Wulfgar dropped his head in his hands, the soft feel of hair reminding him of his new-grown beard. He smoothed both beard and mustache, and rubbed the blurriness from his eyes. He tried not to think of Delly, then, or even of Colson, needing to be free of his regrets and fears for just a brief moment. He envisioned Icewind Dale in his younger days. He had known loss then, too, and had keenly felt the stings of battle. There were no delusions invading his dreams or his memories that presented a softer image of that harsh land. Icewind Dale remained uncompromising, its winter wind more deadly than refreshing.

But there was something simpler about that place, Wulfgar knew. Something purer. Death was a common visitor to the tundra, and monsters roamed freely. It was a land of constant trial, and with no room for error, and even in the absence of error, the result of any decision often proved disastrous.

Wulfgar nodded, understanding the emotional refuge offered by such uncompromising conditions. For Icewind Dale was a land without regret. It simply was the way of things.

Wulfgar pulled himself from his chair and stretched the weariness from his long arms and legs. He felt constricted, trapped, and as the walls seemed to close in on him, he recalled Delly's pleas to him regarding that very feeling.

"Perhaps you were right," Wulfgar said to the empty room.

He laughed then, at himself, as he considered the steps that had brought him back to that place. He had been turned around by a storm.

He, Wulfgar, son of Beornegar, who had grown tall and strong in the brutal winters of frozen Icewind Dale, had been chased back into the dwarven complex by the threat of winter snows!

Then it hit him. All of it. His meandering, empty road for the last eight years of his life, since his return from the Abyss and the torments of the demon, Errtu. Even after he had gathered up Colson from Meralda in Auckney, had retrieved Aegis-fang and his sense of who he was, and had rejoined his friends for the journey back to Mithral Hall, Wulfgar's steps had not been purposeful, had not been driven by a clear sense of where he wanted to go. He had taken Delly as his wife, but had never stopped loving Catti-brie.

Yes, it was true, he admitted. He could lie about it to others, but not to himself.

Many things came clear at last to Wulfgar that morning in his room in Mithral Hall, most of all the fact that he had allowed himself to live a lie. He knew that he couldn't have Catti-brie—her heart was for Drizzt—but how unfair had he been to Delly and to Colson? He had created a facade, an illusion of family and of stability for the benefit of everyone involved, himself included.

Wulfgar had walked his road of redemption, since Auckney, with manipulation and falsity. He understood that finally. He had been so determined to put everything into a neat and trim little box, a perfectly controlled scene, that he had denied the very essence of who he was, the very fires that had forged Wulfgar son of Beornegar.

He looked at Aegis-fang leaning against the wall then hefted the mighty warhammer in his hand, bringing its crafted head up before his icy-blue eyes. The battles he had waged recently, on the cliff above

Keeper's Dale, in the western chamber, and to the east in the breakout to the Surbrin, had been his moments of true freedom, of emotional clarity and inner calm. He had reveled in that physical turmoil, he realized, because it had calmed the emotional confusion.

That was why he had neglected Delly and Colson, throwing himself with abandon into the defenses of Mithral Hall. He had been a lousy husband to her, and a lousy father to Colson.

Only in battle had he found escape.

And he was still engaged in the self-deception, Wulfgar knew as he stared at the etched head of Aegis-fang. Why else had he allowed the trail to Colson to grow stale? Why else had he been turned back by a mere winter storm? Why else . . . ?

Wulfgar's jaw dropped open, and he thought himself a fool indeed. He dropped the hammer to the floor and swept on his trademark gray wolf cloak. He pulled his backpack out from under the bed and stuffed it with his blankets, then slung it over one arm and gathered up Aegis-fang with the other.

He strode out of his room with fierce determination, heading east past Bruenor's audience chamber.

"Where are you going?" he heard, and paused to see Regis standing before a door in the hallway.

"Out to check on the weather and the ferry."

"Drizzt is back."

Wulfgar nodded, and his smile was genuine. "I hope his journey went well."

"He'll be in with Bruenor in a short while."

"I haven't time. Not now."

"The ferry isn't running yet," Regis said.

But Wulfgar only nodded, as if it didn't matter, and strode off down the corridor, turning through the doors that led to the main avenue that would take him over Garumn's Gorge.

Thumbs hooked in his suspenders, Regis watched his large friend go. He stood there for a long while, considering the encounter, then turned for Bruenor's audience chamber.

He paused after only a few steps, though, and looked back again to the corridor down which Wulfgar had so urgently departed.

The ferry wasn't running.

CHAPTER

2

Grguch blinked repeatedly as he moved from the recesses of the cave toward the pre-dawn light. Broad-shouldered and more than seven feet in height, the powerful half-orc, half-ogre stepped tentatively with his thick legs, and raised one hand to shield his eyes. The chieftain of Clan Karuck, like all of his people other than a couple of forward scouts, had not seen the light of day in nearly a decade. They lived in the tunnels, in the vast labyrinth of lightless caverns known as the Underdark, and Grguch had not undertaken his journey to the surface lightly.

Scores of Karuck warriors, all huge by the standards of the orc race—approaching if not exceeding seven feet and weighing in at nearly four hundred pounds of honed muscle and thick bone—lined the cave walls. They averted their yellow eyes in respect as the great warlord Grguch passed. Behind Grguch came the merciless war priest Hakuun, and behind him the elite guard, a quintet of mighty ogres fully armed and armored for battle. More ogres followed the procession, bearing the fifteen-foot *Kokto Gung Karuck,* the Horn of Karuck, a great instrument with a conical bore and a wide, upturned bell. It was fashioned of *shroomwood,* what the orcs named the hard skin of certain species of gigantic Underdark mushrooms. To the orc warriors looking on, the horn was deserving of, and receiving of, the same respect as the chieftain who preceded it.

Grguch and Hakuun, like their respective predecessors, would have had it no other way.

31

Grguch moved to the mouth of the cave, and out onto the mountain-side ledge. Only Hakuun came up beside him, the war priest signaling the ogres to wait behind.

Grguch gave a rumbling laugh as his eyes adjusted and he noted the more typical orcs scrambling among the mountainside's lower stones. For more than two days, the second orc clan had been frantically keeping ahead of Clan Karuck's march. The moment they'd at last broken free of the confines of the Underdark, their desire to stay far, far away from Clan Karuck grew only more apparent.

"They flee like children," Grguch said to his war priest.

"They *are* children in the presence of Karuck," Hakuun replied. "Less than that when great Grguch stands among them."

The chieftain took the expected compliment in stride and lifted his eyes to survey the wider view around them. The air was cold, winter still gripped the land, but Grguch and his people were not caught unprepared. Layers of fur made the huge orc chieftain appear even larger and more imposing.

"The word will spread that Clan Karuck has come forth," Hakuun assured his chieftain.

Grguch considered the fleeing tribe again and scanned the horizon. "It will be known faster than the words of running children," he replied, and turned back to motion to the ogres.

The guard quintet parted to grant passage to *Kokto Gung Karuck*. In moments, the skilled team had the horn set up, and Hakuun properly blessed it as Grguch moved into place.

When the war priest's incantation was complete, Grguch, the only Karuck permitted to play the horn, wiped the shroomwood mouthpiece and took a deep, deep breath.

A great bass rumbling erupted from the horn, as if the largest bellows in all the world had been pumped by the immortal titans. The low-pitched roar echoed for miles and miles around the stones and mountainsides of the lower southern foothills of the Spine of the World. Smaller stones vibrated under the power of that sound, and one field of snow broke free, creating a small avalanche on a nearby mountain.

Behind Grguch, many of Clan Karuck fell to their knees and began swaying as if in religious frenzy. They prayed to the great One-eye, their warlike god, for they held great faith that when *Kokto Gung*

Karuck was sounded, the blood of Clan Karuck's enemies would stain the ground.

And for Clan Karuck, particularly under the stewardship of mighty Grguch, it had never been hard to find enemies.

* * * * *

In a sheltered vale a few miles to the south, a trio of orcs lifted their eyes to the north.

"Karuck?" asked Ung-thol, a shaman of high standing.

"Could it be any other?" replied Dnark, chieftain of the tribe of the Wolf Jaw. Both turned to regard the smugly smiling shaman Toogwik Tuk as Dnark remarked, "Your call was heard. And answered."

Toogwik Tuk chuckled.

"Are you so sure that the ogre-spawn can be bent to your will?" Dnark added, stealing the smile from Toogwik Tuk's ugly orc face.

His reference to Clan Karuck as "ogre-spawn" rang as a clear reminder to the shaman that they were not ordinary orcs he had summoned from the lowest bowels of the mountain range. Karuck was famous among the many tribes of the Spine of the World—or infamous, actually—for keeping a full breeding stock of ogres among their ranks. For generations untold, Karuck had interbred, creating larger and larger orc warriors. Shunned by the other tribes, Karuck had delved deeper and deeper into the Underdark. They were little known in recent times, and considered no more than a legend among many orc tribes.

But the Wolf Jaw orcs and their allies of tribe Yellow Fang, Toogwik Tuk's kin, knew better.

"They are only three hundred strong," Toogwik Tuk reminded the doubters.

A second rumbling from *Kokto Gung Karuck* shook the stones.

"Indeed," said Dnark, and he shook his head.

"We must go and find Chieftain Grguch quickly," Toogwik Tuk said. "The eagerness of Karuck's warriors must be properly steered. If they come upon other tribes and do battle and plunder . . ."

"Then Obould will use that as more proof that his way is better," Dnark finished.

"Let us go," said Toogwik Tuk, and he took a step forward. Dnark moved to follow, but Ung-thol hesitated. The other two paused and regarded the older shaman.

"We do not know Obould's plan," Ung-thol reminded.

"He has stopped," said Toogwik Tuk.

"To strengthen? To consider the best road?" asked Ung-thol.

"To build and to hold his meager gains!" the other shaman argued.

"Obould's consort has told us as much," Dnark added, and a knowing grin crossed his tusky face, his lips, all twisted from teeth that jutted in a myriad of random directions, turning up with understanding. "You have known Obould for many years."

"And his father before him," Ung-thol conceded. "And I have followed him here to glory." He paused and looked around for effect. "We have not known victory such as this—" he paused again and lifted his arms high—"in living memory. It is Obould who has done this."

"It is the start, and not the end," Dnark replied.

"Many great warriors fall along the road of conquest," added Toogwik Tuk. "That is the will of Gruumsh. That is the glory of Gruumsh."

All three started in surprise as the great bass note of *Kokto Gung Karuck* again resonated across the stones.

Toogwik Tuk and Dnark stood quiet then, staring at Ung-thol, awaiting his decision.

The older orc shaman gave a wistful look back to the southwest, the area where they knew Obould to be, then nodded at his two companions and bade them to lead on.

* * * * *

The young priestess Kna curled around him seductively. Her lithe body slowly slid around the powerful orc, her breath hot on the side of his neck, then the back of his neck, then the other side. But while Kna stared intensely at the great orc as she moved, her performance was not for Obould's benefit.

King Obould knew that, of course, so his smile was double-edged as he stood there before the gathering of shamans and chieftains. He had chosen wisely in making the young, self-absorbed Kna his consort replacement for Tsinka Shinriil. Kna held no reservations. She welcomed the stares of all around as she writhed over King Obould. More than welcomed, Obould knew. She craved them. It was her moment of glory, and she knew that her peers across the kingdom clenched their fists in jealousy. That was her paramount pleasure.

Young and quite attractive by the standards of her race, Kna had entered the priesthood of Gruumsh, but was not nearly as devout or fanatical as Tsinka had been. Kna's god—goddess—was Kna, a purely self-centered view of the world that was so common among the young.

And just what King Obould needed. Tsinka had served him well in her tenure, in bed and out, for she had always spoken in the interests of Gruumsh. Feverishly so. Tsinka had arranged the magical ceremony that had imbued in Obould great prowess both physical and mental, but her devotion was absolute and her vision narrow. She had outlived her usefulness to the orc king before she had been thrown from the lip of the ravine, to fall to her death among the stones.

Obould missed Tsinka. For all of her physical beauty, practiced movements and enthusiasm for the position, Kna was no Tsinka in lovemaking. Nor was Kna possessed of Tsinka's intellect and cunning, not by any means. She could whisper nothing into Obould's ear worth listening to, regarding anything other than coupling. And so she was perfect.

King Obould was clear in his vision, and it was one shared by a collection of steady shamans, most notably a small, young orc named Nukkels. Beyond that group, Obould needed no advice and desired no nay-saying. And most of all, he needed a consort he could trust. Kna was too enamored of Kna to worry about politics, plots and varying interpretations of Gruumsh's desires.

He let her continue her display for a short while longer then gently but solidly pried her from his side and put her back to arms' length. He motioned for her to go to a chair, to which she returned an exaggerated pout. He gave her a resigned shrug to placate her and worked hard to keep his utter contempt for her well suppressed. The orc king motioned again to the chair, and when she hesitated, he forcefully guided her to it.

She started to protest, but Obould held up his huge fist, reminding her in no uncertain terms that she was nearing the limits of his patience. As she settled into a quiet pout, the orc king turned back to his audience, and motioned to Tornfang Brakk, a courier from General Dukka, who oversaw the most important military region.

"The valley known as Keeper's Dale is well secured, God-king," Tornfang reported. "The ground has been broken to prevent easy passage and the structures topping the northern wall of the valley are nearly complete. The dwarves cannot come out."

"Even now?" Obould asked. "Not in the spring, but even now?"

"Even now, Greatness," Tornfang answered with confidence, and Obould wondered just how many titles his people would bestow upon him.

"If the dwarves came forth from Mithral Hall's western doors, we would slaughter them in the valley from on high," Tornfang assured the gathering. "Even if some of the ugly dwarves managed to cross the ground to the west, they would find no escape. The walls are in place, and the army of General Dukka is properly entrenched."

"But can we go in?" asked Chieftain Grimsmal of Clan Grimm, a populous and important tribe.

Obould flashed the impertinent orc a less-than-appreciative glare, for that was the most loaded and dangerous question of all. That was the point of contention, the source of all the whispers and all the arguing between the various factions. Behind Obould they had trampled the ground flat and had marched to glory not known in decades, perhaps centuries. But many were openly asking, to what end? To further conquest and plunder? To the caves of a dwarf clan or to the avenues of a great human or elven city?

As he considered things, however, particularly the whispers among the various shamans and chieftains, Obould came to realize that Grimsmal might have just done him a favor, though inadvertently.

"No," Obould declared solidly, before the bristling could really begin. "The dwarves have their hole. They keep their hole."

"For now," the obstinate Grimsmal dared utter.

Obould didn't answer, other than to grin—though whether it was one of simple amusement or agreement, none could tell.

"The dwarves are out of their hole in the east," reminded another of the gathering, a slight creature in a shaman's garb. "They build through the winter along the ridgeline. They now seek to connect and strengthen walls and towers, from their gates to the great river."

"And foundations along the bank," another added.

"They will construct a bridge," Obould reasoned.

"The foolish dwarves do our work for us!" Grimsmal roared. "They will grant us easier passage to wider lands."

The others all nodded and grinned, and a couple slapped each other on the back.

Obould, too, grinned. The bridge would indeed serve the Kingdom of Many-Arrows. He glanced over at Nukkels, who returned his contented look and offered a slight nod in reply.

Indeed, the bridge would serve, Obould knew, but hardly in the manner that Grimsmal and many of the others, so eager for war, now envisioned.

While the chatter continued around him, King Obould quietly imagined an orc city just to the north of the defenses the dwarves were constructing along the mountain ridge. It would be a large settlement, with wide streets to accommodate caravans, and strong buildings suitable for the storage of many goods. Obould would need to wall it in to protect from bandits, or overeager warrior orcs, so that the merchants who arrived from across King Bruenor's bridge would rest easy and with confidence before beginning their return journey.

The sound of his name drew the orc king from his contemplations, and he looked up to see many curious stares aimed at him. Obviously he had missed a question.

It did not matter.

He offered a calm and disarming smile in response and used the hunger for battle permeating the air around him to remind himself that they were a long, long way from constructing such a city.

But what a magnificent achievement it would be.

* * * * *

"The yellow banner of Karuck," Toogwik Tuk informed his two companions as the trio made their way along a winding, snow-filled valley below the cave that served as the primary exit point for orcs leaving the Underdark.

Dnark and Ung-thol squinted in the midday glare, and both nodded as they sorted out the two yellow pennants shot with red that flew in the stiff, wintry wind. They had known they were getting close, for they had crossed through a pair of hastily abandoned campsites in the sheltered valley. Clan Karuck's march had apparently sent other orcs running fast and far.

Toogwik Tuk led the way up the rocky incline that ramped up between those banners. Hulking orc guards stood to block the way, holding pole arms of various elaborate designs, with side blades and angled spear tips. Half axe and half spear, the weight of the weapons was intimidating enough, but just to enhance their trepidation, the approaching trio couldn't miss the ease with which the Karuck guards handled the heavy implements.

"They are as large as Obould," Ung-thol quietly remarked. "And they are just common guards."

"The orcs of Karuck who do not achieve such size and strength are slave fodder, so it is said," Dnark said.

"And so it is true," Toogwik Tuk said, turning back to the pair. "Nor are any of the runts allowed to breed. They are castrated at an early age, if they are fortunate."

"And my eagerness grows," said Ung-thol, who was the smallest of the trio. In his younger years, he had been a fine warrior, but a wound had left him somewhat infirm, and the shaman had lost quite a bit of weight and muscle over the intervening two decades.

"Rest easy, for you are too old to be worth castrating," Dnark chided, and he motioned for Toogwik Tuk to go and announce them to the guards.

Apparently the younger priest had laid the groundwork well, for the trio was ushered along the trail to the main encampment. Soon after, they stood before the imposing Grguch and his war priest advisor, Hakuun. Grguch sat on a chair of boulders, his fearsome double-bladed battle-axe in hand. The weapon, Rampant by name, was obviously quite heavy, but Grguch easily lifted it before him with one hand. He turned it slowly, so that his guests would get a good view, and a good understanding of the many ways Rampant could kill them. The black metal handle of the axe, which protruded up past the opposing "wing" blades, was shaped in the form of a stretching and turning dragon, its small forelegs pulled in close and the widespread horns on its head presenting a formidable spear tip. At the base, the dragon's long tail curved up and over the grip, forming a guard. Spines extended all along the length so that a punch from Grguch would hit like the stab of several daggers.

Most impressive were the blades, the symmetrical wings of the beast. Of shining silver mithral, they fanned out top and bottom, reinforced every finger's-breadth or so by a thin bar of dark adamantine, which created spines top and bottom along each blade. The convex edges were as long as the distance from Dnark's elbow to the tips of his extended fingers, and none of the three visitors had any trouble imagining being cut cleanly in half by a single swipe of Rampant.

"Welcome to Many-Arrows, great Grguch," Toogwik Tuk said with a respectful bow. "The presence of Clan Karuck and its worthy leader makes us greater."

Grguch led his gaze drift slowly across the three visitors then around the gathering to Hakuun. "You will learn the truth of your hopeful claim," he said, his eyes turning back to Toogwik Tuk, "when I have the bones of dwarves and elves and ugly humans to crush beneath my boot."

Dnark couldn't suppress a grin as he looked to Ung-thol, who seemed similarly pleased. Despite their squeamishness at being so badly outnumbered among the fierce and unpredictable tribe, things were going quite well.

* * * * *

Out of the same cavern from which Grguch and Clan Karuck had emerged came a figure much less imposing, save to those folk who held a particular phobia of snakes. Fluttering on wings that seemed more suited to a large butterfly, the reptilian creature wove a swaying, zigzagging course through the chamber, toward the waning daylight.

The twilight was brighter than anything the creature had seen in a century, and it had to set down inside the cave and spend a long, long while letting its eyes properly adjust.

"Ah, Hakuun, why have you done this?" asked the wizard, who was not really a snake, let alone a flying one. Anyone nearby might have thought it a curious thing to hear a winged snake sigh.

He slithered into a darker corner, and peeked out only occasionally to let his eyes adjust.

He knew the answer to his own question. The only reason the brutes of Clan Karuck would come forth would be for plunder and war. And while war could be an interesting spectacle, the wizard Jack, or Jack the Gnome as he had once been commonly called, really didn't have time for it just then. His studies had taken him deep into the bowels of the Spine of the World, and his easy manipulation of Clan Karuck, from Hakuun's father's father's father's father, had provided him with most excellent cover for his endeavors, to say nothing of the glory it had rained upon Hakuun's miserable little family.

Quite a while later, and only with the last hints of daylight left in the air, Jack slipped up to the cavern exit and peered out over the vast landscape. A couple of spells would allow him to locate Hakuun and the others, of course, but the perceptive fellow didn't need any magic to sense that something was . . . different. Something barely distinguishable in the air—a scent or distant sounds, perhaps—pricked at Jack's sensibilities. He had lived on the surface once, far back beyond his memories, before he had fallen in with the illithids and demons in his quest to learn magic more powerful and devious than the typical evocations of mundane spellcasters. He had lived on the surface when he truly was a gnome, something he could hardly claim anymore. He only rarely wore that guise, and had come to understand that physical form really wasn't all that important or defining anyway. He was a blessed thing, he knew, mostly thanks to the illithids, because he had learned to escape the bounds of the corporeal and of the mortal.

A sense of pity came over him as he looked out over the wide lands, populated by creatures so inferior, creatures who didn't understand the truth of the multiverse, or the real power of magic.

That was Jack's armor as he looked out over the land, for he needed such pride to suppress the other, inevitable feelings that whirled in his thoughts and in his heart. For all of his superiority, Jack had spent the last century or more almost completely alone, and while he had found wondrous revelations and new spells in his amazing workshop, with its alchemical equipment and reams of parchments and endless ink and spellbooks he could stack to several times his gnomish height, only by lying to himself could Jack even begin to accept the paradoxical twist of fate afforded him by practical immortality. For while—and perhaps because—he wouldn't die anytime soon of natural causes, Jack was acutely aware that the world was full of mortal danger. Long life had come to mean "more to lose," and Jack had been walled into his secure laboratory as much by fear as by the thick stones of the Underdark.

That laboratory, hidden and magically warded, remained secure even though his unwitting protectors, Clan Karuck, had traveled out of the Underdark. And still, Jack had followed them. He had followed Hakuun, though the pathetic Hakuun was hardly worth following, because, he knew deep inside but wasn't quite ready to admit, he had wanted to come back, to remember the last time he was Jack the Gnome.

He found himself pleasantly surprised by the view. Something tingled in the air around him, something exciting and teeming with possibility.

Perhaps he didn't know the extent of Hakuun's reasoning in allowing Grguch to come forth, Jack thought, and he was intrigued.

CHAPTER

Wulfgar's long, powerful legs drove through the knee-deep—often hip-deep—snow, plowing a path north from the mountain ridge. Rather than perceive the snow as a hindrance, though, Wulfgar considered it a freeing experience. That kind of trailblazing reminded him of the crisp air of home, and in a more practical sense, the snow slowed to a grumbling halt the pair of dwarven sentries who stubbornly pursued him.

More snow fell, and the wind blew cold from the north, promising yet another storm. But Wulfgar did not fear, and his smile was genuine as he drove forward. He kept the river on his immediate right and scrolled through his thoughts all of the landmarks Ivan Bouldershoulder had told him regarding the trail leading to the body of Delly Curtie. Wulfgar had grilled Ivan and Pikel on the details before they had departed Mithral Hall.

The cold wind, the stinging snow, the pressure on his legs from winter's deep . . . it all felt right to Wulfgar, familiar and comforting, and he knew in his heart that his course was the right one. He drove on all the harder, his stride purposeful and powerful, and no snow drift could slow him.

The calls of protest from Bruenor's kin dissipated into nothingness behind him, defeated by the wall of wind, and very soon the fortifications and towers, and the mountain ridge itself became indistinct black splotches in the distant background.

He was alone and he was free. He had no one on whom he could rely, but no one for whom he was responsible. It was just Wulfgar, son of Beornegar, ranging through the deep winter snow, against the wind of the newest storm. He was just a lone adventurer, whose path was his own to choose, and who had found, to his thrill, a road worth walking.

Despite the cold, despite the danger, despite the missing Colson, despite Delly's death and Catti-brie's relationship with Drizzt, Wulfgar knew only simple joy.

He traveled on long after the dim light had waned to darkness, until the cold night air became too intense for even a proud son of the frozen tundra to bear. He set up camp under the lowest boughs of thick pines, behind insulating walls of snow, where the wind could not find him. He passed the night in dreams of the caribou, and the wandering tribes that followed the herd. He envisioned his friends, all of them, beside him in the shadow of Kelvin's Cairn.

He slept well, and went out early the next day, under the gray sky.

The land was not unfamiliar to Wulfgar, who had spent years in Mithral Hall, and even as he had exited the eastern door of the dwarven complex, he had a good idea of where Ivan and Pikel had found the body of poor Delly. He would get there that day, he knew, but reminded himself repeatedly of the need for caution. He had left friendly lands, and from the moment he had crossed the dwarven battlements on the mountain spur, he was outside the realm of civilization. Wulfgar passed several encampments, the dark smoke of campfires curling lazily into the air, and he didn't need to get close enough to see the campers to know their orc heritage and their malicious intent.

He was glad that the daylight was dim.

The snow began again soon after midday, but it was not the driving stuff of the previous night. Puffy flakes danced lightly on the air, trailing a meandering course to the ground, for there was no wind other than the occasional small whisper of a breeze. Despite having to continually watch for signs of orcs and other monsters, Wulfgar made great progress, and the afternoon was still young when he breached one small rocky rise to look down upon a bowl-shaped dell.

Wulfgar held his breath as he scanned the region. Across the way, beyond the opposite rise, rose the smoke of several campfires, and in the small vale itself Wulfgar saw the remains of an older, deserted encampment. For though the dell was sheltered, the wind had found its way in on the previous day, and had driven the snow to the southeastern reaches, leaving a large portion of the bowl practically uncovered. Wulfgar could clearly see a half-covered ring of small stones, the remains of a cooking pit.

Exactly as Ivan Bouldershoulder had described it.

With a great sigh, the barbarian pulled himself over the ridge and began a slow and deliberate trudge into the dell. He slid his feet along slowly rather than lift them, aware that he might trip over a body buried beneath the foot or so of snow that blanketed the ground. He set a path that took him straight to the cooking pit, then lined himself up as Ivan had described and slowly made his way back out. It took him a long while, but sure enough, he noticed a bluish hand protruding from the edge of the snow.

Wulfgar knelt beside it and reverently brushed back the white powder. It was Delly, unmistakably so, for the deep freeze of winter had only intensified after her fall those months before, and little decomposition had set in. Her face was bloated, but not greatly, and her features were not too badly distorted.

She looked as if she were asleep and at peace, and it occurred to Wulfgar that the poor woman had never known such serenity in all of her life.

A pang of guilt stung him at that realization, for in the end, that truth had been no small part his own fault. He recalled their last conversations, when Delly had subtly and quietly begged him to get her out of Mithral Hall, when she had pleaded with him to free her from the confines of the dwarf-hewn tunnels.

"But I am a stupid one," he whispered to her, gently stroking her face. "Would that you had said it more directly, and yet I fear that still I would not have heard you."

She had given up everything to follow him to Mithral Hall. Truly her impoverished life in Luskan had not been an enviable existence. But still, in Luskan Delly Curtie had friends who were as her family, had a warm bed and food to eat. She had abandoned that much at least for Wulfgar and Colson, and had held up her end of that bargain all the way to Mithral Hall and beyond.

In the end, she had failed. Because of Catti-brie's evil and sentient sword, to be sure, but also because the man she had trusted to stand beside her had not been able to hear and recognize her quiet desperation.

"Forgive me," Wulfgar said, and he bent low to kiss her cold cheek. He rose back to his knees and blinked, for suddenly the dim daylight stung his eyes.

Wulfgar stood.

"*Ma la, bo gor du wanak,*" he said, an ancient barbarian way of accepting resignation, a remark without direct translation to the common tongue.

It was a lament that the world "is as it would be," as the gods would have it, and it was the place of men to accept and discover their best path from what was presented them. Hearing the somewhat stilted and less-flowing tongue of the Icewind Dale barbarians rolling so easily from his lips gave Wulfgar pause. He never used that language anymore, and yet it had come back to him so easily just then.

With the winter thick about him, in the crisp and chill air, and with tragedy lying at his feet, the words had come to him, unbidden and irresistible.

"*Ma la, bo gor du wanak,*" he repeated in a whisper as he looked down at Delly Curtie.

His gaze slid across the bowl to the rising lines of campfire smoke. His expression shifted from grimace to wicked grin as he lifted Aegis-fang into his hands, his current "best path" crystallizing in his thoughts.

Beyond the northern rim of the dell, the ground dropped away sharply for more than a dozen feet, but not far from the ridge sat a small plateau, a single flat-topped jut of stone, like the trunk of a gigantic, ancient tree. The main orc encampment encircled the base of that plinth, but the first thing Wulfgar saw when he charged over the rim of the dell was the single tent and the trio of orc sentries stationed there.

Aegis-fang led the way, trailing the leaping barbarian's cry to the war god Tempus. The spinning warhammer took the closest orc sentry in the chest and blew him across the breadth of the ten-foot diameter pillar, spreading the snow cover like the prow of a speeding ship before dropping him off the back side.

Encumbered by layers of heavy clothing and with only slippery footing beneath, Wulfgar didn't quite clear the fifteen-foot distance, and slammed his shins against the ledge of the pillar, which sent him sprawling into the snow. Roaring with battle-frenzy, thrashing about so that he would present no clear target to the remaining two orcs, the barbarian quickly got his hands under him and heaved himself to his feet. His shins were bleeding but he felt no pain, and he barreled forward at the nearest orc, who lifted a spear to block.

Wulfgar slapped the feeble weapon aside and bore in, grasping the front of the orc's heavy fur wrap. As he simply ran the creature over, Wulfgar caught a second grip down by the orc's groin, and he hoisted his enemy up over his head. He spun toward the remaining orc and let fly, but that last orc dropped low beneath the living missile, who went flailing into the small tent and took it with him in his continuing flight over the far side of the pillar.

The remaining orc took up its sword in both hands, lifting the heavy blade over its head, and charged at Wulfgar with abandon.

He had seen such eagerness many times before in his enemies, for, as was often the case, Wulfgar appeared unarmed. But as the orc came in, Aegis-fang magically reappeared in Wulfgar's waiting grasp, and he jabbed it ahead with one hand. The heavy hammerhead connected solidly on the chest of the charging orc.

The creature stopped as though it had rammed into a stone wall.

Wulfgar drew back Aegis-fang and took it up in both hands to strike again, but the orc made no move at all, just stood there staring at him blankly. He watched as the sword slipped from the creature's grasp, to fall to the ground behind it. Then, before he could strike, the orc simply fell over.

Wulfgar sprinted past it to the edge of the pillar. Below him, orcs scrambled, trying to discern the threat that had come so unexpectedly. One orc lifted a bow Wulfgar's way, but too slowly, for Aegis-fang was already spinning its way. The warhammer crashed through the orc's knuckles and laid the archer low.

Wulfgar leaped from the pillar, right over the nearest duo, who had set spears pointed his way. He crashed among a second group, far less prepared, and drove one down below his descending knee, and knocked two others aside with his falling bulk. He managed to keep his footing somehow, and staggered forward, beyond the reach of the spear-wielders.

He used that momentum to flatten the next orc in line with a heavy punch, then grabbed the next and lifted it before him in his run, using its body as a shield as he charged into the raised swords of a pair of confused sentries.

Aegis-fang returned to him, and a mighty strike sent all of that trio flying to the ground. Purely on instinct, Wulfgar halted his momentum and pivoted, Aegis-fang swiping across to shatter the spears and arms of creatures coming in at his back. The overwhelmed orcs fell away in a jumble and Wulfgar, not daring to pause, ran off.

He crashed through the side of a tent, his hammer tearing the deerskin from the wooden supports. He dragged his feet and kicked powerfully, scattering bedrolls and supplies, and a pair of young orcs who crawled off yelping.

That pair was no threat to him, Wulfgar realized, so he didn't pursue, veering instead for the next that raised weapons against him. He came in swinging, rolling his arms in circles above his head. Aegis-fang hummed as it cut through the air. The three orcs fell back, but one tripped and went to the ground. It dropped its weapon and tried to scramble away, but Wulfgar kicked it hard on the hip, sending it sprawling. Stubbornly the orc rolled to its belly and hopped up to all fours, trying to get its feet under it for a dash.

His great muscled arms straining and bulging, Wulfgar halted the spin of Aegis-fang, slid his lead hand up the handle, and jabbed at the orc. The warhammer smacked off the orc's shoulder and cracked into the side of its head, and the creature fell flat to the ground and lay very still.

Wulfgar stomped on it for good measure as he ran past in pursuit of its two companions, who had halted their retreat and stood ready.

Wulfgar roared and lifted Aegis-fang above his head, eagerly accepting the challenge. On he charged . . . but he noted something out of the corner of his eye. He dug in his lead foot, stopped abruptly, and tried to turn. Then he threw himself around, a spear grazing his side painfully. The missile caught in his flying wolf cloak and held fast, hanging awkwardly, its handle dragging on the ground and tangling with Wulfgar's legs as he continued his turn. He could only give it a fraction of his attention, though, for a second spear flew his way. Wulfgar brought

Aegis-fang in close to his chest and turned it down at the last moment to crack the spearhead out of line. Still, the missile flipped over the parry and slapped against Wulfgar's shoulder. As it went over, the back point of the weapon's triangular head cut the barbarian chin to cheek.

And as he lurched away, his leg caught the spear shaft hanging from his cloak.

To his credit, Wulfgar managed to not fall over, but he was off balance, his posture and the positioning of his weapon all wrong, as the two nearer orcs howled and leaped at him.

He drove Aegis-fang across his body, left to right, blocking a sword cut, but more with his arm than with the warhammer. He lifted his lower hand up desperately, turning the warhammer horizontal to parry a spear thrust from the other orc.

But the thrust was a feint, and Wulfgar missed cleanly. As the orc retracted, its smile was all the barbarian needed to see to know that he had no way to stop the second thrust from driving the spear deep into his belly.

He thought of Delly, lying cold in the snow.

* * * * *

Bruenor stood with Catti-brie outside the eastern door of Mithral Hall. North of them, construction was on in full, strengthening the wall that ran from the steep mountainside along the spur all the way to the river. As long as that wall could hold back the orcs, Clan Battlehammer remained connected above ground to the rest of the Silver Marches. The ferry across the River Surbrin, barely a hundred feet from where Bruenor and Catti-brie stood, would be running soon, and it would only be needed for a short while anyway. The abutments of a strong bridge were already in place on both banks.

The orcs could not get at them from the south without many days of forewarning, and such a journey through that broken ground would leave an army vulnerable at many junctures. With the line of catapults, archer posts, and other defensive assault points already set on the banks, particularly across the river, any orc assault using the river for passage would result in utter ruin for the attackers, much as it had for the dwarves of Citadel Felbarr when they had come to join the

Battlehammer dwarves in their attempt to secure that most vital piece of ground.

Neither Bruenor nor Catti-brie were looking at the dwarven handiwork at that point, however. Both had their eyes and thoughts turned farther north, to where Wulfgar had unexpectedly gone.

"Ye ready to walk with him to Silverymoon?" Bruenor asked his adopted daughter after a long and uncomfortable silence, for the dwarf knew that Catti-brie harbored the very same feelings of dread as he.

"My leg hurts with every step," the woman admitted. "The boulder hit me good, and I don't know that I'll ever walk easy again."

Bruenor turned to her, his eyes moist. For she spoke the truth, he knew, and the clerics had told him in no uncertain terms. Catti-brie's injuries would never fully heal. The fight in the western entry hall had left her with a limp that she would carry for the rest of her days, and possibly with more damage still. Priest Cordio had confided to Bruenor his fears that Catti-brie would never bear children, particularly given that the woman was nearing the end of her childbearing years anyway.

"But I'm ready for the walk today," Catti-brie said with determination, and without the slightest hesitation. "If Wulfgar crossed over that wall right as we're speaking, I'd turn him to the river that we could be on our way. It is past time that Colson was returned to her father."

Bruenor managed a wide smile. "Ye be quick to get the girl and get ye back," he ordered. "The snows're letting go early this year, I'm thinking, and Gauntlgrym's waiting!"

"You believe that it really was Gauntlgrym?" Catti-brie dared to ask, and it was the first time anyone had actually put the most important question directly to the driven dwarf king. For on their journey back to Mithral Hall, before the coming of Obould, one of the caravan wagons had been swallowed up by a strange sinkhole, one that led, apparently, to an underground labyrinth. Bruenor had immediately proclaimed the place Gauntlgrym, an ancient and long-lost dwarven city, the pinnacle of power for the clan called Delzoun, a common heritage for all the dwarves of the North, Battlehammer, Mirabarran, Felbarran, and Adbarran alike.

"Gauntlgrym," Bruenor said with certainty, a claim he had been making in that tone since his return from the dead. "Moradin put me back here for a reason, girl, and that reason'll be shown to me when I get meself to Gauntlgrym. There we'll be findin' the weapons we're needing to drive the ugly orcs back to their holes, don't ye doubt."

Catti-brie wasn't about to argue with him, because she knew that Bruenor was in no mood for any debate. She and Drizzt had spoken at length about the dwarf's plan, and about the possibility that the sinkhole had indeed been an entry point to the lost avenues of Gauntlgrym, and she had discussed it at length with Regis, as well, who had been poring over ancient maps and texts. The truth of it was that none of them had any idea whether or not the place was what Bruenor had decided it to be.

And Bruenor wasn't about to argue the point. His litany against the darkness that had settled on the land was a simple one, a single word: Gauntlgrym.

"Durn stubborn fool of a boy," Bruenor muttered, looking back to the north, his mind's eye well beyond the wall that blocked his view. "He's to slow it all down."

Catti-brie started to respond, but found that she could not speak past the lump that welled in her throat. Bruenor was complaining, of course, but in truth, his anger that Wulfgar's rash decision to run off alone into orc-held lands would slow the dwarves' plans was the most optimistic assessment of all.

The woman gave in to her sense of dread for just a moment, and wondered if her duty to her friend would send her off alone across the Surbrin in search of Colson. And in that case, once the toddler had been retrieved, what then?

CHAPTER

BUILDING HIS KINGDOM

The beams creaked for a moment, then a great rush of air swept across the onlookers as the counterweights sent the massive neck of the catapult swinging past. The basket released its contents, tri-pointed caltrops, in a line from the highest peak of the arc to the point of maximum momentum and distance.

The rain of black metal plummeted from sight, and King Obould moved quickly to the lip of the cliff to watch them drop to the floor of Keeper's Dale.

Nukkels, Kna, and some of the others shifted uneasily, not pleased to see their god-king standing so near to a two-hundred-foot drop. Any of General Dukka's soldiers, or more likely, proud Chieftain Grimsmal and his guards, could have rushed over and ended the rule of Obould with a simple shove.

But Grimsmal, despite his earlier rumblings of discontent, nodded appreciatively at the defenses that had been set up on the northern ridge overlooking Mithral Hall's sealed western door.

"We have filled the valley floor with caltrops," General Dukka assured Obould. He motioned to the many baskets set beside the line of catapults, all filled with stones ranging in size from a large fist to twice an orc's head. "If the ugly dwarves come forth, we'll shower them with death."

Obould looked down to the southwest, about two-thirds of the way across the broken valley from the dwarven complex, where a line of orcs chopped at the stone, digging a wide, deep trench. Directly to the king's left, atop the cliff at the end of the trench, sat a trio of catapults, all sighted to rake the length of the ravine should the dwarves try to use it for cover against the orcs positioned in the west.

Dukka's plan was easy enough to understand: he would slow any dwarven advance across Keeper's Dale as much as possible, so that his artillery and archers on high could inflict massive damage on the break-out army.

"They came out of the eastern wall with great speed and cunning," Obould warned the beaming general. "Encased in metal carts. A collapsed mountain wall did not slow them."

"From their door to the Surbrin was not far, my king," Dukka dared reply. "Keeper's Dale offers no such sanctuary."

"Do not underestimate them," Obould warned. He stepped closer to General Dukka as he spoke, and the other orc seemed to shrink in stature before him. His voice ominous and loud, so that all could hear, Obould roared out, "They will come out with *fury*. They will have brooms before them to sweep aside your caltrops, and shielding above to block your arrows and stones. They will have folding bridges, no doubt, and your trench will slow them not at all. King Bruenor is no fool, and does not charge into battle unprepared. The dwarves will know exactly where they need to go, and they will get there with all speed."

A long and uncomfortable silence followed, with many of the orcs looking at each other nervously.

"Do you expect them to come forth, my king?" Grimsmal asked.

"All that I expect from King Bruenor is that whatever he chooses to do, he will do it well, and with cunning," Obould replied, and more than one orc jaw fell open to hear such compliments for a dwarf coming forth from an orc king.

Obould considered those looks carefully in light of his disastrous attempt to break into Mithral Hall. He could not let any of them believe that he was speaking from weakness, from memories of his own bad judgment.

"Witness the devastation of the ridge where you now place your catapults," he said, waving his arm out to the west. Where once had stood a ridge line—one atop which Obould had placed allied frost giants and their huge war engines—loomed a torn and jagged crevice of shattered stones. "The dwarves are on their home ground. They know every stone, every rise, and every tunnel. They know how to fight. But *we* . . ." he roared, striding about for maximum effect, and lifting his clawing hands to the sky. He let the words hang in the air for many heartbeats before continuing, "We do not deny them the credit they deserve. We accept that they are formidable and worthy foes, and in that knowledge, we prepare."

He turned directly to General Dukka and Chieftain Grimsmal, who had edged closer together. "We know them, but even against what we have shown to them in conquering this land, they still do not know us. This"—he swept his arm out to encompass the catapults, archers, and all the rest—"they know, and expect. Your preparations are half done, General Dukka, and half done well. Now envision how King Bruenor will try to counter everything you have done, and complete your preparations to defeat that counter."

"B-but . . . my king?" General Dukka stammered.

"I have all confidence in you," Obould said. "Begin by trapping your own entrenchments on the western side of Keeper's Dale, so that if the dwarves reach that goal, your warriors can quickly retreat and leave them exposed on another battlefield of your choosing."

Dukka began to nod, his eyes shining, and his lips curled into a wicked grin.

"Tell me," Obould bade him.

"I can set a second force in the south to get to the doors behind them," the orc replied. "To cut off any dwarf army that charges across the valley."

"Or a second force that appears to do so," said Obould, and he paused and let all around him digest that strange response.

"So they will turn and run back," Dukka answered at length. "And then have to cross yet again to gain the ground they covet."

"I have never wavered in my faith in you, General Dukka," said Obould, and he nodded and even patted the beaming orc on the shoulder as he walked past.

His smile was twofold, and genuine. He had just strengthened the loyalty of an important general, and had impressed the potentially troublesome Grimsmal in the process. Obould knew what played in Grimsmal's mind as he swept up behind the departing entourage. If

Obould, and apparently his commanders, could think so far ahead of King Bruenor, then what might befall any orc chieftain who plotted against the King of Many-Arrows?

Those doubts were the real purpose of his visit to Keeper's Dale, after all, and not any concerns about General Dukka's readiness. For it was all moot, Obould understood. King Bruenor would never come forth from those western doors. As the dwarf had learned in his breakout to the east—and as Obould had learned in trying to flood into Mithral Hall—any such advance would demand too high a cost in blood.

* * * * *

Wulfgar screamed at the top of his lungs, as if his voice alone might somehow, impossibly, halt the thrust of the spear.

A blue-white flash stung the barbarian's eyes, and for a moment he thought it was the burning pain of the spear entering his belly. But when he came out of his blink, he saw the spear-wielding orc flipping awkwardly in front of him. The creature hit the ground limp, already dead, and by the time Wulfgar turned to face its companion that orc had dropped its sword and grasped and clawed at its chest. Blood poured from a wound, both front and back.

Wulfgar didn't understand. He jabbed his warhammer at the wounded orc and missed—another streaking arrow, a bolt of lightning, soared past Wulfgar and hit the orc in the shoulder, throwing it to the ground near its fallen comrade. Wulfgar knew that tell-tale missile, and he roared again and turned to face his rescuer.

He was surprised to see Drizzt, not Catti-brie, holding Taulmaril the Heartseeker.

The drow sprinted toward him, his light steps barely ruffling the blanket of deep snow. He started to nock another arrow, but tossed the bow aside instead and drew forth his two scimitars. He tossed a salute at Wulfgar then darted to the side as he neared, turning into a handful of battle-ready orcs.

"Biggrin!" Drizzt shouted as Wulfgar charged in his wake.

"Tempus!" the barbarian responded.

He put Aegis-fang up behind his head, and let it fly from both hands, the warhammer spinning end-over-end for the back of Drizzt's head.

Drizzt ducked and dropped to his knees at the last moment. The five orcs, following the drow's movements, had no time to react to the spinning surprise. At the last moment, the orcs threw up their arms defensively and tangled each other in their desperation to get out of the way. Aegis-fang took one squarely, and that flying orc clipped another enough to send both tumbling back.

The remaining three hadn't even begun to re-orient themselves to their opponents when the fury of Drizzt fell over them. He skidded on his knees as the hammer flew past, but leaped right back up to his feet and charged forward with abandon, his deadly blades crossing before him, going out wide, then coming back in another fast cross on the backhand. He counted on confusion, and confusion he found. The three orcs fell away in moments, slashed and stabbed.

Wulfgar, still chasing, summoned Aegis-fang back to his waiting hands, then veered inside the drow's turn so that his long legs brought him up beside Drizzt as they approached the encampment's main area of tents, where many orcs had gathered.

But those orcs would not stand against them, and any indecision the porcine humanoids might have had about running away was snapped away a moment later when a giant panther roared from the side.

Weapons went flying, and orcs went running, scattering to the winter's winds.

Wulfgar heaved Aegis-fang after the nearest, dropping it dead in its tracks. He put his head down and plowed on even faster—or started to, until Drizzt grabbed him by the arm and tugged him around.

"Let them go," the drow said. "There are many more about, and we will lose our advantage in the chase."

Wulfgar skidded to a stop and again called his magical warhammer back to his grasp. He took a moment to survey the dead, the wounded, and the fleeing orcs then met Drizzt's gaze and nodded, his bloodlust sated.

And he laughed. He couldn't help it. It came from somewhere deep inside, a desperate release, a burst of protest against the absurdity of his own actions. It came from those distant memories again, of running free in Icewind Dale. He had caught the "Biggrin" reference so easily, understanding in that single name that Drizzt wanted him to throw the warhammer at the back of the drow's head.

How was that even possible?

"Wulfgar has a desire to die?" Drizzt asked, and he, too, chuckled.

"I knew you would arrive. It is what you do."

* * * * *

Kna curled around his arm, rubbing his shoulder, purring and growling as always. Seated at the table in the tent, King Obould seemed not even to notice her, which of course only made her twist, curl, and growl even more intensely.

Across the table, General Dukka and Chieftain Grimsmal understood all too clearly that Kna was their reminder that Obould was above them, in ways they simply could never hope to attain.

"Five blocks free," General Dukka explained, "block" being the orc military term coined by Obould to indicate a column of one thousand warriors, marching ten abreast and one hundred deep. "Before the turn of Tarsakh."

"You can march them to the Surbrin, north of Mithral Hall, in five days," Chieftain Grimsmal remarked. "Four days if you drive them hard."

"I would drive them through the stones for the glory of King Obould!" Dukka replied.

Obould did not appear impressed.

"There is no need of such haste," he said at length, after sitting with a contemplative stare that had the other two chewing their lips in anticipation.

"The onset of Tarsakh will likely bring a clear path to the dwarven battlements," Chieftain Grimsmal dared to reply.

"A place we will not go."

The blunt response had Grimsmal sliding back in his chair, and brought a stupefied blink from Dukka.

"Perhaps I can free six blocks," the general said.

"Five or fifty changes nothing," Obould declared. "The ascent is not our wisest course."

"You know another route to strike at them?" Dukka asked.

"No," said Grimsmal, shaking his head as he looked knowingly at Obould. "The whispers are true, then. King Obould's war is over."

The chieftain wisely kept his tone flat and non-judgmental, but Dukka's wide eyes betrayed the general's shock, albeit briefly.

"We pause to see how many roads are open to us," Obould explained.

"Roads to victory?" asked General Dukka.

"Victory in ways you cannot yet imagine," said Obould, and he wagged his large head and showed a confident and toothy grin. For greater effect, he brought one of his huge fists up on the table before him, and clenched it tightly so that the muscles of his bare forearm bulged and twisted to proportions that pointedly reminded the other orcs of the superiority of this creature. Grimsmal was large by orc standards, and a mighty warrior, which was how he had attained the leadership of his warrior tribe, of course. But even he blanched before the spectacle of Obould's sheer power. Truly it seemed that if the orc king had been holding a block of granite in that hand, he would have easily ground it to dust.

No less overpowering was Obould's expression of supreme confidence and power, heightened by his disciplined detachment to Kna's writhing and purring at his side.

Grimsmal and General Dukka left that meeting having no idea what Obould was planning, but having no doubt of Obould's certainty in that plan. Obould watched them go with a knowing smile that the two would not plot against him. The orc king grabbed Kna and yanked her around before him, deciding that it was time to celebrate.

* * * * *

The body was frozen solid, and Wulfgar and Drizzt could not bend Delly's arms back down against her. Tenderly, Wulfgar took the blankets from his pack and wrapped them around her, keeping her face exposed to the last, as if he wanted her to see his sincere remorse and sorrow.

"She did not deserve this," Wulfgar said, standing straight and staring down at the poor woman. He looked at Drizzt, who stood with Guenhwyvar at his side, one hand on the tuft at the back of the panther's neck. "She had her life in Luskan before I arrived to steal her from it."

"She chose the road with you."

"Foolishly," Wulfgar replied with a self-deprecating laugh and sigh.

Drizzt shrugged as if the point was moot, which of course it was. "Many roads end suddenly, in the wilds and also in the alleyways of Luskan. There is no way of truly knowing where a road will lead until it is walked."

"Her trust in me was misplaced, I fear."

"You did not bring her out here to die," said Drizzt. "Nor did you drive her from the safety of Mithral Hall."

"I did not hear her calls for help. She told me that she could not suffer the dwarven tunnels, but I would not hear."

"And her way was clear across the Surbrin, had that been the route she truly wanted. You are no more to blame for this than is Catti-brie, who did not anticipate the reach of that wicked sword."

The mention of Catti-brie jolted Wulfgar a bit, for he knew that she felt the weight of guilt indeed about Khazid'hea's apparent role in Delly Curtie's tragic death.

"Sometimes what is, just is," said Drizzt. "An accident, a cruel twist of fate, a conjunction of forces that could not have been anticipated."

Wulfgar nodded, and it seemed as if a great weight had been lifted from his broad shoulders. "She did not deserve this," he said again.

"Nor did Dagnabbit, nor did Dagna, nor did Tarathiel, and so many others, like those who took Colson across the Surbrin," said Drizzt. "It is the tragedy of war, the inevitability of armies crashing together, the legacy of orcs and dwarves and elves and humans alike. Many roads end suddenly—it is a reality of which we should all be aware—and Delly could just as easily have fallen to a thief in the dark of Luskan's night, or have been caught in the middle of a brawl in the Cutlass. We know for certain only one thing, my friend, that we will one day share in Delly's fate. If we walk our roads solely to avoid such an inevitability, if we step with too much caution and concern . . ."

"Then we should just as well lie under the snow and let the cold find our bones," Wulfgar finished. He nodded with every word, assuring Drizzt that he needn't worry about the weight of harsh reality bending Wulfgar low.

"You will go for Colson?" Drizzt asked.

"How could I not? You speak of our responsibility to ourselves in choosing our roads with courage and acceptance, yet there remains our responsibility to others. Mine is to Colson. It is the pact I willingly accepted when I took her from Meralda of Auckney. Even if I were assured that she was safe with the goodly refugees who crossed the Surbrin, I could not abandon my promise to Colson's mother, nor to the girl.

"For yourself there is Gauntlgrym?" Wulfgar asked. "Beside Bruenor?"

"That is his expectation, and my duty to him, yes."

Wulfgar gave a nod and scanned the horizon.

"Perhaps Bruenor is right, and Gauntlgrym will show us an end to this war," said Drizzt.

"There will be another war close behind," Wulfgar said with a helpless shrug and chuckle. "It is the way of things."

"Biggrin," Drizzt said, drawing a smile from his large friend.

"Indeed," said Wulfgar. "If we cannot change the way of things, then we are wise to enjoy the journey."

"You knew that I would duck, yes?"

Wulfgar shrugged. "I figured that if you did not, it was—"

"—the way of things," Drizzt finished with him.

They shared a laugh and Wulfgar looked down at Delly once more, his face somber. "I will miss her. She was so much more than she appeared. A fine companion and mother. Her road was difficult for all her days, but she oft found within herself a sense of hope and even joy. My life is lessened with her passing. There is a hole within me that will not be easily filled."

"Which cannot be filled," Drizzt corrected. "That is the thing of loss. And so you will go on, and you will take solace in your memories of Delly, in the good things you shared. You will see her in Colson, though the girl was not of her womb. You will feel her beside you on occasion, and though the sadness will ever remain, it will settle behind treasured memories."

Wulfgar bent down and gently slid his arms beneath Delly and lifted her. It didn't appear as if he was holding a body, for the frozen form did not bend at all. But he hugged her close to his chest and moisture filled his bright blue eyes.

"Do you now hate Obould as much as I do?" Drizzt asked.

Wulfgar didn't reply, but the answer that came fast into his thoughts surprised him. Obould was just a name to him, not even a symbol on which he could focus his inner turmoil. Somehow he had moved past rage and into acceptance.

It is what it is, he thought, echoing Drizzt's earlier sentiments, and Obould diminished to become a circumstance, one of many. An orc, a thief, a dragon, a demon, an assassin from Calimport—it did not matter.

"It was good to fight beside you again," Wulfgar said, and in such a tone as to give Drizzt pause, for the words sounded more like a farewell than anything else.

Drizzt sent Guenhwyvar out to the point, and side-by-side, he and Wulfgar began their trek back to Mithral Hall, with Wulfgar holding Delly close all the way.

CHAPTER

TAKING ADVANTAGE

5

"Clan Grimm has turned north," Toogwik Tuk told his two companions on a clear, calm morning in the middle of Ches, the third month of the year. "King Obould has granted Chieftain Grimsmal a favorable region, a sheltered and wide plateau."

"To prepare?" asked Ung-thol.

"To build," Toogwik Tuk corrected. "To raise the banner of Clan Grimm beside the flag of Many-Arrows above their new village."

"Village?" Dnark asked, spitting the word with surprise.

"King Obould will claim that this is a needed pause to strengthen the lines of supply," Toogwik Tuk said.

"A reasonable claim," said Dnark.

"But one we know is only half true," Toogwik Tuk said.

"What of General Dukka?" asked an obviously agitated Ung-thol. "Has he secured Keeper's Dale?"

"Yes," the other shaman answered.

"And so he marches to the Surbrin?"

"No," said Toogwik Tuk. "General Dukka and his thousands have not moved, though there are rumors that he will assemble several blocks . . . eventually."

Dnark and Ung-thol exchanged concerned glances.

"King Obould would not allow that collection of warriors to filter back to their tribes," Dnark said. "He would not dare."

"But will he send them around to strike at the dwarves at the

Surbrin?" asked Ung-thol. "The dwarf battlements grow higher with each passing day."

"We expected Obould would not proceed," Toogwik Tuk reminded. "Is that not why we coaxed Grguch to the surface?"

Looking at his co-conspirators, Toogwik Tuk recognized that typical doubt right before the moment of truth. The three had long shared their concerns that Obould was veering from the path of conquest, and that was something they, as followers of Gruumsh One-eye, could not suffer. Their shared expectations, however, were that the war was not quite over, and that Obould would strike hard one more time at least, to gain a more advantageous position before his halt.

Leaving the dwarves open to the Surbrin had seemed a more distinct possibility over the past few months, and particularly the past few tendays. The weather was soon to turn, and the appropriate forces were not being moved into a strike position.

Still, in the face of it, the other two couldn't help but be surprised—and concerned, as the weight of their conspiracy settled more heavily on their shoulders.

"Turn them against the elf raiders in the east," Toogwik Tuk said suddenly, jolting his two companions, both of whom looked at him curiously, almost plaintively.

"We had hoped to use Grguch to force the charge to the Surbrin," Toogwik Tuk explained. "But with Obould's waiting to position the warriors, that is not presently an option. But we must offer Grguch some blood."

"Or he will take ours," Ung-thol muttered.

"There have been reports of elf skirmishers along the Surbrin, north of the dwarves," Dnark said, aiming his comment mostly at Ung-thol.

"Grguch and Clan Karuck will build a reputation that will serve them—and us—well when at last it comes to dealing with King Bruenor's troublesome beasts," Toogwik Tuk nudged. "Let us go and bring the Kingdom of Many-Arrows its newest hero."

* * * * *

Like a leaf fluttering silently on a midnight breeze, the dark elf slipped quietly to the side of the darkened stone and mud structure. The orc guards hadn't noted his quiet passing, nor was he leaving any obvious tracks on the frozen snow.

No corporeal creature could move more stealthily than a trained drow, and Tos'un Armgo was proficient even by the lofty standards of his race.

He paused at the wall and glanced around at the cluster of structures—the village of Tungrush, he knew through the conversations he had overheard from various "villagers." He noted the foundation, even a growing base in several places, of a wall that would eventually ring the compound.

Too late, the drow thought with an evil grin.

He inched toward an opening in the house's back wall, though whether it was an actual window or just a gap that had not yet been properly fitted, he could not tell. Nor did it matter, for the missing stone provided ample egress for the lithe creature. Tos'un slithered in like a snake, walking his hands down the inside of the wall until they braced him against the floor. His roll, like all of his other movements, was executed without a whisper of sound.

The room was nearly pitch black, the meager starlight barely filtering through the many breaks in the stone. A surface dweller would have had little chance of quietly navigating the cluttered place. But to Tos'un, who had lived almost all of his life in the lightless corridors of the Underdark, the place verily glowed with brightness. He stood in the main room, twice the size of the smaller chamber sectioned by an interior wall that extended from the front wall to within three feet of the back. From beyond that partition, he heard snoring.

His two swords, one drow made and the other, the sentient and fabulous Khazid'hea, came out in his hands as he silently approached. At the wall, he peeked in to see a large orc sleeping comfortably, face down on a cot against the house's outer side wall. In the corner near the front of the house rested a large pile of rags.

He meant to quietly slide his sword into the orc's lungs, defeating its shout and finishing it quickly and silently. Khazid'hea, though, had other ideas, and as Tos'un neared and readied the strike, the sword overwhelmed him with a sudden and unexpected burst of sheer outrage.

Down came the blade, through the back of the orc's neck, severing its head and cutting through the wooden frame of the cot with ease, sparking off the floor and drawing a deep line in the hard ground. The cot dropped at the break, clunking down.

Behind Tos'un the rags rose fast, for under them was another orc, a female. Purely on reflex, the drow drove his other arm around, his fine Menzoberranyr sword coming in hard against the female's neck and pinning her up against the wall. That blade could have easily opened her throat, of course, but as he struck, Tos'un, for some reason that had not consciously registered, turned to the flat edge. He had the orc's voice choked off, and a line of blood appeared above the blade, but the creature was not finished.

For Khazid'hea would not suffer that inferior sword to score a kill.

Tos'un shushed the orc, who trembled but did not, could not, resist.

Khazid'hea plunged through her chest, right out her back and into, and through, the stones of the house's front wall.

Surprised by his own movement, Tos'un fast retracted the blade.

The orc stared at him with disbelief. She slipped down to the floor and died with that same expression.

Are you always so hungry? the drow's thoughts asked the sentient sword.

He sensed that Khazid'hea was laughing in response.

It didn't matter anyway, of course. It was just an orc, and even if it had been a superior being, Tos'un Armgo never shied from killing. With the witnesses dispatched, the alarms silenced, the drow went back into the main chamber and found the couple's store of food. He ate and drank, and replenished his pack and his waterskin. He took his time, perfectly at ease, and searched the house for anything that might be of service to him. He even went back into the bedroom, and on a whim, placed the male orc's severed head between its legs, its face pressed into its arse.

He considered his work with a resigned shrug. Like his food, the lonely drow had to take his amusement where he could find it.

He went out soon after, through the same window that had allowed him access. The night was dark—still the time of the drow. He found the orc guards no more alert than when he had come in, and he thought to kill them for their lack of discipline.

A movement in some distant trees caught his attention, however, and the drow was fast to the shadows. It took him some time to realize . . .

There were elves about.

Tos'un wasn't really surprised. Many Moonwood elves had been reconnoitering the various orc settlements and caravan routes. He had been captured by just such a band not so many tendays before, and had thought to join with them after deceiving them into believing that he was not their enemy.

Or was it really a deception? Tos'un hadn't yet decided. Surely a life among the elves would be better than what he had. He'd thought that then, and thought it again with wretched orc food still heavy in his belly.

But it was not an option, he reminded himself. Drizzt Do'Urden was with the elves, and Drizzt knew that he, Tos'un, had been part and party to King Obould's advance. Furthermore, Drizzt would take Khazid'hea from him, no doubt, and without the sword, Tos'un would be vulnerable to the spells of priests, detecting any lies he might need to weave.

Tos'un shook the futile debate from his thoughts before Khazid'hea could weigh in, and tried to get a better idea of how many elves might be watching Tungrush. He tried to pick out more movement, but found nothing substantial. The drow was wiser than to take any sense of relief from that, however, for he knew well that the elves could move with stealth akin to his own. They had, after all, surrounded him once without him ever knowing they were near.

He went out carefully, even calling upon his natural drow abilities and summoning a globe of darkness around him at one point, as he broke past the tree line. He continued his scan afterward, and even did a wide circuit of the village.

The perimeter was thick with elves, so Tos'un melted away into the winter night.

* * * * *

Albondiel's sword cut the air, and cut the throat of the orc. Gasping and clawing, the creature spun and stumbled. An arrow drove into its side, dropping it to the red-stained snow.

Another orc emerged from a house and shouted for the guards.

But the guards were all dead. All of them lay out on the perimeter, riddled with elven arrows. No alarms had sounded. The orcs of the village had not a whisper of warning.

The shouting, frantic orc tried to run, but an arrow drove her to her knees and an elf warrior was fast to her side, his sword silencing her forever.

After the initial assault, no orcs had come out in any semblance of defense. Almost all the remaining orcs were running, nothing more, to the edge of the village and beyond, willy-nilly into the snow. Most soon lay dead well within the village's perimeter, for the elves were ready, and fast and deadly with their bows.

"Enough," Albondiel called to his warriors and to the archers who moved to launch a barrage of death on the remaining fleeing orcs. "Let them run. Their terror works in our favor. Let them spread the word of doom, that more will flee beside them."

"You have little taste for this," noted another elf, a young warrior standing at Albondiel's side.

"I shy not at all from killing orcs," Albondiel answered, turning a stern gaze the upstart's way. "But this is less battle than slaughter."

"Because we were cunning in our approach."

Albondiel smirked and shrugged as if it did not matter. For indeed it did not, the wizened elf understood. The orcs had come, had swept down like a black plague, stomping underfoot all before them. They were to be repelled by any means. It was that simple.

Or was it, the elf wondered as he looked down at his latest kill, an unarmed creature, still gurgling as the last air escaped its lungs. It wore only its nightclothes.

Defenseless and dead.

Albondiel had spoken the truth in his response. He did not shy from battle, and had killed dozens of orcs in combat. Raiding villages, however, left a sour taste in his mouth.

A series of cries from across the way told him that some of the orcs had not fled or come out from their homes. He watched as one emerged from an open door, staggering, bleeding. It fell down dead.

A small one, a child.

With brutal efficiency, the elf raiding party collected the bodies in a large pile. Then they began emptying the houses of anything that would burn, tossing furniture, bedding, blankets, clothes, and all the rest on that same pile.

"Lord Albondiel," one called to him, motioning him to a small house on the village's northern perimeter.

As he approached the caller, Albondiel noted a stain of blood running down the stones at the front of the house, to the left side of the door. Following his summoner's movements, Albondiel saw the hole, a clean gash, through the stones—all the way through to the interior.

"Two were in there, dead before we arrived," the elf explained. "One was beheaded, and the other stabbed against this wall."

"*Inside* the wall," Albondiel remarked.

"Yes, and by a blade that came right through."

"Tos'un," Albondiel whispered, for he had been in Sinnafain's hunting party when she had captured the drow. The drow who carried Khazid'hea, the sword of Catti-brie. A sword that could cut through solid stone.

"When were they killed?" Albondiel asked.

"Before the dawn. No longer."

Albondiel shifted his gaze outward, beyond the limits of the village. "So he is still out there. Perhaps even watching us now."

"I can send scouts . . ."

"No," Albondiel answered. "There is no need, and I would have none of our people confront the rogue. Be on with our business here, and let us be gone."

Soon after, the pile of rags, wood, and bodies was set ablaze, and from that fire, the elves gathered brands with which to light the thatched roofs. Using fallen trees from the nearby woods, the elves battered down the sides of the burning structures, and any stones that could be pried from the smoking piles were quickly carried to the western side of the village, which was bordered by a long, steep slope, and were thrown down.

What the orcs had created on that windswept hilltop, the elves fast destroyed. To the ground. As if the ugly creatures had never been there.

When they left later that same morning, dark smoke still lifting into the air behind them, Albondiel swept his gaze long and wide across the rugged landscape, wondering if Tos'un might be looking back at him.

* * * * *

He was.

Tos'un Armgo let his gaze linger on the thickest line of black smoke drifting skyward and dissipating into the smothering gray of the continuing overcast. Though he didn't know the specific players in that scene—whether or not Albondiel or Sinnafain, or any of the others he had met, even traveled with, might be up there—they were Moonwood elves. Of that he had no doubt.

They were growing bolder, and more aggressive, and Tos'un knew why. The clouds would soon break, and the wind would shift southward, ferrying the milder breezes of spring. The elves sought to create chaos among the orc ranks. They wanted to inspire terror, confusion, and cowardice, to erode King Obould's foundations before the turn of the season allowed for the orc army to march against the dwarves in the south.

Or even across the river to the east, to the Moonwood, their precious home.

A pang of loneliness stabbed at Tos'un's thoughts and heart as he looked back at the burned village. He would have liked to join in that battle. More than that, the drow admitted, he would have liked departing with the victorious elves.

CHAPTER
FAREWELL

A thousand candles flickered on the northern side of the twenty-five foot square chamber, set in rows on a series of steps carved into the wall for just that purpose. A slab of gray stone leaned against the eastern wall, beside the closed wooden door. It had been expertly cut from the center of the floor, and on it, engraved in the Dethek runes of the dwarves:

DELENIA CURTIE OF LUSKAN AND MITHRAL HALL
WIFE OF WULFGAR, SON OF KING BRUENOR
MOTHER OF COLSON
WHO FELL TO THE DARKNESS OF OBOULD
IN THE YEAR OF THE UNSTRUNG HARP
1371 DALERECKONING
TO THIS HUMAN
MORADIN OFFERS HIS CUP
AND DUMATHOIN WHISPERS HIS SECRETS
BLESSED IS SHE

Over the hole that had been made when the slab was removed, a stone sarcophagus rested on two heavy wooden beams. A pair of ropes ran out to either side from under it. The box was closed and sealed after Wulfgar paid his final respects.

Wulfgar, Bruenor, Drizzt, Catti-brie, and Regis stood solemnly in a line before the sarcophagus and opposite the candles, while the other guests attending the small ceremony fanned out in a semi-circle behind them. Across from them, the cleric Cordio Muffinhead read prayers to the dead. Wulfgar paid no heed to those words, but used the rhythms of Cordio's resonant voice to find a state of deep contemplation. He recalled the long and arduous road that had brought him there, from his fall in the grasp of the yochlol in the battle for Mithral Hall, to his years of torment at the hands of Errtu. He looked at Catti-brie only once, and regretted what might have been.

What might have been but could not be reclaimed, he knew. There was an old Dwarvish saying: *k'niko burger braz-pex strame*—"too much rubble over the vein"—to describe the point at which a mine simply wasn't worth the effort anymore. So it was with him and Catti-brie. Neither of them could go back. Wulfgar had known that when he had taken Delly as his wife, and he had been sincere in their relationship. That gave him comfort, but it only somewhat mitigated the pain and guilt. For though he had been sincere with Delly, he had not been much of a husband, had not heard her quiet pleas, had not placed her above all else.

Or could he even do that? Were his loyalties to Delly or to Mithral Hall?

He shook his head and pushed that justification away before it could find root. His responsibility was to bring both of those responsibilities to a place of agreement. Whatever his duties to Bruenor and Mithral Hall, he had failed Delly. To hide from that would be a lie, and a lie to himself would destroy him.

Cordio's chanting anesthetized him. He looked at the casket, and he remembered Delly Curtie, the good woman who had been his wife, and who had done so well by Colson. He accepted his own failure and he moved past it. To honor Delly would be to serve Colson, and to make of himself a better man.

Delly forgave him, he knew in his heart, as he would forgive her if the situation had been reversed. That was all they could do in the end, really. Do their best, accept their mistakes, and go on to a better way.

He felt her spirit all around him, and in him. His mind scrolled through images of the woman, flashes of Delly's smile, the tenderness on her face when they finished making love—a look, he knew without asking, that was reserved for him alone.

He recalled a moment when he had observed Delly dancing with Colson, unaware of his presence. In all the time he had known her, never had Wulfgar seen her so animated, so free, so full of life. It was as if, through Colson, and for just that moment, she had found a bit of her own childhood—or the childhood that harsh circumstances had never allowed her to truly experience. That had been Wulfgar's rawest glance into the soul of Delly Curtie, more so even than in their lovemaking.

That was the image that lingered, the image he burned into his consciousness. Forever after, he decided, when he thought of Delly Curtie, he would first envision her dancing with Colson.

A wistful smile creased his face by the time Cordio stopped his chanting. It took Wulfgar a few moments to realize that everyone was looking at him.

"He asked if you wished to say a few words," Drizzt quietly explained to Wulfgar.

Wulfgar nodded and looked around at the dwarves, and at Regis and Catti-brie.

"This is not where Delly Curtie would have chosen to be buried," he said bluntly. "For all of her love for Clan Battlehammer, she was not fond of the tunnels. But she would be . . . she *is* honored that so fine a folk have done this for her."

He looked at the casket and smiled again. "You deserved so much more than life ever offered to you. I am a better man for having known you, and I will carry you with me forever. Farewell, my wife and my love."

He felt a hand clasp his own, and turned to see Catti-brie beside him. Drizzt put his hand over both of theirs, and Regis and Bruenor moved to join in.

Delly deserved better, Wulfgar thought, and I am not deserving of such friends as these.

* * * * *

The sun climbed into the bright blue sky across the Surbrin before them. To the north along the battlements, the hammers rang out, along with a chorus of dwarf voices, singing and whistling as they went about their important work. Across the Surbrin, too, many dwarves and humans were hard at work, strengthening the bridge abutments and pillars and bringing up many of the materials they'd need to properly construct the bridge that summer. For a strong hint of spring was surely in the air that fifth day of Ches, and behind the five friends, rivulets of water danced down the stony mountainside.

"It will be a short window, I am told," Drizzt said to the others. "The river is not yet swollen with the spring melt, and so the ferry can cross. But once the melt is on in full, the pilots do not expect to execute many crossings. If you cross, you may not be able to get back until after the onset of Tarsakh, at least."

"There is no choice in the matter," said Wulfgar.

"It will take you tendays to get to Silverymoon and Sundabar and back anyway," said Regis.

"Especially since my legs aren't ready for running," said Catti-brie. She smiled as she spoke to let the others know that there was no regret or bitterness in her off-handed comment.

"Well, we ain't waitin' for Ches to become an old man," Bruenor grumbled. "If the weather's holding, then we're out for Gauntlgrym in days. I'm not for knowin' how long that's to take, but it'll be tendays, I'm guessing. Might be the whole durned summer."

Drizzt watched Wulfgar in particular, and noted the distance in the man's blue eyes. Bruenor might as well have been talking about Menzoberranzan or Calimport for all Wulfgar seemed to note or to care. He looked outward—to Colson.

And farther, Drizzt knew. It didn't matter to Wulfgar whether or not the Surbrin could be crossed again.

A few moments of silence slipped past, the five friends standing there in the morning sun. Drizzt knew that he should savor that moment, should burn it into his memory. Across from Bruenor, Regis shifted uneasily, and when Drizzt looked that way, he saw the halfling looking back at him, as if at a loss. Drizzt nodded at him and offered an accepting smile.

"The ferry docks," said Catti-brie, turning their attention to the river, where the boat was being quickly off-loaded. "Our road awaits."

Wulfgar nodded for her to lead on and make the arrangements, and with a curious glance at him, she did so, limping slightly and using Taulmaril as a crutch. As she went, Catti-brie kept glancing back, trying to decipher the curious scene. Wulfgar wore a serious expression as he spoke to the three, then he hugged each of them in turn. He ended with his hand firmly grasping Drizzt's wrist, the drow similarly holding him, and the two staring long at each other, with respect and what seemed to Catti-brie to be solemn agreement.

She suspected what that might foretell, but she turned her attention back to the river and the ferry, and cast those suspicions aside.

* * * * *

"Come on, elf," Bruenor said before Wulfgar had even caught up to Catti-brie at the ferry. "I'm wanting to get our maps in order for the trip. No time for wasting!"

Muttering to himself and rubbing his hands together, the dwarf moved back into the complex. Regis and Drizzt waited just a bit longer then turned and followed. They slowed in unison as they neared the open doors and the darkness of the corridor, and turned to look back to the river, and to the sun climbing into the sky beyond.

"Summer cannot come quickly enough for me," said Regis.

Drizzt didn't answer, but his expression wasn't one of disagreement.

"Though I almost fear it," Regis added, more quietly.

"Because the orcs will come?" asked Drizzt.

"Because others may not," said Regis, and he tossed a glance at the departing duo, who had boarded the ferry and were looking to the east, and not back.

Again, Drizzt didn't disagree. Bruenor was too preoccupied to see it, perhaps, but Regis's fears had confirmed Drizzt's suspicions about Wulfgar.

* * * * *

"Pwent's going with us," Bruenor announced to Drizzt and Regis when they caught up to him in his audience chamber later that day. As he spoke, he reached down to the side of his stone throne, lifted a pack, and tossed it to Drizzt.

"Just you three?" Regis asked, but he bit off the question as Bruenor reached down again and brought up a second pack, and tossed it the halfling's way.

Regis gave a little squeak and managed to get out of the way. The pack didn't hit the floor, though, for Drizzt snapped out his hand and plucked it from the air. The drow kept his arm extended, holding the pack out to the startled halfling.

"I'm needin' a sneak. Yerself's a sneak," Bruenor explained. "Besides, ye're the only one who's been into the place."

"Into the place?"

"Ye fell in the hole."

"I was only in there for a few moments!" Regis protested. "I didn't see anything other than the wag—"

"That makes yerself the expert," stated Bruenor.

Regis looked to Drizzt for help, but the drow just stood there holding out the satchel. With a look back to Bruenor and his unrelenting grin, the halfling gave a resigned sigh and took the pack.

"Torgar's coming, too," said Bruenor. "I'm wantin' them Mirabar boys in this from the beginning. Gauntlgrym's a Delzoun place, and Delzoun's including Torgar and his boys."

"Five, then?" asked Drizzt.

"And Cordio's making it six," Bruenor replied.

"In the morning?" asked Drizzt.

"The spring, the first of Tarsakh," Regis argued—rather helplessly, since he was holding a full pack, and since, as he spoke, he noted that Pwent, Torgar, and Cordio all entered the room from a side door, all with heavy packs slung over their shoulders, and Pwent in his full suit of ridged and spiked armor.

"No time better'n this time," said Bruenor. He stood up and gave a whistle, and a door opposite from the one the three dwarves had just used pushed open and Banak Brawnanvil rolled himself out. Behind him came a pair of younger dwarves, carrying Bruenor's mithral armor, his one-horned helmet, and his old and battle-worn axe.

"Seems our friend has been plotting without us," Drizzt remarked to Regis, who didn't seem amused.

"Yerself's got the throne and the hall," Bruenor said to Banak, and he moved down from the dais and tightly clasped his old friend's offered hand. "Ye don't be too good a steward, so that me folk won't want me back."

"Not possible, me king," said Banak. "I'd make 'em take ye back, even if it's just to guard me throne."

76

Bruenor answered that with a wide, toothy smile, his white teeth shining through his bushy orange-red beard. Few dwarves of Clan Battlehammer, or elsewhere for that matter, would speak to him with such irreverence, but Banak had more than earned the right.

"I'm goin' in peace because I'm knowing that I'm leaving yerself in charge behind me," Bruenor said in all seriousness.

Banak's smile disappeared and he gave his king a grateful nod.

"Come on, then, elf, and yerself, Rumblebelly," Bruenor called, slipping his mithral mail over his head and dropping his battered old one-horned helm on his head. "Me boys've dug us a hole out in the west so that we're not needing to cross all the way back over Garumn's Gorge, then back around the mountain. No time for wasting!"

"Yeah, but I'm not thinking that stoppin' to wipe out a fort o' them orcs is wastin' time," Thibbledorf Pwent remarked as he eagerly led the other two across in front of Drizzt and Regis and over to Bruenor. "Might that we'll find the dog Obould himself and be rid o' the beast all at once."

"Simply wonderful," Regis muttered, taking the pack and slinging it over his shoulder. He gave another sigh, one full of annoyance, when he saw that his small mace was strapped to the flap of the pack. Bruenor had taken care of every little detail, it seemed.

"The road to adventure, my friend," said Drizzt.

Regis smirked at him, but Drizzt only laughed. How many times had he seen that same look from the halfling over the years? Always the reluctant adventurer. But Drizzt knew, and so did everyone else in the room, that Regis was always there when needed. The sighs were just a game, a ritual that somehow allowed Regis to muster his heart and his resolve.

"I am pleased that we have an expert to lead us down this hole," Drizzt remarked quietly as they fell into line behind the trio of dwarves.

Regis sighed.

It occurred to Drizzt as they passed the room where Delly had just been interred that some were leaving who wanted to stay, and some were staying who wanted to leave. He thought of Wulfgar and wondered if that pattern would hold.

CHAPTER

THAT TINGLING FEELING

It looked like a simple bear den, a small hole covered by a crisscross of broken branches blanketed by snow. Tos'un Armgo knew better, for he had built that facade. The bear den was at the end of a long but shallow tunnel, chosen because it allowed Tos'un to watch a small work detail composed mostly of goblins, constructing a bridge over a trench they apparently hoped would serve as an irrigation canal through the melt.

Northeast of that, sheltered in a ravine, the elves of the Moonwood plotted. If they decided on an attack, it would come soon, that night or the next day, for it was obvious that they were running short on supplies, and shorter on arrows. Tos'un, following them south to north then northeast, realized that they were heading for their preferred ford across the Surbrin and back to the sheltering boughs of the Moonwood. The drow suspected that they wouldn't ignore a last chance at a fight.

The sun climbed in the sky behind him, and Tos'un had to squint against the painful glare off the wet snow. He noted movement in the sky to the north, and caught a glimpse of a flying horse before it swerved out of sight behind a rocky mountain jag.

The elves favored midday assaults against the usually nocturnal goblins.

Tos'un didn't have to go far to find a fine vantage point for the coming festivities. He slipped into a recess between a pair of high stones, settling back just in time to see the first volley of elven arrows lead the way into the goblin camp. The creatures began howling, hooting, and running around.

So predictable, Tos'un's fingers signaled in the intricate, silent drow code.

Of course, he had seen many goblins in his decades in the Underdark, in Menzoberranzan, where the ugly things were more numerous among the slaves than any other race—other than the kobolds who lived in the channels along the great chasm known as the Clawrift. Goblins could be molded into fierce fighting groups, but the amount of work that required made it hardly worth the effort. Their natural "fight or flight" balance leaned very heavily in the direction of the latter.

And so it was in the valley below him. Goblins rushed every which way, and on came the skilled and disciplined elf warriors, their fine blades gleaming in the sun. It looked to be a fast and uneventful rout.

But then a yellow banner, shot with red so that it looked like the bloodshot eye of an orc, appeared in the west, moving quickly through a pass between a pair of small, round-topped hills. Tos'un peered hard, and harder still as the standard-bearer and its cohorts came into view. He could almost smell them from his perch. They were orcs, but huge by orc standards, even more broad-shouldered than Obould's elite guards, some even bigger than Obould himself.

So caught up in the spectacle, Tos'un stood up and leaned forward, out of the shelter of the stones. He looked back to the rout, and saw that there, too, things had changed, for other groups of those hulking orcs had appeared, some coming up from under the snow near the center of the battle.

"A trap for the elves," the drow whispered in disbelief. A myriad of thoughts flitted through his mind at that realization. Did he want the elves destroyed? Did he care?

He didn't allow himself time to sort through those emotions, though, for the drow realized that he, too, might get swept up in the tumult— and that was something he most certainly did not want.

He looked back to the approaching banner, then to the fight, then back again, measuring the time. With a quick glance all around to ensure his own safety, he rushed out from his perch and back to the hidden tunnel entrance. When he got there, he saw that the battle had been fully joined, and fully reversed.

The elves, badly outnumbered, were on the run. They didn't flee like the goblins, though, and kept their defenses in place against incursions from the brutish orcs. They even managed a couple of stop-and-pivot maneuvers that allowed them to send a volley of arrows at the orc mass.

But that dark wall rolled on after them.

The winged horse appeared again, flying low over the battlefield then climbing gradually as it passed over the orcs, who of course threw a few spears in its direction. The rider and pegasus went up even higher as they glided over the elves.

The rider meant to direct the retreat, obviously, and good fortune sent the winged horse in Tos'un's general direction. As it neared, the drow's eyes widened, for though looking up at the midday sky surely stung his sensitive eyes, he recognized that elf rider, Sinnafain.

For a moment, the drow held his position just inside the tunnel, not sure whether to retreat through the passage or go back out into Sinnafain's view.

Hardly aware of his movements, he came out of that hole and waved at Sinnafain, and when she didn't look his way, he called out to her.

What are you doing? Khazid'hea imparted to him.

The sudden jerk of the reins had the pegasus banking sharply and told Tos'un that Sinnafain had spotted him. He took some comfort in the fact that her next movement was not to draw out her bow.

You would go back to them? Khazid'hea asked and the telepathic communication was edged with no small amount of anger.

Sinnafain brought the winged horse in a slow turn, her eyes locked on the drow the entire time. She was too far away for Tos'un to see her face or fathom what she might be thinking, but still she did not draw her bow. Nor had she signaled to her retreating friends to veer away.

Drizzt will kill you! Khazid'hea warned. *When he takes me from you, you will find yourself defenseless against the truth-finding spells of elf clerics!*

Tos'un lifted the twig barrier that covered his hole, and began motioning to the entrance.

Sinnafain continued to guide the pegasus in a slow circle. When she at last turned back to her companions, Tos'un sprinted off to the side, disappearing into the shadows of the foothills, much to the relief of his demanding sword.

The drow glanced back only one time, to see the elves filtering into the tunnel. He looked up for the pegasus, but it had flown over the ridge and out of sight at that moment.

But Sinnafain had trusted him.

Unbelievably, Sinnafain had trusted him.

Tos'un wasn't sure whether he should take pride in that, or whether his respect for the elves had just diminished.

Perhaps a bit of both.

* * * * *

Sinnafain couldn't track their progress, nor could she join her comrades in the tunnel, obviously, while riding Sunrise. She came back over the high ridge and flew near the entrance of the small cave. She drew out her bow and began peppering the leading edge of the orc advance.

She kept up her barrage even after all the elves had disappeared underground. But the huge orcs carried heavy shields to frustrate such attacks, and Sinnafain could only hope that she had held them back long enough for her friends to escape. She put Sunrise up higher then, and angled back the other way, over the rise once more. She looked for Tos'un as much as for her friends, but there was no sign of the drow.

A long while later, with Sunrise tiring beneath her, the elf was finally able to breathe a sigh of relief, as a flash of white from a copse of trees some distance to the east signaled to her that Albondiel and the other elves had gotten through the tunnel.

Sinnafain took a roundabout route to get to them, not wanting to tip off any orc spotters who might watch her descending from on high, and by the time she got down to the ground, much activity was already underway. Deep in the woods, in a small clearing, the wounded had been laid out side by side, with priests tending them. Another group carried heavy logs and stones to seal the tunnel exit, and the rest had taken to the trees on the perimeter of the copse, setting up a defensive line that allowed them many overlapping angles of fire on approaching enemies.

As she walked Sunrise along a path through the trees, Sinnafain heard whispers of King Obould over and over again, many of the elves certain that he had come. She found Albondiel near the wounded, standing off to the side of the field and sorting the extra packs and weapons.

"You saved many," Albondiel greeted when she approached. "Had you not directed us to that tunnel, more of us would have fallen. Perhaps a complete rout."

Sinnafain thought to mention that it was not her doing, but that of a certain drow, but she kept the thought to herself. "How many were taken down?"

"Four casualties," Albondiel said grimly. He nodded toward the small field, where the quartet of wounded lay on blankets on the snow. "Two of them were wounded seriously, perhaps mortally."

"We . . . *I,* should have seen the trap from on high," Sinnafain said, turning back to the ridge in the east that blocked the view of the battlefield.

"The orc ambush was well set," Albondiel replied. "Those who prepared this battlefield understood our tactics well. They have studied us and learned to counter our methods. Perhaps it is time for us to head back across the Surbrin."

"We are low on supplies," Sinnafain reminded him.

"Perhaps it is time for us to *stay* across the Surbrin," Albondiel clarified.

Again, thoughts of a certain dark elf popped into Sinnafain's mind. Had Tos'un betrayed them? He had fought beside them for a short while, and he knew much of their tactics. Plus, he was a drow, and no race in all the world knew better how to lay an ambush than the treacherous dark elves. Though of course, he had shown the elves the way to escape. With any other race, that alone might serve to dispel Sinnafain's suspicions. But Sinnafain could not allow herself to forget that Tos'un was a dark elf, and no Drizzt Do'Urden, who had proven himself repeatedly over a matter of years. Perhaps Tos'un was playing the elves and orcs against each other for personal gain, or simply for his own amusement.

"Sinnafain?" Albondiel asked, drawing her from her contemplations. "The Surbrin? The Moonwood?"

"You believe that we are finished here?" Sinnafain asked.

"The weather warms, and the orcs will find it easier to move in the coming days. They will be less isolated from each other and so our work here will become more difficult."

"And they have taken note of us."

"It is time to leave," said Albondiel.

Sinnafain nodded and looked to the east. In the distance, the silvery line of the Surbrin could just be seen, flickering out on the horizon.

"Would that we could collect Tos'un on our way," said Sinnafain. "I have much to ask that one."

Albondiel looked at her with surprise for just a few moments then nodded his agreement. Though seemingly out of context, it sounded like a reasonable desire—of course they both knew that they weren't going to catch a drow in those wilds anytime soon.

* * * * *

I know them, Tos'un assured the doubting Khazid'hea. *Dnark is chieftain of an important tribe. I was the one who coaxed him into Obould's coalition before they ever marched from the Spine of the World.*

Much has happened, Khazid'hea reminded him, *between Tos'un and Obould. If these three know of your last encounter with the orc king, they will not welcome you.*

They were not there, Tos'un assured the sword.

They have not heard of the fall of Kaer'lic Suun Wett? Khazid'hea asked. *Can you be certain?*

Even if they have, they are well aware of Obould's temper, Tos'un imparted. *They will accept that he was outraged at Kaer'lic, and so he killed her. Do you believe that any of these orcs have not lost friends to the temper of Obould? And yet they remain loyal to him.*

You risk much.

I risk nothing, Tos'un argued. *If Dnark and his friends know that Obould hunts for me, or if they have concluded that I am in league with the elves, then I . . . then we, will have to kill them. I did not expect that such a result would displease Khazid'hea.*

There, he had communicated the magic words, he knew, for the sword fell silent in his thoughts, and he even sensed eagerness coming from it. He considered the exchange as he made his way down toward the trio of orcs, who had drifted off to the side of the construction area where the unusually large orcs had gathered. He came to the conclusion that he had been paid a compliment, that Khazid'hea did not want to be pried from his grasp.

He chose his path to the three orcs carefully, allowing himself a fast route of escape should the need arise—and he feared it would. Several times he paused to search the surrounding area for any guards he might have missed.

Still some distance from the three, he called out the expected, respectful refrain to the chieftain. "Hail Dnark, may the Wolf Jaw bite strong," he said in his best Orcish, but with no attempt to hide his Underdark drow accent. He watched carefully then to gauge their initial reaction, knowing that to be the bare truth.

All three turned his way, their expressions showing surprise, even shock. Tellingly, however, not one flinched toward a weapon.

"To the throat of your enemy," Tos'un finished the Wolf Jaw tribe's salute. He continued his approach, noting that Ung-thol, the older shaman, visibly relaxed, but that the younger Toogwik Tuk remained very much on edge.

"Well met, again," Tos'un offered, and he climbed the last small rise to gain the sheltered flat ground the trio had staked out. "We have come far from the holes in the Spine of the World, as I predicted to you those months ago."

"Greetings, Tos'un of Menzoberranzan," said Dnark.

The drow measured the chieftain's voice as cautious, and neither warm or cold.

"I am surprised to see you," Dnark finished.

"We have learned the fate of your companions," Ung-thol added.

Tos'un stiffened, and had to consciously remind himself not to grasp his sword hilts. "Yes, Donnia Soldou and Ad'non Kareese," he said. "I have heard their sad fate, and a curse upon the murderous Drizzt Do'Urden."

The three orcs exchanged smug grins. They knew of the murdered priestess, Tos'un realized.

"And pity to Kaer'lic," he said lightly, as if it didn't really matter. "Foolish was she who angered mighty Obould." He found a surprising response to that from Toogwik Tuk, for the young orc's smile disappeared, and his lips grew tight.

"She and you, so it is said," Ung-thol replied.

"I will prove my value again."

"To Obould?" asked Dnark.

The question caught the drow off-balance, for he had no idea of where the chieftain might be going with it.

"Is there another who would seek that value?" he asked, keeping enough sarcasm out of his tone so that Dnark might seize it as an honest question if he so chose.

"There are many above ground now, and scattered throughout the Kingdom of Many-Arrows," said Dnark. He glanced back at the hulking orcs milling around the construction area. "Grguch of Clan Karuck has come."

"I just witnessed his ferocity in routing the cursed surface elves."

"Strong allies," said Dnark.

"To Obould?" Tos'un asked without hesitation, turning the question back in similar measure.

"To Gruumsh," said Dnark with a toothy grin. "To the destruction of Clan Battlehammer and all the wretched dwarves and all the ugly elves."

"Strong allies," said Tos'un.

They are not pleased with King Obould, Khazid'hea said in the drow's mind. Tos'un didn't respond, other than to not disagree. *An interesting turn.*

Again the drow didn't disagree. A tingling feeling came over him, that exciting sensation that befell many of Lady Lolth's followers when they first discovered that an opportunity for mischief might soon present itself.

He thought of Sinnafain and her kin, but didn't dwell on them. The joy of chaos came precisely from the reality that it was often so very easy, and not requiring too much deep contemplation. Perhaps the coming mayhem would benefit the elves, perhaps the orcs, Dnark or Obould, one or both. That was not for Tos'un to determine. His duty was to ensure that no matter which way the tumult broke, he would be in the best position to survive and to profit.

For all of his time with the elves of late, for all of his fantasies of living among the surface folk, Tos'un Armgo remained, first and foremost, drow.

He sensed clearly that Khazid'hea very much approved.

* * * * *

Grguch was not pleased. He stomped across the hillside before the tunnel entrance and all of Clan Karuck fled before him. All except for Hakuun, of course. Hakuun could not flee before Grguch. It was not permitted. If Grguch decided that he wanted to kill Hakuun then Hakuun had to accept that as his fate. Being the shaman of Clan Karuck carried such a responsibility, and it was one that Hakuun's family had accepted throughout the generations— and was one that had cost more than a few of his family their lives.

He knew that Grguch would not cleave him in half, though. The chieftain was angry that the elves had escaped, but the battle could not be called anything but a victory for Clan Karuck. Not only had they stung a few of the elves, but they had sent them running, and had it not been for that troublesome tunnel, the raiding elf band never would have escaped complete and utter ruin.

The hulking brutes of Clan Karuck could not follow them through that tunnel, however, to Grguch's ultimate frustration.

"This will not end here," he said in Hakuun's face.

"Of course not."

"I desired a greater statement to be made in our first meeting with these ugly faerie folk."

"The fleeing elves wore expressions of terror," Hakuun replied. "That will spread back to their people."

"Right before we fall upon them more decisively."

Hakuun paused, expecting the order.

"Plan it," said Grguch. "To their very home."

Hakuun nodded, and Grguch seemed satisfied with that and turned away, barking orders at the others. Elves were just the sort of cowardly creatures to run away and sneak back for quiet murder, of course, and so the chieftain began setting his defenses and his scouts, leaving Hakuun alone with his thoughts.

Or so Hakuun believed.

He flinched then froze when the foot-long serpent landed on his shoulder, and he held his breath, as he always did on those thankfully rare occasions when he found himself in the company of Jaculi—for that was the name that Jack had given him, the name of the winged serpent that Jack wore as a disguise when venturing out of his private workshops.

"I wish that you had informed me of your departure," Jack said in Hakuun's ear.

"I did not want to disturb you," Hakuun meekly replied, for it was hard for him to hold his steadiness with Jack's tongue flicking in his ear, close enough to send one of his forked lightning bolts right through the other side of poor Hakuun's head.

"Clan Karuck disturbs me often," Jack reminded him. "Sometimes I believe that you have told the others of me."

"Never that, O Awful One!"

Jack's laughter came out as a hiss. When he had first begun his domination and deception of the orcs those decades before, pragmatism alone had ruled his actions. But through the years he had come to accept the truth of it: he liked scaring the wits out of those ugly creatures! Truly, that was one of the few pleasures remaining for Jack the Gnome, who lived a life of simplicity and . . . And what? Boredom, he knew, and it stung him to admit it to himself. In the secret corners of his heart, Jack understood precisely why he had followed Karuck out of the caves: because his fear of danger, even of death, could not surmount his fear of letting everything stay the same.

"Why have you ventured out of the Underdark?" he demanded.

Hakuun shook his head. "If the tidings are true then there is much to be gained here."

"For Clan Karuck?"

"Yes."

"For Jaculi?"

Hakuun gulped and swallowed hard, and Jack hiss-laughed again into his ear.

"For Gruumsh," Hakuun dared whisper.

As weakly as it was said, that still gave Jack pause. For all of his domination of Hakuun's family, their fanatical service to Gruumsh had never been in question. It had once taken Jack an afternoon of torture to make one of Hakuun's ancestors—his grandfather, Jack believed, though he couldn't really remember—utter a single word against Gruumsh, and even then, the priest had soon after passed his duties down to his chosen son and killed himself in Gruumsh's name.

As he had in the cave, the gnome wizard sighed. With Gruumsh invoked, he wasn't about to turn Clan Karuck around.

"We shall see," he whispered into Hakuun's ear, and said to himself as well, a resigned acceptance that sometimes the stubborn orcs had their own agenda.

Perhaps he could find some amusement and profit out of it, and really, what did he have to lose? He sniffed the air again, and again sensed that something was different.

"There are many orcs about," he said.

"Tens of thousands," Hakuun confirmed. "Come to the call of King Obould Many-Arrows."

Many-Arrows, Jack thought, a name that registered deep in his memories of long ago. He thought of Citadel Fel . . . Citadel Felb . . . Fel-something-or-other, a place of dwarves. Jack didn't much like dwarves. They annoyed him at least as much as did the orcs, with their hammering and stupid chanting that they somehow, beyond all reason, considered song.

"We shall see," he said again to Hakuun, and noting that the ugly Grguch was fast approaching, Jack slithered down under Hakuun's collar to nestle in the small of his back. Every now and then, he flicked his forked tongue against Hakuun's bare flesh just for the fun of hearing the shaman stutter in his discussion with the beastly Grguch.

PART 2

GAUNTLGRYM

GAUNTLGRYM

I came from the Underdark, the land of monsters. I lived in Icewind Dale, where the wind can freeze a man solid, or a bog can swallow a traveler so quickly that he'll not likely understand what is happening to him soon enough to let out a cry, unless it is one muffled by loose mud. Through Wulfgar I have glimpsed the horrors of the Abyss, the land of demons, and could there be any place more vile, hate-filled, and tormenting? It is indeed a dangerous existence.

I have surrounded myself with friends who will fearlessly face those monsters, the wind and the bog, and the demons, with a snarl and a growl, a jaw set and a weapon held high. None would face them more fearlessly than Bruenor, of course.

But there is something to shake even that one, to shake us all as surely as if the ground beneath our feet began to tremble and break away.

Change.

In any honest analysis, change is the basis of fear, the idea of something new, of some paradigm that is unfamiliar, that is beyond our experiences so completely that we cannot even truly predict where it will lead us. Change. Uncertainty.

It is the very root of our most primal fear—the fear of death—that one change, that one unknown against which we construct elaborate scenarios and "truisms" that may or may not be true at all. These constructions, I think, are an extension of the routines of our lives. We dig ruts with the sameness of our daily paths, and drone and rail against those routines while we, in fact, take comfort in them. We awake and construct our days of habit, and follow the norms we have built fast, solid, and bending only a bit in our daily existence. Change is the unrolled die, the unused *sava* piece. It is exciting and frightening only when we hold some power over it, only when there is a potential reversal of course, difficult though it may be, within our control.

Absent that safety line of real choice, absent that sense of some control, change is merely frightening. Terrifying, even.

An army of orcs does not scare Bruenor. Obould Many-Arrows does not scare Bruenor. But what Obould represents, particularly if the orc king halts his march and establishes a kingdom, and more especially if the other kingdoms of the Silver Marches accept this new paradigm, terrifies Bruenor Battlehammer to the heart of his being and to the core tenets of his faith. Obould threatens more than Bruenor's kin, kingdom, and life. The orc's designs shake the very belief system that binds Bruenor's kin, the very purpose of Mithral Hall, the understanding of what it is to be a dwarf, and the dwarven concept of where the orcs fit into that stable continuum. He would not say it openly, but I suspect that Bruenor hopes the orcs will attack, that they will, in the end, behave in accordance with his expectations of orcs and of all goblinkind. The other possibility is too dissonant, too upsetting, too contrary to Bruenor's very identity for him to entertain the plausibility, indeed the probability, that it would result in less suffering for all involved.

I see before me the battle for the heart of Bruenor Battlehammer, and for the hearts of all the dwarves of the Silver Marches.

Easier by far to lift a weapon and strike dead a known enemy, an orc.

In all the cultures I have known, with all the races I have walked beside, I have observed that when beset by such dissonance, by events that are beyond control and that plod along at their own pace, the frustrated onlookers often seek out a beacon, a focal point—a god, a person, a place, a magical item—which they believe will set all the world aright. Many are the whispers in Mithral Hall that King Bruenor will fix it, all of it, and make everything as it had been before the onslaught of Obould. Bruenor has earned their respect many times over, and wears the mantle of hero among his kin as comfortably and deservedly as has any dwarf in the history of the clan. For most of the dwarves here, then, King Bruenor has become the beacon and focal point of hope itself.

Which only adds to Bruenor's responsibility, because when a frightened people put their faith in an individual, the ramifications of incompetence, recklessness, or malfeasance are multiplied many times over. And so becoming the focus of hope only adds to Bruenor's tension. Because he knows that it is not true, and that their expectations may well be beyond him. He cannot convince Lady Alustriel of Silverymoon or any of the other leaders, not even King Emerus Warcrown of Citadel Felbarr, to march in force against Obould. And to go out alone with Mithral Hall's own forces would lead to the wholesale slaughter of Clan Battlehammer. Bruenor understands that he has to wear the mantle not only of hero, but of savior, and it is for him a terrible burden.

And so Bruenor, too, has engaged in deflection and wild expectation, has found a focal point on which to pin his hopes. The most common phrase he has spoken throughout this winter has been, "Gauntlgrym, elf."

Gauntlgrym. It is a legend among Clan Battlehammer and all the Delzoun dwarves. It is the name of their common heritage, an immense city of splendor, wealth, and strength that represents to every descendant of the Delzoun tribes the apex of dwarven civilization. It is, perhaps, history wound with myth, a likely unintentional lionizing of that which once was. As heroes of old take on more gigantic proportions with each passing generation, so too does this other focal point of hope and pride expand.

"Gauntlgrym, elf," Bruenor says with steady determination. All of his answers lie there, he is certain. In Gauntlgrym, Bruenor will find a path to unravel the doings of King Obould. In Gauntlgrym, he will discover how to put the orcs back in their holes, and more importantly, how to realign the races of the Silver Marches into proper position, into places that make sense to an old, immovable dwarf.

He believes that we found this magical kingdom on our journey here from the Sword Coast. He has to believe that this unremarkable sinkhole in a long-dead pass was really the entrance to a place where he can find his answers.

Otherwise he has to become the answer for his anxious people. And Bruenor knows that their faith is misplaced, for at present, he has no answer to the puzzle that is Obould.

Thus, he says, "Gauntlgrym, elf," with the same conviction that a devout believer will utter the name of his savior god.

We will go to this place, this hole in the ground in a barren pass in the west. We will go and find Gauntlgrym, whatever that may truly mean. Perhaps Bruenor's instincts are correct—could it be that Moradin told him of this in his days of near death? Perhaps we will find something entirely different, but that will still bring to us, to Bruenor, the clarity he needs to find the answers for Mithral Hall.

Fixated and desperate as he is, and as his people are, Bruenor doesn't yet understand that the name he has affixed to our savior is not the point. The point is the search itself, for solutions and for the truth, and not the place he has determined as our goal.

"Gauntlgrym, elf."

Indeed.

—Drizzt Do'Urden

CHAPTER

The gates of Silverymoon, shining silver and with bars decorated like leafy vines, were closed, a clear signal that things were amiss in the Silver Marches. Stern-faced guards, elf and human, manned all posts along the city's wall and around a series of small stone houses that served as checkpoints for approaching visitors.

Catti-brie—limping more profoundly from her days on the road—and Wulfgar noted the tense looks coming their way. The woman merely smiled, though, understanding that her companion, nearly seven feet tall and with shoulders broad and strong, could elicit such trepidation even in normal times. Predictably, those nervous guards relaxed and even offered waves as the pair neared, as they came to recognize the barbarian in his trademark wolf-skin cloak and the woman who had often served as liaison between Mithral Hall and Silverymoon.

There was no call for the pair to stop or even slow as they passed the stone structures, and the gate parted before them without request. Several of the sentries near that gate and atop the wall even began clapping for Wulfgar and Catti-brie and more than a few "huzzahs" were shouted as they passed.

"With official word or for pleasure alone?" the commander of the guard asked the couple inside the city gates. He looked at Catti-brie with obvious concern. "Milady, are you injured?"

Catti-brie replied with a dismissive look, as if it did not matter, but the guard continued, "I will provide a coach for you at once!"

"I have walked from Mithral Hall through snow and mud," the woman replied. "I would not deny myself the joy of Silverymoon's meandering ways."

"But . . ."

"I will walk," Catti-brie said. "Do not deny me this pleasure."

The guard relented with a bow. "Lady Alustriel will be pleased by your arrival."

"And we will be pleased to see her," said Wulfgar.

"With official word from King Bruenor?" the commander asked again.

"With word more personal, but equally pressing," the barbarian answered. "You will announce us?"

"The courier is already on his way to the palace."

Wulfgar nodded his gratitude. "We will walk the ways of Silverymoon, a course not direct, and will arrive at Lady Alustriel's court before the sun has passed its zenith," he explained. "Pleased we are to be here—truly Silverymoon is a welcomed sight and a welcoming city for road-weary travelers. Our business here might well include you and your men as well, commander. . . ."

"Kenyon," said Catti-brie, for she had met the man on many occasions, though briefly at each.

"I am honored that you remember me, Lady Catti-brie," he said with another bow.

"We arrive in search of refugees who have come from Mithral Hall and may have crossed into your fairest of cities," said Wulfgar.

"Many have come," Kenyon admitted. "And many have left. But of course, we are at your disposal, son of Bruenor, on word of Lady Alustriel. Go and secure that word, I bid you."

Wulfgar nodded, and he and Catti-brie moved past the guard station.

With their road-weathered clothes, one with a magical bow as a crutch and the other a giant of a man with a magnificent warhammer strapped across his back, the pair stood out in the city of philosophers and poets, and many a curious look turned their way as they walked the winding, seemingly aimless avenues of the decorated city. As with every visitor to Silverymoon, no matter how many times one traversed the place, their eyes were continually drawn upward, studying the intricate designs and artwork that covered the walls of every building, and upward still, to the tapering spires that topped every structure. Most communities were an expression of utility, with structures built suitable to the elements of their environment and the threats of regional monsters. Cities of commerce were built with wide avenues, port cities with fortified harbors and breakwaters, and frontier towns with thick walls. Silverymoon stood above all of these, for it was an expression of utility, of course, but more than that, an expression of spirit. Security and commerce were facilitated, but they were not paramount to the needs of the soul, where the library was grander than the barracks and the avenues were designed to turn visitors and residents to the most spectacular of views, rather than as efficient straight lines to the marketplace or the rows of houses and mercantiles.

It was hard to arrive in Silverymoon with urgent business, for few could walk swiftly through those streets, and fewer still could focus the mind sufficiently to defeat the intrusions of beauty.

Contrary to Wulfgar's stated expectations, the sun had passed its zenith before Wulfgar and Catti-brie came in sight of Lady Alustriel's wondrous palace, but that was all right, for the experienced guards had informed the Lady of Silverymoon that such would be the case.

"The finest humans of Clan Battlehammer," said the tall woman, coming out from behind the curtains that separated this private section of her palatial audience chamber from the main, public promenade.

There was no overt malice in her humorous remark, though of course the couple standing before her, the adopted son and daughter of King Bruenor, were the only humans of Clan Battlehammer. Wulfgar smiled and chuckled, but Catti-brie didn't quite find that level of mirth within her.

She stared at the great woman, Lady Alustriel, one of the Seven Sisters and leader of magnificent Silverymoon. She only remembered to offer a bow when Wulfgar dipped beside her, and even then, Catti-brie did not lower her head as she bent, staring intently at Alustriel.

For despite herself, Catti-brie was intimidated. Alustriel was nearly six feet tall and undeniably beautiful, by human standards, by elven standards—by any standards. Even the creatures of the higher planes would be pleased by her presence, Catti-brie knew in her heart, for there was a luminescence and gravity about Alustriel that was somehow beyond mortal existence. Her hair was silver and lustrous, and hung thick to her shoulders, and her eyes could melt a man's heart or strip him of all courage at her will. Her gown was a simple affair, green with golden stitching, and just a few emeralds sewn for effect. Most kings and queens wore robes far more decorated and elaborate, of course, but Alustriel didn't need any ornamentation. Any room that she entered was her room to command.

She had never shown Catti-brie anything but kindness and friendship, and the two had been quite warm on occasion. But Catti-brie hadn't seen Alustriel much of late, and she could not help but feel somewhat smaller in the great woman's presence. Once she had been jealous of the Lady of Silverymoon, hearing rumors that Alustriel had been Drizzt's lover, and she had never discerned whether or not that had been the case.

Catti-brie smiled genuinely and laughed at herself, and pushed all of the negative thoughts aside. She couldn't be jealous where Drizzt was concerned anymore, nor could she feel diminished by anyone when she thought of her relationship with the drow.

What did it matter if the gods themselves bowed to Lady Alustriel? For Drizzt had chosen Catti-brie.

To Catti-brie's surprise, Alustriel walked right over and embraced her, and kissed her on the cheek.

"Too many months pass between our visits, milady," Alustriel said, moving Catti-brie back to arms' length. She reached up and pushed back a thick strand of Catti-brie's auburn hair. "How you manage to stay so beautiful, as if the dirt of the road cannot touch you, I will never know."

Catti-brie hardly knew how to reply.

"You could fight a battle with a thousand orcs," Alustriel went on, "slay them all—of course—and bloody your sword, your fist, and your boots. Not even that stain would diminish your glow."

Catti-brie gave a self-deprecating laugh. "Milady, you are too kind," she said. "Too kind for reason, I fear."

"Of course you do, daughter of Bruenor. You are a woman who grew up among dwarves, who hardly appreciated your charms and your beauty. You have no idea of how tall you would stand among those of your own race."

Catti-brie's face twisted a bit in confusion, not quite knowing how to take that.

"And that, too, is part of the charm of Catti-brie," said Alustriel. "Your humility is not calculated, it is intrinsic."

Catti-brie looked no less confused, and that drew a bit of laughter from Wulfgar. Catti-brie shot him a frown to silence him.

"The wind whispers that you have taken Drizzt as your husband," Alustriel said.

Still glancing Wulfgar's way as Alustriel spoke, Catti-brie noted a slight grimace on the barbarian's face—or maybe it was just her imagination.

"You are married?" Alustriel asked.

"Yes," Catti-brie replied. "But we have not celebrated in formal ceremony yet. We will wait for the darkness of Obould to recede."

Alustriel's face grew very serious. "That will be a long time, I fear."

"King Bruenor is determined that it will not."

"Indeed," said Alustriel, and she offered a hopeful little smile and a shrug. "I do hope you will celebrate your joining with Drizzt Do'Urden soon, both in Mithral Hall, and here in Silverymoon, as my honored guests. I will gladly open the palace to you, for many of my subjects would wish well the daughter of good King Bruenor and that most unusual dark elf."

"And many of your court would prefer that Drizzt remain in Mithral Hall," Catti-brie said, a bit more harshly than she had intended.

But Alustriel only laughed and nodded, for it was true enough, and undeniable. "Well, Fret likes him," she said, referring to her favored advisor, a most unusual and uniquely tidy dwarf. "And Fret likes you, and so do I—both of you. If I spent my time worrying over the pettiness and posturing of court lords and ladies, I would turn endless circles of appeasement and apology."

"When you doubt, then trust in Fret," Catti-brie said. She winked and Alustriel gave a hearty laugh and hugged her again.

As she did, she whispered into Catti-brie's ear, "Come here more often, I beg of you, with or without your stubborn dark elf companion."

She stepped up to Wulfgar then and wrapped him in a warm embrace. When she moved back to arms' length, a curious look came over her. "Son of Beornegar," she said quietly, respectfully.

Catti-brie's mouth dropped open in surprise at that, for only recently had Wulfgar been wearing that title more regularly, and it seemed to her as if Alustriel had somehow just discerned that.

"I see contentment in your blue eyes," Alustriel remarked. "You have not been at peace like this ever before—not even when I first met you, those many years ago."

"I was young then, and too strong of spirit," said Wulfgar.

"Can one ever be?"

Wulfgar shrugged. "Too anxious, then," he corrected.

"You hold your strength deeper now, because you are more secure in it, and in how you wish to use it."

Wulfgar's nod seemed to satisfy Alustriel, but Catti-brie just kept looking from the large man to the tall woman. She felt as if they were speaking in code, or half-saying secrets, the other half of which were known only to them.

"You are at peace," said Alustriel.

"And yet I am not," Wulfgar replied. "For my daugh—the girl, Colson, is lost to me."

"She was slain?"

Wulfgar shook his head immediately to calm the gentle woman. "Delly Curtie was lost to the hordes of Obould, but Colson lives. She was sent across the river in the company of refugees from the conquered northern lands."

"Here to Silverymoon?"

"That is what I would know," Wulfgar explained.

Alustriel nodded and stepped back, taking them both in with her protective stare.

"We could go from inn to inn," Catti-brie said. "But Silverymoon is no small city, nor is Sundabar, and there are many more villages about."

"You will remain right here as my guests," Alustriel insisted. "I will call out every soldier of Silverymoon's garrison, and will speak with the merchant guilds. You will have your answer in short time, I promise."

"You are too generous," Wulfgar said with a bow.

"Would King Bruenor, would Wulfgar or Catti-brie, offer any less to me or one of mine if we similarly came to Mithral Hall?"

That simple truth ended any forthcoming arguments from the two grateful travelers.

"We thought that we might travel to some of the common inns and ask around," Catti-brie said.

"And draw attention to your hunt?" Alustriel replied. "Would this person who has Colson wish to give the child back to you?"

Wulfgar shook his head, but Catti-brie said, "We don't know, but it is possible that she would not."

"Then better for you to remain here, as my guests. I have many contacts who frequent the taverns. It is important for a leader to hear the commoners' concerns. The answers you seek will be easily found—in Silverymoon, at least." She motioned to her attendants. "Take them and make them comfortable. I do believe that Fret wishes to see Catti-brie."

"He cannot suffer the dirt of the road upon me," Catti-brie remarked dryly.

"Only because he cares, of course."

"Or because he so despises dirt?"

"That too," Alustriel admitted.

Catti-brie looked to Wulfgar and offered a resigned shrug. She was pleasantly surprised to see him equally at ease with this arrangement. Apparently he understood that their work was better left to Alustriel, and that they could indeed relax and enjoy the respite at the luxurious palace of the Lady of Silverymoon.

"And she came without proper clothing, I'll wager!" came an obviously annoyed voice, a chant that sounded both melodic and sing-song like an elf, and resonant like the bellow of a dwarf—a most unusual dwarf.

Wulfgar and Catti-brie turned to see the fellow, dressed in a fine white gown with bright green trim, enter the room. He looked at Catti-brie and gave a disapproving sigh and a wag of his meticulously manicured stubby finger. Then he stopped and sighed again, and put his chin in one hand, his fingers stroking the thin line of his well-trimmed silver beard as he considered the task of transforming Catti-brie.

"Well met, Fret," Alustriel said. "It would seem that you have your work cut out for you. Do try not to break this one's spirit."

"You confuse spirit with odor, milady."

Catti-brie frowned, but it was hard for her to cover her inner smile.

"Fret would put perfume and bells on a tiger, I do believe," Alustriel said, and her nearby attendants shared a laugh at the dwarf's expense.

"And colored bows and paint for its nails," the tidy dwarf proudly replied. He walked up to Catti-brie, gave a "tsk tsk," and grabbed her by the elbow, pulling her along. "As we appreciate beauty, so it is our divine task to facilitate it. And so I shall. Now come along, child. You've a long bath to suffer."

Catti-brie flashed her smile back at Wulfgar. After their long and arduous journey, she planned to "suffer" it well.

Wulfgar's returned smile was equally genuine. He turned to Alustriel, saluted, and thanked her.

"What might we do for Wulfgar while my scouts seek word of Colson?" Alustriel asked him.

"A quiet room with a view of your fair city," he replied, and he added quietly, "One that faces to the west."

* * * * *

Catti-brie caught up to Wulfgar early that evening on a high balcony of the main turret—one of a dozen that adorned the palace.

"The dwarf has his talents," Wulfgar said.

Catti-brie's freshly washed hair smelled of lilac and springtime. She almost always kept it loose to bounce over her shoulders, but she had one side tied up and the other had a hint of a curl teased into it. She wore a light blue gown that enhanced and highlighted the hue of her eyes, its straps revealing the smooth skin of her delicate shoulders. A white and gold sash was tied around her waist at an angle and a place to accentuate her shapely body. The dress did not go all the way to the floor, and Wulfgar's surprise showed as a smile when he noted that she wasn't wearing her doeskin boots, but rather a pair of delicate slippers, all lace and fancy trim.

"I found meself a choice to let him do it to me or punch him in the nose," Catti-brie remarked, her self-deprecation exaggerated because she allowed just a hint of her Dwarvish accent to come through.

"There is not a part of you that enjoys it?"

Catti-brie scowled at him.

"You would not wish for Drizzt to see you like this?" the barbarian pressed. "You would take no pleasure in the look upon his face?"

"I'll take me pleasure in killing orcs."

"Stop it."

Catti-brie looked at him as if he had slapped her.

"Stop it," Wulfgar repeated. "You need not your boots or your weapons here in Silverymoon, or your dwarf-bred pragmatism and that long-lost accent. Have you looked in the mirror since Fret worked his magic on you?"

Catti-brie snorted and turned away, or started to, but Wulfgar held her with his gaze and his grin.

"You should," he said.

"You are talking foolishness," Catti-brie replied, and her accent was no more.

"Far from that. Is it foolish to enjoy the sights of Silverymoon?" He half-turned and swept his arm out to the deepening gloom in the west, to the twilit structures of the free-form city, with candles burning in many windows. Glowing flames of harmless faerie fire showed on a few of the spires, accenting their inviting forms.

"Did you not allow your mind to wander as we walked through the avenues to this palace?" Wulfgar asked. "Could you help but feel that way with beauty all around you? So why is it any different with your own appearance? Why are you so determined to hide behind mud and simple clothes?"

Catti-brie shook her head. Her lips moved a few times as if she wanted to reply but couldn't find the words.

"Drizzt would be pleased by the sight before him," Wulfgar stated. "I am pleased, as your friend. Quit hiding behind the gruff accent and the road-worn clothing. Quit being afraid of who you are, of who you might dare to be, deep inside. You do not care if someone sees you after a hard day of labor, sweating and dirty. You don't waste your time primping and prettying yourself, and all of that is to your credit. But in times like this, when the opportunity presents itself, do not shy from it, either."

"I feel . . . vain."

"You should simply feel pretty, and be happy with that. If you really are one who cares not what others may think or say, then why would you hide from pleasant thoughts?"

Catti-brie looked at him curiously for a moment, and a smile spread on her face. "Who are you, and what have you done with Wulfgar?"

"The doppelganger is long dead, I assure you," Wulfgar replied. "He was thrown out with the weight of Errtu."

"I have never seen you like this."

"I have never before felt like this. I am content and I know my road. I answer to no one but myself now, and never before have I known such freedom."

"And so you wish to share that with me?"

"With everyone," Wulfgar replied with a laugh.

"I did look in a mirror . . . or two," Catti-brie said, and Wulfgar laughed harder.

"And were you pleased by what you saw?"

"Yes," she admitted.

"And do you wish that Drizzt was here?"

"Enough," she bade him, which of course meant "yes."

Wulfgar took her by the arm and guided her to the railing of the balcony. "So many generations of men and elves have built this place. It is a refuge for Fret and those akin to him, and it is also a place where we all might come from time to time to simply stand and look, and enjoy. That, I think, is the most important time of all. To look inside ourselves honestly and without regret or fear. I could be battling orcs or dragons. I could be digging mithral from the deep mines. I could be leading the hunt in Icewind Dale. But there are times, too few I fear, when this, when standing and looking and just enjoying, is more important than all of that."

Catti-brie wrapped her arm around Wulfgar's waist and leaned her head against his strong shoulder, standing side-by-side, two friends enjoying a moment of life, of perception, of simple pleasure.

Wulfgar draped his arm across her shoulders, equally at peace, and both of them sensed, deep inside, that the moment would be one they would remember for all their days, a defining and lasting image of all they had been through since that fateful day in Icewind Dale when Wulfgar the young warrior had foolishly smacked a tough old dwarf named Bruenor on the head.

They lingered for some time, but the moment was lost as Lady Alustriel came out onto the balcony. The two turned at the sound of her voice, to see her standing with a middle-aged man dressed in the apron of a tavernkeeper.

Alustriel paused when she looked upon Catti-brie, her eyes roaming the woman's form.

"Fret is full of magic, I am told," Catti-brie said, glancing at Wulfgar.

Alustriel shook her head. "Fret finds the beauty, he does not create it."

"He finds it as well as Drizzt finds orcs to slay, or Bruenor finds metal to mine, to be sure," said Wulfgar.

"He has mentioned that he would like to search for the same in Wulfgar, as well."

Catti-brie laughed as Wulfgar chuckled and shook his head. "I've not the time."

"He will be so disappointed," said Alustriel.

"Next time we meet, perhaps," said Wulfgar, and his words elicited a doubting glance from Catti-brie.

She stared at him deeply for a long while, measuring his every expression and movement, and the inflections of his voice. His offer to Fret may or may not have been disingenuous, she knew, but it was moot in any case because Wulfgar had decided that he would never again visit Silverymoon. Catti-brie saw that clearly, and had been feeling it since before they had departed Mithral Hall.

A sense of dread welled up inside her, mingling with that last special moment she had shared with Wulfgar. There was a storm coming. Wulfgar knew it, and though he hadn't yet openly shared it, the signs were mounting.

"This is Master Tapwell of the Rearing Dragon, a fine establishment in the city's lower ward," Alustriel explained. The short, round-bellied man came forward a step, rather sheepishly. "A common respite for visitors to Silverymoon."

"Well met," Catti-brie greeted, and Wulfgar nodded his agreement.

"And to yerselves, Prince and Princess of Mithral Hall," Tapwell replied, dipping a few awkward bows in the process.

"The Rearing Dragon played host to many of the refugees that crossed the Surbrin from Mithral Hall," Alustriel explained. "Master Tapwell believes that a pair who passed through might be of interest to you."

Wulfgar was already leaning forward eagerly. Catti-brie put her hand on his forearm to help steady him.

"Yer girl, Colson," Tapwell said, rubbing his hands nervously over his beer-stained apron. "Skinny thing with straw hair to here?" He indicated a point just below his shoulder, a good approximation of the length of Colson's hair.

"Go on," Wulfgar bade, nodding.

"She came in with the last group, but with her mother."

"Her mother?" Wulfgar looked to Alustriel for an explanation, but the woman deferred to Tapwell.

"Well, she said she was her mother," the tavernkeeper explained.

"What was her name?" Catti-brie asked.

Tapwell fidgeted as if trying to fathom the answer. "I remember her calling the girl Colson clear enough. Her own name was like that. Same beginning, if ye get my meaning."

"Please remember," Wulfgar prompted.

"Cottie?" Catti-brie asked.

"Cottie, yeah. Cottie," said Tapwell.

"Cottie Cooperson," Catti-brie said to Wulfgar. "She was with the group Delly tended in the hall. She lost her family to Obould."

"And Delly gave her a new one," said Wulfgar, but his tone was not bitter.

"You agree with this assessment?" Alustriel asked.

"It does make sense," said Catti-brie.

"This was the last group that crossed the Surbrin before the ferry was closed down, and not just the last group to arrive in Silverymoon," Alustriel said. "I have confirmed that from the guards of Winter Edge themselves. They escorted the refugees in from the Surbrin— all of them—and they, the guards, remain, along with several of the refugees."

"And have you found those refugees to ask them of Cottie and Colson?" asked Catti-brie. "And are Cottie and Colson among those who remain?"

"Further inquiries are being made," Alustriel replied. "I am fairly certain that they will only confirm what we have already discovered. As for Cottie and the child, they left."

Wulfgar's shoulders slumped.

"For Nesmé," Alustriel explained. "Soon after those refugees arrived, a general call came out from Nesmé. They are rebuilding, and offering homes to any who would go and join with them. The place is secure once more—many of the Knights in Silver stand watch with the Riders of Nesmé to ensure that all of the trolls were destroyed or chased back into the Trollmoors. The city will thrive this coming season, well defended and well supplied."

"You are certain that Cottie and Colson are there?" Wulfgar asked.

"I am certain that they were on the caravan that left for Nesmé, only days after they arrived here in Silverymoon. That caravan arrived, though whether Cottie and the child remained with it through the entirety of the journey, I cannot promise. They stopped at several way stations and villages along the route. The woman could have left at any of those."

Wulfgar nodded and looked to Catti-brie, their road clear before them.

"I could fly you to Nesmé upon my chariot," Alustriel offered. "But there is another caravan leaving by midday tomorrow, one that will follow the exact route that Cottie rode, and one in need of more guards. The drivers would be thrilled to have Wulfgar and Catti-brie along for the journey, and Nesmé is only a tenday away."

"And there is nowhere for Cottie to have gone beyond Nesmé," Wulfgar reasoned. "That will do, and well."

"Very good," said Alustriel. "I will inform the lead driver." She and Tapwell took their leave.

"Our road is clear, then," said Wulfgar, and he seemed content with that.

Catti-brie, though, shook her head.

"The southern road is secured and Nesmé is not so far," Wulfgar said to her doubting expression.

"This is not good news, I fear."

"How so?"

"Cottie," Catti-brie explained. "I happened upon her a few times after my wound kept me in the lower tunnels. She was a broken thing, in spirit and in mind."

"You fear that she would harm Colson?" Wulfgar said, his eyes widening with alarm.

"Never that," said Catti-brie. "But I fear that she will clutch the girl too tightly, and will not welcome the reaching hands of Wulfgar."

"Colson is not her child."

"And for some, truth is no more than an inconvenience," Catti-brie replied.

"I will take the child," Wulfgar stated in a tone that left no room for debate.

Aside from that undeniable determination, it struck Catti-brie that Wulfgar had named Colson as "the child," and not as "my child." She studied her friend carefully for a few moments, seeking a deeper read.

But it was not to be found.

CHAPTER

AT DESTINY'S DOOR

9

I don't like this place."

A trick of the wind, blowing down a channel between a pair of towering snow dunes, amplified Regis's soft-spoken words so that they seemed to fill the space around his four dwarf companions. The words blended with the mourn of the cold breeze, a harmony of fear and lament that seemed so fitting in a place called Fell Pass.

Bruenor, who was too anxious to be anywhere but up front, turned, and appeared as if he was about to scold the halfling. But he didn't. He just shook his head and left it at that, for how could he deny the undeniable?

The region was haunted, palpably so. They had felt it on their journey through the pass the previous spring, moving west to east toward Mithral Hall. That same musty aura remained very much alive in Fell Pass, though the surroundings had been transformed by the season. When they'd first come through, the ground was flat and even, a wide and easily-traversed pass between a pair of distant mountain ranges. Perhaps the winds from both of those ranges continually met here in battle, flattening the ground. Deep snow had since fallen in the teeth of those competing winds, forming a series of drifts that resembled the dunes of the Calim Desert, like a series of gigantic, bright white scallop shells evenly spaced perpendicular to the east-west line that marked the bordering mountain ranges. With the melting and refreezing of the late winter, the top surface of the snow had been crusted with ice, but not enough to bear the weight of a dwarf. Thus they had to make their trudging way along the low points of the still-deep snow, through the channels between the dunes.

Drizzt served as their guide. Running lightly, every now and then chopping a ledge into the snow with one of his scimitars, the drow traversed the dunes as a salmon might skip the waves of a slow river. Up one side and down another he went, pausing at the high points to set his bearings.

It had taken the party of six—Bruenor, Regis, Drizzt, Thibbledorf Pwent, Cordio, and Torgar Hammerstriker—four days to get to the eastern entrance of Fell Pass. They'd kept up a fine pace considering the snow and the fact that they had to circumvent many of King Obould's guard posts and a pair of orc caravans. Once in the pass, even with the scallop drifts, they had continued to make solid progress, with Drizzt scaling the dunes and instructing Pwent where to punch through.

Seven days out, the pace had slowed to a crawl. They were certain they were near to where they'd found the hole that Bruenor believed was the entrance to the legendary dwarven city of Gauntlgrym.

They had mapped the place well on that journey from the west, and had taken note, as Bruenor had ordered, of all the landmarks—the angles to notable mountain peaks north and south, and such. But with the wintry blanket of snow, Fell Pass appeared so different that Drizzt simply could not be certain. The very real possibility that they might walk right past the hole that had swallowed one of their wagons weighed on all of them, particularly Bruenor.

And there was something else there, a feeling hanging in the air that had the hairs on the backs of all their necks tingling. The mournful groan of the wind was full of the laments of the dead. Of that, there was no doubt. The cleric, Cordio, had cast divination spells that told him there was indeed something supernatural about the place, some rift or outsider presence. On the journey to Mithral Hall, Bruenor's priests had urged Drizzt not to call upon Guenhwyvar, for fear of inciting unwanted attention from other extraplanar sources in the process, and once again Cordio had reiterated that point. The Fell Pass, the dwarf priest had assured his companions, was not stable in a planar sense—though even Cordio admitted that he wasn't really sure what that meant.

"Ye got anything for us, elf?" Bruenor called up to Drizzt. His gruff voice, full of irritation, echoed off the frozen snow.

Drizzt came into view atop the drift to the party's left, the west. He shrugged at Bruenor then stepped forward and began a balanced slide down the glistening white dune. He kept his footing perfectly, and slipped right past the halfling and dwarves to the base of the drift on their other side, where he used its sharp incline to halt his momentum.

"I have snow," he replied. "As much snow as you could want, extending as far as I can see to the west."

"We're goin' to have to stay here until the melt, ain't we?" Bruenor grumbled. He put his hands on his hips and kicked his heavy boot through the icy wall of one mound.

"We will find it," Drizzt replied, but his words were buried by the sudden grumbling of Thibbledorf Pwent.

"Bah!" the battlerager snorted, and he banged his hands together and stomped about, crunching the icy snow beneath his heavy steps. While the others wore mostly furs and layers of various fabrics, Pwent was bedecked in his traditional Gutbuster battle mail, a neck-to-toe suit of overlapping ridged metal plates, spiked at all the appropriate strike zones: fists, elbows, shoulders, and knees. His helmet, too, carried a tall, barbed spike, one that had skewered many an orc in its day.

"Ye got no magic to help me?" Bruenor demanded of Cordio.

The cleric shrugged helplessly. "The riddles of this maze extend beyond the physical, me king," he tried to explain. "Questions asked in spells're getting me nothin' but more questions. I'm knowin' that we're close, but more because I'm feeling that rift with me every spellcasting."

"Bah!" Pwent roared. He lowered his head and rammed through the nearest snow drift, disappearing behind a veil of white that fell behind him as he plowed through to the channel on the other side.

"We'll find it, then," said Torgar Hammerstriker. "If it was here when ye came through, then here it is still. And if me king's thinking it's Gauntlgrym, then nothin's stopping meself from seein' that place."

"Aye and huzzah!" Cordio agreed.

They all jumped as the snow erupted from up ahead. Drizzt's scimitars appeared in his hands as if they had been there all along.

From that break in the dune emerged a snow-encrusted Thibbledorf Pwent, roaring still. He didn't slow, but plowed through the dune across the way, crunching through the icy wall with ease and disappearing from sight.

"Will ye stop it, ye durned fool?" Bruenor chastised, but Pwent was already gone.

"I am certain that we're near the entrance," Drizzt assured Bruenor, and the drow slid his blades away. "We are the right distance from the mountains north and south. Of that, I am sure."

"We are close," Regis confirmed, still glancing all around as if he expected a ghost to leap out and throttle him at any moment. In that regard, Regis knew more than the others, for he had been the one who had gone into the hole after the wagon those months before, and who had encountered, down in the dark, what he believed to be the ghost of a long-dead dwarf.

"Then we'll just keep looking," said Bruenor. "And if it stays in hiding under the snow, its secrets won't be holding, for the melt's coming soon."

"Bah!" they heard Pwent growl from behind the dune to the east and they all scrambled, expecting him to burst through in their midst, and likely with that lethal helmet spike lowered.

The dune shivered as he hit it across the way, and he roared again fiercely. But his pitch changed suddenly, his cry going from defiance to surprise. Then it faded rapidly, as if the dwarf had fallen away.

Bruenor looked at Drizzt. "Gauntlgrym!" the dwarf declared.

Torgar and Cordio dived for the point on the drift behind which they had heard Pwent's cry. They punched through and flung the snow out behind them, working like a pair of dogs digging for a bone. As they weakened the integrity of that section of the drift, it crumbled down before them, complicating their dig. Still, within moments, they came to the edge of a hole in the ground, and the remaining pile of snow slipped in, but seemed to fill the crevice.

"Pwent?" Torgar called into the snow, thinking his companion buried alive.

He leaned over the edge, Cordio stabilizing his feet, and plunged his hand down into the snow pile. That blockage, though, was neither solid nor thick, and had merely packed in to seal the shaft below. When

Torgar's hand broke the integrity of the pack, the collected snow broke and fell away, leaving the dwarf staring down into a cold and empty shaft.

"Pwent?" he called more urgently, realizing that his companion had fallen quite far.

"That's it!" Bruenor yelled, rushing up between the kneeling pair. "The wagon went in right there!" As he made the claim, he fell to his knees and brushed aside some more of the snow, revealing a rut that had been made by the wagon wheel those months before. "Gauntl-grym!"

"And Pwent fell in," Drizzt reminded him.

The three dwarves turned to see the drow and Regis feeding out a line of rope that Drizzt had already tied around his waist.

"Get the line, boys!" Bruenor yelled, but Cordio and Torgar were already moving anyway, rushing to secure the rope and find a place to brace their heavy boots.

Drizzt dropped down beside the ledge and tried to pick a careful route, but a cry came up from far below, followed by a high-pitched, siz-zling roar that sounded unlike anything any of them had ever heard, like a cross between the screech of an eagle and the hiss of a gigantic lizard.

Drizzt rolled over the lip, turning and setting his hands, and Bru-enor dived to add his strength to the rope brace.

"Quickly!" Drizzt instructed as the dwarves began to let out the line. Trusting in them, the drow let go of the lip and dropped from sight.

"There's a ledge fifteen feet down," Regis called, scrambling past the dwarves to the hole. He moved as if he would go right over, but he stopped suddenly, just short of the lip. There he held as the seconds passed, his body frozen by memories of his first journey into the place that Bruenor called Gauntlgrym.

"I'm on the ledge," Drizzt called up, drawing him from his trance. "I can make my way, but keep ready on the rope."

Regis peered over and could just make out the form of the drow in the darkness below.

"Ye be guidin' us, Rumblebelly," Bruenor instructed, and Regis found the fortitude to nod.

A loud crash from far below startled him again, though, followed by a cry of pain and another otherworldly shriek. More noise arose, metal scraping on stone, hissing snakes and eagle screams, and Dwarvish roars of defiance.

Then a cry of absolute terror, Pwent's cry, shook them all to their spines, for when had Thibbledorf Pwent ever cried out in terror?

"What do ye see?" Bruenor called out to Regis.

The halfling peered in and squinted. He could just make out Drizzt, inching down the wall below the ledge. As his eyes adjusted to the gloom, Regis realized it wasn't really a ledge, or a wall, but rather a stalagmite mound that had grown up beside the side of the cave below. He looked back to Drizzt, and the drow dropped from sight. The dwarves behind him gave a yelp and fell over backward as the rope released.

"Set it!" Bruenor yelled at Torgar and Cordio, and the dwarf king charged for the hole, yelling, "What do ye see, Rumblebelly?"

Regis pulled back and turned, shaking his head, but Bruenor wasn't waiting for an explanation anyway. The dwarf dived to the ground and grabbed up the rope, and without hesitation, flung himself over the lip, rapidly descending into the gloom. Back from the hole, Torgar and Cordio grunted from the strain and tried hard to dig their boots in.

Regis swallowed. He heard a grunt and a shriek from far below. Images of a dwarf ghost haunted him and told him to run far away. But Drizzt was down there, Bruenor was down there, Pwent was down there.

The halfling swallowed again and rushed to the hole. He fell to the ground atop the rope and with a glance back at Torgar and Cordio, he disappeared from sight.

* * * * *

As soon as he hit the ledge, Drizzt recognized it for what it was. The tall stalagmite mound rose up at an angle, melding with the sheerer stone of the wall behind him.

Even though he was only fifteen feet down from the lip, Drizzt's sensibilities switched to those of the person he used to be, a creature of the Underdark. He started down tentatively, feeding out the rope behind him, for just a couple of steps.

His eyes focused in the gloom, and he saw the contours of the stalagmite and the floor some twenty feet below. On that floor rested the broken remains of the wagon that had been lost in the journey east those months before. Also on that floor, Drizzt saw a familiar boot, hard and wrapped in metal. Below and to the left, he heard a muffled cry, and the sound of metal scraping on stone, as if an armored dwarf was being dragged.

With a flick of his wrist, Drizzt disengaged himself from the rope, and so balanced was he as he ran down the side of the stalagmite that he not only did not bend low and use his hands, but he drew out both his blades as he descended. He hit the floor in a run, thinking to head off down the narrow tunnel he had spotted ahead and to the right. But his left-hand scimitar, Twinkle, glowed with a blue light, and the drow's keen eyes and ears picked out a whisper of movement and a whisper of sound over by the side wall.

Skidding to a stop, Drizzt whirled to meet the threat, and his eyes went wide indeed when he saw the creature, unlike anything he had ever known, coming out fast for him.

Half again Drizzt's height from head to tail, it charged on strong back legs, like a bipedal lizard, back hunched low and tail suspended behind it, counterbalancing its large head—if it could even be called a head. It seemed no more than a mouth with three equidistant mandibles stretched out wide. Black tusks as large as Drizzt's hands curled inward at the tips of those mandibles, and Drizzt could make out rows of long, sharp teeth running back down its throat, a trio of ridged lines.

Even stranger came the glow from the creature's eyes—three of them—each centered on the flap of mottled skin stretched wide between the respective mandibles. The creature bore down on the drow like some triangular-mouthed snake unhinging its jaw to swallow its prey.

Drizzt started out to the left then reversed fast as the creature swerved to follow. Even with his speed-enhancing anklets, though, the drow could not get far enough back to the right to avoid the turning creature.

The mandibles snapped powerfully, but hit only air as Drizzt leaped and tumbled forward, over the top mandible. He slashed down hard with both hands as he went over, and used the contact to push himself even higher as he executed a twist and brought his feet fast under him. The creature issued a strange roaring, hissing protest—a fitting, otherworldly sound for an otherworldly beast, Drizzt thought.

Tucking and turning, Drizzt planted his feet against the side of the creature's shoulder and kicked out, but the beast was more solid than he'd thought. His strike did no more than bend it away from him at the shoulder as he went out to the side. And that bend, of course, again turned the terrible jaws his way.

But Drizzt flew backward with perfect balance and awareness. As the beast swung around he cut his scimitars across, one-two, scoring hits on the thick muscle and skin of the jaws' connecting flap.

The creature howled again and bit down at the passing blades, its three mandible tips not quite aligning as they clicked together. It opened wide its maw again as it turned to face Drizzt.

His blades worked in a flash, the backhand of Icingdeath slicing the opposing skin flap, and a hard strike of Twinkle passing through the muscle and flesh, then turning straight down to slash the base flap that connected the lower two mandible tips. Drizzt turned the blade just a bit as it connected, and leaned forward hard, forcing the jaws to angle down.

The creature snapped its head back up, accepting the cut, and leaped straight up, turning its back end under so that it landed on its out-stretched tail with its hind legs free to claw at its opponent. Formidable indeed were the three claws tipping the feet of those powerful legs, and Drizzt barely dodged back in time to avoid the vicious rake.

Somehow the creature hopped forward in pursuit, using just its tail for propulsion. Its tiny front legs waved frantically in the air as its long, powerful rear legs slashed wildly at the drow.

Drizzt worked his scimitars in a blur to defend, connecting repeatedly, but never too solidly for fear of having a blade torn from his grasp. He retracted a blade and the creature's hind leg flailed free, then he stabbed straight out, piercing its foot.

The creature threw back its head and howled again—from up above there came a crash as a form rolled over the ledge—and Drizzt didn't miss the opportunity offered by the distraction. Rolling around those flailing legs and slashing across with Icingdeath, then with Twinkle in close pursuit, he scored two hits on the creature's thin neck. There was a sucking of air and Drizzt saw the bubbling of blood as his blades passed through flesh.

Not even slowing in his turn as the creature fell silent, then just fell over, the drow sprinted down the tunnel. A roar from behind made him glance back, to see Bruenor flying down the last few feet beside the stalagmite, axe over his head. The dwarf timed his landing perfectly with his overhand chop, driving his axe through the already mortally wounded creature's backbone with a sickening sound.

"Wait here!" Drizzt called to him, and the drow was gone.

* * * * *

Bruenor held on as the creature thrashed in its death throes. It tried to turn around to snap at him, but Drizzt had completely disabled the once-formidable jaws' ability to inflict any real damage. The mandibles flopped awkwardly and without coordination, most of the supporting muscles severed. Similarly, the creature's tail and hind legs exhibited only the occasional spasmodic twitch, for Bruenor's axe had cleaved its spine.

So the dwarf stayed at arms' length, holding his axe out far from his torso to avoid any incidental contact.

"Hurry, elf!" Bruenor called after Drizzt when he glanced to the side and noted Thibbledorf's boot lying on the stone floor. No longer willing to wait out the dying beast, Bruenor leaped atop its back and ripped through tendon and bone as he tugged and yanked his axe free. He thought to run off after Drizzt, but before he even had the weapon set in his hands, a movement to the side caught his eye.

The dwarf watched curiously as a darker patch of shadow coalesced near the side wall and the broken wagon, gradually taking shape—the shape of another of the strange beasts.

It came out hard and fast at him, and Bruenor wisely dropped down behind the fallen creature. On came the second beast, jaws snapping furiously, and the dwarf fell to the stone floor and heaved the fallen creature up as a meaty shield. The dwarf finally saw the damage those strange triangular jaws could inflict, for the ravenous newcomer tore through great chunks of flesh and bone in seconds.

Movement behind Bruenor had him half turning to his right.

"Just me!" Regis called to him before he came around, and the dwarf refocused on the beast before him.

Then Bruenor glanced left, to see Drizzt backing frantically out of the tunnel, his scimitars working fast and independently, each slashing quick lines to hold the snapping mouths of two more creatures at bay.

"Rumblebelly, ye help the elf!" Bruenor called, but when he glanced back, Regis was gone.

Bruenor's foe plowed over its fallen comrade then, and the dwarf king had no time to look for his halfling companion.

* * * * *

Drizzt noticed Regis flattened against the wall as he, and the pair of monsters pursuing him, moved past the halfling.

Regis nodded and waited for a responding nod. As soon as Drizzt offered it, the halfling came out fast and slapped his small mace against the tail of the creature on the left. Predictably, the beast wheeled to snap at this newest foe, but anticipating that, Drizzt moved faster, bringing his right hand blade over and across, cutting a gash across the side of the turning beast's neck.

With a roar of protest, the creature spun back, and the other, seeing the opening, came on suddenly.

But Drizzt was the quicker, and he managed to backstep fast enough to buy the time to realign his blades. He gave an approving nod to Regis as the halfling slipped down the tunnel.

* * * * *

Regis moved deliberately, but nervously, into the darkness, expecting a monster to spring out at him from every patch of shadow. Soon he heard the scraping of metal, and an occasional grumble and Dwarvish curse, and he could tell from the lack of bluster that Thibbledorf Pwent was in serious trouble.

Propelled by that, Regis moved with more speed, coming up to the edge of a side chamber from which issued the terrible, gnashing, metallic sounds. Regis summoned his courage and peeked around the rim of the opening. There in the room, silhouetted by the glow of lichen along the far wall, stood another creature, one larger than the others and easily more than ten feet from maw to tail tip. It stood perfectly still, except that it thrashed its head back and forth. Looking at it from the back, but on a slight angle, Regis could see why it did so. For out of the side of that mouth hung an armored dwarf leg with a dirty bare foot dangling limply at its end. Regis winced, thinking that his friend was being torn apart by that triangular maw. He could picture the black teeth crunching through Pwent's armored shell, tearing his flesh with fangs and ripped metal.

And the dwarf wasn't moving, other than the flailing caused by the limp limbs protruding from the thing's mouth, and no further protests or groans came forth.

Trembling with anger and terror, Regis charged with abandon, leaping forward and lifting high his small mace. But where could he even hit the murderous beast to hurt it?

He got his answer as the creature noticed him, whipping its head around. It was then that the halfling first came to understand the strange head, with its three equidistant eyes set in the middle of each of the skin flaps that connected the mandibles. Purely on instinct, the halfling swung for the nearest eye, and the creature's short forelimbs could not reach forward far enough to block.

The mace hit true, and the flap, taut about the knee and upper leg of the trapped dwarf, had no give that it might absorb the blow. With a sickening *splat,* the eye popped, gushing liquid all over the horrified halfling.

The creature hissed and whipped its head furiously—an attempt to throw the dwarf free.

But Pwent wasn't dead. He had gone into a defensive curl, a "turtle" maneuver that tightened the set of his magnificent armor, strengthening its integrity and hiding its vulnerable seams. As the creature loosened its death grip on him, the dwarf came out of his curl with a defiant snarl. He had no room to punch, or to maneuver his head spike, so he simply thrashed, shaking like a wide-leafed bush in a gale.

The creature lost interest in Regis, and tried to clamp down on the dwarf instead. But too late, for Pwent was in a frenzy, insane with rage.

Finally the creature managed to open wide its maw and angle down, expelling the dwarf. When Pwent came free, Regis's eyes widened to see the amount of damage—torn skin, broken teeth, and blood—the dwarf had inflicted on the beast.

And Pwent was far from done. He hit the ground in a turn that put his feet under him, and his little legs bent, then propelled him right back at the creature, head—and helmet spike—leading. He drove into and through the apex of the jaws, and the dwarf bored on, bending the creature backward. The dwarf punched out, both hands at the same time, launching twin roundhouse hooks that pounded the beast on opposite sides of its neck, fist-spikes digging in. Again and again, the dwarf retracted and punched back hard, both hands together, mashing the flesh.

And the dwarf's legs ground on, pushing the beast backward, up against the side-chamber's wall, and by the time they got there, the creature was not resisting at all, was not pushing back, and without the barrage it would have likely fallen over.

But Pwent kept hitting it, muttering profanities all the while.

* * * * *

Bruenor thrust his axe out horizontally before him, defeating the first attack. He turned the weapon and used it to angle the charging creature aside as he, too, ran ahead, sprinting by the beast to the remains of the wagon. All of the supply crates and sacks had been destroyed, either from the fall or torn apart thereafter, but Bruenor found what he was looking for in an intact portion of the side of the wagon, angling up to about waist height. Knowing the creature to be in full pursuit, the dwarf dived right over that, falling to the floor at its base and rolling to his back, axe up above his head along the ground.

The creature leaped over the planks, not realizing that Bruenor was so close to them until the dwarf's axe hit it hard in the side, cutting a long gash just behind its small, twitching foreleg.

Bruenor fell back flat and continued the momentum to roll him right over, coming back up to his feet. He didn't pause to look over his handiwork, but propelled himself forward, lifting his axe high over one shoulder as he went.

The creature was ready, though, and as the dwarf bore in, it snapped its mouth out at him, and when it had to retract far short of the mark to avoid a swipe of that vicious axe, the creature just fell back on its tail, as the other one had done, and brought up its formidable rear legs.

One blocked Bruenor's next swing, kicking out and catching the axe below the head, while the other lashed out, scraping deep lines on the dwarf's armor. Following that, the creature snapped its upper body forward, the triangular maw biting hard at the dwarf, who only managed at the last instant to get back out of range.

And right back came Bruenor, with a yell and a spit and a downward chop.

The creature rocked back and the axe whipped past cleanly. The creature reversed, coming in behind.

Bruenor didn't stop the axe's momentum and reverse it to parry. Rather, he let it flow through, turning sidelong as the blade came low, then turning some more, daring to roll his back around before the beast in the belief that he would be the quicker.

And so he was.

Bruenor came around, the axe in both hands and at full extension in a great sidelong slash. The creature scrambled to block. Bruenor shortened his grip, bringing the axe head in closer. When the creature kicked out to block, the axe met it squarely, removing one of the three toes and cleaving the blocking foot in half.

The creature threw itself forward, screaming in pain and anger, coming at Bruenor with blind rage. And the dwarf king backed frantically, his axe working to-and-fro to fend off the snapping assaults.

"Elf! I'm needin' ye!" the desperate dwarf bellowed.

* * * * *

Drizzt was in no position to answer. The wound he had inflicted on one of the beasts wasn't quite as serious as he'd hoped, apparently, for that creature showed no signs of relenting. Worse for Drizzt, he had been backed into a wider area, giving the creatures more room to maneuver and spread out before him.

They went wide, left and right, amazingly well coordinated for unthinking beasts—if they were indeed unthinking beasts. Drizzt worked his blades as far to either side as he could, and when that became impractical and awkward, the drow rushed ahead suddenly, back toward the tunnel.

Both creatures turned to chase, but Drizzt reversed even faster, spinning to meet their pursuit with a barrage of blows. He scored a deep gash on the side of one's mouth, and poked the other in its bottom eye.

Up above he heard a crash, and from the side Bruenor called for him. All he could do was look for options.

His gaze followed the trail of falling rocks, to see Torgar Hammerstriker in a wild and overbalanced run down the side of the stalagmite. The dwarf held a heavy crossbow before him, and just before his stumbling sent him into a headlong slide, he let fly a bolt, somehow hitting the creature to Drizzt's right. The crossbow went flying and so did Torgar, crashing and bouncing the rest of the way down.

The creature he had hit stumbled then spun to meet the dwarf's charge. But its jaws couldn't catch up to the bouncing and flailing Torgar, and the dwarf slammed hard against the back and side of the beast, bringing it down in a heap. Dazed beyond sensibility, Torgar couldn't begin to defend himself in that tumble as the creature moved to strike.

But Drizzt moved around the remaining creature and struck hard at the fallen beast, his scimitars slicing at its flesh in rapid succession, tearing deep lines. Drizzt had to pause to fend off the other, but as soon as that attack was repelled, he went back to the first, ensuring that it was dead.

Then the drow smiled, seeing that the tide had turned, seeing the lowered head spike rushing in hard at the standing creature's backside.

Even as Pwent connected, skewering the beast from behind, Drizzt broke off and ran toward the wagon. By the time he got there, he found Bruenor and his opponent in a wild back and forth of snapping and slashing.

Drizzt leaped up to the lip of the wagon side, looking for an opening. Noting him, Bruenor rushed out the other way, and the creature turned with the dwarf.

Drizzt leaped astride its back, his scimitars going to quick and deadly work.

"What in the Nine Hells are them things?" Bruenor asked when the vicious thing at last lay still.

"What *from* the Nine Hells, perhaps," said Drizzt with a shrug.

The two moved back to the center of the room, where Pwent continued pummeling the already dead beast and Regis tended to the dazed and battered Torgar.

"I can't be getting down," came a call from above, and all eyes lifted to see Cordio peering over the entrance, far above. "Ain't no place to set the rope."

"I'll get him," Drizzt assured Bruenor.

With agility that continued to awe, the drow ran up the side of the stalagmite, sliding his scimitars away. At the top, he searched and found his handholds, and between those and the rope, which Cordio had braced once more, Drizzt soon disappeared back out of the hole.

A few moments later, Cordio came down on the rope, gaining to the top of the mound, then, with Drizzt's help, he worked his way gingerly down to the ground. Drizzt came back into the cavern soon after, hanging by his fingertips. He fell purposely, landing lightly atop the stalagmite mound. From there, the drow trotted down to join his friends.

"Stupid, smelly lizards," Pwent muttered as he tried to put his boot back on. The metal bands had been bent, though, crimping the opening in the shoe, and so it was no easy task.

"What were them things?" Bruenor asked any and all.

"Extraplanar creatures," said Cordio, who was inspecting one of the bodies—one of the bodies that was smoking and dissipating before his very eyes. "I'd be keeping yer cat in its statue, elf."

Drizzt's hand went reflexively to his pouch, where he kept the onyx figurine he used to summon Guenhwyvar to the Prime Material Plane. He nodded his agreement with Cordio. If ever he had needed the panther, it would have been in the last fight, and even then, he hadn't dared call upon her. He could sense it, too, a pervasive aura of strange otherworldliness. The place was either truly haunted or somehow dimensionally unstable.

He slipped his hand in the pouch and felt the contours of the panther replica. He hoped the situation wouldn't force him to chance a call to Guenhwyvar, but in glancing around at his already battered companions, he had little confidence that it could be avoided for long.

CHAPTER

10

The orcs of Clan Yellowtusk swept into the forest from the north, attacking trees as if avenging some heinous crime perpetrated upon them by the inanimate plants. Axes chopped and fires flared to life, and the group, as ordered, made as much noise as they could.

On a hillside to the east, Dnark, Toogwik Tuk, and Ung-thol crouched and waited nervously, while Clan Karuck crept along the low ground behind them and to the south.

"This is too brazen," Ung-thol warned. "The elves will come out in force."

Dnark knew that his shaman's words were not without merit, for they'd encroached on the Moonwood, the home of a deadly clan of elves.

"We will be gone across the river before the main groups arrive," Toogwik Tuk replied. "Grguch and Hakuun have planned this carefully."

"We are exposed!" Ung-thol protested. "If we are seen here on open ground . . ."

"Their eyes will be to the north, to the flames that eat their beloved god-trees," said Toogwik Tuk.

"It is a gamble," Dnark interjected, calming both shamans.

"It is the way of the warrior," said Toogwik Tuk. "The way of the orc. It is something Obould Many-Arrows would have once done, but no more."

Truth resonated in those words to both Dnark and Ung-thol. The chieftain glanced down at the creeping warriors of Clan Karuck, many shrouded by branches they had attached to their dark armor and clothing. Further to the side, tight around the trees of a small copse, a band of ogre javelin throwers held still and quiet, atlatl throwing sticks in hand.

The day could bring disaster, a ruination of all of their plans to force Obould forward, Dnark knew. Or it could bring glory, which would then only push their plans all the more. In any event, a blow struck here would sound like the shredding of a treaty, and that, the chieftain thought, could only be a good thing.

He crouched back low in the grass and watched the scene unfolding before him. He wouldn't likely see the approach of the cunning elves, of course, but he would know of their arrival by the screams of Clan Yellowtusk's sacrificed forward warriors.

A moment later, and not so far to the north, one such cry of orc agony rent the air.

Dnark glanced down at Clan Karuck, who continued their methodical encirclement.

* * * * *

Innovindil could only shake her head in dismay to see the dark lines of smoke rising from the northern end of the Moonwood yet again. The orcs were nothing if not stubborn.

Her bow across her saddle before her, the elf brought Sunset up above the treetops, but kept the pegasus low. The forward scouts would engage the orcs before her arrival, no doubt, but she still hoped to get some shots in from above with the element of surprise working for her.

She banked the pegasus left, toward the river, thinking to come around the back of the orc mob so that she could better direct the battle to her companions on the ground. She went even lower as she broke clear of the thick tree line and eased Sunset's reins, letting the pegasus fly full out. The wind whipped through the elf's blond locks, her hair and cape flapping out behind her, her eyes tearing from the refreshingly chilly breeze. Her rhythm held perfect, posting smoothly with the rise and fall of her steed's powerful shoulders, her balance so centered and complete that she seemed an extension of the pegasus rather than a separate being. She let the fingers of one hand feel the fine design of her bow, while her other hand slipped down to brush the feathered fletching of the arrows set in a quiver on the side of her saddle. She rolled an arrow with her fingers, anticipating when she could let it fly for the face of an orc marauder.

Keeping the river on her left and the trees on her right, Innovindil cruised along. She came up on one hillock and had nearly flown over it by the time she noticed carefully camouflaged forms creeping along.

Orcs. South of the fires and the noise. South of the forward scouts.

The veteran elf warrior recognized an ambush when she saw one. A second group of orcs were set to swing against the rear flank of the Moonwood elves, which meant that the noisemakers and fire-starters in the north were nothing more than a diversion.

Innovindil did a quick scan of the forest beyond and the movement before her, and understood the danger. She took up the reins and banked Sunset hard to the right, flying over a copse of trees that left only a short open expanse to the forest proper. She focused on the greater forest ahead, trying to gauge the fight, the location of the orcs and of her people.

Still, the perceptive elf caught the movements around the trees below her, for she could hardly have missed the brutish behemoths scrambling in the leafless copse. They stood twice her height, with shoulders more than thrice her girth.

She saw them, and they saw her, and they rushed around below her, lifting heavy javelins on notched atlatls.

"Fly on, Sunset!" Innovindil cried, recognizing the danger even before one of the missiles soared her way. She pulled back the reins hard, angling her mount higher, and Sunset, understanding the danger, beat his wings with all his strength and speed.

A javelin cracked the air as it flew past, narrowly missing her, and Innovindil couldn't believe the power behind that throw.

She banked the pegasus left and right, not wanting to present an easy target or a predictable path. She and Sunset had to be at their best in the next few moments, and Innovindil steeled her gaze, ready to meet that challenge.

She couldn't know that she had been expected, and she was too busy dodging huge javelins to take note of the small flying serpent soaring along the treetops parallel to her.

* * * * *

Chieftain Grguch watched the darting and swerving pegasus with amusement and grudging respect. It quickly became clear to him that the ogres would not take the flying pair down, as his closest advisor had predicted. He turned to the prescient Hakuun then, his smile wide.

"This is why I keep you beside me," he said, though he doubted that the shaman, deep in the throes of casting a spell he had prepared precisely for that eventuality, even heard him.

The sight of a ridden pegasus over the previous battle with the elves had greatly angered Grguch, for he had thought on that occasion that his ambush had the raiding group fooled. The flyer had precipitated the elves' escape, Grguch believed, and so he had feared it would happen again—and worse, feared that an elf on high might discover the vulnerable Clan Karuck as well.

Hakuun had given him his answer, and that answer played out in full as the shaman lifted his arms skyward and shouted the last few words of his spell. The air before Hakuun's lips shuddered, a wave of shocking energy blaring forth, distorting images like a rolling ball of water or extreme heat rising from hot stone.

Hakuun's spell exploded around the dodging elf and pegasus, the air itself trembling and quaking in shock waves that buffeted and battered both rider and mount.

Hakuun turned a superior expression his beloved chieftain's way, as if to report simply, "Problem solved."

* * * * *

Innovindil didn't know what hit her, and perhaps more importantly, hit Sunset. They held motionless for a heartbeat, sudden, crackling gusts battering them from all sides. Then they were falling, dazed, but only for a short span before Sunset spread his wings and caught the updrafts.

But they were lower again, too near the ground, and with all momentum stolen. No skill, in rider or in mount, could counter that sudden reversal. Luck alone would get them through.

Sunset whinnied in pain and Innovindil felt a jolt behind her leg. She looked down to see a javelin buried deep in the pegasus's flank, bright blood dripping out on the great steed's white coat.

"Fly on!" Innovindil implored, for what choice did they have?

Another spear flew past, and another sent Sunset into a sudden turn as it shot up in front of them.

Innovindil hung on for all her life, knuckles whitening, legs clamping the flying horse's flanks. She wanted to reach back and pull out the javelin, which clearly dragged at the pegasus, but she couldn't risk it in that moment of frantic twisting and dodging.

The Moonwood rose up before her, dark and inviting, the place she had known as her home for centuries. If she could just get there, the clerics would tend to Sunset.

She got hit hard on the side and nearly thrown from her perch, unexpectedly buffeted by Sunset's right wing. It hit her again, and the horse dropped suddenly. A javelin had driven through the poor pegasus's wing, right at the joint.

Innovindil leaned forward, imploring the horse for his own sake and for hers, to fight through the pain.

She got hit again, harder.

Sunset managed to stop thrashing and extend his wings enough to catch the updraft and keep them moving along.

As they left the copse behind, Innovindil believed that they could make it, that her magnificent pegasus had enough determination and fortitude to get them through. She turned again to see to the javelin in Sunset's flank—or tried to.

For as Innovindil pivoted in her saddle, a fiery pain shot through her side, nearly taking her from consciousness. The elf somehow settled and turned just her head, and realized then that the last buffet she had taken hadn't been from Sunset's wing, for a dart of some unknown origin hung from her hip, and she could feel it pulsing with magical energy, beating like a heart and flushing painful acid into her side. The closer line of blood pouring down Sunset's flank was her own and not the pegasus's.

Her right leg had gone completely numb, and patches of blackness flitted about her field of vision.

"Fly on," she murmured to the pegasus, though she knew that every stroke of wings brought agony to her beloved equine friend. But they had to get over the forward elf line. Nothing else mattered.

Valiant Sunset rose up over the nearest trees of the Moonwood, and brave Innovindil called down to her people, who she knew to be moving through the trees. "Flee to the south and west," she begged in a voice growing weaker by the syllable. "Ambush! Trap!"

Sunset beat his wings again then whinnied in pain and jerked to the left. They couldn't hold. Somewhere in the back of her mind, in a place caught between consciousness and blackness, Innovindil knew the pegasus could not go on.

She thought that the way before them was clear, but suddenly a large tree loomed where before there had been only empty space. It made no sense to her. She didn't even begin to think that a wizard might be nearby, casting illusions to deceive her. She was only dimly aware as she and Sunset plowed into the tangle of the large tree, and she felt no real pain as she and the horse crashed in headlong, tumbling and twisting in a bone-crunching descent through the branches and to the ground. At one point she caught a curious sight indeed, though it hardly registered: a little, aged gnome with only slight tufts of white hair above his considerable ears and dressed in beautiful shimmering robes of purple and red sat on a branch, legs crossed at the ankles and rocking childlike back and forth, staring at her with an amused expression.

Delirium, the presage to death, she briefly thought. It had to be.

Sunset hit the ground first, in a twisted and broken heap, and Innovindil fell atop him, her face close to his.

She heard his last breath.

She died atop him.

* * * * *

Back on the hillside, the three orcs lost sight of the elf and her flying horse long before the crash, but they had witnessed the javelin strikes, and had cheered each.

"Clan Karuck!" Dnark said, punching his fist into the air, and daring to believe in that moment of elation and victory that the arrival of the half-ogres and their behemoth kin would indeed deliver all the promises of optimistic Toogwik Tuk. The elves and their flying horses had been a bane to the orcs since they had come south, but would any more dare glide over the fields of the Kingdom of Many-Arrows?

"Karuck," Toogwik Tuk agreed, clapping the chieftain on the shoulder, and pointing below.

There, Grguch stood tall, arms upraised. "Take them!" the half-ogre cried to his people. "To the forest!"

With a howl and hoot that brought goosebumps to the chieftain and shamans, the warriors of Clan Karuck leaped up from their concealment and ran howling toward the forest. From the small copse to the south came the lumbering ogres, each with a throw-stick resting on one shoulder, a javelin set in its Y, angled forward and up, ready to launch.

The ground shook beneath their charge, and the wind itself retreated before the force of their vicious howls.

"Clan Karuck!" Ung-thol agreed with his two companions. "And may all the world tremble."

* * * * *

Innovindil's warning cry had been heard, and her people trusted her judgment enough not to question the command. As word filtered through the trees, the Moonwood elves let fly one last arrow and turned to the southwest, sprinting along from cover to cover. Whatever their anger, whatever the temptation of turning back to strike at the orcs in the north, they would not ignore Innovindil.

And true to their beliefs, within a matter of moments, they heard the roars from the east, and realized the trap that their companion had spied. With expert coordination, they tightened their ranks and moved toward the most defensible ground they could find.

Those farthest to the east, a group of a dozen forest folk, were the first to see the charge of Clan Karuck. The enormous half-breeds ran through the trees with wild abandon and frightening speed.

"Hold them," the leader of that patrol told her fellow elves.

Several others looked at her incredulously, but from the majority came nothing but determination. The charge was too ferocious. The other elves moving tree to tree would be overrun.

The group settled behind an ancient, broken, weatherworn wall of piled stones. Exchanging grim nods, they set their arrows and crouched low.

The first huge orcs came into sight, but the elves held their shots. More and more appeared behind the lead runners, but the elves did not break, and did not let fly. The battle wasn't about them, they understood, but about their kin fleeing behind them.

The nearest Clan Karuck warriors were barely five strides from the rock wall when the elves popped up as one, lowered their bows in unison and launched a volley of death.

Orcs shrieked and fell, and the snow before the wall was splattered with red. More arrows went out, but more and more orcs came on. And leaping out before those orcs came a small flaming sphere, and the elves knew what it portended. As one, they crouched and covered against the fireball—one that, in truth, did more damage to the front rank of the charging orcs than to the covering elves, except that it interrupted the stream of the elves' defense.

Clan Karuck fed on the cries of its dying members. Fear was not known among the warriors, who wanted only to die in the service of Gruumsh and Grguch. In a frenzy they defied the rain of arrows and the burning branches falling from the continuing conflagration on high. Some even grabbed their skewered companions and tugged them along as shields.

Behind the wall, the elves abandoned their bows and drew out long, slender swords. In shining mail and with windblown cloaks, most still trailing wisps of smoke and a couple still burning, they met the charge with splendor, strength, and courage.

But Grguch and his minions overran them and slaughtered them, and their weapons gleamed red, not silver, and their cloaks, weighted with blood, would not flap in the breeze.

Grguch led the warriors through the forest a short distance farther, but he knew that he was traveling on elven ground, where defensive lines of archers would sting his warriors from the tops of hills and the boughs of trees, and where powerful spells would explode without warning. He pulled up and raised his open hand, a signal to halt the charge, then he motioned to the south, sending a trio of ogres forward.

"Take their heads," he ordered to his orcs, and nodded back to the stone wall. "We'll pike them along the western bank of the river to remind the faerie folk of their mistake."

Up ahead, some distance already, an ogre cried out in pain. Grguch nodded his understanding, knowing that the elves would regroup quickly—that they probably already had. He looked around at his charges and grinned.

"To the river," he ordered, confident that his point had been made, to Clan Karuck and to the three emissaries who had brought them forth from their tunnels under the Spine of the World.

He didn't know about the fourth non-Karuck onlooker, of course, who had played a role in it all. Jack was back in his Jaculi form, wrapped around the limb of a tree, watching it all unfold around him with mounting curiosity. He would have to have a long talk with Hakuun, and soon, he realized, and he felt a bit of joy then that he had followed Clan Karuck out of the Underdark.

He had long forgotten about the wide world and the fun of mischief.

Besides, he'd never liked elves.

* * * * *

Toogwik Tuk, Ung-thol, and Dnark beamed with toothy grins as they made their way back to orc-held lands.

"We have brought forth the fury of Gruumsh," Dnark said when the trio stood on the western bank of the Surbrin, looking back east at the Moonwood. The sun was low behind them, dusk falling, and the forest took on a singular appearance, as if its tree line was the defensive wall of an immense castle.

"It will remind King Obould of our true purpose," Ung-thol posited.

"Or he will be replaced," said Toogwik Tuk.

The other two didn't even wince at those words, spoken openly. Not after seeing the cunning, the ferocity, and the power of Grguch and Clan Karuck. Barely twenty feet north of their position, an elf head staked upon a tall pike swayed in the wind.

* * * * *

Albondiel's heart sank when he spotted the flash of white against the forest ground. At first he thought it just another patch of snow, but as he came around one thick tree and gained a better vantage point, he realized the truth.

Snow didn't have feathers.

"Hralien," he called in a voice breaking on every syllable. Time seemed to freeze for the shocked elf, as if half the day slid by, but in only a few moments, Hralien was at Albondiel's side.

"Sunset," Hralien whispered and moved forward.

Albondiel summoned his courage and followed. He knew what they would find.

Innovindil still lay atop the pegasus, her arms wrapped around Sunset's neck, her face pressed close to his. From Albondiel's first vantage point when he came around the tree that had abruptly ended Innovindil and Sunset's flight, the scene was peaceful and serene, almost as if his friend had fallen asleep atop her beloved equine friend. Scanning farther down, though, revealed the truth, revealed the blood and the gigantic javelins, the shattered wings and the magical wound of dissolved flesh behind Innovindil's hip.

Hralien bent over the dead elf and gently stroked her thick hair, and ran his other hand over the soft and muscled neck of Sunset.

"They were ready for us," he said.

"Ready?" said Albondiel, shaking his head and wiping the tears from his cheeks. "More than that. They lured us. They anticipated our counterstrike."

"They are orcs!" Hralien protested, rising fast and turning away.

He brought his arms straight out before him, then slowly moved them out wide to either side then behind him, arching his back and lifting his face to the sky as he went. It was a ritual movement, often used in times of great stress and anguish, and Hralien ended by issuing a high-pitched keen toward the sky, a protest to the gods for the pain visited upon his people that dark day.

He collected himself quickly, his grief thrown out for the moment, and spun back at Albondiel, who still kneeled, stroking Innovindil's head.

"Orcs," Hralien said again. "Have they become so sophisticated in their methods?"

"They have always been cunning," Albondiel replied.

"They know too much of us," Hralien protested.

"Then we must change our tactics."

But Hralien was shaking his head. "It is more, I fear. Could it be that they are guided by a dark elf who knows how we fight?"

"We do not know that," Albondiel cautioned. "This was a simple ambush, perhaps."

"One ready for Innovindil and Sunset!"

"By design or by coincidence? You assume much."

Hralien knelt beside his friends, living and dead. "Can we afford not to?"

Albondiel pondered that for a few moments. "We should find Tos'un."

"We should get word to Mithral Hall," said Hralien. "To Drizzt Do'Urden, who will grieve for Innovindil and Sunset. He will understand better the methods of Tos'un, and has already vowed to find the drow."

A shadow passed over them, drawing their attention skyward.

Sunrise circled above them, tossing his head and crying out pitifully for the lost pegasus.

Albondiel looked at Hralien and saw tears streaking his friend's face. He looked back up at the pegasus, but could hardly make out the flying horse through the glare of his own tears in the morning sunlight.

"Get Drizzt," he heard himself whisper.

CHAPTER

MISDIRECTING CLUES

11

"Pack it up and move it out," Bruenor grumbled, slinging his back-pack over his shoulder. He snatched up his axe, wrapping his hand around the handle just under the well-worn head. He prodded the hard ground with it as if it were a walking stick as he moved away from the group.

Thibbledorf Pwent, wearing much of his lunch in his beard and on his armor, hopped up right behind, eager to be on his way, and Cordio and Torgar similarly rose to Bruenor's call, though with less enthusiasm, even with a wary glance to each other.

Regis just gave a sigh and looked down at the remainder of his meal, a slab of cold beef wrapped with flattened bread, and with a bowl of thick gravy and a biscuit on the side.

"Always in a hurry," the halfling said to Drizzt, who helped him rewrap the remaining food.

"Bruenor is nervous," said Drizzt, "and anxious."

"Because he fears more monsters?"

"Because these tunnels are not to his expectations or to his liking," the drow explained, and Regis nodded at the revelation.

They had come into the hole expecting to find a tunnel to the dwarven city of Gauntlgrym, and at first, after their encounter with the strange beasts, things had seemed pretty much as they had anticipated, including a sloping tunnel with a worked wall. The other side seemed more natural stone and dirt, as were the ceiling and floor, but that one wall had left no doubt that it was more than a natural cave, and the craftsmanship evident in the fitted stones made Bruenor and the other dwarves believe that it was indeed the work of their ancestors.

But that tunnel hadn't held its promise or its course, and though they were deeper underground, and though they still found fragments of old construction, the trail seemed to be growing cold.

Drizzt and Regis moved quickly to close the distance to the others. With the monsters about, appearing suddenly from the shadows as if from nowhere, the group didn't dare separate. That presented a dilemma a hundred feet along, when Bruenor led them all into a small chamber they quickly recognized to be a hub, with no fewer than six tunnels branching out from it.

"Well, there ye be!" Bruenor cried, hefting his axe and punching it into the air triumphantly. "Ain't no river or burrowing beast made this plaza."

Looking around, it was hard for Drizzt to disagree, for other than one side, where dirt had collapsed into the place, the chamber seemed perfectly circular, and the tunnels too equidistant for it to be a random design.

Torgar fell to his knees and began digging at the hard-packed dirt, and his progress multiplied many times over when Pwent dropped down beside him and put his spiked gauntlets to work. In a few moments, the battlerager scraped stone, and as he worked his way out to the sides, it became apparent that the stone was flat.

"A paver!" Torgar announced.

"Gauntlgrym," Bruenor said to Drizzt and Regis with an exaggerated wink. "Never doubt an old dwarf."

"Another one!" Pwent announced.

"Sure'n the whole place is full o' them," said Bruenor. "It's a trading hub for caravans, or I'm a bearded gnome. Yerself's knowing that," he said to Torgar, and the Mirabarran dwarf nodded.

Drizzt looked past the three dwarves to the fourth, Cordio, who had moved to the wall between a pair of the tunnels and was scraping at the wall. The dwarf nodded as his knife sank in deeper along a crease in the stone behind the accumulated dirt and mud, revealing a vertical line.

"What do ye know?" Bruenor asked, leading Torgar and Thibbledorf over to the cleric.

A moment later, as Cordio broke away a larger piece of the covering grime, it became apparent to all that the cleric had found a door. After a few moments, they managed to clear it completely, and to their delight they were able to pry it open, revealing a single-roomed structure behind it. Part of the back left corner had collapsed, taking a series of shelves down with it, but other than that, the place seemed frozen in time.

"Dwarven," Bruenor was saying as Drizzt moved to the threshold.

The dwarf stood off to the side of the small door, examining a rack holding a few ancient metal artifacts. They were tools or weapons, obviously, and Bruenor upended one to examine its head, which could have been the remnants of a pole arm, or even a hoe, perhaps.

"Might be dwarven," Torgar agreed, examining the shorter-handled item beside the one Bruenor had lifted, one showing the clear remains of a spade. "Too old to know for sure."

"Dwarven," Bruenor insisted. He turned and let his gaze encompass the whole of the small house. "All the place is dwarven."

The others nodded, more because they couldn't disprove the theory than because they had reached the same conclusions. The remnants of a table and a pair of chairs might well have been dwarf-made, and seemed about the right size for the bearded folk. Cordio moved around those items to a hearth, and as he began clearing the debris from it and scraping at the stone, that, too, seemed to bolster Bruenor's argument. For there was no mistaking the craftsmanship evident in the ancient fireplace. The bricks had been so tightly set that the passage of time had done little to diminish the integrity of the structure, and indeed it seemed as if, with a bit of cleaning, the companions could safely light a fire.

Drizzt, too, noted that hearth, and paid particular heed to the shallowness of the fireplace, and the funnel shape of the side walls, widening greatly into the room.

"The plaza's a forward post for the city," Bruenor announced as they began moving back out. "So I'm guessing that the city's opposite the tunnel we just came down."

"In the lead!" said Pwent, heading that way at once.

"Good guess on the door," Bruenor said to Cordio, and he patted the cleric on the shoulder before he and Torgar started off after the battlerager.

"It wasn't a guess," Drizzt said under his breath, so that only Regis could hear. And Cordio, for the dwarf glanced back at Drizzt—his expression seeming rather sour, Regis thought—then moved off after his king, muttering, "Wouldn't need pavers this far down."

Regis looked from him to Drizzt, his expression begging answers.

"It was a free-standing house, and not a reinforced cave dwelling," Drizzt explained.

Regis glanced around. "You think there are others, separating the exit tunnels?"

"Probably."

"And what does that mean? There were many free-standing houses in the bowels of Mirabar. Not so uncommon a thing in underground cities."

"True enough," Drizzt agreed. "Menzoberranzan is comprised of many similar structures."

"Cordio's expression spoke of some significance," the halfling remarked. "If this type of structure is to be expected, then why did he wear a frown?"

"Did you note the fireplace?" Drizzt asked.

"Dwarven," Regis replied.

"Perhaps."

"What's wrong?"

"The fireplace was not a cooking pit, primarily," Drizzt explained. "It was designed to throw heat into the room."

Regis shrugged, not understanding.

"We are far enough underground so that the temperature hardly varies," Drizzt informed him, and started off after the others.

Regis paused for just a moment, and glanced back at the revealed structure.

"Should we search this area more completely?" the halfling asked.

"Follow Bruenor," Drizzt replied. "We will have our answers soon enough."

They kept their questions unspoken as they hurried to join up with the four dwarves, which took some time, for the excited Bruenor led them down the tunnel at a hurried pace.

The tunnel widened considerably soon after, breaking into what seemed to be a series of parallel tracks of varying widths continuing in the same general direction. Bruenor moved without hesitation down the centermost of them, but they found it to be a moot choice anyway, since the tunnels interconnected at many junctures. What they soon discerned was that this wasn't so much a series of tunnels as a singular pathway, broken up by pillars, columns, and other structures.

At one such interval, they came upon a low entrance, capped diagonally by a structure that had obviously been made by skilled masons, for the bricks could still be seen, and they held fast despite the passage of centuries and the apparent collapse of the building, which had sent it crashing to the side into another wall.

"Could be a shaft, pitched for a fast descent," Bruenor remarked.

"It's a building that tipped," Cordio argued, and Bruenor snorted and waved his hand dismissively.

But Torgar, who had moved closer, said, "Aye, it is." He paused and looked up. "And one that fell a long way. Or slid."

"And how're ye knowin' that?" Bruenor asked, and there was no mistaking the hint of defiance. He was catching on, obviously, that things weren't unfolding the way he'd anticipated.

Torgar was already motioning them over, and began pointing out the closest corner of the structure, where the edge of the bricks had been rounded, but not by tools.

"We see this in Mirabar all the time," Torgar explained, running a fat thumb over the corner. "Wind wore it round. This place was under the sky, not under the rock."

"There's wind in some tunnels," said Bruenor. "Currents and such blowin' down strong from above."

Torgar remained unconvinced. "This building was up above," he said, shaking his head, "for years and years afore it fell under."

"Bah!" Bruenor snorted. "Ye're guessin'."

"Might be that Gauntlgrym had an aboveground market," Cordio interjected.

Drizzt looked at Regis and rolled his eyes, and as the dwarves moved off, the halfling grabbed Drizzt by the sleeve and held him back.

"You don't believe that Gauntlgrym had an aboveground market?" he asked.

"Gauntlgrym?" Drizzt echoed skeptically.

"You don't believe?"

"More than the market of this place was above ground, I fear," said Drizzt. "Much more. And Cordio and Torgar see it, too."

"But not Bruenor," said Regis.

"It will be a blow to him. One he is not ready to accept."

"You think this whole place was a city above ground?" Regis stated. "A city that sank into the tundra?"

"Let us follow the dwarves. We will learn what we will learn."

The tunnels continued on for a few hundred more feet, but the group came to a solid blockage, one that sealed off all of the nearby corridors. Torgar tapped on that wall repeatedly with a small hammer, listening for echoes, and after inspecting it at several points in all the tunnels, announced to the troop, "There's a big open area behind it. I'm knowin' it."

"Forges?" Bruenor asked hopefully.

Torgar could only shrug. "Only one way we're goin' to find out, me king."

So they set their camp right there, down the main tunnel at the base of the wall, and while Drizzt and Regis went back up the tunnel some distance to keep watch back near the wider areas, the four dwarves devised their plans for safely excavating. Soon after they had shared their next meal, the sound of hammers rang out against the stone, none more urgent than Bruenor's own.

CHAPTER

NESMÉ'S PRIDE

"I had hoped to find the woman before we crossed the last expanse to Nesmé," Wulfgar remarked to Catti-brie. Their caravan had stopped to re-supply at a nondescript, unnamed cluster of houses still a couple of days' travel from their destination, and the last such scheduled stop on their journey.

"There are still more settlements," Catti-brie reminded him, for indeed, the drivers had told them that they would pass more secluded lodges in the next two days.

"The houses of hunters and loners," Wulfgar replied. "No places appropriate for Cottie to remain with Colson."

"Unless all the refugees remained together and decided to begin their own community."

Wulfgar replied with a knowing smile, a reflection of Catti-brie's own feelings on the subject, to be sure. She knew as Wulfgar knew that they would find Cottie Cooperson and Colson in Nesmé.

"Two days," Catti-brie said. "In two days, you will have Colson in your arms once more. Where she belongs."

Wulfgar's grim expression, even a little wince, caught her by surprise.

"We have heard of no tragedies along the road," Catti-brie added. "If the caravan bearing Cottie and the others had been attacked, word would have already spread through these outposts. Since we are so close, we can say with confidence that Cottie and Colson reached Nesmé safely."

"Still, I have no love of the place," he said, "and no desire to see the likes of Galen Firth or his prideful companions ever again."

Catti-brie moved closer and put her hand on Wulfgar's shoulder. "We will collect the child and be gone," she said. "Quickly and with few words. We come with the backing of Mithral Hall, and to Mithral Hall we will return with your child."

Wulfgar's face was unreadable, though that, of course, only reaffirmed Catti-brie's suspicions that something was amiss.

The caravan rolled out of the village before the next dawn, wheels creaking against the uneven strain of the perpetually muddy ground. As they continued west, the Trollmoors, the fetid swamp of so many unpleasant beasts, seemed to creep up toward them from the south. But the drivers and those more familiar with the region appeared unconcerned, and were happy to explain, often, that things had quieted since the rout of the trolls by Alustriel's Knights in Silver and the brave Riders of Nesmé.

"The road's safer than it's been in more than a decade," the lead driver insisted.

"More's the pity," one of the regulars from the second wagon answered loudly. "I been hoping a few trolls or bog blokes might show their ugly faces, just so I can watch the work of King Bruenor's kids!"

That brought a cheer from all around, and a smile did widen on Catti-brie's face. She looked to Wulfgar. If he had even heard the remarks, he didn't show it.

Wulfgar and Catti-brie weren't really sure what they might find when their caravan finally came into view of Nesmé, but they knew at once that it was not the same town through which they had traveled on their long-ago journey to rediscover Mithral Hall. Anticipated images of ruined and burned-out homes and shoddy, temporary shelters did not prepare them for the truth of the place. For Nesmé had risen again already, even through the cold winds of winter.

Most of the debris from the troll rampage had been cleared, and newer buildings, stronger, taller, and with thicker walls, replaced the old structures. The double wall surrounding the whole of the place neared completion, and was particularly fortified along the southern borders, facing the Trollmoors.

Contingents of armed and armored riders patrolled the town, meeting the caravan far out from the new and larger gate.

Nesmé was alive again, a testament to the resiliency and determination, and sheer stubbornness that had marked the frontiers of human advancement throughout Faerûn. For all of their rightful negativity toward the place, given their reception those years before, neither Wulfgar nor Catti-brie could hide their respect.

"So much like Ten-Towns," Catti-brie quietly remarked as their wagon neared the gate. "They will not bend."

Wulfgar nodded his agreement, slightly, but he was clearly distracted as he continued to stare at the town.

"They've more people now than before the trolls," Catti-brie said, repeating something the caravan drivers had told the both of them earlier along the road. "Twice the number, say some."

Wulfgar didn't blink and didn't look her way. She sensed his inner turmoil, and knew that it wasn't about Colson. Not only, at least.

She tried one last time to engage him, saying, "Nesmé might inspire other towns to grow along the road to Silverymoon, and won't that be a fitting response to the march of the murderous trolls? It may well be that the northern border will grow strong enough to build a militia that can press into the swamp and be rid of the beasts once and for all."

"It might," said Wulfgar, in such a tone as to show Catti-brie that he hadn't even registered that to which he agreed.

The town gates, towering barriers thrice the height of a tall man and built of strong black-barked logs banded together with heavy straps of metal, groaned in protest as the sentries pulled them back to allow the caravan access to the town's open courtyard. Beyond that defensive wall, Wulfgar and Catti-brie could see that their initial views of Nesmé were no illusion, for indeed the town was larger and more impressive than it had been those years before. It had an official barracks to support the larger militia, a long, two-story building to their left along the defensive southern wall. Before them loomed the tallest structure in town, aside from a singular tower that was under work somewhere in the northwestern quadrant. Two dozen steps led off the main plaza where the wagons parked, directly west of the eastern-facing gates. At the top of those steps ran a pair of parallel, narrow bridges, just a short and defensible expanse, to the impressive front of the new Nesmian Town Hall. Like all the rest of the town, the building was under construction, but like most of the rest, it was ready to stand against any onslaught the Trollmoors in the south, or King Obould in the north, might throw against it.

Wulfgar hopped down from the back of the wagon, then helped Catti-brie to the ground so that she didn't have to pressure her injured hip. She spent a moment standing there, using his offered arm for support, as she stretched the tightness out of her pained leg.

"The folk ye seek could be anywhere in the town," their wagon driver said to them, walking over and speaking quietly.

He alone among the caravan had been in on the real reason Wulfgar and Catti-brie were journeying to Nesmé, for fear that someone else might gossip and send word to Cottie and her friends to flee ahead of their arrival. "They'll not be in any common rooms, as ye saw in Silverymoon, for Nesmé's being built right around the new arrivals. More than half the folk ye'll find here just came from other parts, mostly from lands Obould's darkened with his hordes. Them and some of the Knights in Silver, who remained with the Lady's blessing so that they could get closer to where the fighting's likely to be. . . ."

"Surely there are scribes making note of who's coming in and where they're settling," said Catti-brie.

"If so, ye'll find them in there," said the driver, motioning toward the impressive town hall. "If not, yer best chance is in frequenting the taverns after work's done. Most all the workers find their way to those places—and there're only a few such establishments, and they're all together on one avenue near the southwestern corner. If any're knowing of Cottie, there's the place to find them."

* * * * *

Word spread fast through Nesmé that the arriving caravan had carried with it a couple of extraordinary guards. When the whispers of Catti-brie and Wulfgar reached the ears of Cottie Cooperson's fellow refugees, they knew at once that their friend was in jeopardy.

So by the time Wulfgar and Catti-brie had made their way to the tavern avenue, a pair of concerned friends had whisked Cottie and Colson to the barracks area and the separate house of the town's current leader, Galen Firth.

"He's come to take the child," Teegorr Reth explained to Galen, while his friend Romduul kept Cottie and Colson out in the anteroom.

Galen Firth settled back in his chair behind his desk, digesting it all. It had come as a shock to him, and not a pleasant one, that the human prince and princess of Mithral Hall had arrived in his town. He had assumed it to be a diplomatic mission, and given the principals involved, he had suspected that it wouldn't be a friendly one. Mithral Hall had suffered losses for the sake of Nesmé in the recent battles. Could it be that King Bruenor sought some sort of recompense?

Galen had never been friendly with the dwarves of Mithral Hall or with these two.

"You cannot let him have her," Teegorr implored the Nesmian leader.

"What is his claim?" Galen asked.

"Begging your pardon, sir, but Cottie's been seeing to the girl since she left Mithral Hall. She's taken Colson as her own child, and she's been hurt."

"The child?"

"No, Cottie, sir," Teegorr explained. "She's lost her own—all her own."

"And the child is Wulfgar's?"

"No, not really. He brought the girl to Mithral Hall, with Delly, but then Delly gave her to Cottie."

"With or without Wulfgar's agreement?"

"Who's to say?"

"Wulfgar, I would assume."

"But . . ."

"You assume that Wulfgar has come here to take the child, but could it be that he is merely passing through to check up on her?" Galen asked. "Or might it be that he is here for different reasons—would he even know that your friend Cottie decided to settle in Nesmé?"

"I . . . I . . . I can't be saying for sure, sir."

"So you presume. Very well, then. Let Cottie stay here for now until we can determine why Wulfgar has come."

"Oh, and I thank you for that!"

"But make no mistake, good Teegorr, if Wulfgar's claim is true and he wants the child back, I am bound to honor his claim."

"Your pardon, sir, but Cottie's got twenty folk with her. Good strong hands, who know the frontier and who know how to fight."

"Are you threatening me?"

"No, sir!" Teegorr was quick to reply. "But if Nesmé's not to protect our own, then how are our own to stay in Nesmé?"

"What are you asking?" Galen replied, standing up forcefully. "Am I to condone kidnapping? Is Nesmé to become an outpost for criminals?"

"It's not so simple as that, is all," said Teegorr. "Delly Curtie gave the girl to Cottie, so she's no kidnapper, and not without claim."

That settled Galen Firth back a bit. He couldn't keep the disdain from his face, for it was not a fight he wanted to entertain just then. Clan Battlehammer and Nesmé were not on good terms, despite the fact that the dwarves had sent warriors down to help the Nesmians. In the subsequent sorting of events, the rebuilding of Nesmé had taken precedence over King Bruenor's desire to take the war back to Obould, something that had clearly simmered behind the angry eyes of the fiery dwarf.

And there remained that old issue of the treatment Bruenor and his friends, including Wulfgar and the drow elf Drizzt, had met with on their initial pass through Nesmé those years ago, an unpleasant confrontation that had set Galen Firth and the dwarf at odds.

Neither could Galen Firth keep the wry grin from breaking through his otherwise solemn expression on occasion as he pondered the possibilities. He couldn't deny that there would be a measure of satisfaction in causing grief to Wulfgar, if the opportunity presented itself.

"Who knows that you came here?" Galen asked.

Teegorr looked at him curiously. "To Nesmé?"

"Who knows that you and your friend brought Cottie and the child here to me?"

"Some of the others who crossed the Surbrin beside us."

"And they will not speak of it?"

"No," said Teegorr. "Not a one of us wants to see the child taken from Cottie Cooperson. She's suffered terribly, and now she's found peace—and one that's better for the girl than anything Wulfgar might be offering."

"Wulfgar is a prince of Mithral Hall," Galen reminded. "A man of great wealth, no doubt."

"And Mithral Hall is no place for a man, or a girl—particularly a girl!" Teegorr argued. "Good enough for them dwarves, and good for them. But it's no place for a human girl to grow."

Galen Firth rose up from his seat. "Keep her here," he instructed. "I will go and see my old friend Wulfgar. Perhaps he is here for reasons other than the girl."

"And if he is?"

"Then you and I never had this discussion," Galen explained.

He set a pair of guards outside the anteroom, with orders that no one should enter, and he gathered up a couple of others in his wake as he headed out across the darkening town to the taverns and the common rooms. As he expected, he found Wulfgar and Catti-brie in short order, sitting at a table near the bar of the largest of the taverns, and listening more than speaking.

"You have come to join our garrison!" Galen said with great exaggeration as he approached. "I always welcome strong arms and a deadly bow."

Wulfgar and Catti-brie turned to regard him, their faces, particularly the large barbarian's, hardening upon recognition.

"We have need for a garrison of our own in Mithral Hall," Catti-brie replied politely.

"The orcs have not been pushed back," Wulfgar added, his sharp tone reminding Galen Firth that Galen himself, and his insistence on Nesmé taking precedence, had played no minor role in the decision to not dislodge King Obould.

The other folk in the town knew that as well, and didn't miss the reference, and all in the tavern hushed as Galen stood before the two adopted children of King Bruenor Battlehammer.

"Everything in its time," Galen replied, after looking around to ensure his support. "The Silver Marches are stronger now that Nesmé has risen from the ruins." A cheer started around him, and he raised his voice in proclamation, "For never again will the trolls come forth from the mud to threaten the lands west of Silverymoon or the southern reaches of your own Mithral Hall."

Wulfgar's jaw tightened even more at the notion that Nesmé was serving as Mithral Hall's vanguard, particularly since Mithral Hall's efforts had preserved what little had remained of Nesmé's population.

Which was exactly the effect Galen Firth had been hoping for, and he grinned knowingly as Catti-brie put her hand on Wulfgar's enormous forearm in an effort to keep him calm.

"We had no word that we would be so graced," Galen said. "Is it customary among Clan Battlehammer for emissaries to arrive unannounced?"

"We are not here on the business of Bruenor," said Catti-brie, and she motioned for Galen Firth to sit down beside her, opposite Wulfgar.

The man did pull out the chair, but he merely turned it and put his foot up on it, which made him tower over the two even more. Until, that is, Wulfgar rose to his feet, his nearly seven foot frame, his giant shoulders, stealing that advantage.

But Galen didn't back down. He stared hard at Wulfgar, locking the man's gaze. "Then why?" he asked, his voice lower and more insistent.

"We came in as sentries for a caravan," Catti-brie said.

Galen glanced down at her. "The children of Bruenor hire out as mercenaries?"

"Volunteers doing our part in the collective effort," Catti-brie answered.

"It was a way to serve others as we served our own needs," Wulfgar said.

"To come to Nesmé?" asked Galen.

"Yes."

"Why, if not for Brue—"

"I have come to find a girl, Colson, who was taken from Mithral Hall," Wulfgar stated.

" 'Taken'? Wrongly?"

"Yes."

Behind Wulfgar, several people bustled about. Galen recognized them as friends of Teegorr and Cottie, and expected that there might soon be trouble—which he didn't think so dire a possibility. In truth, the man was interested in testing his strength against that of the legendary Wulfgar, and besides, he had enough guards nearby to ensure that there would be no real downside to any brawl.

"How is it that a child was abducted from Mithral Hall," he asked, "and ferried across the river by Bruenor's own? What dastardly plot turned that result?"

"The girl's name is Colson," Catti-brie intervened, as Wulfgar and Galen Firth leaned in closer toward each other. "We have reason to believe that she has come to Nesmé. In fact, that seems most assured."

"There are children here," Galen Firth admitted, "brought in with the various groups of displaced people, who have come to find community and shelter."

"No one can deny that Nesmé has opened her gates to those in need," Catti-brie replied, and Wulfgar shot a glare her way. "A mutually beneficial arrangement for a town that grows more grand by the day."

"But there is a child here that does not belong in Nesmé, nor to the woman who brought her here," Wulfgar insisted. "I have come to retrieve that girl."

Someone moved fast behind Wulfgar, and he spun, quick as an elf. He brought his right arm across, sweeping aside a two-handed grab by one of Cottie's friends, then turned the arm down, bringing the fool's arms with it. Wulfgar's left hand snapped out and grabbed the man by the front of his tunic. In the blink of an astonished eye, Wulfgar had the man up in the air, fully two feet off the ground, and shook him with just the one hand.

The barbarian turned back on Galen Firth, and with a flick of his arm sent the shaken fool tumbling aside.

"Colson is leaving with me. She was wrongly taken, and though I bear no ill will"—he paused and turned to let his penetrating gaze sweep the room—"to any of those who were with the woman to whom she was entrusted, and no ill will toward the woman herself—surely not!—I will leave with the girl rightfully returned."

"How did she get out of Mithral Hall, a fortress of dwarves?" an increasingly annoyed Galen Firth asked.

"Delly Curtie," said Wulfgar.

"Wife of Wulfgar," Catti-brie explained.

"Was she not then this child's mother?"

"Adopted mother, as Wulfgar is Colson's adopted father," said Catti-brie.

Galen Firth snorted, and many in the room muttered curses under their breath.

"Delly Curtie was under the spell of a powerful and evil weapon,"

Catti-brie explained. "She did not surrender the child of her own volition."

"Then she should be here to swear to that very thing."

"She is dead," said Wulfgar.

"Killed by Obould's orcs," Catti-brie added. "For after she handed the child to Cottie Cooperson, she ran off to the north, to the orc lines, where she was found, murdered and frozen in the snow."

Galen Firth did grimace a bit at that, and the look he gave to Wulfgar was almost one tinged with sympathy. Almost.

"The weapon controlled her," said Catti-brie. "Both in surrendering the child and in running to certain doom. It is a most foul blade. I know well, for I carried it for years."

That brought more murmurs from around the room and a look of astonishment from Galen. "And what horrors did Catti-brie perpetrate under the influence of such a sentient evil?"

"None, for I controlled the weapon. It did not control me."

"But Delly Curtie was made of stuff less stern," said Galen Firth.

"She was no warrior. She was not raised by dwarves."

Galen Firth didn't miss the pointed reminder of both facts, of who these two were and what they had behind their claim.

He nodded and pondered the words for a bit, then replied, "It is an interesting tale."

"It is a demand that will be properly answered," said Wulfgar, narrowing his blue eyes and leaning even more imposingly toward the leader of Nesmé. "We do not ask you to adjudicate. We tell you the circumstance and expect you to give back the girl."

"You are not in Mithral Hall, son of Bruenor," Galen Firth replied through gritted teeth.

"You deny me?" Wulfgar asked, and it seemed to all that the barbarian was on the verge of a terrible explosion. His blue eyes were wide and wild.

Galen didn't back down, though he surely expected an attack.

And again Catti-brie intervened. "We came to Nesmé as sentries on a caravan from Silverymoon, as a favor to Lady Alustriel," she explained, turning her shoulder and putting her arm across the table to block Wulfgar, though of course she couldn't hope to slow his charge, should it come. "For it was Lady Alustriel, friend of King Bruenor Battlehammer, friend of Drizzt Do'Urden, friend of Wulfgar and of Catti-brie, who told us that Colson would be found in Nesmé."

Galen Firth tried to hold steady, but he knew he was giving ground.

"For she knows Colson well, and well she knows of Colson's rightful father, Wulfgar," Catti-brie went on. "When she heard our purpose in traveling to Silverymoon, she put all of her assets at our disposal, and it was she who told us that Cottie Cooperson and Colson had traveled to Nesmé. She wished us well on our travels, and even offered to fly us here on her fiery chariot, but we felt indebted and so we agreed to travel along with the caravan and serve as sentries."

"Would not a desperate father take the quicker route?" asked Galen Firth, and around him, heads bobbed in agreement.

"We did not know that the caravan bearing Colson made it to Nesmé, or whether perhaps the hearty and good folk accompanying the child decided to debark earlier along the road. And that is not for you to decide in any case, Galen Firth. Do you deny Wulfgar's rightful claim? Would you have us go back to Lady Alustriel and tell her that the proud folk of Nesmé would not accede to the proper claim of Colson's own father? Would you have us return at once to Silverymoon and to Mithral Hall with word that Galen Firth refused to give Wulfgar his child?"

"Adopted child," remarked one of the men across the way.

Galen Firth didn't register that argument. The man had thrown him some support, but only because he obviously needed it at that moment. That poignant reminder had him squaring his shoulders, but he knew that Catti-brie had delivered a death blow to his obstinacy. For he knew that she spoke the truth, and that he could ill afford to anger the Lady of Silverymoon. Whatever might happen between King Bruenor and Galen would not likely ill affect Nesmé, for the dwarves would not come south to do battle, but for Lady Alustriel to take King Bruenor's side was another matter entirely. Nesmé needed Silverymoon's support. No caravan would travel to Nesmé that did not originate in, or at least pass through, the city of Lady Alustriel.

Galen Firth was no fool. He did not doubt the story of Catti-brie and Wulfgar, and he had seen clearly the desperation on Cottie Cooperson's face when he had left her in the barracks. That type of desperation was borne of knowing that she had no real claim, that the child was not hers.

For of course, Colson was not.

Galen Firth looked over his shoulder to his guards. "Go and fetch Cottie Cooperson and the girl," he said.

Protests erupted around the room, with men shaking their fists in the air.

"The child is mine!" Wulfgar shouted at them, turning fiercely, and indeed, all of those in front stepped back. "Would any of you demand any less if she was yours?"

"Cottie is our friend," one man replied, rather meekly. "She means the girl no harm."

"Fetch your own child, then," said Wulfgar. "Relinquish her, or him, to me in trade!"

"What foolish words are those?"

"Words to show you your own folly," said the big man. "However good Cottie Cooperson's heart, and I do not doubt your claim that she is worthy both as a friend and a mother, I cannot surrender to her a girl that is my own. I have come for Colson, and I will leave with Colson, and any man who stands in my way would do well to have made his peace with his god."

He snapped his arm in the air before him and called to Aegis-fang, and the mighty warhammer appeared magically in his grasp. With a flick, Wulfgar rapped the hammer atop a nearby table, shattering all four legs and dropping the kindling to the floor.

Galen Firth gasped in protest, and the one guard behind him reached for his sword—and stared down the length of an arrow set on Catti-brie's Taulmaril.

"Which of you will come forward and deny my claim to Colson?" Wulfgar asked the group, and not surprisingly, his challenge was met with silence.

"You will leave my town," Galen Firth said.

"We will, on the same caravan that brought us in," Catti-brie replied, easing her bow back to a rest position as the guard relinquished his grip on the sword and raised his hands before him. "As soon as we have Colson."

"I intend to protest this to Lady Alustriel," Galen Firth warned.

"When you do," said Catti-brie, "be certain to explain to Lady Alustriel how you almost incited a riot and a tragedy by playing the drama out before the hot humors of men and women who came to your town seeking naught but refuge and a new home. Be certain to tell Lady Alustriel of Silverymoon of your discretion, Galen Firth, and we will do likewise with King Bruenor."

"I grow tired of your threats," Galen Firth said to her, but Catti-brie only smiled in reply.

"And I long ago tired of you," Wulfgar said to the man.

Behind Galen Firth, the tavern door opened, and in came Cottie Cooperson holding Colson and pulled along by a guard. Outside the door two men jostled with another pair of guards, who would not let them enter.

The question of Wulfgar's claim was answered the moment Colson came into the room. "Da!" the toddler cried, verily leaping out of Cottie's grasp to get to the man she had known as her father for all her life. She squealed and squirmed and reached with both her arms for Wulfgar, calling for her "Da!" over and over again.

He rushed to her, dropping Aegis-fang to the ground, and took her in his arms then gently, but forcefully, removed her from Cottie's desperate grasp. Colson made no movement back toward the woman at all, but crushed her da in a desperate hug.

Cottie began to tremble, to cry, and her desperation grew by the second. In a few moments, she went down to her knees, wailing.

And Wulfgar responded, dropping to one knee before her. With his free hand, he lifted her chin and brushed back her hair, then quieted her with soft words. "Colson has a mother who loves her as much as you loved your own children, dear woman," he said.

Behind him, Catti-brie's eyes widened with surprise.

"I can take care o' her," Cottie wailed.

Wulfgar smiled at her, brushed her hair back again, then rose. He called Aegis-fang to his free hand and stalked past Galen Firth, snickering in defiance of the man's glare. As he went through the door, Cottie's two companions, for all their verbal protests, parted before him, for few men in all the world would dare stand before Wulfgar, son of Beornegar, a warrior whose legend had been well earned.

"I will speak with our drivers," Catti-brie informed Wulfgar when they exited the inn, with a chorus of shouts and protests echoing behind them. "We should be on our way as soon as possible."

"Agreed," said Wulfgar. "I will wait for the wagons to depart."

Catti-brie nodded and started for the door of a different tavern, where she knew the lead driver to be. She stopped short, though, as she considered the curious answer, and turned back to regard Wulfgar.

"I will not be returning to Silverymoon," Wulfgar confirmed.

"You can't be thinking of going straight to Mithral Hall with the child. The terrain is too rough, and in the hands of orcs for much of the way. The safest road back to Mithral Hall is through Silverymoon."

"It is, and so you must go to Silverymoon."

Catti-brie stared at him hard. "Are you planning to stay here, that Cottie Cooperson can help with Colson?" she said with obvious and pointed sarcasm. To her ultimate frustration, she couldn't read Wulfgar's expression. "You've got family in the hall. I'll be there for you and for the girl. I'm knowing that it will be difficult for you without Delly, but I won't be on the road anytime soon, and be sure that the girl will be no burden to me."

"I will not return to Mithral Hall," Wulfgar stated bluntly, and a gust of wind would have likely knocked Catti-brie over at that moment. "Her place is with her mother," Wulfgar went on. "Her real mother. Never should I have taken her, but I will correct that error now, in returning her where she belongs."

"Auckney?"

Wulfgar nodded.

"That is halfway across the North."

"A journey I have oft traveled and one not fraught with peril."

"Colson has a home in Mithral Hall," Catti-brie argued, and Wulfgar was shaking his head even as the predictable words left her mouth.

"Not one suitable for her."

Catti-brie licked her lips and looked from the girl to Wulfgar, and she knew that he might as well have been speaking about himself at that moment.

"How long will you be gone from us?" the woman dared to ask.

Wulfgar's pause spoke volumes.

"Ye cannot," Catti-brie whispered, seeming very much like a little girl with a Dwarvish accent again.

"I have no choice before me," Wulfgar replied. "This is not my place. Not now. Look at me!" He paused and swept his free hand dramatically from his head to his feet, encompassing his gigantic frame. "I was not born to crawl through dwarven tunnels. My place is the tundra. Icewind Dale, where my people roam."

Catti-brie shook her head with every word, in helpless denial. "Bruenor is your father," she whispered.

"I will love him to the end of my days," Wulfgar admitted. "His place is there, but mine is not."

"Drizzt is your friend."

Wulfgar nodded. "As is Catti-brie," he said with a wistful smile. "Two dear friends who have found love, at long last."

Catti-brie mouthed, "I'm sorry," but she couldn't bring herself to actually speak the words aloud.

"I am happy for you both," said Wulfgar. "Truly I am. You complement each other's every movement, and I have never heard your laughter more full of contentment, nor Drizzt's. But this was not as I had wanted it. I am happy for you—both, and truly. But I cannot stand around and watch it."

The admission took the woman's breath away. "It doesn't have to be like this," she said.

"Do not be sad!" Wulfgar roared. "Not for me! I know now where my home is, and where my destiny lies. I long for the song of Icewind Dale's chill breeze, and for the freedom of my former life. I will hunt caribou along the shores of the Sea of Moving Ice. I will battle goblins and orcs without the restraints of political prudence. I am going home, to be among my own people, to pray at the graves of my ancestors, to find a wife and carry on the line of Beornegar."

"It is too sudden."

Again Wulfgar shook his head. "It is as deliberate as I have ever been."

"You have to go back and talk to Bruenor," Catti-brie said. "You owe him that."

Wulfgar reached under his tunic, produced a scroll, and handed it to her. "You will tell him for me. My road is easier west from here than from Mithral Hall."

"He will be outraged!"

"He will not even be in Mithral Hall," Wulfgar reminded. "He is out to the west with Drizzt in search of Gauntlgrym."

"Because he is in dire need of answers," Catti-brie protested. "Would you desert Bruenor in these desperate days?"

Wulfgar chuckled and shook his head. "He is a dwarf king in a land of orcs. Every day will qualify as you describe. There will be no end to this, and if there is an end to Obould, another threat will rise from the depths of the halls, perhaps, or from Obould's successor. This is the way of things, ever and always. I leave now or I wait until the situation is settled—and it will only be settled for me when I have crossed to Warrior's Rest. You know the truth of it," he said with a disarming grin, one that Catti-brie could not dismiss. "Obould today, the drow yesterday, and something—of course something—tomorrow. That is the way of it."

"Wulfgar . . ."

"Bruenor will forgive me," said the barbarian. "He is surrounded by fine warriors and friends, and the orcs will not likely try again to capture the hall. There is no good time for me to leave, and yet I know that I cannot stay. And every day that Colson is apart from her mother is a tragic day. I understand that now."

"Meralda gave the girl to you," Catti-brie reminded him. "She had no choice."

"She was wrong. I know that now."

"Because Delly is dead?"

"I am reminded that life is fragile, and often short."

"It is not as dark as you believe. You have many here who support . . ."

Wulfgar shook his head emphatically, silencing her. "I loved you," he said. "I loved you and lost you because I was a fool. It will always be the great regret of my life, the way I treated you before we were to be wed. I accept that we cannot go back, for even if you were able and willing, I know that I am not the same man. My time with Errtu left marks deep in my soul, scars I mean to erase in the winds of Icewind Dale, running beside my tribe, the Tribe of the Elk. I am content. I am at peace. And never have I been more certain of my road."

Catti-brie shook her head with every word, in helpless and futile denial, and her blue eyes grew wet with tears. This wasn't how it was supposed to be. The five Companions of the Hall were together again, and they were supposed to stay that way for all their days.

"You said that you support me, and so I ask you to now," said Wulfgar. "Trust in my judgment, in that I know what course I must follow. I take with me my love for you and for Drizzt and for Bruenor and for Regis. That is ever in the heart of Wulfgar. I will never let the image of you and the others fade from my thoughts, and never let the lessons I have learned from all of you escape me as I walk my road."

"Your road so far away."

Wulfgar nodded. "In the winds of Icewind Dale."

CHAPTER

A CITY UNDWARVEN

13

The six companions stood just inside the opening they had carved through the stone, their mouths uniformly agape. They had their backs to the wall of a gigantic cavern that held a magnificent and very ancient city. Huge structures rose up all around them: a trio of stepped pyramids to their right and a beautifully crafted series of towers to their left, all interconnected with flying walkways, and every edge adorned with smaller spires, gargoyles, and minarets. A collection of smaller buildings sat before them, around an ancient pond that still held brackish water and many plants creeping up around its stone perimeter wall. The plants near the pool and scattered throughout the cavern, the common Underdark luminous fungi, provided a minimal light beyond the torches held by Torgar and Thibbledorf, and of course Regis, who would not let his go. The pool and surrounding architecture hardly held their attention at that moment, though, for beyond the buildings loomed the grandest structure of all, a domed building—a castle, cathedral, or palace. Many stone stairs led up to the front of the place, where giant columns stood in a line, supporting a heavy stone porch. In the shadowy recesses, the six could make out gigantic doors.

"Gauntlgrym," Bruenor mouthed repeatedly, and his eyes were wet with tears.

Less willing to make such a pronouncement, Drizzt instead continued to survey the area. The ground was broken, but not excessively, and he could see that the entire area had been paved with flat stones, shaped and fitted to define specific avenues winding through the many buildings.

"The dwarves had different sensibilities then," Regis remarked, and fittingly, Drizzt thought.

Indeed, the place was unlike any dwarven city he had known. No construction under Kelvin's Cairn in Icewind Dale, or in Mirabar, Felbarr, or Mithral Hall, approached the height of even the smallest of the many grand structures around them, and the main building before them loomed larger even than the individual stalagmite-formed great houses of Menzoberranzan. That building was more suited to Waterdeep, he thought, or to Calimport and the marvelous palaces of the pashas.

As the overwhelming shock and awe faded a bit, the dwarves fanned out and moved away from the wall. Drizzt focused on Torgar, who went down to one knee and began scraping between the edges of two flagstones. He brought up a bit of dirt and tasted it then spat it aside, nodding his head and wearing an expression of concern.

Drizzt looked ahead to Bruenor, who seemed oblivious to his companions, walking zombielike toward the giant structure as if pulled by unseen forces.

And indeed the dwarf king was, Drizzt understood. He was tugged forward by pride and by hope, that it truly was Gauntlgrym, the fabulous city of his ancestors, glorious beyond his expectations, and that he would somehow find answers to the question of how to defeat Obould.

Thibbledorf Pwent walked behind Bruenor, while Cordio moved near to Torgar, the latter two striking up a quiet conversation.

One of doubt, Drizzt suspected.

"Is it Gauntlgrym?" Regis asked the drow.

"We will learn soon enough," Drizzt replied and started after Bruenor.

But Regis grabbed him by the arm, forcing him to turn back around.

"It doesn't sound like you believe it is," the halfling said quietly.

Drizzt scanned the cavern, inviting Regis to follow his gaze. "Have you ever seen such structures as these?"

"Of course not."

"No?" Drizzt asked. "Or is it that you have never seen such structures as these in such an environment as this?"

"What do you mean?" Regis asked, but his voice trailed away and his eyes widened as he finished, and Drizzt knew that he had caught on.

The pair scurried to catch up to Torgar and Cordio, who were fast gaining on the front two.

"Check the buildings as we pass," Bruenor instructed, motioning to Pwent and Torgar. "Elf, ye take the flank, and Rumblebelly come close up to me and Cordio."

As they moved by doorways, Pwent and Torgar alternately kicked them in, or rushed in through those that were already opened, as Bruenor continued his march, but more slowly, toward the huge structure, with Regis seemingly glued to his side. Cordio, though, kept hanging back, close enough to get to any of the other three dwarves in a hurry.

Drizzt, moving out into the shadows on the right flank, watched them all with quick glances while focusing his attention primarily on the deeper shadows. He wanted to unravel the mystery of the place, of course, but his main concern was ensuring that no current monstrous residents of the strange city made a sudden and unexpected appearance. Drizzt had been a creature of the Underdark long enough to know that few places so full of shelter would remain uninhabited for long.

"A forge!" Thibbledorf Pwent called from one building—one that had an open back, Drizzt noted, much like a smithy in the surface communities. "I got me a forge!"

Bruenor paused for just a moment before starting again for the huge building, his grin wide and his pace quicker. The other dwarves and Regis, even the stupidly grinning Pwent, hurried to catch up, and by the time Bruenor put his foot on the bottom step, all five were grouped together.

The stairs were wider than they were tall, and while they rose up a full thirty feet, they extended nearly twice that to Bruenor's left and right. Over at the very edge to the right, Drizzt moved fast to get up ahead of the others. Silent as a shadow and nearly invisible in the dim light, Drizzt rushed along, and Bruenor had barely taken his tenth step up when Drizzt crested the top, coming under the darker shadows of the pillared canopy.

And in there, the drow saw that they were not alone, and that danger was indeed waiting for his friends, for behind one of the centermost pillars loomed a behemoth unlike any Drizzt had even seen.

Tall and sinewy, the hairless humanoid was blacker than a drow, if that was possible. It stood easily thrice Drizzt's height, perhaps four times, and exuded an aura of tremendous power, the strength of a mountain giant, monstrous and brutish despite its lean form.

And it moved with surprising speed.

* * * * *

Perched in the rafters of the canopy behind and above Drizzt, another beast of darkness studied the approaching group. Batlike in appearance, but huge and perfectly black, the nightwing took note of the movements, particularly those of the drow elf and the behemoth, a fellow denizen of the Plane of Shadow, a fearsome creature known as a nightwalker.

* * * * *

"Bruenor!" Drizzt cried as the giant started moving, and at the sound of his warning the dwarves reacted at once, particularly Thibbledorf Pwent, who leaped defensively before his king.

And when the giant, black-skinned nightwalker appeared, twenty feet of muscle and terror, Thibbledorf Pwent met its paralyzing gaze with a whoop of battlerager delight, and charged.

He got about three strides up the stairs before the nightwalker bent and reached forward, with long arms more akin in proportion to those of a great ape than to a human. Giant black hands clamped about the ferocious dwarf, long fingers fully engulfing him. Kicking and thrashing like a child in his father's arms, Pwent lifted off the ground.

Behind him, Bruenor could not move quickly enough to stop the hoist, and Cordio fell to spellcasting, and Regis and Torgar didn't move at all, both of them captured by the magical gaze of the powerful giant, both of them standing and trembling and gasping for breath.

That would have been the sudden end of Thibbledorf Pwent, surely, for the nightwalker could turn solid stone to dust in the crush of its tremendous grasp, but from the stairs above and to the right came Drizzt Do'Urden, leaping high, scimitars drawn. He executed a vicious double slash across the upper left arm of the nightwalker, his magical blades tearing through flesh and muscle.

In its lurch, the nightwalker dropped its left hand away, and so lost half the vice with which to crush the wildly flailing dwarf. So the behemoth took the second best option and instead of crushing Thibbledorf Pwent, it flung him high and far.

Pwent's cry changed pitch like the screech of a diving hawk, and he slammed hard against the front of the porch's canopy, some forty feet from the ground. He somehow kept the presence of mind to smash his spiked gauntlets against that facing, and luck was with him as one caught fast in a seam in the stone and left him hanging helplessly, but very much alive.

Down below, Drizzt landed on the stairs, more than a dozen feet below where he had begun his leap, and only his quickness and great agility kept him from serious harm, as he scrambled down the steps to absorb his momentum, even keeping the presence of mind to swat Torgar with the flat of one blade as he rushed past.

Torgar blinked and came back to his senses, just a bit, and turned to regard the running drow.

Drizzt finally stopped his run and swung around, to see Bruenor darting between the nightwalker's legs, his axe chopping hard against one. The behemoth roared—a strange and otherworldly howl that changed pitch multiple times, as if several different creatures had been given voice through the same horn. Again the nightwalker moved with deceiving speed, twisting and turning, lifting one foot and slamming it down at the dwarf.

But Bruenor saw it coming and threw himself back the other way, and even managed to whack at the other leg as he tumbled past. The nightwalker hit only stone with its stomp, but it cracked and crushed that stone.

Drizzt charged to join his friend, but noted a movement to his right that he could not dismiss. Looking past the thrashing, cursing, hanging Thibbledorf, he saw the gigantic, batlike creature drop from the canopy, spreading black wings fully forty feet across as it commenced its swoop. The air shimmered in front of it before it ever really began, though. It sent forth a wave of devastating magical energy that struck the drow with tremendous force.

Drizzt felt his heart stop as if it had been grabbed by a giant hand. Blood came from his eyes and blackness filled his vision. He staggered and stumbled, and as the nightwing came on, he knew he was helpless. He did see, but didn't consciously register, Thibbledorf Pwent curling up against the canopy, tucking his feet against the stone.

* * * * *

Torgar Hammerstriker, proud warrior from Mirabar, whose family had served the various Marchions of Mirabar for generations, and who had bravely marched from that city to Mithral Hall, pledging allegiance to King Bruenor, could not believe his fright. Torgar Hammerstriker, who had leaped headlong into an army of orcs, who had battled giants and giant mottled worms, who had once fought a dragon, cursed himself for being held in the paralysis of fear from the black-skinned behemoth.

He saw Drizzt stagger and stumble, and noted the swoop of the giant batlike creature. But he went for Bruenor, only for Bruenor, his king, his great-axe held high.

Beside him as he sped past, Cordio Muffinhead cast the first of his spells, throwing a wave of magic out at Bruenor that infused the dwarf king with added strength so that with his next swing, his many-notched axe bit in a little deeper. Cordio, too, turned to meet the rush of the nightwing, and deduced immediately that it had somehow rendered Drizzt helpless. The dwarf began another spell, but doubted he could cast it in time.

But Thibbledorf Pwent loosed his own type of spell, a battlerager dweomer, indeed. With a roar of defiance, the already battered dwarf shoved off with all his strength, his powerful legs tearing free his embedded hand spikes with a terrible screeching noise. Pwent flew out and up backward from the canopy and executed a half-twist, half-somersault as he went.

He came around as the nightwing glided under him, and he punched out, one fist after another, latching on with forged metal spikes.

The nightwing dipped under the dwarf's weight as he crashed down on its back, then it shrieked in protest. It finished with a great intake of breath, and Pwent felt it grow cold beneath him—not as if in death, but magically so, as if he had leaped not on a living, giant bat, but upon the Great Glacier itself.

The nightwing started to swing its head, but Pwent moved faster, tucking his chin and snapping every muscle in his body to propel himself forward and down, driving his head spike into the base of the nightwing's skull. The sheer power of the dwarf's movement straightened the creature's head back out and facing forward as the nightwing executed its magic, breathing a cone of freezing air before it.

Unfortunately for the humanoid giant, it stood right in the path of the devastating cone of cold.

The behemoth roared in protest and thrashed its arms to block the blinding and painful breath. White frost appeared all over the black skin of its head, arms, and chest, and strictly on reflex the giant punched out as the frantic nightwing fluttered past, scoring a solid slam against the base of its wing that sent both bat and dwarf into a fast-spinning plummet. They soared over the stairs and off toward the towers, skipped off the top of one building and barreled into another, crashing down in a tangled heap.

Thibbledorf Pwent never stopped shouting, cursing, or thrashing.

* * * * *

Drizzt fought through the pain and wiped the blurriness from his bloodied eyes. He had no time to go after Pwent and the giant shadowy bat. None of them did, for the black-skinned giant was far from defeated.

Bruenor and Torgar raced across the stairs, swatting at the treelike legs with their masterwork weapons, and indeed several gashes showed on those legs, and from them issued grayish ooze that smoked as it dribbled to the ground. But they would have to hit the giant a hundred times to fell it, Drizzt realized, and if the behemoth connected solidly on either of them but once. . . .

Drizzt winced as the nightwalker kicked out, just clipping the dodging Torgar, but still hitting him hard enough to send him bouncing down the stone stairs, his axe flying from his grasp. Knowing that Bruenor couldn't stand alone against the beast, Drizzt started for him, but stumbled, still weak and wounded, disoriented from the magical attack of the flying creature.

The drow felt another magical intrusion then, a wave of soothing, healing energy, and as he renewed his charge Bruenor's way, he managed a quick glance, a quick nod of appreciation, to Cordio.

As he did, he noted Regis simply walking away, muttering to himself, as if oblivious to the events unfolding around him.

As with Pwent, though, the drow had no time to concern himself with it, and when he refocused on his giant target, he winced in fear, for the behemoth chopped down its huge hand, leaving a trail of blackness hanging in the air, and more than opaque, that blackness had dimension.

A magical gate. And one with shapes already moving within its inviting swirls.

Drizzt took heart as Bruenor scored a solid hit, nearly tripping up the giant as it lifted a foot to stomp at him. The nightwalker howled and grabbed at its torn foot, giving Bruenor time to move safely aside, and more importantly, giving Torgar time to begin his charge back up the stairs, limping though he was.

Drizzt, though, had stopped his own advance. The warnings of the priests echoing in his thoughts, the drow pulled forth his onyx figurine. He could see the dangers clearly, the instability of the region, the appearance of a gate to the Plane of Shadow. But as the first wraithlike form began to slide through that smoky portal, Drizzt knew they could not win without help.

"Come to me, Guenhwyvar!" he yelled, and dropped the statue to the stone. "I need you."

"Drizzt, no!" Cordio cried, but it was too late, already the gray mist that would become the panther had begun to form.

Torgar sprinted by the drow, taking the stairs two at a time. He veered from his path to the behemoth to intercept the first floating, shadowy creature to emerge from the gate, which resembled an emaciated human dressed in tattered dark gray robes. Torgar leaped at it with a great two-handed swipe of his axe, and the creature, a dread wraith, met that with a sweep of its arm, trailing tendrils of smoke.

The axe struck home and the creature's hand slapped across the dwarf's shoulder, its permeating and numbing touch reaching into Torgar and leaching his life-force. Blanching, weaker, Torgar growled through the sudden weariness and pulled back his axe, spinning a complete circuit the other way and coming around with a second chop that bludgeoned the dread wraith straight back into the smoky portal.

But another was taking its place, and Torgar's legs shook beneath him. He hadn't the strength to charge, so he tried to firm himself up to meet the newest wraith's approach.

Leaving Drizzt with a dilemma, to be sure, for while Torgar obviously needed his help, so did Bruenor up above, where the giant was moving deliberately, cutting off the dwarf's avenues of escape.

But the choice didn't materialize, for there came a flash of blackness and time seemed to stand still for many long heartbeats.

Light turned to dark and dark to light, so that the giant seemed to become a brighter gray in hue, as did Drizzt, and the dwarves' faces darkened. Everything reversed, torches flaring black, and the hush of surprise engulfed the creatures of shadow and the companions alike.

Guenhwyvar's roar broke the spell.

When Drizzt turned to see his beloved companion, his hope turned to horror, for Guenhwyvar, whiter than Drizzt or the behemoth, seemed only half-formed, and she elongated as she leaped for the second emerging wraith, as if she were somehow dragging her magical gate with her very form. She hit the wraith and went back into the shadow portal with it, and as those two portals merged into a weird weave of conflicting energies, there came another blinding burst of black energy. The wraith hissed in protest, and Guenhwyvar's roar flooded with pain.

The behemoth howled, too, its agony obvious. The portal stretched, twisted, and reached out to grab at the gigantic creature of shadow, as if to bring it home.

No, Drizzt realized, his eyes straining to make sense through the myriad of free-flowing shapes, not to bring it home but as if to engulf the giant and swallow it, and the behemoth's howls only confirmed that the assault of the twisting portals was no pleasant embrace.

The giant proved the stronger, though, and the portals winked out, and the light returned to normal torch- and lichen light, and all was as it had been before the giant had enacted its gate and Drizzt had responded with one of his own.

Except that the behemoth was clearly wounded, clearly off-balance and staggering. And not everyone had been frozen by the stunning events of the merging gates and the dizzying reversals of light and dark.

Far up the stairs, King Bruenor Battlehammer seized the moment of opportunity. He came down like a rolling boulder, skipped out to the edge of a stair, and leaped as high and as far as his short legs would carry him.

Drizzt charged at the behemoth, demanding its attention with a wild flurry of his blades and a piercing battle cry, and so the giant was fully focused on him when Bruenor's axe, clutched in both his hands, cracked into its spine.

The behemoth threw its shoulders back in pain and surprise, its elbows tucked against its ribs, its forearms and long fingers flailing and grabbing at the empty air.

Drizzt's charge became real, focused, and he went right for the giant's most obviously injured leg, his scimitars digging many lines as he quick-stepped past.

The behemoth whirled to follow the movements of the drow, and Bruenor could not hold on. His axe remained deep into the giant's back as the dwarf flew off down the stairs. He crashed in a twisted mess, but Cordio was there at once, infusing him with waves of magical healing.

The giant grimaced and staggered, and Drizzt easily got out of reach. He turned fast, thinking to charge right back in.

But he paused when he saw a tell-tale mist reappearing by the small figurine lying on the stairs.

The giant set itself again. It tried to reach back to extract the dwarf's axe, but the placement prevented it from getting any grip. Down below, Torgar tried to join in, but his legs gave out and he slumped to the stone. No help would come soon from Bruenor, either, Drizzt could see, nor from Cordio, who attended the dwarf king. And Regis was nowhere to be seen.

Giving up on the axe, the behemoth turned its hateful glare at Drizzt. The drow felt a wave of energy flow forth, and for just an instant, he forgot where he was or what was happening. In that split second, he even thought about leaping down at the dwarves, somehow envisioning them as mortal enemies.

But the spell, a dizzying enchantment of confusion, could not take hold on the veteran dark elf the way it had so debilitated Regis, and Drizzt leaped down to the side, coming to the same level as the giant, surrendering the higher ground to limit the giant's attack options. Better to force it to reach for him, he thought, and better still for it to try to stomp or kick at him.

The giant did just that, lifting its leg, and Guenhwyvar did just as Drizzt wanted and sprang upon the one planted leg, raking at the back of the behemoth's knee.

In charged Drizzt, forcing the giant to twist, or try to twist, to keep pace. The drow's magical anklets allowed him to accelerate suddenly past the stomping foot, and he reversed immediately, spinning and slashing at the back of the leading leg. The giant twisted and tried to kick, but Guenhwyvar clamped powerful jaws on the back of its knee, feline fangs tearing deep into dark muscle.

That leg buckled. Arms flailing, the giant fell over backward down the stairs, landing with a tremendous, stone-crunching crash, and just missing crushing poor unconscious Torgar.

Drizzt sprinted and leaped atop it, running down its length to reach its neck before it could bring its arms in to fend him off. Drizzt found less resistance than he expected, for the giant's fall had driven Bruenor's axe in all the deeper, severing its spine.

The behemoth was helpless, and Drizzt showed it no mercy. He crossed its massive chest. Its head was back due to the angle of the stairs, leaving its neck fully exposed.

He leaped from the gurgling, dying behemoth a moment later, landing gracefully on the stairs in full run, angling toward where the batlike creature and Pwent had tumbled. It was quiet there, the fight apparently ended, and Drizzt winced when he saw a leathery wing flop, thinking the monster still alive.

But it was just Pwent, he saw, grumbling as he extracted himself from the broken body.

Drizzt veered back the way they'd come, thinking to go after Regis, but before he could even begin, Regis appeared between the buildings, walking back swiftly toward the group, his mace in hand, his chubby cheeks flushed with embarrassment.

"It took me strength, me king," Torgar Hammerstriker was saying when Drizzt, Guenhwyvar in tow, moved back to the three dwarves. "Like it pulled me spine right out."

"A wraith," explained Cordio, who was still working on the battered Bruenor, bandaging a cut along the dwarf king's scalp. "Their chilling

R.A. SALVATORE

touch steals yer inner strength—and it can suren kill ye to death if it gets enough o' the stuff from ye! Take heart, for ye'll be fine in a short bit."

"As will me king?" Torgar asked.

"Bah!" Bruenor snorted. "Got me a bigger bounce fallin' off me throne after a proper blessing to Moradin. A night o' the holy mead's hurtin' me more than that thing e'er could!"

Torgar moved over to the dead giant and tried to lift its shoulder. He looked back at the others, shaking his head. "Gonna be a chore for ten in gettin' back yer axe," he said.

"Then take yer own and cut yer way through the durned thing," Bruenor ordered.

Torgar considered the giant, then looked to his great-axe. He gave a "hmm" and a shrug, spat in both his hands, and hoisted the weapon. "Won't take long," he promised. "But take care with yer axe when I get it for ye, for the handle's sure to be slick."

"Nah, it crusts when it dries," came a voice from the side, and the group turned to regard Thibbledorf Pwent, who certainly knew of what he spoke. For Pwent was covered in blood and gore from the thrashing he had given the batlike monster, and a piece of the creature's skull was still stuck to his great head spike, with gobs of bloody brain sliding slowly down the spike's stem. To emphasize his point, Pwent held up his hand and clenched and unclenched his fist, making sounds both sloppy wet and crunchy.

"And what happened to yerself?" Pwent demanded of Regis as the halfling approached. "Ye find something to hit back there, did ye?"

"I don't know," the halfling honestly answered.

"Bah, let off the little one," Bruenor told Pwent, and he included all the others as he swept his gaze around. "Ain't nothing chasing Rumble-belly off."

"I don't know what happened," Regis said to Bruenor, and he looked at the dead giant and shrugged. "For any of it."

"Magic," said Drizzt. "The creatures were possessed of more than physical prowess, as is typical of extraplanar beings. One of those spells attacked the mind. A disorienting dweomer."

"True enough, elf," Cordio agreed. "It delayed me spellcasting."

"Bah, but I didn't feel nothing," said Pwent.

"Attacked the *mind*," Bruenor remarked. "Yerself was well defended."

174

Pwent paused and pondered that for a few moments before bursting into laughter.

"What is this place?" Torgar asked at length, finding the strength to rise and walk, taking in the sights, the sculpture, the strange designs.

"Gauntlgrym," Bruenor declared, his dark eyes gleaming with intensity.

"Then yer Gauntlgrym was a town above the ground," said Torgar, and Bruenor glared at him.

"This place was above ground, me king," Torgar answered that look. "All of it. This building and those, too. This plaza, set with stones to protect from the mud o' the spring melt. . . ." He looked at Cordio, then Drizzt, who nodded his agreement. "Something must've melted the tundra beneath the whole of it. Turned it all to mud and sank this place from sight."

"And the melts bring water, every year," Cordio added, pointing to the north. "Washing away the mud, bucket by bucket, but leaving the stones behind."

"Yer answer's in the ceiling," Torgar explained, pointing up. "Can ye get a light up there, priest?"

Cordio nodded and moved away from Bruenor. He began casting again, gently waving his arms, creating a globe of light up at the cavern's ceiling, right at the point where it joined in with the top of the great building before them. Some tell-tale signs were revealed with that light, confirming Torgar's suspicions.

"Roots," the Mirabarran dwarf explained. "Can't be more than a few feet o' ground between that roof and the surface. And these taller buildings're acting like supports to keep that ceiling up. The tangle o' roots and the frozen ground're doin' the rest. Whole place sank, I tell ye, for these buildings weren't built for the Underdark."

Bruenor looked at the ceiling, then at Drizzt, but the drow could only nod his agreement.

"Bah!" Bruenor snorted. "Gauntlgrym was akin to Mirabar, then, and ye're for knowin' that. So this must be the top o' the place, with more below. All we need be looking for is a shaft to take us to the lower levels, akin to that rope and come-along dumbwaiter ye got in Mirabar. Now let's see what this big place is all about—important building,

I'm thinking. Might be a throne room."

Torgar nodded and Pwent ran up in front of Bruenor to lead the way up the stairs, with Cordio close on his heels. Torgar, though, lagged behind, something Drizzt didn't miss.

"Not akin to Mirabar," the dwarf whispered to Drizzt and Regis.

"A dwarf city above ground?" Regis asked.

Torgar shrugged. "I'm not for knowing." He reached to his side and pulled an item from his belt, one he had taken from the smithy he had found back across the plaza. "Lots of these and little of anything else," he said.

Regis sucked in his breath, and Drizzt nodded his agreement with the dwarf's assessment of the muddy catastrophe that had hit the place. For in his hand, Torgar held an item all too common on the surface and all too rare in the Underdark: a horseshoe.

At Drizzt's insistence, he, and not the noisy Thibbledorf, led the way into the building with Guenhwyvar beside him. The drow and panther filtered out to either side of the massive, decorated doors—doors filled with color and gleaming metal much more indicative of a construction built under the sun. The drow and his cat melted into the shadows of the great hall that awaited them, moving with practiced coordination. They sensed no danger. The place seemed still and long dead.

It was no audience chamber, though, no palace for a dwarf king. When the others came in and they filled the room with torchlight, it became apparent that the place had been a library and gallery, a place of art and learning.

Rotted scrolls filled ancient wooden shelves all around the room and along the walls, interspersed with tapestries whose images had long ago faded, and with sculptures grand and small alike.

Those sculptures set off the first waves of alarm in the companions, particularly in Bruenor, for while some depicted dwarves in their typically heroic battle poses and regalia, others showed orc warriors standing proud. And more than one depicted orcs in other dress, in flowing robes or with pen in hand.

The most prominent of all stood upon a dais at the far end of the room, directly across from the doors. The image of Moradin, stocky and strong, was quite recognizable to the dwarves.

So was the image of Gruumsh One-eye, god of the orcs, standing across from him, and while the two were shown eyeing each other with expressions that could be considered suspicious, the simple fact that they were not shown with Moradin standing atop the vanquished Gruumsh's chest elicited stares of disbelief on the faces of all four dwarves. Thibbledorf Pwent even babbled something undecipherable.

"What place was this?" Cordio asked, giving sound to the question that was on all their minds. "What hall? What city?"

"Delzoun," muttered Bruenor. "Gauntlgrym."

"Then she's no place akin to the tales," said Cordio, and Bruenor shot a glare his way.

"Grander, I'm saying," the priest quickly added.

"Whatever it was, it was grand indeed," said Drizzt. "And beyond my expectations when we set out from Mithral Hall. I had thought we would find a hole in the ground, Bruenor, or perhaps a small, ancient settlement."

"I told ye it was Gauntlgrym," Bruenor replied.

"If it is, then it is a place to do your Delzoun heritage proud," said the drow. "If it is not, then let us discover other accomplishments of which you can be rightly proud."

Bruenor's stubborn expression softened a bit at those words, and he offered Drizzt a nod and moved off deeper into the room, Thibbledorf at his heel. Drizzt looked to Cordio and Torgar, both of whom nodded their appreciation of his handling of the volatile king.

It was not Gauntlgrym, all three of them knew—at least, it was not the Gauntlgrym of dwarven legend. But what then?

There wasn't much to salvage in the library, but they did find a few scrolls that hadn't fully succumbed to the passage of time. None of them could read the writing on the ancient paper, but there were a few items that could give hints about the craftsmanship of the former residents, and even one tapestry that Regis believed could be cleaned enough to reveal some hints of its former depictions. They gathered their hoard together with great care, rolling and tying the tapestry and softly packing the other items in bags that had held the food they had thus far consumed.

They were done scouring the hall in less than an afternoon's time, and finished with a cursory and rather unremarkable examination of the rest of the cavern for just as long after that. Abruptly, and at Bruenor's insistence, so ended their expedition. Soon after, they climbed back up through the hole that had brought them underground and were greeted by a late winter's quiet night. At the next break of dawn they began their journey home, where they hoped to find some answers.

CHAPTER

King Obould normally liked the cheering of the many orcs that surrounded his temporary palace, a heavy tent set within a larger tent, set within a larger tent. All three were reinforced with metal and wood, and their entrances opened at different points for further security. Obould's most trusted guards, heavily armored and with great gleaming weapons, patrolled the two outer corridors.

The security measures were relatively new, as the orc king cemented his grip and began to unfold his strategy—a plan, the cheering that day only reminded him, that might not sit well with the warlike instincts of some of his subjects. He had already waged the first rounds of what he knew would be his long struggle among the stones of Keeper's Dale. His decision to stand down the attack on Mithral Hall had been met with more than a few mutterings of discontent.

And that had only been the beginning, of course.

He moved along the outer ring of his tent palace to the opened flap and looked out on the gathering on the plaza of the nomadic orc village. At least two hundred of his minions were out there, cheering wildly, thrusting weapons into the air, and clapping each other on the back. Word had come in of a great orc victory in the Moonwood, tales of elf heads spiked on the riverbank.

"We should go there and see the heads," Kna said to Obould as she curled at his side. "It is a sight that would fill me with lust."

Obould swiveled his head to regard her, and he offered a smile, knowing that stupid Kna would never understand it to be one of pity.

Out in the plaza, the cheering grew a backbone chant: "Karuck! Karuck! Karuck!"

It was not unexpected. Obould, who had received word of the fight in the east the previous night, before the public courier had arrived, motioned to the many loyalists he had set in place, and on his nod, they filtered into the crowd.

A second chant bubbled up among the first, "Many-Arrows! Many-Arrows! Many-Arrows!" And gradually, the call for kingdom overcame the cheer for clan.

"Take me there and I will love you," Kna whispered in the orc king's ear, tightening her hold on his side.

Obould's bloodshot eyes narrowed as he turned to regard her again. He brought his hand up to grab the back of her hair and roughly bent her head back so that she could see the intensity on his face. He envisioned those elf heads he'd heard of, set on tall pikes. His smile widened as he considered putting Kna's head in that very line.

Misconstruing his intensity as interest, the consort grinned and writhed against him.

With almost godlike strength, Obould tugged her from his side and tossed her to the ground. He turned back to the plaza and wondered how many of his minions—those not in his immediate presence—would add the chant of Many-Arrows to the praises of Clan Karuck as word of the victory spread throughout the kingdom.

* * * * *

The night was dark, but not to the sensitive eyes of Tos'un Armgo, who had known the blackness of the Underdark. He crouched by a rocky jag, looking down at the silvery snake known as the Surbrin River, and more pointedly at the line of poles before it.

The perpetrators had moved to the south, along with the prodding trio of Dnark, Ung-thol, and the upstart young Toogwik Tuk. They had talked of attacking the Battlehammer dwarves at the Surbrin.

Obould would not be pleased to see such independence among his ranks. And strangely, the drow wasn't overly thrilled at the prospect himself. He'd personally led the first orc assault on that dwarven position, infiltrating and silencing the main watchtower before the orc tide swept Clan Battlehammer back into its hole.

It had been a good day.

So what had changed, wondered Tos'un. What had left him with such melancholy when battle was afoot, particularly a battle between orcs and dwarves, two of the ugliest and smelliest races he had ever had the displeasure of knowing?

As he looked down at the river, he came to understand. Tos'un was a drow, had been raised in Menzoberranzan, and held no love for his surface elf cousins. The war between the surface and Underdark elves was among the fiercest rivalries in the world, a long history of dastardly deeds and murderous raids that equaled anything the continually warring demons of the Abyss and devils of the Nine Hells could imagine. Cutting out the throat of a surface elf had never presented Tos'un with a moral dilemma, surely, but there was something about the current situation, about those heads, that unnerved him, that filled him with a sense of dread.

As much as he hated surface elves, Tos'un despised orcs even more. The idea that orcs could have scored such a victory over elves of any sort left the drow cold. He had grown up in a city of twenty thousand dark elves, and with probably thrice that number of orc, goblin, and kobold slaves. Was there, perhaps, a Clan Karuck in their midst, ready to spike the heads of the nobles of House Barrison Del'Armgo or even of House Baenre?

He scoffed at the absurd notion, and reminded himself that surface elves were weaker than their drow kin. This group fell to Clan Karuck because they deserved it, because they were weak or stupid, or both.

Or at least, that's what Tos'un told himself over and over again, hoping that repetition would provide comfort where reason could not. He looked to the south, where the receding pennants of Clan Karuck had long been lost to the uneven landscape and the darkness. Whatever he might tell himself about the slaughter in the Moonwood, deep inside the true echoes of his heart and soul, Tos'un hoped that Grguch and his minions would all die horribly.

* * * * *

The sound of dripping water accompanied the wagon rolling east from Nesmé, as the warm day nibbled at winter's icy grip. Several times the wagon driver grumbled about muddy ruts, even expressing his hope that the night would be cold.

"If the night's warm, we'll be walking!" he warned repeatedly.

Catti-brie hardly heard him, and hardly noticed the gentle symphony of the melt around her. She sat in the bed of the wagon, with her back up against the driver's seat, staring out to the west behind them.

Wulfgar was out there, moving away from her. Away forever, she feared.

She was full of anger, full of hurt. How could he leave them with an army of orcs encamped around Mithral Hall? Why would he ever want to leave the Companions of the Hall? And how could he go without saying farewell to Bruenor, Drizzt, and Regis?

Her mind whirled through those questions and more, trying to make sense of it all, trying to come to terms with something she could not control. It wasn't the way things were supposed to be! She had tried to say that to Wulfgar, but his smile, so sure and serene, had defeated her argument before it could be made.

She thought back to the day when she and Wulfgar had left Mithral Hall for Silverymoon. She remembered the reactions of Bruenor and Drizzt—too emotional for the former and too stoic for the latter, she realized.

Wulfgar had told them. He'd said his good-byes before they set out, whether in explicit terms or in hints they could not miss. It hadn't been an impulsive decision brought about by some epiphany that had come to him on the road.

Catti-brie grimaced through a sudden flash of anger, at Bruenor and especially at Drizzt. How could they have known and not have told her?

She suppressed that anger quickly, and realized that it had been Wulfgar's choice. He had waited to tell her until after they'd recovered Colson. Catti-brie nodded as she considered that. He'd waited because he knew that the sight of the girl, the girl who had been taken from her mother and was to be returned, would make things more clear for Catti-brie.

"My anger isn't for Wulfgar, or any of them," she whispered.

"Eh?" asked the driver, and Catti-brie turned her head and gave him a smile that settled him back to his own business.

She held that smile as she turned back to stare at the empty west, and squinted, putting on a mask that might counter the tears that welled within. Wulfgar was gone, and if she sat back and considered his reasons, she knew she couldn't fault him. He was not a young man any longer. His legacy was still to be made, and time was running short. It would not be made in Mithral Hall, and even in the cities surrounding the dwarven stronghold, the people, the humans, were not kin to Wulfgar in appearance or in sensibility. His home was Icewind Dale. His people were in Icewind Dale. In Icewind Dale alone could he truly hope to find a wife.

Because Catti-brie was lost to him. And though he bore her no ill will, she understood the pain he must have felt when he looked upon her and Drizzt.

She and Wulfgar had had their moment, but that moment had passed, had been stolen by demons, both within Wulfgar and in the form of the denizens of the Abyss. Their moment had passed, and there seemed no other moments for Wulfgar to find in the court of a dwarf king.

"Farewell," Catti-brie silently mouthed to the empty west, and never had she so meant that simple word.

* * * * *

He bent low to bring Colson close to the flowering snowdrops, their tiny white bells denying the snow along the trail. The first flowers, the sign of coming spring.

"For Ma, Dell-y," Colson chattered happily, holding the first syllable of Delly's name for a long heartbeat, which only tugged all the more at Wulfgar's heart. "Flowvers," she giggled, and she pulled one close to her nose.

Wulfgar didn't correct her lisp, for she beamed as brightly as any "flowvers" ever could.

"Ma for flowvers." Colson rambled, and she mumbled through a dozen further sounds that Wulfgar could not decipher, though it was apparent to him that the girl thought she was speaking in cogent sentences. Wulfgar was sure that Colson made perfect sense to Colson, at least!

There was a little person in there—Wulfgar only truly realized at that innocent moment. A thinking, rational individual. She wasn't a baby anymore, wasn't helpless and unwitting.

The joy and pride that brought to Wulfgar was tempered, to be sure, by his realization that he would soon turn Colson over to her mother, to a woman the girl had never known in a land she had never called home.

"So be it," he said, and Colson looked at him and giggled, and gradually Wulfgar's delight overcame his sense of impending dread. He felt the season in his heart, as if his own internal, icy pall had at last been lifted. Nothing could change that overriding sensation. He was free. He was content. He knew in his heart that what he was doing was good, and right.

As he bent lower to the flower, he noted something else: a fresh print in the mud, right on the edge of the hardened snow. It had come from a shoddily-wrapped foot, and since it was so far from any town, Wulfgar recognized it at once as the print of a goblinkin's foot. He stood back up and glanced all around.

He looked to Colson and smiled comfortingly, then hustled along down the broken trail, his direction, fortunately, opposite the one the creature had taken. He wanted no battle that day, or any other day Colson was in his arms.

All the more reason to get the child back where she belonged.

Wulfgar hoisted the girl onto his broad shoulder and whistled quietly for her as his long legs carried them swiftly down the road, to the west.

Home.

* * * * *

North of Wulfgar's position, four dwarves, a halfling, and a drow settled around a small fire in a snowy dell. They had stopped their march early, that they could better light a fire to warm some stones that would get them more comfortably through the cold night. After briskly rubbing their hands over the dancing orange flames, Torgar, Cordio, and Thibbledorf set off to find the stones.

Bruenor hardly noticed their departure, for his gaze had settled on the sack of scrolls and artifacts, and on a tied tapestry lying nearby.

While Regis began preparing their supper, Drizzt just sat and watched his dwarf friend, for he knew that Bruenor was churning inside, and that he would soon enough need to speak his mind.

As if on cue, Bruenor turned to the drow. "Thought I'd find Gauntlgrym and find me answers," he said.

"You don't know whether you've found them or not," Drizzt reminded.

Bruenor grunted. "Weren't Gauntlgrym, elf. Not by any o' the legends o' the place. Not by any stories I e'er heard."

"Likely not," the drow agreed.

"Weren't no place I ever heared of."

"Which might prove even more important," said Drizzt.

"Bah," Bruenor snorted half-heartedly. "A place of riddles, and none that I'm wanting answered."

"They are what they are."

"And that be?"

"Hopefully revealed in the writings we took."

"Bah!" Bruenor snorted more loudly, and he waved his hands at Drizzt and at the sack of scrolls. "Gonna get me a stone to warm me bed," he muttered, and started away. "And one I can bang me head against."

The last remark brought a grin to Drizzt's face, reminding him that Bruenor would follow the clues wherever they led, whatever the implications. He held great faith in his friend.

"He's afraid," Regis remarked as soon as the dwarf was out of sight.

"He should be," Drizzt replied. "At stake are the very foundations of his world."

"What do you think is on the scrolls?" Regis asked, and Drizzt shrugged.

"And those statues!" the halfling went on undeterred. "Orcs and dwarves, and not in battle. What does it mean? Answers for us? Or just more questions?"

Drizzt thought about it for just a moment, and was nodding as he replied, "Possibilities."

PART
3

A WAR WITHIN A WAR

A WAR WITHIN A WAR

We construct our days, bit by bit, tenday by tenday, year by year. Our lives take on a routine, and then we bemoan that routine. Predictability, it seems, is a double-edged blade of comfort and boredom. We long for it, we build it, and when we find it, we reject it.

Because while change is not always growth, growth is always rooted in change. A finished person, like a finished house, is a static thing. Pleasant, perhaps, or beautiful or admirable, but not for long exciting.

King Bruenor has reached the epitome, the pinnacle, the realization of every dream a dwarf could fathom. And still King Bruenor desires change, though he would refuse to phrase it that way, admitting only his love of adventure. He has found his post, and now seeks reasons to abandon that post at every turn. He seeks, because inside of him he knows that he must seek to grow. Being a king will make Bruenor old before his time, as the old saying goes.

Not all people are possessed of such spirits. Some desire and cling to the comfort of the routine, to the surety that comes with the completion of the construction of life's details. On the smaller scale, they become wedded to their daily routines. They become enamored of the predictability. They calm their restless souls in the confidence that they have found their place in the multiverse, that things are the way they are supposed to be, that there are no roads left to explore and no reason to wander.

On the larger scale, such people become fearful and resentful—

sometimes to extremes that defy logic—of anyone or anything that intrudes on that construct. A societal change, a king's edict, an attitude shift in the neighboring lands, even events that have nothing to do with them personally can set off a reaction of dissonance and fear. When Lady Alustriel initially allowed me to walk the streets of Silverymoon openly, she found great resistance. Her people, well protected by one of the finest armies in all the land and by a leader whose magical abilities are renowned throughout the world, did not fear Drizzt Do'Urden. Nay, they feared the change that I represented. My very presence in Silverymoon infringed upon the construct of their lives, threatened their understanding of the way things were, threatened the way things were supposed to be. Even though, of course, I posed no threat to them whatsoever.

That is the line we all straddle, between comfort and adventure. There are those who find satisfaction, even fulfillment, in the former, and there are those who are forever seeking.

It is my guess, and can only be my guess, that the fears of the former are rooted in fear of the greatest mystery of all, death. It is no accident that those who construct the thickest walls are most often rooted firmly, immovably, in their faith. The here and now is as it is, and the better way will be found in the afterlife. That proposition is central to the core beliefs that guide the faithful, with, for many, the added caveat that the afterlife will only fulfill its promise if the here and now remains in strict accord with the guiding principles of the chosen deity.

I count myself among the other group, the seekers. Bruenor, too, obviously so, for he will ever be the discontented king. Catti-brie cannot be rooted. There is no sparkle in her eyes greater than the one when she looks upon a new road. And even Regis, for all his complaints regarding the trials of the road, wanders and seeks and fights. Wulfgar, too, will not be confined. He has seen his life in Mithral Hall and has concluded, rightfully and painfully, that there is for him a better place and a better way. It saddens me to see him go. For more than a score of years he has been my friend and companion, a trusted arm in battle and in life. I miss him dearly, every day, and yet when I think of him, I smile for him. Wulfgar has left Mithral Hall because he has outgrown all that this place can offer, because he knows that in Icewind Dale he will find a home where he will do more good—for himself and for those around him.

I, too, hold little faith that I will live out my days in Bruenor's kingdom. It is not just boredom that propels my steps along paths unknown, but a firm belief that the guiding principle of life must be a search not for what is, but for what could be. To look at injustice or oppression, at poverty or slavery, and shrug helplessly, or worse to twist a god's "word" to justify such states, is anathema to the ideal, and to me, the ideal is achieved only when the ideal is sought. The ideal is not a gift from the gods, but a promise from them.

We are possessed of reason. We are possessed of generosity. We are possessed of sympathy and empathy. We have within us a better nature, and it is one that cannot be confined by the constructed walls of anything short of the concept of heaven itself. Within the very logic of that better nature, a perfect life cannot be found in a world that is imperfect.

So we dare to seek. So we dare to change. Even knowing that we will not get to "heaven" in this life is no excuse to hide within the comfort of routine. For it is in that seeking, in that continual desire to improve ourselves and to improve the world around us, that we walk the road of enlightenment, that we eventually can approach the gods with heads bowed in humility, but with confidence that we did their work, that we tried to lift ourselves and our world to their lofty standards, the image of the ideal.

—Drizzt Do'Urden

CHAPTER

CONVERGENCE OF CRISES

15

Magical horses striding long, the fiery chariot cut a line of orange across the pre-dawn sky. Flames whipped in the driving wind, but for the riders they did not burn. Standing beside Lady Alustriel, Catti-brie felt that wind indeed, her auburn hair flying wildly behind her, but the bite of the breeze was mitigated by the warmth of Alustriel's animated cart. She lost herself in that sensation, allowing the howl of the wind to deafen her thoughts as well. For a short time, she was free to just exist, under the last twinkling stars with all of her senses consumed by the extraordinary nature of the journey.

She didn't see the approaching silver line of the Surbrin, and was only vaguely aware of a dip in altitude as Alustriel brought the conjured chariot down low over the water, and to a running stop on the ground outside the eastern door of Mithral Hall.

Few dwarves were out at that early hour, but those who were, mostly those standing guard along the northern wall, came running and cheering for the Lady of Silverymoon. For of course they knew it was she, whose chariot had graced them several times over the past few months.

Their cheering grew all the louder when they noted Alustriel's passenger, the Princess of Mithral Hall.

"Well met," more than one of the bearded folk greeted.

"King Bruenor's not yet returned," said one, a grizzled old sort, with one eye lost and patched over, and half his great black beard torn away. Catti-brie smiled as she recognized the fierce and fiercely loyal Shingles

McRuff, who had come to Mithral Hall beside Torgar Hammerstriker. "Should be along any day."

"And be knowin' that ye're all welcome, and that ye'll find all the hospitality o' Mithral Hall for yerself," another dwarf offered.

"That is most generous," said Alustriel. She turned and looked back to the east as she continued, "More of my people—wizards from Silverymoon—will be coming in throughout the morn, on all manner of flight, some self-propelled and some riding ebony flies, and two on broomsticks and another on a carpet. I pray your archers will not shoot them down."

"Ebony flies?" Shingles replied. "Flying on bugs, ye mean?"

"Big bugs," said Catti-brie.

"Would have to be."

"We come armed with spells of creation, for we wish to see the bridge across the Surbrin opened and secure as soon as possible," Alustriel explained. "For the sake of Mithral Hall and for all the goodly kingdoms of the Silver Marches."

"More well met, then!" bellowed Shingles, and he led yet another cheer.

Catti-brie moved toward the back edge of the chariot, but Alustriel took her by the shoulder. "We can fly out to the west and seek King Bruenor," she offered.

Catti-brie paused and looked that way, but shook her head and replied, "He will return presently, I'm sure."

Catti-brie accepted Shingles's offered hand, and let the dwarf ease her down to the ground. Shingles was quick to Alustriel, similarly helping her, and the Lady, though not injured as was Catti-brie, graciously accepted. She moved back from her cart and motioned for the others to follow.

Alustriel could have simply dismissed the flaming chariot and the horses made of magical fire. Dispelling her own magic was easy work, of course, and the fiery team and cart alike would have flared for an instant before they winked into blackness, a final puff of smoke drifting and dissipating into the air.

But Lady Alustriel had been using that particular spell for many years, and had put her own flavor into it, both in the construction of the cart and team and in the dismissal of the magic. Figuring that the dwarves could use a bit of spirit-lifting, the powerful wizardess performed her most impressive variation of the dispelling.

The horse team snorted and reared, flames shooting from swirling, fiery nostrils. As one, they leaped into the air, straight up, the cart lurching behind them. Some twenty feet off the ground, the many sinews of fire that held the form broke apart, orange tendrils soaring every which way, and as they reached their limits, exploded with deafening bangs, throwing showers of sparks far and wide.

The dwarves howled with glee, and Catti-brie, for all of her distress, couldn't contain a giggle.

When it ended a few heartbeats later, their ears ringing with the echoes of the retorts, their eyes blinking against the sting of the brilliant flashes, Catti-brie offered an appreciative smile to her friend and driver.

"It was just the enchantment they needed," she whispered, and Alustriel replied with a wink.

They went into Mithral Hall side-by-side.

* * * * *

Early the next morning, Shingles again found himself in the role of official greeter in the region east of the hall's eastern gate, for it was he who first caught up with the six adventurers returning from the place Bruenor had named Gauntlgrym. The old Mirabarran dwarf had directed the watch overnight, and was sorting out assignments for the workday, both along the fortifications on the northern mountain spur and at the bridge. No stranger to the work of wizards, Shingles repeatedly warned his boys to stay well back when Alustriel's gang came out to work their dweomers. When word came that King Bruenor and the others had returned, Shingles moved fast to the south to intercept them.

"Did ye find it, then, me king?" he asked excitedly, giving voice to the thoughts and whispers of all the others around him.

"Aye," Bruenor replied, but in a tone surprisingly unenthusiastic. "We found something, though we're not for knowing if it's Gauntlgrym just yet." He motioned to the large sack that Torgar carried, and the rolled tapestry slung over Cordio's shoulder. "We've some things for Nanfoodle and me scholars to look over. We'll get our answers."

"Yer girl's come home," Shingles explained. "Lady Alustriel flew her in on that chariot o' fire. And the Lady's here, too, along with ten Silverymoon wizards, all come to work on the bridge."

Bruenor, Drizzt, and Regis exchanged glances as Shingles finished.

"Me girl alone?" Bruenor asked.

"With the Lady."

Bruenor stared at Shingles.

"Wulfgar's not returned with 'em," the old Mirabarran dwarf said. "Catti-brie said nothing of it, and I didn't think it me place to ask."

Bruenor looked to Drizzt.

"He is far west," the drow said quietly, and Bruenor inadvertently glanced out that way then nodded.

"Get me to me girl," Bruenor instructed as he started off at a swift pace for Mithral Hall's eastern door.

They found Catti-brie, Lady Alustriel, and the Silverymoon wizards not far down the corridor inside, the lot of them having spent the night in the hall's easternmost quarters. After a quick and polite greeting, Bruenor begged the Lady's pardon, and Alustriel and her wizards quickly departed the hall, heading for the Surbrin bridge.

"Where's he at?" Bruenor asked Catti-brie when it was just the two of them, Drizzt, and Regis.

"You're knowing well enough."

"Ye found Colson, then?"

Catti-brie nodded.

"And he's taking her home," Bruenor stated.

Another nod. "I offered to journey with him," Catti-brie explained, and she glanced at Drizzt and was relieved to see him smile at that news. "But he would not have me along."

"Because the fool ain't for coming back," said Bruenor, and he spat and stalked off. "Durned fool son of an over-sized orc."

Drizzt motioned to Regis to go with Bruenor, and the halfling nodded and trotted away.

"I think Bruenor is right," Catti-brie said, and she shook her head in futile denial, then rushed over and wrapped Drizzt in a tight hug and kissed him deeply. She put her head on his shoulder, not relenting a bit in her embrace. She sniffed back tears.

"He knew that Wulfgar would not likely return," Drizzt whispered.

Catti-brie pushed him back to arms' length. "As did yourself, but you didn't tell me," she said.

"I honored Wulfgar's wishes. He was not sure of where his road would lead, but he did not wish discussion of it all the way to Silverymoon and beyond."

"If I had known along our road, I might've been able to change his mind," Catti-brie protested.

Drizzt gave her a helpless look. "More the reason to not tell you."

"You agree with Wulfgar's choice?"

"I think it is not my place to agree or to argue," Drizzt said with a shrug.

"You think it's his place to be deserting Bruenor at this time of—?"

"This time or any time."

"How can you say that? Wulfgar is family to us, and he just left . . ."

"As you and I did those years ago, after the drow war when Wulfgar fell to the yochlol," Drizzt reminded her. "We longed for the road and so we took to the road, and left Bruenor to his hall. For six years."

That reminder seemed to deflate Catti-brie's ire quite a bit. "But now Bruenor's got an army of orcs on his doorstep," she protested, but with far less enthusiasm.

"An army that will likely be there for years to come. Wulfgar told me that he could not see his future here. And truly, what is there for him here? No wife, no children."

"And it pained him to look upon us."

Drizzt nodded. "Likely."

"He told me as much."

"And so you wear a mantle of guilt?"

Catti-brie shrugged.

"It doesn't suit you," Drizzt said. He drew her in close once more, and gently pushed her head onto his shoulder. "Wulfgar's road is Wulfgar's own to choose. He has family in Icewind Dale, if that is where he decides to go. He has his people there. Would you deny him the chance to find love? Should he not sire children, who will follow his legacy of leadership among the tribes of Icewind Dale?"

Catti-brie didn't respond for a long while then merely said, "I miss him already," in a voice weak with sorrow.

"As do I. And so too for Bruenor and Regis, and all else who knew him. But he isn't dead. He did not fall in battle, as we feared those years ago. He will follow his road, to bring Colson home, as he 'sees fit, and then perhaps to Icewind Dale. Or perhaps not. It might be that when he is away, Wulfgar will come to realize that Mithral Hall truly is his home, and turn again for Bruenor's halls. Or perhaps he'll take another wife, and return to us with her, full of love and free of pain."

He pushed Catti-brie back again, his lavender eyes locking stares with her rich blue orbs. "You have to trust in Wulfgar. He has earned that from us all many times over. Allow him to walk whatever road he chooses, and hold confidence that you and I, and Bruenor and Regis, all go with him in his heart, as we carry him in ours. You carry with you guilt you do not deserve. Would you truly desire that Wulfgar not follow his road for the sake of mending your melancholy?"

Catti-brie considered the words for a few heartbeats, then managed a smile. "My heart is not empty," she said, and she came forward and kissed Drizzt again, with urgency and passion.

* * * * *

"Whate'er ye're needin', ye're gettin'," Bruenor assured Nanfoodle as the gnome gently slid one of the parchment scrolls out of the sack. "Rumblebelly here is yer slave, and he'll be running to meself and all me boys at the command o' Nanfoodle."

The gnome began to unroll the document, but winced and halted, hearing the fragile parchment crackle.

"I will have to brew oils of preservation," he explained to Bruenor. "I dare not put this under bright light until it's properly treated."

"Whate'er ye need," Bruenor assured him. "Ye just get it done, and get it done quick."

"How quick?" The gnome seemed a bit unnerved by that request.

"Alustriel's here now," said Bruenor. "She's to be working on the bridge for the next few days, and I'm thinkin' that if them scrolls're saying what I'm thinkin' they're saying, it might be good for Alustriel to go back to Silverymoon muttering and musing on the revelations."

But Nanfoodle shook his head. "It will take me more than a day to prepare the potions—and that's assuming that you have the ingredients

I will require." He looked to Regis. "Bat guano forms the base."

"Wonderful," the halfling muttered.

"We'll have it or we'll get it," Bruenor promised him.

"It will take more than a day to brew anyway," said Nanfoodle. "Then three days for it to set on the parchment—at least three. I'd rather it be five."

"So four days total," said Bruenor, and the gnome nodded.

"Just to prepare the parchments for examination," Nanfoodle was quick to add. "It could take me tendays to decipher the ancient writing, even with my magic."

"Bah, ye'll be faster."

"I cannot promise."

"Ye'll be faster," Bruenor said again, in a tone less encouraging and more demanding. "Guano," he said to Regis, and he turned and walked from the room.

"Guano," Regis repeated, looking at Nanfoodle helplessly.

"And oil from the smiths," said the gnome. He drew another scroll from the sack and placed it beside the first, then put his hands on his hips and heaved a great sigh. "If they understood the delicacy of the task, they would not be so impatient," he said, more to himself than to the halfling.

"Bruenor is well past delicacy, I'm guessing," said Regis. "Too many orcs about for delicacy."

"Orcs and dwarves," muttered the gnome. "Orcs and dwarves. How is an artist to do his work?" He heaved another sigh, as if to say "if I must," and moved to the side of the room, to the cabinet where he kept his mortar and pestle, and assorted spoons and vials.

"Always rushing, always grumbling," he griped. "Orcs and dwarves, indeed!"

* * * * *

The companions had barely settled into their chambers in the dwarven hall west of Garumn's Gorge when word came that yet another unexpected visitor had arrived at the eastern gate. It wasn't often that elves walked through King Bruenor's door, but those gates were swung wide for Hralien of the Moonwood.

Drizzt, Catti-brie, and Bruenor waited impatiently in Bruenor's audience chamber for the elf.

"Alustriel and now Hralien," Bruenor said, nodding with every word. "It's all coming together. Once we get the words from them scrolls, we'll get both o' them to agree that the time's now for striking them smelly orcs."

Drizzt held his doubts private and Catti-brie merely smiled and nodded. There was no reason to derail Bruenor's optimism with an injection of sober reality.

"We know them Adbar and Felbarr boys'll fight with us," Bruenor went on, oblivious to the detachment of his audience. "If we're getting the Moonwood and Silverymoon to join in, we'll be puttin' them orcs back in their holes in short order, don't ye doubt!"

He rambled on sporadically for the next few moments, until at last Hralien was led into the chamber and formally introduced.

"Well met, King Bruenor," the elf said after the list of his accomplishments and titles was read in full. "I come with news from the Moonwood."

"Long ride if ye've come just to break bread," said Bruenor.

"We have suffered an incursion from the orcs," Hralien explained, talking right past Bruenor's little jest. "A coordinated and cunning attack."

"We know yer pain," Bruenor replied, and Hralien bowed in appreciation.

"Several of my people were lost," Hralien went on, "elves who should have known the birth and death of centuries to come." He looked squarely at Drizzt as he continued, "Innovindil among them."

Drizzt's eyes widened and he gasped and slumped back, and Catti-brie brought her arm across his back to support him.

"And Sunset beneath her," said Hralien, his voice less steady. "It would appear that the orcs had anticipated her arrival on the field, and were well prepared."

Drizzt's chest pumped with strong, gasping breaths. He looked as if he was about to say something, but no words came forth and he had the strength only to shake his head in denial. A great emptiness washed through him, a cold loss and callous reminder of the harsh immediacy of change, a sudden and irreversible reminder of mortality.

"I share your grief," Hralien said. "Innovindil was my friend, beloved by all who knew her. And Sunrise is bereaved, do not doubt, for the loss of Innovindil and of Sunset, his companion for all these years."

"Durned pig orcs," Bruenor growled. "Are ye all still thinkin' we should leave them to their gains? Are ye still o' the mind that Obould's kingdom should stand?"

"Orcs have attacked the Moonwood for years uncounted," Hralien replied. "They come for wood and for mischief, and we kill them and send them running. But their attack was better this time—too much so for the simplistic race, we believe." As he finished, he was again looking directly at Drizzt, so much so that he drew curious stares from Bruenor and Catti-brie in response.

"Tos'un Armgo," Drizzt reasoned.

"We know him to be in the region, and he learned much of our ways in his time with Albondiel and Sinnafain," Hralien explained.

Drizzt nodded, determination replacing his wounded expression. He had vowed to hunt down Tos'un when he and Innovindil had returned Ellifain's body to the Moonwood. Suddenly that promise seemed all the more critical.

"A journey full o' grief is a longer ride by ten, so the sayin' goes," said Bruenor. "Ye make yerself comfortable, Hralien o' the Moonwood. Me boys'll see to yer every need, and ye stay as long as ye're wantin'. Might be that I'll have a story for ye soon enough—one that'll put us all in better stead for ridding ourselves o' the curse of Obould. A few days at the most, me friends're tellin' me."

"I am a courier of news, and have come with a request, King Bruenor," the elf explained, and he gave another respectful and appreciative bow. "Others will journey here from the Moonwood to your call, of course, but my own road is back through your eastern door no later than dawn tomorrow." Again he looked Drizzt in the eye. "I hope I will not be alone."

Drizzt nodded his agreement to go out on the hunt before he even turned to Catti-brie. He knew that she would not deny him that.

* * * * *

The couple were alone in their room soon after, and Drizzt began to fill his backpack.

R. A. SALVATORE

"You're going after Tos'un," Catti-brie remarked, but did not ask.

"Have I a choice?"

"No. I only wish that I were well enough to go with you."

Drizzt paused in his packing and turned to regard her. "In Menzoberranzan, they say, *Aspis tu drow bed n'tuth drow.* 'Only a drow can hunt a drow.' "

"Then hunt well," said Catti-brie, and she moved to the side wardrobe to aid Drizzt in his preparations. She seemed not upset with him in the least, which was why she caught Drizzt completely off his guard when she quietly asked, "Would you have married Innovindil when I am gone?"

Drizzt froze, and slowly mustered the courage to turn and look at Catti-brie. She wore a slight smile and seemed quite at ease and comfortable. She moved to their bed and sat on the edge, and motioned for Drizzt to join her.

"Would you have?" she asked again as he approached. "Innovindil was very beautiful, in body and in mind."

"It is not something I think about," said Drizzt.

Catti-brie's smile grew wider. "I know," she assured him. "But I am asking you to consider it now. Could you have loved her?"

Drizzt thought about it for a few moments then admitted, "I do not know."

"And you never wondered about it at all?"

Drizzt's thoughts went back to a moment he had shared with Innovindil when the two of them were out alone among the orc lines. Innovindil had nearly seduced him, though only to let him see more clearly his feelings for Catti-brie, whom he had thought dead at the time.

"You could have loved her, I think," Catti-brie said.

"You may well be right," he said.

"Do you think she thought of you in her last moments?"

Drizzt's eyes widened in shock at the blunt question, but Catti-brie didn't back down.

"She thought of Tarathiel, likely, and what was," he answered.

"Or of Drizzt and what might have been."

Drizzt shook his head. "She would not have looked there. Not then. Likely her every thought was for Sunset. To be an elf is to find the moment, the here and now. To revel in what is with knowledge and acceptance that what will be, will be, no matter the hopes and plans of any."

"Innovindil would have had a fleeting moment of regret for Drizzt, and potential love lost," Catti-brie said.

Drizzt didn't disagree, and couldn't, given the woman's generous tone and expression. Catti-brie wasn't judging him, wasn't looking for reasons to doubt him. She confirmed that a moment later, when she laughed and put her hand up to stroke his cheek.

"You will outlive me by centuries, in all likelihood," she explained. "I understand the implications of that, my love, and what a selfish fool I would be if I expected you to remain faithful to a memory. Nor would I want—nor do I want—that for you."

"It doesn't mean that we have to speak of it," Drizzt retorted. "We know not where our roads will lead, nor which of us will outlive the other. These are dangerous times in a dangerous world."

"I know."

"Then is this something we should bother to discuss?"

Catti-brie shrugged, but gradually her smile dissipated and a cloud crossed her fair features.

"What is it?" Drizzt asked, and lifted his hand to turn her to face him directly.

"If the dangers do not end our time together, how will Drizzt feel, I wonder, in twenty years? Or thirty?"

The drow wore a puzzled expression.

"You will still be young and handsome, and full of life and love to give," Catti-brie explained. "But I will be old and bent and ugly. You will stay by my side, I am sure, but what life will that be? What lust?"

It was Drizzt's turn to laugh.

"Can you look at a human woman who has seen the turn of seventy years and think her attractive?"

"Are there not couples of humans still in love after so many years together?" Drizzt asked. "Are there not human husbands who love their wives still when seventy is a birthday passed?"

"But the husbands are not usually in the springtime of their lives."

"You err because you pretend that it will happen overnight, in the snap of fingers," Drizzt said. "That is far from the case, even for an elf looking upon the human lifespan. Every wrinkle is earned, my love. Day by day, we spend our time together, and the changes that come will be well earned. In your heart you know that I love you, and I have no doubt but that my love will grow with the passage of years. I know your heart, Catti-brie. You are blissfully predictable to me in some ways, never so in others. I know where your choices will be, time and again, and ever are they on the right side of justice and integrity."

Catti-brie smiled and kissed him, but Drizzt broke it off fast and pushed her back.

"If a dragon's fiery breath were to catch up with me, and scar my skin hideously, blind me, and keep about me a stench of burnt flesh, would Catti-brie still love me?"

"Wonderful thought," the woman said dryly.

"Would she? Would you stand beside me?"

"Of course."

"And if I thought otherwise, at all, then never would I have desired to be your husband. Do you not similarly trust in me?"

Catti-brie grinned and kissed him again, then pushed him on his back on the bed.

The packing could wait.

* * * * *

Early the next morning, Drizzt leaned over the sleeping Catti-brie and gently brushed her lips with his own. He stared at her for a long while, even while he walked from the bed to the door. He at last turned and nearly jumped back in surprise, for set against the door was Taulmaril, the Heartseeker, Catti-brie's bow, and lying below it was her magical quiver, one that never ran out of arrows. For a moment, Drizzt stood confused, until he noticed a small note on the floor by the quiver. From a puncture in its side, he deduced that it had been pressed onto the top of the bow but had not held its perch.

He knew what it said before he ever brought it close enough to read the scribbling.

He looked back at Catti-brie once more. She couldn't be with him in body, perhaps, but with Taulmaril in his hand, she'd be there in spirit.

Drizzt slung the bow over his shoulder then retrieved the quiver and did likewise. He looked back once more to his love then left the room without a sound.

CHAPTER

16

The warriors of Clan Karuck paraded onto the muddy plaza centering a small orc village one rainy morning, the dreary overcast and pounding rain doing nothing to diminish the glory of their thunderous march.

"Stand and stomp!" the warriors sang in voices that resonated deeply from their massive half-ogre chests. "Smash and crush! All for the glory of One-eye Gruumsh!"

Yellow pennants flapping in the wind, waves of mud splattering with every coordinated step, the clan came on in tight and precise formation, their six flags moving, two-by-two, in near perfect synchronization. The curious onlookers couldn't help but notice the stark contrast between the huge half-ogre, half-orcs and the scores of orcs from other tribes that had been swept up into their wake from the first villages through which Chieftain Grguch had marched.

Only one full-blooded orc marched with Grguch, a young and fiery shaman. Toogwik Tuk wasted no time as the villagers gathered. He moved out in front as Grguch halted his march.

"We are fresh from victory in the Moonwood!" Toogwik Tuk proclaimed, and every orc along the eastern reaches of Obould's fledgling kingdom knew well that hated place. Thus, predictably, a great cheer greeted the news.

"All hail Chieftain Grguch of Clan Karuck!" Toogwik Tuk proclaimed, and that was met with an uncomfortable pause until he added, "For the glory of King Obould!"

Toogwik Tuk glanced back to Grguch, who nodded his agreement, and the young shaman started the chant, "Grguch! Obould! Grguch! Obould! Grguch! Grguch! Grguch!"

All of Clan Karuck fell in quickly with the cadence, as did the orcs who had already joined in with the march, and the villagers' doubts were quickly overwhelmed.

"As Obould before him, Chieftain Grguch will bring the judgment of Gruumsh upon our enemies!" Toogwik Tuk cried, running through the mob and whipping them into frenzy. "The snow retreats, and we advance!" With every glorious proclamation, he took care to add, "For the glory of Obould! By the power of Grguch!"

Toogwik Tuk understood well the weight that had settled on his shoulders. Dnark and Ung-thol had departed for the west to meet with Obould regarding the new developments, and it fell squarely upon Toogwik Tuk to facilitate Grguch's determined march to the south. Clan Karuck alone would not stand against Obould and his thousands, obviously, but if Clan Karuck carried along with them the orc warriors from the dozen villages lining the Surbrin, their arrival on the field north of King Bruenor's fortifications would carry great import—enough, so the conspirators hoped, to coerce the involvement of the army Obould had likely already positioned there.

That sort of rabble rousing had been Toogwik Tuk's signature for years. His rise through the ranks to become the chief shaman of his tribe—almost all of whom were dead, crushed in the mysterious, devastating explosion of a mountain ridge north of Keeper's Dale—had been expedited by precisely that talent. He knew well how to manipulate the emotions of the peasant orcs, to conflate their present loyalties with what he wanted their loyalties to be. Every time he mentioned Obould, he was quick to add the name Grguch. Every time he spoke of Gruumsh, he was quick to add the name of Grguch. Mingle them, say them together enough times so that his audience would unwittingly add "Grguch" whenever they heard the names of the other two.

His energy again proved infectious, and he soon had all of the villagers hopping about and chanting with him, always for the glory of Obould, and always by the power of Grguch.

Those two names needed to be intimately linked, the three conspirators had decided before Dnark and Ung-thol had departed. To even hint against Obould after such dramatic and sweeping victories as the orc king had brought would have spelled a fast end to the coup. Even considering the disastrous attempt to enter Mithral Hall's western gate, or the loss of the eastern ground between the dwarven halls and the Surbrin, or the stall throughout winter and the whispers that it might be longer than that, the vast majority of orcs spoke of Obould in the hushed tones usually reserved for Gruumsh himself. But Toogwik Tuk and two companions planned to move the tribes to oppose their king, one baby-step at a time.

"By the power of Grguch!" Toogwik Tuk cried again, and before the cheer could erupt, he added, "Will the dwarven wall hold against a warrior who burned the Moonwood?"

Though he expected a cheer, Toogwik Tuk was answered with looks of suspicion and confusion.

"The dwarves will flee before us," the shaman promised. "Into their hole they will run, and we will control the Surbrin for King Obould! *For the glory of King Obould!*" he finished, screaming with all his power.

The orcs around him cheered wildly, insanely.

"By the power of Grguch!" the not-quite-so-out-of-control Toogwik Tuk cleverly added, and many of the villagers, so used to the chant by then, shouted the words right along beside him.

Toogwik Tuk glanced back at Chieftain Grguch, who wore a most satisfied grin.

Another step taken, Toogwik Tuk knew.

Taking many offered supplies, Clan Karuck soon resumed their march, and a new pennant flew among the many in the mob behind them, and another forty warriors eagerly melded into Chieftain Grguch's trailing ranks. With several larger villages before them, both the chieftain and his shaman spokesman expected that they would number in the thousands when they at last reached the dwarven wall.

Toogwik Tuk held faith that when they smashed that wall, the cries for Grguch would be louder than those for Obould. The next cheers he led would hold fewer references to the glory of Obould and more to the glory of Gruumsh. But he would not lessen the number of his claims that all of it was being wrought by the power of Grguch.

* * * * *

Jack could see that the sprout of hair on one side of Hakuun's mis-shapen, wart-covered nose tingled with nervous energy as he walked out from the main host, among dark pines and broken fir trees.

"By sprockets and elemental essences, that was exciting, wasn't it?"

The orc shaman froze in place at the all-too-familiar voice, composed himself with a deep breath that greatly flared his nostrils, and slowly turned to regard a curious little humanoid in brilliant purple robes sitting on a low branch, swinging his feet back and forth like a carefree child. The form was new to Hakuun. Oh, he knew what a gnome was, indeed, but he had never seen Jaculi in that state before.

"That young priest is so full of spirit," Jack said. "I almost walked out and joined in with Grguch myself! Oh, what a grand march they have planned!"

"I didn't ask you to come up here," Hakuun remarked.

"Did you not?" said Jack, and he hopped down from the tree and brushed the twigs from his fabulous robes. "Tell me, Shaman of Clan Karuck, what am I to think when I peer out from my work to find that the one to whom I have bestowed such great gifts has run off?"

"I did not run off," Hakuun insisted, trying to keep his voice steady, though he was visibly near panic. "Often does Clan Karuck go hunting."

Hakuun gave ground as the gnome walked up to him. Jack continued to advance as Hakuun retreated.

"But this was no ordinary excursion."

Hakuun looked at Jack with dull curiosity, obviously not understanding him.

"No ordinary *hunt,*" Jack explained.

"I have told you."

"Of Obould, yes, and of his thousands," said Jack. "A bit of mischief and a bit of loot to be found, so you said. But it is more than that, is it not?"

Again Hakuun wore a puzzled expression.

Jack snapped his stubby fingers in the air and whirled away. "Do you not feel it, shaman?" he asked, his voice full of excitement. "Do you not recognize that this is no ordinary hunt?"

Jack spun back on Hakuun to measure his response, and still he saw that the shaman wasn't quite catching on. For Jack, so perceptive and cunning, had deduced the subtext of Toogwik Tuk's speech, and the implications it offered.

"Perhaps it is just my own suspicion," the gnome said, "but you must tell me all that you know. Then we should speak with that spirited young priest."

"I have told you . . ." Hakuun protested. His voiced trailed off and he retreated a step, knowing what awful thing was about to befall him.

"No, I mean that you must tell me everything," Jack said, all humor gone from his voice and his expression as he took a step toward the shaman. Hakuun shrank back, but that only made Jack stride more purposefully.

"Ah, you do forget," the gnome said as he closed the gap. "All that I have done for you, and so little have I asked in return. With great power, Hakuun, comes great expectations."

"There is nothing more," the shaman started to plead, and he held up his hands.

Jack the Gnome wore a mask of evil. He said not a word, but pointed to the ground. Hakuun shook his head feebly and continued to wave, and Jack continued to point.

But it was no contest, the outcome never in doubt. With a slight whimper, Hakuun, the mighty shaman of Clan Karuck, the conduit between Grguch and Gruumsh, prostrated himself on the ground, face down.

Jack looked straight ahead and lowered his arms to his sides as he quietly mouthed the words to his spell. He thought of the mysterious illithids, the brilliant mind flayers, who had taught him so much of one particular school of magic.

His robes fluttered only briefly as he shrank, then they and all his other gear melded into his changing form. In an instant Jack the Gnome was gone and a sightless rodent padded across the ground on four tiny feet. He went up to Hakuun's ear and sniffed for a few moments, hesitating simply because he recognized how uncomfortable it was making the cowering creature.

Then Jack the Gnome-cum-brain mole crawled into Hakuun's ear and disappeared from sight.

Hakuun shuddered and jerked in agonized spasms as the creature burrowed deeper, through the walls of his inner ear and into the seat of his consciousness. The shaman forced himself up to all fours as he began to gag. He vomited and spat, though of course the feeble defenses of his physical body could not begin to dislodge his unwelcome guest.

A few moments later, Hakuun staggered to his feet.

There, said the voice of Jack in his head. *Now I better understand the purpose of this adventure, and together we will learn the extent of this spirited young shaman's plans.*

Hakuun didn't argue—there was no way he could, of course. And for all his revulsion and pain, Hakuun knew that with Jack inside him, he was much more perceptive, and many times more powerful.

A private conversation with Toogwik Tuk, Jack instructed, and Hakuun could not disagree.

* * * * *

Even with their sensitive elf ears, Drizzt and Hralien could only make out the loudest chants from the gathered orcs. Still, the purpose of the march became painfully obvious.

"They are the ones," Hralien remarked. "The yellow banner was seen in the Moonwood. It appears that their numbers have . . ."

He paused as he looked over at his companion, who didn't seem to be listening. Drizzt crouched, perfectly still, his head turned back to the south, toward Mithral Hall.

"We have already passed several orc settlements," the drow said a few heartbeats later. "No doubt this march will cross through each."

"Swelling their numbers," Hralien agreed, and Drizzt finally looked at him.

"And they'll continue southward," the drow reasoned.

Hralien said, "This may be renewed aggression brewing. And I fear that there is an instigator."

"Tos'un?" said Drizzt. "I see no dark elf among the gathering."

"He's likely not far afield."

"Look at them," Drizzt said, nodding his chin in the direction of the chanting, cheering orcs. "If Tos'un did instigate this madness, could he still be in control of it?"

It was Hralien's turn to shrug. "Do not underestimate his cunning," the elf warned. "The attack on the Moonwood was well-coordinated, and brutally efficient."

"Obould's orcs have surprised us at every turn."

"And they were not without drow advisors."

The two locked stares at that remark, a cloud briefly crossing Drizzt's face.

"I truly believe that Tos'un orchestrated the attack on the Moonwood," Hralien said. "And that he is behind this march, wherever it may lead."

Drizzt glanced back to the south, toward Bruenor's kingdom.

"It may well be that their destination is Mithral Hall," Hralien conceded. "But I beg you to continue on the road that led you out of Bruenor's depths. For all our sakes, find Tos'un Armgo. I will shadow these orcs, and will give ample warning to King Bruenor should it become necessary—and I will err on the side of caution. Trust me in this, I beg, and free yourself for this most important task."

Drizzt looked from the gathered orcs back toward Mithral Hall yet again. He envisioned a battle fought along the Surbrin, fierce and vicious, and felt the pangs of guilt in considering that Bruenor and Regis, perhaps even Catti-brie and the rest of Clan Battlehammer, would yet again be fighting for their survival without him by their side. He winced as he saw again the fall of the tower at Shallows, with Dagnabbit, whom he had then thought to be Bruenor, tumbling down to his death atop it.

He took a deep breath and turned back to the orc frenzy, the chanting and dancing continuing unabated. If a dark elf from Barrison Del'Armgo, one of the most formidable Houses of Menzoberranzan, was to blame then the orcs would no doubt prove many times more formidable than they appeared. Drizzt nodded grimly, his responsibility and thus his path clear before him.

"Follow their every move," he bade Hralien.

"On my word," the elf replied. "Your friends will not be caught unprepared."

The orcs moved along soon after, and Hralien shadowed their southwestern march, leaving Drizzt alone on the mountainside. He considered going down to the orc village and snooping around, but decided that

Tos'un, if he was about, would likely be along the periphery, among the stones, as was Drizzt.

"Come to me, Guenhwyvar," the drow commanded, drawing forth the onyx figurine. When the gray mist coalesced into the panther, Drizzt sent her out hunting. Guenhwyvar could cover a tremendous amount of ground in short order, and not even a lone drow could escape her keen senses.

Drizzt, too, set off, moving deliberately but with great caution in the opposite direction from the panther, who was already cutting across the wake of the departing army. If Hralien's guess was correct and Tos'un Armgo was directing the orcs from nearby, Drizzt held all faith that he would soon confront the rogue.

His hands went to his scimitars as he considered Khazid'hea, Catti-brie's sword, the weapon that had fallen into the hands of Tos'un. Any drow warrior was formidable. A warrior of a noble House likely more so. Even thinking in those respectful terms, Drizzt consciously reminded himself that the drow noble was even more potent, for those who under-estimated Khazid'hea usually wound up on the ground.

In two pieces.

* * * * *

Interesting, Jack said to Hakuun's mind when they walked away from their quiet little meeting with Toogwik Tuk, one in which Jack had used the power of magical suggestion to complement Hakuun's spells of lie detection, allowing the dual being to extract much more honest answers from Toogwik Tuk than the young shaman had ever meant to offer. *So the conspirators have not brought you here to enhance Obould's forces.*

"We must tell Grguch," Hakuun whispered.

Tell him what? That we have come to do battle?

"That our venture into the Moonwood and now against the dwarves will likely anger Obould."

Inside his head, Hakuun could feel Jack laughing. *Orcs plotting against orcs,* Jack silently related. *Orcs manipulating orcs to plot against orcs. All of this will be surprising news to old Chieftain Grguch, I am sure.*

Hakuun's determined stride slowed, his tailwind stolen by Jack's cynical sarcasm—sarcasm effective only because it held the ring of truth.

Let the play play, said Jack. *The plots of the conspirators will be bent to our favor when we need them to be. For now, all the risk is theirs, for Clan Karuck is unwitting. If they have played the part of fools to even consider such a plot, their fall will be enjoyable to witness. If they are not fools, then all to our gain.*

"Our gain?" said Hakuun, emphasizing Jack's inclusion into it all.

"For as long as I am interested," Hakuun's voice replied, though it was Jack who controlled it.

A not-so-subtle reminder, Hakuun understood, of who was leading whom.

CHAPTER
DEFINING GRUUMSH

Chieftain Dnark did not miss the simmer behind King Obould's yellow eyes whenever the orc king's glance happened his and Ung-thol's way. Obould was continually repositioning his forces, which all of the chieftains understood was the king's way of keeping them in unfamiliar territory, and thus, keeping them dependent upon the larger kingdom for any real sense of security. Dnark and Ung-thol had rejoined their clan, the tribe of the Wolf Jaw, only to learn that Obould had summoned them to work on a defensive position north of Keeper's Dale, not far from where Obould had settled to ride out the fleeting days of winter.

As soon as Obould had met Wolf Jaw at the new site, the wise and perceptive Dnark understood that there had been more to that movement than simple tactical repositioning, and when he'd first met the orc king's gaze, he had known beyond doubt that he and Ung-thol had been the focus of Obould's decision.

The annoying Kna squirmed around his side, as always, and shaman Nukkels kept to a respectful two paces behind and to his god-figure's left. That meant that Nukkels's many shamans were filtered around the common warriors accompanying the king. Dnark presumed that all of the orcs setting up Obould's three-layered tent were fanatics in the service of Nukkels.

Obould launched into his expected tirade about the importance of the mountain ridge upon which the tent was being erected, and how the fate of the entire kingdom could well rest upon the efforts of Clan Wolf Jaw in properly securing and fortifying the ground, the tunnels, and the walls. They had heard it all before, of course, but Dnark couldn't help but marvel at the rapt expressions on the faces of his minions as the undeniably charismatic king wove his spell yet again. Predictability didn't diminish the effect, and that, the chieftain knew, was no small feat.

Dnark purposely focused on the reactions of the other orcs, in part to keep himself from listening too carefully to Obould, whose rhetoric was truly hard to resist—sometimes so much so that Dnark wondered if Nukkels and the other priests weren't weaving a bit of magic of their own behind the notes of Obould's resonating voice.

Wound in his contemplations, it took a nudge from Ung-thol to get Dnark to realize that Obould had addressed him directly. Panic washing through him, the chieftain turned to face the king squarely, and he fumbled for something to say that wouldn't give away his obliviousness.

Obould's knowing smile let him know that nothing would suffice.

"My pennant will be set upon the door of my tent when it is ready for private audience," the orc king said—said again, obviously. "When you see it, you will come for a private parlay."

"Private?" Dnark dared ask. "Or am I to bring my second?"

Obould, his smile smug indeed, looked past him to Ung-thol. "Please do," he said, and it seemed to Dnark the enticing purr of a cat looking to sharpen its claws.

Wearing a smug and superior smile, Obould walked past him, carrying Kna and with Nukkels scurrying in tow. Dnark scanned wider as the king and his entourage moved off to the tent, noting the glances from the king's warriors filtering across his clan, and identifying those likely serving the priests. If it came to blows, Dnark would have to direct his own warriors against the magic-wielding fanatics, first and foremost.

He winced as he considered that, seeing the futility laid bare before him. If it came to blows with King Obould and his guard, Dnark's clan would scatter and flee for their lives, and nothing he could say would alter that.

He looked to Ung-thol, who stared at Obould without blinking, watching the king's every receding step.

Ung-thol knew the truth of it as well, Dnark realized, and wondered—not for the first time—if Toogwik Tuk hadn't led them down a fool's path.

"The flag of Obould is on the door," Ung-thol said to his chieftain a short while later.

"Let us go, then," said Dnark. "It would not do to keep the king waiting."

Dnark started off, but Ung-thol grabbed him by the arm. "We must not underestimate King Obould's network of spies," the shaman said. "He has sorted the various tribes carefully throughout the region, where those more loyal to him remain watchful of others he suspects. He may know that you and I were in the east. And he knows of the attack on the Moonwood, for Grguch's name echoes through the valleys, a new hero in the Kingdom of Many-Arrows."

Dnark paused and considered the words, then began to nod.

"Does Obould consider Grguch a hero?" Ung-thol asked.

"Or a rival?" asked Dnark, and Ung-thol was glad that they were in agreement, and that Dnark apparently understood the danger to them. "Fortunately for King Obould, he has a loyal chieftain"—Dnark patted his hand against his own chest—"and wise shaman who can bear witness here that Chieftain Grguch and Clan Karuck are valuable allies."

With a nod at Ung-thol's agreeing grin, Dnark turned and started for the tent. The shaman's grin faded as soon as Dnark looked away. None of it, Ung-thol feared, was to be taken lightly. He had been at the ceremony wherein King Obould had been blessed with the gifts of Gruumsh. He had watched the orc king break a bull's neck with his bare hands. He had seen the remains of a powerful drow priestess, her throat bitten out by Obould after the king had been taken down the side of a ravine in a landslide brought about by a priestess's earth-shaking enchantment. Watching Grguch's work in the east had been heady, invigorating and inspiring, to be sure. Clan Karuck showed the fire and mettle of the very best orc warriors, and the priest of Gruumsh could not help but feel his heart swell with pride at their fast and devastating accomplishments.

But Ung-thol was old enough and wise enough to temper his elation and soaring hopes against the reality that was King Obould Many-Arrows.

As he and Dnark entered the third and final off-set entrance into Obould's inner chamber, Ung-thol was only reminded of that awful reality. King Obould, seeming very much the part, sat on his throne on a raised dais, so that even though he was seated, he towered over any who stood before him. He wore his trademark black armor, patched back together after his terrific battle with the drow, Drizzt Do'Urden. His greatsword, which could blaze with magical fire at Obould's will, rested against the arm of his throne, within easy reach.

Obould leaned forward at their approach, dropping one elbow on his knee and stroking his chin. He didn't blink as he measured the steps of the pair, his focus almost exclusively on Dnark. Ung-thol hoped that his wrath, if it came forth, would be equally selective.

"Wolf Jaw performs brilliantly," Obould greeted, somewhat dissipating the tension.

Dnark bowed low at the compliment. "We are an old and disciplined clan."

"I know that well," said the king. "And you are a respected and feared tribe. It is why I keep you close to Many-Arrows, so that the center of my line will never waver."

Dnark bowed again at the compliment, particularly the notion that Wolf Jaw was feared, which was about as high as orc praise ever climbed. Ung-thol considered his chieftain's expression when he came back up from that bow. When the smug Dnark glanced his way, Ung-thol shot him a stern but silent retort, reminding him of the truth of Obould's reasoning. He was keeping Wolf Jaw close, indeed, but Dnark had to understand that Obould's aim was more to keep an eye on the tribe than to shore up his center. After all, there was no line of battle, so there was no center to fortify.

"The winter was favorable to us all," said Dnark. "Many towers have been built, and miles of wall."

"Every hilltop, Chieftain Dnark," said Obould. "If the dwarves or their allies come against us, they will have to fight over walls and towers on every hilltop."

Dnark glanced at Ung-thol again, and the cleric nodded for him to let it go at that. There was no need to engage Obould in an argument of defensive versus offensive preparations, certainly. Not with their schemes unfolding in the east.

"You were gone from your tribe," Obould stated, and Ung-thol started and blinked, wondering if the perceptive Obould had just read his mind.

"My king?" Dnark asked.

"You have been away in the east," said Obould. "With your shaman."

Dnark had done a good job keeping his composure, Ung-thol believed, but then the shaman winced when Dnark swallowed hard.

"There are many rogue orcs left over from the fierce battles with the dwarves," Dnark said. "Some strong and seasoned warriors, even shamans, have lost all their kin and clan. They have no banner."

As soon as he spoke the words, Dnark shrank back a step, for a murderous scowl crossed Obould's powerful features. At either side of the tent chamber, guards bristled, a couple even growling.

"They have no banner?" Obould calmly—too calmly—asked.

"They have the flag of Many-Arrows, of course," Ung-thol dared to interject, and Obould's eyes widened then narrowed quickly as he regarded the shaman. "But your kingdom is arranged by tribe, my king. You send tribes to the hills and the vales to do the work, and those who have lost their tribes know not where to go. Dnark and other chieftains are trying to sweep up the rogues to better organize your kingdom, so that you, with great plans opening wide before your Gruumsh-inspired visions, are not cluttered by such minor details."

Obould eased back in his throne and the moment of distress seemed to slip back from the edge of disaster. Of course with Obould, whose temper had left uncounted dead in his murderous wake, none could be sure.

"You were in the east," Obould said after many heartbeats had passed. "Near the Moonwood."

"Not so near, but yes, my king," said Dnark.

"Tell me of Grguch."

The blunt demand rocked Dnark back on his heels and crippled his denial as he replied with incredulity, "Grguch?"

"His name echoes through the kingdom," said Obould. "You have heard it."

"Ah, you mean Chieftain Grguch," Dnark said, changing the inflection of the name to put emphasis on the "Gr," and acting as if

Obould's further remarks had spurred recognition. "Yes, I have heard of him."

"You have met him," said Obould, his tone and the set of his face conveying that his assertion was not assumption, but known fact.

Dnark glanced at Ung-thol, and for a moment the shaman thought his chieftain might just turn on his heel and flee. And indeed, Ung-thol wanted to do the same. Not for the first time and not for the last time, he wondered how they could have been foolish enough to dare conspire against King Obould Many-Arrows.

A soft chuckle from Dnark settled Ung-thol, though, and reminded him that Dnark had risen through difficult trials to become the chieftain of an impressive tribe—a tribe that even then surrounded Obould's tent.

"Chieftain Grguch of Clan Karuck, yes," Dnark said, matching Obould's stare. "I witnessed his movement through Teg'ngun's Dale near the Surbrin. He was marching to the Moonwood, though we did not know that at the time. Would that I had, for I would have enjoyed witnessing his slaughter of the foolish elves."

"You approve of his attack?"

"The elves have been striking at your minions in the east day after day," said Dnark. "I think it good that the pain of battle was taken to their forest, and that the heads of several of the creatures were placed upon pikes at the river's edge. Chieftain Grguch did you a great service. I had thought his assault on the Moonwood to be at your command."

He ended with an inflection of confusion, even suspicion, craftily turning the event back upon the orc king.

"Our enemies do not avoid their deserved punishment," Obould said without hesitation.

At Dnark's side, Ung-thol realized that his companion's quick-thinking had likely just saved both their lives. For King Obould would not kill them and tacitly admit that Grguch had acted independent of the throne.

"Chieftain Grguch and Clan Karuck will serve the kingdom well," Dnark pressed. "They are as fierce as any tribe I have ever seen."

"They breed with ogres, I am told."

"And carry many of the brutes along to anchor their lines."

"Where are they now?"

"In the east, I expect," said Dnark.

"Near the Moonwood still?"

"Likely," said Dnark. "Likely awaiting the response of our enemies. If the ugly elves dare cross the Surbrin, Chieftain Grguch will pike more heads on the riverbank."

Ung-thol eyed Obould carefully through Dnark's lie, and he easily recognized that the king knew more than he was letting on. Word of Grguch's march to the south had reached Obould's ear. Obould knew that the chieftain of Clan Karuck was a dangerous rival.

Ung-thol studied Obould carefully, but the cunning warrior king gave little more away. He offered some instructions for shoring up the defense of the region, included a punishing deadline, then dismissed the pair with a wave of his hand as he turned his attention to the annoying Kna.

"Your hesitance in admitting your knowledge of Grguch warned him," Ung-thol whispered to Dnark as they left the tent and crossed the muddy ground to rejoin their clan.

"He pronounced it wrong."

"You did."

Dnark stopped and turned on the shaman. "Does it matter?"

CHAPTER

The wizard held his hand out, fingers locked as if it were the talon of a great hunting bird. Sweat streaked his forehead despite the cold wind, and he locked his face into a mask of intensity.

The stone was too heavy for him, but he kept up his telekinetic assault, willing it into the air. Down at the riverbank, dwarf masons on the far bank furiously cranked their come-alongs, while others rushed around the large stone, throwing an extra strap or chain where needed. Still, despite the muscle and ingenuity of the dwarf craftsmen, and magical aid from the Silverymoon wizard, the floating stone teetered on the brink of disaster.

"Joquim!" another citizen of Silverymoon called.

"I . . . can't . . . hold . . . it," the wizard Joquim grunted back, each word forced out through gritted teeth.

The second wizard shouted for help and rushed down to Joquim's side. He had little in the way of telekinetic prowess, but he had memorized a dweomer for just that eventuality. He launched into his spellcasting and threw his magical energies out toward the shaking stone. It stabilized, and when a third member of the Silverymoon contingent rushed over, the balance shifted in favor of the builders. It began to seem almost effortless as the combination of dwarf and wizard guided the stone out over the rushing waters of the River Surbrin.

With a dwarf on the end of a beam guiding the way, the team with the come-alongs positioned the block perfectly over the even larger stones that had already been set in place. The guide dwarf called for a hold, rechecked the alignment, then lifted a red flag.

The wizards eased up their magic gradually, slowly lowering the block.

"Go get the next one!" the dwarf yelled to his companions and the wizards on the near bank. "Seems the Lady's almost ready for this span!"

All eyes turned to the work at the near bank, the point closest to Mithral Hall, where Lady Alustriel stood on the first length of span over the river, her features serene as she whispered the words of a powerful spell of creation. Cold and strong she appeared, almost godlike above the rushing waters. Her white robes, highlighted in light green, blew about her tall and slender form. There was hardly a gasp of surprise when a second stone span appeared before her, reaching out to the next set of supports.

Alustriel's arms slipped down to her sides and she gave a deep exhale, her shoulders slumping as if her effort had thrown out more than magical strength.

"Amazing," Catti-brie said, coming up beside her and inspecting the newly conjured slab.

"The Art, Catti-brie," Alustriel replied. "Mystra's blessings are wondrous indeed." Alustriel turned a sly look her way. "Perhaps I can tutor you."

Catti-brie scoffed at the notion, but coincidentally, as she threw her head back, she twisted her leg at an angle that sent a wave of pain rolling through her damaged hip, and she was reminded that her days as a warrior might indeed be at their end—one way or another.

"Perhaps," she said.

Alustriel's smile beamed genuine and warm. The Lady of Silverymoon glanced back and motioned to the dwarf masons, who flooded forward with their tubs of mortar to seal and smooth the newest span.

"The conjured stone is permanent?" Catti-brie asked as she and Alustriel moved back down the ramp to the bank.

Alustriel looked at her as if the question was completely absurd. "Would you have it vanish beneath the wheels of a wagon?"

They both laughed at the flippant response.

"I mean, it is real stone," the younger woman clarified.

"Not an illusion, to be sure."

"But still the stuff of magic?"

Alustriel furrowed her brow as she considered the woman. "The stone is as real as anything the dwarves could drag in from a quarry, and the dweomer that created it is permanent."

"Unless it is dispelled," Catti-brie replied, and Alustriel said, "Ah," as she caught on to the woman's line of thought.

"It would take Elminster himself to even hope to dispel the work of Lady Alustriel," another nearby wizard interjected.

Catti-brie looked from the mage to Alustriel.

"A bit of an exaggeration, of course," Alustriel admitted. "But truly, any mage of sufficient power to dispel my creations would also have in his arsenal evocations that could easily destroy a bridge constructed without magic."

"But a conventional bridge can be warded against lightning bolts and other destructive evocations," Catti-brie reasoned.

"As this one shall be," promised Alustriel.

"And so it will be as safe as if the dwarves had . . ." Catti-brie started, and Alustriel finished the thought with her, "dragged the stones from a quarry."

They shared another laugh, until Catti-brie added, "Except from Alustriel."

The Lady of Silverymoon stopped cold and turned to stare directly at Catti-brie.

"It is an easy feat for a wizard to dispel her own magic, so I am told," Catti-brie remarked. "There will be no wards in place to prevent you from waving your hands and making expanse after expanse disappear."

A wry grin crossed Alustriel's beautiful face, and she cocked an eyebrow, an expression of congratulations for the woman's sound and cunning reasoning.

"An added benefit should the orcs overrun this position and try to use the bridge to spread their darkness to other lands," Catti-brie went on.

"Other lands like Silverymoon," Alustriel admitted.

"Do not be quick to sever the bridge to Mithral Hall, Lady," Catti-brie said.

"Mithral Hall is connected to the eastern bank through tunnels in any case," Alustriel replied. "We will not abandon your father, Catti-brie. We will never abandon King Bruenor and the valiant dwarves of Clan Battlehammer."

Catti-brie's responding smile came easy to her, for she didn't doubt a word of the pledge. She glanced back at the conjured slabs and nodded appreciatively, both for the power in creating them and the strategy of Alustriel in keeping the power to easily destroy them.

* * * * *

The late afternoon sun reflected moisture in Toogwik Tuk's jaundiced brown eyes, for he could hardly contain his tears of joy at the ferocious reminder of what it was to be an orc. Grguch's march through the three remaining villages had been predictably successful, and after Toogwik Tuk had delivered his perfected sermon, every able-bodied orc warrior of those villages had eagerly marched out in Grguch's wake. That alone would have garnered the fierce chieftain of Clan Karuck another two hundred soldiers.

But more impressively, they soon enough discovered, came the reinforcements from villages through which they had not passed. Word of Grguch's march had spread across the region directly north of Mithral Hall, and the war-thirsty orcs of many tribes, frustrated by the winter pause, had rushed to the call.

As he crossed the impromptu encampment, Toogwik Tuk surveyed the scores—no, hundreds—of new recruits. Grguch would hit the dwarven fortifications with closer to two thousand orcs than one thousand, by the shaman's estimation. Victory at the Surbrin was all but assured. Could King Obould hope to hold back the tide of war after that?

Toogwik Tuk shook his head with honest disappointment as he considered the once-great leader. Something had happened to Obould. The shaman wondered if it might have been the stinging defeat Bruenor's dwarves had handed him in his ill-fated attempt to breach Mithral Hall's western door. Or had it been the loss of the conspiring dark elves and Gerti Orelsdottr and her frost giant minions? Or perhaps it had come about because of the loss of his son, Urlgen, in the fight on the cliff tops north of Keeper's Dale.

Whatever the cause, Obould hardly seemed the same fierce warrior who had led the charge into Citadel Adbar, or who had begun his great sweep south from the Spine of the World only a few months before. Obould had lost his understanding of the essence of the orc. He had lost the voice of Gruumsh within his heart.

"He demands that we wait," the shaman mused aloud, staring out at the teeming swarm, "and yet they come by the score to the promise of renewed battle with the cursed dwarves."

Never more certain of the righteousness of his conspiracy, the shaman moved quickly toward Grguch's tent. Obould no longer heard the call of Gruumsh, but Grguch surely did, and after the dwarves were smashed and chased back into their holes, how might King Obould claim dominion over the chieftain of Clan Karuck? And how might Obould secure fealty from the tens of thousands of orcs he had brought forth from their holes with promises of conquest?

Obould demanded they sit and wait, that they till the ground like peasant human farmers. Grguch demanded of them that they sharpen their spears and swords to better cut the flesh of dwarves.

Grguch heard the call of Gruumsh.

The shaman found the chieftain standing on the far side of a small table, surrounded by two of his Karuck warlords and with a much smaller orc standing across from them and manipulating a pile of dirt and stones that had been set upon the table. As he neared, Toogwik Tuk recognized the terrain being described by the smaller orc, for he had seen the mountain ridge that stretched from the eastern end of Mithral Hall down to the Surbrin.

"Welcome, Gruumsh-speaker," Grguch greeted him. "Join us."

Toogwik Tuk moved to an open side of the table and inspected the scout's work, which depicted a wall nearly completed to the Surbrin and a series of towers anchoring it.

"The dwarves have been industrious throughout the winter," said Grguch. "As you feared. King Obould's pause has given them strength."

"They will anticipate an attack like ours," the shaman remarked.

"They have witnessed no large movements of forces to indicate it," said Grguch.

"Other than our own," Toogwik Tuk had to remind him.

But Grguch laughed it off. "Possibly they have taken note of many orcs now moving nearer to their position," he agreed. "They may expect an attack in the coming tendays."

The two Karuck warlords beside the brutish chieftain chuckled at that.

"They will never expect one this very night," said Grguch.

Toogwik Tuk's face dropped into a sudden frown, and he looked down at the battlefield in near panic. "We have not even sorted out our forces . . ." he started to weakly protest.

"There is nothing to sort," Grguch replied. "Our tactic is swarm fodder and nothing more."

"Swarm fodder?" asked the shaman.

"A simple swarm to and through the wall," said Grguch. "Darkness is our ally. Speed and surprise are our allies. We will hit them as a wave flattens the ridge of a boot print on a beach."

"You know not the techniques of the many tribes who have come into the fold."

"I don't need to," Grguch declared. "I don't need to count my warriors. I don't need to place them in lines and squares, to form reserves and ensure that our flanks are protected back far enough to prevent an end run by our enemies. That is the way of the dwarf." He paused and looked around at the stupidly grinning warlords and the excited scout. "I see no dwarves in this room," he said, and the others laughed.

Grguch looked back at Toogwik Tuk. His eyes went wide, as if in alarm, and he sniffed at the air a couple of times. "No," he declared, looking again to his warlords. "I *smell* no dwarves in this room."

The laughter that followed was much more pronounced, and despite his reservations, Toogwik Tuk was wise enough to join in.

"Tactics are for dwarves," the chieftain explained. "Discipline is for elves. For orcs, there is only . . ." He looked directly at Toogwik Tuk.

"Swarm fodder?" the shaman asked, and a wry grin spread on Grguch's ugly face.

"Chaos," he confirmed. "Ferocity. Bloodlust and abandon. As soon as the sun has set, we begin our run. All the way to the wall. All the way to the Surbrin. All the way to the eastern doors of Mithral Hall. Half, perhaps more than half, of our warriors will find tonight the reward of glorious death."

Toogwik Tuk winced at that, and silently berated himself. Was he beginning to think more like Obould?

Grguch reminded him of the words of Gruumsh One-eye. "They will die with joy," the chieftain promised. "Their last cry will be of elation and not agony. And any who die otherwise, with regret or with sorrow or with fear, should have been slaughtered in sacrifice to Gruumsh before our attack commenced!"

The sudden volume and ferocity of his last proclamation set Toogwik Tuk back on his heels and had both the Clan Karuck warlords and guards at the perimeter of the room growling and gnashing their teeth. For a brief moment, Toogwik Tuk almost reconsidered his call to the deepest holes to rouse Chieftain Grguch.

Almost.

"There has been no sign from the dwarves that they know of our march," Grguch told a great gathering later that day, when the sunlight began to wane. Toogwik Tuk noted the dangerous priest Hakuun standing at his side, and that gave the younger shaman pause. He got the feeling that Hakuun had been watching him all along.

"They do not see the doom that has come against them," Grguch ordered. "Do not shout out, but run. Run fast to the wall, without delay, and whispering praise for Gruumsh with every stride."

There were no lines or coordinated movements, just a wild charge begun miles from the goal. There were no torches to light the way, no magical lights conjured by Toogwik Tuk or the other priests of Gruumsh. They were orcs, after all, raised in the upper tunnels of the lightless Underdark.

The night was their ally, the dark their comfort.

* * * * *

Once, when he was a child, Hralien had found a large pile of sand down by one of the Moonwood's two lakes. From a distance, that mound of light-colored sand had seemed discolored with streaks of red, and as he moved closer, young Hralien realized that the streaks weren't discolored sand, but were actually moving upon the surface of the mound. Being young and inexperienced, he had at first feared that he had happened upon a tiny volcano, perhaps.

On closer inspection, though, the truth had come clear to him, for the pile of sand had been an ant mound, and the red streaks were lines of the six-legged creatures marching to and fro.

Hralien thought of that long-ago experience as he witnessed the charge of the orcs, swarming the small, rocky hills north of King

Bruenor's eastern defenses. Their movements seemed no less frenetic, and truly their march appeared no less determined. Given their speed and intensity, and the obstacle that awaited them barely two miles to the south, Hralien recognized their intent.

The elf bit his lip as he remembered his promise to Drizzt Do'Urden. He looked south, sorting out the landscape and recalling the trails that would most quickly return him to Mithral Hall.

Then he was running, and fearing that he could not keep his promise to his drow friend, for the orc line stretched ahead of him and the creatures had not far to travel. With great grace and agility, Hralien sprang from stone to stone. He leaped up and grabbed a low tree branch and swung out across a narrow chasm, landing lightly on the other side and in a full run. He moved with hardly a whisper of sound, unlike the orcs, whose heavy steps echoed in his keen elf's ears.

He knew that he should be cautious, for he could ill afford the delay if he happened into a fight. But neither could he slow his run and carefully pick his path, for some of the orcs were ahead of him, and the dwarves would need every heartbeat of warning he could give them. So he ran on, leaping and scrambling over bluffs and through low dales, where the melting snow had streamed down and pooled in clear, cold pockets. Hralien tried to avoid those pools as much as possible, for they often concealed slick ice. But even with his great dexterity and sharp vision, he occasionally splashed through, cringing at the unavoidable sound.

At one point, he heard an orc cry out, and feared that he had been spotted. Many strides later, he realized that the creature was just calling to a companion, a stark reminder that the lead runners and scouts of the brutish force were all around him.

Finally he left the sounds of orcs behind, for though the brutes could move with great speed, they could not match the pace of a dexterous elf, even across such broken ground.

Soon after, coming up over a rocky rise, Hralien caught sight of squat stone towers in the south, running down from tall mountains to the silvery, moonlit snake that was the River Surbrin.

"Too soon," the elf whispered in dismay, and he glanced back as if expecting Obould's entire army to roll over him. He shook his head and winced, then sprinted off for the south.

* * * * *

"We will have it completed within the tenday," Alustriel said to Catti-brie, the two sitting with some of the other Silverymoon wizards around a small campfire. One of the wizards, a robust human with thick salt and pepper hair and a tightly trimmed goatee, had conjured the flames and was playing with them, casting cantrips to change their color from orange to white to blue and red. A second wizard, a rather eccentric half-elf with shiny black hair magically streaked by a bloom of bright red locks, joined in and wove enchantments to make the red flames form into the shape of a small dragon. Seeing the challenge, the first wizard likewise formed blue flames, and the two spellcasters set their fiery pets into a proxy battle. Almost immediately, several other wizards began excitedly placing their bets.

Catti-brie watched with amusement and interest—more than she would have expected, and Alustriel's words to her about dabbling in the dark arts flitted unbidden through her thoughts. Her experience with wizards was very limited, and mostly involved the unpredictable and dangerously foolish Harpell family from Longsaddle.

"Asa Havel will win," Alustriel whispered to her, leaning in close and indicating the half-elf wizard who had manipulated the red flame. "Duzberyl is far more powerful at manipulating fire, but he has taxed his powers to their limit this day conjuring bright hot flames to seal the stone. And Asa Havel knows it."

"So he challenged," Catti-brie whispered back. "And his friends know, too, so they wager."

"They would wager anyway," Alustriel explained. "It is a matter of pride. Whatever is lost here will be reclaimed soon enough in another challenge."

Catti-brie nodded and watched the unfolding drama, the many faces, elf and human alike, glowing in varying shades and hues in the uneven light, turning blue as the blue dragon leaped atop the red, but then drifting back, green and yellow and toward a feverish red as Asa Havel's drake filtered up through Duzberyl's and gradually gained supremacy. It was all good-natured, of course, but Catti-brie didn't miss the intensity etched onto the faces of the combatants and onlookers alike. It occurred to her that she was looking into an entirely different world. She could relate it to the drinking games, and the arm-wrestling and sparring that so often took place in the taverns of Mithral Hall, for though the venue was different, the emotions were not. Still, there remained enough of a difference to intrigue her. It was a battle of strength, but of mental strength and concentration, and not of muscle and intestinal fortitude.

"Within a month, you could form flames into such shapes, yourself," Alustriel teased.

Catti-brie looked at her and laughed dismissively, but that hardly hid her interest.

She looked back to the fire just in time to see Duzberyl's blue roll over and consume Asa Havel's red, contrary to Alustriel's prediction. The backers of both wizards gasped in surprise and Duzberyl gave a yelp that was more shock than of victory. Catti-brie's gaze turned to Asa Havel, and her surprise turned to confusion.

The half-elf was not looking at the fight, and seemed oblivious to the fact that his dragon had been consumed by the human's blue. He stared out to the north, his sea-blue eyes scanning high above the flames. Catti-brie felt Alustriel turn beside her, then stand. The woman glanced over her shoulder, up at the dark wall, but shook her head slightly in confusion, seeing nothing out of the ordinary. Beside her, Alustriel cast a minor spell.

Other wizards rose and peered out to the north.

"An elf has come," Alustriel said to Catti-brie. "And the dwarves are scrambling."

"It's an attack," Asa Havel announced, rising and moving past the two women. He looked right at Alustriel and the princess of Mithral Hall and asked, "Orcs?"

"Prepare for battle," Alustriel said to her contingent. "Area spells to disrupt any charge."

"We have little left this day," Duzberyl reminded her.

In response, Alustriel reached inside one of the folds of her robes and drew forth a pair of slender wands. She half-turned and tossed one to Duzberyl. "Your necklace, too, if needed," she instructed, and the human nodded and brought a hand to a gaudy choker he wore, its golden links set with large stones like rubies of varying sizes, including one so large that Catti-brie couldn't have closed her fist around it.

"Talindra, to the gates of the dwarven halls," Alustriel said to a young elf female. "Warn the dwarves and help them sort the battle."

The elf nodded and took a few fast steps to the west, then disappeared with a flash of blue-white light. A second flash followed almost instantly, over near the hall's eastern gates, transporting Talindra to her assigned position, the surprised Catti-brie assumed, for she couldn't actually see the young elf.

She turned back to hear Alustriel positioning Asa Havel and another pair. "Secure fast passage to the far bank, should we need it. Prepare enough to carry any dwarves routed from the wall."

Catti-brie heard the first shouts from the wall, followed by the blare of horns, many horns, from beyond to the north. Then came the blare of one that overwhelmed all the others, a resonating, low-pitched grumble that shook the stones beneath Catti-brie's feet.

"Damn Obould to the Nine Hells," Catti-brie whispered, and she grimaced at the realization that she had loaned Taulmaril to Drizzt. She looked over at Alustriel. "I haven't my bow, or a sword. A weapon, please? Conjure one or produce one from a deep pocket."

To Catti-brie's surprise, the Lady of Silverymoon did just that, pulling yet another wand from inside her robes. Catti-brie took it, not knowing what to make of the thing, and when she looked back at Alustriel, the tall woman was tugging a ring from her finger.

"And this," she said, handing over the thin gold band set with a trio of sparkling diamonds. "I trust you are not already in the possession of two magical rings."

Catti-brie took it and held it pressed between her thumb and index finger, her expression dumbfounded.

"The command word for the wand is 'twell-in-sey,'" Alustriel explained. "Or 'twell-in-sey-sey' if you wish to loose two magical bolts."

"I don't know . . ."

"Anyone can use it," Alustriel assured her. "Point it at your target and speak the word. For the bigger orcs, choose two."

"But . . ."

"Put the ring on your finger and open your mind to it, for it will impart to you its dweomers. And know that they are powerful indeed." With that, Alustriel turned away, and Catti-brie understood that the lesson was at its end.

The Lady of Silverymoon and her wizards, except for those working near the river preparing a magical escape to the far bank, headed off for the wall, nearly all of them drawing forth wands or rods, or switching rings and other jewelry. Catti-brie watched it all with an undeniable sense of excitement, so much so that she was trembling so badly she could hardly line up the ring to slip it on her finger.

Finally she did, and she closed her eyes and took a deep breath. She felt as if she were looking up at the heavens, to see stars shooting across the darkened night sky, to see flashes of brilliance so magnificent that it seemed to her as if the gods must be throwing bolts at each other.

The first sounds of battle shook her from her contemplation. She opened her eyes and nearly fell over due to dizziness from the sudden change, as if she had just stepped back to solid ground from the Astral Plane.

She started after Alustriel, inspecting the wand, and garnered quickly which end to hold from a leather strap wrapped diagonally as a hand grip. At least she hoped it was the right end, and she winced at the thought of unloading enchanted bolts of magic into her own face. She dismissed the worry, noting that she wasn't gaining much on Alustriel, and noting more pointedly that the dwarves at the wall scrambled and yelled for support in many places already. She dropped her arms down beside her and ran as fast as her battered hip would allow.

"Twell-in-sey," she whispered, trying to get the inflection correct.

She did.

The wand discharged and a red dart of energy burst forth, snapping into the ground with a hiss right before her running feet. Catti-brie yelped and stumbled, nearly falling over. She caught her balance and her composure, and was glad that no one seemed to notice.

On she ran, or tried to, but a wave of hot fire ran up her leg and nearly toppled her yet again. She looked down to her boot, smoking and charred on the side just back of her little toe. She paused again and composed herself, taking heart that the wound was not too severe, and thanking Moradin himself that Lady Alustriel hadn't given her a wand of lightning bolts.

* * * * *

234

The orc gained the wall in a wild rush, stabbing powerfully at the nearest dwarf, who seemed an easy kill as he was busy driving a second orc back over the wall and into the darkness.

But that dwarf, Charmorffe Dredgewelder of Fine Family Yellowbeard—so named because none of the Dredgewelders was ever known to have a yellow beard—was neither particularly surprised nor particularly impressed by the aggressive move. Trained under Thibbledorf Pwent himself, having served more than a score of years in the Gutbuster Brigade, Charmorffe had faced many a finer foe than that pathetic creature.

As Charmorffe had never gotten familiar with a formal buckler, his plate-shielded arm swooped down to intercept the spear, blocking it solidly and sweeping it back behind him as he turned. That same movement brought his cudgel swinging around, and a quick three-step forward caught the overbalanced orc cleanly in range. The creature grunted, as did the dwarf, as the cudgel slammed it right behind the shoulder, launching it into a dive and spin forward, right off the ten-foot parapet.

As the path before him cleared, Charmorffe looked down the tip of an arrow set on a short bow. He yelped and fell over backward, buckling at both his knees, and as soon as he was clear, Hralien let fly. The missile hummed through the air right above the dwarf, and splattered into the chest of an orc that had been sneaking up on him from behind.

As soon as his back hit the stone, Charmorffe snapped all of his muscles forward, throwing his arms up high, and brought himself right back to his feet.

"That's twice I'm owin' ye, ye durned elf!" the dwarf protested. "First for savin' us all, and now for savin' meself!"

"I did neither, good dwarf," Hralien replied, running across the parapet to the waist-high wall, where he set his bow to work immediately. "I've faith that Clan Battlehammer is more than able to save itself."

He shot off an arrow as he spoke, but as soon as he finished, a large orc rose into the air right before him, sword ready to strike a killing blow. The orc landed lightly on the wall top and struck, but a spinning cudgel hit both the sword and the orc, turning its blow harmlessly short. And when the orc managed to hold its balance and throw itself forward at Hralien, it too was intercepted, by a flying Charmorffe Dredgewelder. The dwarf connected with a shoulder block, driving the orc tight against the wall. The orc began raining ineffective blows upon the dwarf's back for Charmorffe's powerful legs kept grinding, pressing in even tighter.

Hralien stabbed the orc in the eye with an arrow.

The elf jumped back fast, though, set the arrow and let fly, point blank into yet another orc flying up to the top of the wall. Hralien hit it squarely, and though its feet landed atop the narrow rail, the jolt of the hit dropped it right back off.

Charmorffe leaped up and clean-and-jerked the thrashing orc up high over his head. The dwarf threw himself into the wall, which hit him about mid chest, and snapped forward, tossing the orc over. As he went forward, Charmorffe solved the riddle, for just below him, and off to both sides as well, stood ogres, their backs tight against the wall. As each bent low and cupped its hands down near the ground, another orc ran up and stepped into that brace. A slight toss by the ogres had orcs sailing up over the wall.

"Pig-faced goblin kissers," Charmorffe growled. He turned and shouted, "Rocks over the wall, boys! We got ogres playing as ladders!"

Hralien rushed up beside Charmorffe, leaned far out and shot an arrow into the top of the nearest ogre's head. He marveled at his handiwork, then saw it all the more clearly as a fireball lit up the night, down to the east of his position, closer to the Surbrin where the wall was far from complete.

When Hralien looked that way, he thought their position surely lost, for though Alustriel and her wizards had entered the fray, a mass of huge orcs and larger foes swarmed across the defenses.

"Run for Mithral Hall, good dwarf," the elf said.

"That's what I be thinking," said Charmorffe.

* * * * *

Duzberyl ambled toward the wall, grumbling incessantly. "Two hundred pieces of gold for this one alone," he muttered, pulling another glittering red jewel from his enchanted necklace. He reached back and threw it at the nearest orcs, but his estimate of distance in the low light was off and the jewel landed short of the mark. Its fiery explosion still managed to engulf and destroy a couple of the creatures, and the others fell back in full flight, shrieking with every stride.

But Duzberyl griped all the more. "A hundred gold an orc," he grumbled, glancing back at Alustriel, who was far off to the side. "I could hire an army of rangers to kill ten times the number for one-tenth the cost!" he said, though he knew she was too far away to hear him.

And she wasn't listening anyway. She stood perfectly still, the wind whipping her robes. She lifted one arm before her, a jeweled ring on her clenched fist sparking with multicolored light.

Duzberyl had seen that effect before, but still he was startled when a bolt of bright white lightning burst forth from Alustriel's ring, splitting the night. The powerful wizard's aim was, as always, right on target, her bolt slamming an ogre in the face as it climbed over the wall. Hair dancing wildly, head smoking, the brute flew back into the darkness as Alustriel's bolt bounced away to hit another nearby attacker, an orc that seemed to simply melt into the stone. Again and again, Alustriel's chain lightning leaped away, striking orc or ogre or half-ogre, sending foes flying or spinning down with smoke rising from bubbling skin.

But every vacancy was fast-filled, ten attackers for every one that fell, it seemed.

The apparent futility brought a renewed growl to Duzberyl's chubby face, and he stomped along to a better vantage point.

* * * * *

Limping from foot and hip, Catti-brie watched it all with equal if not greater frustration, for at least Alustriel and her wizards were equipped to battle the monsters. The woman felt naked without her bow, and even with the gifts Alustriel had offered, she believed that she would prove more a burden than an asset.

She considered removing herself from the front lines, back to the bridge where she might prove of some use to Asa Havel in directing the retreat, should it come to that. That in mind, she glanced back—and noted a small group of orcs sprinting along the riverbank toward the distracted wizards.

Catti-brie thrust forth the wand, but brought it back and punched out with her other fist instead. The ring's teeming magical energies called out to her and she listened, and though she didn't know exactly the effects of her call, she followed the magical path toward the strongest sensation of stored energy.

The ring jolted once, twice, thrice, each burst sending forth a fiery ball at Catti-brie's targets. Like twinkling little stars, they seemed, as if the ring had reached up to the heavens and pulled celestial bodies down for its wielder to launch at her enemies. At great speed, they shot out across the night, leaving fiery trails, and when they reached the orc group, they exploded into larger blasts of consuming flames.

Orcs shrieked and scrambled frantically, and more than one leaped into the river to be washed away by cold, killing currents. Others rolled on the ground, trying to douse the biting flames, and when that failed, they ran off like living torches into the dark night, only to fall a few steps away, to crumble and burn on the frozen ground.

It lasted only a heartbeat, but seemed like much longer to Catti-brie, who stood transfixed, breathing hard, her eyes wide with shock. With a thought, she had blown apart nearly a score of orcs. As if they were nothing. As if she were a goddess, passing judgment on insignificant creatures. Never had she felt such power!

At that moment, if someone had asked Catti-brie the Elvish name of her treasured longbow, she would not have recalled it.

* * * * *

"It's not to hold!" Charmorffe cried to Hralien, and a swipe of the dwarf's heavy cudgel sent another orc flying aside.

Hralien wanted to shout back words of encouragement, but his view of the battlefield, since he wielded a weapon that made it incumbent upon him to seek a wider perspective, was more complete, and he understood that the situation was even worse than Charmorffe likely believed.

Few dwarves came forth from Mithral Hall and a host of orcs poured through the lower, uncompleted sections of the defensive wall. Huge orcs, some two feet taller and more than a hundred pounds heavier than the dwarves. Among them were true ogres, though it was hard for Hralien to distinguish where some of the orcs ended and the clusters of ogres began.

More orcs came up over the wall, launched by their ogre stepstools, putting pressure on the dwarves and preventing them from organizing a coordinated defense against the larger mass rolling in from the east.

"It's not to hold!" Charmorffe yelled again, and the words rang true. Hralien knew that the end was coming fast. The wizards intervened— one fireball then another, and a lightning chain that left many creatures smoking on the ground. But that wouldn't be enough, and Hralien understood that the wizards had been at their magical work all day long and had little power left to offer.

"Start the retreat," the elf said to Charmorffe. "To Mithral Hall!"

Even as he spoke, the orc mass surged forward, and Hralien feared that he and Charmorffe and the others had waited too long.

* * * * *

"By the gods, and the gemstone vendors!" Duzberyl roared, watching the sudden break in the dwarven line, the bearded folk sprinting back to the west along the wall, leaping down from the parapets and veering straight for Mithral Hall's eastern door. All semblance of a defensive posture had flown, creating a full and frantic retreat.

And it wouldn't be enough, the wizard calculated, for the orcs, hungry for dwarf blood, closed with every stride. Duzberyl grimaced as a dwarf was swallowed in the black cloud of the orc horde.

The portly wizard ran, and he reached up to his necklace, grasping the largest stone of all. He tore it free, cursed the gemstone merchant again for good measure, and heaved it with all his strength.

The magical grenade hit the base of the wall just behind the lead- ing orcs, and exploded, filling the area, even up onto the parapet, with biting, killing fires. Those monsters immediately above and near the blast charred and died, while others scrambled in an agonized and horrified frenzy, flames consuming them as they ran. Panic hit the orc line, and the dwarves ran free.

* * * * *

"Mage," Grguch muttered as he alighted on the wall some distance back of the enormous fireball.

"Of considerable power," said Hakuun, who stood beside him, having blessed himself and Grguch with every conceivable ward and enhancement.

The chieftain turned back and fell prone on the parapet railing. "Hand it up," he called down to the ogre who had flipped him up, indicating a weapon. A moment later, Grguch stood again on the wall, hoisting on one shoulder a huge javelin at the end of an atlatl.

"Mage," Grguch grumbled again with obvious disgust.

Hakuun held up a hand, motioning for the chieftain to pause. Then, from inside the orc priest, Jack the Gnome cast a most devious enchantment on the head of the missile.

Grguch grinned and brought his shoulder back, shifting the angle of the ten-foot missile. As Hakuun cast a second, complimentary spell upon the intended victim, Grguch launched the spear with all his might.

* * * * *

The stubborn orc lurched toward her, one of its legs still showing flashes of biting flame.

Catti-brie didn't flinch, didn't even start as the orc awkwardly threw a spear her way. She kept her eyes locked on the creature, met its gaze and its hate, and slowly lifted her wand.

She wished at that moment that she had Khazid'hea at her side, that she could engage the vile creature in personal combat. The orc took another staggering step, and Catti-brie uttered the command word.

The red missile sizzled into the orc's chest, knocking it backward. Somehow it held its balance and even advanced another step. Catti-brie said the last word of the trigger twice, as she had been schooled, and the first red missile knocked the orc back yet again, and the second dropped it to the ground where it writhed for just a heartbeat before laying very still.

Catti-brie stood calm and motionless for a few moments, steadying herself. She turned back to the wall, and blinked against the bursts of fiery explosions and the sharp cuts of lightning bolts, a fury that truly left her breathless. In her temporary blindness, she almost expected that the battle had ended, that the wizardly barrage had utterly destroyed the attackers as she had laid low the small group by the river.

But there came the largest blast of all, a tremendous fireball some distance back along the wall to the west, toward Mithral Hall. Catti-brie saw the truth of it, saw the dwarves, and one elf, in desperate retreat, saw all semblance of defense stripped from the wall, buried under the trampling boots of a charging orc horde.

The wall was lost. All from Mithral Hall to the Surbrin was lost. Even Lady Alustriel was withdrawing, not quite in full flight, but in a determined retreat.

Looking past Alustriel, Catti-brie noted Duzberyl. For a moment, she wondered why he, too, was not in retreat, until she realized that he stood strangely, leaning too far back for his legs to support him, his arms lolling limply at his sides.

One of the other wizards threw a lightning bolt—a rather feeble one—and in the flash, Catti-brie saw the huge javelin that had been driven half of its ten-foot length through his chest, its tip buried into the ground, pinning the wizard in that curious, angular stance.

* * * * *

"We have them routed! Now is the moment of victory!" a frustrated Hakuun said as he stood alone behind the charging horde. He wanted to go with them, or to serve as Jaculi's conduit, as he often had, to launch a barrage of devastating magic.

But Jaculi would not begin that barrage, and worse, the uninvited parasite interrupted him every time he tried to use his more conventional shaman's magic.

A temporary moment, to be sure, Jack said in his thoughts.

"What foolishness . . . ?"

That is Lady Alustriel, Jack explained. *Alustriel of the Seven Sisters. Do not draw her attention!*

"She is running!" Hakuun protested.

She will know me. She will recognize me. She will turn loose her army and all of her wizards and all of her magic to destroy me, Jack explained. *It is an old grudge, but one that neither I nor she has forgotten! Do nothing to draw her attention.*

"She is running! We can kill her," said Hakuun.

Jack's incredulous laughter filled his head with dizzying volume, so much so that the shaman couldn't even start off after Grguch and the others. He just stood there, swaying, as the battle ended around him.

Inside Hakuun's head, Jack the brain mole breathed a lot easier. In truth, he had no idea if Alustriel remembered the slight he had given her more than a century earlier. But he surely remembered her wrath from that dangerous day, and it was nothing that Jack the Gnome ever wanted to see again.

* * * * *

One of Lady Alustriel's wizards ran past Catti-brie at that moment, shouting, "Be quick to the bridge!"

Catti-brie shook her head, but she knew it to be a futile denial. Mithral Hall hadn't expected an assault of such ferocity so soon. They had been lulled by a winter of inaction, by the many reports that the bulk of the orc army remained in the west, near to Keeper's Dale, and by the widespread rumors that King Obould had settled in place, satisfied with his gains.

"To the Nine Hells with you, Obould," she cursed under her breath. "I pray that Drizzt won't kill you, only that I may find the pleasure myself."

She turned and started for the bridge with as much speed as she could muster, stepping awkwardly, as each time she brought her right foot forward, she felt the pangs from her damaged hip, and each time she placed that foot onto the ground, she was reminded by a burning sting of her foolishness with the magical wand.

When another wizard running by skidded to a stop beside her and offered her shoulder, Catti-brie, for all her pride and all her determination to not be a burden, gratefully accepted. If she had refused a hand, she would have fallen to the back of the line and likely would have never made it to the bridge.

Asa Havel greeted the returning contingent, directing them to floating disks of glowing magic that hovered nearby. As each seat filled, the wizard who had created it climbed aboard, but for a few moments, none started out across the river, for none wanted to leave the fleeing dwarves.

"Be gone!" Alustriel ordered them, coming in at the end of the line and with orc pursuit not far behind. "Because of Duzberyl's sacrifice, the retreating dwarves will make the safety of the hall, and I have sent a whisper on the wind to Talindra to instruct them to hold fast their gates and wait for morning. Across the river for us, to the safety of the eastern bank. Let us prepare our spells for a morning reprisal that will leave our enemies melted between the river and King Bruenor's hall."

Many heads nodded in agreement, and as Alustriel's eyes flashed with the sheerest intensity, Catti-brie could only wonder what mighty dweomers the Lady of Silverymoon would cast upon the foolish orcs when dawn revealed them.

Seated on the edge of a disk, her feet dangling just inches above the cold and dark rushing waters of the Surbrin, Catti-brie stared back at Mithral Hall with a mixture of emotions, not least among them guilt, and fear for her beloved home and for her beloved husband. Drizzt had gone to the north, and the army had descended from that direction. Yet he had not returned in front of the marching force with a warning, she knew, for she had not seen the lightning arrows of Taulmaril streaking through the night sky.

Catti-brie looked down at the water and steeled her thoughts and her heart.

Asa Havel, sitting beside her, put a hand on her shoulder. When she looked at the half-elf, he offered a warm and comforting smile. That smile turned a bit mischievous, and he nodded down to her torn boot. Catti-brie followed his gaze then looked back up at him, her face flushed with embarrassment.

But the elf nodded and shrugged, and lifted his red and black hair by his left ear, turning his head to catch the moonlight so that she could take note of a white scar running up the side of his head. He took her wand and assumed a pensive pose, tapping it against the side of his face, in line with the scar.

"You won't err like that again," he assured her with a playful wink, handing the wand back. "And take heart, for your impressive meteor shower gave us the time to complete the floating disks."

"It wasn't mine. It came from the ring Lady Alustriel loaned to me."

"However you accomplished it, your timing and your calm action saved our efforts. You will find a role in the morning."

"When we avenge Duzberyl," Catti-brie said grimly.

Asa Havel nodded, and added, "And the dwarves who no doubt fell this dark night."

The shouting across the river ended soon after, silenced by a resounding *bang* as Mithral Hall slammed shut her eastern door. But as the wizards and Catti-brie set their camp for the evening, they heard more commotion across the dark water. The orcs scrambled around the towers and the wizards' previous encampment, tearing and smashing and looting, their grunts and assaults punctuated by the occasional *crack* of a thrown boulder hitting the bridge abutments, and bouncing into the water.

Others settled down to sleep, but Catti-brie remained sitting, staring back at the darkness, where an occasional fire sprang to life, consuming a tent or some other item.

"I had an extra spellbook over there," one wizard grumbled.

"Aye, and I, the first twenty pages of a spell I was penning," said another.

"And I, my finest robes," a third wailed. "Oh, but orcs will burn for this!"

A short while later, a rustle from the other direction, back to the east, turned Catti-brie and the few others who hadn't yet settled in for the night. The woman rose and limped across to stand beside Alustriel, who greeted the Felbarran contingent as they rushed in to investigate the night's tumult.

"We'd set off for Winter Edge to quarry more stones," explained the leader, a squat and tough old character with a white beard and eyebrows so bushy that they hid his eyes. "What in the grumble of a dragon's belly hit ye?"

"Obould," Catti-brie said before Alustriel could respond.

"So much then for the good intentions," said the Felbarran dwarf. "Never thought them dogs'd sit quiet on the ground they'd taken. Mithral Hall get breached?"

"Never," said Catti-brie.

"Good enough then," said the dwarf. "We'll push 'em back north o' the wall in short order."

"In the morning," said Alustriel. "My charges are preparing their spells. I have ears and a voice in Mithral Hall to coordinate the counterattack."

"Might be then that we'll kill 'em all and not let any be running," said the dwarf. "More's the fun!"

"Set your camp by the river, and order your forces into small and swift groups," Alustriel explained. "We will open magical gates of transport to the other bank and your speed and coordination in entering the battle-field will prove decisive."

"Pity them orcs, then," said the dwarf, and he nodded and bowed, then stormed off, barking orders at his grim-faced forces.

He had barely gone a few strides, though, when there came a tremendous crash from across the way, followed by wild orc cheering.

"A tower," Alustriel explained to the surprised stares of all around her.

Catti-brie cursed under her breath.

"We will extend our time at Mithral Hall," the Lady of Silverymoon promised her. "Our enemies have exploited a vulnerability that cannot be allowed to hold. We will sweep the orcs back to the north and chase them far from the doors."

"Then finish the bridge," another nearby wizard offered, but Alustriel was shaking her head.

"The wall first," she explained. "Our enemies did us a favor by revealing our weakness. Woe to all in the North if the orcs had taken this ground after the bridge's completion. So our first duty after they are expelled is to complete and fortify that wall. Any orc excursion back to Mithral Hall's eastern door must come at a great cost to them, and must provide the time for us to disassemble the bridge. We will finish the wall and then we will finish the bridge."

"And then?" Catti-brie asked, and Alustriel and the other wizards looked at her curiously.

"You will return to Silverymoon?" Catti-brie asked.

"My duties are there. What else would you suggest?"

"Obould has shown his hand," Catti-brie replied. "There is no peace to be found while he is camped north of Mithral Hall."

"You ask me to rally an army," said Alustriel.

"Have we a choice?"

Alustriel paused and considered the woman's words. "I know not," she admitted. "But let us first concentrate on the battle at hand." She turned to the nearby wizards. "Sleep well, and when you awaken, prepare your most devastating evocations. Join with each other when you open your spellbooks, and coordinate your efforts and complement your spells. I want these orcs utterly destroyed. Let their folly serve as a warning that will keep their kin at bay long enough for us to strengthen the defenses."

Many nods came back at her, along with a sudden and unexpected shout, "For Duzberyl!"

"Duzberyl!" another cried, and another, and even those Silverymoon wizards who had settled down for the night rose and joined in the chant. Soon enough, even the Felbarran dwarves joined in, though none of them knew what a "Duzberyl" might be.

It didn't matter.

More than once that night, Catti-brie awoke to the sound of a thunderous crash from across the river. That only steeled her determination, though, and each time, she fell back asleep with Lady Alustriel's promise in her thoughts. They would pay the orcs back in full, and then some.

The preparations began before dawn, wizards ruffling the pages of their spellbooks, dwarves sharpening weapons. With a wave of yet another wand, Lady Alustriel turned herself into an owl, and flew off silently to scout out the coming battlefield.

She returned in mere moments, and reverted to her human form as the first rays of dawn crept across the Surbrin, revealing to all the others what Alustriel had returned to report.

Spellbooks snapped shut and the dwarves lowered their weapons and tools, moving to the riverbank and staring in disbelief.

Not an orc was to be seen.

Alustriel set them to motion, her minions opening dimensional doors that soon enough got all of them, dwarf, wizard, and Catti-brie alike, across the Surbrin, the last of them crossing even as Mithral Hall's eastern door banged open and King Bruenor himself led the charge out from the stronghold.

But all they found were a dozen dead dwarves, stripped naked, and a dead wizard, still standing, held in place by a mighty javelin.

The wizards' encampment had been razed and looted, as had the small shacks the dwarf builders had used. An assortment of boulders lay around the base of the damaged bridge abutment, and all of the towers and a good portion of the northern wall had been toppled.

And not an orc, dead or alive, was anywhere to be found.

CHAPTER

19

By all the glories of Gruumsh!" Kna squealed happily when the reports of the victory at the Surbrin made their way like wildfire back to King Obould's entourage. "We have killed the dwarves!"

"We have stung them and left them vulnerable," said the messenger who had come from the battle, an orc named Oktule, who was a member of one of the many minor tribes that had been swept up in the march of Chieftain Grguch—a name Oktule used often, Obould had sourly noted. "Their walls are reduced and the winter is fast receding. They will have to work through the summer, building as they defend their position at the Surbrin."

The orcs all around began to cheer wildly.

"We have severed Mithral Hall from their allies!"

The cheering only increased.

Obould sat there, digesting it all. He knew that Grguch hadn't done any such thing, for the cunning dwarves had tunnels under the Surbrin, and many others that stretched far to the south. Still, it was hard to dismiss the victory, from both practical and symbolic terms. The bridge, had it been completed, would have provided a comfortable and easy approach to Mithral Hall from Silverymoon, Winter Edge, the Moonwood, and the other surrounding communities, and an easy way for King Bruenor to continue doing his profitable business.

Of course, one orc's victory was another orc's setback. Obould, too, had wanted to claim a piece of the Surbrin bridge, but not in such a manner, not as an enemy. And certainly not at the cost of assuring the mysterious Grguch all the glory. He fought hard to keep the scowl from his face. To go against the tide of joy then was to invite suspicion, perhaps even open revolt.

"Chieftain Grguch and Clan Karuck did not hold the ground?" he asked, not so innocently, for he knew well the answer.

"Lady Alustriel and a gang of wizards were with the dwarves," Oktule explained. "Chieftain Grguch expected that the whole of the dwarven hall would come forth with the morning light."

"No doubt with King Bruenor, Drizzt Do'Urden, and the rest of that strange companionship at its head," Obould muttered.

"We did not have the numbers to hold against that," Oktule admitted.

Obould glanced past the messenger to the gathered crowd. He saw more trepidation on their faces than anything else, along with an undercurrent of . . . what? Suspicion?

The orc king stood up and stretched to his full height, towering over Oktule. He looked up and let his gaze sweep in the mob then said with a wicked grin, "A great victory anyway!"

The cheering reached new heights, and Obould, his anger beginning to boil within him, used that opportunity to steal off into his tent, the ever-present Kna and the priest Nukkels following close behind.

Inside the inner chamber, Obould dismissed all of his guards.

"You, too," Kna snapped at Nukkels, errantly presuming that the glorious news had excited her partner as it had her.

Nukkels grinned at her and looked to Obould, who confirmed his suspicions.

"You, too," Obould echoed, but aimed the comment at Kna and not the priest. "Be gone until I summon you back to my side."

Kna's yellow eyes widened in shock, and she instinctively moved to Obould's side and began to curl sensually around him. But with one hand, with the strength of a giant, he yanked her away.

"Do not make me ask you again," he said slowly and deliberately, as if he were a parent addressing a child. With a flick of his wrist he sent Kna skipping and tumbling backward, and she kept scrambling away, her eyes wide with shock as she locked her stare on Obould's frightening expression.

"We must commune with Gruumsh to determine the next victory,"

Obould said to her, purposely softening his visage. "You will play with Obould later."

That seemed to calm the idiot Kna a bit, and she even managed a smile as she exited the chamber.

Nukkels started to talk then, but Obould stopped him with an upraised hand. "Give Kna time to be properly away," the king said loudly. "For if my dear consort inadvertently overhears the words of Gruumsh, the One-eye will demand her death."

As soon as he finished, a rustling just to the side of the exit confirmed his suspicions that his foolish Kna had been thinking to eavesdrop. Obould looked at Nukkels and sighed.

"An informative idiot, at least," the priest offered, and Obould could only shrug. Nukkels began spellcasting, waving his arms and releasing wards to silence the area around himself and Obould.

When he finished, Obould nodded his approval and said, "I have heard the name of Chieftain Grguch far too often of late. What do you know of Clan Karuck?"

It was Nukkels's turn to shrug. "Half-ogres, say the rumors, but I cannot confirm. They are not known to me."

"And yet they heard my call."

"Many tribes have come forth from the deep holes of the Spine of the World, seeking to join in the triumph of King Obould. Surely Clan Karuck's priests could have heard of our march through communion with Gruumsh."

"Or from mortal voices."

Nukkels mulled that over for a bit. "There has been a chain of whispers and shouts, no doubt," he replied cautiously, for Obould's tone hinted at something more nefarious.

"He comes forth and attacks the Moonwood then sweeps south and overruns the dwarves' wall. For a chieftain who lived deep in the holes of the distant mountains, Grguch seems to know well the enemies lurking on the borders of Many-Arrows."

Nukkels nodded and said, "You believe that Clan Karuck was called here with purpose."

"I believe I would be a fool not to find out if that was the case," Obould replied. "It is no secret that many have disagreed with my decision to pause in our campaign."

"Pause?"

"As far as they know."

"So they bring forth an instigator, to drive Obould forward?"

"An instigator, or a rival?"

"None would be so foolish!" the priest said with proper and prudent astonishment.

"Do not overestimate the intelligence of the masses," Obould said. "But whether as an instigator or a rival, Grguch has brought trouble to my designs. Perhaps irreparable damage. We can expect a counterattack from King Bruenor, I am sure, and from many of his allies if we are unlucky."

"Grguch stung them, but he left," Nukkels reminded the king. "If they see his strike as bait, Bruenor will not be so foolish as to come forth from his defended halls."

"Let us hope, and let us hope that we can quickly contain this eager chieftain. Send Oktule back to Grguch, with word that I would speak to him. Offer an invitation to Clan Karuck for a great feast in honor of their victories."

Nukkels nodded.

"And prepare yourself for a journey, my trusted friend," Obould went on, and that reference took Nukkels off-guard, for he had only known Obould for a short time, and had only spoken directly to the orc king since Obould had climbed back up from the landslide that had nearly killed him and the dark elf.

"I would go to Mithral Hall itself for King Obould Many-Arrows," Nukkels replied, standing straight and determined.

Obould grinned and nodded, and Nukkels knew that his guess had been correct. And his answer had been sincere and well-placed—and expected, since it had, after all, come from the king's "trusted friend."

"Shall I invite Kna and your private guard to return to you, Great One?" Nukkels asked, bowing low.

Obould paused for a moment then shook his head. "I will call for them when they are needed," he told the priest. "Go and speak with Oktule. Send him on his way, and return to me this night, with your own pack readied for a long and trying road."

Nukkels bowed again, turned, and swiftly departed.

* * * * *

"Ah, but it's good that ye're here, Lady," Bruenor said to Alustriel when they met out by the wall. Catti-brie stood beside the Lady of Silverymoon, with Regis and Thibbledorf Pwent close behind Bruenor.

Not far away, Cordio Muffinhead and another dwarf priest went to work immediately on the poor, impaled Duzberyl, extricating the dead wizard as gently as possible.

"Would that we could have done more," Alustriel replied solemnly. "Like your kin, we were lulled by the passing months of quiet, and so the orc assault caught us by surprise. We had not the proper spells prepared, for our studies have focused on working the Surbrin Bridge to completion."

"Ye did a bit o' damage to the pigs, and got most o' me boys back to the hall," said Bruenor. "Ye did good by us, and we're not for forgettin' that."

Alustriel responded with a bow. "And now that we know, we will not be caught unawares again," she promised. "Our efforts on the bridge will be slowed, of course, as half our magical repertoire each day will be focused on spells for defending the ground and repelling invaders. And indeed, we will have just a small crew at the bridge until the wall and towers are repaired and completed. The bridge will serve no useful purpose until—"

"Bah!" Bruenor snorted. "The point's all moot. We seen the truth o' Obould, suren as there is any. Put all yer spells for orc-killing— excepting them ye'll be needin' to get yer Knights in Silver across the Surbrin. When we're done with the damned orcs, we can worry about the bridge and the wall, though I'm thinkin' we won't be needing much of a wall!"

Behind him, Thibbledorf Pwent snorted, as did several others, but Alustriel just looked at him curiously, as if she didn't understand. As her expression registered to Bruenor, his own face became a scowl of abject disbelief. That look only intensified as he noted Catti-brie's wince at Alustriel's side, confirmation that he wasn't misreading the Lady of Silverymoon.

"Ye're thinkin' we're to dig in and let Obould play it as Obould wants?" the dwarf asked.

"I advise caution, good king," Alustriel said.

"Caution?"

"The orcs did not hold the ground," Alustriel noted. "They struck and then they ran—likely to evoke just such a response from you. They would have you roar out of Mithral Hall, all full of fight and rage. And out there"—she motioned to the wild north—"they would have their battle with you on the ground of their own choosing."

"Her words make sense," Catti-brie added, but Bruenor snorted again.

"And if they're thinking that Clan Battlehammer's to come out alone, then I'm thinkin' their plan to be a good one," Bruenor said. "But what a trap they'll find when the trap they spring closes on all the force o' the Silver Marches. On Alustriel's wizards and the Knights in Silver, on Felbarr's thousands and Adbar's tens o'! On Sundabar's army, guided in on Obould's flank by them Moonwood elves, who're not too fond o' the damned orcs, in case ye're missing the grumbles."

Alustriel drew her lips very tight, as clear a response as she could possibly give.

"What?" Bruenor roared. "Ye're not for calling them? Not now? Not when we seen what Obould's all about? Ye hoped for a truce, and now ye're seein' the truth o' that truce! What more're ye needing?"

"It is not a matter of evidence, good dwarf," Alustriel replied, calmly and evenly, though her voice rang much thinner than usual. "It is a matter of practicality."

"Practicality, or cowardice?" Bruenor demanded.

Alustriel accepted the barb with a light, resigned shrug.

"Ye said ye'd be standin' with me boys when we needed ye," Bruenor reminded.

"They will . . ." Catti-brie started to say, but she shut up fast when Bruenor snapped his scowl her way.

"Ye're friendship's all pretty when it's words and building, but when there's blood. . . ." Bruenor accused, and Alustriel swept her arm out toward Duzberyl, who lay on the ground with Cordio praying over him.

"Bah, so ye got caught in one fight, but I'm not talking about one!" Bruenor kept on. "Lost me a dozen good boys last night."

"All the Silver Marches weep for your dead, King Bruenor."

"I ain't askin' ye to weep!" Bruenor screamed at her, and all around, work stopped, and dwarf, human, and elf—including Hralien—stood and stared at the outraged king of Mithral Hall and the great Lady of Silverymoon, who not a one of them had ever imagined could be yelled at in such a manner. "I'm askin' ye to fight!" the unrelenting Bruenor fumed on. "I'm askin' ye to do what's right and send yer armies—*all* yer durned armies! Obould's belongin' in a hole, and ye're knowing that! So get yer armies, and get all the armies, and let's put him where he belongs, and let's put the Silver Marches back where the Silver Marches're belonging!"

"We will leave all the ground between Mithral Hall and the Spine of the World stained with the blood of dwarves and men and elves," Alustriel warned. "Obould's thousands are well en—"

"And well meaning to strike out until they're stopped!" Bruenor shouted over her. "Ye heared o' the Moonwood and their dead, and now ye're seein' this attack with yer own eyes. Ye can't be doubtin' what that foul orc's got in his head."

"But to go out from defensive positions against that force—"

"Is to be our only choice, now or tomorrow, or me and me boys'll forever be on yer point, fighting Obould one bridge, one door at a time," said Bruenor. "Ye think we're to take their hits? Ye think we can be keeping both our doors always sealed and secured, and our tunnels, too, lest the durned pigs tunnel in and pop up in our middle?"

Bruenor's eyes narrowed, his expression taking on a clear look of suspicion. "Or would that arrangement please Alustriel and all th' others about? Battlehammer dwarves'll die, and that's suitin' ye all, is it?"

"Of course not," Alustriel protested, but her words did little to soften the scowl of King Bruenor.

"Me girl beside ye just got back from Nesmé, and what a fine job yer knights've done pushing them trolls back into the swamp," Bruenor went on. "Seems Nesmé's grander than afore the attacks, mostly because o' yer own work—and don't that make Lady Alustriel proud?"

"Father," Catti-brie warned, shocked by the sarcasm.

"But then, them folk're more akin to yer own, in looks and thoughts."

"We should continue this discussion in private, King Bruenor," said Alustriel.

Bruenor snorted at her and waved his hand, turned on his heel, and stomped away, Thibbledorf Pwent in tow.

Regis remained, and he turned a concerned look at Alustriel then at Catti-brie.

"He will calm down," Regis said unconvincingly.

"Not so sure I'm wantin' him to," Catti-brie admitted, and she glanced at Alustriel.

The Lady of Silverymoon had nothing more than helplessly upraised hands in reply, and so Catti-brie limped off after her beloved father.

"It is a dark day, my friend Regis," Alustriel said when the woman had gone.

Regis's eyes popped open wide, surprised at being directly addressed by one of Alustriel's stature.

"This is how great wars begin," Alustriel explained. "And do not doubt that no matter the outcome, there will be no winners."

* * * * *

As soon as the priest had gone, Obould was glad of his decision not to call in his entourage. He needed to be alone, to vent, to rant, and to think things through. He knew in his heart that Grguch was no ally, and had not arrived by accident. Ever since the disaster in the western antechamber of Mithral Hall and the pushback of Proffit's troll army, the orcs and dwarves had settled into a stalemate—and it was one that Obould welcomed. But one that he welcomed privately, for he knew that he was working against the traditions, instincts, and conditioning of his warrior race. No voices of protest came to him directly, of course—he was too feared by those around him for that kind of insolence—but he heard the rumbles of discontent even in the grating background of praises thrown his way. The restless orcs wanted to march on, back into Mithral Hall, across the Surbrin to Silverymoon and Sundabar, and particularly Citadel Felbarr, which they had once, long ago, claimed as their own.

"The cost . . ." Obould muttered, shaking his head.

He would lose thousands in such an endeavor—even if he only tried to dislodge fierce King Bruenor. He would lose tens of thousands if he went farther, and though he would have loved nothing more than to claim the throne of Silverymoon as his own, Obould understood that if he had gathered all the orcs from all the holes in all the world, he could not likely accomplish such a thing.

Certainly he might find allies—more giants and dark elves, perhaps, or any of the other multitude of races and monsters that lived solely for the pleasure of fighting and destruction. In such an alliance, though, he could never reign, nor could his minions ever gain true freedom and self-determination.

And even if he did manage greater conquests with his orc minions, even if he widened the scope of the Kingdom of Many-Arrows, the lessons of history had taught him definitively that the center of such a kingdom could never hold. His reach was long, his grip iron strong. Long and strong enough to hold the perimeters of the Kingdom of Many-Arrows? Long and strong enough to fend off Grguch and any potential conspirators who had coaxed the fierce chieftain to the surface?

Obould clenched his fist mightily as that last question filtered through his mind, and he issued a long and low growl then licked his lips as if tasting the blood of his enemies.

Were Clan Karuck even his enemies?

The question sobered him. He was getting ahead of the facts, he realized. A ferocious and aggressive orc clan had arrived in Many-Arrows, and had taken up the fight independently, as orc clans often did, and with great and glorious effect.

Obould nodded as he considered the truth of it and realized the limits of his conjecture. In his heart, though, he knew that a rival had come, and a very dangerous one at that.

Reflexively, the orc king looked to the southwest, the direction of General Dukka and his most reliable fighting force. He would need another courier, he realized immediately. As Oktule went to summon Grguch, as Nukkels traveled to King Bruenor's Court with word of truce, so he would need a third, the fastest of the three, to go and retrieve Dukka and the warriors. For the dwarves might soon counter-attack, and likely would be joined by the dangerous and outraged Moonwood elves.

Or more likely, Clan Karuck would need to be taught a lesson.

CHAPTER

With but one hand, for the chieftain was no minor warrior, Dnark pushed Oktule to the side and stepped past him to the edge of a mountain-view precipice overlooking King Obould's encampment. A group of riders exited that camp, moving swiftly to the south, and without the banner of Many-Arrows flying from their midst.

"War pigs, and armored," the shaman Ung-thol remarked. "Elite warriors. Obould's own."

Dnark pointed to a rider in the middle of the pack, and though they were far away and moving farther, his headdress could still be seen.

"The priest, Nukkels," Ung-thol said with a nod.

"What does this mean?" Oktule asked, his tone concurring with his body posture to relate his discomfort. Young Oktule had been chosen as a courier from the east because of his speed and stamina, but he had not the experience or the wisdom to fathom all that was going on around him.

The chieftain and his shaman turned as one to regard the orc. "It means that you should tell Grguch to proceed with all caution," Dnark said.

"I do not understand."

"King Obould might not welcome him with the warmth promised in the invitation," Dnark explained.

"Or might greet him with more warmth than promised," Ung-thol quipped.

Oktule stared at them, his jaw hanging open. "King Obould is angry?"

That brought a laugh from the two older and more worldly orcs.

"You know Toogwik Tuk?" Ung-thol asked.

Oktule nodded. "The preacher orc. His words showed me to the glory of Grguch. He proclaimed the power of Chieftain Grguch and the call of Gruumsh to bring war to the dwarves."

Dnark chuckled and patted the air with his hand, trying to calm the fool. "Deliver your words to Chieftain Grguch as your king demanded," he said. "But seek out Toogwik Tuk first and inform him that a second courier went out from Obould's"—then he quickly corrected himself—"*King* Obould's camp, this one riding to the south."

"What does it mean?" Oktule asked again.

"It means that King Obould expects trouble," Ung-thol interrupted, stopping Dnark before he could respond. "Toogwik Tuk will know what to do."

"Trouble?" asked Oktule.

"The dwarves will likely counterattack, and more furious will they become when they learn that both King Obould and Chieftain Grguch are in the same place."

Oktule began to nod stupidly, catching on.

"Be off at once," Dnark told him, and the young orc spun on his heel and rushed away. A signal from Dnark sent a couple of guards off with him, to escort him on his important journey.

As soon as they were gone, the chieftain and the shaman turned back to the distant riders.

"Do you really believe that Obould would send an emissary to the Battlehammer dwarves?" Ung-thol asked. "Has he become so cowardly as that?"

Dnark nodded through every word, and when Ung-thol glanced over at him, he replied, "We should find out."

* * * * *

"Ye tell Emerus that we'll be lookin' for all he's to bring," Bruenor said to Jackonray Broadbelt and Nikwillig, the emissaries from Citadel Felbarr.

"The bridge'll be ready soon, I'm told," Jackonray replied.

"Forget the durned bridge!" Bruenor snapped, startling everyone in the room with his unexpected outburst. "Alustriel's wizards'll be working more on the wall for the next days. I'm wanting an army here afore the work's even begun on the bridge again. I'm wanting Alustriel to see Felbarr side-by-side with Mithral Hall, that when we're walking out that gate, she'll know the time for talkin's over and the time for fightin's come."

"Ah," Jackonray replied, nodding, a smile spreading on his hairy and toothy face. "So I'm seeing why Bruenor's the king. Ye've got me respect, good King Bruenor, and ye've got me word that I'll shove King Emerus out the durned tunnel door meself if it's needin' to be!"

"Ye're a good dwarf. Ye do yer kin proud."

Jackonray bowed so low that his beard brushed the ground, and he and Nikwillig left in a rush—or started to, until Bruenor's call turned them fast around.

"Go out through the eastern gate, under the open sky," Bruenor instructed with a wry grin.

"Quicker through the tunnels," Nikwillig dared to argue.

"Nah, ye go out and tell Alustriel that I'm wantin' the two o' ye put outside o' Felbarr in a blink," Bruenor explained, and snapped his stubby fingers in the air to accentuate his point. All around Bruenor, dwarves began to chuckle.

"Never let it be said that a Battlehammer don't know a good joke when he's seein' one," Bruenor remarked, and the chuckles turned to laughter.

Jackonray and Nikwillig left in a rush, giggling.

"Let Alustriel play a part in her own trap," Bruenor said to Cordio, Thibbledorf, and Banak Brawnanvil, who had a specially designed throne right beside Bruenor's own, a place of honor for the heroic leader who had been crippled in the orc assault.

"Suren she's to be scrunching up her pretty face," Banak said.

"When Mithral Hall and Citadel Adbar march right past her working wizards, to be sure," Bruenor agreed. "But she'll be seeing, too, that the time's past hiding from Obould's dogs. He's wantin' a fight and we're for givin' him one—one that'll take him all the way back where he came from, and beyond."

The room erupted in cheering, and Banak reached out to grab Bruenor's offered hand, clasping tight in a shake of mutual respect and determination.

"Ye stay here and take the rest o' the audiences," Bruenor instructed Banak. "I'm for seeing Rumblebelly and the littler one. There's clues in them scrolls we brought back, or I'm a bearded gnome, and I'm wantin' all the tricks and truths we can muster afore we strike out against Obould."

He hopped down from his throne and from the dais, motioning for Cordio to follow and for Thibbledorf to stand as Banak's second.

"Nanfoodle told me that the runes on them scrolls weren't nothing he'd e'er seen," Cordio said to Bruenor as they started out of the audience chamber. "Squiggles in places squiggles shouldn't be."

"The littler one'll straighten 'em out, don't ye doubt. As clever as any I've ever seen, and a good friend o' the clan. Mirabar's lost a lot when Torgar and his boys come our way, and they lost a lot when Nanfoodle and Shoudra come looking for Torgar and his boys."

Cordio nodded his agreement and left it at that, following Bruenor down the corridors and stairwells to a small cluster of secluded rooms where Nanfoodle had set up his alchemy lab and library.

* * * * *

No one in the tribe knew if it had gotten its name through its traditional battle tactics, or if the succession of chieftains had fashioned the tactics to fit the name. Whatever the cause-effect, their peculiar battle posture had been perfected through generations. Indeed, the leaders of Wolf Jaw selected orcs at a young age based on size and speed to find the appropriate place in the formation each might best fit.

Choosing the enemy and the battleground was more important even than that, if the dangerous maneuver was to work. And no orc in the tribe's history had been better at such tasks than the present chieftain, Dnark of the Fang. He was descended from a long line of point warriors, the tip of the fangs of the wolf jaw that snapped over its enemies. For years, young Dnark had spearheaded the top line of the V formation, sliding out along the left flank of an intended target, while another orc, often a cousin of Dnark's, led the right, or bottom, jaw. When the lines stretched to their limit, Dnark would swing his assault group to a sharp right, forming a fang, and he and his counterpart would join forces, sealing the escape route at the rear of the enemy formation.

As chieftain, though, Dnark anchored the apex. His jaws of warriors went out north and south of the small encampment, and when the signals came back to the chieftain, he led the initial assault, moving forward with his main battle group.

They did not charge, and did not holler and hoot. Instead, they approached calmly, as if nothing was amiss—and indeed, why would King Obould's shaman advisor suspect anything different?

The camp did stir at the approach of so large a contingent, with calls for Nukkels to come forth from his tent.

Ung-thol put his hand on Dnark's arm, urging restraint. "We do not know his purpose," the shaman reminded.

Nukkels appeared a few moments later, moving to the eastern end of the small plateau he and his warriors had used for their pause. Beside him, Obould's powerful guards lifted heavy spears.

How Dnark wanted to call for the charge! How he wanted to lead the way up the rocky incline to smash through those fools!

But Ung-thol was there, reminding him, coaxing him to patience.

"Praise to King Obould!" Dnark called out, and he took his tribe's banner from an orc to the side and waved it around. "We have word from Chieftain Grguch," he lied.

Nukkels held up his hand, palm out at Dnark, warning him to hold back.

"We have no business with you," he called down.

"King Obould does not share that belief," Dnark replied, and he began his march again, slowly. "He has sent us to accompany you, as more assurance that Clan Karuck will not interfere."

"Interfere with what?" Nukkels shouted back.

Dnark glanced at Ung-thol, then back up the rise. "We know where you are going," he bluffed.

It was Nukkels's turn to look around at his entourage. "Come in alone, Chieftain Dnark," he called. "That we might plot our next move."

Dnark kept moving up the slope, calm and unthreatening, and he did not bid his force to lag behind.

"Alone!" Nukkels called more urgently.

Dnark smiled, but otherwise changed not a thing. The orcs beside Nukkels lifted their spears.

It didn't matter. The bluff had played its part, allowing Dnark's core force to close nearly half the incline to Nukkels. Dnark held up his hands to Nukkels and the guards then turned to address his group—ostensibly to instruct them to wait there.

"Kill them all—except for Nukkels and the closest guards," he instructed instead, and when he turned back, he had his sword in hand, and he raised it high.

The warriors of Clan Wolf Jaw swept past him on either side, those nearest swerving to obstruct their enemies' view of their beloved chieftain. More than one of those shield orcs died in the next moments, as spears flew down upon them.

But the jaws of the wolf closed.

By the time Dnark got up to the plateau, the fighting was heavy all around him and Nukkels was nowhere to be found. Angered by that, Dnark threw himself into the nearest battle, where a pair of his orcs attacked a single guard, wildly and ineffectively.

Obould had chosen his inner circle of warriors well.

One of the Wolf Jaw orcs stabbed in awkwardly with his spear, but the guard's sword swept across and shattered the hilt, launching it out to confuse the attacker's companion. With the opening clear, the guard retracted and stepped forward for the easy kill.

Except that Dnark came in fast from the side and hacked the fool's sword arm off at the elbow.

The guard howled and half-turned, falling to its knees and clutching its stump. Dnark stepped in and grabbed it by the hair, tugging its head back, opening its neck for a killing strike.

And always before, the chieftain of Clan Wolf Jaw would have taken that strike, would have claimed that kill. But he held back his sword and kicked the guard in the throat instead, and as it fell away, he instructed his two warriors to make sure that the fallen enemy didn't die.

Then he went on to the next fight in a long line of battles.

When the skirmish on the plateau ended, though, Shaman Nukkels was not to be found, either among the seven prisoners or the score of dead. He had gone off the back end at the first sign of trouble, so said witnesses.

Before Dnark could begin to curse that news, however, he found that his selections for the fangs of the formation had done his own legacy proud, for in they marched, Nukkels and a battered guard prodded before them with spears.

"Obould will kill you for this," Nukkels said when presented before Dnark.

Dnark's left hook left the shaman squirming on the ground.

* * * * *

"The symbol is correct," Nanfoodle proudly announced. "The pattern is unmistakable."

Regis stared at the large copy of the parchment, its runes separated and magnified. On Nanfoodle's instruction, the halfling had spent the better part of a day transcribing each mark to that larger version then the pair had spent several days cutting out wooden stencils for each—even for those that seemed to hold an obvious correlation to the current Dwarvish writing.

Mistaking that tempting lure, accepting the obvious runes for what they supposed them to be, Dethek runes of an archaic orc tongue called Hulgorkyn, had been their downfall through all of their early translation attempts, and it wasn't until Nanfoodle had insisted that they treat the writing from the lost city as something wholly unrecognizable that the pair had begun to make any progress at all.

If that was indeed what they were making.

Many other stencils had been crafted, multiple representations of every Dwarvish symbol. Then had come the trial and error—and error, and error, and error—for more than a day of painstaking rearranging and reevaluation. Nanfoodle, no minor illusionist, had cast many spells, and priests had been brought in to offer various auguries and inspired insights.

Thirty-two separate symbols appeared on the parchment, and while a thorough statistical analysis had offered hints of potential correlations to the traditional twenty-six runes of Dethek, the fact that none of those promising hints added up to anything substantial made much of that analysis no more than guesswork.

Gradually, though, patterns had taken shape, and spells seemed to confirm the best guesses time and time again.

More than a tenday into the work, an insight from Nanfoodle—after hearing all of Regis's stories of the strange city—proved to be the tipping point. Instead of using Dwarvish as his basis for the analysis, he decided upon a double-basis and began incorporating the Orcish tongue—in which, of course, he was fluent. More stencils were cut, more combinations explored.

Early one morning, Nanfoodle presented Regis with his completed conclusion for translation, a correlative identifying every symbol on the parchment, some that mirrored current Dwarvish or Orcish lettering.

The halfling went to work over the transcribed, larger-lettered parchment, diligently placing above each symbol the stencil Nanfoodle believed correlative. Regis didn't pause at all to consider familiar patterns, but simply placed them all as fast as he could.

Then he stepped back and stood up on the high bench Nanfoodle had placed beside the work table. The gnome was already there, staring back incredulously, his mouth hanging open, and when he took his place beside Nanfoodle, Regis understood.

For the gnome's guesses had been correct, obviously, and the translation of the text was clear to see, and to read. It wasn't unknown for orcs to steal and incorporate Dethek runes, of course, as was most evident with Hulgorkyn. But there was something more than that, a willful blending of related but disparate languages in a balanced manner, one that indicated compromise and coordination between dwarf and orc linguists.

The translation was laid bare for them to see. Digesting the words, however, proved more difficult.

"Bruenor won't like this," Regis remarked, and he glanced around as if expecting the dwarf king to crash into the room in a tirade at any moment.

"It is what it is," Nanfoodle replied. "He will not like it, but he must accept it."

Regis looked back at the translated paragraph and read again the words of the orc philosopher Duugee.

"You place too much value in reason," the halfling muttered.

PART

4

STEPPING BACK

FROM ANGER

STEPPING BACK
FROM ANGER

The questions continue to haunt me. Are we watching the birth of a civilization? Are the orcs, instead of wanting us dead, wishing to become more like us, with our ways, our hopes, our aspirations? Or was that wish always present in the hearts of the primitive and fierce race, only they saw not how to get to it? And if this is the case, if the orcs are redeemable, tamable, how then are we best to facilitate the rise of their more civilized culture? For that would be an act of great self-defense for Mithral Hall and all of the Silver Marches.

Accepting the premise of a universal desire among rational beings, a commonality of wishes, I wonder, then, what might occur should one kingdom stand paramount, should one city-state somehow attain unquestioned superiority over all the rest. What responsibilities might such predominance entail? If Bruenor has his way, and the Silver Marches rise up and drive Obould's orcs from the land and back to their individual tribes, what will be our role, then, in our resulting, unquestioned dominance?

Would the moral road be the extermination of the orcs, one tribe at a time? If my suspicions regarding Obould are correct, then that I cannot reconcile. Are the dwarves to become neighbors or oppressors?

It is all premised on a caveat, of course, on a hunch—or is it a deep-rooted prayer in the renegade soul of Drizzt Do'Urden? I desperately want to be right about Obould—as much as my personal desires might urge me to kill him!—because if I am, if there is in him a glint of rational and acceptable aspirations, then surely the world will benefit.

These are the questions for kings and queens, the principal building blocks of the guiding philosophies for those who gain power over others. In the best of these kingdoms—and I name Bruenor's among that lot—the community moves constantly to better itself, the parts of the whole turn in harmony to the betterment of the whole. Freedom and community live side-by-side, a tandem of the self and the bigger tapestry. As those communities evolve and ally with other like-minded kingdoms, as roads and trade routes are secured and cultures exchanged, what of the diminishing few left behind? It is incumbent, I believe, for the powerful to bend and grasp the hand of the weak, to pull them up, to share in the prosperity, to contribute to the whole. For that is the essence of community. It is to be based on hope and inspiration and not on fear and oppression.

But there remains the truth that if you help an orc to stand, he will likely stab your heart on the way to his feet.

Ah, but it is too much, for in my heart I see the fall of Tarathiel and want to cut the vicious orc king apart! It is too much because I know of Innovindil's fall! Oh, Innovindil, I pray you do not think less of me for my musing!

I feel the sting of paradox, the pain of the irresolvable, the stark and painful imperfections of a world of which I secretly demand perfection. Yet for all the blemishes, I remain an optimist, that in the end the ideal will prevail. And this too I also know, and it is why my weapons sit comfortably in my hands. Only from a position of unquestioned strength can true change be facilitated. For it is not in the hands of a rival to affect change. It is not in the hands of the weaker to grant peace and hope to the stronger.

I hold faith in the kingdom of common voices that Bruenor has created, that Alustriel has similarly created in Silverymoon. I believe that this is the proper order of things—though perhaps with some refining yet to be found—for theirs are kingdoms of freedom and hope, where individual aspirations are encouraged and the common good is shared by all, in both benefit and responsibility. How different are these two places from the darkness of Menzoberranzan, where the power of House presided over the common good of the community, and the aspirations of the individual overwhelmed the liberty, even the life, of others.

My belief in Mithral Hall as nearer the ideal brings with it a sense of Mithral Hall's responsibilities, however. It is not enough to field armies to thwart foes, to crush our enemies under the stamp of well-traveled dwarven boots. It is not enough to bring riches to Mithral Hall, to expand power and influence, if said power and influence is to the benefit only of the powerful and influential.

To truly fulfill the responsibilities of predominance, Mithral Hall must not only shine brightly for Clan Battlehammer, but must serve as a beacon of hope for all of those who glimpse upon it. If we truly believe our way to be the best way, then we must hold faith that all others—perhaps even the orcs!—will gravitate toward our perspectives and practices, that we will serve as the shining city on the hill, that we will influence and pacify through generosity and example instead of through the power of armies.

For if it is the latter, if dominance is attained and then maintained through strength of arm alone, then it is no victory, and it cannot be a permanent ordering. Empires cannot survive, for they lack the humility and generosity necessary to facilitate true loyalty. The wont of the slave is to throw off his shackles. The greatest aspiration of the conquered is to beat back their oppressors. There are no exceptions to this. To the victors I warn without doubt that those you conquer will never accept your dominion. All desire to emulate your better way, even if the conquered agree with the premise, will be overwhelmed by grudge and humiliation and a sense of their own community. It is a universal truth, rooted in tribalism, perhaps, and in pride and the comfort of tradition and the sameness of one's peers.

And in a perfect world, no society would aspire to dominance unless it was a dominance of ideals. We believe our way is the right way, and thus we must hold faith that others will gravitate similarly, that our way will become their way and that assimilation will sheathe the swords of sorrow. It is not a short process, and it is one that will be played out in starts and stops, with treaties forged and treaties shattered by the ring of steel on steel.

Deep inside, it is my hope that I will find the chance to slay King Obould Many-Arrows.

Deeper inside, it is my prayer that King Obould Many-Arrows sees the dwarves standing higher on the ladder in pursuit of true civilization, that he sees Mithral Hall as a shining city on the hill, and that he will have the strength to tame the orcs long enough for them to scale the rungs of that same ladder.

—Drizzt Do'Urden

CHAPTER
PUTTING HIS WORLD TOGETHER

The wagon rocked, sometimes soothing, sometimes jarring, as it rolled along the rocky path, heading north. Sitting on the open bed and looking back the way they had come, Wulfgar watched the skyline of Luskan recede. The many points of the wizard's tower seemed like a single blur, and the gates were too far for him to make out the guards pacing the city wall.

Wulfgar smiled as he considered those guards. He and his accomplice Morik had been thrown out of Luskan with orders never to return, on pain of death, yet he had walked right into the city, and at least one of the guards had surely recognized him, even tossing him a knowing wink. No doubt Morik was in there, too.

Justice in Luskan was a sham, a scripted play for the people to make them feel secure and feel afraid and feel empowered over the specter of death itself, however the authorities decided was timely.

Wulfgar had debated whether or not to return to Luskan. He wanted to join in with a caravan heading north, for that would serve as his cover, but he feared exposing Colson to the potential dangers of entering the forbidden place. In the end, though, he found that he had no real choice. Arumn Gardpeck and Josi Puddles deserved to learn of Delly Curtie's sad end. They had been friends of the woman's for years, and far be it from Wulfgar to deny them the information.

The tears shed by all three—Arumn, Josi, and Wulfgar—had felt right to the barbarian. There was so much more to Delly Curtie than the easy, clichéd idea that many in Luskan had of her, and that Wulfgar had initially bought into himself. There was an honesty and an honor beneath the crust that circumstance had caked over Delly. She'd been a good friend to all three, a good wife to Wulfgar, and a great mother to Colson.

Wulfgar tossed off a chuckle as he considered Josi's initial reaction to the news, the small man practically launching himself at Wulfgar in a rage, blaming the barbarian for the loss of Delly. With little effort, Wulfgar had put him back in his seat, where he had melted into his folded arms, his shoulders bobbing with sobs—perhaps enhanced by too many drinks, but likely sincere, for Wulfgar had never doubted that Josi had secretly loved Delly.

The world rolled along, stamping its events into the books of history. What was, was, Wulfgar understood, and regrets were not to be long held—no longer than the lessons they imparted regarding future circumstance. He was not innocent of Josi's accusations, though not to the extent the distraught man had taken them, surely.

But what was, was.

After one particularly sharp bounce of the wagon, Wulfgar draped his arm over Colson's shoulder and glanced down at the girl, who was busying herself with some sticks Wulfgar had tied together to approximate a doll. She seemed content, or at least unbothered, which was the norm for her. Quiet and unassuming, asking for little and accepting less, Colson just seemed to go along with whatever came her way.

That road had not been fair so far in her young life, Wulfgar knew. She had lost Delly, by all measures her mother, and nearly as bad, Wulfgar realized, she had suffered the great misfortune of being saddled with him as her surrogate father. He stroked her soft, wheat-colored hair.

"Doll, Da," she said, using her moniker for Wulfgar, one that he had heard only a couple of times over the last tendays.

"Doll, yes," he said back to her, and tousled her hair.

She giggled, and if ever a sound could lift Wulfgar's heart. . . .

And he was going to leave her. A momentary wave of weakness flushed through him. How could he even think of such a thing?

"You don't remember your Ma," he said quietly, not expecting a response as Colson went back to her play. But she looked up at him, beaming a huge smile.

"Dell-y. Ma," she said.

Wulfgar felt as if her little hand had just flicked against his heart. He realized how poor a father he had been to her. Urgent business filled his every day, it seemed, and Colson was always placed behind the necessities. She had been with him for many months, and yet he hardly knew her. They had traveled hundreds of miles to the east, and then back west, and only on that return trip had he truly spent time with Colson, had he tried to listen to the child, to understand her needs, to hug her.

He gave a helpless and self-deprecating chuckle and patted her head again. She looked up at him with that unending smile, and went immediately back to her doll.

He hadn't done right by her, Wulfgar knew. As he had failed Delly as a husband, so he had failed Colson as her father. "Guardian" would be a better term to describe his role in the child's life.

So he was on that road that would pain him greatly, but in the end it would give to Colson all that she deserved and more.

"You are a princess," he said to her, and she looked up at him again, though she knew not what it meant.

Wulfgar responded with a smile and another pat, and turned his eyes back toward Luskan, wondering if he would ever travel that far south again.

* * * * *

The village of Auckney seemed to have changed not at all in the three years since Wulfgar had last seen it. Most of his last visit, of course, had been spent in the lord's dungeon, an accommodation he hoped to avoid a second time. It amused him to think of how his time with Morik had so ingratiated him to the towns of that region, where the words "on pain of death" seemed to accompany his every departure.

Unlike those guards in Luskan, though, Wulfgar suspected that Auckney's crew would follow through with the threat if they figured out who he was. So for the sake of Colson, he took great pains to disguise himself as the trading caravan wound its way along the rocky road in the westernmost reaches of the Spine of the World, toward the Auckney gate. He wore his beard much thicker, but his stature alone distinguished him from the great majority of the populace, being closer to seven feet tall than to six, and with shoulders wide and strong.

He bundled his traveling cloak tight around him and kept the cowl up over his head—not an unusual practice in the early spring in that part of the world, where the cold winds still howled from on high. When he sat, which was most of the time, he kept his legs tucked in tight so as not to emphasize the length of the limbs, and when he walked, he crouched and hunched his shoulders forward, not only disguising his true height somewhat, but also appearing older, and more importantly, less threatening.

Whether through his cleverness, or more likely sheer luck and the fact that he was accompanied by an entire parade of merchants in that first post-winter caravan, Wulfgar managed to get into the town easily enough, and once past the checkpoint, he did his best to blend in with the group at the circled wagons, where kiosks were hastily constructed and goods displayed to the delight of the winter-weary townsfolk.

Lord Feringal Auck, seeming as petulant as ever, visited on the first full day of the caravan faire. Dressed in impractical finery, including puffy pantaloons of purple and white, the foppish man strutted with a perpetual air of contempt turning up his thin, straight nose. He glanced at goods but never seemed interested enough to bother—though his attendants often returned to purchase particular pieces, obviously for the lord.

Steward Temigast and the gnome driver—and fine fighter—Liam Woodgate, stood out among those attendants. Temigast, Wulfgar trusted, but he knew that if Liam spotted him, the game was surely up.

"He casts an impressive shadow, don't he?" came a sarcastic voice from behind, and Wulfgar turned to see one of the caravan drivers looking past him to the lord and his entourage. "Feringal Auck. . . ." the man added, chuckling.

"I am told that he has a most extraordinary wife," Wulfgar replied.

"Lady Meralda," the man answered, rather lewdly. "As pretty as the moon and more dangerous than the night, with hair blacker than the darkest of 'em and eyes so green that ye're thinking yerself to be in a summer's meadow whenever she glances yer way. Aye, but every man doing business in Auckney would want to bed that one."

"Have they children together?"

"A son," the man answered. "A strong and sturdy lad, and with features favoring his mother and not the lord, thank the gods. Little lord Ferin. All in the town celebrated his first birthday just a month ago, and from what I'm hearing, they'll be buying extra stores to replenish that which they ate at the feast. Finished off their winter stores, by some accounts, and there's more truth than lie to those, judging by the coins that've been falling all the morning."

Wulfgar glanced back at Feringal and his entourage as they wound their way along the far side of the merchant caravan.

"And here we feared that the market'd be thinner with the glutton Lady Priscilla gone."

That perked up Wulfgar's ears, and he turned fast on the man. "Feringal's . . . ?"

"Sister," the man confirmed.

"Died?"

The man snorted and didn't seem the least bit bothered by that possibility, something that Wulfgar figured anyone who had ever had the misfortune of meeting Priscilla Auck would surely appreciate.

"She's in Luskan—been there for a year. She went back with this same caravan after our market here last year," the man explained. "She never much cared for Lady Meralda, for 'twas said she'd had Feringal's ear until he married that one. I'm not for knowing what happened, but that Priscilla's time in Castle Auck came to an end soon after the marriage, and when Meralda got fat with Feringal's heir, she likely knew her influence here would shrink even more. So she went to Luskan, and there she's living, with enough coin to keep her to the end of her days, may they be mercifully short."

"Mercifully for all around her, you mean?"

"That's the way they tell it, aye."

Wulfgar nodded and smiled, and that genuine grin came from more than the humor at Priscilla's expense. He looked back at Lord Feringal and narrowed his crystalline blue eyes, thinking that one major obstacle, the disagreeable Lady Priscilla, had just been removed from his path.

"If Priscilla was at Castle Auck, as much as he'd be wanting to leave,

Lord Feringal wouldn't dare be out without his wife at his side. He wouldn't leave them two together!" the man said.

"I would expect that Lady Meralda would wish to visit the caravan more than would the lord," Wulfgar remarked.

"Ah, but not until her flowers bloom."

Wulfgar looked at him curiously.

"She's put in beds of rare tulips, and they're soon to bloom, I'm guessing," the man explained. " 'Twas so last year—she didn't come down to the market until our second tenday, not until the white petals were revealed. Put her in a fine, buying mood, and finer still, for by that time, we knew that Lady Priscilla would be journeying from Auckney with us."

He began to laugh, but Wulfgar didn't follow the cue. He stared across the little stone bridge to the small island that housed Castle Auck, trying to remember the layout and where those gardens might be. He took note of a railing built atop the smaller of the castle's square keeps. Wulfgar glanced back at Feringal, to see the man making his way out of the far end of the market, and with the threat removed, Wulfgar also set out, nodding appreciatively at the merchant, to find a better vantage point for scouting the castle.

Not long after, he had his answer, spotting the form of a woman moving along the flat tower's roof, behind the railing.

* * * * *

There were no threats to Auckney. The town had known peace for a long time. In that atmosphere, it was no surprise to Wulfgar to learn that the guards were typically less than alert. Even so, the big man had no idea how he might get across that little stone bridge unnoticed, and the waters roiling beneath the structure were simply too cold for him to try to swim—and besides, both the near bank and the island upon which the castle stood had sheer cliffs that rose too steeply from the pounding surf below.

He lingered long by the bridge, seeking the answer to his dilemma, and he finally came to accept that he might have to simply wait for those flowers to bloom, so he could confront Lady Meralda in the market. That thought didn't sit well with him, for in that setting he would almost surely need to face Lord Feringal and his entourage as well. It would be easier if he could speak with Meralda first, and alone.

He leaned against the wall of a nearby tavern one afternoon, staring out at the bridge and taking note of the guards' maneuvers. They weren't very disciplined, but the bridge was so narrow that they didn't have to be. Wulfgar stood up straight as a coach rambled across the structure, heading out of the castle.

Liam Woodgate wasn't driving. Steward Temigast was.

Wulfgar stroked his beard and weighed his options, and purely on instinct—for he knew that if he considered his movements, he would lose heart—he gathered up Colson and moved out to the road, to a spot where he could intercept the wagon out of sight of the guards at the bridge, and most of the townsfolk.

"Good trader, do move aside," Steward Temigast bade him, but in a kindly way. "I've some paintings to sell and I wish to see the market before the light wanes. Dark comes early to a man of my age, you know."

The old man's smile drifted to nothingness as Wulfgar pulled back the cowl of his cloak, revealing himself.

"Always full of surprises, Wulfgar is," Temigast said.

"You look well," Wulfgar offered, and he meant it. Temigast's white hair had thinned a bit, perhaps, but the last few years had not been rough on the man.

"Is that. . . . ?" Temigast asked, nodding to Colson.

"Meralda's girl."

"Are you mad?"

Wulfgar merely shrugged and said, "She should be with her mother."

"That decision was made some three years ago."

"Necessary at the time," said Wulfgar.

Temigast sat back on his seat and conceded the point with a nod.

"Lady Priscilla is gone from here, I am told," said Wulfgar, and Temigast couldn't help but smile—a reassurance to Wulfgar that his measure of the steward was correct, that the man hated Priscilla.

"To the joy of Auckney," Temigast admitted. He set the reins on the seat, and with surprising nimbleness climbed down and approached Wulfgar, his hands out for Colson.

The girl shoved her hand in her mouth and whirled away, burying her face in Wulfgar's shoulder.

"Bashful," Temigast said. Colson peeked out at him and he smiled all the wider. "And she has her mother's eyes."

"She is a wonderful girl, and sure to become a beautiful woman," said Wulfgar. "But she needs her mother. I cannot keep her with me. I am bound for a land that will not look favorably on a child, any child."

Temigast stared at him for a long time, obviously unsure of what he should do.

"I share your concern," Wulfgar said to him. "I never hurt Lady Meralda, and never wish to hurt her."

"My loyalty is to her husband, as well."

"And what a fool he would be to refuse this child."

Temigast paused again. "It is complicated."

"Because Meralda loved another before him," said Wulfgar. "And Colson is a reminder of that."

"Colson," said Temigast, and the girl peeked out at him and smiled, and the steward's whole face lit up in response. "A pretty name for a pretty girl." He grew more serious as he turned back to Wulfgar, though, and asked bluntly, "What would you have me do?"

"Get us to Meralda. Let me show her the beautiful child her daughter has become. She will not part with the girl again."

"And what of Lord Feringal?"

"Is he worthy of your loyalty and love?"

Temigast paused and considered that. "And what of Wulfgar?"

Wulfgar shrugged as if it did not matter, and indeed, regarding his obligation to Colson, it did not. "If he desires to hang me, he will have to—"

"Not that," Temigast interrupted, and looked at Colson.

Wulfgar's shoulders slumped and he heaved a deep sigh. "I know what is right. I know what I must do, though it will surely break my heart. But it will be a temporary wound, I hope, for in the passing months and years, I will rest assured that I did right by Colson, that I gave her the home and the chance she deserved, and that I could not provide."

Colson looked at Temigast and responded to his every gesture with a delighted smile.

"Are you certain?" the steward asked.

Wulfgar stood very straight.

Temigast glanced back at Castle Auck, at the short keep where Lady Meralda kept her flowers. "I will return this way before nightfall," he said. "With an empty carriage. I can get you to her, perhaps, but I disavow myself of you from that point forward. My loyalty is not to Wulfgar, not even to Colson."

"One day it will be," said Wulfgar. "To Colson, I mean."

Temigast was too charmed by the girl to disagree.

* * * * *

One hand patted the soft soil at the base of the stem, while the fingers of Meralda's other hand gently brushed the smooth petals. The tulips would bloom soon, she knew—perhaps even that very evening.

Meralda sang to them softly, an ancient rhyme of sailors and explorers lost in the waves, as her first love had been taken by the sea. She didn't know all the words, but it hardly mattered, for she hummed to fill in the holes in the verses and it sounded no less beautiful.

A slap on the stone broke her song, though, and the woman stood up suddenly and retreated a fast step when she noted the prongs of a ladder. Then a large hand clamped over the lip of the garden wall, not ten feet from her.

She brushed back her thick black hair, and her eyes widened as the intruder pulled his head up over the wall.

"Who are you?" she demanded, retreating again, and ignoring his shushing plea.

"Guards!" Meralda called, and turned to run as the intruder shifted. But as his other hand came up, she found herself frozen in place, rooted as if she was just another plant in her carefully cultivated garden. In the man's other hand was a young girl.

"Wulfgar?" Meralda mouthed, but had not the breath to say aloud.

He put the girl down inside, and Colson turned shyly away from Meralda. Wulfgar grabbed the wall with both hands and hauled himself over. The girl went to his leg and wrapped one arm around it, the thumb of her other hand going into her mouth as she continued to shy away.

"Wulfgar?" Meralda asked again.

"Da!" implored Colson, reaching up to Wulfgar with both hands. He scooped her up and set her on his hip, then pulled back his cowl, revealing himself fully.

"Lady Meralda," he replied.

"You should not be here!" Meralda said, but her eyes betrayed her words, for she stared unblinkingly at the girl, at her child.

Wulfgar shook his head. "Too long have I been away."

"My husband would not agree."

"It is not about him, nor about me," Wulfgar said, his calm and sure tone drawing her gaze back to him. "It is about her, your daughter."

Meralda swayed, and Wulfgar was certain that a slight breeze would have knocked her right over.

"I have tried to be a good father to her," Wulfgar explained. "I had even found her a woman to serve as her mother, though she is gone now, taken by foul orcs. But it is all a ruse, I know."

"I never asked—"

"Your husband's actions demanded it," Wulfgar reminded her, and she went silent, her gaze locking once more on the shy child, who had buried her face in her da's strong shoulder.

"My road is too arduous," Wulfgar explained. "Too dangerous for the likes of Colson."

"Colson?" Meralda echoed.

Wulfgar merely shrugged.

"Colson . . ." the woman said softly, and the girl looked her way only briefly and flashed a sheepish smile.

"She belongs with her mother," Wulfgar said. "With her real mother."

"I had thought her father had demanded her to raise as his princess in Icewind Dale," came a sharp retort from the side, and all three turned to regard the entrance of Lord Feringal. The man twisted his face tightly as he moved near to his wife, all the while staring hatefully at Wulfgar.

Wulfgar looked to Meralda for a clue, but found nothing on her shocked face. He struggled to figure out which way to veer the conversation, when Meralda unexpectedly took the lead.

"Colson is not his child," the Lady of Auckney said. She grabbed

Feringal by the hands and forced him to look at her directly. "Wulfgar never ravished—"

Before she could finish, Feringal pulled one of his hands free and lifted a finger over her lips to silence her, nodding his understanding.

He knew, Meralda realized and so did Wulfgar. Feringal had known all along that the child was not Wulfgar's, not the product of a rape.

"I took her to protect your wife . . . and you," Wulfgar said after allowing Feringal and Meralda a few heartbeats to stare into each other's eyes. Feringal turned a scowl his way, to which Wulfgar only shrugged. "I had to protect the child," he explained.

"I would not . . ." Feringal started to reply, but he stopped and shook his head then addressed Meralda instead. "I would not have hurt her," he said, and Meralda nodded.

"I would not have continued our marriage, would not have borne you an heir, if I had thought differently," Meralda quietly replied.

Feringal's scowl returned as he glanced back at Wulfgar. "What do you want, son of Icewind Dale?" he demanded.

Some noise to the side clued Wulfgar in to the fact that the Lord of Auckney hadn't come to the garden alone. Guards waited in the shadows to rush out and protect Feringal.

"I want only to do what is right, Lord Feringal," he replied. "As I did what I thought was right those years ago." He shrugged and looked at Colson, the thought of parting with her suddenly stabbing at his heart.

Feringal stood staring at him.

"The child, Colson, is Meralda's," Wulfgar explained. "I would not cede her to another adoptive mother without first determining Meralda's intent."

"Meralda's intent?" Feringal echoed. "Am I to have no say?"

As the lord of Auckney finished, Meralda put a hand to his cheek and turned him to face her directly. "I cannot," she whispered.

Again Feringal silenced her with a finger against her lips, and turned back to Wulfgar. "There are a dozen bows trained upon you at this moment," he assured the man. "And a dozen guards ready to rush out and cut you down, Liam Woodgate among them—and you know that he holds no love for Wulfgar of Icewind Dale. I warned you that you return to Auckney only under pain of death."

A horrified expression crossed Meralda's face, and Wulfgar squared his shoulders. His instincts told him to counter the threat, to bring Aegis-fang magically to his hand and explain to the pompous Feringal in no uncertain terms that in any ensuing fight, he, Feringal, would be the first to die.

But Wulfgar held his tongue and checked his pride. Meralda's expression guided him, and Colson, clutching his shoulder, demanded that he diffuse the situation and not escalate a threat into action.

"For the sake of the girl, I allow you to flee, straightaway," Feringal said, and both Wulfgar and Meralda widened their eyes with shock.

The lord waved his hands dismissively at Wulfgar. "Be gone, foul fool. Over the wall and away. My patience wears thin, and when it is gone, the whole of Auckney will fall over you."

Wulfgar stared at him for a moment then looked at Colson.

"Leave the girl," Feringal demanded, lifting his voice for the sake of the distant onlookers, Wulfgar realized. "She is forfeit, a princess of Icewind Dale no more. I claim her for Auckney, by Lady Meralda's blood, and do so with the ransom of Wulfgar's promise that the tribes of Icewind Dale will never descend upon my domain."

Wulfgar spent a moment digesting the words, shaking his head in disbelief all the while. When it all sorted out, he dipped a quick and respectful bow to the surprising Lord Feringal.

"Your faith in your husband and your love for him were not misplaced," he said quietly to Meralda, and he wanted to laugh out loud and cry all at the same time, for never had he expected to see such growth in the foppish lord of that isolated town.

But for all of Wulfgar's joy at the confirmation that he had been right to return there, the price of his, and Feringal's, generosity could not be denied.

Wulfgar pulled Colson out to arms' length then brought her in and hugged her close, burying his face in her soft hair. "This is your mother," he whispered, knowing that the child wouldn't begin to understand. He was reminding himself, though, for he needed to do that. "Your ma will always love you. I will always love you."

He hugged her even closer and kissed her on the cheek then stood fast and offered a curt nod to Feringal.

Before he could change his mind, before he surrendered to the tearing of his heart, Wulfgar thrust Colson out at Meralda, who gathered her up.

He hadn't even let go of the girl when she began to cry out, "Da! Da!" reaching back at him plaintively and pitifully.

Wulfgar blinked away his tears, turned, and went over the wall, dropping the fifteen feet and landing on the grass below in a run that didn't stop until he had long crossed through Auckney's front gates.

A run that carried with every step the frantic cries of "Da! Da!"

"You did the right thing," he said to himself, but he hardly believed it. He glanced back at Castle Auck and felt as if he had just betrayed the one person in the world who had most trusted him and most needed him.

CHAPTER

THE PRACTICAL MORALITY

Certain that no orcs were about, for he could hear their revelry far over a distant hill, Tos'un Armgo settled against a natural seat of stone. Or perhaps it wasn't natural, he mused, situated as it was in the middle of a small lea, roughly circular and sheltered by ancient evergreens. Perhaps some former occupant had constructed the granite throne, for though there were other such stones scattered around the area, the placement of those two, seat and back, was perhaps a bit too convenient.

Whatever and however it had come to be, Tos'un appreciated the chair and the view it afforded him. He was a creature of the nearly light-less Underdark, where no stars shone, where no ceiling was too far above, too vast and distant, otherworldly or extraplanar, even. The canopy that floated above him every night was far beyond his experience, reaching into places that he did not know he possessed. Tos'un was a drow, and a drow male, and in that role his life remained solidly grounded in the needs of the here-and-now, in the day-to-day practicality of survival. As his goals were ever clear to him, based on simple necessity, so his limitations stayed crystalline clear as well—the boundaries of House walls and the cavern that was Menzoberranzan. For all of his life, the limits of Tos'un's aspirations hung over him as solidly as the ceiling of Menzoberranzan's stone cavern.

But those limitations were one of the reasons he had abandoned his House on their journey back to Menzoberranzan after the stunning defeat at the hands of Clan Battlehammer and Mithral Hall. Aside from the chaos that was surely to ensue following that catastrophe, when Matron Yvonnel Baenre herself had been cut down, Tos'un understood that whatever the reshuffling that chaos resolved, his place was set. Perhaps he would have died in the House warfare—as a noble, he made a fine trophy for enemy warriors, and since his mother thought little of him, he would have no doubt wound up on the front lines of any fight. But even had he survived, even had House Barrison Del'Armgo used the vulnerability of the suddenly matron-less House Baenre to ascend to the top rank in Menzoberranzan's hierarchy, Tos'un's life would be as it had always been, as he could not dare hope it would be anything but.

So he had seized the opportunity and had fled, not in search of any particular opportunity, not to follow any ambition or fleeting dream. Why had he fled, then, he wondered as he sat there under the stars?

You will be king, promised a voice in his head, startling Tos'un from his contemplations.

Without a word, with hardly a thought, the drow climbed out of the seat and took a few steps across the meadow. The snow had settled deep on that spot not long ago, but had melted, leaving spongy, muddy ground behind. A few steps from the throne, Tos'un unstrapped his sword belt and lay it upon the ground, then went back to his spot and leaned back, letting his thoughts soar up among the curious points of light.

"Why did I flee?" he asked himself quietly. "What did I desire?"

He thought of Kaer'lic, Donnia, and Ad'non, the drow trio he had joined up with after wandering aimlessly for tendays. Life with them had been good. He had found excitement and had started a war—a proxy war, which was the best kind, after all. It had been heady and clever and great fun, right up until the beastly Obould had bitten the throat out of Kaer'lic Suun Wett, sending Tos'un on the run for his life.

But even that excitement, even controlling the destiny of an army of orcs, a handful of human settlements, and a dwarven kingdom, had been nothing Tos'un had ever desired or even considered, until circumstance had dangled it before him and his three co-conspirators.

No, he realized in that moment of clarity, sitting under a canopy so foreign to his Underdark sensibilities. No tangible desire had brought him from the ranks of House Barrison Del'Armgo. It was, instead, the desire to eliminate the boundaries, the need to dare to dream, whatever dream may come to him. Tos'un and the other three drow—even Kaer'lic, despite her subservience to Lady Lolth—had run to their freedom for no reason more than to escape from the rigid structure of drow culture.

The irony of that had Tos'un blinking repeatedly as he sat there. "The rigid structure of drow culture," he said aloud, just to bask in the irony. For drow culture was premised on the tenets of Lady Lolth, the Spider Queen, the demon queen of chaos.

"Controlled chaos, then," he decided with a sharp laugh.

A laugh that was cut short as he noted movement in the trees.

Never taking his eyes from that spot, Tos'un rolled backward from the stone seat, flipping to his feet in a crouch with the stone between him and the shadowy form—a large, feline form—filtering in and out of the darker lines of the tree trunks.

The drow eased his way to the edge of the stone nearest his discarded sword belt, preparing his dash. He held still, though, not wanting to alert the creature to his presence.

But then he stood taller, blinking, for the great cat seemed to diminish, to dematerialize into a dark mist that filtered away to nothingness. For just a moment, Tos'un wondered if his imagination was playing tricks on him in that strange environment, under a sky that he had still not grown accustomed to or comfortable with.

When he realized the truth of the beast, when he recalled its origins, the drow leaped out from the stone, dived into a forward roll retrieving his belt as he went, and came up so perfectly that he had already buckled it in place before he stood once more.

Drizzt's cat! his thoughts screamed.

Pray that it is! came the unexpected and unasked for answer from his intrusive sword. *A glorious victory is at hand!*

Tos'un winced at the thought. *In Lolth's favor . . .* he imparted to the sword, recalling Kaer'lic's fears about Drizzt Do'Urden.

The priestess had been terrified at the prospect of battling the rogue from Menzoberranzan, fearing, with solid reasoning, that the trouble Drizzt had brought upon the drow city was just the sort of chaos that pleased Lady Lolth. Add to that Drizzt's uncanny luck and almost supernatural proficiency with the blade, and the idea that he was secretly in the favor of Lolth seemed not so far-fetched.

And Tos'un, for all of his irreverence, understood well that anyone who crossed Lolth's will could meet a most unpleasant end.

All of those thoughts followed his intentional telepathic message to Khazid'hea, and the sword went strangely quiet for the next few moments. Indeed, to Tos'un's sensibilities, everything seemed to go strangely quiet. He strained his eyes in the direction of the pines where he had last seen the feline shape, his hands wringing on the hilt of Khazid'hea and his other, drow-made sword. Every passing moment drew him farther into the shadows. His eyes, his ears, his sense of smell, every instinct within him honed in on that spot where the cat had disappeared as he tried desperately to discern where it had gone.

And so he nearly leaped out of his low, soft boots when a voice behind him, speaking in the drow language with perfect Menzoberranyr inflection, said, "Guenhwyvar was tired, so I sent her home to rest."

Tos'un whirled, slashing the empty air with his blades as if he believed the demon Drizzt to be right behind him.

The rogue drow was many steps away, though, standing easily, his scimitars sheathed, his forearms resting comfortably on their respective hilts.

"A fine sword you carry, son of Barrison Del'Armgo," Drizzt said, nodding toward Khazid'hea. "Not drow made, but fine."

Tos'un turned his hand over and regarded the sentient blade for a moment before turning back to Drizzt. "One I found in the valley, below . . ."

"Below where I fought King Obould," Drizzt finished, and Tos'un nodded.

"You have come for it?" Tos'un asked, and in his head, Khazid'hea simmered and imparted thoughts of battle.

Leap upon him and cut him down! I would drink the blood of Drizzt Do'Urden!

Drizzt noted Tos'un's uncomfortable wince, and suspected that Khazid'hea had been behind the grimace. Drizzt had carried the annoying sentient blade long enough to understand that its ego simply would not let it remain silent through any conversation. The way Tos'un had measured his cadence, as if he was listening to the sound of his own words coming back at him in an echo from a stone wall, revealed the continual intrusions of the ever-present Khazid'hea.

"I have come here to see this curiosity I find before me," Drizzt replied. "A son of Barrison Del'Armgo, living on the surface world, alone."

"Akin to yourself."

"Hardly," Drizzt said with a chuckle. "I carry my surname out of habit alone, and toward no familiarity or relationship with the House of Matron Malice."

"As I have abandoned my own House," Tos'un insisted, again in that stilted cadence.

Drizzt wasn't about to argue with that much of his claim, for indeed it seemed plausible enough—though of course, the events that drove Tos'un from the ranks of his formidable House might be anything but exculpatory. "To trade service to a matron mother for service to a king," Drizzt remarked. "For both of us, it seems."

Whatever Tos'un meant to reply, he bit it back and tilted his head to the side, searching the statement, no doubt.

Drizzt didn't hide his wry and knowing grin.

"I serve no king," Tos'un insisted, and with speed enough and force enough to prevent any interruptions from the intrusive blade.

"Obould names himself a king."

Tos'un shook his head, his face curling into a snarl.

"Do you deny your part in the conspiracy that prompted Obould to come south?" Drizzt asked. "I have had this conversation with two of your dead companions, of course. Or do you deny your partnering with the pair I killed? Recall that I saw you standing with the priestess when I came to battle Obould."

"Where was I, a Houseless rogue, to turn?" Tos'un replied. "I happened upon the trio of which you speak in my wandering. Alone and without hope, they offered me sanctuary, and that I could not refuse. We did not raid your dwarf friends, nor any human settlements."

"You prompted Obould and brought disaster upon the land."

"Obould was coming with his thousands with no prompt from us—from my companions, for I had no part in that."

"So you would have to say."

"So I do say. I serve no orc king. I would kill him if given the chance."

"So you would have to say."

"I watched him bite out the throat of Kaer'lic Suun Wett!" Tos'un roared at him.

"And I killed your other two friends," Drizzt was quick to reply. "By your reasoning, you would kill me if given the chance."

That gave Tos'un pause, but only for a moment. "Not so," he said.

But he winced again as Khazid'hea emphatically shot, *Do not let him strike first!* into his thoughts.

The sword continued its prompting, egging Tos'un to leap forward and dispatch Drizzt, as the drow continued, "There is no honor in Obould, no honor in the smelly orcs. They are *iblith.*"

Again his comments were broken, his cadence uneven, and Drizzt knew that Khazid'hea was imploring him. Drizzt took a slight step and shift to Tos'un's right, for in that hand he held Khazid'hea.

"You may be correct in your assessment," Drizzt replied. "But then, I found little honor in your two friends before I killed them." He half-expected his words to prompt a charge, and shifted his hands appropriately nearer his hilts, but Tos'un stayed in place.

He just stood there, trembling, waging an inner battle against the sword's murderous intent, Drizzt surmised.

"The orcs have gone on the attack once again," Drizzt remarked, and his tone changed, and his thoughts went dark, as he reminded himself of the fate of Innovindil. "In the Moonwood and against the dwarves."

"They are old enemies." Tos'un replied, as if the whole news was matter-of-fact and hardly unexpected.

"Spurred by instigators who revel in chaos—indeed, who worship a demon queen who thrives on a state of utter confusion."

"No," Tos'un answered flatly. "If you are referring to me—"

"Are there other drow about?"

"No, and no," said Tos'un.

"You would have to say that."

"I fought beside the Moonwood elves."

"Why would you not, in the service of chaos? I doubt that you care which side wins this war, as long as Tos'un realizes his gain."

The drow shook his head, unconvinced.

"And in the Moonwood, " Drizzt continued, "the orcs' attacks were cunning and coordinated—more so than one might expect from a band of the dimwitted goblinkin." As he finished, Drizzt's scimitars appeared in his hands as if they had simply materialized there, so fast and fluid was his motion. Again he sidled to his left, reminding himself that

Tos'un was a drow warrior, trained at Melee-Magthere, likely under the legendary Uthegental. House Barrison Del'Armgo's warriors were known for their ferocity and straightforward attacks. Formidable, to be sure, Drizzt knew, and he could not forget for one instant that sword Tos'un carried.

Drizzt went to the right, trying to keep Tos'un using only short strokes with Khazid'hea, a weapon powerful enough to perhaps sever one of Drizzt's enchanted blades if swung with enough weight behind the blow.

"There is a new general among them, an orc most cunning and devious," Tos'un replied, his face twisting with every word—arguing against the intrusions of Khazid'hea, Drizzt clearly recognized.

That obvious truth of Tos'un's inner struggle had Drizzt somewhat hesitant, for why would this drow, if everything Drizzt presumed was true, be arguing against the murderous sword?

Before his thoughts could even go down that road, however, Drizzt thought again of Innovindil, and his face grew very dark. He turned his blades over and back again, anxious to exact revenge for his lost friend.

"More cunning than a warrior trained in Melee-Magthere?" he asked. "More devious than one raised in Menzoberranzan? More hateful of elves than a drow?"

Tos'un shook his head through all of the questions. "I was with the elves," he argued.

"And you deceived them and ran—and ran with knowledge of their tactics."

"I killed none as I left, though I surely could—"

"Because you are more cunning than that," Drizzt interrupted. "I would expect nothing less from a son of House Barrison Del'Armgo. You knew that if you struck and murdered some in your escape, the elves of the Moonwood would have understood the depths of your depravity and would have known that an attack was soon to befall them."

"I did not," Tos'un said, shaking his head helplessly. "None of . . ." He stopped and grimaced as Khazid'hea assaulted his thoughts.

He will take from you his friend's sword! Without me, your lies will not withstand the interrogations of the elf clerics. They would know your heart.

Tos'un found it hard to breathe. He was trapped in a way he never wanted, facing a foe he believed he could not defeat. He couldn't run away from Drizzt as he had Obould.

Kill him! Khazid'hea demanded. *With me in your grasp, Drizzt Do'Urden will fall. Take his head to Obould!*

"No!" Tos'un shot back audibly—and Drizzt smiled in understanding—instinctively recoiling from the orc king, an emotion that Khazid'hea surely understood.

Then take his head to Menzoberranzan, the sword offered, and again Tos'un's reasoning argued, for he hadn't the strength to return to the drow city alone along the unmerciful corridors of the Underdark.

But again the sword had the answers waiting. *Promise Dnark the friendship of Menzoberranzan. He will give you warriors to accompany you to the city, where you will betray them and assume your place as a hero of Menzoberranzan.*

Tos'un tightened his grip on both his swords and thought of Kaer'lic's warning regarding Drizzt. Before Khazid'hea could even begin to argue, though, the drow did it for himself, for Kaer'lic's warning that Drizzt might be in the graces of Lolth had been but a suspicion, and an outlandish one at that, but that mortal predicament standing before him loomed all too real.

And Drizzt watched it all, and recognized many of the fears and emotions playing through Tos'un's thoughts, and so when the son of House Barrison Del'Armgo leaped toward him, his scimitars rose in a sudden and effortless cross before him.

Tos'un executed a double-thrust wide, Khazid'hea and his other sword stabbing past the axis of Drizzt's blades. Drizzt threw his hands out wide to their respective sides, the called-for defense, each of his blades taking one of Tos'un's.

Advantage taken, Drizzt went for the greater stance offered by his curved blades. A more conventional warrior would have reversed the thrust back at his opponent, but Tos'un, expecting that, would have been too quick on the retreat for any real advantage to be realized. So Drizzt turned his scimitars over Tos'un's swords, using the curve of his blades to draw the swords in tighter, that he could send them out with more authority and perhaps even knock his foe off-balance enough that he could score a quick kill.

He rolled the scimitars over with a snap of his wrists.

But Khazid'hea. . . .

Tos'un countered by jamming the powerful sword hard into the hilt of Drizzt's scimitar—and the impossibly sharp blade cut in, catching a hold that halted Drizzt's move. Tos'un pressed forward with his right and stepped back with his left, keeping perfect balance as he disengaged his left from Drizzt's rolling blade.

Seeing disaster, Drizzt reversed suddenly, bringing Icingdeath, his right-hand blade, across hard instead of ahead, which would have left him off-balance and lunging. He drove Twinkle down hard directly away from the terrible blade of Khazid'hea, for that was the only chance to disengage before the mighty sword cut half of Twinkle's crosspiece away. Tos'un followed until the disengagement, then thrust forward at Drizzt, of course, and Icingdeath came across in the last instant, scraping along Khazid'hea's blade, shearing a line of sparks into the air.

Drizzt was half-turned, though, and Tos'un stabbed forward with his left for the ranger's exposed side.

But Twinkle came up from under Drizzt's other arm, neatly picking off the attack, and Drizzt uncrossed his arms suddenly, Icingdeath slashing back across to knock Tos'un's sword aside. Twinkle slapped back against Khazid'hea with equal fury. Tos'un leaped back, as did Drizzt, the two again circling, taking a measure of each other.

He was good, Drizzt realized. Better than he had anticipated. He managed a glance at Twinkle to note the clear tear where Khazid'hea had struck, and noted, too, a nick on Icingdeath's previously unblemished blade.

Tos'un came ahead with a lazy thrust, a feint and a sudden flurry, leading with his left then rattling off several quick blows with Khazid'hea. He moved forward with every strike, forcing Drizzt to block and not dodge. Every time Khazid'hea slapped against one of his blades, Drizzt winced, fearing that the awful sword would cut right through.

He couldn't play it Tos'un's way, he realized. Not with Khazid'hea in the mix. He couldn't use a defensive posture, as he normally would against a warrior who had trained under Uthegental, an overly aggressive sort that would allow him to simply let Tos'un's rage wear him out.

As soon as the attacks of Khazid'hea played out, Drizzt sprang forward, putting his blades up high and rolling his hands in a sudden blur.

Over and over went his scimitars, as he rolled his hands left and right, striking rapidly at Tos'un from varying angles.

Tos'un's defense mirrored Drizzt's movements, hands rolling, blades turning in and out, rolling over each other with equal harmony.

Drizzt kept in tight and kept the strokes short, not willing to let Tos'un put any weight behind Khazid'hea. He thought that to be Tos'un's only possible advantage, the sheer viciousness and power of that sword, and without it, Drizzt, who had defeated the greatest weapons master of Menzoberranzan, would find victory.

But Tos'un matched his rolling fury, anticipated his every move, and even managed several short counterstrikes that interrupted Drizzt's rhythm, and one that nearly got past Drizzt's sudden reversal and defense and would have surely gutted him. Surprised, Drizzt pressed the attack even more, rolling his hands more widely, changing the angles of attack more dramatically.

He slashed—one, two, three—downward at Tos'un's left shoulder, spun suddenly as the last parry sounded, and turned lower as he went so that as he came around, both his swords tore for Tos'un's right side. He expected a down-stroke parry from Khazid'hea, but Tos'un turned inside the attack, bringing his drow blade across to block. As he turned, he stabbed Khazid'hea back and down over his right shoulder.

Drizzt ducked the brunt of it, but felt the bite as the sword sliced down his shoulder blade, leaving a long and painful gash. Drizzt ran straight out from the engagement and dived forward in a roll, turning as he came up to face the pursuing Tos'un.

It was Tos'un's turn, and he came on with fury, stabbing and slashing, spinning completely around and with perfect balance and measured speed.

Ignoring the pain and the warm blood running down the right side of his back, Drizzt matched that intensity, parrying left and right, up and down, the blades ringing in one long note as they clanged and scraped. With every parry of Khazid'hea, Drizzt caught the sword more softly, retreating his own blade upon contact, as he might catch a thrown egg to avoid breaking it. That was more taxing, though, more precise and time-consuming, and the necessity of such a concentrated defense prevented him from regaining the momentum and the offense.

Around and around the sheltered lea they went, Tos'un pressing, not tiring, and growing more confident with every strike.

He had a right to do so, Drizzt had to admit, for he fought brilliantly, fluidly, and only then did Drizzt begin to understand that Tos'un had done with Khazid'hea that which Drizzt had refused to allow. Tos'un was letting the sword infiltrate his thoughts, was following the instincts of Khazid'hea as if they were his own. They had found a complementary relationship, a joining of sword and wielder.

Worse, Drizzt realized, Khazid'hea knew him, knew his movements as intimately as a lover, for Drizzt had wielded the sword in a desperate fight against King Obould.

He understood then, to his horror, how Tos'un had so easily anticipated his rollover and second throw move after the initial cross and parry. He understood then, to his dilemma, his inability to set up a killing strike. Khazid'hea knew him, and though the sword couldn't read his thoughts, it had taken a good measure of the fighting techniques of Drizzt Do'Urden. Just as damaging, since Tos'un had apparently given over to Khazid'hea's every intrusion, the sword and the trained drow warrior had found a symbiosis, a joining of knowledge and instinct, of skill and understanding.

For a fleeting moment, Drizzt wished that he had not dismissed Guenhwyvar, as tired as she had been after finally leading him to Tos'un Armgo.

A fleeting moment indeed, for Tos'un and Khazid'hea came on again, hungrily, the drow stabbing high and low simultaneously then spinning his blades over in a cross, and back again with a pair of backhand slashes.

Drizzt backed as Tos'un pursued. He parried about half the strikes—mostly those of the less dangerous drow blade—and dodged the other half cleanly. He offered no counters, allowing Tos'un to press, as he tried to find the answers to the riddle of the drow warrior and his mighty sword.

Back he stepped, parrying a slash. Back he stepped again, and he knew that he was running out of room, that the stone throne was near. He began to parry more and retreat less, his steps slowing and becoming more measured, until he felt at last the thick granite of the throne behind his trailing heel.

Apparently sensing that Drizzt had run out of room, Tos'un came forward more aggressively, executing a double thrust low. Surprised by the maneuver, Drizzt launched a double-cross down, the appropriate parry, where he crossed his scimitars down over the two thrusting swords. Drizzt had long ago solved the riddle of that maneuver. Before, the defender could hope for no advantage beyond a draw.

Tos'un would know that, he realized in the instant it took him to begin the second part of his counter, kicking his foot through the upper cross of his down-held blades, and so when Tos'un reacted, Drizzt already had his improvisation ready.

He kicked for Tos'un's face, so it appeared. Tos'un leaned back and drove his swords straight up, his intent to knock the kicking Drizzt, already in an awkward maneuver, off his balance.

But Drizzt shortened his kick, which could have no more than glanced Tos'un's face anyway, and changed the angle of his momentum upward then used Tos'un's push from below to bolster that directional change. Drizzt leaped right up and tucked in a tight turn that spun him head-over-heels to land lightly atop the seat of the stone throne, and it was Tos'un who overbalanced as the counterweight disappeared in a back flip, the drow staggering back a step.

Typical of an Armgo, Tos'un growled and came right back in, slashing across, which Drizzt hopped easily. Up above, Drizzt had the advantage, but Tos'un tried to use sheer aggressiveness to dislodge him from the seat, slashing and stabbing with abandon. One swipe cut across short of Drizzt, who threw back his hips, and sent Khazid'hea hard into the back of the stone throne. With a crack and a spark, the sword slashed through, leaving a gouge in the granite.

"I will not let you win, and I will not let you flee!" Drizzt cried in that moment, when the stone, though it hadn't stopped the sword, surely broke Tos'un's rhythm.

Drizzt went on the offensive, hacking down at Tos'un with powerful and straightforward strokes, using his advantageous angle to put his weight behind every blow. Tos'un tried to not retreat as a drum roll of bashing blades landed against his upraised swords, sending shivers of numbness down his arms, but Drizzt had him defending against angles varying too greatly for him to ever get his feet fully under him. Soon he had no choice but to fall back, stumbling, and Drizzt was there, leaping from the seat and coming down with a heavy double chop of his blades that nearly took Tos'un's swords from his hands.

"I will not let you win!' Drizzt cried again, throwing out the words in a release of all his inner strength as he backhanded across with Icingdeath, smashing Tos'un's drow-made sword out to the side.

And that was the moment when Drizzt could have ended it, for Twinkle's thrust, turn, and out-roll had Khazid'hea too far to the side to stop the second movement of Icingdeath, a turn and stab that would have plunged the blade deep into Tos'un's chest.

Drizzt didn't want the kill, for all the rage inside him for Innovindil. He played his trump.

"I will again wield the magnificent Khazid'hea!" he cried, disengaging instead of pressing his advantage. He went back just a couple of steps, and only for a few heartbeats—long enough to see a sudden wave of confusion cross Tos'un's face.

"Give me the sword!" Drizzt demanded.

Tos'un cringed, and Drizzt understood. For he had just given Khazid'hea what it had long desired, had just spoken the words Khazid'hea could not ignore. Khazid'hea's loyalty was to Khazid'hea alone, and Khazid'hea wanted, above all else, to be wielded by Drizzt Do'Urden.

Tos'un stumbled, hardly able to bring his blades up in defense as Drizzt charged in. In came Twinkle, in came Icingdeath, but not the blades. The hilts smashed Tos'un's face, one after another. Both Tos'un's swords went flying, and he went with them, back and to the ground. He recovered quickly, but not quickly enough. Drizzt's boot slammed down upon his chest and Icingdeath came to rest against his neck, its diamond edge promising him a quick death if he struggled.

"You have so much to answer for," Drizzt said to him.

Tos'un fell back and gave a great exhale, his whole body relaxing with utter resignation, for he could not deny that he was truly doomed.

CHAPTER

BLACK AND WHITE

23

Nanfoodle lifted one foot and drew little circles on the floor with his toes. Standing with his hands clasped behind his back, the gnome presented an image of uncertainty and trepidation. Bruenor and Hralien, who had been sitting discussing their next moves when Nanfoodle and Regis had entered the dwarf's private quarters, looked at each other with confusion.

"Well if ye can't get it translated, then so be it," Bruenor said, guessing at the source of the gnome's consternation. "But ye're to keep working on it, don't ye doubt!"

Nanfoodle looked up, glanced at Regis, then bolstered by Regis's nod, turned back to the dwarf king and squared his shoulders. "It is an ancient language, based on the Dwarvish tongue," he explained. "It has roots in Hulgorkyn, perhaps, and Dethek runes for certain."

"Thought I'd recognized a couple o' the scribbles," Bruenor replied.

"Though it is more akin to the proper Orcish," Nanfoodle explained, and Bruenor gasped.

"Dworcish?" Regis remarked with a grin, but he was the only one who found any humor in it.

"Ye're telling me that the durned orcs took part of me Delzoun ancestors' words?" Bruenor asked.

Nanfoodle shook his head. "How this language came about is a mystery whose answer is beyond the parchments you brought to me.

From what I can tell of the proportion of linguistic influence, you've juxtaposed the source and add."

"What in the Nine Hells are ye babblin' about?" Bruenor asked, his voice beginning to take on an impatient undercurrent.

"Seems more like old Dwarvish with added pieces from old Orcish," Regis explained, drawing Bruenor's scowl his way and taking it off of Nanfoodle, who seemed to be withering before the unhappy dwarf king with still the most important news forthcoming.

"Well, they needed to talk to the dogs to tell them what's what," said Bruenor, but both Regis and Nanfoodle shook their heads with every word.

"It was deeper than that," Regis said, stepping up beside the gnome. "The dwarves didn't borrow orc phrases, they integrated the language into their own."

"Something that would have taken years, even decades, to come into being," said Nanfoodle. "Such language blending is common throughout the history of all the races, but it occurs, every time, because of familiarity and cultural bonds."

Silence came back at the pair, and Bruenor and Hralien looked to each other repeatedly. Finally, Bruenor found the courage to ask directly, "What are ye saying?"

"Dwarves and orcs lived together, side-by-side, in the city you found," said Nanfoodle.

Bruenor's eyes popped open wide, his strong hands slapped against the arms of his chair, and he came forward as if he meant to leap out and throttle both the gnome and the halfling.

"For years," Regis added as soon as Bruenor settled back.

The dwarf looked at Hralien, seeming near panic.

"There is a town called Palishchuk in the wastes of Vaasa on the other side of Anauroch," the elf said with a shrug, as if the news was not as unexpected and impossible as it seemed. "Half-orcs, one and all, and strong allies with the goodly races of the region."

"Half-orcs?" Bruenor roared back at him. "Half-orcs're half-humans, and that lot'd take on a porcupine if the durned spines didn't hurt so much! But we're talkin' me kin here. Me ancestors!"

Hralien shrugged again, as if it wasn't so shocking, and Bruenor stopped sputtering long enough to catch the fact that the elf might be having a bit of fun with the revelation, at the dwarf's expense.

"We don't know that these were your ancestors," Regis remarked.

"Gauntlgrym's the home o' Delzoun!" Bruenor snapped.

"This wasn't Gauntlgrym," said Nanfoodle, after clearing his throat. "It wasn't," he reiterated when Bruenor's scowl fell over him fully.

"What was it, then?"

"A town called Baffenburg," said Nanfoodle.

"Never heared of it."

"Nor had I," the gnome replied. "It probably dates from around the time of Gauntlgrym, but it was surely not the city described in your histories. Not nearly that size, or with that kind of influence."

"That which we saw of it was probably the extent of the main town," Regis added. "It wasn't Gauntlgrym."

Bruenor fell back in his seat, shaking his head and muttering under his breath. He wanted to argue, but had no facts with which to do so. As he considered things, he recognized that he'd never had any evidence that the hole in the ground led to Gauntlgrym, that he had no maps that indicated the ancient Delzoun homeland to be anywhere near that region. All that had led him to believe that it was indeed Gauntlgrym was his own fervent desire, his faith that he had been returned to Mithral Hall by the graces of Moradin for that very purpose.

Nanfoodle started to talk, but Bruenor silenced him and waved both him and Regis away.

"This does not mean that there is nothing of value . . ." Regis started to say, but again, Bruenor waved his hand, dismissing them both—then dismissing Hralien with a gesture, as well, for at that terrible moment of revelation, with orcs attacking and Alustriel balking at decisive action, the crestfallen dwarf king wanted only to be alone.

* * * * *

"Still here, elf?" Bruenor asked when he saw Hralien inside Mithral Hall the next morning. "Seeing the beauty o' dwarf ways, then?"

Hralien shared the dwarf king's resigned chuckle. "I am interested in watching the texts unmasked. And I would be re—" He stopped and studied Bruenor for a moment then added, "It is good to see you in such fine spirits this day. I·had worried that the gnome's discovery from yesterday would cloak you in a dour humor."

Bruenor waved a hand dismissively. "He's just scratched the scribblings. Might be that some dwarves were stupid enough to trust the damned orcs. Might be that they paid for it with their city and their lives—and that might be a lesson for yer own folk and for Lady Alustriel and the rest of them that's hesitating in driving Obould back to his hole. Come with me, if ye're wantin', for I'm on me way to the gnome now. He and Rumblebelly have worked the night through, on me orders. I'm to take their news to Alustriel and her friends out working on the wall. Speak for the Moonwood in that discussion, elf, and let's be setting our plans together."

Hralien nodded and followed Bruenor through the winding tunnels and to the lower floors, and a small candlelit room where Regis and Nanfoodle were hard at work. Parchment had been spread over several tables, held in place by paperweights. The aroma of lavender permeated the room, a side-effect from Nanfoodle's preservation potions that had been carefully applied to each of the ancient writings, and to the tapestry, which had been hung on one wall. Most of its image remained obscured, but parts of it had been revealed. That vision made Bruenor cringe, for the orcs and dwarves visible in the drawing were not meeting in battle or even in parlay. They were together, intermingled, going about their daily business.

Regis, who sat off to the side transcribing some text, greeted the pair as they entered, but Nanfoodle didn't even turn around, hunched as he was over a parchment, his face pressed close to the cracked and faded page.

"Ye're not looking so tired, Rumblebelly," Bruenor greeted accusingly.

"I'm watching a lost world open before my eyes," he replied. "I'm sure that I will fall down soon enough, but not now."

Bruenor nodded. "Then ye're saying that the night showed ye more o' the old town," he said.

"Now that we have broken the code of the language, the pace improves greatly," said Nanfoodle, never turning from the parchment he was studying. "You retrieved some interesting texts on your journey."

Bruenor stared at him for a few heartbeats, expecting him to elaborate, but soon realized that the gnome was fully engulfed by his work once more. The dwarf turned to Regis instead.

"The town was mostly dwarves at first," Regis explained. He hopped up from his chair and moved to one of the many side tables, glanced at the parchment spread there, and moved along to the next in line. "This one," he explained, "talks about how the orcs were growing more numerous. They were coming in from all around, but most of the dwarven ties remained to places like Gauntlgrym, which was of course belowground and more appealing to a dwarf's sensibilities."

"So it was an unusual community?" Hralien asked.

Regis shrugged, for he couldn't be certain.

Bruenor looked to Hralien and nodded smugly in apparent vindication, and certainly the elf and the halfling understood that Bruenor did not want his history intertwined with that of the foul orcs!

"But it was a lasting arrangement," Nanfoodle intervened, finally looking up from the parchment. "Two centuries at least."

"Until the orcs betrayed me ancestors," Bruenor insisted.

"Until something obliterated the town, melting the permafrost and dropping the whole of it underground in a sudden and singular catastrophe," Nanfoodle corrected. "And not one of orc making. Look at the tapestry on the wall—it remained in place after the fall of Baffenburg, and certainly it would have been removed if that downfall had been precipitated by one side or the other. I don't believe that there were 'sides,' my king."

"And how're ye knowing that?" Bruenor demanded. "That scroll tellin' ye that?"

"There is no indication of treachery on the part of the orcs—at least not near the end of the arrangement," the gnome explained, hopping down from his bench and moving to yet another parchment across from the table where Regis stood. "And the tapestry . . . Early on, there were problems. A single orc chieftain held the orcs in place beside the dwarves. He was murdered."

"By the dwarves?" Hralien asked.

"By his own," said Nanfoodle, moving to another parchment. "And a time of unrest ensued."

"Seemin' to me that the whole time was a time of unrest," Bruenor said with a snort. "Ye can't be living with damned orcs!"

"Off and on unrest, from what I can discern," Nanfoodle agreed. "And it seemed to get better through the years, not worse."

"Until the orcs brought an end to it," Bruenor grumbled. "Suddenly, and with orc treachery."

"I do not believe . . ." Nanfoodle started to reply.

"But ye're guessin', and not a thing more," said Bruenor. "Ye just admitted that ye don't know what brought the end."

"Every indication—"

"Bah! But ye're guessing."

Nanfoodle conceded the point with a bow. "I would very much like to go to this city and build a workshop there, in the library. You have uncovered something fascinating, King Bru—"

"When the time's for it," Bruenor interrupted. "Right now I'm seeing the call of them words. Get rid of Obould and the orcs'll fall apart, as we were expecting from the start. This is our battle call, gnome. This is why Moradin sent me back here and told me to go to that hole, Gauntlgrym or not!"

"But that's not . . ." Nanfoodle started to argue, but his voice trailed away, for it was obvious that Bruenor paid him no heed.

His head bobbing with excitement and vigor, Bruenor had already turned to Hralien. He swatted the elf on the shoulder and swept Hralien up in his wake as he quick-stepped from the room, pausing only to berate Nanfoodle, "And I'm still thinking it's Gauntlgrym!"

Nanfoodle looked helplessly at Regis. "The possibilities. . . ." the gnome remarked.

"We've all our own way of looking at the world, it would seem," Regis answered with a shrug that seemed almost embarrassed for Bruenor.

"Is this find not an example?"

"Of what?" asked Regis. "We do not even know how it ended, or why it ended."

"Drizzt has whispered of the inevitability of Obould's kingdom," Nanfoodle reminded him.

"And Bruenor is determined that it will not be. The last time I looked, Bruenor, and not Drizzt, commanded the army of Mithral Hall and the respect of the surrounding kingdoms."

"A terrible war is about to befall us," said the gnome.

"One begun by King Obould Many-Arrows," the halfling replied.

Nanfoodle sighed and looked at the many parchment sheets spread around the room. It took all his willpower to resist the urge to rush from table to table and crumble them to dust.

* * * * *

"His name was Bowug Kr'kri," Regis explained to Bruenor, presenting more of the deciphered text to the dwarf king.

"An orc?"

"An orc philosopher and wizard," the halfling replied. "We think the statues we saw in the library were of him, and maybe his disciples."

"So he's the one who brought the orcs into the dwarf city?"

"We think."

"The two of ye do a lot o' thinking for so little answering," Bruenor growled.

"We have only a few old texts," Regis replied. "It's all a riddle, still."

"Guesses."

"Speculation," said Regis. "But we know that the orcs lived there with the dwarves, and that Bowug Kr'kri was one of the leaders of the community."

"Any better guesses on how long that town lived? Ye said centuries, but I'm not for believin' ye."

Regis shrugged and shook his head. "It had to be over generations. You saw the structures, and the language."

"And how many o' them structures were built by the dwarfs afore the orcs came in?" Bruenor asked with a sly smile.

Regis had no answer.

"Might've been a dwarf kingdom taken down by trusting the damned orcs," Bruenor said. "Fool dwarfs who took much o' the orc tongue to try to be better neighbors to the treacherous dogs."

"We don't think—"

"Ye think too much," Bruenor interrupted. "Yerself and the gnome're all excited about finding something so different than that which we're knowin' to be true. If ye're just finding more o' the same, then it's just more o' the same. But if ye're findin' something to make yer eyes go wide enough to fall out o' their holes, then that's something to dance about."

"We didn't invent that library, or the statues inside it," Regis argued, but he was talking into as smug and sure an expression as he had ever seen. And he wasn't sure, of course, that Bruenor's reasoning was wrong, for indeed, he and Nanfoodle were doing a lot of guessing. The final puzzle picture was far from complete. They hadn't even yet assembled the borders of the maze, let alone filled in the interior details.

Hralien walked into the room then, answering a summons Bruenor had sent out for him earlier.

"It's coming clear, elf," Bruenor greeted him. "That town's a warning. If we're following Alustriel's plans, we're to wind up a dead and dust-covered artifact for a future dwarf king to discover."

"My own people are as guilty as is Alustriel in wanting to find a stable division, King Bruenor," Hralien admitted. "The idea of crossing the Surbrin to do battle with Obould's thousands is daunting—it will not be attempted without great sorrow and great loss."

"And what's to be found by sitting back?" Bruenor asked.

Hralien, who had just lost a dozen friends in an orc assault on the Moonwood, and had just witnessed first-hand the attack on the dwarven wall, didn't need to use his imagination to guess the answer to that question.

"We can't be fightin' them straight up," Bruenor reasoned. "That's the way o' doom. Too many o' the stinking things." He paused and grinned, nodding his hairy head. "Unless they're attacking us, and in bits and pieces. Like the group that went into the Moonwood and the one that come over me wall. If we were ready for them, then there'd be a lot o' dead orcs."

Hralien gave a slight bow in agreement.

"So Drizzt was right," said Bruenor. "It's all about the one on top. He tried to get rid of Obould, and almost did. That'd've been the answer, and still is. If we can just get rid o' the durned Obould, we'll be tearing it all down."

"A difficult task," said Hralien.

"It's why Moradin gave me back to me boys," said Bruenor. "We're goin' to kill him, elf."

" 'We're'?" asked Hralien. "Are you to spearhead an army to strike into the heart of Obould's kingdom?"

"Nah, that's just what the dog's wantin'. We'll do it the way Drizzt tried it. A small group, better'n . . ." He paused and a cloud passed over his face.

"Me girl won't be going," Bruenor explained. "Too hurt."

"And Wulfgar has left for the west," said Hralien, catching on to the source of Bruenor's growing despair.

"They'd be helpin', don't ye doubt."

"I do not doubt at all," Hralien assured him. "Who, then?"

"Meself and yerself, if ye're up for the fight."

The elf gave a half-bow, seeming to agree but not fully committing, and Bruenor knew he'd have to be satisfied with that.

The dwarf looked over to Regis, who nodded with increased determination, his face as grim as his cherubic features would allow.

"And Rumblebelly there," the dwarf said.

Regis took a step back, shifting uncomfortably as Hralien cast a doubtful look his way.

"He's knowing how to find his place," Bruenor assured the elf. "And he's knowin' me fightin' ways, and them o' Drizzt."

"We will collect Drizzt on our road?"

"Can ye think o' anyone ye'd want beside ye more than the drow?"

"Indeed, no, unless it was Lady Alustriel herself."

"Bah!" Bruenor snorted. "Ye won't be getting that one to agree. Meself and a few o' me boys, yerself and Drizzt, and Rumblebelly."

"To kill Obould."

"Crush his thick skull," said Bruenor. "Me and some o' me best boys. We'll be cuttin' a quiet way, right to the head o' th' ugly beast, and then let it fall where it may."

"He is formidable," Hralien warned.

"Heared the same thing about Matron Baenre o' Menzoberranzan," Bruenor replied, referring to his own fateful strike that had decapitated the drow city and ended the assault on Mithral Hall. "And we got Moradin with us, don't ye doubt. It's why he sent me back."

Hralien's posture and expression didn't show him to be completely convinced by any of it, but he nodded his agreement just the same.

"Ye help me find me drow friend," Bruenor said to him, seeing that unspoken doubt. "Then ye make yer mind up."

"Of course," Hralien agreed.

Off to the side, Regis shifted nervously. He wasn't afraid of adventuring beside Bruenor and Drizzt, even if it would be behind orc lines. But he did fear that Bruenor was reading it all wrong, and that their mission would turn out badly, for them perhaps, and for the world.

* * * * *

The gathering fell quiet when Banak Brawnanvil looked Bruenor in the eye and declared, "Ye're bats!"

Bruenor, however, didn't blink. "Obould's the one," he said evenly.

"Not doubtin' that," replied the irrepressible Banak, who seemed to tower over Bruenor at that moment despite the fact that he was confined to a sitting position because of his injury in the orc war. "So send Pwent and yer boys to go and get him, like ye're wantin'."

"It's me own job."

"Only because ye're a thick-headed Battlehammer!"

A few gasps filtered about the room at that proclamation, but they were diffused by a couple of chortles, most notably from the priest Cordio. Bruenor turned on Cordio with a scowl, but it fast melted against the reality of Banak's words. Truer words regarding the density of Bruenor's skull, Cordio—and Bruenor—knew, had never been spoken.

"Was meself that went to Gauntlgrym," Bruenor said. He snapped his head to Regis's direction, as if expecting the halfling to argue that it wasn't Gauntlgrym. Regis, though, wisely stayed silent. "Was meself that anchored the retreat from Keeper's Dale. Was meself that battled Obould's first attack in the north." He was gaining speed and momentum, not to *bang drums for meself*, as the dwarven saying went, but to justify his decision that he would personally lead the mission. "Was meself that went to Calimport to bring back Rumblebelly. Was meself that cut the damned Baenre in half!"

"I drunk enough toasts to ye to appreciate the effort," said Banak.

"And now I'm seeing one more task afore me."

"The King o' Mithral Hall's plannin' to march off behind an orc army and kill the orc king," Banak remarked. "And if ye're caught on the way? Won't yer kin here be in fine straits then in trying to bargain with Obould?"

"If ye're thinkin' I'm to be caught livin', then ye're not knowing what it is to be a Battlehammer," Bruenor retorted. "Besides, ain't no different than if Drizzt got himself caught already, or any o' the rest of us. Ye're not for changing yer ways with orcs for meself any more than ye would for any of our boys."

Banak started to respond, but really had no answer for that.

"Besides, besides," Bruenor added, "once I'm walking out that gate, I'm not the king o' Mithral Hall, which is the whole point in us being here, now ain't it?"

"I'll be yer steward, but no king is Banak," the crippled Brawnanvil argued.

"Ye'll be me steward, but if I'm not returning then yerself is the Ninth King o' Mithral Hall and don't ye be doubting it. And not a dwarf here would agree with ye if ye were."

Bruenor turned and led Banak's gaze around the room with his own, taking in the solemn nods of all the gathering, from Pwent and his Gutbusters to Cordio and the other priests to Torgar and the dwarves from Mirabar.

"This is why Moradin sent me back," Bruenor insisted. "It's me against Obould, and ye're a fool betting if ye're betting on Obould!"

That elicited a cheer around the room.

"Yerself and the drow?" Banak asked.

"Me and Drizzt," Bruenor confirmed. "And Rumblebelly's up for it, though me girl's in no place for it."

"Ye telled her that, have ye?" Banak asked with a snicker that was echoed around the room.

"Bah, but she can't be running, if running we're needing, and she'd not ever put her friends in a spot o' staying behind to protect her," said Bruenor.

"Then ye ain't telled her," said Banak, and again came the snorts.

"Bah!" Bruenor said, throwing up his hands.

"So yerself, Drizzt, and Regis," said Banak. "And Thibbledorf Pwent?"

"Try to stop me," Pwent replied, and the Gutbuster brigade cheered.

"And Pwent," said Bruenor, and the Gutbusters cheered again. Nothing seemed to excite that group quite so much as the prospect of one of their own walking off on an apparent suicide mission.

R. A. SALVATORE

"Begging yer pardon, King Bruenor," Torgar Hammerstriker said from the other side of the room. "But me thinking is that the Mirabar boys should be represented on yer team, and me thinking's that meself and Shingles here"—he reached to the side and pulled forward the scarred old warrior, Shingles McRuff—"be just the two to do Mirabar proud."

As he finished, the other five Mirabarran dwarves in the room exploded into cheers for their mighty leader and the legendary Shingles.

"Make it seven, then," Cordio Muffinhead added. "For ye can't be goin' on a march for Moradin without a priest o' Moradin, and I'm that priest."

"Eight, then," Bruenor corrected, "for I'm thinking that Hralien o' the Moonwood won't be leaving us after we find Drizzt."

"Eight for the road and eight for Obould!" came the cheer, and it grew louder as it was repeated a second then a third time.

Then it ended abruptly, as a scowling Catti-brie came in through the door, staring hard at Bruenor with a look that had even the doubting Banak Brawnanvil looking at the dwarf king with sympathy.

"Go and do what needs doin'," Bruenor instructed them all, his voice suddenly shaky, and as the others scattered through every door in the room, Catti-brie limped toward her father.

"So you're going for Obould's head, and you're to lead it?" she asked.

Bruenor nodded. "It's me destiny, girl. It's why Moradin put me back here."

"Regis brought you back, with his pendant."

"Moradin let me go from his hall," Bruenor insisted. "And it was for a reason!"

Catti-brie stared at him long and hard. "So now you're to go out, and to take my friend Regis with you, and to take my husband with you. But I'm not welcome?"

"Ye can't run!" Bruenor argued. "Ye can hardly walk more than a few dozen yards. If we're turning from orcs, then are we to wait for yerself?"

"There'll be less turning from orcs if I'm there."

"Not for doubtin' that," said Bruenor. "But ye know ye can't do it. Not now."

"Then wait for me."

Bruenor shook his head. Catti-brie's lips grew tight and she blinked her blue eyes as if fighting back tears of frustration.

"I could lose all of you," she whispered.

Bruenor caught on then that part of her difficulty at least had to do with Wulfgar. "He'll come back," the dwarf said. "He'll walk the road that's needin' walking, but don't ye doubt that Wulfgar'll be coming back to us."

Catti-brie winced at the mention of his name, and her expression showed her to be far less convinced of that than was her father.

"But will you?" she asked.

"Bah!" Bruenor snorted, throwing up a hand as if the question was ridiculous.

"And will Regis come back? And Drizzt?"

"Drizzt is out there already," Bruenor argued. "Are ye doubtin' him?"

"No."

"Then why're ye doubting me?" asked Bruenor. "I'm out for doing the same thing Drizzt set out to do afore the winter. And he went out alone! I won't be out there alone, girl, and ye'd be smarter if ye was worrying about the damned orcs."

Catti-brie continued to look at him, and had no answer.

Bruenor opened wide his arms, inviting her to a hug that she could not resist. "Ye won't be alone, girl. Ye won't ever be alone," he whispered into her ear.

He understood fully her frustration, for would his own have been any less if he was to be left out of such a mission, when all of his friends were to go?

Catti-brie pulled back from him far enough to look him in the eye and ask, "Are you sure of this?"

"Obould's got to die, and I'm the dwarf to kill him," said Bruenor.

"Drizzt tried, and failed."

"Well Drizzt'll try again, but this time he's got friends trying with him. When we come back to ye, the orc lines'll be breaking apart. Ye'll find plenty o' fighting then, to be sure, and most of it outside our own doors. But the orcs'll be scattered and easy to kill. Take me bet now, girl, that I'll kill more than yerself."

"You're going out now, and getting a head start," Catti-brie answered, her face brightening a bit.

"Bah, but I won't count the ones I'm killing on the road," said Bruenor. "When I get back here and the orcs come on, as they're sure'n to do when Obould's no more, then I'll be killing more orcs than Catti-brie's to fell."

Catti-brie wore a sly grin. "I'll have me bow back from Drizzt then," she said, assuming a Dwarvish accent as she threw out the warning. "Every arrow's taking one down. Some'll take down two, or might even be three."

"And every swipe o' me axe is cutting three in half," Bruenor countered. "And I'm not for tiring when there're orcs to cut."

The two stared at each other without blinking as each extended a hand to shake on the bet.

"The loser represents Mithral Hall at the next ceremony in Nesmé," Catti-brie said, and Bruenor feigned a grimace, as though he hadn't expected the stakes to be quite so high.

"Ye'll enjoy the journey," the dwarf said. He smiled and tried to pull back, but Catti-brie held his hand firmly and stared him in the eye, her expression solemn.

"Just get back to me, alive, and with Drizzt, Regis, and the others alive," she said.

"Plannin' on it," said Bruenor, though he didn't believe it any more than did Catti-brie. "And with Obould's ugly head.

Catti-brie agreed. "With Obould's head."

CHAPTER

24

Clan Wolf Jaw lined both sides of the trail, their formidable array of warriors stretching out for hundreds of feet, beyond the bend and out of Chieftain Grguch's line of sight. None moved to block the progress of Clan Karuck, or to threaten the hulking orcs in any way, and Grguch recognized the pair who did step out in the middle of the trail.

"Greetings again, Dnark," Grguch said. "You have heard of our assault on the ugly dwarves?"

"All the tribes of Many-Arrows have heard of the glory of Grguch's march," Dnark answered, and Grguch smiled, as did Toogwik Tuk, who stood to the side and just behind the ferocious chieftain.

"You march west," remarked Dnark, glancing back over his shoulder. "To the invitation of King Obould?"

Grguch spent a few moments looking over Dnark and his associate, the shaman Ung-thol. Then the huge orc warrior glanced back at Toogwik Tuk and beyond him, motioning to a trio of soldiers, two obviously of Clan Karuck, with wide shoulders and bulging muscles, and a third that Dnark and Ung-thol had parted company with just a few days earlier.

"Obould has sent an emissary, requesting parlay," Grguch explained. Behind him, Oktule saluted the pair and bowed repeatedly.

"We were there among King Obould's entourage when Oktule was sent forth," Dnark replied. "Know you, though, that he was not the only emissary sent out that day." He finished and met Grguch's hard stare for

313

a few heartbeats, then motioned behind to the Wolf Jaw ranks. Several warriors stepped out, dragging a beaten and battered orc. They took him around Dnark, and on his signal closed half the distance to Grguch before dropping their living cargo unceremoniously onto the dirt.

Priest Nukkels groaned as he hit the ground, and squirmed a bit, but Ung-thol and Dnark had done their work extremely well and there was no chance of him getting up from the ground.

"An emissary sent to you?" Grguch asked. "But you said that you were with Obould."

"No," Toogwik Tuk explained, reading correctly the smug expressions worn by his co-conspirators. He stepped forward, daring to pass Grguch as he moved toward the battered priest. "No, this is Nukkels," he explained, looking back at Grguch.

Grguch shrugged, for the name meant nothing to him.

"King Obould's advisor," Toogwik Tuk explained. "He would not be sent to deliver a message to Chieftain Dnark. No, not even to Chieftain Grguch."

"What?" Grguch demanded, and though his tone was calm and even, there remained behind it a hint of warning to Toogwik Tuk to tread lightly, where he seemed on the verge of insult.

"This emissary was for no orc," Toogwik Tuk explained. He looked to Dnark and Ung-thol. "Nor was he heading north, to Gerti Orelsdottr, was he?"

"South," Dnark answered.

"Southeast, precisely," added Ung-thol.

Toogwik Tuk could barely contain his amusement—and his elation that King Obould had so perfectly played into their plans. He turned to Grguch, certain of his guess. "Priest Nukkels was sent by King Obould to parlay with King Bruenor Battlehammer."

Grguch's face went stone cold.

"We believe the same," said Dnark, and he moved forward to stand beside Toogwik Tuk—and to ensure that Toogwik Tuk did not claim an overdue amount of the credit for that revelation. "Nukkels has resisted our . . . methods," he explained, and to accentuate his point, he stepped over and kicked the groaning Nukkels hard in the ribs, sending him into a fetal curl. "He has offered many explanations for his journey, including that of going to King Bruenor."

"This pathetic dwarf-kisser in the dirt was sent by Obould to meet with Bruenor?" Grguch asked incredulously, as if he could not believe his ears.

"So we believe," Dnark answered.

"It is easy enough to discern," came a voice from behind, among Clan Karuck's ranks. All turned, Grguch with a wide, knowing smile, to see Hakuun step forward to stand beside his chieftain. "Would you like me to question the emissary?" Hakuun asked.

Grguch laughed and glanced around, motioning at last to a dark cluster of trees off to the side of the path. Dnark began signaling to his ranks for orcs to drag the prisoner over, but Grguch cut him short as Hakuun launched into a spell. Nukkels contorted as if in pain, and curled up on the ground—until he was not on the ground, but floating in the air. Hakuun walked for the trees, and Nukkels drifted behind him.

* * * * *

Away from the others, Hakuun obediently put his ear in line with that of Nukkels. The transfer took only a moment, with Jack the brain mole slipping out of Hakuun's ear and into Nukkels's.

As he realized what was happening to him, Nukkels began thrashing wildly in the air, but with nothing to orient him, with no pull of gravity to keep him upright or even on his side, he began to spin—which dizzied him, of course, and only made Jack's intrusion that much easier.

Jack came back out, and back into his more usual host a short while later, having ripped Nukkels's brain of every detail. He knew, and soon Hakuun knew, of Obould's true designs, confirming the fears of the trio who had summoned Clan Karuck from the bowels of the Spine of the World.

"Obould seeks peace with the dwarves," Hakuun remarked in disbelief. "He wants the war to be at its end."

A very un-orc orc, said the voice in his head.

"He defiles the will of Gruumsh!"

As I said.

Hakuun stalked out of the tree cluster, Jack's magic yanking the shivering, slobbering, floating Nukkels along behind him. When Hakuun got back to the others on the trail, he waved Nukkels in and let him drop hard to the ground.

"He was bound for King Bruenor," the shaman of Clan Karuck stated. "To undo the damage wrought by Chieftain Grguch and Clan Karuck."

"Damage?" Grguch asked, furrowing his thick brow. "Damage!"

"As we explained to you upon your arrival," said Ung-thol.

"It is as our friends have told us," Hakuun confirmed. "King Obould has lost his heart for war. He wishes no further battle with Clan Battlehammer."

"Cowardice," spat Toogwik Tuk.

"Has he found enough spoils to return to his home?" Grguch asked, his tone mocking and derogatory.

"He has conquered empty rocks," Dnark proclaimed. "All that is of value lies within the halls of the Battlehammer dwarves, or across the river in the realm of Silverymoon. But Obould—" he paused, turned, and kicked Nukkels hard—"Obould would parlay with Bruenor. He would seek a treaty!"

"With *dwarves?*" Grguch bellowed.

"Exactly that," said Hakuun, and Grguch nodded, having seen Hakuun at his work too many times to doubt a word he spoke.

Ung-thol and Toogwik Tuk exchanged knowing grins. It was all for show, all to rouse the rabble around the two chieftains, to garner outrage at the utter ridiculousness of the apparent designs of Obould.

"And he would parlay with Grguch," Dnark reminded the ferocious orc chieftain. "He would summon you to his side to gain your approval. Or perhaps to scold you for attacking the elves and dwarves."

Grguch's bloodshot eyes opened wide and a great snarl rumbled behind his trembling lips. He seemed as if he would leap forward and bite off Dnark's head, but the Chieftain of Wolf Jaw did not relent. "Obould intends to show Grguch who controls the Kingdom of Many-Arrows. He will coax you to join his way, so certain is he that he follows the true vision of Gruumsh."

"To parlay with dwarves?" Grguch roared.

"Cowardice!" Dnark cried.

Grguch stood there, clenching his fists, the muscles in his neck straining, his chest and shoulders bulging as if their sinewy power could not be contained by the orc's skin.

"Oktule!" he cried, wheeling to face the orc who had arrived with

King Obould's invitation.

The emissary shrank back, as did every orc around him.

"Come here," Grguch demanded.

Oktule, trembling and sweating, gave a quick shake of his head and stumbled back even more—or would have, had not a pair of Clan Karuck's powerful warriors grabbed him by the arms and walked him forward. He tried to dig his feet in, but they just dragged him, depositing him before the wild gaze of Chieftain Grguch.

"King Obould would scold me?" Grguch asked.

A line of wetness ran down poor Oktule's leg, and he shook his head again—though whether in response to the question or in simple, desperate denial, no one around could tell. He focused on Dnark, pleading with the chieftain who knew that his role was unwitting.

Dnark laughed at him.

"He would scold me?" Grguch said again, louder. He leaned forward, towering over the trembling Oktule. "You did not tell me that."

"He would not . . . he . . . he . . . he told me to come to get you," Oktule stammered.

"That he might scold me?" Grguch demanded, and Oktule seemed about to faint.

"I did not know," the pathetic courier protested meekly.

Grguch whirled to regard Dnark and the others, his expression brightening as if he had just sorted everything out. "To gain the favor of Bruenor, Obould would have to offer something," Grguch realized. He spun back on Oktule and slapped him with a backhand across the face, launching him to the side and to the ground.

Grguch turned on Dnark again, his smile wry, nodding his head knowingly. "He would offer to Bruenor the head of the warrior who struck against Mithral Hall, perhaps."

Behind him, Oktule gulped.

"Is there truth in that?" Dnark asked Nukkels, and he kicked the prone orc hard again.

Nukkels grunted and groaned, but said nothing decipherable.

"It is reasonable," Ung-thol said, and Dnark quickly nodded, neither of them wishing to let Grguch calm from his self-imposed frenzy. "If Obould wishes to convince Bruenor that the attack was not of his doing, he would have to prove his claim."

"With the head of Grguch?" the chieftain of Clan Karuck asked as he turned to Hakuun, and Grguch laughed as if it was all absurd.

"The foolish priest showed me nothing of this," Hakuun admitted. "But if Obould truly wishes peace with Bruenor, and he does, then Chieftain Grguch has quickly become . . . an inconvenience."

"It is past time I meet this Obould fool, that I can show him the truth of Clan Karuck," said Grguch, and he gave a little laugh, clearly enjoying the moment. "It may be unfortunate that you interrupted the journey of the one in the dirt," he said, nodding toward the still-squirming Nukkels. "Greater would be King Bruenor's surprise and fear when he looked into that basket, I say! I would pay in women and good gold to see the face of the dwarf when he pulled out Obould's head!"

The orcs of Clan Karuck began to howl at that, but Dnark, Ung-thol, and Toogwik Tuk just looked at each other solemnly and with nods of understanding. For there it was, the conspiracy spoken clearly, openly proclaimed, and there could be no turning back. They offered their nods of thanks to Hakuun, who remained impassive, the part of him that was Jack the Gnome not wishing to even acknowledge their existence, let alone allow them the illusion that they were somehow his peers.

Grguch hoisted his two-bladed axe, but paused then set it aside. Instead, he drew a long and wicked knife from his belt and glanced back to the Karuck orcs standing around Oktule. His smile was all the impetus those orcs needed to drag the poor courier forward.

Oktule's feet dug small trenches in the wet spring ground. He shook his head in denial, crying, "No, no, please no!"

Those pleas only seemed to spur Grguch on. He strode behind Oktule and grabbed a handful of the fool's hair, roughly yanking his head back, exposing his throat.

Even the orcs of Oktule's own clan joined in the cheering and chanting, and so he was doomed.

He screamed and shrieked in tones preternatural in their sheer horror. He thrashed and kicked and fought as the blade came against the soft skin of his throat.

Then his screams became watery, and Grguch bore him to the ground, face down, the chieftain's knees upon his back, pinning him, while Grguch's arm pumped furiously.

When Grguch stood up again, presenting Oktule's head to the

frenzied gathering, the three conspirators shared another glance, and each took a deep and steadying breath.

Dnark, Toogwik Tuk, and Ung-thol had made a deal with as brutal a creature as any of them had ever known. And they knew, all three, that there was more than a passing chance that Chieftain Grguch would one day present their heads for the approval of the masses.

They had to be satisfied with the odds, however, because the other choice before them was obedience to Obould, and Obould alone. And that course of cowardice they could not accept.

* * * * *

"There will be nothing subtle about Grguch's challenge to Obould," Ung-thol warned his comrades when the three were alone later that same night. "Diplomacy is not his way."

"There is no time for diplomacy, nor is there any need," said Toogwik Tuk, who clearly stood as the calmest and most confident of the trio. "We know the options before us, and we chose our road long ago. Are you surprised by Grguch and Clan Karuck? They are exactly as I portrayed them to you."

"I am surprised by their . . . efficiency," said Dnark. "Grguch walks a straight line."

"Straight to Obould," Toogwik Tuk remarked with a snicker.

"Do not underestimate King Obould," warned Dnark. "That he sent Nukkels to Mithral Hall tells us that he understands the true threat of Grguch. He will not be caught unawares."

"We cannot allow this to become a wider war," Ung-thol agreed. "Grguch's name is great among the orcs in the east, along the Surbrin, but the numbers of warriors there are few compared to what Obould commands in the west and the north. If this widens in scope, we will surely be overwhelmed."

"Then it will not," Toogwik Tuk said. "We will confront Obould with his small group around him, and Clan Karuck will overwhelm him and be done with it. He does not have the favor of Gruumsh—have we any doubt of that?"

"His actions do not echo the words of Gruumsh," Ung-thol reluctantly agreed.

"If we are certain of his actions," said Dnark.

"He will not march against Mithral Hall!" Toogwik Tuk snarled at them. "You have heard the whimpers of Nukkels! Grguch's priest confirmed it."

"Did he? Truly?" Dnark asked.

"Or is it all a ruse?" Ung-thol posed. "Is Obould's pause a feint to fully unbalance our enemies?"

"Obould will not march," Toogwik Tuk protested.

"And Grguch will not be controlled," said Dnark. "And are we to believe that this half-ogre creature will hold the armies of Many-Arrows together in a unified march for wider glory?"

"The promise of conquest will hold the armies together far better than the hope of parlay with the likes of King Bruenor of the dwarves," Toogwik Tuk argued.

"And that is the truth," said Dnark, ending the debate. "And that is why we brought Clan Karuck forth. It unfolds before us now exactly as we anticipated, and Grguch meets and exceeds every expectation. Now that we are finding that which we decided we wished to find, we must hold fast to our initial beliefs that led us to this point. It is not the will of Gruumsh that his people should pause when great glory and conquest awaits. It is not the will of Gruumsh that his people should parlay with the likes of King Bruenor of the dwarves. Never that! Obould has pushed himself beyond the boundaries of decency and common sense. We knew that when we called to Clan Karuck, and we know that now." He turned his head and spat upon Nukkels, who lay unconscious and near death in the mud. "We know that with even more certainty now."

"So let us go and witness Grguch as he answers the summons of Obould," said Toogwik Tuk. "Let us lead the cheers to King Grguch, as he leads our armies against King Bruenor."

Ung-thol still wore doubts on his old and wrinkled face, but he looked to Dnark and shared in his chieftain's assenting nod.

In a tree not far away, a curious winged snake listened to it all with amusement.

CHAPTER

25

Raised in Menzoberranzan, a male drow in the matriarchal city of Menzoberranzan, Tos'un Armgo didn't as much as grimace when Drizzt tugged his arms back hard and secured the rope on the other side of the large tree. He was caught, with nowhere to run or hide. He glanced to the side—or tried to, for Drizzt had expertly looped the rope under his chin to secure him against the tree trunk—where Khazid'hea rested, stabbed into a stone by Drizzt. He could feel the sword calling to him, but he couldn't reach out to it.

Drizzt studied Tos'un as if he understood the silent pleas exchanged between drow and sentient sword—and likely, he did, Tos'un realized.

"You have nothing further to gain or lose," Drizzt said. "Your day in the service of Obould is done."

"I have not been in his service for many tendays," Tos'un stubbornly argued. "Not since before the winter. Not since that day you battled him, and even before that, truth be told."

"Truth told by a son of House Barrison Del'Armgo?" Drizzt asked with a scoff.

"I have nothing to gain or lose, just as you said."

"A friend of mine, a dwarf named Bill, would speak with you about that," Drizzt said. "Or whisper at you, I should say, for his throat was expertly cut to steal the depth of his voice."

Tos'un grimaced at that inescapable truth, for he had indeed cut a dwarf's throat in preparation for Obould's first assault on Mithral Hall's eastern door.

"I have other friends who might have wished to speak with you, too," said Drizzt. "But they are dead, in no small part because of your actions."

"I was fighting a war," Tos'un blurted. "I did not understand—"

"How could you not understand the carnage to which you contributed? Is that truly your defense?"

Tos'un shook his head, though it would hardly turn to either side.

"I have learned," the captured drow added. "I have tried to make amends. I have aided the elves."

Despite himself and his intentions that he would bring no harm to his prisoner, Drizzt slapped Tos'un across the face. "You led them to the elves," he accused.

"No," said Tos'un. "No."

"I have heard the details of the raid."

"Facilitated by Chieftain Grguch of Clan Karuck, and a trio of conspirators who seek to force Obould back to the road of conquest," said Tos'un. "There is more afoot here than you understand. Never did I side with those who attacked the Moonwood, and who have marched south, I am sure, with intent to strike at Mithral Hall."

"Yet you just said that you were no ally of Obould," Drizzt reasoned.

"Not of Obould, nor of any other orc," said Tos'un. "I admit my role, though it was a passive one, in the early stages, when Donnia Soldou, Ad'non Kareese, and Kaer'lic Suun Wett decided to foster an alliance between Obould and his orcs, Gerti Orelsdottr and her giants, and the two-headed troll named Proffit. I went along because I did not care—why would I care for dwarves, humans, and elves? I am drow!"

"A point I have never forgotten, I assure you."

The threat took much of Tos'un's bluster, but he pressed on anyway. "The events surrounding me were not my concern."

"Until Obould tried to kill you."

"Until I was chased away by the murderous Obould, yes," said Tos'un. "And into the camp of Albondiel and Sinnafain of the Moonwood."

"Whom you *betrayed,*" Drizzt shouted in his face.

"From whom I escaped, though I was not their captive," Tos'un yelled back.

"Then why did you run?"

"Because of you!" Tos'un cried. "Because of that sword I carried, who knew that Drizzt Do'Urden would never allow me to keep it, who knew that Drizzt Do'Urden would find me among the elves and strike me down for possessing a sword that I had found abandoned in the bottom of a ravine."

"That is not why, and you know it," said Drizzt, backing off just a step. " 'Twas I who lost the sword, recall?"

As he spoke he glanced over at Khazid'hea, and an idea came to him. He wanted to believe Tos'un, as he had wanted to believe the female, Donnia, when he had captured her those months before.

He looked back at Tos'un, smiled wryly, and said, "It is all opportunity, is it not?"

"What do you mean?"

"You ally with Obould as he gains the upper hand. But he is held at bay, and you face his wrath. So you find your way to Sinnafain and Albondiel and the others and think to create new opportunities where your old ones have ended. Or to recreate the old ones, at the expense of your new 'friends.' Once you have gained their trust and learned their ways, you again have something to offer to the orcs, something that will perhaps bring Obould back to your side."

"By helping Grguch? You do not understand."

"But I shall," Drizzt promised, moving off to the side, toward Khazid'hea. Without hesitation, he grabbed the sword by the hilt. Metal scraped and screeched as he withdrew the blade from the stone, but Drizzt didn't hear that, for Khazid'hea already invaded his thoughts.

I had thought you lost to me.

But Drizzt wasn't listening to any of that, had not the time for it. He forced his thoughts into the sword, demanding of Khazid'hea a summary of its time in the hands of Tos'un Armgo. He did not coddle the sword with promises that together they would find glory. He did not offer to the sword anything. He simply asked of it, *Were you in the Moonwood? Have you tasted the blood of elves?*

Sweet blood . . . Khazid'hea admitted, but with that thought came to Drizzt a sense of a time long past. And the sword had not been in the Moonwood. Of that much, the drow was almost immediately certain.

In light of Khazid'hea's open admission of its fondness for elf blood, Drizzt considered the unlikely scenario that Tos'un could have been an integral part of the planning for that raid and yet still have remained on the western side of the Surbrin. Would Khazid'hea have allowed that participation from afar, knowing that blood was to be spilled, and particularly since Khazid'hea had been in Tos'un's possession when he had been with the elves?

Drizzt glanced back at the captured drow and considered the relationship between Tos'un and the sword. Had Tos'un so dominated Khazid'hea?

As that very question filtered through Drizzt's thoughts, and thus was offered to the telepathic sword, Khazid'hea's mocking response chimed in.

Drizzt put the sword down for a few moments to let it all sink in. When he retrieved the blade, he directed his questioning toward the newcomer.

Grguch, he imparted.

A fine warrior. Fierce and powerful.

A worthy wielder for Khazid'hea? Drizzt asked.

The sword didn't deny it.

More worthy than Obould? Drizzt silently asked.

The feeling that came back at him seemed not so favorably impressed. And yet, Drizzt knew that King Obould was as fine a warrior as any orc he had ever encountered, as fine as Drizzt himself, whom the sword had long coveted as a wielder. Though not of that elite class, Catti-brie, too, was a fine warrior, and yet Drizzt knew from his last experience with the sword that she had fallen out of Khazid'hea's favor, as she opted to use her bow far too often for Khazid'hea's ego.

A long time passed before Drizzt set the sword down once again, and he was left with the impression that the ever-bloodthirsty Khazid'hea clearly favored Grguch over Obould, and just for the reasons that Tos'un had said. Obould was not pressing for conquest and battle.

Drizzt looked at Tos'un, who rested as comfortably as could be expected given his awkward position tied to the tree. Drizzt could not dismiss the plausibility of Tos'un's claims, all of them, and perhaps, whether through heartfelt emotion or simple opportunity, Tos'un was not now an enemy to him and his allies.

But after his experiences with Donnia Soldou—indeed, after his experiences with his own race from the earliest moments of his conscious life, Drizzt Do'Urden wasn't about to take that chance.

* * * * *

The sun had long set, the dark night made murkier by a fog that curled up from the softening snow. Into that mist disappeared Bruenor, Hralien, Regis, Thibbledorf Pwent, Torgar Hammerstriker and Shingles McRuff of Mirabar, and Cordio the priest.

On the other side of the ridgeline, behind the wall where Bruenor's dwarves and Alustriel's wizards worked vigilantly, Catti-brie watched the receding group with a heavy heart.

"I should be going with them," she said.

"You cannot," said her companion, Lady Alustriel of Silverymoon. The tall woman moved nearer to Catti-brie and put her arm around the woman's shoulders. "Your leg will heal."

Catti-brie looked up at her, for Alustriel was nearly half a foot taller than she.

"Perhaps this is a sign that you should consider my offer," Alustriel said.

"To train in wizardry? Am I not too old to begin such an endeavor?"

Alustriel laughed dismissively at the absurd question. "You will take to it naturally, even though you were raised by the magically inept dwarves."

Catti-brie considered her words for a moment, but soon turned her attention to the view beyond the wall, where the fog had swallowed her father and friends. "I had thought that you would walk beside my father, as he bade," she said, and glanced over at the Lady of Silverymoon.

"As you could not, neither could I," Alustriel replied. "My position prevented me from it as fully as did your wounded leg."

"You do not agree with Bruenor's goal? You would side with Obould?"

"Surely not," said Alustriel. "But it is not my place to interject Silverymoon in a war."

"You did exactly that when you and your Knights in Silver rescued the wandering Nesmians."

"Our treaties with Nesmé demanded no less," Alustriel explained. "They were under attack and running for their lives. Small friends we would be if we did not come to them in their time of need."

"Bruenor sees it just that way right now," said Catti-brie.

"Indeed he does," Alustriel admitted.

"So he plans to eradicate the threat. To decapitate the orc army and send them scattering."

"And I hope and pray that he succeeds. To have the orcs gone is a goal agreed upon by all the folk of the Silver Marches, of course. But it is not my place to bring Silverymoon into this provocative attack. My council has determined that our posture is to remain defensive, and I am bound to abide by their edicts."

Catti-brie shook her head and did not hide her disgusted look. "You act as if we are in a time of peace, and Bruenor is breaking that peace," she said. "Does a needed pause in the war because of the winter's snows cancel what has gone before?"

Alustriel hugged the angry woman a bit tighter. "It is not the way any of us wish it to be," she said. "But the council of Silverymoon has determined that Obould has stopped his march, and we must accept that."

"Mithral Hall was just attacked," Catti-brie reminded. "Are we to sit back and let them strike at us again and again?"

Alustriel's pause showed that she had no answer for that. "I cannot go after Obould now," she said. "In my role as leader of Silverymoon, I am bound by the decisions of the council. I wish Bruenor well. I hope with all my heart and soul that he succeeds and that the orcs are chased back to their holes."

Catti-brie calmed, more from the sincerity and regret in Alustriel's tone than from her actual words. Alustriel had helped, despite her refusal to go along, for she had given to Bruenor a locket enchanted to lead the dwarf toward Drizzt, an identical locket to the one she had given to Catti-brie many years before when she, too, had gone off to find a wandering Drizzt.

"I hope that Bruenor is correct in his guess," Alustriel went on, trepidation in her voice. "I hope that killing Obould will bring the results he desires."

Catti-brie didn't reply, but just stood there and absorbed the words. She couldn't bring herself to believe that Obould, who had started the war, might actually have become a stabilizing force, and yet she could not deny her doubts.

* * * * *

The two orcs stood under a widespread maple, the sharp, stark lines of its branches not yet softened by the onset of buds. They talked and chuckled at their own stupidity, for they were completely lost, and far separated from their kin at the small village. A wrong turn on a trail in the dark of night had put them far afield, and they had long ago abandoned the firewood they had come out to collect.

One lamented that his wife would beat him red, to warm him up so he could replace the fire that wouldn't last half the night.

The other laughed and his smile lingered long after his mirth was stolen by an elven arrow, one that neatly sliced into his companion's temple. Standing in confusion, grinning simply because he hadn't the presence of mind to remove his own smile, the orc didn't even register the sudden *thump* of heavy boots closing in fast from behind him. He was caught completely unawares as the sharp tip of a helmet spike drove into his spine, tearing through muscle and bone, and blasted out the front of his chest, covered in blood and pieces of his torn heart.

He was dead before Thibbledorf Pwent straightened, lifting the orc's flopping body atop his head. The dwarf hopped around, looking for more enemies. He saw Bruenor and Cordio scrambling in the shadows south of the maple, and noted Torgar and Shingles farther to the east. With Hralien in the northwest, and Regis following in the shadows behind Pwent, the group soon surmised that the pair had been out alone.

"Good enough, then," said Bruenor, nodding his approval. He held up the locket Alustriel had given him. "Warmer," he explained. "Drizzt is nearby."

"Still north?" Hralien asked, coming in under the maple to stand beside Bruenor.

"Back from where ye just walked," Bruenor confirmed, holding forth his fist, which held the locket. "And getting warmer by the step."

A curious expression showed on Bruenor's face. "And getting warmer as we're standin' here," he explained to the curious glances that came his way.

"Drizzt!" Regis cried an instant later.

Following the halfling's pointing finger, the others spied a pair of dark elves coming toward them, with Tos'un bound and walking before their friend.

"Taked ye long enough to find him, eh?" Thibbledorf Pwent said with a snort. He bent and slapped his leg for effect, which sent the dead orc flopping weirdly.

Drizzt stared at the bloody dwarf, at the cargo he carried on his helmet spike. Realizing that there was simply nothing he might say against the absurdity of that image, he just prodded Tos'un on, moving to the main group.

"They hit the wall east of Mithral Hall," Hralien explained to Drizzt. "As you had feared."

"Aye, but know that we sent them running," Bruenor added.

Drizzt's confused expression didn't change as he scanned the group.

"And now we're out for Obould," Bruenor explained. "I'm knowing ye were right, elf. We got to kill Obould and break it all apart, as ye thought afore when ye went after him with me girl's sword."

"*We're* out for him?" Drizzt asked doubtfully, looking past the small group. "You've brought no army, my friend."

"Bah, an army'd just muddle it all," Bruenor said with a wave of his hand.

It wasn't hard for Drizzt to catch the gist of that, and in considering it for a moment, in considering Bruenor's leadership methodology, he realized that he should not be the least bit surprised.

"We wish to get to Obould, and it seems that we have a captive who might aid in exactly that," Hralien remarked, stepping up before Tos'un.

"I have no idea where he is," Tos'un said in his still-stinted command of the Elvish tongue.

"You would have to say that," said Hralien.

"I helped you . . . your people," Tos'un protested. "Grguch had them caught in the failed raid and I showed them the tunnel that took them to safety."

"True," Hralien replied. "But then, isn't that what a drow would do? To gain our trust, I mean?"

Tos'un's shoulders sagged and he lowered his eyes, for he had just fought that same battle with Drizzt, and there seemed no way for him to escape it. Everything he had done leading up to that point could be interpreted as self-serving, and for the benefit of a larger and more nefarious plot.

"Ye should've just killed him and been done with it," Bruenor said to Drizzt. "If he's not for helping us then he's just slowing us down."

"Meself'll be there for the task in a heartbeat, me king!" Pwent shouted from the side, and all eyes turned to see the dwarf, bent low with head forward, backing through the narrow opening between a pair of trees. Pwent set the back of the dead orc's thighs against one trunk, the poor creature's shoulder blades against another, and with a sudden burst, the dwarf tugged backward. Bones and gristle popped and ground as the barbed spike tore back through, freeing the dwarf of his dead-weight burden.

Pwent stumbled backward and fell to his rump, but hopped right back to his feet and bounced around to face the others, shaking his head so vigorously that his lips flapped. Then, with a smile, Pwent brought his hands up before him, palms facing out, extended thumbs touching tip-to-tip, lining up his charge.

"Turn the dark-skinned dog just a bit," he instructed.

"Not just yet, good dwarf," Drizzt said, and Pwent straightened, disappointment clear on his face.

"Ye thinkin' to take him along?" Bruenor asked, and Drizzt nodded.

"We could divert our course to the Moonwood, or back to Mithral Hall," Hralien offered. "We would lose no more than a day or so, and would be rid of our burden."

But Drizzt shook his head.

"Easier just to kill him," said Bruenor, and to the side, Pwent began scraping his feet across the ground like a bull readying for a charge.

"But not wiser," Drizzt said. "If Tos'un's claims are true, he might prove to be a valuable asset to us. If not, we have lost nothing because we have risked nothing." He looked to his fellow drow. "If you do not deceive us, on my word I will let you leave when we are done."

"You cannot do this," said Hralien, drawing all eyes his way. "If he has committed crimes against the Moonwood, his fate is not yours alone to decide."

"He has not," Drizzt assured the elf. "He was not there, for Khazid'hea was not there."

Bruenor yanked Drizzt aside, pulling him away from the others. "How much o' this is yer way o' hoping for a drow akin to yerself?" the dwarf asked bluntly.

Drizzt shook his head, with sincerity and certainty. "On my word, Bruenor, this I do because I think it best for us and our cause—whatever that cause may be."

"What's that meaning?" the dwarf demanded. "We're for killing Obould, don't ye doubt!" He raised his voice with the proclamation, and the others all looked his way.

Drizzt didn't argue. "Obould would kill Tos'un if given the chance, as Obould murdered Tos'un's companion. We will gamble nothing with Tos'un, I promise you, my friend, and the possibility of gain cannot be ignored."

Bruenor looked long and hard at Drizzt then glanced back at Tos'un, who stood calmly, as if resigned to his fate—whatever that fate may be.

"On my word," Drizzt said.

"Yer word's always been good enough, elf," said Bruenor. He turned and started back for the others, calling to Torgar and Shingles as he went. "Think yerselves are up to guardin' a drow?" he asked, or started to, for as soon as his intent became clear, Drizzt interrupted him.

"Let Tos'un remain my responsibility," he said.

Again Bruenor granted Drizzt his wish.

CHAPTER

CROSSROAD

26

Wulfgar lingered around the outskirts of Auckney for several days. He didn't dare show his face in the town for fear that connecting himself to the new arrival at Castle Auck would put undue pressure on Lord Feringal, and create dangerous ramifications for Colson. But Wulfgar was a man comfortable in the wilds, who knew how to survive through the cold nights, and who knew how to keep himself hidden.

Everything he heard about the lord and lady's new child brought him hope. One of the prevalent rumors whispered by excited townsfolk hinted that the girl was Feringal's and Meralda's own, and that she had been born in a sleep-state from which they had never expected her to awaken. And what joy now for the couple and the town that the child had recovered!

Another rumor attached Colson to barbarian nobility, and claimed that her presence with Lord Feringal ensured security for the folk of Auckney—a wonderful thing in the tough terrain of the frozen North.

Wulfgar absorbed it all with a growing sense that he had done well for Colson, for himself, and for Delly. Truly he had a hole in his heart that he never expected to fill, and truly he vowed that he would visit Auckney and Colson in the coming years. Feringal would have no reason to dismiss him or arrest him as time passed, after all, and indeed Wulfgar might find a level of bargaining power in the future, since he knew the truth of the girl's parentage. Lord Feringal wouldn't want him for an enemy, physically or politically.

That was the barbarian's hope, the one thing that kept him from breaking down and rushing back into the town to "rescue" Colson.

He continued to linger, to listen and to watch, for on more than one occasion he chanced to see Colson out with her new parents. He was truly amazed and heartened to see how quickly the young girl had adapted to her new surroundings and new parents, from afar at least. Colson smiled as often as she had in Mithral Hall, and she seemed at ease holding Meralda's hand and walking along in the woman's shadow.

Similarly, the love Meralda held for her could not be denied. The look of serenity on her face was everything Wulfgar had hoped it would be. She seemed complete and content, and in addition to those promising appearances, what gave Wulfgar more hope still was the posture of Lord Feringal whenever he was near to the girl. There could be no doubt that Feringal had grown greatly in character over the years. Perhaps it was due to the support of Meralda, a woman Wulfgar knew to be possessed of extraordinary integrity, or perhaps it was due to the absence of Feringal's shrill sister.

Whatever the cause, the result was clear for him to see and hear, and every day he lingered near to Auckney was a day in which he grew more certain of his decision to return the child to her rightful mother. It did Wulfgar's heart good, for all the pain still there, to think of Colson in Meralda's loving arms.

So many times he wanted to run into Auckney to tell Colson that he loved her, to crush her close to him in his arms and assure her that he would always love her, would always protect her. So many times he wanted to go in and simply say goodbye. Her cries of "Da!" still echoed in his mind and would haunt him for years and years, he knew.

But he could not go in, and so as the days became a tenday, Wulfgar melted away down the mountain road to the east, the way he had come. The next day, he arrived at the end of the eastern pass, where the road ran south through the foothills to Luskan, and north to the long dale that traversed the Spine of the World and opened up into Icewind Dale.

Wulfgar turned neither way at first. Instead he crossed the trail and scaled a rocky outcropping that afforded him a grand view of the rolling lands farther to the east. He perched upon the stone and let his mind's eye rove beyond the physical limitations of his vision, imagining the landscape as it neared Mithral Hall and his dearest friends. The place he had called home.

He turned suddenly back to the west, thinking of his daughter and realizing just how badly he missed her—much more so than he'd anticipated.

Then back to the east went his thoughts and his eyes, to the tomb of Delly, lying cold in Mithral Hall.

"I only ever tried to do the best I could," he whispered as if talking to his dead wife.

It was true enough. For all of his failures since his return from the Abyss, Wulfgar had tried to do the best he could manage. It had been so when he'd first rejoined his friends, when he'd failed and assaulted Catti-brie after a hallucinatory dream. It had been so during his travels with Morik, through Luskan and up to Auckney. So many times had he failed during those dark days.

Looking west then looking east, Wulfgar accepted the responsibility for all of those mistakes. He did not couch his admission of failure with self-serving whining about the trials he had suffered at the claws of Errtu. He did not make excuses for any of it, for there were none that could alter the truth of his behavior.

All he could do was do the best he could in all matters before him. That was what had led him to retrieve Delly's body. It was the right thing to do. That was what had led him not only to retrieve Colson from Cottie and the refugees, but to bring her home to Meralda. It was the right thing to do.

And now?

Wulfgar had thought he'd sorted it all out, had thought his plans and road determined. But with the stark reality of those plans before him, he was unsure. He knelt upon the stone and prayed to Delly for guidance. He called upon her ghost to show him the way.

Was Obould pounding on the doors of Mithral Hall yet again?

Bruenor might need him, he knew. His adoptive father, who had shown him nothing but love for all those years, might need his strength in the coming war. Wulfgar's absence could result in Bruenor's death!

The same could be true of Drizzt, or Regis, or Catti-brie. They might find themselves in situations in the coming days where only Wulfgar could save them.

"Might," Wulfgar said, and as he heard the word, he recognized that that would forever be the case. They might need him as he might need any of them, or all of them. Or perhaps even all of them together would one day soon be overcome by a black tide like the one of Obould.

"Might," he said again. "Always might."

Aside from the grim possibilities offered by the nearly perpetual state of war, however, Wulfgar had to remind himself of important questions. What of his own needs? What of his own desires? What of his own legacy?

He was approaching middle age.

Reflexively, Wulfgar turned from the east to face north, looking up the trail that would lead him to Icewind Dale, the land of his ancestors, the land of his people.

Before he could fully turn that way, however, he looked back to the east, toward Mithral Hall, and envisioned Obould the Awful towering over Bruenor.

CHAPTER

T his Toogwik Tuk is aggressive," Grguch said to Hakuun, and to Jack,
though of course Grguch didn't know that. They stood off to the side
of the gathering force as it realigned itself for a march to the west. "He
would have us wage war with Obould."

"He claims that Obould would wage war with us," the shaman agreed
after a quick internal dialogue with Jack.

Grguch grinned as if nothing in the world would please him more. "I
like this Toogwik Tuk," he said. "He speaks with Gruumsh."

"Are you not curious as to why Obould halted his march?" Hakuun
asked, though the question had originated with Jack. "His reputation is
for ferocity, but he builds walls instead of tearing them down."

"He fears rivals," Grguch assumed. "Or he has grown comfortable.
He walks away from Gruumsh."

"You do not intend to convince him otherwise."

Grguch grinned even more wickedly. "I intend to kill him and take
his armies. I speak to Gruumsh, and I will please Gruumsh."

"Your message will be blunt, or coaxed at first?"

Grguch looked at the shaman curiously then motioned with his chin
toward a bag set off to the side, a sack that held Oktule's head.

A wry smile widened on Hakuun's face. "I can strengthen the message," he promised, and Grguch was pleased.

Hakuun looked back over his shoulder and spoke a few arcane words,
strung together with dramatic inflection. Jack had predicted all of it, and

had already worked the primary magic for it. Out of the shadows walked Oktule, headless and grotesque. The animated zombie strode stiff-legged to the sack and shifted aside the flaps. It stood straight a moment later and moved slowly toward the pair, cradling its lost head in both hands at its midsection.

Hakuun looked to Grguch and shrugged sheepishly. The chieftain laughed.

"Blunt," he said. "I only wish that I might view Obould's face when the message is delivered."

Inside Hakuun's head, Jack whispered, and Hakuun echoed to Grguch, "It can be arranged."

Grguch laughed even louder.

With a bellow of *"Kokto Gung Karuck,"* Grguch's orc force, a thousand strong and growing, began its march to the west, the clan of the Wolf Jaw taking the southern flank, Clan Karuck spearheading the main mass.

In the very front walked the zombie Oktule, holding a message for Obould.

* * * * *

They heard the resonating grumble of *"Kokto Gung Karuck,"* and from a high mountain ridge not far northeast of Mithral Hall, Drizzt, Bruenor, and the others saw the source of that sound, the march of Clan Karuck and its allies.

"It is Grguch," Tos'un told the group. "The conspirators are leading him to Obould."

"To fight him?" Bruenor asked.

"Or to convince him," said Tos'un.

Bruenor snorted at him, but Tos'un just looked at Drizzt and Hralien and shook his head, unwilling to concede the point.

"Obould has shown signs that he wishes to halt his march," Drizzt dared say.

"Tell it to the families of me boys who died at the wall a couple o' nights ago, elf," Bruenor growled.

"That was Grguch, perhaps," Drizzt offered, careful to add the equivocation.

"That was orcs," Bruenor shot back. "Orcs is orcs is orcs, and th' only thing they're good for is fertilizing the fields. Might that their rotting bodies'll help grow trees to cover the scars in yer Moonwood," he added, addressing Hralien, who blanched and rocked back on his heels.

"To cover the blood of Innovindil," Bruenor added, glaring at Drizzt.

But Drizzt didn't back from the stinging comment. "Information is both our weapon and our advantage," he said. "We would do well to learn more of this march, its purpose, and where it might turn next." He looked down and to the north, where the black swarm of Grguch's army was clear to see along the rocky hills. "Besides, our trails parallel anyway."

Bruenor waved his hand dismissively and turned away, Pwent following him back to the food spread out at the main encampment.

"We need to get closer to them," Drizzt told the remaining half a dozen. "We need to learn the truth of their march."

Regis took a deep breath as Drizzt finished, for he felt the weight of the task on his shoulders.

"The little one will be killed," Tos'un said to Drizzt, using the drow language, Low Drow, that only he and Drizzt understood.

Drizzt looked at him hard.

"They are warriors, fierce and alert," Tos'un explained.

"Regis is more than he seems," Drizzt replied in the same Underdark language.

"So is Grguch." As he finished, Tos'un glanced at Hralien, as if to invite Drizzt to speak to the elf for confirmation.

"Then I will go," said Drizzt.

"There is a better way," Tos'un replied. *"I know of one who can walk right in and speak with the conspirators."*

That gave Drizzt pause, an expression of doubt clouding his face and obvious to everyone nearby.

"Ye plannin' to tell us what ye're talking about?" Torgar said impatiently.

Drizzt looked at him then back at Tos'un. He nodded, to both.

After a brief private conversation with Cordio, Drizzt pulled Tos'un off to the side to join the priest.

"Ye sure?" Cordio asked Drizzt when they were alone. "Ye're just gonna have to kill him."

Tos'un tensed at the words, and Drizzt fought hard to keep the smile from his face.

"He might be full o' more information that we can coax out o' him," Cordio went on, playing his role perfectly. "Might be that a few tendays o' torture'll bring us answers about Obould."

"Or lies to stop the torture," Drizzt replied, but he ended the forthcoming debate with an upraised hand, for it didn't matter anyway. "I am sure," he said simply, and Cordio heaved an "oh-if-I-must" sigh, the perfect mix of disgust and resignation.

Cordio began to chant and slowly dance around the startled Tos'un. The dwarf cast a spell—a harmless dweomer that would have cured any diseases that Tos'un might have contracted, though of course, Tos'un didn't know that, and recognized only that the dwarf had sent some magical energy into his body. Another harmless spell followed, then a third, and with each casting, Cordio narrowed his eyes and sharpened his inflection just a bit more, making it all seem quite sinister.

"The arrow," the dwarf commanded, holding a hand out toward Drizzt though his intense stare never left Tos'un.

"What?" Drizzt asked, and Cordio snapped his fingers impatiently. Drizzt recovered quickly and drew an arrow from his magical quiver, handing it over as demanded.

Cordio held it up before his face and chanted. He waggled the fingers of his free hand over the missile's wicked tip. Then he moved it toward Tos'un, who shrank back but did not retreat. The dwarf lifted the arrow up to Tos'un's head then lowered it.

"The head, or the heart?" he asked, turning to Drizzt.

Drizzt looked at him curiously.

"Telled ye it was a good spell," Cordio lied. "Not that it'll much matter with that durned bow o' yers. Blast his head from his shoulders or take out half his chest? Yer choice."

"The head," said the amused drow. "No, the chest. Shoot center mass. . . ."

"Ye can't miss either way," the dwarf promised.

Tos'un stared hard at Drizzt.

"Cordio has placed an enchantment upon you," Drizzt explained as Cordio continued to chant and wave the arrow before Tos'un's slender chest. The dwarf ended by tapping the arrowhead against the drow, right over his heart.

"This arrow is now attuned to you," Drizzt said, taking the arrow from the dwarf. "If it is shot, it will find your heart, unerringly. You cannot dodge it. You cannot deflect it. You cannot block it."

Tos'un's look was skeptical.

"Show 'im, elf," Cordio said.

Drizzt hesitated for effect.

"We're shielded from the damned orcs," the priest insisted. "Show 'im."

Looking back at Tos'un, Drizzt still saw doubt, and that he could not allow. He drew Taulmaril from his shoulder, replaced the "enchanted" arrow in his quiver and took out a different one. As he set it, he turned and targeted, then let fly at a distant boulder.

The magical bolt split the air like a miniature lightning bolt, flashing fast and true. It cracked into the stone and blasted through with a sharp retort that had Regis and the other dwarves jumping with surprise. It left only a smoking hole in the stone where it had hit.

"The magic of the surface dwellers is strange and powerful, do not doubt," Drizzt warned his fellow drow.

"Ye ain't got a chest plate thick enough," Cordio added, and he tossed an exaggerated wink at Tos'un then turned with a great laugh and ambled away.

"What is this about?" Tos'un asked in the drow tongue.

"You wish to play the role of scout, so I will let you."

"But with the specter of death walking beside me."

"Of course," said Drizzt. *"Were it just me, I might trust you."*

Tos'un tilted his head, curious, trying to get a measure of Drizzt.

"Fool that I am," Drizzt added. *"But it is not just me, and if I am to entrust you with this, I need to ensure that my friends will not be harmed by my decision. You hinted that you can walk right into their camp."*

"The conspirators know that I am no friend of Obould's."

"Then I will allow you to prove your worth. Go and learn what you may. I will be near, bow in hand."

"To kill me if I deceive you."

"To ensure the safety of my friends."

Tos'un began to slowly shake his head.

"You will not go?" Drizzt asked.

"You need not do any of this, but I understand," Tos'un replied. *"I will go as I offered. You will come to know that I am not deceiving you."*

By the time the two dark elves got back to the rest of the group, Cordio had informed the others of what had transpired, and of the plan going forward. Bruenor stood with his hands on his hips, clearly unconvinced, but he merely gave a "harrumph" and turned away, letting Drizzt play out his game.

* * * * *

The two drow set off from the others after nightfall, moving through the shadows with silent ease. They picked their way toward the main orc encampment, dodging guards and smaller camps, and always with Tos'un several steps in the lead. Drizzt followed with Taulmaril in hand, the deadly "enchanted" arrow set on its string—at least, Drizzt hoped he had taken out the same arrow Cordio had played with, or that if he had not, Tos'un hadn't noticed.

As they neared the main group, crossing along the edge of a clearing that was centered by a large tree, Drizzt whispered for Tos'un to stop. Drizzt paused for a few heartbeats, hearing the rhythm of the night. He waved for Tos'un to follow out to the tree. Up Drizzt went, so gracefully that it seemed as if he had walked along a fallen log rather than up a vertical trunk. On the lowest branch, he paused and looked around then turned his attention on Tos'un below.

Drizzt dropped a sword belt, both of Tos'un's weapons sheathed.

You would trust me? the son of House Barrison Del'Armgo signaled up with his fingers, using the intricate silent language of the drow.

Drizzt's answer was simple, and reflected on his impassive expression. *I have nothing to lose. I care nothing for that sword—it destroys more than it helps. You will drop it and your other blade to the ground when you return to the tree, or I will retrieve it from the grasp of the dying orc who took it from you after I put an arrow through your heart.*

Tos'un stared at him long and hard, but had no retort against the simple and straightforward logic. He looked down at the sword belt, at the hilt of Khazid'hea, and truly he was glad to have the sword back in hand.

He disappeared into the darkness a moment later, and Drizzt could only hope that his guess regarding Tos'un's veracity had been correct. For there had been no spell, of course, Cordio's grand exhibition being no more than an elaborate ruse.

* * * * *

Tos'un was truly torn as he crossed the orc lines to the main encampment. Known by the Wolf Jaw orcs sprinkled among the Clan Karuck sentries, he had no trouble moving in, and found Dnark and Ung-thol easily enough.

"I have news," he told the pair.

Dnark and Ung-thol exchanged suspicious looks. "Then speak it," Ung-thol bade him.

"Not here." Tos'un glanced around, as if expecting to find spies behind every rock or tree. "It is too important."

Dnark studied him for a few moments. "Get Toogwik . . ." he started to say to Ung-thol, but Tos'un cut him short.

"No. For Dnark and Ung-thol alone."

"Regarding Obould."

"Perhaps," was all the drow would answer, and he turned and started away. With another look at each other, the two orcs followed him into the night, all the way back to the edge of the field where Drizzt Do'Urden waited in a tree.

"My friends are watching," Tos'un said, loudly enough for Drizzt, with his keen drow senses, to hear.

Drizzt tensed and drew back Taulmaril, wondering if he was about to be revealed.

Tos'un would die first, he decided.

"Your friends are dead," Dnark replied.

"Three are," said Tos'un.

"You have made others. I salute you."

Tos'un shook his head with disgust at the pathetic attempt at sarcasm, wondering why he had ever suffered such creatures to live.

"There is a sizable drow force beneath us," he explained, and the two orcs, predictably, blanched. "Watching us—watching you."

He let that hang there for a few heartbeats, watching the two shift uncomfortably.

"Before she died, Kaer'lic called to them, to Menzoberranzan, my home. There was glory and wealth to be found, she promised them, and that call from a priestess of Lady Lolth could not go unheeded. And so they have come, to watch and to wait, at first. You are advancing toward Obould."

"Ob—*King* Obould," Dnark corrected rather stiffly, "has summoned Chieftain Grguch to his side."

Tos'un wore a knowing grin. "The drow hold no love for Obould," he explained, and indeed, it seemed to Drizzt as if the orc chieftain relaxed a bit at that.

"You go to pay fealty? Or to wage war?"

The two orcs looked at each other again.

"King Obould summoned Clan Karuck, and so we go," Ung-thol said with clear determination.

"Grguch attacked the Moonwood," Tos'un replied. "Grguch attacked Mithral Hall. Without Obould's permission. He will not be pleased."

"Perhaps . . ." Dnark started.

"He will not be pleased at all," Tos'un interrupted. "You know this. It is why you brought Clan Karuck forth from their deep hole."

"Obould has no heart for the fight," Dnark said with a sudden sneer. "He has lost the words of Gruumsh. He would barter and . . ." He stopped and took a deep breath, and Ung-thol picked up the thought.

"Perhaps the presence of Grguch will inspire Obould and remind him of his duty to Gruumsh," the shaman said.

"It will not," said Tos'un. "And so my people watch and wait. If Obould wins, we will travel back to the lower Underdark. If Grguch prevails, perhaps there is cause for us to come forth."

"And if Obould and Grguch join together to sweep the northland?" Dnark asked.

Tos'un laughed at the preposterous statement.

Dnark laughed, too, after a moment.

"Obould has forgotten the will of Gruumsh," Dnark said bluntly. "He sent an emissary to parlay with the dwarves, to beg forgiveness for Grguch's attack."

Tos'un could not hide his surprise.

"An emissary who never arrived, of course," the orc chieftain explained.

"Of course. And so Grguch and Dnark will remind Obould?"

The orc didn't reply.

"You will kill Obould, and replace him with Grguch, for the will of Gruumsh?"

No answer again, but it was apparent from the posture and expressions of the two orcs that the last remark hit closer to the truth.

Tos'un smiled at them and nodded. "We will watch, Chieftain Dnark. And we will wait. And I will take great pleasure in witnessing the death of Obould Many-Arrows. And greater pleasure in taking the head of King Bruenor and crossing the River Surbrin to lay waste to the wider lands beyond."

The drow gave a curt bow and turned away. "We are watching," he warned as he started off. "All of it."

"Listen for the Horn of Karuck," Dnark said. "When you hear it blow, know that King Obould nears the end of his reign."

Tos'un didn't so much as offer a glance up at Drizzt as he crossed the clearing to the far side, but soon after the orcs had headed back to their encampment, the rogue drow returned to the base of the tree.

"Your belt," Drizzt whispered down, but Tos'un was already undoing it. He let it fall to the ground and stepped back.

Drizzt hopped down and retrieved it.

"You might have prepared them to say as much," Drizzt remarked.

"Ask the sword."

Drizzt looked down at Khazid'hea skeptically. "It is not to be trusted."

"Then demand of it," said Tos'un.

But Drizzt merely slung the sword belt over his shoulder, motioning for Tos'un to lead the way back to the waiting dwarves.

Whatever Tos'un's position, whether it was out of a change of heart or simple pragmatism, Drizzt had no reason to doubt what he had heard, and one statement in particular kept repeating in his thoughts, the orc's claim that Obould had "sent an emissary to parlay with the dwarves, to beg forgiveness for Grguch's attack."

Obould would not march. For the orc king, the war was at its end. But for many of his subjects, apparently, that was not so pleasing a thought.

CHAPTER

28

The scout pointed to a trio of rocky hills in the northwest, a few miles away. "Obould's flag flies atop the centermost," he explained to Grguch, Hakuun, and the others. "He has rallied his clan around him in a formidable defense."

Grguch nodded and stared toward his distant enemy. "How many?"

"Hundreds."

"Not thousands?" the chieftain asked.

"There are thousands south of his position, and thousands north," the scout explained. "They could close before us and shield King Obould."

"Or swing around and trap us," said Hakuun, but in a tone that showed he was not overly concerned—for Jack, answering that particular question through Hakuun's mouth, held little fear of being trapped by orcs.

"If they remain loyal to King Obould," Toogwik Tuk dared interject, and all eyes turned his way. "Many are angry at his decision to halt his march. They have come to know Grguch as a hero."

Dnark started as if to speak, but changed his mind. He had caught Grguch's attention, though, and when the fierce half-orc, half-ogre turned his gaze Dnark's way, Dnark said, "Do we even know that Obould intends to do battle? Or will he just posture and paint with pretty words? Obould rules through wit and muscle. He will see the wisdom of coaxing Grguch."

"To build walls?" the chieftain of Clan Karuck said with a dismissive snicker.

"He will not march!" Toogwik Tuk insisted.

"He will speak enough words of war to create doubt," said Dnark.

"The only word I wish to hear from the coward Obould is 'mercy,'" Grguch stated. "It pleases me to hear a victim beg before he is put to my axe."

Dnark started to respond, but Grguch held up his hand, ending any further debate. With a scowl that promised only war, Grguch nodded to Hakuun, who commanded forth the grotesque zombie of Oktule, still holding its head before it.

"This is our parlay," Grguch said. He swung his gaze out to the side, where the battered Nukkels hung by his ankles from poles suspended across the broad shoulders of a pair of ogres. "And our advanced emissary," Grguch added with a wicked grin.

He took up his dragon-fashioned axe and stalked toward Nukkels, who was too beaten and dazed to even register his approach. Nukkels did see the axe, though, at the last moment, and he gave a pathetic yelp as Grguch swung it across, cleanly severing the rope and dropping Nukkels on his head to the ground.

Grguch reached down and hoisted the shaman to his feet. "Go to Obould," he ordered, turning Nukkels around and shoving him toward the northwest so ferociously that the poor orc went flying headlong to the ground. "Go and tell Obould the Coward to listen for the sound of *Kokto Gung Karuck.*"

Nukkels staggered back to his feet and stumbled along, desperate to be away from the brutal Karuck orcs.

"Tell Obould the Coward that Grguch has come and that Gruumsh is not pleased," Grguch shouted after him, and cheers began to filter through all of the onlookers. "I will accept his surrender . . . perhaps."

That sent the Karuck orcs and ogres into a frenzy, and even Toogwik Tuk beamed in anticipation. Dnark, though, looked at Ung-thol.

This conspiracy had been laid bare, to the ultimate fruition. This was real, suddenly, and this was war.

* * * * *

"Grguch comes with many tribes in his wake," Obould said to General Dukka. "To parlay?"

He and Obould's other commanders stood on the centermost of the three rocky hills. The foundations of a small keep lined the ground behind the orc leader, and three low walls of piled stones ringed the hill. The other two hills were similarly outfitted, though the defenses were hardly complete. Obould looked over his shoulder and motioned to his attendants, who brought forth the battered, nearly dead Nukkels.

"He's already spoken, it would seem," the orc king remarked.

"Then it will be war within your kingdom," the general replied, and his doubts were evident for all to hear.

Doubts offered for his benefit, Obould recognized. He didn't blink as he stared at Dukka, though others around him gasped and whispered.

"They are well-supported at their center," Dukka explained. "The battle will be fierce and long."

They are well-supported indeed, Obould thought but did not say.

He offered a slight nod of appreciation to Dukka, for he read easily enough between Dukka's words. The general had just warned him that Grguch's fame had preceded him, and that many in Obould's ranks had grown restless. There was no doubt that Obould commanded the superior forces. He could send orcs ten-to-one against the march of Clan Karuck and its allies. But with the choice laid bare before them, how many of those orcs would carry the banner of Obould, and how many would decide that Grguch was the better choice?

But there was no question among those on the three hills, Obould understood, for there stood Clan Many-Arrows, his people, his slavish disciples, who would follow him into Lady Alustriel's own bedroom if he so commanded.

"How many thousands will die?" he asked Dukka quietly.

"And will not the dwarves come forth when the opportunity is seen?" the general bluntly replied, and again Obould nodded, for he could not disagree.

A part of Obould did want to reach out and throttle Dukka for the assessment and for the lack of complete obedience and loyalty, but he knew in his heart that Dukka was right. If Dukka's force, more than two thousand strong, joined battle on the side of Clan Karuck and her allies, the fight could well shift before first blood was spilled.

Obould and his clan would be overwhelmed in short order.

"Hold my flank from the orcs who are not Karuck," Obould asked of his general. "Let Gruumsh decide which of us, Obould or Grguch, is more worthy to lead the kingdom forward."

"Grguch is strong with Gruumsh, so they say," Dukka warned, and a cloud crossed over Obould's face. But Dukka broke a smile before that cloud could become a full scowl. "You have chosen wisely, and for the good of the Kingdom of Many-Arrows. Grguch is strong with Gruumsh, it is said, but Obould protects the minions of the One-eye."

"Grguch is strong," the orc king said, and he brought his greatsword from its scabbard strapped diagonally across his back. "But Obould is stronger. You will learn."

General Dukka eyed that sword for a long while, recalling the many occasions when he had seen it put to devastating use. Gradually, he began to nod then to grin.

"Your flanks will be secure," he promised his king. "And any fodder prodded before Grguch's clan will be swept clean before they reach the hill. Clan Karuck alone will press the center."

* * * * *

"Ye lost yer wits, ye durned orc-brained, pointy-eared elf!" Bruenor bellowed and stomped the ground in frustration. "I come out here to kill the beast!"

"Tos'un speaks the truth."

"I ain't for trusting drow elfs, exceptin' yerself!"

"Then trust me, for I overheard much of his conversation with the orc conspirators. Obould dispatched an emissary to Mithral Hall to forbid the attack."

"Ye don't know what Tos'un told them orcs to say afore they got out to ye."

"True enough," Drizzt conceded, "but I suspected that which Tos'un reports long before I ever caught up to him. Obould's pause has run too long."

"He attacked me wall! And the Moonwood. Are ye so quick in forgetting Innovindil?"

The accusation rocked Drizzt back on his heels, and he winced, profoundly stung. For he had not forgotten Innovindil, not at all. He could still hear her sweet voice all around him, coaxing him to explore his innermost thoughts and feelings, coaching him on what it was to be an elf. Innovindil had given to him a great and wondrous gift, and in that gift, Drizzt Do'Urden had found himself, his heart and his course. With her lessons, offered in the purest friendship, Innovindil had solidified the sand beneath Drizzt' Do'Urden's feet, which had been shifting unsteadily for so many years.

He hadn't forgotten Innovindil. He could see her. He could smell her. He could hear her voice and the song of her spirit.

But her demise was not the work of Obould, he was certain. That terrible loss was the consequence of the *absence* of Obould, a prelude to the chaos that would ensue if that new threat, the beast Grguch, assumed command of Obould's vast and savage army.

"What are ye askin' me for, elf?" Bruenor said after the long and uncomfortable pause.

"It wasn't Gauntlgrym."

Bruenor locked his gaze, unblinking.

"But it was beautiful, was it not?" Drizzt asked. "A testament—"

"An abomination," Bruenor interrupted.

"Was it? Would Dagna and Dagnabbit think it so? Would Shoudra?"

"Ye ask me to dishonor them!"

"I ask you to honor them with the most uncommon courage, will and vision. In all the recorded and violent histories of all the races, there are few who could claim such."

Bruenor tightened his grip on his many-notched axe and lifted it before him.

"No one doubts the courage of King Bruenor Battlehammer," Drizzt assured the dwarf. "Any who witnessed your stand against the tide of orcs on the retreat into Mithral Hall places you among the legends of dwarf warriors, and rightly so. But I seek in you the courage *not* to fight."

"Ye're bats, elf, and I knowed ye'd be nothing but trouble when I first laid eyes on ye on the side o' Kelvin's Cairn."

Drizzt drew out Twinkle and Icingdeath and tapped them on either side of Bruenor's axe.

"I'll be watchin' the fight afore us," Bruenor promised. "And when I find me place in it, don't ye be blocking me axe, where'er it's aimed."

Drizzt snapped his scimitars away and bowed before Bruenor. "You are my king. My counsel has been given. My blades are ready."

Bruenor nodded and started to turn away, but stopped abruptly and swiveled his head back at Drizzt, a sly look in his eye. "And if ye send yer durned cat to pin me down, elf, I'll be cooking kitty, don't ye doubt."

Bruenor stomped away and Drizzt looked back at the probable battlefield, where the distant lines of orcs were converging. He pulled the onyx figurine from his belt pouch and summoned Guenhwyvar to his side, confident that the fight would ensue long before the panther began to tire.

Besides, he needed the surety of Guenhwyvar, the nonjudgmental companionship. For as he had asked for courage from Bruenor, so Drizzt had demanded it of himself. He thought of Tarathiel and Shoudra and all the others, dead now because of the march of Obould, dead at Obould's own hand. He thought of Innovindil, always he thought of Innovindil, and of Sunset, and he knew that he would carry that pain with him for the rest of his life. And though he could logically remove that last atrocity from the bloody hands of Obould, would any of it have happened in the Moonwood, in Mithral Hall, in Shallows and Nesmé, and all throughout the Silver Marches, had not Obould come forth with designs of conquest?

And yet, there he was, asking for uncommon courage from Bruenor, betting on Tos'un, and gambling with all the world, it seemed.

He brought his hand down to stroke Guenhwyvar's sleek black coat, and the panther sat down then collapsed onto her belly, her tongue hanging out between her formidable fangs.

"If I am wrong, Guenhwyvar, my friend, and to my ultimate loss, then I ask of you this one thing: dig your claws deep into the flesh of King Obould of the orcs. Leave him in agony upon the ground, dying of mortal wounds."

Guenhwyvar gave a lazy growl and rolled to her side, calling for a scratching on her ribs.

But Drizzt knew that she had understood every word, and that she, above all others, would not let him down.

CHAPTER

DWARVEN KING, DWARVEN ARROW

29

Shingles and Torgar stood quietly, staring at Bruenor, letting him lead without question, while an eager Pwent hopped around them. Cordio kept his eyes closed, praying to Moradin—and to Clangeddin, for he understood that the road to battle was clear. For Hralien, there showed only grim determination, and beside him, the bound Tos'un matched that intensity. Regis shifted from foot to foot nervously. And Drizzt, who had just delivered the assessment that battle was soon to be joined, and that the time had come for them to either leave or engage, waited patiently.

All focus fell to Bruenor, and the weight of that responsibility showed clearly on the face of the agitated dwarf. He had brought them there, and on his word they would either flee to safety or leap into the jaws of a tremendous battle—a battle they could not hope to win, or likely even survive, but one that they might, if their gods blessed them, influence.

* * * * *

To the south, Obould saw Dukka's force rolling forward like a dark cloud, streaming toward a line of orcs moving west to flank the hills. The clan of the Wolf Jaw, he knew, and he nodded and growled softly, imagining all the horrors he would inflict upon Dnark when his business with Grguch was over.

Confident that General Dukka would keep Wolf Jaw at bay, Obould focused his gaze directly to the east, where rising dust showed the approach of a powerful force, and yellow banners shot with red proclaimed Clan Karuck. The orc king closed his eyes and fell within his thoughts, imagining again his great kingdom, full of walls and castles, and teeming cities of orcs living under the sun and sharing fully in the bounty of the world.

Kna's shriek brought him from his quiet meditation, and as soon as he opened his eyes, Obould understood her distress.

An orc approached, a zombie orc, holding its head plaintively in its hands before it. Before any of his warriors and guards could react, Obould leaped the low wall before him and charged down, drawing his greatsword as he went. A single swing cleaved the zombie in half and sent the head flying.

So it was, the orc king knew as he executed the swing. Grguch had stated his intent and Obould had answered. There was no more to be said.

Not so far to the east, a great horn blared.

* * * * *

From over the very next ridge came the sound of a skirmish, orc against orc.

"Obould and Grguch," Tos'un stated.

In the distance to the northeast, a great horn, *Kokto Gung Karuck*, sounded.

"Grguch," Drizzt agreed.

Bruenor snorted. "I can't be asking any o' ye to come with me," he started.

"Bah, but just ye try to stop us," said Torgar, with Shingles nodding beside him.

"I would travel to the Abyss itself for a try at Obould," Hralien added.

Beside him, Tos'un shook his head.

"Obould's to be found on them hills," Bruenor said, waving his axe in the general direction of the trio of rocky mounds they had determined to be Obould's main encampment. "And I'm meaning to get there. Right through, one charge, like an arrow shot from me girl's bow. I'm not for knowing how many I'll be leavin' in me wake. I'm not for knowin' how I'm getting back out after I kill the dog. And I'm not for caring."

Torgar slapped the long handle of his greataxe across his open palm, and Shingles banged his hammer against his shield.

"We'll get ye there," Torgar promised.

The sounds of battle grew louder, some close and some distant. The great horn blew again, its echoes vibrating the stones beneath their feet.

Bruenor nodded and turned to the next ridge, but hesitated and glanced back, focusing his gaze on Tos'un. "Me elf friend told me that ye done nothing worth killin' ye over," he said. "And Hralien's agreeing. Get ye gone, and don't ye e'er give me a reason to regret me choice."

Tos'un held his hands out wide. "I have no weapons."

"There'll be plenty for ye to find in our wake, but don't ye be following too close," Bruenor replied.

With a helpless look to Drizzt, then to all the others, Tos'un gave a bow and walked back the way they had come. *Grguch is your nightmare, now,* he called to Drizzt, in the drow tongue.

"What's that?" Bruenor asked, but Drizzt only smiled and walked over to Hralien.

"I'll be moving fast beside Bruenor," the drow explained, handing Tos'un's weapon belt over. "If any are to escape this, it will be you. Beware this sword. Keep it safe." He glanced over at Regis, clearly nervous. "This will not unravel the way we had intended. Our run will be frantic and furious, and had we known the lay of the land and the orc forces, Bruenor and I would have come out—"

"Alone, of course," finished the elf.

"Keep the sword safe," Drizzt said again, though he looked not at Khazid'hea, but at Regis as he spoke, a message all too clear for Hralien.

"And live to tell our tale," the drow finished, and he and Hralien clasped hands.

"Come on, then!" Bruenor called.

He scraped his boots in the dirt to clear them of mud, and adjusted his one-horned helmet and his foaming mug shield. He started off at a brisk walk, but Thibbledorf Pwent rushed up beside him, and past him, and swept Bruenor up in his eagerness.

They were in full charge before they crested the ridge.

They found the fighting to the west of them, back toward Obould's line, but there were orcs aplenty right below, running eagerly to battle—so eagerly that Pwent had already lowered his head spike before the nearest one turned to regard the intruders.

That orc's scream became a sudden gasp as the helmet spike prodded through its chest, and a lip-flapping head wag from Pwent sent the mortally wounded creature flying aside. The next two braced for the charge, ready to dive aside, but Pwent lifted his head and leaped at them, spiked gauntlets punching every which way.

* * * * *

Drizzt and Bruenor veered to the right, where orc reinforcements rushed past the trees and the stones. Torgar and Shingles ran straight ahead off their wake, following Pwent in his attempt to punch through this thin flank and toward the main engagement, which was still far to the north.

With his long strides, Drizzt moved ahead of Bruenor. He lifted Taulmaril, holding the bow horizontal before his chest, for the orcs were close enough and plentiful enough that he didn't even need to aim. His first shot took one in the chest and blasted it backward and to the ground. His second went through another orc so cleanly that the creature hardly jerked, and Drizzt thought for a moment that he had somehow missed—he even braced for a counter.

But blood poured forth, chest and back, and the creature died where it stood, too fast for it to even realize that it should fall over.

"Bend right!" Bruenor roared, and Drizzt did, sidestepping as the dwarf charged past him, barreling into the next group of orcs, shield bashing and axe flying left, right, and center.

With a single fluid movement, Drizzt shouldered the bow and drew forth his scimitars, and went in right behind Bruenor. Dwarf and drow found themselves outnumbered three to one in short order.

The orcs never had a chance.

* * * * *

Regis didn't argue as Hralien pulled him to the side, still well behind the other six and moving from cover to cover.

"Protect me," the elf bade as he put up his longbow and began streaming arrows at the plentiful orcs.

His little mace in hand, Regis was in no position to argue—though he suspected that Drizzt had arranged it for his protection. For Hralien, Regis knew, was the one Drizzt most expected to escape the insanity.

His anger at the drow for pushing him to the side of the fight lasted only the moment it took Regis to view the fury of the engagement. To the right, Pwent spun, punched, butted, kicked, kneed, and elbowed with abandon, knocking orcs aside with every twist and turn.

But they were orcs of Wolf Jaw, warriors all, and not all of the blood on the battlerager was from an orc.

Back-to-back behind him, Torgar and Shingles worked with a precision wrought of years of experience, a harmony of devastating axe-work the pair had perfected in a century of fighting together as part of Mirabar's vaunted watch. Every routine ended with a step—either left or right, it didn't seem to matter—as each dwarf behind moved in perfect complement to keep the defense complete.

"Spear, down!" Torgar yelled.

He ducked, unable to deflect the missile. It flew over his head, apparently to crack through the back of Shingles's skull, but hearing the warning, old Shingles threw his shield up behind his head at the last instant, turning the crude spear aside.

Shingles had to fall away as the orc before him seized the opening.

But of course there was no opening, as Shingles rolled out to the side and Torgar came in behind him with a two-handed slash that disemboweled the surprised creature.

Two orcs took its place and Torgar got stabbed in the upper arm—which only made him madder, of course.

Regis swallowed hard and shook his head, certain that if he'd followed the charge, he'd already have been dead. He nearly fainted as he saw an orc, stone axe high for a killing blow, close in on Shingles, an angle that neither dwarf could possibly block.

But the orc fell away, an arrow deep in its throat.

That startled Regis from his shock, and he looked up to Hralien, who had already set another arrow and swiveled back the other way.

For there Bruenor and Drizzt worked their magic, as only they could. Drizzt's scimitars spun in a blur, too quick for Regis to follow their movements, which he measured instead by the angles of the orcs falling away from the furious drow. What Bruenor couldn't match in finesse, he made up for with sheer ferocity, and it occurred to Regis that if Thibbledorf Pwent and Drizzt Do'Urden collided with enough force to meld them into a single warrior, the result would be Bruenor Battlehammer.

The dwarf sang as he cut, kicked, and bashed. Unlike the other trio, who seemed stuck in a morass and tangle of orcs, Drizzt and Bruenor kept moving across and to the north, chopping and slashing and dancing away. At one point, a group of orcs formed in their path, and it seemed as if they would be stopped.

But Hralien's arrows broke the integrity of the orc line, and a flying black panther crashed into the surprised creatures, scattering them and sending them flying.

Drizzt and Bruenor ran by, breaking clear of the conflict.

At first, that thought panicked Regis. Shouldn't the two turn back to help Pwent and the others? And shouldn't he and Hralien hurry to keep up?

He looked at the elf and realized it wasn't about them, any of them. It was about Bruenor getting to Obould, about Bruenor killing Obould.

Whatever the cost.

* * * * *

Cordio wanted to keep up with Bruenor, to protect his beloved king at all costs, but the priest could not pace the fiery dwarf and his drow companion, and once he noted the harmony of their movements, attacks and charges, he recognized that he would likely only get in their way.

He turned for the dwarf trio instead, angling to get into the melee near to Torgar, whose right arm drooped low from a nasty stab.

Still fighting fiercely, the Mirabarran dwarf nevertheless grunted his approval as Cordio reached toward him, sending waves of magical healing energy into him. When Torgar turned to note his appreciation more directly, he saw that Cordio's help hadn't come without cost, for the priest had sacrificed his own position against one particularly large and nasty orc for the opportunity to help Torgar. Cordio bent low under the weight of a rain of blows against his fine shield.

"Pwent!" Torgar roared, motioning for the priest as the battlerager turned his way.

"For Moradin!" came Pwent's roar and he disengaged from the pair he was battering and charged headlong for Cordio.

The two orcs gave close chase, but Torgar and Shingles intercepted and drove them aside.

By the time Pwent reached Cordio, the priest was back to an even stance against the orc. No novice to battle, Cordio Muffinhead had covered himself with defensive enchantments and had brought the strength of his gods into his arms, swinging his flail with powerful strokes.

That didn't slow Pwent, of course, who rushed past the startled priest and leaped at the orc.

The orc's sword screeched against Pwent's wondrous armor, but it hardly bit through before Pwent slammed against the orc and began to thrash, the ridges on his plate mail tearing apart the orc's leather jerkin and slicing into its flesh beneath. With a howl of pain, the orc tried to disengage, but a sudden left and right hook from Pwent's spiked gauntlets held it in place like harvest corn.

Cordio used the opportunity to cast some healing magic into the battlerager, though he knew that Pwent wouldn't feel any difference. Pwent didn't really seem to feel pain.

* * * * *

The back of the small clearing dipped even lower, down into a dell full of boulders and a few scraggly tree skeletons. Drizzt and Bruenor rushed through, leaving their fighting companions behind, and with his longer strides, Drizzt took the lead.

Their goal was to avoid battle while they closed the ground to the trio of rocky hills and King Obould. As they came up the far side of the dell, they saw the orc king, picking him out from the flames engulfing his magical greatsword.

An ogre tumbled away from him then he shifted back and stabbed up over his shoulder, skewering another ten-foot behemoth. With strength beyond all reason, Obould used his sword to pull that ogre right over his shoulder and send it spinning down the side of the hillock.

All around him the battle raged, as Clan Karuck and Clan Many-Arrows fought for supremacy.

And in truth, with Obould and his minions holding the high ground, it didn't seem as if it would be much of a fight.

But then a fireball exploded, intense and powerful, right behind the highest wall on the hill to Obould's left, the northernmost of the three, and all of the Many-Arrows archers concealed there flailed about, immolated by the magical flames. They shrieked and they died, curling up on the ground in blackened, smoking husks.

Clan Karuck warriors swarmed over the stones.

"What in the Nine Hells . . . ?" Bruenor asked Drizzt. "Since when are them orcs throwing fireballs?"

Drizzt had no answer, other than to reinforce his feelings about the entire situation, simply by stating, "Grguch."

"Bah!" Bruenor snorted, so predictably, and the pair ran on.

* * * * *

"Keep to the high ground," Hralien instructed Regis as he led the halfling along to the east. They pulled up amidst a boulder tumble, beside a single maple tree, Hralien sighting targets and lifting his bow.

"We have to go and join them!" Regis cried, for the four dwarves moved out of sight over the near ridge of the dell.

"No time!"

Regis wanted to argue, but the frantic hum of Hralien's bowstring, the elf firing off arrow after arrow, denied him his voice. More orcs swarmed along before them from the east, and a darker cloud had formed in the west as a vast army began its approach.

Regis cast a plaintive gaze to the north, where Drizzt and Bruenor had gone, where Cordio, Pwent, and the others had run. He believed that he would never see his friends again. Drizzt had done it, he knew. Drizzt had put him with Hralien, knowing that the elf would likely find a way out, where there could be no retreat for Drizzt and Bruenor.

Bitterness filled the back of Regis's throat. He felt betrayed and abandoned. In the end, when the circumstances had grown darkest, he had been set aside. Logically he could understand it all—he was, after all, no hero. He couldn't fight like Bruenor, Drizzt, and Pwent. And with so many orcs around, there really wasn't any way for him to hide and strike from points of opportunity.

But that did little to calm the sting.

He nearly jumped out of his boots when a form rose up beside him, an orc springing from concealment. Purely on instinct, Regis squealed and shouldered the thing, knocking it off-balance just enough so that its stab at Hralien only grazed the distracted archer.

Hralien turned fast, smashing his bow across the orc's face. The bow flew free as the orc tumbled, Hralien going for his sword.

Regis lifted his mace to finish the orc first, except that as he retracted his arm for the strike, something grabbed him and yanked that arm back viciously. He felt his shoulder pop out of joint. His hand went numb as his mace fell away. He managed to half turn then to duck, bringing his other arm up over his head defensively as he noted the descent of a stone hammer.

A blinding explosion spread over the back of his head, and he had no idea of whether his legs had buckled or simply been driven straight into the ground as he fell face-down in the stony dirt. He felt a soft boot come in tight against his ear and heard Hralien battling above him.

He tried to put his hands under him, but one arm would not move to his call, and the attempt sent waves of nauseating agony through him. He managed to lift his head, just a bit, and tasted the blood streaming down from the back of his skull as he half-turned to try to get his bearings.

He was back on the ground again, though he knew not how. Cold fingers reached up at him, as if from the ground itself. He had his eyes open, but the darkness crept in from the edges.

The last thing he heard was his own ragged breathing.

* * * * *

R. A. SALVATORE

Orc armor proved no match for the fine elven sword as Hralien slid the blade deep into the chest of the newest attacker, who held a stone hammer wet with Regis's blood.

The elf slashed out to the side, finishing the first one, who stubbornly tried to regain its footing, then spun to meet the charge of a third creature coming in around the tree. His sword flashed across, turning the orc's spear in against the bark and knocking the creature off balance. The tree alone stopped it from falling aside, but that proved an unfortunate thing for the orc, as Hralien leaped out to the side and stabbed back in, catching the creature through the armpit.

It shrieked and went into a frenzy, spinning and stumbling away, grabbing at the vicious wound.

Hralien let it go, turning back to Regis, who lay so very still on the cold ground. More orcs had spotted him, he knew. He had no time. He grabbed the halfling as gently as he could and slid him down into a depression at the base of the maple, between two large roots. He kicked dirt and twigs and leaves, anything he could find to disguise the poor halfling. Then, for the sake of the fallen Regis, Hralien grabbed up his bow and sprang away, running again to the east.

Orcs closed on him from behind and below. More rose up before him, running at an angle to prevent him from going over the ridge to the south.

Hralien dropped his second sword belt, the one Drizzt had given him, and threw aside his bow, needing to be nimble.

He charged ahead, desperate to put as much ground between himself and Regis as possible, in the faint hope that the orcs would not find the wounded halfling. The run lasted only a few strides, though, as Hralien skidded to a stop, turning frantically to bring his sword around to deflect a flying spear. Swords came in at him from every angle, orcs closing for the kill. Hralien felt the hot blood of his elders coursing through his veins. All the lessons he had learned in two centuries of life flooded through him, driving him on. There was no thought, only instinct and reaction, his shining sword darting to block, angling to turn a spear and stabbing ahead to force an attacker into a short retreat.

Beautiful was his dance, magnificent his turns, and lightning-quick his thrusts and ripostes.

But there were too many—too many for him to even consider

them separately as he tried to find some answer to the riddle of the battle.

Images of Innovindil flitted through his mind, along with those others he had lost so recently. He took hope in the fact that they had gone before him, that they would greet him in Arvandor when a single missed block let a sword or a spear slip through.

Behind him, back the way he had come, Regis sank deeper into the cold darkness. And not so far away, perhaps halfway to the tree, a black hand closed over Khazid'hea's hilt.

* * * * *

They had intended to follow in the wake of Bruenor and Drizzt, but the four dwarves found the route blocked by a wall of orcs. They came out of the dell to the east instead, and there, too, they met resistance.

"For Mirabar and Mithral Hall!" Torgar Hammerstriker called, and shoulder to shoulder with his beloved and longtime friend Shingles, the leader of the Mirabarran exodus met the orcs.

To the side of them, Thibbledorf Pwent snarled and bit and found within himself yet another frenzy. Flailing his arms and legs, and butting his head so often that his forward movements seemed the steps of a gawky, long-necked seabird, Pwent had the orcs on that side of the line in complete disarray. They threw spears at him, but so intent were they on getting out of his way that they threw as they turned, and thus with little or no effect.

It couldn't hold, though. Too many orcs stood before them, and they would have to pile the orc bodies as thick as the walls of a dwarf-built keep before they could even hope to find a way through.

Bruenor and Drizzt were lost to them, as was any route that would get them back to the south and the safety of Mithral Hall. So they did what dwarves do best, they fought to gain the highest ground.

Cordio wanted to tap some offensive magic, to stun the orcs with a blast of shocking air, perhaps, or to hold a group in place so that Torgar and Shingles could score quick kills. But blood flowed freely from all the dwarves in short order, and the priest could not keep up with the wounds, though his every spell cast was one of healing. Cordio was filled with Moradin's blessing, a priest of extraordinary power and piety. It occurred to him, though, that Moradin himself was not possessed of enough magical healing to win that fight. They were known, the clear spectacle of the most-hated enemy in the midst of the orcs, and behind the immediate fighting, the ugly creatures stalked all around them, preparing to overwhelm them.

Not a dwarf was afraid, though. They sang to Moradin and Clangeddin and Dumathoin. They sang of bar wenches and heavy mugs of ale, of killing orcs and giants, of chasing dwarf ladies.

And Cordio led a song to King Bruenor, of the fall of Shimmergloom and the reclamation of Mithral Hall.

They sang and they fought. They killed and they bled, and they looked continually to the north, where Bruenor their king had gone.

For all that mattered was that they had served him well that day, that they had given him enough time and enough of a distraction to get to the hills and to end, once and for all, the threat of Obould.

* * * * *

Hralien felt the sting of a sword across his forearm, and though the wound was not deep, it was telling. He was slowing, and the orcs had caught on to the rhythms of his dance.

He had nowhere to run.

An orc to his right came on suddenly, he thought, and he spun to meet the charge—then saw that it was no charge at all, for the tip of a sword protruded from the falling creature's chest.

Behind the orc, Tos'un Armgo retracted Khazid'hea and leaped out to the side. An orc lifted its shield to block, but the sword went right through the shield, right through the arm, and right through the side of the creature's chest.

Before it had even fallen away, another orc fell to Tos'un's second weapon, an orc-made sword.

Hralien had no time to watch the spectacle or to even consider the insanity of it all. He spun back and took down the nearest orc, who seemed dumbfounded by the arrival of the drow. On the elves pressed, light and dark, and orcs fell away, or threw their weapons and ran away, and soon the pair faced off, Hralien drawing a few much-needed deep breaths.

"Clan Wolf Jaw," Tos'un explained to Hralien. "They fear me."

"With good reason," Hralien replied.

The sound of battle to the north, and the sound of dwarf voices lifted in song, stole their conversation, and before Tos'un could begin to clarify, he found that he did not have to, for Hralien led their run down from the ridgeline.

It had to come down to the two of them, for among the orcs, struggles within and among tribes were ultimately personal.

King Obould leaped atop a stone wall and plunged his sword into the belly of a Karuck ogre. He stared the behemoth in the face, grinning wickedly as he called upon his enchanted sword to burst into flame.

The ogre tried to scream. Its mouth stretched wide in silent horror.

Obould only smiled wider and held his sword perfectly still, not wanting to hurry the death of the ogre. Gradually, the dimwitted behemoth leaned back, back, then slid off the blade, tumbling down the hill, wisps of smoke coming from the already cauterized wound.

Looking past it, Obould saw one of his guards, an elite Many-Arrows warrior, go flying aside, broken and torn. Tracing its flight back to the source, he saw another of his warriors, a young orc who had shown great promise in the battles with the Battlehammer dwarves, leap back. The warrior stood still for a curiously long time, his arms out wide.

Obould stared at his back, shaking his head, not understanding, until a huge axe swept up from in front of the warrior, then cut down diagonally with tremendous, jolting force, cleaving the warrior in half, left shoulder to right hip. Half the orc fell away, but the other half stood there for a few long heartbeats before buckling to the ground.

And there stood Grguch, swinging his awful axe easily at the end of one arm.

Their eyes met, and all the other orcs and ogres nearby, Karuck and Many-Arrows alike, took their battles to the side.

Obould stretched his arms out wide, fires leaping from the blade of his greatsword as he held it aloft in his right hand. He threw back his head and bellowed.

Grguch did likewise, axe out wide, his roar echoing across the stones, the challenge accepted. Up the hill he ran, hoisting his axe in both hands and bringing it back over his left shoulder.

Obould tried for the quick kill, feigning a defensive posture, but then leaping down at the approaching chieftain and stabbing straight ahead. Across came Grguch's axe with brutal and sudden efficiency, the half-ogre chopping short to smash his dragon-winged weapon against Obould's blade. He turned it sidelong as he swiped, the winged blades perpendicular to the ground, but so strong was the beast that the resistance as he brought the axe across didn't slow his swing in the least. By doing it that way, his blade obscuring nearly three feet top-to-bottom, Grguch prevented Obould from turning his greatsword over the block.

Obould just let his sword get knocked out to his left, and instead of letting go with his right hand, as would be expected, the cunning orc let go with his left, allowing him to spin in behind the cut of Grguch's axe. He went forward as he went around, lowering his soon-leading left shoulder as he collided with Grguch.

The pair slid down the stony hill, and to Obould's amazement, Grguch did not fall. Grguch met his heavy charge with equal strength.

He was taller than Obould by several inches, but Obould had been blessed by Gruumsh, had been given the strength of the bull, a might of arm that had allowed him to bowl over Gerti Orelsdottr of the frost giants.

But not Grguch.

The two struggled, their weapon arms, Obould's right and Grguch's left, locked at one side. Obould slugged Grguch hard in the face, snapping his head back, but as he recoiled from that stinging blow, Grguch snapped his head forward, inside the next punch, and crunched his forehead into Obould's nose.

They clutched, they twisted, and they postured, and both tried to shove back at the same time, sending themselves skidding far apart.

Right back they went with identical blows, axe and sword meeting with tremendous force, so powerfully that a gout of flames flew free of Obould's sword and burst into the air.

* * * * *

"As Tos'un told us," Drizzt said to Bruenor as they slipped between fights to come in view of the great struggle.

"Think they'd forget each other and turn on us, elf?" Bruenor asked hopefully.

"Likely not—not Obould, at least," Drizzt replied dryly, stealing Bruenor's mirth, and he led the dwarf around a pile of stones that hadn't yet been set on the walls.

"Bah! Ye're bats!"

"Two futures clear before us," Drizzt remarked. "What does Moradin say to Bruenor?"

Before Bruenor could answer, as Drizzt came around the pile, a pair of orcs leaped at him. He snapped up both his blades and threw himself backward, quickstepping across Bruenor's field of vision and dragging the bloodthirsty orcs with him.

The dwarf's axe came crashing down, and then there was one.

And that orc twisted and half-turned, startled by Bruenor and never imagining that Drizzt could be nimble enough to reverse his field so quickly.

The orc got hit four times by Drizzt's scimitars, and Bruenor creased its skull for good measure, and the pair rambled along.

Before them, much closer, Obould and Grguch clutched again, and traded a series of brutal punches that splattered blood from both faces.

"Two roads before us," Drizzt said, and he looked at Bruenor earnestly.

The dwarf shrugged then tapped his axe against Drizzt's scimitars. "For the good o' the world, elf," he said. "For the kids o' me kin and me trust for me friends. And ye're still bats."

* * * * *

Every swing brought enough force to score a kill, every cut cracked through the air. They were orcs, one half ogre, but they fought as giants, titans even, gods among their respective people.

Bred for battle, trained in battle, hardened as his skin had calloused, and propped by magical spells from Hakuun, and secretly from Jack the Gnome, Grguch moved his heavy axe with the speed and precision with which a Calimport assassin might wield a dagger. None in Clan Karuck, not the largest and the strongest, questioned Grguch's leadership role, for none in that clan would dare oppose him. With good reason, Obould understood all too quickly, as the chieftain pressed him ferociously.

Blessed by Gruumsh, infused with the strength of a chosen being, and veteran of so many battles, Obould equaled his opponent, muscle for muscle. And unlike so many power-driven warriors who could smash a weapon right through an opponent's defenses, Obould combined finesse and speed with that sheer strength. He had matched blades with Drizzt Do'Urden, and overmatched Wulfgar with brawn. And so he met Grguch's heavy strikes with powerful blocks, and so he similarly pressed Grguch with mighty counterstrikes that made the chieftain's arms strain to hold back the deadly greatsword.

Grguch rushed around to Obould's left, up the hill a short expanse. He turned back from that higher ground and drove a tremendous overhand chop down at the orc king, and Obould nearly buckled under the weight of the blow, his feet sliding back dangerously beneath him.

Grguch struck again, and a third time, but Obould went out to the side suddenly, and that third chop cut nothing but air, forcing Grguch down the hill a few quick steps.

They stood even again, and with the miss, Obould gained an offensive posture. Both hands grasping his sword, he smashed it in from the right then the left then right again. Grguch moved to a solely defensive posture, axe darting left and right to block.

Obould quickened the pace, slashing with abandon, allowing Grguch no chance for a counter. He brought forth fire on his blade then winked it out with a thought—and brought it forth again, just to command more of his opponent's attention, to further occupy Grguch.

Left and right came the greatsword, then three overhead chops, battering Grguch's blocking blade, sending shivers through the chieftain's muscled arms. Obould did not tire, and more furious came his strikes, backing his opponent.

Grguch was no longer looking for an opening to counter, Obould knew. Grguch tried only to find a way to disengage, to put them back on even ground.

Obould wouldn't give it to him. The chieftain was worthy, indeed, but in the end, he was no Obould.

A blinding flash and a thunderous retort broke the orc king's momentum and rhythm, and as he recovered from the initial, stunning shock of it, he realized that he had lost more than advantage. His legs twitched and could hardly hold him upright. His greatsword trembled violently and his teeth chattered so uncontrollably that he tore strips of skin from the inside of his mouth.

A wizard's lightning bolt, he understood somewhere deep in the recesses of his dazed mind, and a mighty one.

His block of Grguch's next attack was purely coincidental, his greatsword fortunately in the way of the swing. Or maybe Grguch had aimed for the weapon, Obould realized as he staggered back from the weight of the blow, fighting to hold his balance with every stumbling, disoriented step.

He offered a better attempt to block the next sidelong swing, turning to the left and presenting his sword at a perfect angle to intercept the flying axe.

A perfect parry, except that Obould's twitching legs gave out under the weight of the blow. He skidded half-backward and half-sidelong down the hill and went down to one knee.

Grguch hit his sword again, knocking it aside, and as the chieftain stepped forward, bringing his blade back yet again, Obould realized that he had little defense.

A booted foot stomped hard on the back of Obould's neck, driving him low, and he tried to turn and lash out at what he deemed to be a new attacker.

But Bruenor Battlehammer's target was not Obould, and he had used the battered and dazed orc king merely as a springboard to launch himself at his real quarry.

Grguch twisted frantically to get his axe in line with the dwarf's weapon, but Bruenor, too, turned as he flew, and his buckler, emblazoned with the foaming mug of Clan Battlehammer, crashed hard into Grguch's face, knocking him back.

Grguch leaped up and came right back at Bruenor with a mighty chop, but Bruenor rushed ahead under the blow, butting his one-horned helmet into Grguch's belly and sweeping his axe up between the orc chieftain's legs. Grguch leaped, and Bruenor grabbed and leaped back and over with him, the pair flying away and tumbling down the hill. As they unwound, Grguch, caught with his back to the dwarf, rushed away and shoulder-rolled over the hill's lowest stone wall.

Bruenor pursued furiously, springing atop the wall, then leaping from it, swooping down from on high with a mighty chop that sent the blocking Grguch staggering backward.

The dwarf pressed, axe and shield, and it took Grguch many steps before he could begin to attain even footing with his newest enemy.

Back on the hill, Obould stubbornly gained his feet and tried to follow, but another crackling lightning bolt flattened him.

* * * * *

Hralien darted out in front as the pair crossed the narrow channel. He leaped a stone, started right, then rolled back left around the trunk of a dead tree, coming around face up against an unfortunate orc, whose sword was still angled the other way to intercept his charge. The elf struck hard and true, and the orc fell away, mortally wounded.

Hralien retracted the blade as he ran past the falling creature, which left his sword arm out behind him.

As his sword pulled free, a sudden sting broke the elf's grasp on it, and he glanced back in shock to see Tos'un flipping the blade over between his two swords. With amazing dexterity, the drow slid his own sword into its sheath and caught Hralien's flipping weapon by the hilt.

"Treacherous dog!" Hralien protested as the dark elf moved in behind him, prodding him along.

"Just shut up and run," Tos'un scolded him.

Hralien stopped, though, and the tip of Khazid'hea nicked him. Tos'un's hand came against his back then, and shoved him roughly forward.

"Run!" he demanded.

Hralien stumbled forward and Tos'un didn't let him dig in, keeping up and pushing him along with every stride.

* * * * *

Drizzt hated breaking away from Bruenor with both the orc leaders so close, but the magic-using orc, nestled in a mixed copse of evergreen and deciduous trees to the east of Obould's defenses, demanded his attention. Having lived and fought beside the wizards of the drow school Sorcere, who were skilled in the tactics of wizardry combined with sword-fighters, Drizzt understood the danger of those thunderous, blinding lightning bolts.

And there was something more, some nagging suspicion in Drizzt's thoughts. How had the orcs taken Innovindil and Sunset from the sky? That puzzle had nagged at Drizzt since Hralien had delivered the news of their fall. Did he have his answer?

The wizard wasn't alone, for he had set other orcs, large Karuck half-ogre orcs, around the perimeter of the copse. One of them confronted Drizzt as he reached the tree line, leaping forward with a growl and a thrusting spear.

But Drizzt had no time for such nonsense, and he shifted, throwing himself to the left, and brought both of his scimitars down and back to the right, double-striking the spear and driving it harmlessly aside. Drizzt continued right past the off-balance spear-wielder, lifting Twinkle expertly to slash a line across the orc's throat.

As that one fell away, though, two more charged at the drow, from left and right, and the commotion also drew the attention of the wizard, still some thirty feet away.

Drizzt pasted an expression of fear on his face, for the benefit of the wizard, then darted out to the right, quick-stepping to intercept the charging orc. He turned as they came together, rolling right around and to the left, tilting his shoulders out of horizontal as he turned so that his sweeping blades lifted the orc's sword up high.

Drizzt sprinted right for the trunk of a nearby tree, both orcs closing. He ran up it and leaped off, threw his head and shoulders back, and tucked into a tight somersault. He landed lightly, exploding into a barrage of whirling blades, and one orc fell away, the other running off to the side.

Drizzt came out from behind the tree as he pursued, to see the orc wizard waggling his fingers in spellcasting, aiming his way.

It was exactly as Drizzt had planned, for the surprise on the wizard orc's face was both genuine and delicious as Guenhwyvar crashed in from the side, bearing the creature to the ground.

* * * * *

"For the lives of your dwarven friends," Tos'un explained, pushing the stubborn elf forward. The surprising words diminished Hralien's resistance, and he did not fight against the shift when the flat of Tos'un's blade turned him, angling him more directly to the east.

"The Wolf Jaw standard," Tos'un explained to the elf. "Chieftain Dnark and his priest."

"But the dwarves are in trouble!" Hralien protested, for not far away, Pwent and Torgar and the others fought furiously against an orc force thrice their number.

"To the head of the serpent!" Tos'un insisted, and Hralien could not disagree.

He began to understand as they passed several orcs, who glanced at the dark elf deferentially and did not try to intercept them.

They sprinted around some boulders and broken ground, down past a cluster of thick pines and across a short expanse to the heart of Dnark's army. Tos'un spotted the chieftain immediately, Toogwik Tuk and Ungthol at his side as expected.

"A present for Dnark," the drow called at the stunned expressions, and he pushed Hralien harder, nearly toppling the elf.

Dnark waved some guards toward Hralien to take the elf from Tos'un.

"General Dukka and his thousands approach," Dnark called to the drow. "But we will not fight until it is settled between the chieftains."

"Obould and Grguch," Tos'un agreed, and as the orc guards approached, he went past Hralien.

"Left hip," the dark elf whispered as he crossed past Hralien, and he brushed close enough for the surface elf to feel the hilt of his own belted sword.

Tos'un paused and nodded at both the orcs, drawing their attention and giving Hralien ample time to draw forth the blade. And so Hralien did, and even as the orc guards noted it and called out in protest, the flash of elven steel left them dead.

Tos'un stumbled away from Hralien, stumbled toward Dnark's group, looking back and scrambling as if fleeing the murderous elf. He turned fully as he put his feet under him, and saw that Toogwik Tuk had begun spellcasting, with Dnark directing other orcs toward Hralien.

"Back to the elf and finish him!" Dnark protested as Tos'un continued his flight. "Dukka is coming and we must prepare . . ."

But Dnark's voice trailed off as he finished, as he came to realize that Tos'un, that treacherous drow, wasn't running away from the elf, but was, in fact, charging at him.

Standing at Dnark's left, Toogwik Tuk gasped as Khazid'hea rudely interrupted his spellcasting, biting deep into his chest. To Chieftain Dnark's credit, he managed to get his shield up to block Tos'un's other blade as it came in at him. He couldn't anticipate the power of Khazid'hea, though, for instead of yanking the blade out of Toogwik Tuk's chest, Tos'un just drove it across, the impossibly fine edge of the sword known as Cutter slicing through bone and muscle as easily as if it were parting water. The blade came across just under Dnark's shoulder, and before the chieftain even realized the attack enough to spin away, his left arm was taken, falling free to the ground.

Dnark howled and dropped his weapon, reaching across to grab at the blood spurting from his stumped shoulder. He fell back and to the ground, thrashing and roaring empty threats.

But Tos'un wasn't even listening, turning to strike at the nearest orcs. Not Ung-thol, though, for the shaman ran away, taking a large portion of Dnark's elite group with him.

"The dwarves!" Hralien called to the drow, and Tos'un followed the Moonwood elf. He forced back his nearest attackers with a blinding, stabbing routine, then angled away, turning back toward Hralien, who had already swung around in full charge toward the dell in the west.

* * * * *

Bruenor rolled his shield forward, picking off a swing, then advanced, turning his shoulders and rolling his axe at the dodging Grguch. He swung his shield arm up to deflect the next attack, and swiped his axe across underneath it, forcing Grguch to suck in his gut and throw back his hips.

On came the dwarf, pounding away with his shield, slashing wildly with his axe. He had the much larger half-ogre off balance, and knew from the craftsmanship and sheer size of Grguch's axe that he would do well to keep it that way!

The song of Moradin poured from his lips. He swung across and reversed in a mighty backhand, nearly scoring a hit, then charged forward, shield leading. That is why he had been returned to his people, Bruenor knew in his heart. That was the moment when Moradin needed him, when Clan Battlehammer needed him.

He threw out the confusion of the lost city and its riddles, of Drizzt's surprising guesses. None of that mattered—it was he and that newest, fiercest foe, battling to the death, old enemies locked in mortal combat. It was the way of Moradin and the way of Gruumsh, or at least, it was the way it had always been.

Light steps propelled the dwarf, spinning, advancing and retreating out of every swing and every block with perfect balance, using his speed to keep his larger, stronger foe slightly off balance.

Every time Grguch tried to wind up for a mighty stroke of that magnificent axe, Bruenor moved out of range, or came in too close, or too far to the same side as the retracted weapon, shortening Grguch's strike and stealing much of its power.

And always Bruenor's axe slashed at the orc. Always, the dwarf had Grguch twisting and dodging, and cursing.

Like sweet music to Bruenor's ears did those orc curses sound.

In utter frustration, Grguch leaped back and roared in protest, bringing his axe up high. Bruenor knew better than to pursue, dropping one foot back instead, then rushing back and to the side, under the branch of a leafless maple.

Grguch, too outraged by the frustrating dwarf to hold back, rushed forward and swung with all his might anyway—and the dragon-axe crashed right through that thick limb, splintering its base and driving it back at the dwarf. Bruenor threw up his shield at the last second, but the weight of the limb sent him staggering backward.

By the time he recovered, Grguch was there, roaring still, his axe cutting a line for Bruenor's skull.

Bruenor ducked and threw up his shield, and the axe hit it solidly—too solidly! The foaming mug shield, that most recognizable of Mithral Hall's artifacts, split in half, and below it, the bone in Bruenor's arm cracked, the weight of the blow driving the dwarf to his knees.

Agony burned through Bruenor's body, and white flashes filled his vision.

But Moradin was on his lips, and Moradin was in his heart, and he scrambled forward, slashing his axe with all his might, forcing Grguch before him in his frenzy.

* * * * *

Pwent, Torgar, and Shingles formed a triangle around Cordio. The priest directed their movements, mostly coordinating Shingles and Torgar with the wild leaps and surges of the unbridled fury that was Thibbledorf Pwent. Pwent had never viewed battle in terms of defensive formations. To his credit, though, the wild-eyed battlerager did not completely compromise the integrity of their defensive stand, and the bodies of dead orcs began to pile up around them.

But more took the places of the fallen—many more, an endless stream. As weapon arms drooped from simple weariness, the three frontline dwarves took more and more hits, and Cordio's spells of healing came nearly constant from his lips, depleting his magical energies.

They couldn't keep it up for much longer, all three knew, and even Pwent suspected that it would be their last, glorious stand.

The orc immediately before Torgar rushed forward suddenly. The Mirabarran dwarf turned the long handle of his axe at the last moment to deflect the creature aside, and only when it started to fall away did Torgar recognize that it was already mortally wounded, blood pouring from a deep wound in its back.

As the dwarf turned to face any other nearby orcs, he saw the way before him cleared of enemies, saw Hralien and Tos'un fighting side by side. They backed as Torgar shifted to his right, moving beside

Shingles, and the defensive triangle became two, two and one, and with an apparent escape route open to the east. Hralien and Tos'un started that flight, Cordio bringing the others in behind.

But they became bogged down before they had ever really started, as more and more orcs joined the fray—orcs thirsty for vengeance for their fallen chieftain, and orcs simply thirsty for the taste of dwarf and elf blood.

* * * * *

The panther's claws raked the fallen orc's body, but Jack's wards held strong and Guenhwyvar did little real damage. Even as Guenhwyvar thrashed, Hakuun began to mouth the words of a spell as Jack took control.

Guenhwyvar understood well the power of wizards and priests, though, and the panther clamped her jaws over the orc's face, pressing and twisting. Still the wizard's defensive wards held, diminishing the effect. But Hakuun began to feel the pain, and knowing that the magical shields were being torn asunder, the orc panicked.

That mattered little to Jack, safe within Hakuun's head. Wise old Jack was worldly enough to recognize Guenhwyvar for what she was. In the shelter of Hakuun's thick skull, Jack calmly went about his task. He reached into the Weave of magical energy, found the nearby loose ends of enchanting emanations, and tied them together, filling the area with countering magical force.

Hakuun screamed as panther claws tore through his leather tunic and raked lines of blood along his shoulder. The cat retracted her huge maw, opened wide and snapped back at his face, and Hakuun screamed louder, certain that the wards were gone and that the panther would crush his skull to dust.

But that head dissipated as the panther bit down, and gray mist replaced the dispelled Guenhwyvar.

Hakuun lay there, trembling. He felt some of the magical wards being renewed about his disheveled frame.

Get up, you idiot! Jack screamed in his thoughts.

The orc shaman rolled to his side and up to one knee. He struggled to stand then stumbled away and back to the ground as a shower of sparks exploded beside him, a heavy punch knocking him backward.

He collected his wits and looked back in surprise to see the drow lifting a bow his way.

A second lightning-arrow streaked in, exploding, throwing him backward. But inside of Hakuun, Jack was already casting, and while the shaman struggled, one of his hands reached out, answering the drow's third shot with a bolt of white-hot lightning.

When his blindness cleared, Hakuun saw that his enemy was gone. Destroyed to a smoking husk, he hoped, but only briefly, as another arrow came in at him from a different angle.

Again Jack answered with a blast of his own, followed by a series of stinging magical missiles that weaved through the trees to strike at the drow.

Dual voices invaded Hakuun's head, as Jack prepared another evocation and Hakuun cast a spell of healing upon himself. He had just finished mending the panther's fleshy tear when the stubborn drow hit him with another arrow.

He felt the magical wards flicker dangerously.

"Kill him!" Hakuun begged Jack, for he understood that one of those deadly arrows, maybe the very next one, was going to get through.

* * * * *

They had fought minor skirmishes, as anticipated, but nothing more, as word arrived along the line that Grguch and Obould had met in battle. Never one to play his hand fully, General Dukka moved his forces deliberately and with minimal risk. However things turned out, he intended to remain in power.

The Wolf Jaw orcs gave ground to Dukka's thousands, rolling down the channel on Obould's southern flank like floodwaters.

Always ready for a fight, Dukka stayed near the front, and so he was not far away when he heard a cry from the south, along the higher ridge, and when he heard the sound of battle to the northeast, and to the north, where he knew Obould to be. Lightning flashes filled the air up there, and Dukka could only imagine the carnage.

* * * * *

His arm ached and hung practically useless, and Bruenor understood that if he lost his momentum, he would meet a quick and unpleasant end. So he didn't relent. He drove on and on, slashing away with his many-notched axe, driving the oversized orc before him.

The orc could hardly keep up, and Bruenor scored minor hits, clipping him across one hand and nicking his thigh as he spun away.

The dwarf could win. He knew he could.

But the orc began calling out, and Bruenor understood enough Orcish to understand that he called for help. Not just orc help, either, the dwarf saw, as a pair of ogres moved over at the side of his vision, lifting heavy weapons.

Bruenor couldn't hope to win against all three. He thought to drive the orc leader back before him, then break off and head back the other way—perhaps Drizzt was finished with the troublesome wizard.

But the dwarf shook his head stubbornly. He had come to win against Obould, of course, until his dark-skinned friend had shown him another way. He had never expected to return to Mithral Hall, had guessed from the start that his reprieve from Moradin's halls had been temporary, and for a single purpose.

That purpose stood before him in the form of one of the largest and ugliest orcs he had ever had the displeasure to lay eyes on.

So Bruenor ignored the ogres and pressed his attack with even more fury. He would die, and so be it, but that bestial orc would fall before him.

His axe pounded with wild abandon, cracking against the blocking weapon of his opponent. He drew a deep line in one of the heads on Grguch's axe then nearly cracked through the weapon's handle when the orc brought it up horizontally to intercept a cut.

Bruenor had intended that cut to be the coup de grace, though, and he winced at the block, expecting that his time was over, that the ogres would finish him. He heard them off to the side, stalking in, growling . . . screaming.

Before him, the orc roared in protest, and Bruenor managed to glance back as he wound up for another strike.

One of the ogres had fallen away, its leg cleaved off at the hip. The other had turned away from Bruenor, to battle King Obould.

"Bah! Haha!" Bruenor howled at the absurdity of it all, and he brought his axe in at the same chopping downward angle, but more to his right, more to his opponent's left. The orc shifted appropriately and blocked, and Bruenor did it again, and again more to his right.

The orc decided to change the dynamics, and instead of just presenting the horizontal handle to block, he angled it down to his left. Since Bruenor was already leaning that way, there was no way for him to avoid the rightward slide.

The huge orc howled, advantage gained.

* * * * *

The orc had dispelled Guenhwyvar! From its back, claws and fangs digging at it, the orc had sent Drizzt's feline companion back to the Astral Plane.

At least, that's what the stunned drow prayed had happened, for when he had finished with the pair of orcs at the trees, he had come in sight just in time to watch his friend dissolve into smoky nothingness.

And that orc, so surprising, so unusual for one of the brutish race, had taken the hits of Drizzt's arrows, and had met his barrage with lightning-bolt retorts that had left Drizzt dazed and wounded.

Drizzt continued to circle, firing as he found opportunities between the trees. Every shot hit the mark, but every arrow was stopped just short, exploding into multicolored sparks.

And every arrow was met with a magical response, lightning and insidious magic missiles, from which Drizzt could not hide.

He went into the thickness of some evergreens, only to find other orcs already within. Bow in hand instead of his scimitars, and still dazed from the magical assaults, Drizzt had no intention of joining combat at that difficult moment, and so he cut to his right, back away from the magic-using orc, and ran out of the copse.

And just in time, for without regard to its orc comrades, the wizard dropped a fireball on those trees, a tremendous blast that instantly consumed the copse and everyone within.

Drizzt continued his run farther to the side before turning back at the orc. He dropped Taulmaril and drew forth his blades, and he thought of Guenhwyvar, and called out plaintively for his lost cat.

In sight of the wizard again, Drizzt dived behind a tree.

A lightning bolt split it down the middle before him, opening the ground to the orc wizard again, stealing Drizzt's protective wall, and so he ran on, to the side again.

"I won't run out of magic, foolish drow!" the orc called—and in High Drow, with perfect inflection!

That unnerved Drizzt almost as much as the magical barrage, but Drizzt accepted his role, and suspected that Bruenor was no less hard-pressed.

He swung out away from the orc wizard then veered around, finding a direct path to his enemy that would take him under a widespread maple and right beside another cluster of evergreens.

He roared and charged. He saw a tell-tale movement beside him, and grinned as he recognized it.

Drizzt reached inside himself as the wizard began casting, and summoned a globe of absolute darkness before him, between him and the mage.

Into the darkness went Drizzt. To his right, the evergreens rustled, as if he had cut fast and leaped out that way.

* * * * *

Dull pain and cold darkness filled Regis's head. He was far from consciousness, and sliding farther with every passing heartbeat. He knew not where he was, or what had put him there, in a deep and dark hole.

Somewhere, distantly, he felt a heavy thud against his back, and the jolt sent lines of searing pain into the halfling.

He groaned then simply let it all go.

The sensation of flying filled him, as if he had broken free of his mortal coil and was floating . . . floating.

* * * * *

"Not so clever, drow," Jack said through Hakuun's mouth as they both noted the movement in the limbs of the evergreens. A slight turn had the fiery pea released from Jack's spell lofting out that way, and an instant later, those evergreens exploded into flames, with, Jack and Hakuun both presumed, the troublesome drow inside.

But Drizzt had not gone out to his right. That had been Guenhwyvar, re-summoned from the Astral Plane by his call, heeding his quiet commands to serve her role as diversion. Guenhwyvar had gone across right behind Drizzt to leap into the evergreens, while Drizzt had tumbled headlong, gaining momentum, into the darkness.

In there, he had leaped straight up, finding the maple's lowest branch.

"Be gone, Guen," he whispered as he ran along that branch, feeling the heat of the flames to his side. "Please be gone," he begged as he came out of the blackness, bearing down on the wizard, who was still looking at the evergreens, still apparently oblivious to Drizzt.

The drow came off the branch in a leaping somersault, landing lightly in a roll before the orc, who nearly jumped out of his boots and threw his hands up defensively. As Drizzt came out of that roll, he sprang and rolled again, going right past the orc, right over the orc's shoulder as he turned back upright.

Anger drove him, memories of Innovindil. He told himself that he had solved the riddle, that that creature had been the cause.

Fury driving his arms, he slashed back behind him and down with Icingdeath as he landed, and felt the blade slash hard through the orc's leather tunic and bite deeply into flesh. Drizzt skidded to an abrupt stop and pirouetted, slashing hard with Twinkle, gashing the back-bending orc across the shoulder blades. Drizzt stepped back toward him, moving around him on the other side, and cut Twinkle down hard across the creature's exposed throat, driving it to the ground on its back.

He moved for the kill, but stopped short, realizing that he needn't bother. A growl from over by the burning pines showed him that Guenhwyvar hadn't heeded his call to be gone, but neither had the panther, so swift and clever, been caught in the blast.

Relief flooded through Drizzt, but with the diversion, he didn't take notice of a small winged snake slithering out of the dead orc's ear.

* * * * *

Bruenor's axe slid down hard to the side, and Bruenor stumbled that way. He saw the huge orc's face twist in glee, in the belief of victory.

But that was exactly the look he had hoped for.

For Bruenor was not stumbling, and had forced the angled block for that very reason, to disengage his axe quickly and down to the side, far to the right of his target. In his stumble, Bruenor was really just re-setting his stance, and he spun away from the orc, daring to turn his back on it for a brief moment.

In that spin, Bruenor sent his axe in a roundabout swing at the end of his arm, and the orc, readying a killing strike, could not redirect his heavy two-bladed axe in time.

Bruenor whirled around, his axe flying out wide to the right, setting himself in a widespread stance, ready to meet any attack.

None came, for his axe had torn the orc's belly as it had come around, and the creature crumbled backward, holding its heavy axe in its right hand, but clutching at its spilling entrails with its left.

Bruenor stalked forward and began battering it once more. The orc managed to block a blow, then a second, but the third slipped past and gashed its forearm, tearing its hand clear of its belly.

Guts spilled out. The orc howled and tried to back away.

But a flaming sword swept in over Bruenor's one-horned helmet and cut Grguch's misshapen head apart.

* * * * *

Guenhwyvar's roar saved him, for Drizzt glanced back at the last moment, and ducked aside just in time to avoid the brunt of the winged snake's murderous lightning strike. Still the bolt clipped the drow, and lifted him into the air, flipping him over more than a complete rotation, so that he landed hard on his side.

He bounced right back up, though, and the winged snake dropped to the ground and darted for the trees.

But the curved edge of a scimitar hooked under it and flipped it into the air, where Drizzt's other blade slashed against it.

Against it, but not through it, for a magical ward prevented the cut—though the force of the blade surely bent the serpent over it!

Undeterred, for that mystery within a mystery somehow confirmed to Drizzt his suspicions about Innovindil's fall, the drow growled and pushed on. Whether his guess was accurate or not hardly mattered, for

Drizzt transformed that rage into blinding, furious action. He flipped the serpent again, then went into a frenzy, slashing left, right, left, right, over and over again, holding the serpent aloft by the sheer speed and precision of his repeated hits. He didn't slow, he didn't breathe, he simply battered away with abandon.

The creature flapped its wings, and Drizzt scored a hit at last, cutting up and nearly severing one where it met the serpent's body.

Again the drow went into a fury, slashing back and forth, and he ended by turning one blade around the torn snake. He fell into a short run and turn behind that strike and used his scimitar to fling the snake out far.

In mid-air, the snake transformed, becoming a gnome as it hit the ground in a roll, turning as it came up and slamming its back hard against a tree.

Drizzt relaxed, convinced that the tree was the only thing holding the surprising creature upright.

"You summoned . . . the panther . . . back," the gnome said, his voice weak and fading.

Drizzt didn't reply.

"Brilliant diversion," the gnome congratulated.

A curious expression came over the diminutive creature, and it held up one trembling hand. Blood poured from out of his robe's voluminous sleeve, though it did not stain the material—material that showed not a tear from the drow's assault.

"Hmm," the gnome said, and looked down, and so did Drizzt, to see more blood pouring out from under the hem of the robe, pooling on the ground between the little fellow's boots.

"Good garment," the gnome noted. "Know you a mage worthy?"

Drizzt looked at him curiously.

Jack the Gnome shrugged. His left arm fell off then, sliding out of his garment, the tiny piece of remaining skin that attached it to his shoulder tearing free under the dead weight.

Jack looked at it, Drizzt looked at it, and they looked at each other again.

And Jack shrugged. And Jack fell face down. And Jack the Gnome was dead.

CHAPTER
GARUMN'S GORGE

Bruenor tried to stand straight, but the pain of his broken arm had him constantly twitching and lowering his left shoulder. Directly across from him, King Obould stared hard, the fingers of his hand kneading the hilt of his gigantic sword. Gradually that blade inched down toward the ground, and Obould dismissed its magical flames.

"Well, what of it, then?" Bruenor asked, feeling the eyes of orcs boring into him from all around.

Obould let his gaze sweep across the crowd, holding them all at bay. "You came to me," he reminded the dwarf.

"I heared ye wanted to talk, so I come to talk."

Obould's expression showed him to be less than convinced. He glanced up the hill, motioning to Nukkels the priest, the emissary, who had never made it near to Bruenor's court.

Bruenor, too, looked up at the battered shaman, and the dwarf's eyes widened indeed when Nukkels was joined by another orc, dressed in decorated military garb, who carried a bundle of great interest to Bruenor. The two orcs walked down to stand beside their king, and the second, General Dukka, dropped his cargo, a bloody and limp halfling, at Obould's feet.

All around them, the orcs stirred, expecting the fight to erupt anew.

But Obould silenced them with an upraised hand, as he looked Bruenor in the eye. Before him, Regis stirred, and Obould reached down and with surprising gentleness, lifted the halfling to his feet.

Regis could not stand on his own, though, his knees buckling. But Obould held him upright and motioned to Nukkels. Immediately, the shaman cast a spell of healing over the halfling, and though it only marginally helped, it was enough for Regis to stand at least. Obould pushed him toward Bruenor, but again, without any evident malice.

"Grguch is dead," Obould proclaimed to all around, ending as he locked stares with Bruenor. "Grguch's path is not the way."

Beside Obould, General Dukka stood firm and nodded, and Bruenor and Obould both understood that the orc king had all the support he needed, and more.

"What are you wantin', orc?" Bruenor asked, and he held his hand up as he finished, looking past Obould.

Many orcs turned, Obould, Dukka, and Nukkels included, to see Drizzt Do'Urden standing calmly, Taulmaril in hand, arrow resting at ease on its string, and with Guenhwyvar beside him.

"What are ye wanting?" Bruenor asked again as Obould turned back.

The dwarf already knew, of course, and the answer was one that filled him with both hope and dread.

Not that he was in any position to bargain.

* * * * *

"It won't make her more than a surcoat, elf," Bruenor said as Drizzt folded up the fabulous garment of Jack the Gnome, wrapping it over a few rings and other trinkets he had taken from the body.

"Give it to Rumblebelly," said Bruenor, and he propped Regis up a bit more, for the halfling leaned on him heavily.

"A wizard's . . . robe," the still-groggy Regis slurred. "Not for me."

"Not for me girl, neither," Bruenor declared.

But Drizzt only smiled and tucked the fairly won gains into his pack.

Somewhere in the east, fighting erupted again, a reminder to them all that not everything was settled quite yet, with remnants of Clan Karuck still to be rooted out. The distant battle sounds also reminded them that their friends were still out there, and though Obould, after conferring with Dukka, had assured them that four dwarves, an elf, and a drow had gone back over the southern ridge when Dukka's force had sent Wolf Jaw running, the relief of the companions showed clearly on their faces when they came in sight of the bedraggled, battered, and bloody sextet.

Cordio and Shingles ran to take Regis off of Bruenor's hands, while Pwent fell all over himself, hopping around Bruenor with unbridled glee.

"Thought ye was sure'n dead," Torgar said. "Thought we were suren dead, to boot. But them orcs held back and let us run south. I'm not for knowin' why."

Bruenor looked at Drizzt then at Torgar and the others. "Not sure that I'm knowin' why, meself," he said, and he shook his head helplessly, as if none of it made any sense to him. "Just get me home. Get us all home, and we'll figure it out."

It sounded good, of course, except that one of the group had no home to speak of, none in the area, at least. Drizzt stepped past Bruenor and the others and motioned for Tos'un and Hralien to join him off to the side.

Back with the others, Cordio tended to Bruenor's broken arm, which of course had Bruenor cursing him profusely, while Torgar and Shingles tried to figure out the best way to repair the king's broken shield, an artifact that could not be left in two pieces.

"Is it in your heart, or in your mind?" Drizzt asked his fellow drow when the three of them were far enough away.

"Your change, I mean," Drizzt explained when Tos'un did not immediately answer. "This new demeanor you wear, these possibilities you see before you—are they in your heart, or in your mind? Are they born of feelings, or is it pragmatism that guides your actions?"

"He was dismissed and running free," Hralien said. "Yet he came back to save me, perhaps to save us all."

Drizzt nodded his acceptance of that fact, but it didn't change his posture as he continued to stare at Tos'un.

"I do not know," Tos'un admitted. "I prefer the elves of the Moonwood to Obould's orcs. That much I can tell you. And I will not go against the Moonwood elves, on my word."

"The word of a drow," Drizzt remarked, and Hralien snorted at the absurdity of the statement, given the speaker.

Drizzt held his hand out, and motioned toward the sentient sword belted on Tos'un's hip. With only a moment's hesitation, Tos'un drew the blade and handed it over.

"I cannot allow him to keep it," Drizzt explained to Hralien.

"It is Catti-brie's sword," the elf agreed, but Drizzt shook his head.

"It is a corrupting, evil, sentient being," Drizzt said. "It will feed the doubts of Tos'un and play into his fears, hoping to incite him to spill blood." To Hralien's surprise, Drizzt handed it over to him. "Nor does Catti-brie wish it returned to Mithral Hall. Take it to the Moonwood, I beg, for your wizards and priests are better able to deal with such weapons."

"Tos'un will be there," Hralien warned, and he glanced at the wandering drow and nodded, and relief showed clearly on Tos'un's face.

"Perhaps your wizards and priests will be better able to discern the heart and mind of the dark elf, too," said Drizzt. "If trust is gained then return the sword to him. It is a choice beyond my judgment."

"Elf! Ye done jabberin'?" Bruenor called. "I'm wanting to go see me girl."

Drizzt looked to Hralien and Tos'un in turn. "Indeed," he offered. "Let us all go home."

* * * * *

The wind howled out its singular, mournful note, a constant blow that sounded to Wulfgar of home.

He stood on the northeastern slopes of Kelvin's Cairn, not far below the remnants of the high ridge once known as Bruenor's Climb, looking out over the vast tundra, where the snows had receded once more.

Slanting light crossed the flat ground, the last rays of day sparkling in the many puddles dotting the landscape.

Wulfgar stayed there, unmoving, as the last lights faded, as the stars began to twinkle overhead, and his heart leaped again when a distant campfire appeared out in the north.

His people.

His heart was full. This was his place, his home, the land where he would build his legacy. He would assume his rightful place among the Tribe of the Elk, would take a wife and live as his father, his grandfather, and all of his ancestors had lived. The simplicity of it, the lack of the deceitful trappings of civilization, welcomed him, heart and soul.

His heart was full.

The son of Beornegar had come home.

*****

The dwarven hall in the great chamber known as Garumn's Gorge, with its gently arcing stone bridge and the new statue of Shimmergloom the shadow dragon, ridden to the bottom of the gorge to its death by heroic King Bruenor, had never looked so wondrous. Torches burned throughout the hall, lining the gorge and the bridge, their firelight changing through the spectrum of colors due to the enchantments of Lady Alustriel's wizards.

On the western side of the gorge before the bridge stood hundreds of Battlehammer dwarves, all dressed in their full, shining armor, pennants flying, spear tips gleaming in the magical light. Across from them stood a contingent of orc warriors, not nearly as well-outfitted, but standing with equal discipline and pride.

Dwarf masons had constructed a platform at the center of the long bridge, and on it had built a three-tiered fountain. Nanfoodle's alchemy and Alustriel's wizards had done their work there, as well, for the water danced to the sound of haunting music, its flowing streams glowing brightly and changing colors.

Before the fountain, on a mosaic of intricate tiles fashioned to herald that very day, stood a mithral podium, and on it rested a pile of identical parchments, pinned by weights sculpted into the form of a dwarf, an elf, a human, and an orc. The bottom paper of that pile had been sealed atop the podium, to remain there throughout the coming decades.

Bruenor stepped out from his line and walked the ten strides to the podium. He looked back to his friends and kin, to Banak in his chair, sitting impassive and unconvinced, but unwilling to argue with Bruenor's decision. He matched stares with Regis, who solemnly nodded, as did Cordio. Beside the priest, Thibbledorf Pwent was too distracted to return Bruenor's look. The battle-rager, as clean as anyone in the hall had ever seen him, swiveled his head around, sizing up any threats that might materialize from the strange gathering—or maybe, Bruenor thought with a grin, looking for Alustriel's dwarf friend, Fret, who had forced a bath upon Pwent.

To the side lay Guenhwyvar, majestic and eternal, and beside her stood Drizzt, calm and smiling, his mithral shirt, his belted weapons, and Taulmaril over his shoulder, reminding Bruenor that no dwarf had ever known a better champion. In looking at him, Bruenor was amazed yet again at how much he had come to love and trust that dark elf.

Just as much, Bruenor knew, as his gaze slipped past Drizzt to Catti-brie, his beloved daughter, Drizzt's wife. Never had she looked as beautiful to Bruenor as she did just then, never more sure of herself and comfortable in her place. She wore her auburn hair up high on one side, hanging loosely on the other, and it caught the light of the fountain, reflected off the rich, silken colors of her blouse, the garment of the gnome wizard. It had been a full robe on the gnome, of course, but it reached only to mid-thigh on Catti-brie, and while the sleeves had nearly covered the gnome's hands, they flared halfway down Catti-brie's delicate forearms. She wore a dark blue dress under the blouse, a gift from Lady Alustriel, her new tutor—working through Nanfoodle—that reached to her knees and matched exactly the blue trim of her blouse. High boots of black leather completed the outfit, and seemed so appropriate for Catti-brie, as they were both delicate and sturdy all at once.

Bruenor chuckled, recalling so many images of Catti-brie covered in dirt and in the blood of her enemies, dressed in simple breeches and tunic, and fighting in the mud. Those times were gone, he knew, and he thought of Wulfgar.

So much had changed.

Bruenor looked back to the podium and the treaty, and the extent of the change weakened his knees beneath him.

Along the southern rim of the center platform stood the other dignitaries: Lady Alustriel of Silverymoon, Galen Firth of Nesmé, King Emerus Warcrown of Citadel Felbarr—looking none too pleased, but accepting King Bruenor's decision—and Hralien of the Moonwood. More would join in, it was said, including the great human city of Sundabar and the largest of the dwarven cities in the region, Citadel Adbar.

If it held.

That thought made Bruenor look across the podium to the other principal, and he could not believe that he had allowed King Obould Many-Arrows to enter Mithral Hall. Yet there stood the orc, in all his terrible splendor, with his black armor, ridged and spiked, and his mighty greatsword strapped diagonally across his back.

Together they walked to opposite sides of the podium. Together they lifted their respective quills.

Obould leaned forward, but even though he was a foot and a half taller, his posture did not diminish the splendor and strength of King Bruenor Battlehammer.

"If ye're e'er to deceive . . ." Bruenor started to whisper, but he shook his head and let the thought drift away.

"It is no less bitter for me," Obould assured him.

And still they signed. For the good of their respective peoples, they put their names to the Treaty of Garumn's Gorge, recognizing the Kingdom of Many-Arrows and forever changing the face of the Silver Marches.

Calls went out from the gorge, and horns blew along the tunnels of Mithral Hall. And there came a greater blast, a rumble and resonance that vibrated through the stones of the hall and beyond, as the great horn once known as *Kokto Gung Karuck,* a gift from Obould to Bruenor, sounded from its new perch on the high lookout post above Mithral Hall's eastern door.

The world had changed, Bruenor knew.

EPILOGUE

"How different might the world now be if King Bruenor had not chosen such a course with the first Obould Many-Arrows," Hralien asked Drizzt. "Better, or worse?"

"Who can know?" the drow replied. "But at that time, a war between Obould's thousands and the gathered armies of the Silver Marches would have changed the region profoundly. How many of Bruenor's people would have died? How many of your own, who now flourish in the Glimmerwood in relative peace? And in the end, my friend, we do not know who would have prevailed."

"And yet here we stand, a century beyond that ceremony, and can either of us say with absolute truth that Bruenor chose correctly?"

He was right, Drizzt knew, to his ultimate frustration. He reminded himself of the roads he had walked over the last decades, of the ruins he had seen, of the devastation of the Spellplague. But in the North, instead of that, because of a brave dwarf named Bruenor Battle-hammer, who threw off his baser instincts, his hatred and his hunger for revenge, in light of what he believed to be the greater good, the region had known a century and more of relative peace. More peace than ever it had known before. And that while the world around had fallen to shadow and despair.

Hralien started away, but Drizzt called after him.

"We both supported Bruenor on that day when he signed the Treaty of Garumn's Gorge," he reminded. Hralien nodded as he turned.

"As we both fought alongside Bruenor on the day he chose to stand beside Obould against Grguch and the old ways of Gruumsh," Drizzt added. "If I recall that day correctly, a younger Hralien was so taken by the moment that he chose to place his trust in a dark elf, though that same drow had marched to war against Hralien's people only months before."

Hralien laughed and held up his hands in surrender.

"And what resulted from that trust?" Drizzt asked. "How fares Tos'un Armgo, husband of Sinnafain, father of Teirflin and Doum'wielle?"

"I will ask him when I return to the Moonwood," the beaten Hralien replied, but he managed to get in the last arrow when he directed Drizzt's gaze to the prisoners they had taken that day.

Drizzt conceded the point with a polite nod. It wasn't over. It wasn't decided. The world rolled on around him, the sand shifted under his feet.

He reached down to pet Guenhwyvar, needing to feel the comfort of his panther friend, the one constant in his surprising life, the one great hope along his ever-winding road.

PRAISE FOR *EMERGING*

"Engaging students and helping them see the relevance between what they read in class and what they experience in society is critical for effective learning. The selections are fresh and original, and I think that my students would enjoy reading them."
— Barbara B. Booker, *Pasco-Hernando Community College*

"This innovative book prepares students for the complex task of critical thinking in the modern world."
— Roberta Stagnaro, *San Diego State University*

"*Emerging* asks students to engage with a number of recent concerns raised in the public sphere. Its contribution is unique in that it asks students to use the tools they are learning in the university — critical thinking, close reading, and lucid writing — to construct intelligent, articulate arguments that might be of interest to a broader literate public 'beyond' the university."
— John Champagne, *Penn State Erie, The Behrend College*

"This is an exciting collection of readings and writing sequences that I think students would really sink their academic teeth into!"
— Sonja L. Andrus, *Collin College*

"*Emerging* brings together a series of lively, complex thinkers whose multidisciplinary approaches to global problem-solving serve as models for the types of inquiry, evaluation, and synthesis that we want to inculcate in first-year students. The sequences and assignments ask students to draw meaningful connections among their own writing, the larger discourse within the academy, and the international marketplace of ideas."
— Gina Maranto, *University of Miami*

tradition religion community identity culture family death kins

change loss globalization ethics social terrorism international policy mora

knowledge responsibility human dignity biotechnology civil rights diplom

conversation technology surrogates art performance aesthe

boundaries creativity censorship diversity integration education cosmopolitan

supply chains ethnic conflict collaboration economics politics multitask

body objectification research adoption media makeovers melting pot rac

ethnicity descent faith groups Wikipedia collaborative holons r

About this book

Your students are themselves emerging as thinkers and writers. The readings and assignments in *Emerging* are designed to introduce important issues and thinkers in a way that helps students understand how to work with them. In so doing, your students will gain the critical reading, thinking, and writing skills that will help them succeed.

The selections and assignment sequences in *Emerging* include descriptive "tags" such as those on this page to highlight key concepts and show connections.

personal individu

assignments expl

role play politi

exploring relationsh

introduction sequen

examine help identi

consider quinceañe

self-identity analy

national turn diffic

rite final idea

determine families assignment paper community write argument expl

question context concepts cultural critical thinking questio

self-identity passage similar different essay shaping work read

effect definition concerned author ethical global world order problems a

authors working essays tools locally develop extend consider

create drawing limits discussion primacy achieving HIV/AIDS preventi

individuals practices response mitigate propose strategies technologi

science scientific group concerns conversations system genetics econor

EMERGING

CONTEMPORARY READINGS FOR WRITERS

EMERGING

CONTEMPORARY READINGS FOR WRITERS

BARCLAY BARRIOS
Florida Atlantic University

BEDFORD/ST. MARTIN'S
Boston ◆ New York

For Bedford/St. Martin's

Senior Executive Editor: Leasa Burton
Executive Editor: John E. Sullivan III
Production Editor: Kendra LeFleur
Production Supervisor: Jennifer Peterson
Marketing Manager: Molly Parke
Editorial Assistant: Alicia Young
Copyeditor: Arthur Johnson
Senior Art Director: Anna Palchik
Text Design: Henry Rachlin
Cover Design: Sara Gates
Cover Art: Stefana McClure, *Map of the World*, 2005–06. Josée Bienvenu Gallery.
Composition: MPS Limited, A Macmillan Company
Printing and Binding: Haddon Craftsmen, Inc., an RR Donnelley & Sons Company

President: Joan E. Feinberg
Editorial Director: Denise B. Wydra
Editor in Chief: Karen S. Henry
Director of Marketing: Karen R. Soeltz
Director of Editing, Design, and Production: Marcia Cohen
Assistant Director of Editing, Design, and Production: Elise S. Kaiser
Managing Editor: Elizabeth M. Schaaf

Library of Congress Control Number: 2009934716

Manufactured in the United States of America.

5   4   3   2   1   0
f   e   d   c   b   a

For information, write: Bedford/St. Martin's, 75 Arlington Street, Boston, MA 02116 (617-399-4000)

ISBN-10: 0–312–47444–X
ISBN-13: 978–0–312–47444–7

Acknowledgments

Madeleine Albright, "Faith and Diplomacy." Chap. 5 from *The Mighty and the Almighty: Reflections on America, God, and World Affairs* by Madeleine Albright, pp. 65–78. Copyright © 2006 by Madeleine Albright. Reprinted by permission of HarperCollins Publishers.

Acknowledgments and copyrights are continued at the back of the book on pages 515–17, which constitute an extension of the copyright page. It is a violation of the law to reproduce these selections by any means whatsoever without the written permission of the copyright holder.

PREFACE FOR INSTRUCTORS

Emerging/Thinking

One of the fundamental facts of teaching writing is that when students leave our classrooms, they go back to their increasingly busy lives: They go to other classes, go to their jobs after school, go hang out with friends, go into their disciplines, go into their careers, go into the world. The challenge for us as instructors is to help students acquire the skills of critical reading, thinking, and writing that will allow them to succeed in these diverse contexts.

Emerging seeks to address this challenge. It offers sustained readings that present complex ideas in approachable language; it encourages critical thinking and writing skills by prompting students to make connections among readings; it draws from a broad cross section of disciplines in order to present students with numerous points of entry and identification; and it introduces emerging problems — such as globalization (in both its economic and its political dimensions), the impact of technology (from Wikipedia to brain science), and the dilemmas of ethics (including genetic engineering and the relations between religion and foreign politics) — that students, as agents in the public sphere, will be asked to address. More enduring issues are broached in this collection as well, such as concerns about aesthetics, community, race, and death.

The readings are organized alphabetically to showcase them and open up possibilities for connections. Because they consist of entire book chapters or complete articles, readings can stand on their own as originally intended. However, the readings in *Emerging* were chosen because they connect to each other in interesting and illuminating ways. The issues under discussion resonate across readings, prompting students to think about each selection in multiple dimensions. These resonant connections are shown through *tags*. About a half-dozen tags for each piece are listed in the table of contents, in each headnote, and for each assignment sequence — highlighting concepts such as *community, diversity, identity, culture,* and *technology*. The readings' central concepts are most prominent in the tags, with larger and darker type. Thus one can see at a glance the thematic connections among the readings and assignment sequences as well as the degree of those connections. Connections are also highlighted through the assignment sequences included at the back of the book (see p. 491). The assignment sequences suggest a succession of readings that are linked conceptually so that one assignment sequence provides the structure for an entire semester. (Sequences are further explained below.)

Emerging/Reading

Because students ultimately enter diverse disciplines, the readings are drawn from across fields of knowledge located both inside and outside the academy. Political science, sociology, anthropology, economics, and art are some of the disciplines one might expect to find in such a collection, but *Emerging* also includes readings from diplomacy, public health, psychology, business, technology, and law. The author of each selection addresses his or her concerns to an audience outside the discipline — a useful model for students who eventually will need to communicate beyond the boundaries of their chosen fields. Many of the readings also represent cross-disciplinary work — an economist thinking about politics, an anthropologist thinking about education — since the walls between departments in academia are becoming increasingly permeable.

Yet despite this disciplinary grounding, the readings, though challenging, are accessible, written as they are with a general, informed, and educated audience in mind. The readings thus demonstrate multiple ways in which complex ideas and issues can be presented in formal yet approachable language. The accessible nature of the essays also allows for readings longer than those typically seen in first-year composition anthologies, because the level of writing makes them comprehensible to students. Their length, moreover, means that these readings are substantive, providing greater opportunities for nuanced arguments — both in the readings themselves and in the writing students will in turn produce about them. Each essay serves as an opportunity for students to join important contemporary conversations.

Of course, in addition to referencing emerging issues, the title of this collection refers also to the students in first-year composition courses who themselves are emerging as readers, thinkers, and writers. By providing them with challenging texts along with the tools needed to decode, interpret, and deploy those texts, *Emerging* helps college readers to develop the skills they will need as they move into working with the difficult theoretical texts presented in their choice of majors — and ultimately into their twenty-first-century careers.

Beyond simply indexing developing sociocultural concerns, the title of the collection further refers directly to the concept of *emergence*. An idea taken from chaos/complexity theory, emergence pertains to the intricate and related patterns that materialize spontaneously from the interactions among independent, adaptive agents. In a famous example, emergence explains how a butterfly flapping its wings in China can cause a tornado in Texas; the concept also explains how individual neurons operating in the brain can produce consciousness. Though technically a branch of mathematics, complexity theory has been applied to multiple fields and phenomena, from economics to the Web. Indeed, it is present, implicitly or explicitly, in many of the readings gathered here.

Emerging/Writing

One of the philosophical tenets supporting *Emerging* is that students need to be prepared to deal with emerging issues in their jobs and lives, and to do so, they not only require information about those issues (since such information will continually change) but also must possess an ability to think critically in relation to them. The editorial apparatus in *Emerging* includes the following features that will help students develop the skills needed to become fluid, reflective, and critically self-aware writers:

▶ **General Introduction.** The introduction presents six key skills of academic success and global citizenship: the ability to read critically, think critically, synthesize, argue, support, and revise.

▶ **Assignment Sequences.** In order to stress the iterative processes of thinking and writing, ten assignment sequences are included in the back of the book, each of which uses multiple selections to engage students' thinking about a central theme, issue, or problem. Each sequence frames a project extensive enough for an entire semester's work and can be easily adapted for individual classes.

Additionally, apparatus accompanying each reading provides substantial help for students while featuring innovative approaches to understanding the essays and their relation to the world outside the classroom:

▶ **Headnotes.** A headnote before each reading selection provides biographical information about the author and describes the context of the larger work from which the reading has been taken.

▶ **Questions for Critical Reading.** These questions at the end of each reading direct students to central concepts, issues, and ideas from the essay in order to prompt a directed rereading of the text while providing a guide for the student's own interpretive moves.

▶ **Exploring Context.** In order to leverage students' existing literacies with digital technologies, these questions ask students to use the Web and other electronic sources to contextualize each reading further. Besides sites that might be familiar to students, such as Facebook or Wikipedia, these questions also feature emerging tools such as Twitter and Digg.

▶ **Questions for Connecting.** Because thinking across essays provides particular circumstances for critical thinking, these opportunities for writing ask students to make connections between essays and to apply and synthesize authors' ideas.

▶ **Language Matters.** The Language Matters questions are a unique feature of this reader. These questions address issues of grammar and writing through the context of the essays, presenting language not as a set of rules to be memorized but as a system of meaning-making that can also be used as a tool for analysis.

▶ **Assignments for Writing.** Each reading has three Assignments for Writing questions that ask students to build on the work they've done in the other questions of the apparatus and create a piece of writing with a sustained argument supported by textual engagement.

You Get More Choices with *Emerging*

Emerging doesn't stop with this book. Online, you'll find both free and affordable premium resources to help students get even more out of the book and your course. You'll also find convenient instructor resources, such as download-able sample syllabi, classroom activities, and even a nationwide community of teachers. To learn more about or order any of the products below, contact your Bedford/St. Martin's sales representative, e-mail sales support (sales_support@bfwpub.com), or visit the Web site at bedfordstmartins.com/emerging/catalog.

Student Resources

Send students to free and open resources, upgrade to an expanding collection of innovative digital content, or package a stand-alone CD-ROM for free with *Emerging*.

Re:Writing, the best free collection of online resources for the writing class, offers clear advice on citing sources in *Research and Documentation Online* by Diana Hacker, thirty sample papers and designed documents, and over nine thousand writing and grammar exercises, with immediate feedback and report-ing, in *Exercise Central*. Updated and redesigned, *Re:Writing* also features five free videos from *VideoCentral* and five new tutorials on visual analysis from our popu-lar *ix visual exercises* by Cheryl Ball and Kristin Arola. *Re:Writing* is completely free and open (no codes required) to ensure access to all students.

VideoCentral is a growing collection of videos for the writing class that captures real-world, academic, and student writers talking about how and why they write. Writer and teacher Peter Berkow interviewed hundreds of people — from Michael Moore to Cynthia Selfe — to produce fifty brief videos about topics such as revising and getting feedback. *VideoCentral* can be pack-aged with *Emerging* at a significant discount. An activation code is required. To order *VideoCentral* packaged with the print book, use ISBN-10: 0–312–64258–X or ISBN-13: 978–0–312–64258–7.

Re:Writing Plus gathers all of Bedford/St. Martin's premium digital content for composition into one online collection. It includes hundreds of model docu-ments, the first-ever peer review game, and *VideoCentral*. *Re:Writing Plus* can be purchased separately or packaged with the print book at a significant discount. An activation code is required. To order *Re:Writing Plus* packaged with the print book, use ISBN-10: 0–312–62463–8 or ISBN-13: 978–0–312–62463–7.

i-series on CD-ROM presents multimedia tutorials in a flexible CD-ROM format — because there are things you can't do in a book.

- **ix visual exercises** help students visualize and put into practice key rhetorical and visual concepts. To order *ix visual exercises* packaged with the print book, use ISBN-10: 0–312–62462–X or ISBN-13: 978–0–312–62462–0.

- **i·claim visualizing argument** offers a new way to see argument and includes six tutorials, an illustrated glossary, and over seventy multimedia arguments. To order *i·claim visualizing argument* packaged with the print book, use ISBN-10: 0–312–62453–0 or ISBN-13: 978–0–312–62453–8.

- **i·cite visualizing sources** brings research to life through an animated introduction, four tutorials, and hands-on source practice. To order *i·cite visualizing sources* packaged with the print book, use ISBN-10: 0–312–62452–2 or ISBN-13: 978–0–312–62452–1.

Instructor Resources

You have a lot to do in your course. Bedford/St. Martin's wants to make it easy for you to find the support you need and to get it quickly.

The ***Resources for Teaching Emerging*** is available in PDF files that can be downloaded from the Bedford/St. Martin's online catalog. In addition to chapter overviews and teaching tips, the Instructor's Manual includes sample syllabi, correlations to the Council of Writing Program Administrators' Outcomes Statement, and suggestions for classroom activities.

TeachingCentral offers the entire list of Bedford/St. Martin's print and online professional resources in one place. You'll find landmark reference works, sourcebooks on pedagogical issues, award-winning collections, and practical advice for the classroom—all free for instructors.

Bits collects creative ideas for teaching a range of composition topics in an easily searchable blog. A community of teachers—leading scholars, authors, and editors—discuss revision, research, grammar and style, technology, peer review, and much more. Take, use, adapt, and share the ideas. Then come back to the site to comment or to contribute your own suggestions.

Content cartridges for the most common course management systems—Blackboard, WebCT, Angel, and Desire2Learn—allow you to easily download Bedford/St. Martin's digital materials for your course.

Acknowledgments

This collection itself has been a long time emerging, and I would be remiss not to thank the many people who contributed their time, energy, feedback, and support throughout the course of this project.

I would first like to acknowledge past and current colleagues who have played a role in developing this text. Richard E. Miller and Kurt Spellmeyer, both of Rutgers University, through their mentorship and guidance laid the foundations for my approach to composition as reflected in this reader. My department chairs during my time here at Florida Atlantic University, Andrew Furman and Wenying Xu, provided reassurance and support as I balanced the work of this text and the work of serving as Director of Writing Programs. The members of the Writing Committee for Florida Atlantic University's Department of English—Jeff Galin, Joanne Jasin, Jennifer Low, Julia Mason, Daniel Murtaugh, and Magdalena Ostas—generously allowed me to shape both this reader and the writing program. The Dean's office of the Dorothy F. Schmidt College of Arts and Letters of Florida Atlantic University provided a Summer Teaching Development Award, which aided in the creation of the materials that form the core of the Instructor's Manual.

All the teachers in the writing program at Florida Atlantic University had a role to play in this text by teaching possible selections and offering feedback on what did or did not work in the classroom; I regret I cannot list them all. Some of these teachers deserve special mention, including Amy Letter and Brian Spears, who offered suggestions on readings as well as friendship and dinners, and those teachers who crafted assignments and sequences included in this edition, specifically Jennifer Brachfeld, Michael Buso, Skye Cervone, Daniel Creed, Ryan Dessler, Valorie Ebert, Margaret Feeley, Elizabeth Kelly, Gloria Panzera, Tracy Stone, Courtney Watson, and Scott Wood.

This project could not possibly have been completed without the relentless help of my assistant Alison Amato, who scanned essays into electronic format, edited and composed headnotes and assignments, handled all the details that threatened to overwhelm me, and kept me laughing all the while. Also deserving special mention: Paul Ardoin who brilliantly crafted much of the headnotes, Mike Shier who lifted my spirits and lent a keen eye to the manuscript proofs, and Mellissa Carr and Adam Berzak who helped proofread the manuscript.

I am grateful to the reviewers who examined the manuscript and provided valuable feedback: Sonja Andrus, Collin County Community College; Susan Bailor, Front Range Community College; Barbara Booker, Pasco-Hernando Community College; John Champagne, Penn State Erie, The Behrend College; Michael Cripps, York College/CUNY; Brock Dethier, Utah State University; Kimberly Harrison, Florida International University; Karen Head, the Georgia Institute of Technology; Virginia Scott Hendrickson, Missouri State University; Lindsay Lewan, Arapahoe Community College; April Lewandowski, Front Range Community College–Westminster; Gina Maranto, University of Miami; Erica Messenger, Bowling Green State University–Main Campus; Beverly Neiderman, Kent State University; Jill Onega, Calhoun Community College; Roberta Stagnaro, San Diego State University; Melora G. Vandersluis, Azusa Pacific University; and Patricia Webb Boyd, Arizona State University.

I cannot say enough about the support I have received from Bedford/St. Martin's. Joan Feinberg's enthusiasm for this project was always appreciated. Leasa Burton's ability to handle all the small details was essential. And my editor John Sullivan patiently pushed me to make the best book possible and provided vital encouragement whenever my spirits drooped. Thanks, too, to Alicia Young, for getting to me what I needed when I needed it. I am grateful to Sandy Schechter and Barbara Rodriguez for clearing text permissions and to Martha Friedman and Constance Gardner for obtaining art permissions. Kendra LeFleur expertly guided the manuscript through production, assisted by copyeditor Arthur Johnson. I appreciate their help.

Finally, a special thanks to those who kept me centered and strong, including Chris Larkin and Brian Ouellette but above all my partner Joseph Tocio, who offered not only love and support but a compelling reason to be in Boston so that I could meet with the publisher.

CONTENTS

THE READINGS

A former secretary of state argues, "The challenge for policy-makers is to harness the unifying potential of faith, while containing its capacity to divide."

▶ TAGS: *faith*, *diversity*, *conflict*, *religion*, *community*, *diplomacy*

A novelist examines a coming-of-age cultural ritual and asserts, "The quinceañera is like a rehearsal wedding without a groom, and it sends a clear message to the Latina girl: we expect you to get married, have children, devote yourself to your family."

▶ TAGS: *tradition*, *rites*, *identity*, *culture*, *gender*, *race*

A prominent philosopher argues, "In the wake of 9/11, there has been a lot of fretful discussion about the divide between 'us' and 'them.' What's often taken for granted is a picture of a world in which conflicts arise, ultimately, from conflicts between values. This is what we take to be good; that is what they take to be good. That picture of the world has deep philosophical roots; it is thoughtful, well worked out, plausible. And, I think, wrong."

▶ TAGS: *human dignity*, *community*, *globalization*, *identity*, *conversation*, *obligation*

The spiritual leader of the Tibetan people and winner of the Nobel Peace Prize cautions, "If we examine the philosophical basis underlying much of human ethics, a clear recognition of the principle that correlates greater knowledge and power with a greater need for moral responsibility serves as a key foundation. Until recently we could say that this principle had been highly effective."

▶ TAGS: *research*, *social changes*, *biotechnology*, *human dignity*, *ethics*

A noted essayist and novelist writes, "Nine months and five days ago, at approximately nine o'clock on the evening of December 30, 2003, my husband, John Gregory Dunne, appeared to (or did) experience, at the table where he and I had just sat down to dinner in the living room of our apartment in New York, a sudden massive coronary event that caused his death."

▶ TAGS: *loss*, *mourning*, *kinship*, *language*, *death*, *change*

A biologist and expert in public health examines a new approach to preventing AIDS: "LoveLife's media campaign . . . was positive and cheerful, and resembled the bright, persuasive modern ad campaigns that many South African kids were very much attracted to."

▶ TAGS: *community*, *research*, *conversation*, *technology*, *social change*, *media*

A Pulitzer Prize–winning journalist advances a novel geopolitical theory: "No two countries that are both part of a major global supply chain, like Dell's, will ever fight a war against each other as long as they are both part of the same global supply chain."

▶ TAGS: *politics*, *globalization*, *economics*, *knowledge*, *supply chains*, *collaboration*

A prominent political scientist says, "What the demand for equality of recognition implies is that when we strip all of a person's contingent and accidental characteristics away, there remains some essential human quality underneath that is worthy of a certain minimal level of respect — call it Factor X."

▶ TAGS: *civil rights*, *morality*, *human dignity*, *biotechnology*, *ethics*

much more fluid and ambiguous — something more like the social structures that have emerged in Hawaii as intermarriage has accelerated."

▶ TAGS: *research*, *race*, *community*, *diplomacy*, *diversity*, *ethnicity*, *bioethics*, *integration* alteration. One consequence of this change is that we face constant challenges to our ability to focus our attention."

▶ TAGS: *education*, *feedback*, **technology**, *creativity*, **multitasking**

A science writer says, "It is an unfortunate given of human trauma research that the things most likely to accidentally maim or kill people—things we most need to study and understand—are also the things most likely to mutilate research cadavers: car crashes, gunshots, explosions, sporting accidents. There is no need to use cadavers to study stapler injuries."

▶ TAGS: *research*, surrogates, *death*, **ethics**, *morality*

A noted advertising critic claims that "language experts know that America's language wouldn't be what it is—and certainly wouldn't pop as much—without black English."

▶ TAGS: *conversation*, *diversity*, **race**, media, *culture*, **language**, collaboration, *creativity*

An evolutionary and developmental biologist writes, "I would argue that the major reason that plastic surgeries, gastric bypasses, and sex reassignments are all given similar sensationalistic treatments is because the subjects cross what is normally considered an impenetrable class boundary: from unattractive to beautiful, from fat to thin, and in the case of transsexuals, from male to female, or from female to male."

▶ TAGS: *technology*, **gender**, objectification, *research*, **class**, *human dignity*

An expert in global commerce writes, "On one side are those who see adoption as a purely social interaction: It is about building families and rescuing children and assuaging the pain of missing people. . . . From the other side, however, adoption is not only a market but indeed a market of the worst possible sort. It is a market that sells innocent children, putting a price on their heads without any concern for their well-being or for the toll imposed by being treated as trade."

▶ TAGS: *community*, **family**, *culture*, supply chains, *human dignity*, **ethics**, *morality*

ASSIGNMENT SEQUENCES

Assignments

Life is filled with rites of passage—attending college, for example. Many such rites—as is the case with the quinceañera—are located at the intersection of the personal and the social, the individual and the community. These assignments explore the role that such rites play in the political sphere by exploring their relationship to rights.

▶ TAGS: *kinship*, *family*, *change*, *tradition*, *loss*, *religion*, *community*, *mourning*, *culture*, *death*, *identity*

Surviving Alone, Surviving Together: Ethical Conflict in a Global Economy

KWAME ANTHONY APPIAH, Making Conversation *and* The Primacy of Practice • **HELEN EPSTEIN,** AIDS, Inc • **THOMAS FRIEDMAN,** The Dell Theory of Conflict Prevention • **DEBORA L. SPAR,** Trading Places: The Practice and Politics of Adoption

Assignments

Living in a globalized world doesn't mean we all have to get along; it does mean, however, that we must learn how to mediate cultural differences in order to solve the problems we face in common with others. This sequence of assignments examines authors' writing and thinking about an array of global problems. The essays and assignments suggest tools and concepts needed to advocate for change not only globally but locally as well.

▶ TAGS: *international policy*, *globalization*, *ethics*, *terrorism*, *community*, *social change*

We tend to think of science as the neutral search for truth, but as the readings in this sequence make clear, scientific endeavors are enmeshed in political and ethical concerns. This sequence explores the relationship between science and politics in order to foster conversations about the ethics of a broad spectrum of scientific and technological research.

▶ TAGS: *diplomacy*, *morality*, *biotechnology*, *knowledge and responsibility*, *human dignity*, *ethics*, *civil rights*

Psychotherapy is called the "talking cure" since it allows people to talk through and resolve their inner conflicts with the help of a trained professional. But can conversation function more generally as a kind of social medicine? Can talking about things make them better? The authors in this sequence all explore the value of conversation in a variety of contexts. These assignments explore the potential for spoken exchanges to create personal and social change.

▶ TAGS: *conversation*, *social change*, *technology*, *surrogates*

We often think of art as rarefied and separated from our lives—that which hangs on a wall in a museum. But this sequence asks us to think about the ways in which art, performance, and aesthetics have very real effects on our lives and on culture. These effects force us to ask questions about the limits of creative expression, the rights of individuals and of communities in relation to art, and the future of aesthetics itself.

▶ TAGS: *culture, art, performance, aesthetic boundaries, censorship, creativity, technology*

What role does diversity play in forming a community? This sequence explores the answer to that question by looking at diversity on college campuses and across the globe. It also considers the risks of diversity and the possibilities of community in the present and the future.

▶ TAGS: *research, body, economics, media, adoption, objectification, makeovers*

The United States is often described as a "melting pot," a country in which different ethnicities, cultures, and other social identities are united into a diverse but cohesive whole. But differences may instead lead to tensions in society, blocking any true community. This sequence explores the possibility and reality of a melting pot society.

▶ TAGS: *melting pot, diversity, religion, faith, diplomacy, community of descent, ethnicity, race, education*

What makes collaboration so powerful? This sequence examines the potential and dangers of collaboration, from small group efforts to Wikipedia to global supply chains. But it also considers the role of the individual in these collaborative processes, using an examination of organic farming to understand the relationship between individuals and the group, or parts and the whole.

▶ TAGS: *holons*, *technology*, *groups*, *Wikipedia*, *knowledge*, *collaboration*, *supply chains*

EMERGING

CONTEMPORARY READINGS FOR WRITERS

INTRODUCTION
THINKING GLOBALLY, READING CRITICALLY

IN SOME CLASSES, such as biology, sociology, economics, or chemistry, what you learn and what you're tested on is content—a knowledge of terms and concepts. In contrast, what you need to learn in a composition class is a *process*—a process of reading and writing that you will practice with the essays of this book, in class discussions, and by responding to essay assignments. This class is not just about the readings in this book but also about what you can do with them. What you will do with them, of course, is write. And yet it's not entirely accurate to say you're here to learn how to write, either. After all, you already did a lot of writing in high school, and if you couldn't write you couldn't have gotten into college. But you will learn a particular *kind* of writing in this class, one which may be new to you: academic writing—researching, weighing, and incorporating what others say into your own work. It is the type of writing you'll be expected to do throughout your college career. The skills you learn in this class will also help you throughout your life. That's because academic writing involves critical thinking, and critical thinking is an essential skill no matter what career you choose. Thriving in a career—any career—is never about how much you know but about what you can do with the knowledge you have. College will prepare you for your career by providing you with knowledge (your job here is part memorization), but college will also help you learn how to evaluate knowledge, how to apply it, and how to create it; those are the skills of critical thinking.

The readings gathered here were all chosen to provide you fertile ground in which to practice critical thinking through academic writing. Each is a chapter from a current book, usually written by an expert in a particular field communicating to people outside that field. These readings are effective in a writing course because each contains a complex argument, which is why the readings might feel long and therefore why they might seem "hard" to you. You'll notice, though, that it's not the individual sentences that feel difficult. If you find these readings challenging, it's because you have to do a lot of thinking about what they say.

Take, for example, Thomas Friedman's chapter "The Dell Theory of Conflict Prevention" (p. 121), taken from his best-selling book *The World Is Flat*. Friedman is an expert in foreign relations, but he writes not to academics or economists or political theorists but to people like you and me. Yet his argument—that worldwide business supply chains bring political stability—requires a lot of thinking. Comprehension is not so much the issue. Friedman lays out his argument logically and supports it with many kinds of evidence (as you will learn to do as well). But the ideas he proposes about the relationship between economics and geopolitics, as well as his ideas about war, peace, and terrorism, will require you to think about the implications of his argument, and that kind of work is the start of critical thinking. Figuring out what's in the text is challenging, but even more challenging is figuring out what's not in the text: the examples that would challenge Friedman's argument, or new areas where his ideas have value, or modifications of his argument based on your experience or on other things you have read. That's critical thinking. *Emerging* will help you learn how to do it.

The headnotes that appear before each reading, for example, provide context. Besides finding out about the author, you'll learn about the larger argument of the book from which each reading is taken so that you can have a sense of the author's overall project. In reading the headnotes, you may find that you have already developed questions about the selection you're about to read, questions that can serve as the basis of your critical thinking. Your own questions can be supplemented by those at the end of each reading, which are more specifically designed to focus your reading and thinking in ways that will develop your critical thinking while helping you to produce the writing asked of you in this class. The Exploring Context questions use technology to deepen your understanding of the essay and its context in the world. These questions also underscore the fact that the readings have a life outside of this text where their ideas are discussed, developed, refuted, and extended—a life that you will contribute to through your work in this class. Questions for Critical Reading invite you to enter that process as well by returning you to key moments of the text and encouraging you to think more critically about specific aspects of the author's argument. Once you've flexed your critical thinking muscles in the context of the reading, Questions for Connecting then prompt you to apply those skills by relating the current reading to other selections in the book, and Assignments for Writing provide opportunities to join the conversation of these essays. All of these questions require you to use your skills with critical thinking.

The Language Matters questions ask you to do the same, but in the specific context of writing, grammar, and language. Academic writing is formal writing, and that means you need to pay attention to issues of grammar. Error-free writing should always be your goal. Proofreading is an important technique in meeting that goal, and you might also want to work with a handbook, which can give you specific guidance on issues of correctness. But in the end language is not about learning rules, though it might feel that way. Language is about creating meaning. The Language Matters questions at the end of each reading will help you practice skills with language and grammar by asking you to look at how meaning is made in these readings. Thinking critically about the language used by these authors will help you think critically about the language you use in your writing as well, so that you can take these insights back to your own writing.

But critical thinking is not just something you practice when you answer questions in response to texts like Friedman's. It's something we all do all the time. For instance, I asked one of the student workers in our department office, Sherline, about a recent problem she had to solve: buying a car. As a junior at our school Sherline was ready to move off campus, but that meant she needed a reliable means of transportation to make it to class and to work on time; relying on public transportation (especially in southern Florida) wouldn't be enough. The problem she needed to solve was which car to buy. *Whenever we solve problems or make decisions we use critical thinking because we gather, evaluate, and apply knowledge to the situation at hand.* So Sherline started by gathering information. She talked to friends and asked for recommendations about what car she should purchase, and she did some research on Web sites such as Cars.com and Kelly Blue Book. Then she applied that information to her specific context. For example, she had to work within a specific budget because she didn't want to finance. And, being a student, she knew she needed a car that wouldn't require a lot of expensive maintenance. In assessing the information she had gathered—discarding options she couldn't afford, deciding which of her friends had the best recommendation, assessing the

> **Whenever we solve problems or make decisions we use critical thinking because we gather, evaluate, and apply knowledge to the situation at hand.**

value of what each Web site had to say—Sherline exercised critical thinking, and that helped her to make a decision and buy her car. (She got a 1999 Acura TL.)

Thinking about buying a car and thinking about geopolitical stability might seem like very different processes, but both involve very similar skills. And that's a key point: *The skills you need for academic writing are skills you already use in your life.* When you choose your career you use those skills. When you decide to help a disaster relief effort at home or abroad you use those skills. When you vote in an election you use those skills. And when you decide which cell phone plan is right for you, you use them too. Part of what you will gain through this class is an awareness of those skills. What you'll also gain is a translation of those skills into an academic context—taking everyday decision-making skills used for things like buying a car and applying them to things like the Friedman reading. As you refine those skills in an academic context, you also strengthen them for use in the rest of your life. Thus critical thinking is not simply a skill for college success; it's the cornerstone of the skills you will need to survive in the kind of globalized world that Friedman describes. You might call the skills of critical thinking the survival skills for global citizenship—not because you politically are a global citizen but because the world is now "flat." What makes the world flat for Friedman is not geography but the fact that economies are so interconnected that everyone everywhere is competing with everyone everywhere else. And as you enter the job market, that will include you too. But you're already participating in the global citizenship engendered by the flat world. If you need to consider gas mileage when buying a car or if you wince at the price of gas while filling up the car you own, you're reflecting what it means to live in a world where everyone competes for a limited resource. Similarly, if you chat online with someone who lives in another country, you're making connections through the global culture enabled by the flat world.

Skills for Global Citizenship and Academic Success

Fortunately, just as you've entered class with many writing skills, so too do you enter with skills in global citizenship and thus in critical thinking. Critical thinking, after all, is fully concerned with processing information, and we live in an information-rich world. So chances are many of the things you do every day involve some kind of critical thinking; this class will hone those skills and translate them into the academic realm.

For now, it might be helpful to focus on six skills you might already use that correspond to aspects of academic writing and that also will enable you to thrive in the world at large. Those skills are the abilities to search, to connect, to mash, to post, to sample, and to version. They are all familiar in some form to anyone living in a digital age. In academic terms, you will build them into the abilities to read critically, think critically, synthesize, argue, support, and revise.

Skills for Global Citizenship		Skills for Academic Success
Search	→	Read Critically
Connect	→	Think Critically
Mash	→	Synthesize
Post	→	Argue
Sample	→	Support
Version	→	Revise

Search, or Read Critically

We live in a world saturated with information—so much so that Richard Restak notes in "Attention Deficit: The Brain Syndrome of Our Era" (p. 332) that our brains are being rewired by the multiple and competing demands information makes on our attention. Mastering the ability to search is crucial to managing those demands since searching allows us to select just the information we're looking for. So basic is this skill to our survival today that we don't even think about it anymore. Indeed, you probably search for information on the Web every day, and you probably find what you need, too. Yet, while it seems intuitive, searching involves a kind of critical thinking. For starters, you have to do some thinking about what terms to use to find what you're looking for. And even then, Google and most other search engines return thousands or even millions of results when we search; we must evaluate those results in order to find the right one.

In an academic context, searching happens whenever you read critically. After all, reading is a way to find information. But you may find it difficult to locate information in these readings. They likely are not the kind of texts you've read previously in your life or educational career, and so they might feel very hard. That's OK; they're supposed to be hard because dealing with difficulty is the best way to develop your skills with critical thinking. In other words, if you didn't have to think about what you read in this class you wouldn't be doing any critical thinking at all.

Though these readings might seem hard they don't have to feel impossible. There are a number of strategies you can use to deal with their difficulty. The first step is to acknowledge the difficulty—recognizing it forces you to consciously activate your skills with critical thinking. The second step is just to keep reading, even if you feel you don't understand what you're reading. Often, the opening of an essay might be confusing or disorienting, but as you continue to read you start to see the argument emerge. Similarly, the author might repeat key points throughout the essay, and so by the time you complete the reading what seemed impossible to understand begins to make sense. After you've completed the reading, you might still feel confused. Write down what you *did* understand—no matter how little that might be and no matter how unsure you are of your understanding. Recognizing what you know is the best way to figure out what you need to learn. Identifying specific passages that you did not understand is an important strategy too. In locating any points of confusion, you can focus your critical thinking skills on those passages in order to begin to decode them. Make a list of specific questions you have, too, and then bring those questions to class as a way of guiding the class's discussion in ways that will enhance your understanding. The questions following the reading will give you some help, but your peers are another valuable resource. Discussing the reading with them allows you to pool your comprehension—the section you didn't understand might be the one your peer did, and vice versa. Finally, reread the essay. Reading, like writing, is an iterative process. We read and reread, just as we write and revise, and each time, we get a little more out of it.

Understand too that when you read the selections for this class, you'll be doing a kind of searching. As with the Web, you'll want to have some idea of what you're looking for before you start. The headnotes before each selection will guide you in that process by giving an overview of the author and the argument. While reading, one of the things you'll want to search for is the author's argument, the point he or she is trying to make in the selection. In addition, you'll want to search for concepts, terms, or ideas that are unique or central to the author's argument. Reading with a pen, highlighter, or sticky notes at hand will help you as you find this information. Marking places that strike you or that feel key to the author's argument is akin to bookmarking a Web site you want to find again—it shortcuts the search process when you return by making it easier to find the information again. In academic terms we

DEALING WITH DIFFICULTY

- Acknowledge that the reading is hard.
- Keep reading the essay.
- Write down what you *did* understand.
- Identify specific passages that confused you.
- Make a list of specific questions.
- Use the questions that follow the reading.
- Discuss the reading with peers.
- Reread the essay at least once, or more.

ANNOTATING THE TEXT

- Read with a pen, highlighter, or sticky notes at hand.
- Look for the author's argument.
- Mark key terms, concepts, and ideas.
- Mark information you will need again.
- Mark words you don't understand.
- Ask questions in reaction to the text.
- Summarize key points in the margin.

call this process annotating the text; it's the start of critical reading because it identifies the most important information in the essay, and that's exactly the information you need to think about.

Let's look at an example, an annotated excerpt from "What's Black, Then White, and Said All Over?" (p. 363), Leslie Savan's essay about the use of black slang in advertising and pop talk:

> Wannabe or crossover talk didn't begin with hip-hop, nor is lingo-lending from one group to another confined to blacks and whites in America. Whites talking some black is part of an apparently universal phenomenon that sociolinguists call covert prestige. This means that speakers of a "standard" language (whatever the language) "have favorable attitudes toward lower-class, nonstandard speech forms," explains the linguist Margaret Lee. "However, these attitudes are not always overtly expressed, and they may be subconscious, because they stray from mainstream—or overt—values about the perceived superior status of the standard forms." This occurs, she adds, "for the most part throughout the world—when new forms enter the mainstream, in fact, they usually come from nonstandard speech." (p. 377)

Margin notes:
So then how is Savan's argument unique? Sounds like this happens all the time.

Note to self: look up this word

Definition of "covert prestige"

What would overt prestige look like? Could there be such a thing?

Again, if this happens all over, then how can Savan be making this argument?

In annotating the text, you will want to deploy several search strategies. The first of these involves marking information you will need again, such as the definition of "covert prestige," which is underlined in the passage above to lend it visual importance. You will also want to mark any terms you don't understand, such as *sociolinguist*. Another set of strategies, though, involves questions you have in reaction to the text, each of which can serve as a point for re-searching the text. Each question you ask during your initial reading of the text gives you a new direction for searching the text again—both for an answer to your question and for support for any alternative position you want to take.

That's because—just like when you are searching the Web—sometimes you don't find what you need the first time around. Returning to the text and reading it again refines your searching, helping you find what you missed the first time, and it provides an opportunity to briefly summarize key points. Rereading is not something we usually do if we're just reading for comprehension; generally we understand enough of what we read that we don't have to read it again. But in an academic context rereading is essential, because critical reading goes beyond comprehension to evaluation, and before we can evaluate we have to know the key points that need evaluation. The Questions for Critical Reading located at the end of each selection will help you in this process by focusing your rereading on a significant point in the essay—a particular term, concept, or idea that will allow you to read and think critically. Rereading Savan's essay with the above questions might cause you to pay attention to those parts of the essay where Savan explains why black talk uniquely impacts white language. For example, Savan talks about African American history in the United States, from slavery to minstrel shows and on through jazz and beyond. Taking note of those sections in rereading makes it clear why covert prestige is such a useful idea for Savan in making her argument: It explains how black talk "as the original flipside to the voice of the Man" enables "pop talk's crush on everything 'alternative' and 'outsider'" (p. 365).

It's important to note that searching is not *researching*. Searching finds what information is there; researching—in academic terms—means generating new knowledge. In this sense, researching a car purchase is very different from researching a paper topic. In the first case you're just using the information available; in the second you're applying the available information to create new information and ideas. Researching in an everyday context means gathering information, but researching in an academic context means producing new information. For instance, if a medical researcher only duplicated the information already available on a disease, no progress would be made toward a cure. At the same time, all research begins with a search because you need to know what information is available before you generate new knowledge. When you read these essays you will be searching, but when you write about them you will be doing a kind of research. Summarizing the reading won't be sufficient for this class since doing so only provides the search results, the information we already know. By thinking critically about what you found in your search of the text, you begin to move toward research because your critical thinking will generate something new, the unique product of your thoughts.

> In an academic context rereading is essential, because critical reading goes beyond comprehension to evaluation.

You'll be researching these essays when you respond to the Exploring Context questions, which often ask you to use the Web to elaborate your understanding of the text. However, before you use any Web site in an academic setting, you will want to make sure you evaluate it. You start that process by asking yourself how you want to use the site. Any site on the Web can be used as an example of your ideas or the ideas of any essay; thus, Savan uses Black People Love Us! (blackpeopleloveus.com) as an illustration of her ideas about how whites treat African Americans. What's clear in Savan's argument, though, is that the site is an example of her own idea—she doesn't use it to *provide* an idea. Whenever you take ideas or evidence from Web sites you need to be careful about which sites you use. Ask yourself questions about who wrote the material (a government organization? an individual?), what qualifications the source has, when the site was last updated, and how stable the address or URL is (is it hosted on a free site like geocities or through a domain name?). *Any Web site can be used as an example, but only those Web sites that establish their authority should be used for ideas or evidence.*

That's because research has such a specific meaning in the context of the academic world. When you generate new ideas in your writing for this class, you'll be doing a kind of research, but research also involves working with academic sources to support your points. For this class, those sources are largely provided for you by the essays in this book. If your argument needs support beyond that you will need to find valid and reliable evidence, and that will involve more than what you can find through Google or Wikipedia. Academic research demands academic sources, the kind you will find through the library in books and journals across the disciplines. You will need to move your Web-searching skills into the electronic interfaces that can help you find those sources. Once you do, you will need to search and re-search them through reading just as you would do with Savan's essay. This is what we mean when we say that academic writing is an iterative process — you do it, and then you do it again.

Connect, or Think Critically

Connecting is another skill that translates into an academic context. You already connect all the time because it too is an essential skill for surviving in the world today. In part, connecting means going online and connecting to static information on the Web, but it also means connecting to others, through the dynamic social networks you form through sites like Facebook or MySpace or through your friends, family, coworkers, and communities.

Connecting is also a method of critical thinking. Each of the essays you will read here is already connected to the rest of the book it originally appeared in and thus to that author's larger argument as well as to the conversation taking place around that author's particular topic. When you read, you will infer many of these connections, but as you think critically about these readings you will make new connections of your own, which is essential to critical thinking. You'll start by connecting what you read to your own life, to what you know and think and how you feel. Your instructor might ask you to keep a reading journal or a blog where you can record these initial connections.

These personal reactions will help you to think about the ideas of each essay. What will help you even more is connecting ideas *between* the essays. The strongest way to evaluate the information in an essay is to test it against other information, such as the ideas expressed in another essay. Connecting the readings might mean using a concept from one piece, such as Francis Fukuyama's idea of "Factor X," to explain another essay such as Mary Roach's "The Cadaver Who Joined the Army." But it might also mean using the ideas from one essay to modify the ideas in another: elaborating Michael Pollan's idea of the "holon" through Daniel Gilbert's concept of "super-replicators," for example. (See Figure 1.)

Connecting is a kind of critical thinking used by the authors of the essays in this book, too. We've already seen how Leslie Savan connects the concept of "covert prestige" to pop talk and black talk. In "AIDS, Inc." (p. 106), Helen Epstein does something similar in discussing HIV prevention programs in Africa:

> . . . Ugandans are more likely to know their neighbors and to live near members of their extended families. This in turn may have contributed to what sociologists call "social cohesion" — the tendency of people to talk openly with one another and form trusted relationships. Perhaps this may have facilitated more realistic and open discussion of AIDS, more compassionate attitudes toward infected people, and pragmatic behavior change. (p. 113)

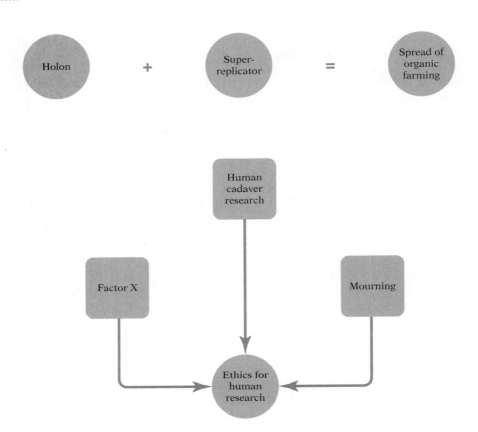

Figure 1   Clustering
Connecting and synthesizing are crucial ways of thinking critically about what you read.

Epstein, a molecular biologist and specialist in public health, connects a concept from sociology, "social cohesion," with HIV prevention in Uganda. In making that connection, she uses the idea to support her argument and to create a new idea about what an effective prevention program should look like. It's the connections between ideas that allow authors like Savan and Epstein — and *you* — to make an argument.

In working with these readings you might feel like there simply are no connections between them, that the topic of each essay is unique. But keep in mind that a connection is not something you find; it's something you *make*. If the connections were already sitting there in the essays, then there wouldn't be much critical thinking involved because there wouldn't be much thinking involved at all. The process of making connections between disparate ideas is part of critical thinking. Sociology and public health might not seem to have much in common, but when we make connections between them we generate a new understanding of how a search operates.

When making connections between the readings for this class, you might want to start by listing the important terms, concepts, and ideas from each essay. Once you've done that, you can literally draw lines between ideas that have some relation. You might also try a technique called *clustering*. Put the main concept of each essay in a circle on a sheet of paper. Draw other circles containing related or subsidiary ideas and connect them with lines to the circles containing the main ideas of the readings. When you find ways to connect the branches of these separate groups, you're locating relationships between the essays that you might want to pursue. Figuring out exactly what those relationships are not only utilizes critical thinking but also starts the process of forming your own ideas, which you will express in the writing of this class. The Questions for Connecting at the end of each reading will also help in this process by asking you to think specifically about one essay in terms of another. These questions, then, will give you a direction to think about both essays, using each to test the concepts and ideas of the other. The "tags" for each essay show key concepts, some of which overlap with the tags for other selections.

Mash, or Synthesize

Connecting defines relationships—in your life, between two people; in this class, between two ideas. Mashing—and its academic equivalent, synthesis—goes one step further by combining different sources of information to generate something new. In digital culture, mashing involves integrating two or more sources of information. For example, a DJ named Danger Mouse created quite a stir a few years back by taking music from The Beatles' *The White Album* and combining it with the vocals from Jay-Z's *The Black Album* to create *The Grey Album*, a new musical composition synthesized from the two sources. Similarly, the Kleptones use instrumentation from one source and vocals from another; the resulting mashup produces new music. Mashing happens on the Web, too, when different sources of data are combined into a new tool. You might have used mashups of Google Maps or Flickr. For example, Weather Underground's WunderMap (wunderground. com/wundermap) combines Google maps with National Weather Service data, satellite cloud images, and weather station information.

But mashing is not just a recreational activity for the digital world. It is a form of synthesis, a central component of critical thinking that you will use throughout your life and career. A doctor might combine test results, a patient's medical history, and her or his own knowledge to reach a diagnosis; a businessperson might use a marketing report, recent sales figures, a demographic study, and data on the current economic outlook to craft a business strategy. Whenever you combine multiple sources of information to create new information or ideas, you're mashing. When you do it in an academic context, you're synthesizing. Synthesis always creates something new; because you'll be using it in this class to create new ideas and thus new knowledge, you'll use it to show your critical thinking.

Steve Olson, for example, synthesizes information about genetics, history, and marriage in Hawaii to examine "The End of Race" (p. 250). In her essay

"The Boundaries of Design" (p. 296), Virginia Postrel synthesizes information about law and aesthetics to consider the boundary between the two. As we've seen, Helen Epstein synthesizes ideas from sociology and public health, while Leslie Savan synthesizes concepts from sociolinguistics with pop talk. All of the authors in this text use synthesis because all of them are working from what's already been said and written about a subject to say and write something new. You'll do the same. After you've read a piece and connected its ideas to other contexts, you will synthesize the ideas into a new idea, your own idea. That idea will form the center of the writing you do in this class.

There are several techniques you can use to synthesize the ideas of these readings. You might, for example, use ideas from two authors and combine them into a new concept that you use in your paper. Or you might use a concept from one essay to show the limitations of another author's argument. You might even invent a term all your own, defining and deploying it through the essays. When synthesizing or mashing, you want to ask yourself not simply how the two elements you're working with are alike but also how they're different. Paying attention to both similarities and differences allows you to find out how different ideas fit together in different ways.

Post, or Argue

All the processes we've discussed so far take place before you actually start writing in response to an assignment. You need to search (and re-search), connect, and mash in order to begin the process of critical thinking that forms the core of academic writing. Once you've done all that, it's time to post. If you've ever joined a discussion online or kept a blog, then you're familiar with posting. Posting involves joining a conversation, taking a stand, or making a point. When you write in this class you'll be doing all of those things.

In the academic world, making an argument is a form of posting—you take a position and defend it. But that sounds antagonistic, and academic arguments are not about fighting, or winning, really. After all, *argument* can mean several different things—an argument between lovers is quite different from an argument in a courtroom, which is also different from a scientific argument. Rather than thinking of a post as the position you defend, as an army would, it might be useful to think of it as the words you send out into the world, as in posting a letter in the mail. Posting in this sense has many academic equivalents: hypothesis, argument, thesis. In the sciences, for example, a hypothesis is an idea you test through an experiment, using the evidence from that experiment to prove the hypothesis true or false or, more generally, to modify the hypothesis in some way. In an academic sense, an argument is the primary point to be proven through evidence collected through research. *Thesis* might generally mean "theme," but it also has a similar meaning to *post*—the central point around which all the evidence is gathered. It is the claim you make, the point you want to prove. More generally, posts in the academic world and beyond have projects; when you post you're trying to *accomplish something*. Online, that might be trying to answer someone's questions about *World of Warcraft* in a discussion forum, but in this class it means making a specific contribution to the conversation around a subject.

Every paper you write is a post. You take a position in the paper and state that position in your argument or thesis. The point of the paper, your post, is to lay out your thinking regarding that position in order to persuade your reader of the validity of your ideas.

Sample, or Support

As you lay out your thinking, you'll need proof to support your point, which in academic writing happens through working with quotations from the texts. Using the text as support for your argument is similar to something you might know as sampling. In musical terms, sampling involves using part of one recording as an element in a whole new recording. For example, you're probably not familiar with James Brown's 1970 recording "Funky Drummer," but you may know its drum beat from songs by artists as diverse as Public Enemy, Dr. Dre, Big Daddy Kane, the Beastie Boys, Sinéad O'Connor, George Michael, and Dido. The "Amen Break," from the Winstons' 1960 song "Amen, Brother," is another famous drum loop used in a wide variety of songs today (see Figure 2). When artists sample music, they use a piece of another musical composition to support the music they want to make.

Figure 2   Sampling
Part of the waveform for the "Amen Break," including the cymbal crash at the end.

Quotation serves the same function in an academic context. When you use quotation in your writing, you support your words and ideas through the words and ideas of others. Quotation supports critical thinking in two ways. First, it provides evidence for your argument, thesis, or position, showing the reader how and why you thought that way and reached the conclusions that led to your argument. But beyond that, integrating quotation into your text itself requires some critical thinking. That's the difference between "having" quotations in your paper and "using" them. It's not enough to drop in a quotation every now and then, just as it wouldn't make sense to have drum loops randomly sprinkled throughout a song. You need to think about the function of every quotation you use, its purpose in your paper: Is it defining a term? supporting an assertion? connecting ideas? To make that function clear, you will want to explain each quotation you use. That doesn't mean you should summarize or reiterate each quotation; it means you should write about what that piece of text does for your overall project. Think of it as connecting that text to your own text. You might also analyze the quotation in this process. Analyzing a quotation means explaining what it says and what it means.

> **When you use quotation in your writing, you support your words and ideas through the words and ideas of others.**

Here's a pattern you can use to incorporate quotation into your paragraphs in ways that show your critical thinking through connection. Begin your paragraph with a sentence that contains the main idea you want to make or the connection you want to show between two essays. Introduce the first quotation, provide it, and then perhaps add a sentence that explains that quotation. After a brief transition, move to the second quotation. Then add several sentences that explain the connection you see between the quotations. These sentences should also explain how the relationship between the quotations supports your argument. These sentences record your critical thinking, allowing you to use the connection you've made between these two authors to support your project for the paper.

Crucially, as sampling has evolved as a musical technique, acknowledgment has become paramount. That is, artists can't take a sample without properly recognizing (and paying) the original artist. Similarly, it is absolutely essential that you acknowledge the words of others when you use them. In the real world, failure to do so can result in expensive lawsuits and ruined careers. In the academic world, failure to do so is considered plagiarism. Every time you use the words or ideas of another, you must provide a citation. Once you enter your major you'll learn a specific system for providing that citation — every discipline has its own system. In this class, the system you will likely use is MLA citation, developed through the Modern Language Association, the governing body for the discipline of English. You will probably spend time in class learning the intricacies of this system, but for now remember the basics: Every time you use a quotation or paraphrase, include the author's name and the page number in parentheses at the end of the sentence, just before the period. Publication information for all of your sources should be listed of the end of your paper.

Version, or Revise

So far we've discussed all the stages of critical thinking you'll need to exercise in order to produce a draft of your paper. Each stage relates to a skill you might already use, and each, too, will have value in your future career. Once you've written a draft, making an argument that contributes to the larger conversation and supporting it by working with quotation, there is still more work to be done, because every good piece of writing goes through at least one revision. This is the eighth draft of this introduction, for example.

Software goes through revision, too. Nearly every piece of software you use exists in multiple versions. Right now I'm writing what you're reading in Word 2008 for Mac, version 12.1.5, on a computer running Mac OS X version 10.5.6, while I listen to some music in iTunes 8.0.2 and chat online through Firefox 3.1b2 and Yahoo! Messenger version 3.0 beta 3. Most of the time we don't think about which version of a piece of software we're using — we just use it. But inevitably we will need to upgrade that software at some point, which involves moving to a new version. And when companies release a new version of software, they don't start from scratch — they begin with the previous version, adding what's needed, moving perhaps in a new direction with a novel feature, fixing what doesn't work.

When we write, we do the same thing: We produce new versions of our product through revision. Often students think of revision as "fixing" their papers — just correcting all the errors. But as with versions of software, that's only part of the process. Revision involves making substantive changes and should produce something new. Again, when we produce something new in the realm of ideas, we're doing critical thinking; revision, then, is also a form of critical thinking. Instead of thinking about the readings of the class, though, revision asks you to think critically about — to evaluate, test, and assess — your own writing.

When we discussed connecting, we said that it's easier to evaluate ideas against something else. The same is true with revision. Often when we write our initial draft looks fine to us; it seems like our best thinking. This is where connecting with others — in this case, through the process of peer revision — is again useful. As part of my job coordinating the writing classes at my university, I read the class evaluations for all of the writing courses, and one thing students say over and over is that they feel peer review is useless — *but really it's one of the most practical things you'll learn in this class.* In the rest of your life you won't be asked to write papers, but you will be asked to work with others on committees or teams again and again. Learning to work well with others — to recognize valuable feedback and to give it in turn — is essential, since, as James Surowiecki shows in "Committees, Juries, and Teams: The *Columbia* Disaster and How Small Groups Can Be Made to Work" (p. 440), the failure of small groups can lead to disaster.

Peer review gives you practice in testing your ideas with actual readers. Software makers don't just write some code and send it out into the world; they test it first (often through a "beta" version). And they test it with actual end users, the audience for the final product. Similarly, other students in your class—and not just your instructor—are actual end users for your writing. Every piece of writing has an audience, and your peers form part of that audience. Since the goal of each paper is to contribute to the conversation started in the texts, and since your classmates have also read and written about the texts, they are the interlocutors for your written conversation.

That process works in reverse, too. When you read your peers' writing you will want to bring all your critical thinking skills to bear. You might be tempted to just write "Good job!" no matter what you think about the writing, from fear of being critical, but that shows no critical thinking. Critical thinking is not the same as being critical. When you offer valuable feedback you're helping your classmates, no matter how strong that feedback is. Start by reading your peer's paper, using the same skills with search and research that you used when you read the texts of this class. Then think critically about what they are saying, using the skills you have with connection—connect what they say about the text to what you know about the text as well as to what you think and have written about the text. Then post your response.

Bringing It Together

It might be useful for you to see how this all comes together in an actual student paper. Let's start with the assignment, taken from one of my recent classes:

> In "What's Black, Then White, and Said All Over?" Leslie Savan explores the appropriation of black language into pop culture and its use in advertising and marketing. Locate your own example of a word or phrase that has entered pop culture from a racial, ethnic, or cultural group and then **write an essay in which you extend or complicate Savan's argument through this example.**
>
> Does your example participate in "cool"? Does it offer an alternative template for pop talk? Is it modeled on the dominant language or does it create a new model for others to follow? Has it been commercialized or does it resist that kind of appropriation? How? Does it participate in "covert prestige"?

You can apply your same skills with critical thinking to this assignment; treat it as you would one of the readings in this text. For starters, searching the assignment will help you locate key information in writing your response, and you should annotate it as you would a reading. Notice, for example, that the middle section is in bold, highlighting the main task of the assignment: "write an essay in which you extend or complicate Savan's argument through this example." That's the central task for your paper. If we search for the key terms in that core, we find *extend, complicate,* and *example.* You would need then to *use* the example you find to say something about Savan's argument. To do so you will need to mash the ideas from Savan and your own example, synthesizing them into a position that you will argue and support in the post that is your paper.

Here is one student's response to the assignment:

What's Geek, Then Sleek, and Read All Over?

In "What's Black, Then White, and Said All Over?" Leslie Savan argues that "African American vernacular" has been influencing pop culture for years, and recently, pop culture has been using this "black talk" in advertisements. Not only does black culture have a strong influence on pop culture, but — one could argue — it *defines* pop culture. Our society both knowingly and subconsciously uses words and phrases of African American origin on a regular basis. Just as African American vernacular has been infiltrating the English language for decades, Internet-inspired words and phrases are also beginning to influence our language, primarily with the help of video games and text messaging. It is undeniable that Internet-inspired words and phrases are becoming more and more popular. Internet slang is becoming more widespread, it is being used as a marketing tool, and it is even used by individuals to gain acceptance within certain communities.

As Savan points out in the text, black talk has proven to be an effective marketing tool for many products. When advertising for a video game system, the black talk might not appeal to the average video game consumer, so it seems that the geeks have created their own dialect. There are many popular initialisms used by nerds such as *ctf, ftw, orz, gg,* and *irl.* It is also common for nerds to substitute numbers for letters or even totally replace letters with numbers altogether. This mannerism is called 1337 5P34K (leet speak). It seems that in the gaming community, a gamer's coolness is directly proportional to how few letters he uses.

One form of leet speak has already been used as advertisement by Sony. Sony's Playstation has four main buttons on its controller: x, circle, triangle, and square. The Playstation slogan is "Live in your world. Play in ours," but some of the letters are cleverly replaced with the aforementioned shapes on the controller. This is an example of a major corporation using a form of Internet slang as a marketing tool. Savan says "at white society's major intersection with black language — that is, in entertainment — white society has gone from mocking black talk, as in minstrel shows, to marketing it, as in hip-hop" (Savan 48). Similarly, white society's major intersection with Internet talk is also in entertainment, with video games being a part of entertainment. Also, like black talk, society has gone from mocking geeks to using their language as advertisement.

Not all of the Internet slang words have nerdy connotations; some popular examples are *lol, bff, brb, g2g, idk,* and *ttyl*. These notations along with many other similar ones can be seen in just about any text message or instant message. They are widely used and accepted among America's youth, male and female, nerd and non-nerd. Some tech-savvy middle-aged adults might even recognize some of these notations. In early 2007 AT&T/Cingular released a commercial of a young girl who communicated with her mother solely using this jargon. Later in 2007 the company released a similar commercial. In both commercials there were subtitles translating the jargon and introducing many ignorant watchers to the phenomenon.

Even though I see many of these initialisms every day — and even hear them out loud occasionally — they are not words. Most of them are unpronounceable combinations of consonants. "Lol" is the only exception. It is always unexpected to hear "lol" in an out-loud or over-the-phone conversation, mainly because it is used to signify laughter. In a face-to-face conversation, it is just more natural to laugh out loud instead of saying "lol."

However, there are two words coined by video gamers that are both slowly gaining momentum in pop culture. One of them is "noob." It evolved from "newbie" and is sometimes spelled "newb." Thefreedictionary.com defines newbie as "one that is new to something, especially a novice at using computer technology or the Internet." Gamers have taken this definition a step further. Wikipedia accurately defines a noob as someone with "the sole purpose of annoying others." Wikipedia goes on to say that a noob is "someone who did something stupid, or asked an obvious question." Both of these definitions are applicable. Consequently, it is quite a degrading insult to be called a *noob* when playing an online game.

The second word to be adopted by video gamers is any variation of the word "own" (commonly misspelled and pronounced as "pwn"). Yes, this has always been a word, but video gamers have given it a new definition. To put things in perspective, our wallets are getting owned by gas prices. When my team wins a capture the flag game three to zero, that is an instance of *ownage*. Only *noobs* get *owned*.

As previously stated, both of these words are seeping into mainstream pop culture. I once saw someone wearing a shirt that simply said "GET OWNED" on it. At one point in time, only the hardcore computer nerds knew these words and how to use them. Slowly over time, as online gaming has boomed, these terms have become more widespread. Now, even casual video gamers call each other *noobs* and *own* each other. Even though it is uncommon, non-video gamers sometimes use these words in their nerdy contexts.

When playing a video game, it seems that the more nerdy lingo someone uses, the more accepted he will become. This is called covert prestige. As defined by Savan, covert prestige is when "speakers of a 'standard' language (whatever the language) have favorable attitudes toward lower-class, nonstandard speech forms'" (Savan 65). With black talk, covert prestige demonstrates coolness or toughness. When someone uses hip-hop language, it is easier to become accepted by the in-crowd whether the person is hip-hop or not. That is why Savan says that "it usually allows whites to feel good about themselves without having to do anything particularly worthwhile" (73). White people can put on a facade to appear hip-hop. The same is true with any community. Insecure individuals are willing to go great distances to feel accepted by people they admire. Although it's not the only reason, this might be part of the reason why Facebook walls, instant messages, and Internet forums are saturated with abbreviations and slang derived from Internet users. People imitate what they see in online communities to gain acceptance in that community. Savan observes that "a large number of male speakers, it seems, are more concerned with acquiring *covert prestige* than with obtaining social status" (65). This is true because often times, covert prestige has *become* social status. Many young people do not find themselves attractive or fun or cool, so they act like someone who *does* find himself cool and attractive and fun. That is probably why "pop is modeled on black and not the other way around" (47). Black people are at home with who they are. They do what they want and break the rules sometimes. They spell how they want and have fun with it too. If admired individuals use Internet-inspired initialisms on Facebook, then everyone who looks up to that person may start using the same initialisms. Also, if someone who is exceptionally good at Halo 3 uses words like *pwn* and *noob,* other Halo players will use those words.

As an avid gamer and Internet user, I enjoy seeing Internet lingo expand into pop culture. Because the Internet is such a vital part of our society, I think that Internet language has no choice but to become more popular. I expect to see more advertisements using Internet jargon in the coming years, and I expect that people will continue to use it as covert prestige.

Every paper needs an argument, the main point that the author is posting. This student makes that argument clear in the introduction: "Internet slang is becoming more widespread, it is being used as a marketing tool, and it is even used by individuals to gain acceptance within certain communities." Notice how the paper responds to the assignment: It *extends* Savan's argument through a new example. In order to reach that argument, the paper's author had to connect what Savan says about black language and pop talk to Internet talk. What's synthesized out of that is a new idea about how advertisers use Internet language to market products as well.

That argument, of course, needs to be proven through work with the text, and so the author uses quotations from Savan's text to support the argument. The third paragraph provides a particularly good example of this kind of work, showing how textual support can illustrate the kind of critical thinking that happens with connection and synthesis. The author begins with an example of Internet language in advertising and then uses a quotation from Savan to connect this ad to Savan's argument about companies using pop talk to sell products. Notice how the paragraph draws from the pattern described above in the discussion of sampling.

This is the second version of the paper — there was a prior initial draft — and though the author has improved many parts of the paper through revision, you may also notice that there are still some issues that could be resolved with additional revision to produce a new version of the paper. For instance, though there are several good examples of Internet language, not all of the examples are connected; that is, it's not clear how all of them support the argument. Some additional attention could also be paid to language matters; addressing those would make the argument stronger by making the meaning clearer.

Despite these shortcomings, this paper does demonstrate critical thinking through a clear argument supported with specific examples and quotations from the text. Your work in this class may look very different (in part because the writing prompts you work with may look very different), but the skills will remain the same. For, in the end, those skills are what matter — not just in this class and not just in college, but in your career and your life as well.

THE READINGS

Madeleine Albright

Madeleine Albright is the Mortara Distinguished Professor of Diplomacy at Georgetown University, but she is more widely known for being the first woman to serve as U.S. secretary of state, a position she held under President Bill Clinton from 1997 to 2001 and a role for which she was confirmed unanimously by the Senate. She has also served as the U.S. ambassador to the United Nations and as a member of the board of directors for the Council on Foreign Relations, a nonpartisan foreign policy think tank. Albright attended Wellesley College, Johns Hopkins University, and Columbia University, where she earned a Ph.D. in public law in government. She has written a number of books, including *The Mighty and the Almighty: Reflections on America, God, and World Affairs* (2006), from which the following chapter is taken, and, most recently, *Memo to the President Elect: How We Can Restore America's Reputation and Leadership* (2008).

The Mighty and the Almighty explores the role of religion in government affairs. As a former government official and a person whose identity was shaped dramatically by religion (she was raised Catholic but discovered her Jewish heritage when she was an adult), Albright is able to offer a unique perspective on the power and place of religion in politics.

In "Faith and Diplomacy," Albright suggests that religion's influence on world events is inherent and persistent. Our government, she argues, must recognize this reality and adjust its diplomatic strategy accordingly. Albright proposes concrete steps the government can take to prepare itself for the religious dimensions of inter- and intranational disputes, but she also advises that religiously informed diplomacy will not always solve the complicated problems of a complicated world.

Albright's aim, then, is to remind us that while dividing the religious from the political has fostered peace and stability here at home, we must keep in mind that religion often plays a much more central role in the affairs of nations abroad. Attending to that fact, Albright shows us, should be central to U.S. foreign policy.

▶ TAGS: *faith*, *diversity*, *conflict*, *religion*, *community*, *diplomacy*

Faith and Diplomacy

"This would be the best of all possible worlds if there were no religion in it!!" So wrote John Adams to Thomas Jefferson. The quotation, well known to proselytizing atheists, appears differently when placed in context. The full passage reads:

> Twenty times in the course of my late reading have I been on the point of breaking out, "This would be the best of all possible worlds if there were no religion in it!!" But in this exclamation I would have been . . .

fanatical. . . . Without religion this world would be something not fit to be mentioned in polite company, I mean hell.

In his song "Imagine," John Lennon urged us to dream of a world free of religious doctrines. For many nonbelievers, religion is not the solution to anything. For centuries, they argue, people have been making each other miserable in the name of God. Studies indicate that wars with a religious component last longer and are fought more savagely than other conflicts. As the acerbic liberal columnist I. F. Stone observed, "Too many throats have been cut in God's name through the ages, and God has enlisted in too many wars. War for sport or plunder has never been as bad as war waged because one man's belief was theoretically 'irreconcilable' with another."

The fault in such logic is that, although we know what a globe plagued by religious strife is like, we do not know what it would be like to live in a world where religious faith is absent. We have, however, had clues from Lenin, Stalin, Mao Zedong, and, I would also argue, the Nazis, who conjured up a soulless Christianity that denied and defamed the Jewish roots of that faith. It is easy to blame religion—or, more fairly, what some people do in the name of religion—for all our troubles, but that is too simple. Religion is a powerful force, but its impact depends entirely on what it inspires people to do. The challenge for policy-makers is to harness the unifying potential of faith, while containing its capacity to divide. This requires, at a minimum, that we see spiritual matters as a subject worth studying. Too often, as the Catholic theologian Bryan Hehir notes, "there is an assumption that you do not have to understand religion in order to understand the world. You need to understand politics, strategy, economics, and law, but you do not need to understand religion. If you look at standard textbooks of international relations or the way we organize our foreign ministry, there's no place where a sophisticated understanding of religion as a public force in the world is dealt with."

> **It is easy to blame religion . . . for all our troubles, but that is too simple.**

To anticipate events rather than merely respond to them, American diplomats will need to take Hehir's advice and think more expansively about the role of religion in foreign policy and about their own need for expertise. They should develop the ability to recognize where and how religious beliefs contribute to conflicts and when religious principles might be invoked to ease strife. They should also reorient our foreign policy institutions to take fully into account the immense power of religion to influence how people think, feel, and act. The signs of such influence are all around us in the lives of people of many different faiths. By way of illustration, I offer three stories.

In 1981, I visited Poland; it was during the second year of the uprising by the Solidarity movement against the communist government. I had long studied central and eastern Europe, where, for decades, very little had changed. Now the entire region was awakening, as from a deep slumber. A large part of the reason was that Pope John Paul II had earlier returned for the first time to Poland, his native land. Formerly Karol Wojtyla, a teacher, priest, and bishop of Kraków, the pope exemplified the pervasive role that religion had played in the history of Poland. While communist leaders in Warsaw dictated what Poles could do, parish priests in every corner of the country still spoke to what Poles believed. The government, alarmed by the prospect of the pope's pilgrimage, sent a memorandum to schoolteachers identifying John Paul II as "our enemy" and warning of the dangers posed by "his uncommon skills and great sense of humor." The authorities nevertheless made a tactical mistake by allowing church officials to organize the visit, giving them a chance to schedule a series of direct contacts between the "people's pope" and the pope's people.

One of the titles of the bishop of Rome is pontifex maximus, or "greatest bridge-builder." In Poland, John Paul II helped construct a bridge that would ultimately restore the connection between Europe's East and West. For bricks, he used words carefully chosen to expose the void at the heart of the communist system, arguing that if people were to fulfill their responsibility to live according to moral principles, they must first have the right to do so. He made plain his conviction that the totalitarian regime could not survive if Poles had the courage to withhold their cooperation. Above all, he urged his countrymen not to be afraid—a simple request with enormous impact. Slowly at first, but with gathering momentum, the pope's listeners drew strength from one another. No longer were they separated into small, controllable groups; the communists' obsession with isolating dangerous ideas had met its match. Standing amid huge crowds, the listeners recognized in each other once again the qualities that made them proud to be Polish—faith in God and a willingness to run risks for freedom. The pope's visits—for he made more than one—sparked a revolution of the spirit that liberated Poland, brought down the Berlin Wall, reunited Europe, and transformed the face of the world.

The pope helped the people of Poland to overcome their fear. Bob Seiple, who served with me in the State Department as the first American ambassador-at-large for international religious freedom, tells a second story, this one about overcoming hate. It concerns Mary, a young Lebanese woman he encountered while working as the head of World Vision, a Christian relief and development agency. In the 1980s, Lebanon had been the scene of a destructive and multi-sided civil war. Mary lived in a mostly Christian village; and when a Muslim militia invaded it, everyone fled. Mary tripped on a root, plunging face-first to the ground. As she scrambled to her knees, a young man of no more than twenty pressed the barrel of a pistol into the side of her head and demanded, "Renounce the cross or die." Mary did not flinch. "I was born a Christian," she said. "I will die a Christian." The pistol fired, propelling a bullet through Mary's neck and spine. Remorselessly, the militiaman carved a cross on her chest with his bayonet, then left her to die.

The following day, the militia returned and prepared to occupy the village. As they carted off the dead, a few of them came across Mary, still alive but unable to move; she was paralyzed. Instead of finishing her off, the militiamen improvised a stretcher out of wood and cloth and took her to a hospital. Seiple continues:

> And I'm talking to Mary, sitting across from her, and I said, "Mary, this makes absolutely no sense. These are people who tried to kill you. Why in the world would they take you to the hospital the next day?"
>
> She says, "You know, sometimes bad people are taught to do good things."
>
> And I said, "Mary, how do you feel about the person who pulled the trigger? Here you are, an Arab woman in a land twice occupied at that time—the Israelis in the south, the Syrians every place else—strapped to a wheelchair, held hostage by your own body, a ward of the state for the rest of your life. How do you feel about the guy who pulled the trigger?"
>
> She said, "I have forgiven him."
>
> "Mary, how in the world could you forgive him?"
>
> "Well, I forgave him because my God forgave me. It's as simple as that."

In Seiple's view, there are two lessons in this story. The first is that there are people who are willing to die—and kill—for their faith. This was true thousands of years ago and is no less true today. The second lesson is that religion at its best teaches forgiveness and reconciliation, not only when those acts are relatively easy but also when they are almost unbelievably difficult. (Mary, I need hardly add, is a more forgiving person than most—including me.)

The third story involves a boy with haunted eyes whom I met on a blisteringly hot afternoon in December 1997 during my first trip to Africa as secretary of state. The youngster looked about five years old and spoke softly, in a voice drained of emotion. He told me that, two weeks earlier, the small village where his family lived had been attacked. His mother had thrown him to the ground, shielding him with her body. When it was quiet, he wriggled his way out from under her and looked. His mother was dead. The bodies of other women were nearby, more than a dozen, drenched in blood. The boy then heard an infant crying; it was his sister, lying among the corpses. He gathered the baby into his arms and started walking. For hours, as the youngster stumbled along over hills and rocks, the infant wailed. Eventually they came to a place where the boy knew from experience that they would be welcomed and kept safe.

That place was Gulu, a town in a remote part of northern Uganda. World Vision ran the camp and hospital there—a haven for local villagers, who were being terrorized by an outlaw militia group. During the previous decade, an estimated 8,000 children had been kidnapped; most were presumed dead. Boys who survived and did not escape were impressed into rebel units; girls were taken as servants or "wives."

Camp officials blamed rebel leaders who had twisted religion into something grotesque. The tragedy had begun in 1986, when a change in government threatened the privileges of a previously dominant tribe, the Acholi.

Fear is a powerful motivator, and the Acholi feared retribution for the many abuses they had committed while in power. A potential savior arrived in the unlikely form of a thirty-year-old woman, Alice Auma, who said that she was able to commune with spirits—a rare but by no means unique claim in her culture. She told her companions that she had been possessed by a deceased Italian military officer who had instructed her to organize an army and retake Kampala, the Ugandan capital. Once victory was achieved, commanded the spirit, the Acholi should cleanse themselves by seeking forgiveness. Auma's sacred campaign was launched but lacked the military clout to match its supernatural inspiration. After some initial successes, the movement—armed only with sticks, stones, and voodoo dolls—was crushed. Auma, her mind no longer host to the Italian officer, found refuge across the border in Kenya.

That would have ended the story had not Joseph Kony, Auma's nephew, decided to take up the cause of holy war. Piecing together a small force from various rebel groups, he assembled what came to be known as the Lord's Resistance Army (LRA). From 1987 on, the LRA has attacked villagers throughout the region, also targeting local governments and aid workers. Because Kony finds adults hard to control and reluctant to enlist, he kidnaps children as a means of procuring troops. Once captured, the children are forced to obey or be put to death; and obedience demands a willingness to kill anyone, including one another. Discipline is administered in the form of beatings, lashings, and amputations predicated on their leader's reading of the Old Testament. The LRA's professed goal is to overthrow the Ugandan government and replace it with one based on the Ten Commandments—or actually ten plus one. The eleventh, added by Kony to restrict the movements of adversaries, is "Thou shalt not ride a bicycle."

Itself a product of fear, the LRA has survived twenty years by instilling fear in others. The Ugandan government has veered between efforts to make peace with the LRA and efforts to destroy it, but officials lack the resources to protect those living in the vicinity of the rebel force. That task has been left to World Vision and similar groups whose resources are also limited, as I saw during my tour of the camp in Gulu. The surroundings reminded me of pictures I had seen of the Crimean War. The camp hospital smelled of disinfectant and human waste. Ancient IVs dripped. Mosquitoes were buzzing everywhere. There were hundreds of patients, most of them children, many covered with welts and scars, some missing a limb. I met a group of teenage girls sitting on mattresses, braiding each other's hair. They looked as if they belonged in junior high school, yet several were already mothers, their babies sired by LRA rapists. "Even if you are a very young girl," said one, who was wearing a Mickey Mouse T-shirt, "you would be given to a man who was the age of my father."

As I started to leave, a young man came up to me holding an infant. "This is the girl that little boy brought to us, his little sister. Her name is Charity." As I cradled the tiny orphan, I was told that the girl had been named for one of the volunteers at the mission. There were many such volunteers. It was a place filled with terrible suffering but also a resilient joy. Patients and volunteers laughed, sang, played games, and cared for each other. The Italian doctor who ran the facility had been in Gulu for more than twenty years. What a contrast between the faith that manifests itself in such love and the twisted fantasies pursued by the LRA.*

One insight that is present in these stories and often in religious faith more generally is that we share a kinship with one another, however distant it may sometimes seem; we are all created in the image of God. This in turn places upon us a responsibility to our neighbors. That principle provides both a solid foundation for religion and a respectable basis for organizing the affairs of secular society. What complicates matters is that religion can be interpreted in ways that exclude large numbers of people from any claim to kinship. Those truly imbued with religious faith—such as Pope John Paul II, Bob Seiple's Mary, and the volunteers in Gulu—may affirm "We are all God's children"; but others may follow their convictions to a more argumentative conclusion—"I am right, you are wrong, go to hell!"

When I appeared on a panel with the Jewish writer and thinker Elie Wiesel, a survivor of the Holocaust, he recalled how a group of scholars had once been asked to name the unhappiest character in the Bible. Some said Job, because of the trials he endured. Some said Moses, because he was denied entry to the promised land. Some said the Virgin Mary, because she witnessed the death of her son. The best answer, Wiesel suggested, might in fact be God, because of the sorrow caused by people fighting, killing, and abusing each other in His name.

This is why so many practitioners of foreign policy—including me—have sought to separate religion from world politics, to liberate logic from beliefs that transcend logic. It is, after all, hard enough to divide land between two groups on the basis of legal or economic equity; it is far harder if one or both claim that the land in question was given to them by God. But religious motivations do not disappear simply because they are not mentioned; more often they lie dormant only to rise up again at the least convenient moment. As our experience in Iran reflected, the United States has not always understood this well enough. To lead internationally, American policy-makers must learn as much as possible about religion, and then incorporate that knowledge in their strategies. Bryan Hehir has compared this challenge to brain surgery—a necessary task, but fatal if not done well.

In any conflict, reconciliation becomes possible when the antagonists cease dehumanizing each other and begin instead to see a bit of themselves in their enemy. That is why it is a standard negotiating technique to ask each side to stand in the shoes of the other. Often this is not as difficult as it might seem. The very fact that adversaries have been fighting over the same issue or prize can furnish a common ground. For centuries, Protestants and Catholics competed for religious ascendancy in Europe. That was a point of similarity: wanting to be number one. For even longer, Christians, Muslims, and Jews have pursued

---

* In October 2005, the International Criminal Court issued arrest warrants for Joseph Kony and four other LRA leaders on the charge of crimes against humanity. The court does not, however, have any independent capacity to enforce those warrants.

rival claims in Jerusalem; that, too, is a point of similarity—wanting to occupy the same space. In parts of Asia and Africa, Christians and Muslims are fighting, but they share a desire to worship freely and without fear. When people are pursuing the same goal, each side should be able to understand what motivates the other. To settle their differences, they need only find a formula for sharing what both want—a tricky task, but one that can at least be addressed through an appeal to reason.

Not all conflicts lend themselves to this sort of negotiation. During World War II, the Axis and the Allies were fighting for two entirely different visions of the future. Today, Al Qaeda's lust for a war of vengeance fought with the tools of terror cannot be accommodated. Some differences are too great to be reconciled. In most situations, however, reconciliation will be eminently preferable to continued stalemate or war. But how is reconciliation achieved?

When participants in a conflict claim to be people of faith, a negotiator who has the credentials and the credibility to do so might wish to call their bluff. If the combatants argue the morality of their cause, how is that morality reflected in their actions? Are they allowing their religion to guide them or using it as a debating point to advance their interests? Has their faith instilled in them a sense of responsibility toward others or a sense of entitlement causing them to disregard the rights and views of everyone else?

Effective foreign policy requires that we comprehend why others act as they do.

If I were secretary of state today, I would not seek to mediate disputes on the basis of religious principles any more than I would try to negotiate alone the more intricate details of a trade agreement or a pact on arms control. In each case, I would ask people more expert than I to begin the process of identifying key issues, exploring the possibilities, and suggesting a course of action. It might well be that my involvement, or the president's, would be necessary to close a deal, but the outlines would be drawn by those who know every nuance of the issues at hand. When I was secretary of state, I had an entire bureau of economic experts I could turn to, and a cadre of experts on nonproliferation and arms control whose mastery of technical jargon earned them a nickname, "the priesthood." With the notable exception of Ambassador Seiple, I did not have similar expertise available for integrating religious principles into our efforts at diplomacy. Given the nature of today's world, knowledge of this type is essential.

If diplomacy is the art of persuading others to act as we would wish, effective foreign policy requires that we comprehend why others act as they do. Fortunately, the constitutional requirement that separates state from church in the United States does not also insist that the state be ignorant of the church, mosque, synagogue, pagoda, and temple. In the future, no American ambassador should be assigned to a country where religious feelings are strong unless he or she has a deep understanding of the faiths commonly practiced there. Ambassadors and their representatives, wherever they are assigned, should establish relationships with local religious leaders. The State Department should hire or train a core of specialists in religion to be deployed both in Washington and in key embassies overseas.

In 1994, the Center for Strategic and International Studies published *Religion, the Missing Dimension of Statecraft.* The book makes a compelling case for recognizing the role of religion in affecting political behavior and for using spiritual tools to help resolve conflicts. Douglas Johnston, the book's coauthor, subsequently formed the International Center for Religion and Diplomacy (ICRD), which has continued to study what it calls "faith-based diplomacy" while also playing an important mediating role in Sudan and establishing useful relationships in Kashmir, Pakistan, and Iran. Johnston, a former naval officer and senior official in the Defense Department, believes that, ordinarily, everyone of influence in a given situation is not necessarily bad, and those who are bad aren't bad all the time. He argues that a faith-based mediator has means that a conventional diplomat lacks, including prayers, fasting, forgiveness, repentance, and the inspiration of scripture.

The ICRD is not alone in its efforts. After leaving the State Department, Bob Seiple founded the Institute for Global Engagement, which is working to improve the climate for religious liberty in such volatile nations as Uzbekistan and Laos. The institute's mantra is, "Know your faith at its deepest and richest best, and enough about your neighbor's faith to respect it." [25]

While in office, I had occasion to work closely with the Community of Sant'Egidio, a lay movement that began in Rome in the 1960s, inspired by the Second Vatican Council of Pope John XXIII. Over a period of years, Sant'Egidio successfully brokered negotiations ending a long and bloody civil war in Mozambique. It has also played a constructive role in, among other places, Kosovo, Algeria, Burundi, and Congo. The community sees prayer, service to the poor, ecumenism, and dialogue as the building blocks of interreligious cooperation and problem solving.

Numerous other faith-based organizations, representing every major religion, are in operation. They are most effective when they function cooperatively, pooling their resources and finding areas in which to specialize. Some are most skilled at mediation; others are best at helping former combatants readjust to civilian life. Still others emphasize prevention, addressing a problem before it can explode into violence. Many are experts in economic development or building democracy, both insurance policies against war. Together, these activists have more resources, more skilled personnel, a longer attention span, more experience, more dedication, and more success in fostering reconciliation than any government.

The most famous example of faith-based peacemaking was orchestrated by President Jimmy Carter at Camp David in 1978. Most observers acknowledge that the peace agreement between Egypt and Israel would never have come about if not for Carter's ability to understand and appeal to the deep religious convictions of President Sadat and Prime Minister Begin. I recently asked the former president how policy-makers should think about religion as part of the foreign policy puzzle. He told me that it is not possible to separate what people feel and believe in the spiritual realm from what they will do as a matter of public policy. "This is an opportunity," he argued, "because the basic elements of the major religious faiths are so similar—humility, justice, and peace." He said that in the unofficial diplomacy he is often asked to conduct through the Carter Center, one of the first aspects he investigates is whether the parties to a dispute represent the same faith. He said it is often simpler to deal with people of completely different faiths than with those who share a religion but disagree about how it should be interpreted. As a moderate Baptist, Carter said he found it less complicated to have a conversation with a Catholic than with a Baptist fundamentalist; with the Catholic it was easier simply to accept the differences and not feel obliged to argue about them.

When I broached this same subject with Bill Clinton, he stressed two points. First, religious leaders can help to validate a peace process before, during, and after negotiations; through dialogue and public statements, they can make peace easier to achieve and sustain. Second, persuading people of different faiths to work cooperatively requires separating what is debatable in scripture from what is not. "If you're dealing with people who profess faith," he said, "they must believe there is a Creator; if they believe that, they should agree that God created everyone. This takes them from the specific to the universal. Once they acknowledge their common humanity, it becomes harder to kill each other; then compromise becomes easier because they've admitted that they are dealing with people like themselves, not some kind of Satan or subhuman species."

Faith-based diplomacy can be a useful tool of foreign policy. I am not arguing, however, that it can replace traditional diplomacy. Often the protagonists in a political drama are immune to, or deeply suspicious of, appeals made on religious or moral grounds. But if we do not expect miracles, little is lost in making the attempt. The resurgence of religious feeling will continue to influence world events. American policy-makers cannot afford to ignore this; on balance they should welcome it. Religion at its best can reinforce the core values necessary for people from different cultures to live in some degree of harmony; we should make the most of that possibility.

Questions for Critical Reading

1. According to Albright, does religion ultimately help or hinder diplomacy? Reread Albright's text, searching for quotations that support your interpretation.

2. Although Albright closely examines the role religion should play in diplomacy she does not provide a clear picture of what a faith-inflected diplomacy would look like. Craft an argument about the role religion should play in foreign policy, locating quotations from her text that would support your argument.

3. Is faith-based diplomacy best pursued through the government or through private organizations? Reread Albright's text looking for passages that support your position.

Exploring Context

1. Using Flickr (flickr.com), search for images that illustrate Albright's argument. Paste these images into a document to create a visual montage of this essay.

2. Visit the Web site for the U.S. Department of State at state.gov. Explore the site, reading it critically to determine the role that religion currently plays in U.S. foreign policy. Does this Web site support your response to Question 3 of Questions for Critical Reading?

3. The International Center for Religion and Diplomacy (icrd.org) is an organization that seems to pursue Albright's goals of considering religion in diplomacy. Search through the center's Web site for evidence that would support Albright's arguments. Does it reflect your vision of faith-inflected diplomacy from Question 2 of Questions for Critical Reading?

Questions for Connecting

1. How would the primacy of practice, as described by Kwame Anthony Appiah in "Making Conversation" (p. 57) and "The Primacy of Practice" (p. 63), complicate Albright's vision of diplomacy? Would Appiah's understanding of cosmopolitanism enhance a faith-based diplomacy, or do political practices resist the kinds of changes Albright suggests? How can you synthesize their positions to argue for an effective diplomacy?

2. Is Kenji Yoshino's vision of civil rights in "Preface" (p. 479) and "The New Civil Rights" (p. 481) compatible with Albright's call for taking religion into consideration in foreign policy? Is the diplomacy described by Albright akin to a liberty or equality paradigm? Synthesize the ideas of these two authors and support your argument with quotations from both texts.

3. Which author provides a better strategy for reaching peace, Albright or Thomas Friedman in "The Dell Theory of Conflict Prevention" (p. 121)? Are their proposals concerning religion and economics and the roles each plays in global politics compatible? Is it possible to synthesize their ideas?

Language Matters

1. Varying your word choice adds interest for the reader, but it can be a particularly challenging task. Look back through Albright's essay. How does she vary her word choice to convey meaning? How many different words for "diplomacy" or "faith" does she use? How does she handle the implications of these terms? How might you vary your word choice in your own writing?

2. Select a key passage from Albright and replace all the verbs with blanks ("_____"). Working in small groups, fill in the blanks with verbs and then reflect on which verbs you chose and why. How does the context of each sentence determine which word to use? More important, how significant are verbs to the meaning of a sentence? Could you change Albright's entire argument by changing the verbs?

3. Constellations help us to make sense out of the stars — they give the stars meaning by grouping them into meaningful patterns. Examine how sentence

structure does the same with words. Select a key quotation from Albright's essay and then create a map of its different parts. How did you choose to break up the sentence? What relationships can you find between the parts? Are some connections more important than others? That is, if you took out certain parts of the sentence, would it still have the same meaning?

Assignments for Writing

1. Albright's essay makes it clear that faith can both unite and divide people. Write a paper in which you argue for faith's potential to enable political unification. Draw from your work on the role of religion in diplomacy from Question 1 in Questions for Critical Reading as well as the current political climate — both domestic and international — in your discussion. The goal of this assignment is for you to synthesize your experiences and observations of faith's function in current political climates with Albright's arguments. Consider, for example, what Albright says about a world without political doctrine; also, pay close attention to the stories she shares and the examples she offers the reader.

2. Albright finds a shared sense of humanity through religion, but the idea of a common sense of humanity extends to other fields of knowledge and experience. Write a paper in which you identify another avenue through which humans might find commonalities. Extend Albright's insights to those other instances of shared humanity, synthesizing her arguments with your examples. You may wish to use your work with one of the authors from Questions for Connecting in formulating your argument. To begin thinking critically about this assignment, consider these questions: In the end, is religion the only thing that binds humans together? Is religion the only thing that separates humans from everything else in existence?

3. Albright stresses that ignorance must be overcome in order for all of us to find common political ground. Although her essay focuses specifically on religious ignorance, her position could be the foundation for a much more comprehensive conversation on the matter. Write an essay in which you examine the possibilities of overcoming ignorance in relation to diplomacy. Must we overcome ignorance — religious or otherwise — in order to achieve productive international relations? If so, how do we overcome this ignorance? You may wish to incorporate the work you did in Question 3 of Exploring Context.

Julia Alvarez

Julia Alvarez was born in New York. Shortly afterward, her family returned to the Dominican Republic, where they lived under the infamous Trujillo dictatorship. Alvarez's father became involved with the underground resistance, and eventually the family was forced to flee the country and return to the United States, an experience which led Alvarez to write the 1994 novel *In the Time of the Butterflies*. She has written many other novels, including *How the Garcia Girls Lost Their Accents* (1991), as well as essays, poetry, and children's literature. She earned her B.A. from Middlebury College and an M.A. in creative writing from Syracuse University. Alvarez has received numerous awards and honors, including the Latina Leader Award in Literature from the Congressional Hispanic Caucus Institute in

2007. Her nonfiction book *Once Upon a Quinceañera: Coming of Age in the USA*, from which the following selection is taken, was a 2007 finalist for a National Book Critics Circle Award.

In *Once Upon a Quinceañera* Alvarez follows the female coming-of-age tradition known among Hispanic communities as quinceañera (or *quince*, for short). Throughout the book, Alvarez spends time with Monica, who is preparing for her quinceañera, as well as other teen girls and their families. Through her journey with these girls and their families Alvarez is able to explore the history and evolution of the quince tradition in the context of immigration, culture, class, and gender. In addition, Alvarez looks to the influences of religion, cultural tradition, and American consumerism for reasons this ritual is able to thrive throughout generations. Overall, while the book closely examines the motions and traditions of quinces, Alvarez pushes readers and herself to interrogate cultural perceptions of gender, as well as rituals and rites of passage, and how these perceptions might be influenced when crossing cultural boundaries.

In the following selections, Alvarez touches on various aspects of the quinceañera. While some view the quince as the initiation of a young girl into a community of womanhood and culture of responsibility, Alvarez wonders if such arguments merely provide an illusion of female power within a traditionally patriarchal system. Though Alvarez is continually skeptical of the quince craze, she often finds herself caught up in the excitement. Moments such as these lead Alvarez to a new stage of investigation in which she explores the social, familial, and economic implications of the quince tradition. Perhaps as Isabella, founder of bellaquinceanera.com, suggests, quinceañeras in the twenty-first century are an opportunity to offer young Latina women a sense of empowerment and individual importance. In order to do this, the tradition must be redefined in a way that reflects and embodies the values and desires of women today. Alvarez addresses the idea of whether and how this redefining might occur by leading readers and herself to consider the meaning of tradition and gender as they are practiced today. How can traditions be redefined in the spirit of these changing values and desires? Is it possible to redefine traditions without losing the original ties to them? How is it possible for traditions to offer a means of crossing cultural and social boundaries? What role does gender play in the preservation of cultural traditions, and how might these traditions differ according to gender? In what ways has consumerism affected the importance of quinceañeras and other traditions?

▶ TAGS: *tradition*, *rites*, *identity*, *culture*, gender, *race*

Selections from
Once Upon a Quinceañera

Every Girl Should Have One

I wish I'd had Isabella Martínez Wall to call up and talk to back when I was a young teen in need of rescue and an infusion of self-esteem.

Based in Los Angeles, Isabella is the founder of a one-stop quinceañera Web site cum advice column, bellaquinceañera.com. She's also an actress, a former Miss Dominican Republic, a successful fashion model, and founder of Someone Cares International, a nonprofit that is described on her Web site as "benefiting needy children" in her native country. Speaking by phone with this passionate and inspirational woman, I feel the same unsettling mixture of amazement, caution, and yearning that I feel toward televangelists. Can somebody really believe this? And if so, why can't I?

I learned about Isabella from a Dominican contact at Disney World, whom I had called to find out more about the Disney quince package. She described Isabella as an "awesome, full-bodied Latina" who is doing amazing things for young Hispanic girls. According to my contact, Isabella had actually found that young girls who had quinceañeras didn't drop out of school, didn't get pregnant, didn't get in trouble.

"Really? I mean, statistically?" I shot back. Here you go, I thought, peppering these kids with questions. But a quinceañera panacea seemed too good to be true. I'd just barely surfaced from *The State of Hispanic Girls** with a sense of dread in my heart, which was also making me want to grab for a cure.

"I don't know," my contact said. "Talk to Isabella, she'll tell you."

Ah, my people, I thought. Statistics are for the gringos. We trust testimonials, what our hearts and telenovelas tell us. I had just attended a lecture by Dr. James Martin titled "The Meaning of the 21st Century." Solutions to world problems didn't have to be costly or complex, the information technology guru

5

---

*A study published by the National Coalition of Hispanic Health and Human Services Organizations in 1999 that documented the high rates of teen pregnancy, substance abuse, school dropouts, and suicide attempts by young Latinas.

explained. In Mexico, a vanguard group of TV producers who understood the dangers of population explosion had started a campaign to bring down the birthrate by introducing female leads who practiced birth control into popular telenovelas. Initial results showed the campaign was working. Better than pamphlets or science classes or lectures like Dr. Martin's.

When I reached Isabella, after the initial honorifics, "So you're the author!" "So you're the beauty queen!" I asked her about this claim I'd heard that quinceañeras really turn girls around. Not that I wanted an analysis or anything academic, I added, thinking maybe I was sounding too much like a doubting-Thomas gringa. But with all those statistics still heavy in my heart, I wanted to hear why she thought quinceañeras were so effective. "Well, let me tell you." Isabella laughed right out. "There's nothing academic about a quinceañera!

"What I mean is there's no textbook about how you have to do a quinceañera," Isabella went on to explain. She hears from a lot of young ladies on her Web site, where she offers free advice, a kind of Ann Landers to Latina girls.

"They write me, and they ask, can I wear a short dress? Does it have to be white? Can I have a court with only my best friend and my sister? I tell them, listen, there are no rules. The most important thing is to make this celebration yours, totally yours. I try to educate them, I talk to them, the site is highly interactive. Quinceañeras are about creating strong women. Our girls need all the help we can give them."

The most important thing is to make this celebration yours, totally yours.

It's funny how you are sure you are going to end up on the other side of an opinion from someone, and it turns out you're in each other's court. Never would I have guessed that a former beauty queen promoting a princessy fantasy would turn out to be a crown-carrying feminist. But how on earth can this quasi beauty pageant cum mini wedding make an Amazon out of a stardust girl? 10

"I have seen it happen!" In fact, it happened to Isabella herself. As a teenager growing up in the Dominican Republic, she hit a wall. "I was smoking, drinking, I had body issues and identity problems." I'm dying to ask her to be specific, but she is on a roll. "When I turned fifteen, everybody started having quinceañeras. I mean everybody. Quinceañeras know no social or class boundaries. You might not have the money but you have a quinceañera for your daughter. The family is making that statement. We might not be rich but we value our daughter."

Isabella's quinceañera turned her around. "It made me feel so special." In fact, she credits it with leading her down the path to being crowned Miss Dominican Republic. "I've been there," Isabella says. "I had that moment. But how many women in the world get to feel like a queen? How many?"

Not this skinny, undersized Latina for sure, I have to agree.

"Well, that's the first reason to have a quinceañera," Isabella says. "To have that experience and not because you're marrying someone."

The second reason comes from her own experience. "Being fifteen, let's face it, it's a tough age. Your body is all over the map. You wonder who you are. Who 15 your friends are. Where you're going. You can get lost for sure. What better time in your life to have your family, friends, community come together and create a support system for you for the rest of your life?"

Isn't that asking an awful lot of a quinceañera?

But Isabella dismisses my skepticism. "About two years ago, I realized that I had a mission: to promote this important ritual. And yes, I've seen it turn girls around. I don't have statistics, this is not academic, like I said, but girls who have quinces, think about it, they're spending a lot of time with their moms, shopping, talking about life. Their friends are coming over to do rehearsals. I mean, a room full of fifteen-year-olds learning dance steps right under your nose. Parents are always complaining they don't know what to do when their daughters hit puberty. *Hel-*lo?! Here's something to do. Give her a wishing well.

"Of course, we've got to take the quinceañera a step forward," Isabella adds. Before, the whole quinceañera thing was about a girl being of marriageable age, goods to be displayed. But now we can invest this old tradition with new meaning.

"We can create a support platform for that young lady that she can have to look back upon for the rest of her life. That moment when she stands dressed like a queen with her mom beside her looking in the mirror, for that moment, if only that moment, she knows she is all right just as she is. She is the queen of her life if she can hold on to that feeling."

In fact, Isabella thinks quinces are so special, the tradition should come out   20 of its ethnic closet and become an American phenomenon. "I don't care what class or group you come from," Isabella claims. "Every girl should have one."

When I hang up I feel that uplifted feeling that must be why folks pick up the phone after watching a TV evangelist and put a donation on their charge card.

One-(Very Small)-Size-Fits-All Script

My first year at Abbot* did for me what Isabella Martínez Wall's year of going to quinceañeras and having her own quinceañera did for her. It gave me a new community to belong to, a narrative I could follow into adulthood. Instead of a family and community rallying around the quinceañera's transformation into a woman, planning and preparing sometimes for a year for that symbolic pageant marking her passage, I had a community of classmates and female teachers and coaches and housemothers honing my skills, encouraging my talents, preparing me for being what Isabella Martínez Wall would call "queen of my own life."

Incidentally, I was also turning from fourteen to fifteen, and, needless to say, away at a school where we were the only Latinas (the closest thing to us was a German girl whose parents lived in Guatemala and an American girl whose father was posted in Venezuela), I did not have a quinceañera. Nor was much made of my fifteenth birthday: a cake in the dorm, a phone call from my parents, a card with a check for twenty-five dollars. My older sister had already

---

*Abbot Academy: A private boarding school for girls in Massachusetts.

gotten my mother's ring, and away at school I could shave my legs and wear makeup without asking anyone for permission.

But although some psychological elements of the American quinceañera and my first Abbot year were the same — a community grooming a young lady for her entry into womanhood — the content of that grooming was significantly different. We Abbot girls were encouraged to develop our minds, not leave our brains parked at the door of our gender. In fact, the plaque at the front gate encouraged us to ENTER INTO UNDERSTANDING, SO YOU MAY GO FORTH TO NOBLER LIVING. Nobler living! True, many of my Abbot classmates would eventually marry and have children (this was, after all, the mid-sixties), but it was assumed we would all go to college first. (Out of a class of seventy-eight girls, only one, my room-mate, did not go to college, but married her longtime boyfriend instead.) And since many of our teachers were unmarried women, making their own way in the world, the subliminal message was clear: We were to be smart, resourceful, independent women.

This new narrative of female possibility was groundbreaking and bracing even for my American classmates. "Although Columbus and Cabot never heard of Abbot," one of our school songs began. A good thing, too. Those old-world explorers would not have approved of young women taking over the helm of their journey through life and discovering their own new worlds.

In contrast, the typical quinceañera enacts a traditional narrative that is, let's face it, a one-(very small)-size-fits-all script corseting a full-bodied female life. The young Latina is dressed up in finery not unlike a bride, her father is changing her shoes, claiming that first waltz, then passing her on to a brother or uncle or grandfather, until finally she ends up in the arms of her escort to a round of applause. The quinceañera is like a rehearsal wedding without a groom, and it sends a clear message to the Latina girl: We expect you to get married, have children, devote

It's no wonder that girls end up getting pregnant soon after celebrating their quinces.

yourself to your family. It's no wonder that girls end up getting pregnant soon after celebrating their quinces. Jaider Sánchez, a hairdresser and dance coach for quinceañeras in Denver, mentioned in a recent interview that out of seven quinceañeras he instructed in 2005, four have already invited them to their baby showers.

And so, although it gives her a momentary illusion of power (the princess rhetoric, the celebration of her sexual power, her youth, her beauty), in fact, the ritual enacts an old paradigm of the patriarchy increasingly (in the U.S.A.) pumped up by a greedy market. In a fascinating book titled *Emerging from the Chrysalis: Studies in Rituals of Women's Initiations*, Bruce Lincoln, who teaches at the University of Chicago Divinity School, amplifies Arnold van Gennep's classic theory about rites of passage as they apply to females. According to van Gennep, who coined the term, rites of passage are ceremonies within cultures that enable an individual to pass from one well-defined role to another. Male initiation rites of passage involve the stripping, testing, and reintegration of the young man into the sociopolitical adult society.

But what Bruce Lincoln found was that female initiations follow a different pattern: The girl is decked in ceremonial finery, often layer on layer is piled on her, a magnification that confers on her cosmic status and participation in a mythic drama. "Rituals of women's initiation claim to transform a girl into a woman, [they] claim to renew society by providing it with a new productive member." During the ceremonies, the initiant is "regarded as having become a deity, a culture heroine, the link between past and future." So far so good, but Bruce Lincoln goes on to suggest that this mythic power is a substitution for actual power, a pie in the sky versus options and opportunities in the here and now:

> The strategy of women's initiation is to lead a woman's life . . . away from the sociopolitical arena, introducing her to the real or imagined splendors of the cosmos instead. To put it in different terms, women's initiation offers a religious compensation for a sociopolitical deprivation. Or to put it differently still, it is an opiate for an oppressed class. . . .
>
> Cosmic claims notwithstanding, the desired result of the ritual is to make a girl ready and willing to assume the traditional place of a woman as defined within a given culture. . . . The strategy is that of placing women on a pedestal, carried to its outermost possibilities: speak of her as a goddess to make of her a drudge.

Although the young quinceañera is being crowned queen, the ritual doesn't change anything. It merely casts its net of glittering meaning over what might be a dismal situation: "It is rare that a ritual can alter the basic ways in which a society is organized," Bruce Lincoln concludes. "Nor do rituals shape the way in which people live as much as they shape the way people understand the lives they would lead in any event."

Even if she is at the bottom of the American heap, if the young Latina girl can believe the fantasy—that her condition is temporary, that she is a Cinderella waiting for that fairy godmother or husband to endow her with their power—then she can bear the burden of her disadvantage. And as years go by, and the probability of her dream becoming true lessens, she can at least pass on the story to her daughter.

Maybe that is why I get tearful at quinceañeras. I'm watching the next 30 generation be tamed into a narrative my generation fought so hard to change. Why I feel like a snake in the garden, because here I sit in their living rooms or in their rented halls, eating their catered food, celebrating with la familia, and I am thinking, Why spend all this money enacting a fantasy that the hard numbers out there say is not going to come true?

Quinceañera Expo

At the Quinceañera Expo in the Airport Convention Center in San Antonio, little girls are walking around with tiaras in their hair, oohing and ahing at the fancy dresses, the pink balloons, the wedding-cake-size cakes, the last dolls encased in plastic, the fluffy pillows with straps for securing the heels in case the page trips as he bears them to the altar to be blessed by the priest.

At a cordoned-off area at the rear of the hall, Victoria Acosta, a fourteen-year-old local pop sensation, is singing into a microphone as she dances and gestures with her free hand. "Crazy, crazy, crazy, I think the world's gone crazy!" Her next song, "Once Upon a Time," is dedicated to "all of you out there who have had your hearts broken." "All of you out there" is a semicircle of pudgy pre-teens sitting on the floor, mesmerized by the slender, glamorous Victoria with her long mascara'd lashes, her glittery eye shadow, her slinky black outfit and sparkly silver tie. "You bet I'm going to have a quince," she tells me during a break between songs, although I don't see why. She seems to have already made her passage into womanhood quite successfully.

There isn't a male shopper in sight. In fact, the only men around are manning booths or working the floor:

> a couple of boy models, one in a white tuxedo with a pale pink vest, the other in a white suit with a yellow vest;
>
> a grown man in a military uniform, a popular escort outfit with some girls, he tells me;
>
> a dj in a cowboy hat who plays loud music while his sidekick, a skinny boy, hands out flyers;
>
> Seve, the clown (who come to think of it might be female under all that face paint and bulbous, attached nose);
>
> Dale of Awesome Ice Designs (for $350 you can have the "Fire & Ice Sculpture" with the quinceañera's picture embedded in a central medallion of ice);
>
> Ronny of VIP Chocolate Fountains, whose wife, Joanne, does most of the talking. (Did you know that you can run chili con queso through the fountains for a Mexican theme at your daughter's quinceañera? The young people still prefer chocolate, as you can imagine);
>
> and Tony Guerrero, the owner of Balloons Over San Antonio ("We Blow for u").

Add the two photographers at Tilde (Photography, Invitations, Videography), Mr. Acosta (Victoria's manager-dad), the guy with a Starbucks urn strapped to his back, and Manuel Villamil at the Primerica Financial Services booth — and that makes for just over a dozen men in a crowd of about three hundred women of all ages here to shop for some member of their family's quinceañera. The hall is so girl-packed that the discreetly curtained BABY CHANGING/NURSING booth seems extraneous. You could breast-feed your baby out in the open and still be within the strict bounds of modesty, like peeing without shutting your stall door in the ladies' room because everyone inside except the little toddler in Mommy's arms is female.

I feel as if I've wandered into the back room where the femaleness of the next generation of Latinas is being manufactured, displayed, and sold. A throwback vision, to be sure. Lots of pink-lacey-princessy-glittery-glitzy stuff. One little girl wheels a large última muñeca around while her mother follows, carting the baby sister, who has ceded her stroller to a doll bigger than she is. "How beautiful!" I bend down to admire the little girl's proud cargo. "Is that for your quince?" The little girl looks pleadingly toward her mom. "It's her cousin's," the mom says, gesturing with her head toward a chunky teenager carting a large shopping bag and lolling at Joanne and Ronny's booth, scooping her toothpick of cake into the chocolate fountain. The little girl looks forlorn. "I'm sure you'll have a last doll, too, when you have your quince," I console her. She gives me a weak smile in return. Why on earth am I encouraging her?

Crazy, crazy, crazy, I think the world's gone crazy.

It's not that. It's that after an hour roaming up and down the aisles, I fall in with the spirit of the expo. There is a contagious, evangelical air to the whole thing that sweeps you up and makes you want to be part of the almost religious fervor that surrounds this celebration. I half expect to find Isabella Martínez Wall here, addressing a crowd of wide-eyed teens.

In fact, my guide, Priscilla Mora, reminds me of Isabella. Both women share a crusading enthusiasm for a tradition they believe is one of the best things going for Latina womanhood. Plump and pretty with the sunny face of someone perennially in a good mood, Priscilla has organized six of these expos, and even though some have not been as well attended as she would have liked, her faith is undimmed. When not organizing these expos, she is a quinceañera planner, an author of the *Quinceañera Guide and Handbook,* and most of all a passionate promoter of the tradition. She actually thought up this business at a workshop where participants had to write down their dreams on little pieces of paper. Then they all put their pieces of paper in a fire and let their dreams go up to God. This isn't just a business, Priscilla explains, it's a calling, part of God's plan for her.

It's from Priscilla that I first hear that when the quinceañera makes her vow in the church, "it's about chastity. You're promising God that you're not going to have sex till you're back at the altar, getting married. That's why it's important that these girls learn all about the meaning," Priscilla insists. Otherwise, the quinceañera "is nothing but a party."

Priscilla's missionary zeal seems to be shared by many of the providers, who tell inspirational stories of why they got involved in quinces. Take Tony Guerrero of Balloons Over San Antonio. Tony grew up real poor in a family of four boys and four girls. ("Are you kidding?" he replies when I ask if the girls had quinceañeras.) A few years ago, Tony gave up his office job to do this because "I just wanted the opportunity to give back something to my community." He loves seeing people having fun, being happy, and hey, if nothing else, "I got myself another entry once I go over to the other side." "Another" because he already has a great-aunt over there. "She promised me she was going to have a spot waiting for me." Ruby of Great Expectations (a photography studio) thinks it's "a privilege" to share this special day with a girl. "I love the idea of rededicating your life to the Lord." (Echoes of Priscilla.) Curiously, the nuns' booth next to Ruby's is empty. "They told me they were coming." Priscilla looks momentarily nonplussed. But her sunny personality bounces back. "Maybe they'll be by later after Mass." This is Sunday, after all. The sisters, it turns out, are the Missionary

Catechists of Divine Providence, the first and only religious order of Mexican American women founded in the United States. Their focus on the quinceañera is part of their larger mission as "evangelizadoras del barrio and transmitters of a rich Mexican American faith to the universal Church."

The only heavy hitter at the expo is Sunita Trevino, who was born in Bombay but is married to a Hispanic. At her seminar on financing a quinceañera, Sunita gives us the opposite of the hard sell: the watch-your-financial-back-as-a-minority-woman talk that has me sitting at the edge of my chair. As she talks, Sunita paces up and down the raised platform stage like a lion trapped in a too-small cage.

Sunita works for Primerica Financial Services, but her training is in clinical psychology, which she ends up using a lot as she counsels families about their finances. "I'll tell you," she tells the audience of about a dozen, mostly grandmothers, as this is the only area of the whole hall where there are chairs to sit down, "quinceañeras are high-stress times." A lot of couples come to see her for extra sessions. But the majority of Sunita's clients are single women who are in financial trouble. They don't budget. They overspend. They get into debt. She knows women in their seventies still paying off second mortgages they took out for their daughter's quinceañera. She finds this devastating.

"Nobody sits down to talk to us women! We are playing a money game but no one taught us the rules!" Sunita's own mother came from Bombay to America, thinking her husband would always be there to take care of her, and then her parents separated, and her mother was lost. She had no idea how to take care of herself. Sunita doesn't want to see this happen to any woman. We women are sinking into a hole of debt and the quinceañera is often where we get in over our heads.

Her recommendation to all of us sitting in the audience: pay cash. "If you budget eighteen hundred dollars for flowers, and what you pick amounts to double that, don't do it. DON'T DO IT! Stay within your budget. A lot of women get in trouble at the last minute. They think, oh, I'll go ahead, just this once."

If you end up borrowing money, "please," Sunita pleads with us, "read the terms, read them carefully. What the big print giveth, the small print taketh away. Educate yourselves! Don't think banks and savings accounts are there to do you a favor. Okay, let's see, who can tell me what banks do with your money?" she asks. [45]

None of us grown women in the audience would dare hazard a guess. But a young girl about eleven years old raises her hand and says proudly, "They save it for you."

Sunita shakes her head fondly. "Out of the mouths of babes." She sighs. Nobody laughs. Nobody seems to get the biblical reference that Sunita is misusing anyway. Out of the mouths of babes usually the truth comes. But this young girl is headed for that sinkhole of debt unless Sunita can steer her away from the dangers of borrowing. "No, honey, that's not what they do. They use your money to make money."

The girl sits back in her chair, a chastened, embarrassed expression on her face. Her tiara glints as Sunita explains to her that what she just said is what most people think. But that's why Sunita is here today. To tell us the truth no one else is going to tell us. To get us thinking about these things. "Two hundred fifty families declare bankruptcy every hour of every day in the U.S.A. I know a seventy-nine-year-old retired guy who is now bagging groceries. People don't plan to fail," Sunita explains. "They fail to plan. So, get mad. Get mad and learn the rules."

The girl squirms in her chair, as do the rest of us. After all, we came here in a party mood, not to feel that at the end of our adult lives we will end up as bag ladies, wishing we hadn't started down the road of debt with our own or our daughters' quinceañeras.

Throwing the House Out the Window

So, how much does a quinceañera cost? You ask any of the party planners and they'll tell you the same thing—anywhere from a hundred bucks for a cookout in the backyard and a stereo booming music for the young lady and her friends to fifty grand and up in a hall with a party planner, a limo, dinner for a hundred or more.

Everyone talks about this range, but after interviewing dozens of quinceañeras and talking to as many party planners, events providers, choreographers, caterers, I have to conclude that the cookout quinceañeras are becoming the exception. In the past, perhaps they were the rule. In the old countries, of course. In small homogenous pockets—a border town in Texas, a barrio composed solely of Central Americans; in other words, a group still largely out of the mainstream loop, perhaps. But now, as one quinceañera remarked, "If I had to be that cheap I just wouldn't have one. What for?" It is in the nature of the beast to be a splurge, an extravaganza. More than one person describing a recent quinceañera used the Spanish expression for an over-the-top expense: *throwing the house out the window*. They threw the house out the window for that girl's quinceañera.

They threw the house out the window. In a country where the rate of poverty is growing (12.7 percent of U.S. citizens were living below the poverty line in 2004, up from 11.3 percent in 2000), with Latinos forming a sizeable portion of those impoverished numbers (21.9 percent of the Hispanic population was living below the poverty line in 2004 according to a U.S. census survey). Sunita, it turns out, was not exaggerating.

They threw the house they probably didn't own out the window.

Monica's quinceañera was actually quite modest if her estimate of "maybe three thousand dollars" is correct. Why don't I have an exact number? Let me just come right out and say that talking to my people about money is not easy. Maybe if I were an Americana reporter with a stenographic notebook and only a sprinkling of classroom Spanish, I could get away with asking the parents how much they paid for the party. But I'm a Latina. I know the rules. They know I know the rules. To ask my host for the price tag of the fiesta would be una falta de vergüenza. And so, I learned any number of discreet ways to approach the topic. Aproximadamente, how much does a quinceañera cost in your experience? If someone were to throw a party not unlike this one, how much would that quinceañera cost them?

50

The one person I could openly ask this question turned out to be the   55
quinceañera herself. But though fifteen-year-old girls are really good at knowing how much their dress or makeup session cost, they're not so good at knowing the charges for halls, or what it costs to have beef Wellington instead of
Swedish meatballs for a hundred people, or what additional charge was made
for the linen napkins and tablecloths or the chairs draped in white covers and
tied with satin bows, which seem to be de rigueur for anything but the cheapest
quinceañera. Fifteen-year-old girls like to throw out huge numbers to impress
their friends, but they are not so good at addition — that is, if they paid $250 for
a dress, and $250 for the limo, and the hall with a catered meal was $2,500 for
one hundred people, not counting the cake made up of four cakes, which was
no less than $300, and let's throw in another $100 to $200 for sessions at the
beauty parlor, and at least $300 for the photographer and pictures, and because
things always come up at the last minute and Mami definitely needs a new dress
herself and Papi will probably have to rent a tux and some family members will
need help with travel costs, another $500 to $1,000 more — anyhow, I've gone
way over the low-end figure of $3,000 that Monica Ramos with uncharacteris-
tic teenage understatement calculated.

And her father was not working.

They threw the rented apartment out the window. Why not? It's not theirs
to keep anyhow, just as this American dream isn't as easy to achieve as it seems,
so why not live it up, give your little girl a party she won't forget, enjoy the only
thing you really have, tonight's good time, before the bills start rolling in.

When Abuelita Is No Longer a Resource

Will Cain is president and founder of *Quince Girl,* a new national magazine targeting the more than four hundred thousand Latinas in the United States who
turn fifteen every year. Early in 2006, the magazine sent out a survey asking its
readers how much they had spent or were planning to spend on their quinces.
The resulting average was $5,000.

I confess to Will that I find that average low given the figures events planners and quinceañeras and their families have been quoting me. I'm thinking
of Idalia's quinceañera, which cost her affluent Dominican family $80,000,
not surprising given a guest list of more than five hundred and a fully choreo-
graphed performance by her court of twenty-eight couples (double the usual
number so as not to leave out any friends or cousins) with special effects to
rival a Broadway show and mermaid dresses for the girls designed by Leonel
Lirio, renowned for Miss Universe Amelia Vega's gown. Granted that's the top
end of the Q-scale, but the low end is rising. In Miami, Sofía's dad apologeti-
cally confessed that he was "only" spending about $12,000 on his daugh-
ter's quince, though his wife corrected him by appending, "Twelve thousand
dollars not counting all the food and goodies we fed twenty-eight kids for three
months of rehearsals."

"You have to remember that $5,000 takes into account the full spectrum,"   60
Will Cain reminds me about the *Quince Girl* average. "It includes the girl who is
spending $25,000 with the one who might spend $1,000. The point is that even

working-class folks who don't have a whole lot of purchasing power are going to devote a significant portion of their resources to this one tradition. It cuts across a wide range of strata."

Will himself did the numbers before he decided to launch his magazine. The Latino population is exploding, and it is mostly a young population. "I don't have to tell you about the demographics," Will tells me. "One out of every five teens is Hispanic. And that population is growing at the rate of 30 percent, while the non-Hispanic population rate is just 8 percent."

I'm trying to follow what Will is saying, but the question that keeps tugging at my curiosity is not about Hispanic demographics but about Will himself. Will Cain does not sound even close to a Hispanic name. How did "your run-of-the-mill white boy," as he describes himself when I ask him about his background, end up founding a magazine for young Latinas celebrating their quinceañeras?

Will, who is all of thirty-one—just over twice a quinceañera's age—grew up in Texas surrounded by Mexican Americans and has always been interested in the Hispanic culture. He was also interested in media. So, he decided to put the two things together and came up with the idea of *Quince Girl*. Though it's a shrewd economic decision, Will believes he's also providing an important service for Hispanics in this country.

"The Hispanic community is this very fractured community," he explains. "You have your Mexican Americans and your Puerto Ricans and your Cuban Americans. And the only thing that ties all these separate nationalities together— no, it's not Spanish," he says, anticipating what I might think, "in fact, many in the second and third generation don't even speak Spanish. What ties them together, the one single tie that binds all these cultures . . ."

As he drumrolls toward his conclusion, I'm thinking that Will Cain learned   65
something from growing up surrounded by a Hispanic community: a sense of drama.

". . . is this tradition celebrated across the whole diverse group: the quinceañera. I mean, it is big! And the rest of America is starting to pay attention to it."

"Amen," I say. I'm writing a whole book about it.

As if he can hear my mind thinking, Will adds, "We would not be having this conversation right now if this were not so."

What Will realized was that there was no magazine out there that these girls could consult about the tradition and trends and fashions. "Girls were in chat rooms asking each other about the ceremony, what to do. It used to be you could learn these things from your grandmother . . ." But with immigration and the amount of mobility in this country, la abuelita is not always a resource. Plus it's a different world from the one she grew up in. A different budget. Five thousand dollars is probably more than the grandparents earned in a year back in their home countries.

Does he think the tradition is becoming more popular here?   70

"Well." Will hesitates. He is rightly cautious about delivering opinions beyond what the numbers can tell him. "The quince tradition has always been important, but there's this retroculturation going on right now—"

"Retroculturation?" This is the first I've heard of the term.

"It's a pattern that's been happening with the Hispanic community," Will goes on to explain. "First generation comes to the United States, and they push to assimilate. They adopt the American culture and norms. Second generation, they want to be all-American. Many don't even speak Spanish. They aren't that familiar with the culture. By the third generation, they're born and bred here, but they have this special something that makes them unique, their Hispanic culture. They want to learn Spanish—many, in fact, speak more Spanish than the second generation. They make a concerted effort to hold on to their traditions, to establish cultural ties with their past."

Will quotes a study on Hispanic teens "just released today" by the Cheskin Group, an international consulting and marketing firm that has done a great deal of research on Hispanics. The study confirms Will's point that the up-and-coming generation of Hispanic teens is "predominantly bilingual and bicultural," celebrating its ethnic identity and combining it with mainstream teen culture. "They live on MySpace.com and shop at Abercrombie, but they listen to Spanish radio and embrace diversity," a summary of the study reads. Most important for businesses that are considering purchasing the full report with its $5,850 price tag—the cost of your average quinceañera—is that Hispanic teens are

> a bellwether for one of the most important trends shaping the future of the United States—the growth of the U.S. Hispanic population. Clearly, the future is theirs and they know it.

The future is ours and we know it. Meanwhile the present needs to be lived through and paid for.   75

The Difference between Boys and Girls

How did the quinceañera get to be so expensive? Even the *Quince Girl* average of five thousand dollars is a lot of money to blow on a birthday party.

Kern's Nectar, which has developed a niche market of "untraditional" juices (guava, papaya, mango) popular among Latinos, sponsors a yearly Dulce Quinceañera Sweepstakes: "Fifteen lucky Quinceañeras will be awarded $1,000 each plus a year's supply of Kern's Nectars; the grand prize winner selected at random from this group takes home $15,000."

Why did Kern's Nectar single out this one tradition? "Next to marriage, a quinceañera is perhaps the most meaningful moment in a young woman's life," the press announcement reads. Given such claims, perhaps five thousand dollars is not a lot to spend on a girl's coming-of-age.

I decide to ask the girls themselves about such claims.

In the wood-paneled faculty lounge at Lawrence High School I speak with   80
a gathering of a dozen girls who have volunteered to be interviewed about the tradition. Light streams down from a magnificent stained-glass window, giving the room the hallowed feel of a chapel. At first glance, the robed scholar portrayed in the window could be Aristotle or Plato, but on closer inspection it turns out to be a woman. With one hand clutching a book, the other lifted, palm out, she seems to be setting the example of telling the truth, the whole truth,

and nothing but, which is precisely what I am after. Later I find out that this testifying woman is Emily Greene Weatherbee, the first female principal of the high school, in the 1880s.

A century and a quarter later, the room fills with the likes of students that Miss Emily could never have imagined. The young Latinas present are mostly of Dominican and Puerto Rican descent, though one junior varsity softball player in sweatpants and sweatshirt whom it's a stretch to imagine in the girly-girl getup of a quinceañera is of Ecuadorian parentage. Except for one girl who feels "really gypped" that she didn't have one (her mother said the expense was too high), the other eleven girls have all had or will be having quinceañeras before the year is out. A few days before my visit they were reminded to bring their albums along to school. They file in, lugging large pink or white wedding-type albums of what amounts to extensive photo shoots. A few of the empty-handed girls confess they left their albums at home so as not to have to haul such a heavy weight around all day.

After paging through several of these albums, I ask the girls if they consider their quinceañeras as important as their eventual marriages. "I mean if you get married," I add. I do not want to be pushing any assumptions on their life stories.

"That's the thing," Soraya pipes up. Hers is among the largest albums, borne in by her brother, who has carted it around all day for her. "You don't ever know if you're going to get married. I mean you hope you will, but that's not for sure. But you are going to turn fifteen no matter what." The other girls agree.

But if it's just about turning fifteen, boys turn fifteen, too. Why not give them a quinceañera?

"Boys don't need a quinceañera," Madeline, who left her heavy album at home, explains. "Boys are born men but girls turn into women."

I have pondered that statement many times in the last year. The comment highlights that very deep, heavily guarded (at least traditionally) divide in a young Latina's life when she goes from niña to señorita and becomes sexualized. In her memoir, *Silent Dancing: A Partial Remembrance of a Puerto Rican Childhood*, Judith Ortiz Cofer describes how when she became una señorita, she was watched closely as if she "carried some kind of time-bomb in [my] body that might go off any minute . . . Somehow my body with its new contours and new biological powers had changed everything: Half the world had now become a threat, or felt threatened by its potential for disaster."

"We never touch the girls," more than one male photographer told me when I interviewed them about the very popular photo shoots in Miami. The full package features young quinceañeras in a variety of provocative poses and outfits, including teensy bikinis. "We tell the mothers, 'Mami, there's a little masita that needs tucking in.' We let the mothers do it." Why was I being assured of this sexual delicacy over and over? Girls hitherto blithely living inside children's bodies turn into women with sexy, enticing cuerpos, and suddenly, it's open season. Meanwhile, boys, born men, who have been taught since day one to prove themselves as healthy machos, are going to prey on them.

When I make these observations to the Lawrence group, the roomful of young girls erupts into excited giggles. Obviously, I'm onto something.

All the girls admit that once they started developing, their parents, especially their papis, were like, *Who are you going out with? Who was that that just called? Whose parents will be there?*

These girls are on the receiving end of the ill effects of machismo, no arguing with that. But what of those poor boys having to perform from day one, if Madeline is to be believed? Often at quinceañeras, I'd spot some little tyke in a teensy tuxedo pushed and prodded to pick up some girl at a dance or given a shot of rum and encouraged to strut around. Contrary to how it's often described, machismo oppresses not just the girls but also the boys. And yet, understandably, would you want your pubescent daughter to be in the company of a grown version of this little macho, unsupervised? 90

"The quinceañera is the sanctioned way that a nice family says, okay, now my daughter may receive male attention," Gloria González, a Spanish professor at Middlebury College, explains to me about her experience growing up in Guadalajara, Mexico. "We are permitting this and we are monitoring it." That *is* a big moment. In fact, in his song "De Niña a Mujer," which is arguably *the* quinceañera anthem of all time, Julio Iglesias bewails how as a father he has been anticipating this moment when his little girl disappears forever inside a woman. The lament goes on for six pained stanzas. The song makes a daughter's growing up sound like something that's going to break her father's heart.

If so, then why celebrate this loss?

Enter the mothers.

If the father is losing his little girl, the mother is gaining a potential girlfriend. More than one girl in the Lawrence group mentions—and when she does the others agree—that planning their quinceañeras really brought them and their moms close together. "We were deciding about what dress and what decorations and addressing all the invitations. I'd say that I was spending most of my time when I wasn't in school with my mom," Soraya recalls about the months of preparations. "We were already close, but we got even closer."

Even if the ceremony itself focuses on the father-daughter transaction (he changes her flat shoes to heels, he dances her first grown-up dance in public with her), the months of preparations are intense mother-daughter time. Inevitably, this causes fights and disagreements, but even those moments offer opportunities for negotiation and bonding. And it's not just mothers and daughters, but the extended familia of tías, abuelitas, primas who often get involved. Sofía's mom in Miami, Consuelo, explained how in deciding each detail of her daughter's quinceañera her mother, her sisters, and Sofía's girl cousins would all vote. "We'd go into a store and try on dresses or pick out decorations and the whole gang would be giving their opinions." As her mom recounted how special it had been for her to share this experience with her only daughter, Sofía, who had been sitting quietly beside her, began to cry. 95

"Are you okay?" her father, who had come along for the interview, asked from the other end of the couch. "What's wrong?"

Consuelo, who had been distracted talking to me, turned to her daughter. In profile they were time-lapsed copies of each other. Consuelo understood.

Tears filled her own eyes as she reached over and the two women joined hands like little girls who were going to be best friends for life.

Remote Control

Another factor that has upped the price tag of this traditional celebration is that tricky word "traditional."

Más católico que el Papa, goes a Dominican saying, more Catholic than the pope. Our exported *tradiciones* mix and combine with those of other Latin American and Caribbean countries stateside and become more elaborate, more expensive, more traditional than they ever were back home.

In fact, to have a full-blown traditional quinceañera in our Pan-Hispanic United States is to have adopted every other Latino group's little traditions and then some. So that now, Cuban quinceañeras in Miami are hiring Mexican mariachis to sing the traditional "Las Mañanitas." The full court of fourteen *damas* and *chambelanes*, "each couple representing a year of the quinceañera's life," a mostly Mexican practice, is now a traditional must. As is the changing of the shoes to heels, which seems to originally have been a Puerto Rican embellishment. From the Puerto Ricans as well, though some say from the Mexicans, came the tradition of la última muñeca, a "last doll" dressed exactly like the quinceañera, which the girl cradles to symbolize the "end of her childhood" or "the child that she herself will be having in the not-too-distant future" (both explanations given to me by different events planners). The quinceañera might keep this last doll as a keepsake or give it away to a younger member of the family. In one celebration, perhaps inspired by the wedding bouquet, the quinceañera threw her last doll over her shoulder to be caught by a screaming group of little girls, anticipating their own future quinceañeras.

This symbol of bygone childhood is also mirrored in a Central American or Puerto Rican custom (I've heard both) of having a very little girl dress up in a minuscule version of the quinceañera's dress and be "the symbol of innocence." Sometimes she is accompanied by a little escort, though the tradition has now been further elaborated so that "the symbol of innocence" as well as a little prince and princess (slightly older) are part of a full traditional court.

There is also always some sort of photo session to commemorate the event. This is not a custom exclusive to quinceañeras. In our old countries every important life event is marked by a photograph. Your First Communion photo, your quince photo, your graduation photo, your wedding photo. Even in my husband's old German-Nebraskan family, there were the formal portraits shot in a studio, the principals in dress clothes, hair combed and tamped down: a wedding, a christening, a son shipping off to war. Of course, now there are whole albums of the young lady in different outfits, in different locations, a practice that seems to have started with the Cuban community in Miami, where girls sometimes just have the photo shoot and forego the party. Many girls also have videos made, recounting their lives since birth, with still shots and footage of themselves at different ages and credits rolling as if this were a real movie with the quinceañera playing the lead and her parents starring as "padre" and "madre" and Julio Iglesias's "De Niña a Mujer" as the score, of course. Clearly, the old-country portrait tradition has arrived stateside and, as one Cuban friend put it, "taken steroids."

The tradition of crowning the young girl is often ascribed to the Mexicans, who seem to be the group that has most ritualized the ceremony. But here in America, every quinceañera gets her tiara. The bouquet the quinceañera carries to put at the Virgin Mary's statue at the Mass is also part of the Mexican and Central American tradition, as is the Mass, which our more hedonistic Caribbean party-cultures dispensed with back home. But now the Mass and the Virgin's bouquet have become part of our Dominican and Puerto Rican and Cuban "tradition" in the United States.

One economically sensible and emotionally gratifying tradition that has not been picked up by other Hispanic groups is the Mexican custom of sponsorships by madrinas and padrinos. In a Mexican quince, every aspect of the fiesta from the cake to the dj has a sponsor, which spreads the cost of the celebration around. It is also a touching symbol of the emotional, spiritual, as well as financial investment of a whole community in this young person. Why aren't others adopting this custom?

"It's a point of pride not to go begging for your party," my Cuban friend Carmel 105 confided. But in fact, a lot of informal sponsorships are going on. The grandmother who buys the quinceañera's earrings and necklace, the brother who gives her the birthday gift of paying for the limo, the sister who contributes to the dress. Still, when the twenty or more names of sponsors are read out in a Mexican-American quinceañera, there is a sense of public participation

> **They threw the house out the window for that girl's quinceañera.**

that is not lost on the young lady. "Everybody I knew contributed something," Verónica Fajardo remembers about her quinceañera fifteen years ago. "I felt like I received so many bendiciones, my whole community made it happen!" In actual fact, Verónica's family is from Nicaragua, but she grew up in a Mexican American neighborhood in Los Angeles, so though sponsorships were not part of the custom back home, by the time her quince came around, her family had adopted that tradition.

Sometimes these cultural borrowings are not even coming from fellow Latinos. The tradition of lighting and dedicating candles, for example, seems to have been lifted from the Bar and Bat Mitzvah. In fact many critics see the quinceañera as going the same route as the Jewish celebration. Rabbi Jeffrey Salkin, author of *Putting God on the Guest List: How to Reclaim the Spiritual Meaning of Your Child's Bar or Bat Mitzvah*, compares this moment in time for the Hispanic community to the early 1960s for the Jewish community, when the Bar and Bat Mitzvah ceremonies became increasingly secular and extravagant. "These rites of passage are a way for a minority group to demonstrate that they have succeeded in America."

But given the statistics, our Hispanic community cannot yet lay claim to such wholesale success. For many, the quinceañera becomes an extravaganza that, as Sunita warned, puts the family further into the hole. Marie Arana of the *Washington Post* shared with me stories of visiting migrant camps in the Maryland and Virginia countryside where families with almost nothing would put out hundreds of dollars to throw their girls' quinceañeras. Perhaps these are the cookout parties everybody talks about, the ones that are under the radar because they are taking place in segregated, often undocumented populations? If you do the numbers, several hundred dollars for a migrant worker with no citizenship or papers or cushion of savings might as well be several thousand for a working-class family that owns a car and has access to unemployment benefits and credit cards.

"Today, it's all about supersizing," Nina Diaz, the executive producer of *My Super Sweet 16*, told *U.S. News & World Report*. (The price tag for a recent quince party featured in one of the episodes was $180,000.) One quince site I happened upon in cruising the Web for Q-lore — just Google "quinceañera" and you will get 8,230,000 hits (if you put the tilde over the "n") or 4,220,000 hits (if you dispense with the tilde) — urged providers to register with their site. "The Hispanic population's buying power is expected to reach $300 billion by 2006. Timing is prime to begin your Sweet 16 and Quinceañera advertising campaign. The demand for more vendors that cater to Latinos is of epic proportions."

Epic proportions; the house out the window; 8,230,000 hits and rising.

"Upholding this coming of age celebration is definitely expensive," Kimberly García concluded in her 1999 article: "Sweet 15: A Financial Affair." In the seven years since her article was published in *Hispanic Magazine*, the trend is growing. Her shocking high-end figure of $15,000 for a celebration would not raise an eyebrow now. More likely, it would elicit an apology, as with Sofía's dad. "Hispanics are likely to make a big spending decision no matter their income level," Lisa Holton reported in an article about quinceañeras for the *Chicago Sun-Times*.

At Disneyland, Denny Nicholas, manager of corporate and wedding sales, says he has seen anything from a modest $5,000 to $50,000 for a quinceañera, the average nowadays being about $12,000 to $15,000. When I ask Denny if he doesn't find this *average* shocking given that the poverty threshold for a family of three is $15,277, he laughs. "By the time families come to me, they've already made the decision that this is what they want. All I do is provide the elements they need to make their dreams come to life." It's just a different world, Denny reminds me. "Kids are growing up expecting so much more." He chuckles, sounding a lot more cheerful about this than I obviously feel. "I joke with my two boys that when I was growing up, the remote control was me standing by the TV and my dad saying, 'Change it to such and such a channel'!"

Dinero vs. Money

The supersizing of the tradition might well be blamed on U.S. consumerism, but the spending of money now instead of mañana seems to be our very own bagaje.

"Hispanics tend to make immediate use of their money," writes Rose Carbonell in her article "Dinero vs. Money." As part of her graduate research in Hispanic Marketing Communication at Florida State University, Carbonell studied the different attitudes of Hispanics toward money. She found that "capital accumulation is not a characteristic of Hispanics, especially because being wealthy has a negative connotation . . . as the masses of Hispanics have endured slavery and endemic poverty over the past 500 years, the meaning of wealth has been associated with the experience of others, not oneself."

Initially, I dismissed this as a kind of cultural profiling we do to ourselves as it hath been done unto us, until I found this point curiously echoed by none other than Octavio Paz, the seminal writer on Mexican identity and thought and the 1990 winner of the Nobel Prize in Literature. "Our poverty can be measured by the frequency and luxuriousness of our holidays. Fiestas are our only luxury," Paz writes in *The Labyrinth of Solitude*. "Wasting money and expending energy affirms the community's wealth in both. When life is thrown away it increases. What is sought is potency, life, health. In this sense the fiesta . . . is one of the most ancient economic forms."

Another way of understanding this phenomenon is an interesting term I found bandied about in academic articles: "cultural capital." The term, originally coined by French social theorist Pierre Bourdieu, describes other kinds of assets, not monetary, that are important for status in a community. A family's throwing its daughter a lavish quinceañera represents a kind of cultural statement that counts for a lot more than the dollar cost. Thinking only of "how much it cost" in dollar amount is to simplify a much more complex and layered transaction. Patricia Saldarriaga, a professor of Spanish at Middlebury College, turned fifteen in 1975 in the port city of Talara, Peru, where her father was mayor. Although she did not want one, she was obligated to have a big quince party because of her father's position.

"*Somos decentes* is a very important concept in our communities," Eduardo Béjar, also a Spanish professor at Middlebury, explains. Eduardo, who grew up in Cuba in the forties and fifties, recalls how fiestas de quince años were a family's way of maintaining status. "Ser una familia decente. You work hard, you do things for the welfare of your family. La quinceañera reflects that: a way of saying we are decentes."

But why not have both? After all, being Latina/o is about being a hybrid, a made-in-the-U.S.A. sancocho of all our different cultures and races and histories and nationalities. Why not be una familia decente that celebrates a daughter's quinceañera without going into debt? Throw a fiesta, not the house, out the window? Our cultural habits and traditions can be revised to work better for us in the new realities we are facing right now.

But whenever I've suggested restraint to quinceañera parents and events providers, the refrain I often hear is, "We love to party!" That's the way we are.

This ethnic profiling persists both internally within our communities and without. It's a reductionist either/or way of thinking about ourselves that ill prepares us for this new millennium in which the world is shrinking and we are all becoming ever more permeable mixtures of traditions and cultures.

Mami, too, always maintained we couldn't have it both ways. We couldn't   120
be both girls from una familia decente and little Americanitas with minds (and
bodies) of our own.

"Why not?" I would challenge. "'I resist anything better than my own
diversity.'"

"Don't you answer me back!" she'd scold. "Don't you be fresh with me!"

"But that's Walt Whitman. We're reading him in English class."

That always made her stop.

"You live in this house, you respect our rules!" she'd grumble, more quietly   125
now. What monster had she created by sending her daughter to Abbot? "Who
do you think you are?"

"'I am large, I contain multitudes.'" I was finding a new way to defend myself. Technically, it was not "answering back" if I was reciting poetry.

Questions for Critical Reading

1. What is "retroculturation"? Reread Alvarez's text to locate passages that define
   the term. Can you think of additional examples? Do these examples support
   Alvarez's argument?

2. How does Alvarez feel about quinces? Search the texts for passages that reveal
   the author's stand on this cultural practice.

3. What is the value of tradition? Find quotations from Alvarez that support your
   position. Are the economic costs of traditions like quinces worth their cultural
   value?

Exploring Context

1. *My Super Sweet 16* is a television show chronicling a coming-of-age ritual similar
   to the quinceañera. Explore the Web site for the series at mtv.com/ontv/dyn/
   sweet_16/series.jhtml and connect what you find there to Alvarez's text. In what
   ways does the series reflect the issues and concerns about quinces that Alvarez
   explores? You might want to use your work on Alvarez's feelings about quinces
   from Question 2 of Questions for Critical Reading in making your response.

2. This selection opens with Alvarez's visit to Isabella Martínez Wall, who runs the
   Web site Bella Quinceañera (bellaquinceanera.com). How does the Web site, in
   its design and advertising, reflect the points that Alvarez wants to make about
   this ritual? Does the Web site reflect Alvarez's arguments about quinces? How
   does the Web site support or complicate your response to Question 3 of Questions for Critical Reading about the value of tradition?

3. What coming-of-age rituals exist in other cultures? Use the Web to search for
   information on another ritual, perhaps one from your own cultural, national,
   ethnic, or religious background. How is it preserved today? Does it have the
   same economic implications of the quince? In what ways is it connected to
   quinceañeras?

Questions for Connecting

1. Daniel Gilbert's essay "Reporting Live from Tomorrow" (p. 169) is about predicting our future happiness. How can his ideas help explain the features of
   quinces that Alvarez explores? Is the quinceañera a super-replicator? Does it
   function as a kind of cultural surrogate for womanhood? Is it possible to synthesize Gilbert's concepts with Alvarez's examples?

2. Retroculturation seems to promote diversity. How might colleges and universities promote retroculturation on their campuses? Would such a strategy solve
   the problems with community and diversity that Rebekah Nathan notes in
   "Community and Diversity" (p. 228)? Draw on your definition of the term from
   Question 1 in Questions for Critical Reading.

3. In "False Identifications: Minority Populations Mourn Diana" (p. 454), Diana
   Taylor examines the performance of grief by looking at how minority populations mourn celebrity figures such as Princess Diana. How do quinces also act
   as a cultural performance? Do they perform some sort of social drama? What
   is the "hauntology" of the quince? Synthesize these two cultural performances
   in order to argue for the function of social rituals. Support your argument with
   quotations from the texts.

Language Matters

1. Each discipline has a specific approach to evidence. Start by finding information
   on how research is done in your intended major or field. How would you pursue
   Alvarez's arguments through that field? How would that discipline make this
   argument?

2. In small groups, select a common grammatical error, such as sentence fragments or subject-verb agreement problems. Select a key quotation from
   Alvarez's text and then change it to represent the error. Share the original
   and altered quotations in small groups to create a list of error examples and
   corrections using this essay.

3. Spanish has a unique punctuation mark—an inverted question mark at the
   start of a question. In small groups, create your own punctuation marks and
   apply them to passages from Alvarez. What do you want your punctuation to
   do? What does any punctuation mark do?

Assignments for Writing

1. How do quinceañeras help to define self-identity in the Hispanic community?
   Write a paper in which you define the relationship between these rituals and
   self-identity. In making your argument you may want to use the other rituals you
   explored in Question 3 of Exploring Context or some of the concepts you synthesized in Questions for Connecting, such as super-replicators or cultural performance. To help you begin your critical thinking on this assignment, consider

these questions: How do traditions, both native and acquired, contribute to the development of identity? How does gender determine self-identity in the Hispanic community? Why do only girls receive quinceañeras? What part does retroculturation play in the establishing of self-identity? Is this rite of passage similar or different to rites of passage in other cultures? Does the commercialization of the quinceañera affect its overall value in establishing a girl's self-worth and self-identity? If so, how?

2. Alvarez examines the expanding marketplace emerging around the quinceañera. What role does business play in developing ideas of femininity? Write an essay in which you explore the intersection of commercialism and gender. In making your argument, draw not only from Alvarez's text but also from your work on the value of tradition in Question 3 of Questions for Critical Reading or your responses to the questions in Exploring Context. The following questions might help you locate a focus for your response; use them to think critically about this assignment: Does the quinceañera lend itself to the promotion of a specific view of femininity? What function does the Quinceañera Expo play in manufacturing femininity? How does the media shape perceptions of femininity in the Hispanic community? Is there still a generational gap in determining the social position of women?

3. Quinceañeras have an important role to play not simply in the lives of individuals but also, as Alvarez makes clear, in the lives of families and communities. Using Alvarez's text and your response to Question 3 of Questions for Critical Reading on the value of tradition and/or Question 3 of Questions for Connecting on cultural performances, determine the function of social rituals like the quinceañera in the lives of communities. Write a paper in which you specify the role of social ritual in community life, using Alvarez as well as your own experiences. Consider: What is the role of the individual in a community effort? What is the effect on a community when cultural events absorb outside cultural influences? How does retroculturation revitalize communities?

KWAME ANTHONY APPIAH

Kwame Anthony Appiah was born in London, grew up in Ghana, and earned a Ph.D. at Cambridge University. He is the Laurance S. Rockefeller University Professor of Philosophy and the University Center for Human Values at Princeton University. He has also taught at Duke, Harvard, Yale, Cornell, Cambridge, and the University of Ghana. He serves as an editor for *Transition Magazine* and has published numerous academic books and articles as well as three detective novels. In 2008, Appiah was recognized for his contributions to racial, ethnic, and religious relations when Brandeis University awarded him the first Joseph B. and Toby Gittler Prize.

Appiah's *Cosmopolitanism: Ethics in a World of Strangers* (2006) was one of the first books published in Henry Louis Gates Jr.'s "Issues of Our Time" series, which aims to tackle the important concerns of the information age. With *Cosmopolitanism*, Appiah examines the imaginary boundaries that have separated people around the world and the ways we can redraw those boundaries. Appiah claims with the book's title that we are all citizens of the world. In the time of al Qaeda, we can no longer afford to draw significant lines between different groups and regions. Humanity has fundamental commonalities, Appiah suggests, and we should embrace them.

The following selections, "Making Conversation" and "The Primacy of Practice," appear in *Cosmopolitanism* as the introduction and one of the book's chapters. Appiah first defines *cosmopolitanism* and its problems but ultimately determines that practicing a citizenship of the world is not only helpful in a post-9/11 world, but necessary. There is no divide between "us" and "them," he suggests, only a basic moral obligation we have to each other. It is not necessary for people to agree to behave morally for the right reason, or the right god, or the right country or custom. It is only necessary that they agree to behave morally. Conversation, Appiah writes, is the best starting point.

It's tempting to reduce what follows to something as simple as "We should all just get along," but Appiah is also challenging us to think about how we can make that happen. How primal is practice in your own life? Is what you do more important than why you do it?

▶ TAGS: *human dignity*, **community**, *globalization*, *identity*, *conversation*, *obligation*

Making Conversation

Our ancestors have been human for a very long time. If a normal baby girl born forty thousand years ago were kidnapped by a time traveler and raised in a normal family in New York, she would be ready for college in eighteen years. She would learn English (along with — who knows? — Spanish or Chinese), understand trigonometry, follow baseball and pop music; she would probably want a pierced tongue and a couple of tattoos. And she would be unrecognizably different from the brothers and sisters she left behind. For most of human history, we were born into small societies of a few score people, bands of hunters and gatherers, and would see, on a typical day, only people we had known most of our lives. Everything our long-ago ancestors ate or wore, every tool they used, every shrine at which they worshipped, was made within that group. Their knowledge came from their ancestors or from their own experiences. That is the world that shaped us, the world in which our nature was formed.

Now, if I walk down New York's Fifth Avenue on an ordinary day, I will have within sight more human beings than most of those prehistoric hunter-gatherers saw in a lifetime. Between then and now some of our forebears settled down and learned agriculture; created villages, towns, and, in the end, cities; discovered the power of writing. But it was a slow process. The population of classical Athens when Socrates died, at the end of the fifth century BC, could have lived in a few large skyscrapers. Alexander set off from Macedon to conquer the world three-quarters of a century later with an army of between thirty and forty thousand, which is far fewer people than commute into Des Moines every Monday morning. When, in the first century, the population of Rome reached a million, it was the first city of its size. To keep it fed, the Romans had had to build an empire that brought home grain from Africa. By then, they had already worked out how to live cheek by jowl in societies where most of those who spoke your language and shared your laws and grew the food on your table were people you would never know. It is, I think, little short of miraculous that brains shaped by our long history could have been turned to this new way of life.

Even once we started to build these larger societies, most people knew little about the ways of other tribes, and could affect just a few local lives. Only in the past couple of centuries, as every human community has gradually been drawn into a single web of trade and a global network of information, have we come to a point where each of us can realistically imagine contacting any other of our six billion conspecifics and sending that person something worth having: a radio, an antibiotic, a good idea. Unfortunately, we could also send, through negligence as easily as malice, things that will cause harm: a virus, an airborne pollutant, a bad idea. And the possibilities of good and of ill are multiplied beyond all measure when it comes to policies carried out by governments in our name. Together, we can ruin poor farmers by dumping our subsidized grain into their markets, cripple industries by punitive tariffs, deliver weapons that will kill thousands upon thousands. Together, we can raise standards of living by adopting new policies on trade and aid, prevent or treat diseases with vaccines and pharmaceuticals, take measures against global climate change, encourage resistance to tyranny and a concern for the worth of each human life.

And, of course, the worldwide web of information—radio, television, telephones, the Internet—means not only that we can affect lives everywhere but that we can learn about life anywhere, too. Each person you know about and can affect is someone to whom you have responsibilities: To say this is just to affirm the very idea of morality. The challenge, then, is to take minds and hearts formed over the long millennia of living in local troops and equip them with ideas and institutions that will allow us to live together as the global tribe we have become.

Under what rubric to proceed? Not "globalization"—a term that once referred to a   5 marketing strategy, and then came to designate a macroeconomic thesis, and now can seem to encompass everything, and nothing. Not "multiculturalism," another shape shifter, which so often designates the disease it purports to cure. With some ambivalence, I have settled on "cosmopolitanism." Its meaning is equally disputed, and celebrations of the "cosmopolitan" can suggest an unpleasant posture of superiority toward the putative provincial. You imagine a Comme des Garçons–clad sophisticate with a platinum frequent-flyer card regarding, with kindly condescension, a ruddy-faced farmer in workman's overalls. And you wince.

Maybe, though, the term can be rescued. It has certainly proved a survivor. Cosmopolitanism dates at least to the Cynics of the fourth century BC, who first coined the expression cosmopolitan, "citizen of the cosmos." The formulation was meant to be paradoxical, and reflected the general Cynic skepticism toward custom and tradition. A citizen—a *politēs*—belonged to a particular *polis*, a city to which he or she owed loyalty. The cosmos referred to the world, not in the sense of the earth, but in the sense of the universe. Talk of cosmopolitanism originally signaled, then, a rejection of the conventional view that every civilized person belonged to a community among communities.

The creed was taken up and elaborated by the Stoics, beginning in the third century BC, and that fact proved of critical importance in its subsequent intellectual history. For the Stoicism of the Romans—Cicero, Seneca, Epictetus, and the emperor Marcus Aurelius—proved congenial to many Christian intellectuals, once Christianity became the religion of the Roman Empire. It is profoundly ironic that, though Marcus Aurelius sought to suppress the new Christian sect, his extraordinarily personal *Meditations*, a philosophical diary written in the second century AD as he battled to save the Roman Empire from barbarian invaders, has attracted Christian readers for nearly two millennia. Part of its appeal, I think, has always been the way the Stoic emperor's cosmopolitan conviction of the oneness of humanity echoes Saint Paul's insistence that "there is neither Jew nor Greek, there is neither bond nor free, there is neither male nor female: for ye are all one in Christ Jesus."[1]

Cosmopolitanism's later career wasn't without distinction. It underwrote some of the great moral achievements of the Enlightenment, including the 1789 "Declaration of the Rights of Man" and Immanuel Kant's work proposing a "league of nations." In a 1788 essay in his journal *Teutscher Merkur*, Christoph

Martin Wieland—once called the German Voltaire—wrote, in a characteristic expression of the ideal, "Cosmopolitans . . . regard all the peoples of the earth as so many branches of a single family, and the universe as a state, of which they, with innumerable other rational beings, are citizens, promoting together under the general laws of nature the perfection of the whole, while each in his own fashion is busy about his own well-being."[2] And Voltaire himself—whom nobody, alas, ever called the French Wieland—spoke eloquently of the obligation to understand those with whom we share the planet, linking that need explicitly with our global economic interdependence. "Fed by the products of their soil, dressed in their fabrics, amused by games they invented, instructed even by their ancient moral fables, why would we neglect to understand the mind of these nations, among whom our European traders have traveled ever since they could find a way to get to them?"[3]

So there are two strands that intertwine in the notion of cosmopolitanism. One is the idea that we have obligations to others, obligations that stretch beyond those to whom we are related by the ties of kith and kind, or even the more formal ties of a shared

> **Cosmopolitanism is the name not of the solution but of the challenge.**

citizenship. The other is that we take seriously the value not just of human life but of particular human lives, which means taking an interest in the practices and beliefs that lend them significance. People are different, the cosmopolitan knows, and there is much to learn from our differences. Because there are so many human possibilities worth exploring, we neither expect nor desire that every person or every society should converge on a single mode of life. Whatever our obligations are to others (or theirs to us) they often have the right to go their own way. As we'll see, there will be times when these two ideals—universal concern and respect for legitimate difference—clash. There's a sense in which cosmopolitanism is the name not of the solution but of the challenge.

A citizen of the world: How far can we take that idea? Are you really supposed to abjure all local allegiances and partialities in the name of this vast abstraction, humanity? Some proponents of cosmopolitanism were pleased to think so; and they often made easy targets of ridicule. "Friend of men, and enemy of almost every man he had to do with," Thomas Carlyle memorably said of the eighteenth-century physiocrat the Marquis de Mirabeau, who wrote the treatise *L'Ami des hommes* when he wasn't too busy jailing his own son. "A lover of his kind, but a hater of his kindred," Edmund Burke said of Jean-Jacques Rousseau, who handed each of the five children he fathered to an orphanage.

Yet the impartialist version of the cosmopolitan creed has continued to hold a steely fascination. Virginia Woolf once exhorted "freedom from unreal loyalties"—to nation, sex, school, neighborhood, and on and on. Leo Tolstoy, in the same spirit, inveighed against the "stupidity" of patriotism. "To destroy war, destroy patriotism," he wrote in an 1896 essay—a couple of decades before the tsar was swept away by a revolution in the name of the international working class. Some contemporary philosophers have similarly urged that the boundaries of nations are morally irrelevant—accidents of history with no rightful claim on our conscience.

But if there are friends of cosmopolitanism who make me nervous, I am happy to be opposed to cosmopolitanism's noisiest foes. Both Hitler and Stalin—who agreed about little else, save that murder was the first instrument of politics—launched regular invectives against "rootless cosmopolitans"; and while, for both, anti-cosmopolitanism was often just a euphemism for anti-Semitism, they were right to see cosmopolitanism as their enemy. For they both required a kind of loyalty to one portion of humanity—a nation, a class—that ruled out loyalty to all of humanity. And the one thought that cosmopolitans share is that no local loyalty can ever justify forgetting that each human being has responsibilities to every other. Fortunately, we need take sides neither with the nationalist who abandons all foreigners nor with the hardcore cosmopolitan who regards her friends and fellow citizens with icy impartiality. The position worth defending might be called (in both senses) a partial cosmopolitanism.

There's a striking passage, to this point, in George Eliot's *Daniel Deronda*, published in 1876, which was, as it happens, the year when England's first—and, so far, last—Jewish prime minister, Benjamin Disraeli, was elevated to the peerage as Earl of Beaconsfield. Disraeli, though baptized and brought up in the Church of England, always had a proud consciousness of his Jewish ancestry (given the family name, which his father spelled D'Israeli, it would have been hard to ignore). But Deronda, who has been raised in England as a Christian gentleman, discovers his Jewish ancestry only as an adult; and his response is to commit himself to the furtherance of his "hereditary people":

> It was as if he had found an added soul in finding his ancestry—his judgment no longer wandering in the mazes of impartial sympathy, but choosing, with the noble partiality which is man's best strength, the closer fellowship that makes sympathy practical—exchanging that bird's-eye reasonableness which soars to avoid preference and loses all sense of quality, for the generous reasonableness of drawing shoulder to shoulder with men of like inheritance.

Notice that in claiming a Jewish loyalty—an "added soul"—Deronda is not rejecting a human one. As he says to his mother, "I think it would have been right that I should have been brought up with the consciousness that I was a Jew, but it must always have been a good to me to have as wide an instruction and sympathy as possible." This is the same Deronda, after all, who has earlier explained his decision to study abroad in these eminently cosmopolitan terms: "I want to be an Englishman, but I want to understand other points of view. And I want to get rid of a merely English attitude in studies." [4] Loyalties and local allegiances determine more than what we want; they determine who we are. And Eliot's talk of the "closer fellowship that makes sympathy practical" echoes Cicero's claim that "society and human fellowship will be best served if we confer the most kindness on those with whom we are most closely associated." [5] A creed that disdains the partialities of kinfolk and community may have a past, but it has no future.

In the final message my father left for me and my sisters, he wrote, "Remember you are citizens of the world." But as a leader of the independence movement in what was then the Gold Coast, he never saw a conflict between local partialities and a universal morality—between being part of the place you were and a part of a broader human community. Raised with this father and an English mother, who was both deeply connected to our family in England and fully rooted in Ghana, where she has now lived for half a century, I always had a sense of family and tribe that was multiple and overlapping: Nothing could have seemed more commonplace.

Surely nothing *is* more commonplace. In geological terms, it has been a blink of an eye since human beings first left Africa, and there are few spots where we have not found habitation. The urge to migrate is no less "natural" than the urge to settle. At the same time, most of those who have learned the languages and customs of other places haven't done so out of mere curiosity. A few were looking for food for thought; most were looking for food. Thoroughgoing ignorance about the ways of others is largely a privilege of the powerful. The well-traveled polyglot is as likely to be among the worst off as among the best off—as likely to be found in a shantytown as at the Sorbonne. So cosmopolitanism shouldn't be seen as some exalted attainment: It begins with the simple idea that in the human community, as in national communities, we need to develop habits of coexistence: conversation in its older meaning, of living together, association.

And conversation in its modern sense, too. The town of Kumasi, where I grew up, is the capital of Ghana's Asante region, and, when I was a child, its main commercial thoroughfare was called Kingsway Street. In the 1950s, if you wandered down it toward the railway yards at the center of town, you'd first pass by Baboo's Bazaar, which sold imported foods and was run by the eponymous Mr. Baboo—a charming and courteous Indian—with the help of his growing family. Mr. Baboo was active in the Rotary and could always be counted on to make a contribution to the various charitable projects that are among the diversions of Kumasi's middle class, but the truth is that I remember Mr. Baboo mostly because he always had a good stock of candies and because he was always smiling. I can't reconstruct the tour down the rest of the street, for not every store had bonbons to anchor my memories. Still, I remember that we got rice from Irani Brothers; and that we often stopped in on various Lebanese and Syrian families, Muslim and Maronite, and even a philosophical Druze, named Mr. Hanni, who sold imported cloth and who was always ready, as I grew older, for a conversation about the troubles of his native Lebanon. There were other "strangers" among us, too: In the military barracks in the middle of town, you could find many northerners among the "other ranks," privates and NCOs, their faces etched in distinctive patterns of ethnic scarification. And then there was the occasional European—the Greek architect, the Hungarian artist, the Irish doctor, the Scots engineer, some English barristers and judges, and a wildly international assortment of professors at the university, many of whom, unlike the colonial officials, remained after independence. I never thought to wonder, as a child, why these people traveled so far to live and work in my hometown; still, I was glad they did. Conversations across boundaries can be fraught, all the more so as the world grows smaller and the stakes grow larger. It's therefore worth remembering that they can also be a pleasure. What academics sometimes dub "cultural otherness" should prompt neither piety nor consternation.

Cosmopolitanism is an adventure and an ideal: But you can't have any respect for human diversity and expect everyone to become cosmopolitan. The obligations of those who wish to exercise their legitimate freedom to associate with their own kind—to keep the rest of the world away as the Amish do in the United States—are only the same as the basic obligations we all have: to do for others what morality requires. Still, a world in which communities are neatly hived off from one another seems no longer a serious option, if it ever was. And the way of segregation and seclusion has always been anomalous in our perpetually voyaging species. Cosmopolitanism isn't hard work; repudiating it is.

In the wake of 9/11, there has been a lot of fretful discussion about the divide between "us" and "them." What's often taken for granted is a picture of a world in which conflicts arise, ultimately, from conflicts between values. This is what we take to be good; that is what they take to be good. That picture of the world has deep philosophical roots; it is thoughtful, well worked out, plausible. And, I think, wrong.

I should be clear: This book is not a book about policy, nor is it a contribution to the debates about the true face of globalization. I'm a philosopher by trade, and philosophers rarely write really useful books. All the same, I hope to persuade you that there are interesting conceptual questions that lie beneath the facts of globalization. The cluster of questions I want to take up can seem pretty abstract. How real are values? What do we talk about when we talk about difference? Is any form of relativism right? When do morals and manners clash? Can culture be "owned"? What do we owe strangers by virtue of our shared humanity? But the way these questions play out in our lives isn't so very abstract. By the end, I hope to have made it harder to think of the world as divided between the West and the Rest; between locals and moderns; between a bloodless ethic of profit and a bloody ethic of identity; between "us" and "them." The foreignness of foreigners, the strangeness of strangers: These things are real enough. It's just that we've been encouraged, not least by well-meaning intellectuals, to exaggerate their significance by an order of magnitude.

As I'll be arguing, it is an error—to which we dwellers in a scientific age   20
are peculiarly prone—to resist talk of "objective" values. In the absence of a natural science of right and wrong, someone whose model of knowledge is physics or biology will be inclined to conclude that values are not real; or, at any rate, not real like atoms and nebulae. In the face of this temptation, I want to hold on to at least one important aspect of the objectivity of values: that there are some values that are, and should be, universal, just as there are lots of values that are, and must be, local. We can't hope to reach a final consensus on how to rank and order such values. That's why the model I'll be returning to is that of conversation—and, in particular, conversation between people from different

ways of life. The world is getting more crowded: In the next half a century the population of our once foraging species will approach nine billion. Depending on the circumstances, conversations across boundaries can be delightful, or just vexing: What they mainly are, though, is inevitable.

The Primacy of Practice

Local Agreements

Among the Asante, you will be glad to hear, incest between brothers and sisters and parents and children is shunned as *akyiwadeε*. You can agree with an Asante that it's wrong, even if you don't accept his explanation of why. If my interest is in discouraging theft, I needn't worry that one person might refrain from theft because she believes in the Golden Rule; another because of her conception of personal integrity; a third because she thinks God frowns on it. I've said that value language helps shape common responses of thought, action, and feeling. But when the issue is what to do, differences in what we think and feel can fall away. We know from our own family lives that conversation doesn't start with agreement on principles. Who but someone in the grip of a terrible theory would want to insist on an agreement on principles before discussing which movie to go to, what to have for dinner, when to go to bed?

Indeed, our political coexistence, as subjects or citizens, depends on being able to agree about practices while disagreeing about their justification. For many long years, in medieval Spain under the Moors and later in the Ottoman Near East, Jews and Christians of various denominations lived under Muslim rule. This modus vivendi was possible only because the various communities did not have to agree on a set of universal values. In seventeenth-century Holland, starting roughly in the time of Rembrandt, the Sephardic Jewish community began to be increasingly well integrated into Dutch society, and there was a great deal of intellectual as well as social exchange between Christian and Jewish communities. Christian toleration of Jews did not depend on express agreement on fundamental values. Indeed, these historical examples of religious toleration—you might even call them early experiments in multiculturalism—should remind us of the most obvious fact about our own society.

Americans share a willingness to be governed by the system set out in the U.S. Constitution. But that does not require anyone to agree to any particular claims or values. The Bill of Rights tells us, "Congress shall make no law respecting an establishment of religion, or prohibiting the free exercise thereof. . . ." Yet we don't need to agree on what values underlie our acceptance of the First Amendment's treatment of religion. Is it religious toleration as an end in itself? Or is it a Protestant commitment to the sovereignty of the individual conscience? Is it prudence, which recognizes that trying to force religious conformity on people only leads to civil discord? Or is it skepticism that any religion has it right? Is it to protect the government from religion? Or religion from the government? Or is it some combination of these, or other, aims?

Cass Sunstein, the American legal scholar, has written eloquently that our understanding of Constitutional law is a set of what he calls "incompletely theorized agreements."[6] People mostly agree that it would be wrong for the Congress to pass laws prohibiting the building of mosques, for example, without agreeing exactly as to why. Many of us would, no doubt, mention the First Amendment (even though we don't agree about what values it embodies). But others would ground their judgment not in any particular law but in a conception, say, of democracy or in the equal citizenship of Muslims, neither of which is explicitly mentioned in the Constitution. There is no agreed-upon answer — and the point is there doesn't need to be. We can live together without agreeing on what the values are that make it good to live together; we can agree about what to do in most cases, without agreeing about why it is right.

I don't want to overstate the claim. No doubt there are widely shared values that help Americans live together in amity. But they certainly don't live together successfully because they have a shared theory of value or a shared story as to how to bring "their" values to bear in each case. They each have a pattern of life that they are used to; and neighbors who are, by and large, used to them. So long as this settled pattern is not seriously disrupted, they do not worry over-much about whether their fellow citizens agree with them or their theories about how to live. Americans tend to have, in sum, a broadly liberal reaction when they *do* hear about their fellow citizens' doing something that they would not do themselves: They mostly think it is not their business and not the government's business either. And, as a general rule, their shared Americanness matters to them, although many of their fellow Americans are remarkably unlike themselves. It's just that what they do share can be less substantial than we're inclined to suppose.

Changing Our Minds

It's not surprising, then, that what makes conversation across boundaries worthwhile isn't that we're likely to come to a reasoned agreement about values. I don't say that we can't change minds, but the reasons we exchange in our conversations will seldom do much to persuade others who do not share our fundamental evaluative judgments already. (Remember: The same goes, mutatis mutandis, for factual judgments.)

When we offer judgments, after all, it's rarely because we have applied well-thought-out principles to a set of facts and deduced an answer. Our efforts to justify what we have done — or what we plan to do — are typically made up after the event, rationalizations of what we have decided intuitively. And a good deal of what we intuitively take to be right, we take to be right just because it is what we are used to. If you live in a society where children are spanked, you will probably spank your children. You will believe that it is a good way to teach them right from wrong and that, despite the temporary suffering caused by a beating, they will end up better off for it. You will point to the wayward child and say, sotto voce, that his parents do not know how to discipline him; you will mean that they do not beat him enough. You will also, no doubt, recognize that there are people who beat their children too hard or too often. So you will recognize that beating a child can sometimes be cruel.

Much the same can be said about the practice of female genital cutting. . . . If you've grown up taking it for granted as the normal thing to do, you will probably respond at first with surprise to someone who thinks it is wrong. You will offer reasons for doing it—that unmodified sexual organs are unaesthetic; that the ritual gives young people the opportunity to display courage in their transition to adulthood; that you can see their excitement as they go to their ceremony, their pride when they return. You will say that it is very strange that someone who has not been through it should presume to know whether or not sex is pleasurable for you. And, if someone should try to force you to stop from the outside, you may decide to defend the practice as an expression of your cultural identity. But this is likely to be as much a rationalization as are the arguments of your critics. They say it is mutilation, but is that any more than a reflex response to an unfamiliar practice? They exaggerate the medical risks. They say that female circumcision demeans women, but do not seem to think that male circumcision demeans men.

I am not endorsing these claims, or celebrating the argumentative impasse, or, indeed, the poverty of reason in much discussion within and across cultures. But let's recognize this simple fact: A large part of what we do we do because it *is* just what we do. You get up in the morning at eight-thirty. Why *that* time? You have coffee and cereal. Why not porridge? You send the kids to school. Why not teach them at home? You have to work. Why that job, though? Reasoning—by which I mean the public act of exchanging stated justifications—comes in not when we are going on in the usual way, but when we are thinking about change. And when it comes to change, what moves people is often not an argument from a principle, not a long discussion about values, but just a gradually acquired new way of seeing things.

My father, for example, came from a society in which neither women nor men were traditionally circumcised. Indeed, circumcision was *akyiwadeɛ*; and since chiefs were supposed to be unblemished, circumcision was a barrier to holding royal office. Nevertheless, as he tells us in his autobiography, he decided as a teenager to have himself circumcised.

> As was the custom in those happy days, the young girls of Adum would gather together in a playing field nearby on moonlight nights to regale themselves by singing traditional songs and dancing from about 7 PM until midnight each day of the week.
>
> . . . On one such night, these girls suddenly started a new song that completely bowled us over: Not only were the words profane in the extreme, but they also constituted the most daring challenge to our manhood and courage ever flung at us. More than that, we were being invited to violate an age-old tradition of our ancestors, long respected among our people, namely the taboo on circumcision. Literally translated the words were:

"An uncircumcised penis is detestable, and those who are uncircumcised should come for money from us so that they can get circumcised. We shall never marry the uncircumcised."[7]

To begin with, my father and his friends thought the girls would relent. But they were wrong. And so, after consultation with his mates, my father found himself a *wansam*—a Muslim circumcision specialist—and had the operation performed. (It was, he said, the most painful experience of his life and, if he'd had it to do again, he would have refrained. He did not, of course, have the advantage of the preparation, the companionship of boys of his own age, and the prestige of suffering bravely that would have come if the practice had been an Akan tradition.)

My father offered a reason for this decision: He and his friends conceded that "as our future sweethearts and wives, they were entitled to be heard in their plea in favor of male circumcision, even though they were not prepared to go in for female circumcision, which was also a taboo among our people." This explanation invites a question, however. Why did these young women, in the heart of Asante, decide to urge the young men of Adum to do what was not just untraditional but taboo? One possibility is that circumcision somehow became identified in their minds with being modern. If that was the point, my father would have been sympathetic. He was traditional in some ways; but like many people in Kumasi in the early twentieth century, he was also excited by a modern world that was bringing new music, new technology, new possibilities. To volunteer for circumcision in his society he surely had not just to hear the plea of the young women of Adum but to understand—and agree with—the impulse behind it. And, as I say, it may have been exactly the fact that it was untraditional that made it appealing. Circumcision—especially because it carried with it exclusion from the possibilities of traditional political office—became a way of casting his lot with modernity.

This new fashion among the young people of Adum was analogous to, if more substantial than, the change in taste that has produced a generation of Americans with piercings and tattoos. And that change was not simply the result of argument and debate, either (even though, as anyone who has argued with a teenager about a pierced belly button will attest, people on both sides can come up with a whole slew of arguments). There's some social-psychological truth in the old Flanders & Swann song "The Reluctant Cannibal," about a young "savage" who pushes away from the table and declares, "I won't eat people. Eating people is wrong." His father has all the arguments, such as they are. ("But people have always eaten people, / What else is there to eat? / If the Juju had meant us not to eat people, / He wouldn't have made us of meat!") The son, though, just repeats his newfound conviction: Eating people is wrong. He's just sure of it, he'll say so again and again, and he'll win the day by declamation.

Or take the practice of foot-binding in China, which persisted for a thousand years—and was largely eradicated within a generation. The anti-foot-binding campaign, in the 1910s and 1920s, did circulate facts about the disadvantages of bound feet, but those couldn't have come as news to most people. Perhaps more effective was the campaign's emphasis that no other country went in for the practice; in the world at large, then, China was "losing face" because of it. Natural-foot societies were formed, with members forswearing the practice and further pledging that their sons would not marry women with bound feet. As the movement took hold, scorn was heaped on older women with bound feet, and they were forced to endure the agonies of unbinding. What had been beautiful became ugly; ornamentation became disfigurement. (The success of the anti-foot-binding campaign was undoubtedly a salutary development, but it was not without its victims. Think of some of the last women whose feet were bound, who had to struggle to find husbands.) The appeal to reason alone can explain neither the custom nor its abolition.

So, too, with other social trends. Just a couple of generations ago, in most of the industrialized world, most people thought that middle-class women would ideally be housewives and mothers. If they had time on their hands, they could engage in charitable work or entertain one another; a few of them might engage in the arts, writing novels, painting, performing in music, theater, and dance. But there was little place for them in the "learned professions"—as lawyers or doctors, priests or rabbis; and if they were to be academics, they would teach young women and probably remain unmarried. They were not likely to make their way in politics, except perhaps at the local level. And they were not made welcome in science. How much of the shift away from these assumptions is the result of arguments? Isn't a significant part of it just the consequence of our getting used to new ways of doing things? The arguments that kept the old pattern in place were not—to put it mildly—terribly good. If the *reasons* for the old sexist way of doing things had been the problem, the women's movement could have been done with in a couple of weeks. There are still people, I know, who think that the ideal life for any woman is making and managing a home. There are more who think that it is an honorable option. Still, the vast majority of Westerners would be appalled at the idea of trying to force women back into these roles. Arguments mattered for the women who made the women's movement and the men who responded to them. This I do not mean to deny. But their greatest achievement has been to change our habits. In the 1950s, if a college-educated woman wanted to go to law or business school, the natural response was "Why?" Now the natural response is "Why not?"

> **Reasoning . . . comes in not when we are going on in the usual way, but when we are thinking about change.**

Or consider another example: In much of Europe and North America, in places where a generation ago homosexuals were social outcasts and homosexual acts were illegal, lesbian and gay couples are increasingly being recognized by their families, by society, and by the law. This is true despite the continued opposition of major religious groups and a significant and persisting undercurrent of social disapproval. Both sides make arguments, some good, most bad, if you apply a philosophical standard of reasoning. But if you ask the social scientists what has produced this change, they will rightly not start with

35

a story about reasons. They will give you a historical account that concludes with a sort of perspectival shift. The increasing presence of "openly gay" people in social life and in the media has changed our habits. Over the last thirty or so years, instead of thinking about the private activity of gay *sex*, many Americans started thinking about the public category of gay *people*. Even those who continue to think of the sex with disgust now find it harder to deny these people their respect and concern (and some of them have learned, as we all did with our own parents, that it's better not to think too much about other people's sex lives anyway).

Now, I don't deny that all the time, at every stage, people were talking, giving each other reasons to do things: accept their children, stop treating homosexuality as a medical disorder, disagree with their churches, come out. Still, the short version of the story is basically this: People got used to lesbians and gay people. I am urging that we should learn about people in other places, take an interest in their civilizations, their arguments, their errors, their achievements, not because that will bring us to agreement, but because it will help us get used to one another. If that is the aim, then the fact that we have all these opportunities for disagreement about values need not put us off. Understanding one another may be hard; it can certainly be interesting. But it doesn't require that we come to agreement.

Fighting for the Good

I've said we can live in harmony without agreeing on underlying values (except, perhaps, the cosmopolitan value of living together). It works the other way, too: We can find ourselves in conflict when we do agree on values. Warring parties are seldom at odds because they have clashing conceptions of "the good." On the contrary, conflict arises most often when two peoples have identified the same thing as good. The fact that both Palestinians and Israelis—in particular, that both observant Muslims and observant Jews—have a special relation to Jerusalem, to the Temple Mount, has been a reliable source of trouble. The problem isn't that they disagree about the importance of Jerusalem: The problem is exactly that they both care for it deeply and, in part, for the same reasons. Muhammad, in the first years of Islam, urged his followers to turn toward Jerusalem in prayer because he had learned the story of Jerusalem from the Jews among whom he lived in Mecca. Nor is it an accident that the West's fiercest adversaries among other societies tend to come from among the most Westernized of the group. *Mon semblable mon frère?* Only if the *frère* you have in mind is Cain. We all know now that the foot soldiers of al Qaeda who committed the mass murders at the Twin Towers and the Pentagon were not Bedouins from the desert; not unlettered fellahin.

Indeed, there's a wider pattern here. Who in Ghana excoriated the British and built the movement for independence? Not the farmers and the peasants. Not the chiefs. It was the Western-educated bourgeoisie. And when in the 1950s Kwame Nkrumah—who went to college in Pennsylvania and lived in London—created a nationalist mass movement, at its core were soldiers who had returned from fighting a war in the British army, urban market women who traded Dutch prints, trade unionists who worked in industries created by colonialism, and the so-called veranda boys, who had been to colonial secondary schools, learned English, studied history and geography in textbooks written in England. Who led the resistance to the British Raj? An Indian-born South African lawyer, trained in the British courts, whose name was Gandhi; an Indian named Nehru who wore Savile Row suits and sent his daughter to an English boarding school; and Muhammad Ali Jinnah, founder of Pakistan, who joined Lincoln's Inn in London and became a barrister at the age of nineteen.

In Shakespeare's *Tempest*, Caliban, the original inhabitant of an island   40
commandeered by Prospero, roars at his domineering colonizer, "You taught me language and my profit on't / Is, I know how to curse." It is no surprise that Prospero's "abhorred slave" has been a figure of colonial resistance for literary nationalists all around the world. And in borrowing from Caliban, they have also borrowed from Shakespeare. Prospero has told Caliban,

> When thou didst not, savage,
> Know thine own meaning, but wouldst gabble like
> A thing most brutish, I endowed thy purposes
> With words that made them known.

Of course, one of the effects of colonialism was not only to give many of the natives a European language, but also to help shape their purposes. The independence movements of the post-1945 world that led to the end of Europe's African and Asian empires were driven by the rhetoric that had guided the Allies' own struggle against Germany and Japan: democracy, freedom, equality. This wasn't a conflict between values. It was a conflict of interests couched in terms of the same values.

The point applies as much within the West as elsewhere. Americans disagree about abortion, many vehemently. They couch this conflict in a language of conflicting values: They are pro-life or pro-choice. But this is a dispute that makes sense only because each side recognizes the very values the other insists upon. The disagreement is about their significance. Both sides respect something like the sanctity of human life. They disagree about such things as why human life is so precious and where it begins. Whatever you want to call those disagreements, it's just a mistake to think that either side doesn't recognize the value at stake here. And the same is true about choice: Americans are not divided about whether it's important to allow people, women and men, to make the major medical choices about their own bodies. They are divided about such questions as whether an abortion involves two people—both fetus and mother—or three people, adding in the father, or only one. Furthermore, no sane person on either side thinks that saving human lives or allowing people medical autonomy is the only thing that matters.

Some people will point to disputes about homosexuality and say that there, at least, there really is a conflict between people who do and people who don't regard homosexuality as a perversion. Isn't that a conflict of values? Well, no. Most Americans, on both sides, have the concept of perversion: of sexual acts that are wrong because their objects are inappropriate objects of sexual desire. But not everyone thinks that the fact that an act involves two women or two men makes it perverted. Not everyone who thinks these acts are perverse thinks they should be illegal. Not everyone who thinks they should be illegal thinks that gay and lesbian people should be ostracized. What is at stake, once more, is a battle about the meaning of perversion, about its status as a value, and about how to apply it. It is a reflection of the essentially contestable character of perversion as a term of value. When one turns from the issue of criminalization of gay sex—which is, at least for the moment, unconstitutional in the United States—to the question of gay marriage, all sides of the debate take seriously issues of sexual autonomy, the value of the intimate lives of couples, the meaning of family, and, by way of discussions of perversion, the proper uses of sex.

What makes these conflicts so intense is that they are battles over the meaning of the *same* values, not that they oppose one value, held exclusively by one side, with another, held exclusively by their antagonists. It is, in part, because we have shared horizons of meaning, because these are debates between people who share so many other values and so much else in the way of belief and of habit, that they are as sharp and as painful as they are.

Winners and Losers

But the disputes about abortion and gay marriage divide Americans bitterly   45
most of all because they share a society and a government. They are neighbors and fellow citizens. And it is laws governing all of them that are in dispute. What's at stake are their bodies or those of their mothers, their aunts, their sisters, their daughters, their wives, and their friends; those dead fetuses could have been their children or their children's friends.

We should remember this when we think about international human rights treaties. Treaties are law, even when they are weaker than national law. When we seek to embody our concern for strangers in human rights law and when we urge our government to enforce it, we are seeking to change the world of law in every nation on the planet. We have outlawed slavery not just domestically but in international law. And in so doing we have committed ourselves, at a minimum, to the desirability of its eradication everywhere. This is no longer controversial in the capitals of the world. No one defends enslavement. But international treaties define slavery in ways that arguably include debt bondage; and debt bondage is a significant economic institution in parts of South Asia. I hold no brief for debt bondage. Still, we shouldn't be surprised if people whose income and whose style of life depend upon it are angry. Given that we have neighbors—even if only a few—who think that the fact that abortion is permitted in the United States turns the killing of the doctors who perform them into an act of heroism, we should not be surprised that there are strangers—even if only a few—whose anger turns them to violence against us.

I do not fully understand the popularity among Islamist movements in Egypt, Algeria, Iran, and Pakistan of a high-octane anti-Western rhetoric. But I do know one of its roots. It is, to use suitably old-fashioned language, "the woman question." There are Muslims, many of them young men, who feel that forces from outside their society—forces that they might think of as Western or, in a different moment, American—are pressuring them to reshape relations between men and women. Part of that pressure, they feel, comes from our media. Our films and our television programs are crammed with indescribable indecency. Our fashion magazines show women without modesty, women whose presence on many streets in the Muslim world would be a provocation, they think, presenting an almost irresistible temptation to men. Those magazines influence publications in their own countries, pulling them inevitably in the same direction. We permit women to swim almost naked with strange men, which is our business; but it is hard to keep the news of these acts of immodesty from Muslim women and children or to protect Muslim men from the temptations they inevitably create. As the Internet spreads, it will get even harder, and their children, especially their girls, will be tempted to ask for these freedoms too. Worse, they say, we are now trying to force our conception of how women and men should behave upon them. We speak of women's rights. We make treaties enshrining these rights. And then we want their governments to enforce them.[8]

Like many people in every nation, I support those treaties, of course; I believe that women, like men, should have the vote, should be entitled to work outside their homes, should be protected from the physical abuse of men, including their fathers, brothers, and husbands. But I also know that the changes that these freedoms would bring will change the balance of power between men and women in everyday life. How do I know this? Because I have lived most of my adult life in the West as it has gone through the latter phases of just such a transition, and I know that the process is not yet complete.

The recent history of America does show that a society can radically change its attitudes—and more importantly, perhaps, its habits—about these issues over a single generation. But it also suggests that some people will stay with the old attitudes, and the whole process will take time. The relations between men and women are not abstractions: They are part of the intimate texture of our everyday lives. We have strong feelings about them, and we have inherited many received ideas. Above all, we have deep *habits* about gender. A man and a woman go out on a date. Our habit is that, even if the woman offers, the man pays. A man and a woman approach an elevator door. The man steps back. A man and a woman kiss in a movie theater. No one takes a second look. Two men walk hand in hand in the high street. People are embarrassed. They hope their children don't see. They don't know how to explain it to them.

Most Americans are against gay marriage, conflicted about abortion, and   50
amazed (and appalled) that a Saudi woman can't get a driver's license. But my guess is that they're not as opposed to gay marriage as they were twenty years ago. Indeed, twenty years ago, most Americans would probably just have thought the whole idea ridiculous. On the other hand, those Americans who are in favor of recognizing gay marriages probably don't have a simple set of reasons why. It just seems right to them, probably, in the way that it just seems wrong to those who disagree. (And probably they're thinking not about couples

in the abstract but about Jim and John or Jean and Jane.) The younger they are, the more likely it is that they think that gay marriage is fine. And if they don't, it will often be because they have had religious objections reinforced regularly through life in church, mosque, or temple.

I am a philosopher. I believe in reason. But I have learned in a life of university teaching and research that even the cleverest people are not easily shifted by reason alone—and that can be true even in the most cerebral of realms. One of the great savants of the postwar era, John von Neumann, liked to say, mischievously, that "in mathematics you don't understand things, you just get used to them." In the larger world, outside the academy, people don't always even care whether they *seem* reasonable. Conversation, as I've said, is hardly guaranteed to lead to agreement about what to think and feel. Yet we go wrong if we think the point of conversation is to persuade, and imagine it proceeding as a debate, in which points are scored for the Proposition and the Opposition. Often enough, as Faust said, in the beginning is the deed: Practices and not principles are what enable us to live together in peace. Conversations across boundaries of identity—whether national, religious, or something else—begin with the sort of imaginative engagement you get when you read a novel or watch a movie or attend to a work of art that speaks from some place other than your own. So I'm using the word "conversation" not only for literal talk but also as a metaphor for engagement with the experience and the ideas of others. And I stress the role of the imagination here because the encounters, properly conducted, are valuable in themselves. Conversation doesn't have to lead to consensus about anything, especially not values; it's enough that it helps people get used to one another.

NOTES

1. Galatians 3:28. In quoting the Bible, I have used the King James version, except for the Pentateuch, where I have used Robert Alter's powerful modern translation, *The Five Books of Moses* (New York: Norton, 2004).
2. Christoph Martin Wieland. "Das Geheimniß des Kosmopolitenordens," *Teutscher Merkur,* August 1788, p. 107. (Where I give a reference only to a source that is not in English, the translation is mine.)
3. *Essai sur les mœurs et l'esprit des nations,* vol. 16 of *Oeuvres complètes de Voltaire* (Paris: L'Imprimerie de la Société Litteraire-Typographique, 1784), p. 241. Voltaire is speaking specifically here of "the Orient," and especially of China and India, but he would surely not have denied its more general application.
4. George Eliot, *Daniel Deronda* (London: Penguin, 1995), pp. 745, 661–62, 183.
5. Cicero, *De officiis* 1.50.
6. Cass R. Sunstein, "Incompletely Theorized Agreements," *Harvard Law Review* 108 (1995): 1733–72.
7. Joseph Appiah, *Joe Appiah: The Autobiography of an African Patriot* (New York: Praeger, 1990), p. 22.
8. I have put this complaint in the mouth of a Muslim. But the truth is you could hear it from non-Muslims in many places as well. It is less likely to be heard in non-Muslim Africa, because there, by and large (as Amartya Sen has pointed out), women have a less unequal place in public life. See Jean Drèze and Amartya Sen, *Hunger and Public Action* (Oxford: Clarendon Press, 1989).

Questions for Critical Reading

1. What does Appiah mean by "cosmopolitanism"? Use his text to create a definition, working with quotations from Appiah that support your interpretation. Then apply this definition to a current national or world situation. How does it show cosmopolitanism at work, or how might embracing this concept help resolve the situation?

2. According to Appiah, what are some crucial tools needed to enact his vision of cosmopolitanism? Reread his essay to locate quotations in which Appiah discusses these tools. How realistic is his vision? Based on the examples he offers, do you think these tools would be effective? Why or why not?

3. In order to make his argument Appiah includes some stories from his own life. How does he use these stories? What sort of evidence do they provide? What other forms of evidence does he use? Support your answers by searching for specific examples from the text.

Exploring Context

1. Appiah uses the term *cosmopolitanism* to describe an ability to get along with others in a globalized and deeply connected world, an ability he relates to having conversation. Locate a Web site that you think represents Appiah's understanding of "cosmopolitan." What makes it so? What kinds of conversations happen on this site? Locate passages from Appiah's text that support your interpretation of the Web site as an example of cosmopolitanism. Does the site fit the definition you created in Question 1 of Questions for Critical Reading?

2. Appiah looks at a number of culturally specific practices, including foot-binding in China and circumcision in African nations. Select one of Appiah's examples and use information from the Web to prepare a short report on how the practice has changed in its home culture. Are the reasons for these changes consistent with Appiah's arguments?

3. Visit a social networking site such as MySpace (myspace.com) or Facebook (facebook.com). If you don't currently have a profile on either site, create one. Explore the site and consider the role it might play in Appiah's vision of cosmopolitanism. Does it promote that ideal? What sorts of conversations does the site allow? Is it the kind of tool you described in Question 2 of Questions for Critical Reading?

Questions for Connecting

1. How do Appiah's insights about conversation confirm Helen Epstein's findings in "AIDS, Inc." (p. 106)? How can AIDS prevention be further promoted in Africa despite differences in values and practices? Synthesize the ideas of these authors to suggest strategies for halting the spread of HIV.

2. In "Community and Diversity" (p. 228), Rebekah Nathan explores the idea and the reality of community and diversity on college campuses. Can Appiah's ideas about cosmopolitanism be applied to educational settings to redress the problems that Nathan sees? Use your work on Appiah's concepts from Questions for Critical Reading or your findings from Exploring Context in composing your response.

3. What sorts of values are at play in the international adoption business as it is described by Debora L. Spar in "Trading Places: The Practice and Politics of Adoption" (p. 402)? Do these adoptions reflect cosmopolitanism or more local values?

Language Matters

1. Transition words or phrases help readers move from one idea or unit in an essay to another. In order to practice using transitions, locate a passage in Appiah that you found difficult or confusing. To clarify the thinking of your selected passages, write a short paragraph that could precede your selection using transitions to ease the difficulty of the passage from Appiah. Think about what Appiah is trying to do in that part of his essay and then clarify that purpose with transition words or phrases. How might the paragraph you write work as a transitional paragraph for Appiah's ideas? How can you more effectively use transitions in your own writing?

2. As an exercise in being concise, summarize Appiah's argument in a haiku, a Japanese form of nonrhyming poetry that has three lines with five syllables in the first line, seven syllables in the second line, and five in the third. For example:

> Language matters much.
> Working on a haiku can
> Clarify this text.

Use the haiku to express Appiah's argument in the fewest number of words.

3. Locate materials on simple sentences, then choose one of the key sentences of Appiah's text. Transform this sentence into a simple sentence or into a series of simple sentences. Does breaking down Appiah's sentence into simple sentences make his ideas easier to understand? When are simple sentences useful? Why didn't Appiah write this whole essay in simple sentences? When should you use these in your own writing? What makes them useful?

Assignments for Writing

1. For Appiah, cosmopolitanism is as much a challenge as a solution to the problems of a globalized world. Using Appiah's sense of the term *cosmopolitanism*, locate the challenges presented by the examples he uses to illustrate his arguments. Then write a paper in which you propose the best strategies for overcoming the challenges presented by cosmopolitanism. In what way does Appiah

offer a solution to facing these challenges in an increasingly diverse world? Is the solution Appiah finds in cosmopolitanism adequate in addressing these challenges in a way that respects the diversity of local populations? Use your work in Exploring Context to offer specific examples of successful strategies.

2. Appiah discusses his choice of cosmopolitanism as a rubric for moving forward. At the same time, he discusses the problems of realizing social change. Based on his discussion of the primacy of practice, how can we advocate for change in social practices? Write a paper in which you identify the best tools for achieving social change. In constructing and supporting your argument, you may wish to build on the cultural practice you explored in Question 2 of Exploring Context.

3. Appiah is invested in conversation as an engagement with others, but has this engagement been constructive in the ideological conflicts Appiah discusses? Using one of the examples Appiah describes in "Changing Our Minds" and "Fighting for the Good," write a paper in which you determine whether conversation has helped to resolve the conflict Appiah describes, and if so, how.

THE DALAI LAMA

Tenzin Gyatso is the fourteenth Dalai Lama and the leader of the Central Tibetan Administration — the government-in-exile of Tibet. Gyatso was declared at two years old to be the reincarnation of an earlier Dalai Lama; at the age of fifteen he assumed the roles of religious and political leader of the Tibetan people. The only Dalai Lama to visit the West, Gyatso has become notable for gaining Western sympathy for the cause of a free Tibet and for authoring or coauthoring more than fifty books. Among his many honors are the Nobel Peace Prize (1989) and the U.S. Congressional Gold Medal (2006).

In *The Universe in a Single Atom* (2005), the Dalai Lama tries to reconcile religion with science, claiming that religion and science are parts of the same path to ultimate truth. Relying on just one, he suggests, is incomplete at best and "impoverishing" at worst. Simply following the rationale of science that everything "is reducible to matter and energy leaves out a huge range of human experience," and the opposite approach "can lock us into fundamentalist cages" that deny proven facts. According to the Dalai Lama, we must attempt to bridge this gap between our different ways of thinking.

In "Ethics and the New Genetics," a chapter from *The Universe in a Single Atom*, the Dalai Lama focuses on the field of genetic engineering. The potential benefits of this area of science are enormous, but the Dalai Lama reminds us to bear the potential costs in mind: "The higher the level of knowledge and power," he writes, "the greater must be our sense of moral responsibility." He argues that the speed of scientific progress in recent years has outpaced our society's ethical development, raising questions of what to do about possible breakthroughs in the future, when to trust our instinctual reactions, and what consequences science can have on culture and society.

In an age when stem cell research is passionately argued from both sides, the Dalai Lama urges us in this essay to craft ethical standards that can guide us in the complex decisions involved when technology intersects with life.

▶ TAGS: *research*, *social changes*, *biotechnology*, *human dignity*, *ethics*

Ethics and the New Genetics

Many of us who have followed the development of the new genetics are aware of the deep public disquiet that is gathering around the topic. This concern has been raised in relation to everything from cloning to genetic manipulation. There has been a worldwide outcry over the genetic engineering of foodstuffs. It is now possible to create new breeds of plants with far higher yields and far lower susceptibility to disease in order to maximize food production in a world where the increasing population needs to be fed. The benefits are obvious and wonderful. Seedless watermelons, apples that have longer shelf lives, wheat and other grains that are immune to pests when growing in the field — these are no longer science fiction. I have read that scientists are even experimenting to develop farm products, such as tomatoes, injected with genes from different species of spiders.

But by doing these things, we are changing the genetic makeup, and do we really know what the long-term impact will be on the species of plants, on the soil, on the environment? There are obvious commercial benefits, but how do we judge what is really useful? The complex web of interdependence that characterizes the environment makes it seem beyond our capacity to predict.

Genetic changes have happened slowly over hundreds of thousands of years of natural evolution. The evolution of the human brain has occurred over millions of years. By actively manipulating the gene, we are on the cusp of forcing an unnaturally quick rate of change in animals and plants as well as our own species. This is not to say that we should turn our backs on developments in this area — it is simply to point out that we must become aware of the awesome implications of this new area of science.

The most urgent questions that arise have to do more with ethics than with science per se, with correctly applying our knowledge and power in relation to the new possibilities opened by cloning, by unlocking the genetic code and other advances. These issues relate to the possibilities for genetic manipulation not only of human beings and animals but also of plants and the environment of which we are all parts. At heart the issue is the relationship between our knowledge and power on the one hand and our responsibility on the other.

Any new scientific breakthrough that offers commercial prospects attracts 5 tremendous interest and investment from both the public sector and private enterprise. The amount of scientific knowledge and the range of technological possibilities are so enormous that the only limitations on what we do may be the results of insufficient imagination. It is this unprecedented acquisition of knowledge and power that places us in a critical position at this time. The higher the level of knowledge and power, the greater must be our sense of moral responsibility.

If we examine the philosophical basis underlying much of human ethics, a clear recognition of the principle that correlates greater knowledge and power with a greater need for moral responsibility serves as a key foundation. Until recently we could say that this principle had been highly effective. The human capacity for moral reasoning has kept pace with developments in human knowledge and its capacities. But with the new era in biogenetic science, the gap between moral reasoning and our technological capacities has reached a critical point. The rapid increase of human knowledge and the technological possibilities emerging in the new genetic science are such that it is now almost impossible for ethical thinking to keep pace with these changes. Much of what is soon going to be possible is less in the form of new breakthroughs or paradigms in science than in the development of new technological options combined with the financial calculations of business and the political and economic calculations of governments. The issue is no longer whether we should or should not acquire knowledge and explore its technological potentials. Rather, the issue is how to use this new knowledge and power in the most expedient and ethically responsible manner.

The area where the impact of the revolution in genetic science may be felt most immediately at present is medicine. Today, I gather, many in medicine believe that the sequencing of the human genome will usher in a new era, in which it may be possible to move beyond a biochemical model of therapy to a genetically based model. Already the very definitions of many diseases are changing as illnesses are found to be genetically programmed into human beings and animals from their conception. While successful gene therapy for some of these conditions may be some way off, it seems no longer beyond the bounds of possibility. Even now, the issue of gene therapy and the associated question of genetic manipulation, especially at the level of the human embryo, are posing grave challenges to our capacity for ethical thinking.

A profound aspect of the problem, it seems to me, lies in the question of what to do with our new knowledge. Before we knew that specific genes caused senile dementia, cancer, or even aging, we as individuals assumed we wouldn't be afflicted with these problems, but we responded when we were. But now, or at any rate very soon, genetics can tell individuals and families that they have genes which may kill or maim them in childhood, youth, or middle age. This knowledge could radically alter our definitions of health and sickness. For example, someone who is healthy at present but has a particular genetic predisposition may come to be marked as "soon to be sick." What should we do with such knowledge, and how do we handle it in a way that is most compassionate? Who should have access to such knowledge, given its social and personal implications in relation to insurance, employment, and relationships, as well as reproduction? Does the individual who carries such a gene have a responsibility to reveal this fact to his or her potential partner in life? These are just a few of the questions raised by such genetic research.

To complicate an already intricate set of problems, I gather that genetic forecasting of this kind cannot be guaranteed to be accurate. It is sometimes certain that a particular genetic disorder observed in the embryo will give rise to disease in the child or adult, but it is often a question of relative probabilities. Lifestyle, diet, and other environmental factors come into play. So while we may know that a particular embryo carries a gene for a disease, we cannot be certain that the disease will arise.

People's life choices and indeed their very self-identity may be significantly affected by their perception of genetic risk, but those perceptions may not be correct and the risk may not be actualized. Should we be afforded such probabilistic knowledge? In cases where one member of the family discovers a genetic disorder of this type, should all the other members who may have inherited the same gene be informed? Should this knowledge be made available to a wider community — for instance, to health insurance companies? The carriers of certain genes may be excluded from insurance and hence even from access to health care all because there is a possibility of a particular disease manifesting itself. The issues here are not just medical but ethical and can affect the psychological well-being of the people concerned. When genetic disorders are detected in the embryo (as will increasingly be the case), should parents (or society) make the decision to curtail the life of that embryo? This question is further complicated by the fact that new methods of dealing with genetic disease and new medications are being found as swiftly as the genes carrying individual disease are identified. One can imagine a scenario in which a baby whose disease may manifest in twenty years is aborted and a cure for the disease is found within a decade.

Many people around the world, especially practitioners of the newly emerging discipline of bioethics, are grappling with the specifics of these problems. Given my lack of expertise in these fields, I have nothing concrete to offer in regard to any specific question — especially as the empirical facts are changing so rapidly. What I wish to do, however, is think through some of the key issues which I feel every informed person in the world needs to reflect upon, and to suggest some general principles that can be brought to bear in dealing with these ethical challenges. I believe that at heart the challenge we face is really a question of what choices we make in the face of the growing options that science and technology provide us.

At heart the challenge we face is really a question of what choices we make in the face of growing options that science and technology provide us.

Attendant on the new frontiers of genetically based medicine there is a series of further issues which again raise deep and troubling ethical questions. Here I am speaking primarily of cloning. It has now been several years since the world was introduced to a completely cloned sentient being, Dolly, the famous sheep. Since then there has been a huge amount of coverage of human cloning. We know that the first cloned human embryos have been created. The media frenzy aside, the question of cloning is highly complex. I am told there are two quite different kinds of cloning — therapeutic and reproductive. Within therapeutic cloning, there is the use of cloning technology for the reproduction of cells and the potential creation of semi-sentient beings purely for the purpose of harvesting body parts for transplantation. Reproductive cloning is basically the creation of an identical copy.

In principle, I have no objection to cloning as such — as a technological instrument for medical and therapeutic purposes. As in all these cases, what must govern one's decisions is the question of compassionate motivation. However, regarding the idea of deliberately breeding semi-human beings for spare parts, I feel an immediate, instinctive revulsion. I once saw a BBC documentary which simulated such creatures through computer animation, with some distinctively recognizable human features. I was horrified. Some people might feel this is an irrational emotional reaction that need not be taken seriously. But I believe we must trust our instinctive feelings of revulsion, as these arise out of our basic humanity. Once we allow the exploitation of such hybrid semi-humans, what is to stop us from doing the same with our fellow human beings whom the whims of society may deem deficient in some way? The willingness to step across such natural thresholds is what often leads humanity to the commission of horrific atrocities.

Although reproductive cloning is not horrifying in the same way, in some respects its implications may be more far-reaching. Once the technology becomes feasible, there could be parents who, desperate to have children and unable to do so, may seek to bear a child through cloning. What would this practice do to the future gene pool? To the diversity that has been essential to evolution?

There could also be individuals who, out of a desire to live beyond biological possibility, may choose to clone themselves in the belief that they will continue to live in the new cloned being. In this case, I find it difficult to see any justifiable motives — from the Buddhist perspective, it may be an identical body, but there will be two different consciousnesses. They will still die.

One of the social and cultural consequences of new genetic technologies is their effect on the continuation of our species, through interference with the reproductive process. Is it right to select the sex of one's child, which I believe is possible now? If it is not, is it right to make such choices for reasons of health (say, in couples where a child is at serious risk of muscular dystrophy or hemophilia)? Is it acceptable to insert genes into human sperm or eggs in the lab? How far can we go in the direction of creating "ideal" or "designer" fetuses — for instance, embryos that have been selected in the lab to provide particular molecules or compounds absent in genetically deficient siblings in order that the children born from such embryos may donate bone marrow or kidneys to cure siblings? How far can we go with the artificial selection of fetuses with desirable traits that are held to improve intelligence or physical strength or specific color of eyes for instance?

When such technologies are used for medical reasons — as in the curing of a particular genetic deficiency — one can deeply sympathize. The selection of particular traits, however, especially when done for primarily aesthetic purposes, may not be for the benefit of the child. Even when the parents think they are selecting traits that will positively affect their child, we need to consider whether this is being done out of positive intention or on the basis of a particular society's prejudices at a particular time. We have to bear in mind the long-term impact of this kind of manipulation on the species as a whole, given that its effects will be passed on to following generations. We need also to consider the effects of limiting the diversity of humanity and the tolerance that goes with it, which is one of the marvels of life.

Particularly worrying is the manipulation of genes for the creation of children with enhanced characteristics, whether cognitive or physical. Whatever inequalities there may be between individuals in their circumstances — such as wealth, class, health, and so on — we are all born with a basic equality of our human nature, with certain potentialities; certain cognitive, emotional, and physical abilities; and the fundamental disposition — indeed the right — to seek happiness and overcome suffering. Given that genetic technology is bound to remain costly, at least for the foreseeable future, once it is allowed, for a long period it will be available only to a small segment of human society, namely the rich. Thus society will find itself translating an inequality of circumstance (that is, relative wealth) into an inequality of nature through enhanced intelligence, strength, and other faculties acquired through birth.

The ramifications of this differentiation are far-reaching — on social, political, and ethical levels. At the social level, it will reinforce — even perpetuate — our disparities, and it will make their reversal much more difficult. In political matters, it will breed a ruling elite, whose claims to power will be invocations of an intrinsic natural superiority. On the ethical level, these kinds of pseudo-nature-based differences can severely undermine our basic moral sensibilities insofar as these sensibilities are based on a mutual recognition of shared humanity. We cannot imagine how such practices could affect our very concept of what it is to be human.

When I think about the various new ways of manipulating human genetics, I can't help but feel that there is something profoundly lacking in our appreciation of what it is to cherish humanity. In my native Tibet, the value of a person rests not on physical appearance, not on intellectual or athletic achievement, but on the basic, innate capacity for compassion in all human beings. Even modern medical science has demonstrated how crucial affection is for human beings, especially during the first few weeks of life. The simple power of touch is critical for the basic development of the brain. In regard to his or her value as a human being, it is entirely irrelevant whether an individual has some kind of disability — for instance, Down syndrome — or a genetic disposition to develop a particular disease, such as sickle-cell anemia, Huntington's chorea, or Alzheimer's. All human beings have an equal value and an equal potential for goodness. To ground our appreciation of the value of a human being on genetic makeup is bound to impoverish humanity, because there is so much more to human beings than their genomes.

> We cannot imagine how such practices could affect our very concept of what it is to be human.

For me, one of the most striking and heartening effects of our knowledge of the genome is the astounding truth that the differences in the genomes of the different ethnic groups around the world are so negligible as to be insignificant. I have always argued that the differences of color, language, religion, ethnicity, and so forth among human beings have no substance in the face of our basic sameness. The sequencing of the human genome has, for me, demonstrated this in an extremely powerful way. It has also helped reinforce my sense of our basic kinship with animals, who share very large percentages of our genome. So it is conceivable if we humans utilize our newly found genetic knowledge skillfully, it could help foster a greater sense of affinity and unity not only with our fellow human beings but with life as a whole. Such a perspective could also underpin a much more healthy environmental consciousness.

In the case of food, if the argument is valid that we need some kind of genetic modification to help feed the world's growing population, then I believe that we cannot simply dismiss this branch of genetic technology. However, if, as suggested by its critics, this argument is merely a front for motives that are primarily commercial — such as producing food that will simply have a longer lasting shelf life, that can be more easily exported from one side of the world to the other, that is more attractive in appearance and more convenient in consumption, or creating grains and cereals engineered not to produce their own seeds so that farmers are forced to depend entirely upon the biotech companies for seeds — then clearly such practices must be seriously questioned.

Many people are becoming increasingly worried by the long-term consequences of producing and consuming genetically modified produce. The gulf between the scientific community and the general public may be caused in part by the lack of transparency in the companies developing these products. The onus should be on the biotech industry both to demonstrate that there are no long-term negative consequences for consumers of these new products and to adopt complete transparency on all the possible implications such plants may have for the natural environment. Clearly the argument that if there is no conclusive evidence that a particular product is harmful then there is nothing wrong with it cannot be accepted.

The point is that genetically modified food is not just another product, like a car or a portable computer. Whether we like it or not, we do not know the long-term consequences of introducing genetically modified organisms into the wider environment. In medicine, for instance, the drug thalidomide was found to be excellent for the treatment of morning sickness in pregnant women, but its long-term consequences for the health of the unborn child were not foreseen and proved catastrophic.

Given the tremendous pace of development in modern genetics, it is urgent now to refine our capacity for moral reasoning so that we are equipped to address the ethical challenges of this new situation. We cannot wait for a series of responses to emerge in an organic way. We need to confront the reality of our potential future and tackle the problems directly.

I feel the time is ripe to engage with the ethical side of the genetic revolution in a manner that transcends the doctrinal standpoints of individual religions. We must rise to the ethical challenge as members of one human family, not as a Buddhist, a Jew, a Christian, a Hindu, a Muslim. Nor is it adequate to address these ethical challenges from the perspective of purely secular, liberal political ideals, such as individual freedom, choice, and fairness. We need to examine the questions from the perspective of a global ethics that is grounded in the recognition of fundamental human values that transcend religion and science.

It is not adequate to adopt the position that our responsibility as a society is simply to further scientific knowledge and enhance our technological power. Nor is it sufficient to argue that what we do with this knowledge and power should be left to the choices of individuals. If this argument means that society at large should not interfere with the course of research and the creation of new technologies based on such research, it would effectively rule out any significant role for humanitarian or ethical considerations in the regulation of scientific development. It is essential, indeed it is a responsibility, for us to be much more critically self-aware about what we are developing and why. The basic principle is that the earlier one intervenes in the causal process, the more effective is one's prevention of undesirable consequences.

In order to respond to the challenges in the present and in the future, we need a much higher level of collective effort than has been seen yet. One partial solution is to ensure that a larger segment of the general public has a working grasp of scientific thinking and an understanding of key scientific discoveries, especially those which have direct social and ethical implications. Education needs to provide not only training in the empirical facts of science but also an examination of the relationship between science and society at large, including the ethical questions raised by new technological possibilities. This educational imperative must be directed at scientists as well as laypeople, so that scientists retain a wider understanding of the social, cultural, and ethical ramifications of the work they are doing.

Given that the stakes for the world are so high, the decisions about the course of research, what to do with our knowledge, and what technological possibilities should be developed cannot be left in the hands of scientists, business interests, or government officials. Clearly, as a society we need to draw some lines. But these deliberations cannot come solely from small committees, no matter how august or expert they may be. We need a much higher level of public involvement, especially in the form of debate and discussion, whether through the media, public consultation, or the action of grassroots pressure groups.

Today's challenges are so great — and the dangers of the misuse of technology so global, entailing a potential catastrophe for all humankind — that I feel we need a moral compass we can use collectively without getting bogged down in doctrinal differences. One key factor that we need is a holistic and integrated outlook at the level of human society that recognizes the fundamentally interconnected nature of all living beings and their environment. Such a moral compass must entail preserving our human sensitivity and will depend on us constantly bearing in mind our fundamental human values. We must be willing to be revolted when science — or for that matter any human activity — crosses the line of human decency, and we must fight to retain the sensitivity that is otherwise so easily eroded.

How can we find this moral compass? We must begin by putting faith in the basic goodness of human nature, and we need to anchor this faith in some fundamental and universal ethical principles. These include a recognition of the preciousness of life, an understanding of the need for balance in nature and the employment of this need as a gauge for the direction of our thought and action, and — above all — the need to ensure that we hold compassion as the key motivation for all our endeavors and that it is combined with a clear awareness of the wider perspective, including long-term consequences. Many will agree with me that these ethical values transcend the dichotomy of religious believers and nonbelievers, and are crucial for the welfare of all humankind. Because of the profoundly interconnected reality of today's world, we need to relate to the challenges we face as a single human family rather than as members of specific nationalities, ethnicities, or religions. In other words, a necessary principle is a spirit of oneness of the entire human species. Some might object that this is unrealistic. But what other option do we have?

I firmly believe it is possible. The fact that, despite our living for more than half a century in the nuclear age, we have not yet annihilated ourselves is what gives me great hope. It is no more coincidence that, if we reflect deeply, we find these ethical principles at the heart of all major spiritual traditions.

In developing an ethical strategy with respect to the new genetics, it is vitally important to frame our reflection within the widest possible context. We must first of all remember how new this field is and how new are the possibilities it offers, and to contemplate how little we understand what we know. We have now sequenced the whole of the human genome, but it may take decades for us fully to understand the functions of all the individual genes and their interrelationships, let alone the effects of their interaction with the environment. Too much of our current focus is on the feasibility of a particular technique, its immediate or short-term results and side effects, and what effect it may have on individual liberty. These are all valid concerns, but they are not sufficient. Their purview is too narrow, given that the very conception of human nature is at stake. Because of the far-reaching scope of these innovations, we need to examine all areas of human existence where genetic technology may have lasting implications. The fate of the human species, perhaps of all life on this planet, is in our hands. In the face of the great unknown, would it not be better to err on the side of caution than to transform the course of human evolution in an irreversibly damaging direction?

In a nutshell, our ethical response must involve the following key factors. First, we have to check our motivation and ensure that its foundation is compassion. Second, we must relate to any problem before us while taking into account the widest possible perspective, which includes not only situating the issue within the picture of wider human enterprise but also taking due regard of both short-term and long-term consequences. Third, when we apply our reason in addressing a problem, we have to be vigilant in ensuring that we remain honest, self-aware, and unbiased; the danger otherwise is that we may fall victim to self-delusion. Fourth, in the face of any real ethical challenge, we must respond in a spirit of humility, recognizing not only the limits of our knowledge (both collective and personal) but also our vulnerability to being misguided in the context of such a rapidly changing reality. Finally, we must all — scientists and society at large — strive to ensure that whatever new course of action we take, we keep in mind the primary goal of the well-being of humanity as a whole and the planet we inhabit.

The earth is our only home. As far as current scientific knowledge is concerned, this may be the only planet that can support life. One of the most powerful visions I have experienced was the first photograph of the earth from outer space. The image of a blue planet floating in deep space, glowing like the full moon on a clear night, brought home powerfully to me the recognition that we are indeed all members of a single family sharing one little house. I was flooded with the feeling of how ridiculous are the various disagreements and squabbles within the human family. I saw how futile it is to cling so tenaciously to the differences that divide us. From this perspective one feels the fragility, the vulnerability of our planet and its limited occupation of a small orbit sandwiched between Venus and Mars in the vast infinity of space. If we do not look after this home, what else are we charged to do on this earth?

Questions for Critical Reading

1. The Dalai Lama calls for an ethics to match our rapidly evolving technologies in areas such as genetic engineering. What might such an ethics look like? As you reread his essay to compose your response, locate quotations that support your proposed system of ethics.

2. What are the keys to developing an ethics apart from religion? Search the Dalai Lama's essay for quotations that support your position.

3. According to the Dalai Lama, when should we use genetic technologies? Reread his text for specific quotations that suggest the conditions necessary for the use of such technology.

Exploring Context

1. Visit the home page for the Human Genome Project (ornl.gov/sci/techresources/ Human_Genome/home.shtml). How does the project address the kinds of ethical problems that concern the Dalai Lama? Is it consistent with your proposed system of ethics from Question 1 of Questions for Critical Reading?

2. Explore the Web site for the President's Council on Bioethics (bioethics.gov). Are government organizations equipped to answer the Dalai Lama's call for a new ethics governing these technologies? Does the Council reflect your argument about a nonreligious ethics from Question 2 of Questions for Critical Reading?

3. London's Science Museum has an online exhibit about Dolly the sheep, the first cloned animal. Visit the site at sciencemuseum.org.uk/antenna/dolly/index.asp. In the aftermath of Dolly's life and death, what new ethical concerns should we consider?

Questions for Connecting

1. Francis Fukuyama's "Human Dignity" (p. 142) is also concerned about the potential of biotechnologies. How does Fukuyama's exploration of the matter complicate the Dalai Lama's call for a new ethics? What are their respective positions on genetic technologies? Does Fukuyama answer the Dalai Lama's call for a "moral compass"? You may wish to draw from your work on the use of genetic technologies from Question 3 of Questions for Critical Reading.

2. How can we apply the Dalai Lama's call for a new ethics to the use of human cadavers? Apply his concepts to Mary Roach's exploration of the subject in "The Cadaver Who Joined the Army" (p. 347). Can you synthesize their respective positions on ethics into a position of your own?

3. The Dalai Lama is a world religious figure. How can we account for his authority on the subject of genetics and ethics using the insights provided by Madeleine Albright in "Faith and Diplomacy" (p. 23)?

Language Matters

1. The Dalai Lama uses a clear, simple style of writing to discuss a very complex subject. Select a key quotation from his text and break down the parts of each sentence. How does he use language to express difficult concepts clearly? How can you do the same in your writing?

2. In a small group discuss what revision means. If you were going to revise this text, where would you start? What areas need more development?

3. If you were going to include images with this text, which ones would you choose? How would adding images change the meaning of the text? How does the visual support an argument?

Assignments for Writing

1. The Dalai Lama uses the complex ethical dilemma of genetic technologies to make his argument about the necessity for a moral compass to guide us in relation to knowledge and scientific discovery. Write a paper in which you extend the Dalai Lama's argument using your own example of a technology or discovery that demands a moral compass. You may want to use your example to discuss how to utilize new knowledge and power in the most expedient and ethically responsible manner. In composing your essay, consider the gap between moral reasoning and technological capacity. Should different approaches be taken when developing ethical standards for the two different types of cloning? Why? What are the implications of probabilistic knowledge?

2. In this essay the Dalai Lama discusses potential consequences of people being able to forecast genetic predispositions in their children and to alter their children's genetic makeup accordingly. Write a paper in which you propose a standard for when such forecasting should be used. Is such a technology ever ethical? Is it ever accurate? Why must relative probabilities be taken into consideration when thinking about genetic forecasting? To what degree must self-determination be considered a factor? You may wish to discuss the correlation of greater knowledge with a greater need for moral responsibility, and you may wish to draw from your exploration of the Web sites in Exploring Context and your understanding of the Dalai Lama's concepts from Questions for Connecting.

3. The possible consequences of genetic manipulation reach far beyond the sphere of science. Consider, for example, the role of national and global politics in relation to scientific breakthroughs that have the potential to literally change the face of humanity but will almost certainly not be available to everyone. Write a paper in which you examine the consequences of technology in terms of social and economic stability. How does the Dalai Lama characterize the relationship between knowledge and responsibility? In what ways does genetic engineering have the potential to perpetuate our disparities on social, political and ethical levels? Should new technologies be available to everyone?

Joan Didion

Joan Didion is a noted and versatile writer—a novelist, a screenwriter, an essayist, and a journalist. She began her career at *Vogue* magazine, where she worked as an associate features editor until the late 1960s. Since then, she has been a contributor to both the *New Yorker* and the *New York Review of Books*. However, she is perhaps best known for her collections of essays, including *Slouching Towards Bethlehem* (1968) and *The White Album* (1979). The following selection appeared in a different form in her nonfiction book *The Year of Magical Thinking* (2005), which won the National Book Award. Didion's memoir was later adapted into a one-woman show that ran on Broadway for twenty-four weeks and starred award-winning actress Vanessa Redgrave.

In *Magical Thinking*, Didion records the year after the death of her husband, John Gregory Dunne, with whom she wrote multiple screenplays, including 1996's *Up Close and Personal*. In December 2003, Didion's daughter Quintana fell into a coma, and just a few days later Didion's husband died from a massive heart attack. With this book, Didion details the "weeks and then months that cut loose any fixed idea I had ever had about death, about illness."

"After Life" deals with the immediate aftermath of Dunne's death. Didion recalls the moment his heart attack occurred (she first suspected he was joking), the arrival of the paramedics, and her realization that he was dead, which came when she met the social worker assigned to her at the hospital. In an instant, Didion finds herself answering questions about autopsies and funerals and deciding what to do with this bad news, whom to wake, and whom to leave undisturbed. And she deals with this grief while her daughter lies in a hospital room of her own. "You sit down to dinner and life as you know it ends," Didion writes. This, she adds, was not "the kind of conclusion [she] anticipated."

Grief and mourning are intensely personal and often private experiences. By inviting us in to these processes, Didion allows us to explore what happens to life in the wake of death.

▶ TAGS: *loss*, **mourning**, *kinship*, *language*, **death**, *change*

After Life

1

Life changes fast.
Life changes in the instant.
You sit down to dinner and life as you know it ends.
The question of self-pity.

Those were the first words I wrote after it happened. The computer dating on the   5
Microsoft Word file ("Notes on change.doc") reads "May 20, 2004, 11:11 PM,"
but that would have been a case of my opening the file and reflexively pressing
save when I closed it. I had made no changes to that file in May. I had made no
changes to that file since I wrote the words, in January 2004, a day or two or
three after the fact.
    For a long time I wrote nothing else.
Life changes in the instant.
The ordinary instant.
    At some point, in the interest of remembering what seemed most strik-
ing about what had happened, I considered adding those words, "the ordinary instant." I saw immediately that there would be no need to add the word
"ordinary," because there would be no forgetting it: The word never left my
mind. It was in fact the ordinary nature of everything preceding the event
that prevented me from truly believing it had happened, absorbing it, incorporating it, getting past it. I recognize now that there was nothing unusual
in this: Confronted with sudden disaster, we all focus on how unremarkable
the circumstances were in which the unthinkable occurred, the clear blue
sky from which the plane fell, the routine errand that ended on the shoulder
with the car in flames, the swings where the children were playing as usual
when the rattlesnake struck from the ivy. "He was on his way home from
work—happy, successful, healthy—and then, gone," I read in the account of
a psychiatric nurse whose husband was killed in a highway accident. In 1966 I
happened to interview many people who were living in Honolulu on the morning of December 7, 1941; without exception, these people began their accounts
of Pearl Harbor by telling me what an "ordinary Sunday morning" it had been.
"It was just an ordinary beautiful September day," people still say when asked
to describe the morning in New York when American Airlines 11 and United
Airlines 175 got flown into the World Trade towers. Even the report of the 9/11
Commission opened on this insistently premonitory and yet still dumbstruck
narrative note: "Tuesday, September 11, 2001, dawned temperate and nearly
cloudless in the eastern United States."
    "And then—gone." *In the midst of life we are in death,* Episcopalians say at   10
the graveside. Later I realized that I must have repeated the details of what
happened to everyone who came to the house in those first weeks, all those
friends and relatives who brought food and made drinks and laid out plates

on the dining-room table for however many people were around at lunch or dinner, all those who picked up the plates and froze the leftovers and ran the dishwasher and filled our (I could not yet think *my*) otherwise empty apartment even after I had gone into the bedroom (our bedroom, the one in which there still lay on a sofa a faded terry-cloth XL robe bought in the 1970s at Richard Carroll in Beverly Hills) and shut the door. Those moments when I was abruptly overtaken by exhaustion are what I remember most clearly about the first days and weeks. I have no memory of telling anyone the details, but I must have done so, because everyone seemed to know them. At one point I considered the possibility that they had picked up the details of the story from one another, but immediately rejected it: The story they had was in each instance too accurate to have been passed from hand to hand. It had come from me.

Another reason I knew that the story had come from me was that no version I heard included the details I could not yet face, for example the blood on the living room floor that stayed there until José came in the next morning and cleaned it up.

José. Who was part of our household. Who was supposed to be flying to Las Vegas later that day, December 31, but never went. José was crying that morning as he cleaned up the blood. When I first told him what had happened he had not understood. Clearly I was not the ideal teller of this story, something about my version had been at once too offhand and too elliptical, something in my tone had failed to convey the central fact in the situation (I would encounter the same failure later when I had to tell our daughter Quintana), but by the time José saw the blood he understood.

I had picked up the abandoned syringes and ECG electrodes before he came in that morning but I could not face the blood.

In outline.

It is now, as I begin to write this, the afternoon of October 4, 2004.   15

Nine months and five days ago, at approximately nine o'clock on the evening of December 30, 2003, my husband, John Gregory Dunne, appeared to (or did) experience, at the table where he and I had just sat down to dinner in the living room of our apartment in New York, a sudden massive coronary event that caused his death. Our only child, Quintana, then 37, had been for the previous five nights unconscious in an intensive care unit at Beth Israel Medical Center's Singer Division, at that time a hospital on East End Avenue (it closed in August 2004), more commonly known as "Beth Israel North" or "the old Doctors' Hospital," where what had seemed a case of December flu sufficiently severe to take her to an emergency room on Christmas morning had exploded into pneumonia and septic shock. This is my attempt to make sense of the period that followed, weeks and then months that cut loose any fixed idea I had ever had about death, about illness, about probability and luck, about good fortune and bad, about marriage and children and memory, about grief, about the ways in which people do and do not deal with the fact that life ends, about the shallowness of sanity, about life itself.

I have been a writer my entire life. As a writer, even as a child, long before what I wrote began to be published, I developed a sense that meaning itself was resident in the rhythms of words and sentences and paragraphs, a technique for withholding whatever it was I thought or believed behind an increasingly impenetrable polish. The way I write is who I am, or have become, yet this is a case in which I wish I had instead of words and their rhythms a cutting room, equipped with an Avid, a digital editing system on which I could touch a key and collapse the sequence of time, show you simultaneously all the frames of memory that come to me now, let you pick the takes, the marginally different expressions, the variant readings of the same lines. This is a case in which I need more than words to find the meaning. This is a case in which I need whatever it is I think or believe to be penetrable, if only for myself.

2

December 30, 2003, a Tuesday.

We had seen Quintana in the sixth-floor ICU at Beth Israel North.

We had come home.   20

We had discussed whether to go out for dinner or eat in.

I said I would build a fire, we could eat in.

I built the fire, I started dinner, I asked John if he wanted a drink.

I got him a Scotch and gave it to him in the living room, where he was reading in the chair by the fire where he habitually sat.

The book he was reading was by David Fromkin, a bound galley of *Europe's*   25
Last Summer: Who Started the Great War in 1914?

I finished getting dinner. I set the table in the living room where, when we were home alone, we could eat within sight of the fire. I find myself stressing the fire because fires were important to us. I grew up in California, John and I lived there together for twenty-four years, in California we heated our houses by building fires. We built fires even on summer evenings, because the fog came in. Fires said we were home, we had drawn the circle, we were safe through the night. I lighted the candles. John asked for a second drink before sitting down. I gave it to him. We sat down. My attention was on mixing the salad.

John was talking, then he wasn't.

At one point in the seconds or minute before he stopped talking he had asked me if I had used single-malt Scotch for his second drink. I had said no, I used the same Scotch I had used for his first drink. "Good," he had said. "I don't know why but I don't think you should mix them." At another point in those seconds or that minute he had been talking about why World War I was the critical event from which the entire rest of the twentieth century flowed.

I have no idea which subject we were on, the Scotch or World War I, at the instant he stopped talking.

I only remember looking up. His left hand was raised and he was slumped   30
motionless. At first I thought he was making a failed joke, an attempt to make the difficulty of the day seem manageable.

I remember saying *Don't do that.*

When he did not respond my first thought was that he had started to eat and choked. I remember trying to lift him far enough from the back of the chair to give him the Heimlich. I remember the sense of his weight as he fell forward, first against the table, then to the floor. In the kitchen by the telephone I had taped a card with the New York–Presbyterian ambulance numbers. I had not taped the numbers by the telephone because I anticipated a moment like this. I had taped the numbers by the telephone in case someone in the building needed an ambulance.

Someone else.

I called one of the numbers. A dispatcher asked if he was breathing. I said *Just come.* When the paramedics came I tried to tell them what had happened but before I could finish they had transformed the part of the living room where John lay into an emergency department. One of them (there were three, maybe four, even an hour later I could not have said) was talking to the hospital about the electrocardiogram they seemed already to be transmitting. Another was opening the first or second of what would be many syringes for injection. (Epinephrine? Lidocaine? Procainamide? The names came to mind but I had no idea from where.) I remember saying that he might have choked. This was dismissed with a finger swipe: The airway was clear. They seemed now to be using defibrillating paddles, an attempt to restore a rhythm. They got something that could have been a normal heartbeat (or I thought they did, we had all been silent, there was a sharp jump), then lost it, and started again.

"He's still fibbing," I remember the one on the telephone saying.   35

"V-fibbing," John's cardiologist said the next morning when he called from Nantucket. "They would have said 'V-fibbing.' V for ventricular."

Maybe they said "V-fibbing" and maybe they did not. Atrial fibrillation did not immediately or necessarily cause cardiac arrest. Ventricular did. Maybe ventricular was the given.

I remember trying to straighten out in my mind what would happen next. Since there was an ambulance crew in the living room, the next logical step would be going to the hospital. It occurred to me that the crew could decide very suddenly to go to the hospital and I would not be ready. I would not have in hand what I needed to take. I would waste time, get left behind. I found my handbag and a set of keys and a summary John's doctor had made of his medical history. When I got back to the living room the paramedics were watching the computer monitor they had set up on the floor. I could not see the monitor, so I watched their faces. I remember one glancing at the others.

When the decision was made to move it happened very fast. I followed them to the elevator and asked if I could go with them. They said they were taking the gurney down first, I could go in the second ambulance. One of them waited with me for the elevator to come back up. By the time he and I got into the second ambulance the ambulance carrying the gurney was pulling away from the front of the building. The distance from our building to the part of New York–Presbyterian that used to be New York Hospital is six crosstown blocks. I have no memory of sirens. I have no memory of traffic. When we arrived at the emergency entrance to the hospital the gurney was already disappearing into the building. A man was waiting in the driveway. Everyone else in sight was wearing scrubs. He was not. "Is this the wife?" he said to the driver, then turned to me. "I'm your social worker," he said, and I guess that is when I must have known.

"I opened the door and I seen the man in the dress greens and I knew. I immediately knew." This was what the mother of a nineteen-year-old killed by a bomb in Kirkuk said on an HBO documentary quoted by Bob Herbert in the *New York Times* on the morning of November 12, 2004. "But I thought that if, as long as I didn't let him in, he couldn't tell me. And then it—none of that would've happened. So he kept saying, 'Ma'am, I need to come in.' And I kept telling him, 'I'm sorry, but you can't come in.'"   40

When I read this at breakfast almost eleven months after the night with the ambulance and the social worker I recognized the thinking as my own.

Inside the emergency room I could see the gurney being pushed into a cubicle, propelled by more people in scrubs. Someone told me to wait in the reception area. I did. There was a line for admittance paperwork. Waiting in the line seemed the constructive thing to do. Waiting in the line said that there was still time to deal with this. I had copies of the insurance cards in my handbag, this was not a hospital I had ever negotiated—New York Hospital was the Cornell part of New York–Presbyterian, the part I knew was the Columbia part, Columbia-Presbyterian, at 168th and Broadway, twenty minutes away at best, too far in this kind of emergency—but I could make this unfamiliar hospital work, I could be useful, I could arrange the transfer to Columbia-Presbyterian once he was stabilized. I was fixed on the details of this imminent transfer to Columbia (he would need a bed with telemetry, eventually I could also get Quintana transferred to Columbia, the night she was admitted to Beth Israel North I had written on a card the beeper numbers of several Columbia doctors, one or another of them could make all this happen) when the social worker reappeared and guided me from the paperwork line into an empty room off the reception area. "You can wait here," he said. I waited. The room was cold, or I was. I wondered how much time had passed between the time I called the ambulance and the arrival of the paramedics. It had seemed no time at all (*a mote in the eye of God* was the phrase that came to me in the room off the reception area) but it must have been at the minimum several minutes.

I used to have on a bulletin board in my office, for reasons having to do with a plot point in a movie, a pink index card on which I had typed a sentence from *The Merck Manual* about how long the brain can be deprived of oxygen. The image of the pink index card was coming back to me in the room off the reception area: "Tissue anoxia for > 4 to 6 min. can result in irreversible brain damage or death." I was telling myself that I must be misremembering the sentence when the social worker reappeared. He had with him a man he introduced as "your husband's doctor." There was a silence. "He's dead, isn't he," I heard myself say to the doctor. The doctor looked at the social worker. "It's okay," the social worker said. "She's a pretty cool customer." They took me into the curtained cubicle where John lay, alone now. They asked if I wanted a priest. I said yes. A priest appeared and said the words. I thanked him. They gave me the silver clip in which John kept his driver's license and credit cards. They gave me the cash that had been in his pocket. They gave me his watch. They gave me his cell phone. They gave me a plastic bag in which they said I would find his clothes. I thanked them. The social worker asked if he could do anything more for me. I said he could put me in a taxi. He did. I thanked him. "Do you have money for the fare?" he asked. I said I did, the cool customer. When I walked into the apartment and saw John's jacket and scarf still lying on the chair where he had dropped them when we came in from seeing Quintana at Beth Israel North (the red cashmere scarf, the Patagonia windbreaker that had been the crew jacket on *Up Close and Personal*), I wondered what an uncool customer would be allowed to do. Break down? Require sedation? Scream?

I remember thinking that I needed to discuss this with John.

There was nothing I did not discuss with John.   45

Because we were both writers and both worked at home our days were filled with the sound of each other's voices.

I did not always think he was right nor did he always think I was right but we were each the person the other trusted. There was no separation between our investments or interests in any given situation. Many people assumed that we must be, since sometimes one and sometimes the other would get the better review, the bigger advance, in some way "competitive," that our private life must be a minefield of professional envies and resentments. This was so far from the case that the general insistence on it came to suggest certain lacunae in the popular understanding of marriage.

That had been one more thing we discussed.

What I remember about the apartment the night I came home alone from New York Hospital was its silence.

In the plastic bag I had been given at the hospital there were a pair of corduroy pants, a wool shirt, a belt, and I think nothing else. The legs of the corduroy pants had been slit open, I supposed by the paramedics. There was blood on the shirt. The belt was braided. I remember putting his cell phone in the charger on his desk. I remember putting his silver clip in the box in the bedroom in which we kept passports and birth certificates and proof of jury service. I look now at the clip and see that these were the cards he was carrying: a New York State driver's license, due for renewal on May 25, 2004; a Chase ATM card; an American Express card; a Wells Fargo MasterCard; a Metropolitan Museum card; a Writers Guild of America West card (it was the season before Academy voting, when you could use a WGAW card to see movies free, he must have gone to a movie, I did not remember); a Medicare card; a MetroCard; and a card issued by Medtronic with the legend "I have a Kappa 900 SR pacemaker implanted," the serial number of the device, a number to call for the doctor who implanted it, and the notation "Implant Date: 03 Jun 2003." I remember combining the cash

50

that had been in his pocket with the cash in my own bag, smoothing the bills, taking special care to interleaf twenties with twenties, tens with tens, fives and ones with fives and ones. I remember thinking as I did this that he would see that I was handling things.

When I saw him in the curtained cubicle in the emergency room at New York Hospital there was a chip in one of his front teeth, I supposed from the fall, since there were also bruises on his face. When I identified his body the next day for the undertaker the bruises were not apparent. It occurred to me that masking the bruises must have been what the undertaker meant when I said no embalming and he said "in that case we'll just clean him up." The part with the undertaker remains remote. I had arrived to meet him so determined to avoid any inappropriate response (tears, anger, helpless laughter at the Oz-like hush) that I had shut down all response. After my mother died the undertaker who picked up her body left in its place on the bed an artificial rose. My brother had told me this, offended to the core. I would be armed against artificial roses. I remember making a brisk decision about a coffin. I remember that in the office where I signed the papers there was a grandfather clock, not running. John's nephew Tony, who was with me, mentioned to the undertaker that the clock was not running. The undertaker, as if pleased to elucidate a decorative element, explained that the clock had not run in some years but was retained as "a kind of memorial" to a previous incarnation of the firm. He seemed to be offering the clock as a lesson. I concentrated on Quintana. I could shut out what the undertaker was saying, but I could not shut out the lines I was hearing as I concentrated on Quintana: *Full fathom five thy father lies/Those are pearls that were his eyes.*

3

Eight months later I asked the manager of our apartment building if he still had the log kept by the doormen for the night of December 30. I knew there was a log, I had been for three years president of the board of the building, the door log was intrinsic to building procedure. The next day the manager sent me the page for December 30. According to the log, the doormen that night were Michael Flynn and Vasile Ionescu. I had not remembered that. Vasile Ionescu and John had a routine with which they amused themselves in the elevator, a small game, between an exile from Ceaucescu's Romania and an Irish Catholic from West Hartford, Connecticut, based on a shared appreciation of political posturing. "So where is bin Laden?" Vasile would say when John got onto the elevator, the point being to come up with ever more improbable suggestions: "Could bin Laden be in the penthouse?" "In the maisonette?" "In the fitness room?" When I saw Vasile's name on the log it occurred to me that I could not remember if he had initiated this game when we came in from Beth Israel North in the early evening of December 30. The log for that evening showed only two entries, fewer than usual, even for a time of the year when most people in the building left for more clement venues:

NOTE: Paramedics arrived at 9:20 PM for Mr. Dunne. Mr. Dunne was taken to hospital at 10:05 PM.

NOTE: Lightbulb out on A-B passenger elevator.

The A-B elevator was our elevator, the elevator in which the paramedics came up at 9:20 PM, the elevator in which they took John (and me) downstairs to the ambulance at 10:05 PM, the elevator in which I returned alone to our apartment at a time not noted. I had not noticed a lightbulb being out in the elevator. Nor had I noticed that the paramedics were in the apartment for forty-five minutes. I had always described it as "fifteen or twenty minutes." *If they were here that long does it mean that he was alive?* I put this question to a doctor I knew. "Sometimes they'll work that long," he said. It was a while before I realized that this in no way addressed the question.

The death certificate, when I got it, gave the time of death as 10:18 PM, December 30, 2003.

I had been asked before I left the hospital if I would authorize an autopsy. I had said yes. I later read that asking a survivor to authorize an autopsy is seen in hospitals as delicate, sensitive, often the most difficult of the routine steps that follow a death. Doctors themselves, according to many studies (for example, Katz, J., and Gardner, R., "The Intern's Dilemma: The Request for Autopsy Consent," *Psychiatry in Medicine* 3:197–203, 1972), experience considerable anxiety about making the request. They know that autopsy is essential to the learning and teaching of medicine, but they also know that the procedure touches a primitive dread. If whoever it was at New York Hospital who asked me to authorize an autopsy experienced such anxiety I could have spared him or her: I actively wanted an autopsy. I actively wanted an autopsy even though I had seen some, in the course of doing research. I knew exactly what occurs, the chest open like a chicken in a butcher's case, the face peeled down, the scale on which the organs are weighed. I had seen homicide detectives avert their eyes from an autopsy in progress. I still wanted one. I needed to know how and why and when it had happened. In fact I wanted to be in the room when they did it (I had watched those other autopsies with John, I owed him his own, it was fixed in my mind at that moment that he would be in the room if I were on the table) but I did not trust myself to rationally present the point so I did not ask.

If the ambulance left our building at 10:05 PM, and death was declared at 10:18 PM, the thirteen minutes in between were just bookkeeping, bureaucracy, making sure the hospital procedures were observed and the paperwork was done and the appropriate person was on hand to do the sign-off, inform the cool customer.

The sign-off, I later learned, was called the "pronouncement," as in "Pronounced: 10:18 PM."

I had to believe he was dead all along.

If I did not believe he was dead all along I would have thought I should have been able to save him.

Until I saw the autopsy report I continued to think this anyway, an example 60
of delusionary thinking, the omnipotent variety.

A week or two before he died, when we were having dinner in a restaurant,
John asked me to write something in my notebook for him. He always carried
cards on which to make notes, three-by-six-inch cards printed with his name
that could be slipped into an inside pocket. At dinner he had thought of something he wanted to remember but when he looked in his pockets he found no
cards. I need you to write something down, he said. It was, he said, for his new
book, not for mine, a point he stressed because I was at the time researching a
book that involved sports. This was the note he dictated: "Coaches used to go
out after a game and say, 'You played great.' Now they go out with state police,
as if this were a war and they the military. The militarization of sports." When I
gave him the note the next day he said "You can use it if you want to."

What did he mean?

Did he know he would not write the book?

Did he have some apprehension, a shadow? Why had he forgotten to bring
note cards to dinner that night? Had he not warned me when I forgot my own
notebook that the ability to make a note when something came to mind was
the difference between being able to write and not being able to write? Was
something telling him that night that the time for being able to write was running out?

One summer when we were living in Brentwood Park we fell into a pattern of 65
stopping work at four in the afternoon and going out to the pool. He would stand
in the water reading (he reread *Sophie's Choice* several times that summer, trying
to see how it worked) while I worked in the garden. It was a small, even miniature,
garden with gravel paths and a rose arbor and beds edged with thyme and san-
tolina and feverfew. I had convinced John a few years before that we should tear
out a lawn to plant this garden. To my surprise, since he had shown no previous
interest in gardens, he regarded the finished product as an almost mystical gift.
Just before five on those summer afternoons we would swim and then go into the
library wrapped in towels to watch *Tenko*, a BBC series, then in syndication, about
a number of satisfyingly predictable English women (one was immature and selfish, another seemed to have been written with *Mrs. Miniver* in mind) imprisoned
by the Japanese in Malaya during World War II. After each afternoon's *Tenko* segment we would go upstairs and work another hour or two, John in his office at
the top of the stairs, me in the glassed-in porch across the hall that had become
my office. At seven or seven thirty we would go out to dinner, many nights at
Morton's. Morton's felt right that summer. There was always shrimp quesadilla,
chicken with black beans. There was always someone we knew. The room was
cool and polished and dark inside but you could see the twilight outside.

John did not like driving at night by then. This was one reason, I later
learned, that he wanted to spend more time in New York, a wish that at the
time remained mysterious to me. One night that summer he asked me to drive
home after dinner at Anthea Sylbert's house on Camino Palmero in Hollywood.
I remember thinking how remarkable this was. Anthea lived less than a block
from the house on Franklin Avenue in which we had lived from 1967 until

1971, so it was not a question of reconnoitering a new neighborhood. It had occurred to me as I started the ignition that I could count on my fingers the number of times I had driven when John was in the car; the single other time I could remember that night was once spelling him on a drive from Las Vegas to Los Angeles. He had been dozing in the passenger seat of the Corvette we then had. He had opened his eyes. After a moment he had said, very carefully, "I might take it a little slower." I had no sense of unusual speed and glanced at the speedometer: I was doing 120.

Yet.

A drive across the Mojave was one thing. There had been no previous time when he asked me to drive home from dinner in town: This evening on Camino Palmero was unprecedented. So was the fact that at the end of the forty-minute drive to Brentwood Park he pronounced it "well driven."

He mentioned those afternoons with the pool and the garden and *Tenko* several times during the year before he died.

Philippe Ariès, in *The Hour of Our Death,* points out that the essential char-   70
acteristic of death as it appears in the *Chanson de Roland* is that the death, even if sudden or accidental, "gives advance warning of its arrival." Gawain is asked: "Ah, good my lord, think you then so soon to die?" Gawain answers: "I tell you that I shall not live two days." Ariès notes: "Neither his doctor nor his friends nor the priests (the latter are absent and forgotten) know as much about it as he. Only the dying man can tell how much time he has left."

You sit down to dinner.

"You can use it if you want to," John had said when I gave him the note he had dictated a week or two before.

And then—gone.

4

Grief, when it comes, is nothing we expect it to be. It was not what I felt when my parents died: My father died a few days short of his eighty-fifth birthday and my mother a month short of her ninety-first, both after some years of increasing debility. What I felt in each instance was sadness, loneliness (the loneliness of the abandoned child of whatever age), regret for time gone by, for things unsaid, for my inability to share or even in any real way to acknowledge, at the end, the pain and helplessness and physical humiliation they each endured. I understood the inevitability of each of their deaths. I had been expecting (fearing, dreading, anticipating) those deaths all my life. They remained, when they did occur, distanced, at a remove from the ongoing dailiness of my life. After my mother died I received a letter from a friend in Chicago, a former Maryknoll priest, who precisely intuited what I felt. The death of a parent, he wrote, "despite our preparation, indeed, despite our age, dislodges things deep in us, sets off reactions that surprise us and that may cut free memories and feelings that we had thought gone to ground long ago. We might, in that indeterminate period they call mourning, be in a submarine, silent on the ocean's bed, aware of the depth charges, now near and now far, buffeting us with recollections."

My father was dead, my mother was dead, I would need for a while to watch   75
for mines, but I would still get up in the morning and send out the laundry.

I would still plan a menu for Easter lunch.

I would still remember to renew my passport.

Grief is different. Grief has no distance. Grief comes in waves, paroxysms, sudden apprehensions that weaken the knees and blind the eyes and obliterate the dailiness of life. Virtually everyone who has ever experienced grief mentions this phenomenon of "waves." Erich Lindemann, who was chief of psychiatry at Massachusetts General Hospital in the 1940s and interviewed many family members of those killed in the 1942 Cocoanut Grove fire, defined **Grief, when it comes, is nothing we expect it to be.** the phenomenon with absolute specificity in a famous 1944 study: "sensations of somatic distress occurring in waves lasting from twenty minutes to an hour at a time, a feeling of tightness in the throat, choking with shortness of breath, need for sighing and an empty feeling in the abdomen, lack of muscular power and an intense subjective distress described as tension or mental pain."

Tightness in the throat.

Choking, need for sighing.   80

Such waves began for me on the morning of December 31, 2003, seven or eight hours after the fact, when I woke alone in the apartment. I do not remember crying the night before; I had entered at the moment it happened a kind of shock in which the only thought I allowed myself was that there must be certain things I needed to do. There had been certain things I had needed to do while the ambulance crew was in the living room. I had needed for example to get the copy of John's medical summary, so I could take it with me to the hospital. I had needed for example to bank the fire, because I would be leaving it. There had been certain things I had needed to do at the hospital. I had needed for example to stand in the line. I had needed for example to focus on the bed with telemetry he would need for the transfer to Columbia-Presbyterian.

Once I got back from the hospital there had again been certain things I needed to do. I could not identify all of these things, but I did know one of them: I needed, before I did anything else, to tell John's brother Nick. It had seemed too late in the evening to call their older brother Dick on Cape Cod (he went to bed early, his health had not been good, I did not want to wake him with bad news) but I needed to tell Nick. I did not plan how to do this. I just sat on the bed and picked up the phone and dialed the number of his house in Connecticut. He answered. I told him. After I put down the phone, in what I can only describe as a new neural pattern of dialing numbers and saying the words, I picked it up again. I could not call Quintana (she was still where we had left her a few hours before, unconscious in the ICU at Beth Israel North), but I could call Gerry, her husband of five months, and I could call my brother, Jim, who would be at his house in Pebble Beach. Gerry said he would come over. I said there was no need to come over, I would be fine. Jim said he would get a flight. I said there was no need to think about a flight, we would talk in the morning. I was trying to think what to do next when the phone rang. It was John's and my agent, Lynn Nesbit, a friend since I suppose the late '60s. It was not clear to me at the time how she knew but she did (it had something to do with a mutual friend to whom both Nick and Lynn seemed in the last minute to have spoken), and she was calling from a taxi on her way to our apartment. At one level I was relieved (Lynn knew how to manage things, Lynn would know what it was that I was supposed to be doing) and at another I was bewildered: How could I deal at this moment with company? What would we do, would we sit in the living room with the syringes and the ECG electrodes and the blood still on the floor, should I rekindle what was left of the fire, would we have a drink, would she have eaten?

Had I eaten?

The instant in which I asked myself whether I had eaten was the first intimation of what was to come: If I thought of food, I learned that night, I would throw up.

Lynn arrived.

We sat in the part of the living room where the blood and electrodes and syringes were not.

I remember thinking as I was talking to Lynn (this was the part I could not say) that the blood must have come from the fall: He had fallen on his face, there was the chipped tooth I had noticed in the emergency room, the tooth could have cut the inside of his mouth.

Lynn picked up the phone and said that she was calling Christopher.

This was another bewilderment: The Christopher I knew best was in either Paris or Dubai and in any case Lynn would have said Chris, not Christopher. I found my mind veering to the autopsy. It could even be happening as I sat there. Then I realized that the Christopher to whom Lynn was talking was Christopher Lehmann-Haupt, who was the chief obituary writer at the *New York Times*. I remember a sense of shock. I wanted to say *not yet* but my mouth had gone dry. I could deal with "autopsy" but the notion of "obituary" had not occurred to me. "Obituary," unlike "autopsy," which was between me and John and the hospital, meant it had happened. I found myself wondering, with no sense of illogic, if it had also happened in Los Angeles. I was trying to work out what time it had been when he died and whether it was that time yet in Los Angeles. (Was there time to go back? Could we have a different ending on Pacific time?) I recall being seized by a pressing need not to let anyone at the *Los Angeles Times* learn what had happened by reading it in the *New York Times*. I called our closest friend at the *Los Angeles Times*. I have no memory of what Lynn and I did then. I remember her saying that she would stay the night, but I said no, I would be fine alone.

And I was.

Until the morning. When, only half awake, I tried to think why I was alone in the bed. There was a leaden feeling. It was the same leaden feeling with which I woke on mornings after John and I had fought. Had we had a fight? What about, how had it started, how could we fix it if I could not remember how it started?

Then I remembered.

For several weeks that would be the way I woke to the day.

I wake and feel the fell of dark, not day.

One of several lines from different poems by Gerard Manley Hopkins that John strung together during the months immediately after his younger brother committed suicide, a kind of improvised rosary.

O the mind, mind has mountains; cliffs of fall
Frightful, sheer, no-man-fathomed. Hold them cheap
May who ne'er hung there.
I wake and feel the fell of dark, not day.
And I have asked to be
Where no storms come.

I see now that my insistence on spending that first night alone was more complicated than it seemed, a primitive instinct. Of course I knew John was dead. Of course I had already delivered the definitive news to his brother and to my brother and to Quintana's husband. The *New York Times* knew. The *Los Angeles Times* knew. Yet I was myself in no way prepared to accept this news as final: There was a level on which I believed that what had happened remained reversible. That was why I needed to be alone.

After that first night I would not be alone for weeks (Jim and his wife would fly in from California the next day, Nick would come back to town, Tony and his wife would come down from Connecticut, José would not go to Las Vegas, our assistant Sharon would come back from skiing, there would never not be people in the house), but I needed that first night to be alone.

I needed to be alone so that he could come back.

5

Grief turns out to be a place none of us know until we reach it. We anticipate (we know) that someone close to us could die, but we do not look beyond the few days or weeks that immediately follow such an imagined death. We misconstrue the nature of even those few days or weeks. We might expect if the death is sudden to feel shock. We do not expect this shock to be obliterative, dislocating to both body and mind. We might expect that we will be prostrate, inconsolable, crazy with loss. We do not expect to be literally crazy, cool customers who believe that their husband is about to return. In the version of grief we imagine, the model will be "healing." A certain forward movement will prevail. The worst days will be the earliest days. We imagine that the moment to most severely test us will be the funeral, after which this hypothetical healing will take place.

When we anticipate the funeral we wonder about failing to "get through it," rise to the occasion, exhibit the "strength" that invariably gets mentioned as the correct response to death. We anticipate needing to steel ourselves for the moment: Will I be able to greet people, will I be able to leave the scene, will I be able even to get dressed that day? We have no way of knowing that this will not be the issue. We have no way of knowing that the funeral itself will be anodyne, a kind of narcotic regression in which we are wrapped in the care of others and the gravity and meaning of the occasion. Nor can we know ahead of the fact (and here lies the heart of the difference between grief as we imagine it and grief as it is) the unending absence that follows, the void, the very opposite of meaning, the relentless succession of moments during which we will confront the experience of meaninglessness itself.

As a child I thought a great deal about meaninglessness, which seemed at the time the most prominent negative feature on the horizon. After a few years of failing to find meaning in the more commonly recommended venues I learned that I could find it in geology, so I did. This in turn enabled me to find meaning in the Episcopal litany, most acutely in the words *as it was in the beginning, is now and ever shall be, world without end,* which I interpreted as a literal description of the constant changing of the earth, the unending erosion of the shores and mountains, the inexorable shifting of the geological structures that could throw up mountains and islands and could just as reliably take them away. I found earthquakes, even when I was in them, deeply satisfying, abruptly revealed evidence of the scheme in action. That the scheme could destroy the works of man might be a personal regret but remained, in the larger picture I had come to recognize, a matter of abiding indifference. No eye was on the sparrow. No one was watching me. *As it was in the beginning, is now and ever shall be, world without end.* On the day it was announced that the atomic bomb had been dropped on Hiroshima those were the words that came immediately to my ten-year-old mind. When I heard a few years later about mushroom clouds over the Nevada test site those were again the words that came to mind. I began waking before dawn, imagining that the fireballs from the Nevada test shots would light up the sky in Sacramento.

Later, after I married and had a child, I learned to find equal meaning in the repeated rituals of domestic life. Setting the table. Lighting the candles. Building the fire. Cooking. All those soufflés, all that crème caramel, all those daubes and albóndigas and gumbos. Clean sheets, stacks of clean towels, hurricane lamps for storms, enough water and food to see us through whatever geological event came our way. *These fragments I have shored against my ruins,* were the words that came to mind then. These fragments mattered to me. I believed in them. That I could find meaning in the intensely personal nature of my life as a wife and mother did not seem inconsistent with finding meaning in the vast indifference of geology and the test shots; the two systems existed for me on parallel tracks that occasionally converged, notably during earthquakes.

In my unexamined mind there was always a point, John's and my death, at which the tracks would converge for a final time. On the Internet I recently found aerial photographs of the house on the Palos Verdes Peninsula in which we had lived when we were first married, the house to which we had brought Quintana home from St. John's Hospital in Santa Monica and put her in her bassinet by the wisteria in the box garden. The photographs, part of the California

Coastal Records Project, the point of which was to document the entire California coastline, were hard to read conclusively, but the house as it had been when we lived in it appeared to be gone. The tower where the gate had been seemed intact but the rest of the structure looked unfamiliar. There seemed to be a swimming pool where the wisteria and box garden had been. The area itself was identified as "Portuguese Bend landslide." You could see the slumping of the hill where the slide had occurred. You could also see, at the base of the cliff on the point, the cave into which we used to swim when the tide was at exactly the right flow.

The swell of clear water.

That was one way my two systems could have converged.

We could have been swimming into the cave with the swell of clear water and the entire point could have slumped, slipped into the sea around us. The entire point slipping into the sea around us was the kind of conclusion I anticipated. I did not anticipate cardiac arrest at the dinner table.

Questions for Critical Reading

1. What does Didion mean by the "ordinary instant"? Develop a definition of that term supported with quotations from her text and then provide an example of an "ordinary instant" from your own life.

2. Grief plays a central role in Didion's essay. What does grief mean to Didion? Reread Didion's text, locating quotations that support your understanding of the term.

3. Didion examines death in this essay but she is also concerned with creating meaning in life. Locate passages that show how Didion believes meaning can be created despite—or perhaps even because of—death's inevitability.

Exploring Context

1. The book from which this essay was taken, *The Year of Magical Thinking*, was turned into a Broadway play. Visit the Web site for the play at magicalthinkingonbroadway.com/about.html. How does the design of the site reflect or complicate the meaning of Didion's text? Use your response to Question 3 of Questions for Critical Reading on creating meaning in life in making your response.

2. Research the stages of grief on the Web. Does Didion go through these stages as evidenced by this essay? Does the essay seem to suggest that Didion is stuck in a particular stage? How do these stages relate to the definition of grief you developed in your response to Question 2 of Questions for Critical Reading?

3. Using the Web, locate information on the decline in the number of autopsies. Why is Didion so insistent on having an autopsy? Why are autopsies occurring less frequently? Should they be performed more regularly?

Questions for Connecting

1. Daniel Gilbert's essay "Reporting Live from Tomorrow" (p. 169) is about the failure of our imaginations to predict our future happiness. Given Didion's essay, how well do our imaginations predict our future *unhappiness*? Use Gilbert's ideas to explore the process of grief documented by Didion.

2. How is an individual's response to death different from a community's response? Use Diana Taylor's "False Identifications: Minority Populations Mourn Diana" (p. 454) to examine the relationship between the mourning of individuals and the sorrowing of groups, synthesizing Taylor's ideas about grief and mourning with Didion's.

3. Mary Roach, in "The Cadaver Who Joined the Army" (p. 347), examines the ethics of using human cadavers. Expand her analysis by using Didion's experience. Is Didion concerned with medical knowledge when she asks for an autopsy to be performed on her husband? Does her experience of grief give us reason to avoid using cadavers in research? You may wish to use your research on autopsies from Question 3 of Exploring Context in composing your answer.

Language Matters

1. Ellipses and brackets are useful punctuation marks when using quotations. Select a long quotation from Didion that represents an important part of her essay. How would you use these punctuation marks to incorporate the quotation into your own writing? How might they be instead used, even unintentionally, to misrepresent the meaning of the quotation? How can you be sure you're using these punctuation marks correctly?

2. The most solid transitions come from a statement that directly ties together two paragraphs. Select two paragraphs from Didion's essay. Write a one-sentence summary of the first paragraph and then another one-sentence summary of the second paragraph. Then combine these two sentences into one to form a new transition between the paragraphs. How does it differ from Didion's transition? How can you use this skill in your own writing?

3. Using section headings or subtitles can help a reader understand the organization of your writing. Didion numbers her sections; provide descriptive subtitles for each section instead. Why might Didion have chosen numbers instead of subtitles? In what situations might you use these elements in your own writing?

Assignments for Writing

1. Given Didion's retelling of the events before and after her husband's death, write an essay that examines the relationship between trauma and memory. What does Didion remember about that night? About her husband? How does trauma shape those memories? You may want to use your response about mourning from Question 2 of Questions for Connecting to support your argument.

2. Didion authorized an autopsy of her husband because she needed to know more about her husband's death, so much so that she wanted to be present during the autopsy. Write a paper that evaluates Didion's decision to authorize an autopsy. Was she in the right frame of mind when she made her decision? What should she have considered that she did not when making her decision? Are autopsies immoral? Are they unethical? How does Didion justify her decision? Is there a need to justify such a decision? Does information beyond personal experience help the grieving process? Why is Didion more concerned about the obituary than the autopsy? Why do doctors feel anxiety about asking for an autopsy? You may want to use your research on autopsies from Question 3 of Exploring Context and your work with Roach's essay from Question 3 of Questions for Connecting in making your argument.

3. At times Didion wants to be alone—especially on the night of her husband's death—but at other times she seems surrounded by people. Using Didion's experience, write a paper in which you evaluate the need to be alone after a traumatic event such as the loss of a loved one. Consider: Why does Didion feel differently about the obituary than she does about the autopsy? What is the difference between grief as we imagine it and grief as it really is? Was Didion ever as alone as she really thought? Is grief strictly a private matter? Does it help to make grief public? What value is there in allowing others into our lives as we grieve?

Helen Epstein

After earning a Ph.D. in molecular biology from Cambridge University, **Helen Epstein** attended the London School of Hygiene and Tropical Medicine, where she earned an M.Sc. in public health in developing countries. In 1993, while working as a scientist for a biotechnology company in search of an AIDS vaccine, Epstein moved to Uganda, where she witnessed the suffering caused by the virus. Epstein still works in public health care in developing countries. She has had articles published in magazines such as the *New York Review of Books* and in 2007 published her book *The Invisible Cure: Africa, the West, and the Fight against AIDS.*

Epstein compiled the information she had gathered in her years as a scientist in Africa, along with her personal observations, to write *The Invisible Cure.* In it she explores the reasons behind the unprecedented AIDS epidemic in Africa and suggests ways to reduce infection rates on that continent. Along the way she corrects the misinformation and misconceptions that Westerners have been using as a guide for aiding Africans who suffer from or are at risk for AIDS/HIV. She points out that programs for prevention might need to be in the hands of Africans themselves in order to account for local cultures. For instance, while campaigns promoting condom usage might be successful in Western countries, this does not mean such campaigns will succeed within other cultures. Instead, listening to and understanding the traditions and customs of individual cultures might lead to more successful approaches to the AIDS epidemic.

In "AIDS, Inc," a chapter from *The Invisible Cure,* Epstein examines HIV and AIDS prevention programs in Africa. In South Africa, Epstein witnesses a government-run campaign that focuses on creating conversations about sexual activity among the nation's youth in order to help them create informed decisions about sex. However, many of the conversations stop there, leaving out any talk of people who already have AIDS. While the campaign may open up new avenues for youth in terms of sexual responsibility and respect, the lack of conversation surrounding AIDS perpetuates the social stigmas of infected peoples as well as an "out of sight, out of mind" attitude toward the virus. Perhaps, as Epstein points out, campaigns are only as successful as the conversations surrounding them. She points to Uganda — one of the few countries in Africa where the rate of infection has dropped precipitously — as an example of effective conversation. Open conversation among Ugandans about personal experiences with the virus has succeeded in preventing its spread by breaking the cycle of social stigmas surrounding those infected.

What social stigmas concerning HIV and AIDS exist locally and globally? How do these social stigmas interfere with campaigns to successfully prevent the spread of the virus? How might class, race, gender, and religion contribute to the way prevention is approached? While Epstein points out how important conversation is among communities, is it possible to create a global conversation about HIV and AIDS?

▶ TAGS: *community, research, conversation, technology, social change, media*

AIDS, Inc.

In response to government prevarication over HIV treatment, a vigorous AIDS activist movement emerged in South Africa and a fierce public relations battle ensued. The Treatment Action Campaign, or TAC, along with other activist groups, accused the South African health minister, Manto Tshabalala-Msimang, of "murder" for denying millions of South Africans access to medicine for AIDS. A spokesman from the ANC Youth League then called the activists "paid marketing agents for toxic AIDS drugs from America."[1] An official in the Department of Housing accused journalists who defended the AIDS activists of fanaticism, and quoted Lenin on how the "press in bourgeois society . . . deceive[s], corrupt[s], and fool[s] the exploited and oppressed mass of the people, the poor."

Meanwhile, across the nation thousands of people were becoming infected daily, from the rural homesteads of the former Bantustans to the peri-urban townships and squatter camps to the formerly all-white suburbs, now home to a growing black middle class. By 2005, the death rate for young adults had tripled.[2] Surveys showed that nearly everyone in South Africa knew that HIV was sexually transmitted and that it could be prevented with condoms, abstinence, and faithfulness to an uninfected partner. Children were receiving AIDS education in school and condoms were widely available, but these programs made little difference. In the din of the battle between the activists and the government, the deeper message, that HIV was everyone's problem, was lost.

In 1999, a group of public health experts sponsored by the U.S.-based Kaiser Family Foundation stepped into this fray. They were concerned about the worsening AIDS crisis in South Africa and wanted to launch a bold new HIV prevention program for young people. They also knew they had to take account of the South African government's attitudes toward AIDS and AIDS activists. Their program, called loveLife, would soon become South Africa's largest and most ambitious HIV prevention campaign. It aimed both to overcome the limitations of similar campaigns that had failed in the past and, at the same time, to avoid dealing with the issues of AIDS treatment and care that had become so controversial.

Could this work? I wondered. Was it possible to reduce the spread of HIV without involving HIV-positive people and the activists and community groups that supported them? LoveLife had been endorsed at one time or another by the archbishop of Cape Town; Nelson Mandela; the king of the Zulu tribe; Jacob

Zuma, South Africa's former deputy president; and even Zanele Mbeki, the wife of the president. In 2003, loveLife's annual $20 million budget was paid for by the South African government, the Kaiser Family Foundation, UNICEF, the Bill and Melinda Gates Foundation, and the Global Fund to Fight AIDS, Tuberculosis, and Malaria. At least South Africa's leaders were beginning to take AIDS seriously, I thought, but what kind of program was this?

"What we want to do is create a substantive, normative shift in the way young people behave," explained loveLife's director, David Harrison, a white South African doctor, when I met him in his Johannesburg office. The average age at which young South Africans lose their virginity—around seventeen—is not much different from the age at which teenagers in other countries do. What's different, Harrison said, was that many of the young South Africans who were sexually active were very sexually active. They were more likely to start having sex at very young ages, even below the age of fourteen—well below the national average. Those vulnerable young people were more likely to have more than one sexual partner, and they were less likely to use condoms. South African girls were more likely to face sexual coercion or rape, or to exchange sex for money or gifts, all of which placed them at greater risk of HIV infection. For Harrison, the trick was to "get inside the head-space of these young people . . . we have to understand what is driving them into sex—they know what HIV is, but they don't internalize it," he said.

LoveLife's aim was to get young people talking, to each other and to their parents, so they would really understand and act on what they knew. But to reach out to them, you had to use a special language that young people could relate to. According to Harrison, traditional HIV prevention campaigns were too depressing: They tried to scare people into changing their behavior, and this turned kids off. LoveLife's media campaign, on the other hand, was positive and cheerful, and resembled the bright, persuasive modern ad campaigns that many South African kids were very much attracted to.

In the past couple of years, nearly a thousand loveLife billboards had sprouted all along the nation's main roads. They were striking. For example, on one of them, the hands of four women of different races caressed the sculpted back and buttocks of a young black man as though they were appraising an antique newel post. The caption read, "Everyone he's slept with, is sleeping with you." On another, a gorgeous mixed-race couple—the boy looked like Brad Pitt, the girl like an Indian film star—lay in bed, under the caption "No Pressure." Some people told me they found these ads oversexualized and disturbing, but it is hard to see why. On the same roads, there are torsos advertising sexy underwear and half-naked actresses advertising romantic movies. Sex is a potent theme in marketing all sorts of products; loveLife, according to its creators, tries to turn that message around to get young people thinking and talking about sex in more responsible ways and convince them of the virtues of abstinence, fidelity, and the use of condoms.

Harrison calls loveLife "a brand of positive lifestyle." The sexy billboards and similar ads on TV and radio, as well as newspaper inserts that resemble teen gossip magazines, with articles and advice columns about clothes, relationships, and sexual health, were designed, Harrison says, to persuade young people to avoid sex in the same way a sneaker ad tries to seduce them into buying new sneakers, because the players in the ads look so cool. The idea is "to create a brand so strong that young people who want to be hip and cool and the rest of it want to associate with it," Harrison told an interviewer in 2001.[3]

The concept of a "lifestyle brand" originated with the rise of brand advertising in the 1960s, when ads for such products as Pepsi-Cola and Harley-Davidson began to promote not only soft drinks and motorcycles, but also a certain style or aesthetic. People were urged to "join the Pepsi generation" or ride a Harley-Davidson not just to get around, but to embrace a certain attitude. A Harley wasn't just a bike; it was a macho rebellion, an escape from the workaday world to the open road. In the 1970s, family-planning programs also tried to

> **Harrison calls loveLife "a brand of positive lifestyle."**

promote contraceptives in developing countries by tapping into poor people's aspirations for a glamorous Western lifestyle. Campaigns depicted small, well-dressed families surrounded by sleek new commodities, including televisions and cars. Harrison predicted that young South Africans would readily respond to this approach too.

"Kids have changed," Harrison explained. Today's young South Africans weren't like the activists who risked their lives in the anti-apartheid demonstrations at Sharpeville and Soweto. "Seventy-five percent of South African teenagers watch TV every day," Harrison informed me. "Their favorite program is *The Bold and the Beautiful*" — an American soap opera in which glamorous characters struggle with personal crises while wearing and driving some very expensive gear. "They are exposed to the global youth culture of music, fashion, pop icons, and commercial brands. They talk about brands among themselves, even if they can't afford everything they see."

The Kaiser Foundation's Michael Sinclair told me that loveLife drew much of its inspiration from the marketing campaign for the soft drink Sprite.[4] In the mid-1990s, sales of Sprite were flagging until the company began an aggressive campaign to embed Sprite in youth culture by sponsoring hip-hop concerts and planting attractive, popular kids in Internet chat rooms or college dormitories and paying them to praise or distribute Sprite in an unobtrusive way. Sprite is now one of the most profitable drinks in the world because it managed to exploit what marketing experts call "the cool effect" — meaning the influence that a small number of opinion leaders can have on the norms and behavior of large numbers of their peers. So far, corporate marketers had made the greatest use of the cool effect, but there was speculation that small numbers of trendsetters could change more complex behavior than shopping, such as criminality, suicide, and sexual behavior.[5]

For this reason, loveLife had established a small network of recreation centers for young people, known as Y-Centers, throughout the country. At Y-Centers, young people could learn to play basketball, volleyball, and other sports, as well as learn break dancing, radio broadcasting, and word processing. All Y-Center activities were led by "loveLife GroundBreakers"—older youths, usually in their early twenties, who, like the kids who made Sprite cool, were stylish and cheerful and enthusiastic about their product, in this case, loveLife and its program to encourage safer sexual behavior. If abstinence, monogamy, and condoms all happened to fail, each Y-Center was affiliated with a family-planning clinic that offered contraceptives and treatment for sexually transmitted diseases such as syphilis and gonorrhea. The centers offered no treatment for AIDS symptoms, however, and when I visited, none of them offered HIV testing either.

Any young person could become a Y-Center member, but in order to fully participate in its activities, he or she had to complete a program of seminars about HIV, family planning, and other subjects related to sexuality and growing up. The seminars emphasized the biological aspects of HIV and its prevention, but not the experience of the disease and its effects on people's lives. Members also received training to raise their self-esteem, because, as Harrison told an interviewer in 2001,

> there is a direct correlation between young people's sexual behavior and their sense of confidence in the future. Those young people who feel motivated, who feel that they have something to look forward to—they are the ones who protect themselves, who ensure that they do not get HIV/AIDS. . . . It's all about the social discount rates that young people apply to future benefits.[6]

Dr. Harrison arranged for me to visit a loveLife Y-Center in the archipelago of townships in the flat scrubland south of Johannesburg known as the Vaal Triangle. Millions of people live in these townships, many of them recent migrants from rural South Africa or from neighboring countries. The Vaal, once a patchwork of white-owned farms, is now a residential area for poor blacks. At first, only a few families moved here, because the apartheid government used the notorious pass laws to restrict the tide of impoverished blacks seeking a better life in Johannesburg. But when the apartheid laws were scrapped, people poured in. Today, the roads and other services in the area are insufficient for its huge and growing population, and many people have no electricity and lack easy access to clean water and sanitation. Unemployment exceeds 70 percent and the crime rate is one of the highest in South Africa.[7]

The loveLife Y-Center was a compound of two small lavender buildings surrounded by an iron fence and curling razor wire. Inside the compound, a group of young men in shorts and T-shirts were doing warm-up exercises on the outdoor basketball court, while girls and barefoot children looked on. Inside the main building, another group of boys in fashionably droopy jeans and dreadlocks practiced a hip-hop routine, and two girls in the computer room experimented with Microsoft Word.

Valentine's Day was coming up, and the Y-Center had organized a group discussion for some of its members. About thirty teenagers, most of them in school uniforms, sat around on the floor of a large seminar room and argued about who should pay for what on a Valentine's Day date. A GroundBreaker in a love-Life T-shirt and with a loveLife kerchief tied pirate-style on her head officiated. "I go with my chick and I spend money on her and always we have sex," said a husky boy in a gray school uniform. "And I want to know, what's the difference between my chick and a prostitute?" As we have seen, long-term transactional relationships—in which money or gifts are frequently exchanged—may not be the same as prostitution, but they nevertheless put many township youths at risk of HIV.[8]

"Boys, they are expecting too much from us. They say we are parasites if we don't sleep with them," said a plump girl in the uniform of a local Catholic school.

"The girls, they ask for a lot of things," another boy chimed in.

"Me, I think it is wrong. If most of the boys think Valentine's Day is about buying sex, the boys must stop," a girl said. "We girls must hold our ground."

These young people were certainly talking openly about sexual relation-   20
ships all right, just as Harrison prescribed. Nevertheless, I felt something was missing. "Do you ever talk about AIDS in those discussion groups?" I asked the GroundBreaker afterward. "We do it indirectly," she replied. "We know that if we just came out and started lecturing them about AIDS, they wouldn't listen. They would just turn off. So we talk about positive things, like making informed choices, sharing responsibility, and positive sexuality."

Was this true? Do young people in South Africa, like their politicians, really want to avoid the subject of AIDS? I wanted to meet young people outside the Y-Center and ask them what they thought about that. A few hundred yards away from the Y-Center stood the headquarters of St. Charles Lwanga, a Catholic organization that carries out a number of activities in the township. Their AIDS program, called Inkanyezi, meaning "star" in Zulu, provides counseling to young people about AIDS and also brings food and other necessities to some four hundred orphans and people living with AIDS in the Vaal.

St. Charles Lwanga was independent of loveLife, and its budget was modest, less than a tenth of what loveLife spent on its billboards alone. The Inkanyezi program was staffed almost entirely by volunteers, whose only compensation was that they were allowed to eat some of the food—usually rice and vegeta-bles—that they prepared for the patients. Lack of funding greatly limited the help that Inkanyezi was able to provide. Although Inkanyezi nurses were able to dispense tuberculosis medicine, antiretroviral drugs were as yet unavailable. Indeed, many of the patients they visited lacked some of the most basic neces-sities for life and human dignity. Sometimes destitute patients had their water and electricity cut off. But the worst thing was that many of the patients were socially isolated and lived alone in flimsy shacks. The doors were easily broken down and at night neighborhood thugs sometimes came in and stole what little they had. Sometimes the patients were raped.

Justice Showalala, who ran Inkanyezi, organized a meeting for me with a group of about twenty-five young people from Orange Farm. The HIV rate in the area was not known, but several people explained to me how their lives had been changed by the virus. They said they had witnessed extreme prejudice and discrimination against people with AIDS, and they did not know where to turn when they learned that a relative or friend was HIV positive. "People say you shouldn't touch someone with HIV," said one girl. "I have a friend at school who disclosed she has HIV, and the others won't even walk with her." Justice explained how he had offered to introduce some teachers from a local school to some of his HIV-positive clients. "They said, 'If you want me to meet people with AIDS, you better give me a rubber suit.'"

The loveLife Y-Center did little to help young people deal with such confusion, stigma, and shame. "I learned basketball at the Y-Center," one girl told me, "and at meetings we talked about resisting peer pressure, [like when] your friends advise you to break your virginity, to prove you are girl enough. But I was afraid the people there would find out my sister had HIV. We talked about it as though it was someone else's problem."

In general, although sex was openly discussed at the Y-Center, the experience of AIDS was not. The Y-Center offered individual counseling for a small number of young people with HIV, but those who were hungry, homeless, or destitute, or were suffering from the symptoms of AIDS, were told to consult other organizations, including Inkanyezi.

It turns out that talking about the pain, both physical and emotional, that the disease creates is far more difficult than getting over the embarrassment of talking about sex. "I had heard about HIV before," said an Inkanyezi girl, wearing a bright blue T-shirt and matching headband. "But then I found out my mother was HIV positive. I was so shocked, so shocked. I even talked to my teacher about it. She said it can happen to anyone; it must have been from mistakes my mother made, and that I shouldn't make those mistakes in my own life."

"Sometimes, women have no choice," said the older woman sitting next to the girl in blue. She was thin, with intense dark eyes and a deep, wry smile. She was dressed entirely in black, except for a baseball cap with a red ribbon on it—the universal symbol of solidarity with HIV-positive people. "They get infected because of their husbands, and there's nothing they can do.

"It happened like this," the older woman went on. "It was back when we were living in Soweto, before we moved here. One day my daughter and I were washing clothes together," she said, nodding at the girl in blue. "She said she'd had a dream that I was so sick, that I had cancer and I was going to die. I waited until we were done with the washing, and then I told her that I was HIV positive. She said, 'I knew it, you were always sick and always going to support groups.' She was so down, she just cried all day and all night after that. I told her, 'Only God knows why people have this disease. Don't worry, I won't die right away.'

"Once I visited the loveLife Y-Center," the woman continued, "but I just saw children playing. I sat and talked with them, and they were shocked when I said I was HIV positive. I told them about what it was like, and one of them said she would ask the managers whether I could come and talk to a bigger group. But that was about six months ago and they haven't called me. I haven't moved and my number hasn't changed. I don't know why they haven't called."

"I think there should be more counseling and support groups for people   30
who find out their parents are HIV positive," the girl in blue said. "It puts you
down, it really gets to you, it haunts you. When you are standing in class and
you have to recite a poem or something, I find I can't get anything out of my
mouth. I can't concentrate. [The problem] here is ignorance. I didn't care about
HIV until I found out about my mother. Then I started to care about these
people. I wish many people in our country would also think like that."

In 2003, the only African country that had seen a nationwide decline in HIV
prevalence was Uganda. Since 1992 the HIV rate had fallen by some two-
thirds, a success that saved perhaps a million lives. The programs and policies
that led to this success [are discussed elsewhere], but the epidemiologists Rand
Stoneburner and Daniel Low-Beer have argued that a powerful role was played
by the ordinary, but frank, conversations people had with family, friends, and
neighbors—not about sex, but about the frightening, calamitous effects of
AIDS itself.[9] Stoneburner and Low-Beer maintain that these painful personal
conversations did more than anything else to persuade Ugandans to come to
terms with the reality of AIDS, care for the afflicted, and change their behavior.
This in turn led to declines in HIV transmission. The researchers found that
people in other sub-Saharan African countries were far less likely to have such
discussions.

In South Africa, people told Stoneburner and Low-Beer that they had heard
about the epidemic from posters, radio, newspapers, and clinics, as well as from
occasional mass rallies, schools, and village meetings; but they seldom spoke
about it with the people they knew. They were also far less likely to admit knowing someone with AIDS or to be willing to care for an AIDS patient. It may be
no coincidence that the HIV rate in South Africa rose higher than it ever did in
Uganda, and has taken far longer to fall.

When I was in Uganda during the early 1990s, the HIV rate was already
falling, and I vividly recall how the reality of AIDS was alive in people's minds.
Kampala taxi drivers talked as passionately about AIDS as taxi drivers elsewhere discuss politics or football. And they talked about it in a way that would
seem foreign to many in South Africa because it was so personal: "my sister,"
"my father," "my neighbor," "my friend."[10]

Ugandans are not unusually compassionate people, and discrimination
against people with AIDS persists in some families and institutions. But Ugandans do seem more willing to openly address painful issues in their lives. This
courage owes much to the AIDS information campaigns launched by the government of Uganda early on in the epidemic. But it may have other sources as
well. Maybe the difference between the ways South Africa and Uganda have
dealt with AIDS has historical roots. Both South Africa and Uganda have bitter
histories of conflict. But while Uganda was terrorized for decades by a series of
brutal leaders, they could not destroy the traditional rhythms of rural family
life. Uganda is one of the most fertile countries in Africa; there is enough land
for everyone, and most people live as their ancestors did, as peasant farmers
and herders. No large settler population displaced huge numbers of people or

set up a system to exploit and humiliate them, as happened in South Africa and in many other African countries. This means Ugandans are more likely to know their neighbors and to live near members of their extended families. This in turn may have contributed to what sociologists call "social cohesion" — the tendency of people to talk openly with one another and form trusted relationships. Perhaps this may have facilitated more realistic and open discussion of AIDS, more compassionate attitudes toward infected people, and pragmatic behavior change.

Perhaps many attempts to prevent the spread of HIV fail because those in charge of them don't recognize that the decisions people make about sex are usually a matter of feeling, not calculation. In other words, sexual behavior is determined less by what Dr. Harrison called "discount rates" that young people "apply to future benefits" than by emotional attachments. I thought of the South African girls who said they had lost a sister or a friend to AIDS. If one of them was faced with a persistent, wealthy seducer, what would be more likely to persuade her to decline? The memory of a loveLife billboard, with its flashy, beautiful models? Or the memory of a person she had known who had died?

On the morning before I left South Africa, I attended a loveLife motivational seminar at a school not far from Orange Farm. "These seminars help young people see the future, identify choices, and identify the values that underpin those choices," Harrison had told me. "We help them ask themselves, 'What can you do to chart life's journey and control it as much as possible?'" The seminars were based on Success by Choice, a series devised by Marlon Smith, a California-based African-American motivational speaker. How was Mr. Smith's message of personal empowerment translated to South Africa, I wondered, where children have to contend with poverty, the risk of being robbed or raped, and a grim future of likely unemployment?

About twenty-five children aged ten to fourteen were in the class, and the GroundBreaker asked them to hold their hands out in front of them, pretend they were looking in a mirror, and repeat the following words:

"You are intelligent!"

"You are gifted!"

"There is no one in the world like you!"

"I love you!"

The children spoke quietly at first, then louder, as though they were being hypnotized. The GroundBreaker urged them to talk more openly with their parents, to keep themselves clean, and to make positive choices in their lives, especially when it came to sexuality. There was little mention of helping other people, nor was there much advice about how to avoid being raped or harassed by other students as well as teachers, relatives, or strangers, or how to plan a future in a country where unemployment for township blacks was so high.

Then something really odd occurred. One of the GroundBreakers asked the children to stand up because it was time for an "Icebreaker." "This is a little song-and-dance thing we do, to give the children a chance to stretch. It improves their concentration," another GroundBreaker told me. The words of the song were as follows:

> *Pizza Hut*
> *Pizza Hut*
> *Kentucky Fried Chicken and a Pizza Hut*
> *McDonald's*
> *McDonald's*
> *Kentucky Fried Chicken and a Pizza Hut.*

In the dance, the children spread their arms out as though they were rolling out a pizza, or flapped their elbows like chickens.

What kinds of choices was Dr. Harrison really referring to? I wondered. The techniques of marketing attempt to impose scientific principles on human choices. But it seemed a mad experiment to see whether teenagers living through very difficult times could be persuaded to choose a new sexual lifestyle as they might choose a new brand of shampoo, or whether children could be trained to associate safe sex with pizza and self-esteem.

Afterward, I spoke to some of the children who had participated in the seminar. They all knew how to protect themselves from HIV, and they were eager to show off their knowledge about condoms, abstinence, and fidelity within relationships. But they all said they didn't personally know anyone with AIDS; nor did they know of any children who had lost parents to AIDS. They did mention Nkosi Johnson, the brave HIV-positive twelve-year-old boy who became world-famous in 2000 when he stood up at an International Conference on AIDS and challenged the South African president, Thabo Mbeki, to do more for people living with the virus.

In fact, their principal would tell me later, more than twenty children at the school were AIDS orphans, and many more had been forced to drop out because there was no one to pay their expenses after their parents died. The children I spoke to seemed not to know why some of their classmates wore ragged uniforms or had no shoes or stopped showing up at all.

The week before, I had met some teenage girls in Soweto and I had asked them the same question. They answered in the same way: The only person they knew with AIDS was Nkosi Johnson, the famous boy at the AIDS conference. Just as Harrison had warned me, these girls said they were tired of hearing about AIDS. The girls were orphans, although they said their parents had not died of AIDS. I later discovered that, in another part of that same orphanage, there was a nursery where thirty babies and small children, all of them HIV positive, all abandoned by their parents, lay on cots or sat quietly on the floor, struggling for life. No wonder those girls were tired of hearing about HIV. It was right in their midst, within earshot, but the world around them was telling them to look the other way.

A couple of years later, I would meet a group of primary-school students in Kigali, Rwanda. By then, the HIV infection rate in Rwanda had fallen steeply, just as it had in Uganda years earlier. The school was a typical single-story line of classrooms in one of the poorest sections of Kigali. I spoke to the principal first, and he showed me the government-issued manual used for teaching about AIDS, which contained the usual information about abstinence and condoms. The school day had just ended, and he went outside and asked a few students to stay behind and chat with me.[11]

The Rwandan students had no idea in advance what I wanted to talk to them about. But when I asked them the same question I had asked the South African children, "Do you know anyone with AIDS?" their answers floored me. Every one of them had a story about someone they knew who was HIV positive or suffering from AIDS. "I knew a man who had bad lips [sores] and tears all over his skin," said a fourteen-year-old boy. "People stigmatized him and he died because no one was caring for him." Another boy described a woman who was "so thin, she almost died." But then her relatives took her to the hospital, where she was given AIDS treatment. "She got better because people cared for her," he said.

When I asked the Rwandan children whether they had any questions for me, all they wanted to know was what they could do to help people with AIDS. The responses of the South African children were strikingly different. When I asked them if they had questions for me, they quickly changed the subject from AIDS and asked me what America was like and whether I knew any of the pop stars they admired on TV.

The persistent denial of AIDS in South Africa was deeply disturbing. People liked the colorful, frank advertising and the basketball games sponsored by loveLife. But its programs seemed to me to reinforce the denial that posed so many obstacles to preventing HIV in the first place. In 2005, the Global Fund to Fight AIDS, Tuberculosis, and Malaria would come to similar conclusions and terminate its multimillion-dollar grant to loveLife.[12]

> **The persistent denial of AIDS in South Africa was deeply disturbing.**

Epidemiologists are equivocal about whether loveLife had any effect on HIV transmission in South Africa, but during the program's first seven years, HIV infection rates continued to rise steadily.[13]

A more realistic HIV prevention program would have paid less attention to aspirations and dreams unattainable for so many young people, and greater attention to the real circumstances in people's lives that make it hard for them to avoid infection. It would also have been more frank about the real human consequences of the disease. But that would have meant dealing with some very painful matters that South Africa's policy-makers seemed determined to evade.

It was heartening that Western donors were now spending so much money on AIDS programs in Africa. But the problem with some large foreign-aid programs was that distributing the funds often involved negotiating with governments with a poor record of dealing with AIDS. In addition, the huge sums of money involved were often very difficult to manage, so that small community-based groups that need thousands of dollars, rather than millions—like Inkanyezi in Orange Farm—were often overlooked in favor of overly ambitious megaprojects, whose effectiveness had not been demonstrated and whose premises were open to question. It seemed clear to me that more could be learned from Inkanyezi's attempt to help people deal with the reality of AIDS than from loveLife's attempt to create a new consumerist man and woman for South Africa.

NOTES

1. Helen Schneider, "On the fault-line: The politics of AIDS policy in contemporary South Africa," *Afr Stud* 61:1 (July 1, 2002), 145–67; Samantha Power, "The AIDS Rebel," *New Yorker*, May 19, 2003, pp. 54–67.
2. Rob Dorrington et al., "The Impact of HIV/AIDS on Adult Mortality in South Africa" (Cape Town: Burden of Disease Research Unit, Medical Research Council of South Africa, September 2001); "Mortality and causes of death in South Africa, 2003 and 2004," Statistics South Africa, May 2006.
3. Richard Delate, "The Struggle for Meaning: A Semiotic Analysis of Interpretations of the loveLife His&Hers Billboard Campaign," November 2001, http://www.comminit.com/stlovelife/sld-4389.html.
4. Personal communication, February 2003.
5. For more about this, see Malcolm Gladwell, *The Tipping Point* (Boston: Little, Brown, 2000), and Everett Rogers, *Diffusion of Innovations* (New York: Free Press, 1983).
6. Delate, "Struggle for Meaning."
7. See Prishani Naidoo, "Youth Divided: A Review of loveLife's Y-Centre in Orange Farm" (Johannesburg: CADRE Report, 2003).
8. Nancy Luke and Kathleen M. Kurtz, "Cross-Generational and Transactional Sexual Relations in Sub-Saharan Africa: Prevalence of Behavior and Implications for Negotiating Safer Sexual Practices," International Center for Research on Women, 2002, http://www.icrw.org/docs/CrossGenSex_ Report_902.pdf; J. Swart-Kruger and L. M. Richter, "AIDS-related knowledge, attitudes and behaviour among South African street youth: Reflections on power, sexuality and the autonomous self," *Soc Sci Med* 45:6 (1997), 957–66; Editorial, "Reassessing priorities: Identifying the determinants of HIV transmission," *Soc Sci Med* 36:5 (1993), iii–viii.
9. Daniel Low-Beer and Rand Stoneburner, "Uganda and the Challenge of AIDS," in *The Political Economy of AIDS in Africa*, ed. Nana Poku and Alan Whiteside (London: Ashgate, 2004).
10. See Helen Epstein, "Fat," *Granta* 49 (1995). Low-Beer and Stoneburner make this observation, too, as do Janice Hogle et al. in *What Happened in Uganda? Declining HIV Prevalence, Behavior Change and the National Response* (USAID, 2002).
11. In 2006, the *Washington Post* reported that the HIV infection rate in Rwanda, once estimated to be 15 percent, was now estimated to be 3 percent. See Craig Timberg, "How AIDS in Africa Was Overstated: Reliance on Data from Urban Prenatal Clinics Skewed Early Projections," *Washington Post*, April 6, 2006, p. A1. Timberg attributed the downward revision to a new U.S. government survey and suggested that the earlier estimate, issued by the UNAIDS program, had been inflated, perhaps to raise money or appease AIDS activists. Although the old UNAIDS statistics were in need of correction, there clearly had been a decline in the true infection rate. A population-based survey carried out in

Rwanda in 1986 found that prevalence was 17.8 percent in urban areas and 1.3 percent in rural areas. (Rwandan HIV Seroprevalence Study Group, "Nationwide community-based serological survey of HIV-1 and other human retrovirus infections in a country," *Lancet* 1 (ii) (1989), 941–43.

12. A. E. Pettifor et al., "Young people's sexual health in South Africa: HIV prevalence and sexual behaviors from a nationally representative household survey," *AIDS* 19:14 (September 23, 2005), 1525–34; but see R. Jewkes, "Response to Pettifor et al.," *AIDS* 20:6 (April 4, 2006), 952–53; author reply, 956–58; and W. M. Parker and M. Colvin, "Response to Pettifor et al.," *AIDS* 20:6 (April 4, 2006), 954–55.

13. In 2005, an article in the prestigious medical journal *AIDS* reported that young people who had attended at least one loveLife program were slightly, but significantly, less likely to be HIV positive than those who had not. The author argued that this was consistent with the possibility that loveLife reduced risky sexual behavior. However, there could well be another explanation. From what I saw, loveLife attracted young people who would have been at lower risk of infection in the first place, either because they were wealthier or better educated or less vulnerable to abuse. (While the loveLife study attempted to control for education and wealth, it did not do so rigorously.) Indeed, the tendency to avoid the subject of AIDS would seem to discourage HIV-positive young people from attending loveLife's programs, and this could make it look as though loveLife protected young people when in fact it merely alienated those most at risk. Most loveLife materials were in English, and thus accessible only to young people with higher social status. This would have sent a clear signal to those — often marginalized and vulnerable young people — who could not speak English well that loveLife was not for them. The main author of the article reporting lower HIV rates among young people exposed to loveLife admitted to me in an interview that an anthropologist hired by loveLife itself had come to these same conclusions, but her results remain unpublished. See Pettifor et al., "A community-based study to examine the effect of a youth HIV prevention intervention on young people aged 15–24 in South Africa: results of the baseline survey," *Trop Med Int Health* 10:10 (October 2005), 971–80; but see also Jewkes, "Response to Pettifor et al.," author reply, and Parker and Colvin, "Response to Pettifor." Information re the loveLife anthropologist from Pettifor, personal communication, April 2006.

Questions for Critical Reading

1. What is a "lifestyle brand"? Define the term using Epstein's text. Then find an example of a lifestyle brand from popular culture. How might such an approach be used in health education? How effective might it be? How effective was it in South Africa?

2. Define *social cohesion* using Epstein's text. What role did it play in HIV infection rates in Uganda? How might that role be extended to other countries, including the United States?

3. Given Epstein's argument, what would an effective HIV prevention program look like in Africa? How about the United States? Would the same strategies be effective in those two different cultural contexts? Support your responses with passages from the essay.

Exploring Context

1. The (PRODUCT) RED campaign (joinred.com) pairs popular products with fundraising in the fight against AIDS in Africa. Explore the (PRODUCT) RED Web site. Given Epstein's argument, how successful might this campaign be? How does your work with lifestyle brands from Question 1 of Questions for Critical Reading inform your answer?

2. Use the Web to locate information on current HIV infection rates in Africa. Has the situation improved since Epstein wrote her essay, or is it continuing to get worse? What might account for this trend, given Epstein's argument?

3. One of Epstein's central arguments is the usefulness of conversation in combating HIV infection in Africa. How might social networking technologies like Facebook or MySpace help in such a campaign?

Questions for Connecting

1. Leslie Savan, in "What's Black, Then White, and Said All Over?" (p. 363), explores the role of black talk in mainstream advertising. How do her arguments help explain the loveLife campaign that Epstein examines? What are the limits of advertising? What role does race play in the production of cultural change? You may want to draw from your work on lifestyle brands from Question 1 of Questions for Critical Reading.

2. What role should religion play in HIV education in Africa and elsewhere? Use Madeleine Albright's arguments in "Faith and Diplomacy" (p. 23) to determine the best functions of religion in HIV prevention campaigns. You may want to use your work imagining a prevention program from Question 3 of Questions for Critical Reading in composing your response. Should faith be a determining factor when lives are at stake? Would taking religion into account produce better prevention campaigns? What do Epstein's experiences in Uganda and South Africa suggest?

3. Kenji Yoshino, in "Preface" (p. 479) and "The New Civil Rights" (p. 481), suggests that conversation has an important role to play in producing change around civil rights. How does Epstein's argument confirm or complicate Yoshino's ideas? What makes conversation useful in producing social change?

Language Matters

1. Periods are important marks of punctuation, denoting the units of meaning we call sentences. Select a key passage from Epstein's text and type it into a word processor without any capital letters or periods. In class, trade these never-ending sentences and work on replacing the missing punctuation marks. How can you tell when a period is needed in Epstein's text? How can you tell when one is needed in your own text?

2. Outlines can be helpful in creating organization before we start writing, but they can also help us see the organization of any existing piece of writing. Create a "postdraft outline" of Epstein's piece, using a one-sentence summary of each major move of her argument. What sections do you see in her essay? How do they relate to each other? How can you use postdraft outlines of your own papers to check your organization?

3. Because it is sexually transmitted, AIDS/HIV is a delicate issue for many people. What sort of tone and language does Epstein use to discuss the disease and its transmission? How do her choices reflect both her audience and the delicacy of the subject matter? When would you make similar choices in your own writing?

Assignments for Writing

1. Epstein explores the way children and families address the AIDS crisis in Africa. In a short paper, examine the generational response to HIV/AIDS using Epstein's essay. Here are some questions to help your critical thinking: How do adults handle the discussion of AIDS? Is this separate from the discussion of other sexually transmitted diseases? How do children and young adults handle this topic? How do *you* handle it? You might want to draw from your work on social cohesion from Question 2 of Questions for Critical Reading or your analysis of conversation's potential for combating HIV from Question 3 of Exploring Context.

2. Epstein evaluates a number of approaches to HIV prevention, both formal and informal campaigns. Write a paper in which you assess the role of government in the prevention of diseases like HIV. Consider: What should the role of the government be in addressing the HIV/AIDS crisis? Both loveLife and Inkanyezi are private organizations that address sexually transmitted diseases and HIV/AIDS; should there be a similar government outreach program? What role would that program play? Are ordinary people better at preventing disease? How can a government promote the kind of strategies that were effective in Uganda?

3. South Africa's loveLife relies heavily on an advertising campaign. Write an essay in which you evaluate the role of commercial culture in addressing national crises such as HIV/AIDS. What role should companies and advertisers take upon themselves? How does that differ from what they appear to do? Are they really just out for profit, or do companies have a conscience? Should or can they act on issues that affect national health? You might want to reference your work on Product (Red) from Question 1 in Exploring Context in making your argument.

THOMAS FRIEDMAN

Journalist and author **Thomas L. Friedman** holds a B.A. in Mediterranean studies from Brandeis University and an M.A. in Middle Eastern studies from Oxford University. Friedman joined the *New York Times* in 1981 and has won three Pulitzer Prizes since. His foreign affairs column appears in more than seven hundred newspapers, and his books *From Beirut to Jerusalem* (1989), *The Lexus and the Olive Tree: Understanding Globalization* (1999), *Longitudes and Attitudes: Exploring the World after September 11* (2002), *The World Is Flat: A Brief History of the Twenty-first Century* (2005), and *Hot, Flat, and Crowded: Why We Need a Green Revolution—and How It Can Renew America* (2008) have been national best-sellers.

The World Is Flat examines the impact of the "flattening" of the globe, an international leveling of business competition enabled by increasing interconnectedness. Friedman argues that globalized trade, outsourcing, offshoring, supply-chaining, and six other economic, technological, and political forces have changed the world permanently. He examines the positive and negative effects flattening has had and will continue to have on global politics and business.

In "The Dell Theory of Conflict Prevention," which is the penultimate chapter in *The World Is Flat*, Friedman explores the future of war in a globalized economy. Updating a concept he first introduced in *The Lexus and the Olive Tree*—the "Golden Arches Theory of Conflict Prevention," which suggested that citizens in societies economically developed enough to support a McDonald's lose interest in fighting wars—Friedman proposes with the "Dell Theory of Conflict Prevention" that countries will hesitate to risk their place in the global supply chain by fighting a nonessential war. He warns, though, that his new theory does not apply to every kind of modern threat, for terrorists, too, have learned how to use global supply chains.

The flat world will have an impact on you directly as you compete for work with others around the world. This new business environment presents tremendous opportunities for us all; but what are the geopolitical consequences of this new economic reality, and will those consequences generate peace or more conflict?

▶ TAGS: *politics*, *globalization*, *economics*, *knowledge*, *supply chains*, *collaboration*

The Dell Theory of Conflict Prevention

> Free Trade is God's diplomacy. There is no other certain way of uniting
> people in the bonds of peace.
> —BRITISH POLITICIAN RICHARD COBDEN, 1857

Before I share with you the subject of this chapter, I have to tell you a little bit
about the computer that I wrote this book on. It's related to the theme I am
about to discuss. This book was largely written on a Dell Inspiron 600m notebook, service tag number 9ZRJP41. As part of the research for this book, I visited with the management team at Dell near Austin, Texas. I shared with them
the ideas in this book and in return I asked for one favor: I asked them to trace
for me the entire global supply chain that produced my Dell notebook. Here is
their report:

My computer was conceived when I phoned Dell's 800 number on April
2, 2004, and was connected to sales representative Mujteba Naqvi, who immediately entered my order into Dell's order management system. He typed in
both the type of notebook I ordered as well as the special features I wanted,
along with my personal information, shipping address, billing address, and
credit card information. My credit card was verified by Dell through its work
flow connection with Visa, and my order was then released to Dell's production system. Dell has six factories around the world—in Limerick, Ireland;
Xiamen, China; Eldorado do Sul, Brazil; Nashville, Tennessee; Austin, Texas; and
Penang, Malaysia. My order went out by e-mail to the Dell notebook factory in
Malaysia, where the parts for the computer were immediately ordered from the
supplier logistics centers (SLCs) next to the Penang factory. Surrounding every
Dell factory in the world are these supplier logistics centers, owned by the different suppliers of Dell parts. These SLCs are like staging areas. If you are a Dell
supplier anywhere in the world, your job is to keep your SLC full of your specific
parts so they can constantly be trucked over to the Dell factory for just-in-time
manufacturing.

"In an average day, we sell 140,000 to 150,000 computers," explained Dick
Hunter, one of Dell's three global production managers. "Those orders come in
over Dell.com or over the telephone. As soon as these orders come in, our suppliers know about it. They get a signal based on every component in the machine
you ordered, so the supplier knows just what he has to deliver. If you are supplying power cords for desktops, you can see minute by minute how many power
cords you are going to have to deliver." Every two hours, the Dell factory in
Penang sends an e-mail to the various SLCs nearby, telling each one what parts
and what quantities of those parts it wants delivered within the next ninety
minutes—and not one minute later. Within ninety minutes, trucks from the
various SLCs around Penang pull up to the Dell manufacturing plant and unload the parts needed for all those notebooks ordered in the last two hours. This
goes on all day, every two hours. As soon as those parts arrive at the factory, it
takes thirty minutes for Dell employees to unload the parts, register their bar

codes, and put them into the bins for assembly. "We know where every part in every SLC is in the Dell system at all times," said Hunter.

So where did the parts for my notebook come from? I asked Hunter. To begin with, he said, the notebook was codesigned in Austin, Texas, and in Taiwan by a team of Dell engineers and a team of Taiwanese notebook designers. "The customer's needs, required technologies, and Dell's design innovations were all determined by Dell through our direct relationship with customers," he explained. "The basic design of the motherboard and case—the basic functionality of your machine—was designed to those specifications by an ODM [original design manufacturer] in Taiwan. We put our engineers in their facilities and they come to Austin and we actually codesign these systems. This global teamwork brings an added benefit—a globally distributed virtually twenty-four-hour-per-day development cycle. Our partners do the basic electronics and we help them design customer and reliability features that we know our customers want. We know the customers better than our suppliers and our competition, because we are dealing directly with them every day." Dell notebooks are completely redesigned roughly every twelve months, but new features are constantly added during the year—through the supply chain—as the hardware and software components advance.

It happened that when my notebook order hit the Dell factory in Penang, one part was not available—the wireless card—due to a quality control issue, so the assembly of the notebook was delayed for a few days. Then the truck full of good wireless cards arrived. On April 13, at 10:15 AM, a Dell Malaysia worker pulled the order slip that automatically popped up once all my parts had arrived from the SLCs to the Penang factory. Another Dell Malaysia employee then took out a "traveler"—a special carrying tote designed to hold and protect parts—and started plucking all the parts that went into my notebook.

> This supply chain symphony . . . is one of the wonders of the flat world.

Where did those parts come from? Dell uses multiple suppliers for most of the thirty key components that go into its notebooks. That way if one supplier breaks down or cannot meet a surge in demand, Dell is not left in the lurch. So here are the key suppliers for my Inspiron 600m notebook: The Intel microprocessor came from an Intel factory either in the Philippines, Costa Rica, Malaysia, or China. The memory came from a Korean-owned factory in Korea (Samsung), a Taiwanese-owned factory in Taiwan (Nanya), a German-owned factory in Germany (Infineon), or a Japanese-owned factory in Japan (Elpida). My graphics card was shipped from either a Taiwanese-owned factory in China (MSI) or a Chinese-run factory in China (Foxconn). The cooling fan came from a Taiwanese-owned factory in Taiwan (CCI or Auras). The motherboard came from either a Korean-owned factory in Shanghai (Samsung), a Taiwanese-owned factory in Shanghai (Quanta), or a Taiwanese-owned factory in Taiwan (Compal or Wistron). The keyboard came from either a Japanese-owned company in Tianjin, China (Alps), a Taiwanese-owned factory in Shenzen, China (Sunrex), or a Taiwanese-owned factory in Suzhou, China (Darfon). The LCD display was made in either South Korea (Samsung or LG.Philips LCD), Japan (Toshiba or Sharp), or Taiwan (Chi Mei Optoelectronics, Hannstar Display, or AU Optronics). The wireless card came from either an American-owned factory in China (Agere) or Malaysia (Arrow), or a Taiwanese-owned factory in Taiwan (Askey or Gemtek) or China (USI). The modem was made by either a Taiwanese-owned company in China (Asustek or Liteon) or a Chinese-run company in China (Foxconn). The battery came from an American-owned factory in Malaysia (Motorola), a Japanese-owned factory in Mexico or Malaysia or China (Sanyo), or a South Korean or Taiwanese factory in either of those two countries (SDI or Simplo). The hard disk drive was made by an American-owned factory in Singapore (Seagate), a Japanese-owned company in Thailand (Hitachi or Fujitsu), or a Japanese-owned factory in the Philippines (Toshiba). The CD/DVD drive came from a South Korean–owned company with factories in Indonesia and the Philippines (Samsung); a Japanese-owned factory in China or Malaysia (NEC); a Japanese-owned factory in Indonesia, China, or Malaysia (Teac); or a Japanese-owned factory in China (Sony). The notebook carrying bag was made by either an Irish-owned company in China (Tenba) or an American-owned company in China (Targus, Samsonite, or Pacific Design). The power adapter was made by either a Thai-owned factory in Thailand (Delta) or a Taiwanese, Korean, or American-owned factory in China (Liteon, Samsung, or Mobility). The power cord was made by a British-owned company with factories in China, Malaysia, and India (Volex). The removable memory stick was made by either an Israeli-owned company in Israel (M-System) or an American-owned company with a factory in Malaysia (Smart Modular).

This supply chain symphony—from my order over the phone to production to delivery to my house—is one of the wonders of the flat world.

"We have to do a lot of collaborating," said Hunter. "Michael [Dell] personally knows the CEOs of these companies, and we are constantly working with them on process improvements and real-time demand/supply balancing." Demand shaping goes on constantly, said Hunter. What is "demand shaping"? It works like this: At 10 AM Austin time, Dell discovers that so many customers have ordered notebooks with 40-gigabyte hard drives since the morning that its supply chain will run short in two hours. That signal is automatically relayed to Dell's marketing department and to Dell.com and to all the Dell phone operators taking orders. If you happen to call to place your Dell order at 10:30 AM, the Dell representative will say to you, "Tom, it's your lucky day! For the next hour we are offering 60-gigabyte hard drives with the notebook you want—for only $10 more than the 40-gig drive. And if you act now, Dell will throw in a carrying case along with your purchase, because we so value you as a customer." In an hour or two, using such promotions, Dell can reshape the demand for any part of any notebook or desktop to correspond with the projected supply in its global supply chain. Today memory might be on sale, tomorrow it might be CD-ROMs.

Picking up the story of my notebook, on April 13, at 11:29 AM, all the parts had been plucked from the just-in-time inventory bins in Penang, and the computer was assembled there by A. Sathini, a team member "who manually screwed together all of the parts from kitting as well as the labels needed for Tom's system," said Dell in their production report to me. "The system was then sent down the conveyor to go to burn, where Tom's specified software was downloaded." Dell has huge server banks stocked with the latest in Microsoft, Norton Utilities, and other popular software applications, which are downloaded into each new computer according to the specific tastes of the customer.

"By 2:45 PM, Tom's software had been successfully downloaded, and [was] manually moved to the boxing line. By 4:05 PM, Tom's system [was] placed in protective foam and a shuttle box, with a label, which contains his order number, tracking code, system type, and shipping code. By 6:04 PM, Tom's system had been loaded on a pallet with a specified manifest, which gives the Merge facility visibility to when the system will arrive, what pallet it will be on (out of 75+ pallets with 152 systems per pallet), and to what address Tom's system will ship. By 6:26 PM, Tom's system left [the Dell factory] to head to the Penang, Malaysia, airport."

Six days a week Dell charters a China Airlines 747 out of Taiwan and flies it from Penang to Nashville via Taipei. Each 747 leaves with twenty-five thousand Dell notebooks that weigh altogether 110,000 kilograms, or 242,500 pounds. It is the only 747 that ever lands in Nashville, except Air Force One, when the president visits. "By April 15, 2004, at 7:41 AM, Tom's system arrived at [Nashville] with other Dell systems from Penang and Limerick. By 11:58 AM, Tom's system [was] inserted into a larger box, which went down the boxing line to the specific external parts that Tom had ordered."

That was thirteen days after I'd ordered it. Had there not been a parts delay in Malaysia when my order first arrived, the time between when I phoned in my purchase, when the notebook was assembled in Penang, and its arrival in Nashville would have been only four days. Hunter said the total supply chain for my computer, including suppliers of suppliers, involved about four hundred companies in North America, Europe, and primarily Asia, but with thirty key players. Somehow, though, it all came together. As Dell reported: On April 15, 2004, at 12:59 PM, "Tom's system had been shipped from [Nashville] and was tenured by UPS shipping LTL (3-5-day ground, specified by Tom), with UPS tracking number 1Z13WA374253514697. By April 19, 2004, at 6:41 PM, Tom's system arrived in Bethesda, MD, and was signed for."

I am telling you the story of my notebook to tell a larger story of geopolitics in the flat world. To all the forces . . . that are still holding back the flattening of the world, or could actually reverse the process, one has to add a more traditional threat, and that is an outbreak of a good, old-fashioned, world-shaking, economy-destroying war. It could be China deciding once and for all to eliminate Taiwan as an independent state; or North Korea, out of fear or insanity, using one of its nuclear weapons against South Korea or Japan; or Israel and a soon-to-be-nuclear Iran going at each other; or India and Pakistan finally nuking it out. These and other classic geopolitical conflicts could erupt at any time and either slow the flattening of the world or seriously unflatten it.

The real subject of this chapter is how these classic geopolitical threats might be moderated or influenced by the new forms of collaboration fostered and demanded by the flat world—particularly supply-chaining. The flattening of the world is too young for us to draw any definitive conclusions. What is certain, though, is that as the world flattens, one of the most interesting dramas to watch in international relations will be the interplay between the traditional global threats and the newly emergent global supply chains. The interaction between old-time threats (like China *versus* Taiwan) and just-in-time supply chains (like China *plus* Taiwan) will be a rich source of study for the field of international relations in the early twenty-first century.

In *The Lexus and the Olive Tree* I argued that to the extent that countries tied their economies and futures to global integration and trade, it would act as a restraint on going to war with their neighbors. I first started thinking about this in the late 1990s, when, during my travels, I noticed that no two countries that both had McDonald's had ever fought a war against each other since each got its McDonald's. (Border skirmishes and civil wars don't count, because McDonald's usually served both sides.) After confirming this with McDonald's, I offered what I called the Golden Arches Theory of Conflict Prevention. The Golden Arches Theory stipulated that when a country reached the level of economic development where it had a middle class big enough to support a network of McDonald's, it became a McDonald's country. And people in McDonald's countries didn't like to fight wars anymore. They preferred to wait in line for burgers. While this was offered slightly tongue in cheek, the serious point I was trying to make was that as countries got woven into the fabric of global trade and rising living standards, which having a network of McDonald's franchises had come to symbolize, the cost of war for victor and vanquished became prohibitively high.

This McDonald's theory has held up pretty well, but now that almost every country has acquired a McDonald's, except the worst rogues like North Korea, Iran, and Iraq under Saddam Hussein, it seemed to me that this theory needed updating for the flat world. In that spirit, and again with tongue slightly in cheek, I offer the Dell Theory of Conflict Prevention, the essence of which is that the advent and spread of just-in-time global supply chains in the flat world are an even greater restraint on geopolitical adventurism than the more general rising standard of living that McDonald's symbolized.

The Dell Theory stipulates: No two countries that are both part of a major global supply chain, like Dell's, will ever fight a war against each other as long as they are both part of the same global supply chain. Because people embedded in major global supply chains don't want to fight old-time wars anymore. They want to make just-in-time deliveries of goods and services—and enjoy the rising standards of living that come with that. One of the people with the best feel for the logic behind this theory is Michael Dell, the founder and chairman of Dell.

"These countries understand the risk premium that they have," said Dell of the countries in his Asian supply chain. "They are pretty careful to protect the equity that they have built up or tell us why we should not worry [about their doing anything adventurous]. My belief after visiting China is that the change that has occurred there is in the best interest of the world and China. Once people get a taste for whatever you want to call it—economic independence, a better lifestyle, and a better life for their child or children—they grab on to that and don't want to give it up."

Any sort of war or prolonged political upheaval in East Asia or China "would have a massive chilling effect on the investment there and on all the progress that has been made there," said Dell, who added that he believes the governments in that part of the world understand this very clearly. "We certainly make clear to them that stability is important to us. [Right now] it is not a day-to-day worry for us . . . I believe that as time and progress go on there, the chance for a really disruptive event goes down exponentially. I don't think our industry gets enough credit for the good we are doing in these areas. If you are making money and being productive and raising your standard of living, you're not sitting around thinking, Who did this to us? or Why is our life so bad?"

There is a lot of truth to this. Countries whose workers and industries are   20
woven into a major global supply chain know that they cannot take an hour, a week, or a month off for war without disrupting industries and economies around the world and thereby risking the loss of their place in that supply chain for a long time, which could be extremely costly. For a country with no natural resources, being part of a global supply chain is like striking oil—oil that never runs out. And therefore, getting dropped from such a chain because you start a war is like having your oil wells go dry or having someone pour cement down them. They will not come back anytime soon.

"You are going to pay for it really dearly," said Glenn E. Neland, senior vice president for worldwide procurement at Dell, when I asked him what would happen to a major supply-chain member in Asia that decided to start fighting with its neighbor and disrupt the supply chain. "It will not only bring you to your knees [today], but you will pay for a long time—because you just won't have any credibility if you demonstrate you are going to go [off] the political deep end. And China is just now starting to develop a level of credibility in the business community that it is creating a business environment you can prosper in—with transparent and consistent rules." Neland said that suppliers regularly ask him whether he is worried about China and Taiwan, which have threatened to go to war at several points in the past half century, but his standard response is that he cannot imagine them "doing anything more than flexing muscles with each other." Neland said he can tell in his conversations and dealings with companies and governments in the Dell supply chain, particularly the Chinese, that "they recognize the opportunity and are really hungry to participate in the same things they have seen other countries in Asia do. They know there is a big economic pot at the end of the rainbow and they are really after it. We will spend about $35 billion producing parts this year, and 30 percent of that is [in] China."

If you follow the evolution of supply chains, added Neland, you see the prosperity and stability they promoted first in Japan, and then in Korea and Taiwan, and now in Malaysia, Singapore, the Philippines, Thailand, and Indonesia. Once countries get embedded in these global supply chains, "they feel part of something much bigger than their own businesses," he said. Osamu Watanabe, the CEO of the Japan External Trade Organization (JETRO), was explaining to me one afternoon in Tokyo how Japanese companies were moving vast amounts of low- and middle-range technical work and manufacturing to China, doing the basic fabrication there, and then bringing it back to Japan for final assembly. Japan was doing this despite a bitter legacy of mistrust between the two countries, which was intensified by the Japanese invasion of China in the last century. Historically, he noted, a strong Japan and a strong China have had a hard time coexisting. But not today, at least not for the moment. Why not? I asked. The reason you can have a strong Japan and a strong China at the same time, he said, "is because of the supply chain." It is a win-win for both.

Obviously, since Iraq, Syria, south Lebanon, North Korea, Pakistan, Afghanistan, and Iran are not part of any major global supply chains, all of them remain hot spots that could explode at any time and slow or reverse the flattening of the world. As my own notebook story attests, the most important test case of the Dell Theory of Conflict Prevention is the situation between China and Taiwan—since both are deeply embedded in several of the world's most important computer, consumer electronics, and, increasingly, software supply chains. The vast majority of computer components for every major company comes from coastal China, Taiwan, and East Asia. In addition, Taiwan alone has more than $100 billion in investments in mainland China today, and Taiwanese experts run many of the cutting-edge Chinese high-tech manufacturing companies.

It is no wonder that Craig Addison, the former editor of *Electronic Business Asia* magazine, wrote an essay for the *International Herald Tribune* (September 29, 2000), headlined "A 'Silicon Shield' Protects Taiwan from China." He argued that "Silicon-based products, such as computers and networking systems, form the basis of the digital economies in the United States, Japan, and other developed nations. In the past decade, Taiwan has become the third-largest information technology hardware producer after the United States and Japan. Military aggression by China against Taiwan would cut off a large portion of the world's supply of these products . . . Such a development would wipe trillions of dollars off the market value of technology companies listed in the United States, Japan, and Europe." Even if China's leaders, like former president Jiang Zemin, who was once minister of electronics, lose sight of how integrated China and Taiwan are in the world's computer supply chain, they need only ask their kids for an update. Jiang Zemin's son, Jiang Mianheng, wrote Addison, "is a partner in a wafer fabrication project in Shanghai with Winston Wang of Taiwan's Grace T.H.W. Group." And it is not just Taiwanese. Hundreds of big American tech companies now have R&D operations in China; a war that disrupted them could lead not only to the companies moving their plants elsewhere but also to a significant loss of R&D investment in China, which the Beijing government has been betting on to advance its development. Such a war could also, depending on how it started, trigger a widespread American boycott of Chinese goods—if China were to snuff out the Taiwanese democracy—which would lead to serious economic turmoil inside China.

The Dell Theory had its first real test in December 2004, when Taiwan   25
held parliamentary elections. President Chen Shui-bian's pro-independence
Democratic Progressive Party was expected to win the legislative runoff over
the main opposition Nationalist Party, which favored closer ties with Beijing.
Chen framed the election as a popular referendum on his proposal to write a
new constitution that would formally enshrine Taiwan's independence, ending the purposely ambiguous status quo. Had Chen won and moved ahead on
his agenda to make Taiwan its own motherland, as opposed to maintaining
the status quo fiction that it is a province of the mainland, it could have led to a
Chinese military assault on Taiwan. Everyone in the region was holding his or
her breath. And what happened? *Motherboards won over motherland.* A majority
of Taiwanese voted against the pro-independence governing party legislative
candidates, ensuring that the DPP would not have a majority in parliament.
I believe the message Taiwanese voters were sending was not that they never
want Taiwan to be independent. It was that they do not want to upset the status
quo right now, which has been so beneficial to so many Taiwanese. The voters
seemed to understand clearly how interwoven they had become with the mainland, and they wisely opted to maintain their de facto independence rather than
force de jure independence, which might have triggered a Chinese invasion and
a very uncertain future.

Warning: What I said when I put forth the McDonald's theory, I would repeat even more strenuously with the Dell Theory: It does not make wars obsolete. And it does not guarantee that governments will not engage in wars of
choice, even governments that are part of major supply chains. To suggest so
would be naive. It guarantees only that governments whose countries are enmeshed in global supply chains will have to think three times, not just twice,
about engaging in anything but a war of self-defense. And if they choose to go
to war anyway, the price they will pay will be ten times higher than it was a
decade ago and probably ten times higher than whatever the leaders of that
country think. It is one thing to lose your McDonald's. It's quite another to fight
a war that costs you your place in a twenty-first-century supply chain that may
not come back around for a long time.

While the biggest test case of the Dell Theory is China versus Taiwan, the fact is
that the Dell Theory has already proved itself to some degree in the case of India
and Pakistan, the context in which I first started to think about it. I happened
to be in India in 2002, when its just-in-time services supply chains ran into
some very old-time geopolitics—and the supply chain won. In the case of India
and Pakistan, the Dell Theory was working on only one party—India—but it
still had a major impact. India is to the world's knowledge and service supply
chain what China and Taiwan are to the manufacturing ones. By now readers
of this book know all the highlights: General Electric's biggest research center
outside the United States is in Bangalore, with seventeen hundred Indian engineers, designers, and scientists. The brain chips for many brand-name cell
phones are designed in Bangalore. Renting a car from Avis online? It's managed
in Bangalore. Tracing your lost luggage on Delta or British Airways is done

from Bangalore, and the backroom accounting and computer maintenance for scores of global firms are done from Bangalore, Mumbai, Chennai, and other major Indian cities.

Here's what happened: On May 31, 2002, State Department spokesman Richard Boucher issued a travel advisory saying, "We urge American citizens currently in India to depart the country," because the prospect of a nuclear exchange with Pakistan was becoming very real. Both nations were massing troops on their borders, intelligence reports were suggesting that they both might be dusting off their nuclear warheads, and CNN was flashing images of people flooding out of India. The global American firms that had moved their back rooms and R&D operations to Bangalore were deeply unnerved.

"I was actually surfing on the Web, and I saw a travel advisory come up on India on a Friday evening," said Vivek Paul, president of Wipro, which manages backroom operations from India of many American multinationals. "As soon as I saw that, I said, 'Oh my gosh, every customer that we have is going to have a million questions on this.' It was the Friday before a long weekend, so over the weekend we at Wipro developed a fail-safe business continuity plan for all of our customers." While Wipro's customers were pleased to see how on top of things the company was, many of them were nevertheless rattled. This was not in the plan when they decided to outsource mission-critical research and operations to India. Said Paul, "I had a CIO from one of our big American clients send me an e-mail saying, 'I am now spending a lot of time looking for alternative sources to India. I don't think you want me doing that, and I don't want to be doing it.' I immediately forwarded his message to the Indian ambassador in Washington and told him to get it to the right person." Paul would not tell me what company it was, but I have confirmed through diplomatic sources that it was United Technologies. And plenty of others, like American Express and General Electric, with back rooms in Bangalore, had to have been equally worried.

For many global companies, "the main heart of their business is now sup- 30 ported here," said N. Krishnakumar, president of MindTree, another leading Indian knowledge outsourcing firm based in Bangalore. "It can cause chaos if there is a disruption." While not trying to meddle in foreign affairs, he added, "What we explained to our government, through the Confederation of Indian Industry, is that providing a stable, predictable operating environment is now the key to India's development." This was a real education for India's elderly leaders in New Delhi, who had not fully absorbed how critical India had become to the world's knowledge supply chain. When you are managing vital backroom operations for American Express or General Electric or Avis, or are responsible for tracing all the lost luggage on British Airways or Delta, you cannot take a month, a week, or even a day off for war without causing major disruptions for those companies. Once those companies have made a commitment to outsource business operations or research to India, they expect it to stay there. That is a major commitment. And if geopolitics causes a serious disruption, they will leave, and they will not come back very easily. When you lose this kind of service trade, you can lose it for good.

"What ends up happening in the flat world you described," explained Paul, "is that you have only one opportunity to make it right if something [goes] wrong. Because the disadvantage of being in a flat world is that despite all the nice engagements and stuff and the exit barriers that you have, every customer has multiple options, and so the sense of responsibility you have is not just out of a desire to do good by your customers, but also a desire for self-preservation."

The Indian government got the message. Was India's central place in the world's services supply chain the only factor in getting Prime Minister Vajpayee to tone down his rhetoric and step back from the brink? Of course not. There were other factors, to be sure—most notably the deterrent effect of Pakistan's own nuclear arsenal. But clearly, India's role in global services was an important additional source of restraint on its behavior, and it was taken into account by New Delhi. "I think it sobered a lot of people," said Jerry Rao, who, as noted earlier, heads the Indian high-tech trade association. "We engaged very seriously, and we tried to make the point that this was very bad for Indian business. It was very bad for the Indian economy . . . [Many people] didn't realize till then how suddenly we had become integrated into the rest of the world. We are now partners in a twenty-four by seven by three-sixty-five supply chain."

Vivek Kulkarni, then information technology secretary for Bangalore's regional government, told me back in 2002, "We don't get involved in politics, but we did bring to the government's attention the problems the Indian IT industry might face if there were a war." And this was an altogether new factor for New Delhi to take into consideration. "Ten years ago, [a lobby of IT ministers from different Indian states] never existed," said Kulkarni. Now it is one of the most important business lobbies in India and a coalition that no Indian government can ignore.

"With all due respect, the McDonald's [shutting] down doesn't hurt anything," said Vivek Paul, "but if Wipro had to shut down we would affect the day-to-day operations of many, many companies." No one would answer the phones in call centers. Many e-commerce sites that are supported from Bangalore would shut down. Many major companies that rely on India to maintain their key computer applications or handle their human resources departments or billings would seize up. And these companies did not want to find alternatives, said Paul. Switching is very difficult, because taking over mission-critical day-to-day backroom operations of a global company takes a great deal of training and experience. It's not like opening a fast-food restaurant. That was why, said Paul, Wipro's clients were telling him, " 'I have made an investment in you. I need you to be very responsible with the trust I have reposed in you.' And I think that created an enormous amount of back pressure on us that said we have to act in a responsible fashion . . . All of a sudden it became even clearer that there's more to gain by economic gains than by geopolitical gains. [We had more to gain from building] a vibrant, richer middle class able to create an export industry than we possibly could by having an ego-satisfying war with Pakistan." The Indian government also looked around and realized that the vast majority of India's billion people were saying, "I want a better future, not more territory." Over and over again, when I asked young Indians working at call centers how they felt about Kashmir or a war with Pakistan, they waved me off with the same answer: "We have better things to do." And they do. America needs to keep this in mind as it weighs its overall approach to outsourcing. I would never advocate shipping some American's job overseas just so it will keep Indians and Pakistanis at peace with each other. But I would say that to the extent that this process happens, driven by its own internal economic logic, it will have a net positive geopolitical effect. It will absolutely make the world safer for American kids.

Each of the Indian business leaders I interviewed noted that in the event of some outrageous act of terrorism or aggression from Pakistan, India would do whatever it takes to defend itself, and they would be the first to support that—the Dell Theory be damned. Sometimes war is unavoidable. It is imposed on you by the reckless behavior of others, and you have to just pay the price. But the more India and, one hopes, soon Pakistan get enmeshed in global service supply chains, the greater disincentive they have to fight anything but a border skirmish or a war of words.

The example of the 2002 India-Pakistan nuclear crisis at least gives us some hope. That cease-fire was brought to us not by General Powell but by General Electric.

We bring good things to life.

Infosys versus al Qaeda

Unfortunately, even GE can do only so much. Because, alas, a new source for geopolitical instability has emerged only in recent years, for which even the updated Dell Theory can provide no restraint. It is the emergence of mutant global supply chains—that is, nonstate actors, be they criminals or terrorists, who learn to use all the elements of the flat world to advance a highly destabilizing, even nihilistic agenda. I first started thinking about this when Nandan Nilekani, the Infosys CEO, was giving me [a] tour . . . of his company's global videoconferencing center at its Bangalore headquarters. As Nandan explained to me how Infosys could get its global supply chain together at once for a virtual conference in that room, a thought popped into my head: Who else uses open-sourcing and supply-chaining so imaginatively? The answer, of course, is al Qaeda.

Al Qaeda has learned to use many of the same instruments for global collaboration that Infosys uses, but instead of producing products and profits with them, it has produced mayhem and murder. This is a particularly difficult problem. In fact, it may be the most vexing geopolitical problem for flat-world countries that want to focus on the future. The flat world—unfortunately—is a friend of both Infosys and al Qaeda. The Dell Theory will not work at all against these informal Islamo-Leninist terror networks, because they are not a state with a population that will hold its leaders accountable or with a domestic business lobby that might restrain them. These mutant global supply chains are formed for the purpose of destruction, not profit. They don't need investors, only recruits, donors, and victims. Yet these mobile, self-financing mutant supply chains use all the tools of collaboration offered by the flat world—open-sourcing to raise money, to recruit followers, and to stimulate and disseminate ideas; outsourcing to train recruits; and supply-chaining to distribute the tools and the suicide bombers to undertake operations. The U.S. Central Command has a name for this whole underground network: the Virtual Caliphate. And its leaders and innovators understand the flat world almost as well as Wal-Mart, Dell, and Infosys do.

In the previous chapter, I tried to explain that you cannot understand the rise of al Qaeda emotionally and politically without reference to the flattening of the world. What I am arguing here is that you cannot understand the rise of al Qaeda technically without reference to the flattening of the world, either. Globalization in general has been al Qaeda's friend in that it has helped to solidify a revival of Muslim identity and solidarity, with Muslims in one country much better able to see and sympathize with the struggles of their brethren in another country—thanks to the Internet and satellite television. At the same time, . . . this flattening process has intensified the feelings of humiliation in some quarters of the Muslim world over the fact that civilizations to which the Muslim world once felt superior—Hindus, Jews, Christians, Chinese—are now all doing better than many Muslim countries, and everyone can see it. The flattening of the world has also

In the flat world it is much more difficult to hide, but much easier to get connected.

led to more urbanization and large-scale immigration to the West of many of these young, unemployed, frustrated Arab-Muslim males, while simultaneously making it much easier for informal open-source networks of these young men to form, operate, and interconnect. This certainly has been a boon for underground extremist Muslim political groups. There has been a proliferation of these informal mutual supply chains throughout the Arab-Muslim world today—small networks of people who move money through *hawalas* (hand-to-hand financing networks), who recruit through alternative education systems like the madrassas, and who communicate through the Internet and other tools of the global information revolution. Think about it: A century ago, anarchists were limited in their ability to communicate and collaborate with one another, to find sympathizers, and to band together for an operation. Today, with the Internet, that is not a problem. Today even the Unabomber could find friends to join a consortium where his "strengths" could be magnified and reinforced by others who had just as warped a worldview as he did.

What we have witnessed in Iraq is an even more perverse mutation of this mutant supply chain—the suicide supply chain. Since the start of the U.S. invasion in March 2002, more than two hundred suicide bombers have been recruited from within Iraq and from across the Muslim world, brought to the Iraqi front by some underground railroad, connected with the bomb makers there, and then dispatched against U.S. and Iraqi targets according to whatever suits the daily tactical needs of the insurgent Islamist forces in Iraq. I can understand, but not accept, the notion that more than thirty-seven years of Israeli occupation of the West Bank might have driven some Palestinians into a suicidal rage.

But the American occupation of Iraq was only a few months old before it started to get hit by this suicide supply chain. How do you recruit so many young men "off the shelf" who are ready to commit suicide in the cause of jihad, many of them apparently not even Iraqis? And they don't even identify themselves by name or want to get credit—at least in this world. The fact is that Western intelligence agencies have no clue how this underground suicide supply chain, which seems to have an infinite pool of recruits to draw on, works, and yet it has basically stymied the U.S. armed forces in Iraq. From what we do know, though, this Virtual Caliphate works just like the supply chains I described earlier. Just as you take an item off the shelf in a discount store in Birmingham and another one is immediately made in Beijing, so the retailers of suicide deploy a human bomber in Baghdad and another one is immediately recruited and indoctrinated in Beirut. To the extent that this tactic spreads, it will require a major rethinking of U.S. military doctrine.

The flat world has also been such a huge boon for al Qaeda and its ilk because of the way it enables the small to act big, and the way it enables small acts—the killing of just a few people—to have big effects. The horrific video of the beheading of *Wall Street Journal* reporter Danny Pearl by Islamist militants in Pakistan was transmitted by the Internet all over the world. There is not a journalist anywhere who saw or even just read about that who was not terrified. But those same beheading videos are also used as tools of recruitment. The flat world makes it much easier for terrorists to transmit their terror. With the Internet they don't even have to go through Western or Arab news organizations but can broadcast right into your computer. It takes much less dynamite to transmit so much more anxiety. Just as the U.S. Army had embedded journalists, so the suicide supply chain has embedded terrorists, in their own way, to tell us their side of the story. How many times have I gotten up in the morning, fired up the Internet, and been confronted by the video image of some masked gunman threatening to behead an American—all brought to me courtesy of AOL's home page? The Internet is an enormously useful tool for the dissemination of propaganda, conspiracy theories, and plain old untruths, because it combines a huge reach with a patina of technology that makes anything on the Internet somehow more believable. How many times have you heard someone say, "But I read it on the Internet," as if that should end the argument? In fact, the Internet can make things worse. It often leads to more people being exposed to crazy conspiracy theories.

"The new system of diffusion—the Internet—is more likely to transmit irrationality than rationality," said political theorist Yaron Ezrahi, who specializes in the interaction between media and politics. "Because irrationality is more emotionally loaded, it requires less knowledge, it explains more to more people, it goes down easier." That is why conspiracy theories are so rife in the Arab-Muslim world today—and unfortunately are becoming so in many quarters of the Western world, for that matter. Conspiracy theories are like a drug that goes right into your bloodstream, enabling you to see "the Light." And the Internet is the needle. Young people used to have to take LSD to escape. Now they just go online. Now you don't shoot up, you download. You download the precise point of view that speaks to all your own biases. And the flat world makes it all so much easier.

Gabriel Weimann, a professor of communication at Haifa University, Israel, did an incisive study of terrorists' use of the Internet and of what I call the flat world, which was published in March 2004 by the United States Institute of Peace and excerpted on YaleGlobal Online on April 26, 2004. He made the following points:

> While the danger that cyber-terrorism poses to the Internet is frequently debated, surprisingly little is known about the threat posed by terrorists' use of the Internet. A recent six-year-long study shows that terrorist organizations and their supporters have been using all of the tools that the Internet offers to recruit supporters, raise funds, and launch a worldwide campaign of fear. It is also clear that to combat terrorism effectively, mere suppression of their Internet tools is not enough. Our scan of the Internet in 2003–04 revealed the existence of hundreds of websites serving terrorists in different, albeit sometimes overlapping, ways . . . There are countless examples of how [terrorists] use this uncensored medium to spread disinformation, to deliver threats intended to instill fear and helplessness, and to disseminate horrific images of recent actions. Since September 11, 2001, al Qaeda has festooned its websites with a string of announcements of an impending "large attack" on U.S. targets. These warnings have received considerable media coverage, which has helped to generate a widespread sense of dread and insecurity among audiences throughout the world and especially within the United States. . . .
>
> The Internet has significantly expanded the opportunities for terrorists to secure publicity. Until the advent of the Internet, terrorists' hopes of winning publicity for their causes and activities depended on attracting the attention of television, radio, or the print media. The fact that terrorists themselves have direct control over the content of their websites offers further opportunities to shape how they are perceived by different target audiences and to manipulate their image and the images of their enemies. Most terrorist sites do not celebrate their violent activities. Instead—regardless of their nature, motives, or location—most terrorist sites emphasize two issues: the restrictions placed on freedom of expression; and the plight of their comrades who are now political prisoners. These issues resonate powerfully with their own supporters and are also calculated to elicit sympathy from Western audiences that cherish freedom of expression and frown on measures to silence political opposition. . . .
>
> Terrorists have proven not only skillful at online marketing but also adept at mining the data offered by the billion-some pages of the World Wide Web. They can learn from the Internet about the schedules and locations of targets such as transportation facilities, nuclear power plants, public buildings, airports and ports, and even counterterrorism

measures. According to Secretary of Defense Donald Rumsfeld, an al Qaeda training manual recovered in Afghanistan tells its readers, "Using public sources openly and without resorting to illegal means, it is possible to gather at least 80 percent of all information required about the enemy." One captured al Qaeda computer contained engineering and structural architecture features of a dam, which had been downloaded from the Internet and which would enable al Qaeda engineers and planners to simulate catastrophic failures. In other captured computers, U.S. investigators found evidence that al Qaeda operators spent time on sites that offer software and programming instructions for the digital switches that run power, water, transportation, and communications grids.

Like many other political organizations, terrorist groups use the Internet to raise funds. Al Qaeda, for instance, has always depended heavily on donations, and its global fund-raising network is built upon a foundation of charities, nongovernmental organizations, and other financial institutions that use websites and Internet-based chat rooms and forums. The fighters in the Russian breakaway republic of Chechnya have likewise used the Internet to publicize the numbers of bank accounts to which sympathizers can contribute. And in December 2001, the U.S. government seized the assets of a Texas-based charity because of its ties to Hamas.

In addition to soliciting financial aid online, terrorists recruit converts by using the full panoply of website technologies (audio, digital video, etc.) to enhance the presentation of their message. And like commercial sites that track visitors to develop consumer profiles, terrorist organizations capture information about the users who browse their websites. Visitors who seem most interested in the organization's cause or well suited to carrying out its work are then contacted. Recruiters may also use more interactive Internet technology to roam online chat rooms and cyber cafes, looking for receptive members of the public, particularly young people. The SITE Institute, a Washington, D.C.–based terrorism research group that monitors al Qaeda's Internet communications, has provided chilling details of a high-tech recruitment drive launched in 2003 to recruit fighters to travel to Iraq and attack U.S. and coalition forces there. The Internet also grants terrorists a cheap and efficient means of networking. Many terrorist groups, among them Hamas and al Qaeda, have undergone a transformation from strictly hierarchical organizations with designated leaders to affiliations of semi-independent cells that have no single commanding hierarchy. Through the Internet, these loosely interconnected groups are able to maintain contact with one another — and with members of other terrorist groups. The Internet connects not only members of the same terrorist organizations but also members of different groups. For instance, dozens of sites supporting terrorism in the name of jihad permit terrorists in places as far-removed from one another as Chechnya and Malaysia to exchange ideas and practical information about how to build bombs, establish terror cells, and carry out attacks . . . Al Qaeda operatives relied heavily on the Internet in planning and coordinating the September 11 attacks.

For all of these reasons we are just at the beginning of understanding the geopolitical impact of the flattening of the world. On the one hand, failed states and failed regions are places we have every incentive to avoid today. They offer no economic opportunity and there is no Soviet Union out there competing with us for influence over such countries. On the other hand, there may be nothing more dangerous today than a failed state with broadband capability. That is, even failed states tend to have telecommunications systems and satellite links, and therefore if a terrorist group infiltrates a failed state, as al Qaeda did with Afghanistan, it can amplify its power enormously. As much as big powers want to stay away from such states, they may feel compelled to get even more deeply embroiled in them. Think of America in Afghanistan and Iraq, Russia in Chechnya, Australia in East Timor.

In the flat world it is much more difficult to hide, but much easier to get connected. "Think of Mao at the beginning of the Chinese communist revolution," remarked Michael Mandelbaum, the Johns Hopkins foreign policy specialist. "The Chinese Communists had to hide in caves in northwest China, but they could move around in whatever territory they were able to control. Bin Laden, by contrast, can't show his face, but he can reach every household in the world, thanks to the Internet." Bin Laden cannot capture any territory but he can capture the imagination of millions of people. And he has, broadcasting right into American living rooms on the eve of the 2004 presidential election.

Hell hath no fury like a terrorist with a satellite dish and an interactive Web site.

Too Personally Insecure

In the fall of 2004, I was invited to speak at a synagogue in Woodstock, New York, home of the famous Woodstock music festival. I asked my hosts how was it that they were able to get a synagogue in Woodstock, of all places, big enough to support a lecture series. Very simple, they said. Since 9/11, Jews, and others, have been moving from New York City to places like Woodstock, to get away from what they fear will be the next ground zero. Right now this trend is a trickle, but it would become a torrent if a nuclear device were detonated in any European or American city.

Since this threat is the mother of all unflatteners, this book would not be complete without a discussion of it. We can live with a lot. We lived through 9/11. But we cannot live with nuclear terrorism. That would unflatten the world permanently.

The only reason that Osama bin Laden did not use a nuclear device on 9/11 was not that he did not have the intention but that he did not have the capability. And since the Dell Theory offers no hope of restraining the suicide supply chains, the only strategy we have is to limit their worst capabilities. That means a much more serious global effort to stanch nuclear proliferation by limiting the supply — to buy up the fissile material that is already out there, particularly in the former Soviet Union, and prevent more states from going nuclear. Harvard University international affairs expert Graham Allison, in his book *Nuclear Terrorism: The Ultimate Preventable Catastrophe*, outlines just such a strategy for denying terrorists access to nuclear weapons and nuclear materials. It can be done, he insists. It is a challenge to our will and convictions, but *not to our capabilities.* Allison proposes a new American-led international security order to deal with this problem based on what he calls "a doctrine of the Three No's: No loose nukes, No new nascent nukes, and No new nuclear states." No loose nukes, says Allison, means locking down all nuclear weapons and all nuclear material from which bombs could be made — in a much more serious way than we have done up till now. "We don't lose gold from Fort Knox," says Allison. "Russia doesn't lose treasures from the Kremlin armory. So we both know how to prevent theft of those things that are super valuable to us if we are determined to do it." No new nascent nukes means recognizing that there is a group of actors out there who can and do produce highly enriched uranium or plutonium, which is nothing more than nuclear bombs just about to hatch. We need a much more credible, multilateral nonproliferation regime that soaks up this fissile material. Finally, no new nuclear states means "drawing a line under the current eight nuclear powers and determining that, however unfair and unreasonable it may be, that club will have no more members than those eight," says Allison, adding that these three steps might then buy us time to develop a more formal, sustainable, internationally approved regime.

It would be nice also to be able to deny the Internet to al Qaeda and its ilk, but that, alas, is impossible — without undermining ourselves. That is why limiting their capabilities is necessary but not sufficient. We also have to find a way to get at their worst intentions. If we are not going to shut down the Internet and all the other creative and collaborative tools that have flattened the world, and if we can't restrict access to them, the only thing we can do is try to influence the imagination and intentions that people bring to them and draw from them. When I raised this issue, and the broad themes of this book, with my religious teacher, Rabbi Tzvi Marx from Holland, he surprised me by saying that the flat world I was describing reminded him of the story of the Tower of Babel.

How so? I asked. "The reason God banished all the people from the Tower of Babel and made them all speak different languages was not because he did not want them to collaborate per se," answered Rabbi Marx. "It was because he was enraged at what they were collaborating on — an effort to build a tower to the heavens so they could become God." This was a distortion of the human capacity, so God broke their union and their ability to communicate with one another. Now, all these years later, humankind has again created a new platform for more people from more places to communicate and collaborate with less friction and more ease than ever: the Internet. Would God see the Internet as heresy?

"Absolutely not," said Marx. "The heresy is not that mankind works to-gether—it is to what ends. It is essential that we use this new ability to commu-nicate and collaborate for the right ends—for constructive human aims and not megalomaniacal ends. Building a tower was megalomaniacal. Bin Laden's insistence that he has the truth and can flatten anyone else's tower who doesn't heed him is megalomaniacal. Collaborating so mankind can achieve its full potential is God's hope."

Questions for Critical Reading

1. Much of Friedman's focus in this chapter is on collaboration. What role does collaboration play in economic and terroristic systems of production? You will need to analyze his text to determine a response; reread it to find supporting quotations.

2. What is the Dell Theory of Conflict Prevention? Reread Friedman's text to locate a quotation that defines this concept. Can you offer any examples from current events that show the Dell Theory's success or failure in relation to conflicts around the world?

3. What are mutant global supply chains? What makes them so successful and thus so dangerous? Locate passages from Friedman that support your answer.

Exploring Context

1. Friedman opens this chapter by tracing the assembly of his Dell notebook. Explore Dell's Web site (dell.com). Does it provide any sense of the global supply chains that are vital to the creation of its computers? Why would Dell highlight or obscure these global supply chains on its Web site? What global images and what national images are created? How does the site reflect your response to Question 1 of Questions for Critical Reading about collaboration?

2. Infosys, headquartered in Bangalore, India, is one of the companies that Fried-man mentions. The Web site for Infosys has a special section about the flat world (infosys.com/flat-world/business/default.asp). How does the information on this site reflect Friedman's arguments?

3. Visit the Federal Bureau of Investigation's counterterrorism Web site at fbi.gov/terrorinfo/counterrorism/waronterrorhome.htm. Does it reflect the global nature of terror networks as explained by Friedman? How does Friedman propose we fight terrorism? Are such strategies being pursued by organizations like the FBI? You may want to draw from your work on collaboration and mutant global supply chains from Questions 1 and 3 of Questions for Critical Reading.

Questions for Connecting

1. Michael Pollan, in "The Animals: Practicing Complexity" (p. 281), describes a very different, very local economic system. What parallels can you find between

Pollan's and Friedman's ideas about the collateral effects of economic systems? Do "holons" have a role to play in the global supply chain? Are integrated and organic farming systems a kind of supply chain? Use your work defining Friedman's concepts from Questions for Critical Reading to help make your argument.

2. Like Friedman, James Surowiecki focuses on collaboration in "Committees, Juries, and Teams: The *Columbia* Disaster and How Small Groups Can Be Made to Work" (p. 440). How might some of the pitfalls of small groups noted by Surowiecki endanger the Dell Theory? Are small-group dynamics applicable to global collaborative systems? How can the lessons learned from Surowiecki's analysis help in the fight against mutant supply chains and terrorism? Use your work on collaboration from Question 1 of Questions for Critical Reading.

3. Leslie Savan examines the economic appropriation of black talk in "What's Black, Then White, and Said All Over?" (p. 363). Should there be limits on economic systems or global supply chains? Must we limit their effects? Or, based on the ideas of Friedman and Savan, is it in our best interests to give economic systems free reign? Drawing from your work in Exploring Context, can you use Dell or Infosys as an example for your argument?

Language Matters

1. Integrating the words of other authors into your writing is an essential skill. In small groups, select a key quotation from Friedman's text and then create three different sentences that integrate that quotation. Have different groups share their results. What general techniques or strategies did people use?

2. Systems of citation are a central aspect of academic writing. In this class, you may be asked to use MLA, APA, or some other format for in-text citations. Develop your own system and illustrate it by citing a quotation from Friedman's essay. What kind of information would it have to include? What does this then say about how citation systems work? Why are there so many citation systems?

3. Strong organization is self-evident. That is, when a paper is well organized each paragraph clearly has a place in the whole. Imagine a different order for Friedman's essay. What sections would you have placed first and why? What transitions would you need? Why do you think Friedman organized his essay the way he did?

Assignments for Writing

1. According to Friedman's theory, global supply chains promote geopolitical stability. But Friedman is careful to say that they do not guarantee peace. Write a paper in which you determine the limitations of Friedman's theory. What would cause the Dell Theory of Conflict Prevention to fail? Are there specific supply chains or commodities (oil, gas, natural resources) that fall outside this theory? You may want to build your argument using your work on the Dell Theory from Question 2 of Questions for Critical Reading.

2. Both Friedman's Dell Theory of Conflict Prevention and his earlier Golden Arches Theory seem to rely on the spread of American culture. Can we reap the benefits of globalized economics without sacrificing local culture? Write a paper in which you suggest strategies for balancing globalization with localization. You might want to draw from your work with Leslie Savan's essay from Question 3 of Questions for Connecting in making your argument. Consider, too, these questions: Are terrorist supply chains an attempt to preserve local cultures? Must global economics mean global culture?

3. As you learned in Question 1 of Questions for Critical Reading, collaboration is one of Friedman's central concerns in this essay. Write a paper in which you use Friedman's ideas to suggest the key factors for making collaboration a success. You might also want to draw from your work with James Surowiecki's essay from Question 2 of Questions for Connecting.

FRANCIS FUKUYAMA

Francis Fukuyama holds a B.A. in classics from Cornell University and a Ph.D. in political science from Harvard University. He is currently the Bernard L. Schwartz Professor in International Political Economy at Johns Hopkins University. As a prominent neoconservative thinker, Fukuyama signed letters to both President Bill Clinton (in 1998) and President George W. Bush (in 2001) advocating the overthrow of Saddam Hussein (at the time, the president of Iraq). However, Fukuyama ultimately disapproved of the 2003 invasion of Iraq, writing publicly that neoconservative ideas had changed and were no longer supportable. Fukuyama is the author of multiple books of political philosophy advocating liberal democracy, including his 2006 publication *America at the Crossroads*, which deals directly with his departure from the neoconservative agenda.

In *Our Posthuman Future: Consequences of the Biotechnology Revolution* (2002), Fukuyama updates an earlier proposal. Fukuyama had, in his book *The End of History and the Last Man* (1992), suggested that the history of humanity is an ideological struggle that is pretty much settled now, with liberal democracy as the eventual and destined end point, an argument he clarified in *America at the Crossroads*, stating that modernization is what wins the ideological struggle and that liberal democracy is merely one of the outcomes of modernization. In *Our Posthuman Future*, he reexamines this argument, taking into account the potential effects of biotechnology on liberal democracy. Now that human behavior can potentially be modified and DNA can be manipulated, Fukuyama asks, how will a political order based on natural equality survive?

In "Human Dignity," a chapter from *Our Posthuman Future*, Fukuyama examines the idea of "Factor X," an "essential human quality . . . that is worthy of a certain minimal level of respect" regardless of our varying individual characteristics, such as skin color, looks, or social class. Modern science, particularly the science of genetic engineering, Fukuyama claims, tends to disagree with the very idea of an essential human quality like Factor X. From this scientific perspective, human beings are the end result of genetic accidents and environmental influences. Fukuyama, however, finds merit in Pope John Paul II's assertion that science can't fully explain how human beings emerge from simple components. If that assertion is correct, Fukuyama speculates, what does this imply about science's ability to understand other complex systems? What does this mean for the future of human consciousness and political systems? With "Human Dignity," Fukuyama asks the reader to consider what happens to the idea of universal human equality when genetic engineering can be used to "improve" human genes.

Given the seemingly inevitable progress of science, which undoubtedly will influence you throughout your life, what does it mean to be human, and how can we preserve the qualities that make us so?

▶ TAGS: *civil rights*, *morality*, *human dignity*, *biotechnology*, *ethics*

Human Dignity

> Is it, then, possible to imagine a new Natural Philosophy, continually conscious that the "natural object" produced by analysis and abstraction is not reality but only a view, and always correcting the abstraction? I hardly know what I am asking for. . . . The regenerate science which I have in mind would not do even to minerals and vegetables what modern science threatens to do to man himself. When it explained it would not explain away. When it spoke of parts it would remember the whole. . . . The analogy between the *Tao* of Man and the instincts of an animal species would mean for it new light cast on the unknown thing, Instinct, by the inly known reality of conscience and not a reduction of conscience to the category of Instinct. Its followers would not be free with the words *only* and *merely*. In a word, it would conquer Nature without being at the same time conquered by her and buy knowledge at a lower cost than that of life.
>
> —C. S. LEWIS, *THE ABOLITION OF MAN*[1]

According to the Decree by the Council of Europe on Human Cloning, "The instrumentalisation of human beings through the deliberate creation of genetically identical human beings is contrary to human dignity and thus constitutes a misuse of medicine and biology."[2] Human dignity is one of those concepts that politicians, as well as virtually everyone else in political life, like to throw around, but that almost no one can either define or explain.

Much of politics centers on the question of human dignity and the desire for recognition to which it is related. That is, human beings constantly demand that others recognize their dignity, either as individuals or as members of religious, ethnic, racial, or other kinds of groups. The struggle for recognition is not economic: What we desire is not money but that other human beings respect us in the way we think we deserve. In earlier times, rulers wanted others to recognize their superior worth as king, emperor, or lord. Today, people seek recognition of their equal status as members of formerly disrespected or devalued groups—as women, gays, Ukrainians, the handicapped, Native Americans, and the like.[3]

The demand for an equality of recognition or respect is the dominant passion of modernity, as Tocqueville noted over 170 years ago in *Democracy in America*.[4] What this means in a liberal democracy is a bit complicated. It is not necessarily that we think we are equal in all important respects, or demand that our lives be the same as everyone else's. Most people accept the fact that a Mozart or an Einstein or a Michael Jordan has talents and abilities that they don't have, and receives recognition and even monetary compensation for what he accomplishes with those talents. We accept, though we don't necessarily like, the fact that resources are distributed unequally based on what James Madison called the "different and unequal faculties of acquiring property." But we also believe that people deserve to keep what they earn and that the faculties for working and earning will not be the same for all people. We also accept the fact that we look different, come from different races and ethnicities, are of different sexes, and have different cultures.

Factor X

What the demand for equality of recognition implies is that when we strip all of a person's contingent and accidental characteristics away, there remains some essential human quality underneath that is worthy of a certain minimal level of respect—call it Factor X. Skin color, looks, social class and wealth, gender, cultural background, and even one's natural talents are all accidents of birth relegated to the class of nonessential characteristics. We make decisions on whom to befriend, whom to marry or do business with, or whom to shun at social events on the basis of these secondary characteristics. But in the political realm we are required to respect people equally on the basis of their possession of Factor X. You can cook, eat, torture, enslave, or render the carcass of any creature lacking Factor X, but if you do the same thing to a human being, you are guilty of a "crime against humanity." We accord beings with Factor X not just human rights but, if they are adults, political rights as well—that is, the right to live in democratic political communities where their rights to speech, religion, association, and political participation are respected.

The circle of beings to whom we attribute Factor X has been one of the most contested issues throughout human history. For many societies, including most democratic societies in earlier periods of history, Factor X belonged to a significant subset of the human race, excluding people of certain sexes, economic classes, races, and tribes and people with low intelligence, disabilities, birth defects, and the like. These societies were highly stratified, with different classes possessing more or less of Factor X, and some possessing none at all. Today, for believers in liberal equality, Factor X etches a bright red line around the whole of the human race and requires equality of respect for all of those on the inside, but attributes a lower level of dignity to those outside the boundary. Factor X is the human essence, the most basic meaning of what it is to be human. If all human beings are in fact equal in dignity, then X must be some characteristic universally possessed by them. So what is Factor X, and where does it come from?

For Christians, the answer is fairly easy: It comes from God. Man is created in the image of God, and therefore shares in some of God's sanctity, which entitles human beings to a higher level of respect than the rest of natural creation. In the words of Pope John Paul II, what this means is that "the human individual cannot be subordinated as a pure means or a pure instrument, either to the species or to society; he has value per se. He is a person. With his intellect and his will, he is capable of forming a relationship of communion, solidarity, and self-giving with his peers . . . It is by virtue of his spiritual soul that the whole person possesses such dignity even in his body."[5]

Supposing one is not a Christian (or a religious believer of any sort), and doesn't accept the premise that man is created in the image of God. Is there a secular ground for believing that human beings are entitled to a special moral status or dignity? Perhaps the most famous effort to create a philosophical basis for human dignity was that of Kant, who argued that Factor X was based on the human capacity for moral choice. That is, human beings could differ in intelligence, wealth, race, and gender, but all were equally able to act according to moral law or not. Human beings had dignity because they alone had free will—not just the subjective illusion of free will but the actual ability to transcend natural determinism and the normal rules of causality. It is the existence of free will that leads to Kant's well-known conclusion that human beings are always to be treated as ends and not as means.

It would be very difficult for any believer in a materialistic account of the universe—which includes the vast majority of natural scientists—to accept the Kantian account of human dignity. The reason is that it forces them to accept a form of dualism—that there is a realm of human freedom parallel to the realm of nature that is not determined by the latter. Most natural scientists would argue that what we believe to be free will is in fact an illusion and that all human decision making can ultimately be traced back to material causes. Human beings decide to do one thing over another because one set of neurons fires rather than another, and those neuronal firings can be traced back to prior material states of the brain. The human decision-making process may be more complex than that of other animals, but there is no sharp dividing line that distinguishes human moral choice from the kinds of choices that are made by other animals. Kant himself does not offer any proof that free will exists; he says that it is simply a necessary postulate of pure practical reason about the nature of morality—hardly an argument that a hard-bitten empirical scientist would accept.

Seize the Power

The problem posed by modern natural science goes even deeper. The very notion that there exists such a thing as a human "essence" has been under relentless attack by modern science for much of the past century and a half. One of the most fundamental assertions of Darwinism is that species do not have essences.[6] That is, while Aristotle believed in the eternity of the species (i.e., that what we have been labeling "species-typical behavior" is something unchanging), Darwin's theory maintains that this behavior changes in response to the organism's interaction with its environment. What is typical for a species represents a snapshot of the species at one particular moment of evolutionary time; what came before and what comes after will be different. Since Darwinism maintains that there is no cosmic teleology guiding the process of evolution, what seems to be the essence of a species is just an accidental by-product of a random evolutionary process.

In this perspective, what we have been calling human nature is merely the species-typical human characteristics and behavior that emerged about 100,000 years ago, during what evolutionary biologists call the "era of evolutionary adaptation"—when the precursors of modern humans were living and breeding on the African savanna. For many, this suggests that human nature

10

has no special status as a guide to morals or values because it is historically contingent. David Hull, for example, argues,

> I do not see why the existence of human universals is all that important. Perhaps all and only people have opposable thumbs, use tools, live in true societies, or what have you. I think that such attributions are either false or vacuous, but even if they were true and significant, the distributions of these particular characters is largely a matter of evolutionary happenstance.[7]

The geneticist Lee Silver, trying to debunk the idea that there is a natural order that could be undermined by genetic engineering, asserts,

> Unfettered evolution is never predetermined [toward some goal], and not necessarily associated with progress—it is simply a response to unpredictable environmental changes. If the asteroid that hit our planet 60 million years ago had flown past instead, there would never have been any human beings at all. And whatever the natural order might be, it is not necessarily good. The smallpox virus was part of the natural order until it was forced into extinction by human intervention.[8]

This inability to define a natural essence doesn't bother either writer. Hull, for example, states that "I, for one, would be extremely uneasy to base something as important as human rights on such temporary contingencies [as human nature]. . . I fail to see why it matters. I fail to see, for example, why we must all be essentially the same to have rights."[9] Silver, for his part, pooh-poohs fears about genetic engineering on the part of those with religious convictions or those who believe in a natural order. In the future, man will no longer be a slave to his genes, but their master:

> Why not seize this power? Why not control what has been left to chance in the past? Indeed, we control all other aspects of our children's lives and identities through powerful social and environmental influences and, in some cases, with the use of powerful drugs like Ritalin and Prozac. On what basis can we reject positive genetic influences on a person's essence when we accept the rights of parents to benefit their children in every other way?[10]

Why not seize this power, indeed?

Well, let us begin by considering what the consequences of the abandonment of the idea that there is a Factor X, or human essence, that unites all human beings would be for the cherished idea of universal human equality—an idea to which virtually all of the debunkers of the idea of human essences are invariably committed. Hull is right that we don't all need to be the same in order to have rights—but we need to be the same in some one critical respect in order to have *equal* rights. He for one is very concerned that basing human rights on human nature will stigmatize homosexuals, because their sexual orientation differs from the heterosexual norm. But the only basis on which anyone can make an argument in favor of equal rights for gays is to argue that whatever their sexual orientation, *they are people too* in some other respect that is more essential than their sexuality. If you cannot find this common other ground, then there is no reason not to discriminate against them, because in fact they are different creatures from everyone else.

Similarly, Lee Silver, who is so eager to take up the power of genetic engineering to "improve" people, is nonetheless horrified at the possibility that it could be used to create a class of genetically superior people. He paints a scenario in which a class called the GenRich steadily improve the cognitive abilities of their children to the point that they break off from the rest of the human race to form a separate species.

Silver is not horrified by much else that technology may bring us by way of unnatural reproduction — for example, two lesbians producing genetic offspring, or eggs taken from an unborn female fetus to produce a child whose mother had never been born. He dismisses the moral concerns of virtually every religion or traditional moral system with regard to future genetic engineering but draws the line at what he perceives as threats to human equality. He does not seem to understand that, given his premises, there are no possible grounds on which he can object to the GenRich, or the fact that they might assign themselves rights superior to those of the GenPoor. Since there is no stable essence common to all human beings, or rather because that essence is variable and subject to human manipulation, why not create a race born with metaphorical saddles on their backs, and another with boots and spurs to ride them? Why not seize *that* power as well?

The bioethicist Peter Singer, whose appointment to Princeton University caused great controversy because of his advocacy of infanticide and euthanasia under certain circumstances, is simply more consistent than most people on the consequences of abandoning the concept of human dignity. Singer is an unabashed utilitarian: He believes that the single relevant standard for ethics is to minimize suffering in the aggregate for all creatures. Human beings are part of a continuum of life and have no special status in his avowedly Darwinian worldview. This leads him to two perfectly logical conclusions: the need for animal rights, since animals can experience pain and suffering as well as humans, and the downgrading of the rights of infants and elderly people who lack certain key traits, like self-awareness, that would allow them to anticipate pain. The rights of certain animals, in his view, deserve greater respect than those of certain human beings.

But Singer is not nearly forthright enough in following these premises through to their logical conclusion, since he remains a committed egalitarian. What he does not explain is why the relief of suffering should remain the only moral good. As usual, the philosopher Friedrich Nietzsche was much more clear-eyed than anyone else in understanding the consequences of modern natural science and the abandonment of the concept of human dignity. Nietzsche had the great insight to see that, on the one hand, once the clear red line around the whole of humanity could no longer be drawn, the way would be paved for a return to a much more hierarchical ordering of society. If there is a continuum of gradations between human and nonhuman, there is a continuum within the type human as well. This would inevitably mean the liberation of the strong from the constraints that a belief in either God or Nature had placed on them. On the other hand, it would lead the rest of mankind to demand health and safety as the only possible goods, since all the higher goals that had once been set for them were now debunked. In the words of Nietzsche's Zarathustra, "One has one's little pleasure for the day and one's little pleasure for the night: But one has a regard for health. 'We have invented happiness,' say the last men, and they blink."[11] Indeed, both the return of hierarchy and the egalitarian demand for health, safety, and relief of suffering might all go hand in hand if the rulers of the future could provide the masses with enough of the "little poisons" they demanded.

It has always struck me that one hundred years after Nietzsche's death, we are much less far down the road to either the superman or the last man than he predicted. Nietzsche once castigated John Stuart Mill as a "flathead" for believing that one could have a semblance of Christian morality in the absence of belief in a Christian God. And yet, in a Europe and an America that have become secularized over the past two generations, we see a lingering belief in the concept of human dignity, which is by now completely cut off from its religious roots. And not just lingering: The idea that one could exclude any group of people on the basis of race, gender, disability, or virtually any other characteristic

> So what is Factor X, and where does it come from?

from the charmed circle of those deserving recognition for human dignity is the one thing that will bring total obloquy on the head of any politician who proposes it. In the words of the philosopher Charles Taylor, "We believe it would be utterly wrong and unfounded to draw the boundaries any narrower than around the whole human race," and should anyone try to do so, "we should immediately ask what distinguished those within from those left out."[12] The idea of the equality of human dignity, deracinated from its Christian or Kantian origins, is held as a matter of religious dogma by the most materialist of natural scientists. The continuing arguments over the moral status of the unborn (about which more later) constitute the only exception to this general rule.

The reasons for the persistence of the idea of the equality of human dignity are complex. Partly it is a matter of the force of habit and what Max Weber once called the "ghost of dead religious beliefs" that continue to haunt us. Partly it is the product of historical accident: The last important political movement to explicitly deny the premise of universal human dignity was Nazism, and the horrifying consequences of the Nazis' racial and eugenic policies were sufficient to inoculate those who experienced them for the next couple of generations.

But another important reason for the persistence of the idea of the universality of human dignity has to do with what we might call the nature of nature itself. Many of the grounds on which certain groups were historically denied their share of human dignity were proven to be simply a matter of prejudice, or else based on cultural and environmental conditions that could be changed. The notions that women were too irrational or emotional to participate in politics, and that immigrants from southern Europe had smaller head sizes and were less intelligent than those from northern Europe, were overturned on the basis of sound, empirical science. That moral order did not completely break down in the West in the wake of the destruction of consensus over traditional religious values should not surprise us either, because moral order comes from within human nature itself and is not something that has to be imposed on human nature by culture.[13]

All of this could change under the impact of future biotechnology. The most clear and present danger is that the large genetic variations between individuals will narrow and become clustered within certain distinct social groups. Today, the "genetic lottery" guarantees that the son or daughter of a rich and successful parent will not necessarily inherit the talents and abilities that created conditions conducive to the parent's success. Of course, there has always been a degree of genetic selection: Assortative mating means that successful people will tend to marry each other and, to the extent that their success is genetically based, will pass on to their children better life opportunities. But in the future, the full weight of modern technology can be put in the service of optimizing the kinds of genes that are passed on to one's offspring. This means that social elites may not just pass on social advantages but embed them genetically as well. This may one day include not only characteristics like intelligence and beauty, but behavioral traits like diligence, competitiveness, and the like.

The genetic lottery is judged as inherently unfair by many because it condemns certain people to lesser intelligence, or bad looks, or disabilities of one sort or another. But in another sense it is profoundly egalitarian, since everyone, regardless of social class, race, or ethnicity, has to play in it. The wealthiest man can and often does have a good-for-nothing son; hence the saying "Shirtsleeves to shirtsleeves in three generations." When the lottery is replaced by choice, we open up a new avenue along which human beings can compete, one that threatens to increase the disparity between the top and bottom of the social hierarchy.

What the emergence of a genetic overclass will do to the idea of universal human dignity is something worth pondering. Today, many bright and successful young people believe that they owe their success to accidents of birth and upbringing but for which their lives might have taken a very different course. They feel themselves, in other words, to be lucky, and they are capable of feeling sympathy for people who are less lucky than they. But to the extent that they become "children of choice" who have been genetically selected by their parents for certain characteristics, they may come to believe increasingly that their success is a matter not just of luck but of good choices and planning on the part of their parents, and hence something deserved. They will look, think, act, and perhaps even feel differently from those who were not similarly chosen, and may come in time to think of themselves as different kinds of creatures. They may, in short, feel themselves to be aristocrats, and unlike aristocrats of old, their claim to better birth will be rooted in nature and not convention.

Aristotle's discussion of slavery in Book I of the *Politics* is instructive on this score. It is often condemned as a justification of Greek slavery, but in fact the discussion is far more sophisticated and is relevant to our thinking about genetic classes. Aristotle makes a distinction between conventional and natural slavery.[14] He argues that slavery would be justified by nature if it were the case that there were people with naturally slavish natures. It is not clear from his discussion that he believes such people exist: Most actual slavery is conventional—that is, it is the result of victory in war or force, or based on the wrong opinion that barbarians as a class should be slaves of Greeks.[15] The noble-born think their nobility comes from nature rather than acquired virtue and that they can pass it on to their children. But, Aristotle notes, nature is "frequently unable to bring this about."[16] So why not, as Lee Silver suggests, "seize this power" to give children genetic advantages and correct the defect of natural equality?

The possibility that biotechnology will permit the emergence of new genetic classes has been frequently noted and condemned by those who have speculated about the future.[17] But the opposite possibility also seems to be entirely plausible—that there will be an impetus toward a much more genetically egalitarian society. For it seems highly unlikely that people in modern democratic societies will sit around complacently if they see elites embedding their advantages genetically in their children.

Indeed, this is one of the few things in a politics of the future that people are likely to rouse themselves to fight over. By this I mean not just fighting metaphorically, in the sense of shouting matches among talking heads on TV and debates in Congress, but actually picking up guns and bombs and using them on other people. There are very few domestic political issues today in our rich, self-satisfied liberal democracies that can cause people to get terribly upset, but the specter of rising genetic inequality may well get people off their couches and into the streets.

If people get upset enough about genetic inequality, there will be two alternative courses of action. The first and most sensible would simply be to forbid the use of biotechnology to enhance human characteristics and decline to compete in this dimension. But the notion of enhancement may become too powerfully attractive to forgo, or it may prove difficult to enforce a rule preventing people from enhancing their children, or the courts may declare they have a right to do so. At this point a second possibility opens up, which is to use that same technology to raise up the bottom.[18]

This is the only scenario in which it is plausible that we will see a liberal democracy of the future get back into the business of state-sponsored eugenics. The bad old form of eugenics discriminated against the disabled and less intelligent by forbidding them to have children. In the future, it may be possible to breed children who are more intelligent, more healthy, more "normal." Raising the bottom is something that can only be accomplished through the intervention of the state. Genetic enhancement technology is likely to be expensive and involve some risk, but even if it were relatively cheap and safe, people who are poor and lacking in education would still fail to take advantage of it. So the bright red line of universal human dignity will have to be reinforced by allowing the state to make sure that no one falls outside it.

The politics of breeding future human beings will be very complex. Up to now, the Left has on the whole been opposed to cloning, genetic engineering, and similar biotechnologies for a number of reasons, including traditional humanism, environmental concerns, suspicion of technology and of the corporations that produce it, and fear of eugenics. The Left has historically sought to play down the importance of heredity in favor of social factors in explaining human outcomes. For people on the Left to come around and support genetic engineering for the disadvantaged, they would first have to admit that genes are important in determining intelligence and other types of social outcomes in the first place.

The Left has been more hostile to biotechnology in Europe than in North America. Much of this hostility is driven by the stronger environmental movements there, which have led the campaign, for example, against genetically modified foods. (Whether certain forms of radical environmentalism will translate into hostility to human biotechnology remains to be seen. Some environmentalists see themselves defending nature from human beings, and seem to be more concerned with threats to nonhuman than to human nature.) The Germans in particular remain very sensitive to anything that smacks of eugenics. The philosopher Peter Sloterdijk raised a storm of protest in 1999 when he suggested that it will soon be impossible for people to refuse the power of selection that biotechnology provides them, and that the questions of breeding something "beyond" man that were raised by Nietzsche and Plato could no longer be ignored.[19] He was condemned by the sociologist Jürgen Habermas, among others, who in other contexts has also come out against human cloning.[20]

On the other hand, there are some on the Left who have begun to make the case for genetic engineering.[21] John Rawls argued in *A Theory of Justice* that the unequal distribution of natural talents was inherently unfair. A Rawlsian should therefore want to make use of biotechnology to equalize life chances by breeding the bottom up, assuming that prudential considerations concerning safety, cost, and the like would be settled. Ronald Dworkin has laid out a case for the right of parents to genetically engineer their children based on a broader concern to protect autonomy,[22] and Laurence Tribe has suggested that a ban on cloning would be wrong because it might create discrimination against children who were cloned in spite of the ban.[23]

It is impossible to know which of these two radically different scenarios — one of growing genetic inequality, the other of growing genetic equality — is more likely to come to pass. But once the technological possibility for biomedical enhancement is realized, it is hard to see how growing genetic inequality would fail to become one of the chief controversies of twenty-first-century politics.

Human Dignity Redux

Denial of the concept of human dignity — that is, of the idea that there is something unique about the human race that entitles every member of the species to a higher moral status than the rest of the natural world — leads us down a very perilous path. We may be compelled ultimately to take this path, but we should do so only with our eyes open. Nietzsche is a much better guide to what lies down that road than the legions of bioethicists and casual academic Darwinians that today are prone to give us moral advice on this subject.

To avoid following that road, we need to take another look at the notion of human dignity, and ask whether there is a way to defend the concept against its detractors that is fully compatible with modern natural science but that also does justice to the full meaning of human specificity. I believe that there is.

In contrast to a number of conservative Protestant denominations that continue to hold a brief for creationism, the Catholic Church by the end of the twentieth century had come to terms with the theory of evolution. In his 1996 message to the Pontifical Academy of Sciences, Pope John Paul II corrected the encyclical *Humani generis* of Pius XII, which maintained that Darwinian evolution was a serious hypothesis but one that remained unproven. The pope stated, "Today, almost half a century after the publication of the Encyclical, new knowledge has led to the recognition of the theory of evolution as more than a hypothesis. It is indeed remarkable that this theory has been progressively accepted by researchers, following a series of discoveries in various fields of knowledge. The convergence, neither sought nor fabricated, of the results of work that was conducted independently is in itself a significant argument in favor of this theory."[24]

But the pope went on to say that while the church can accept the view that man is descended from nonhuman animals, there is an "ontological leap" that occurs somewhere in this evolutionary process.[25] The human soul is something directly created by God: Consequently, "theories of evolution which, in accordance with the philosophies inspiring them, consider the mind as emerging from the forces of living nature, or as a mere epiphenomenon of this matter, are incompatible with the truth about man." The pope continued, "Nor are they able to ground the dignity of the person."

The pope was saying, in other words, that at some point in the 5 million years between man's chimplike forebears and the emergence of modern human beings, a human soul was inserted into us in a way that remains mysterious. Modern natural science can uncover the time line of this process and explicate its material correlates, but it has not fully explained either what the soul is or how it came to be. The church has obviously learned a great deal from modern natural science in the past two centuries and has adjusted its doctrines accordingly. But while many natural scientists would scoff at the idea that they have anything to learn from the church, the pope has pointed to a real weakness in the current state of evolutionary theory, which scientists would do well to ponder. Modern natural science has explained a great deal less about what it means to be human than many scientists think it has.

Parts and Wholes

Many contemporary Darwinians believe that they have demystified the problem of how human beings came to be human through the classical reductionist methods of modern natural science. That is, any higher-order behavior or characteristic, such as language or aggression, can be traced back through the firing of neurons to the biochemical substrate of the brain, which in turn can be understood in terms of the simpler organic compounds of which it is composed. The brain arrived at its present state through a series of incremental evolutionary changes that were driven by random variation, and a process of natural selection by which the requirements of the surrounding environment selected for certain mental characteristics. Every human characteristic can thus be traced back to a prior material cause. If, for example, we today love to listen to Mozart or Beethoven, it is because we have auditory systems that were evolved, in the environment of evolutionary adaptation, to discriminate between certain kinds of sounds that were necessary perhaps to warn us against predators or to help us on a hunt.[26]

The problem with this kind of thinking is not that it is necessarily false but that it is insufficient to explain many of the most salient and unique human traits. The problem lies in the methodology of reductionism itself for understanding complex systems, and particularly biological ones.

Reductionism constitutes, of course, one of the foundations of modern natural science and is responsible for many of its greatest triumphs. You see before you two apparently different substances, the graphite in your pencil lead and the diamond in your engagement ring, and you might be tempted to believe that they were essentially different substances. But reductionist chemistry has taught us that in fact they are both composed of the same simpler substance, carbon, and that the apparent differences are not ones of essence but merely of the way the carbon atoms are bonded. Reductionist physics has been busy over the past century tracing atoms back to subatomic particles and thence back to an even more reduced set of basic forces of nature.

But what is appropriate for domains in physics, like celestial mechanics and fluid dynamics, is not necessarily appropriate for the study of objects at the opposite end of the complexity scale, like most biological systems, because the behavior of complex systems cannot be predicted by simply aggregating or scaling up the behavior of the parts that constitute them.* The distinctive and easily recognizable behavior of a flock of birds or a swarm of bees, for example, is the product of the interaction of individual birds or bees following relatively simple behavioral rules (fly next to a partner, avoid obstacles, and so on), none of which encompasses or defines the behavior of the flock or swarm as a whole. Rather, the group behavior "emerges" as a result of the interaction of the individuals that make it up. In many cases, the relationship between parts and wholes is nonlinear: That is, increasing input A increases output B up to a certain point, whereupon it creates a qualitatively different and unexpected output C. This is true even of relatively simple chemicals like water: H_2O undergoes a phase transition from liquid to solid at 32 degrees Fahrenheit, something that one would not necessarily predict on the basis of knowledge of its chemical composition.

---

*The determinism of classical Newtonian mechanics is based in large measure on the parallelogram rule, which says that the effects of two forces acting on a body can be summed as if each were acting independently of the other. Newton shows that this rule works for celestial bodies like planets and stars, and assumes that it will also work for other natural objects, like animals.

That the behavior of complex wholes cannot be understood as the aggregated behavior of their parts has been understood in the natural sciences for some time now,[27] and has led to the development of the field of so-called nonlinear or "complex adaptive" systems, which try to model the emergence of complexity. This approach is, in a way, the opposite of reductionism: It shows that while wholes can be traced back to their simpler antecedent parts, there is no simple predictive model that allows us to move from the parts to the emergent behaviors of the wholes. Being nonlinear, they may be extremely sensitive to small differences in starting conditions and thus may appear chaotic even when their behavior is completely deterministic.

This means that the behavior of complex systems is much more difficult to understand than the founders of reductionist science once believed. The eighteenth-century astronomer Laplace once said that he could precisely predict the future of the universe on the basis of Newtonian mechanics, if he could know the mass and motion of the universe's constituent parts.[28] No scientist could make this claim today—not just because of the inherent uncertainties introduced by quantum mechanics but also because there exists no reliable methodology for predicting the behavior of complex systems.[29] In the words of Arthur Peacocke, "The concepts and theories . . . that constitute the content of the sciences focusing on the more complex levels are often (not always) logically not reducible to those operative in the sciences that focus on their components."[30] There is a hierarchy of levels of complexity in the sciences, with human beings and human behavior occupying a place at the uppermost level.

Each level can give us some insight into the levels above it, but understanding the lower levels does not allow one to fully understand the higher levels' emergent properties. Researchers in the area of complex adaptive systems have created so-called agent-based models of complex systems, and have applied them in a wide variety of areas, from cell biology to fighting a war to distributing natural gas. It remains to be seen, however, whether this approach constitutes a single, coherent methodology applicable to all complex systems.[31] Such models may tell us only that certain systems will remain inherently chaotic and unpredictable, or that prediction rests on a precise knowledge of initial conditions that is unavailable to us. The higher level must thus be understood with a methodology appropriate to its degree of complexity.

We can illustrate the problematic relationship of parts to wholes by reference to one unique domain of human behavior, politics.[32] Aristotle states that man is a political animal by nature. If one were to try to build a case for human dignity based on human specificity, the capability of engaging in politics would certainly constitute one important component of human uniqueness. Yet the idea of our uniqueness in this regard has been challenged. . . . [C]himpanzees and other primates engage in something that looks uncannily like human politics as they struggle and connive to achieve alpha male status. They appear, moreover, to feel the political emotions of pride and shame as they interact with other members of their group. Their political behavior can also apparently be transmitted through nongenetic means, so that political culture would not seem to be the exclusive preserve of human beings.[33] Some observers gleefully cite examples like this to deflate human feelings of self-importance relative to other species.

But to confuse human politics with the social behavior of any other species is to mistake parts for wholes. Only human beings can formulate, debate, and modify abstract rules of justice. When Aristotle asserted that man is a political animal by nature, he meant this only in the sense that politics is a potentiality that emerges over time.[34] He notes that human politics did not begin until the first lawgiver established a state and promulgated laws, an event that was of great benefit to mankind but that was contingent on historical developments. This accords with what we know today about the emergence of the state, which took place in parts of the world like Egypt and Babylonia perhaps 10,000 years ago and was most likely related to the development of agriculture. For tens of thousands of years before that, human beings lived in stateless hunter-gatherer societies in which the largest group numbered no more than 50 to 100 individuals, most of them related by kinship.[35] So in a certain sense, while human sociability is obviously natural, it is not clear that humans are political animals by nature.

But Aristotle insists that politics is natural to man despite the fact that it did not exist at all in early periods of human history. He argues that it is human language that allows human beings to formulate laws and abstract principles of justice that are necessary to the creation of a state and of political order. Ethologists have noted that many other species communicate with sounds, and that chimpanzees and other animals can learn human language to a limited extent. But no other species has *human* language—that is, the ability to formulate and communicate abstract principles of action. It is only when these two natural characteristics, human sociability and human language, come together that human politics emerges. Human language obviously evolved to promote sociability, but it is very unlikely that there were evolutionary forces shaping it to become an enabler of politics. It was rather like one of Stephen Jay Gould's spandrels,* something that evolved for one reason but that found another key purpose when combined in a human whole.[36] Human politics, though natural in an emergent sense, is not reducible to either animal sociability or animal language, which were its precursors.

Consciousness

The area in which the inability of a reductionist materialist science to explain observable phenomena is most glaringly evident is the question of human consciousness. By consciousness I mean subjective mental states: not just the thoughts and images that appear to you as you are thinking or reading this page, but also the sensations, feelings, and emotions that you experience as part of everyday life.

---

*A spandrel is an architectural feature that emerges, unplanned by the architect, from the intersection of a dome and the walls that support it.

There has been a huge amount of research and theorizing about consciousness over the past two generations, coming in equal measure from the neurosciences and from studies in computer and artificial intelligence (AI). Particularly in the latter field there are many enthusiasts who are convinced that with more powerful computers and new approaches to computing, such as neural networks, we are on the verge of a breakthrough in which mechanical computers will achieve consciousness. There have been conferences and earnest discussions devoted to the question of whether it would be moral to turn off such a machine if and when this breakthrough occurs, and whether we would need to assign rights to conscious machines.

The fact of the matter is that we are nowhere close to a breakthrough; consciousness remains as stubbornly mysterious as it ever was. The problem with the current state of thinking begins with the traditional philosophical problem of the ontological status of consciousness. Subjective mental states, while produced by material biological processes, appear to be of a very different, nonmaterial order from other phenomena. The fear of dualism—that is, the doctrine that there are two essential types of being, material and mental—is so strong among researchers in this field that it has led them to palpably ridiculous conclusions. In the words of the philosopher John Searle,

> Seen from the perspective of the last fifty years, the philosophy of mind, as well as cognitive science and certain branches of psychology, present a very curious spectacle. The most striking feature is how much of mainstream philosophy of mind of the past fifty years seems obviously false . . . in the philosophy of mind, obvious facts about the mental, such as that we all really do have subjective conscious mental states and that these are not eliminable in favor of anything else, are routinely denied by many, perhaps most, of the advanced thinkers in the subject.[37]

An example of a patently false understanding of consciousness comes from one of the leading experts in the field, Daniel Dennett, whose book *Consciousness Explained* finally comes to the following definition of consciousness: "Human consciousness is *itself* a huge complex of memes (or more exactly, meme-effects in brains) that can best be understood as the operation of a *'von Neumannesque'* virtual machine *implemented* in the *parallel architecture* of a brain that was not designed for any such activities."[38] A naive reader may be excused for thinking that this kind of statement doesn't do much at all to advance our understanding of consciousness. Dennett is saying in effect that human consciousness is simply the by-product of the operations of a certain type of computer, and if we think that there is more to it than that, we have a mistakenly old-fashioned view of what consciousness is. As Searle says of this approach, it works only by denying the existence of what you and I and everyone else understand consciousness to be (that is, subjective feelings).[39]

Similarly, many of the researchers in the field of artificial intelligence side-step the question of consciousness by in effect changing the subject. They assume that the brain is simply a highly complex type of organic computer that

50

can be identified by its external characteristics. The well-known Turing test asserts that if a machine can perform a cognitive task such as carrying on a conversation in a way that from the outside is indistinguishable from similar activities carried out by a human being, then it is indistinguishable on the inside as well. Why this should be an adequate test of human mentality is a mystery, for the machine will obviously not have any subjective awareness of what it is doing, or feelings about its activities.* This doesn't prevent such authors as Hans Moravec [40] and Ray Kurzweil [41] from predicting that machines, once they reach a requisite level of complexity, will possess human attributes like consciousness as well.[42] If they are right, this will have important consequences for our notions of human dignity, because it will have been conclusively proven that human beings are essentially nothing more than complicated machines that can be made out of silicon and transistors as easily as carbon and neurons.

The likelihood that this will happen seems very remote, however, not so much because machines will never duplicate human intelligence—I suspect they will probably be able to come very close in this regard—but rather because it is impossible to see how they will come to acquire human emotions. It is the stuff of science fiction for an android, robot, or computer to suddenly start experiencing emotions like fear, hope, even sexual desire, but no one has come remotely close to positing how this might come about. The problem is not simply that, like the rest of consciousness, no one understands what emotions are ontologically; no one understands why they came to exist in human biology.

There are of course functional reasons for feelings like pain and pleasure. If we didn't find sex pleasurable we wouldn't reproduce, and if we didn't feel pain from fire we would be burning ourselves constantly. But state-of-the-art thinking in cognitive science maintains that the particular subjective form that the emotions take is not necessary to their function. It is perfectly possible, for example, to design a robot with heat sensors in its fingers connected to an actuator that would pull the robot's hand away from a fire. The robot could keep itself from being burned without having any subjective sense of pain, and it could make decisions on which objectives to fulfill and which activities to avoid on the basis of a mechanical computation of the inputs of different electrical impulses. A Turing test would say it was a human being in its behavior, but it would actually be devoid of the most important quality of a human being, feelings. The actual subjective form that emotions take are today seen in evolutionary biology and in cognitive science as no more than epiphenomenal to their underlying function; there are no obvious reasons this form should have been selected for in the course of evolutionary history.[43]

As Robert Wright points out, this leads to the very bizarre outcome that what is most important to us as human beings has no apparent purpose in the material scheme of things by which we became human.[44] For it is the distinctive human gamut of emotions that produces human purposes, goals, objectives,

---

*Searle's critique of this approach is contained in his "Chinese room" puzzle, which raises the question of whether a computer could be said to understand Chinese any more than a non-Chinese-speaking individual locked in a room who received instructions on how to manipulate a series of symbols in Chinese. See Searle (1997), p. 11.

wants, needs, desires, fears, aversions, and the like and hence is the source of human values. While many would list human reason and human moral choice as the most important unique human characteristics that give our species dignity, I would argue that possession of the full human emotional gamut is at least as important, if not more so.

The political theorist Robert McShea demonstrates the importance of human emotions to our commonsense understanding of what it means to be human by asking us to perform the following thought experiment.[45] Suppose you met two creatures on a desert island, both of which had the rational capacity of a human being and hence the ability to carry on a conversation. One had the physical form of a lion but the emotions of a human being, while the other had the physical form of a human being but the emotional characteristics of a lion. Which creature would you feel more comfortable with, which creature would you be more likely to befriend or enter into a moral relationship with? The answer, as countless children's books with sympathetic talking lions suggest, is the lion, because species-typical human emotions are more critical to our sense of our own humanness than either our reason or our physical appearance. The coolly analytical Mr. Spock in the TV series *Star Trek* appears at times more likable than the emotional Mr. Scott only because we suspect that somewhere beneath his rational exterior lurk deeply buried human feelings. Certainly many of the female characters he encountered in the series hoped they could rouse something more than robotic responses from him.

> We would regard a Mr. Spock who was truly devoid of any feelings as a psychopath and a monster.

On the other hand, we would regard a Mr. Spock who was truly devoid of any feelings as a psychopath and a monster. If he offered us a benefit, we might accept it but would feel no gratitude because we would know it was the product of rational calculation on his part and not goodwill. If we double-crossed him, we would feel no guilt, because we know that he cannot himself entertain feelings of anger or of having been betrayed. And if circumstances forced us to kill him to save ourselves, or to sacrifice his life in a hostage situation, we would feel no more regret than if we lost any other valuable asset, like a car or a teleporter.[46] Even though we might want to cooperate with this Mr. Spock, we would not regard him as a moral agent entitled to the respect that human beings command. The computer geeks in AI labs who think of themselves as nothing more than complex computer programs and want to download themselves into a computer should worry, since no one would care if they were turned off for good.

So there is a great deal that comes together under the rubric of consciousness that helps define human specificity and hence human dignity, which nonetheless cannot currently be fully explicated by modern natural science. It is not sufficient to argue that some other animals are conscious, or have culture, or have language, for their consciousness does not combine human reason, human language, human moral choice, and human emotions in ways that are capable of producing human politics, human art, or human religion. All of the nonhuman precursors of these human traits that existed in evolutionary history, and all of the material causes and preconditions for their emergence, collectively add up to much less than the human whole. Jared Diamond in his book *The Third Chimpanzee* notes the fact that the chimpanzee and human genomes overlap by more than 98 percent, implying that the differences between the two species are relatively trivial.[47] But for an emergent complex system, small differences can lead to enormous qualitative changes. It is a bit like saying there is no significant difference between ice and liquid water because they differ in temperature by only 1 degree.

Thus one does not have to agree with the pope that God directly inserted a human soul in the course of evolutionary history to acknowledge with him that there was a very important qualitative, if not ontological, leap that occurred at some point in this process. It is this leap from parts to a whole that ultimately has to constitute the basis for human dignity, a concept one can believe in even if one does not begin from the pope's religious premises.

What this whole is and how it came to be remain, in Searle's word, "mysterious." None of the branches of modern natural science that have tried to address this question have done more than scratch the surface, despite the belief of many scientists that they have demystified the entire process. It is common now for many AI researchers to say that consciousness is an "emergent property" of a certain kind of complex computer. But this is no more than an unproven hypothesis based on an analogy with other complex systems. No one has ever seen consciousness emerge under experimental conditions, or even posited a theory as to how this might come about. It would be surprising if the process of "emergence" didn't play an important part in explaining how humans came to be human, but whether that is all there is to the story is something we do not at present know.

This is not to say that the demystification by science will never happen. Searle himself believes that consciousness is a biological property of the brain much like the firing of neurons or the production of neurotransmitters and that biology will someday be able to explain how organic tissue can produce it. He argues that our present problems in understanding consciousness do not require us to adopt a dualistic ontology or abandon the scientific framework of material causation. The problem of how consciousness arose does not require recourse to the direct intervention of God.

It does not, on the other hand, rule it out, either.

60

What to Fight For

If what gives us dignity and a moral status higher than that of other living creatures is related to the fact that we are complex wholes rather than the sum of simple parts, then it is clear that there is no simple answer to the question, What is Factor X? That is, Factor X cannot be reduced to the possession of moral choice, or reason, or language, or sociability, or sentience, or emotions, or consciousness, or any other quality that has been put forth as a ground for human dignity. It is all of these qualities coming together in a human whole that make up Factor X. Every member of the human species possesses a genetic endowment that allows him or her to become a whole human being, an endowment that distinguishes a human in essence from other types of creatures.

A moment's reflection will show that none of the key qualities that contribute to human dignity can exist in the absence of the others. Human reason, for example, is not that of a computer; it is pervaded by emotions, and its functioning is in fact facilitated by the latter.[48] Moral choice cannot exist without reason, needless to say, but it is also grounded in feelings such as pride, anger, shame, and sympathy.[49] Human consciousness is not just individual preferences and instrumental reason, but is shaped intersubjectively by other consciousnesses and their moral evaluations. We are social and political animals not merely because we are capable of game-theoretic reason, but because we are endowed with certain social emotions. Human sentience is not that of a pig or a horse, because it is coupled with human memory and reason.

This protracted discussion of human dignity is intended to answer the following question: What is it that we want to protect from any future advances in biotechnology? The answer is, we want to protect the full range of our complex, evolved natures against attempts at self-modification. We do not want to disrupt either the unity or the continuity of human nature, and thereby the human rights that are based on it.

If Factor X is related to our very complexity and the complex interactions of uniquely human characteristics like moral choice, reason, and a broad emotional gamut, it is reasonable to ask how and why biotechnology would seek to make us less complex. The answer lies in the constant pressure that exists to reduce the ends of biomedicine to utilitarian ones—that is, the attempt to reduce a complex diversity of natural ends and purposes to just a few simple categories like pain and pleasure, or autonomy. There is in particular a constant predisposition to allow the relief of pain and suffering to automatically trump all other human purposes and objectives. For this will be the constant trade-off that biotechnology will pose: We can cure this disease, or prolong this person's life, or make this child more tractable, at the expense of some ineffable human quality like genius, or ambition, or sheer diversity.

That aspect of our complex natures most under threat has to do with our emotional gamut. We will be constantly tempted to think that we understand what "good" and "bad" emotions are, and that we can do nature one better by suppressing the latter, by trying to make people less aggressive, more sociable, more compliant, less depressed. The utilitarian goal of minimizing suffering is itself very problematic. No one can make a brief in favor of pain and suffering, but the fact of the matter is that what we consider to be the highest and most admirable human qualities, both in ourselves and in others, are often related to the way that we react to, confront, overcome, and frequently succumb to pain, suffering, and death. In the absence of these human evils there would be no sympathy, compassion, courage, heroism, solidarity, or strength of character.* A person who has not confronted

65

---

*The Greek root of *sympathy* and the Latin root of *compassion* both refer to the ability to feel another person's pain and suffering.

suffering or death has no depth. Our ability to experience these emotions is what connects us potentially to all other human beings, both living and dead.

Many scientists and researchers would say that we don't need to worry about fencing off human nature, however defined, from biotechnology, because we are a very long way from being able to modify it, and may never achieve the capability. They may be right: Human germ-line engineering and the use of recombinant DNA technology on humans is probably much further off than many people assume, though human cloning is not.

But our ability to manipulate human behavior is not dependent on the development of genetic engineering. Virtually everything we can anticipate being able to do through genetic engineering we will most likely be able to do much sooner through neuropharmacology. And we will face large demographic changes in the populations that find new biomedical technologies available to them, not only in terms of age and sex distributions, but in terms of the quality of life of important population groups.

The widespread and rapidly growing use of drugs like Ritalin and Prozac demonstrates just how eager we are to make use of technology to alter ourselves. If one of the key constituents of our nature, something on which we base our notions of dignity, has to do with the gamut of normal emotions shared by human beings, then we are *already* trying to narrow the range for the utilitarian ends of health and convenience.

Psychotropic drugs do not alter the germ line or produce heritable effects in the way that genetic engineering someday might. But they already raise important issues about the meaning of human dignity and are a harbinger of things to come.

When Do We Become Human?

In the near term, the big ethical controversies raised by biotechnology will not be threats to the dignity of normal adult human beings but rather to those who possess something less than the full complement of capabilities that we have defined as characterizing human specificity. The largest group of beings in this category are the unborn, but it could also include infants, the terminally sick, elderly people with debilitating diseases, and the disabled. 70

This issue has already come up with regard to stem cell research and cloning. Embryonic stem cell research requires the deliberate destruction of embryos, while so-called therapeutic cloning requires not just their destruction but their deliberate creation for research purposes prior to destruction. (As bioethicist Leon Kass notes, therapeutic cloning is not therapeutic for the embryo.) Both activities have been strongly condemned by those who believe that life begins at conception and that embryos have full moral status as human beings.

I do not want to rehearse the whole history of the abortion debate and the hotly contested question of when life begins. I personally do not begin with religious convictions on this issue and admit to considerable confusion in trying to think through its rights and wrongs. The question here is, What does the natural-rights approach to human dignity outlined here suggest about the moral status of the unborn, the disabled, and so on? I'm not sure it produces a definitive answer, but it can at least help us frame an answer to the question.

At first blush, a natural-rights doctrine that bases human dignity on the fact that the human species possesses certain unique characteristics would appear to allow a gradation of rights depending on the degree to which any individual member of that species shares in those characteristics. An elderly person with Alzheimer's, for example, has lost the normal adult ability to reason, and therefore that part of his dignity that would permit him to participate in politics by voting or running for office. Reason, moral choice, and possession of the species-typical emotional gamut are things that are shared by virtually all human beings and therefore serve as a basis for universal equality, but individuals possess these traits in greater or lesser amounts: Some are more reasonable, have stronger consciences or more sensitive emotions than others. At one extreme, minute distinctions could be made between individuals based on the degree to which they possess these basic human qualities, with differentiated rights assigned to them on that basis. This has happened before in history; it is called natural aristocracy. The hierarchical system it implies is one of the reasons people have become suspicious of the very concept of natural rights.

There is a strong prudential reason for not being too hierarchical in the assignment of political rights, however. There is, in the first place, no consensus on a precise definition of that list of essential human characteristics that qualify an individual for rights. More important, judgments about the degree to which a given individual possesses one or another of these qualities are very difficult to make, and usually suspect, because the person making the judgment is seldom a disinterested party. Most real-world aristocracies have been conventional rather than natural, with the aristocrats assigning themselves rights that they claimed were natural but that were actually based on force or convention. It is therefore appropriate to approach the question of who qualifies for rights with some liberality.

Nonetheless, every contemporary liberal democracy does in fact differentiate rights based on the degree to which individuals or categories of individuals share in certain species-typical characteristics. Children, for example, do not have the rights of adults because their capacities for reason and moral choice are not fully developed; they cannot vote and do not have the freedom of person that their parents do in making choices about where to live, whether to go to school, and so on. Societies strip criminals of basic rights for violating the law, and do so more severely in the case of those regarded as lacking a basic human moral sense. In the United States, they can be deprived even of the right to life for certain kinds of crimes. We do not officially strip Alzheimer's patients of their political rights, but we do restrict their ability to drive and make financial decisions, and in practice they usually cease to exercise their political rights as well.

From a natural-rights perspective, then, one could argue that it is reasonable to assign the unborn different rights from those of either infants or children. A day-old infant may not be capable of reason or moral choice, but it already possesses important elements of the normal human emotional gamut—it can get upset, bond to its mother, expect attention, and the like, in ways that a day-old embryo cannot. It is the violation of the natural and very powerful bonding that takes place between parent and infant, in fact, that makes infanticide such a heinous crime in most societies. That we typically hold funerals after the deaths of infants but not after miscarriages is testimony to the naturalness of this distinction. All of this suggests that it does not make sense to treat embryos as human beings with the same kinds of rights that infants possess.

Against this line of argument, we can pose the following considerations, again not from a religious but from a natural-rights perspective. An embryo may be lacking in some of the basic human characteristics possessed by an infant, but it is also not just another group of cells or tissue, because it has the *potential* to become a full human being. In this respect, it differs from an infant, which also lacks many of the most important characteristics of a normal adult human being, only in the degree to which it has realized its natural potential. This implies that while an embryo can be assigned a lower moral status than an infant, it has a higher moral status than other kinds of cells or tissue that scientists work with. It is therefore reasonable, on nonreligious grounds, to question whether researchers should be free to create, clone, and destroy human embryos at will.

Ontogeny recapitulates phylogeny. We have argued that in the evolutionary process that leads from prehuman ancestor to human beings, there was a qualitative leap that transformed the prehuman precursors of language, reason, and emotion into a human whole that cannot be explained as a simple sum of its parts, and that remains an essentially mysterious process. Something similar happens with the development of every embryo into an infant, child, and adult human being: What starts out as a cluster of organic molecules comes to possess consciousness, reason, the capacity for moral choice, and subjective emotions, in a manner that remains equally mysterious.

Putting these facts together—that an embryo has a moral status somewhere between that of an infant and that of other types of cells and tissue, and that the transformation of the embryo into something with a higher status is a mysterious process—suggests that if we are to do things like harvest stem cells from embryos, we should put a lot of limits and constraints around this activity to make sure that it does not become a precedent for other uses of the unborn that would push the envelope further. To what extent are we willing to create and grow embryos for utilitarian purposes? Supposing some miraculous new cure required cells not from a day-old embryo, but tissue from a month-old fetus? A five-month-old female fetus already has in her ovaries all the eggs she will ever produce as a woman; supposing someone wanted access to them? If we get too used to the idea of cloning embryos for medical purposes, will we know when to stop?

If the question of equality in a future biotech world threatens to tear up 80 the Left, the Right will quite literally fall apart over questions related to human dignity. In the United States, the Right (as represented by the Republican Party) is divided between economic libertarians, who like entrepreneurship and technology with minimal regulation, and social conservatives, many of whom are religious, who care about a range of issues including abortion and the family. The coalition between these two groups is usually strong enough to hold up during elections, but it papers over some fundamental differences in outlook. It is not clear that this alliance will survive the emergence of new technologies that, on the one hand, offer enormous health benefits and money-making opportunities for the biotech industry, but, on the other, require violating deeply held ethical norms.

We are thus brought back to the question of politics and political strategies. For if there is a viable concept of human dignity out there, it needs to be defended, not just in philosophical tracts but in the real world of politics, and protected by viable political institutions. . . .

NOTES

1. Clive Staples Lewis, *The Abolition of Man* (New York: Touchstone, 1944), p. 85.
2. Counsel of Europe, Draft Additional Protocol to the Convention on Human Rights and Biomedicine, On the Prohibiting of Cloning Human Beings, Doc. 7884, July 16, 1997.
3. This is the theme of the second part of Francis Fukuyama, *The End of History and the Last Man* (New York: Free Press, 1992).
4. For an interpretation of this passage in Tocqueville, see Francis Fukuyama, "The March of Equality," *Journal of Democracy* 11 (2000): 11–17.
5. John Paul II, "Message to the Pontifical Academy of Sciences," October 22, 1996.
6. Daniel C. Dennett, *Darwin's Dangerous Idea: Evolution and the Meanings of Life* (New York: Simon and Schuster, 1995), pp. 35–39; see also Ernst Mayr, *One Long Argument: Charles Darwin and the Genesis of Modern Evolutionary Thought* (Cambridge, Mass.: Harvard University Press, 1991), pp. 40–42.
7. Michael Ruse and David L. Hull, *The Philosophy of Biology* (New York: Oxford University Press, 1998), p. 385.
8. Lee M. Silver, *Remaking Eden: Cloning and Beyond in a Brave New World* (New York: Avon, 1998), pp. 256–57.
9. Ruse and Hull (1998), p. 385.
10. Silver (1998), p. 277.
11. Friedrich Nietzsche, *Thus Spoke Zarathustra*, First part, section 5, from *The Portable Nietzsche*, ed. Walter Kaufmann (New York: Viking, 1968), p. 130.
12. Charles Taylor, *Sources of the Self: The Making of the Modern Identity* (Cambridge, Mass.: Harvard University Press, 1989), pp. 6–7.
13. For a fuller defense of this proposition, see Francis Fukuyama, *The Great Disruption: Human Nature and the Reconstitution of Social Order*, part II (New York: Free Press, 1999).
14. Aristotle, *Politics* I.2.13, 1254b, 16–24.
15. Ibid., I.2.18, 1255a, 22–38.
16. Ibid., I.2.19, 1255b, 3–5.
17. See, for example, Dan W. Brock, "The Human Genome Project and Human Identity," in *Genes, Humans, and Self-Knowledge*, eds. Robert F. Weir and Susan C. Lawrence et al. (Iowa City: University of Iowa Press, 1994), pp. 18–23.
18. This possibility has already been suggested by Charles Murray. See his "Deeper into the Brain," *National Review* 52 (2000): 46–49.

19. Peter Sloterdijk, "Regeln für den Menschenpark: Ein Antwortschreiben zum Brief über den Humanismus," *Die Zeit*, no. 38, September 16, 1999.

20. Jürgen Habermas, "Nicht die Natur verbietet das Klonen. Wir müssen selbst entscheiden. Eine Replik auf Dieter E. Zimmer," *Die Zeit*, no. 9, February 19, 1998.

21. For a discussion of this issue, see Allen Buchanan and Norman Daniels et al., *From Chance to Choice: Genetics and Justice* (New York and Cambridge: Cambridge University Press, 2000), pp. 17–20. See also Robert H. Blank and Masako N. Darrough, *Biological Differences and Social Equality: Implications for Social Policy* (Westport, Conn.: Greenwood Press, 1983).

22. Ronald M. Dworkin, *Sovereign Virtue: The Theory and Practice of Equality* (Cambridge, Mass.: Harvard University Press, 2000), p. 452.

23. Laurence H. Tribe, "Second Thoughts on Cloning," *New York Times*, December 5, 1997, p. A31.

24. John Paul II (1996).

25. On the meaning of this "ontological leap," see Ernan McMullin, "Biology and the Theology of the Human," in Phillip R. Sloan, ed., *Controlling Our Desires: Historical, Philosophical, Ethical, and Theological Perspectives on the Human Genome Project* (Notre Dame, Ind.: University of Notre Dame Press, 2000), p. 367.

26. It is in fact very difficult to come up with a Darwinian explanation for the human enjoyment of music. See Steven Pinker, *How the Mind Works* (New York: W. W. Norton, 1997), pp. 528–38.

27. See, for example, Arthur Peacocke, "Relating Genetics to Theology on the Map of Scientific Knowledge," in Sloan, ed. (2000), pp. 346–50.

28. Laplace's exact words were: "We ought then to regard the present state of the universe [not just the solar system] as the effect of its anterior state and as the cause of the one which is to follow. Given an intelligence that could comprehend at one instant all the forces by which nature is animated and the respective situation of the beings who compose it—an intelligence sufficiently vast to submit these data [initial conditions] to analysis—it would embrace in the same formula the movements of the greatest bodies in the universe and those of the lightest atom; for it, nothing would be uncertain and the future, as the past, would be present to its eyes . . . The regularity which astronomy shows us in the movements of the comets doubtless exists also in all phenomena. The curve described by a simple molecule of air or vapor is regulated in a manner just as certain as the planetary orbits; the only difference between them is that which comes from our ignorance." Quoted in *Final Causality in Nature and Human Affairs*, ed. Richard F. Hassing (Washington, D.C.: Catholic University Press, 1997), p. 224.

29. Hassing, ed. (1997), pp. 224–26.

30. Peacocke, in Sloan, ed. (2000), p. 350.

31. McMullin, in Sloan, ed. (2000), p. 374.

32. On this question, see Roger D. Masters, "The Biological Nature of the State," *World Politics* 35 (1983): 161–93.

33. Andrew Goldberg and Christophe Boesch, "The Cultures of Chimpanzees," *Scientific American* 284 (2001): 60–67.

34. Larry Arnhart, *Darwinian Natural Right: The Biological Ethics of Human Nature* (Albany, N.Y.: State University of New York Press, 1998), pp. 61–62.

35. One exception to this appears to be the indigenous peoples of the American Pacific Northwest, a hunter-gatherer society that seems to have developed a

state. See Robert Wright, *Nonzero: The Logic of Human Destiny* (New York: Pantheon Books, 2000), pp. 31–38.

36. Stephen Jay Gould and R. C. Lewontin, "The Spandrels of San Marco and the Panglossian Paradigm: A Critique of the Adaptionist Programme," *Proceedings of the Royal Society of London* 205 (1979): 81–98.

37. John R. Searle, *The Mystery of Consciousness* (New York: New York Review Books, 1997).

38. Daniel C. Dennett, *Consciousness Explained* (Boston: Little, Brown, 1991), p. 210.

39. John R. Searle, *The Rediscovery of the Mind* (Cambridge, Mass.: MIT Press, 1992), p. 3.

40. Hans P. Moravec, *Robot: Mere Machine to Transcendent Mind* (New York: Oxford University Press, 1999).

41. Ray Kurzweil, *The Age of Spiritual Machines: When Computers Exceed Human Intelligence* (London: Penguin Books, 2000).

42. For a critique, see Colin McGinn, "Hello HAL," *New York Times Book Review*, January 3, 1999.

43. On this point, see Wright (2000), pp. 306–8.

44. Ibid., pp. 321–22.

45. Robert J. McShea, *Morality and Human Nature: A New Route to Ethical Theory* (Philadelphia: Temple University Press, 1990), p. 77.

46. Daniel Dennett makes the following bizarre statement in *Consciousness Explained:* "But why should it matter, you may want to ask, that a creature's desires are thwarted if they aren't conscious desires? I reply: Why would it matter more if they were conscious—especially if consciousness were a property, as some think, that forever eludes investigation? Why should a 'zombie's' crushed hopes matter less than a conscious person's crushed hopes? There is a trick with mirrors here that should be exposed and discarded. Consciousness, you say, is what matters, but then you cling to doctrines about consciousness that systematically prevent us from getting any purchase on *why* it matters" (p. 450). Dennett's question begs a more obvious one: What person in the world would care about crushing a zombie's hopes, except to the extent that the zombie was instrumentally useful to that person?

47. Jared Diamond, *The Third Chimpanzee* (New York: HarperCollins, 1992), p. 23.

48. The dualism between reason and emotion—that is, the idea that these are distinct and separable mental qualities—can be traced to Descartes (see *The Passions of the Soul*, Article 47). This dichotomy has been widely accepted since then but is misleading in many ways. The neurophysiologist Antonio Damasio points out that human reasoning invariably involves what he labels somatic markers—emotions that the mind attaches to certain ideas or options in the course of thinking through a problem—that help speed many kinds of calculations. Antonio R. Damasio, *Descartes' Error: Emotion, Reason, and the Human Brain* (New York: Putnam, 1994).

49. That is, the Kantian notion that moral choice is an act of pure reason overriding or suppressing natural emotions is not the way that human beings actually make moral choices. Human beings more typically balance one set of feelings against another and build character by strengthening the pleasurability of good moral choices through habit.

Questions for Critical Reading

1. What is "Factor X"? Reread Fukuyama to locate quotations where he defines this term and then provide a definition of the concept in your own words.

2. Do humans have an "essence"? Locate passages from Fukuyama that support your analysis. Does he think there is a human essence? What quotations make his position clear? You will need to read his text closely and critically to determine his position.

3. As the title of this selection suggests, Fukuyama is centrally concerned with the concept of human dignity in this chapter. Define human dignity, using quotations from Fukuyama that support your definition.

Exploring Context

1. Fukuyama opens this chapter by quoting from a decree from the Council of Europe. Visit the Council's Web site at coe.int and search for information on cloning. What else does the council have to say on the issue? How does its position reflect or complicate Fukuyama's argument?

2. Fukuyama turns to complexity theory to recuperate an understanding of the human essence. Conway's Game of Life is a classic mathematical model illustrating how simple rules governing individual parts can combine into very complex wholes. Play the Game of Life at bitstorm.org/gameoflife. Does it reflect the evolution of consciousness? How often does a stable pattern emerge in the game? How does it support or undercut Fukuyama's arguments about Factor X?

3. Fukuyama asks, "What is it that we want to protect from any future advances in biotechnology?" (p. 159). Visit the Web site of the *American Journal of Bioethics* at bioethics.net. In browsing through the site, what answers to Fukuyama's question can you find? How can we decide which biotechnologies should be pursued and which would cause us to lose our humanity?

Questions for Connecting

1. Michael Pollan's discussion of "holons" in "The Animals: Practicing Complexity" (p. 281) seems closely related to Fukuyama's use of complexity theory. In what ways are humans and organic farms similar? What insight does Pollan's essay provide on Fukuyama's argument?

2. In "The End of Race: Hawaii and the Mixing of Peoples" (p. 250), Steve Olson suggests that, as a result of intermarriage, race no longer has a genetic basis. Is race part of "Factor X"? How does Fukuyama's essay support or complicate Olson's argument about race? Is race part of being human? Is it part of human dignity? You may want to use the definition of human dignity you developed in Question 3 of Questions for Critical Reading in making your argument.

3. According to Richard Restak in "Attention Deficit: The Brain Syndrome of Our Era" (p. 332), our brains are being rewired to produce Attention Deficit Disorder. Is multitasking a threat to human dignity as well? If culture can change the wiring of our brains, then is that, too, a kind of biotechnology?

Language Matters

1. Select a key paragraph from the essay and then reduce each sentence of the paragraph down to a single subject and verb. What's lost by condensing the sentences in this way? What other grammatical constructions help carry the meaning of a sentence?

2. The best way to avoid awkward sentences in your own writing is to say what you mean. You can also use this technique when dealing with difficult readings like Fukuyama's. Select a particularly complex sentence from this essay. If you could make Fukuyama say what he meant, what would the sentence look like? Begin by breaking down his writing into several smaller sentences. Try substituting simpler vocabulary too. Once you've absorbed the ideas through this process, try stating out loud a summary of what Fukuyama is trying to communicate and then write down what you say. Try these same strategies in your own writing.

3. You're probably familiar with common parts of speech like nouns and verbs. Using Fukuyama's text, create new parts of speech from common combinations of the usual parts of speech. For example, a noun and a verb together might form a "quarplat," an adverb and an adjective might be a "jerbad." Create rules for your parts of speech. When does Fukuyama use the kinds of constructions you've named? When might you?

Assignments for Writing

1. Write a paper in which you explain what it means to be human. In making your argument, you should account for the fact that Fukuyama identifies many different qualities as being necessary to "Factor X." Why, then, does he call them collectively "Factor X"? How do you account for the seemingly infinite number of divergent views on what it is to be human? Use your definition of "Factor X" from Question 1 of Questions for Critical Reading.

2. Fukuyama acknowledges the difficulties that a vision of human equality presents when dealing with specific populations, including the elderly, disabled, and terminally ill. Write a paper in which you suggest standards for dealing with these boundary populations in relation to medical advances such as biotechnology. How might you change Fukuyama's working definitions of Factor X to be more inclusive? Consider using any specific examples you located from your work with the *American Journal of Bioethics* Web site in Question 3 of Exploring Context.

3. Fukuyama stresses the centrality of human nature in current political and ethical debate. Some environmentalists would consider his discussion anthropocentric. What about natural life beyond human beings? Write a paper in which

you extend Fukuyama's discussion of human dignity to account for the natural environment, ecosystems, and other forms of life. You may want to identify those parts of Fukuyama's essay that deal directly with the distinction between the "natural" and "human" worlds as a point of departure for this discussion. What happens when we extend the concept of dignity beyond humans? Would it change the way we acquire our food or what we eat? Consider your work with Michael Pollan from Question 1 of Questions for Connecting.

Daniel Gilbert

Daniel Gilbert is a professor of psychology at Harvard University. He has won a Guggenheim fellowship, as well as the American Psychological Association's Distinguished Scientific Award for an Early Career Contribution to Psychology. In 2002, *Personality and Social Psychology Bulletin* named him one of the fifty most influential social psychologists of the decade. In addition to his book *Stumbling on Happiness* (2006) and his scholarly publications, Gilbert has published works of science fiction as well as contributed to the *New York Times*, the *Los Angeles Times*, *Forbes*, and *Time*.

Stumbling on Happiness, a *New York Times* best-seller, applies Gilbert's expertise to the study of happiness itself. Gilbert argues that people are rarely able to predict with any accuracy how they will feel in the future, and so are often quite wrong about what will make them happy.

In "Reporting Live from Tomorrow," a chapter from *Stumbling on Happiness*, Gilbert suggests that beliefs, just like genes, can be "super-replicators," given to spreading regardless of their usefulness. Thus even beliefs that are based on inaccurate information can provide the means for their own propagation. Gilbert explains why humans, with our unreliable memories and imaginations, are so easily susceptible to such beliefs. Though "the best way to predict our feelings tomorrow is to see how others are feeling today," most people are unwilling to make use of the experiences of others because they mistakenly believe themselves to be unique.

The pursuit of happiness is central to our understanding of America—we all want to be happy. But this selection cautions us about predicting our future happiness and in the process provides the tools we need to correct our misapprehensions.

▶ TAGS: *research*, *happiness*, surrogates, *identity*, *decision making*

Reporting Live from Tomorrow

In Alfred Hitchcock's 1956 remake of *The Man Who Knew Too Much*, Doris Day sang a waltz whose final verse went like this:

> When I was just a child in school,
> I asked my teacher, "What will I try?
> Should I paint pictures, should I sing songs?"
> This was her wise reply:
> "*Que sera, sera*. Whatever will be, will be.
> The future's not ours to see. *Que sera, sera*."[1]

Now, I don't mean to quibble with the lyricist, and I have nothing but fond memories of Doris Day, but the fact is that this is *not* a particularly wise reply. When a child asks for advice about which of two activities to pursue, a teacher should be able to provide more than a musical cliché. Yes, of *course* the future is hard to see. But we're all heading that way anyhow, and as difficult as it may be to envision, we have to make *some* decisions about which futures to aim for and which to avoid. If we are prone to mistakes when we try to imagine the future, then how *should* we decide what to do?

Even a child knows the answer to that one: We should ask the teacher. One of the benefits of being a social and linguistic animal is that we can capitalize on the experience of others rather than trying to figure everything out for ourselves. For millions of years, human beings have conquered their ignorance by dividing the labor of discovery and then communicating their discoveries to one another, which is why the average newspaper boy in Pittsburgh knows more about the universe than did Galileo, Aristotle, Leonardo, or any of those other guys who were so smart they only needed one name. We all make ample use of this resource. If you were to write down everything you know and then go back through the list and make a check mark next to the things you know only because somebody told you, you'd develop a repetitive-motion disorder because almost *everything* you know is secondhand. Was Yury Gagarin the first man in space? Is *croissant* a French word? Are there more Chinese than North Dakotans? Does a stitch in time save nine? Most of us know the answers to these questions despite the fact that none of us actually witnessed the launching of *Vostok I*, personally supervised the evolution of language, hand-counted all the people in Beijing and Bismarck, or performed a fully randomized double-blind study of stitching. We know the answers because someone shared them with us. Communication is a kind of "vicarious observation"[2] that allows us to learn about the world without ever leaving the comfort of our Barcaloungers. The six billion interconnected people who cover the surface of our planet constitute a leviathan with twelve billion eyes, and anything that is seen by one pair of eyes can potentially be known to the entire beast in a matter of months, days, or even minutes.

The fact that we can communicate with one another about our experiences should provide a simple solution to the core problem with which this book has been concerned. Yes, our ability to imagine our future emotions is flawed—but that's okay, because we don't have to imagine what it would feel like to marry a lawyer, move to Texas, or eat a snail when there are so many people who have *done* these things and are all too happy to tell us about them. Teachers, neighbors, coworkers, parents, friends, lovers, children, uncles, cousins, coaches, cabdrivers, bartenders, hairstylists, dentists, advertisers—each of these folks has something to say about what it would be like to live in this future rather than that one, and at any point in time we can be fairly sure that one of these folks has actually *had* the experience that we are merely contemplating. Because we are the mammal that shows and tells, each of us has access to information about almost any experience we can possibly imagine—and many that we can't. Guidance counselors tell us about the best careers, critics tell us about the best restaurants, travel agents tell us about the best vacations, and friends tell us about the best travel agents. Every one of us is surrounded by a platoon of Dear Abbys who can recount their own experiences and in so doing tell us which futures are most worth wanting.

Given the overabundance of consultants, role models, gurus, mentors, yentas, and nosy relatives, we might expect people to do quite well when it comes to making life's most important decisions, such as where to live, where to work, and whom to marry. And yet, the average American moves more than six times,[3] changes jobs more than ten times,[4] and marries more than once,[5] which suggests that most of us are making more than a few poor choices. If humanity is a living library of information about what it feels like to do just about anything that can be done, then why do the people with the library cards make so many bad decisions? There are just two possibilities. The first is that a lot of the advice we receive from others is bad advice that we foolishly accept. The second is that a lot of the advice we receive from others is good advice that we foolishly reject. So which is it? Do we listen too well when others speak, or do we not listen well enough? As we shall see, the answer to that question is *yes*.

Super-Replicators

The philosopher Bertrand Russell once claimed that believing is "the most mental thing we do."[6] Perhaps, but it is also the most *social* thing we do. Just as we pass along our genes in an effort to create people whose faces look like ours, so too do we pass along our beliefs in an effort to create people whose minds think like ours. Almost any time we tell anyone anything, we are attempting to change the way their brains operate—attempting to change the way they see the world so that their view of it more closely resembles our own. Just about every assertion—from the sublime ("God has a plan for you") to the mundane ("Turn left at the light, go two miles, and you'll see the Dunkin' Donuts on your right")—is meant to bring the listener's beliefs about the world into harmony with the speaker's. Sometimes these attempts succeed and sometimes they fail. So what determines whether a belief will be successfully transmitted from one mind to another?

The principles that explain why some genes are transmitted more successfully than others also explain why some beliefs are transmitted more successfully than others.[7] Evolutionary biology teaches us that any gene that promotes its own "means of transmission" will be represented in increasing proportions in the population over time. For instance, imagine that a single gene were responsible for the complex development of the neural circuitry that makes orgasms feel so good. For a person having this gene, orgasms would feel . . . well, orgasmic. For a person lacking this gene, orgasms would feel more like sneezes—brief, noisy, physical convulsions that pay rather paltry hedonic dividends. Now, if we took fifty healthy, fertile people who had the gene and fifty healthy, fertile people who didn't, and left them on a hospitable planet for a million years or so, when we returned we would probably find a population of thousands or millions of people, almost all of whom had the gene. Why? Because a gene that made orgasms feel good would tend to be transmitted from generation to generation simply because people who enjoy orgasms are inclined to do the thing that transmits their genes. The logic is so circular that it is virtually inescapable: Genes tend to be transmitted when they make us do the things that transmit genes. What's more, even *bad* genes—those that make us prone to cancer or heart disease—can become super-replicators if they compensate for these costs by promoting their own means of transmission. For instance, if the gene that made orgasms feel delicious also left us prone to arthritis and tooth decay, that gene might still be represented in increasing proportions because arthritic, toothless people who love orgasms are more likely to have children than are limber, toothy people who do not.

The same logic can explain the transmission of beliefs. If a particular belief has some property that facilitates its own transmission, then that belief tends to be held by an increasing number of minds. As it turns out, there are several such properties that increase a belief's transmissional success, the most obvious of which is accuracy. When someone tells us where to find a parking space downtown or how to bake a cake at high altitude, we adopt that belief and pass it along because it helps us and our friends do the things we want to do, such as parking and baking.

> Do we listen too well when others speak, or do we not listen well enough? As we shall see, the answer to that question is *yes*.

As one philosopher noted, "The faculty of communication would not gain ground in evolution unless it was by and large the faculty of transmitting true beliefs."[8] Accurate beliefs give us power, which makes it easy to understand why they are so readily transmitted from one mind to another.

It is a bit more difficult to understand why *inaccurate* beliefs are so readily transmitted from one mind to another—but they are. False beliefs, like bad genes, can and do become super-replicators, and a thought experiment illustrates how this can happen. Imagine a game that is played by two teams, each of which has a thousand players, each of whom is linked to teammates by a telephone. The object of the game is to get one's team to share as many accurate beliefs as possible. When players receive a message that they believe to be accurate, they call a teammate and pass it along. When they receive a message that they believe to be inaccurate, they don't. At the end of the game, the referee blows a whistle and awards each team a point for every accurate belief that the entire team shares and subtracts one point for every inaccurate belief the entire team shares. Now, consider a contest played one sunny day between a team called the Perfects (whose members always transmit accurate beliefs) and a team called the Imperfects (whose members occasionally transmit an inaccurate belief). We should expect the Perfects to win, right?

Not necessarily. In fact, there are some special circumstances under which the Imperfects will beat their pants off. For example, imagine what would happen if one of the Imperfect players sent the false message "Talking on the phone all day and night will ultimately make you very happy," and imagine that other Imperfect players were gullible enough to believe it and pass it on. This message is inaccurate and thus will cost the Imperfects a point in the end. But it may have the compensatory effect of keeping more of the Imperfects on the telephone for more of the time, thus increasing the total number of accurate messages they transmit. Under the right circumstances, the costs of this inaccurate belief would be outweighed by its benefits, namely, that it led players to behave in ways that increased the odds that they would share other accurate beliefs. The lesson to be learned from this game is that inaccurate beliefs can prevail in the belief-transmission game if they somehow facilitate their own "means of transmission." In this case, the means of transmission is not sex but communication, and thus any belief—even a false belief—that increases communication has a good chance of being transmitted over and over again. False beliefs that happen to promote stable societies tend to propagate because people who hold these beliefs tend to live in stable societies, which provide the means by which false beliefs propagate.

Some of our cultural wisdom about happiness looks suspiciously like a super-replicating false belief. Consider money. If you've ever tried to sell anything, then you probably tried to sell it for as much as you possibly could, and other people probably tried to buy it for as little as they possibly could. All the parties involved in the transaction assumed that they would be better off if they ended up with more money rather than less, and this assumption is the bedrock of our economic behavior. Yet, it has far fewer scientific facts to substantiate it than you might expect. Economists and psychologists have spent decades studying the relation between wealth and happiness, and they have generally concluded that wealth increases human happiness when it lifts people out of abject poverty and into the middle class but that it does little to increase happiness thereafter.[9] Americans who earn $50,000 per year are much happier than those who earn $10,000 per year, but Americans who earn $5 million per year are not much happier than those who earn $100,000 per year. People who live in poor nations are much less happy than people who live in moderately wealthy nations, but people who live in moderately wealthy nations are not much less happy than people who live in extremely wealthy nations. Economists explain that wealth has "declining marginal utility," which is a fancy way of saying that it hurts to be hungry, cold, sick, tired, and scared, but once you've bought your way out of these burdens, the rest of your money is an increasingly useless pile of paper.[10]

So once we've earned as much money as we can actually enjoy, we quit working and enjoy it, right? Wrong. People in wealthy countries generally work long and hard to earn more money than they can ever derive pleasure from.[11] This fact puzzles us less than it should. After all, a rat can be motivated to run through a maze that has a cheesy reward at its end, but once the little guy is all topped up, then even the finest Stilton won't get him off his haunches. Once we've eaten our fill of pancakes, more pancakes are not rewarding, hence we stop trying to procure and consume them. But not so, it seems, with money. As Adam Smith, the father of modern economics, wrote in 1776: "The desire for food is limited in every man by the narrow capacity of the human stomach; but the desire of the conveniences and ornaments of building, dress, equipage, and household furniture, seems to have no limit or certain boundary."[12]

If food and money both stop pleasing us once we've had enough of them, then why do we continue to stuff our pockets when we would not continue to stuff our faces? Adam Smith had an answer. He began by acknowledging what most of us suspect anyway, which is that the production of wealth is not necessarily a source of personal happiness.

> In what constitutes the real happiness of human life, [the poor] are in no respect inferior to those who would seem so much above them. In ease of body and peace of mind, all the different ranks of life are nearly upon a level, and the beggar, who suns himself by the side of the highway, possesses that security which kings are fighting for.[13]

That sounds lovely, but if it's true, then we're all in big trouble. If rich kings are no happier than poor beggars, then why should poor beggars stop sunning themselves by the roadside and work to become rich kings? If no one wants to be rich, then we have a significant economic problem, because flourishing economies require that people continually procure and consume one another's goods and services. Market economies require that we all have an insatiable hunger for *stuff*, and if everyone were content with the stuff they had, then the economy would grind to a halt. But if this is a significant *economic* problem, it is not a significant *personal* problem. The chair of the Federal Reserve may wake up every morning with a desire to do what the economy wants, but most of us get up with a desire to do what *we* want, which is to say that the fundamental needs of a vibrant economy and the fundamental needs of a happy individual are not necessarily the same. So what motivates people to work hard every day to do things that will satisfy the economy's needs but not their own? Like so many thinkers, Smith believed that people want just one thing—happiness—hence economies can blossom and grow only if people are deluded into believing that the production of wealth will make them happy.[14] If and only if people hold this false belief will they do enough producing, procuring, and consuming to sustain their economies.

> The pleasures of wealth and greatness . . . strike the imagination as something grand and beautiful and noble, of which the attainment is well worth all the toil and anxiety which we are so apt to bestow upon it. . . . It is this deception which rouses and keeps in continual motion the industry of mankind. It is this which first prompted them to cultivate the ground, to build houses, to found cities and commonwealths, and to invent and improve all the sciences and arts, which ennoble and embellish human life; which have entirely changed the whole face of the globe, have turned the rude forests of nature into agreeable and fertile plains, and made the trackless and barren ocean a new fund of subsistence, and the great high road of communication to the different nations of the earth.[15]

In short, the production of wealth does not necessarily make individuals happy, but it does serve the needs of an economy, which serves the needs of a stable society, which serves as a network for the propagation of delusional beliefs about happiness and wealth. Economies thrive when individuals strive, but because individuals will only strive for their own happiness, it is essential that they mistakenly believe that producing and consuming are routes to personal well-being. Although words such as *delusional* may seem to suggest some sort of shadowy conspiracy orchestrated by a small group of men in dark suits, the belief-transmission game teaches us that the propagation of false beliefs does not require that anyone be *trying* to perpetrate a magnificent fraud on an innocent populace. There is no cabal at the top, no star chamber, no master manipulator whose clever program of indoctrination and propaganda has duped us all into believing that money can buy us love. Rather, this particular false belief is a super-replicator because holding it causes us to engage in the very activities that perpetuate it.[16]

The belief-transmission game explains why we believe some things about happiness that simply aren't true. The joy of money is one example. The joy of children is another that for most of us hits a bit closer to home. Every human culture tells its members that having children will make them happy. When people think about their offspring—either imagining future offspring or thinking about their current ones—they tend to conjure up images of cooing babies smiling from their bassinets, adorable toddlers running higgledy-piggledy across the lawn, handsome boys and gorgeous girls playing trumpets and tubas in the school marching band, successful college students going on to have beautiful weddings, satisfying careers, and flawless grandchildren whose affections can be purchased with candy. Prospective parents know that diapers will need changing, that homework will need doing, and that orthodontists will go to Aruba on their life savings, but by and large, they think quite happily about parenthood, which is why most of them eventually leap into it. When parents look back on parenthood, they remember feeling what those who are looking forward to it expect to feel. Few of us are immune to these cheery contemplations. I have a twenty-nine-year-old son, and I am absolutely convinced that he is and always has been one of the greatest sources of joy in my life, having only recently been eclipsed by my two-year-old granddaughter, who is equally adorable but who has not yet asked me to walk behind her and pretend we're unrelated. When people are asked to identify their sources of joy, they do just what I do: They point to their kids.

> If parenting is such difficult business, then why do we have such a rosy view of it?

Yet if we measure the *actual* satisfaction of people who have children, a very different story emerges. As Figure 1 shows, couples generally start out quite happy in their marriages and then become progressively less satisfied over the course of their lives together, getting close to their original levels of satisfaction only when their children leave home.[17] Despite what we read in the popular press, the only known symptom of "empty nest syndrome" is increased smiling.[18] Interestingly, this pattern of satisfaction over the life cycle describes women (who are usually the primary caretakers of children) better than men.[19] Careful studies of how women feel as they go about their daily activities show that they are less happy when taking care of their children than when eating,

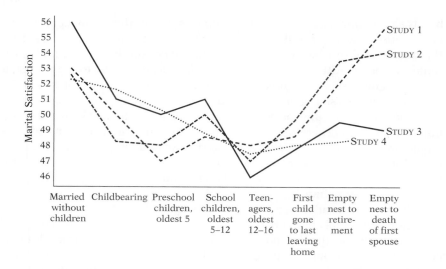

Figure 1

As the four separate studies in this graph show, marital satisfaction decreases dramatically after the birth of the first child and increases only when the last child leaves home.

exercising, shopping, napping, or watching television.[20] Indeed, looking after the kids appears to be only slightly more pleasant than doing housework.

None of this should surprise us. Every parent knows that children are a lot of work—a lot of really *hard* work—and although parenting has many rewarding moments, the vast majority of its moments involve dull and selfless service to people who will take decades to become even begrudgingly grateful for what we are doing. If parenting is such difficult business, then why do we have such a rosy view of it? One reason is that we have been talking on the phone all day with society's stockholders—our moms and uncles and personal trainers—who have been transmitting to us an idea that they *believe* to be true but whose accuracy is not the cause of its successful transmission. "Children bring happiness" is a super-replicator. The belief-transmission network of which we are a part cannot operate without a continuously replenished supply of people to do the transmitting, thus the belief that children are a source of happiness becomes a part of our cultural wisdom simply because the opposite belief unravels the fabric of any society that holds it. Indeed, people who believed that children bring misery and despair—and who thus stopped having them—would put their belief-transmission network out of business in around fifty years, hence terminating the belief that terminated them. The Shakers were a utopian farming community that arose in the 1800s and at one time numbered about six thousand. They approved of children, but they did not approve of the natural act that creates them. Over the years, their strict belief in the importance of celibacy caused their network to contract, and today there are just a few elderly Shakers left, transmitting their doomsday belief to no one but themselves.

The belief-transmission game is rigged so that we *must* believe that children and money bring happiness, regardless of whether such beliefs are true. This doesn't mean that we should all now quit our jobs and abandon our families. Rather, it means that while we *believe* we are raising children and earning paychecks to increase our share of happiness, we are actually doing these things for reasons beyond our ken. We are nodes in a social network that arises and falls by a logic of its own, which is why we continue to toil, continue to mate, and continue to be surprised when we do not experience all the joy we so gullibly anticipated.

The Myth of Fingerprints

My friends tell me that I have a tendency to point out problems without offering solutions, but they never tell me what I should do about it. In one chapter after another, I've described the ways in which imagination fails to provide us with accurate previews of our emotional futures. I've claimed that when we imagine our futures we tend to fill in, leave out, and take little account of how differently we will think about the future once we actually get there. I've claimed that neither personal experience nor cultural wisdom compensates for imagination's shortcomings. I've so thoroughly marinated you in the foibles, biases, errors, and mistakes of the human mind that you may wonder how anyone ever manages to make toast without buttering their kneecaps. If so, you will be heartened to learn that there *is* a simple method by which anyone can make strikingly accurate predictions about how they will feel in the future. But you may be disheartened to learn that, by and large, no one wants to use it.

Why do we rely on our imaginations in the first place? Imagination is the poor man's wormhole. We can't do what we'd really *like* to do—namely, travel through time, pay a visit to our future selves, and *see* how happy those selves are—and so we imagine the future instead of actually going there. But if we cannot travel in the dimensions of time, we can travel in the dimensions of space, and the chances are pretty good that somewhere in those other three dimensions there is another human being who is actually *experiencing* the future event that we are merely thinking about. Surely we aren't the first people ever to consider a move to Cincinnati, a career in motel management, another helping of rhubarb pie, or an extramarital affair, and for the most part, those who have already tried these things are more than willing to tell us about them. It is true that when people tell us about their past experiences ("That ice water wasn't really so cold" or "I love taking care of my daughter"), memory's peccadilloes may render their testimony unreliable. But it is also true that when people tell us about their *current* experiences ("How am I feeling right now? I feel like pulling my arm out of this freezing bucket and sticking my teenager's head in it instead!"), they are providing us with the kind of report about their subjective state that is considered the gold standard of happiness measures. If you believe (as I do) that people can generally say how they are feeling at the moment they are asked, then one way to make predictions about our own emotional futures is to find someone who is having the experience we are contemplating and ask them how they feel. Instead of remembering our past experience in order to simulate our future experience, perhaps we should simply ask other people to introspect on their inner states. Perhaps we should give up on remembering and imagining entirely and use other people as *surrogates* for our future selves.

This idea sounds all too simple, and I suspect you have an objection to it that goes something like this: *Yes, other people are probably right now experiencing the very things I am merely contemplating, but I can't use other people's experiences as proxies for my own because those other people are not me. Every human being is as unique as his or her fingerprints, so it won't help me much to learn about how others feel in the situations that I'm facing. Unless these other people are my clones and have had all the same experiences I've had, their reactions and my reactions are bound to differ. I am a walking, talking idiosyncrasy, and thus I am better off basing my predictions on my somewhat fickle imagination than on the reports of people whose preferences, tastes, and emotional proclivities are so radically different from my own.* If that's your objection, then it is a good one — so good that it will take two steps to dismantle it. First let me prove to you that the experience of a single randomly selected individual can sometimes provide a better basis for predicting your future experience than your own imagination can. And then let me show you why you — and I — find this so difficult to believe.

Finding the Solution

Imagination has three shortcomings, and if you didn't know that then you may be reading this book backward. If you did know that, then you also know that imagination's first shortcoming is its tendency to fill in and leave out without telling us (which we explored in the section on *realism*). No one can imagine every feature and consequence of a future event, hence we must consider some and fail to consider others. The problem is that the features and consequences we fail to consider are often quite important. You may recall the study in which college students were asked to imagine how they would feel a few days after their school's football team played a game against its archrival.[21] The results showed that students overestimated the duration of the game's emotional impact because when they tried to imagine their future experience, they imagined their team winning ("The clock will hit zero, we'll storm the field, everyone will cheer . . .") but failed to imagine what they would be doing afterward ("And then I'll go home and study for my final exams"). Because the students were focused on the game, they failed to imagine how events that happened *after* the game would influence their happiness. So what *should* they have done instead?

They should have abandoned imagination altogether. Consider a study that put people in a similar predicament and then forced them to abandon their imaginations. In this study, a group of volunteers (reporters) first received a delicious prize — a gift certificate from a local ice cream parlor — and then performed a long, boring task in which they counted and recorded geometric shapes that appeared on a computer screen.[22] The reporters then reported how they felt. Next, a new group of volunteers was told that they would also receive a prize and do the same boring task. Some of these new volunteers (simulators) were told what the prize was and were asked to use their imaginations to

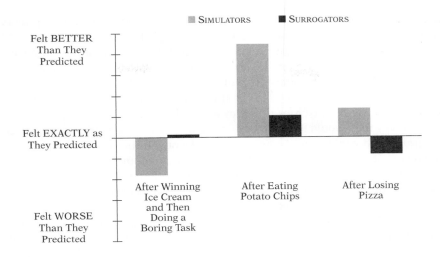

Figure 2

Volunteers made much more accurate predictions of their future feelings when they learned how someone else had felt in the same situation (surrogators) than when they tried to imagine how they themselves would feel (simulators).

predict their future feelings. Other volunteers (surrogators) were not told what the prize was but were instead shown the report of a randomly selected reporter. Not knowing what the prize was, they couldn't possibly use their imaginations to predict their future feelings. Instead, they had to rely on the reporter's report. Once all the volunteers had made their predictions, they received the prize, did the long, boring task, and reported how they actually felt. As the leftmost bars in Figure 2 show, simulators were not as happy as they thought they would be. Why? Because they failed to imagine how quickly the joy of receiving a gift certificate would fade when it was followed by a long, boring task. This is precisely the same mistake that the college-football fans made. But now look at the results for the surrogators. As you can see, they made extremely accurate predictions of their future happiness. These surrogators didn't know what kind of prize they would receive, but they did know that someone who had received that prize had been less than ecstatic at the conclusion of the boring task. So they shrugged and reasoned that they too would feel less than ecstatic at the conclusion of the boring task—and they were right!

Imagination's second shortcoming is its tendency to project the present onto the future (which we explored in the section on *presentism*). When imagination paints a picture of the future, many of the details are necessarily missing, and imagination solves this problem by filling in the gaps with details that it borrows from the present. Anyone who has ever shopped on an empty stomach, vowed to quit smoking after stubbing out a cigarette, or proposed marriage while on shore leave knows that how we feel now can erroneously influence how we *think* we'll feel later. As it turns out, surrogation can remedy this shortcoming too. In one study, volunteers (reporters) ate a few potato chips and reported how much they enjoyed them.[23] Next, a new group of volunteers was fed pretzels, peanut-butter cheese crackers, tortilla chips, bread sticks, and melba toast, which, as you might guess, left them thoroughly stuffed and with little desire for salty snack foods. These stuffed volunteers were then asked to predict how much they would enjoy eating a particular food the next day. Some of these stuffed volunteers (simulators) were told that the food they would eat the next day was potato chips, and they were asked to use their imaginations to predict how they would feel after eating them. Other stuffed volunteers (surrogators) were not told what the next day's food would be but were instead shown the report of one randomly selected reporter. Because surrogators didn't know what the next day's food would be, they couldn't use their imaginations to predict their future enjoyment of it and thus they had to rely on the reporter's report. Once all the volunteers had made their predictions, they went away, returned the next day, ate some potato chips, and reported how much they enjoyed them. As the middle bars in Figure 2 show, simulators enjoyed eating the potato chips more than they thought they would. Why? Because when they made their predictions they had bellies full of pretzels and crackers. But surrogators—who were equally full when they made their predictions—relied on the report of someone without a full belly and hence made much more accurate predictions. It is important to note that the surrogators accurately predicted their future enjoyment of a food despite the fact that they didn't even know what the food was!

Imagination's third shortcoming is its failure to recognize that things will look different once they happen—in particular, that bad things will look a whole lot better (which we explored in the section on *rationalization*). When we imagine losing a job, for instance, we imagine the painful experience ("The boss will march into my office, shut the door behind him . . .") without also imagining how our psychological immune systems will transform its meaning ("I'll come to realize that this was an opportunity to quit retail sales and follow my true calling as a sculptor"). Can surrogation remedy this shortcoming? To find out, researchers arranged for some people to have an unpleasant experience. A group of volunteers (reporters) was told that the experimenter would flip a coin, and if it came up heads, the volunteer would receive a gift certificate to a local pizza parlor. The coin was flipped and—*oh, so sorry*—it came up tails and the reporters received nothing.[24] The reporters then reported how they felt. Next, a new group of volunteers was told about the coin-flipping game and was asked to predict how they would feel if the coin came up tails and they didn't get the pizza gift certificate. Some of these volunteers (simulators) were told the precise monetary value of the gift certificate, and others (surrogators) were instead shown the report of one randomly selected reporter. Once the volunteers had made their predictions, the coin was flipped and—*oh, so sorry*—came up tails. The volunteers then reported how they felt. As the rightmost bars in Figure 2 show, simulators felt better than they predicted they'd feel if they lost the coin flip. Why? Because simulators did not realize how quickly and easily they would rationalize the loss ("Pizza is too fattening, and besides, I don't like that restaurant anyway"). But surrogators—who had nothing to go on except the report of another randomly selected individual—assumed that they wouldn't feel too bad after losing the prize, hence made more accurate predictions.

Rejecting the Solution

This trio of studies suggests that when people are deprived of the information [25] that imagination requires and are thus *forced* to use others as surrogates, they make remarkably accurate predictions about their future feelings, which suggests that the best way to predict our feelings tomorrow is to see how others are feeling today.[25] Given the impressive power of this simple technique, we should expect people to go out of their way to use it. But they don't. When an entirely new group of volunteers was told about the three situations I just described—winning a prize, eating a mystery food, or failing to receive a gift certificate—and was then asked whether they would prefer to make predictions about their future feelings based on *(a)* information about the prize, the food, and the certificate; or *(b)* information about how a randomly selected individual felt after winning them, eating them, or losing them, virtually

> **If you are like most people,
> then like most people, you don't
> know you're like most people.**

every volunteer chose the former. If you hadn't seen the results of these studies, you'd probably have done the same. If I offered to pay for your dinner at a restaurant if you could accurately predict how much you were going to enjoy it, would you want to see the restaurant's menu or some randomly selected diner's review? If you are like most people, you would prefer to see the menu, and if you are like most people, you would end up buying your own dinner. Why?

Because if you are like most people, then like most people, you don't know you're like most people. Science has given us a lot of facts about the average person, and one of the most reliable of these facts is that the average person doesn't see herself as average. Most students see themselves as more intelligent than the average student,[26] most business managers see themselves as more competent than the average business manager,[27] and most football players see themselves as having better "football sense" than their teammates.[28] Ninety percent of motorists consider themselves to be safer-than-average drivers,[29] and 94 percent of college professors consider themselves to be better-than-average teachers.[30] Ironically, the bias toward seeing ourselves as better than average causes us to see ourselves as less biased than average too.[31] As one research team concluded, "Most of us appear to believe that we are more athletic, intelligent, organized, ethical, logical, interesting, fair-minded, and healthy—not to mention more attractive—than the average person."[32]

This tendency to think of ourselves as better than others is not necessarily a manifestation of our unfettered narcissism but may instead be an instance of a more general tendency to think of ourselves as *different* from others—often for better but sometimes for worse. When people are asked about generosity, they claim to perform a greater number of generous acts than others do; but when they are asked about selfishness, they claim to perform a greater number of selfish acts than others do.[33] When people are asked about their ability to perform an easy task, such as driving a car or riding a bike, they rate themselves as better than others; but when they are asked about their ability to perform a difficult task, such as juggling or playing chess, they rate themselves as worse than others.[34] We don't always see ourselves as *superior*, but we almost always see ourselves as *unique*. Even when we do precisely what others do, we tend to think that we're doing it for unique reasons. For instance, we tend to attribute other people's choices to features of the chooser ("Phil picked this class because he's one of those literary types"), but we tend to attribute our own choices to features of the options ("But I picked it because it was easier than economics").[35] We recognize that our decisions are influenced by social norms ("I was too embarrassed to raise my hand in class even though I was terribly confused"), but fail to recognize that others' decisions were similarly influenced ("No one else raised a hand because no one else was as confused as I was").[36] We know that our choices sometimes reflect our aversions ("I voted for Kerry because I couldn't stand Bush"), but we assume that other people's choices reflect their appetites ("If Rebecca voted for Kerry, then she must have liked him").[37] The list of differences is long but the conclusion to be drawn from it is short: The self considers itself to be a very special person.[38]

What makes us think we're so darned special? Three things, at least. First, even if we aren't special, the way we know ourselves is. We are the only people in the world whom we can know from the inside. We *experience* our own thoughts and feelings but must *infer* that other people are experiencing theirs. We all trust that behind those eyes and inside those skulls, our friends and neighbors are having subjective experiences very much like our own, but that trust is an article of faith and not the palpable, self-evident truth that our own subjective experiences constitute. There is a difference between making love and reading about it, and it is the same difference that distinguishes our knowledge of our own mental lives from our knowledge of everyone else's. Because we know ourselves and others by such different means, we gather very different kinds and amounts of information. In every waking moment we monitor the steady stream of thoughts and feelings that runs through our heads, but we only monitor other people's words and deeds, and only when they are in our company. One reason why we seem so special, then, is that we learn about ourselves in such a special way.

The second reason is that we *enjoy* thinking of ourselves as special. Most of us want to fit in well with our peers, but we don't want to fit in too well.[39] We prize our unique identities, and research shows that when people are made to feel too similar to others, their moods quickly sour and they try to distance and distinguish themselves in a variety of ways.[40] If you've ever shown up at a party and found someone else wearing exactly the same dress or necktie that you were wearing, then you know how unsettling it is to share the room with an unwanted twin whose presence temporarily diminishes your sense of individuality. Because we *value* our uniqueness, it isn't surprising that we tend to overestimate it.

The third reason why we tend to overestimate our uniqueness is that we tend to overestimate everyone's uniqueness—that is, we tend to think of people as more different from one another than they actually are. Let's face it: All people are similar in some ways and different in others. The psychologists, biologists, economists, and sociologists who are searching for universal laws of human behavior naturally care about the similarities, but the rest of us care mainly about the differences. Social life involves selecting particular individuals to be our sexual partners, business partners, bowling partners, and more. That task requires that we focus on the things that distinguish one person from another and not on the things that all people share, which is why personal ads are much more likely to mention the advertiser's love of ballet than his love of oxygen. A penchant for respiration explains a great deal about human behavior—for example, why people live on land, become ill at high altitudes, have lungs, resist suffocation, love trees, and so on. It surely explains more than does a person's penchant for ballet. But it does nothing to distinguish one person from another, and thus for ordinary folks who are in the ordinary business of selecting others for commerce, conversation, or copulation, the penchant for air is stunningly irrelevant. Individual similarities are vast, but we don't care much about them because they don't help us do what we are here on earth to do, namely, distinguish Jack from Jill and Jill from Jennifer. As such, these individual similarities are an inconspicuous backdrop against which a small number of relatively minor individual differences stand out in bold relief.

Because we spend so much time searching for, attending to, thinking about, and remembering these differences, we tend to overestimate their magnitude and frequency, and thus end up thinking of people as more varied than they actually are. If you spent all day sorting grapes into different shapes, colors, and kinds, you'd become one of those annoying grapeophiles who talks endlessly about the nuances of flavor and the permutations of texture. You'd come to think of grapes as infinitely varied, and you'd forget that almost all of the really *important* information about a grape can be deduced from the simple fact of its grapehood. Our belief in the variability of others and in the uniqueness of the self is especially powerful when it comes to emotion.[41] Because we can *feel* our own emotions but must *infer* the emotions of others by watching their faces and listening to their voices, we often have the impression that others don't experience the same intensity of emotion that we do, which is why we expect others to recognize our feelings even when we can't recognize theirs.[42] This sense of emotional uniqueness starts early. When kindergarteners are asked how they and others would feel in a variety of situations, they expect to experience unique emotions ("Billy would be sad but I wouldn't") and they provide unique reasons for experiencing them ("I'd tell myself that the hamster was in heaven, but Billy would just cry").[43] When adults make these same kinds of predictions, they do just the same thing.[44]

Our mythical belief in the variability and uniqueness of individuals is the main reason why we refuse to use others as surrogates. After all, surrogation is only useful when we can count on a surrogate to react to an event roughly as we would, and if we believe that people's emotional reactions are more varied than they actually are, then surrogation will seem less useful to us than it actually is. The irony, of course, is that surrogation is a cheap and effective way to predict one's future emotions, but because we don't realize just how similar we all are, we reject this reliable method and rely instead on our imaginations, as flawed and fallible as they may be.

Onward

Despite its watery connotation, the word *hogwash* refers to the feeding — and not to the bathing — of pigs. Hogwash is something that pigs eat, that pigs like, and that pigs need. Farmers provide pigs with hogwash because without it, pigs get grumpy. The word *hogwash* also refers to the falsehoods people tell one another. Like the hogwash that farmers feed their pigs, the hogwash that our friends and teachers and parents feed us is meant to make us happy; but unlike hogwash of the porcine variety, human hogwash does not always achieve its end. As we have seen, ideas can flourish if they preserve the social systems that allow them to be transmitted. Because individuals don't usually feel that it is their personal duty to preserve social systems, these ideas must disguise themselves as prescriptions for individual happiness. We might expect that after spending some time in the world, our experiences would debunk these ideas, but it doesn't always work that way. To learn from our experience we must remember it, and for a variety of reasons, memory is a faithless friend. Practice and coaching get us out of our diapers and into our britches, but they are not enough to get us out of our presents and into our futures. What's so ironic about this predicament is that the information we need to make accurate predictions of our emotional futures is right under our noses, but we don't seem to recognize its aroma. It doesn't always make sense to heed what people tell us when they communicate their beliefs about happiness, but it does make sense to observe how happy they are in different circumstances. Alas, we think of ourselves as unique entities — minds unlike any others — and thus we often reject the lessons that the emotional experience of others has to teach us.

NOTES

1. J. Livingston and R. Evans, "Whatever Will Be, Will Be (Que Sera, Sera)" (1955).
2. W. V. Quine and J. S. Ullian, *The Web of Belief*, 2nd ed. (New York: Random House, 1978), 51.
3. Half of all Americans relocated in the five-year period of 1995–2000, which suggests that the average American relocates about every ten years; B. Berkner and C. S. Faber, *Geographical Mobility, 1995 to 2000* (Washington, D.C.: U.S. Bureau of the Census, 2003).
4. The average baby boomer held roughly ten jobs between the ages of eighteen and thirty-six, which suggests that the average American holds at least this many in a lifetime. Bureau of Labor Statistics, *Number of Jobs Held, Labor Market Activity, and Earnings Growth among Younger Baby Boomers: Results from More than Two Decades of a Longitudinal Survey*, Bureau of Labor Statistics news release (Washington, D.C.: U.S. Department of Labor, 2002).

5. The U.S. Census Bureau projects that in the coming years, 10 percent of Americans will never marry, 60 percent will marry just once, and 30 percent will marry at least twice. R. M. Kreider and J. M. Fields, *Number, Timing, and Duration of Marriages and Divorces, 1996* (Washington, D.C.: U.S. Bureau of the Census, 2002).

6. B. Russell, *The Analysis of Mind* (New York: Macmillan, 1921), 231.

7. The biologist Richard Dawkins refers to these beliefs as *memes*. See R. J. Dawkins, *The Selfish Gene* (Oxford: Oxford University Press, 1976). See also S. Blackmore, *The Meme Machine* (Oxford: Oxford University Press, 2000).

8. D. C. Dennett, *Brainstorms: Philosophical Essays on Mind and Psychology* (Cambridge, Mass.: Bradford/MIT Press, 1981), 18.

9. R. Layard, *Happiness: Lessons from a New Science* (New York: Penguin, 2005); E. Diener and M. E. P. Seligman, "Beyond Money: Toward an Economy of Well-Being," *Psychological Science in the Public Interest* 5: 1–31 (2004); B. S. Frey and A. Stutzer, *Happiness and Economics: How the Economy and Institutions Affect Human Well-Being* (Princeton, N.J.: Princeton University Press, 2002); R. A. Easterlin, "Income and Happiness: Towards a Unified Theory," *Economic Journal* 111: 465–84 (2001); and D. G. Blanchflower and A. J. Oswald, "Well-Being over Time in Britain and the USA," *Journal of Public Economics* 88: 1359–86 (2004).

10. The effect of declining marginal utility is slowed when we spend our money on the things to which we are least likely to adapt. See T. Scitovsky, *The Joyless Economy: The Psychology of Human Satisfaction* (Oxford: Oxford University Press, 1976); L. Van Boven and T. Gilovich, "To Do or to Have? That Is the Question," *Journal of Personality and Social Psychology* 85: 1193–1202 (2003); and R. H. Frank, "How Not to Buy Happiness," *Daedalus: Journal of the American Academy of Arts and Sciences* 133: 69–79 (2004). Not all economists believe in decreasing marginal utility: R. A. Easterlin, "Diminishing Marginal Utility of Income? Caveat Emptor," *Social Indicators Research* 70: 243–326 (2005).

11. J. D. Graaf et al., *Affluenza: The All-Consuming Epidemic* (New York: Berrett-Koehler, 2002); D. Myers, *The American Paradox: Spiritual Hunger in an Age of Plenty* (New Haven: Yale University Press, 2000); R. H. Frank, *Luxury Fever* (Princeton, N.J.: Princeton University Press, 2000); J. B. Schor, *The Overspent American: Why We Want What We Don't Need* (New York: Perennial, 1999); and P. L. Wachtel, *Poverty of Affluence: A Psychological Portrait of the American Way of Life* (New York: Free Press, 1983).

12. Adam Smith, *An Inquiry into the Nature and Causes of the Wealth of Nations* (1776), book 1 (New York: Modern Library, 1994).

13. Adam Smith, *The Theory of Moral Sentiments* (1759; Cambridge: Cambridge University Press, 2002).

14. N. Ashraf, C. Camerer, and G. Loewenstein, "Adam Smith, Behavorial Economist," *Journal of Economic Perspectives* 19: 131–45 (2005).

15. Smith, *The Theory of Moral Sentiments.*

16. Some theorists have argued that societies exhibit a cyclic pattern in which people do come to realize that money doesn't buy happiness but then forget this lesson a generation later. See A. O. Hirschman, *Shifting Involvements: Private Interest and Public Action* (Princeton, N.J.: Princeton University Press, 1982).

17. C. Walker, "Some Variations in Marital Satisfaction," in *Equalities and Inequalities in Family Life,* ed. R. Chester and J. Peel (London: Academic Press, 1977), 127–39.

18. D. Myers, *The Pursuit of Happiness: Discovering the Pathway to Fulfillment, Well-Being, and Enduring Personal Joy* (New York: Avon, 1992), 71.

19. J. A. Feeney, "Attachment Styles, Communication Patterns and Satisfaction Across the Life Cycle of Marriage," *Personal Relationships* 1: 333–48 (1994).

20. D. Kahneman et al., "A Survey Method for Characterizing Daily Life Experience: The Day Reconstruction Method," *Science* 306: 1776–80 (2004).

21. T. D. Wilson et al., "Focalism: A Source of Durability Bias in Affective Forecasting," *Journal of Personality and Social Psychology* 78: 821–36 (2000).

22. R. J. Norwick, D. T. Gilbert, and T. D. Wilson, "Surrogation: An Antidote for Errors in Affective Forecasting" (unpublished manuscript, Harvard University, 2005).

23. Ibid.

24. Ibid.

25. This is also the best way to predict our future behavior. For example, people overestimate the likelihood that they will perform a charitable act but correctly estimate the likelihood that others will do the same. This suggests that if we would base predictions of our own behavior on what we see others do, we'd be dead-on. See N. Epley and D. Dunning, "Feeling 'Holier Than Thou': Are Self-Serving Assessments Produced by Errors in Self- or Social Prediction?" *Journal of Personality and Social Psychology* 79: 861–75 (2000).

26. R. C. Wylie, *The Self-Concept: Theory and Research on Selected Topics*, vol. 2 (Lincoln: University of Nebraska Press, 1979).

27. L. Larwood and W. Whittaker, "Managerial Myopia: Self-Serving Biases in Organizational Planning," *Journal of Applied Psychology* 62: 194–98 (1977).

28. R. B. Felson, "Ambiguity and Bias in the Self-Concept," *Social Psychology Quarterly* 44: 64–69.

29. D. Walton and J. Bathurst, "An Exploration of the Perceptions of the Average Driver's Speed Compared to Perceived Driver Safety and Driving Skill," *Accident Analysis and Prevention* 30: 821–30 (1998).

30. P. Cross, "Not Can but Will College Teachers Be Improved?" *New Directions for Higher Education* 17: 1–15 (1977).

31. E. Pronin, D. Y. Lin, and L. Ross, "The Bias Blind Spot: Perceptions of Bias in Self versus Others," *Personality and Social Psychology Bulletin* 28: 369–81 (2002).

32. J. Kruger, "Lake Wobegon Be Gone! The 'Below-Average Effect' and the Egocentric Nature of Comparative Ability Judgments," *Journal of Personality and Social Psychology* 77: 221–32 (1999).

33. J. T. Johnson et al., "The 'Barnum Effect' Revisited: Cognitive and Motivational Factors in the Acceptance of Personality Descriptions," *Journal of Personality and Social Psychology* 49: 1378–91 (1985).

34. Kruger, "Lake Wobegon Be Gone!"

35. E. E. Jones and R. E. Nisbett, "The Actor and the Observer: Divergent Perceptions of the Causes of Behavior," in *Attribution: Perceiving the Causes of Behavior*, ed. E. E. Jones et al. (Morristown, N.J.: General Learning Press, 1972); and R. E. Nisbett and E. Borgida, "Attribution and the Psychology of Prediction," *Journal of Personality and Social Psychology* 32: 932–43 (1975).

36. D. T. Miller and C. McFarland, "Pluralistic Ignorance: When Similarity Is Interpreted as Dissimilarity," *Journal of Personality and Social Psychology* 53: 298–305 (1987).

37. D. T. Miller and L. D. Nelson, "Seeing Approach Motivation in the Avoidance Behavior of Others: Implications for an Understanding of Pluralistic Ignorance," *Journal of Personality and Social Psychology* 83: 1066–75 (2002).

38. C. R. Snyder and H. L. Fromkin, "Abnormality as a Positive Characteristic: The Development and Validation of a Scale Measuring Need for Uniqueness," *Journal of Abnormal Psychology* 86: 518–27 (1977).

39. M. B. Brewer, "The Social Self: On Being the Same and Different at the Same Time," *Personality and Social Psychology Bulletin* 17: 475–82 (1991).

40. H. L. Fromkin, "Effects of Experimentally Aroused Feelings of Undistinctiveness upon Valuation of Scarce and Novel Experiences," *Journal of Personality and Social Psychology* 16: 521–29 (1970); and H. L. Fromkin, "Feelings of Interpersonal Undistinctiveness: An Unpleasant Affective State," *Journal of Experimental Research in Personality* 6: 178–85 (1972).

41. R. Karniol, T. Eylon, and S. Rish, "Predicting Your Own and Others' Thoughts and Feelings: More Like a Stranger Than a Friend," *European Journal of Social Psychology* 27: 301–11 (1997); J. T. Johnson, "The Heart on the Sleeve and the Secret Self: Estimations of Hidden Emotion in Self and Acquaintances," *Journal of Personality* 55: 563–82 (1987); and R. Karniol, "Egocentrism versus Protocentrism: The Status of Self in Social Prediction," *Psychological Review* 110: 564–80 (2003).

42. C. L. Barr and R. E. Kleck, "Self-Other Perception of the Intensity of Facial Expressions of Emotion: Do We Know What We Show?" *Journal of Personality and Social Psychology* 68: 608–18 (1995).

43. R. Karniol and L. Koren, "How Would You Feel? Children's Inferences Regarding Their Own and Others' Affective Reactions," *Cognitive Development* 2: 271–78 (1987).

44. C. McFarland and D. T. Miller, "Judgments of Self-Other Similarity: Just Like Other People, Only More So," *Personality and Social Psychology Bulletin* 16: 475–84 (1990).

Questions for Critical Reading

1. What is a "super-replicator"? Develop a definition by rereading Gilbert's text and then offer an example not included in his essay. What function does this concept serve in Gilbert's argument?

2. What does Gilbert mean by *surrogate*? Gilbert never explicitly defines the term. Instead, you should read his text critically and construct a definition out of quotations you find that discuss the idea.

3. Using Gilbert's text, define *happiness*. As with *surrogate*, you will need to analyze Gilbert's text to construct this definition. What does it mean in the context of this essay, and what does it mean for you?

Exploring Context

1. Visit PikiStrips.com and make a comic strip that represents the argument of Gilbert's essay. Incorporate representations for your definitions of the terms in Questions for Critical Reading.

2. What is "happiness"? Put *happy*, *happiness*, and related terms into Google or another search engine. What sort of results do you get? What if you search for

images? What does "happiness" look like on the Web? Does it match the definition you developed in Question 3 of Questions for Critical Reading?

3. Gilbert suggests that if we want to know how happy we will be in the future we should ask someone who's already living our goals. Use Yahoo! Answers (answers.yahoo.com) to ask questions about possible plans for your future. Can the Web function as a surrogate? Use the definition of *surrogate* that you developed in Questions for Critical Reading in your answer.

Questions for Connecting

1. Gilbert examines the happiness produced by both money and children. How does Debora L. Spar's discussion of adoption in "Trading Places: The Practice and Politics of Adoption" (p. 402) challenge these findings? Can adopting children make people happy? You may want to use the definition of happiness you developed in Questions for Critical Reading and Exploring Context.

2. What role does feedback play in the spread of super-replicators? Consider the impact of Steven Johnson's ideas in "Listening to Feedback" (p. 191) on what Gilbert has to say about both super-replicators and happiness, drawing from the understanding of those terms that you developed in Questions for Critical Reading.

3. Gilbert suggests that surrogates can help us predict our future happiness, but can surrogates help us in dealing with other emotions as well? To what extent does Joan Didion function as a surrogate in "After Life" (p. 88)? Does it match your definition from Questions for Critical Reading?

Language Matters

1. Locate information on sentence diagrams. Then select a key sentence from Gilbert's text and diagram the sentence. What are the different parts of the sentence, and how are they related?

2. Locate a sentence in Gilbert's essay that uses *I* as the subject. When does Gilbert use *I*? When doesn't he? When should you?

3. Take a key sentence from Gilbert. Summarize it and then paraphrase it. What's the difference between a summary, a paraphrase, and a quotation? When would you use each in your writing, and what citation does each need?

Assignments for Writing

1. According to Gilbert, surrogates can offer us an accurate sense of our future happiness. Write a paper in which you assess the potential of the kind of surrogates that Gilbert describes. You will want to extend, complicate, or refute Gilbert's argument for surrogates and their reliability in predicting the future. Think about these questions: What role does individuality have in our future

happiness? Is Gilbert correct in claiming that we are not as unique as we believe? Can surrogates be used to examine all future events? How can surrogates be used to control social processes? If we are not unique, why do we see ourselves as individuals? Use your definition of *surrogate* from Question 2 of Questions for Critical Reading as well as your work with Yahoo! Answers from Question 3 of Exploring Context.

2. Write a paper in which you evaluate Gilbert's argument about surrogates and their reliability in predicting the future by finding an appropriate surrogate for you and your future happiness. You may wish to use your experience finding a surrogate on the Web from Question 3 of Exploring Context in making your argument. Also consider: What role does individuality have in our future happiness? Are surrogate examples more accurate than our imagination? What event in your life did you imagine was going to make you happier than it did?

3. Gilbert defines *super-replicators* as genes or beliefs that are given to transmission regardless of their usefulness. Write a paper in which you extend Gilbert's argument through your own example of a super-replicator that persists in society. How do we communicate our ideas to others? What super-replicators are we passing along to those we come into contact with? Does the validity of a belief correlate to its speed of transmission? What is the role of super-replicators in communicating cultural ideas? Use your definition of the term from Question 1 of Questions for Critical Reading.

STEVEN JOHNSON

Steven Johnson is currently serving as the Distinguished Writer in Residence in the journalism department at New York University. He has published five books: *Interface Culture: How New Technology Transforms the Way We Create and Communicate* (1997); *Emergence: The Connected Lives of Ants, Brains, Cities, and Software* (2001); *Mind Wide Open: Your Brain and the Neuroscience of Everyday Life* (2004); *Everything Bad Is Good For You: How Today's Popular Culture Is Actually Making Us Smarter* (2005); and *The Ghost Map: The Story of London's Most Terrifying Epidemic—and How it Changed Science, Cities, and the Modern World* (2006). Johnson has worked as a columnist for multiple magazines, and he is the founder of outside.in, a Web site that collects local information about individual neighborhoods.

Johnson calls *Emergence* "the story of bottom-up intelligence, from slime mold to Slashdot" and reports that it has influenced fields as far-ranging as "political campaigns, Web business models, urban planning, [and] the war on terror." In the book, Johnson explores the impact emergence theory already has had on the construction of neighborhoods, the World Wide Web, and media events, and he predicts that, fueled by the connectedness of the Internet, this power of self-organization will prompt further and fundamental revolutions, akin to those that followed the discovery of electricity.

"Listening to Feedback," an excerpt from *Emergence*, shows the impact of emergence theory in the world of television news media. Formerly structured in a hierarchical, top-down model, television news has increasingly transitioned into "a more bottom-up distributed model." Johnson uses the "positive feedback" model of local and national news outlets as a springboard into a discussion about the consequences of feedback loops and explores as well a different kind of feedback, one that can change "a complex system into a complex *adaptive* system." Johnson investigates the "lack of fatigue" detectable in television news feedback that seems to break the rules of natural feedback loops, the amplification of that same lack of fatigue through the Web, and the positive results that can come from a "mix of hierarchy and heterarchy." Ultimately, Johnson is concerned with finding the correct type and amount of feedback necessary to effectively regulate a complex system; the origins and potential of Slashdot.org and Amazon.com, Johnson suggests, might hold the answer. That answer has something to say to you, since through blogging and sites like YouTube, we all are playing a part in the larger systems of news and, through that, cultural power.

▶ TAGS: *collaboration*, **technology**, *social change*, *conversation*, **community**, *media*

Listening to Feedback

Late in the afternoon of January 23, 1992, during a campaign stop at the American Brush Company in Claremont, New Hampshire, the ABC political reporter Jim Wooten asked then-candidate Bill Clinton about allegations being made by an ex–cabaret singer named Gennifer Flowers. While rumors of Clinton's womanizing had been rampant among the press corps, Wooten's question was the first time the young Democratic front-runner had been asked about a specific woman. "She claims she had a long-standing affair with you," Wooten said with cameras running. "And she says she tape-recorded the telephone conversations with you in which you told her to deny you had ever had an affair."[1]

Wooten said later that Clinton took the question as though he'd been practicing his answer for months. "Well, first of all, I read the story. It isn't true. She has obviously taken money to change the story, a story she felt so strongly about that she hired a lawyer to protect her good name not very long ago. She did call me. I never initiated any calls to her. . . ." The candidate's denials went on for another five minutes, and then the exchange was over. Clinton had responded to the question, but was it news? Across the country, a furious debate on journalistic ethics erupted: Did unproven allegations about the candidate's sex life constitute legitimate news? And did it matter that the candidate himself had chosen to deny the allegations on camera? A cabaret singer making claims about the governor's adulterous past was clearly tabloid material—but what happened when the governor himself addressed the story?

After two long hours of soul-searching, all three major television networks —along with CNN and PBS's MacNeil/Lehrer show—chose not to mention Wooten's question on their national news broadcast, or to show any of the footage from the exchange. The story had emphatically been silenced by some of the most influential figures in all of mass media. The decision to ignore Gennifer Flowers had been unanimous—even at the network that had originally posed the question. Made ten or twenty years before, a decision of that magnitude could have ended a story in its tracks (assuming the *Washington Post* and the *New York Times* followed suit the next morning). For the story to be revived, it would need new oxygen—some new development that caused it to be reevaluated. Without new news, the Flowers story was dead.

And yet the following day, all three networks opened with Gennifer Flowers as their lead item. Nothing had happened to the story itself: None of the protagonists had revealed any additional information; even Clinton's opponents were surprisingly mute about the controversy. The powers that be in New York and Washington had decided the day before that there was no story—and yet here were Peter Jennings and Tom Brokaw leading their broadcasts with the tale of a former Arkansas beauty queen and her scandalous allegations.

How did such a reversal come to pass? It's tempting to resort to the usual hand-wringing about the media's declining standards, but in this case, the most powerful figures in televised media had at first stuck to the high road. If they had truly suffered from declining standards, the network execs would have put Jim

Wooten on the first night. Something pushed them off the high road, and that something was not reducible to a national moral decline or a prurient network executive. Gennifer Flowers rode into the popular consciousness via the *system* of televised news, a system that had come to be wired in a specific way.

What we saw in the winter of 1992 was not unlike watching Nixon sweat his way through the famous televised debate of 1960. As countless critics have observed since, we caught a first glimpse in that exchange of how the new medium would change the substance of politics: Television would increase our focus on the interpersonal skills of our politicians and diminish our focus on the issues. With the Flowers affair, though, the medium hadn't changed; the underlying system had. In the late eighties, changes in the flow of information—and particularly the raw footage so essential to televised news—had pushed the previously top-down system toward a more bottom-up, distributed model. We didn't notice until Jim Wooten first posed that question in New Hampshire, but the world of televised news had taken a significant first step toward emergence. In the hierarchical system of old, the network heads could willfully suppress a story if they thought it was best for the American people not to know, but that privilege died with Gennifer Flowers, and not because of lowered standards or sweeps week. It was a casualty of feedback.

It is commonplace by now to talk about the media's disposition toward feeding frenzies, where the coverage of a story naturally begets more coverage, leading to a kind of hall-of-mirrors environment where small incidents or allegations get amplified into Major Events. You can normally spot one of these feedback loops as it nears its denouement, since it almost invariably triggers a surge of self-loathing that washes through the entire commentariat. These self-critical waters seem to rise on something like an annual cycle: Think of the debate about the paparazzi and Princess Di's death, or the permanent midnight of "Why Do We Care So Much About O.J.?" But the feedback loops of the 1990s weren't an inevitability; they came out of specific changes in the underlying system of mass media, changes that brought about the first stirrings of emergence—and foreshadowed the genuinely bottom-up systems that have since flourished on the Web. That feedback was central to the process should come as no surprise: All decentralized systems rely extensively on feedback, for both growth and self-regulation.

Consider the neural networks of the human brain. On a cellular level, the brain is a massive network of nerve cells connected by the microscopic passageways of axons and dendrites. A flash of brain activity—thinking of a word, wrestling with a concept, parsing the syntax of the sentence you're reading now—triggers an array of neuronal circuits like traffic routes plotted on the map of the mind. Each new mental activity triggers a new array, and an unimaginably large number of possible neuronal circuits go unrealized over the course of a human life (one reason why the persistent loss of brain cells throughout our adult years isn't such a big deal). But beneath all that apparent diversity, certain circuits repeat themselves again and again.[2] One of the most tantalizing hypotheses in neuroscience today is that the cellular basis of learning lies in the repetition of those circuits. As neurologist Richard Restak explains, "Each thought and behavior is embedded within the circuitry of the neurons, and . . . neuronal activity accompanying or initiating an experience persists in the form of reverberating neuronal circuits, which become more strongly defined with repetition. Thus habit and other forms of memory may consist of the establishment of permanent and semipermanent neuronal circuits." A given circuit may initially be associated with the idea of sandwiches, or the shape of an isosceles triangle—and with enough repetition of that specific circuit, it marks out a fixed space in the brain and thereafter becomes part of our mental vocabulary.[3]

Why do these feedback loops and reverberating circuits happen? They come into being because the neural networks of the brain are densely interconnected: Each individual neuron contains links—in the form of axons and synapses—to as many as a thousand other neurons. When a given neuron fires, it relays that charge to all those other cells, which, if certain conditions are met, then in turn relay the charge to their connections, and so on. If each neuron extended a link to one or two fellow neurons, the chance of a reverberating loop would be greatly reduced. But because neurons reach out in so many directions simultaneously, it's far more likely that a given neuron firing will wind its way back to the original source, thus starting the process all over again. The likelihood of a feedback loop correlates directly to the general interconnectedness of the system.[4]

By any measure, the contemporary mediasphere is a densely interconnected system, even if you don't count the linkages of the online world. Connected not just in the sense of so many homes wired for cable and so many rooftops crowned by satellite dishes, but also in the more subtle sense of information being plugged into itself in ever more baroque ways. Since Daniel Boorstin first analyzed the television age in his still-invaluable 1961 work, *The Image*, the world of media journalism has changed in several significant ways, with most of the changes promoting an increase of relays between media outlets. There are far more agents in the system (twenty-four-hour news networks, headline pagers, newsweeklies, Web sites), and far more repackagings and repurposings of source materials, along with an alarming new willingness to relay uncritically other outlets' reporting. Mediated media-critique, unknown in Boorstin's less solipsistic times, and formerly quarantined to early-nineties creations such as CNN's *Reliable Sources* and the occasional Jeff Greenfield segment on *Nightline*, is now regularly the lead story on *Larry King* and *Hardball*. The overall system, in other words, has shifted dramatically in the direction of distributed networks, away from the traditional top-down hierarchies. And the more the media contemplates its own image, the more likely it is that the system will start looping back on itself, like a Stratocaster leaning against the amp it's plugged into.

The upshot of all this is that—in the national news cycle at least—there are no longer any major stories in which the media does not eventually play an essential role, and in many cases the media's knack for self-reflection creates the story itself. You don't need much of an initial impulse to start the whole circuit reverberating. The Gennifer Flowers story is the best example of this process at work. As Tom Rosenstiel reported in a brilliant *New Republic* piece several years ago, the Flowers controversy blossomed because of a shift in the relationship between the national news networks and their local affiliates, a shift that made the entire system significantly more interconnected. Until the late eighties, local news (the six- and eleven-o'clock varieties) relied on the national network for thirty minutes of national news footage, edited according to the august standards of the veterans in New York. Local affiliates could either ignore the national stories or run footage that had been supplied to them, but if the network decided the story wasn't newsworthy, the affiliates couldn't cover it.

All this changed when CNN entered the picture in the mideighties. Since the new network lacked a pool of affiliates to provide breaking news coverage when local events became national stories, Ted Turner embarked on a strategy of wooing local stations with full access to the CNN news feed. Instead of a tightly edited thirty-minute reel, the affiliates would be able to pick and choose from almost anything that CNN cameras had captured, including stories that the executive producers in Atlanta had decided to ignore. The Flowers episode plugged into this newly rewired system, and the results were startling. Local news affiliates nationwide also had access to footage of Clinton's comment, and many of them

The system began calling the shots.

chose to jump on the story, even as the network honchos in New York and Washington decided to ignore it. "When NBC News political editor Bill Wheatley got home and turned on the eleven PM local news that night, he winced: The station NBC owned in New York ran the story the network had chosen not to air the same evening," Rosenstiel writes. "By the next afternoon, even Jim Lehrer of the cautious *MacNeil/Lehrer NewsHour* on PBS told the troops they had to air the Flowers story against their better judgment. 'It's out of my hands,' he said."[5]

The change was almost invisible to Americans watching at home, but its consequences were profound. The mechanism for determining what constituted a legitimate story had been reengineered, shifting from a top-down system with little propensity for feedback, to a kind of journalistic neural net where hundreds of affiliates participated directly in the creation of the story. And what made the circuit particularly vulnerable to reverberation was that the networks themselves mimicked the behavior of the local stations, turning what might have been a passing anomaly into a full-throttle frenzy. That was the moment at which the system began to display emergent behavior. The system began calling the shots, instead of the journalists themselves. Lehrer had it right when he said the Gennifer Flowers affair was "out of my hands." The story was being driven by feedback.

The Flowers affair is a great example of why emergent systems aren't intrinsically good. Tornadoes and hurricanes are feedback-heavy systems too, but that doesn't mean you want to build one in your backyard. Depending on their component parts, and the way they're put together, emergent systems can work toward many different types of goals: some of them admirable, some more destructive. The feedback loops of urban life created the great bulk of the world's most dazzling and revered neighborhoods—but they also have a hand in the self-perpetuating cycles of inner-city misery.[6] Slums can also be emergent phenomena. That's not an excuse to resign ourselves to their existence or to write them off as part of the "natural" order of things. It's reason to figure out a better system. The Flowers affair was an example of early-stage emergence—a system of local agents driving macrobehavior without any central authority calling the shots. But it was not necessarily *adaptive*.

Most of the time, making an emergent system more adaptive entails tinker- 15 ing with different kinds of feedback. In the Flowers affair, we saw an example of what systems theorists call positive feedback—the sort of self-fueling cycles that cause a note strummed on a guitar to expand into a howling symphony of noise.[7] But most automated control systems rely extensively on "negative feedback" devices. The classic example is the thermostat, which uses negative feedback to solve the problem of controlling the temperature of the air in a room. There are actually two ways to regulate temperature. The first would be to design an apparatus capable of blowing air at various different temperatures; the occupant of the room would simply select the desired conditions and the machine would start blowing air cooled or heated to the desired temperature. The problem with that system is twofold: It requires a heating/cooling apparatus capable of blowing air at precise temperatures, and it is utterly indifferent to the room's existing condition. Dial up seventy-two degrees on the thermostat, and the machine will start pumping seventy-two-degree air into the room—even if the room's ambient temperature is already in the low seventies.

The negative feedback approach, on the other hand, provides a simpler solution, and one that is far more sensitive to a changing environment. (Not surprisingly, it's the technique used by most home thermostats.) Instead of pumping precisely calibrated air into the room, the system works with three states: hot air, cool air, and no air. It takes a reading of the room's temperature, measures that reading against the desired setting, and then adjusts its state accordingly. If the room is colder than the desired setting, the hot air goes on. If it is warmer, the cool air flows out. The system continuously measures the ambient temperature and continuously adjusts its output, until the desired setting has been reached—at which point it switches into the "no air" state, where it remains until the ambient temperature changes for some reason. The system uses negative feedback to home in on the proper conditions—and for that reason it can handle random changes in the environment.

Negative feedback, then, is a way of reaching an equilibrium point despite unpredictable—and changing—external conditions. The "negativity" keeps the system in check, just as "positive feedback" propels other systems onward. A thermostat with no feedback simply pumps seventy-two-degree air into a room, regardless of the room's temperature. An imaginary thermostat driven by positive feedback might evaluate the change in room temperature and follow that lead: If the thermostat noted that the room had grown warmer, it would start pumping hotter air, causing the room to grow even warmer, causing the device to pump hotter air. Next thing you know, the water in the goldfish bowl is boiling. Negative feedback, on the other hand, lets the system find the right balance, even in a changing environment. A cold front comes in, a window is opened, someone lights a fire—any of these things can happen, and yet the temperature remains constant. Instead of amplifying its own signal, the system regulates itself.

We've been wrestling with information as a medium for negative feedback ever since Norbert Wiener published *Cybernetics* in 1949, and Wiener himself had been thinking about the relationship between control and feedback since his war-related research of the early forties. After the Japanese bombed Pearl Harbor and the United States joined the war in earnest, Wiener was asked by the army to figure out a way to train mechanical guns to fire automatically at their targets. The question Wiener found himself answering was this: Given enough information about the target's location and movement, could you translate that data into something a machine could use to shoot a V-2 out of the sky?

The problem was uniquely suited for the adaptability of negative feedback: The targets were a mixture of noise and information, somewhat predictable but also subject to sudden changes. But as it happened, to solve the problem Wiener also needed something that didn't really exist yet: a digital computer capable of crunching the flow of data in real time. With that need in mind, Wiener helped build one of the first modern computers ever created. When the story is told of Wiener's war years, the roots of the modern PC are usually emphasized, for legitimate reasons. But the new understanding of negative feedback that emerged from the ENIAC effort had equally far-reaching consequences, extending far beyond the vacuum tubes and punch cards of early computing.[8]

For negative feedback is not solely a software issue, or a device for your home furnace. It is a way of indirectly pushing a fluid, changeable system toward a goal. It is, in other words, a way of transforming a complex system into a complex *adaptive* system. Negative feedback comes in many shapes and sizes. You can build it into ballistic missiles or circuit boards, neurons or blood vessels. It is, in today's terms, "platform agonistic." At its most schematic, negative feedback entails comparing the current state of a system to the desired state, and pushing the system in a direction that minimizes the difference between the two states. As Wiener puts it near the outset of *Cybernetics*: "When we desire a motion to follow a given pattern, the difference between this pattern and the actually performed motion is used as a new input to cause the part regulated to move in such a way as to bring its motion closer to that given by the pattern."[9] Wiener gave that knack for self-regulation a name: homeostasis.[10]

Your body is a massively complex homeostatic system, using an intricate network of feedback mechanisms to keep itself stable in the midst of dynamically changing situations.[11] Many of those feedback mechanisms are maintained by the brain, which coordinates external stimuli received by sensory organs and responds by triggering appropriate bodily actions. Our sleep cycles, for instance, depend heavily on negative feedback. The body's circadian rhythms— accumulated after millions of years of life on a planet with a twenty-four-hour day—flow out of the central nervous system, triggering regular changes in urine formation, body temperature, cardiac output, oxygen consumption, cell division, and the secretions of endocrine glands. But for some reason, our body clocks are set a little slow: The human circadian cycle is twenty-five hours, and so we rely on the external world to reset our clock every day, both by detecting patterns of light and darkness, and by detecting the more subtle change in the earth's magnetic field, which shifts as the planet rotates. Without that negative feedback pulling our circadian rhythms back into sync, we'd find ourselves sleeping through the day for two weeks out of every month. In other words, without that feedback mechanism, it would be as though the entire human race were permanently trapped in sophomore year of college.

Understanding the body and the mind as a feedback-regulated homeostatic system has naturally encouraged some people to experiment with new forms of artificial feedback. Since the seventies, biofeedback devices have reported changes in adrenaline levels and muscle tension in real time to individuals wired up to special machines. The idea is to allow patients to manage their anxiety or stress level by letting them explore different mental states and instantly see the physiological effects. With a little bit of practice, biofeedback patients can easily "drive" their adrenaline levels up or down just by imagining stressful events, or reaching a meditative state. Our bodies, of course, are constantly adjusting adrenaline levels anyway — the difference with biofeedback is that the conscious mind enters into that feedback process, giving patients more direct control over the levels of the hormone in their system. That can be a means of better managing your body's internal state, but it can also be a process of self-discovery. The one time I tried conventional biofeedback, my adrenaline levels hovered serenely at the middle of the range for the first five minutes of the session; the doctor actually complimented me on having such a normal and well-regulated adrenal system. And then, in the course of our conversation, I made a joke — and instantly my adrenaline levels shot off the charts. At the end of my visit, the therapist handed me a printout of the thirty-minute session, with my changing adrenaline levels plotted as a line graph. It was, for all intents and purposes, a computer graph of my attempts at humor over the preceding half hour: a flat line interrupted by six or seven dramatic spikes, each corresponding to a witticism that I had tossed out to the therapist.

I walked away from the session without having improved myself in any noticeable way, and certainly I hadn't achieved more control over my adrenaline levels. But I'd learned something nonetheless: that without consciously realizing it, I'd already established a simple feedback circuit for myself years ago, when my body had learned that it could give itself a targeted adrenaline rush by making a passing joke in conversation. I thought of all those office meetings or ostensibly serious conversations with friends where I had found myself compulsively making jokes, despite the inappropriate context; I thought of how deeply ingrained that impulse is in my day-to-day personality — and suddenly it seemed closer to a drug addiction than a personality trait, my brain scrambling to put together a cheap laugh to secure another adrenaline fix. In a real sense, our personalities are partially the sum of all these invisible feedback mechanisms; but to begin to understand those mechanisms, you need additional levels of feedback — in this case, a simple line graph plotted by an ordinary PC.

If analyzing indirect data such as adrenaline levels can reveal so much about the mind's ulterior motives, imagine the possibilities of analyzing the brain's activity directly.[12] That's the idea behind the technology of neurofeedback: Rather than measure the *results* of the brain's actions, neurofeedback measures brain waves themselves and translates them into computer-generated images and sounds. Certain brain-wave patterns appear in moments of intense concentration; others in states of meditative calm; others in states of distraction, or fear. Neurofeedback — like so many of the systems we've seen — is simply a pattern amplification and recognition device: A series of EEG sensors applied to your skull registers changes in the patterns of your brain waves and transforms them into a medium that you can perceive directly, often in the form of audio tones or colors on a computer screen. As your brain drifts from one state to another, the tone or the image changes, giving you real-time feedback about your brain's EEG activity. With some practice, neurofeedback practitioners can more readily drive their brains toward specific states — because the neurofeedback technology supplies the brain with new data about its own patterns of behavior. Once you've reached a meditative state using neurofeedback, devotees claim, the traditional modes of meditation seem like parallel parking without a rearview mirror — with enough practice, you can pull it off, but you're missing a lot of crucial information.[13]

> **Feedback, after all, is usually not a television thing. You need the Web to hear it wail.**

Were he alive today, I suspect Wiener would be surprised to find that biofeedback [25] and neurofeedback technology are not yet mainstream therapeutic practices. But Wiener also recognized that homeostasis was not exclusively the province of individual human minds and bodies. If systems of neurons could form elaborate feedback mechanisms, why couldn't larger human collectivities? "In connection with the effective amount of communal information," Wiener wrote, "one of the most surprising facts about the body politic is its extreme lack of efficient homeostatic processes."[14] He would have diagnosed the pathology of Gennifer Flowers in a heartbeat.[15] The Flowers episode was an instance of pure positive feedback, unchecked by its opposing force. Each agent's behavior encouraged more like-minded behavior from other agents. There was nothing homeostatic about the process, only the "ever-widening gyre" of positive feedback.

But if positive feedback causes such a ruckus in the media world, how can the brain rely so heavily on the reverberating circuits of neurons? One answer is a familiar term from today's media: *fatigue*. Every neuron in the brain suffers from a kind of regulated impotence: After firing for a stretch, the cell must go through a few milliseconds of inaction, the "absolute refractory period," during which it is immune to outside stimulation. Along with many other ingenious inhibiting schemes that the brain relies on, fatigue is a way of shorting out the reverberating circuit, keeping the brain's feeding frenzy in check.

It is this short circuit that is lacking in the modern media's vast interconnectedness. Stories generate more stories, which generate stories about the coverage of the stories, which generate coverage about the meta-coverage. (Here the brain science seems wonderfully poetic: What better diagnosis for the 24/7 vertigo of media feedback than "lack of fatigue"?) A brain that can't stop reverberating is one way of describing what happens during an epileptic fit; the media version is something like Steven Brill's epic critique of the Lewinsky coverage in the first issue of *Content*: a high-profile media critic launching a new magazine with a high-profile indictment of the media's obsession with its own reporting. If the problem stemmed from errors of judgment made by individual reporters, then a media critique might make sense. But since the problem lies in the media's own tendency for self-amplification, it only makes the problem worse to cover the coverage. It's like firing a pistol in the air to stop a fusillade. Once again, the Flowers affair illustrates the principle: The story wasn't "real news" — according to the network wise men — until other outlets started covering it. The newsworthiness of a given story can't be judged by the play the story is getting on the other channels. Otherwise the gravitational pull of positive feedback becomes too strong, and the loop starts driving the process, more than the reporters *or* the event itself.

It's not overstating things to say that the story that emerged from this loop was a milestone in American history. It's entirely possible that the Flowers controversy would have subsided had Clinton's answer to Jim Wooten been ignored; the Clintons would never have gone on *60 Minutes*, and a whole series of tropes that appeared around the couple (Clinton's philandering, Hillary's anti–Tammy Wynette feminism) might never have found their way into the public mind. Without Gennifer Flowers in Clinton's past, would the Monica Lewinsky affair have played out the same way? Probably not. And if that's the case, then we must ask: What really brought this chain of events about? On the one hand, the answer is simple: Individual life choices made by individual people — Clinton's decision to have an affair, and to break it off, Flowers's decision to go public, Clinton's decision to answer the question — result in a chain of events that eventually stirs up an international news story. But there is another sine qua non here, which is the decision made several years before, somewhere in an office complex in Atlanta, to share the entire CNN news feed with local affiliates. That decision was not quite a "pseudo event," in Boorstin's famous phrase. It was a "system event": a change in the way information flowed through the overall news system. But it was a material change nonetheless.

If you think that Clinton's remarks on Gennifer Flowers should never have been a story, then who are the culprits? Whom do we blame in such a setting? The traditional critiques don't apply here: There's no oak-paneled, cigar-smoke-filled back room where the puppeteers pull their invisible strings; it's not that the television medium is particularly "hot" or "cold"; there was a profit motive behind CNN's decision to share more footage, but we certainly can't write off the Flowers episode as just another tribute to the greed of the network execs. Once again, we return to the fundamental laws of emergence: The behavior of individual agents is less important than the overall system. In earlier times, the channels that connected politicians, journalists, and ordinary citizens were one-way and hierarchical; they lacked the connections to generate true feedback; and too few agents were interacting to create any higher-level order. But the cable explosion of the eighties changed all that. For the first time, the system started to reverberate on its own. The sound was quiet during those initial years and may not have crossed into an audible range until Jim Wooten asked that question. And yet anyone who caught the nightly news on January 24, 1992, picked up its signal loud and clear.

Still, the top-heavy structure of mass media may keep those loops relatively muted for the foreseeable future, at least where the tube is concerned. Feedback, after all, is usually not a television thing. You need the Web to hear it wail.

In June of 1962, a full year after the appearance of *The Death and Life of Great American Cities*, Lewis Mumford published a scathing critique of Jane Jacobs's manifesto in his legendary *New Yorker* column, "The Sky Line." In her prescriptions for a sidewalk-centric urban renewal, "Mother Jacobs"—as Mumford derisively called her—offered a "homemade poultice for the cure of cancer." The *New Yorker* critic had been an early advocate of Jacobs's work, encouraging her to translate her thoughts into a book while she was a junior editor at *Architecture Forum* in the midfifties. But the book she eventually wrote attacked Mumford's much-beloved Ebenezer Howard and his "garden cities," and so Mumford struck back at his onetime protégé with full fury.[16]

At over ten thousand words, Mumford's critique was extensive and wide-ranging, but the central message came down to the potential of metropolitan centers to self-regulate. Jacobs had argued that large cities can achieve a kind of homeostasis through the interactions generated by lively sidewalks; urban planning that attempted to keep people off the streets was effectively destroying the lifeblood of the urban system. Without the open, feedback-heavy connections of street culture, cities quickly became dangerous and anarchic places. Building a city without sidewalks, Jacobs argued, was like building a brain without axons or dendrites. A city without connections was no city at all, at least in the traditional sense of organic city life. Better to build cities that encouraged the feedback loops of sidewalk traffic by shortening the length of blocks and supporting mixed-use zoning.[17]

Mumford was no fan of the housing projects of the postwar era, but he had lost faith in the self-regulatory powers of massive urban systems. Cities with populations in the millions simply put too much stress on the natural homeostatic tendencies of human collectives. In *The City in History*, published around the same period, Mumford had looked back at the Greek city-states, and their penchant for founding new units once the original community reached a certain size—the urban equivalent of reproducing by spores. His attachment to Ebenezer Howard also stemmed from the same lack of confidence in metropolitan self-regulation: The Garden City movement—not entirely unlike the New Urbanist movement of today—was an attempt to provide the energy and dynamism of city life in smaller doses.[18] The Italian hill towns of the Renaissance had achieved an ideal mix of density and diversity while keeping their overall population within reasonable bounds (reined in largely by the walls that surrounded them). These were street-centric spaces with a vibrant public culture, but they remained knowable communities too: small enough to foster a real sense of civic belonging. That kind of organic balance, Mumford argued, was impossible in a city of 5 million people where the noise and congestion—the sensory overload of it all—drained out the "vitality" from the city streets. "Jacobs forgets that in organisms there is no tissue growth quite as 'vital' or 'dynamic' as cancer growths. . . . The author has forgotten the most essential characteristic of all organic growth—to maintain diversity and balance, the organism must not exceed the norm of its species. Any ecological association eventually reaches the 'climax stage,' beyond which growth without deterioration is not possible."[19]

Like many debates from the annals of urban studies, the Mumford/Jacobs exchange over the "climax stage" of city life mirrors recent developments in the digital realm, as Web-based communities struggle to manage the problems of runaway growth.[20] The first generation of online hangouts—dial-up electronic bulletin boards like ECHO or the Well—were the equivalent of those Italian hill towns: lively, innovative, contentious places, but also places that remained within a certain practical size. In their heyday before the Web's takeoff, both services hovered around five thousand members, and within that population, community leaders and other public characters naturally emerged: the jokers and the enablers, the fact checkers and the polemicists. These characters—many of them concealed behind playful pseudonyms—served as the equivalent of Jacobs's shopkeepers and bartenders, the regular "eyes on the street" that give the neighborhood its grounding and its familiarity.

These online communities also divided themselves into smaller units organized around specific topics. Like the trade-specific clusters of Savile Row and the Por Santa Maria, these divisions made the overall space more intelligible, and their peculiarities endowed each community with a distinctive flavor. (For the first few years of its existence, the Grateful Dead discussion area on the Well was larger than all the other areas combined.) Because each topic area attracted a smaller subset of the overall population, visiting each one felt like returning to an old block in a familiar part of town, and running into the same cast of characters that you had found there the last time you visited.

ECHO and the Well had a certain homeostatic balance in those early years—powerfully captured in Howard Rheingold's book *The Virtual Community*—and part of that balance came from the community's own powers of self-organization. But neither was a pure example of bottom-up behavior: The topic areas, for instance, were central-planning affairs, created by fiat and not by footprints; both communities benefited from the strong top-down leadership of their founders. That their overall populations never approached a "climax stage" reflected the slow modem-adoption curve of the general public, and the limited marketing budgets at both operations. More important, the elements of each community that did self-regulate had little to do with the underlying software. Anyone who spent any time on those services in the early nineties will tell you that community leaders and other recognizable figures emerged, but that status existed only in the perceptions of the users themselves. The software itself was agnostic when it came to status, but because the software brought hominid minds together—minds that are naturally inclined to establish hierarchies in social relationships—leaders and pariahs began to appear. The software did recognize official moderators for each discussion area, but those too were appointments handed down from above; you applied to the village chieftain for the role that you desired, and if you'd been a productive member of the society, your wish might be granted. The[re] were plenty of unofficial leaders, to be sure—but where the code was concerned, the only official moderators came straight from the top.

This mix of hierarchy and heterarchy was well suited to ECHO's and the Well's stage of growth. At five thousand members, the community was still small enough to be managed partially from above, and small enough that groups and recognizable characters naturally emerged. At that scale, you didn't need to solve the problem of self-regulation with software tools: All you needed was software that connected people's thoughts—via the asynchronous posts of a threaded discussion board—and the community could find its own balance. If something went wrong, you could always look to the official leaders for guidance. But even in those heady early days of the virtual community, the collective systems of ECHO and the Well fell short of achieving real homeostasis, for reasons that would become endemic to the next generation of communities then forming on the Web itself.

A threaded discussion board turns out to be an ideal ecosystem for that peculiar species known as the crank—the ideologue obsessed with a certain issue or interpretive model, who has no qualms about interjecting his or her worldview into any discussion, and apparently no day job or family life to keep him from posting voluminous commentary at the slightest provocation. We all know people like this, the ones grinding their ax from the back of the seminar room or the coffee shop: the conspiracy theorist, the rabid libertarian, the evangelist—the ones who insist on bringing all conversations back to their particular issue, objecting to any conversation that doesn't play by their rules. In real life, we've developed a series of social conventions that keep the crank from dominating our conversations. For the most pathological cases, they simply don't get invited out to dinner very often. But for the borderline case, a subtle but powerful mechanism is at work in any face-to-face group conversation: If an individual is holding a conversation hostage with an irrelevant obsession, groups can naturally establish a consensus—using words, body language, facial expressions, even a show of hands—making it clear that the majority of the group feels their time is being wasted. The face-to-face world is populated by countless impromptu polls that take the group's collective pulse. Most of them happen so quickly that we don't even know that we're participating in them, and that transparency is one reason why they're as powerful as they are. In the face-to-face world, we are all social thermostats: reading the group temperature and adjusting our behavior accordingly.

Some of those self-regulatory social skills translate into cyberspace—particularly in a threaded discussion forum or an e-mail exchange, where participants have the time and space to express their ideas in long form, rather than in the spontaneous eruptions of real-time chat. But there is a crucial difference in an environment like ECHO or the Well—or in the discussion areas we built at *FEED*. In a public discussion thread, not all the participants are visible. A given conversation may have five or six active contributors and several dozen "lurkers" who read through the posts but don't chime in with their own words. This creates a fundamental imbalance in the system of threaded discussion and gives the crank an opportunity to dominate the space in a way that would be much more difficult offline. In a threaded discussion, you're speaking both to the other active participants and to the lurkers, and however much you might offend or bore your direct interlocutors, you can always appeal to that silent majority out there—an audience that is both present and absent at the same time. The crank can cling to the possibility that everyone else tuning in is enthralled by his prose, while the active participants can't turn to the room and say, "Show of hands: Is this guy a lunatic or what?"

The crank exploits a crucial disparity in the flow of information: While 40 we conventionally think of threaded discussions as two-way systems, for the lurkers that flow follows a one-way path. They hear us talking, but we hear nothing of them: no laughs, no hisses, no restless stirring, no snores, no rolling eyeballs. When you factor in the lurkers, a threaded discussion turns out to be less interactive than a traditional face-to-face lecture, and significantly less so than a conversation around a dinner table, where even the most reticent participants contribute with gestures and facial expressions. Group conversations in the real world have an uncanny aptitude for reaching a certain kind of homeostasis: The conversation moves toward a zone that pleases as much of the group as possible and drowns out voices that offend. A group conversation is a kind of circuit board, with primary inputs coming from the official speakers, and secondary inputs coming from the responses of the audience and other speakers. The primary inputs adjust their signal based on the secondary inputs of group feedback. Human beings . . . are exceptionally talented at assessing the mental states of other people, both through the direct exchanges of spoken language and the more oblique feedback mechanisms of gesture and intonation. That two-way exchange gives our face-to-face group conversations precisely the flexibility and responsiveness that Wiener found lacking in mass communications.

I suspect Wiener would immediately have understood the virtual community's problem with cranks and lurkers. Where the Flowers affair was a case of runaway positive feedback, the tyranny of the crank results from a scarcity of feedback: a system where the information flows are unidirectional, where the audience is present and at the same time invisible. These liabilities run parallel to the problems of one-way linking. . . . Hypertext links and virtual communities were supposed to be the advance guard of the interactive revolution, but in a real sense they only got halfway to the promised land. (Needless to say, the ants were there millions of years ago.) And if the cranks and obsessive-compulsives flourish in a small-scale online community of several thousand members, imagine the anarchy and noise generated by a million community members. Surely there is a "climax stage" on that scale where the online growth turns cancerous, where the knowable community becomes a nightmare of overdevelopment. If feedback couldn't help regulate the digital villages of early online communication, what hope can it possibly have on the vast grid of the World Wide Web?

The sleepy college town of Holland, Michigan, might seem like the last place you'd expect to generate a solution for the problem of digital sprawl, but the Web has never played by the rules of traditional geography. Until recent years, Holland had been best known for its annual tulip festival. But it is increasingly recognized as the birthplace of Slashdot.org—the closest thing to a genuinely self-organizing community that the Web has yet produced.

Begun as a modest bulletin board by a lifetime Hollander named Rob Malda, Slashdot came into the world as the ultimate in knowable communities: just Malda and his friends, discussing programming news, Star Wars rumors, video games, and other geek-chic marginalia. "In the beginning, Slashdot was small," Malda writes. "We got dozens of posts each day, and it was good. The signal was high, the noise was low."[21] Before long, though, Slashdot floated across the rising tsunami of Linux and the Open Source movement and found itself awash in thousands of daily visitors. In its early days, Slashdot had felt like the hill towns of ECHO and the Well, with strong leadership coming from Malda himself, who went by the handle Commander Taco. But the volume of posts became too much for any single person to filter out the useless information. "Trolling and spamming became more common," Malda says now, "and there wasn't enough time for me to personally keep them in check and still handle my other responsibilities."

Malda's first inclination was to create a Slashdot elite: twenty-five hand-picked spam warriors who would sift through the material generated by the community, eliminating irrelevant or obnoxious posts. While the idea of an elite belonged to a more hierarchical tradition, Malda endowed his lieutenants with a crucial resource: They could rate other contributions, on a scale of −1 to 5. You could browse through Slashdot.org with a "quality filter" on, effectively telling the software, "Show me only items that have a rating higher than 3." This gave his lieutenants a positive function as well as a negative one. They could emphasize the good stuff and reward users who were productive members of the community.

Soon, though, Slashdot grew too large for even the elites to manage, and Malda went back to the drawing board. It was the kind of thing that could only have happened on the Web. A twenty-two-year-old college senior, living with a couple of buddies in a low-rent house—affectionately dubbed Geek House One—in a nondescript Michigan town, creates an intimate online space for his friends to discuss their shared obsessions, and within a year fifty thousand people each day are angling for a piece of the action. Without anything resembling a genuine business infrastructure, much less a real office, Malda needed far more than his twenty-five lieutenants to keep the Slashdot community from descending into complete anarchy. But without the resources to hire a hundred full-time moderators, Slashdot appeared to be stuck at the same impasse that Mumford had described thirty years before: stay small and preserve the quality of the original community; keep growing and sacrifice everything that had made the community interesting in the first place. Slashdot had reached its "climax stage."

What did the Commander do? Instead of expanding his pool of special authorized lieutenants, he made *everyone* a potential lieutenant. He handed over the quality-control job to the community itself. His goals were relatively simple, as outlined in the Frequently Asked Questions document on the site:

1. Promote quality, discourage crap.
2. Make Slashdot as readable as possible for as many people as possible.
3. Do not require a huge amount of time from any single moderator.
4. Do not allow a single moderator a "reign of terror."

Together, these objectives define the parameters of Slashdot's ideal state. The question for Malda was how to build a homeostatic system that would naturally push the site toward that state without any single individual being in control. The solution that he arrived at should be immediately recognizable by now: a mix of negative and positive feedback, structured randomness, neighbor interactions, and decentralized control. From a certain angle, Slashdot today resembles an ant colony. From another, it looks like a virtual democracy. Malda himself likens it to jury duty.

Here's how it works: If you've spent more than a few sessions as a registered Slashdot user, the system may on occasion alert you that you have been given moderator status (not unlike a jury summons arriving in your mailbox). As in the legal analogy, moderators only serve for a finite stretch of time, and during that stretch they have the power to rate contributions made by other users, on a scale of −1 to 5.[22] But that power diminishes with use: Each moderator is endowed only with a finite number of points that he or she can distribute by rating user contributions. Dole out all your ratings, and your tenure as a moderator comes to an end.

Those ratings coalesce into something that Malda called karma: If your contributions as a user are highly rated by the moderators, you earn karma in the system, giving you special privileges. Your subsequent posts begin life at a higher rating than usual, and you are more likely to be chosen as a moderator in future sessions. This last privilege exemplifies meta-feedback at work, the ratings snake devouring its own tail: Moderators rate posts, and those ratings are used to select future moderators. Malda's system not only encouraged quality in the submissions to the site; it also set up an environment where community leaders could naturally rise to the surface. That elevation was specifically encoded in the software. Accumulating karma on Slashdot was not just a metaphor for winning the implicit trust of the Slashdot community; it was a quantifiable number. Karma had found a home in the database.

Malda's point system brings to mind the hit points of Dungeons & Dragons ⁵⁰ and other classics of the role-playing genre. (That the Slashdot crowd was already heavily versed in the role-playing idiom no doubt contributed a great deal to the rating system's quick adoption.) But Malda had done something more ambitious than simply porting gaming conventions to the community space. He had created a kind of currency, a pricing system for online civics. By ensuring that the points would translate into special privileges, he gave them value. By making one's moderation powers expendable, he created the crucial property of scarcity. With only one or the other, the currency is valueless; combine the two, and you have a standard for pricing community participation that actually works.

The connection between pricing and feedback is itself more than a metaphor. As a character in Jane Jacobs's recent Socratic dialogue, *The Nature of Economies*, observes: "Adam Smith, back in 1775, identified prices of goods and rates of wages as feedback information, although of course he didn't call it that because the word *feedback* was not in the vocabulary at the time. But he understood the idea. . . . In his sober way, Smith was clearly excited about the marvelous form of order he'd discovered, as well he should have been. He was far ahead of naturalists in grasping the principle of negative feedback controls."[23]

Malda himself claims that neither *The Wealth of Nations* nor *The Dungeon Master's Guide* were heavy in his thoughts in Geek House One. "There wasn't really anything specific that inspired me," Malda says now. "It was mostly trial and error. The real influence was my desire to please users with very different expectations for Slashdot. Some wanted it to be Usenet: anything goes and unruly. Others were busy people who only wanted to read three to four comments a day."[24] You can see the intelligence and flexibility of the system firsthand: Visit the Slashdot site and choose to view all the posts for a given conversation. If the conversation is more than a few hours old, you'll probably find several hundred entries, with at least half of them the work of cranks and spammers. Such is the fate of any Web site lucky enough to attract thousands of posts an hour.

Set your quality threshold to four or five, however, and something miraculous occurs. The overall volume drops precipitously—sometimes by an order of magnitude—but the dozen or two posts that remain will be as stimulating as anything you've read on a traditional content site where the writers and the editors are actually paid to put their words and arguments together. It's a miracle not so much because the quality is lurking there somewhere in the endless flood of posting. Rather, it's a miracle because the community has collectively done such an exceptional job at bringing that quality to light. In the digital world, at least, there is life after the climax stage.

Slashdot is only the beginning. In the past two years, user ratings have become the kudzu of the Web, draping themselves across pages everywhere you look. Amazon had long included user ratings for all the items in its inventory, but in 1999 it began to let users rate the reviews of other users. An ingenious site called Epinions cultivates product reviews from its audience and grants "trust" points to contributors who earn the community's respect. The online auction system of eBay utilizes two distinct feedback mechanisms layered on top of each other: the price feedback of the auction bids coupled to the user ratings that evaluate buyers and sellers. One system tracks the value of stuff; the other tracks the value of people.

Indeed, the adoption rate for these feedback devices is accelerating so rapidly that I suspect in a matter of years a Web page without a dynamic rating system attached will trigger the same response that a Web page without hyperlinks triggers today: Yes, it's technically possible to create a page without these features, but what's the point? The Slashdot system might seem a little complex, a little esoteric for consumers who didn't grow up playing D&D, but think of the millions of people who learned how to use a computer for the first time in the past few years, just to get e-mail or to surf the Web. Compared to that learning curve, figuring out the rules of Slashdot is a walk in the park.

And rules they are. You can't think of a system like the one Malda built at Slashdot as a purely *representational* entity, the way you think about a book or a movie. It is partly representational, of course: You read messages via the Slashdot platform, and so the components of the textual medium that Marshall McLuhan so brilliantly documented in *The Gutenberg Galaxy* are on display at Slashdot as well. Because you are reading words, your reception of the information behind those words differs from what it would have been had that information been conveyed via television. The medium is still the message on Slashdot—it's just that there's another level to the experience, a level that our critical vocabularies are only now finding words for.

In a Slashdot-style system, there is a medium, a message, and an audience. So far, no different from television. The difference is that those elements exist alongside a set of rules that govern the way the messages flow through the system. "Interactivity" doesn't do justice to the significance of this shift. A button that lets you e-mail a response to a published author; a tool that lets you build your own home page; even a collection of interlinked pages that let you follow your own path through them—these are all examples of interactivity, but they're in a different category from the self-organizing systems of eBay or Slashdot. Links and home-page-building tools are cool, no question. But they are closer to a newspaper letters-to-the-editor page than Slashdot's collective intelligence.

First-generation interactivity may have given the consumer a voice, but systems like Slashdot force us to accept a more radical proposition: To understand how these new media experiences work, you have to analyze the message, the medium, *and the rules*. Think of those thousand-post geek-Dionysian frenzies transformed into an informative, concise briefing via the Slashdot quality filters. What's interesting here is not just the medium, but rather the rules that govern what gets selected and what doesn't. It's an algorithmic problem, then, and not a representational one. It is the difference between playing a game of Monopoly and hanging a Monopoly board on your wall. There are representational forces unleashed by a game of Monopoly (you have to be able to make out the color coding of the various properties and to count your money) but what makes the game interesting — indeed, what makes it a game at all — lies in the instruction set that you follow while playing. Slashdot's rules are what make the medium interesting — so interesting, in fact, that you can't help thinking they need their own category, beyond message *and* medium.

Generically, you can describe those rules as a mix of positive and negative feedback pushing the system toward a particular state based on the activities of the participants. But the mix is different every time. The edge cities of Paul Krugman's model used feedback to create polycentric clusters, while other metropolitan systems collapse into a single, dense urban core. The networks in CNN-era television have engendered runaway positive feedback loops such as the Gennifer Flowers story, while a system like Slashdot achieves homeostatic balance, at least when viewed at level 5. Different feedback systems produce different results — even when those systems share the same underlying medium. In the future, every Web site may well be connected to a rating mechanism, but that doesn't mean all Web sites will behave the same way. There may be homeostasis at Slashdot's level 5, but you can always choose to read the unfiltered, anarchic version at level –1.

Is there a danger in moving to a world where all our media responds directly to user feedback? Some critics, such as *The Control Revolution*'s Andrew Shapiro, worry about the tyranny of excessive user personalization, as in the old Nicholas Negroponte vision of the *Daily Me*, the newspaper perfectly custom-tailored to your interests — so custom-tailored, in fact, that you lose the serendipity and surprise that we've come to expect from reading the newspaper. There's no stumbling across a different point of view, or happening upon an interesting new field you knew nothing about — the *Daily Me* simply feeds back what you've instructed the software to find, and nothing more. It's a mind-narrowing experience, not a mind-expanding one. That level of personalization may well be around the corner. . . . But for now, it's worth pointing out that the Slashdot system is indifferent to your personal interests — other than your interest in a general level of quality. The "ideal state" that the Slashdot system homes in on is not defined by an individual's perspective; it is defined by the overall group's perspective. The collective decides what's quality and what's crap, to use Rob Malda's language. You can tweak the quality-to-crap ratio based on your individual predilections, but the ratings themselves emerge through the actions of the community at large. It's more groupthink than *Daily Me*.

Perhaps, then, the danger lies in too much groupthink. Malda designed his system to evaluate submissions based on the average Slashdot reader — although the karma points tend to select moderators who have a higher-than-average reputation within the community. It's entirely possible that Malda's rules have created a tyranny of the majority at Slashdot, at least when viewed at level 5. Posts that resonate with the "average" Slashdotter are more likely to rise to the top, while posts that express a minority viewpoint may be demoted in the system. (Technically, the moderation guidelines suggest that users should rate posts based purely on quality, not on whether they agree with the posts,

60

but the line is invariably a slippery one.) From this angle, then, Slashdot bears a surprising resemblance to the old top-down universe of pre-cable network television. Both systems have a heavy center that pulls content toward the interests of the "average user"—like a planet pulling satellites into its orbit. In the days before cable fragmentation, the big three networks were competing for the entire television-owning audience, which encouraged them to serve up programming designed for the average viewer rather than for a particular niche. (McLuhan observed how this phenomenon was pushing the political parties toward the center as well.) The network decision to pursue the center rather than the peripheries was invariably made at the executive level, of course—unlike at Slashdot, where the centrism comes from below. But if you're worried about suppressing diversity, it doesn't really matter whether it comes from above or below. The results are the same, either way. Majority viewpoints get amplified, while minority viewpoints get silenced.

This critique showcases why we need a third term beyond *medium* and *message*. While it's true that Slashdot's filtering software creates a heavy center, that tendency is not inherent to the Web medium, or even the subset of online communities. You could just as easily build a system that would promote both quality *and* diversity, simply by tweaking the algorithm that selects moderators. Change a single variable in the mix, and a dramatically different system emerges. Instead of picking moderators based on the average rating of their posts, the new system picks moderators whose contributions have triggered the greatest range of responses. In this system, a member who was consistently rated highly by the community would be unlikely to be chosen as a moderator, while a member who inspired strong responses either way—both positive and negative—would be first in line to moderate. The system would reward controversial voices rather than popular ones. You'd still have moderators deleting useless spam and flamebait, and so the quality filters would remain in place. But the fringe voices in the community would have a stronger presence at level 5, because the feedback system would be rewarding perspectives that deviate from the mainstream, that don't aim to please everyone all the time. The cranks would still be marginalized, assuming their polemics annoyed almost everyone who came across them. But the thoughtful minorities—the ones who attract both admirers *and* detractors—would have a place at the table.

There's no reason why centrist Slashdot and diverse Slashdot can't coexist. If you can adjust the quality filters on the fly, you could just as easily adjust the diversity filters. You could design the system to track the ratings of both popular and controversial moderators; users would then be able to view Slashdot through the lens of the "average" user on one day, and through the lens of a more diverse audience the next. The medium and the message remain the same; only the rules change from one system to the other. Adjust the feedback loops, and a new type of community appears on the screen. One setting gives you Gennifer Flowers and cyclone-style feeding frenzies, another gives you the shapeless datasmog of Usenet. One setting gives you an orderly, centrist community strong on shared values, another gives you a multiculturalist's fantasy. As Wiener recognized a half century ago, feedback systems come in all shapes and sizes. When we come across a system that doesn't work well, there's no point in denouncing the use of feedback itself. Better to figure out the specific rules of the system at hand and start thinking of ways to wire it so that the feedback routines promote the values we want promoted. It's the old sixties slogan transposed into the digital age: If you don't like the way things work today, change the system.

BIBLIOGRAPHY

Dean, Katie. "Attention Kids: Play This Game." *Wired News.* December 19, 2000.

De Landa, Manuel. *A Thousand Years of Nonlinear History.* New York: Zone Books, Swerve Editions, 1997.

Edelman, Gerald M. *Bright Air, Brilliant Fire: On the Matter of Mind.* New York: Basic Books, 1992.

Jacobs, Jane. *The Death and Life of Great American Cities.* New York: Vintage, 1961.

———. *The Nature of Economies.* New York: Modern Library Original, 2000.

Kurzweil, Ray. *The Age of Spiritual Machines: When Computers Exceed Human Intelligence.* New York: Penguin Books, 1999.

Mumford, Lewis. *The City in History: Its Origins, Its Transformations and Its Prospects.* New York and London: Harcourt, Brace, Jovanovich, 1961.

Ridley, Matt. *Genome: The Autobiography of a Species in 23 Chapters.* New York: HarperCollins, 1999.

Rosenstiel, Tom. *Strange Bedfellows: How Television and the Presidential Candidates Changed American Politics, 1992.* New York: Hyperion, 1993.

Wiener, Norbert. *Cybernetics: or, Control and Communication in the Animal and the Machine.* Cambridge, Mass.: MIT Press, 1948.

Wright, Robert. *NonZero: The Logic of Human Destiny.* New York: Pantheon Books, 2000.

NOTES

1. Rosenstiel, 55–65.
2. This is true also for the interaction between the brain and the rest of the body. "Nervous system behavior is to some extent self-generated in loops; brain activity leads to movement, which leads to further sensation and perception and still further movement. The layers and the loops between them are the most intricate of any object we know, and they are dynamic; they continually change." Edelman, 1992, 29.
3. "What is learning? What changes occur to nerve cells when the brain (or the abdominal ganglion) acquires a new habit or a change in its behavior? The central nervous system consists of lots of nerve cells, down each of which electrical signals travel; and synapses, which are junctions between nerve cells. When an electrical nerve signal reaches a synapse, it must transfer to chemical agent, like a train passenger catching a ferry across a sea channel, before resuming its electrical journey. Kandel's attention quickly focused on these synapses between neurons. Learning seems to be a change in their properties. Thus when a sea slug habituates to a false alarm, the synapse between the

receiving, sensory neuron and the neuron that moves the gill is somehow weakened. Conversely, when the sea slug is sensitized to the stimulus, the synapse is strengthened." Ridley, 223.

4. Edelman has a far more precise variation on this theme, which he calls "reentry." "To explain how categorization may occur, we can use the workings of what I have called a 'classification couple' in the brain. This is a minimal unit consisting of two functionally different maps made up of neuronal groups and connected by reentry. Each map independently receives signals from other brain maps or from the world (in this example the signals come from the world). Within a certain time period, reentrant signaling strongly connects certain active combinations of neuronal groups in one map to different combinations in the other map." Edelman, 1992, 87.

5. Rosenstiel, 63.

6. Jacobs wrote about this in *Death and Life* as the tendency for successful cities to destroy themselves: "These forces, in the form that they work for ill, are: the tendency for outstandingly successful diversity in cities to destroy itself; the tendency for massive single elements in cities (many of which are necessary and otherwise desirable) to cast a deadening influence; the tendency for population instability to counter the growth of diversity; and the tendency for both public and private money either to glut or to starve development and change." Jacobs, 1961, 242.

7. . . . Positive feedback is also an important tool for understanding social or technological revolutions: "These meshworks of mutually supporting innovations (coal-iron-steam-cotton) are well-known to historians of technology. They existed long before the nineteenth century (e.g., the interlocking web formed by the horseshoe, the horse harness, and triennial rotation which was behind the agricultural intensification at the turn of the millennium), and they occurred afterward, as in the meshwork of oil, electricity, steel, and synthetic materials that contributed to the second industrial revolution. Nonetheless, as important as they were, autocatalytic loops of technologies were not complex enough to create a self-sustained industrial takeoff. Before the 1800s, as we noted, these intensifications often led back to depictions of resources and diminishing returns. Negative feedback eventually checked the turbulent growth generated by positive feedback." De Landa, 1997, 77.

8. As usual, Jane Jacobs was quick to adapt these new ideas to her understanding of the city: "The analogy that comes to mind is faulty feedback. The conception of electronic feedback has become familiar with the development of computers and automated machinery, where one of the end products of an act or series of acts by the machine is a signal which modifies and guides the next act. A similar feedback process, regulated chemically rather than electronically, is now believed to modify some of the behavior of cells. A report in the *New York Times* explains it thus:

> " 'The presence of an end product in the milieu of a cell causes the machinery that produces the end product to slow down or to stop. This form of cell behavior Dr. [Van R.] Potter [of the University of Wisconsin Medical School] characterized as "intelligent." In contrast, a cell that has changed or mutated behaves like an "idiot" in that it continues without feedback regulation to produce even materials that it does not require.'
>
> "I think that last sentence is a fair description of the behavior of city localities where the success of diversity destroys itself.

"Suppose we think of successful city areas, for all their extraordinary and intricate economic and social order, as faulty in this fashion. In creating city success, we human beings have created marvels, but we left out feedback. What can we do with cities to make up for this omission?" Jacobs, 1961, 251–52.

9. Wiener, 7.

10. "In short, our inner economy must contain an assembly of thermostats, automatic hydrogen-ion-concentration controls, governors, and the like, which would be adequate for a great chemical plant. These are what we know collectively as our homeostatic mechanism." Ibid., 115.

11. Ecosystems too abound with feedback systems. As one of the characters in Jane Jacobs's latest book says, "Here's a pleasing example of this category—a positive loop in a California coastal redwood forest. Mature redwoods require enormous amounts of water, about twice as much, on average, as rainfall delivers to their habitats. . . . A coastal redwood lives to an age of about two thousand years; quite a demonstration of successful survival. Here's how their seemingly inadequate supply situation is overcome. With their fine and luxuriant needles, the trees intercept fog and strip its moisture; in effect, they take water straight from clouds. During a dry but foggy night, each tall redwood douses the ground beneath it with as much water as if there had been a drenching rainstorm. This beneficent process works as a loop. The growth of the trees is fed in good part from the fog. Taller growth gives trees access to higher—hence additional—fog. Additional fog feeds still higher growth. And so on. Because of the height-fog loop, the trees themselves participate in keeping their environment stable." Jacobs, 2000, 93.

12. Dean.

13. "There is already one technology that appears to generate at least one aspect of a spiritual experience. This experimental technology is called Brain Generated Music (BGM), pioneered by NeuroSonics, a small company in Baltimore, Maryland, of which I am a director. BGM is a brain-wave biofeedback system capable of evoking an experience called the Relaxation Response, which is associated with deep relaxation. The BGM user attaches three disposable leads to her head. A personal computer then monitors the user's brain waves to determine her unique alpha wavelength. Alpha waves, which are in the range of eight to thirteen cycles per second (cps), are associated with a deep meditative state, as compared to beta waves (in the range of thirteen to twenty-eight cps), which are associated with routine conscious thought. Music is then generated by the computer, according to an algorithm that transforms the user's own brain-wave signal." Kurzweil,157.

14. Wiener, 158.

15. ". . . One of the directions of work which the realm of ideas of the Macy meetings has suggested concerns the importance of the notion and the technique of communication in the social system. It is certainly true that the social system is an organization like the individual, that it is bounded together by a system of communication, and that it has a dynamics in which circular processes of a feedback nature play an important part." Ibid., 24.

16. "The program he proposed in 1898 was to halt the growth of London and also repopulate the countryside, where villages were declining, by building a new kind of town—the Garden City, where the city poor might again live close to

nature. So they might earn their livings, industry was to be set up in the Garden City, for while Howard was not planning cities, he was not planning dormitory suburbs either. His aim was the creation of self-sufficient small towns, really very nice towns if you were docile and had no plans of your own and did not mind spending your life among others who had no plans of their own. As in all Utopias, the right to have plans of any significance belonged only to the planners in charge." Jacobs, 1961, 17.

17. "Ebenezer Howard's vision of the Garden City would seem almost feudal to us. He seems to have thought that members of the industrial working classes would stay neatly in their class, and even at the same job within their class; that agricultural workers would stay in agriculture; that businessmen (the enemy) would hardly exist as a significant force in his Utopia; and that planners could go about their good and lofty work, unhampered by rude nay-saying from the untrained." Ibid., 289.

18. "Howard's greatest contribution was less in recasting the physical form of the city than in developing the organic concepts that underlay this form; for though he was no biologist like Patrick Geddes, he nevertheless brought to the city the essential biological criteria of dynamic equilibrium and organic balance: balance as between city and country in a larger ecological pattern, and balance between the varied functions of the city: above all, balance through the positive control of growth in the limitation in area, number, and density of occupation, and the practice of reproduction (colonization) when the community was threatened by such an undue increase in size as would lead only to lapse of function." Mumford, 1961, 516.

19. Mumford, 1962, 148–77.

20. Wiener had made the same connection a decade before in *Cybernetics*: "It has been commented on by many writers, such as D'Arcy Thompson, that each form of organization has an upper limit of size, beyond which it will not function. Thus the insect organization is limited by the length of tubing over which the spiracle method of bringing air by diffusion directly to the breathing tissues will function; a land animal cannot be so big that the legs or other portions of contact with the ground will be crushed by the weight; a tree is limited by the mechanism for transferring water and minerals from the roots to the leaves, and the products of photosynthesis from the leaves to the roots, and so on." Wiener, 150.

21. Posted on the Slashdot site: www.slashdot.org.

22. Technically, Slashdot moderators don't give each post a grade on the scale. Posts start out life at 0 or 1 (depending on whether their authors are registered users of the system). Moderators can then "spend" a moderation point rating a post either up or down. A post that starts life at 1, and receives three positive points and one negative point would be at Level 3, because 1 plus 3 minus 1 equals 3.

23. Jacobs, 2000, 154. A related idea is the pricing mechanism of market economies as an information-processing system, as described by the libertarian demigod Friedrich von Hayek. "Long before the fall of communism, Hayek identified its oft-overlooked weakness: Not only did it fail to offer an incentive to work hard; it forced signals connecting supply and demand to travel a tortuous path that invited distortion." Wright, 199.

24. Interview conducted with Rob Malda, April 2000.

Questions for Critical Reading

1. As Johnson's title might suggest, "feedback" plays a central role in this essay. What does Johnson mean by *feedback*? What definitions seem to be in operation in his text? Perform a critical reading of his text to develop a definition and provide citations to support your understandings of the term.

2. What is "homeostasis"? What role does it play in the media? in our bodies? Develop an understanding of the term by locating specific quotations from Johnson's text.

3. According to Johnson, what makes user-generated content systems like Slashdot successful? Can you think of other examples of self-regulating online communities?

Exploring Context

1. Spend some time exploring Slashdot (slashdot.org). Does it continue to exhibit the qualities that Johnson delineates? Is it still a successful self-regulating community? What makes it successful? Use your response to Question 3 of Questions for Critical Reading in evaluating the site.

2. The Stack tool of Digg Labs (labs.digg.com/stack) provides a real-time visual representation of the kind of feedback systems Johnson discusses in relation to the news and media. Based on what you see in the Stack, does Digg use a positive or negative feedback system? Does it reach homeostasis? Apply your definition of *homeostasis* from Question 2 of Questions for Critical Reading.

3. According to Johnson, CNN's decision to share its news feed with local affiliates changed the entire media system, making it more bottom-up than top-down. Visit CNN's Web site at cnn.com; does it suggest a bottom-up system?

Questions for Connecting

1. How can Johnson's insights about feedback help explain the success and failure of small groups, as explored by James Surowiecki in "Committees, Juries, and Teams: The *Columbia* Disaster and How Small Groups Can Be Made to Work" (p. 440)? Do groups achieve homeostasis? What happens when groups experience positive or negative feedback? Use your definition of *homeostasis* from Question 2 of Questions for Critical Reading.

2. Does Leslie Savan's description of advertising and pop talk in "What's Black, Then White, and Said All Over?" (p. 363) reflect a top-down or bottom-up system? How can systems like Slashdot change cultural practices like pop talk? Use your work with Slashdot from Question 3 of Questions for Critical Reading and Question 1 of Exploring Context as you consider these questions.

3. Marshall Poe in "The Hive" (p. 264) examines another popular Web publication, Wikipedia. In what ways is that site similar to Slashdot? What systems of

feedback are at work? What makes these sites so successful? Incorporate your responses about Slashdot from Questions for Critical Reading and Exploring Context.

Language Matters

1. At one point in this selection Johnson uses a sentence fragment (see if you can find it!). Why does Johnson use it? In what situations might a sentence fragment be acceptable?

2. Quotations in academic writing must be of appropriate length. Find a significant passage from the essay and choose the shortest and longest useful quotations from the passage. How short is *too* short? How long is too long? How might you use quotations of different lengths for different ends?

3. The classic rhetorical triangle is composed of receiver, sender, and message. Using this essay, design a new shape to explain this rhetorical situation: What additional elements should be considered? Would the inclusion of style make a rhetorical square? What elements would be in a rhetorical hexagon?

Assignments for Writing

1. Using Johnson's observations on the working rules of Slashdot, write a paper in which you propose strategies for incorporating feedback systems into news media. Incorporate your work with Slashdot from Questions for Critical Reading and Exploring Context, and consider these questions: Why is Slashdot "a virtual democracy," and why isn't the news media one? Is the news now a bottom-up system? Is it possible to incorporate feedback systems into the news?

2. Throughout this essay Johnson is concerned with making information networks successful. Drawing from Johnson's ideas, write a paper that determines the best practices for organizing and administering an information network. You may either choose a specific type of network, like a news organization or an online wiki, or write of practices that would work for many types of networks. What role should self-reflection play in an information network? What is the role of the individual in a decentralized system? How can a system promote a diverse perspective? You might want to construct your argument using your work with Wikipedia from Question 3 of Questions for Connecting.

3. What are the key factors to a successful collaboration? Write a paper in which you specify the crucial elements in the success of collaborative efforts, using Johnson's ideas about feedback in your argument. Consider: What is the function of a feedback loop? What is the role of self-regulation in a successful collaboration? You may want to use your response about feedback from Question 1 of Questions for Connecting in making your argument.

MICHAEL KIMMELMAN

Michael Kimmelman, the chief art critic for the *New York Times*, believes "art is too important and interesting to be left to the art world." A Harvard and Yale graduate and a Pulitzer Prize finalist, Kimmelman has contributed to *Egg: The Art Show* as well as the *New York Review of Books*, and in 1998 he published *Portraits: Talking with Artists at the Met, the Modern, the Louvre, and Elsewhere*. Kimmelman is currently working in Europe and writes the column "Abroad" for the *New York Times*, in which he explores culture and society all across Europe—from the cultural and societal ties of bullfighting in Spain to the anxieties of Russian artists and writers about artistic freedom under the current government. The selection printed here comes from his 2005 book, *The Accidental Masterpiece: On the Art of Life and Vice Versa*.

The Accidental Masterpiece
On the Art of Life and Vice Versa
Michael Kimmelman

As Kimmelman explains in the book's introduction, *The Accidental Masterpiece* is "about how creating, collecting, and even just appreciating art can make living a daily masterpiece," since "even the most ordinary daily affair . . . is enriched by the lessons that can be gleaned from art." He also offers the same argument in reverse—that the world of art can be enriched by even the most ordinary daily affair: There is an art to collecting lightbulbs. "Good art," Kimmelman said in a 2005 interview, is "about encouraging people to look more closely at what's around them."

"The Art of Collecting Lightbulbs" tells the story of Hugh Francis Hicks, a dentist who has assembled an astonishing collection of lightbulbs and lightbulb-related objects. Kimmelman examines more collectors of the ordinary and not-so-ordinary and the art that has emerged from their work. "Serious obsessives," motivated more by an appreciation of their objects than by the desire for fame and fortune often present in the professional art world, have made extraordinary contributions to art through their ordinary collections. Kimmelman proposes that all modern collections, whether lightbulbs in a basement or paintings in a museum, owe a debt to pioneers of the practice who assembled "wonder cabinets." These "cabinets of curiosities . . . meant to encapsulate the world in microcosm," composed order and art from the chaos of everyday life.

▶ TAGS: *technology*, *aesthetic boundaries*, **art**, *creativity*

The Art of Collecting Lightbulbs

A few years ago I met Hugh Francis Hicks, a dentist in downtown Baltimore with an office on the parlor floor of a big old brownstone just up the street from the Walters Art Museum. One afternoon he took me into his building's basement to show me a collection he has been putting together for nearly seventy years. Dr. Hicks, who died at the age of seventy-nine in 2002, collected lightbulbs.

He had 75,000 of them. You probably won't be surprised to learn that this was the largest collection of lightbulbs in the world. Dr. Hicks had officially turned it into a museum, the Mount Vernon Museum of Incandescent Lighting. It contained what used to be the world's biggest bulb (at 50,000 watts and four feet high, it was the size of a shrub) and also the smallest, which you could see only by looking through a microscope. Edison's early experimental bulbs were there, with their original Bristol-board filaments. One of them still worked. The bulbs were decoratively arranged in crowded glass-and-wood cases, like the ones that turn-of-the-previous-century museums used to have, the cases accompanied by yellowed typewritten labels full of arcane information, detailing the source of the name Mazda (a Zoroastrian sun god) and the history of tungsten filaments. Dr. Hicks had what lightbulb collectors evidently considered to be an incredible collection of "B" type Mazdas. He amassed a definitive variety of switches, sockets, and adapters, and he also had many one-of-a-kind, or nearly one-of-a-kind, treasures: the headlamps from Himmler's Mercedes and three lights from the *Enola Gay*. There were also joke bulbs shaped like Dick Tracy and Betty Boop, men's ties that lighted up, and a display documenting the history of Christmas lighting. A kind of rabbit warren, the basement included a room at the end with a big round table covered by a plastic flowered tablecloth where Dr. Hicks served cookies to visiting schoolchildren. Before visiting, I phoned ahead, and he met me in his office—there were no patients around—then took me downstairs and turned on the lights.

Why do people collect? The consolation of art comes in many forms. For some it is making, for others it is having. For Dr. Hicks, it was the hunting and gathering of illuminating trophies. For many of us it may simply be appreciating what people like Dr. Hicks have collected—it may be just looking at constellations of someone else's extraordinary things. Dr. Hicks said that his obsession began in the crib. His mother noticed one day that he was bored with his toys, so for some reason she gave him an old lightbulb to play with. He survived this brush with danger and began devising school projects entailing electricity. In time, he discovered other bulb enthusiasts and began to trade. He was not above thievery. Once, on vacation in Paris, he spotted a row of 1920s tungsten bulbs along a wall of a Metro station and hurriedly swiped one, whereupon the whole station went pitch-black because the bulbs were wired so that if one were removed, they would all go out. Unable to fit the stolen bulb back into the socket, he decided to flee. At his museum, he displayed his booty in a case marked "Hot Types."

Psychiatrists came to interview him about why he collected, and he told them about William j. Hammer, one of Edison's engineers, who before 1900 collected 130,000 different electric bulbs, which were evidently later dispersed. Hammer died the month that Dr. Hicks was born. "Do you believe in reincarnation?" he asked the psychiatrists. They seemed stupefied.

Some people collect because collecting can be a great art if earnestly engaged in. That is why we enjoy looking at great collections, even if we are not collectors. Collecting is a way to bring order to the world, which is what museums, our public collectors, do. It is also a way to define some idiosyncratic niche for the collector, as art does for an artist. There are people who collect candy wrappers without the candy, thimbles, and inedible food. If you look up Dr. Hicks's museum on the Internet, you will find links to various collections of technological artifacts, from slide rules to chopsticks to pocket calculators to mimeograph machines. Over the years, I have visited a museum of trash and the basement of a churchgoing teetotaler in New Jersey who had collected several thousand miniature liquor bottles and several dozen miniature Vargas pinups from old cigarette packs. (He didn't smoke, either.) I have toured the Nicholas Roerich Museum on the Upper West Side of Manhattan, an obscure shrine to a once-famous Russian mystic (or charlatan, depending on which accounts of him you read), which collects his eccentric paintings. I have seen a few of the cars and planes that James Turrell, the sculptor of light, has collected in Arizona. Turrell is like Donald Judd and Dan Flavin, archetypal American minimalists, purveyors of the sparest sort of modern art, who were in their private lives aspiring packrats. Like the teetotaler who loved liquor bottles, Turrell is the quintessential paradoxical collector. His art consists of the most ephemeral and insubstantial thing of all, light, while

Collecting is a way to bring order to the world, which is what museums, our public collectors, do.

his collecting entails big bulky machines, which I must assume fill some private need, aside from the practical one of getting him from one place to another, and this other need may be partly aesthetic but is also, no doubt, psychological. Judd collected cars, modern furniture (a warehouse full of it), Indian crafts, and buildings along with books; Flavin, who also made art out of the light cast by colored fluorescent tubes, collected Stickley furniture, Rembrandt etchings, Asian pottery, Indian jewelry, nineteenth-century American drawings, Japanese prints, and sketches by modernists he admired, like Brancusi and Malevich.

It is taken for granted that Rembrandts are worth collecting because they are art and expensive, but collectors, as Dr. Hicks proves, will collect pretty much everything, without necessarily thinking that what they collect has aesthetic or monetary value. Prestige, like taste in art, is often in the eye of the collector, and true value may be greatest when the value is only symbolic. Collected objects become symbolic when they lose their utilitarian purpose. A former prisoner in a Stalinist labor camp, for example, collected keys to locks that were no longer in use. A key is no longer just a key if it belonged to the Bastille, nor a sewing kit just a sewing kit if Betsy Ross sewed with it. As Philipp Blom, a writer on collecting, has put it: "As often as not the objects collected are the cast-offs of society, overtaken by technological advance, used and disposable, outmoded, disregarded, unfashionable." Their uselessness becomes their asset: They turn into totems and fragments of the lost worlds they came from. So the arm of Teresa of Avila is prized not because it is practical to medical science as a specimen of muscle and bone but because it is connected, as Blom says, "with otherworldliness, as a key to heaven, to a world infinitely richer than our everyday existence." It becomes a holy relic.

Just as art promises wonderment—an access to a realm beyond the everyday, through the experience of which we may understand the everyday better—a collection of things, even everyday things, promises wonderment, too, as these things become no longer everyday, having been enshrined by a collector. Walter Benjamin, who collected books, said that "one of the finest memories of a collector is the moment when he rescued a book to which he might never have given a thought, much less a wishful look, because he found it lonely and abandoned on the marketplace and bought it to give it its freedom—the way the prince bought a beautiful slave girl in 'The Arabian Nights.'" He added, "To a book collector, you see, the true freedom of all books is somewhere on his shelves."

For Benjamin, collecting makes sense of a senseless world. Collectors take up "arms against dispersal. The great collector is touched to the core by the confusion and the dispersal in which things are found in this world." Collectors impose their own private rationale on what they own. They make order out of chaos. Albert C. Barnes made a fortune at the turn of the last century with an over-the-counter antiseptic remedy called Argyrol, and with the money he made put together one of the world's most spectacular and idiosyncratic collections: He amassed great Cézannes, Matisses, and African art, along with metal knickknacks and folk doodads like door locks and a tiny acorn sculpture in the shape of a cricket. Famously, he displayed these all together at a mansion outside Philadelphia, in odd, mixed-up arrangements, seemingly arbitrary to the uninitiated—arrangements he vigorously explained according to an elaborate private dogma of decoration, partly inspired by John Dewey, which he and his cultish disciples, at a school he founded on the premises specifically to perpetuate his artistic beliefs, preached with a kind of quasi-religious fervor through pamphlets and books. Pictures might be put together to convey a triangular or diagonal scheme that Dr. Barnes thought he perceived in their compositions. A great Seurat could thereby share real estate with *Balloon Man*, a painting by somebody Dr. Barnes came across named Liz Clark. Works that looked optimistically attributed to El Greco, along with dozens of pinheaded Renoirs, mostly awful but some great, hung with sublime landmarks of the most intelligent sort of modern art like the mural by Henri Matisse that Barnes, in a stroke of genius, commissioned. Matisse evidently enjoyed Barnes's eccentricity. He declared the weird juxtapositions a help to the public, since people could "understand a lot of things that the academics don't teach," which was true. Nobody else looked at art the way Barnes did. Self-taught in this regard, from a working-class background, having earned his way through medical school playing professional baseball, he developed a notorious chip on his shoulder toward what he considered the art establishment, and he feuded publicly with anyone he thought hoity-toity. His collection was only open to "the plain people, that is men and women who gain their livelihood by daily toil in shops, factories, schools, stores, and similar places." The eminent art historian Erwin Panofsky supposedly had to dress up like a chauffeur to sneak in.

Nine months before he died in 1951 at the age of seventy-nine, when his Packard collided with a ten-ton truck, Barnes decided, in another stroke of eccentric philanthropy, to bequeath everything to a small, historically black school in Chester County, Pennsylvania, called Lincoln University, which had

little, if any, experience with art collecting. He stipulated that the school maintain the museum untouched where it was, ensuring years of legal wrangling,
financial crisis, and limited access for almost everyone, including plain people,
to some of the most important modern art in the world—that is, until 2004.
Overriding Barnes's will, a judge ordered the straitened museum to be recon-
stituted in Philadelphia, as a partial simulacrum of itself, more convenient
to tourists and with money from several local foundations that had made its
move downtown a condition of their support. The decision would have horrified Dr. Barnes, who acted, you could say, like a jealous lover (the erotic aspect
of collecting has always been much commented on): He wanted to control
these objects of his desire, even beyond the grave.

He was not merely being perverse. His collection, he realized, was itself
a novel expression of creativity. You might never have noticed a connection between Persian miniature painting and the early American modernist
painter Marsden Hartley unless Barnes had put them together. His unorthodox installations, so unlike what other museums did, inclined you to look
at his art fresh, which is what museums should do. Barnes imposed himself onto great works of Georges
Seurat and Matisse by insisting **Not all collectors are eccentrics,**
they be viewed only as he saw **of course.**
fit, which meant that a colorful
and ornery former baseball player and medical entrepreneur declared a kind
of aesthetic authority over cultural figures of enduring consequence—not
a perfectly defensible position for advocates of serious art who believe art
should really be as accessible as reasonably possible to the public. But Barnes
(whose Argyrol, by the way, was a remedy for conjunctivitis in newborns, an
aid to seeing) opened more than a few eyes with his display techniques while
demonstrating that there was an art to collecting—and, by extension, to appreciating a great collection.

It is a fair question to ask whether collectors like Barnes devise their own
museums because they are exhibitionists or promoters of some private philosophy or have a sense of civic responsibility, or all of the above. Not all
collectors are eccentrics, of course. Most aren't, although the best often are:
Out of passion and private conviction, they collect what may not yet be ratified, as opposed to what fashion and the market already prize, in the belief
that public taste should someday catch up. The combination of public service
and the strength of one's conviction is what defines an admirable collector.
Like artists, collectors may also collect in a vain hope of achieving immortality. Collections, as Blom says (and this certainly pertains to Barnes's), "have
always had overtones of burial and interment. Graves are filled with objects
symbolic of future use, shoring up the deceased against irrevocable loss,
allowing him a symbolic afterlife with all the comforts of the here and now.
The greater a collection, the more precious its contents, the more it must be
reminiscent of a mausoleum, left behind by a ruler determined not to be forgotten, not to have his memory squabbled over and his most immediate self
disintegrate to dust."

This even applies to benign collectors like Dr. Hicks, whose museums of artifacts can have a fascination that is indistinguishable from that of art museums. I don't mean that, aesthetically, lightbulbs or slide rules are as compelling as paintings. I mean that the museum, whether it is a collection of art or something else, derives from the old *Kunst- und Wunderkammern*, or art and wonder cabinets, and it retains its original aspirations to wonderment.

Kunst- und Wunderkammern began to proliferate more or less in the sixteenth century, the result of humanist curiosity, technological advances in things like optics and engineering, a revival of interest in antique texts that were preoccupied with the marvelous, and global exploration, which exposed Europe to what seemed like a strange new world. Sophisticated banking systems also made the exchange of rare and precious worldly goods easier. Trading empires, like the Dutch and Venetian, fostered and facilitated rich collectors who sought the most wonderful objects. Wonderment in the sixteenth and seventeenth centuries came to be perceived as a kind of middle state between ignorance and knowledge, and wonder cabinets were theaters of the marvelous, museums of accumulated curiosities, proving God's ingenuity. They contained whatever was the biggest, the smallest, the rarest, the most exquisite, the most bizarre, the most grotesque. Art, astrolabes, armor — man-made wonders — were cheek by jowl with monkeys' teeth and pathological anomalies like human horns. A German doctor named Lorenz Hoffman had a typical *Kunst- und Wunderkammer*: He owned paintings by Albrecht Dürer and Lucas Cranach, a skeleton of a newborn, two dozen miniature spoons hidden within a cherry pit, an armband made of elks' hooves, mummies, and various rare musical instruments. In the middle of the sixteenth century the Dutch collector Hubert Goltzius could list 968 collections he knew of in the Low Countries, Germany, Austria, Switzerland, France, and Italy. In Amsterdam, nearly 100 private cabinets of curiosities were documented between 1600 and 1740. Calvinist propriety discouraged the Dutch from displays of wealth in public, but in the privacy of their homes they stuffed fancy mahogany cupboards with coins, cameos, and statues, capped off by precious porcelain, the archetype for modern bourgeois drawing rooms with their obligatory glass-fronted cabinet in which to show off the family china.

Wonder cabinets of the past were, in part, meant to encapsulate the world in microcosm: again, order from chaos. Blom reminds us about Philipp Hainhofer, the great Augsburg envoy and collector, who, in designing various cabinets for princes, devised one of the most extraordinary pieces of seventeenth-century furniture: a vast chest, topped by a huge rare Seychelle nut, in which objects were methodically arranged to represent the animal, plant, and mineral worlds, the four continents, and various human activities, with painted *vanitas* scenes on the front to remind everyone that death is part of life. The drawers contained exotica like bezoars, calcareous concretions from the stomachs of Persian goats, believed to be antidotes to poison, vastly expensive; musk pouches; cups of *lignum Guaiacum*, a West Indian wood of medicinal powers, and objects "for vexation," like gloves with no openings for the hands, fake fruit, and pictures that came into focus only when viewed through special mirrors.

CHARLES WILLSON PEALE, *The Artist in His Museum*

These early cabinets of wonderment became occasions for collectors to exercise their artistic skills at display. The art of museum exhibition has its roots in this impulse. Frederik Ruysch, a Dutch anatomist and famous collector, concocted wild tableaux made of flowers, skulls, kidney stones, and diseased organs in his *Wunderkammer* in Amsterdam. One of the first museums in the United States, which belonged to the Philadelphia artist Charles Willson Peale, was a kind of *Wunderkammer,* containing fossils and stuffed birds as well as paintings. In 1822, Peale did a painting of himself holding open a curtain onto his museum, like a carnival barker inviting visitors into the big top. Collecting, for Peale and the others, put the world together like pieces of a puzzle.

While driving to Dr. Hicks's in Baltimore, I noticed a sign on the highway for 15 a museum of hunting decoys in Havre de Grace, Maryland, so I pulled off at the exit for a visit. Havre de Grace is a sleepy place on the Susquehanna Flats, where the Susquehanna River meets the Chesapeake Bay. It is duck hunter's nirvana, although a series of laws during the 1930s and '40s curtailed market-gunning or hunting ducks for restaurants. The Decoy Museum preserves hundreds of duck decoys by local carvers. Astonishingly, the carvers are also preserved behind glass, right there in life-size, full-length polyvinylacetate figures, like decoys, you might say, of the decoy makers. There's a big tableau that lights up when you press a button, à la Madame Tussaud's, showing local carvers sitting around a stove in one of the town's decoy shops in 1942. Display cases are dedicated to different expert decoy makers. At a glance, I couldn't always tell the difference between the works of R. Madison Mitchell, a local funeral director, who was evidently the Giotto of Havre de Grace, and the works of Bob McGaw, who perfected a way of decorating his decoys that, I learned, is called scratch painting. But no doubt the distinctions are obvious to the people who have looked at the decoys a lot longer than I did. Connoisseurship entails making distinctions through slow, comparative observation, whether it involves paintings or wooden ducks.

Partly it was a desire for a more methodical approach to collected objects, a system for spreading connoisseurship, that ushered in a new age of museums two centuries ago. Museums began to specialize. Elks' hooves went one way, paintings another. The balance tipped from delight toward instruction. The new museums set out more systematically to categorize things, to create order, or at least to imply that there is an order to life. René Descartes, who called wonderment the first of all the passions, also wrote that an excess of wonder can "pervert the use of reason." The age of wonder cabinets turned into the age of Descartes and the encyclopedists.

But the spirit of the wonder cabinets never altogether died. Art museums, and even modern collections of light bulbs, though they may not be true wonder cabinets, preserve what's marvelous to show us what is rare and what we can't see otherwise, and thereby help us see, with heightened curiosity, what is around us. Thomas Dent Mütter was a Philadelphia surgeon who went to Paris in the 1830s, when it was the medical mecca. There he saw hospital wards arranged according to diseases, so that doctors could compare the conditions of patients suffering from the same things; he also saw collections of tumors, aneurysms, bones, and so on. He returned to Philadelphia inspired by the systematic connection of morbid anatomy and clinical pathology. Soon he began to build his own teaching collection of anatomical and pathological specimens for the benefit of medical students. In the nineteenth century, medical students regularly learned about scientific anomalies like human horns or conjoined twins by looking at collections of dried dissections, wax models of skin diseases, and papier-mâché models of reproductive organs. To this end, Mütter accumulated hundreds of air-dried specimens, specimens preserved in alcohol, plaster casts, watercolors, and oil paintings—1,344 items—all of which he bequeathed in 1858 to the College of Physicians of Philadelphia, a private medical society with some of its own oddments whose founders included lettered men like Benjamin Rush, a signer of the Declaration of Independence.

Mütter understood novelty as a kind of collector's bait. So he also collected the bladder stones removed from Chief Justice John Marshall by Philip Syng Physick, the father of American surgery, in 1831, and the deformed skeleton of

> **The balance tipped from delight toward instruction.**

a woman whose rib cage had been compressed by tying her corset too tightly. In time, the college added to his oddments. The Mütter Museum, as it came to be called, now occupies part of a big, somewhat forbidding Georgian building behind a tall iron gate in the center of the city. A two-story anachronism of polished wood cases, thick burgundy curtains, and brass lamps, it looks much as one imagines Peale's museum to have looked. In recent years it has streamlined its display, making it more attractive to tourists but somewhat skewing the public's perception of the historic function of the museum by showing only what's most striking or unusual or catchy. The collection today boasts of having the connected livers of the Siamese twins Chang and Eng; a piece of the thorax of John Wilkes Booth; a tumor removed from the jaw of President Grover Cleveland; the skeleton of a seven-foot-six-inch man from Kentucky who suffered from a condition called acromegaly, a hyperactive pituitary gland; a bound foot from China; the remains of the so-called Soap Lady, whose corpse decomposed into a grayish white fatty, soapy wax substance called adipocere; and more than two thousand objects removed from choking victims, the objects carefully arranged in narrow drawers in a filing cabinet according to type: meat, nuts, pins, buttons, toy jacks. These last items came to the museum in 1924 from a pioneering bronchoesophagologist named Chevalier Jackson, who devised a technique for extracting them from patients' throats.

J. DENNIS WELSCH
Dr. Chevalier Jackson pointing to diagram of safety pin lodged in throat

In the collection is also a photograph of Dr. Jackson himself, looking a bit like Sigmund Freud, unsmiling, in bow tie and a white doctor's gown with natty trim, stiffly pointing to a large diagram on an easel showing a safety pin stuck in a throat.

It is now possible to see much of what the Mütter keeps on view as art: Théodore Géricault, the great French Romantic artist, painted severed limbs; Kiki Smith, the contemporary artist, has made sculptures of flayed figures; Nayland Blake and Damien Hirst have in recent years devised artful arrangements of medical instruments; and to see the Soap Lady, her mouth wide open, is to be put in mind of the paintings by Zoran Music, a Holocaust survivor who became a painter in Paris, of screaming figures. The Mütter's dried skeleton of a newborn child, hanging by its outstretched arms, head back, can even make you think of some great crucifixion by Peter Paul Rubens, with Jesus's eyes upturned, as if in a state of spiritual ecstasy.

20

But I wouldn't want to push the connection too far; I only wish to stress how a place like the Mütter, notwithstanding its original medical function, can seem neatly to blur the distinction between science and art by dwelling in the marvelous. Its collection causes us to react in a way that, like art, goes beyond reason and touches our nerves. Was Dr. Mütter motivated merely by scientific inquiry? Maybe he was, but many collections, including his, suggest an obsession on the part of the collector that exceeds practicality. A Manhattan psychoanalyst, Werner Muensterberger, once wrote a book called *Collecting: An Unruly Passion*, in which he argued that collecting is, among other things, more or less a form of displaced childhood in which the collector longs for parental comfort, his or her collected objects becoming, like sucked thumbs, stand-ins for a mother's breast. They are the lightbulb in Dr. Hicks's crib. I am not a collector. I can't say. Collecting, the issue of financial investment aside, is clearly some form of consolation to many collectors, as is its appreciation by others. Beyond that, it can be a wonder and a mystery.

In his prologue to *Invisible Man*, Ralph Ellison wrote, "In my hole in the basement there are exactly 1,369 lights. I've wired the ceiling, every inch of it. And not with fluorescent bulbs, but with the older, more expensive-to-operate kind, the filament kind. . . . When I finish all four walls, then I'll start on the floor. Just how that will go, I don't know. Yet when you have lived invisible for as long as I have you develop a certain ingenuity."

Dr. Hicks, our lightbulb man with his basement museum, told me about those psychiatrists who came to interview him. "They were something," he said. "They didn't blink their eyes. They were interviewing collectors from all over the world. After spending $4 million, they concluded that collectors collect for the fascination of an object and for no other reason. Heck, I would have told them that for $1 million."

Questions for Critical Reading

1. In what ways is collecting an art form? You will need to reread this essay closely to form your response. Look for passages from the essay that illustrate Kimmelman's points about the connection between collecting and art to support your response.

2. According to Kimmelman, what is the connection between wonder cabinets and art? Can you locate any modern equivalent to the wonder cabinet? Is your example also a form of art?

3. What connection does Kimmelman suggest between medicine and art? Does such a connection still exist today? What makes art "art"? What connection does it have to science?

Exploring Context

1. Spend some time on eBay (ebay.com) browsing through the categories. Given all the objects collected there, could you argue that eBay is a kind of virtual museum? Locate passages from Kimmelman to support your position, and draw from your understanding of collecting as art from Question 1 of Questions for Critical Reading.

2. Visit a local museum, and then visit the Web site for that museum. How is collecting represented differently in the real and virtual spaces?

3. PostSecret (postsecret.blogspot.com) is a public art project in which people design postcards that reveal a secret about themselves. Review the most recent collection of postcards. How does each card function as art, and how does the collection as a whole function as art? Is the group of cards more of an art form than one individual postcard? Use Kimmelman's essay to support your position.

Questions for Connecting

1. Kimmelman discusses the Mütter Museum's display of medical anomalies. How can Kimmelman's analysis further explain people's fascination with before and after photos as explored by Julia Serano in "Before and After: Class and Body Transformations" (p. 392)? Do such photos function as a kind of art? Do collections like the Mütter Museum's participate in systems of class? Explain your responses. You may want to use your experience visiting a museum from Question 2 of Exploring Context.

2. What is the role of human dignity in collecting? Apply Francis Fukuyama's discussion of human dignity in his essay of the same title (p. 142) to Kimmelman's analysis. Does Fukuyama's discussion of complexity, in which the whole is greater than the sum of its parts, underscore the power of collecting as Kimmelman describes it?

3. The wonder cabinets that Kimmelman discusses seem related to the public display of Evita's corpse examined by Diana Taylor in "False Identifications: Minority Populations Mourn Diana" (p. 454). In what ways do art and mourning perform similar social functions? Extend Taylor's analysis to Kimmelman's essay. Use your work on wonder cabinets, medicine, and art from Questions 2 and 3 of Questions for Critical Reading.

Language Matters

1. Select a section of the essay and then locate and remove the topic sentence of each paragraph in that section. What strategies did you use to find the topic sentences? How does removing a paragraph's topic sentence affect the meaning of the paragraph?

2. Introductions do a lot of important work in your papers: They introduce the authors, the essays, and, most important, your position or argument. How does Kimmelman introduce this chapter? How effective is it as an introduction? Why would you want (or not want) to open your paper that way?

3. Photocopy a couple of pages from Kimmelman's essay and then cut out each individual paragraph with a pair of scissors. Trade these in small groups. Can everyone put the paragraphs back in the right order? How strong is Kimmelman's organization? What elements of the paragraphs indicate their order within the piece?

Assignments for Writing

1. Kimmelman states that the great collector is touched to the core by the confusion and dispersal in which things are found in this world. Locate your own example of a "wonder cabinet" and write an essay in which you extend or complicate Kimmelman's argument through this example. Does your example participate in finding order out of chaos? Can a collection of dissimilar objects in itself be considered ordered? What is the purpose of collecting? Does collecting make sense of a senseless world? In making your argument, consider using your exploration of eBay in Question 1 of Exploring Context.

2. In this essay Kimmelman states that a collection can blur the distinction between science and art by "dwelling in the marvelous." Write an essay exploring the role that a collection can play in science. Can a medical collection indeed serve to teach something to students? Can science be an art? Is there a place for art in science? You may want to incorporate your work on the relationship between medicine and art from Question 3 of Questions for Critical Reading in supporting your argument.

3. For Kimmelman, collecting art is itself an art form; his essay thus asks us to rethink what we mean by *art*. Working from Kimmelman's argument, write an essay in which you create a definition of *art* that encompasses collection and display. Consider these questions: Can a collection of ordinary objects be art? Why or why not? Is something artistic only after it loses its utilitarian or everyday purpose? Is a collection artistic only after it is displayed? What role does display have in art? In your response, draw from your work on collecting from Question 1 of Questions for Critical Reading.

REBEKAH NATHAN

Rebekah Nathan is a pseudonym for Cathy Small, an anthropology professor at North Arizona University. When Small went undercover to write her second book, *My Freshman Year: What a Professor Learned by Becoming a Student* (2005), she took on the pseudonym to protect the identity of her students and her university. Small previously published *Voyages: From Tongan Villages to American Suburbs* (1997), an ethnographical study of immigrants in their old and new homelands.

My Freshman Year is the result of a two-semester study by Small of all aspects of freshman life at her university. She applied to the university, enrolled in classes, moved into the student dorms, and even ate with students in the resident dining hall, hoping with her experiment to become a better teacher. After so long in the field, Small had found herself disconnected from the average student at her university, unable to understand why her students seemed so uninterested in and unprepared for class. She reveals in *My Freshman Year* that the demands on freshmen are much more varied and pressing than she had realized and that her initial assessment of her students had not been completely accurate.

"Community and Diversity," a chapter from *My Freshman Year*, deals with the difference between a university's stated goals for both community and diversity and their realization on campus, as well as the perpetual confusion among educators and administrators about why the image and the reality don't align. Small investigates low attendance at dorm events, patterns of freshman friendship, and the eating habits of ethnic and gender groups to reach some conclusions about the reality behind the lofty unmet intentions and the necessity of having such intentions at all.

As a student, you've undoubtedly encountered the call for community and diversity. It's likely, too, that you've seen this call go unanswered. You are in a unique position to continue Small's work on the possibilities of forming community and fostering diversity on the college campus.

▶ TAGS: *community*, *diversity*, integration, *research*, *education*, *conversation*

Community and Diversity

One would be hard-pressed to find words more widespread in university rhetoric than "community" and "diversity." As a student, one is immediately enlisted to join the group, to get involved, to realize that one has become a part of the AnyU "community."

It starts during Previews and Welcome Week. We sing the AnyU alma mater with leaders; we learn the AnyU cheer. At the convocation that commences our freshman year, we are welcomed to AnyU with some statistics about our class, and then an entertaining PowerPoint presentation with voice-over begins: "In the year that you were born . . ."—it goes back eighteen years and shows a baby—"Ronald Reagan was president, AnyU was building its South Campus, and the movie that won the Academy Award was *Out of Africa*." We see graphics of all this, and AnyU history, at least for the past eighteen years, is interspersed with the shared "history" of the audience, which consists primarily of movies, TV shows, and dramatic historical events. "In 1986," the story continues, "the Emmy goes to *L.A. Law*, and the explosion of the *Challenger* saddens the American public." The presentation takes us briefly through all eighteen years of the baby-who-is-us.

By 1991 we have torn down the Berlin Wall, constructed the new AnyU library, and arrived at the same year that *Seinfeld* begins. There is silence, clapping, or booing as the event being described moves us. Our history continues, year by year, to mention, among other things, the end of the TV series *Cheers* in 1993, the Monica Lewinsky scandal in 1998, the beginning of *Friends* in 1994 (to thunderous applause), and the September 11, 2001, attack. By 2002 we are eighteen and ready to go to college, and—the lights come on—here we are, part of the AnyU family.

The presentation works; it is relatively short, and students leave mildly entertained and energized, having experienced a compressed version of our joint heritage and our shared place at the starting line of something new. It is clear what the common heritage has been constructed to be. What holds students together, really, is age, pop culture, a handful of (recent) historical events, and getting a degree. No one ever remembers the institutional history or the never-sung alma mater.

How Community Works at AnyU

Youth, pop culture, and getting a degree are pretty accurately the ties that bind   5
together a public state university "community." Unless it offers a big-time (and winning) sports team that draws large attendance and loyalty, there is little in the way of shared first-year experiences that three thousand or so freshmen will have in common. AnyU did have a Freshman Colloquium course that was mandatory for all first-year students. It was designed to be just such a community builder, one that required students to complete a summer reading assignment—usually a provocative contemporary novel chosen collectively by the participating faculty—that would be discussed in small seminars before classes formally began.

The faculty had an ambitious, and what they thought exciting, intellectual agenda in mind. Students would read the same book, and then their academic career would start with a stimulating seminar-style discussion with only twenty or so participants. The entire freshman class would be engaged in the same reading, and thus have a common basis for debate and dialogue. Freshmen would then meet the book's author, who had been invited at great expense to give a talk following their small-group discussions. This experience would jump-start the colloquium that would follow: a small, seminar-based fresh-man course centered on readings about community and citizenship, diversity, environment, and technology, designed to help them explore their journeys as "thinking persons," including the purpose of the liberal education they had begun. For the administration, the course was also a way to build a sense of loyalty and community, and thus, according to official belief, to retain freshmen as paying students.

I was in one of the last freshman classes to take the course. It was nullified as a requirement because the university faculty and administration concluded that it wasn't working. For one thing, only about a third of the students actually did the summer reading. My own pre-course seminar was led by an impressive instructor who practically pulled teeth trying to get a response to questions raised by our reading: "Does a common enemy help to make people a community? What is a typical American or an ideal citizen? Can anyone think of places within America that seem like a different country? Does technology bring you closer to or farther away from other people—does it separate or connect?" She ended up letting us go a half-hour early because, I surmised, of our silence. Very few in my seminar had read the book, at least "all the way through," as one student qualified it.

According to student surveys, many disliked the course that followed, in particular the idea that they "had no choice and that they *had* to take it," but also because it was abstract and impractical, and they didn't learn anything "related to their interests." The requirement, designed as the only common academic experience the freshmen would have, was accordingly wiped from the books, leaving an elective course, chosen separately by each student, in its place.

One can learn from the fate of the freshman seminar. It is a good example of what happens nowadays when efforts at building community compete with the demand for choice. The freshman course had been designed and initiated at AnyU as part of a nationwide agenda, begun in the early 1990s, to engage students in their freshman year and quickly establish a "learning community." It was one local response to what educational policy analysts identified as a crisis in community that left the university to be experienced in "momentary and marginal ways." "Not only has cultural coherence faded," reads the thoughtful and influential 1990 report from the Carnegie Foundation for the Advancement of Teaching, "but the very notion of commonalities seems strikingly inapplicable to the vigorous diversity of contemporary life." Titled *Campus Life: In Search of Community*, the report called for a renewal of community in higher learning. Its authors wrote:

> It is of special significance, we believe, that higher learning institutions, even the big, complex ones, continue to use the familiar rhetoric of "community" to describe campus life and even use the metaphor of "family." Especially significant, 97 percent of the college and university presidents we surveyed said they "strongly believe in the importance

of community." Almost all the presidents agreed that "community is appropriate for my campus" and also support the proposition that "administrators should make a greater effort to strengthen common purposes and shared experiences."[1]

It is a cry that has been taken up in earnest by university presidents around   10
the country. Because *requiring* common experiences is vastly unpopular, and efforts often meet the fate of the freshman seminar, AnyU, like many universities today, encourages community through elective participation. "If you don't see what you like," said one Welcome Week booster, "start your own club." The 158 registered student organizations on campus don't tell the full story of the options that confront a student in a single week, from salsa dancing night at a downtown club, to the regular pickup game of coed volleyball, to the Overeaters Anonymous meeting, to the self-defense lesson in the dorm, to the plethora of academic events that are part of lecture and film series.

Every week the hall bulletin boards are plastered with notices about new events to attend, new music groups in town, or organizations offering enthusiastic invitations to their open house. The proliferation of event choices, together with the consistent message to "get involved," and the ever available option of dropping out, creates a self-contradictory system. Students are confronted

> AnyU, like many universities today, encourages community through elective participation.

with an endless slate of activities vying for their time. Every decision not to join but to keep one's time for oneself is interpreted as "student apathy" or "program irrelevance," and ever more activities are designed to remedy them. Each decision to join something new pulls at another commitment, fragmenting the whole even further. Not only people but also community are spread thin.

In my life as a student this process of community building through elective involvement was repeated numerous times and in numerous places within the university. On my dorm floor alone, where we had not done much together as a group during my first semester, the process worked like this. To begin our second semester and usher in a renewed spirit of community, our enthusiastic RA devised an "interest survey," which she administered at the first mandatory hall meeting of that period. (Since it was second semester, the turnout was decidedly sparse: Only six people attended.) "Let's do more things together," the RA suggested, and we agreed. It would be desirable, the collective thinking seemed to be, to have more "community" in the dorm.

"What would we like to do this semester?" she asked us. To find out, she distributed the survey with a written checklist that would assist her in launching new dorm programs that fit our interests and schedules. There were sixty-four activities suggested on the checklist in ten categories (community living, health/wellness, social awareness, employment skills, academic programs, relationship issues . . .), which ranged from presentation and panels, to group games and activities, to participatory workshops. We could write in activities if the ones presented did not suit. There was also an availability section of the form, where we were asked to check our preferred times—which evenings, which hours—for the activities. Because the showing at the meeting was so meager, our RA placed questionnaires under each of the doors on the wing, to be returned to her by a specified date. I asked whether I could see the final tallies.

A total of 304 selections were made by all hall mates, with eighteen of the sixty-four listed activities chosen by approximately half of all respondents. The most popular choice was not an activity at all but an expressed interest in buying floor T-shirts or boxer shorts. Among activities, several—including swing or salsa dancing and playing board games—were high on the list, but the RA decided to start her local "community" program with the biggest vote-getter, "Movie Night," endorsed by about three-quarters of the voting residents on the floor.

Movie Night was an activity whereby once every other week we would come to our RA's room, as in Welcome Week, to watch a movie on video while sharing popcorn and other snacks provided by the RA or anted up by the residents. The preferred time, according to the questionnaires, was 8 PM on Tuesday. And so Movie Night was instituted twice a month on Tuesday nights, and slips of paper appeared under our doors to announce the first movie. On the first Tuesday, two people showed, besides the RA. The second time nobody showed. The RA moved the night to Sunday. Still nobody showed. The program was canceled, leaving the RA wondering what she could do to "really involve" her corridor.

Two organizational levels up from the corridor was the dorm. Here RAs and dorm officers attempted more extensive full-dorm programs that would get the residents involved. There were dozens of them, in addition to the corridor or floor-level activities devised by individual RAs. The most residents I ever saw attend any single event in our dormitory, housing about four hundred people, was for the talent show, where there were about twenty-one people—mostly the talent—and the "How to Make Edible Underwear" program around Valentine's Day, which drew twenty-three people.

With varying degrees of success, this was the pattern of "community involvement" that operated at various levels of the university: a multiplicity of voluntary activities, a handful of participants at each, and renewed efforts to create new activities that were more relevant and attractive, resulting in an even greater proliferation of choices and fragmentation of the whole.

The American Way: The Individualism in Community

To university administrators my story of Movie Night would be yet one more example of failing involvement and community on the contemporary college campus. By 1990 it was already becoming clear that few students participate in campus events; 76 percent of college and university presidents called non-participation a moderate to major problem on campuses.[2] An RA might count Movie Night as a personal failure, and become dispirited by the apathy of residents, or perhaps hear a call to invent more and better activities.

Students, I imagine, would see it a little differently. The activities chosen were not the "wrong" ones, nor were their RAs remiss. Nor had students been insincere in their desire for more community life in the dorm. If you had asked most students what happened with Movie Night, they would have answered, "I wanted to go, but when the time came, I didn't," or "I forgot." They genuinely want to have a close community, while at the same time they resist the claims that community makes on their schedule and resources in the name of individualism, spontaneity, freedom, and choice.

This is exactly how many students talk about sororities and fraterni- 20 ties. Fewer than 10 percent of AnyU residents are members of either. When I asked students whether they'd considered "rushing," instead of mentioning the "elitism" or "conservative politics" that dominated Greek critique in my day, students complained about "conformity" and "control of my life." Judy explained that she had almost rushed but then changed her mind because "you become lost. It's hard to know all ninety girls in a sorority. You become the same rather than an individual in a group. It can get, you know, almost cult-like, and you spend all your time there. You can't live in other dorms, or meet new people."

I found that students' greatest objections to the Greek system were its steep demands—that it required so much time ("I can't give up that many nights a week to one organization") and so many resources ("Why should I pay all that money to a fraternity to have friends when I can make friends for free?"), all of them mandatory ("I don't want people telling me what to do and where I have to be all the time"; "I'm an individual, not a group person"). Yet, the one AnyU student in ten who did join a fraternity or sorority was, according to 2003 surveys conducted by the Office of Student Life, much less likely to drop out of school and much more likely to report the highest level of satisfaction with campus life.

There is a familiar dilemma here. "The very organizations that give security to students," concluded national policy analysts in 1990, "can also create isolation and even generate friction on the campus."[3] More than half of university presidents were reported to view Greek life as a problem, largely because it creates "little loyalties" that isolate students, removing them from the mainstream life of the university. It is not just Greek groups that operate this way. They are only illustrative of what one university president saw as "a great deal of 'orbital energy' among the many subgroups, a magnetism that tugs at these groups, pulling them away from any common agenda."[4]

Struggling with community in this way is, as observers of American life have pointed out, the American way.[5] The same things that make us feel connected and protected are the things that make us feel obligated and trapped as individuals and/or cut off from other groups with different agendas. For most students, as for most Americans in general, the "big community" has a dual connotation that includes both a warm and fuzzy side, all about "oneness" or "togetherness" or "common purpose," and a negative side that tends to surface with reference to government regulations, Big Brother images, and fears of conformity. When students talk about their educational community, these contradictory ideas of community are reproduced, bouncing between an entity that provides love and a sense of belonging and one that limits freedom and imposes new obligations.

I initially encountered student thoughts about community on "introduction sheets," tellingly titled "IT'S ALL ABOUT ME," that the RA had asked us to fill out and hang on our doors. Aimed at "community building," the sheets posed questions designed to acquaint others on the hall with our opinions and personality. After blanks for our major, hometown, and favorite color, and prompts to name our distinctive qualities, "the things I like to do for fun," and "what makes you unique," was the question, "What does community mean to you?"

For half the students, community was a somewhat naïve amalgam of love, belonging, sharing, and togetherness—all the things we would want community to do for us with none of its obligations. It was, in their words, "respect; caring, open people" who would be "sharing together, always there for me"; a place where there are "pillows on the floor" and "everybody leaves their door open," where you can "crash on your neighbor's floor if you're too tired to go home." My favorite answer in this category was "Community means being able to fart comfortably," because it so perfectly ignores the possibility of being the one at the other end of the farting freedom who has to put up with her flatulent neighbors. Only one person, in fact, mentioned any kind of responsibility when defining community, stating that she would "pick up garbage when I see it on the ground."

The downside of the community coin was also well represented, with some students balking at the idea of community or making jokes: "Community means Communism"; "Community means dirt—do you realize how many germs infest close-proximity living quarters?"; "Community means I can do whatever annoying habits I want and if my neighbors don't like it they can move out."

What I saw in student responses, as well as in student behavior, was a profound ambivalence about community life, resulting in a tentative, often conflicted relationship to the collective life of the university. Not only did campus participation suffer from this conflict, but also it was difficult to create mutual commitments and agreements among people whose connection to community was so hesitant.

One of the most interesting community ventures at AnyU came in the form of our second hall meeting in each semester, where we devised our "Community Living Agreement." Initiated by the RAs, these were to be the local agreements that each wing lived by, the "dos and don'ts" of hall life, fashioned by the residents themselves. The agreement for the first semester was drafted at a "mandatory" hall meeting at which seven people on the wing showed, one of whom left almost immediately because it was her birthday and she was too drunk to pay attention. After pizza, M&Ms, and yet another icebreaker game, the RA introduced our charge of creating a joint compact and handed out cards and pens, asking each person to write down something in the way of a rule or a "don't" that she would like to obtain for the hall. When we'd finished, the RA taped an enormous blank sheet of white paper to the wall, stood next to it with a marker, and said, "Tell me some of your items." Reluctantly and slowly, each person volunteered some rule. "Don't be too loud at night"; "Close the shower curtain so it doesn't flood the little anteroom"; "Don't leave your hair in the drain"; "Keep your door open when you're in your room (unless you're studying/sleeping)"; "Wipe your hair off of the shower walls"; "Don't take showers too long if there are people waiting."

There was no real discussion of any of the items. After everyone contributed, the RA took the sheet off the wall and left us to our candy. About one week later a large printed poster appeared on the hall, titled "Community Living Agreement," listing eight items, half of them pertaining to showers and a few to hair.

The same process occurred during the second semester, although shower   30 etiquette had a lower priority. Six items were posted in the hall for our second semester community agreement:

Keep hair off the shower walls.
Keep doors open while you're chillin'.
Sleepovers and parties on the hall are cool.
Yell "flushing" if there's someone in the shower [because the shower water turned scalding during the flush].
No writing on the bathroom stall walls [this was the RA's].
Say "hi" to people to be friendly.

Although the agreement no doubt reflected some important values held by the residents, including sociability, courtesy, and cleanliness, it was the relationship of the individuals to the community agreement that interested me most. There had been no road map for actually creating an agreement, no mechanism for turning individual opinions into a community document. No one, including the RA, was comfortable suggesting that we might modify, prioritize, or remove individuals' suggestions from the list. While the seven students in attendance were considered to "represent" the others, because the latter did not show up to participate, there was no means for making the "agreement" binding on hall residents. As a result, the list remained posted for a semester, but each student on the hall decided whether she would abide by the agreement or not.

I never once heard anyone yell "flushing" in the bathroom, nor did I ever see a "cool sleepover" or public party on the hall. It seemed to me that the same people who kept their doors open prior to the agreement, including me, were the ones who kept their doors open afterward. There was never any follow-up or discussion about whether our agreement was being honored.

Community in the American university is paradoxically a private and an individual decision. As Robert Putnam documents in his history of community in the United States, *Bowling Alone*, the private decision to participate in community life is one that individuals in recent U.S. history are making less and less. From civic and religious life to political participation and informal social connections, there is an increasing individualism in American life that is evident in our universities as well.[6]

In such a historical light, the trends in dormitory living are thought-provoking. The newest dormitories being built across the country are both higher in amenities and lower in density than those of the past. It is no longer considered a viable model of campus life to have a hall full of people sharing a communal bathroom, lounge, and washing machine. The old blueprint of collective living has given way to much more individualized and opulent arrangements. Put in student lingo, individualism "rules."

At AnyU, new dorms are all built "suite-style," with four students shar-   35 ing a huge apartment with four bedrooms and two bathrooms, as well as its own living room, kitchen, and washer-dryer units. The private bedrooms and semi-private bathrooms are more acceptable to contemporary students, who are no longer accustomed in childhood to sharing a room with a sibling. In fact, according to AnyU's Office of Residence Life, the number one reason why students move out of traditional dormitories is that they do not like sharing a communal bathroom. Dormitories, like campus life as a whole, are increasingly privatized, well appointed, and focused on an ever smaller network of people that constitutes the significant living community of the student.

These national trends bring into clearer focus the use of space in my own dormitory, a building constructed in the 1940s for a 1940s student. One can see how new students with new values have refashioned the existing space. The dormitory includes big, cushy public spaces filled with overstuffed furniture which appear to be expecting a crowd. There are lounges on each floor, one with a fireplace and some with large outside terraces; they have tables and chairs, community TVs and VCRs.

After using these spaces as a student, I began to realize something that I subsequently checked by monitoring more public lounges in my dorm and others: Fellow students didn't really use these areas as social space. With the exception of the cleaning staff on their lunch breaks, I never saw students bring food and eat together, sit and socialize together, or even watch television together in our local lounge. During the course of an entire semester, what could be called "community life" or even "social activity" was extremely sparse. I saw one or two card games in the lounge on my floor, one simulation game meeting, scattered study groups that assembled in the dorm to work on a class project, and a Christian group who occasionally used the space to work on volunteer projects.

My observations of lounges in other dormitories were not significantly different. These spaces often sat empty. During the day, no one used them at all. On most nights, the overstuffed couches and chairs in our largest lounge would be draped with one to three students who had positioned themselves as far as possible from one another. Interviews with the few students who *were* in the lounges during my observations revealed that the majority came there to "get away" — from a gathering in their room, music blasting on the hall, or a roommate with a guest. In other words, the community spaces were often a *retreat* from social interaction, a way to create more private options. They were no longer, as their builders had probably envisioned, primarily a place for people to come together and participate in joint activities.

One of my greatest epiphanies about community life in the dorm came on Super Bowl Sunday. I had sneaked home Saturday night, intending to stay at my own house until Sunday night, when I realized that on Sunday afternoon at 2 PM Super Bowl coverage would begin, and I needed to be at the dorm. The event had been advertised heavily in the hall for weeks. "Free Ticket," the flyers read, and the "ticket" entitled one to good company, free pizza, and drinks during the game. The large lobby had been set up with two big-screen TVs so as to accommodate viewers from any vantage point.

I arrived a little early to get a good seat and waited for the lobby lounge to   40
fill, but by game time there were only five other people in the space. One had tuned the second TV set to a different program, so I and four others watched the opening kickoff together. A couple of months earlier, when I had been the only one in the lounge for the World Series, I simply assumed that the event was under-advertised and that this generation had no love of baseball. When I saw that the same no-show pattern had occurred with the well-publicized football event, I decided to investigate further. Where were the other students? I left at halftime.

Many, I surmised, had gone to sports bars. But as I wandered the floors of my dorm, I could hear the game playing from numerous rooms. On my corridor alone, where there were two open doors, I could see clusters of people in each room eating and drinking as they watched the game together on their own sizable television sets. It seemed telling to me that so many dormitory residents were watching the same game in different places, the great majority preferring to pass the time with a carefully chosen group of personal friends in their own private space. It spoke in a more general way to how community really worked in the university.

Rather than being located in its shared symbols, meetings, activities, and rituals, the university for an undergraduate was more accurately a world of self-selected people and events. The university community was experienced by most students as a relatively small, personal network of people who did things together. This "individual community" was bolstered by a university system that honors student choice, as well as a level of materialism in the larger society that, by enabling students to own their own cars, computers, TV sets, and VCRs, renders collective resources and spaces superfluous. These characteristics of American university life—individualism, choice, and materialism—stand out even more clearly in chapter 4, where foreign students at AnyU describe and compare their own educational systems.

AnyU's Real Community: The Ego-Centered Network

When I asked students in interviews whether they felt they had a "community" at AnyU, most said yes. But what they meant by community were these personal networks of friends that some referred to as my "homeys." It was these small, ego-centered groups that were the backbone of most students' social experience in the university.

On a daily basis these personal networks were easily recognizable within the dorm and on campus. "Where are you now?" says the cell phone caller walking back to the dorm from class. "I'm on my way home, so ask Jeffrey and Mark to come, and I'll meet you at my room at 8." Such conversations are everywhere. In the dorm, residents can be heard discussing the timing and location of dinners and after-dinner plans, and message boards record the social negotiations: "Be home by 5:30. What about Mexican? Call me—P." Creating one's community involved very conscious choices to make one's leisure hours jibe with selected others'. There were few open invitations in these exchanges. Unless the RA had planned an activity, there was no general call to join in on dinner plans or come watch a video in someone's room.

Among members of the same network, however, there were constant inter-actions, ranging from borrowing detergent and snacks, to arranging social and shopping trips, to watching TV or videos together, to working out. The communications among network members occurred both publicly, like the planning just noted, and privately, as I saw in student diaries, where frequent cell phone contact and Instant Messaging sessions were the norm.

The intense reciprocity of ego-based groups helped explain a problem about campus traffic that had long puzzled me. As a professor, I could never under-stand why campus roads were so hopelessly jammed between classes. After all, AnyU had a campus bus system, and students had parking permits only for the lots adjacent to their dorms. They couldn't legally park at classroom building lots and would receive a hefty ticket if they did. When I pasted my student park-ing pass on my car, I found myself basically grounded—able to drive off campus and back to my dorm but nowhere else. Why, then, were the roads so crowded with cars seemingly traveling from dorms to classes?

It wasn't long before I saw message boards with reminders such as "Tara, don't forget to pick me up 10 AM at the Social Science building.—L." Or "Be out in the Education Parking Lot at 3:10—Nick." As I walked or took the bus to class, I began to pay more attention to the non-dormitory parking lots and real-ized that there was a vast web of personal relationships activated for dropping and picking up passengers. It was network reciprocity at work.

These personal networks grew in importance to me as I realized their salience in the life of my fellow students, and in the life of the university. I became increasingly interested in how friends are made, how groups are formed, and how activities are coordinated. I built these queries in to my interviews and discovered much that observation alone did not tell me.

Student networks, like family relations, are ego based. In a family, even your first cousin will have relatives that you don't have in common, and the same is true of two students who are in each other's networks. Pam and Terry are part of the same social network, but when they separately name their own closest friends, the names are not exactly the same. Pam includes her boyfriend and his roommate along with Alice and Marie in her close net-work, while Terry includes Alice, Marie, and Pam but also a friend from class whom Pam barely knows. And Pam's boyfriend shares only a few of Pam's friends. One student's network, although it may overlap with those of others, is essentially personal; no two people share the exact same group of friends. This is what is meant by ego based: Even these intimate forms of community are quite individual.

Most students, I found, had established a network of two to six friends who 50
formed their core university community. From the "native" point of view, they
got together because "we like each other." Students regularly named personality traits and attitudes to explain their attraction to friends: "They're outspo-
ken"; "We're all a little weird"; "We like to have fun"; they're "strong-minded
and focused like me"; they're "up for anything, and pretty laid back"; "We're the
same when it comes to school, not big party-ers"; or they're "real friendly, open,
responsible people."

To an outsider, especially an outsider who is looking at the points of convergence among a number of students, student networks have less to do with
personality than with shared circumstances and shared demographics. Kyle,
a Christian student on the floor, had a network of close friends for whom being
Christian was very important. They'd met while they were still in high school,
after attending several retreats that happened to be held at AnyU. By the time
they came to AnyU as freshmen, they were already friends. The close networks
of five of the six minority students in my sample contained several other minority students. A number of them had met their closest friends in an intensive
pre-college summer program for first-generation students, where there had
been a sizable percentage of minority students. One of the most surprising findings to me was the discovery that eight of fourteen students interviewed about
the subject of social networks had one or more people in their close personal
networks whom they knew from high school or their hometown. In all, then,
many of the networks that endured through college were based on experiences
before college, and these were conditioned by demographic characteristics such
as religion, race, ethnicity, and/or hometown (itself a function of race, ethnicity,
religion, and class).

Once in school, it was also edifying to learn how early the enduring friend-
ships occurred in students' college life, and how little they drew on academic
interests and contacts. Most students whose friends were cultivated after
college began had met their closest friends by virtue of living in the same freshman dorm or floor. Classroom contacts figured relatively little in the social
networks of students; fewer than one-quarter of my interview students had
met a member of their network in an academic class or in an activity or club
related to their major, while almost as many had met a close friend through
ROTC or work.

Despite the belief that college expands our social horizons and extends
our experience to include new and different types of people, the findings
suggest otherwise. The most significant relationships are formed either
before college or very early in one's college career, most often in some shared
affiliation, whether voluntary or not, such as freshman dorm assignment,
special freshman summer program, ROTC, ethnic club, or sorority and fraternity rush.

Diaries and interviews confirmed that for many students, their social lives
at the university consisted of repeated contacts with the same people, who
constituted that student's personal network. Once networks were formed, usually by the end of the freshman year, students tended to stay with their groups,

maintaining intense and frequent interactions with their network and more superficial and sparse contacts with others. The way that student social life is formed necessarily affects issues of diversity.

Diversity at AnyU?

Student networks may be able to explain, at least in part, the failed diversity efforts at many universities, and certainly at AnyU. About 22 to 25 percent of AnyU students are considered "minority" by federal standards, and minority students appear approximately in these percentages in AnyU dorms and classes. What makes diversity a "success" in a state university, however, is not only that the university population reflects the diversity of the general population but also that students become more involved in the lives and issues of that diverse population. Part of that diversity ideal is the hope that all students will develop friends and have important conversations with those of backgrounds and ethnicities different from their own.

The National Survey of Student Engagement tries to capture this information by asking a student to self-report as to whether he or she has "had serious conversations with students of a different race or ethnicity than your own." In 2003, fifty percent of college seniors nationwide indicated

Most students, but white students predominantly, ended up becoming close friends with people of their own ethnicity.

that they "often" or "very often" had such conversations, while only 13 percent said they did not.

This jibed with the information I initially was getting from my interviews about social networks, where I was finding that many students named someone from a different ethnic group within their close circle of friends. The interview information, though, did not match my direct observations, and this led me to probe further by fiddling with my interview questions and format. I soon realized that if I started, as I had, by asking informants whether they had close friends from other ethnic groups, the majority of students would say that they did. If I questioned them further, they would name that man from a class, or woman on the same intramural volleyball team, with whom they had close contact and describe how they met.

If, however, I started by asking informants to name their closest friends and then later asked them to identify the ethnicity of the named people, it turned out that most students, but white students predominantly, ended up becoming close friends with people of their own ethnicity. Since I thought that this "names first, ethnicity later" approach was more accurate, I changed the order of my questions and arrived at a very different picture. Five out of six white students I interviewed in this way about their networks had no members of another racial or ethnic group in their close social circle; the networks of five of the six minority students contained one or more minorities (more on the details of this later).

One can see from the descriptions of how networks form why this might be true. Many students are building on contacts developed before they entered college, contacts that have strong demographic and social components. If many student networks begin with hometown contacts, what is the likelihood that they will cross class, ethnic, race, or even religious lines when the United States is demographically divided along precisely these lines? Although there was one instance in my data of a cross-racial network pair with its origin in high school, the probabilities in this country work strongly the other way because of de facto neighborhood and school segregation. All other examples I found of high school or hometown friends in an AnyU network involved a woman or man of the same ethnicity as the person interviewed.

Even many relationships developed early in college contain a built-in bias. Although classes and interest clubs may be ethnically well mixed, this is not where students make their earliest school contacts. Freshman dorms are generally well integrated, but not several of the early programs and events that help introduce and acclimate new students, including Previews weekends designated for particular ethnic groups, pre-college "outdoor adventure" trips that cost extra money, a summer program for first-generation college students, or the opening round of sorority and fraternity mixers. Some institutional structures like these may encourage the early formation of same-ethnicity relationships. 60

There is no doubt that active racism also plays a part in the lack of diversity on college campuses. Yet, race or ethnicity is typically ignored as a topic of conversation in mainstream college culture, treated as an invisible issue and with silence. As Levine and Cureton (1998) found in their nationwide survey, students were "more willing to tell intimate details of their sex lives than discuss race relations on campus."[7] When the subject *is* raised, as in the occasional class, students of color report being continually expected to educate whites about minority issues or speak "as a representative of their race."

Despite the general invisibility of the subject of race in informal student culture, there was not a single minority student I interviewed who hadn't experienced racism.[8] Few openly complained, but everyone had at least one story to tell of comments made in class, rude remarks on the street, or just hostile looks. When I asked Pat, a Hispanic–Native American woman, whether she had ever considered rushing a sorority, she told me that she had in her freshman year, but "I could see that it wasn't really right for me, because I'd pass by all the sorority tables—you know how they call out to girls to come over and take a look—well, I saw they called out to other girls but not to me. They just kinda ignored me, not hostile or anything, but not interested either."

"It's just how it is," another female student explained. "There are some good people and some not so good people, and you deal with it."

Who Eats with Whom: A Study of Student Dining

My very small sample of student networks and interviews was suggestive to me but not convincing that diversity in student relationships was in serious question. So I decided to conduct a larger observational study of students' informal social behavior. I chose eating as the focus, one of my favorite social activities, and asked the research question "Who eats with whom?" This seemed a fair and appropriate inquiry into diversity, to determine the range of people with whom one breaks bread.

It was my most extensive and longest-running "mini-study" of campus life. For five months I directly observed and recorded the dining behavior of fellow students during randomly selected periods of the day at optional dining areas on campus.[9] Although some patrons carried out their food, returning to their dorms or outside benches to eat, many ate and drank singly or in groups at the various tables provided in one of five eating areas I surveyed. Sitting at a different table in the room, I would record who sat at each table by gender and, as much as outward appearances can signal, ethnicity.

It is always problematic to do research like this, because there is a wide range of appearances for all ethnicities, and many sticky issues. My interest, however, *was* in appearances, and in seeing to what extent students chose to share food and conversation with people who looked like them (or, more accurately, seemed to belong in the same broad ethnic category that an observer would attribute to them). Although there are other kinds of diversity (e.g., age), I recorded only the data reflecting each person's gender and, to the extent possible, his or her category of ethnicity such as white non-Hispanic, Hispanic, Asian, African American, Native American, and so on. These were not easy calls. Sometimes I could tell only that someone was not a white non-Hispanic but couldn't identify the more specific group to which she or he belonged; at other times I could not tell whether a person was white and non-Hispanic or something else.

In gathering this information I had these questions in mind: To what extent did informal university activities (e.g., eating together) convey diversity? Did students eat in same or mixed ethnic and gender groups? Were there differences in the eating patterns of dominant (defined as white non-Hispanic) and non-dominant (defined as people of color) ethnic groups? Did any ethnic group or category eat alone more often than others?

I analyzed the data with regard to these questions but took care to analyze by person rather than by table in order to try to see the data through the eyes of the particular diner. For instance, if there were a table consisting of four people—a white male, two white women, and one Hispanic woman—each would have a different reality at the table: The male is eating with a table of all women of mixed ethnicity; both white women are eating at a table of mixed gender and mixed ethnicity; and the Hispanic woman is eating at a mixed-gender table where everyone is of a different ethnicity from herself. I recorded the data, preserving the perspective of each diner, and then analyzed the data in ten different categories that allowed me to examine the relationship of each table diner to the rest.[10] In this way, I tracked almost 1,500 examples of dining behavior.

What I found was interesting. It showed not only an overall lack of diversity, as national studies report,[11] but also the existence of huge differences in the diversity experiences of dominant and non-dominant groups. Minorities (people of color) ate alone only slightly more often: one-quarter of minority women and more than one-third of minority men sitting in public spaces ate alone, a rate greater than that for white women and men by 3 percent and 5 percent, respectively. But of all those who ate with others, only 10 percent of white men and 14 percent of white women ate at a table where there was anyone of a different color from themselves. Only 2.6 percent and 3.5 percent of white men and women, respectively, ate at a table of two or more where they were the only white person. The statistics were strikingly different for people of color: 68 percent of women and 58 percent of men ate with "mixed groups." People of color were ten times more likely than whites to eat in a group in which they were the only person of a different race/ethnicity at the table.

The same patterns I saw in the dining spaces proved true in the composition of personal networks when I compared a group of twelve students on my hall, six whites and six students of color. Although the networks of Caucasian students included more whites, and those of people of color more minorities, the total networks of minority students were primarily "mixed," comprising people of various ethnicities, including whites. One student of color was in an all-white network, while another had friends of only her own ethnicity. By contrast, five of the six white students had networks that were solidly white; only one white student had a mixed network, and none was the only Caucasian.

Seen in this context, minority ethnic clubs, dorms, and student unions have a clearer meaning. Ethnic-based groups are often clouded by perceptions that they, like the Greek system, remove their members from the mainstream and surround them with people of the same background. What the data suggest to me is that people of color are already heavily involved in interethnic and interracial relationships on campus. In fact, most of their informal dining contacts, as well as personal networks, included people who were ethnically different from them. Under these circumstances, an ethnic-based club—which half of the minorities in my sample thought was important in their lives—is better understood as a needed respite from difference, a chance to rest comfortably with others who share similar experiences in the world.

It was white students, most markedly males, whose social lives suffered from a lack of diversity. When white men *did* eat with those of different ethnicities, the majority of tables were "cross-gender." In other words, white men socialized at meals to a greater degree with nonwhite women or with groups that included nonwhite women. There was extremely little contact between white and nonwhite men. Only 4 of 489 white males, fewer than 1 percent, ate with (only) males of a different ethnicity, but 31 ate in different or mixed ethnic groups in which women were present. Men of color, while much more diverse in their dining, followed a similar pattern, tending to have fewer cross-ethnic male-only eating partners (7 of 79) while favoring cross-ethnic tables where women were eating too (24 of 79). The same pattern was not true of women. For both white women and women of color, their cross-color contact was primarily with other women.

One of the more disturbing but confusing findings was how few people of color, proportionally, used the common eating spaces. Only 13 percent of the entire dining sample was nonwhite, while 22 percent of full-time students were nonwhite. This left more than 40 percent of the minority population unaccounted for. There are certainly many ways to interpret what was going on. Perhaps this eyeballing approach to minority status simply fails to recognize many who are legal minorities. Perhaps there are economic factors at work that bear on having a meal ticket or buying food during the day that disadvantage some minority students. Perhaps the difference is explained by the larger percentage of minority students who enroll in off-campus programs. But there is another possibility that I entertained, which was related to my finding that more minority students eat alone.

My evidence is only anecdotal because I didn't formally monitor what I thought I was seeing, but this is what I noticed. I would observe the food court area as people got their food and stood in line to pay, watching each person leave the register to see where he or she went to sit in order to mark it in my book. I often found that instead of going to a table, however, a person of color would go to a condiment area, pack up a napkin and the food in a bag, and leave. It seemed to me that a greater proportion of minorities was leaving.

One day, as I was just finishing an observation session, an African American woman left the register and headed for a table. She would be the last diner to enter my monitored space in the set time period. I prepared to mark her table choice, but instead of sitting down, she readjusted her backpack, took her food, and left. Where is she going? I asked myself. To meet a friend in a different area? To eat outside? I felt a bit like a stalker as I followed her out of the dining area and out of the building. She passed the outdoor tables and kept walking until she entered one of the freshman dorms, went through the lobby, and up the stairs. My guess was that she had returned to eat in her dorm room.

I will never know for sure what lay behind that one observation, or what I perceived to be the larger proportion of students of color who did not stay to eat. But it left me with the uncomfortable feeling that I was witnessing the effect of a "white space"—which I had never noticed because I am white—where people of color could eat alone publicly, or eat with people different from themselves, or go home to their rooms. Perhaps, many times, the dorm room just seems the most comfortable option, and this may have explained some of the missing 40 percent of minority students in the dining areas.

The ideals of community and diversity are certainly in place at AnyU and remain important components of stated university policy. Yet neither is fully realized in university culture, as I believe I have illustrated in this chapter. What I also hope I've illustrated, though, is what anthropologists mean when they say that a culture cannot really be divided into its parts; one part of a culture cannot be understood in isolation from its other parts, and all must be contextualized within the larger whole. Culture, we argue, is both integrated and holistic.

In just this way "community" and "diversity" are parts of university culture, but they are not intelligible on their own. As the descriptions of student life attest, diversity is one part of college culture that is intimately tied to community, another part. And both parts are ultimately conditioned by structures in the larger American society—including values of individualism and choice, materialism, and the realities of U.S. demographics—that may seem, at first, to have little bearing on whether college diversity increases because freshmen Joe and Juan truly become friends, or whether Jane strengthens community by deciding to attend Movie Night. But they do. Not understanding this leads to a reality about diversity and community in university culture that does not match its rhetoric, and a persistent confusion about why this is so.

NOTES

1. Carnegie Foundation for the Advancement of Teaching 1990, 64, 63.
2. Ibid., 48.
3. Ibid., 49.
4. Ibid., 50
5. Varenne 1977.
6. Putnam 2000.
7. Levine and Cureton 1998, 72.
8. My brief section here hardly does justice to the urgency of race and ethnicity issues on campus or, for that matter, to the active discrimination experienced by gay and transgendered individuals. For more on the thoughts and experiences of minority and gay students, see Lesage et al. 2002 and Howard and Stevens 2000, and see Tusmith and Reddy 2002 for teachers' challenges with teaching diversity to students.
9. To mitigate such factors as meal plans and off-campus versus on-campus living, which may draw differentially on class and ethnicity, I confined my observations to tables shared in the optional dining areas on campus where either a meal plan card or cash was accepted. I made observations only during the day and from Monday to Friday, when most classes were in session, because these were the times and meals, I figured, that would be least affected by demographic and economic differences among students.
10. Each diner ("who," according to gender and ethnicity) and the number at the table (#) were recorded. Then each person sitting at the table was recorded by gender and specific ethnicity, where possible. The data were then sorted and analyzed by looking at the composition of the table from the diner's point of view and marked as to whether the diner was eating with: (1) no one (the person was sitting alone); (2) females of the same ethnic/power group (SF), males of the same ethnic/power group (SM), or a mixed-gender table of the same ethnic/power group (SX); (2) females (OF) or males (OM) of a different ethnic/power group, a mixed-gender table comprising members of a different ethnic/power group (OX); or (3) a mixed ethnic/power group that was all female (MxF), all male (MxM), or mixed gender (MxX). The term "ethnic/power group" is used because, for purposes of this section, people's ethnicities were analyzed in two broad categories that are more than ethnic designations: dominant (white non-Hispanic) and minority (people of color) groups. More detailed ethnic information was recorded and reviewed, but the comparisons here focused on dominant and non-dominant groups.
11. "Walk into the cafeteria in most colleges and universities," write Levine and Cureton, "and the tables are separated by race and ethnicity. The larger the campus, the sharper the divisions" (1998, 86).

BIBLIOGRAPHY

Carnegie Foundation for the Advancement of Teaching. 1990. *Campus Life: In Search of Community*. Princeton: Carnegie Foundation for the Advancement of Teaching.

Howard, Kim, and Annie Stevens. 2000. *Out and About Campus: Personal Accounts by Lesbian, Gay, Bisexual, and Transgendered College Students.* Los Angeles: Alyson Books.

Lesage, Julia, Abby L. Ferber, Debbie Storrs, and Donna Wong. 2002. *Making a Difference: University Students of Color Speak Out.* Lanham, Md.: Rowman & Littlefield.

Levine, Arthur, and Jeanette S. Cureton. 1998. *When Hope and Fear Collide: A Portrait of Today's College Student.* San Francisco: Jossey-Bass.

Putnam, Robert D. 2000. *Bowling Alone: The Collapse and Revival of American Community.* New York: Simon & Schuster.

Tusmith, Bonnie, and Maureen T. Reddy, eds. 2002. *Race in the College Classroom: Pedagogy and Politics.* New Brunswick: Rutgers University Press.

Varenne, Hervé. 1977. *Americans Together: Structured Diversity in a Midwestern Town.* New York: Teachers College Press.

Questions for Critical Reading

1. What does Nathan mean by *ego-centered network*? Develop a definition of the term by locating passages where Nathan discusses this concept. What role do these networks play in community? Support your answer with examples from the essay.

2. Most of Nathan's essay is concerned with the failures of both community and diversity at AnyU. Reread her essay critically to locate passages in which Nathan indicates the main reasons for the lack of both at her school.

3. Submerged in Nathan's analysis are the requirements for successfully promoting community and diversity. Look back through her essay and find quotations that provide the tools needed to promote these ideals.

Exploring Context

1. In this selection Nathan is interested in exploring the gap between her school's stated goals for community and diversity and the actuality of these ideals in student life. What are your school's objectives in these two areas? Generate a sense of how your school approaches community and diversity by searching for these terms in your institution's Web site, and then prepare a short report on what you find in this search. Do you find the same gap between image and reality that Nathan finds at her institution? If not, what might account for the success of community and diversity in your school? How does your work on failures of community and diversity from Question 2 of Questions for Critical Reading apply to your school's Web site?

2. Nathan opens by recounting the time line presentation that students at AnyU watch during orientation. Use the Web to research significant national or world events that took place at different stages of your own life. Share these time lines in small groups. Do you and your classmates share the same historical sense?

Did you look up the same years or dates? How might such a time line produce community, and why might you and your classmates have different events listed? Do the differences in your apprehensions of the past create challenges to forming community? Does the diversity of your class play any role?

3. At the heart of Nathan's analysis are the very definitions of community and diversity. Search for blog entries on "community" and "diversity" using BlogPulse (blogpulse.com), a search engine for blogs. Based on the blog postings you read, what do these terms mean to people in general? How do they talk about them? Do they value them? How are they viewed differently in the blogosphere and at AnyU? What might account for this difference?

Questions for Connecting

1. How can Leslie Savan's analysis of pop talk in "What's Black, Then White, and Said All Over?" (p. 363) help explain the failure of diversity on college campuses? What role might "paying the dues" have in achieving true diversity? Relate your answer to your work on this issue from Questions for Critical Reading.

2. Given Steve Olson's argument in "The End of Race: Hawaii and the Mixing of Peoples" (p. 250) about the end of any genetic basis for race, how important is diversity? Does Hawaii serve as a model for college communities? Or does Nathan help explain why notions of race persist even without a genetic basis?

3. Michael Pollan examines the complex ecosystems of organic farming in "The Animals: Practicing Complexity" (p. 281). Might those ecosystems provide a model for community and diversity in education? How can individuals serve as holons on the college campus? Use your work on your school's Web site from Question 1 of Exploring Context in considering your own school as an ecosystem. What might be a holon for your campus?

Language Matters

1. Sentences can be written in either active or passive voice. If you're not sure what these terms mean, look up *active* and *passive voice* in a grammar handbook or reference guide. Then select a quotation from Nathan's essay that you think is key to her argument. Identify whether it is written in active or passive voice, noting how you know this to be the case. Then rewrite the sentence in the opposite voice. Is the argument weaker in passive voice or in active voice? Are concepts clearer in one voice or the other? Why or why not? Why might you choose active or passive voice in your own writing?

2. Word choice and tone are important in your writing. Select a significant quotation from Nathan's text, type it into a blank document in a word processor, and, using a thesaurus (the word processor's, one online, or a printed one), replace every significant word in the sentence with a synonym. Does the sentence still work? How does word choice influence tone and meaning? Why didn't Nathan

use "fancier" or more "academic" language in this text? Based on what you have discovered, what sort of tone do you think you should use in your writing for this class?

3. Drafting and revising are crucial components of the writing process. We often see a published piece of writing as perfect, but imagine earlier drafts of Nathan's text. How do you think she started this piece? What areas do you think Nathan revised the most? Where do you think you should do the most revision as you draft your own papers?

Assignments for Writing

1. Nathan notes that despite AnyU's best efforts to unite the university's population, students who make up the different communities within the school would rather bond within their own social groups than venture outside of them. Assess the situation Nathan talks about in her essay. Thinking beyond Nathan's findings, write a paper in which you examine the possibilities of communities becoming fully integrated. Is such integration even possible in a world made up of so many diverse and differing communities? The purpose of this essay is for you to apply the concepts in Nathan's essay to your own specific observations and experiences. Rather than simply writing a story about your own opinions, you should instead use your experiences and observations among diverse communities, on an academic campus or elsewhere, to explore the possibilities of a truly integrated community. You may also want to use your responses to Questions for Critical Reading and Exploring Context in supporting your argument.

2. Nathan decides going undercover is the only way to understand why university social life has not become what university presidents want. This reflects her belief that these leaders are out of touch with students' perspectives on community. So, although university presidents want the best for their schools, in fact it seems like their actions have had little impact. Write a paper in which you examine why it is important for university and college leaders to share the same outlook as their students in terms of community building. To help you complete your essay successfully, you may want to closely read specific passages from Nathan's essay that outline the perspectives university presidents and students have. Why is it so important to understand the differences in those perspectives?

3. How does individuality inhibit community building within diverse populations? Write a paper in which you assess the potential for balancing the needs of individuals and communities. Use your responses to Questions for Critical Reading as well as to Question 3 of Questions for Connecting to support your argument. Are ego-centered networks inevitable? Are diversity and community mutually exclusive goals?

Steve Olson

Journalist **Steve Olson**, who holds a B.S. in physics from Yale University, has reported for the *Atlantic Monthly*, *Science*, and *Scientific American* and has published multiple books, including *Mapping Human History: Discovering the Past through Our Genes* (2002), which was a finalist for the National Book Award, and *Count Down* (2004), about teens at the International Mathematical Olympiad.

In *Mapping Human History*, the source of the following selection, Olson studies the path of our species through genes and continents, tracking all of humanity back to a small group that lived in eastern Africa, debunking racial myths along the way. Regardless of what appear to be differences among us, suggests Olson, biologically we are all basically the same. Our group origins and differences, which were superficial to begin with, lose importance as time goes by.

In "The End of Race: Hawaii and the Mixing of Peoples," Olson considers centuries of intermarriage between native and nonnative races in the Hawaiian islands. Although this extensive "mixing of peoples" has led some to propose Hawaii as an example of interracial harmony, Olson acknowledges that such claims are not entirely true. Though the majority of those born and raised in Hawaii come from a complex racial and ethnic makeup, social, political, and historical influences have contributed to deep cultural divides among the various island populations. Now, in the aftermath of European colonization, the preservation of Hawaiian culture as well as the definition of what it means to be a native Hawaiian are pressing questions with no easy genetic or biological answers. Thus Olson ultimately questions whether racial and cultural identity are rooted in biology or affiliation. The "end of race" is, perhaps, no end at all.

What defines race? And given how complicated such a definition must inevitably be, how can we end racism and promote racial harmony?

▶ TAGS: *research*, *race*, *community*, *diplomacy*, *diversity*, *ethnicity*, *bioethics*, *integration*

The End of Race: Hawaii and the Mixing of Peoples

> He loved everything, he was full of joyous love toward everything that
> he saw. And it seemed to him that was just why he was previously so
> ill—because he could love nothing and nobody.
>
> —HERMANN HESSE, *Siddhartha*

On the morning of November 26, 1778, the 100-foot-long, three-masted ship
Resolution, captained by the fifty-year-old Englishman James Cook, sailed
into view off the northeast coast of the Hawaiian island of Maui. The island's
Polynesian inhabitants had never seen a European sailing ship before. The
sight of the *Resolution* just beyond the fierce windward surf must have looked
as strange to them as a spaceship from another planet. Yet they responded
without hesitation. They boarded canoes and paddled to the ship. From atop
the rolling swells they offered the sailors food, water, and, in the case of the
women, themselves.

One can easily imagine the contrast: the European sailors—gaunt, dirty,
many bearing the unmistakable signs of venereal disease—and the Polynesians, a people who abided by strict codes of personal hygiene, who washed every
day and plucked the hair from their faces and underarms, whose women had
bodies "moulded into the utmost perfection," in the words of one early admirer.
At first Cook forbade his men to bring the women on board the ship "to prevent
as much as possible the communicating [of the] fatal disease [gonorrhea] to
a set of innocent people." In the weeks and months to come, as the *Resolution*
lingered offshore, Cook was far less resolute. Toward the end of 1779, the first of
what are today called *hapa haoles*—half European, half non-European—were
born on the island of Maui.

The nineteenth-century stereotype of the South Pacific as a sexual paradise owes as much to the feverish imaginations of repressed Europeans as to
the actions of the Polynesians. The young women who swam out to the ships in
Hawaii, Tahiti, and other South Pacific islands were from the lower classes, not
from the royalty, which carefully guarded its legitimacy. Many were training to
be dancers in religious festivals. They would rise in status by exchanging their
sexual favors for a tool, a piece of cloth, or an iron nail.

The Polynesians paid dearly for their openness. At least 300,000 people,
and possibly as many as 800,000, lived on the Hawaiian islands when Captain
Cook first sighted them (today the total population of the state is about 1.2 million). Over the course of the next century, diseases introduced by Europeans
reduced the native population to fewer than 50,000. By the time the painter
Paul Gauguin journeyed to the Pacific in 1891, the innocence that Europeans
had perceived among the Polynesians was gone. "The natives, having nothing,
nothing at all to do, think of one thing only, drinking," he wrote. "Day by day
the race vanishes, decimated by the European diseases. . . . There is so much
prostitution that it does not exist. . . . One only knows a thing by its contrary,

and its contrary does not exist." The women in Gauguin's paintings are beautiful yet defeated, without hope, lost in a vision of the past.

Today visitors to Maui land on a runway just downwind from the shore where Captain Cook battled the surf eleven generations ago. Once out of the airport, they encounter what is probably the most genetically mixed population in the world. To the genes of Captain Cook's sailors and the native Polynesians has been added the DNA of European missionaries, Mexican cowboys, African American soldiers, and plantation workers from throughout Asia and Europe. This intense mixing of DNA has produced a population of strikingly beautiful people. Miss Universe of 1997 and Miss America of 2001 were both from Hawaii. The former, Brook Mahealani Lee, is a classic Hawaiian blend. Her ancestors are Korean and Hawaiian, Chinese and European.

Bernie Adair—who was selling candles at a swap meet in Kahului, Maui's largest town, when I met her—told me that her family's history was typical. Adair, whose ancestors came to Hawaii from the Philippines, married a Portuguese man in the 1960s. In the 1980s their daughter Marlene married a man of mixed Hawaiian, Chinese, and Portuguese descent. Adair's granddaughter Carly, peeking shyly at me from under a folding table, therefore embodies four different ethnicities. "These children have grandparents with so many different nationalities you can't tell what they are," Adair said.

> **Hawaii's high rates of intermarriage have fascinated academics for decades.**

Almost half the people who live in Hawaii today are of "mixed" ancestry. What it means to be mixed is not at all obvious genetically, but for official purposes it means that a person's ancestors fall into more than one of the four "racial" categories identified on U.S. census forms: black, white, Native American, and Asian or Pacific Islander. Intermarriage is a cumulative process, so once an individual of mixed ancestry is born, all of that person's descendants also will be mixed. As intermarriage continues in Hawaii—and already almost half of all marriages are between couples of different or mixed ethnicities—the number of people who will be able to call themselves pure Japanese, or pure Hawaiian, or pure white (*haole* in Hawaiian), will steadily decline.

Hawaii's high rates of intermarriage have fascinated academics for decades. The University of Hawaii sociologist Romanzo Adams wrote an article titled "Hawai'i as a Racial Melting Pot" in 1926, and many scholars since then have extolled Hawaii as a model of ethnic and racial harmony. The researchers have always been a bit vague about the reasons for all this intermarriage; explanations have ranged from the benign climate to the "aloha spirit" of the Native Hawaiians. But their lack of analytic rigor hasn't damped their enthusiasm. One of the goals of the former Center for Research on Ethnic Relations at the University of Hawaii was "to determine why ethnic harmony exists in Hawai'i" and "to export principles of ethnic harmony to the mainland and the world."

The rest of the United States has a smaller percentage of mixed marriages than does Hawaii. But given recent trends, one might wonder if the country as a whole is headed down a road Hawaii took long ago. According to the 2000 census, one in twenty children under the age of eighteen in the United States is mixed, in that their parents fall into more than one racial category. Between the 1990 and 2000 censuses, the number of interracial couples quadrupled. This number—about 1.5 million of 55 million married couples—is not yet high, but because of kinship ties, American families are already much more mixed than they look. Demographer Joshua Goldstein of Princeton University has calculated that about 20 percent of Americans are already in extended families with someone from a different racial group—that is, they or their parents, uncles and aunts, siblings, or children have married someone classified as a member of a different race.

The rapid growth of interracial marriages in the United States and else-where marks a new phase in the genetic history of humanity. Since the appearance of modern humans in Africa more than 100,000 years ago, human groups have differentiated in appearance as they have expanded across the globe and have undergone some measure of reproductive isolation. This differentiation has always been limited by the recentness of our common ancestry and by the powerful tendency of groups to mix over time. Still, many human populations have remained sufficiently separate to develop and retain the distinctive physical characteristics we recognize today.

In Hawaii this process is occurring in reverse. It's as if a videotape of our species' history were being played backward at a fantastically rapid speed. Physical distinctions that took thousands of generations to produce are being wiped clean with a few generations of intermarriage.

The vision of the future conjured up by intermarriage in Hawaii can be seductive. When everyone is marrying everyone else, when the ethnic affiliation of most people can no longer be ascertained at a glance, one imagines that ethnic and racial tensions would diminish. But spending some time in Hawaii shows that the future will not be that simple. Despite the high rate of intermarriage here, ethnic and racial tensions haven't really disappeared. They have changed into something else, something less threatening, perhaps, but still divisive. Hawaii may well be a harbinger of a racially mixed future. But it won't be the future many people expect.

Many of the harshest conflicts in the world today are between people who are physically indistinguishable. If someone took a roomful of Palestinians and Israelis from the Middle East, or of Serbs and Albanians from the Balkans, or of Catholics and Protestants from Ireland, or of Muslims and Hindus from northern India, or of Dayaks and Madurese from Indonesia, gave them all identical outfits and haircuts, and forbade them to speak or gesture, no one could distinguish the members of the other group—at least not to the point of being willing to shoot them. The antagonists in these conflicts have different ethnicities, but they have been so closely linked biologically throughout history that they have not developed marked physical differences.

Yet one of the most perverse dimensions of ethnic thinking is the "racialization" of culture—the tendency to think of another people as not just culturally but genetically distinct. In the Yugoslavian war, the Croats caricatured their

Serbian opponents as tall and blond, while the Serbs disparaged the darker hair and skin of the Croats—even though these traits are thoroughly intermixed between the two groups. During World War II the countries of Europe fiercely stereotyped the physical attributes of their enemies, despite a history of inter-marriage and migration that has scrambled physical characteristics through-out the continent. In Africa the warring Tutsis and Hutus often call attention to the physical differences of their antagonists, but most observers have trouble distinguishing individual members of the two groups solely on the basis of appearance.

The flip side of this biological stereotyping is the elevation of one's own an-   15 cestry. The Nazis were the most notorious believers in the purity of their past, but many other groups have similar beliefs. They proclaim themselves to be descended from ancient tribes of noble warriors, or from prominent families in the distant past, or even from famous individuals.

Genetics research has revealed the flaw inherent in any such belief. Every group is a mixture of many previous groups, a fleeting collection of genetic variants drawn from a shared genetic legacy. The Polynesian colonizers of the Hawaiian archipelago are a good example. In 1795 the German anatomist J. F. Blumenbach proposed that the "Malays"—a collection of peoples, including

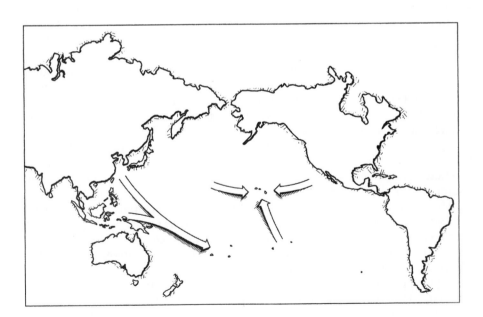

The Polynesian inhabitants of Hawaii are descended from people who lived both in southeastern Asia and in Melanesia, which includes New Guinea and nearby islands. The Polynesians migrated first to the South Pacific islands of Fiji, Tonga, and Samoa, with later migrations taking their descendants from the Marquesas islands to Hawaii. More recent migrants have included people from Asia, the Americas, and Europe.

the Polynesians, from southeastern Asia and Oceania—were one of the five races of humanity, in addition to Africans, Caucasians, Mongoloids, and Native Americans. But all of these groups (to the extent that they can be defined) are genetic composites of previous groups. In the case of the Polynesians, this mixing was part of the spread of humans into the Pacific. The last major part of the world to be occupied by humans was Remote Oceania, the widely separated islands scattered in a broad crescent from Hawaii to New Zealand. Before that, humans had been living only in Near Oceania, which includes Australia, Papua New Guinea, and the Bismarck Archipelago. The humans who settled these regions were adept at short ocean crossings, but they never developed the kinds of boats or navigation skills needed to sail hundreds of miles to Fiji, Samoa, and beyond.

Then, about 6,000 years ago, rice and millet agriculture made the leap across the Formosa Strait from the mainland of southeastern Asia to Taiwan. From there, agriculture began to spread, island by island, to the south and southeast. With it came two important cultural innovations. The first was the Austronesian language family, which eventually spread halfway around the world, from Madagascar to Easter Island. The second was a suite of new technologies—pottery, woodworking implements, and eventually the outrigger canoe and ways of using the stars to navigate across large expanses of open water. Archaeological evidence shows that people first reached the previously uninhabited island of Fiji about 3,000 years ago. They sailed to Easter Island, their farthest point east, in about AD 300 and to New Zealand, their farthest point south, in about 800.

One hypothesis, known as the express-train model of Polynesian origins, claims that both the knowledge of agriculture and Austronesian languages were carried into the Pacific by people descended almost exclusively from the first farmers who set sail from Taiwan. But genetic studies have revealed a much more complex picture. Mitochondrial and Y-chromosome haplotypes among today's Polynesians show that there was extensive mixing of peoples in Near Oceania, which eventually produced the groups that set sail for the remote islands. Though many of the mitochondrial haplotypes and Y chromosomes of the Polynesians do seem to have come from the mainland of southeastern Asia and Taiwan, others originated in New Guinea and its nearby islands—a geographic region known as Melanesia (named for the generally dark skin of its inhabitants). Geneticists Manfred Kayser and Mark Stoneking of the Max Planck Institute for Evolutionary Anthropology in Leipzig have dubbed the resulting synthesis the "slow-boat model." According to this model, today's Polynesians can trace their ancestry both to the Austronesian speakers who moved out of southeastern Asia and to the people who already occupied Melanesia.

The Polynesians first reached the Hawaiian islands around AD 400, probably in a migration from the Marquesas islands. A subsequent wave of people migrated to Hawaii from Tahiti between the twelfth and the fourteenth century. Then the islands saw no more newcomers until Captain Cook's arrival four centuries later.

The discovery of Hawaii by Europeans did not result in an immediate influx   20
of colonists. The early decades of the nineteenth century brought just a trickle
of settlers to the islands—washed-up sailors, retired captains, British and
Russian traders, missionaries. Large-scale migration began only after the first
sugar plantations were established around the middle of the century. In 1852,
three hundred Chinese men arrived to work the plantations. Over the next century nearly half a million more workers followed. They came from China, Japan,
Korea, Puerto Rico, Spain, Poland, Austria, Germany, Norway, and Russia.
Some of these groups have long since disappeared, blending into the genetic
background. Others still have a significant ethnic presence on the islands.

A few miles from the Honolulu airport is a vivid reminder of those times.
Hawaii's Plantation Village is one of the few tourist attractions designed as
much for the locals as for mainlanders. It meticulously recreates a camp town
of the type that once dotted the islands, housing the workers who toiled each
day in the sugar and pineapple fields. Each house along the main avenue reflects
the ethnicity of the workers who lived there: A large bread oven sits next to
the Portuguese house, rice cookers dominate the kitchen of the Chinese house,
crucifixes adorn the walls of the Puerto Rican house. A Japanese shrine is a few
doors away from the Chinese society building. Down the hill by the taro fields is
a *dohyo*, a sumo ring, where the workers wrestled every Sunday afternoon.

Mike Hama showed me around the day I was there. The descendant of
Japanese, German, Hawaiian, and Irish grandparents, Hama grew up on a plantation camp in the 1940s. "Kids of all different nationalities played together in
these camps," he told me. "We didn't know we were different." They communicated using a pidgin that combined words from many languages. The German
kids taught the other kids to polka in the camp social halls. The Japanese kids
taught their friends sumo wrestling. When the Japanese emperor visited Hawaii
after World War II, according to a widely told if hard-to-verify story, he was so
impressed to see wrestlers of all different nationalities in the *dohyo* that when he
returned to Japan he opened the country's sumo rings to foreigners.

When Hama was eighteen, he joined the military and was stationed in
California. "That was a real awakening for me," he recalls. "For the first time I
saw the bigotry that was going on outside Hawaii." He moved back to Hawaii as
soon as he could and married a woman of mixed ancestry. His four daughters
think of themselves as nothing other than local Hawaiians.

The camp towns disappeared decades ago in Hawaii, yet they have left a
remarkable legacy. Large-scale segregation in housing remains rare on the
islands. People of all ethnic backgrounds live side by side, just as they did in
the camp towns. The only people who live in ghettos are the soldiers on military bases and wealthy haoles who wall themselves off in gated communities.
Because neighborhoods are integrated in Hawaii, so are most of the schools.
Children of different ethnicities continue to grow up together and marry, just as
they did in the camps.

Integrated neighborhoods, integrated schools, high rates of intermarriage—the   25
islands sound as if they should be a racial paradise. But there's actually a fair

amount of prejudice here. It pops up in novels, politics, the spiels of standup comics. And it's especially prominent in everyday conversation—"talk stink" is the pidgin term for disrespecting another group.

Some of the prejudice is directed toward haoles, who continue to occupy many of the positions of social and economic prominence on the islands (though their days as plantation overlords are long gone). Nonwhites label haoles as cold, self-serving, arrogant, meddling, loud, and even that old stereotype—smelly (because, it is held, they still do not bathe every day). White kids say they'll get beat up if they venture onto certain nonwhite beaches. Occasionally a rumor sweeps through a school about an upcoming "Kill a Haole" day. The rumors are a joke meant to shock the prevailing sensibilities. But one would not expect such a joke where racial tensions are low.

Other groups come in for similarly rough treatment. The Japanese are derided as clannish and power-hungry, the Filipinos as ignorant and under-handed, the Hawaiians as fat, lazy, and fun-loving. And, as is true of stereotypes everywhere, the objects of them have a tendency to reinforce them, either by too vigorously denying or too easily repeating them.

"Intermarriage may indicate tolerance," says Jonathan Okamura, an anth-ropologist at the University of Hawaii, "but it doesn't mean we have an egal-itarian society on a larger scale." Though he calls his viewpoint a "minority position," Okamura holds that racial and ethnic prejudice is deeply ingrained in the institutional structures of everyday life in Hawaii. For example, the integration of the public schools is deceptive, he says. Well-off haoles, Chinese, and Japanese send their children to private schools, and the public schools are underfunded. "We've created a two-tiered system that makes inequality increasingly worse rather than better," says Okamura. Meanwhile the rapid growth of the tourism industry in Hawaii has shut off many traditional routes to economic betterment. Tourism produces mostly low-paying jobs in sales, service, and construction, Okamura points out, so people have few opportunities to move up career ladders.

Of course, talented and lucky individuals still get ahead. "Students with parents who didn't go to college come to the university and do well—that hap-pens all the time," Okamura says. "But it doesn't happen enough to advance socioeconomically disadvantaged groups in society."

Several ethnic groups occupy the lower end of the socioeconomic scale, but one in particular stands out: the people descended from the island's original inhabitants. Native Hawaiians have the lowest incomes and highest unemploy-ment rates of any ethnic group. They have the most health problems and the shortest life expectancy. They are the least likely to go to college and the most likely to be incarcerated.

Then again, applying statistics like these to a group as large and diverse as Native Hawaiians is inevitably misleading. Individuals with some Hawaiian ancestry make up a fifth of the population in Hawaii. Some are successful; some are not. Some are consumed by native issues; others pay them no mind. And Native Hawaiians are much less marginalized in Hawaii than are, for example, Native Americans in the rest of the United States. Hawaiian words, names, and outlooks have seeped into everyday life on the islands, producing a cultural amalgam that is one of the state's distinct attractions.

Native Hawaiians should not be seen as simply another ethnic group, the leaders of their community point out. Other cultures have roots elsewhere; people of Japanese, German, or Samoan ancestry can draw from the traditions of an ancestral homeland to sustain an ethnic heritage. If the culture of the Native Hawaiians disappears, it will be gone forever. Greater recognition of the value and fragility of this culture has led to a resurgence of interest in the Hawaiian past. Schools with Hawaiian language immersion programs have sprung up around the islands to supplement the English that children speak at home. Traditional forms of Hawaiian dance, music, canoeing, and religion all have undergone revivals.

This Hawaiian Renaissance also has had a political dimension. For the past several decades a sovereignty movement has been building among Native Hawaiians that seeks some measure of political autonomy and control over the lands that the U.S. government seized from the Hawaiian monarchy at the end of the nineteenth century. Reflecting the diversity of the native population, several sovereignty organizations have carried out a sometimes unseemly struggle over strategies and goals. One radical faction advocates the complete independence of the islands from the United States. More moderate groups have called for the establishment of a Native Hawaiian nation modeled on the Indian tribes on the mainland. Native Hawaiians would have their own government, but it would operate within existing federal and state frameworks, and its citizens would remain Americans.

Native Hawaiian sovereignty faces many hurdles, and it is premature to harp on exactly how it would work. But whenever the topic comes up in discussion, a question quickly surfaces: Exactly who is a Native Hawaiian? "Pure" Hawaiians with no non-Hawaiian ancestors probably number just a few thousand. Many Native Hawaiians undoubtedly have a preponderance of Hawaiian ancestors, but no clear line separates natives from nonnatives. Some people who call themselves Native Hawaiians probably have little DNA from Polynesian ancestors.

Past legislation has waffled on this issue. Some laws define Native Hawaiians as people who can trace at least half their ancestry to people living in Hawaii before the arrival of Captain Cook. Others define as Hawaiian anyone who has even a single precontact Hawaiian ancestor. These distinctions are highly contentious for political and economic as well as cultural reasons. Many state laws restrict housing subsidies, scholarships, economic development grants, and other benefits specifically to Native Hawaiians.

As the study of genetics and history has progressed, an obvious idea has arisen. Maybe science could resolve the issue. Maybe a genetic marker could be found that occurs only in people descended from the aboriginal inhabitants of Hawaii. Then anyone with that marker could be considered a Native Hawaiian.

No one is better qualified to judge this idea than Rebecca Cann, a professor of genetics at the University of Hawaii. Cann was the young graduate student at the University of California at Berkeley who, with Mark Stoneking, did much of the work that led to the unveiling of mitochondrial Eve. She haunted hospital delivery rooms to obtain mitochondrion-rich placentas, which at that time was the only way to get enough mitochondrial DNA to sequence. She ran gels and compared nucleotides. Her faculty adviser, Allan Wilson, landed mitochondrial Eve on the cover of *Newsweek*, but Cann did the footwork.

She moved to Hawaii even before mitochondrial Eve made headlines, responding to an ad in *Science* magazine for a job. She's been here ever since, though her flat American accent still betrays a childhood spent in Iowa. She met me at the door of her office, in the foothills above Honolulu, dressed in sandals and a patterned Hawaiian dress. "I think we correctly anticipated many of the applications and potential problems of this research," she said, "right down to people wanting to clone Elvis from a handkerchief he'd used to wipe his brow. What we didn't understand was the degree to which religious and cultural beliefs would dictate attitudes toward genetic materials. In Hawaii, for instance, there's a very strong belief in *mana*, in the power of the spirit, which is contained in the remains of a person's ancestors. The absolute disgust that many people have toward the desecration of a grave—that was a cultural eye-opener for me."

Despite the occasional cultural difficulties, Cann has continued her study of human genetics in Hawaii and has played an important role in piecing together the prehistory of the Pacific. By comparing the mitochondrial

Exactly who is a Native Hawaiian?

DNA sequences of people on various islands, she has traced the gradual eastward spread of modern humans from southeastern Asia and Melanesia. She has discovered that men and women had different migration patterns into the Pacific and has even detected tantalizing evidence, still unconfirmed, of genetic contacts between Pacific Islanders and South Americans. "I'm convinced that our history is written in our DNA," she told me.

Yet she cautioned against using genetics to determine ethnicity. "I get people coming up to me all the time and saying, 'Can you prove that I'm a Hawaiian?'" She can't, she said, at least not with a high degree of certainty. A given individual might have a mitochondrial haplotype that is more common among Native Hawaiians. But the ancestors of the aboriginal Hawaiians also gave rise to other Pacific populations, so a mitochondrial sequence characteristic of Native Hawaiians could have come from a Samoan or Filipino ancestor.

Also, a person's mitochondrial DNA is not necessarily an accurate indication of ancestry. The only way for a person to have mitochondrial DNA from a woman who lived in Hawaii before the arrival of Captain Cook is for that person to have an unbroken line of grandmothers dating back to that woman. But because groups have mixed so much in Hawaii, mitochondrial lineages have become thoroughly tangled. People who think of themselves as Native Hawaiian could easily have had non-Hawaiian female ancestors sometime in the past eleven generations, which would have given them mitochondrial DNA from another part of the world.

These genetic exchanges are also common elsewhere in the world, even in populations that think of themselves as less mixed. Most native Europeans, for example, have mitochondrial DNA characteristic of that part of the world. But some have mitochondrial DNA from elsewhere—southern Africa, or eastern Asia, or even Polynesia—brought to Europe over the millennia by female immigrants. The British matron who has a mitochondrial haplotype found most often in southern Africans is not an African, just as the Native Hawaiian with mitochondrial DNA from a German great-great-grandmother does not automatically become German.

This confusion of genetic and cultural identities becomes even greater with the Y chromosome, given the ease with which that chromosome can insert itself into a genealogy. Most of the early migrants to Hawaii, for example, were males, especially the plantation workers. Those males mated with native women more often than native men mated with immigrant women, so nonnative Y chromosomes are now more common in mixed populations than nonnative mitochondrial DNA. In some populations in South America, virtually all the Y chromosomes are from Europe and all the mitochondrial DNA is from indigenous groups.

The mixing of genes can cause great consternation, but it is the inevitable consequence of our genetic history. Several years ago a geneticist in Washington, D.C., began offering to identify the homelands of the mitochondrial DNA and Y chromosomes of African Americans. The service foundered for several reasons, but one was that 30 percent of the Y chromosomes in African American males come from European ancestors.

Within a few years geneticists will be able to use DNA sequences from all the chromosomes to trace ancestry. But these histories will be just as convoluted as those of mitochondrial DNA and the Y. Granted, geneticists will be able to make statistical assessments. They will be able to say, for instance, that a given person has such and such a probability of descent from a Native Hawaiian population, and in some cases the probability will be very high. But probabilities don't convey the cold, hard certainties that people want in their genealogies.

Beyond the purely genetic considerations are the social ones. When children are adopted from one group into another, they become a member of that group socially, yet their haplotypes and those of their descendants can differ from the group norm. Rape is another way in which the genetic variants of groups mix. And sometimes people from one group make a conscious decision to join another and are gladly accepted, despite their different genetic histories.

"I get nervous when people start talking about using genetic markers to prove ethnicity," Cann told me. "I don't believe that biology is destiny. Allowing yourself to be defined personally by whatever your DNA sequence is, that's insane. But that's exactly what some people are going to be tempted to do."

When geneticists look at our DNA, they do not see a world of rigidly divided groups each going its own way. They see something much more fluid and ambiguous—something more like the social structures that have emerged in Hawaii as intermarriage has accelerated.

The most remarkable aspect of ethnicity in Hawaii is its loose relation to biology. Many people have considerable latitude in choosing their ethnic affiliations. Those of mixed ancestry can associate with the ethnicity of a parent, a grandparent, or a more distant ancestor. They can partition their ethnic affiliations: They can be Chinese with their Chinese relatives; Native Hawaiian with their native kin; and just plain local with their buddies. The community of descent that a person associates with has become more like a professional or religious affiliation, a connection over which a person has some measure of control.

People whose ancestors are from a single ethnic group have fewer options, but they, too, can partake of at least some of Hawaii's ethnic flexibility. Young whites, for example, sometimes try to pass themselves off as mixed by maintaining an especially dark tan. Among many young people, dating someone from a different ethnic group is a social asset rather than a liability, in part because of the doors it opens to other communities. Many prospective students at the University of Hawaii simply mark "mixed" in describing their ethnicity on application forms, even if both parents have the same ethnic background. "My students say they don't want to be pigeonholed," says Okamura. "That way they can identify with different groups." 50

Hawaii's high rates of intermarriage also contribute greatly to the islands' ethnic flux. Ethnicity is not defined just by who one's ancestors were. It also is defined prospectively—by the group into which one is expected to marry. For most young people in Hawaii, the pool of marriageable partners encompasses the entire population. Relations among groups are inevitably less fractious when their members view each other as potential mates.

Of course, ethnic and even "racial" groups still exist in Hawaii, and they will for a long time. Despite the rapid growth of intermarriage in Hawaii and elsewhere, the mixing of peoples takes generations, not a few years or even decades. Most people around the world still choose marriage partners who would be classified as members of the same "race." In many parts of the world—the American Midwest, China, Iceland—few other options are available. Five hundred years from now, unless human societies undergo drastic changes, Asians, Africans, and Europeans still will be physically distinguishable.

But the social effects of intermarriage are much more immediate than are the biological effects. Socially, intermarriage can quickly undermine the idea that culture has biological roots. When a substantial number of mixed individuals demonstrate, by their very existence, that choices are possible, that biology is not destiny, the barriers between groups become more permeable. Ethnicity in Hawaii, for example, seems far less stark and categorical than it does in the rest of the United States. The people of Hawaii recognize overlaps and exceptions. They are more willing to accept the haole who claims to have non-European ancestors or the Native Hawaiian who affiliates with Filipinos. It's true that people talk about the differences among groups all the time, but even talking about these differences, rather than rigidly ignoring them, makes them seem less daunting. Expressions of social prejudice in Hawaii are more like a form of social banter, like a husband and wife picking at each other's faults.

The logical endpoint of this perspective is a world in which people are free to choose their ethnicity regardless of their ancestry. Ethnicity is not yet *entirely* voluntary in Hawaii, but in many respects the islands are headed in that direction. State law, for example, is gradually coming to define a Native Hawaiian as anyone with a single Hawaiian ancestor. But at that point ethnicity becomes untethered from biology—it is instead a cultural, political, or historical distinction. People are no longer who they say they are because of some mysterious biological essence. They have chosen the group with which they want to affiliate.

Genetically, this view of ethnicity makes perfect sense. Our DNA is too tightly interconnected to use biology to justify what are essentially social distinctions. Our preferences, character, and abilities are not determined by the biological history of our ancestors. They depend on our individual attributes, experiences, and choices. As this inescapable conclusion becomes more widely held, our genetic histories inevitably will become less and less important. When we look at another person, we won't think Asian, black, or white. We'll just think: person.

In his novel *Siddhartha*, Hermann Hesse tells the story of a young man in ancient India, a disciple of an inspired teacher, who sets out to find the reality beneath the world of appearance. After years of study and wandering, Siddhartha becomes a ferryman, learning from his predecessor how to listen to the voices in the passing river. One day a childhood friend named Govinda comes to the river. Siddhartha and Govinda have a long conversation about the interdependence of illusion and truth, about the existence of the past and future in the present, about the need not just to think about the world but to love it. Finally Govinda asks Siddhartha how he has achieved such peace in his life. Siddhartha replies, "Kiss me on the forehead, Govinda." Govinda is surprised by the request, but out of respect for his friend he complies. When he touches Siddhartha's forehead with his lips, he has a wondrous vision:

> He no longer saw the face of his friend Siddhartha. Instead he saw other faces, many faces, a long series, a continuous stream of faces— hundreds, thousands, which all came and disappeared and yet all seemed to be there at the same time, which all continually changed and renewed themselves and which were all yet Siddhartha. . . . He saw the face of a newly born child, red and full of wrinkles, ready to cry. He saw the face of a murderer, . . . He saw the naked bodies of men and women in the postures and transports of passionate love. . . . Each one was mortal, a passionate, painful example of all that is transitory. Yet none of them died, they only changed, were always reborn, continually had a new face; only time stood between one face and another.

I began this book [*Mapping Human History*] by calling attention to the different appearances of human beings. I conclude it now by calling attention to the opposite. Throughout human history, groups have wondered how they are related to one another. The study of genetics has now revealed that we all are linked: the Bushmen hunting antelope, the mixed-race people of South Africa, the African Americans descended from slaves, the Samaritans on their mountain stronghold, the Jewish populations scattered around the world, the Han Chinese a billion strong, the descendants of European settlers who colonized the New World, the Native Hawaiians who look to a cherished past. We are members of a single human family, the products of genetic necessity and chance, borne ceaselessly into an unknown future.

Questions for Critical Reading

1. What is a "community of descent"? Develop a definition by rereading Olson's text to locate quotations that define the concept. Offer, too, an example of a community of descent from your own experience.

2. How does Olson define *race*? Create a definition and support it using quotations from Olson's essay. To do so, you will need to reread his essay critically, paying close attention to what Olson has to say about the concept of race.

3. If race no longer has a biological basis, as Olson claims, why do ethnicities continue to function in society? Use Olson's text to propose reasons why race persists.

Exploring Context

1. Read the U.S. Census Bureau's explanation of the racial categories used in the census taken every ten years: census.gov/population/www/socdemo/race/racefactcb.html. How do these categories relate to Olson's argument? Relate your response to your work on the persistence of race from Question 3 of Questions for Critical Reading.

2. Visit Hawaii's official state government Web site at hawaii.gov and then visit the official Hawaii tourism Web site at gohawaii.com. How is race represented on these sites? What races do you see in the images? Is the representation of race the same for residents and for tourists? Why might there be differences? Use the definition of race you developed in Question 2 of Questions for Critical Reading to support your position.

3. One place that race persists in Hawaii, according to Olson, is in schools. Locate the Web site for some schools in Hawaii. Do you find evidence to support Olson's argument or to complicate it?

Questions for Connecting

1. If Olson is right in discounting the genetic basis of race, why do racial categories persist? Does Leslie Savan's analysis of the economic value of pop talk and its relation to black talk in "What's Black, Then White, and Said All Over?" (p. 363) offer some reasons? Apply your analysis of race from Question 3 of Questions for Critical Reading in making your response.

2. How does the quinceañera reflect a "community of descent"? Using your defini-tion of the term from Question 1 of Questions for Critical Reading as well as Olson's other concepts, explain the widespread popularity of quinces as demon-strated by Julia Alvarez in "Selections from *Once Upon a Quinceañera*" (p. 35). Is retroculturation a hindrance to the end of race?

3. Does Hawaii offer a model for the new civil rights that Kenji Yoshino advocates in "Preface" (p. 479) and "The New Civil Rights" (p. 481)? Given the end of race, should we pursue a liberty or an equality paradigm?

Language Matters

1. Choose a key quotation from Olson. Revise it to make it less effective but still grammatically correct. Would making it a question blunt its force? What about changing it to passive voice? Draw some general conclusions from this experi-ment. What makes a sentence effective?

2. Locate materials in a reference book or online on writing a résumé and then make a résumé for this essay. What would be this essay's "career objective"? What would be its "experience"? Who would it list for references?

3. How would you "grade" Olson's essay? In small groups, develop a set of grading criteria and then apply those criteria to Olson's text. What does your group value in writing? What does this class value in writing?

Assignments for Writing

1. Can there be an end to race? Engage Olson's essay by writing a paper in which you examine the possibility of an end to race. Why does race persist? Can or should we move beyond concepts of race? Would something replace the idea of race, or has something replaced it already? You may want to draw on your responses to the Questions for Critical Reading as well as your examination of the census from Question 1 of Exploring Context in making your argument.

2. Olson's argument is based in part on advances in genetic technologies. Write a paper in which you evaluate the relationship between technology and race. Consider: Is race itself a kind of technology? Can technology move us beyond race? You may want to use the definition of race you developed in Question 2 of Questions for Critical Reading in making your argument.

3. Race is not the only factor in determining group identity; Olson discusses com-munities of descent as well. Using Olson's essay, write a paper in which you determine the relationship between race and cultural identity. Does the history of a particular race dictate its importance as a cultural identity? Can a particular race have ownership over its cultural aspects? Can an individual choose a racial or cultural identity? In making your argument, you may want to use the defini-tion of communities of descent that you developed in Questions for Critical Reading.

Marshall Poe

Marshall Poe, a historian who has published numerous books on Russian and Soviet history and has held fellowships at Harvard and Columbia universities, is currently associate professor of history at the University of Iowa. In addition to his work in history, Poe is also interested in the intersections of technology, publishing, and memory. He is the creator of MemoryArchive (memoryarchive.org), a Wikipedia-modeled "encyclopedia of memories," where users can post their memories of personal or historical events and others can read them. As a journalist, Poe worked for the *Atlantic Monthly*, where he published the following article, "The Hive," in September 2006.

"The Hive" tells a number of stories about Wikipedia (wikipedia.org), the collaboratively written and edited online encyclopedia, in order to tell a larger story about collaborative knowledge in general. Poe details his embarrassing attempt to add his own biography to the site's archives, the early role-playing game and discussion-board lives of the site's founders, and the fate of Wikipedia's predecessor. He also documents the site's birth pangs, revealing the influences and motivating factors behind its rapid growth and rapidly growing importance.

"Wikipedia," Poe claims, "has the potential to be the greatest effort in collaborative knowledge gathering the world has ever known, and it may well be the greatest effort in voluntary collaboration of any kind." The epistemological questions offered by "The Hive" go beyond merely what people know to whether collective knowledge is valid, what motivates people to share their knowledge, and what can be gained from what Poe calls "the wisdom of crowds."

Each of you has the opportunity to contribute or edit entries in Wikipedia. But what is the ultimate value of Wikipedia's collective knowledge, and what are the keys to Wikipedia's success?

▶ TAGS: *diplomacy*, *groups*, *technology*, *community*, *collaboration*, *education*, *feedback*

The Hive

Several months ago, I discovered that I was being "considered for deletion." Or rather, the entry on me in the Internet behemoth that is Wikipedia was.

For those of you who are (as uncharitable Wikipedians sometimes say) "clueless newbies," Wikipedia is an online encyclopedia. But it is like no encyclopedia Diderot could have imagined. Instead of relying on experts to write articles according to their expertise, Wikipedia lets anyone write about anything. You, I, and any wired-up fool can add entries, change entries, even propose that entries be deleted. For reasons I'd rather not share outside of therapy, I created a one-line biographical entry on "Marshall Poe." It didn't take long for my tiny article to come to the attention of Wikipedia's self-appointed guardians. Within a week, a very active—and by most accounts responsible—Scottish Wikipedian named "Alai" decided that . . . well, that I wasn't worth knowing about. Why? "No real evidence of notability," Alai cruelly but accurately wrote, "beyond the proverbial average college professor."

Wikipedia has the potential to be the greatest effort in collaborative knowledge gathering the world has ever known, and it may well be the greatest effort in voluntary collaboration of any kind. The English-language version alone has more than a million entries. It is consistently ranked among the most visited Web sites in the world. A quarter century ago it was inconceivable that a legion of unpaid, unorganized amateurs scattered about the globe could create anything of value, let alone what may one day be the most comprehensive repository of knowledge in human history. Back then we knew that people do not work for free; or if they do work for free, they do a poor job; and if they work for free in large numbers, the result is a muddle. Jimmy Wales and Larry Sanger knew all this when they began an online encyclopedia in 1999. Now, just seven years later, everyone knows different.

The Moderator

Jimmy Wales does not fit the profile of an Internet revolutionary. He was born in 1966 and raised in modest circumstances in Huntsville, Alabama. Wales majored in finance at Auburn, and after completing his degree enrolled in a graduate program at the University of Alabama. It was there that he developed a passion for the Internet. His entry point was typical for the nerdy set of his generation: fantasy games.

In 1974, Gary Gygax and Dave Arneson, two gamers who had obviously   5
read *The Lord of the Rings,* invented the tabletop role-playing game Dungeons & Dragons. The game spread largely through networks of teenage boys, and by 1979, the year the classic *Dungeon Master's Guide* was published, it seemed that every youth who couldn't get a date was rolling the storied twenty-sided die in a shag-carpeted den. Meanwhile, a more electronically inclined crowd at the University of Illinois at Urbana-Champaign was experimenting with moving fantasy play from the basement to a computer network. The fruit of their labors was the unfortunately named MUD (Multi-User Dungeon). Allowing masses of players to create virtual fantasy worlds, MUDs garnered a large audience in the 1980s and 1990s under names like Zork, Myst, and Scepter of Goth. (MUDs came to be known as "Multi-Undergraduate Destroyers" for their tendency to divert college students from their studies.)

Wales began to play MUDs at Alabama in the late 1980s. It was in this context that he first encountered the power of networked computers to facilitate voluntary cooperation on a large scale. He did not, however, set up house in these fantasy worlds, nor did he show any evidence of wanting to begin a career in high tech. He completed a degree in finance at Auburn, received a master's in finance at the University of Alabama, and then pursued a Ph.D. in finance at Indiana University. He was interested, it would seem, in finance. In 1994, he quit his doctoral program and moved to Chicago to take a job as an options trader. There he made (as he has repeatedly said) "enough."

Wales is of a thoughtful cast of mind. He was a frequent contributor to the philosophical "discussion lists" (the first popular online discussion forums) that emerged in the late '80s as e-mail spread through the humanities. His particular passion was objectivism, the philosophical system developed by Ayn Rand. In 1989, he initiated the Ayn Rand Philosophy Discussion List and served as moderator—the person who invites and edits e-mails from subscribers. Though discussion lists were not new among the technorati in the 1980s, they were unfamiliar territory for most academics. In the oak-paneled seminar room, everyone had always been careful to behave properly—the chairman sat at the head of the table, and everyone spoke in turn and stuck to the topic. E-mail lists were something altogether different. Unrestrained by convention and cloaked by anonymity, participants could behave very badly without fear of real consequences. The term for such poor comportment—*flaming*—became one of the first bits of net jargon to enter common usage.

Wales had a careful moderation style:

> First, I will frown—very much—on any flaming of any kind whatsoever. . . . Second, I impose no restrictions on membership based on my own idea of what objectivism really is. . . . Third, I hope that the list will be more "academic" than some of the others, and tend toward discussions of technical details of epistemology. . . . Fourth, I have chosen a "middle-ground" method of moderation, a sort of behind-the-scenes prodding.

Wales was an advocate of what is generically termed "openness" online. An "open" online community is one with few restrictions on membership or posting—everyone is welcome, and anyone can say anything as long as it's generally on point and doesn't include gratuitous ad hominem attacks. Openness fit not only Wales's idea of objectivism, with its emphasis on reason and rejection of force, but also his mild personality. He doesn't like to fight. He would rather suffer fools in silence, waiting for them to talk themselves out, than confront them. This patience would serve Wales well in the years to come.

Top-Down and Bottom-Up

In the mid-1990s, the great dream of Internet entrepreneurs was to create *the* entry point on the Web. "Portals," as they were called, would provide everything: e-mail, news, entertainment, and, most important, the tools to help users find what they wanted on the Web. As Google later showed, if you build the best "finding aid," you'll be a dominant player. In 1996, the smart money was on "Web directories," man-made guides to the Internet. Both Netscape and Yahoo relied on Web directories as their primary finding aids, and their IPOs in the

Resources for Teaching

Barclay Barrios

with Elizabeth Kelly

EMERGING

Contemporary Readings for Writers

Resources for Teaching

EMERGING

CONTEMPORARY READINGS FOR WRITERS

BARCLAY BARRIOS
Florida Atlantic University

with ELIZABETH KELLY
Florida Atlantic University

BEDFORD/ST. MARTIN'S
Boston ◆ New York

4   3   2   1   0   9
f   e   d   c   b   a

For information write: Bedford/St. Martin's, 75 Arlington Street, Boston MA 02116
(617-399-4000)

ISBN-10: 0–312–53555–4
ISBN-13: 978–0–312–53555–1

Instructors who have adopted *Emerging: Contemporary Readings for Writers* as a
textbook for a course are authorized to duplicte portions of this manual for
their students.

The Instructor's Manual that follows draws from our experience in the classroom and presents a complete approach to conceptualizing, designing, and implementing a first-year writing course using *Emerging* as the primary text. Part I, Syllabi and Course Philosophy, offers immediate and practical guidance for using this textbook. We know that at the top of most teachers' practical concerns is developing syllabi; thus, we have included several sample syllabi in the beginning of this manual that demonstrate how this text can be used in the classroom. These syllabi, based on a modified portfolio system and class-tested at Florida Atlantic University, can be adapted to meet your institutional and departmental requirements and goals in teaching writing courses. Because syllabi always embody a certain philosophy, we also offer the philosophy, pedagogical approach, and goals that drive our courses at FAU.

The second section of this manual, Part II, General Approaches to Teaching, gathers our experience in the classroom to offer advice and guidance to the new teacher in particular. We provide an extensive selection of class activities and guidance on core elements of the writing classroom such as peer revision, commenting, and grading. We invite seasoned teachers to explore this section in the hope that they might find new techniques to add to their pedagogical repertoire.

Since all of the readings in the text were class-tested at FAU, guidance on teaching each selection is provided in Part III, Approaches to Teaching *Emerging*. This section gives detailed information on each reading and includes common problems students might encounter with some of the readings. We also provide information on our approach to sequencing and writing assignments. Sample student papers provide a specific sense of the work our students have produced.

Throughout this material we have tried to share our excitement for this text, for these readings, and for teaching. We hope you share that excitement with us.

This project is the culmination of several years of development and revision, and we would like to thank FAU's Writing Committee; the many teachers who tested these readings and have contributed syllabi, activities, and worksheets to this project; and the students who have taught us so much about the process of teaching writing. It is our hope that our collective experience can be of use to you as you step into the writing classroom.

Brief Contents

Contents

Chapter 1
Sample Syllabi

Introduction

We offer here four sample syllabi to suggest multiple possibilities for using *Emerging* in first-year writing courses. We invite you to adapt these as needed for your own courses and programs.

Sample Syllabus 1, based on a modified portfolio-driven system, is the template we use at Florida Atlantic University and includes course schedules for classes that meet either two or three times per week. Sample Syllabus 2 is an adapted version of this template that suggests a specific schedule for a discussion-driven approach to teaching a writing course. Sample Syllabus 3 focuses heavily on the writing and revision processes. This format provides a schedule for twice weekly class meetings and suggests specific approaches for working with revision and portfolios and encourages students to recognize each step they make in forming a completed paper. The final Sample Syllabus we have included presents a language-driven approach to teaching this type of course. This syllabus schedules the course around three weekly class meetings, a heavy reading component, specific grammar lessons, and quizzes.

Sample Syllabus 1
Modified Portfolio, 2 or 3 Class Meetings per Week

Course Title
Section | Day/Time | Location | Semester

Information

Instructor:	Name
Office:	Location
Office Hours:	Days and Times (at least 2 hours per week)
Office Phone:	
E-mail:	E-mail is checked approximately [Days and Times}
Mailbox:	
Class Web site:	

Course Objectives

At the end of this course you should be able to:

- Produce clear and appropriate writing that performs the specific rhetorical tasks of analytic discourse.
- Produce both finished writing and preparatory writing (e.g., multiple drafts of formal writing, journal writing, and written responses to other texts).
- Employ critical thinking based on well-reasoned assumptions.
- Read and respond critically to a variety of professional and other student texts in order to position your ideas and arguments relative to the arguments and strategies of others.
- Incorporate and cite external sources in your writing.
- Use writing not only to communicate, but also to generate thinking and examine intellectual and/or cultural assumptions that emerge in the readings and in your own writing.
- Use an academically acceptable ethos (i.e., the ability of writers to effect credibility in their writing).
- Recognize and practice writing as a recursive process that demands substantial reworking of drafts to revise content, organization, clarity, argument structures, and so on (global revision), as distinct from editing and correction of surface error (local revision).
- Demonstrate enhanced learning through global and local revisions that are based on "learning-centered" grading criteria.
- Work effectively with other students in peer-group sessions to critique the substance of each other's work, focusing primarily on issues that would be addressed by global revision.
- Demonstrate the abilities to identify, understand, and edit for global organization, style, and the patterns of error recurrent in your own writing. To help you achieve this goal, you will learn a system of error tracking to identify and correct your patterns of error.

Texts and Materials

List all course materials

Assignments and Grading

We will be using a modified portfolio system. Each portfolio will consist of two major papers, each undergoing a draft and revision process, as well as an additional significant revision of a previous paper. Clear, written descriptions of all writing assignments will be distributed to the class, as well as the evaluation criteria that will be used. Response papers and other writing assignments will be reflected in your class participation grade. The grade break down is:

Portfolio One:

Paper One	10% of final grade
Paper Two	10% of final grade
Revision	15% of final grade
Portfolio	4% of final grade

Portfolio Two:

Paper Three	16% of final grade
Paper Four	16% of final grade
Revision	20% of final grade
Portfolio	4% of final grade

Class Participation   5% of final grade

You will receive substantive comments on all written work through both instructor and peer comments.

Policies

List all institutional, departmental, and individual policies here.

Version A
Schedule of Classes: Two days per week

Week 1, Day 1

Introductions
Writing Sample

Week 1, Day 2

RESPONSE ONE DUE
Discuss Reading One
Discuss assignment prompt

Week 2, Day 1

POLICY SHEETS DUE
Pre-draft workshop

Week 2, Day 2

ROUGH DRAFT ONE DUE
Peer revision

Week 3, Day 1

Drafts returned
Sample work

Week 3, Day 2

FINAL DRAFT ONE DUE
READING TWO RESPONSE DUE
Discuss Reading Two
Discuss assignment prompt

Week 4, Day 1

Discuss Reading Two and Reading One
Pre-draft workshop

Week 4, Day 2

ROUGH DRAFT TWO DUE
Peer revision

Week 5, Day 1
Drafts returned
Sample work

Week 5, Day 2
FINAL DRAFT TWO DUE
Return to the essays

Week 6, Day 1
Discuss Revision Project
Revision workshop or
MLA Review/Elements/Grammar

Week 6, Day 2
FIRST DRAFT REVISION PROJECT DUE
Peer revision

Week 7, Day 1
Drafts returned
Sample work
Discuss portfolios

Week 7, Day 2
FINAL DRAFT REVISION PROJECT DUE
READING THREE RESPONSE DUE
Discuss Reading Three
Discuss assignment prompt

Week 8, Day 1
NO CLASS: CONFERENCES

Week 8, Day 2
NO CLASS: CONFERENCES

Week 9, Day 1
NO CLASS: MIDSEMESTER BREAK

Week 9, Day 2
NO CLASS: MIDSEMESTER BREAK

Week 10, Day 1
Continue Reading Three discussion
Continue prompt discussion
Pre-draft workshop

Week 10, Day 2
ROUGH DRAFT THREE DUE
Peer revision

Week 11, Day 1
Drafts returned
Sample work

Week 11, Day 2
FINAL DRAFT THREE DUE
READING FOUR RESPONSE DUE

Week 12, Day 1
Discuss Reading Four
Discuss assignment prompt

Week 12, Day 2
ROUGH DRAFT FOUR DUE
Peer revision

Week 13, Day 1
Drafts returned
Sample work

Week 13, Day 2
FINAL DRAFT FOUR DUE
Return to readings

Week 14, Day 1
Discuss Revision Project

Week 14, Day 2
Pre-draft workshop

Week 15, Day 1
FIRST DRAFT REVISION PROJECT DUE

Week 15, Day 2
Peer revision
In-class revision workshop
Review

Week 16, Day 1
FINAL DRAFT REVISION PROJECT DUE
Wrap-up
FINAL PORTFOLIOS DUE ON FINAL
EXAM DATE

Version B
Schedule of Classes: Three days per week

Week 1, Day 1

Introductions
Writing sample

Week 1, Day 2

RESPONSE ONE DUE
Discuss Reading One

Week 1, Day 3

Discuss Reading One
Discuss assignment prompt

Week 2, Day 1

POLICY SHEETS DUE
Pre-draft workshop

Week 2, Day 2

Revision workshop or
MLA Review/Grammar

Week 2, Day 3

ROUGH DRAFT ONE DUE
Peer revision

Week 3, Day 1

Sample work

Week 3, Day 2

Drafts returned
Global comments
Continue discussion

Week 3, Day 3

FINAL DRAFT ONE DUE
MLA Review/Grammar

Week 4, Day 1

READING TWO RESPONSE DUE
Discuss Reading Two

Week 4, Day 2

Discuss Reading Two and Reading One
Discuss assignment prompt

Week 4, Day 3

ROUGH DRAFT TWO DUE
Peer revision

Week 5, Day 1

Sample work
In-class workshop

Week 5, Day 2

Revision workshop or
MLA Review/Grammar

Week 5, Day 3

FINAL DRAFT TWO DUE
Peer revision

Week 6, Day 1

Return to the essays

Week 6, Day 2

Revision workshop or
MLA Review/Grammar

Week 6, Day 3

FIRST DRAFT REVISION PROJECT DUE
Peer revision

Week 7, Day 1

Drafts returned
Sample work

Week 7, Day 2

Discuss portfolios
Revision workshop or
MLA Review/Grammar

Week 7, Day 3

FINAL DRAFT REVISION PROJECT DUE
READING THREE RESPONSE DUE
Discuss Reading Three

Week 8, Day 1

NO CLASS: CONFERENCES

5

Week 8, Day 2
NO CLASS: CONFERENCES

Week 8, Day 3
NO CLASS: CONFERENCES

Week 9, Day 1
NO CLASS: MIDSEMESTER BREAK

Week 9, Day 2
NO CLASS: MIDSEMESTER BREAK

Week 9, Day 3
NO CLASS: MIDSEMESTER BREAK

Week 10, Day 1
Discuss Reading Three and Readings
One and Two

Week 10, Day 2
Discuss Reading Three and Readings
One and Two
Pre-draft workshop

Week 10, Day 3
ROUGH DRAFT THREE DUE
Peer Revision

Week 11, Day 1
Revision workshop or
MLA Review/Grammar

Week 11, Day 2
Return drafts
Sample work

Week 11, Day 3
FINAL DRAFT THREE DUE
READING FOUR RESPONSE DUE
Discuss Reading Four

Week 12, Day 1
Discuss Reading Four and Readings
One, Two, and Three
Discuss assignment prompt

Week 12, Day 2
Discuss Reading Four and Readings
One, Two, and Three
Pre-draft workshop

Week 12, Day 3
ROUGH DRAFT FOUR DUE
Peer revision

Week 13, Day 1
Return drafts
Sample work

Week 13, Day 2
Revision workshop or
MLA Review/ Grammar

Week 13, Day 3
FINAL DRAFT FOUR DUE
Return to readings

Week 14, Day 1
Return papers
Discuss revision project

Week 14, Day 2
Revision workshop or
MLA Review/Elements/Grammar
Workshop

Week 14, Day 3
FIRST DRAFT REVISION PROJECT DUE
Peer revision

Week 15, Day 1
Drafts returned
Sample work

Week 15, Day 2
Discuss portfolios
Revision workshop or
MLA Review/Elements/Grammar

Week 15, Day 3
FIRST DRAFT REVISION PROJECT DUE
Wrap-up
FINAL PORTFOLIOS DUE ON FINAL
EXAM DATE

Sample Syllabus 2
Discussion-Driven Approach

Course Title
Section Numbers | Meeting Times | Locations

Information

Instructor:
Office & Mailbox:
Office Hours:
Office Phone:
E-mail:
Class Web site:

Course Objectives: At the end of this course you should be able to:

- Produce clear and appropriate writing that performs the specific rhetorical tasks of analytic discourse.
- Produce both finished writing and preparatory writing (e.g., multiple drafts of formal writing, journal writing, written responses to other texts).
- Employ critical thinking based on well-reasoned assumptions.
- Read and respond critically to a variety of professional and other student texts in order to position your own ideas and arguments relative to the arguments and strategies of others.
- Incorporate and cite external sources in your writing.
- Use writing not only to communicate, but also to generate thinking and examine intellectual and/or cultural assumptions that emerge in the readings and in your own writing.
- Use an academically acceptable ethos (i.e., the ability of writers to effect credibility in their writing).
- Recognize and practice writing as a recursive process that demands substantial reworking of drafts to revise content, organization, clarity, argument structures, and so on (global revision), as distinct from editing and correction of surface error (local revision).
- Demonstrate enhanced learning through global and local revisions that are based on "learning-centered" grading criteria.
- Work effectively with other students in peer-group sessions to critique the substance of each other's work, focusing primarily on issues that would be addressed by global revision.
- Demonstrate the abilities to identify, understand, and edit for global organization, style, and the patterns of errors recurrent in your own writing. To help you achieve this goal, you will learn a system of error tracking to identify and correct your patterns of error.

Texts and Materials

- Barrios, *Emerging: Contemporary Readings for Writers*
- A handbook is also recommended

Assignments and Grading

Clear, written descriptions of all writing assignments, as well as the evaluation criteria that will be used, will be distributed to the class. Drafts, peer reviews, class activities, and participation in class discussion will be reflected in your class participation grade. The grade break down is:

Paper One	10% of final grade	Paper Three	15% of final grade
Paper Two	12% of final grade	Paper Four	17% of final grade
Midterm Assignment 9% of final grade		Revision Project	22% of final grade
*Class Participation 15% of final grade			

*Your class participation grade includes attendance, participation in discussions, group activities, discussion boards and in-class writing assignments, peer reviews, and reading responses.

Policies

Include all pertinent institutional, departmental, and individual policies here. PLEASE NOTE THAT THIS SCHEDULE IS SUBJECT TO CHANGE AS NEEDED.

Schedule of Classes

Week One

Monday: Introductions, course requirements, writing sample assignment
Wednesday: Read and be prepared to discuss Reading One. For all reading discussions, bring at least one question about the reading to discuss in class. **Writing Sample Due**.
Friday: Continue discussion of Reading One

Week Two

Monday: Class review of course policies and citation formatting. Discussion of Paper One Prompt. [Use an Assignment for Writing]
Wednesday: Reading Response One Due. [Use a Question for Critical Reading or Question for Exploring Context]
Friday: Paper One Rough Draft Due. Bring two copies for peer revision and two copies of peer review sheet. This is the only draft I will comment on directly.

Week Three

Monday: In-class workshop on Revision
Wednesday: Paper One Final Draft Due. All final drafts must be submitted in class with rough drafts and all comments you have received.
Friday: Read and be prepared to discuss Reading Two. For all reading discussions, bring at least one question about the reading to discuss in class.

Week Four

Monday: Reading Response Two Due. [Use a Question for Critical Reading or Exploring Context]. Class discussion on the reading and prompt for Paper Two [Use a Question for Connecting or Assignment for Writing.]
Wednesday: In-class workshop activity
Friday: Paper Two Rough Draft Due. Bring two copies for peer revision and two copies of peer review sheet.

Week Five

Monday: Review of the readings and prompt for Paper Two
Wednesday: Workshop on developing an argument and handling two texts
Friday: Paper Two Final Draft Due. All final drafts must be submitted in class with rough drafts and all comments you have received. In-class workshop activity

Week Six

Monday: Read and be prepared to discuss Reading Three. For all reading discussions, bring at least one question about the reading to discuss in class.
Wednesday: Reading Response Three Due. [Use a Question for Critical Reading or Exploring Context.] Discussion of Reading Three
Friday: Discussion on connecting the readings and Midterm Assignment Prompt

Week Seven

Monday: Midterm Assignment Rough Draft Due. Bring two copies for peer revision and two copies of peer review sheet specified on *Blackboard*.
Wednesday: In-class workshop activity on developing a clear thesis
Friday: Midterm Assignment Final Draft Due

Week Eight

Midterm Conferences in Lieu of Class

Week Nine

Monday: In-class review of the readings
Wednesday: Paper Three Rough Draft Due. Bring two copies for peer revision and two copies of peer review sheet specified on *Blackboard*.
Friday: In-class workshop on concise writing

Week Ten

Monday: Paper Three Final Draft Due. All final drafts must be submitted with rough drafts and all comments you have received. The final draft must be uploaded to our *Blackboard* site as well. In-class workshop activity
Wednesday: In-class workshop on logical fallacy and sequence of ideas
Friday: Read and be prepared to discuss Reading Four. For all reading discussions, bring at least one question about the reading to discuss in class.

Week Eleven

Monday: Class discussion on the reading and prompt for Paper Four
Wednesday: Workshop and discussion of the relationships between the readings
Friday: In-class thesis workshop

Week Twelve

Monday: Paper Four Rough Draft Due. Bring two copies for peer revision and two copies of peer review sheet specified on *Blackboard*.
Wednesday: In-class essay organization review
Friday: Paper Four Final Draft Due. All final drafts must be submitted with rough drafts and all comments you have received. The final draft must be uploaded to our *Blackboard* site as well. In-class workshop activity

Week Thirteen

Monday: Discussion on Revision Project Prompt
Wednesday: Review of the readings, in-class review workshop
Friday: Discussion Board Participation Required in Lieu of Class

Week Fourteen

Monday: Revision Project Rough Draft Due. Bring Two copies for peer revision and two copies of peer review sheet specified on *Blackboard*.
Wednesday: Writing Day
Friday: In-class discussion on revision process

Week Fifteen

Monday: Revision Project Final Draft Due. All final drafts must be submitted with rough drafts and all comments you have received, and your revision project must be submitted with the Final Draft of the Paper you are revising. In addition, upload your Revision Final Draft ONLY on *Blackboard*. In-class workshop activity
Wednesday: Last class. Wrap-up.
Exam date: Office hours to pick up finals

Sample Syllabus 3
Writing and Revision Focus

Semester | Course Number Information

Week 1

Introductions
Overview of the class and discussions on what makes a good paper, or *"How to get an A in this class."*

Week 2

Homework Due:
Read and understand the course policies on plagiarism and attendance.
Note: You can obtain these documents [on our course or departmental Web site].

Week 3

Part 1:
Reading One

Homework Due:
Read, re-read, and analyze the introduction to Reading One. Write a 300-word response to the essay using at least one quote from the text. Topics may include, but are not limited to:
- [You may choose to list topics from Themes and Concepts for this essay.]

Week 4

Homework Due:
Create an outline of your first paper consisting of at least 300-words and defining your thesis, your points, your supporting quotes, and your conclusion. This outline must obey the rules discussed in weeks 1 and 2 (such as what makes a good thesis and how to organize an argument).

Week 5

Homework Due:
Using the short paper and outline due in weeks 3 and 4, write a 1000-word essay responding to the prompt you will receive. [This can be based on any of the Questions for Exploring Context or Assignments for Writing.] Your paper must obey the rules discussed in weeks 1 and 2 (such as what makes a good thesis and how to organize an argument).

Homework Due (2nd class of the week):
Revision of paper you turned in this week along with a
revision report detailing at least three changes you made to
your paper and why. The report must explain the changes you
have made, including all grammatical errors, misspellings,
organizational issues, rewrites, and so on. This report must
obey the rules discussed in weeks 1 and 2 (such as what
makes a good thesis and how to organize an argument).

Week 6

Part 2:
Reading Two

Homework Due:
Read, re-read, and analyze the introduction to and the essay
for Reading Two. Using the outline you wrote in week 4 as
a starting point, create a new 300-word outline that incorporates this reading into your first paper, defining your thesis,
your points, your supporting quotes, and your conclusion.

You may *not* simply add Reading Two to your previous outline;
the authors' points must be incorporated into your key
argument. You may do so in several ways, including but not
limited to answering the following:
- [You may choose to draw on Questions for Connecting to
  create points for this section.]

Week 7

Homework Due:
Using your previous essays as a staring point, write a 1000-
word essay using Reading Two to complicate the argument
you made in your Reading One paper, creating a new essay to
address Question Two. [You may choose to use a Question for
Exploring Context, Question for Connecting, or Assignment
for Writing]. You may *not* take your first paper and simply add
paragraphs concerning the second reading; you must integrate ideas from Reading Two into your original argument and
create a new paper. Your paper must obey the rules discussed
in weeks 1 and 2 (such as what makes a good thesis and how
to organize an argument).
Homework Due (2nd class of the week):
Revision of paper you turned in this week along with a
revision report detailing at least three changes you made to
your paper and why. The report must explain the changes you
have made, including all grammatical errors, misspellings,
organizational issues, rewrites, and so on. This report must
obey the rules discussed in weeks 1 and 2 (such as what
makes a good thesis and how to organize an argument).

Week 8

Mid-Semester Meetings

Class meeting are cancelled all this week in order to accommodate personal meetings. Students will sign up for 15-minute meetings, which will take place in [specify location]. **Note:** Tardiness of more than five minutes late will result in an absence. Please be on time and prepared to discuss your papers.

Homework Due:

Portfolio One's Revision Project. This includes:

- A revision of either Paper One or Paper Two, whichever received the lowest grade. This assignment will not replace the original grade but is designed to help you improve your skills.
- A cumulative revision report detailing the three major errors you have tracked during your first two papers, along with a description of what they are and how you plan to fix them during the second half of the semester.

Week 9

Part 3: Reading Three

Homework Due:

Read, re-read, and analyze the introduction to and the essay for Reading Three. Write a 300-word essay examining the key concepts of this essay using at least one quote from the text. Topics may include, but are not limited to:

- [List Concepts from Annotated Bibliography.]

Week 10

Homework Due:

Create an outline of your third paper consisting of at least 300 words and defining your thesis, your points, your supporting quotes, and your conclusion. The outline should also define the link between [add author] and the two other authors you intend to use. This outline must obey the rules discussed in weeks 1 and 2 (such as what makes a good thesis and how to organize an argument).

Week 11

Homework Due:

Using each reading from this semester, write a 1000-word essay exploring [choose a topic from Questions for Connecting or Assignments for Writing]. All three authors must be quoted and be equally represented in your essay.

Homework Due (2nd class of the week):
Revision of Paper Three along with a revision report detailing at least three changes you made to your paper and why. The report must explain the changes you have made, including all grammatical errors, misspellings, organizational issues, rewrites, and so on. This report must obey the rules discussed in weeks 1 and 2 (such as what makes a good thesis and how to organize an argument).

Week 12

Part 4:
Reading Four

Homework Due:
Read, re-read, and analyze the introduction to and the essay for Reading Four, and write a 300-word response applying the authors' ideas on [choose a theme or concept] to one other author that we have discussed in class. Topics may include, but are not limited to:
- [Provide a list of possible topics.]

Week 13

Homework Due:
Create an outline of Paper Four consisting of at least 300 words and defining your thesis, your points, and your conclusion. The outline should define the link between Reading Four and the previous reading you intend to use, using quotes from both readings to define the link. This outline must obey the rules discussed in weeks 1 and 2 (such as what makes a good thesis and how to organize an argument).

Week 14

Homework Due:
Write a 1000-word essay in which you revisit one of your major papers in this class using the terms and arguments found in Reading Four. Does your old thesis still hold true using this author's ideas? Why or why not?

If Reading Four disproves one of your previous papers, then how does it do so? Can you counter the arguments in Reading Four?

If Reading Four supports your previous thesis, how does it do so? What points does the author make supporting your arguments?

Treat your old essay as a source on this assignment; quote from your old essay and incorporate it into your argument as you would any other text. This essay must obey the rules discussed in weeks 1 and 2 (such as what makes a good thesis and how to organize an argument).

Homework Due (2nd class of the week):
Revision of paper you turned in this week along with a revision report detailing at least three changes you made to your paper and why. The report must explain the changes you have made, including all grammatical errors, misspellings, organizational issues, rewrites, and so on. This report must obey the rules discussed in weeks 1 and 2 (such as what makes a good thesis and how to organize an argument).

Week 15

End-of-Semester Meetings (Optional)

Class meetings are cancelled in order to accommodate optional personal meetings. You may come during specified times to discuss Portfolio Two and any other concerns you may have with the class.

Finals

As per the official final exam schedule, Portfolio Two's Revision Project is due on the following days.

[List exam dates]

I will be in my office on [Available Dates and Times]. You may come in during these times to discuss Portfolio Two and any other concerns you may have with the class.

Portfolio Two's Revision Project:
* A revision of either Paper Three or Paper Four. This assignment will not replace the original grade but is designed to help you improve your skills.
* A cumulative revision report detailing the three major errors you have tracked during the semester, along with explanations describing what they are and how you have fixed them, quoting from your own work to show your progress.
* A short paragraph identifying the skills you have learned in this class and how you plan to use them in your academic career.

Sample Syllabus 4
Language-Driven Approach

Course Title

Section Numbers | Meeting Times | Locations

Information

Instructor:
Office:
Office Hours:
Office Phone:
E-mail:
Mailbox:
Class Web site:

Course Objectives

At the end of this course you should be able to:

- Produce clear and appropriate writing that performs the specific rhetorical tasks of analytic discourse.
- Produce both finished writing and preparatory writing (e.g., multiple drafts of formal writing, journal writing, written responses to other texts).
- Employ critical thinking based on well-reasoned assumptions.
- Read and respond critically to a variety of professional and other student texts in order to position your own ideas and arguments relative to the arguments and strategies of others.
- Incorporate and cite external sources in your writing.
- Use writing not only to communicate, but also to generate thinking and examine intellectual and/or cultural assumptions that emerge in the readings and in your own writing.
- Use an academically acceptable ethos (i.e., the ability of writers to effect credibility in their writing).
- Recognize and practice writing as a recursive process that demands substantial reworking of drafts to revise content, organization, clarity, and argument structures, and so on (global revision) as distinct from editing and correction of surface error (local revision).
- Demonstrate enhanced learning through global and local revisions that are based on "learning-centered" grading criteria.
- Work effectively with other students in peer-group sessions to critique the substance of each other's work, focusing primarily on issues that would be addressed by global revision.
- Demonstrate the abilities to identify, understand, and edit for global organization, style, and the patterns of errors recurrent in your own writing. To help you achieve this goal, you will learn a system of error tracking to identlify and correct your patterns of error.

Texts and Materials

- List any supplemental texts you are using.

Assignments and Grading

A student is assessed by performance on assignments. The point vales for the various assignments are below.

Assignments	Point Value
15 Reading Quizzes	150
Lecture Rosponse	25
Paper 1	75
Paper 2	100
Paper 3	125
Paper 4	125
Revision Paper	175
Final Exam	150
Revision Paper Proposal	25
Writing Sample	25
Class Participation	25
Total	**1000**

The final grade will be the sum of the student's total points earned throughout the semester computed on the following scale:

Final Grade	Total Points
Success	
A	1000–940
A–	939–900
B+	899–870
B	869–840
B–	839–800
C+	799–770
C	769–740
Delayed Success	
C–	739–700
D+	699–670
D	669–640
D–	639–600
F	599–0

Assignment Descriptions

Reading Quizzes: All reading quizzes are 10 points apiece; however, seventeen quizzes are assigned, and only 150 points are required. Thus, 20 quiz points of grace are built into the syllabus.

Writing Sample: This practice paper is a way for the instructor to assess the student's initial level and for the student to learn the grading practices of the instructor. Only the introduction and first body paragraph are submitted. Topic TBA.

Lecture Response: Students may either attend the lecture and write a one-page response or write a two-page response to [Reading Related to Visiting Lecturer].

Paper 1: (All paper topics and themes tentative)

TOPIC:
METHOD:
REQUIRED READING:
SUPPLEMENTARY READINGS:

Paper 2

TOPIC:
METHOD:
REQUIRED READING:
SUPPLEMENTARY READINGS:

Paper 3

TOPIC:
METHOD:
REQUIRED READING:
SUPPLEMENTARY READINGS:

Paper 4

TOPIC:
METHOD:
REQUIRED READING:
SUPPLMENTARY READINGS:

Revision Paper Proposal

A short one-page proposal in which the student lays out the direction that will be taken within the revision paper. Points are awarded upon approval.

Revision Paper

TOPIC: Revisit one of papers 1–4 with a new direction to the argument with the added freedom to display your finest work.

Final Exam

An objective exam covering all the readings. Questions will be drawn from the reading quizzes.

Class Participation

A measure of the student's engagement throughout the semester (see policies for definition of engagement).

Policies

List all institutional, departmental, and personal policies here, including plagiarism, attendance and so on. You may also want to list specific requirements for format and submission of papers, class participation, quizzes and homework, and any other specific issues you feel are prudent to address.

Schedule

Week 1

Monday: Introduction
Wednesday: Writing Basics: Thesis
Reading Quiz: 1 on Syllabus
Friday: Writing Basics: Organization

Week 2

Monday: Labor Day—No Class
Wednesday: Writing Basics: Quotation
Elements Forms Due
Friday: Writing Basics: Formatting

Week 3

Monday: Supplementary Reading 1, first 3rd
Reading Quiz 2
Wednesday: Supplementary Reading 1, second 3rd
Reading Quiz 3
Friday: Supplementary Reading, last 3rd
Reading Quiz 4

Week 4

Monday: Primary Reading 1
Reading Quiz 5
Wednesday: Supplementary Reading 2, first half
Reading Quiz 6
Friday: Supplementary Reading 2, second half
Writing Sample Due
Reading Quiz 7

Week 5

Monday: Draft Day
Wednesday: Workshop: Commas
Reading Quiz 8
Friday: Paper 1 Due

Week 6

Monday: Primary Reading 2
Reading Quiz 9
Reading Response Due
Wednesday: Supplementary Reading 3
Reading Quiz 10
Friday: Supplementary Reading 4
Reading Quiz 11

Week 7

Monday: Draft Day
Wednesday: Workshop: Misused Words
Reading Quiz 12
Friday: Paper 2 Due

Week 8

Monday: Conference Week
NO CLASS
Wednesday: Conference Week
NO CLASS
Friday: Conference Week
NO CLASS

Week 9

Monday: Primary Reading 3
Reading Quiz 13
Wednesday: Supplementary Reading 5, first half
Reading Quiz 14
Friday: Supplementary Reading 5, second half
Reading Quiz 15

Week 10

Monday: Draft Day
Wednesday: Workshop: Semicolons and Dashes
Reading Quiz 16
Friday: Paper 3 Due

Week 11

Monday: Primary Reading 4
Reading Quiz 17
Wednesday: Supplementary Reading 6
Reading Quiz 18
Friday: Supplementary Reading 7
Reading Quiz 19

Week 12

Monday: Draft Day
Wednesday: Workshop: TBA
Friday: Paper 4 Due

Week 13

Monday: Revision Project Assigned
Wednesday: Workshop: TBA
Friday: Revision Proposol Due

Week 14

Monday: Library Day
Wednesday: Draft Day
Friday: Workshop: TBA

Week 15

Monday: Draft Day Two
Wednesday: Revision Paper Due
Friday: Final Exam Date and Time

Chapter 2
Philosophy and Pedagogy

A Philosophy for Teaching Writing

The sample syllabi in this manual reflect a particular philosophy for teaching writing. At Florida Atlantic University, we explicitly offer this philosophy for teaching writing to our students to help them better understand their role in the learning experience and the underlying expectations and assumptions we bring to the table:

> The work of learning to write and read is a life-long process. No matter where you are now in your abilities to write and read as ways to think, you will always be capable of more than you have already accomplished. Whether you come with a great deal of formal training in academic writing, or very little, all of you bring with you more writing and reading experience than you realize.

> It should not be surprising, then, that instructors at FAU understand the work of writing as a great deal more than the acquisition of skills. You will be reading complex texts and essays. And, you will be writing complex papers and discussing the ideas and experiences they represent.

> The class operates like a seminar at some times and a workshop at others. Often you will work with small groups of students, within which each student is expected to develop his or her ideas about a particular subject and share them with the group. There will be times when you will be reading each others' papers and making suggestions for revision. And there will also be times when you will discuss a single paper or reading as a class and everyone will be expected to contribute to the discussion.

> You will find first and foremost that the assignments in this course are designed to encourage you to re-imagine the work of reading and writing as opportunities to develop new ways of seeing, knowing, and making meaning. They are designed as invitations for you to question habitual ways of thinking, to move beyond obvious responses, and to develop your own strategies for posing questions about the reading, writing, and thinking you do. (wise.fau.edu/english/writingprogram/wpenc1101syllabuselements.php)

Every educational institution espouses a different approach to teaching writing, and teachers and students alike may contribute to developing an approach that addresses specific pedagogical issues and needs within individual institutions. Sharing a clear, specific philosophy with students is an effective way to include them in this process of development and to communicate your expectations to them. Some ways to share this information are posting it on departmental Web sites and including it in standard syllabi for writing courses.

The Philosophy Behind the Philosophy

So what does our philosophy of our composition courses mean? Here are some points to keep in mind:

- **These courses teach critical thinking.** Critical thinking begins with critical reading: the ability to comprehend complex and subtle arguments in lengthy and complicated readings. Critical thinking, then, demands that students also acquire the ability to evaluate these arguments, to enter into the conversations formed by these texts with confidence and authority. In staking their own positions within this field of ideas, students express their critical thinking through well-written papers with a central argument supported by close interpretive work with the texts.

- **These courses teach writing as a process, and they teach revision as central to that process.** Writing begins with reading and thinking, proceeds through pre-drafting and drafting, but then also includes revision: the refinement of thought, argument, support, and organization in writing. Revision is never approached as editing or correction, though your students will most probably think of it this way when they enter your class. Teaching revision as a core component of the process, as a method of re-seeing thoughts and arguments and making substantive changes to writing are useful approaches to including a revision component to writing courses.

- **These courses do not focus on content; that is, students are not here to learn the content of these particular readings but instead the processes of writing and critical thinking.** We do not expect students to perfectly comprehend the argument made in any essay they approach. We do not administer exams on the readings. Indeed, we could teach different kinds of readings (and we do) because the readings are only the raw material with which students practice the processes that are central to the course. This is, then, a workshop course, and the difference might best be expressed by analogy to art. An art history class teaches content. Students learn and work with this content. An art course, in sculpture perhaps, provides raw materials for students to learn a process. They are not graded on what they know about clay but on what they can do with it. So is the case with composition courses.

Goals and Outcomes

At FAU, we find it helpful to understand and communicate the purpose of our writing courses. Information about our goals, included on our Web site and our syllabi, is on the following page.

Our goal is for students who have completed college writing coursework to be able to:

- produce clear and appropriate writing that performs the specific rhetorical tasks of analytic discourse.
- produce both finished writing and preparatory writing (e.g., multiple drafts of formal writing, journal writing, written responses to other texts, etc.).
- employ critical thinking based on well-reasoned assumptions.
- read and respond critically to a variety of professional and other student texts in order to position their own ideas and arguments relative to the arguments and strategies of others.
- incorporate and cite external sources in their writing.
- use writing not only to communicate, but also to generate thinking and examine intellectual and/or cultural assumptions that emerge in the readings and in their own writing.
- use an academically acceptable ethos (i.e., the ability of writers to effect credibility in their writing).
- recognize and practice writing as a recursive process that demands substantial reworking of drafts to revise content, organization, clarity, argument structures, etc. (global revision), as distinct from editing and correction of surface error (local revision).
- demonstrate enhanced learning through global and local revisions that are based on "learning-centered" grading criteria.
- work effectively with other students in peer-group sessions to critique the substance of each other's work, focusing primarily on issues that would be addressed by global revision.
- demonstrate the abilities to identify, understand, and edit for global organization, style, and the patterns of error recurrent in their own writing. (wise.fau.edu/english/writingprogram/wpenc1101syllabuselements.php).

The Pedagogy of This Course

Given this philosophy and these goals, certain pedagogical practices are central to these courses:

- **Discussion, not lecture.** You should never lecture your class. Because the central goal of these courses is the development of critical thinking skills, you should rely on discussion instead, which allows students to practice these thinking skills. Lectures instead provide students with *your* thoughts on the material. Lectures, too, focus on the content of the essays, while the goal of these courses is the acquisition of skills in the processes of reading and writing critically.
- **Groups, not classes.** Because our focus is on helping students to help themselves, giving them practice in acquiring the skills of critical thinking, we often use small-group work in the classroom. Working in small groups allows students to participate more fully in these processes while helping them to learn from their peers. Rather than promoting a dependence on the teacher, small-group work promotes independence. It also

offers practice in the kinds of collaborative work that students will en-counter in a variety of careers. Having groups report back to the class forms a link between the small groups and the class as a whole.

- **Feedback, not assessment.** Grading is a necessary evil, one that neither we nor our students relish. But more important than the grade is the feedback given by written comments. Our comments are never directed towards justifying a grade; instead, our comments are intended to help students take the next step in their development as writers. What grades are given reflect the progress students are making and offer them a standard to measure their development. By keeping feedback front and center in our response to student writing, we maintain a focus on the skills of writing and thinking that drive the course.

PART II
GENERAL APPROACHES TO TEACHING

Chapter 3
Class Activities

Introduction

For many new teachers, one of the most intimidating aspects of planning a course is filling class time with structured activities that will help students engage the texts and the process of writing, get them involved in active class participation, and provide alternatives for decentering the classroom.

General Strategies

You will find the following general strategies useful in thinking about class activities.

- **Text is central.** No matter what activity you choose to do, you will want to make sure that it involves text. Normally, that will mean making sure that the activity is tied in some way to the text under discussion, but it might also mean using student text and sample work as an opportunity for students to think about their own writing. You should also always provide some chance for students to generate text out of class activity; the most satisfying, energetic, and insightful whole class discussion becomes useless if students leave the classroom and forget everything that was said.
- **The seven-second rule.** If you open your class with a question intended to prompt discussion, do not be surprised if you are met with deafening silence. Keep in mind that students will *always* find this silence more uncomfortable than you do. Try waiting at least seven seconds. Chances are someone will say something just to break the silence.
- **When in doubt, use small groups.** Small-group work never fails. Students often feel more comfortable speaking in groups of 3–5 and the physical activity required for them to shift desks and form groups can get lethargic classes, literally, moving. If nothing else is working, break the class into small groups and give them some task related to the work at hand. But whenever you use small groups be sure to also return to a larger class discussion by having the groups report their findings back to the class.

Working with a New Reading

One of the very first class activities you will need to plan for the semester is working with a new reading. As the semester progresses, you will return to this type of activity with each new essay. Within this category, there are several types of activities you may find useful, each with a particular goal.

Comprehension

Goal: To help students understand the argument of the essay.

The readings in *Emerging* can be challenging, especially for new students. One of the first tasks of any class that involves a new reading, then, is to make sure students have a grasp of the central argument of the reading. You can use a number of activities to accomplish this goal:

1. **Response Papers.** When you assign a reading, also assign a short response paper that asks students to account for the argument of the essay. Ideally, these response papers will begin to point the student toward the next paper and focus, for example, on a crucial section or concept to be used in the next assignment. Consider using any of the questions that follow each reading for short response assignments.

2. **Class Discussion.** While lectures are inappropriate, discussions are not. On the first day of a new reading, you might start a general class discussion by asking students what they thought of the essay and then draw out their reactions to the argument. In these discussions, prompt students to locate passages that support their opinions as a way of grounding the discussion in the text. Keep in mind the seven second rule; it may be difficult to get the class started with such a discussion, but keep at it until they begin to open up.

3. **Draw the Argument.** This is an exercise that works surprisingly well. In small groups, ask students to draw the argument of the essay. Each group should select a representative to reproduce the group's drawing on the board. Then, the group should explain their representation to the class. It is crucial that each group also identify passages in the text that support their interpretation.

4. **Key Passages.** Bring in to class (or have students do so) key passages that relate to the argument of the essay. Discuss these passages as a class or have students work in small groups to create paraphrases of the passages to share with the class. (You can use this as an opportunity to incorporate a discussion of how and when to paraphrase.)

5. **Outline the Argument.** Either before class or in small groups, have students prepare a rough outline of the reading. Use these in class to track the overall movement of the author's argument.

6. **Slanging the Essay.** Ask students to recast the author's argument using slang. What's lost in the translation, and why did the author use the language she or he did?

Reading skills

Goal: To help students refine their skills with reading, particularly their skills in decoding complex passages.

Once students have a basic grasp of an argument, you will want to push them past this zone of relative comfort to deal with the complexities of any argument and any piece of writing. For example:

1. **Confusing Passages.** You might ask students to identify a particularly confusing passage before coming to class. Select a number of passages, and then have students work in small groups to decode the author's meaning in these selections. Have the groups share their findings with the class as a whole. Alternatively, have students come to class with passages they feel are particularly crucial to the author's argument, and then have the groups create paraphrases of these passages to share with the class.

2. **Defining Terms.** Bring in a list of key terms or concepts from the essay. In small groups, have students work on developing definitions of these terms. Each group should be able to present the class a paraphrased definition of the term, a passage from the text that supports that paraphrase, and a statement about how the term relates to the larger argument.

3. **Focusing on Neglected Sections.** In any essay, students will be quick to latch onto certain key areas of the text. These may be the areas they best understand or the ones that feel most central to the argument. Ask students to "dig into" the text by having them focus on the "unimportant" or otherwise neglected areas of the text.

4. **Close Reading.** Ask small groups to select an important passage and then write a short paragraph that performs a close reading of the passage, referencing specific words and phrases that support their analysis.

Continuing Discussion

Discussion of an essay is never completed in one day. As discussion continues, you will want to incorporate a discussion of previous essays by asking students to consider how the ideas of the new essay relate to other texts they've read in the semester. A number of activities can help you accomplish this:

Connection

Goal: To help students see the relationships between a new reading and other essays they have read in the semester.

Critical thinking is best practiced across essays. After all, each piece of writing feels whole in itself, but when examined in the light of other writings and other ideas, students can begin to work their way into the conversation between the texts. Concepts from one essay, for example, can be tested or applied using the materials of a second essay. We call this kind of work connection, and it's a useful way for students to practice critical thinking in class and in their papers. Some activities you can use to promote connective thinking include:

1. **Practice Paragraphs.** Come to class with a series of quotations from the current or previous essay(s). In small groups, have students locate pas-

sages from the other essay that somehow relate to the quotations you have provided. Then, as a group, students should write a paragraph using both pieces of text to explain the connection between the two. Groups then share these paragraphs with the class.

2. **Relation Lists.** In small groups, have students make a list of all connections they see between the essays. Each group then writes their list on the board. This activity lets the entire class see the multiple ways that ideas can relate between the essays.

3. **Conjunction Function.** Ask students to make a list of concepts from each essay and then express the relationship between two of these concepts using a single conjunction. For example, "cosmopolitanism but few loyalties."

4. **Synthetic Writing.** Ask small groups to write a sentence that uses parts of two authors' texts, integrating the two quotations into a single sentence that expresses the relationship between the authors' ideas.

5. **Larger Conversations.** Ask students to list what larger conversations both essays might participate in. For example, immigration, globalization, networks.

Pre-drafting

Goal: To move students toward the first draft of the next paper assignment.

Working in class on activities that prepare students to write their papers gives double practice: practice in the processes of writing and drafting and practice in using the essays. For example:

1. **Imagining the Assignment.** One interesting way to get students thinking about drafts is to ask them to create their own version of the next assignment. For homework, have each student imagine the next assignment. In class, have them work in small groups to compare their imagined assignments—which seems most likely? Which seems hardest? Each group should select the best assignment and then share it with the class. What makes a good assignment?

2. **Sample Arguments.** In small groups, have students come up with a possible argument for the next assignment. Though you will find that some students, perhaps weaker students in particular, will then use these arguments in their actual papers, this remains a useful way to help the class consider the work of these courses.

3. **Sample Introductions.** After students have written sample arguments, ask them to write a sample introduction. Use this as an opportunity to discuss the key elements of any introduction.

4. **Revisited Responses.** For homework, have students revise a previous response paper to include the new essay. How might their response change given the ideas of the new essay? Use these revised responses to prompt class or small-group discussion.

5. **Paper Plans.** Sometimes students have time management issues. As a class or individually, ask them to draft out a plan for writing their paper. What do they need to do first? And then? And then? Also use this as a chance to discuss components of the writing process.

Quotation

Too often, students just sprinkle quotations throughout their text without providing any sense of how those pieces of text relate to their larger argument. Here are some strategies you can use to get them to engage the text closely in ways that support what they want to say:

1. **The Super Secret Formula.** This activity is designed to help students build a paragraph that works with two authors in support of the paper's argument. The Super Secret Formula is:

$$C_l > I > Q_1 > E > T > Q_2 > C_e$$

Students start their paragraphs with "C_l," a sentence that states the *claim* of the paragraph. Then with "I" they *introduce* a quotation from the first author, adding a sentence that *explains* it ("E"). The next sentence makes a *transition* ("T") to a *quotation* from a different author, "Q_2." Finally, students take a sentence or two to explain the *connection* between the two quotations ("C_e") and how it supports the argument they're making in the paper.

   The concrete structure of a "formula" provides good scaffolding for students to build a solid paragraph that works with quotations, but the risk is, of course, that all their paragraphs will becomes (literally) formulaic. When using this exercise, start by having groups use the formula to make a sample paragraph. Then challenge groups to come up with other formulas for working with quotations.

2. **Close Reading.** Sometimes students have difficulty analyzing a quotation; pieces of text will be sprinkled through a paper seemingly with the assumption that their relationship to the argument is self-evident. Here's an exercise that can help students with this problem: Ask students to write or type a quotation they want to work with. Then ask them to underline the key sentences or phrases of the quotation, the parts that they feel are most important for the point they're trying to make. Then have them construct sentences that use these pieces of the quotation and that explain how they relate to their arguments.

3. **Facts and Ideas.** Quotations that only contain statements of fact provide little opportunity for analysis; quotations with ideas do. Bring in examples of each kind for discussion and then during peer review, ask students to identify each quotation in the papers they're reading as either fact or idea. This exercise will give them practice distinguishing between the two and will provide useful feedback for students on what type of quotation they're favoring.

4. **Short and Long.** Another problem students seem to have in working with quotations is choosing quotations of appropriate length: They might choose quotations that are too short and thus don't provide enough support, or they might choose very long quotations and then say little about them. Have students look through their drafts and determine the length of each quotation by noting how many typed lines it takes. They can use

the resulting report to reflect on their tendencies with quotation: Do they always use very short ones? Always use very long ones? After the exercise, challenge students to use a variety of quotation lengths in their papers.
5. **Peer Review Boost.** During peer review, ask students to suggest at least three quotations that could be added to support the paper. This exercise will encourage authors of student papers to use more quotations while helping peer editors to dig deeper into the text to locate quotations that can help the student writers.

Organization

Students often have trouble writing papers with strong organization. Sometimes, in fact, it feels like they could swap around all the body paragraphs and it would be the same paper—the paragraphs don't logically lead one to the other. Here are some exercises to help students focus on the organization of their papers:
1. **Paragraph-to-Paragraph Transition.** The most solid transitions come from a statement that directly ties two paragraphs together. Have students take two paragraphs from their drafts. Ask them to write a one-sentence summary of the first paragraph and then another one-sentence summary of the second paragraph. Students should combine these two sentences into one, forming a strong and specific transition.
2. **Rearrange the Order.** Strong organization is self-evident. That is, when a paper is well-organized each paragraph clearly has a place in the whole. Have students test their organization by bringing in a draft for peer revision with the paragraph order switched around. If their peers cannot reassemble the original order, then they need to work on transitions and organization.
3. **Model Transitions.** Have students locate examples of effective transitions in the current reading. Discuss what makes them effective—is it just the use of transitional words and phrases or is there a sentence pattern at work here? Have students apply what they learn by modeling one of these effective transitions in their current drafts.
4. **Trail Markers.** Trail markers make sure you don't get lost in the woods; students can use the same technique to mark the trail of their arguments in their papers. Have students underline key sentences in each paragraph that "point the way" to the larger argument and/or to the next paragraph. If they can't find sentences that work in that way, then that paragraph might represent someplace their readers might get lost.
5. **All Outta Outlines.** The strongest organization feels inevitable. Help students to locate that level of organization by having them produce multiple pre- or post-draft outlines, each with a different possible organization; you might even ask them to outline until they can't outline any more. Do some points always need to come before others? Do they need to introduce a term, for example, before discussing it? Looking at multiple organizations can help students see the one that makes the most sense, the one that seems most inevitable.

Avoiding Plagiarism

Sometimes discussing plagiarism at the start of the semester is not enough. You might also try some of these class activities:

1. **Seeing Notes in a Draft.** As writing becomes more and more an electronic activity, some students are using computers for all stages of the composition process. While it's great to see students practicing these electronic literacies, their reliance on word processing programs entails some new risks of plagiarism. More than one recent instance of plagiarism in our program at FAU has involved students who had been taking notes in the same document that they were using to compose their draft. Fortunately, word processors include a number of tools students can use to separate out their notes and textual references from their drafts. Encourage students to use different fonts, different colors, or a highlighting feature to make it clear to themselves what they've pasted in from different sources. Visually separating these notes helps remind them that they will need to provide citation for that material in the draft.

2. **File Naming.** Another consequence of word processing is that students have started turning in the wrong file, often an earlier work in progress without citation. In order to make sure that students turn in the correct file, encourage them to name their files specifically by including *draft* in all draft files and only changing the name to *final* when they are ready to turn the paper in.

3. **Paraphrase-O-Meter.** When does a paraphrase become a paraphrase? It's a tricky question but a vital one when it comes to questions of plagiarism. As a useful exercise you can work on successive paraphrases in class. Split the class into groups and give them all a single quotation from the text. Ask each group to paraphrase the quotation so that it's just *barely* a paraphrase. Have the groups share, and then discuss whether or not these paraphrases would be considered plagiarism or not. Have the groups paraphrase the quotation repeatedly, changing it more each time. At what point does it become a legitimate alternative to the quotation? What are the key factors that make a paraphrase a paraphrase? Does it involve changing words, word order, or some combination of those and more?

4. **Jeopardy!** Plagiarism, of course, represents real academic jeopardy, but you can explore some of plagiarism's gray areas by playing a game of *Jeopardy!* in the classroom. In this version, there are only two primary answers, *"What is, plagiarism?"* and *"What is, OK?"* Split the class into teams and create questions that explore tricky questions of academic honesty. For example, "You use *Wikipedia* in your essay. Since this is an encyclopedia, you don't provide a citation." *"What is, plagiarism?"*

5. **Peer Advice.** Ask students to write advice to their peers on how to avoid plagiarism. In doing so, encourage them to consider their own lives and the lives of their peers more than pat notions of honesty. For example, how do they handle situations where they just want to give up and turn something from the Web in as their work? What strategies do they use to make sure their work is *their* work?

Working with Student Samples

Student sample work is a crucial resource. Bringing in full or partial drafts of student papers emphasizes the workshop nature of these courses. Given the limitations of most photocopying budgets, you may want to devise strategies to incorporate drafts into your class with a minimum of paper. Asking students to e-mail you all drafts (or to deliver them to you via a course management system like *Blackboard* if you are using it) is a big help. You can, for instance, strip off a student's name from the text and then e-mail the draft to all students, asking them to read it before class so that you can discuss it. Similarly, you can copy and paste sections from the electronic versions of the drafts, print out a copy, and then copy this onto an overhead to be used in class. How you choose to use and distribute sample work will depend on the technology and budget available to you.

Micro issues

Goal: To help students reflect on issues of language and writing.

At times you will want to bring in drafts or even sentences from drafts in order to focus on sentence level issues. For example:

1. **Group Corrections.** Bring in several sentences from drafts with either the same error or with multiple representative errors. In groups, have students first identify the error, then locate the section of the handbook or a grammar reference that addresses the error, and then correct the error. Groups report their activities to the class.

2. **Grammar Hunt.** Bring in a sample paragraph with several errors in it. Have small groups locate all of the errors in the paragraph. The group that catches all the errors without misidentifying correct uses of grammar as error wins. This activity is especially useful for having students consider issues of style and syntax. Often, groups will want to identify syntactically awkward but grammatically correct sentences as errors. You can use this to begin a discussion on what an error is and isn't as well as a discussion of revising for fluidity.

3. **Verb: That's What's Happening.** Bring in a passage from a promising draft and then have the students work in groups to identify the verbs in every sentence of the passage. Use this to prompt a discussion: What are the key verbs? What is the action of these sentences? Are there more verbs used in clauses? What are the implications of where the verb is for the author of the paper and for the student's own writing?

4. **Judging Arguments.** You might also bring in a series of arguments from drafts and have the class consider the strength of each as well as their potential for the papers as a whole. Groups can work on revising weaker arguments.

5. **Citing Error.** Bring in several sentences with errors and then have students work in groups to not only correct the errors but to locate the specific part of the handbook or a grammar reference that addresses the error, citing the page of the resource used with a properly formatted MLA citation.

Macro issues

At times you might find it most useful to examine a whole draft in order to ad-dress macro issues ranging from argument to support to organization. Working with a whole draft also creates a model for revision; rather than looking at the "corrections" that need to be made, the class can discuss the *content* of the paper and what changes are needed to make it stronger. For example:

1. **Group Peer Revision.** Have students read a draft from the class. Some students are highly uncomfortable having their work discussed by the class, so before selecting a draft, first check for a student who has ex-pressed a willingness to share his or her work. Even then, check with the student and ask if he or she would like you to present the draft anony-mously or openly as the student's draft. In discussion, stress that as with grading, comments should always point out both what works in the draft and what needs improvement.

2. **Finding Keys.** When discussing a whole draft, have small groups locate the key success of the paper and the key weakness. Then have these groups share their "keys." The similarities and differences between these "keys" will help underscore both the value of peer revision as well as how to figure out which peer comments to pay attention to.

3. **Response (to) Papers.** Papers in these classes should be moments in a conversation. After reading a draft, have small groups compose a short reply to the draft that responds to it in order to extend the conversation. Small groups should locate quotations that support their contention in relation to the draft. After discussing all of these responses as a class, discuss too how the author of the draft might revise her or his argument to take the class's responses into account.

4. **What/What Not to Take.** When using a full draft in class you may want to have a discussion about what students can and can not take from the sample work. As a class, make a list of what students might take—organi-zational principles, paragraphing structures, effective methods of using quotation—as well as a list of what cannot be taken (actual sentences, for example).

The Writing Process

At times you will want to focus directly on issues related to the writing process:

1. **Class Generated Criteria.** As a way of assessing how well your class is learning the elements of academic writing, you can have small groups work directly on criteria for the elements you identify as important in the type of writing they are doing. For example, ask small groups to generate a definition of a strong argument or a checklist for proofreading their drafts. Use these small-group discussions to generate a larger discussion about what makes an argument strong or what elements are most impor-tant to check while proofreading.

2. **Examining Readings.** To help students think about their own writing pro-cesses while also working with the current essay, you might ask the class

to create an outline of the current reading. Similarly, you could have students locate the central statement of the argument. In looking at the essays as end results of a writing process, you will want to point out to students that the authors had different goals and different audiences than students in these courses have; thus, their papers will be different in form, style, and content. Use this as an opportunity to discuss issues such as audience.

3. **Thinking about Revision.** Have students review the sections of the handbook on editing and proofreading. Use this to open a discussion about the differences between editing, proofreading, and revising. How are they different? Are they all necessary? Which do they tend to do in their own writing?

4. **Introducing . . .** Open a discussion in groups about what makes an effective introduction, what elements are required by this course in particular, and what variations might be effective. As a class, create a checklist for introductions.

5. **Check!** In small groups, have students make a checklist of elements needed for a successful paper. As a class, discuss each group's list and consolidate them into a single list that everyone agrees includes key elements for every paper. Repeat this exercise with a process checklist, asking groups to detail each step needed to draft a paper successfully.

Language and Grammar

It is helpful to include a handbook in the required texts for freshman writing classes. While there are several online resources for grammar exercises, the following are suggestions for how to incorporate a grammar handbook in class activities:

1. **Search/Find/Replace/Correct.** Review with the class the section of the handbook on apostrophes. Afterwards, tell them to use their word processor's "find and replace" function to replace *it's* with *it is*. Have them re-read their papers—all misuses of *it's* will be very obvious.

2. **Grammar Hunt.** Bring in sentences from drafts that have errors or are syntactically strained. Put the class into groups and have each group work on first identifying the error, then finding the section of the handbook that addresses it, then correcting it. The group with the most correct answers (and corrections) gets a "prize" (chocolate is a good motivator).

3. **It's Not Just Error.** Have students identify what they feel is their strongest statement/sentence in the paper. Then have them write about the sentence using the handbook and its terms. For example, "My sentence uses two clauses, both with active verbs. . . ." The goal is to have students see how grammar is not just about being "wrong," but is an active force in helping them make strong sentences, better papers, and better grades.

4. **Weak Revision.** Choose a sentence from the essay the class is reading. Have students revise it using the grammatical resources in the handbook to make the sentence less effective, though still correct. Discuss as a class what sentence elements make it less effective.

5. **Babel Grammar.** Have students take a sentence from their drafts and translate it into another language using an online tool such as Babel Fish (babelfish.altavista.com/) or Google's Language Tools (google.com/ language_tools). Students might even choose to translate it several times (from English to French to German to Chinese); in the end, translate it back into English. The resulting sentence will be a mess. Have students use the handbook to determine where the mess happened and why (e.g.: "The verb shifted in tense and number").

6. **Close Reading/Close Attention.** When looking at quotations from the essays under discussion, incorporate a discussion of grammar. Examine the verb, subject, and object of a crucial sentence by having students identify each term using the handbook. How does sentence structure make argument?

7. **Checker Challenge.** Go over the material on grammar checkers in the handbook. Have students pay attention to the sentences that are flagged by their word processor's grammar checker. The challenge is to come in with a sentence the grammar checker thought was wrong that isn't. Students should use the handbook, comparing what the grammar checker says is wrong to the handbook definition.

8. **Below the Surface.** In small groups, have students develop a definition of *surface error.* Ask them to come up with its opposite term too; "deep error"? "sub-surface error"? "serious error"? What marks the difference between the two terms? Which one do they need to pay more attention to? At which stage of drafting should they focus on one or the other? And what parts of the handbook will help them with both?

9. **Analyzing the Grammar of Prompts.** When giving a new writing prompt, have the students analyze its sentence structure using the handbook. Are there clues to approaching the prompt in this structure? What sentences seem to be emphasized based simply on the use of verbs or nouns or clauses?

Introduction

Peer revision is one of the most practical skills students will learn in these courses. After all, in their careers, students will never be asked to write a 4–6 page paper connecting two disparate essays; however, no matter what career they choose, they will be expected to work effectively with others, to offer valuable feedback, and to work from the feedback of others. Peer revision is a vital start to these collaborative work processes, and it should in no way be short-changed in our classrooms.

Thus, we must emphasize for students the importance of peer revision. It is not busywork nor is it a less valuable form of feedback compared to your comments. To the contrary, peer revision helps both the author and the reviewer. The student author receives feedback from a real audience; the reviewer enacts an awareness of what's important in a paper in choosing where and how to comment. Every paper should go through at least one peer revision session.

Commenting on Drafts

Because students have neither practiced the skills of peer revision nor experienced the expectations of these courses, you might find it useful to provide full comments on students' drafts of the first paper. These comments should be focused on the elements of the draft that the student needs to work on to pass the first paper or for a passing draft, to move to the next grade level. Thus they will probably be more focused and less extensive than the comments on a revised draft, which is tied to a grade. You should still make both marginal and end comments, but you will probably want to edit these down to the comments most essential for the student to significantly improve the draft.

Many teachers are tempted to continue the practice of full comments on rough drafts throughout the rest of the semester. However, you may wish to avoid doing so because providing comments on all rough drafts for all papers:

- Completely devalues peer revision; students will not take the practice seriously because they will feel the "real" comments come from you.
- Fosters dependence; students may succeed in your class but may not do as well in future classes because they have not learned to work with the feedback of their peers. In some cases, students may even contact you for comments on papers written in other classes, continuing their dependence on your input.
- Contributes to teacher burnout; commenting on papers every week of the semester (rough and then draft) creates a nearly unmanageable workload.

Your students will clamor for your comments on every draft; you will be tempted to provide them. However, have faith in the process of peer revision. When students realize it functions as a primary mechanism of feedback, they will take the process more seriously, both when they review comments from their peers and when they make comments on their peers' papers.

Rather than commenting on every draft for subsequent assignments, you might instead read through all drafts, identify the most common issues in the class as a whole, and then provide "global comments" for the class that are tied into sample work in the classroom. In addition to these global comments, you should make sure your students know that you will always read through a draft and offer feedback during your office hours.

Sources of Feedback

Peer revision thus serves as the foundation of feedback on student work, though students will have many sources of feedback on their work. You should make it clear to them that they should revise based on:

- Peer review comments
- Your global comments on the entire set of drafts
- Comments gathered while meeting with you during office hours

Making Peer Revision Count

Initially, students will probably not take peer revision very seriously. They tend to believe that their peers don't know anything and so can't offer any help and, consequently, they will turn to you for the "right" feedback on their work. There are a few strategies you can use to stress the importance of peer revision:

1. **Full Comments Only on the First Draft.** Provide full comments for student papers only on the drafts for the first paper. For the second paper and beyond, tell students that you will only produce "global" comments concerning common problems you saw across the set of papers. This practice makes it clear that peer revision is important, since it becomes the primary means of feedback for students on their initial drafts, though interested students may still come to your office for individual feedback.

2. **Homework.** From their years of high school education, students have been conditioned to take homework more seriously than class work, which they often imagine is just "busywork." Thus, you might assign peer revision as homework, having each student take one draft home to work on. These drafts and accompanying revision sheets can be e-mailed to the student author or can be returned at the next class.

3. **Comments.** To stress the usefulness of peer comments to student authors, you might incorporate observations about peer revision into your end comments on a draft. For example, "I'm glad you followed Kiran's comments about your argument. That made a big difference" or "Please notice that both of your peers made the same comment on your draft."

4. **Grading.** You might also "grade" peer comments, by using a check-plus, check, check-minus system and then factoring these grades into a class participation component of the final grade.

5. **Sample Peer Comments.** On the day you do sample work from drafts you might also look at sample peer comments. Use this as a chance to model effective peer commenting.

Peer Revision Activities

Generally, peer revision takes place in groups of three students, so be sure to remind students that they should bring in three copies of their drafts—one for you and two for their peers. When you collect revised drafts, collect the peer commented drafts and revision sheets as well.

Some other activities you might consider include:

1. **Grading Drafts.** This activity is particularly useful at the start of the semester. Bring in copies of your grading criteria and then break the students into groups. Ask each group to use the criteria to determine the key factors for not passing, for a "C" range grade, for a "B" range grade, and for an "A" range grade. Groups then share these key components with the class. Then ask the peers to "grade" the drafts in their group, tying their comments into specific pieces of the criteria. This activity not only provides peer feedback but also helps students understand the expectations for papers and helps them understand their own grades as well.

2. **Colorful Drafts.** Ask each student to bring in different colors of highlighter and, as a backup, bring in a collection as well. Ask each peer to use different colors to highlight two different elements of a draft. For example, have them highlight summary in one color and analysis in another or material on one author in one color and material on another in a second color. When student authors get their drafts back, they will have a quick visual assessment of their papers.

3. **Post-Draft Outline.** Have students bring in a "post-draft outline," composed of a single sentence that summarizes each paragraph of the paper. In peer revision groups, have each peer commenter do the same post-draft outline. The author of the paper should then compare his or her own understanding of what each paragraph does with that of her or his peers. Use these collected post-draft outlines to work on organization in revision.

4. **Channeling You.** One of the challenges in peer revision is getting students to be properly critical. Students too often are too generic or too kind because they don't want to offend or upset their peers/friends. One way to get them to be more rigorous in peer revision is to ask them to comment on drafts the way *you* would, making the comments they think *you* would make. This exercise is especially effective toward the middle of the semester after they've seen how you comment on their own drafts and papers. Students can either step into your voice in this exercise or speculate what you would say (e.g., "I think Barclay would want you to use a quotation here.").

Chapter 5
Commenting and Grading

Commenting

Commenting on student work is one of the central tasks of teaching. It is also the most time-consuming one. As you start your teaching career, you should expect to spend at least one half hour commenting on and grading each paper. As you gain experience and your skills with commenting improve, you might find you can provide quality comments in half that time—even though some papers will always take more time. In any case, in scheduling your own time, you will want to make sure you provide a generous period for any commenting or grading task.

Goals

The goal of commenting is always the same: to show the student what he or she is doing well and to focus the student on the next skill that needs to be acquired. The grade for any work emerges from the interplay of these two factors. Comments thus drive grades; grades do not drive comments.

It is perhaps best, then, to think of commenting as an engaged conversation with students rather than as solely a mechanism of assessment, and this conversation takes place on two levels. On one level, you are a reader interested in what the student has to say. On this level you might find yourself writing comments that ask the student to consider the implications of her or his argument or that question the points made in the paper. On a second level, you are an instructor invested in helping the student grow as a writer. On this level, you might find yourself asking the student questions about his or her use of support in an argument or the overall organization of the paper.

This is, to the greatest extent possible, a collegial conversation. Because our goal in commenting is to help students develop, we should avoid demeaning or extreme comments—the kind that would shut down any conversation. This is not to say that we should not be demanding of students or in our comments. Instead, it is to suggest that the way to spur students to meet those demands is by offering balanced comments written in a professional tone.

Methods

Some general points to keep in mind when commenting include:
- Use a pen or pencil that you find comfortable, since you will be doing a lot of writing. Some people like to avoid red since they feel students shut down at the sight of a page filled with red ink. However, any color will do.
- Avoid abbreviations unless you go over what they mean with students (and unless you do so repeatedly). For example, *awk* may clearly mean "awkward" to you but will mean only "awk" to your students.

- If your handwriting is difficult to read, consider providing typed comments instead.
- You may want to provide your students with a printed commenting guide that details and explains any proof marks or commenting shorthand you will use.
- If you wish to comment electronically, avoid inserting your comments directly into the student's text, which makes them more difficult to read. Consider instead the Comment feature in Microsoft Word, which generates marginal comments tied directly to the text.

In all cases you will want to make comments in three places: in the margins of the paper, in the sentences, and especially at the end. These three locations can contain two types of comments, local and global.

Local comments/global comments

Local comments are directed to a specific section or piece of the draft; global comments reflect on the draft as a whole. Locally, you might point out an awkward sentence. Globally, you might suggest that the awkwardness of the sentence is related to a larger issue in the thinking behind the argument as a whole. Similarly, a poor use of quotation may be a local concern—occurring only within that paragraph—or a global one, part of a larger pattern of difficulty using quotations effectively in the student's writing.

As you comment, you most likely will move between local and global concerns. Having both of them is important. If you only direct students to the larger issues in a draft, then they might not see how their writing fits into this global concern. On the other hand, if you focus only on local concerns you might give students the impression that they only need to "fix" these "errors" in order to get an A. Regularly tying the two together provides students the best perception of their own work: They can see the larger issues, but can also then see how these larger issues are manifested directly in their writing.

Marginal comments/sentence comments/end comments

You should expect to write at least one marginal comment for each paragraph in the draft. Sometimes these will be local comments that emerge from your experience as a reader—questions, for example, about what the student means by a certain claim. More often, though, placing a marginal comment at the end of a paragraph allows you to reflect on the success of that one paragraph in the paper as a whole. For example, you might find yourself writing "I'm not sure how this paragraph supports your argument" or "This is a great use of quotation here . . . notice how it connects the texts back into your argument" or "This paragraph feels out of place . . . can you move it further up in the paper?"

Sentence comments frequently involve reactions to student writing. As we will discuss in the section just below on dealing with error, you may want to restrain yourself from over-commenting at the level of the sentence, for both your sake and the student's. An overabundance of sentence-level comments can overwhelm the student who may be unable to see what issues to focus on in the face of so many comments. For your part, too many sentence-level comments can tire you in the commenting process while making it more difficult for you to follow the student's argument and hence determine a sense of the grade. For techniques to balance these kinds of comments, see the next section in this chapter, Dealing with error.

End comments are in many ways the most important; they should not be given short shrift. Expect to write, at the very least, a short paragraph of 5–6 sentences at the end of each draft. Comments should not be much shorter than this. Nor, usually, should they be significantly longer. While you might assume that a full page of detailed comments is particularly useful to students, they often have trouble digesting that much feedback. Excessive comments may also lead to instructor burnout.

The best formula for end comments is a "sandwich": open with what the student is doing well, move on to the *one* writing issue the student needs to focus on for the next paper, and then close with another positive comment. For example:

> This paper shows that you have a really great grasp of both authors' arguments and you've managed to locate a very solid argument of your own, although it's not clearly expressed until the end of the paper. For your next paper you will want to make sure you articulate your argument right at the start but, even more importantly, you will want to focus on your use of quotation. See the paragraph marked * on p. 3—here you tie your discussion of the quotations back to the argument. Contrast that to the other paragraphs. For the next paper, keep up the work with argument but concentrate on improving your use of quotation.

Note that the end comments are tied directly back into the paper. This is an important strategy, since students often cannot connect what you say at the end to what they're doing in the paper. Directing them back to a specific moment, whether a strong or weak one, lets them see what you mean in the context of their own writing.

Notice, too, that the comment directs the student to one skill to work on for the next paper. In almost all cases, students will have multiple weaknesses: argument, use of text, organization. You should prioritize these and other concerns for your class and then direct your comments to the next most important skill. Thus, for example, if you feel students must locate an argument and then learn to support it, early comments might praise the understanding of text and then ask students to work on making an argument. Later papers might then praise the ability to formulate an argument but move students to the next task: supporting it.

Strong papers need similar end comments. It's tempting to just put "Great job!" and move on to the next paper, but students will need, first of all, to know *what* in the paper made it great and then they will need to know how to keep improving—by forming a more complex or nuanced argument, for example.

Dealing with error

You will most likely encounter a great deal of error in student work, ranging from typographical errors to grammatical ones to serious language concerns. "Correcting" all these errors reduces commenting to editing, which is beneficial to neither you nor your students.

As a general practice, you will want to go over proofreading techniques with your students. You may even allow a small amount of class time for students to do a final proofread, particularly for the early papers. Techniques to cover when discussing proofreading include reading the draft out loud, taking a break before proofreading, getting a fresh set of eyes to look at the draft, and using the tools available in most word processors.

No doubt some error will remain after proofreading. For repeated errors, such as problems with parenthetical citation, mark the error once and then note marginally that it occurs throughout the paper. You might then also refer to this pattern of minor error in the end comments.

Language concerns are more serious. See the section on Language and Grammar.

Managing the workload

Commenting is a lot of work. You will want to find techniques that help you manage this workload. For example:

- You might skim through all drafts once without commenting, placing them into piles that roughly correspond to grades. Then, start with the weakest papers and work your way to the strongest. That way, you will encounter the most difficult and time-consuming work while you have the most energy and the work will become less demanding as you continue.
- If you decide to type your end comments, you might keep a file with common comments that you can then copy and paste into your comments for each draft.
- Divide the work evenly over time. Rather than trying to comment on all drafts in one sitting, distribute your work over several days, setting a firm goal of working through a set number of drafts each day.

Grading Criteria Glossary

The following is an example of how we clarify our grading criteria at FAU for our students and instructors. Since our grading criteria make use of some terms that can be interpreted in multiple ways, we have constructed a glossary of our understanding of these terms, available at wise.fau.edu/english/writingprogram/wpenc1101gradingcriteria.php.

Argument

This is perhaps the most ambiguous term in freshman writing classrooms and one of the most difficult terms for students to comprehend. When we use the term *argument* at FAU, we mean the central, problem-solving idea that drives the paper, a concept that many of us learned to think of as a "thesis." We might also think of this as a "position" or as a "project," all of which suggest that there is a central point the student is trying to make in the paper. The argument will usually show up in a thesis statement on the first page of the paper, but this is not the sole defining characteristic of an argument.

The student should have a goal in a paper, something he or she is trying to accomplish, which is often defined by a specific, argumentative statement. But even when this statement is absent, the goal is often still apparent, whether as a summation in the conclusion or an underlying/recurring theme of the paper.

An ideal argument will be spelled out in a clear thesis statement and will provide both a direction for the paper and a motivation for that direction (a problem to solve, a goal to accomplish, a position to defend, a project to complete, and so on).

Evidence

If an argument presents a problem and a potential solution, the evidence attempts to prove the urgency of that problem and the validity of that solution. Evidence consists of examples, details, and quotations (gleaned from the assigned texts) that work together to support the argument.

The most important concerns of evidence relate to relevance and quantity. Strong evidence is directly related to the argument, correctly interpreted and applied from the text, and presented alongside enough similar evidence to ensure the persuasiveness of the argument. Strong use of evidence also often includes the consideration of possible counter-examples.

Student papers should demonstrate this relevant, clear, accurately interpreted and applied, and sufficient use of evidence in every paragraph, as each paragraph will have a point to make and will need evidence to prove that point.

Primarily this will be achieved through strong use of quotation. When a quotation is provided in the text, the student will provide some analysis of that quotation and will indicate how that quotation and its analysis relate to the larger argument.

Connection is the term we use when students bring together the ideas of different texts by relating quotations from two different authors and using that analysis to say something about one or both authors in the context of the argument.

Organization

Organization refers to the way the evidence of the paper is presented. A strong paper will demonstrate organization at the paper level, the paragraph level, and the sentence level. Perhaps most importantly, though, a strong paper will demonstrate a logical kind of cohesiveness that demonstrates organization between the paragraphs.

Student papers should have a clear sense of purpose indicated by their argument, but they should also have a clear plan of action for solving the problem they have presented. Often, strong writers will make use of an organizational statement that specifically lays out this plan toward the beginning of the paper. With or without an organizational statement, though, the direction of the paper should be clear to the reader.

Strong organization at the paper level will make purpose and direction clear. Surprises and unpredictable changes of direction are often characteristics of weak organization. In a strongly organized paper, each paragraph logically connects to and follows from the previous paragraphs. Sentences flow in a way that builds on preceding information, and paragraphs do the same. Lesser organizational patterns rely on listing, a familiar structure for many high-school writers.

Attention to audience

Attentiveness to the reading audience is an element of writing that will be new to most of our students. In the past, they have written for teachers and for grades. Our intention is to teach them to write for real readers. Our peer review process gives students an opportunity to see the reaction of like-minded student writer/readers, and this reaction should be a consideration during all stages of the writing process.

A paper indicates attention to audience by doing much of what was mentioned in the other categories: presenting a strong argument with sufficient evidence to support the claims and organizing the paper in a logical way. Attention to audience involves the additional efforts of ensuring that clarity and logic is present in every part of the paper, anticipating and addressing audience questions and concerns, and leading the audience through difficult concepts.

Confused readers often signal confusing papers, a malady that attention to audience should remedy. Maintaining a consistent tone and plan throughout a paper can make it more palatable. Offering enough contextual information does the same. It is a strong writer's responsibility to make sure the paper is understandable to the audience and, if necessary, to prepare or educate the reader in order to ensure that the paper is understandable.

Attention to audience also means ensuring that the audience cares about the paper. A readable, easy to navigate paper is part of this, but it is also necessary to create a paper that the audience will care about. It is the writer's job to create that relevance, to ensure that the reader understands why the issue/argument is universally important.

Grammar and format

FAU's writing program makes use of standard written English. Grammar and spelling in student papers should follow these conventions. A required handbook is available to clarify student questions.

Students are expected to write all work in MLA (Modern Language Association) format. The purpose here, aside from universality across the program, is not so much to teach MLA format as it is to ensure that students are able to work within an assigned format in general. In this way, we prepare them for the work they will do in their eventual majors and disciplines, each of which uses its own system of citation. MLA is used, then, to give students practice in this convention of academic writing and to underscore its importance in the creation of knowledge.

Grading Criteria

These grading criteria began as a wiki-powered project driven by the teachers of our program. They have been refined by the FAU's Writing Committee and adopted by the faculty of the department of English (wise.fau.edu/english/writingprogram/wpenc1101gradingcriteria.php). Papers are evaluated in five categories: thesis/argument/reasoning, evidence/quotation/support, organization, audience, and grammar/language/formatting. We have found it very helpful to use these criteria and to share it with our students. Should you choose to use a similar system of standardizing evaluation, you will want to spend some time developing and becoming familiar with the criteria you choose. We have also found it helpful to develop a rubric to help us apply our criteria in grading.

The criteria used at FAU are:

Plagiarism and academic irregularity

Issues of academic irregularity such as plagiarism supersede these criteria; any work that has been plagiarized in whole or in part will result in a failing grade for the course as a whole and a notation of academic irregularity on the student's transcript.

Not Passing

NOTE: Papers that are Not Passing may exhibit many of the characteristics described by the criteria below. However, papers that have any one of the following elements cannot pass: no argument, no attention to the assignment, or egregious error to the degree that meaning is severely impeded.

Thesis/Argument/Reasoning

Not Passing papers have little or no sense of argument, thesis, position, or purpose, thus suggesting that the student is unable to think critically in relation to the readings or unable to reproduce that critical thinking in writing. Specifically:
- The paper does not address the prompt.
- The paper contains no clear argument.
- The paper contains a narrative instead of expository essay.

Evidence/Quotation/Support

Not Passing papers generally avoid close engagement with the readings; what engagement there is might suggest significant misreading. In other words, the use of text suggests that the student is unable to read critically or unable to connect critical reading to independent and original thinking. Specifically:
- The paper includes no textual support, no quotation at all.
- The paper includes textual support, but indicates a misreading or haphazard reading of the text.
- The paper includes quotation or summary but fails to use it to support any argument.
- The paper has so many quotations that it seems the student is using quotation and summary to "write" the paper instead of providing his or her own analysis.

Organization

Not Passing papers often have serious problems with organization, reflected either in a failure to meet minimum requirements for length or in a level of disconnection that hinders the comprehension of the reader. Specifically:
- The paper is not sufficiently developed and often will therefore not meet minimum length requirements.

- In the paper, there is no clear relationship between the paragraphs, the ideas expressed, the quotations used, or the summaries presented.
- The paper has no clear pattern of organization, thus impeding meaning and comprehension.

Audience

- The paper adopts an inappropriate tone by using slang, informal English, or nonacademic prose.
- The paper shows little or no awareness of the reader's need for contextual information.

Grammar/Language/Formatting

Not Passing papers pay little attention to issues of grammar, language, and presentation. At times, this will reflect serious language concerns in a student; however, it may also reflect severe carelessness on the part of the student. Specifically:

- The paper contains grammatical errors that impede meaning, including repeated significant errors (subject/verb agreement, sentence boundary issues) and/or convoluted syntax that makes it difficult to understand what the student is trying to say.
- The paper shows that the student made little or no attempt to conform to MLA rules of documentation.

C range (C or C+)

Note: C– papers are not passing; however, the use of C– is often intended to indicate that a student has progressed significantly or is producing work that is almost but not quite passing.

Thesis/Argument/Reasoning

"C" or "C+" papers show that the student can articulate a position in relation to a set of readings. That articulation—which we might variously call the paper's argument, thesis, or project—represents the start of critical thinking. Specifically:

- The paper addresses the prompt.
- The paper has an argument, even though that argument may not be stated in the introduction or may not ever be stated clearly.
- In C+ papers, the argument is stated clearly but reflects only what was discussed in class, thus showing no original thought.

Evidence/Quotation/Support

"C" or "C+" papers demonstrate that students are acquiring skills with critical reading, reflected through their ability to work with texts in support of their position. Specifically:

- The paper has quotations that relate to the topic and argument, but the relationship is often not explained.
- Particularly for low-level C papers, the paper has some quotations that do not support (and may even contradict) the assertions made in the paper.
- Particularly for C+ papers, the paper has original ideas, but these ideas tend to be dropped or repeated rather than developed.

- In assignments that ask students to work with more than one text, the paper provides quotations from all required texts but uses them in isolation, hence weakening the connection between the ideas of those two authors.

Organization

"C" or "C+" papers have a basic sense of organization; that is, the student substantially controls the shape of the paper, though some areas may interrupt the flow of the paper. Specifically:

- The paper includes leaps in logic and expects readers to follow implicit patterns of thought.
- The paper may have some paragraphs that include unrelated ideas and lose argumentative focus.
- The paper offers no link between the ideas expressed in each individual paragraph; transitions between paragraphs are nonexistent or forced.
- The introduction and conclusion are often formulaic; that is, they do not seem uniquely connected to the body paragraphs.
- Particularly in C+ papers, the order of some paragraphs could be changed without changing what the paper is saying.

Audience

- The paper adopts an appropriate tone but may sometimes lapse into slang, informal English, or nonacademic prose.
- The paper shows some awareness of the reader's need for contextual information.

Grammar/Language/Presentation

"C" or "C+" papers reflect less skill with language and presentation. Though errors remain, there is clear evidence that the student is working to improve these issues. Specifically:

- The paper may show patterns of error, but these errors generally do not impede meaning; they may instead represent errors such as article usage, punctuation, or missing words.
- The paper attempts to follow rules of MLA documentation, but errors or omissions are evident.

B range (B–, B, B+)

B–, B, B+ papers have all the elements of papers in the "C" range and have most of these additional elements as well

Thesis/Argument/Reasoning

"B–," "B," and "B+" papers show the student performing solid and original critical thinking, reflected in a clearly stated position (argument, thesis, project) that is in some way original, moving beyond class discussion. Specifically:

- The paper has an argument that shows some originality by expressing ideas that were not expressed in class.

- The paper's purpose is clearly and authoritatively stated from the beginning; that is, it is possible to identify a sentence or group of sentences that contain the purpose or project of the paper.
- The paper has an argument that moves beyond what the readings have said while also clearly engaging with the readings.
- The paper has an argument that avoids absolute claims (with terms like *all*, *never*, *always*) and that acknowledges its limits.
- B+ papers tend to have particularly original, thoughtful, or authoritative arguments.

Evidence/Quotation/Support

"B−," "B," and "B+" papers demonstrate that the student is increasingly comfortable with the text, as shown by an ability to use close textual engagement in support of the argument; B+ papers, in addition, show a kind of authority in relation to the text or a particularly original or insightful reading. Specifically:

- For B− papers, the paper has clear connections between two or more texts, but more development may be needed to show how those connections support the argument.
- Although all paragraphs provide support of the argument, they still include more summary of the text than analysis.
- The paper contains quotations that clearly support the argument, and the student is able to explain the how those quotations provide that support; however, the use of quotation and accompanying explanation may be repetitive throughout the paper.
- Quotation is used in a way that demonstrates thorough understanding of text.
- The paper may, however, avoid possible counter-arguments; portions of the texts that may not support (or may completely go against) the argument are avoided.

Organization

"B−," "B," and "B+" papers have solid organization. That is, there is a clear order to the paper even if some transitions are rough or missing. B+ papers tend to have an especially strong, fluid, or complex organization that may fall short in one or two moments. Specifically:

- The paper's paragraphs follow a logical order, building on each other as the argument unfolds.
- There is an attempt made at transitions between paragraphs, even if some of these transitions are rough, awkward, or implicit.
- The introduction clearly sets forth what the body paragraphs will accomplish.
- The conclusion states the implications of what the body paragraphs have accomplished (answers the question "so what?"), though it may lapse into partial restatement of the introduction.

Audience

- The paper adopts an appropriate tone by avoiding slang, informal English, or nonacademic prose.
- The paper shows a consistent awareness of contextual information needed by readers both inside and outside the class.

Grammar/Language/Formatting

"B−," "B," and "B+" papers show the student attaining increased control over problems of presentation and language. Specifically:

- There is clear evidence that the paper has been proofread and that patterns of error have been addressed, resulting in infrequent error (typographical or grammatical).
- Paper adheres to MLA style and quotations are properly documented.

A range (A−, A)

"A−" and "A" papers have all the elements of papers in the "B" range and have these additional elements as well.

Thesis/Argument/Reasoning

"A−" and "A" papers demonstrate strong critical thinking. The student is able to respond to the readings and to the assignment with originality and authority. Specifically:

- The paper presents an original and compelling argument that addresses the prompt fully and avoids absolute claims.
- The argument is aware of its underlying assumptions and acknowledges its limits.
- The argument is stated with such authority that the order of its statements and the linkages between them seem inevitable.

Evidence/Quotation/Support

"A−" and "A" papers reflect the student's depth of critical reading. Rather than being subject to the texts and their authors, the student begins to assume more and more authority in relation to these texts, both through insightful analysis and through deft use of quotation in support of the argument. Specifically:

- The paper works closely with quotation in multiple ways; it connects quotations from different essays within a paragraph in unique and fluid ways and/or returns to the language of a quotation in the analysis of another quotation or reading.
- Quotations are introduced, discussed, clearly related to the argument, and properly cited.
- Quotations are incorporated seamlessly into grammatically correct sentences (that is, the sentence that includes a quotation works grammatically even with the quotation marks removed).
- The paper considers and responds to possible counter-arguments.

Organization
- Paragraphs contain well-developed subtopics; they have enough information to stand alone but also relate to each other in that they all support the argument.
- Transitions between paragraphs are not forced or confusing. The next paragraph always seems like the next logical step to support the argument.
- Conclusion draws from the main ideas of the essay and opens up new ideas for further research/development.

Audience
- The paper inspires confidence in the audience, addresses significant issues, and leaves the reader with the sense of having learned something.
- The paper anticipates the audience's questions and needs for contextual information.

Grammar/Language/Presentation
- The paper is virtually free of grammatical and typographical errors.
- The paper adheres to MLA style.

Grading Rubric

The following is the rubric developed by FAU's Writing Committee for use in conjunction with our grading criteria. We include these guidelines for its use:

Instructions
1. The rubric is meant as a tool for visualizing, interpreting, and applying the grading criteria. **In no cases should the rubric be used without the grading criteria.**
2. **Do not use the rubric as a substitute for commenting directly on the paper.** A good strategy is to comment directly on the draft first, then fill out the rubric score and comments, referring back to your comments on the draft (i.e., "Work on strengthening intrinsic transitions. See comment on page 3, para 2").
3. **Never leave the comments section on the rubric blank.** This will give your students the idea that writing an essay is formulaic. The comments are the most important part.
4. You are not required to use a rubric. Indeed, as you work with the criteria you will find that you do not need the rubric to determine the proper comments on a paper or its grade. You might, at that point, use the rubric as a peer revision exercise or to help you on particularly borderline papers.
5. The rubric is meant to be an aid to understanding the more elaborate set of guidelines. Like all simplifications, though, it is indeed a simplification. It cannot cover everything, and you cannot expect it to.

	Outstanding	Strong	Adequate	Unacceptable
1. Argument: Argument directly and fully answers prompt. Is clearly stated early in paper. Is original, compelling, and logical and avoids absolute claims.	Comments:			
Argument Score:				
2. Evidence: Appropriate amount of relevant, accuate, and justifiably interpreted quotation. Quotation thoroughly introduced, explained, analyzed, and connected to argument/ other texts. Possible counter-arguments considered.	Comments:			
Evidence Score:				
3. Organization: Paragraphs maintain argumentative focus, exclude extraneous information, appear in a logical order, and transition smoothly. Introduction sets forth argument and goals of essay. Conclusion opens up avenues for future research.	Comments:			
Organization Score:				
4. Attention to Audience: Consistent, academic tone. Appropriate amount of con-textual information, anti-cipating audience questions. Addresses significant issues and makes them important to audience.	Comments:			
Attention to Audience Score:				
5. Grammar and Format: Errors in grammar, spelling, and usage limited or non-existent. Correct MLA format, including proper quotation citation.	Comments:			
Grammar and Format Score:				
Additional Comments:				

Issues in the First Paper

The first paper in our writing classes is unique for several reasons. In general, we are asking students to perform a task that we don't expect them to know how to do until the end of the semester. That is, even though they are taking these courses to learn how to write this kind of paper, it is something we ask them to do right away. Second, all the other papers ask students to work with at least two sustained pieces of writing and thinking. Working across essays provides more opportunities for the kinds of critical thinking we value since ideas are best unpacked in relation to other ideas. Finally, coming at the start of the semester, the first paper confronts students before they have settled into the rhythm of the course and of university life.

Nevertheless, the goals and expectations of the first paper are the same as any of the papers in the course. We should do all we can to prepare students to succeed in this first writing task by maximizing class time to help them understand the essay under discussion as well as the demands of college-level writing. Yet we should not be more lenient with this paper in grading—the criteria remain the same for all papers in these courses.

Returning Student Work

Because comments are central to a student's growth in these courses, *it is essential that you return student work before the next assignment is due.* Thus, if a draft is due on Thursday and the next draft or assignment is due the following Thursday, you should return commented drafts on Tuesday. *In no case should you wait more than a week to return student work.*

Chapter 6
Dealing with Error

English as an Other Language

We used to use the term "English as a Second Language" (ESL) to describe those students whose native language is not English. These days, however, it is far more accurate to speak of English as an Other Language. Not only will you have in your classes international students who grew up speaking another language, but you will also have students who have spoken English all their lives, whose first language *is* English, but who nevertheless exhibit language concerns because multiple languages are spoken in their homes. In South Florida, for example, it is not unusual to have a student whose household speaks Haitian Creole and whose use of English is impacted by that language.

Your institution might have specific resources for such students. At FAU, our goal is to provide as much support as we can for such students by helping them to refine their skills with English as we help them refine their skills in thinking and writing. Let's be clear: Although our courses focus on writing, it is also our responsibility (and not the responsibility of the community colleges, or high schools, or the writing center) to teach students how to recognize and correct their errors in language.

In the past we've offered separate sections of these courses for multiple-language students. However, the data we have been able to collect suggests that these sections are of no particular benefit for this student population at our school. Indeed, it may be more beneficial to these students to be in the standard writing classroom, immersed in the language with native speakers.

One thing to keep in mind when dealing with students whose native language is not English is that they are most likely weak writers and thinkers in their native language as well. Consider any of your native English students; they, too, make numerous errors. Therefore we should disabuse ourselves of the notion that English is the only impediment for multiple-language students. Thinking and writing are equally critical issues.

Patterns of Error

With all students, when approaching error it is best to think not in terms of individual errors in a paper but in terms of *patterns of error*. Looking at one page of a student paper, you may see ten errors, but, looking more closely, you might find instead one error made ten times. That is, if a student has a problem with subject-verb agreement, then she or he will manifest that misunderstanding frequently. Rather than pointing the student to each individual error, it will be more useful to teach him or her to identify this pattern of error.

For students with serious errors, look for the most prominent patterns. In helping students to identify and work through these patterns, focus on one pattern at a time. Keep in your mind a hierarchical list of the student's errors and prioritize this list. Ask them to focus on identifying the most serious error in their writing; once they have a handle on this error, ask them to work on the next most serious one, and so on.

Some errors will seem to follow no pattern, and these we should address as best we can in and out of the classroom. However, one of the key goals for language skills in these courses is teaching students how to become responsible for their own learning. Teaching them proofreading skills and instructing them on how to use a handbook or a grammar reference are important strategies in accomplishing this goal.

You might find that student language will break down in isolated sentences. Often, these are sentences in which students are attempting to convey important critical thoughts. Student language can disintegrate at these moments as the student reaches for the words to express a complex thought. A good strategy for correcting this kind of error is prompting the student to slow down in the most important moments of her or his paper, using several simple sentences to convey the thought that might then be combined into a series of more complex sentences.

Error Tracking System

Error sheets are a formal mechanism for dealing with error and a useful tool to help students reflect on their writing and identify and track their errors. Grammatical errors in academic papers generally follow a specific logic that is traceable and identifiable. That is, students can use error tracking to figure out what mistaken rule they been following, and you can intervene to change that faulty logic. Error sheets are designed to help students identify patterns of sentence-level error in order to prepare them to proofread their work as part of their revision process. By identifying the common mistakes they make, taking the time to record them, and then proofreading for them in future work, students develop an error roadmap that should help them avoid that particular pattern of error again.

Another system you might use is a customized checklist, which should be turned in with every paper. You might begin with several elements particular to your demands for the paper and then provide spaces for students to add their specific patterns of error throughout the semester. In checking off each item, students assert that they have checked their paper specifically for that error. Take a look at the Proofreading and Error checklist on the following page for an example of a customized checklist.

Proofreading and Error Checklist

☐ Proper header on each page

☐ Introduction includes names of all authors, titles of all essays, and clear statement of argument

☐ Pattern of error:_____
  Handbook reference page: _____

☐ Pattern of error:_____
  Handbook reference page: _____

☐ Pattern of error:_____
  Handbook reference page: _____

☐ Pattern of error:_____
  Handbook reference page: _____

☐ Pattern of error:_____
  Handbook reference page: _____

While there are many systems for tracking error, at FAU we have adopted the following guidelines for our instructors who choose to develop error tracking systems:

- Ask students to take responsibility for their own skills with language.
- Give students a means to record and track their persistent patterns of error.
- Incorporate the handbook so that students can understand the grammatical issues involved with the error.
- Provide students a means of continuing to work on language issues beyond these courses.

Grammar Expectations and Fatal Errors

We do not expect students to be perfect writers or to have fully mastered the intricacies of English by the time they leave our classrooms. In part, this reflects the limited time we have within a semester, but it also reflects the fact that learning any language, even your native one, is a lifelong process. Our goal instead is twofold:

- Students should leave our classrooms knowing how to recognize, track, and correct their most serious patterns of error.
- Students should have tools to accomplish and continue this task, primarily error sheets.

Some patterns of error are more serious than others. The most serious of these we might call "fatal errors":

- **Sentence integrity and boundary errors.** These errors suggest that students cannot identify a complete sentence. Fragments, run-ons, and comma splices are included in the category.
  Strategy to correct this error: Strategies for these errors depend on the particular issue in question. Fragments often follow a specific pattern, occurring, for example, directly after a quotation. Ask students to locate these trigger points and pay extra attention to them. Run-ons require students to identify each complete thought in a sentence. Comma splice errors can be approached by asking students to examine each use of the comma either in the entire paper or in key sections.
- **Subject-verb agreement.** Subject-verb agreement is central to the function of any sentence. Students should be able to write sentences in which the subject and verb agree.
  Strategy to correct this error: Ask students who are prone to this error to identify each subject and verb in their sentences, either in key paragraphs or in their entire papers. This will force them to pay close attention to questions of agreement.
- **Convoluted syntax.** Sentences in which the syntax is so awkward as to impede meaning are a serious error. Students should be able to convey meaning in each sentence, even if that sentence has some error.
  Strategy to correct this error: If you cannot understand the idea of a sentence, then ask the student to break it down into smaller syntactical units, such as shorter and simpler sentences.

At FAU, students with persistent fatal errors are at risk of failing these courses. As you will have noted in the sample grading criteria provided, papers with "error to the degree that meaning is severely impeded" cannot pass.

In contrast, we are more lenient with certain other errors:

- **Article usage.** The rules for the use of articles in English are obtuse. Students who are not native speakers might have particular difficulties with articles, especially those students whose native language uses no articles. While we should ask these students to work on their mastery of articles, we should not fail them for this error alone.
- **Apostrophes.** The apostrophe often seems to be in severe jeopardy of disappearing. Native speakers use apostrophes inconsistently if at all, a surprising fact given that we live in a culture so invested in possessions. So entrenched is this error that you may find it difficult to eradicate it in student writing; while we will strive to do so, we shall not fault ourselves or our students for a failure to succeed.
- **Pronoun/antecedent agreement.** In an effort to remain gender neutral and to avoid the awkwardness of "he or she," English speakers increasingly use a plural pronoun to refer to a singular antecedent: "The student turned in their paper late." This construction is erroneous, yet it may be that as our language evolves it will not remain so. While pointing out the error to students, we should also keep in mind that it is, at least, an effort to write without a gendered bias.

- **Commas, periods, and quotation marks.** Commas and periods go inside quotation marks; semicolons and colons go outside of them. Students have enormous difficulty with this simple rule of typography. However, since it does involve only typography, it is not considered a serious error.

Using a Handbook

At FAU, we have found it helpful to incorporate a writer's handbook in freshman writing courses because they are valuable resources for addressing issues with language and error. The following are examples of how we have incorporated the handbooks into our commenting and error tracking systems at FAU:

1. When identifying an error in a student paper, note the pages of the handbook that address the error. You might want to create a quick reference of the most common errors and corresponding page numbers at the start of the semester to have handy as you grade.
2. Ask students to bring the handbook to class whenever a draft is due. They can then use the handbook when proofreading their drafts before turning them in.
3. Second language students, in particular, should be familiar with the handbook. When working with them during office hours, make sure they learn how to look up specific errors in the handbook that correspond to their particular weaknesses with language.

Madeleine Albright

Faith and Diplomacy

(text pp. 23–33)

Selection Overview

In "Faith and Diplomacy," Madeleine Albright builds a case for considering religious influence in diplomatic efforts. She begins by acknowledging that religion has an ever-present and unavoidable influence on people, and thus must be recognized as a factor that affects both individuals and the governments that represent them. Albright outlines religion's influence through three examples: The first centers on Pope John Paul II's role in reuniting Eastern and Western Europe; the second involves a Lebanese woman ready to die for her faith and willing to forgive her tormentors; the last and perhaps most complex example involves the use of religion in a rebellion led by Uganda's LRA and the role of a mission in saving Ugandan war orphans. Albright uses these examples to note the massive influence of religion in both fueling and quelling worldwide conflict. Despite its misuse in various conflicts, Albright finds that some aspects of religious belief can serve to resolve conflict. In taking religious belief into consideration, Albright believes that political leaders and diplomats can harness religion's influence to further their efforts. She furthers this argument by citing examples of religious organizations, including the ICRD, that study faith-based diplomacy and the peacemaking efforts of Jimmy Carter at Camp David. Albright concludes her argument by reaffirming the possibility of continuing to use faith-based diplomacy in conjunction with more traditional efforts.

Concepts include: faith-based diplomacy
Themes include: diplomacy, faith, kinship, mediation, religion, secularism, world politics
Works best with: Appiah, Epstein, Friedman, Fukuyama, Taylor, Yoshino

Questions and Assignments

Students will be tempted to flatten Albright's argument into a pro- or anti-religion stance. The Questions for Critical Reading are designed to help them resist this movement by asking them to account for the nuances of Albright's argument. Question 1 asks students to determine Albright's own position on the ultimate role of religion in diplomacy and to locate quotations that reveal that position. Questions 2 and 3 then ask students to engage the complexities of Albright's argument by first imagining what faith-based diplomacy would look like in practice and then expanding the analysis to consider whether such a diplomatic strategy is best pursued by government or private agencies.

The Exploring Context questions help students gain a visual understanding of terms like *diplomacy*, which might be abstract to them. The first question asks them to visualize this essay literally by using a Web site they may already be familiar with—photo storage site Flickr—to create a visual representation of the essay. The other questions in this section help students explore Albright's argument by grounding them in actual practices of the U.S. State Department and a non-profit center for religion and diplomacy. These Web sites should provide students with other examples of these concepts beyond Albright's text.

The three Questions for Connecting use other essays with stronger theoretical engines in order to provide students a critical framework for imagining how Albright's vision for diplomacy might (or might not) be implemented. Appiah's concept of cosmopolitanism, for example, would work very well with Albright's ideas, allowing students to begin critical thinking by synthesizing these concepts. Similarly, in moving to a discussion of civil rights, students can consider how political concepts such as Yoshino's equality and liberty paradigms can be applied to the larger arena of foreign affairs. This project is more explicitly offered in the third question, since Friedman's clear concept, the Dell Theory of Conflict Prevention, aims towards the same goal as Albright's faith-based diplomacy but pursues that goal through economic channels.

The Assignments for Writing ask students to test, revise, and extend Albright's rather abstract vision. The first allows students to examine both the potential of religion to unite and its potential to divide, requiring students to develop their own conclusion about the possibility of faith-based diplomacy succeeding in the current political climate. This essay is essentially an application of Albright's ideas and centers on critically examining the examples Albright provides. In doing so, students will be able to draw from much of the work they have already done in responding to this selection. Question 2 of Assignments for Writing asks students to explore an alternate model for diplomacy, in theory one that would have similar or greater potential than religion to resolve conflict. This prompt encourages students to explore the functional capabilities of faith-based diplomacies and attempts to apply them to another influential factor in global conflicts. The third and final Assignment for Writing for "Faith and Diplomacy" deals with an underlying theme of Albright's work: the ignorance surrounding religion that must be overcome in order to move forward in faith-based diplomacy. Students are asked to parallel the ignorance surrounding religion that Albright identifies with another form of ignorance, which must be overcome in order to resolve conflict. The task of this question is to understand and relate the underlying themes of the essay to one other attitude or belief that may hold us back from resolving conflict.

Julia Alvarez

Selections from
Once Upon a Quinceañera

(text pp. 34–55)

Selection Overview

In these excerpts from *Once Upon a Quinceañera*, Julia Alvarez takes a closer look at the quinceañera, or quinces, a coming-of-age ritual that means many different things to different members of her community. Alvarez finds that the quinceañera can be a positive experience for girls, linking it to self-esteem, strength, and power. Alvarez also recognizes its historical linkages to the tradition of introducing a marriageable girl to the community and symbolically presenting the girl as a woman to be passed from her father to other male family members. She also cites the arguments of divinity scholars that coming-of-age rituals symbolically empower girls but proposes that this empowerment is a poor substitute for any real empowerment the girl might have as a woman. Alvarez also relates another point of view surrounding quinceañeras: Some quinceañera supporters view their meaning as a religiously motivated symbolic vow of chastity until marriage. Because of changing cultural circumstances, Alvarez also finds new meaning in the tradition, including introducing young women to a lifelong support system of other women. In analyzing the overall value of the quinceañera, Alvarez also explores the financial burdens of the tradition. Although she finds families hesitant to discuss the cost associated with these elaborate celebrations, she outlines some of the prohibitive costs of quinces. Despite the financial burden of these celebrations, the popularity of the quinceañera is steadily growing. One of the explanations Alvarez gives for this trend is retroculturation, a growing emphasis on culture, heritage, and tradition common to third-generation Hispanic Americans. She finds that retroculturation does not replace an interest in popular culture, but rather it becomes part of an aspect of popular culture for many teens. In celebrating quinces, Alvarez notes that *traditional* has become a relative term because families tend to export traditions from individual Latin American traditions as well as from American pop culture. While Alvarez recognizes both American consumerism and culturally specific spending habits as part of why quinces carry such a hefty price tag, she also suggests that the "cultural capital," or its non-monetary value within the community, may be well worth their cost for teenage girls and their families.

Concepts include: coming-of-age rituals, cultural capital, quinceañeras or quinces, retroculturation
Themes include: commercialism, community, ethnicity, gender, identity, ritual, tradition
Works best with: Appiah, Didion, Epstein, Gilbert, Olson, Savan, Serano, Taylor, Yoshino

Questions and Assignments

Because Alvarez explores several points of view in assessing the quinceañera, students may have some difficulty determining her argument in this passage. The Questions for Critical Reading break down key ideas in her text to help students pin down Alvarez's concerns. Question 1 asks students to define *retroculturation* and locate examples outside the text to see if those examples support Alvarez's argument. Retroculturation is a clear and portable concept that students will be able to use to analyze Alvarez's text and several others in *Emerging*. In question 2, students are asked to extend Alvarez's work to determine her attitudes toward quinces as a cultural practice. Finally, in the third question, students are asked to broadly explore the value of tradition by looking into their cultural importance and economic cost.

As many students will have difficulty relating to the phenomenon of the quinceañera, the Exploring Context section extends Alvarez's discussion to similar traditions in non-Hispanic cultures. In the first Exploring Context question, students are asked to review the Web site for the television show *My Super Sweet 16* to apply Alvarez's argument to a more common tradition in American pop culture, drawing on their work in Questions for Critical Reading. The second Exploring Context question refers students to a Web site Alvarez discusses and asks them to evaluate the Web site's design and advertising in terms of the issues Alverez links to quinceañeras. Students will further explore the value of tradition they have identified in question 3 of Questions for Critical Reading. The final Exploring Context question asks students to relate the quinceañera to coming-of-age rituals in other cultures in order to establish whether the issues Alvarez identifies are consistent in the practices of other cultures.

The Questions for Connecting for this essay link the very specific cultural phenomena Alvarez discusses with larger trends in culture, gender, class, race, and identity and allow students to link her argument to the ideas of other authors in *Emerging*. The first question asks students to apply Daniel Gilbert's ideas in "Reporting Live from Tomorrow" (p. 169) to Alvarez's argument by asking how quinces affect girls' ability to predict future happiness and questioning whether they function as super-replicators or as a form of surrogation. The second question looks at the relationship between retroculturation and diversity through the lens of Rebekah Nathan's argument in "Community and Diversity" (p. 228) by asking students to consider whether retroculturation could resolve some of the issues Nathan identifies as obstacles to building community and promoting diversity on college campuses. Cultural performance is also at the root of Alvarez's argument; hence, the final question asks students to examine quinces in light of

Diana Taylor's arguments about cultural performance, social drama, and "hauntology" in "False Identifications: Minority Populations Mourn Diana" (p. 454).

The first question in Assignments for Writing help students extend Alvarez's argument by considering the relationship between quinceañeras and self-identity and expand on their work on rituals in question 3 of Exploring Context. Question 2 of Assignments for Writing examines the commercial aspects of the quinceañera by asking students to think about the role of commercialism in forming gender identity. The final Assignment for Writing question asks students to expand on their work in question 3 of Questions for Critical Reading on the value of tradition and/or question 3 of Questions for Connecting to explore the function of social rituals like the quinceañera in the lives of communities, in particular addressing the role of the individual within a community, the presence of cultural performance and tradition, and the effect of retroculturation on a community.

Kwame Anthony Appiah

Making Conversation *and* The Primacy of Practice

(text pp. 56–75)

Selection Overview

Kwame Anthony Appiah begins "Making Conversation" by exploring the benefits and ramifications of an increasingly global society. In order to mediate our changing world, Appiah argues that we must consider the theoretical framework we engage to mediate our relationships with others. He favors cosmopolitanism, which he defines as encompassing the obligations we have to local communities and those we have to the world. Appiah provides a brief history of the term to sketch out the meanings he wishes to highlight in his definition of cosmopolitanism. In order to illustrate his ideal of cosmopolitanism, Appiah turns to a discussion of his hometown, Kumasi, arguing that conversation (by which he means association) has led to a culture there that espouses his ideas of cosmopolitanism. Appiah recognizes that although values are never objective, we can learn to live together and create common value systems by taking the time to associate closely with others across cultural lines. He argues that although these associations are often fraught with discomfort, they are absolutely necessary in order to move forward in global culture. In "The Primacy of Practice," Appiah turns to a more specific discussion of morals and values. Noting that there is little we can do to resolve differences in underlying values, he points out that we can learn to live together through engaging in common practices, regardless of the reasons for our participation. In part, our values are decided by our habits, and our habits can be changed through conversation. Appiah uses several striking examples to illustrate this assertion, including discussions about incest and male and female circumcision. He also applies this paradigm to considering the increasing social acceptance of homosexuals in the United States and the debate over abortion. These examples lead to Appiah's assertions that the same values underlie both sides of these issues, and that through making conversation, we can begin to affect social change.

> **Concepts include:** conversation, cosmopolitanism, primacy of practice
> **Themes include:** conversations across boundaries, cultural change, globalism, habits of coexistence, human community, local allegiance, multiculturalism, nationalism, respect for individual difference, shared citizenship, social change, universal moral obligation
> **Works best with:** Albright, Alvarez, Dalai Lama, Friedman, Gilbert, Johnson, Nathan, Olson, Poe, Pollan, Postrel, Spar, Surowiecki, Taylor, Yoshino

Questions and Assignments

Despite the number and variety of examples Appiah provides, students may have some difficulty in addressing the abstract nature of the approaches he discusses. The Questions for Critical Reading are geared toward helping students firmly grasp the conceptual discussion in these excerpts. Question 1 challenges students to clarify Appiah's definition of *cosmopolitanism* and apply it to a current situation with which they are familiar. This assignment can be specified even further by using question 2 of Questions for Critical Reading to move students from the abstract argument Appiah makes to the more concrete tools he suggests for enacting a cosmopolitan approach. Question 3 ties in Appiah's use of examples by encouraging students to explore his use of particular evidence in making his argument. In working with these questions, students will develop a nuanced understanding of the key concepts of this excerpt.

Students may find Appiah's overall argument simple and idealistic. The Exploring Context questions for this essay help students to overcome these misconceptions by applying his ideas to the world around them. Questions 1 and 3 of Exploring Context use technology to illustrate one form of cosmopolitanism by asking students to analyze Web sites as a space for making conversation. Question 2 challenges students to research one of the cultural practices Appiah identifies in his essay to further apply Appiah's points about changing values.

The three Questions for Connecting challenge students to apply Appiah's theories and concepts to other essays that provide more in-depth, tangible examples that relate to Appiah's points. Question 1 requires an application of Appiah's discussion of conversation and values to Epstein's research in "AIDS, Inc.," a reading that describes AIDS prevention projects in South Africa and Uganda. Question 2 brings Appiah's argument closer to home for students by asking them to look at cosmopolitanism in light of Rebekah Nathan's research on community involvement and diversity on college campuses. This question allows students to critically engage Appiah's assertions in a familiar playing field and bridges the gap many students find between their own experience and Appiah's examples. Question 3 examines the value system at play in Debora L. Spar's essay on adoption by asking students to consider the difference between local and universal values as they apply to her discussion.

Once students have had the opportunity to work with practical applications of Appiah's argument, the Assignments for Writing help them engage in a theoretical discussion of cosmopolitanism. Question 1 of Assignments for Writing asks students to locate the challenges inherent in cosmopolitanism and then propose strategies to overcome these challenges. This question will prevent oversimplification of Appiah's ideas, but it will also test students' ability to work with abstract concepts. Similarly, question 2 unites the concept of cosmopolitanism with more concrete mechanisms for achieving social change by asking students to expand upon the tools they have identified in question 2 of Questions for Critical Reading. The third Assignments for Writing question gives students the opportunity to critique Appiah's assertion that conversation helps us move forward in ideological conflicts.

The Dalai Lama

Ethics and the New Genetics

(text pp. 76–86)

Selection Overview

In "Ethics and the New Genetics," the Dalai Lama argues that we are changing the pace of evolution in our own species and others through genetic manipulation of cells. Although the Dalai Lama recognizes the potential benefits of genetic alteration, he argues that with our new ability to affect genetic development, we have a much greater power than even before to exercise responsibility. Unfortunately, our capacity for ethical consideration of the implications of developments in genetics has not kept pace with the developments themselves. The Dalai Lama expresses the concern that our definitions of disease and health, and ultimately our identities, will change as a result of this technology. He uses cloning as an example to begin discussion on the larger effects of biotechnology on the continuation of the human species. The Dalai Lama argues that both cloning and other types of genetic manipulation have the potential to destroy our diversity and our ability to tolerate each other. Although he finds some merit in genetically modifying food in order to feed the world, the Dalai Lama asserts that we do not yet know the longterm consequences or potentials of biotechnology. It is for this reason that the Dalai Lama argues that it is time to begin serious consideration of its ethical concerns. He recommends public education about new developments in biogenetics, broader public involvement in the decision making process surrounding bioethics, and the development of a moral compass against which to measure our ethics and values. This moral compass must be based on specific principles, including valuing life, compassion, natural balance, and concern for longterm consequence. While the Dalai Lama does not recommend specific ethical guidelines, he does note that we must use compassion as our foundation in considering bioethics, look at the larger picture of implications as clearly as we can, and remain unbiased and humble in our consideration of ethical issues.

> **Concepts include:** bioethics, moral compass
> **Themes include:** cloning, global consequence, genetic engineering, morality, responsibility, scientific progress, self-identity, technology
> **Works best with:** Appiah, Fukuyama, Pollan, Roach, Spar, Yoshino

Questions and Assignments

Since the Dalai Lama offers few specific examples in this essay, students may have a difficult time locating specific ideas and concepts within the text. Question 1 of Questions for Critical Reading asks students to extrapolate the types of ethics the Dalai Lama calls for in light of recent developments in bioengineering. This will help them to pinpoint the ethical considerations he recommends. Students may also have a difficult time framing ethical concerns outside their own moral and religious approaches. Question 2 explores the necessities involved in developing ethics apart from religion while the third question challenges students to outline the specific limitations the Dalai Lama calls for in considering genetic technologies. Using quotations from the text will help to keep students rooted in the text, rather than in their own opinions on biotechnology.

The Exploring Context questions offer students specific focal points within the text from which they can begin to apply the Dalai Lama's argument to current issues in biotechnology. The discoveries made through the Human Genome Project have generated a great deal of genetic research. Question 1 of Exploring Context asks students to research the project online to examine the ways it addresses the Dalai Lama's ethical concerns and their own approach in question 1 of Questions for Critical Reading. Question 2 asks students to explore the President's Council on Bioethics in order to assess whether government agencies are able to address the need for ethical consideration of technologies. Part of this assessment should involve evaluating whether the Council's findings are consistent with a nonreligious approach to ethics, building on question 2 of Questions for Critical Reading. Question 3 of Exploring Context involves identifying ethical concerns about cloning through exploring the London Science Museum's online exhibit about Dolly the sheep, the first cloned animal. This question provides students a concrete example through which they can determine specific concerns raised by cloning.

The Questions for Connecting for this excerpt help students consider the Dalai Lama's argument in light of other authors who explore the changing effects of technology and religion on the world. Question 1 links the Dalai Lama's excerpt to Francis Fukuyama's "Human Dignity" (p. 142), an essay also concerned about the potential of biotechnologies. In this question students are asked to evaluate both authors' positions on ethical practices in genetic technologies by exploring whether Fukuyama answers the Dalai Lama's call for a "moral compass." As the "moral compass" is the crux of the Dalai Lama's argument, students will find it helpful to explore this concept through Fukuyama's more concrete discussion of the ethical concerns surrounding biotechnology. Question 2 of Questions for Connecting extends the Dalai Lama's call for a new ethics to the use of human cadavers for research, as described in Mary Roach's "The Cadaver Who Joined the Army" (p. 347). This question will help students locate the very portable argument in the Dalai Lama's work. The final question challenges students to examine the Dalai Lama's authority as a religious leader by using Madeleine Albright's "Faith and Diplomacy" (p. 23) to explore the usefulness of religion to mediate ethical decisions in diplomacy and in developing technologies.

Because of the broad approach the Dalai Lama uses in this essay, students may have some difficulty extending his ideas beyond the examples he discusses specifically. Question 1 of Assignments for Writing asks students to locate another example of technology or scientific discovery that calls for the development of a "moral compass." This will allow students to understand the specific needs the Dalai Lama works to address while encouraging them to extend key concepts of his excerpt to areas he does not specifically cover. Question 2 addresses the Dalai Lama's concerns about forecasting genetic predispositions and asks students to propose standards (and/or limitations) for when such forecasting should be used. These standards should arise from ethical and practical consideration of this particular technology and should be rooted in the concerns the Dalai Lama notes in his text. The final question asks students to look beyond the sphere of science by examining the consequences in technology in terms of social and economic concerns. This question allows students to question the Dalai Lama's underlying assumption that ethical concerns are of primary interest to humanity as we move ahead in developing technologies.

Joan Didion

After Life
(text pp. 87–104)

Selection Overview
Joan Didion's "After Life" explores her experience of living through the death of her husband. In her writings, Didion refers to her husband's sudden death as having happened in "the ordinary instant," a phenomenon she finds to be commonly referred to by survivors of life-changing incidents. Didion recounts being unable to recall initially telling the details of her husband's death to others and admits to having some difficulty recounting the graphic and painful memories that followed. Throughout the selection, Didion flashes back and forth between the events leading up to her husband's cardiac arrest, the days that immediately followed his death, and her reflections almost a year after the death. While Didion describes

several "ordinary instances" of her day-to-day existence after her husband's passing, she focuses closely on the specific details of dealing with her husband's death, including authorizing an autopsy, analyzing signs that her husband may have in some way anticipated his death, and details of her life with him. Didion notes that we cannot anticipate what grief feels like and describes her grief as affecting her physically and emotionally coming in waves that she relates to the recollections of other survivors of tragedy. Didion also finds that the most difficult aspect of grief is the perception of meaninglessness that accompanies it. For Didion there is some possibility of finding meaning in the convergence of these two tracks despite the unanticipated event of her husband's death.

Concepts include: the ordinary instant
Themes include: change, death, emotion, finding meaning, grief, loss, memorial, mourning
Works best with: Alvarez, Fukuyama, Gilbert, Kimmelman, Restak, Roach, Serano, Taylor

Questions and Assignments

Because of the highly personalized nature of this excerpt, students may have some difficulty drawing out the themes and argument that drive Didion's work. Question 1 of Questions for Critical Reading asks students to locate Didion's definition of the "ordinary instant," the most recognizable concept her excerpt. To help them relate to this concept, students are also encouraged to relate that definition to an example from their own experience. Next, question 2 explores the concept of grief, identifying both Didion's and students' own understanding of the term through a close reading of the text. Since Didion's essay is concerned with creating meaning in life, question 3 asks students to analyze moments in which Didion finds this meaning.

The Exploring Context questions for this essay help students relate this personal account to larger issues surrounding grief and mourning. Because Didion's writing is intimate and moving, students are likely to relate to it on a personal level, often ignoring the subtleties of Didion's discussion and the larger concepts that arise from it. The first question of Exploring Context asks students to visit the Web site for *The Year of Magical Thinking*, a play developed from Didion's work in the book that contains this essay. In particular, students are asked to assess whether the site is consistent with Didion's goals in the text, particularly those explored in question 3 of Questions for Critical Reading. The second Exploring Context question asks students to research online the stages of grief. This question will encourage them to relate Didion's writing to other analyses of the grieving process and place her work within the larger discourse surrounding death and mourning. The last Exploring Context question asks students to look into Didion's insistence on having an autopsy performed, an often uncomfortable subject for students. Through researching the decline in the number of autopsies, students are asked to explore Didion's attitude towards autopsy in order to make their own assertions about the overall trends in autopsy.

This essay is unique because of its reliance on personal narrative. The Questions for Connecting will help students relate Didion's argument to those of other authors included in this text, despite their dissimilar structures. In doing so, students can see how seemingly dissimilar narratives can also contain parallel concepts and ideas. These questions also help to extend the larger themes of Didion's work into other areas explored within *Emerging*. Question 1 of Questions for Connecting asks students to apply Daniel Gilbert's argument in "Reporting Live from Tomorrow" (p. 169) to Didion's essay by asking whether our imaginations can accurately predict our future happiness. This question encourages students to apply the concrete examples found in Gilbert's essay to the more abstract themes of Didion's work. In the second question, students are asked to look at the relationship between individual and community mourning through exploring Didion's essay in conjunction with Diana Taylor's "False Identifications: Minority Populations Mourn Diana" (p. 454), which explores the effects of social issues on mourning. Question 3 asks students to draw on their research for question 3 of Exploring Context to expand Mary Roach's assertion of ethical treatment of cadavers in "The Cadaver Who Joined the Army" (p. 347) and exploring Didion's treatment of her husband's body in requiring an autopsy.

Didion's essay is an exercise in reconciling memory with grief and trauma. Students may have some difficulty in connecting personal memories and trauma with larger issues surrounding death and mourning. Question 1 of Assignments for Writing challenges students to examine the relationship between memory and trauma in light of Didion's retelling of her husband's death. Question 2 asks students to examine Didion's decision to have an autopsy performed on her husband, looking at her justification for that decision, its ethical implications, and the other aspects of autopsy and trauma that affected her decision. This question draws on students' responses to question 3 of Exploring Context and question 3 of Questions for Connecting. The final Assignment for Writing question asks students to consider Didion's experience in wishing to be alone after her husband's death, the value of public and private grief, and her reactions to her husband's autopsy and obituary.

Helen Epstein

AIDS, Inc.

(text pp. 105–119)

Selection Overview

In "AIDS, Inc." Helen Epstein explores the success of different types of HIV/AIDS prevention programs in South Africa and Uganda where rates of HIV infection reached epidemic proportions in the 1990s. Epstein notes that the South African government has been unable to effectively address prevention and unwilling to discuss myriad issues facing South Africa's population dealing with with HIV and AIDS. LoveLife, a private organization, initiated an AIDS prevention program that deliberately worked to prevent HIV/AIDS without acknowledging the difficulties faced by people living with the disease. The prevention program uses a "lifestyle brand" that attracts young people by marketing a specific lifestyle. LoveLife's goal was to get young people more interested in participating in general sexual health programs by making discussions about safer sexual practices "cool." Epstein compares loveLife to another South African program that focuses on HIV prevention and assistance for people with AIDS, noting that despite its less costly budget, this program answers a clear need for open discussions about HIV/AIDS among young people. Epstein also explores more successful prevention programs in Uganda and credits their success to the "social cohesion" of the Ugandan people, arguing that it fosters an atmosphere of open discussion and community that paved the road for a realistic approach to HIV/AIDS. Epstein ultimately argues that although the South African government supports efforts like loveLife that focus on heavily commercialized lifestyle branding, they have not proven as effective in South Africa as initiatives that focus on the realities of HIV/AIDS in South African communities.

Concepts include: lifestyle brands, social cohesion
Themes include: advertising, AIDS prevention, commercialization, community, cultural difference, lifestyle brands, social taboo
Works best with: Albright, Alvarez, Appiah, Friedman, Savan, Spar, Taylor, Yoshino

Questions and Assignments

Students may have some difficulty sorting out the nuts and bolts of Epstein's argument and locating and defining the portable concepts Epstein discusses. Question 1 of Questions for Critical Reading asks students to define the term *lifestyle brand* using Epstein's text and relate their definition to an example from popular culture that could be used successfully in health education. This will help them to understand Epstein's argument in a context they are more likely to relate to. In question 2, students are challenged to define *social cohesion* and identify its role in HIV infection rates in Uganda by extrapolating how that role might be extended to other areas of the world. Because Epstein's discussion of the term is brief, this question will help students to think about the concept in a broader context. Question 3 asks students to consider what strategies would be effective for HIV prevention in Africa and the United States and whether the same program would be efective in the two cultures. Students are asked to support their responses with passages from Epstin's essay.

Students may not be familiar with the specific issues involved in addressing the AIDS epidemic in Africa. In order to help students gain a clearer understanding of the obstacles to successful HIV prevention, the Exploring Context questions require students to engage in contemporary research on HIV prevention in Africa by looking at current projects that address this issue. Question 1 of Exploring Context requires students to explore the (PRODUCT) RED campaign, which focuses on joining popular products with fundraising to support AIDS prevention and treatment in Africa. Students are asked to evaluate the possible success of this effort using Epstein's text and their work with lifestyle brands from question

1 of Questions for Critical Reading. Question 2 of Exploring Context involves researching current rates of HIV infection in Africa to assess whether Epstein's argument continues to explain these trends. The final Exploring Context question looks at conversation as a tool in combating HIV infection in Africa and asks students to evaluate how social networking technologies like Facebook or MySpace can function to help campaigns for HIV education and prevention.

Since Epstein's excerpt discusses specific efforts in AIDS prevention in a very distinct setting, students may find it challenging to relate her ideas to more abstract themes and understand their implications in areas outside of her subject matter. The Questions for Connecting link Epstein's argument to broader issues of media, race, and culture, which should help students relate to this reading more effectively. Question 1 of Questions for Connecting asks students to apply Leslie Savan's discussion of black talk in advertising from "What's Black, Then White, and Said All Over?" (p. 363) to examine the loveLife campaign Epstein describes. This question will challenge students to think about the roles of race, popular culture, and media in influencing cultural change, and will draw on their work on lifestyle brands from question 1 of Questions for Critical Reading. Because many of the controversies surrounding AIDS prevention in the United States are related to religion, question 2 of Questions for Connecting looks at the role religion should play in HIV education by using Madeleine Albright's arguments in "Faith and Diplomacy" (p. 23) in order to determine the best functions of religion in HIV prevention campaigns. Finally, because Epstein considers social change necessary in developing successful AIDS prevention programs in Africa, question 3 of Questions for Connecting challenges students to explore the value of conversation to assess whether Epstein's argument works as an example of Kenji Yoshino's applications of conversation in "Preface" (p. 479) and "The New Civil Rights" (p. 481). This question will allow students to consider conversation as a tool for promoting social change.

The Assignments for Writing for this selection are designed to help students grasp the factors that play a major role in the success of the types of AIDS prevention programs Epstein describes. They work to open up the specific concepts Epstein develops in her text. Question 1 of Assignments for Writing encourages students to extend Epstein's discussion of how children and families address the AIDS crisis in Africa, looking at the differences in response to HIV/AIDS in different age groups. This question will help students consider the impact of age on social cohesion, a concept they defined in question 2 of Questions for Critical Reading. Because Epstein's argument centers around private organizations, the second question of Assignments for Writing asks students to assess the role of the government in promoting HIV prevention, exploring how government programs can succeed using the kind of strategies that Epstein found effective in Uganda. In contrast, the final Assignment for Writing question asks students to evaluate the role of commercial culture in addressing HIV/AIDS prevention, expanding their work on question 1 of Exploring Context. This will challenge students to understand the possible motives of private companies, and analyze whether these motives can be reconciled with humanitarian goals like HIV/AIDS prevention.

Thomas Friedman

The Dell Theory of Conflict Prevention
(text pp. 120–140)

Selection Overview

This excerpt introduces Friedman's assertion that participation in global supply chains makes countries less likely to involve themselves in conflict. Friedman illustrates global supply chains by researching the origins of his computer's components. He identifies a long list of locations involved in manufacturing and assembling these components and notes that such supply chains are only possible because of technologies that allow us to communicate and collaborate with others around the world. Friedman explains his previous theory of conflict prevention, the Golden Arches Theory, which argued that countries with a sufficient middle class to support McDonald's franchises were unlikely to get involved in conflicts and risk their rising quality of life. The Dell Theory of Conflict Prevention links conflict prevention not only to rising quality of life, but also to preventing larger economic risks that would occur if any member of a global supply chain came into conflict with another member of the same chain. To support his theory, Friedman cites several examples of countries like China, Japan, India, Pakistan, and Taiwan that have resisted involvement in conflict in order to keep their economic standing and their place in supply chains. Friedman notes that several countries that are not part of supply chains are more prone to war. He also points out an alternative use of supply chaining in some global terror networks and identifies parallel uses of flat-world communications systems in terrorist networks. Despite this destructive use of supply chains, Friedman argues that they are useful in connecting us and working towards conflict prevention. He closes this excerpt with an appeal to nonproliferation of nuclear arms and a warning that the flat world has the potential to lead us down ever more destructive paths if we do not learn how to harness its beneficial capabilities.

> **Concepts include:** Dell Theory of Conflict Prevention, demand shaping, global supply chain, Golden Arches Theory of Conflict Prevention, suicide supply chain
> **Themes include:** collaboration, cyberterrorism, economic interdependence, geopolitics, globalization, government, service trade, technology
> **Works best with:** Albright, Appiah, Epstein, Johnson, Poe, Pollan, Spar, Taylor

Questions and Assignments

Students may get distracted by the details in this essay and may not firmly grasp its larger concepts. By focusing on issues of collaboration, the Questions for Critical Reading provide students a contextual theme for understanding the link Friedman makes between the global supply chains that prevent conflict and the mutant supply chains that bolster global terrorism. Question 1 of Questions for Critical Reading helps students assess that collaboration is the overarching linkage between the two. This will encourage students to critically examine the underlying similarity in each. Question 2 requires a clear definition of the Dell Theory of Conflict Prevention and prompts students to apply this theory to current events by assessing its efficacy in contemporary conflicts. The final question explores mutant global supply chains and allows students to further engage what is generally the most controversial portion of this excerpt.

In order to fully understand the implications of Friedman's argument, the Exploring Context questions encourage students to work more closely with the examples Friedman utilizes in making his argument. Question 1 asks students to extend Friedman's first example, the assembly of his Dell notebook. In researching Dell's Web site, students are asked to analyze the information on global production provided by the company and look into both the reasons for its presentation (or lack thereof) and its articulation of collaboration and extend their work in question 1 of Questions for Critical Reading. In order to examine Friedman's argument in light of Internet technologies, question 2 asks students to research Infosys, a company Friedman discusses, to explore whether or not its Web site is consistent with Friedman's argument. The final Exploring Context question challenges students to explore counterterrorism initiatives on the Federal Bureau of Investigation's Web site by focusing on whether the FBI pursues strategies that address the mutant global supply chains Friedman describes.

Since Friedman's argument centers on the negative and positive aspects of collaboration, the Questions for Connecting link his work to examinations of collaboration that help to extend his argument into areas with which students can more readily relate. Question 1 ties Friedman's work with Michael Pollan's "The Animals: Practicing Complexity" (p. 281) by asking students to describe the similarities between the complex global economy Friedman describes and the concrete, localized economic system of Polyface Farm. Question 2 explores collaborative efforts by applying James Surowiecki's ideas in "Committees, Juries, and Teams: The *Columbia* Disaster and How Small Groups Can Be Made to Work" (p. 440) to Friedman's argument and drawing on their analysis of collaboration in question 1 of Questions for Critical Reading. The last Question for Connecting requires a more abstract application of Friedman's argument and urges students to explore issues of global economy in Leslie Savan's "What's Black, Then White, and Said All Over?" (p. 363). This question will be challenging to students because they will need to consider Savan's work in light of economic systems, which is a connection that will require significant critical engagement with both texts. Students may want to extend their work in the Exploring Context section in order to address this question.

The Assignments for Writing extend the Questions for Critical Reading into a more in-depth critical approach to Friedman's work. Question 1 challenges students to explore the limitations of Friedman's theory by expanding upon their work in question 2 of Questions for Critical Reading. Question 2 of Assignments for Writing asks students to consider local culture in light of global economic structures and engage Friedman's assertions about global supply chains and terrorist supply chains by analyzing the possibility that both types of supply chains affect local cultures. In order to further consider the collaborative aspects of global supply chains, question 3 of Assignments for Writing builds upon question 1 of Questions for Critical Reading and question 2 of Questions for Connecting in asking students to identify the components of successful collaboration.

Francis Fukuyama

Human Dignity

(text pp. 141–168)

Selection Overview

In "Human Dignity," Francis Fukuyama explores the human essence that entitles us to respect. The excerpt's introduction outlines the need for a concept of human dignity in terms of the political demands of liberal democracy. Next, Fukuyama introduces the idea of Factor X, his designated term for human essence. Factor X is firmly rooted for Fukuyama in philosophical origins and acts as a basis for social equality. Fukuyama reviews the history of morality in natural science and argues that in many cases natural science ignores human dignity. He proposes that both the increasingly secular framing of natural science and the egalitarian demands of modernity spark a new discourse surrounding human dignity, particularly in light of the future of biotechnology. Fukuyama finds that "the genetic lottery" of natural reproduction enforces equality on a genetic level that genetic manipulation could easily destroy. He then sketches the interdependent parts that together make up Factor X, juxtaposing this model with a classical reductionist model of human essence. The components of Factor X include political behavior, abstract and moral thought, reason, human language, and consciousness for which Fukuyama encompasses emotion (hence separating human consciousness from artificial intelligence). These parts working together as a whole constitute Fukuyama's basis for human dignity. Inherent in such a complex, holistic sense of human essence is the necessity of preserving our complex, unique essence in the face of biotechnologies that could alter us. Fukuyama points out that ethics demand that we consider our treatment of humans who do not possess all aspects of Factor X, including the mentally disabled, the elderly, children, and the unborn. He argues that these groups, and in particular the unborn, still possess the potential to develop Factor X. Hence, we must be extremely cautious of intervening with the unborn in order to protect our future and its potential from a loss of human essence.

Concepts include: Factor X, GenRich and GenPoor, natural rights, reductionism

Themes include: bioethics, class, complexity, consciousness, equality, genetic manipulation, human dignity, human essence, human language, human political behavior, human rights, morality, science, technology
Works best with: Appiah, Dalai Lama, Didion, Poe, Pollan, Restak, Roach, Spar, Yoshino

Questions and Assignments

Although Fukuyama's style is very accessible, his ideas are much more complex than they may at first appear. Students tend to get lost in Fukuyama's extensive review of natural philosophy and in the complex structure of his argument. The Questions for Critical Reading emphasize the key points in this selection to steer students towards the fundamental critical issues of this text. Question 1 asks students to define Factor X, a task that requires recognition of the complex relationship between the parts Fukuyama identifies. Question 2 requires an engagement of Fukuyama's assertion that there is a definable human essence, an underlying assumption of this text that students often accept without question. Question 3 sets the task of isolating and exploring Fukuyama's concept of human dignity by encouraging students to focus on Fukuyama's primary argument within the text.

Biotechnology is a relatively specialized and quickly changing field, and students may not be aware of current issues in the field that Fukuyama seeks to address. Exploring Context for this selection challenges students to research current online information about biotechnology and consciousness in order to help them effectively apply Fukuyama's argument to the world around them. Question 1 centers on the Council of Europe and asks students to explore whether the Council's position on advances in biotechnology is consistent with Fukuyama's concerns. Because Fukuyama's discussion of reductionism is abstract and complex, question 2 involves students in the "Game of Life" in order to help them further understand reductionism by applying it as a paradigm for understanding human consciousness. The last Exploring Context question urges students to explore the *American Journal of Bioethics* Web site for information or examples to which Fukuyama's argument can be applied.

Fukuyama's excerpt contains several themes and concepts that can be easily applied to biotechnology as well as to other aspects of modern life that he does not overtly discuss in this section. Although students may get mired in the extensive vocabulary and complex organization of this essay, the Questions for Connecting engage several different approaches to Fukuyama's excerpt that can help students focus on the larger implications of his argument. Question 1 looks at the role of complexity in Factor X by relating it to complex systems in Pollan's "The Animals: Practicing Complexity" (p. 281) by requiring students to apply Pollan's concrete discussion of complexity to the more abstract discussion of complexity in Fukuyama's definition of Factor X. This question draws on their work in question 1 of Questions for Critical Reading, and it will help students relate Fukuyama's abstract discussion to more concrete examples of complexity. Question 2 of Questions for Connecting explores the role of race in human essence and asks students to examine the effect of Fukuyama's conclusions on Steve Olson's argument in "The End of Race: Hawaii and the Mixing of Peoples" (p. 250). Although race has historically been considered an essential human characteristic, this question may help students consider the possibility that race may not be a key factor in shaping humanity. Question 3 considers the possibility that multitasking, the subject of Restak's "Attention Deficit: The Brain Syndrome of Our Era" (p. 332), can be analyzed as a form of biotechnology. Students are required to apply Fukuyama's argument to Restak's assertions. This question gives students the opportunity to consider other technologies in light of human evolution.

In struggling to understand Fukuyama's challenging, complex definition of human essence, students may lose sight of the possibilities he presents for applying human essence in order to further human equality. Question 1 of Assignments for Writing builds upon questions 1 and 2 of Questions for Critical Reading in asking students to identify what it means to be human. This question encourages students to pin down the fundamental concept upon which Fukuyama's argument centers. Equally important for Fukuyama is the issue of populations that are commonly considered unequal in some way because of illness, age, and other incapacity. Question 2 sets the task of extrapolating standards for equal treatment of these populations in light of advances in medicine and technology. Since Fukuyama clarifies that the distinction of human essence entitles humans to equality, question 3 investigates the boundaries between humans who are afforded dignity and creatures that may not be. This assignment calls for an extension of Fukuyama's argument in the natural world, and it may draw on responses to question 1 of Questions for Critical Reading.

Daniel Gilbert

Reporting Live from Tomorrow

(text pp. 169–189)

Selection Overview

Gilbert opens this selection by questioning the ways in which we envision the future and acquire knowledge. Arguing that we gain most of our knowledge through the experience of others, Gilbert suggests that we would be better served by relying on others in considering decisions that affect our future. In looking at how we transmit beliefs, Gilbert turns to the concept of super-replicators—ideas that, like genes, transmit themselves and pass on their means of transmission, regardless of their accuracy. Gilbert argues that we rely on super-replicators to make decisions that we think will further our happiness, such as making money and having children. Noting that super-replicators often promote social agenda, Gilbert presents evidence that these beliefs, although widely held, are not supportable through research. Gilbert proposes that while the actual happiness that results from having children is verifiable, it is a different kind of happiness than expectant parents had previously imagined. Because we think of ourselves as consistently unique, Gilbert argues that we rely on our imaginations rather than the experience of others, a process complicated by our imaginations' incompleteness, its roots in present conditions, and its short-sighted nature. As a solution to the inadequacy of imagination, Gilbert suggests that we could more successfully rely on others as surrogates for our future selves. He illustrates the difference between surrogation and simulation through several experiments that involve groups with various levels of secondhand knowledge predicting their emotional responses to specified situations. Ultimately, because of this imagined difference, we allow ourselves to be lead into false beliefs that promote social stability but not necessarily our own best interests or happiness.

> **Concepts include:** simulators, super-replicators, surrogators
> **Themes include:** decision making, happiness, predicting the future, the shortcomings of imagination, social norms, social order, uniqueness
> **Works best with:** Alvarez, Appiah, Didion, Johnson, Kimmelman, Olson, Pollan, Restak, Taylor

Questions and Assignments

Although Gilbert's examples are easy for students to relate to, the larger concepts that his argument rests upon are more complex. The Questions for Critical Reading for this selection encourage students to use Gilbert's examples to develop definitions of his terms that can be used to draw out his larger argument. Question 1 asks students to explore the term *super-replicator*, piecing together a definition from the text and applying that definition to an example from outside the text in order to examine how the term functions in Gilbert's argument and how it can be applied to other social phenomena. Question 2 engages Gilbert's surrogates by asking students to work out a concrete definition of the term. Question 3 asks students to engage Gilbert's concept of happiness to assess whether Gilbert's concept of happiness is consistent with their own.

While students may be relatively confident in exploring Gilbert's generalized examples surrounding having children and gaining financial success, they may have some difficulty interpreting the results of Gilbert's research on simulators and surrogators and comprehending the overall structure of the excerpt. The first Exploring Context question encourages students to work with the definitions they developed in their responses to the Questions for Critical Reading in order to make a comic strip that depicts the argument of Gilbert's essay. This exercise will also help students in understanding the overall structure of Gilbert's argument by encouraging them to create a visual reference for the text. Building on question 3 of Questions for Critical Reading, question 2 of Exploring Context challenges students to research definitions of happiness in order to understand the different perceptions of happiness. The final Exploring Context question asks students to make use of Yahoo! Answers as an Internet surrogate to expand Gilbert's work with surrogates by evaluating whether the Internet functions as the same type of surrogate Gilbert promotes.

Because the most accessible examples in Gilbert's excerpt are also the broadest, students may have some difficulty transporting the underlying concepts of Gilbert's arguments to more specific issues surrounding social issues. In question 1 of Questions for Connecting, students are asked to apply Gilbert's argument about the happiness people believe children will bring them to Debora Spar's discussion of adoption in "Trading Places: The Practice and Politics of Adoption" (p. 402). This question engages both essays by requiring students to extrapolate from Spar's research while working with the definition of happiness developed in question 3 of Questions for Critical Reading and question 2 of Exploring Context. Question 2 of Questions for Connecting asks students to engage Johnson's discussion of feedback loops in "Listening to Feedback" (p. 191) and Gilbert's arguments about happiness and super-replicators. This question encourages students to look at the process of surrogation rather than just the end results of using surrogates. The last question of Questions for Connecting asks students to apply Gilbert's conclusions about surrogates to emotions other than happiness and challenges students to build upon their definition of surrogates in question 2 of Questions for Critical Reading by considering the possibility of Joan Didion's role as a surrogate in "After Life" (p. 88).

Since Gilbert's discussion of social perceptions of happiness is easy to relate to, students will tend to focus on the most easily accessible themes in his excerpt. In order to understand the intricacies of Gilbert's argument, the Assignments for Writing for this selection ask students to challenge Gilbert's assertions. Question 1 challenges students to build on their work in question 2 of Questions for Critical Reading to assess the potential of surrogates to offer us a sense of our future happiness. This question asks students to consider Gilbert's overall argument in support of using surrogates, possibly by examining surrogation through examples from outside the text. Question 2 asks students to apply Gilbert's argument by proposing an appropriate surrogate for them in seeking their own future happiness. This will allow students to consider both their own perception of happiness and the possibility of applying Gilbert's concept of surrogates to an example of their own. Question 3 asks students to extend Gilbert's argument about super-replicators, building on question 1 of Questions for Critical Reading to form an argument surrounding the function of super-replicators.

Steven Johnson

Listening to Feedback

(text pp. 190–215)

Selection Overview

In "Listening to Feedback," Johnson describes media treatment of Gennifer Flowers' allegations against Bill Clinton, arguing that the story was amplified through inflated media attention that resulted from feedback loops. These loops are the result of a shift from hierarchical decision making in the media to a bottom-up system controlled by feedback. Johnson links media feedback with feedback in the brain where feedback loops repeat information indefinitely. Johnson argues that because of the relationships between local and national news media, the media's feedback system itself becomes a controlling factor in deciding what gets reported. In order to fully understand this type of feedback, Johnson explains the difference between positive feedback systems, in which self-fueling cycles amplify the original stimulus, and negative feedback systems, in which the system responds to changing stimulus to keep equilibrium. In the human body, this equilibrium self-regulates to achieve homeostasis. Johnson points out that other systems, including the media, urban planning, and virtual communities, can be modeled using artificial feedback systems. Johnson points out that early virtual communities, like ECHO and the Well made use of feedback systems by employing a mix of hierarchy and heterarchy; that is, they were top-down systems in which users had a great deal of input. Johnson points out that the characteristics of online communities and their users can limit the regulating feedback of such a system. When this happens, a system enters a "climax stage" in which it ceases to grow. Johnson introduces *Slashdot.org* as an online community that overcame the "climax stage" by developing into a bottom-up system through which every user earns the rights to moderate and rate contributions through a user feedback system. Several larger online communities, including Amazon and eBay, have developed similar feedback systems. Slashdot and these other systems are not purely representational, but they do present the collective effort of an entire community. Johnson suggests that there are other ways of negotiating feedback in Slashdot that would promote more diversity in the postings; feedback systems give us the opportunity to adjust "the rules" in order to give us whatever results we desire.

> **Concepts include:** bottom-up systems, complex adaptive systems, fatigue, hierarchy/heterarchy, homeostasis, positive/negative feedback loops, top-down systems
> **Themes include:** biology, communication, complexity, information management, media, online community, technology
> **Works best with:** Appiah, Friedman, Gilbert, Kimmelman, Nathan, Poe, Pollan, Restak, Savan, Surowiecki, Yoshino

Questions and Assignments

Because Johnson's text includes discussion on several complex and varying examples of feedback, students may have some difficulty engaging the concept of feedback that Johnson applies to media and virtual communities. To help students isolate the concept of feedback, question 1 of Questions for Critical Reading asks students to define feedback and explore its role in the essay. In order to do so, students will need to discuss the specific examples of feedback Johnson introduces and extrapolate an overall concept that connects them. As Johnson argues that the goal of feedback loops is homeostasis, question 2 encourages students to take a closer look at the concept of homeostasis as it relates to Johnson's text. Finally, in question 3, students are asked to apply their work on feedback and homeostasis to explore what makes user-generated content systems like Slashdot successful, linking Slashdot to other examples of self-regulating online communities.

Because students may have very little experience in examining Web site and feedback design, the Exploring Context questions for this selection encourage students to take a look at specific examples of systems that utilize feedback in order to evaluate Johnson's argument in light of recent uses of technologies and organizations that incorporate feedback. Question 1 prompts students to evaluate Slashdot to assess whether it still engages the processes Johnson recognizes in self-regulating communities and expand on their responses to question 3 of Questions for Critical Reading. Question 2 of Exploring Context asks students to examine a visual representation of feedback by looking at the Stack tool of Digg Lab. This exploration provides students with a more accessible way of engaging the type of feedback system Johnson discusses, expanding on their work on homeostasis in question 2 of Questions for Critical Reading. The third Exploring Context question challenges students to assess the difference between top-down and bottom-up systems by evaluating CNN's Web site to see which model it most clearly follows.

Since much of his discussion is fairly technical, students may have some difficulty following Johnson's application of feedback systems to the media. One way to help them make the connections Johnson suggests is to challenge them to relate feedback systems to other types of collaborative efforts. The first Question for Connecting exercise asks students to apply Johnson's arguments about feedback and homeostasis to James Surowiecki's analysis of small groups in "Committees, Juries, and Teams: The *Columbia* Disaster and How Small Groups Can Be Made to Work" (p. 440). Students may find Surowiecki's text more accessible because the types of collaboration he discusses are less technologically driven; hence, his text provides a useful gateway to engaging the concept of feedback outside of scientific discussions of biology and information technology. As Johnson begins his discussion by looking at the media, question 2 of Questions for Connecting encourages students to relate it to the types of advertising and pop talk described in Leslie Savan's "What's Black, Then White, and Said All Over?" (p. 363). This will help students expand upon the difference between top-down and bottom-up systems, building on their work on Slashdot in question 3 of Questions for Critical Reading and question 1 of Exploring Context, particularly in examining the possibility that groups like Slashdot could affect social change. Question 3 examines the relationship between Wikipedia, as described in Marshall Poe's "The Hive" (p. 264) and Slashdot, applying Johnson's discussion of the uses of feedback to the possibilities of tracing feedback through user input on Wikipedia.

The Assignments for Writing in this section ask students to explore the implications of Johnson's argument by examining the possibilities inherent in using feedback systems. Question 1 of Assignments for Writing asks students to consider how feedback systems could be incorporated into the news media by looking at the qualities that make Slashdot a virtual democracy and comparing that system with current news media systems. This will help students grasp the argument Johnson makes about feedback systems and his application of such systems to the media. Question 2 asks students to determine successful practices in organizing and administering information networks, by looking specifically at self-reflection and the role of the individual in such networks. This question allows students to expand upon their work on Wikipedia in question 3 of Questions for Connecting and extend Johnson's argument. The final Assignment for Writing asks students to incorporate Johnson's ideas about feedback into building an argument surrounding the key factors to successful collaboration.

Michael Kimmelman

The Art of Collecting Lightbulbs

(text pp. 216–227)

Selection Overview

Michael Kimmelman begins this excerpt by introducing the Mount Vernon Museum of Incandescent Lighting, a collection of lightbulbs amassed by Francis Hicks. Kimmelman uses this exhibit to examine the possibility of collections as a form of art. He argues that people collect items to bring order to the world, engage in the symbolism of objects that no longer retain their use, make icons and relics from the mundane, and access a realm beyond the ordinary. Kimmelman references Walter Benjamin, who argued that collectors are people who are particularly sensitive to confusion in the world and thus attempt to establish their own system of order. One of the collections Kimmelman explores is Albert Barnes' art collection, which he describes as appearing to be randomly ordered but having been specifically and meticulously arranged. Because of the sheer eccentricity of such a collection, Kimmelman notes that Barnes believed that the juxtaposition of objects could teach the public something beyond the appreciation of the objects themselves. Kimmelman argues that collections are of value not only to the collector but also to those who view and enjoy collections. Because people build collections for different reasons, Kimmelman identifies strength of conviction and public service as the definitive qualities of an admirable collector. He traces collection back to the *Kunst-und Wunderhammen* ("art and wonder cabinets") in the sixteenth century when collections of rare objects were displayed in private homes according to the collectors' creative and aesthetic tastes. Kimmelman points out that the contemporary museum display took shape from the wonder cabinet; both forms of collections seek to order a disordered universe. Kimmelman argues that as museums and connoisseurship developed, collections began to further specialize, creating methodical categories to place objects into a more stringent sense of order. Despite our tendency toward meticulous distinction between types of objects, Kimmelman cites several examples of collections of unusual objects including the Mütter Museum, which houses preserved anatomical oddities. Kimmelman argues that such collections help us redefine what we think of as art.

Concepts include: ordinary collections, promise of wonderment, symbolic value

Themes include: aesthetics, art, collecting, connoisseurship, display, expressions of creativity, juxtaposition, order/chaos, prestige, wonder cabinets

Works best with: Didion, Gilbert, Johnson, Pollan, Postrel

Questions and Assignments

Kimmelman covers a variety of examples in this essay and students may have some difficulty following the conceptual connections he makes between collecting, art, and medicine. They may tend to focus more on the anecdotes and examples Kimmelman discusses than on his ideas about the value of collections. For this reason, question 1 of Questions for Critical Reading explores the heart of Kimmelman's argument by asking students to address the overall issue of collection as a form of art. Because students may not readily relate to the use of wonder cabinets, question 2 challenges students to locate a modern equivalent and to explore them as forms of art as well. Kimmelman moves from viewing wonder cabinets as an art form to examining their use in early medical research; hence question 3 asks students to explore the connection Kimmelman suggests between medicine and art, prompting them to engage larger connections among art, medicine, and science.

As students may have limited interest in museums and difficulty relating to art, the Exploring Context questions offer several types of collections with which students may be more readily able to identify. Most students have more experience in accessing collections than they realize; question 1 of Exploring Context challenges them to browse through the categories on eBay to build an argument that applies Kimmelman's ideas to the collection of objects found there. It may be helpful for students to draw on their responses to question 1 of Questions for Critical Reading. Because Kimmelman's discussion can be best understood by experiencing an arranged collection firsthand, question 2 of Exploring Context encourages students to visit a local museum and its Web site to compare the representations of collecting in real and virtual spaces. The final Exploring Context question asks students to review PostSecret, a Web site that hosts a collection of personalized postcards that reveal secrets of their designers. This Web site's content can be used to open a dialogue about the function of art both in individual pieces and in the whole of the collection.

Having thoroughly examined collections from several points of view, students may begin to develop an understanding of the effects of collections on their viewers. Part of the viewers' role in collections is an active interest in the objects and collections, an interest that is intricately related to aesthetic, social, and political concerns. One of the underlying themes in Kimmelman's discussion of the Mütter Museum's display of medical anomalies is people's fascination with the human body. Question 1 of Questions for Connecting asks students to use Kimmelman's analysis of this fascination to discuss Julia Serano's assertions in "Before and After: Class and Body Transformations" (p. 392), looking at the ways in which such a collection might participate in systems of class. Although

Kimmelman's excerpt is fairly accessible, the argument he makes is far more complex than the simple anecdotes he presents seem to imply. Question 2 of Questions for Connecting asks students to apply Francis Fukuyama's discussion in "Human Dignity" (p.142) to Kimmelman's analysis of collecting, with particular attention to Fukuyama's discussion of complexity and the ways it complicates Kimmelman's argument. Question 3 of Questions for Connecting asks students to look at the intersection between art and mourning through forging a connection between the wonder cabinets that Kimmelman discusses and the public display of Evita's corpse as described in Diana Taylor's "False Identifications: Minority Populations Mourn Diana" (p. 454). This will help to develop their analysis of wonder cabinets, medicine, and art from questions 2 and 3 of Questions for Critical Reading.

The Assignments for Writing for this selection help students extend Kimmelman's arguments by expanding upon their work in the Questions for Critical Reading. Question 1 asks students to locate their own example of a wonder cabinet and discuss it in light of Kimmelman's arguments about collections and order, building upon their exploration of eBay in question 1 of Exploring Context. Question 2 of Assignments for Writing asks students to explore the interdisciplinary applications of Kimmelman's text through examining the role of collections in science, teaching, and art to find ways that the three disciplines can be connected through Kimmelman's argument. Although students may not have previously thought about what they consider to be art, question 3 asks them to develop a definition of art that encompasses Kimmelman's discussion of display and order, drawing on their work in question 1 of Questions for Critical Reading.

Rebekah Nathan

Community and Diversity

(text pp. 228–248)

Selection Overview

In "Community and Diversity," Rebekah Nathan poses as a college freshman to explore the practical applications of university rhetoric surrounding community and diversity. Nathan notes that members of a university community generally share youth, popular culture, and their status at the university. She begins by exploring institutional efforts at building community including freshman curricula, which seek to build community through mandatory programs. Recognizing that students resisted these mandatory attempts, Nathan sought out efforts to build community through voluntary activities—including dormitory events—which ultimately failed because of a lack of student involvement. Nathan notes that individualism within such settings detracts from students' ability and desire to build community. Upon interviewing students, Nathan finds that the basis for community for students was in "ego-centered networks," small groups formed from shared circumstances and similar demographics. Thus, these small groups impede attempts to emphasize diversity on college campuses. Nathan extends her exploration of diversity through studying student dining arrangements and notes that demographics also play a role in the level of diversity any given student is likely to experience. She concludes her argument by recognizing that community and diversity are intimately linked to each other on college campuses.

> **Concepts include:** individual community and ego-centered networks, little loyalties
> **Themes include:** building community, diversity, gender, individualism, race, representative samples
> **Works best with:** Appiah, Olson, Poe, Pollan, Savan, Surowiecki, Taylor, Yoshino

Questions and Assignments

Students generally relate well to Rebekah Nathan's research because it is directly linked to their own experience. At times this can lead to neglecting important points in her work that students may not relate to as readily. Question 1 of Questions for Critical Reading asks students to define Nathan's "ego-centered networks" and explore their functions through close examination of the text. Because Nathan argues that attempts to promote community and diversity at AnyU have failed, question 2 prompts students to retrace the points that lead to this conclusion. Alternately, question 3 asks students to extrapolate what might promote ideals of community and diversity, extending more subtle portions of Nathan's argument.

In this excerpt, Nathan points out some fairly obvious examples of efforts to build community and promote diversity, but students may not always recognize these efforts in their own institutional environments. The Exploring Context questions help students to further relate Nathan's argument to their own experience by directing them to evaluate their own schools' approaches to community and diversity in light of Nathan's findings, continuing their work on question 2 of Questions for Critical Reading. Because popular culture is so ingrained in students' lives, students may not realize that their relationship with it varies from individual to individual. Question 2 challenges students to interact with each other to determine whether the aspects of student life and popular culture Nathan identifies as the basis for community and diversity at AnyU apply to them as individuals. This will help students apply her argument to their own bases for community and diversity. The final Exploring Context question expands upon Nathan's assumptions about defining community and diversity through blogs by encouraging students to examine the similarities and differences between Nathan's definitions and those that are popularized through blogging.

The Questions for Connecting focus on factors in a larger social context that affect community and diversity on college campuses. Many students will have fairly recent and limited experience of campus life, but may be more able to relate to this essay through looking at the larger social context they have experienced throughout their lives. Question 1 challenges students to use Savan's argument in "What's Black, Then White, and Said All Over?" (p. 363) to help explain the failure of diversity on college campuses. Although discussions of race and diversity may be uncomfortable for students, question 2 challenges them to examine the underlying assumptions of Nathan's discussion of racial diversity in light of Olson's discussion in "The End of Race: Hawaii and the Mixing of Peoples" (p. 250). This question, along with question 3 of Questions for Connecting, requires students to consider other types of communities by analyzing the similarities and differences between Nathan's sense of community and those found in other communal situations.

While Nathan outlines the difficulties of establishing strong communities and promoting diversity, she leaves the task of finding solutions to these problems up to the reader. Question 1 of Assignments for Writing challenges students to look for a solution to the difficulties Nathan identifies in building community on college campuses, applying the concepts in Nathan's essay to their own specific observations and experiences, expanding upon question 3 of Questions for Critical Reading. The second Assignment for Writing asks students to engage Nathan's research methods by challenging them to explore how research like Nathan's can be an effective tool for university administrators to gain a student's perspective on community and diversity. Question 3 asks students to extend their work in question 1 of Questions for Critical Reading by examining the interaction between individuality and community.

Steve Olson

The End of Race: Hawaii and the Mixing of Peoples

(text pp. 249–263)

Selection Overview

Steve Olson's "The End of Race: Hawaii and the Mixing of Peoples" focuses on considering the implications of defining race through culture and genetics. Using Hawaii as an example, Olson first traces the history of European settlement in the South Pacific, noting that since Europeans first came to the South Pacific, Hawaii has become home to one of the most racially mixed populations in the world. He thus uses Hawaii as a model for imagining the future of race. Olson argues that racial similarity does not lead to cultural harmony, pointing out that the racialization of culture leads to conflicts waged in the name of race between groups that are not racially distinct. Olson also finds that neither culture nor genetic research can adequately determine a person's race, making the concept of race both useless and obscure. Although students may tend to focus on Hawaii as a utopia of racial harmony, Olson describes the racial stereotyping that still occurs in Hawaii. He also notes that both individual and institutional racism are readily visible in Hawaii, despite its increasingly multi-racial populations. Despite the racially mixed population of Hawaii, the resurgence of Hawaiian culture has given rise to the attempt to identify native Hawaiians as racially distinct from other populations. This distinction is difficult if not impossible to determine conclusively through using genetic haplotyping. Because of this difficulty, Olson turns to social factors to try to explain the persistence of race in Hawaii. He offers the idea of communities of descent as one possible explanation, ultimately finding racial identification to be a matter of choice.

> **Concepts include:** communities of descent, haplotyping, racialization of culture
> **Themes include:** class, culture, discrimination, ethnicity, genetics, identity, race
> **Works best with:** Appiah, Gilbert, Nathan, Savan, Serano, Taylor, Yoshino

Questions and Assignments

Given the persistence of racial identification, racial stereotyping, and racism in the United States, many students will find it difficult to understand the implications of Olson's argument or to suspend predetermined notions of race in order to work with Olson's essay. A good place to start to address this issue is to spend some time discussing the differences among race, ethnicity, and culture. Question 1 of Questions for Critical Reading can help lead to understanding Olson's definition of race. Encouraging further exploration of Olson's concept of "community of descent" as suggested in question 2 will help address the difficulty students may have in understanding Olson's assertion that ethnic identity can be considered a matter of choice. Question 3 requires students to account for the persistence of race despite its lack of a biological basis.

The Exploring Context questions for this selection challenge students to closely examine the evidence Olson uses in building his argument. Question 1 of Exploring Context asks students to relate the U.S. Census Bureau's racial categories to Olson's argument by building on the work they did in question 3 of Questions for Critical Reading. The second Exploring Context question asks students to research the representations of race on Hawaii's government and tourism Web site and incorporate their definition of race from question 2 of Questions for Critical Reading. The final question of Exploring Context considers issues of race in the Hawaiian education system, one of the areas Olson identifies as a remaining site where race persists.

Olson's work can be used to discuss a number of issues that lead to critical engagement with other essays within this reader including race, class, ethnicity, culture, and discrimination. Question 1 of Questions for Connecting challenges students to explore the possibility of Olson's argument for an end to race. Linking Olson's essay with Leslie Savan's "What's Black, Then White, and Said All Over?" (p. 363) allows students to connect the persistence of race in Hawaii to issues of language and race that are generally more recognizable in the context of their own experience. Olson also challenges us to think about racial identification, a topic that links his essay to Serano's "Before and After: Class and Body Transformations" (p. 392). Both essays ask the reader to consider whether ethnic identification moves us toward or away from an end to race, which is a question also raised in question 2 of Questions for Connecting. Question 3 raises the issue of race in terms of Yoshino's argument for a liberty paradigm for civil rights in featured in "Preface" and "The New Civil Rights" (p. 479).

The Assignments for Writing for Olson's "The End of Race: Hawaii and the Mixing of Peoples" ask students to engage Olson's argument by expanding first upon the possibility of an end to race in the first Assignment for Writing, furthering arguments they may have developed in Question 1 of Questions for Critical Reading. The second Assignment for Writing prompts students to consider the relationship between race and technology, exploring the possibilities of considering race as a form of technology and examining technology's ability to help us move beyond current conceptions of race. Finally, the third Assignment for Writing furthers discussion raised in question 1 of Questions for Critical Reading and question 3 of Questions for Connecting.

Marshall Poe

The Hive

(text pp. 264–279)

Selection Overview

Marshall Poe's "The Hive" traces the history of Wikipedia in order to discuss the role of collaboration in sharing and developing knowledge. Poe begins by introducing Wikipedia as one of the most successful collaborative efforts in history. In providing a brief biographical sketch of Wikipedia's founders, Poe notes that Wikipedia developed from gaming sites and discussion lists that served as early attempts at collaborative efforts. During the rise of Internet search engines, Poe posits that two major models for building universal directories developed: the top-down and bottom-up paradigms. Jimmy Wales, a former gamer and the co-founder of Wikipedia, expanded upon the concept of collaborative development through using Web rings, a bottom-up system that allowed users to construct their own systems of categorizing information. Using such systems, he and Larry Sanger founded a Web-based encyclopedia system known as NuPedia. NuPedia was founded on the "cathedral model," which meant that all information added to the site was carefully monitored by a board of experts who controlled the information. After NuPedia proved slow to catch on, the development of the wiki paved the way for Sanger to develop Wikipedia, a system founded on the "bazaar model" that allowed for end users to create, edit, and monitor its information. Poe traces several difficulties in negotiating the rapid growth of Wikipedia, ultimately finding that Wales's hands-off approach to the development of collaborative knowledge proved extremely effective in the rise of Wikipedia. Through examining Wikipedia, Poe finds unparalleled value in the power of the community, or the wisdom of crowds, to develop common knowledge and argues that the accuracy and reach of Wikipedia have begun to redefine our conceptions of truth and knowledge.

Concepts include: cathedral and bazaar models, open-content, neutral point of view (NPOV), top-down and bottom-up models, wikis
Themes include: collaboration, common knowledge, epistemology, governing knowledge, information technology, voluntary cooperation
Works best with: Appiah, Friedman, Johnson, Nathan, Pollan, Restak, Savan, Surowiecki, Yoshino

Questions and Assignments

Because students most likely have some practical experience with using Wikipedia, they may tend to brush past the larger argument Poe makes about redefining knowledge. The Questions for Critical Reading for "The Hive" are meant to help students engage with the complex and subtle concepts Poe considers, including isolating specific structural elements and other characteristics of collaboration that lend themselves to successful collaborative efforts. For example, question 1 explores the factors that Poe considers vital to Wikipedia's success and requires close reading and analysis of the text. This will help students identify the specific qualities Poe favors in making his argument. Question 2 assigns the task of comparing top-down and bottom-up systems in order to extrapolate the potential of each. This will help students understand the structural differences Poe discusses between the two types of systems. The final question examines a conflict that arises on Wikipedia in the penultimate section of the excerpt and questions whether such conflict aids or impedes Wikipedia's success. This question gives students an entry into some of the complexity in Poe's discussion.

Exploring Context allows students to work more closely with Wikipedia and wiki-based Web sites in order to develop their own conclusions about Poe's assertions. Question 1 examines the collaborative process involved in Wikipedia by challenging students to gain hands-on experience in editing entries and explore Poe's analysis through their own experience. Similarly, question 2 directs students to use a wiki-based site that houses memories and examine the collaborative knowledge found there in light of Poe's analysis of similar knowledge on Wikipedia. This question draws on question 1 of Questions for Critical Reading in order to examine the success of such sites. The third question asks students to continue the conversation Poe begins in "The Hive" about his own Wikipedia entry by exploring the changes in his entry and extrapolating whether or not those changes are consistent with Poe's argument for the success of Wikipedia.

The Questions for Connecting for this essay focus on linking this essay's themes of collaboration and truth to other essays with interacting arguments. Question 1 asks students to apply Steven Johnson's argument in "Listening to Feedback" (p. 191) to Poe's discussion of collaborative knowledge. Question 2 focuses on applying the redefinition of truth that Wikipedia promotes to the Dalai Lama's "Ethics and the New Genetics" (p. 76), considering whether socially constructed knowledge is useful in developing systems of ethics. Collaborative efforts are further explored in question 3, in which students seek solutions to the difficulties in collaboration James Surowiecki outlines in "Committees, Juries, and Teams: The *Columbia* Disaster and How Small Groups Can Be Made to

Work" (p. 440). Students are asked to extend the exploration they began in question 1 of Questions for Critical Reading and question 3 of Exploring Context.

The Assignments for Writing allow for more flexible close examination of Poe's assertions. The first Assignment for Writing explores the role of collaboration in the production of knowledge and extends the discussion of wikis in Exploring Context and Poe's concepts from questions 1 and 3 of Questions for Connecting. Building upon question 2 of Questions for Connecting, the second Assignment for Writing asks students to consider the implications of ownership rights that arise in Wikipedia's redefinition of knowledge. The final Assignment for Writing considers Poe's discussion of cathedral and bazaar models by requiring students to suggest proper boundaries between experts and crowds in the development and dissemination of knowledge.

Michael Pollan

The Animals: Practicing Complexity

(text pp. 280–295)

Selection Overview

In "The Animals: Practicing Complexity," Pollan examines Polyface Farm, an organic farm that successfully uses complex systems by taking full advantage of the relationships between their component parts. First Pollan describes the beauty and apparent simplicity of the organic farm, noting that it is both environmentally sound and technologically simple. Pollan describes a number of processes that contribute to the farm's production, each of which is part of a larger ecological system in which everything is connected—the cows, their waste, the chickens, their waste, the grass, and even the chemical balance in the air. Pollan notes that in such a system, all of the parts are interdependent; changing any factor involved would throw off its balance. He then turns to a close examination of the idea of efficiency, arguing that industrial efficiency tends to include repeated simple actions resulting in monoculture, while natural efficiency is produced by complexity. Polyface imitates nature in that its complex systems lead to efficiency, particularly through eliminating the environmental and economic costs associated with industrial farming. Part of this efficiency for Polyface comes from "stacking," which Pollan defines as working with time and space to create a system as close to nature as possible. Pollan uses the concept of the holon to describe each component of the layers, defining holons as entities that can be regarded simultaneously as interdependent parts and wholes. Pollan explains that these holons, with a measure of human intervention and ingenuity, make Polyface an efficient, productive, and humane environment.

Concepts include: efficiency, holons, industrial models vs. biological/ecological models, stacking

Themes include: complexity, economy, interdependence, monoculture, organic farming, self-sufficiency and sustainability, symbiosis

Works best with: Appiah, Dalai Lama, Friedman, Fukuyama, Gilbert, Johnson, Kimmelman, Nathan, Poe, Roach, Surowiecki

Questions and Assignments

Because many students will not have considered the processes of organic farming, they may get lost in the detailed explanations of its practices without paying as much attention to the larger issues at stake in Pollan's work. In addition, students may mistake Pollan's accessible writing style for a simplistic narrative and ignore the complexity that is at the center of Pollan's argument. For this reason, the Questions for Critical Reading focus heavily on complexity. Question 1 requires a broad engagement with the text and asks students to locate moments in the text that describe the reasons for Polyface's success. Next, question 2 works with Pollan's holons by asking students to both define the term and then apply it to another example outside of the text. Since holons are somewhat paradoxical, the exercise of applying the holons on the farm to an example that students can more easily relate to will help them clarify the concept. The final question asks students to engage the theme of complexity and examine passages that describe complexity in action at Polyface.

Exploring Context asks students to research the real-world experience of Polyface Farm by reviewing Polyface's Web site to locate concrete examples of the concepts in Pollan's essay, drawing on question 1 of Questions for Critical Reading. Next, question 2 of Exploring Context asks students to examine the U.S. Department of Agriculture's National Organic Program to question the meaning of *organic* by comparing their philosophy to the philosophy of Polyface Farm. Finally, in question 3 students are asked explore Michael Pollan's Web site to determine whether his own interests affect his discussion of Polyface Farm. This is a good exercise to begin a discussion of authorship and authority.

Students may have some difficulty in transporting the conceptual implications of Pollan's work into other areas. The Questions for Connecting can help by asking students to compare the complexity demonstrated in Polyface Farm with that of other complex systems. In the first question, students are asked to consider the relationship between the ecologically interdependent system of Polyface Farm and the economically interdependent system Thomas Friedman locates in global supply chains in "The Dell Theory of Conflict Prevention" (p. 121). Question 2 asks students to apply Steven Johnson's ideas in "Listening to Feedback" (p. 191) to explaining the success of Polyface Farm and draw on questions 1 and 3 of Questions for Critical Reading. The last question in Questions for Connecting asks students to evaluate Polyface Farm from the point of view of Michael Kimmelman's argument in "The Art of Collecting Lightbulbs" (p. 216) and, in doing so, attempt to view Polyface as a collection of sorts and possibly as a form of art.

The Assignments for Writing ask students to explore the broader implications of Pollan's argument, first requiring students to formulate an argument on the relationship between food production methods and health. In order to do so, it is necessary to look at the effects of industrial trends and organic systems to explore the impact of food production on the health of farmers, animals, and consumers, which also builds upon their exploration of complexity in question 3 of Questions for Critical Reading. The second Assignment for Writing question explores Pollan's definition of efficiency by looking at the benefits and disadvantages of biotechnology-based farming. The third Assignment for Writing delves further into Pollan's assertions about monoculture and multiculture, again considering the benefits and potential of systems like Pollan's at Polyface Farm.

Virginia Postrel

The Boundaries of Design

(text pp. 296–330)

Selection Overview

In "The Boundaries of Design," Virginia Postrel explores the increasing regulation of design as it applies to private and public spaces and argues that design can serve a number of aesthetic and pragmatic purposes. She begins her argument by citing a number of attempts to establish "aesthetic boundaries" that regulate architectural design in private and public spaces because people consistently demand limitations on the aesthetic choices of others. She links these types of regulations to decisions that reflect other types of aesthetic choice, including employers' regulations and preferences surrounding employees' personal appearance. Postrel questions the relevance of aesthetic considerations, offering that while limitations to aesthetics in architectural design are generally supported by legal institutions, regulation of personal appearance is not. One of Postrel's most accessible examples is in her discussion of the legal case and corresponding media treatment of an overweight woman who sued Jazzercise for discrimination because they would not hire her as an instructor. The EEOC ruled that this decision was based on aesthetics rather than function, and the media's commentary on the case sparked a great deal of public disapproval of Jazzercise's position. Postrel argues that Jazzercise's aesthetic choice did not prove to be a successful business decision, since many commentators completely disagreed. Although Postrel notes that we can never really agree on aesthetic issues, she argues that our propensity to judge aesthetics limits our ability to understand the aesthetic values that others hold. She also finds regulating along aesthetic lines narrows the full range of aesthetic value, disallowing the creation of new pleasure and meaning through aesthetic development. We must consider all of the costs and benefits involved in aesthetic choices in order to make decisions that are the most beneficial to everyone involved. Ultimately we can only establish design boundaries in smaller units rather than regulate aesthetic principles on a larger scale. One of the concerns Postrel addresses is "spillover," or the collateral aesthetic cost that one area may face because of the aesthetic decisions made in a neighboring area. For Postrel, regulation of design assumes that people's aesthetics needs can be generalized and tend to promote consistent, unvaried aesthetics. On the other hand, specialization encourages designers to create unique communities, according to individual or small groups' tastes.

> **Concepts include:** aesthetic imperative, aesthetic personality, design boundaries, homogeneity, New Urbanism, spillover, visual pollution
> **Themes include:** aesthetic value, community, design, government, law and regulation
> **Works best with:** Appiah, Kimmelman, Savan, Serano, Taylor, Yoshino

Questions and Assignments

Postrel's essay is complex and may feel long to students. The Questions for Critical Reading give students specific points of focus and concentrate on Postrel's terms and concepts and help them develop the language to discuss the concepts she uses in this excerpt. Question 1 of Questions for Critical Reading challenges students to explore the concept of aesthetic boundaries and extend Postrel's argument about their influence on design. Question 2 asks students to use Postrel's examples to determine an appropriate role of legislation in aesthetics, particularly looking at the types of examples (architecture and personal appearance) that Postrel highlights in her essay. The last critical concept addressed in this section is Postrel's idea of "spillovers." Question 3 asks students to define the term and its function in determining aesthetic boundaries.

Students may have very limited experience in discussing and considering aesthetic issues. The Questions for Exploring Context for this selection direct students toward concrete examples of aesthetic regulation in order to help them further understand the conceptual argument Postrel makes. Question 1 asks students to research Princeton University's Frist Campus Center, an example that Postrel uses to discuss aesthetic conflict. This question encourages students to explore the center's Web site and examine how it is now viewed, paying particular attention to aesthetic boundaries in its presentation on the Web and references to the original dispute surrounding the building's design. Question 2 of Exploring Context ask students to look up local design ordinances in their own communities to apply Postrel's argument to local examples and discuss the specific role of local legislation and build on their responses to question 2 of Questions for Critical Reading. Question 3 of Exploring Context asks students to apply Postrel's analysis to aesthetic boundaries in virtual space by locating an example on MySpace of a page that lacks aesthetic value. Students are then asked to analyze the presence of that space using Postrel's text and their discussion of aesthetic boundaries from question 1 of Questions for Critical Reading.

Because aesthetics may seem esoteric to students, the Questions for Connecting help students to link Postrel's discussion of aesthetics into broader themes of art, beauty, and social interaction. Question 1 challenges students to use Postrel's arguments about aesthetics and Michael Kimmelman's discussion of collections as an art form to develop a definition of art and discuss its boundaries. This assignment encourages students to think about the implications of Postrel's argument in a larger framework than she provides within the text. Students generally relate most clearly to Postrel's discussion of personal aesthetics in evaluating the Jazzercise lawsuit; question 2 of Questions for Connecting encourages students to explore personal aesthetics by applying Postrel's ideas to Serano's discussion of beauty in "Before and After: Class and Body Transformations" (p. 392). In order to help students understand Postrel's conclusion, question 3 asks students to examine the pluralism that Postrel identifies in design in light of Kwame Anthony Appiah's ideas in "Making Conversation" (p. 57) and "The Primacy of Practice" (p. 63), exploring the application of "primacy of practice" to conflicts in aesthetic values.

The Assignments for Writing help students focus more clearly on larger concepts in the text with which they can more easily relate. Question 1 challenges students to explore the conflict between the imposition of others' creativity (or aesthetic values) and individual expressions of creativity by asking them whether freedom of expression in design could cause subjective harm. While Postrel acknowledges individuals' desire for creative freedom, she notes that people also tend to be offended by others' aesthetic choices. Question 2 asks students to approach the conflict Postrel identifies between aesthetic expression and aesthetic control in terms of individuality, creativity, and conformity. While students may have some trouble relating to design in architecture, most will take an active interest in these issues that can be then channeled into a productive engagement of this excerpt. Finally, the boundaries of design can be considered an ethical issue in that they affect individual freedom of expression. The third assignment asks students to explore the ethics of legislative regulation of aesthetics and build on their discussion of the role of legislation in design in question 2 of Questions for Critical Reading.

Richard Restak

Attention Deficit: The Brain Syndrome of Our Era

(text pp. 331–346)

Selection Overview

In "Attention Deficit: The Brain Syndrome of Our Era," Restak argues that exposure to technology is reshaping the functions of our brains. Restak begins by describing the effect of crawlers (moving type across the screen during newscasts), one of many technological advances that force us to divide our focus in order to compile information. Such technologies also split our attention, moving us into a hyperactive state of being. While Restak argues that people have always needed to multitask, advances in technology and in the roles we play force us to split our attention even further, giving rise to Attention Deficit Disorder (ADD) and Attention Deficit Hyperactivity Disorder (ADHD). After defining these disorders as they occur in children and adults, Restak points out that they arise without hereditary disposition, suggesting that they are culturally produced. Restak cites several experts on ADD and ADHD who argue that the constant noise of modern life, the contemporary pressure to listen and speak quickly, and the rise of technologies that keep us in perpetual contact with the world all contribute to the changing functions of our brains. In considering the affects of these pressures on our brains and personalities, Restak also points out that communication technologies affect our identity and behavior. Social critics and historians alike have noted the rise of "modern nerves" and the quick rhythm of modern life, both of which require the brain to adjust to take in an increasingly large amount of information at ever faster speeds. For Restak, telecommunications also allow us to exist in several locations at once, conflating our sense of time and place. Restak does offer some solution to the problems that arise from our constant pressure to multitask, including researching cerebral geography to find ways to activate different parts of the brain simultaneously rather than attempting to engage the same part of the brain in more than one activity.

> **Concepts include:** attention disorders, cerebral geography, cognitive style, modern nerves
> **Themes include:** attention, biology, brain science, evolution, modern life, multitasking, technology
> **Works best with:** Didion, Friedman, Fukuyama, Gilbert, Johnson, Poe

Questions and Assignments

Because Restak writes about a phenomenon that is widely apparent in modern life, students may have difficulty seeing the disadvantages of split attention and the emphasis on multitasking. The first Question for Critical Reading asks students to engage Restak's text to understand his assertions about the problematic nature of multitasking and relate the phenomenon to their own experience. Question 2 broadly asks how culture affects biology and asks students to look for the particular aspects of modern culture that Restak identifies as causing change in who and what we are. The final question asks students to analyze the term *modern nerves* using Restak's excerpt and their own experience. Students may not have a clear reference for anything other than what Restak refers to as the modern condition. This question may help them grasp the elements of change Restak identifies with relatively recent technologies.

Because technology is so integral to their lives, students today have experience with the assumptions behind Restak's arguments, and the Questions for Exploring Context for this section help students relate their own experience to the phenomena Restak describes. Question 1 asks students to take an online ADD/ADHD assessment to evaluate whether their score is consistent with Restak's argument. Their responses are connected to their work on question 1 of Questions for Critical Reading. Question 2 of Exploring Context asks students to consider blogging in light of Restak's argument by asking them to consider the relationship between constant connection through the Internet and "modern nerves," a concept explored in question 3 of Questions for Critical Reading. The final Exploring Context question challenges students to play a multitasking game online in order to determine whether their own experience of multitasking is consistent with Restak's argument. In order to do this, they will need to refer to their work in question 1 of Questions for Critical Reading.

Although Restak uses clear, straightforward examples, it may be difficult for students to grasp the larger implications of his argument. One way to extend Restak's assertions beyond the text is to look at its connections to other themes, specifically globalization, ethics, and evolution. Question 1 of Questions for Connecting asks students to link multitasking to Kwame Anthony Appiah's arguments in "Making Conversation" (p. 57) and "The Primacy of Practice" (p. 63) by considering how Appiah's understanding of primacy of practice can explain and resolve the difficulties Restak sees in our brains' abilities to cope with technology. The second question asks students to consider multitasking as an ethical issue in light of the Dalai Lama's discussion of the ethical implications of new technologies in "Ethics and the New Genetics" (p. 76). The third question asks students to consider the affects of culture on our bodies by looking at Restak's argument in tandem with Julia Serano's ideas in "Before and After: Class and Body Transformations" (p. 392).

Having had the opportunity to explore the specific examples Restak uses in the Questions for Critical Reading and Exploring Context, the Assignments for Writing encourage students to assess the broader implications of Restak's argument. Question 1 challenges students to examine the potential benefits that could result from changes in our brain functions that arise from technology. Restak provides a clear discussion of the types of changes technology has produced in our brain functions, but he does not necessarily find these changes helpful or productive. This question allows students to continue Restak's discussion of looking at how we might embrace and utilize these changes in the future. The next Assignment for Writing asks students to use Restak's work and their own experience to look at the role of emerging forms of media in shaping our attention. Restak's text gives several examples of media that split our attention; since media technologies have expanded and become more common, students should be able to relate well to this assignment. Finally, the last question asks students to draw on their work in Questions for Critical Reading 1 and question 3 of Exploring Context in order to use their own experience to assess the effects of multitasking on our brains.

Mary Roach

The Cadaver Who Joined the Army

(text pp. 347–362)

Selection Overview

In "The Cadaver Who Joined the Army," Mary Roach examines the history of the use of cadavers in ballistics research. She describes the humanitarian goals of this research as attempting to facilitate efficiency in halting an enemy. Through interviewing several specialists in cadaver research, Roach traces the history of researching "stopping power" on both hanging cadavers and on animals. While Roach points out that there are bases for considering "stopping power" as a by-product of neurology and of psychology, neither of these possibilities can be accurately assessed in research on animals. In order to test physical ballistics damage, researchers have developed new technologies using gelatin to simulate body parts. Proponents of this type of technology expressed reluctance to discuss with Roach similar research on cadavers. Despite this reluctance, researchers who develop gelatin models for the military are not concerned with humanitarian goals and are aiming instead to inflict as much damage as possible. Researchers' reluctance to use cadavers in ballistics research is partially due to the difficulties involved in negotiating what constitutes informed consent. Most of the researchers Roach spoke to did not consider it necessary to inform subjects and their families of the details of the research that would be done on a cadaver, but they stopped short of including ballistics research in this assessment. Ultimately, Roach notes that she, like many researchers involved in cadaver research, would not hesitate to donate her own body for research of this kind.

> **Concepts include:** informed consent, humanitarian research, stopping power
> **Themes include:** biomedical ethics, cadaver rights, cost vs. benefit, death, morality, public relations, research
> **Works best with:** Dalai Lama, Didion, Fukuyama, Pollan, Taylor, Yoshino

Questions and Assignments

Because Roach's research is graphic and deals with sensitive material, it is necessary to move students beyond emphasizing the grotesque aspects. The Questions for Critical Reading help students to focus on issues of research and science and move them away from concentrating on the gory and emotional aspects of the essay. Question 1 asks students to consider whether publicly funded ballistics research should be permitted on cadavers, challenging students to identify and engage Roach's argument. Question 2 asks students to decipher Roach's definition of informed consent and the conditions necessary for its validity. This will help students to explore a key issue in this essay that they may tend to overlook. The final question asks the broader question of how we should limit scientific research and expand on Roach's text to develop a concrete recommendation for how to move forward. This question will help students consider Roach's discussion in light of other types of scientific research.

Because students have most likely never encountered this type of research, Exploring Context questions challenge students to better understand the current issues surrounding ballistics research in order to consider Roach's argument as it relates to the very specific field she discusses. Question 1 prompts students to research the Bodies Exhibition Web site, asking students what role ethics play in the controversy surrounding the use of human bodies for this purpose. While Roach's essay may be shocking to students, visiting the Web site for Bodies . . . The Exhibition may be a good entry point to looking at the use of cadavers in a less violent setting. Question 2 asks students to research the Armed Forces Institute of Pathology, a research center that Roach describes, to explore the information provided on ballistics trauma research. Students are then asked to connect this information to their responses to questions 1 and 3 of Questions for Critical Reading. The final Exploring Context question asks students to look further into the production of ballistics gel and explore the attitude of its manufacturers toward it use.

The Questions for Connecting emphasize the particular considerations involved in how we treat our bodies. This will help students contextualize the use of human bodies in research in the larger discussion provided by other authors in *Emerging* surrounding the treatment of living and dead bodies in other settings. Question 1 of Questions for Connecting asks students to explore Roach's text in terms of the notion of human dignity, as explained by Francis Fukuyama (p. 142). Question 2 encourages students to explore the cultural roles the body can play after death through comparing Roach's analysis with Diana Taylor's exploration of death and mourning in "False Identifications: Minority Populations Mourn Diana" (p. 454). Finally, the third question prompts students to consider the donation of a body to science in terms of Daniel Gilbert's "Reporting Live from Tomorrow" (p. 169) by exploring the possibility of determining future happiness, the use of surrogation, and the definition of informed consent they developed in question 2 of Questions for Critical Reading.

The Assignments for Writing focus on specific themes in Roach's work, including objectification of the body, the relationship between science and ethics, and the possibility of considering the greater good involved in scientific research. Question 1 asks students to locate an example of objectification of the human body and explore Roach's assertions that researchers tend to approach cadavers as objects in ballistics research. One place to begin is with their work on the Web site for Bodies . . . The Exhibition in question 1 of Exploring Context. Question 2 of Assignments for Writing asks students to use Roach's work to evaluate the relationship between scientific research and ethical beleifs, building on question 3 of Questions for Critical Reading and question 1 of Exploring Context. The final question of Assignments for Writing asks students to consider Roach's argument in the context of a current conflict and asks them to explore the idea that the greater good may be at stake in research on cadavers.

Leslie Savan

What's Black, Then White, and Said All Over?

(text pp. 363–390)

Selection Overview

In "What's Black, Then White, and Said All Over?" Leslie Savan explores the appropriation of African American vernacular (AAVE), or "black talk," by the media and mainstream culture in America. While arguing that black talk has been extremely influential in the development of American English, Savan also points out that black talk, traditionally a language of the excluded, has had nearly as great an influence on pop culture as it has on language. Black talk has introduced the iconic "cool," creating a template for pop culture and its language. *Cool* is heavily intertwined with identity; for Savan, mainstream America's emphasis on "cool" is part and parcel of identification with the excluded. Savan points out that historically the intersection of mainstream America and black culture in entertainment has been fraught with racism. Black talk has made a major entrance into the media scene through hiphop, appropriating its language for commercial profit. Savan defines black talk as not simply words that *originate* in black talk, but rather phrases whose popular meaning was created by African Americans, and she points out that most black talk has roots in standard American English and gains meaning through nuance. Savan identifies wannabes, specifically in terms of linguistics, arguing that with the rising popularity of black talk, many whites have reversed the traditional field of wannabes by emulating black talk. For Savan, this emulation is inextricably linked to the history of racism in the United States. Savan extends her argument into the realm of spelling, arguing that abbreviation, codes, and deliberate changes in spelling are also linked to black talk and have been just as readily appropriated into popular culture. Savan finds all of these uses of black talk participating in "covert prestige," the attitude she identifies in speakers of standard English who appropriate black terms. The appropriation of black language for Savan is characterized by an underlying theme of racism. It is perhaps because of this covert prestige that black talk has been so successful in the media, where it is constantly appropriated, even to the point of copyrighting specific phrases. Savan points out that even in cases where black talk is merely "borrowed" by the media or by mainstream speakers, each profits without having originated anything of use. This excerpt ends in a discussion of mainstream resistance to black talk in the classroom, where black talk and the identity that comes with it are still met with discrimination.

Concepts include: black talk, covert prestige, the evolution of cool, fetishization
Themes include: appropriation, dialects, discrimination, exclusion, hiphop, language, the media, popular culture, race, slang
Works best with: Alvarez, Epstein, Johnson, Nathan, Olson, Poe, Postrel, Serano, Spar, Taylor, Yoshino

Questions and Assignments

Because use of black language in the media and popular culture has been so prevalent and widely accepted in the last twenty years, the topics in Savan's essay are so close to students' lived experience that they may need help achieving a critical distance from the essay's content in order fully engage her argument about racism and appropriation. The first Question for Critical Reading asks students to define *covert prestige* using Savan's text and then extend their defini-tion into an example outside the text. Question 2 asks students to explore "pay-ing the dues" in order to understand Savan's discussion of ownership and credit for black language. Finally, the last question asks students to suggest why black talk in particular is so widely used in advertising. This will help students to en-gage the text on a deeper level and fully comprehend Savan's discussion of black identity and the history of racism in the United States.

In order to help students understand Savan's discussion in terms of the perasiveness of media that has most likely gone unnoticed, question 1 of Ex-ploring Context prompts students to explore advertising on the Web to locate uses of slang and then apply Savan's argument to these examples. The second question asks students to visit the Web site Black People Love Us, and use its content to extend Savan's brief discussion of the site, building on their re-sponses to questions 1 and 3 of Questions for Critical Reading. The last question requires students to research local initiatives surrounding Ebonics to discover contemporary discourse on black language and analyze whether Savan's discus-sion of Ebonics at the end of the excerpt still applies to popular perceptions of Ebonics.

The Questions for Connecting help students engage Savan's discussion of commercial and media interests in black language. The first question asks students to consider the successful use of language in Helen Epstein's "AIDS, Inc." (p. 106) in light of Savan's argument and tie them together by examining the means of advertising discussed in each. The second question focuses on Julia Alvarez's discussion of retroculturation in "Selections from *Once Upon a Quinceañera*" (p. 35) to examine the relationship among covert prestige, pay-ing the dues, and retroculturation in order to discuss whether retroculturation affects these phenomena. The final question asks students to use Savan's argu-ment to complicate the globalization discussed in Thomas Friedman's "The Dell Theory of Conflict Prevention" (p. 121) and explore issues of culture and com-mercialization in both essays.

The Assignments for Writing help students extend Savan's arguments into arenas outside popular culture that Savan identifies as having been affected by attitudes towards black talk. First, students are asked to evaluate educational standards of language in order to evaluate the efficacy of current treatment of Ebonics in the classroom, drawing on their responses to question 3 of Explor-ing Context. Question 2 of Assignments for Writing asks students to apply the basis of Savan's argument to another example of culture that has been appro-priated by mainstream America, looking specifically at the issues Savan locates in uses of black talk in popular culture and the media. The last assignment asks students to explore the broader cultural implications of Savan's argument by forming an argument about the ideal of the American "melting pot." Re-sponses to this assignment should include discussion of cultural identity and appropriation.

Julia Serano

Before and After:
Class and Body Transformations
(text pp. 391–400)

Selection Overview

In "Before and After: Class and Body Transformations," Julia Serano argues that media treatment of transsexuals focuses exclusively on physical transformations, rather than emphasizing the cultural, psychological, and social aspects of transition. Describing her own experiences in coming out as a transsexual, Serano notes that others questioned the physical aspect of her experience the most. She also links her experience to television shows about procedures like plastic surgeries and gastric bypass, which also highlight subjects undergoing bodily transformations through surgical procedures; she argues that the sensationalistic presentation of such shows is different than shows depicting makeovers. For Serano, there is no element of voyeurism in the presentation of a subject who has merely changed their appearance without altering his or her body. At the core of the sensationalism surrounding plastic surgeries, gastric bypasses, and sex reassignment is the idea that people who undergo these procedures cross what Serano terms "class boundaries," which include the unstated borders between fat and thin, male and female, and ugly and beautiful. Serano argues that we derive social status from our attractiveness, and notes that witnessing a drastic change in attractiveness can alter our response to the idea of beauty. Similarly, she notes that people realize their attitudes surrounding gender when in contact with another person who has crossed the boundaries of gender. Because most people act to reinforce class boundaries, we tend to play up the artificial characteristics of such a transformation, even though the class systems themselves are inherently artificial. Serano points out that highlighting the artificiality of sex reassignment through depicting a variation of medical and nonmedical procedures dismisses the large number of transgendered people who pass without these procedures and who are, prior to their transition, already permeating gender barriers. Serano finds that these depictions of exaggerated artificiality serve to reinforce gender stereotypes and objectify transgendered bodies.

> **Concepts include:** assigned sex vs. subconscious sex, class boundaries, gender identity, gender transition
> **Themes include:** authenticity, beauty, class, gender categories, gender relations, sensationalism, social fabric
> **Works best with:** Alvarez, Olson, Postrel, Savan, Taylor, Yoshino

Questions and Assignments

Students may tend to focus on Serano's transsexualism, which may feel alien or threatening to them. Such focus obscures Serano's discussion of class and gender, which are key elements in this excerpt. To help students focus on a critical approach to these ideas, the Questions for Critical Reading give students clear entries into the issues that drive this essay, including beauty, gender, and class. Question 1 asks students to explore the relationship between physical appearance and class and to relate this discussion in Serano's text to additional examples that support her argument. Question 2 addresses Serano's discussion of nature and gender, another portion of the essay students may have some difficulty engaging. This question encourages students to use Serano's text to explore gender as a natural phenomenon. The third question asks students to evaluate Serano's assertion that people are fascinated with before-and-after photos of physical transformations and asks students to explain the reasoning behind this assertion.

The Exploring Context questions for this essay give students the opportunity to visually explore the issues of representation that are so vital to Serano's argument, while keeping their focus on her arguments about gender and beauty. The first question directs students to Julia Serano's Web site to evaluate whether its content reflects the arguments she makes about representation in her essay. In order to help students relate to the assertions Serano makes about viewing before-and-after pictures, the second question asks them to research Serano's suggestion that before-and-after pictures of plastic surgery patients are a source of fascination. This question challenges students to explore such images online to see if their presentation fits in with Serano's arguments about viewer fascination. Students are to use their responses to class boundaries in questions 1 and 3 of Questions for Critical Reading. The final question builds on the issue of nature and gender in question 2 of Questions for Critical Reading by prompting students to research the recent "pregnant man" controversy to explore the sensationalism Serano identifies surrounding gender.

The Questions for Connecting offer several ways to look at Serano's very specific subject matter in light of broader global issues, including morality, culture, and social change. The first question asks students to apply Albright's arguments in "Faith and Diplomacy" (p. 23) in considering whether transsexualism should be approached from a religious or diplomatic point of view. This question can help students gain critical distance from the issue of transsexualism and can help diffuse tensions surrounding this issue in the classroom. Question 2 links the idea of class boundaries in Serano's work to Julia Alvarez's "Selections from *Once Upon a Quinceañera*" (p. 35) by asking students to consider whether class boundaries are crossed in Alvarez's work. This question should build from the work done on class boundaries in question 1 of Questions for Critical Reading. Question 3 of Questions for Connecting asks students to consider Kwame Anthony Appiah's "Making Conversation" (p. 57) and "The Primacy of Practice" (p. 63) in terms of learning to accept radical body transformations.

Implicit in Serano's work is the idea that physical transformations are inextricably linked to challenging class boundaries. The first Assignment for Writing asks students to explore this linkage by engaging the larger argument of Serano's text. Question 2 asks students to explore gender rights in the United States by researching transgender advocacy organizations and combining that research with the experience Serano relates in order to understand the issues transsexuals face and the ways in which these issues reflect popular perceptions of gender. Similarly, the final assignment asks students to explore the complex systems of sex and gender identity in the United States, drawing on their work in question 2 of Questions for Critical Reading.

Debora L. Spar

Trading Places: The Practice and Politics of Adoption

(text pp. 401–438)

Selection Overview

Debora L. Spar begins "Trading Places: The Practice and Politics of Adoption" by examining Rainbow Kids, an international adoption agency that she argues is representative of the growing market for adoption. Spar believes that the international adoption system often commodifies children. Tracing the development of adoption, Spar finds that the practice was historically motivated by economic concerns. Despite early hesitations about placing children from low-income homes into middle- and upper-class homes, the apparent success of shipping poor and possibly orphaned children to midwestern farms in the late nineteenth and early twentieth centuries motivated several changes in the practice of adoption, including the rise of private brokers. Spar argues that this shift signaled a boom in the business of adoption, putting an overt price tag on obtaining children that persists today. Several social factors have affected the development of the adoption industry in the United States and have motivated the growth of a market for foreign adoption as well. Spar argues that international, or cross-border adoption, is more complicated than domestic adoption because of its complex legal system and diverse population of children. Spar also points out that international adoption gives rise to a black market that occurs outside of licensed trade, places no limits on payment, and can lead to baby-selling and baby-stealing. Although these issues are specifically linked to black-market international adoption, Spar asserts that we should question the role of adoption in the broader context of the baby business. While ethical considerations fall on both sides of the discourse on commercialized adoption, a variety of options are available in how to respond to current adoption practices. The process could be placed in the hands of the government, placed in the private sector, regulated in the international market, or completely separated from the market. Recognizing that an adoption market does work well for many birth mothers, adoptive parents, and children, Spar ultimately notes that the U.S. adoption market could be seen as a model for the larger baby business because it combined for-profit and nonprofit segments and government oversight and private services.

Concepts include: adoption, black market
Themes include: class, commercialization, commodification, ethics, race
Works best with: Appiah, Dalai Lama, Epstein, Friedman, Fukuyama, Savan, Taylor, Yoshino

Questions and Assignments

Students may have trouble maintaining focused attention on Spar's argument in this long and detailed excerpt. The Questions for Critical Reading help students hone in on the specific arguments Spar makes throughout this chapter. Question 1 asks students to evaluate adoption as a compassionate social practice, a troubling economic market, or both. Because Spar's historical evidence is extensive, question 2 prompts students to consider the organization of her essay by asking them to consider why she includes historical background and how it supports her argument. Question 3 challenges students to assess the role of race in adoption and its economic function by exploring one of the crucial arguments of Spar's essay.

The Exploring Context questions encourage students to take a closer look at the adoption market and at Spar's point of view in writing this essay. Question 1 asks students to review the Rainbow Kids Web site to explore whether the representations on the Web site support Spar's argument and to assess the role of race in adoption, which expands upon question 3 of Questions for Critical Reading. Question 2 of Exploring Context directs students to analyze the representation of adoption on Adoption.com, building on their argument in question 1 of Questions for Critical Reading. Question 3 of Exploring Context requires students to explore Spar's larger work by examining her page on Barnard College's Web site.

The Questions for Connecting ask students to explore several of the aspects of adoption Spar discusses, including its economic impact and ethical considerations. Because the commercial aspects of adoption are so crucial to Spar's argument, question 1 challenges students to explore adoption as an economic practice by applying Thomas Friedman's ideas about global economics in "The Dell Theory of Conflict Prevention" (p. 121) to Spar's discussion of international adoption. This question extends their work on adoption and economy in question 1 of Questions for Critical Reading and question 2 of Exploring Context. Question 2 of Questions for Connecting challenges students to look at ethical concerns surrounding adoption in terms of the Dalai Lama's discussion of ethics in biotechnology in "Ethics and the New Genetics" (p. 76). Question 3 of Questions for Connecting also asks students to grapple with the ethical quandary of adoption, this time framing adoption in terms of Francis Fukuyama's definition of human essence in "Human Dignity" (p. 142).

The Assignments for Writing for this excerpt ask students to form their own analyses of adoption through critical examination of Spar's discussion. Question 1 asks students to explore the risks, costs, and benefits of assisted reproduction versus adoption. This question will require students to think about the ethical implications of adoption, the options that parents are faced with, and the processes that both parents and children go through in adoption. Spar is particularly concerned with international adoption. Question 2 asks students to evaluate the ethics of international adoption and expand on their work in question 1 of Questions for Critical Reading, question 1 of Exploring Context, and question 2 of Questions for Connecting. In order to understand the full implications of Spar's argument, students are asked in question 3 of Assignments for Writing to propose the most effective and humanitarian means of regulating adoption. This question will also help students think creatively about the issues Spar raises and read her text closely for examples of different types of existing regulation.

James Surowiecki

Committees, Juries, and Teams: The *Columbia* Disaster and How Small Groups Can Be Made to Work

(text pp. 439–452)

Selection Overview

James Surowiecki begins his discussion of small-group decision making by describing the failure of the Mission Management Team (MMT) to prevent the space shuttle *Columbia* catastrophe in 2003. Surowiecki notes that while the flight team noted several concerns about the foam debris that caused the disaster, the larger committee did not act on their findings, and as a result the shuttle was lost. Surowiecki admits that the *Columbia*'s MMT as whole serves as an example of the counterproductive possibilities of group-based decision making. However, he also notes that group decision making is an integral part of American life and provides a forum for people to have clear and direct influence over others' judgments. While this influence can lead to poor decision making, it can also result in the group becoming more than the sum of its parts. Part of a small group's success is due to its "swing," or the synchronization of components. For Surowiecki, another reason for the failure of small groups can be, as in the MMT's case, that they operate on faulty assumptions that create "confirmation bias," a phenomenon that predisposes a group to come up with specific decisions by discouraging debate and dissention. The MMT also lacked a full knowledge of the problem it was supposed to address, and therefore could not make an informed decision. Surowiecki also points out that hierarchy, lack of structure, and lack of cognitive diversity also contributed to this group's poor decision making. Without cognitive diversity, groups may also tend to focus on consent rather than dissent, and members of such groups will quickly fall prey to "group polarization," prompting members to come to radically different assessments because individuals tend to align themselves with one pole or another out of a tendency to rely on "social comparison." While Surowiecki acknowledges that all of these factors might lead us to abandon using small groups to make decisions, he argues that under optimal conditions, small-group interaction has been shown to produce better results than those of individuals acting alone. He finds that small groups are not inefficient, and if groups are strictly nonhierarchical, they can be much more successful in their endeavors.

> **Concepts include:** cognitive diversity, confirmation bias, group polarization, intellectual swing, social comparison
> **Themes include:** collaboration, collective wisdom, diversity, efficiency, group-based decision making
> **Works best with:** Appiah, Johnson, Nathan, Poe, Pollan

Questions and Assignments

Surowiecki presents so many concepts in this essay that students may find it difficult to understand the argument he makes within the text. Question 1 of Questions for Critical Reading helps students begin to understand and organize Surowiecki's concepts by identifying the elements and conditions necessary for small groups to make successful decisions. In question 2, students are asked to use the text to define and give an example of "group polarization," a specific concept that Surowiecki presents in detail as a factor in the success of small groups. Finally, in the third question, students are prompted to assess whether Surowiecki finds small groups to be worth the risk and form their own argument about small-group viability.

The Exploring Context questions encourage students to look further into the background of several of the issues Surowiecki discusses. The first question asks students to research NASA's Web site to evaluate whether there is evidence of changing conditions in NASA's decision making that could prevent such a disaster from happening again. Juries are another example of small groups that we rely on to make decisions; the second question of Exploring Context asks students to visit the Web site for the Advocates, a jury consulting firm, to evaluate their approach to small-group dynamics of a jury. The third question asks students to consider the technology that facilitates small-group work online, with particular attention to whether that interface lends more to their success than the examples Surowiecki provides.

The Questions for Connecting extend Surowiecki's assessment of small groups to the other types and functions of small groups in contemporary culture. Question 1 asks students to use Surowiecki's argument to explain the failure of community and diversity on college campuses that Rebekah Nathan describes in "Community and Diversity" (p. 228). In Michael Pollan's "The Animals: Practicing Complexity" (p. 281), we are presented with a very different model of small groups. Question 2 prompts students to extrapolate the aspects of organic farming that facilitate its success and apply their findings to Surowiecki's discussion. Students are to build on their work in question 1 of Questions for Critical Reading. Another facet of small groups can be located in Thomas Friedman's discussion of global supply chains in "The Dell Theory of Conflict Prevention" (p. 121). Question 3 asks students to look at the economic risks and benefits of small groups in this context.

The Assignments for Writing ask students to expand upon their work in Questions for Critical Reading. Building on the first Question for Critical Reading, the first Assignment for Writing requires students to determine the best practices for organizing and running a small group by using the characteristics of small groups that Surowiecki describes.

As any small group is made up of individuals, question 2 of Assignments for Writing asks students to assess the influence of an individual in a group setting by using their response to question 2 of Questions for Critical Reading, as well as other examples from the text. Question 3 of Assignments for Writing asks students to evaluate Surowiecki's description of the Mission Management Team's dynamics and components, looking in particular for the errors and flaws in judgment and logic that led to its failure.

Diana Taylor

False Identifications: Minority Populations Mourn Diana

(text pp. 453–478)

Selection Overview

Taylor begins this selection by describing her experience with watching Princess Diana's funeral procession and the conflicting emotions of being caught in its drama and grief. Taylor points out that the spectacle of Diana's death was particularly problematic for minorities and questions the mechanism that gave Diana such popular appeal, arguing that a number of issues associated with the iconic Diana gave her life and death a veneer of universal appeal. Taylor argues that this appeal is a product of staging and social drama. She also explains that Victor Turner's four stages of "social drama" (social rupture, crisis, redressive action, and reintegration) gave Diana's life and death theatricality, and this social drama participates in surrogation, particularly because the patterns of social drama are repetitive. Noting that the "ontology of performance" is absolutely linked to the present, Taylor suggests that its opposite, "hauntology," brings the past into the present by repeating, making sacred, and resuscitating something that has already disappeared. Taylor argues against other perceptions of performance as being purely in the present, instead noting that performance brings out the invisible concepts, influences, and "ghosts" and plays an integral role in the future. Because visibility is necessary to produce these aspects of performance, Taylor examines the preservation of Evita's corpse, which she argues anchored Evita's specter by keeping her "ghost" alive in Argentine politics long after her death. Taylor finds that Diana's mourning has been universalized in ways that the deaths of minority figures, like Selena and Evita, have not. For Taylor, this lasting specter has to do with the extremely publicized social drama surrounding Diana's life and death, her ever-present royalty, her iconic qualities, and the various social agendas Diana was linked to in the public eye. Taylor also argues that minority identification with and mourning of Diana places her death within local communities, moving the dialogue surrounding economic, transnational, and colonial subjectivity into a new arena.

> **Concepts include:** ghosting, hauntology, ontology of performance, social drama
> **Themes include:** class, cultural values, cultural dominance, death, gender, iconography, identification, mourning, performance, race, spectacle, theatricality
> **Works best with:** Albright, Alvarez, Appiah, Didion, Epstein, Friedman, Gilbert, Nathan, Olson, Postrel, Roach, Savan, Serano, Spar

Questions and Assignments

As Taylor's argument rests on a series of terms she creates and defines, the Questions for Critical Reading for this selection help students to understand the particular terms Taylor uses in making her argument. Since these terms are also related to common usage, students will need to closely read her essay to understand the significance Taylor lends to these terms. Question 1 asks students to use Taylor's text to define "social drama" and to link their definition to an example from outside the text. Question 2 prompts students to look at Taylor's very specific uses of the term *ghosting,* first defining it according to the text and then assessing the role it plays in Taylor's argument. Question 3 asks students to answer the overall question that concerns Taylor: why minority populations mourn figures like Princess Diana.

The Exploring Context questions challenge students to explore the contemporary pop culture surrounding iconic figures. Question 1 prompts students to visit a tribute site for Princess Diana to assess how well it reflects Taylor's argument and to pay close attention to the demographics of the populations that still continue to mourn. This question builds on the exploration of public mourning begun in question 3 of Questions for Critical Reading. Question 2 of Exploring Context requires students to research another Web site commemorating a famous death. In particular, students will want to explore the ways mourning is presented online, the populations represented, and the social drama or ghosting that is apparent by applying their work in questions 1 and 2 of Questions for Critical Reading and Taylor's argument to this new example. Question 3 of Exploring Context asks students to use Google Fight to compare the results from searching two public figures and comparing the search results. Since Taylor argues that some aspects of public mourning for Diana do not hold true for other public figures, this question is intended to evaluate the resonance of Taylor's arguments in relation to other public figures and builds on the definitions and terms addressed in the Questions for Critical Reading.

In many ways, Taylor is concerned with the appropriation of identification in racialized and colonial subjects. Question 1 of Questions for Connecting prompts students to use Taylor's text to further explain the appropriation of black talk as explained by Leslie Savan in "What's Black, Then White, and Said All Over?" (p. 363), using definitions of Taylor's terms from Questions for Critical Reading to see if Taylor's arguments about them can be applied to Savan's discussion. Question 2 of Questions for Connecting calls for an application of Kwame Anthony Appiah's ideas in "Making Conversation" (p. 57) and "The Primacy of Practice" (p. 63) to Taylor's argument, with particular attention to primacy of practice in mourning and the possibility that the identifications Taylor examines can be read as cosmopolitan. Question 3 of Questions for Connecting asks students to examine Taylor's concepts of hauntology and social drama in light of Debora L. Spar's commentary on adoption in "Trading Places: The Practice and Politics of Adoption" (p. 402). This question transports the idea of false identification into the arena of international adoption.

The Assignments for Writing ask students to frame Taylor's arguments in terms of broader issues surrounding pop culture, celebrity, and tragedy. The first Assignment for Writing directs students to evaluate the relationship between culture and politics by evaluating the role of popular culture in political discourse. This will help students to extend Taylor's discussion of mass appeal, false identification, and performance. The second Assignment for Writing prompts students to expand Taylor's discussion of Princess Diana into a larger argument about the power of celebrity by looking at the public's positive and negative identifications with celebrities and evaluating the influence of location, religion, nationality, gender, and race on individual and group reaction to celebrity. The final Assignment for Writing asks students to develop Taylor's arguments about why different people identify with Diana and her tragic death. In particular, this question asks students to consider individual and group identities, social drama, and collective imagining in order to build a successful argument about this phenomenon.

Kenji Yoshino

Preface *and* The New Civil Rights

(text pp. 479–490)

Selection Overview

In his "Preface" to *Covering: A Hidden Assault on Our Civil Rights,* Kenji Yoshino begins by defining *covering* as concealing a portion of one's identity to meet mainstream expectations. Yoshino cites several examples of covering, including celebrities and politicians who assume different names and appearances to downplay traits like race, ethnicity, disability, and gender. Linking covering to assimilation, he argues that despite the evolution of American culture from "the melting pot" to a celebration of diversity, we are now undergoing a return to assimilation that is both unhealthy for the individual and constitutes a hidden assault on our civil rights. In "The New Civil Rights," Yoshino describes D. W. Winicott's distinction between the True Self and the False Self, who interact together in order to support a healthy psyche. The False Self in a healthy individual should only present itself enough to allow the True Self to meet its full potential. Yoshino argues that the pressure on any individual to assimilate should be minimized to promote the individual's health and happiness and to fully respect the individuals' civil rights. He further suggests that civil rights must expand to encompass individual authenticity, citing several Supreme Court rulings on suits brought by members of disenfranchised groups and that these cases are about the rights of all individuals and not the rights related to any particular group of individuals. Such decisions constitute what Yoshino refers to as "liberty claims." These differ from "equality claims" in that they are not based in group membership but consider the needs of every individual. Yoshino argues that liberty claims are not only consistent with the philosophical origins of the civil rights movement in the United States but also moved us away from essentializing identity. Although Yoshino argues that changing the basis for civil rights will move us away from demands to assimilate, he also recognizes that the real, practical task of civil rights must happen outside of the courtroom in reason-forming conversations that allow humanity to flourish.

> **Concepts include:** assimilation, covering, group-based equality paradigm, true self and false self, universal liberty paradigm
> **Themes include:** the American melting pot, authenticity, civil rights, disability, ethnicity, gender, government, multiculturalism, race
> **Works best with:** Albright, Alvarez, Appiah, Dalai Lama, Esptein, Fukuyama, Johnson, Nathan, Olson, Poe, Postrel, Savan, Serano, Spar

Questions and Assignments

While most students can easily relate to the concept of covering, they may have some difficulty in conceptualizing the difference between the civil rights models Yoshino describes. Question 1 of Questions for Critical Reading directs students to use the text to define the "new" civil rights and in particular explain how they differ from previous conceptions of civil rights and how they address liberty and equality paradigms. Question 2 asks students to define *covering* using the text, and then apply the concept to their own example. Students should highlight the persistence and frequency of covering in contemporary society. Question 3 builds on both of the previous questions by asking students to read closely for Yoshino's recommendations for how we can achieve the new civil rights.

The Exploring Context questions encourage students to closely examine the legal context for civil rights in the United States. Students may have a hard time grasping the complexity of the conceptual framework Yoshino suggests for civil rights, so looking at concrete examples of civil rights in action will help students connect more closely with Yoshino's overall argument. The first Exploring Context question asks students to use the Web site for the U.S. Commission on Civil Rights to extend their definitions from question 1 of Questions for Critical Reading into current views on civil rights in the United States. In order to understand Yoshino's use of law suits as examples in his argument, the second question of Exploring Context directs students to research recent civil rights cases and explore how they relate to Yoshino's argument. The final Exploring Context question asks students to examine Yoshino's assertion that civil rights should be addressed through conversation by searching BlogPulse's trend tool for discussions about civil rights and connecting their results to the ideas developed in question 3 of Questions for Critical Reading.

Since Yoshino's argument centers around changing the way we view civil rights, the Questions for Connecting encourage students to look at social and philosophical discussions surrounding social change. This will help students connect with the conceptual grounds upon which change begins and link these grounds to the arguments of other authors whose work focuses on related fields. The first Question for Connecting asks students to explore "conversation" as a tool in Kwame Anthony Appiah's "Making Conversation" (p. 57) and "The Primacy of Practice" (p. 63) and Yoshino's excerpts to explore whether Yoshino argues in favor of a cosmopolitan approach and whether civil rights can be considered in the same light as other changing social practices. Question 2 of Questions for Connecting considers Virginia Postrel's assertions about aesthetics in "The Boundaries of Design" (p. 296) in light of civil rights and individual liberties and asks students to connect her ideas about aesthetics to Yoshino's new civil rights by building on their understanding of the new civil rights from question 1 of Questions for Critical Reading. This question will also help students understand the role of legislation as a determining factor in the lives of individuals. The final Question for Connecting asks students to explore the role Francis Fukuyama's concept of human dignity plays in civil rights.

The Assignments for Writing on this selection help students extend Yoshino's ideas into their experience of contemporary society. First, students are asked to work out the relationship between covering and civil rights by exploring their own example of covering (this can be done by building on the second question in Questions for Critical Reading). Next, the second assignment asks students to suggest changes that need to be made in civil rights and the ways in which we could go about making these changes by building on their discussion of liberty and equality paradigms in questions 1 and 3 of Questions for Critical Reading and question 2 of Exploring Context. Finally, the third assignment asks students to expand upon their work in question 2 of Exploring Context in order to build an argument about the role of conversation in social change.

Chapter 8
Sequences and Assignments

Introduction to Sequencing

Sequencing is a key feature of our pedagogy at FAU. By *sequencing*, we mean that the assignments of the semester build on each other, often by developing a common theme. Thus, while the first paper focuses only on the first reading, subsequent assignments work with multiple readings, continually returning to previous essays.

We believe that using a sequenced approach to writing assignments emphasizes process-centered strategies for writing since students return not only to their drafts but to the ideas and texts on which those drafts are based, encouraging them to revise not simply words but positions, ideas, and thinking. Sequencing also shows students how ideas reverberate across readings and disciplines by providing students a more complete model of how knowledge is created and circulated both inside and outside the academy.

Overview of Sequences in *Emerging*

The ten sequences included in *Emerging* cover a broad spectrum of themes from self-identity and community, to ethics, to technology, to art and aesthetics. We consciously designed these sequences to cover all of the readings of the text and, more importantly, to suggest the multiple ways in which these readings could be sequences to highlight particular issues in each reading.

Each sequence contains 4–6 assignments that work together and work with four readings to introduce, explore, and develop a central theme. The "tags" that accompany each reading provide a quick sense of the issues at play, while the description and introduction offer a full sense of the movement of thought and writing that students will experience.

Take, for example, the sequence "Wonderful Displays: Revelations of Art and Culture: Kimmelman, Taylor, Postrel, Restak," which focuses on the ways in which art, aesthetics, and performance operate on and in cultures. Students begin by working with Michael Kimmelman's ideas about art and the art of collecting by locating their own example of a "wonder cabinet." The second assignment, which focuses on Diana Taylor's exploration of public mourning, asks students to extend their work by considering the same issues in relation to performance. The third assignment brings Virginia Postrel into the discussion and focuses on the relation between the rights of communities and of individuals in relation to art and aesthetics. The next assignment extends that work by looking at the role of order and chaos in art and communities, which leads into the fifth assignment focusing on the ethics of censorship. To end the sequence, students use Richard Restak's discussion of brain science to determine the impact that technology has on creativity.

Throughout the sequence, students consider multiple aspects of several issues: art and aesthetics, communities and individuals, ethics and rights, and technology. With each assignment, their thinking on these issues becomes more complex as they return to previous ideas looking through new lenses.

Using Sequences in Your Classroom

Generally speaking, you will only be able to complete one sequence of assignments in the course of a semester. You may want to select a sequence based on the readings, the theme, or current events in the world. All of the included sequences have 4–6 assignments, which represent the minimum and maximum requirements for our writing courses at FAU. Four assignments allow for more revision; six assignments provide constant practice with writing. Given the demands of your program you may want to adapt your selected sequence, adding or removing assignments as needed.

Designing Your Own Sequences

Theoretically, any two randomly selected readings can be sequenced; however, you will probably find it more useful to think in terms of a developing theme around which to organize your sequence. For example, you might select a theme of globalization, death and mourning, science and ethics, networks and communities, or political processes.

A more practical method of building a sequence is to start with an essay you would enjoy teaching and then to add essays that work with that selection, letting the theme emerge as you write the accompanying assignments.

Introduction to Writing Assignments

A writing assignments is part art, part science, part experiment, and part luck. No matter how much teaching experience you have, it's always a surprisingly difficult task. Moreover, the work always remains unpredictable—what you're certain will be a successful assignment may turn out to be a disaster, in which case you adjust as needed and move on. Like the writing we ask our students to do, constant revision is essential.

However, there are some good general guidelines you can follow when working on your assignments. We'll start by thinking about sequences—why we use them, what they are, how to choose one—and then we'll cover some practices you might find useful in writing assignments of your own.

Three Types of Readings

One way to think about how to use these essays in constructing a sequence is to consider the broad general categories within which these readings fall. In this sense, we might think of three kinds of readings available:

- **Narrative.** These readings have very few ideas themselves but provide fruitful ground for testing and expanding the ideas of others. For example, Joan Didion's exploration of mourning has few concepts in itself, yet it can serve as fruitful ground for testing Daniel Gilbert's concepts about happiness.
- **Conceptual.** These readings are primarily theoretical in that they present ideas, and often these ideas are "sitting on the surface." These readings are useful because they provide students with analytical tools with which to explore other readings and with which to make arguments. Francis Fukuyama's essay, for example, is centrally concerned with the "Factor X" that makes humans human. Students can grapple with Fukuyama's text to comprehend this idea and then use that idea in the context of other essays, such as Mary Roach's "The Cadaver Who Joined the Army."
- **Mixed.** Mixed readings fall somewhere between the first two categories. While appearing to be largely narrative, they nevertheless contain useful ideas. Students, however, may have to "dig into" the text to locate and deploy these ideas. For example, Debora Spar's essay about adoption offers students ideas about ethics, globalization, and economics, though embedded in a larger narrative are ideas about adoption.

In considering a sequence, all of these types of readings are useful and you will find it fruitful to include a good mix in your sequence. For first papers, you may wish to avoid a narrative essay, since it will be difficult for students to see the essay as a piece of analytical writing and to respond with a proper argument of their own; conceptual or mixed essays tend to function better for first-paper assignments. Similarly, you may wish to avoid a paper that asks students to work with two narrative essays, since it will be difficult for them to generate ideas and form an argument centered on those ideas. The best pairings are conceptual/narrative, conceptual/conceptual, and conceptual/mixed. After all, since we are trying to get students to develop their critical thinking skills, readings that have ideas provide the best material for them to do so.

Types of Readings in *Emerging*

Madeleine Albright, Faith and Diplomacy	Narrative
Julia Alvarez, *Selections from* Once Upon a Quinceañera	Mixed
Kwame Anthony Appiah, Making Conversation *and* The Primacy of Practice	Mixed
Dalai Lama, Ethics and the New Genetics	Mixed
Joan Didion, After Life	Narrative
Helen Epstein, AIDS, Inc.	Mixed
Thomas Friedman, The Dell Theory of Conflict Prevention	Mixed
Francis Fukuyama, Human Dignity	Conceptual
Daniel Gilbert, Reporting Live from Tomorrow	Conceptual

Steven Johnson, Listening to Feedback	Mixed
Michael Kimmelman, The Art of Collecting Lightbulbs	Narrative
Rebekah Nathan, Community and Diversity	Mixed
Steve Olson, The End of Race: Hawaii and the Mixing of Peoples	Mixed
Marshall Poe, The Hive	Mixed
Michael Pollan, The Animals: Practicing Complexity	Mixed
Virginia Postrel, The Boundaries of Design	Mixed
Richard Restak, Attention Deficit: The Brain Syndrome of Our Era	Narrative
Mary Roach, The Cadaver Who Joined the Army	Narrative
Leslie Savan, What's Black, Then White, and Said All Over?	Mixed
Julia Serano, Before and After: Class and Body Transformations	Conceptual
Debora L. Spar, Trading Places: The Practice and Politics of Adoption	Narrative
James Surowiecki, Committees, Juries, and Teams: The *Columbia* Disaster and How Small Groups Can Be Made to Work	Conceptual
Diana Taylor, False Identifications: Minority Populations Mourn Diana	Mixed
Kenji Yoshino, Preface *and* The New Civil Rights	Conceptual

Skeleton Assignment

After you have selected the readings for your sequence, you will want to begin drafting the paper assignments. These assignments should always ask students to produce expository writing; that is, we wish students to make arguments in their papers. While the format of your assignments will vary according to your individual teaching style, it might be useful to consider the components of a typical assignment:

- **Introduction.** Many assignments open with some sort of introductory paragraph. You may, for example, open with a quotation from the current essay (though, should you choose to do so, be prepared to read that quotation in every paper you get), or you may introduce the topic of the assignment in relation to the reading. A good rule of thumb is to make sure you include the full name of each author in this introductory section as well as the full name of all essays involved in the assignment. That way, students will have a ready reference for the proper spelling and punctuation of both in their papers (though most surprisingly will still make errors in either or both).
- **Core.** Every assignment has a core. The core is the sentence or series of sentences that specifies what students need to do in the paper and is the exact topic on which they should write. It is generally a good idea to visually identify the core either by using bold or italics and/or by placing it in a separate paragraph.

- **Entry.** The entry section provides students ways to begin thinking about the assignment. You might provide a series of questions that point students toward possible arguments or you might provide specific warnings concerning likely but unproductive responses.
- **Apparatus.** The apparatus contains supporting information and requirements such as length requirements and due dates as well as formatting specifications.

Of course, you might choose very different ways to present your assignments. The above categories are suggested as useful guidelines only.

Choosing Verbs

However you write assignments, you will want to pay particular attention to the verbs you use. Often, the difference between a successful and unsuccessful assignment hinges on the choice of a verb. Of course, the success of any given assignment depends on a number of factors; however, in writing assignments you might want to consider the possible implications of using certain verbs. For example:

- **Explore.** *Explore* is a useful verb in assignments because it asks students to use analytical skills. However, you might find that assignments using this verb produce papers that are meandering, since "exploring" does not require students to locate a central argument.
- **Reflect.** *Reflect* implies both regurgitation and interiorization, neither of which is consistent with the goals of these courses. Just as importantly, this verb does not ask student to enter the conversation of the texts.
- **Discuss.** Like *explore*, the verb *discuss* may produce papers without any clear focus. These papers may be more generalized too.
- **Argue.** Certainly we wish students to have arguments in their papers, but using the verb *argue* suggests a black-or-white, win-or-lose position. Students are more likely to use personal attacks against the author with this verb and are more likely to force the evidence or ignore contravening pieces of text in the pursuit of arguing their case.
- **Defend.** Like *argue*, *defend* can be very combative.
- **Refute.** *Refute* is another very combative verb.

You might find other verbs more useful:

- **Extend.** *Extend* is a useful word because it encourages students to enter the conversation of the texts and to literally extend it. However, students may remain within the arguments presented by the authors by simply extending them to new contexts.
- **Examine.** *Examine* is a useful verb because it encourages students to use analytical skills.
- **Evaluate.** *Evaluate* is an excellent verb because it directly encourages critical thinking and, in the process, encourages students to take a position or to make a central point.
- **Propose.** *Propose* can be very useful because students will need to enter the conversation of the texts.
- **Assess.** Like *examine* or *evaluate*, the verb *assess* encourages critical thinking.

Ultimately, you will locate the verbs most useful to you through experience. This list is intended only to give you practice in thinking about how the verb chosen directs the response students create.

Assignment Worksheet

One way to conceive your assignments is to ask yourself a series of questions:
1. What are the issues of the previous essay?
2. What are the issues of the current essay?
3. What are the issues of the next essay?
4. What are the terms and concepts available?
5. What are the problems to be worked?
6. What are the challenges for this assignment?
7. What is the goal?

Weaker Papers

Ashley Torresani, Paper One, Rough Draft*

What's Geek, Then Sleek, and Read All Over?

In "What's Black, Then White, and Said All Over," Leslie Savan argues that "African-American vernacular" has been influencing pop culture for years, and recently, pop culture has been using this "black talk" in advertisements. Not only does black culture have a strong influence on pop culture, but—one could argue—it *defines* pop culture. Our society regularly and unknowingly uses words and phrases of African American origin. Just as African-American vernacular has been infiltrating the English language for decades, Internet-inspired words and phrases are also beginning to influence our language.

As Savan points out in the text, black talk has proven to be an effective marketing tool for many products. When advertising for a video game system, the black talk might not appeal to the average video game consumer, so it seems that the geeks have created their own dialect. There are many popular initialisms used by nerds such as: *ctf, ftw, orz, gg,* and *irl*. It is also common to substitute numbers for letters or even totally re-place letters with numbers altogether. This mannerism is called *1337 5P34K* (leet speak).

One form of leet speak has already been used as advertisement by Sony. Sony's Playstation has four main buttons on its controller: *x, circle, triangle,* and *square*. The Playstation slogan is "Live in your world, play in ours," but some of the letters are cleverly replaced with the aforementioned shapes on the controller. Savan says "at white society's major intersection with black language—that is, in entertainment—white society has gone from mocking black talk, as in minstrel shows, to marketing it, as in hip-hop" (Savan 48). Maybe one day society will go from mocking geek talk to marketing it.

Not all of the Internet slang words have nerdy connotations; some popular examples are *lol, bff, brb, g2g, idk* and *ttyl*. These notations along with many other similar ones can be seen in just about any text message or instant message. They are widely used and accepted among America's youth, male and female, nerd and non-nerd. In early 2007 AT&T/Cingular released a commercial of a young girl who communicated with her mother solely using this jargon. Later in 2007 the company released a similar commercial. In both commercials there were subtitles translating the jargon and introducing many ignorant watchers to the phenomenon.

*See revision on p. 17 in the Introduction to *Emerging*.

Another common Internet-generated initialism is "FAQ" (Frequently Asked Questions). There are many professional web sites that have a FAQ page. "FAQ" may one day even replace its ancestor, "Q&A."

Even though I see many of these initialisms every day—and even hear them out loud occasionally—they are not words. Most of them are unpronounceable combinations of consonants. "Lol" is the only exception. It is always unexpected to hear "lol" in an out-loud or over-the-phone conversation, mainly because it is used to signify laughter. In a face-to-face conversation, it is just more natural to laugh out loud instead of saying "lol."

However, there are two words coined by video gamers that are both slowly gaining momentum in pop culture. One of them is "noob." It evolved from "newbie" and is sometimes spelled "newb." Thefreedictionary.com defines newbie as "one that is new to something, especially a novice at using computer technology or the Internet." It is quite a degrading insult to be called a *noob* when playing a video game.

The second word to be adopted by video gamers is any variation of the word "own" (commonly misspelled and pronounced as "pwn"). Yes, this has always been a word, but video gamers have given it a new definition. To put things in perspective, our wallets are getting owned by gas prices. When my team wins a capture the flag game three to zero, that is an instance of *ownage*. Only noobs get *owned*.

Both of these words are seeping into mainstream pop culture. I once saw someone wearing a shirt that simply said "GET OWNED" on it. At one point in time, only the hardcore computer nerds knew these words and how to use them. Slowly over time, as online gaming has boomed, these terms have become more widespread. Now, even casual video gamers call each other *noobs* and *own* each other. Even though it is uncommon, non-video gamers sometimes use these words in their nerdy contexts.

As defined by Savan, covert prestige is when "speakers of a 'standard' language [whatever the language] 'have favorable attitudes toward lower-class, nonstandard speech forms'" (Savan 65). Because the majority of English-speaking people do not favor the word *noob* or *own*, these words have not become a part of mainstream covert prestige. However, nerds seem to have an affinity for these words, especially when surrounded by other nerds.

Jessica Scouse, Paper Two

Basic Language and Racial Conflict

Without language there would be no possible way of coexistence amongst humans, but to live in the world we live in today there must be something more to coexisting with one another than just the use of language. Race is, and has become a major factor influenced by this concept of coexisting with each other. Author Leslie Savan writes about black vernacular influencing pop culture, and pointing out the outcomes and changes of standard language, in Chapter 3 "What's Black, Then White, and Said All Over?" featured in her book "*Slam Dunks and No-Brainers.*" To illustrate further-

more this concept of influence and role of language, would be the way Chris Hedges*
suggests the concepts of "mythic reality" or sense of what people want to hear and
not necessarily the actuality of situations also known as the "sensory reality", for
example, war. The author's concepts show that in time, people mostly rely on what
they have been taught, and by the knowledge that has been passed down through
various generations. This effect of language being used in non-standard and nontraditional ways could definitely bring an uprising in racial conflict and construction,
by the usage of false stories and fraudulent or "wannabe" people (Savan 54). It could
eventually demonstrate to becoming such a mockery throughout mankind.

Generally speaking, black vernacular or hip-hop slang has become a part of
everyday life it is just something most people say and do on a regular bases. Could
the same be said about people, do they think about the war everyday on a regular
base? The majority of populace would be safe to say that war is not thought of
everyday, or even a concern in people's daily lives. Chris Hedges uses war as his
example of how people do not really want to understand what is in reality happening, so the media converts true to life story and sugar coats it to the public. For
example "in mythic war we imbue events with meanings they do not have" (Hedges
21). Besides the example of this mythic reality seen told through war stories, there
is also Savan's argument about black talk almost becoming a ridicule of its original
roots and its establishment. "Black talk has openly joined the sales force—whites
society's major intersection with black language—that is, in entertainment—white
society has gone form mocking black talk, as in minstrel shows, to marketing it, as
in hip-hop" (Savan 48). Consequently, these examples that are being shown, both
war chronicles and black slang, relate to the deconstruction of cultures, races, and
originality. The racial construct of African-American slang language plays a major role
in community when being used by other ethnicities, and the same goes for the mythic
reality of war tales, creating a position for people to expand on trying to justify what
Hedges calls "organized murder" (21). Extending that a little further, this concept
could be thought of when trying to justify things such as abortion, gay marriage, and
religious rights. As a matter of fact this "mythic reality" that is being exploited, occurs
in everyday changing lives, and could potentially up bring more bias into the multicultural world, all done through the language that is being vocalized.

Therefore, media is controlling a big aspect of society's thoughts especially
about war, and actions particularly on the coolest words that are a must say in
everyone's vocabulary. Race and racial construction all have specific origins and
diversities that are up held within each ethnicity, but when the media begins to
control the knowledge and is the source of the stories, aspects begin to change
as well. For example Savan brings into play this method of covert prestige, stating
that "whites talking some black is part of an apparently universal phenomenon that
sociolinguists call covert prestige" (Savan 65). Now considering that whites did not

*The Hedges Selection was class-tested at FAU but does not appear in *Emerging*. "The Myth of War"
is from *War Is a Force that Gives Us Meaning*.

relay this sort of speech in the construction of their race, this use of black vernacular has adapted its way into mainstream language and seeped into other races and their languages. Ideally this building and constructing of languages meshing together develops new origins for people and forms even more diverse cultures. For example, the reconfiguration of language in armed conflicts within Bosnia has shown a vast sense of division. As Hedges articulates that "the Croats, Muslims, and Serbs, who speak the same language and are nearly indistinguishable, were different people" (20). As humans we thrive on differences among each other, and utilize these differences to create backgrounds for race. Beginning with something as minor as the different kinds of clothes a race wears, to something as major as the different verbal communication or languages spoken.

Consequently these major concepts driven throughout the argument, that the role of language does in fact construct race and potentially commits racial conflict. Language is a device used to connect one another, and the fact that we have diversity within languages keeps everyone separate, but to sum it all up were actually similar. By interchanging slang with other races and using mythic reality to make a sense of belonging, races borrow. For instance Savan shows this when she says, "the human species can't help but borrow after all, that's how languages develop" (Savan 55). Another illustration of this would be similar to when movie stars wear designer clothes and then the pop culture populace tries to mimic their styles, it is trying to be different but also part of a whole. The big way of getting this language out and about and used in people's vocabulary, is once again influence from the media. Hedge's writes that, "mythic war reporting sells papers and boosts ratings. Real reporting, sensory reporting, does not" (Hedges 22). Races want to be different and construct themselves in their own manner, but everyone is told by what the media states, and the media tells the people what they want to hear. Now this false language assembles conflict in how society views situations and creates the wrong messages being portrayed to the populace. So although everyone is culturally and racially different, everyone receives the same influence from the pop culture world we live it today as well as the prevailing false stories that catch headlines in our news.

With that in mind, the world would be pandemonium if every story that was told was verbatim to its exact truth, and language would be boring without using the newest, latest and coolest words. Some might say that if we did not have this pop culture outbreak and only on need to know basis stories, the world wouldn't be as peaceful. These concepts and connections with maintaining the role of language in race has promoted peace, and again a sense of coexistence. Tom Dalzell states in Savans chapter that "'one cannot help but be struck by the powerful influence of African American vernacular on the slang of all 20th-century youth'" (Savan 45). If the youth of nations are coexisting with one another with racial conflict involved, then countries are progressing into a more peaceful world already, and language will continue to participate in the structure of race.

Therefore, race is and has become a major factor influenced by this concept of coexisting with each other. Language is a key factor in determining and building different races and construction separate racial conflicts. Savans concept of the influence of pop culture is just one of the many different influences on race, alongside with the mythic and sensory reality that Hedges mentions in his essay on war. For instance, mythic reality could be something so minor like telling your best friend a story, but not telling her exact in depth details and maybe throwing in a few extra details. Also pop talk doesn't have to be only something that is heard through the media or the television, it could something of self creative or constructed. Language will only rely on the races that commend it, wanting differences in race, borrowing others racial characteristics and also still being a part of a whole or similar to one another are all important aspects that define human beings. Judging from my generation, phases of cool come and go and there will always be some new word or phrase better then the next, and their will always be stories that people would rather hear than the actual true to self stories, but that is just how language has developed over time. Language is the component of race, and alters racial conflict exceedingly through concepts such as pop culture and media.

Madhu Rajma, Paper One

Pop Culture's Slang is Cool

Language over the years has changed drastically to include several slang terms which are used in today's society. Author Leslie Savan describes these changes in her book entitled, *Slam Dunks and No-Brainers*. Within this piece, Savan sets aside a chapter, "What's Black, Then White, and Said All Over?", which describes the transformation and alterations of word meanings which are expressed along with the widespread use of slang and black vernacular. The use of black slang has greatly influenced pop culture and the media and has been included in many advertisements, marketing a variety of different products. A popular example of this is displayed through the use of the words 'cool' and 'wicked' which have changed to mean the same. By using terms such as 'cool' and 'wicked' Savan's argument is extended through the media, advertising and entertainment.

Black slang has changed society's vernacular to include common slang phrases in everyday language. Slang has also become the language of entertainment for all races and ethnic groups. Moreover, slang has put new flavor into words in order to have different meanings that are commonly used in a different perspective. "Yet linguists and other language experts know that America's language wouldn't be what it is—and certainly wouldn't pop as much—without black English" (Savan 45). This is due to the fact that black language has become the new trend of society. Black vernacular represents what is 'cool', popular and reflects an entire different attitude. This attitude displays how individuals try to connect with one another, by being able to share similar ideas and expressing themselves in similar manners including fashion, and speech.

Likewise, black slang is used in everyday speech and allows common words to have new lively meanings. The black experience has influenced many to adopt new current trends which are commonly used amongst the public. Savan states, "...the black experience, publicized more widely than ever now through hip-hop and its celebrities, has encouraged everyone else to more vigorously adopt the style" (47). Hip-hop's style has become more popular because its style is new and trendy, which is what society chooses to take part in, including new phrases and fashion styles. Within the past few years, pop music and its culture have been redefined with new vocabulary and trends.

The word 'cool' has been used for hundreds of years and has gradually become more popular because it has been included into slang and pop culture. As Savan states, "Cool is the tent pole of pop culture. Uttered by folks from two to seventy, cool is both one of the most expressive concepts of our time and one of the emptiest" (Savan 74). This word has become so common that it is used in almost any response. Also, the word cool can be used to describe anything trendy or hip. Cool has become very popular because it has been used by so many. Therefore, individuals tend to follow the trend of others in order to feel accepted and a part of the crowd.

Also, words that have become a part of slang no longer mean the same thing as they did before. The ever-popular word 'cool' has over the years changed its meaning to move along with society and pop culture. As society's standard and entertainment changes, so does language and communication. Cool, which in reality means cold, chilly, or the opposite of hot now means neat, trendy or hip. Cool has been used as an adjective for something good and has found its way into standard vocabulary due to its popularity within society and pop culture. "Today cool has everything to do with mainstream fashions, styles, and trends ..." (Savan 76). The word cool has been used in the media and is used everywhere in entertainment. It is used on popular television shows and are used by famous actors and actresses in movies. Society is very interested in these new trends because they are what now defines popularity, what determines fitting in with the crowd. These new trends originate from famous artists and actors which younger audiences especially, adopt to fit into their own style because it is what everyone else is doing, it is 'cool'. Doing what is 'cool' allows individuals to become a part of a larger community, and also allows them to feel accepted into society.

Along with the common use of 'cool' there are also several other slang words and phrases which now have the same meaning as cool , including the new widely-used term, 'wicked'. Morris states, "A new slang sense of 'wicked,' analogous to the current slang use of 'bad' to mean 'good' does not in any way preclude the use of the word's original meaning of 'evil' or 'cruel'" (Morris). However, the word 'wicked' is now used as a response very similarly to 'cool' and is used within standard speech to mean good or great. The use of these words has spread throughout different communities to enable greater communication. This is because there are several words from pop culture which can be used to relate to others such as teenagers communicating with slang.

In addition to alterations of word meanings, African Americans have also used coded language and misspelled words as a part of their vernacular. A popular example is using the letter X in placement for any word with the prefix –ex. This has become extremely popular in advertising when trying to appeal to the public. Right Guard used this concept when they introduced their new product, Right Guard Xtreme Sport. Furthermore, other popular hip-hop artists have also used this concept within their names and their music. Some of these artists include Mystikal, Xzibit, and Soulja Boy which have all become very popular because of their unique styles, including the spelling of their names. Savan states, "Hip-hop and R&B singers and groups have long been seizing the Z crossing an X or otherwise kurupting the language" (Savan 59). Because these artists have set new trends and styles, audiences will also follow them to become a part of what is 'cool' and trendy. Audiences continue to follow new trends to model famous artists and feel accepted into pop culture society even when these trends include doing something out of the norm such as purposely misspelling words.

Different methods of advertising have also used misspelled words and coded language as a way to attain the attention of consumers. These common catchphrases allow society's involvement with products which they have been exposed to, whether on TV or even on the radio. "A Burger King TV commercial had it both ways, with nods to hip-hop and electronics: 'B Real. B Good,' voiceovers sang as the lyrics were spelled out on-screen to make sure we C the Bs. '2 Go. BK4U'" (Savan 64). This advertising slogan is a very easy way for consumers to be attracted to this company because it is catchy and also easy to remember and therefore would cause consumers to choose this company over others marketing the same products.

Artists such as Paul Wall and Flo' Rida have also advertised products within their music. These products have now become fashion statements and are worn by the public because of the influences these artists have made on the public. Paul Wall's song "Grillz" was a very catchy song which displayed his array collection of gold teeth. Due to the popularity of this song, many decided to get a grill for themselves, becoming the new trend of that time. Another current fashion statement has also been emphasized with Flo' Rida's hit song "Low". This fashion style includes Apple Bottom jeans and boots with fur which are described in this song as the outfit of a very attractive young lady at a club. Due to the success of this hit song, many young ladies now include Apple Bottom jeans in their wardrobe and include it as a part of their fashion style.

Entertainment and the media have had such a huge impact on the public it is very easy to find out where these influences are coming from. Connie Elbe states from her findings, "After researching it, I found that hardly any black slang entered the white vocabulary because a white student has encountered a black student. They've learned it from MTV, the movies, and rap songs" (Savan 73). Society has begun certain trends such as using slang words and wearing certain clothes because of the standards and popularity entertainment has displayed. Pop culture on a whole has changed the way society runs. The desire to be popular while using the same styles as popular pop icons has greatly increased.

Pop culture has been greatly influenced by black slang and will continue to change as society changes. Advertising has allowed the public to now use common slang words and phrases due to their popularity from famous artists. Savan and Morris both describe these current changes in slang and word meanings which have influenced society and entertainment. Words such as 'cool' and 'wicked' now have new meanings and are used in everyday vernacular assisting with communication between different communities. Black slang has significantly contributed a lot to pop culture including style, trends and fashion through entertainment and advertising.

Stronger Papers

Michael Caldosa, Paper Two

Language Shapes Who We Are

Language has an enormous impact on young individuals' lives throughout the world. Both Chris Hedges in "The Myth of War"* and Leslie Savan in "What's Black, Then White, and Said All Over" discuss the role of language in the construction of race and racial conflict. The way that individuals speak impacts the way in which society will view them; for example, it is human nature to automatically categorize those individuals one meets into racial categories. A person's race is in no way genetically influenced. Rather, it is solely socially constructed. Society places individuals into racial categories depending on their appearance as well as their linguistics. Individuals take on this socially constructed race as a way to identify themselves. With the race one takes on, also comes a form of language. Language constructs race and racial conflict both positively and negatively because language is a form of self-identification.

Identity is an issue that individuals, especially the young, constantly struggle with. The reason for this struggle is because there is such great influences on how people are supposed to look, act, and talk. The influence comes from both the media as well as one's peers. Leslie Savan states, "To the young, advertising has become an acceptable—nay, desirable—part of cool life they aspire to" (49). The young observe the actions of those they want to fit in with and pick up on their linguistic style. One begins to talk and act similar to the race they want to be categorized with as seen on television advertisements. Individuals feel constant pressure to speak like the race they want to be categorized with because society is constantly placing individuals into these racial categories. One's constructed race, because of their phenotype, may be different from the racial category that they want to be associated

---

*From *War Is a Force that Gives Us Meaning*. The chapter was class-tested at FAU but does not appear in *Emerging*.

with, which is why "white attempts to *yo* here and *dis* there are an important piece of identity-and-image building" (Savan 49). People have to attempt to break their socially constructed racial category to fit into the racial category they feel the most connection with. Because race is socially constructed, it is easy for people to slightly change the way they speak, behave, and who they associate with and convert in a different racial category. As easy as it is to try and convert, it is not so easy to be accepted by the other group.

Racial Identity is an issue some individuals take very seriously and with great pride. It is quite common for people of different races to have conflict and tension with one another. When there are individuals trying to become a member of a race that they are not classified to because of their outward appearance, they are referred to as wannabes. "*Wannabe* originally referred to people who wanted to be something they weren't," explains Savan (54). These wannabes would begin to dress-like, act-like, and mostly try to speak-like a race that they were not. For example there is a growing trend in pop culture today of white rappers. Although there are more Caucasian rappers than there were years ago, they are still not living up to the standards of the original African American founders of rap music. These white rappers are taking the language of the black race and attempting to make it there own which is not working. It does not work because a word with the origin belonging to black linguistics does not have the same meaning and impact as it would coming out of a black rapper. Some people believe that one should not try to merge into another race or become "wannabes," but should stick with their socially constructed racial category and adapt the behavior and language of that category. Although not all individuals of a racial category are opposed to the fusion with other races, they often feel the pressure from their society to be against it because, "those individuals who understand other cultures, speak other languages, and find richness in diversity are shunted aside" (Hedges 24). Although there is the potential for the acceptance of convergence, social groups are not allowing it. When individuals begin to merge with a different race, conflict may begin.

The conflict begins because the merging race does not appreciate the customs and linguistics of the race they are merging into. Savan mentions, "white people (and not just the young) draw from a black lexicon every day, sometimes unaware of the words' origins" (46). This exemplifies a race merging with another and causing problems. The people taking the language of a different race use the words causally and with no meaning behind them, which often offends those that know the origin of the word. For example the extremely common word "bro." This word is most fre-quently used and recognized with ones typical Orange County surfer boy. Although most would think that the word originated with the surfers, one would be shocked to find out that African Americans were the ones to create it. The stealing of the word "bro" and in a way taking credit for its origin often angers the creators of the word. The individuals are stealing the language because, "whites talking some black is part of an apparently universal phenomenon that sociologists call covert prestige"

(Savan 65). Covert prestige not only applies to black and whites but to all races. Linguist Margaret Lee explains in Savan's book that covert prestige "means that speakers of a 'standard' language (whatever the language) 'have favorable attitudes toward lower-class, nonstandard speech form'" (65). Individuals are taking the speech form from other social groups and are using the words without knowing where it came from and the true meaning behind them.

Although the stealing of another race's language happens quite frequently, it is still not greatly accepted because the individual merging over is seen as a *wannabe* that is attempting to live a mythic reality identity rather than of sensory reality. The individuals living within this mythic reality are living a false identity. These individuals are attempting to "imbue events with meaning they do not have" (Hedges 21). They feel that by simply throwing in words from a different race into their vocabulary they can be classified in that race. Just as explained earlier, white rappers are trying to be something they are not. They feel that by simply being titled as a rapper they are now seen as equals to the original black rappers. Those that live with the sensory reality are able to better understand themselves and are, therefore, confident about their self-identify. Hedges explains, "in sensory reality we see events for what they are" (21). Individuals are not trying to convert to a race that they are not; however, one takes on their constructed race with pride. These people are not taking the language of a different race in order to fit in and live a mythic lifestyle. They are appreciative of their original race and accept it with great pride.

The role language plays in the construction of ones race is extremely complicated, which is why it often leads to racial conflict. Individuals feel the constant pressure from the media as well as society to fit in-to a racial category depending on their linguistics. If one does not want to be classified with their socially constructed race it is very difficult for them to convert to another race. It is difficult to convert because it is not well accepted and the individual will be known as *wannabes*. Those classified as *wannabes* are accused of using convert prestige as well as living in mythic reality. The most obvious example of covert prestige would be young teens today. These people tend to take the words of a lower class and make them their own. It is important to allow language to impact one's race but be cautious to not allow it to lead to racial conflict.

Christopher Socca, Paper Four

Can Cultures Benefit From False Reality?

Today the world consists of various cultures that all have different beliefs and practices. However, the one thing these diverse cultures have in common is the basic will to survive. To accomplish this, all cultures need to form a stable society in which its members can help to spread common beliefs and practices that will allow the culture to succeed throughout generations. For instance, in the past many cultures have grown and influenced individuals; however, due to a lack of stability those once powerful cultures disappeared completely and have long been forgotten. In order to gain the stability they need, cultures must learn from mistakes that other cultures have made in order to fix the problems they themselves might face. In the short excerpt "Reporting Live from Tomorrow," Daniel Gilbert explains how today, communication is used as a way for individuals to pass along true as well as false beliefs. He also explains how people who believe in false beliefs normally live in stable societies because the shared beliefs help to make their society safe from the harsh reality of life while still maintaining stability. To further explain the role false reality has on individuals, Chris Hedges in "The Myth of War,"* writes about people suffering from "mythic reality" also known as false reality which is brought on by greed and the corruption of the media. Hedges also discussed the harsh reality of "sensory reality" and how individuals felt once they found out the truth about the lies the media feeds people. Overall, by embracing the "mythic reality" that the media uses to entice individuals with and by using cultural surrogates in order to learn from the mistakes that other cultures have made, many cultures would be able to thrive, expand, and obtain the futures that they plan for themselves.

In order to increase profits, many media outlets use their influence on the general public by incorporating all aspects of communication, including magazines and television shows, to spread false beliefs throughout mainstream America. These false beliefs or "mythic reality" are then spread throughout different cultures and are either accepted into the culture or set aside and replaced by other beliefs. The media spreads these beliefs because as Hedges states, "nearly every reporter has seen his or her mission as sustaining civilian and army morale" (22.) In other words, for individuals that generally refuse to accept reality, the media will make it their job to tell those people what they want to hear, even if it is false. The accepted false beliefs or "super-replicators" are then further influenced and increased when individuals do activities that help to support the belief. To better explain the concept of "super-replicator" Gilbert states that, "rather, this particular belief is a super-replicator because holding it causes us to engage in the very activities that perpetuate it" (220.) For instance, the belief that Las Vegas is the city of sin is one example of a "super-replicator." Of course Las Vegas has a lot of establishments that deal with gambling, prostitution, and other sinfully illegal businesses, but the entire city does not consist of it. There are several professional establishments such as schools and hospitals as well as normal homes that occupy Las Vegas. However, the belief that Las Vegas is sin city continues to spread because of individuals who go to the city and choose to participate in activities, such as gambling and drug rings, which support the myth.

"Mythic reality" and "super-replicators" may seem to have many negative impacts on society; however, the truth is that these false beliefs can help both societies and cultures tremendously. Gilbert states that, "false beliefs that happen to promote

---

*Though class-tested, this piece does not appear in *Emerging*.

stable societies tend to propagate because people who hold these beliefs tend to live in stable societies, which provide the means by which false beliefs propagate" (217.) When a culture believes in a false belief, the culture is able to form a stable society. As the result of a stable society, more false beliefs are formed and are further spread to other cultures that will in turn be able to form stable societies. Gilbert also writes, "the production of wealth does not necessarily make individuals happy, but it does serve the needs of an economy, which serves the needs of a stable society, which serves as a network for the propagation of delusional beliefs about happiness and wealth (219.) By incorporating media based "mythic reality" into different cultures the individuals would be able to form a stable society based on shared beliefs. In turn, those beliefs would continue to grow and maintain the societies and cultures success for the future. Even if the shared beliefs are false, the cultures would still be allowed to depend on, learn from, and benefit from each one economically.

A culture's overall economy depends on the spreading of "mythic reality." Without the myth, individuals would not want to buy many products that are essential to the cultures survival, stability, and future success. For instance, if Las Vegas did not have the mythic title of being the sin city then many tourists would not be drawn to the cities many businesses and attractions. Without a steady flow of people many of the large casinos as well as other operations would shut down due to the lack of money and the cultures economy would suffer greatly. Gilbert explains that, "market economies require that we all have an insatiable hunger for stuff, and if everyone were content with the stuff they had, then the economy would grind to a halt" (219.) If there is no myth to lure people into buying things or going places, then the economy would stop completely. In his excerpt Hedges further analyzes the need for the myth by stating that, "'mythic war' reporting sells papers and boosts ratings" (22.) Without the "mythic reality" a lot of individuals would not be interested in many of the products or places that are advertised in magazines and movies because they would be too busy with the "sensory reality" or true reality of life. As a result, the economy would be in ruin and the culture itself would not be able to embrace the future it envisioned for itself due to a lack of economic stability.

Many people want to know what is happening throughout their culture; however, sometimes the knowledge of true reality has negative effects. For instance, there are many families in the United States who have loved ones fighting in the war against terrorism. At times the media will report positive news about the soldiers in Iraq without mentioning the death and destruction that constantly plague the people there. The families are constantly fooled into thinking that the soldiers are safe. However, when the hideous truth is revealed and the media reports the mayhem occurring on the front lines, the families begin to panic and start conflicts against the leaders of their culture. In "sensory reality" Hedges states that, "we see events for what they are" (21.) When the lies the media fed the culture are finally revealed, the individuals in the culture realize that everything the media told them was false. In this situation, the internal conflicts from within a culture can become further influenced by "sensory reality," which may get out of hand, and result in an unstable society. In some situations the truth is better left unsaid.

In addition to embracing media based "mythic reality" many societies could also use "surrogates" to maintain stability throughout their cultures. A "surrogate" is an individual who shares experiences and spreads his or her feelings as well as beliefs to other individuals. In order to aid in cultural stability, one culture could observe or communicate with another culture that has been through a certain experience. By doing this, the inexperienced culture could learn important facts and lessons that can help to aid in its future problems and overall cultural survival. However, sometimes many people might not use the knowledge they are given because of every human beings desire to be different. Many people choose to experience the situations themselves based on the belief that only they can predict their futures. Yet Gilbert states that the, "experience of a single randomly selected individual can sometimes provide a better basis for predicting your future experiences than your own imagination can" (224.) In other words, one person might do a better job at predicting another individual's future because that person would be less likely to ignore consequences or miss necessary details. Other people are also more likely to see the positive outcomes of situations the individual might face.

There are plenty of factors that allow cultures to accomplish many necessary goals. The truth is however, that without stability and the will to survival many cultures would not exist today. In order for cultures to survive, succeed, and obtain their preferred futures, each culture must use the knowledge that people are willing to share in order to learn from past mistakes. These cultures must also use media based "mythic reality" to maintain the stability and balance that is necessary for every individuals well being and the societies cultural future as well as economic survival. If false reality is not embraced then mass hysteria could occur and many conflicts would break out within the culture itself. Such conflicts are never essential when it comes to survival. In fact, it could tremendously harm the economy and can possibly result in the entire culture disappearing all together.

mid-1990s suggested a bright future. In 1996, Wales and two partners founded a Web directory called Bomis.

Initially, the idea was to build a universal directory, like Yahoo's. The question was how to build it. At the time, there were two dominant models: top-down and bottom-up. The former is best exemplified by Yahoo, which began as *Jerry's Guide to the World Wide Web*. Jerry—in this case Jerry Yang, Yahoo's cofounder—set up a system of categories and began to classify Web sites accordingly. Web surfers flocked to the site because no one could find anything on the Web in the early 1990s. So Yang and his partner, David Filo, spent a mountain of venture capital to hire a team of surfers to classify the Web. Yahoo ("Yet Another Hierarchical Officious Oracle") was born.

Other would-be classifiers approached the problem of Web chaos more democratically. Beginning from the sound premise that it's good to share, a seventeen-year-old Oregonian named Sage Weil created the first "Web ring" at about the time Yang and Filo were assembling their army of paid Web librarians. A Web ring is nothing more than a set of topically related Web sites that have been linked together for ease of surfing. Rings are easy to find, easy to join, and easy to create; by 1997, they numbered 10,000.

Wales focused on the bottom-up strategy using Web rings, and it worked. Bomis users built hundreds of rings—on cars, computers, sports, and especially "babes" (e.g., the Anna Kournikova Web ring), effectively creating an index of the "laddie" Web. Instead of helping all users find all content, Bomis found itself positioned as the *Playboy* of the Internet, helping guys find guy stuff. Wales's experience with Web rings reinforced the lesson he had learned with MUDs: Given the right technology, large groups of self-interested individuals will unite to cre-

> **Wales is of a thoughtful cast of mind.**

ate something they could not produce by themselves, be it a sword-and-sorcery world or an index of Web sites on Pamela Anderson. He saw the power of what we now call "peer-to-peer," or "distributed," content production.

Wales was not alone: Rich Skrenta and Bob Truel, two programmers at Sun Microsystems, saw it too. In June 1998, along with three partners, they launched GnuHoo, an all-volunteer alternative to the Yahoo Directory. (GNU, a recursive acronym for "GNUs Not Unix," is a free operating system created by the über-hacker Richard Stallman.) The project was an immediate success, and it quickly drew the attention of Netscape, which was eager to find a directory capable of competing with Yahoo's index. In November 1998, Netscape acquired GnuHoo (then called NewHoo), promising to both develop it and release it under an "open content" license, which meant anyone could use it. At the date of Netscape's acquisition, the directory had indexed some 100,000 URLs; a year later, it included about a million.

Wales clearly had the open-content movement in mind when, in the fall of 1999, he began thinking about a "volunteer-built" online encyclopedia. The idea—explored most prominently in Stallman's 1999 essay "The Free Universal Encyclopedia and Learning Resource"—had been around for some time. Wales says he had no direct knowledge of Stallman's essay when he embarked on his encyclopedia project, but two bits of evidence suggest that he was thinking of Stallman's GNU free documentation license. First, the name Wales adopted for his encyclopedia — Nupedia.org — strongly suggested a Stallman-esque venture. Second, he took the trouble of leasing a related domain name, GNUpedia.org. By January 2000, his encyclopedia project had acquired funding from Bomis and hired its first employee: Larry Sanger.

The Philosopher

Sanger was born in 1968 in Bellevue, Washington, a suburb of Seattle. When he was seven, his father, a marine biologist, moved the family to Anchorage, Alaska, where Sanger spent his youth. He excelled in high school, and in 1986 he enrolled at Reed College. Reed is the sort of school you attend if you are intelligent, are not interested in investment banking, and wonder a lot about truth. There Sanger found a question that fired his imagination: What is knowledge? He embarked on that most unremunerative of careers, epistemology, and entered a doctoral program in philosophy at Ohio State.

Sanger fits the profile of almost every Internet early adopter: He'd been a good student, played Dungeons & Dragons, and tinkered with PCs as a youth — going so far as to code a text-based adventure game in BASIC, the first popular programming language. He was drawn into the world of philosophy discussion lists and, in the early 1990s, was an active participant in Wales's objectivism forum. Sanger also hosted a mailing list as part of his own online philosophy project (eventually named the Association for Systematic Philosophy). The mission and mien of Sanger's list stood in stark contrast to Wales's Rand forum. Sanger was far more programmatic. As he wrote in his opening manifesto, dated March 22, 1994:

> The history of philosophy is full of disagreement and confusion. One reaction by philosophers to this state of things is to doubt whether the truth about philosophy can ever be known, or whether there is any such thing as the truth about philosophy. But there is another reaction: One may set out to think more carefully and methodically than one's intellectual forebears.

Wales's Rand forum was generally serious, but it was also a place for philosophically inclined laypeople to shoot the breeze: Wales permitted discussion of "objectivism in the movies" or "objectivism in Rush lyrics." Sanger's list was more disciplined, but he soon began to feel it, too, was of limited philosophical worth. He resigned after little more than a year. "I think that my time could really be better spent in the real world," Sanger wrote in his resignation letter, "as opposed to cyberspace, and in thinking to myself, rather than out loud to a bunch of other people." Sanger was seriously considering abandoning his academic career.

As the decade and the century came to a close, another opportunity arose, one that would let Sanger make a living away from academia, using the acumen he had developed on the Internet. In 1998, Sanger created a digest of news reports relating to the "Y2K problem." *Sanger's Review of Y2K News Reports* became a staple of IT managers across the globe. It also set him to thinking about how he might make a living in the new millennium. In January 2000, he sent Wales a business proposal for what was in essence a cultural news blog. Sanger's timing was excellent.

The Cathedral

Wales was looking for someone with good academic credentials to organize Nupedia, and Sanger fit the bill. Wales pitched the project to Sanger in terms of Eric S. Raymond's essay (and later book) "The Cathedral and the Bazaar." Raymond sketched two models of software development. Under the "cathedral model," source code was guarded by a core group of developers; under the "bazaar model," it was released on the Internet for anyone to tinker with. Raymond argued that the latter model was better, and he coined a now-famous hacker aphorism to capture its superiority: "Given enough eyeballs, all bugs are shallow." His point was simply that the speed with which a complex project is perfected is directly proportional to the number of informed people working on it. Wales was enthusiastic about Raymond's thesis. His experience with MUDs and Web rings had demonstrated to him the power of the bazaar. Sanger, the philosopher, was charier about the wisdom-of-crowds scheme but drawn to the idea of creating an open online encyclopedia that would break all the molds. Sanger signed on and moved to San Diego.

According to Sanger, Wales was very "hands-off." He gave Sanger only the loosest sketch of an open encyclopedia. "Open" meant two things: First, anyone, in principle, could contribute. Second, all of the content would be made freely available. Sanger proceeded to create, in effect, an online academic journal. There was simply no question in his mind that Nupedia would be guided by a board of experts, that submissions would be largely written by experts, and that articles would be published only after extensive peer review. Sanger set about recruiting academics to work on Nupedia. In early March 2000, he and Wales deemed the project ready to go public, and the Nupedia Web site was launched with the following words:

> Suppose scholars the world over were to learn of a serious online encyclopedia effort in which the results were not proprietary to the encyclopedists, but were freely distributable under an open content license in virtually any desired medium. How quickly would the encyclopedia grow?

The answer, as Wales and Sanger found out, was "not very." Over the first several months little was actually accomplished in terms of article assignment, writing, and publication. First, there was the competition. Wales and Sanger had the bad luck to launch Nupedia around the same time as *Encyclopedia Britannica* was made available for free on the Internet. Then there was the real problem: production. Sanger and the Nupedia board had worked out a multistage editorial system that could have been borrowed from any scholarly journal. In a sense, it worked: Assignments were made, articles were submitted and evaluated, and copyediting was done. But, to both Wales and Sanger, it was all much too slow. They had built a cathedral.

The Bazaar

In the mid-1980s, a programmer named Ward Cunningham began trying to create a "pattern language" for software design. A pattern language is in essence a common vocabulary used in solving engineering problems—think of it as best practices for designers. Cunningham believed that software development should have a pattern language, and he proposed to find a way for software developers to create it.

Apple's Hypercard offered inspiration. Hypercard was a very flexible database application. It allowed users to create records ("cards"), add data fields to them, and link them in sets. Cunningham created a Hypercard "stack" of software patterns and shared it with colleagues. His stack was well liked but difficult to share, since it existed only on Cunningham's computer. In the 1990s, Cunningham found himself looking for a problem-solving technique that would allow software developers to fine-tune and accumulate their knowledge collaboratively. A variation on Hypercard seemed like an obvious option.

Cunningham coded and, in the spring of 1995, launched the first "wiki," calling it the "WikiWikiWeb." (*Wiki* is Hawaiian for "quick," which Cunningham chose to indicate the ease with which a user could edit the pages.) A wiki is a Web site that allows multiple users to create, edit, and hyperlink pages. As users work, a wiki can keep track of all changes; users can compare versions as they edit and, if necessary, revert to earlier states. Nothing is lost, and everything is transparent.

The wiki quickly gained a devoted following within the software community. And there it remained until January 2001, when Sanger had dinner with an old friend named Ben Kovitz. Kovitz was a fan of "extreme programming." Standard software engineering is very methodical—first you plan, then you plan and plan and plan, then you code. The premise is that you must correctly anticipate what the program will need to do in order to avoid drastic changes late in the coding process. In contrast, extreme programmers advocate going live with the earliest possible version of new software and letting many people work simultaneously to rapidly refine it.

Over tacos that night, Sanger explained his concerns about Nupedia's lack of progress, the root cause of which was its serial editorial system. As Nupedia was then structured, no stage of the editorial process could proceed before the previous stage was completed. Kovitz brought up the wiki and sketched out "wiki magic," the mysterious process by which communities with common interests work to improve wiki pages by incremental contributions. If it worked for the rambunctious hacker culture of programming, Kovitz said, it could work for any online collaborative project. The wiki could break the Nupedia bottleneck by permitting volunteers to work simultaneously all over the project. With Kovitz in tow, Sanger rushed back to his apartment and called Wales to share the idea.

Over the next few days he wrote a formal proposal for Wales and started a page on Cunningham's wiki called "WikiPedia."

Wales and Sanger created the first Nupedia wiki on January 10, 2001. The initial purpose was to get the public to add entries that would then be "fed into the Nupedia process" of authorization. Most of Nupedia's expert volunteers, however, wanted nothing to do with this, so Sanger decided to launch a separate site called "Wikipedia." Neither Sanger nor Wales looked on Wikipedia as anything more than a lark. This is evident in Sanger's flip announcement of Wikipedia to the Nupedia discussion list. "Humor me," he wrote. "Go there and add a little article. It will take all of five or ten minutes." And, to Sanger's surprise, go they did. Within a few days, Wikipedia outstripped Nupedia in terms of quantity, if not quality, and a small community developed. In late January, Sanger created a Wikipedia discussion list (Wikipedia-L) to facilitate discussion of the project. At the end of January, Wikipedia had seventeen "real" articles (entries with more than 200 characters). By the end of February, it had 150; March, 572; April, 835; May, 1,300; June, 1,700; July, 2,400; August, 3,700. At the end of the year, the site boasted approximately 15,000 articles and about 350 "Wikipedians."

Setting the Rules

Wikipedia's growth caught Wales and Sanger off guard. It forced them to make quick decisions about what Wikipedia would be, how to foster cooperation, and how to manage it. In the beginning it was by no means clear what an "open" encyclopedia should include. People posted all manner of things: dictionary definitions, autobiographies, position papers, historical documents, and original research. In response, Sanger created a "What Wikipedia Is Not" page. There he and the community defined Wikipedia by exclusion—not a dictionary, not a scientific journal, not a source collection, and so on. For everything else, they reasoned that if an article could conceivably have gone in *Britannica*, it was "encyclopedic" and permitted; if not, it was "not encyclopedic" and deleted.

Sanger and Wales knew that online collaborative ventures can easily slide into a morass of unproductive invective. They had already worked out a solution for Nupedia, called the "lack of bias" policy. On Wikipedia it became NPOV, or the "neutral point of view," and it brilliantly encouraged the work of the community. Under NPOV, authors were enjoined to present the conventionally acknowledged "facts" in an unbiased way, and, where arguments occurred, to accord space to both sides. The concept of neutrality, though philosophically unsatisfying, had a kind of everybody-lay-down-your-arms ring to it. Debates about what to include in the article were encouraged on the "discussion" page that attends every Wikipedia article.

The most important initial question, however, concerned governance. When Wikipedia was created, wikis were synonymous with creative anarchy. Both Wales and Sanger thought that the software might be useful, but that it was no way to build a trusted encyclopedia. Some sort of authority was assumed to be essential. Wales's part in it was clear: He owned Wikipedia. Sanger's role was murkier.

Citing the communal nature of the project, Sanger refused the title of "editor   30
in chief," a position he held at Nupedia, opting instead to be "chief organizer."
He governed the day-to-day operations of the project in close consultation with
the "community," the roughly two dozen committed Wikipedians (most of them
Nupedia converts) who were really designing the software and adding content
to the site. Though the division of powers between Sanger and the community
remained to be worked out, an important precedent had been set: Wikipedia
would have an owner, but no leader.

The Cunctator

By October 2001, the number of Wikipedians was growing by about fifty
a month. There were a lot of new voices, among them a user known as "The
Cunctator" (Latin for "procrastinator" or "delayer"). "Cunc," as he was called,
advocated a combination of anarchy (no hierarchy within the project) and radical openness (few or no limitations on contributions). Sanger was not favorably
disposed to either of these positions, though he had not had much of a chance to
air his opposition. Cunc offered such an opportunity by launching a prolonged
"edit war" with Sanger in mid-October of that year. In an edit war, two or more
parties cyclically cancel each other's work on an article with no attempt to find
the NPOV. It's the wiki equivalent of "No, *your* mother wears combat boots."

With Cunc clearly in mind, Sanger curtly defended his role before the
community on November 1, 2001:

> I need to be granted fairly broad authority by the community—by you,
> dear reader—if I am going to do my job effectively. Until fairly recently,
> I was granted such authority by Wikipedians. I was indeed not infre-
> quently called to justify decisions I made, but not constantly and nearly
> always respectfully and helpfully. This place in the community did not
> make me an all-powerful editor who must be obeyed on pain of ousting;
> but it did make me a leader. That's what I want, again. This is my job.

Seen from the trenches, this was a striking statement. Sanger had so far said he
was primus inter pares; now he seemed to be saying that he was just primus.
Upon reading this post, one Wikipedian wrote: "Am I the only person who
detects a change in [Sanger's] view of his own position? Am I the only person
who fears this is a change for the worse?"

On November 4, the Sanger-Cunc contretemps exploded. Simon Kissane, a
respected Wikipedian, accused Sanger of capriciously deleting pages, including
some of Cunc's work. Sanger denied the allegation but implied that the excised
material was no great loss. He then launched a defense of his position in words
that bled resentment:

> I do reserve the right to permanently delete things—particularly when
> they have little merit and when they are posted by people whose main
> motive is evidently to undermine my authority and therefore, as far as
> I'm concerned, damage the project. Now suppose that, in my experi-
> ence, if I make an attempt to justify this or other sorts of decisions, the

people in question will simply co-opt huge amounts of my time and will never simply say, "Larry, you win; we realize that this decision is up to you, and we'll have to respect it." Then, in order to preserve my time and sanity, I have to act like an autocrat. In a way, I am being trained to act like an autocrat. It's rather clever in a way—if you think college-level stunts are clever. Frankly, it's hurting the project, guys—so stop it, already. Just write articles—please!

The blowup disturbed Wales to no end. As a list moderator, he had tried hard to keep his discussants out of flame wars. He weighed in with an unusually forceful posting that warned against a "culture of conflict." Wikipedia, he implied, was about building an encyclopedia, not about debating how to build or govern an encyclopedia. Echoing Sanger, he argued that the primary duty of community members was to contribute—by writing code, adding content, and editing. Enough talk, he seemed to be saying: We know what to do, now let's get to work. Yet he also seemed to take a quiet stand against Sanger's positions on openness and on his own authority:

> Just speaking off the top of my head, I think that total deletions seldom make sense. They should be reserved primarily for pages that are just completely mistaken (typos, unlikely misspellings), or for pages that are nothing more than insults.

Wales also made a strong case that anyone deleting pages should record his or her identity, explain his or her reasons, and archive the entire affair.

Within several weeks, Sanger and Cunc were at each other's throats again. Sanger had proposed creating a "Wikipedia Militia" that would deal with issues arising from sudden massive influxes of new visitors. It was hardly a bad idea: Such surges did occur (they're commonly called "slash-dottings"). But Cunc saw in Sanger's reasonable proposition a very slippery slope toward "central authority." "You start deputizing groups of people to do necessary and difficult tasks," he wrote, "fast-forward two/three years, and you have pernicious cabals."

Given the structure of Wikipedia there was little Sanger could do to defend himself. The principles of the project denied him real punitive authority: He couldn't ban "trolls"—users like Cunc who baited others for sport—and deleting posts was evidence of tyranny in the eyes of Sanger's detractors. A defensive strategy wouldn't work either, as the skilled moderator's tactic for fighting bad behavior—ignoring it—was blunted by the wiki. On e-mail lists, unanswered inflammatory posts quickly vanish under layers of new discussion; on a wiki, they remain visible to all, often near the tops of pages. Sanger was trapped by his own creation.

The "God-King"

Wales saw that Sanger was having trouble managing the project. Indeed, he seems to have sensed that Wikipedia really needed no manager. In mid-December 2001, citing financial shortfalls, he told Sanger that Bomis would be cutting its staff and that he should look for a new job. To that point, Wales and his partners had supported both Nupedia and Wikipedia. But with Bomis suffering in the Internet bust, there was financial pressure. Early on, Wales had said that advertising was a possibility, but the community was now set against any commercialization. In January 2002, Sanger loaded up his possessions and returned to Ohio.

Cunc responded to Sanger's departure with apparent appreciation:

> I know that we've hardly been on the best of terms, but I want you to know that I'll always consider you one of the most important Wikipedians, and I hope that you'll always think of yourself as a Wikipedian, even if you don't have much time to contribute. Herding cats ain't easy; you did a good job, all things considered.

Characteristically, Sanger took this as nothing more than provocation: "Oh, how nice and gracious this was. Oh, thank you SO much, Cunctator. I'm sure glad I won't have to deal with you anymore, Cunctator. You're a friggin' piece of work." The next post on the list is from Wales, who showed a business-as-usual sangfroid: "With the resignation of Larry, there is a much less pressing need for funds."

Sanger made two great contributions to Wikipedia: He built it, and he left it. After forging a revolutionary mode of knowledge building, he came to realize—albeit dimly at first—that it was not to his liking. He found that he was not heading a disciplined crew of qualified writers and editors collaborating on authoritative statements (the Nupedia ideal), but trying to control an ill-disciplined crowd of volunteers fighting over ever-shifting articles. From Sanger's point of view, both the behavior of the participants and the quality of the scholarship were wanting. Even after seeing Wikipedia's explosive growth, Sanger continued to argue that Wikipedia should engage experts and that Nupedia should be saved.

Wales, though, was a businessman. He wanted to build a free encyclopedia, and Wikipedia offered a very rapid and economically efficient means to that end. The articles flooded in, many were good, and they cost him almost nothing. Why interfere? Moreover, Wales was not really the meddling kind. Early on, Wikipedians took to calling him the "God-King." The appellation is purely ironic. Over the past four years, Wales has repeatedly demonstrated an astounding reluctance to use his power, even when the community has begged him to. He wouldn't exile trolls or erase offensive material, much less settle on rules for how things should or should not be done. In 2003, Wales diminished his own authority by transferring Wikipedia and all of its assets to the nonprofit Wikimedia Foundation, whose sole purpose is to set general policy for Wikipedia and its allied projects. (He is one of five members of the foundation's board.)

Wales's benign rule has allowed Wikipedia to do what it does best: grow. The numbers are staggering. The English-language Wikipedia alone has well more than a million articles and expands by about 1,700 a day. (*Britannica*'s online version, by comparison, has about 100,000 articles.) As of mid-February 2006, more than 65,000 Wikipedians—registered users who have made at least ten edits since joining—had contributed to the English-language Wikipedia. The number of registered contributors is increasing by more than 6,000 a month; the number of unregistered contributors is presumably much larger. Then there are the 200-odd non-English-language Wikipedias. Nine of them already have more than 100,000 entries each, and nearly all of the major-language versions are growing on pace with the English version.

What Is Wikipedia?

The Internet did not create the desire to collect human knowledge. For most of history, however, standardizing and gathering knowledge was hard to do very effectively. The main problem was rampant equivocation. Can we all agree on what an apple is exactly, or the shades of the color green? Not easily. The wiki offered a way for people to actually decide in common. On Wikipedia, an apple is what the contributors say it is *right now*. You can try to change the definition by throwing in your own two cents, but the community—the voices actually negotiating and renegotiating the definition—decides in the end. Wikipedia grew out of a natural impulse (communication) facilitated by a new technology (the wiki).

The power of the community to decide, of course, asks us to reexamine what we mean when we say that something is "true." We tend to think of truth as something that resides in the world. The fact that two plus two equals four is written in the stars—we merely discovered it. But Wikipedia suggests a different theory of truth. Just think about the way we learn what words mean. Generally speaking, we do so by listening to other people (our parents, first). Since we want to communicate with them (after all, they feed us), we use the words in the same way they do. Wikipedia says judgments of truth and falsehood work the same way. The community decides that two plus two equals four the same way it decides what an apple is: by consensus. Yes, that means that if the community changes its mind and decides that two plus two equals five, then two plus two does equal five. The community isn't likely to do such an absurd or useless thing, but it has the ability.

> The Internet did not create the desire to collect human knowledge.

Early detractors commonly made two criticisms of Wikipedia. First, unless experts were writing and vetting the material, the articles were inevitably going to be inaccurate. Second, since anyone could edit, vandals would have their way with even the best articles, making them suspect. No encyclopedia produced in this way could be trusted. Last year, however, a study in the journal *Nature* compared *Britannica* and Wikipedia science articles and suggested that the former are usually only marginally more accurate than the latter. *Britannica* demonstrated that *Nature*'s analysis was seriously flawed ("Fatally Flawed" was the fair title of the response), and no one has produced a more authoritative study of Wikipedia's accuracy. Yet it is a widely accepted view that Wikipedia is comparable to *Britannica*. Vandalism also has proved much less of an issue than originally feared. A study by IBM suggests that although vandalism does occur (particularly on high-profile entries like "George W. Bush"), watchful members of the huge Wikipedia community usually swoop down to stop the malfeasance shortly after it begins.

There are, of course, exceptions, as in the case of the journalist John   45
Seigenthaler, whose Wikipedia biography long contained a libel about his supposed complicity in the assassinations of John F. and Robert Kennedy. But even this example shows that the system is, if not perfect, at least responsive. When Seigenthaler became aware of the error, he contacted Wikipedia. The community (led in this instance by Wales) purged the entry of erroneous material, expanded it, and began to monitor it closely. Even though the Seigenthaler entry is often attacked by vandals, and is occasionally locked to block them, the page is more reliable precisely because it is now under "enough eyeballs." The same could be said about many controversial entries on Wikipedia: The quality of articles generally increases with the number of eyeballs. Given enough eyeballs, all errors are shallow.

Common Knowledge

In June 2001, only six months after Wikipedia was founded, a Polish Wikipedian named Krzysztof Jasiutowicz made an arresting and remarkably forward-looking observation. The Internet, he mused, was nothing but a "global Wikipedia without the end-user editing facility." The contents of the Internet — its pages — are created by a loose community of users, namely those on the Web. The contents of Wikipedia — its entries — are also created by a loose community of users, namely Wikipedians. On the Internet, contributors own their own pages, and only they can edit them. They can also create new pages as they see fit. On Wikipedia, contributors own *all* of the pages collectively, and each can edit nearly every page. Page creation is ultimately subject to community approval. The private-property regime that governs the Internet allows it to grow freely, but it makes organization and improvement very difficult. In contrast, Wikipedia's communal regime permits growth *plus* organization and improvement. The result of this difference is there for all to see: Much of the Internet is a chaotic mess and therefore useless, whereas Wikipedia is well ordered and hence very useful.

Having seen all of this in prospect, Jasiutowicz asked a logical question: "Can someone please tell me what's the end point/goal of Wikipedia?" Wales responded, only half jokingly, "The goal of Wikipedia is fun for the contributors." He had a point. Editing Wikipedia *is* fun, and even rewarding. The site is huge, so somewhere on it there is probably something you know quite a bit about. Imagine that you happen upon your pet subject, or perhaps even look it up to see how it's being treated. And what do you find? Well, this date is wrong, that characterization is poor, and a word is mispelled. You click the "edit" tab and make the corrections, and you've just contributed to the progress of human knowledge. All in under five minutes, and at no cost.

Yet Wikipedia has a value that goes far beyond the enjoyment of its contributors. For all intents and purposes, the project is laying claim to a vast region of the Internet, a territory we might call "common knowledge." It is the place where all nominal information about objects of widely shared experience will be negotiated, stored, and renegotiated. When you want to find out *what something is,* you will go to Wikipedia, for that is where common knowledge will, by convention, be archived and updated and made freely available. And while you are there, you may just add or change a little something, and thereby feel the pride of authorship shared by the tens of thousands of Wikipedians.

Keeper

One of the objects of common knowledge in Wikipedia, I'm relieved to report, is "Marshall Poe." Recall that the Scottish Wikipedian Alai said that I had no "notability" and therefore couldn't really be considered encyclopedic. On the same day that Alai suggested my entry be deleted, a rather vigorous discussion took place on the "discussion" page that attended the Marshall Poe entry. A Wikipedian who goes by "Dlyons493" discovered that I had indeed written an obscure dissertation on an obscure topic at a not-so-obscure university. He gave the article a "Weak Keep." Someone with the handle "Splash" searched Amazon and verified that I had indeed written books on Russian history, so my claim to be a historian was true. He gave me a "Keep." And finally, my champion and hero, a Wikipedian called "Tupsharru," dismissed my detractors with this:

> Keep. Obvious notability. Several books published with prestigious academic publishers. One of his books has even been translated into Swedish. I don't know why I have to repeat this again and again in these deletion discussions on academics, but don't just use Amazon when the Library of Congress catalogue is no farther than a couple of mouse clicks away.

Bear in mind that I knew none of these people, and they had, as far as I   50
know, no interest other than truth in doing all of this work. Yet they didn't stop with verifying my claims and approving my article. They also searched the Web for material they could use to expand my one-line biography. After they were done, the Marshall Poe entry was two paragraphs long and included a good bibliography. Now that's wiki magic.

Questions for Critical Reading

1. What makes Wikipedia so successful? Reread Poe's text to locate quotations that demonstrate the key qualities of Wikipedia's success.

2. Poe examines top-down and bottom-up systems. Find passages from his text that show the advantages of each system. Is one inherently better than the other? In what contexts does each work best?

3. Poe spends time discussing the conflict between Cunc and Larry Sanger. Is such conflict beneficial or detrimental to the kind of system Wikipedia represents? Locate quotations from Poe's text that support your position.

Exploring Context

1. This essay is about the collaborative process behind the creation of entries in the online encyclopedia Wikipedia (wikipedia.org). Visit Wikipedia and find an entry you feel qualified to write about. Register at the site and participate in the authorship process by editing your selected entry. What's the process like? Is it consistent with Poe's description? Relate your experience to your work on the key factors in Wikipedia's success from Question 1 of Questions for Critical Reading.

2. Poe is the creator of MemoryArchive (memoryarchive.org), whose wiki-like format allows users to create an encyclopedia of memories. Explore the site and perhaps contribute a memory of your own. Does this site harness the same collective power that Poe locates in Wikipedia? What makes it different? Use your response on Wikipedia's success from Question 1 of Questions for Critical Reading to support your answer.

3. Poe opens this essay by discussing his own entry in Wikipedia. Visit his entry on the site at en.wikipedia.org/wiki/Marshall_Poe and then examine the history of changes to the entry by clicking on the history tab at the top of the page. How has his entry changed? What reasons can you find for those changes? Does the entry reflect the success of the kind of process Poe describes?

Questions for Connecting

1. In what ways is Wikipedia like Slashdot? What systems of feedback are needed for Wikipedia's success? Apply Steven Johnson's ideas in "Listening to Feedback" (p. 191) to Poe's discussion of collaborative knowledge. You may want to use your experience with wikis from Exploring Context in composing your response.

2. In "Ethics and the New Genetics" (p. 76), the Dalai Lama argues for a moral compass to guide us around scientific developments such as genetic technologies, but how can we develop a system of ethics when knowledge itself is coming to be socially constituted? Is ethics possible without transcendent truths? Does Wikipedia threaten the idea of "truth," or can its collaborative model be used to create the ethical system the Dalai Lama calls for?

3. James Surowiecki outlines the many dangers of small groups in "Committees, Juries, and Teams: The *Columbia* Disaster and How Small Groups Can Be Made to Work" (p. 440). Are the same dangers present in a large-scale group project like Wikipedia? How can the pitfalls that Surowiecki details be avoided? Use your responses from Questions for Critical Reading and Exploring Context to support your position.

Language Matters

1. Select a key quotation from Poe's text and then translate it into another language using an online tool such as Babel Fish (babelfish.yahoo.com) or Google's Language Tools (google.com/language_tools). You might even choose

to translate it several times (from English to French to German to Chinese). Then translate it back into English. The resulting sentence will probably make little sense. Describe what happened to the sentence. Did translation change parts of speech? Verb tense? The sentence structure? What elements of the sentence are key to transmitting Poe's meaning? Do they survive translation? What parts of your own sentences should you then pay attention to the most?

2. Draw the argument of Poe's essay, either by hand or with a graphics program on your computer. How would the inclusion of this drawing affect Poe's text? What elements of visual argument do you use to convey Poe's meaning?

3. Locate a key passage from Poe's text and then revise the quotation you've selected using more informal language or slang. How does this revision change the meaning of the quotation? What audience would be most receptive to your revision? Why did Poe choose the tone he used in this essay, and what tone might you choose in your own writing for this class?

Assignments for Writing

1. Write a paper in which you determine the role of collaboration in the production of knowledge. Does a consensus determine the truth? Is knowledge created by individuals? Does society have the right to determine that "two plus two equals five," as noted in the selection from Poe? Use your experience with wikis in Exploring Context and your work with Poe's concepts from Questions 1 and 3 of Questions for Connecting in making your argument.

2. Though Poe's explicit concern is Wikipedia, his essay is also concerned with the circulation of knowledge. Write a paper in which you determine who owns knowledge. Can knowledge be owned? Is it common property or the property of academics or other experts? Consider the ethical implications by drawing from your work with the Dalai Lama's essay from Question 2 of Questions for Connecting.

3. What is the power of experts? Does a consensus determine the truth? Poe's essay asks us to consider these questions, since the collaborative authorship of Wikipedia suggests that experts are not vital in the creation of knowledge. Write a paper in which you suggest the proper boundaries between experts and nonexperts in relation to knowledge. What role does technology play in this process? Should experts be granted special status in relation to knowledge? What makes an expert "expert" anyway?

Michael Pollan

Michael Pollan is Knight Professor of Journalism at the University of California at Berkeley as well as the author of five books: *Second Nature: A Gardener's Education* (1991), *A Place of My Own* (1997), *The Botany of Desire: A Plant's-Eye View of the World* (2001), *The Omnivore's Dilemma: A Natural History of Four Meals* (2006), and *In Defense of Food: An Eater's Manifesto* (2008). A graduate of Bennington College and Columbia University, Pollan has won multiple journalism awards, and his writing has appeared in *The Norton Book of Nature Writing* (1990), *Best American Essays* (1990 and 2003), and *Best American Science Writing* (2004). Pollan's work can often be seen in the *New York Times,* where he is a contributing writer.

The *Omnivore's Dilemma,* declared by the *New York Times* to be one of 2006's best nonfiction books, traces three different food chains—the industrial, the pastoral, and the personal—from nature to table. Ultimately, the book is about the politics of eating: what we should eat, why we should eat it, and what impact our eating decisions have.

In "The Animals: Practicing Complexity" from *The Omnivore's Dilemma,* Pollan writes about an alternative to traditional agribusiness and profiles farmer Joel Salatin. With few outside raw materials, Salatin is able to run an incredibly productive farm that mimics a natural ecosystem in which nothing goes to waste. Pollan shows how order arises from the complex system of Salatin's farm, where everything plays a part, from a tree to a cow to the cow's manure, in a system—described as "holon"-based—in which each element is simultaneously an individual whole and an active part in a complex system.

For Pollan, the omnivore's dilemma is one we face each day: what to have for dinner? This selection suggests that providing a healthy and sustainable answer to that question might come not from rejecting agribusiness entirely for an idealized agrarian past but from rethinking the intersection of business, farming, and food.

▶ TAGS: *tradition, technology, collaboration, feedback, supply chains, biotechnology*

The Animals: Practicing Complexity

1. Tuesday Morning

It's not often I wake up at six in the morning to discover I've overslept, but by the time I had hauled my six-foot self out of the five-foot bed in Lucille's microscopic guest room, everyone was already gone and morning chores were nearly done. Shockingly, chores at Polyface commence as soon as the sun comes up (five-ish this time of year) and always before breakfast. Before coffee, that is, not that there was a drop of it to be had on this farm. I couldn't recall the last time I'd even attempted to do anything consequential before breakfast, or before caffeine at the very least.

When I stepped out of the trailer into the warm early morning mist, I could make out two figures—the interns, probably—moving around up on the broad shoulder of hill to the east, where a phalanx of portable chicken pens formed a checkerboard pattern on the grass. Among other things, morning chores consist of feeding and watering the broilers and moving their pens one length down the hillside. I was supposed to be helping Galen and Peter do this, so I started up the path, somewhat groggily, hoping to get there before they finished.

As I stumbled up the hill, I was struck by how very beautiful the farm looked in the hazy early light. The thick June grass was silvered with dew, the sequence of bright pastures stepping up the hillside dramatically set off by broad expanses of blackish woods. Birdsong stitched the thick blanket of summer air, pierced now and again by the wood clap of chicken pen doors slamming shut. It was hard to believe this hillside had ever been the gullied wreck Joel had described at dinner, and even harder to believe that farming such a damaged landscape so intensively, rather than just letting it be, could restore it to health and yield this beauty. This is not the environmentalist's standard prescription. But Polyface is proof that people can sometimes do more for the health of a place by cultivating it rather than by leaving it alone.

By the time I reached the pasture Galen and Peter had finished moving the pens. Fortunately they were either too kind or too timid to give me a hard time for oversleeping. I grabbed a pair of water buckets, filled them from the big tub in the center of the pasture, and lugged them to the nearest pen. Fifty of these pens were spread out across the damp grass in a serrated formation that had been calibrated to cover every square foot of this meadow in the course of the fifty-six days it takes a broiler to reach slaughter weight; the pens moved ten feet each day, the length of one pen. Each ten-by-twelve, two-foot-tall floorless pen houses seventy birds. A section of the roof is hinged to allow access, and a five-gallon bucket perched atop each unit fed a watering device suspended inside.

Directly behind each pen was a perfectly square patch of closely cropped grass resembling a really awful Jackson Pollock painting, thickly spattered with chicken crap in pigments of white, brown, and green. It was amazing what a

5

mess seventy chickens could make in a day. But that was the idea: Give them twenty-four hours to eat the grass and fertilize it with their manure, and then move them onto fresh ground.

Joel developed this novel method for raising broiler chickens in the 1980s and popularized it in his 1993 book, *Pastured Poultry Profit$*, something of a cult classic among grass farmers. (Joel has self-published four other how-to books on farming, and all but one of them has a $ stepping in for an S somewhere in its title.) Left to their own devices, a confined flock of chickens will eventually destroy any patch of land, by pecking the grass down to its roots and poisoning the soil with their extremely "hot," or nitrogenous, manure. This is why the typical free-range chicken yard quickly winds up bereft of plant life and hard as brick. Moving the birds daily keeps both the land and the birds healthy; the broilers escape their pathogens and the varied diet of greens supplies most of their vitamins and minerals. The birds also get a ration of corn, toasted soybeans, and kelp, which we scooped into long troughs in their pens, but Joel claims the fresh grass, along with the worms, grasshoppers, and crickets they peck out of the grass, provides as much as 20 percent of their diet—a significant savings to the farmer and a boon to the birds. Meanwhile, their manure fertilizes the grass, supplying all the nitrogen it needs. The chief reason Polyface Farm is completely self-sufficient in nitrogen is that a chicken, defecating copiously, pays a visit to virtually every square foot of it at several points during the season. Apart from some greensand (a mineral supplement to replace calcium lost in the meadows), chicken feed is the only important input Joel buys, and the sole off-farm source of fertility. ("The way I look at it, I'm just returning some of the grain that's been extracted from this land over the last 150 years.") The chicken feed not only feeds the broilers but, transformed into chicken crap, feeds the grass that feeds the cows that, as I was about to see, feeds the pigs and the laying hens.

After we had finished watering and feeding the broilers, I headed up to the next pasture, where I could hear a tractor idling. Galen had told me Joel was moving the Eggmobile, an operation I'd been eager to watch. The Eggmobile, one of Joel's proudest innovations, is a ramshackle cross between a henhouse and a prairie schooner. Housing four hundred laying hens, this rickety old covered wagon has hinged nesting boxes lined up like saddlebags on either side, allowing someone to retrieve eggs from the outside. I'd first laid eyes on the Eggmobile the night before, parked a couple of paddocks away from the cattle herd. The hens had already climbed the little ramp into the safety of the coop for the night, and before we went down to dinner Joel had latched the trapdoor behind them. Now it was time to move them into a fresh paddock, and Joel was bolting the Eggmobile to the hitch of his tractor. It wasn't quite 7:00 AM yet, but Joel seemed delighted to have someone to talk to, holding forth being one of his greatest pleasures.

"In nature you'll always find birds following herbivores," Joel explained, when I asked him for the theory behind the Eggmobile. "The egret perched on the rhino's nose, the pheasants and turkeys trailing after the bison—that's a symbiotic relationship we're trying to imitate." In each case the birds dine on the insects that would otherwise bother the herbivore; they also pick insect larvae and parasites out of the animal's droppings, breaking the cycle of infestation and disease. "To mimic this symbiosis on a domestic scale, we follow the cattle in their rotation with the Eggmobile. I call these gals our sanitation crew."

Joel climbed onto the tractor, threw it into gear, and slowly towed the rickety contraption fifty yards or so across the meadow to a paddock the cattle had vacated three days earlier. It seems the chickens eschew fresh manure, so he waits three or four days before bringing them in—but not a day longer. That's because the fly larvae in the manure are on a four-day cycle, he explained. "Three days is ideal. That gives the grubs a chance to fatten up nicely, the way the hens like them, but not quite long enough to hatch into flies." The result is prodigious amounts of protein for the hens, the insects supplying as much as a third of their total diet—and making their eggs unusually rich and tasty. By means of this simple little management trick, Joel is able to use his cattle's waste to "grow" large quantities of high-protein chicken feed for free; he says this trims his cost of producing eggs by twenty-five cents per dozen. (Very much his accountant father's son, Joel can tell you the exact economic implication of every synergy on the farm.) The cows further oblige the chickens by shearing the grass; chickens can't navigate in grass more than about six inches tall.

> I began to understand just how radically different this sort of farming is from the industrial models I'd observed before.

After Joel had maneuvered the Eggmobile into position, he opened the trapdoor, and an eager, gossipy procession of Barred Rocks, Rhode Island Reds, and New Hampshire Whites filed down the little ramp, fanning out across the pasture. The hens picked at the grasses, especially the clover, but mainly they were all over the cowpats, doing this frantic backward-stepping break-dance with their claws to scratch apart the caked manure and expose the meaty morsels within. Unfolding here before us, I realized, was a most impressive form of alchemy: Cowpatties in the process of being transformed into exceptionally tasty eggs.

"I'm convinced an Eggmobile would be worth it even if the chickens never laid a single egg. These birds do a more effective job of sanitizing a pasture than anything human, mechanical, or chemical, and the chickens love doing it." Because of the Eggmobile, Joel doesn't have to run his cattle through a headgate to slather Ivomectrin, a systemic paraciticide, on their hides or worm them with toxic chemicals. This is what Joel means when he says the animals do the real work around here. "I'm just the orchestra conductor, making sure everybody's in the right place at the right time."

That day, my second on the farm, as Joel introduced me to each of his intricately layered enterprises, I began to understand just how radically different this sort of farming is from the industrial models I'd observed before, whether in an Iowa cornfield or an organic chicken farm in California. Indeed, it is so different that I found Polyface's system difficult to describe to myself in an orderly way. Industrial processes follow a clear, linear, hierarchical logic that is fairly easy to put into words, probably because words follow a similar logic: First this, then that; put this in here, and then out comes that. But the relationship between cows and chickens on this farm (leaving aside for the moment the other creatures and relationships present here) takes the form of a loop rather than a line, and that makes it hard to know where to start, or how to distinguish between causes and effects, subjects and objects.

Is what I'm looking at in this pasture a system for producing exceptionally tasty eggs? If so, then the cattle and their manure are a means to an end. Or is it a system for producing grass-fed beef without the use of any chemicals, in which case the chickens, by fertilizing and sanitizing the cow pastures, comprise the means to that end. So does that make their eggs a product or a by-product? And is manure—theirs or the cattle's—a waste product or a raw material? (And what should we call the fly larvae?) Depending on the point of view you take—that of the chicken, cow, or even the grass—the relationship between subject and object, cause and effect, flips.

Joel would say this is precisely the point, and precisely the distinction between a biological and industrial system. "In an ecological system like this everything's connected to everything else, so you can't change one thing without changing ten other things.

"Take the issue of scale. I could sell a whole lot more chickens and eggs than I do. They're my most profitable items, and the market is telling me to produce more of them. Operating under the industrial paradigm, I could boost production however much I wanted—just buy more chicks and more feed, crank up that machine. But in a biological system you can never do just one thing, and I couldn't add many more chickens without messing up something else. 15

"Here's an example: This pasture can absorb four hundred units of nitrogen a year. That translates into four visits from the Eggmobile or two passes of a broiler pen. If I ran any more Eggmobiles or broiler pens over it, the chickens would put down more nitrogen than the grass could metabolize. Whatever the grass couldn't absorb would run off, and suddenly I have a pollution problem." Quality would suffer, too. Unless he added more cattle, to produce more grubs for the chickens and to keep the grass short enough for them to eat it, those chickens and eggs would not taste nearly as good as they do.

"It's all connected. This farm is more like an organism than a machine, and like any organism it has its proper scale. A mouse is the size of a mouse for a good reason, and a mouse that was the size of an elephant wouldn't do very well."

Joel likes to quote from an old agricultural textbook he dug out of the stacks at Virginia Tech many years ago. The book, which was published in 1941 by a Cornell Ag professor, offers a stark conclusion that, depending on your point of view, will sound either hopelessly quaint or arresting in its gnomic wisdom: "Farming is not adapted to large-scale operations because of the following reasons: Farming is concerned with plants and animals that live, grow, and die."

"Efficiency" is the term usually invoked to defend large-scale industrial farms, and it usually refers to the economies of scale that can be achieved by the application of technology and standardization. Yet Joel Salatin's farm makes the case for a very different sort of efficiency—the one found in natural systems, with their coevolutionary relationships and reciprocal loops. For example, in nature there is no such thing as a waste problem, since one creature's waste becomes another creature's lunch. What could be more efficient than turning cow pies into eggs? Or running a half-dozen different production systems—cows, broilers, layers, pigs, turkeys—over the same piece of ground every year?

Most of the efficiencies in an industrial system are achieved through simplification: doing lots of the same thing over and over. In agriculture, this usually means a monoculture of a single animal or crop. In fact, the whole history of agriculture is a progressive history of simplification, as humans reduced the biodiversity of their landscapes to a small handful of chosen species. (Wes Jackson calls our species "homo the homogenizer.") With the industrialization of agriculture, the simplifying process reached its logical extreme—in monoculture. This radical specialization permitted standardization and mechanization, leading to the leaps in efficiency claimed by industrial agriculture. Of course, how you choose to measure efficiency makes all the difference, and industrial agriculture measures it, simply, by the yield of one chosen species per acre of land or farmer.

By contrast, the efficiencies of natural systems flow from complexity and interdependence—by definition the very opposite of simplification. To achieve the efficiency represented by turning cow manure into chicken eggs and producing beef without chemicals you need at least two species (cows and chickens), but actually several more as well, including the larvae in the manure and the grasses in the pasture and the bacteria in the cows' rumens. To measure the efficiency of such a complex system you need to count not only all the products it produces (meat, chicken, eggs) but also all the costs it eliminates: antibiotics, wormers, paraciticides, and fertilizers.

Polyface Farm is built on the efficiencies that come from mimicking relationships found in nature, and layering one farm enterprise over another on the same base of land. In effect, Joel is farming in time as well as in space—in four dimensions rather than three. He calls this intricate layering "stacking" and points out that "it is exactly the model God used in building nature." The idea is not to slavishly imitate nature, but to model a natural ecosystem in all its diversity and interdependence, one where all the species "fully express their physiological distinctiveness." He takes advantage of each species' natural proclivities in a way that not only benefits that animal but other species as well. So instead of treating the chicken as a simple egg or protein machine, Polyface honors—and exploits—"the innate distinctive desires of a chicken," which include pecking in the grass and cleaning up after herbivores. The chickens get to do, and eat, what they evolved to do and eat, and in the process the farmer and his cattle both profit. What is the opposite of zero-sum? I'm not sure, but this is it.

Joel calls each of his stacked farm enterprises a "holon," a word I'd never encountered before. He told me he picked it up from Allan Nation; when I asked Nation about it, he pointed me to Arthur Koestler, who coined the term in *The Ghost in the Machine.* Koestler felt English lacked a word to express the complex relationship of parts and wholes in a biological or social system. A holon (from the Greek *holos,* or whole, and the suffix *on,* as in proton, suggesting a particle) is an entity that from one perspective appears a self-contained whole, and from another a dependent part. A body organ like the liver is a holon; so is an Eggmobile.

At any given time, Polyface has a dozen or more holons up and running, and on my second day Joel and Daniel introduced me to a handful of them. I visited the Raken House, the former toolshed where Daniel has been raising rabbits for the restaurant trade since he was ten. ("Raken?" "Half rabbit, half chicken," Daniel explained.) When the rabbits aren't out on the pasture in portable hutches, they live in cages suspended over a deep bedding of woodchips, in which I watched several dozen hens avidly pecking away in search of earthworms. Daniel explained that the big problem in raising rabbits indoors is their powerful urine, which produces so much ammonia that it scars their lungs and leaves them vulnerable to infection. To cope with the problem most rabbit farmers add antibiotics to their feed. But the scratching of the hens turns the nitrogenous rabbit pee into the carbonaceous bedding, creating a rich compost teeming with earthworms that feed the hens. Drugs become unnecessary and, considering how many rabbits and chickens lived in it, the air in the Raken was, well, tolerable. "Believe me," Daniel said, "if it weren't for these chickens, you'd be gagging right about now, and your eyes would sting something awful."

Before lunch I helped Galen and Peter move the turkeys, another holon. Moving the turkeys, which happens every three days, means setting up a new "feathernet"—a paddock outlined by portable electric fencing so lightweight I could carry and lay out the entire thing by myself—and then wheeling into it the shademobile, called the Gobbledy-Go. The turkeys rest under the Gobbledy-Go by day and roost on top of it at night. They happily follow the contraption into the fresh pasture to feast on the grass, which they seemed to enjoy even more than the chickens do. A turkey consumes a long blade of grass by neatly folding it over and over again with its beak, as if making origami. Joel likes to run his turkeys in the orchard, where they eat the bugs, mow the grass, and fertilize the trees and vines. (Turkeys will eat much more grass than chickens, and they don't damage crops the way chickens can.) "If you run turkeys in a grape orchard," Joel explained, "you can afford to stock the birds at only seventy percent of normal density, and space the vines at seventy percent of what's standard, because you're getting two crops off the same land. And at seventy percent you get much healthier birds and grapevines than you would at one hundred percent. That's the beauty of stacking." By industry standards, the turkey and grape holon are each less than 100 percent efficient; together, however, they produce more than either enterprise would yield if fully stocked, and they do so without fertilizer, weeding, or pesticide.

I had witnessed one of the most winning examples of stacking in the cattle barn during my first visit to Polyface back in March. The barn is an unfancy open-sided structure where the cattle spend three months during the winter, each day consuming twenty-five pounds of hay and producing fifty pounds of manure. (Water makes up the difference.) But instead of regularly mucking out the barn, Joel leaves the manure in place, every few days covering it with another layer of woodchips or straw. As this layer cake of manure, woodchips, and straw gradually rises beneath the cattle, Joel simply raises the adjustable feed gate from which they get their ration of hay; by winter's end the bedding, and the cattle, can be as much as three feet off the ground. There's one more secret ingredient Joel adds to each layer of this cake: a few bucketfuls of corn. All winter long the layered bedding composts, in the process generating heat to warm the barn (thus reducing the animals' feed requirements), and fermenting the corn. Joel calls it his cattle's electric blanket.

Why the corn? Because there's nothing a pig enjoys more than forty-proof corn, and there's nothing he's better equipped to do than root it out with his powerful snout and exquisite sense of smell. "I call them my pigaerators," Salatin said proudly as he showed me into the barn. As soon as the cows head out to pasture in the spring, several dozen pigs come in, proceeding systematically to turn and aerate the compost in their quest for kernels of alcoholic corn. What had been an anaerobic decomposition suddenly turns aerobic, which dramatically heats and speeds up the process, killing any pathogens. The result, after a few weeks of pigaerating, is a rich, cakey compost ready to use.

> **These were the happiest pigs I'd ever seen.**

"This is the sort of farm machinery I like: never needs its oil changed, appreciates over time, and when you're done with it you eat it." We were sitting on the rail of a wooden paddock, watching the pigs do their thing—a thing, of course, we weren't having to do ourselves. The line about the pigaerators was obviously well-worn. But the cliché that kept banging around in my head was "happy as a pig in shit." Buried clear to their butts in composting manure, a bobbing sea of wriggling hams and corkscrew tails, these were the happiest pigs I'd ever seen.

I couldn't look at their spiraled tails, which cruised above the earthy mass like conning towers on submarines, without thinking about the fate of pigtails in industrial hog production. Simply put, there *are* no pigtails in industrial hog production. Farmers "dock," or snip off, the tails at birth, a practice that makes a certain twisted sense if you follow the logic of industrial efficiency on a hog farm. Piglets in these CAFOs* are weaned from their mothers ten days after birth (compared with thirteen weeks in nature) because they gain weight faster on their drug-fortified feed than on sow's milk. But this premature weaning leaves the pigs with a lifelong craving to suck and chew, a need they gratify in confinement by biting the tail of the animal in front of them. A normal pig would fight off his molester, but a demoralized pig has stopped caring. "Learned helplessness" is the psychological term, and it's not uncommon in CAFOs, where tens of thousands of hogs spend their entire lives ignorant of earth or straw or

---

*CAFOs: Confined Animal Feeding Operations.

sunshine, crowded together beneath a metal roof standing on metal slats suspended over a septic tank. It's not surprising that an animal as intelligent as a pig would get depressed under these circumstances, and a depressed pig will allow his tail to be chewed on to the point of infection. Since treating sick pigs is not economically efficient, these underperforming production units are typically clubbed to death on the spot.

Tail docking is the USDA's recommended solution to the porcine "vice" of tail chewing. Using a pair of pliers and no anesthetic, most—but not quite all—of the tail is snipped off. Why leave the little stump? Because the whole point of the exercise is not to remove the object of tail biting so much as to render it even more sensitive. Now a bite to the tail is so painful that even the most demoralized pig will struggle to resist it. Horrible as it is to contemplate, it's not hard to see how the road to such a hog hell is smoothly paved with the logic of industrial efficiency.

A very different concept of efficiency sponsors the hog heaven on display here in Salatin's barn, one predicated on what he calls "the pigness of the pig." These pigs too were being exploited—in this case, tricked into making compost as well as pork. What distinguishes Salatin's system is that it is designed around the natural predilections of the pig rather than around the requirements of a production system to which the pigs are then conformed. Pig happiness is simply the by-product of treating pigs as pigs rather than as "a protein machine with flaws"—flaws such as pigtails and a tendency, when emiserated, to get stressed.

Salatin reached down deep where his pigs were happily rooting and brought a handful of fresh compost right up to my nose. What had been cow manure and woodchips just a few weeks before now smelled as sweet and warm as the forest floor in summertime, a miracle of transubstantiation. As soon as the pigs complete their alchemy, Joel will spread the compost on his pastures. There it will feed the grasses, so the grasses might again feed the cows, the cows the chickens, and so on until the snow falls, in one long, beautiful, and utterly convincing proof that in a world where grass can eat sunlight and food animals can eat grass, there is indeed a free lunch.

2. Tuesday Afternoon

After our own quick lunch (ham salad and deviled eggs), Joel and I drove to town in his pickup to make a delivery and take care of a few errands. It felt sweet to be sitting down for a while, especially after a morning taken up with loading the hay we'd baled the day before into the hayloft. For me this rather harrowing operation involved attempting to catch fifty-pound bales that Galen tossed in my general direction from the top of the hay wagon. The ones that didn't completely knock me over I hoisted onto a conveyor belt that carried them to Daniel and Peter, stationed up in the hayloft. It was an assembly line, more or less, and as soon as I fell behind (or just fell, literally) the hay bales piled up fast at my station; I felt like Lucille Ball at the candy factory. I joked to Joel that, contrary to his claims that the animals did most of the real work on this farm, it seemed to me they'd left plenty of it for us.

On a farm, complexity sounds an awful lot like hard work, Joel's claims to the contrary notwithstanding. As much work as the animals do, that's still us humans out there moving the cattle every evening, dragging the broiler pens across the field before breakfast (something I'd pledged I'd wake up in time for the next day), and towing chicken coops hither and yon according to a schedule tied to the life cycle of fly larvae and the nitrogen load of chicken manure. My guess is that there aren't too many farmers today who are up for either the physical or mental challenge of this sort of farming, not when industrializing promises to simplify the job. Indeed, a large part of the appeal of industrial farming is its panoply of labor- and thought-saving devices: machines of every description to do the physical work, and chemicals to keep crops and animals free from pests with scarcely a thought from the farmer. George Naylor works his fields maybe fifty days out of the year; Joel and Daniel and two interns are out there every day sunrise to sunset for a good chunk of the year.

Yet Joel and Daniel plainly relish their work, partly because it is so varied from day to day and even hour to hour, and partly because they find it endlessly interesting. Wendell Berry has written eloquently about the intellectual work that goes into farming well, especially into solving the novel problems that inevitably crop up in a natural system as complex as a farm. You don't see much of this sort of problem-solving in agriculture today, not when so many solutions come ready-made in plastic bottles. So much of the intelligence and local knowledge in agriculture has been removed from the farm to the laboratory, and then returned to the farm in the form of a chemical or machine. "Whose head is the farmer using?" Berry asks in one of his essays. "Whose head is using the farmer?"

"Part of the problem is, you've got a lot of D students left on the farm today," Joel said, as we drove around Staunton running errands. "The guidance counselors encouraged all the A students to leave home and go to college. There's been a tremendous brain drain in rural America. Of course that suits Wall Street just fine; Wall Street is always trying to extract brainpower and capital from the countryside. First they take the brightest bulbs off the farm and put them to work in Dilbert's cubicle, and then they go after the capital of the dimmer ones who stayed behind, by selling them a bunch of gee-whiz solutions to their problems." This isn't just the farmer's problem, either. "It's a foolish culture that entrusts its food supply to simpletons."

It isn't hard to see why there isn't much institutional support for the sort of low-capital, thought-intensive farming Joel Salatin practices: He buys next to nothing. When a livestock farmer is willing to "practice complexity"—to choreograph the symbiosis of several different animals, each of which has been allowed to behave and eat as they evolved to—he will find he has little need for machinery, fertilizer, and, most strikingly, chemicals. He finds he has no sanitation problem or any of the diseases that result from raising a single animal in a crowded monoculture and then feeding it things it wasn't designed to eat. This is perhaps the greatest efficiency of a farm treated as a biological system: health.

I was struck by the fact that for Joel abjuring agrochemicals and pharmaceuticals is not so much a goal of his farming, as it so often is in organic agriculture, as it is an indication that his farm is functioning well. "In nature health is the default," he pointed out. "Most of the time pests and disease are just nature's way of telling the farmer he's doing something wrong."

At Polyface no one ever told me not to touch the animals, or asked me to put on a biohazard suit before going into the brooder house. The reason I had to wear one at Petaluma Poultry is because that system—a monoculture of chickens raised in close confinement—is inherently precarious, and the organic rules' prohibition on antibiotics puts it at a serious disadvantage. Maintaining a single-species animal farm on an industrial scale isn't easy without pharmaceuticals and pesticides. Indeed, that's why these chemicals were invented in the first place, to keep shaky monocultures from collapsing. Sometimes the large-scale organic farmer looks like someone trying to practice industrial agriculture with one hand tied behind his back.

By the same token, a reliance on agrochemicals destroys the information feedback loop on which an attentive farmer depends to improve his farming. "Meds just mask genetic weaknesses," Joel explained one afternoon when we were moving the cattle. "My goal is always to improve the herd, adapt it to the local conditions by careful culling. To do this I need to know: Who has a propensity for pinkeye? For worms? You simply have no clue if you're giving meds all the time." 40

"So you tell me, who's really *in* this so-called information economy? Those who learn from what they observe on their farm, or those who rely on concoctions from the devil's pantry?"

Of course the simplest, most traditional measure of a farm's efficiency is how much food it produces per unit of land; by this yardstick too Polyface is impressively efficient. I asked Joel how much food Polyface produces in a season, and he rattled off the following figures:

30,000 dozen eggs
10,000 broilers
800 stewing hens
50 beeves (representing 25,000 pounds of beef)
250 hogs (25,000 pounds of pork)
1,000 turkeys
500 rabbits

This seemed to me a truly astonishing amount of food from one hundred acres of grass. But when I put it that way to Joel that afternoon—we were riding the ATV up to the very top of the hill to visit the hogs in their summer quarters—he questioned my accounting method. It was far too simple.

"Sure, you can write that we produced all that food from a hundred open acres, but if you really want to be accurate about it, then you've got to count the four hundred and fifty acres of woodlot too." I didn't get that at all. I knew the woodlot was an important source of farm income in the winter—Joel and Daniel operate a small sawmill from which they sell lumber and mill whatever wood they need to build sheds and barns (and Daniel's new house). But what in the world did the forest have to do with producing food?

Joel proceeded to count the ways. Most obviously, the farm's water sup- 45
ply depended on its forests to hold moisture and prevent erosion. Many of the farm's streams and ponds would simply dry up if not for the cover of trees. Nearly all of the farm's 550 acres had been deforested when the Salatins arrived; one of the first things Bill Salatin did was plant trees on all the north-facing slopes.

"Feel how cool it is in here." We were passing through a dense stand of oak and hickory. "Those deciduous trees work like an air conditioner. That reduces the stress on the animals in summer."

Suddenly we arrived at a patch of woodland that looked more like a sa-vanna than a forest: The trees had been thinned and all around them grew thick grasses. This was one of the pig paddocks that Joel had carved out of the woods with the help of the pigs themselves. "All we do to make a new pig pad-dock is fence off a quarter acre of forest, thin out the saplings to let in some light, and then let the pigs do their thing." Their thing includes eating down the brush and rooting around in the stony ground, disturbing the soil in a way that in-duces the grass seed already present to germinate. Within several weeks, a lush stand of wild rye and foxtail emerges among the trees, and a savanna is born. Shady and cool, this looked like ideal habitat for the sunburn-prone pigs, who were avidly nosing through the tall grass and scratching their backs against the trees. There is something viscerally appealing about a savanna, with its pleasing balance of open grass and trees, and something profoundly hearten-ing about the idea that, together, farmer and pigs could create such beauty here in the middle of a brushy second-growth forest.

But Joel wasn't through counting the benefits of woodland to a farm; idyllic pig habitat was the least of it.

"There's not a spreadsheet in the world that can measure the value of main-taining forest on the northern slopes of a farm. Start with those trees easing the swirling of the air in the pastures. That might not seem like a big deal, but it reduces evaporation in the fields—which means more water for the grass. Plus, a grass plant burns up fifteen percent of its calories just defying gravity, so if you can stop it from being wind whipped, you greatly reduce the energy it uses keeping its photovoltaic array pointed toward the sun. More grass for the cows. That's the efficiency of a hedgerow surrounding a small field, something every farmer used to understand before 'fencerow to fencerow' became USDA mantra."

Then there is the water-holding capacity of trees, he explained, which on a 50
north slope literally pumps water uphill. Next was all the ways a forest multiples a farm's biodiversity. More birds on a farm mean fewer insects, but most birds won't venture more than a couple hundred yards from the safety of cover. Like many species, their preferred habitat is the edge between forest and field. The biodiversity of the forest edge also helps control predators. As long as the wea-sels and coyotes have plenty of chipmunks and voles to eat, they're less likely to venture out and prey on the chickens.

There was more. On a steep northern slope trees will produce much more biomass than will grass. "We're growing carbon in the woods for the rest of the farm—not just the firewood to keep us warm in the winter, but also the wood-chips that go into making our compost." Making good compost depends on the proper ratio of carbon to nitrogen; the carbon is needed to lock down the more volatile nitrogen. It takes a lot of woodchips to compost chicken or rabbit waste. So the carbon from the woodlots feeds the fields, finding its way into the grass and, from there, into the beef. Which it turns out is not only grass fed but tree fed as well.

These woods represented a whole other order of complexity that I had failed to take into account. I realized that Joel didn't look at this land the same way I did, or had before this afternoon: as a hundred acres of productive grassland patchworked into four hundred and fifty acres of unproductive forest. It was all of a biological piece, the trees and the grasses and the animals, the wild and the domestic, all part of a single ecological system. By any conventional accounting, the forests here represented a waste of land that could be put to productive use. But if Joel were to cut down the trees to graze more cattle, as any conventional accounting would recommend, the system would no longer be quite as whole or as healthy as it is. *You can't just do one thing.*

For some reason the image that stuck with me from that day was that slender blade of grass in a too big, wind-whipped pasture, burning all those calories just to stand up straight and keep its chloroplasts aimed at the sun. I'd always thought of the trees and grasses as antagonists—another zero-sum deal in which the gain of the one entails the loss of the other. To a point, this is true: More grass means less forest; more forest less grass. But either-or is a construction more deeply woven into our culture than into nature, where even antagonists depend on one another and the liveliest places are the edges, the in-betweens or both-ands. So it is with the blade of grass and the adjacent forest as, indeed, with all the species sharing this most complicated farm. Relations are what matter most, and the health of the cultivated turns on the health of the wild. Before I came to Polyface I'd read a sentence of Joel's that in its diction had struck me as an awkward hybrid of the economic and the spiritual. I could see now how characteristic that mixing is, and that perhaps the sentence isn't so awkward after all: "One of the greatest assets of a farm is the sheer ecstasy of life."

Questions for Critical Reading

1. What makes Polyface so successful? Locate passages where Pollan describes the key features of this farm, reading this essay critically to abstract the key factors to the farm's success.

2. What is a "holon"? Use Pollan's text to define this term and to offer examples. Then apply the concept to another area by locating your own example of a holon.

3. Pollan subtitles this essay "Practicing Complexity." Use his text to explain what this means, referring to specific quotations or passages that show complexity in practice. You will need to read critically to determine your answer since Pollan never explains the relationship between this subtitle and his essay.

Exploring Context

1. Learn more about Polyface Farm by visiting its Web site at polyfacefarms.com. Look under "Products" for pictures of the Eggmobile and the Gobbledygo. You can also learn more about the farm by checking the sections on "Principles" and "Our Story." How do you see the ideas that Pollan discusses at work in the farm's Web site? Use your work on the success of Polyface from Question 1 of Questions for Critical Reading in making your response.

2. Visit the Web site for the U.S. Department of Agriculture's National Organic Program at ams.usda.gov/nop. What differences can you locate between the philosophy of organic farming at Polyface and that of the U.S. government? Which seems like a better standard for "organic," and why?

3. Spend some time at Michael Pollan's home page, michaelpollan.com. How does this essay fit into Pollan's other writing? What biases do you think he might have based on the information you find on his site? Do these biases make a difference in this essay?

Questions for Connecting

1. Pollan's description of Polyface Farm reveals a complex economic and ecological system. In what ways is this system consistent with the global supply chains that Thomas Friedman explores in "The Dell Theory of Conflict Prevention" (p. 121)? Can local and global economic systems work together?

2. What role does feedback play in ecological systems? Use Steven Johnson's ideas about feedback in "Listening to Feedback" (p. 191) to explain the success of Polyface Farm. Connect your response to the work you did on Polyface and complexity in Questions 1 and 3 of Questions for Critical Reading.

3. Michael Kimmelman explores collections in "The Art of Collecting Lightbulbs" (p. 216). How can we view farming as a kind of art? What sort of collection is necessary for a successful organic farm like Polyface?

Language Matters

1. Find a passage in Pollan's text that you think is central to his argument. Identify each of the verbs in your selected passage. What are the key verbs? What is the *action* of these sentences? Are there more verbs used in clauses? What are the implications of where each verb is located and what kind of verb is used? How can you apply these insights to your own writing?

2. Knowing your audience is a crucial factor in the success of any piece of writing. Looking at Pollan's writing, what audience do you think he has in mind? How do you know that? What audience should you keep in mind when writing in this class? How can you make sure that your writing reflects that audience?

3. Conjunctions are words that join nouns, phrases, or clauses. Find two quotations that seem to have some relation in Pollan's essay (or choose one from Pollan and one from another essay you've read for this class). Express the relationship between the two quotations using only one conjunction. When might you want to use this same conjunction in your own writing?

Assignments for Writing

1. Pollan reviews farmer Joel Salatin's alternative farming methods, in the process prompting us to question the very nature of farming. By attempting to simplify and sanitize farming, have we moved away from the health and efficiency inherent in a natural system? Can the benefits of biotechnology outweigh the benefits of symbiosis and nature? As biotechnology pushes science and food toward new frontiers, will we find that the old ways of farming are the better, more healthful ways, or is technologically engineered food simply a measurement of healthy progress, no different than progress in any other arena? Using Pollan's essay, formulate an argument on the relationship between food production methods and health. To support your position, consider the alternatives to Salatin's farming methods, the effect of farming practices on our health, and how the interdependence among the different parts of the farming process affects not only the farmer, the animals, and the farm's products but the consumer as well. Use your work with complexity from Question 3 of Questions for Critical Reading.

2. Using Pollan's essay, write a paper in which you evaluate the efficiency of nature-based farming methods versus the efficiency of biotechnology-based farming methods in food production. What does Pollan mean when he describes Salatin's methods as "holon"-based? Why don't we all still farm in the traditional, interdependent manner practiced by Salatin? What are the benefits and disadvantages to "alternative," natural farming? What are the benefits and disadvantages to farming with biotechnology? Do complexity and multiculture lead to better efficiency? Are complexity and multiculture more or less efficient than simplicity and monoculture? Use your work with Pollan's essay from Questions for Critical Reading to support your argument.

3. As agribusiness continues to expand in a global economy, will we find that the old ways of farming are the more effective ways, or will we find current monoculture practices are needed to keep up with the demands of an ever-expanding world population? Using Pollan's essay, write a paper in which you evaluate the advantages of monoculture-based farming methods versus multiculture-based farming methods in food production. What are the benefits and disadvantages to "alternative," natural farming, or what Pollan calls "coevolutionary

relationships"? What are the benefits and disadvantages to farming with biotechnology in the form of vaccines, disease-resistant crop varieties, chemical
fertilizers, and genetically modified seeds? Are complexity and multiculture
necessary to feed the modern world? Are complexity and multiculture more or
less efficient than simplicity and monoculture? Draw from your work on complexity from Question 3 of Questions for Critical Reading.

VIRGINIA POSTREL

Virginia Postrel, who holds a B.A. in English literature from Princeton University, is a writer on politics, economics, and culture. She regularly contributes to the "Culture & Commerce" column in the *Atlantic Monthly* and has also written for *Forbes*, the *New York Times*, and the *Wall Street Journal*. Known for her libertarian philosophy, Postrel served as editor of *Reason* magazine for more than a decade, during which she won a Free Press Association Mencken Award. She also serves on the board of directors of the Foundation for Individual Rights in Education (FIRE), an organization concerned with civil liberties on college campuses.

Postrel has published two books: *The Future and Its Enemies: The Growing Conflict over Creativity, Enterprise, and Progress* (1998) and *The Substance of Style: How the Rise of Aesthetic Value Is Remaking Commerce, Culture, and Consciousness* (2003), from which "The Boundaries of Design" is drawn. In *The Substance of Style*, Postrel argues that aesthetic value is growing in importance and is changing the personal and professional lives of Americans. This growth, though, is not something to fear—it is a symptom of a vibrant, dynamic society. This outlook reflects Postrel's similarly forward-looking philosophy, dynamism, which she examined in her first book.

"The Boundaries of Design" addresses the role of aesthetics in public life and, more important, the role of the public in shaping aesthetics. The democratization of taste has created a nation of experts, argues Postrel, each of whom holds an opinion about the design of public buildings, a neighbor's house, even a neighbor's outfit. Postrel also addresses the issues facing a society in which others—from community organizations to government agencies—impose taste on individuals.

Few of us consider the impact aesthetics has had on our everyday lives. But Postrel suggests that it is an essential component of our world, one closely tied to systems of cultural and political power, making it an important concern for us all.

▶ TAGS: *social change*, *identity*, ***aesthetic boundaries***, *community*, *diplomacy*, *diversity*

The Boundaries of Design

Los Angeles artist Mike McNeilly was up high on the wall of a ten-story Westwood office building, painting a mural, when a building inspector showed up and ordered him to stop.[1] McNeilly, who had permission from the building owner but no permit from the city, kept going. Then the cops showed up. "I was told in no uncertain terms from LAPD, 'You either stop painting or you're going to jail,'" he later recalled. With no desire to spend his weekend in the slammer, McNeilly quit working. He was charged with five misdemeanors.

For more than a year thereafter, a striking monument stared west down Wilshire Boulevard: a jaggedly incomplete Statue of Liberty, her face vanishing below her eyes. McNeilly had inadvertently created a graphic symbol of the intensifying conflicts between aesthetic expression and aesthetic control.

When "design is everywhere, and everywhere is now designed," whoever determines look and feel controls a great deal of economic and personal value. As our surroundings get more aesthetically pleasing, the things we find ugly or disconcerting stand out. We demand better design, and that demand inevitably generates conflict. "Design" implies a single set of purposes served by a coherent aesthetic. But not everyone has the same purposes or finds the same elements enjoyable. Identities differ and so do tastes, including the taste for variety versus consistency. Depending on its boundaries, then, design can be satisfying or tyrannical. It ranges from the individualistic, expressing one identity among many possibilities, to the totalitarian, subordinating all particulars to a unitary vision.

Does the aesthetic imperative mean letting all of us pursue our individual aesthetic dreams? Or does it demand that we eliminate stylistic oddities to maintain a consistent theme? Both approaches generate meaning and pleasure. Both create aesthetic value. The challenge is to keep each in its place. To avoid design tyranny, we need to find the right boundaries — to discover rules that preserve aesthetic discovery and diversity, accommodating plural identities and tastes, while still allowing the pleasures of consistency and coherence.

Aesthetics may be a form of expression, but it doesn't enjoy the laissez-faire status accorded speech or writing. To the contrary, the more significant look and feel become, the more they tend to be restricted by law. The very power of beauty encourages people to become absolutists — to insist that other people's stylistic choices, or their trade-offs between aesthetics and other values, constitute environmental crimes. Individuals may expect more expressive freedom for themselves, but they often feel affronted and victimized by the aesthetic choices of others. This is particularly true for places, the touchstone category of our aesthetic era.

The desire for attractive, controlled, immersive environments extends beyond the walls of shopping malls or restaurants. When designer Karim Rashid says, "Our entire physical landscape has improved, and that makes people more critical as an audience," he's thinking of the market for products like his. But that critical audience doesn't just shop for trash cans and furniture. It buys houses and drives down city streets. And it has opinions about how the landscape should look, opinions that increasingly shape not only personal choices but the rules governing the built environment. Instead of tolerating sights they don't like, from tacky porch furniture to innovative architecture, more and more people are demanding a world free of "visual pollution."

Home owners take offense at their neighbors' paint colors, their window frames, even their kids' play equipment. "The 'not in my backyard' creed, so deftly applied to public works, has been given a new kicker: 'and not in yours either,'" wrote a *New York Times* reporter after her backyard neighbors objected to the swing set she and her husband had put up for their young son.[2] Following zoning regulations, the couple had placed the swing set well inside their yard, shielded by trees and bushes. But the neighbors complained they could see it from their bathroom window. "We like to think of your yard as an extension of ours," they said, voicing an increasingly common attitude. "People are definitely less tolerant than they used to be," says a suburban New York building inspector.

Over the past two decades, master-planned communities with standardized styles and prescriptive "pattern books" have become the norm for large-scale home developments. These communities sell predictability. While old-line suburbs started out fairly uniform to keep down construction costs, owners could (and did) dramatically transform their homes over time. Master-planned developments, by contrast, seek to control changes. Buyers are bound by contract to abide by rules designed to preserve a certain look and feel.

The Highlands Ranch community in Colorado, for instance, limits house numbers to no more than six inches tall and kids' backyard clubhouses to no more than twenty-four square feet.[3] No white picket fences are allowed in most neighborhoods. An enforcement team cruises the streets looking for such offenses as deviant home colors. (A light purple house got neighbors particularly riled up.) A competing community, Prospect New Town, takes a contrasting tack, going so far as to require striking colors on its houses—no Highlands Ranch neutrals allowed. Prospect, too, tightly regulates its environment. The developers require changes on 95 percent of the new house plans submitted for their approval. "It sounds harsh," says one. "But somebody's taste has to prevail, or else it would be anarchy."

No white picket fences are allowed.

In this case, the taste enforcement occurs within a voluntary profit-sensitive development that has to compete with nearby alternatives offering radically different design philosophies. Home buyers select the design regime that fits their personalities and lifestyles, and business success depends on design rules that please potential residents. But design restrictions aren't limited to competing contractual communities. The public sector has jumped into the act, bringing similarly uniform standards to property owners who don't necessarily want them.

Building appearance is getting the sort of government scrutiny once reserved for public health and safety. A 1993 survey found that 83 percent of American cities and towns had some form of design review to control building looks, usually on purely aesthetic (as opposed to historic preservation) grounds.[4] Three-quarters of these regulations, covering 60 percent of cities and towns, were passed after 1980, an adoption rate survey author Brenda Case Scheer compares to "zoning in the 1930s." The trend appears to have accelerated in the late nineties.

Some communities prescribe design rules in detailed *dos* and *don'ts*. Others use general terms like *appropriate* and *compatible*, illustrated with drawings showing acceptable and unacceptable examples. Scheer recalls a suburb that had no specific rules at all, allowing the design review board to outlaw whatever members happened to dislike. The result was an ad hoc checklist of idiosyncratic no-nos—"the *strangest* things," she says, "like they didn't want to have any windows with round tops on them. The decking on a deck couldn't run diagonally. If you had shutters, your shutters had to be able to close."[5]

This town isn't an isolated example. Architectural review boards, planning commissions, and city councils often have broad discretion to determine and enforce taste standards, from mandating rooflines and window styles to specifying what kinds of trees can be planted. Minutes of routine meetings record officials opining that the red leaves of ornamental bushes will clash with the brick of a shopping center sign and instructing a housing developer to build more single-story homes on certain streets.[6] In one town, a city council member praised the beauty of Bradford pear trees, while in another an official condemned them as an "epidemic."

In Eden Prairie, Minnesota, authorities ordered a Caribbean restaurant to cut down its summertime palm trees because they undercut the downtown's "visual theme."[7] Savannah, Georgia, told a hotel's owners they could not use a half-inch brick veneer to remodel the building but would have to use full-size bricks, reducing the size of the rooms.[8] Mequon, Wisconsin, ordered McDonald's to keep its building beige and tan, rejecting the restaurant's plan to adopt a retro look with the chain's original red, yellow, and white color scheme.[9] In Fairfax, Virginia, the owner of a golf driving range spent ninety-seven days in jail after refusing to plant nearly three hundred trees and shrubs ordered by local zoning officials.[10]

In Portland, Oregon, you can no longer build a new home whose front is less than 15 percent windows and doors or whose garage takes up more than half the façade.[11] The front door must be within eight feet of the longest street-facing wall. The goal of the ordinance, said a local official in response to critics, was to "put a stop to the ugly and stupid houses that we see going up."[12] Environmental policy is not just about clean air and water anymore. It is, increasingly, about legislating tastes.

"To feel secure in a changing and diverse society, we seem to need consistency, neatness, and 'quality,' wrapped in a reassuring, even sentimental typology," writes Scheer, an architect and urban planning professor who has grown skeptical of the design-review process she once championed.[13] "We are tired of ravaged commercial corridors, garish billboards, the ubiquitous and ever-changing steel-framed buildings coated in the flavor of the month. We want our neighbor to mow his lawn and keep his whirligigs out of sight in his own backyard."

Neither environmental aesthetics nor aesthetic conflict is limited to the outdoors, however. Personal appearance also sparks disputes, particularly within the workplace. Today's tolerance for divergent styles makes conflict more apparent. With less social consensus to dictate the proper appearance, workers sometimes expect more expressive freedom than the boss's standards allow. When style is strategy and hotels have "casting directors," how employees look can be as much a part of the atmosphere as the grain of the furniture or the beat of the background music. To create its signature environment, Starbucks not only controls the look, feel, sound, and smell of its stores. It also gives employees a uniform and requires them to cover tattoos and remove most piercings—a rule whose existence demonstrates how common those once-transgressive adornments have become. "I just take it as a protocol," says a seven-year Starbucks veteran who hides his tattoos under wristbands. "It's a business."[14]

Not all workers are so agreeable. Today's dress codes may be more about interior decorating than authority and conformity, but they can still provoke rebellion. Employees take their appearance as seriously as employers do, and they're especially likely to protest when the rules change. When Harrah's casino in Reno, Nevada, began requiring female employees to sign a promise to wear mascara, blush, powder, and lipstick to work, one bartender refused, was fired, and sued.[15] When the Dallas Police Department began enforcing a long-ignored hairstyle policy, two officers refused to cut their dreadlocks and were fired.[16] One filed a complaint with the Equal Employment Opportunity Commission; the other sued, alleging wrongful discharge.

At first glance, it may seem that only the employees in these cases are arguing for free expression, objecting to rules that violate their sense of identity. In fact, both sides want the freedom to establish an aesthetic personality. For the employee, that identity is personal; for the employer it's organizational. The employer is using how employees look to create a particular atmosphere or suggest what sort of place it is.

The two sides may even agree on what employees' appearance should signal and disagree only on the interpretation. To the cops who wouldn't cut their hair, dreadlocks are natural, practical hairstyles that represent honesty and strength. To the police department, by contrast, dreadlocks signify insensitivity and insubordination, violating the department's need to present a "neutral and uniform image, to effectively relate to all segments of the population." A significant minority of the public sees locked hair as a sign of rebellion or racial separatism, inappropriate messages for a police officer to send. The problem is that dreadlocks do mean all these different, contradictory things. Both sides are right. Even more than beauty, meaning is in the eye of the beholder.

The policy question isn't whether freedom of expression is good but where the design boundaries should be. Who gets to decide which aesthetic matches which purposes? Forcing an employer to accept an unwanted style is in some sense like forcing a newspaper to publish articles that disagree with its editorial viewpoint, or like redesigning a magazine or reediting a film against the will of its owners. Authors, graphic designers, and movie directors have freedom of expression, but they can't require businesses to use their work. They have to compete with others offering different visions and talents, and they often have to alter their creations to suit their clients, or to quit jobs they believe are making unreasonable demands. And, of course, they're free to raise a public fuss about their would-be employers' bad judgment.

Such disputes are more amenable to the give-and-take of negotiation than to the black and white of law, which must operate without the parties' intimate knowledge of particulars. Successful managers will avoid driving off valued employees simply on the basis of looks, one reason for the spread of "business casual" dress and for the adoption of more stylish and personalizable uniforms everywhere from McDonald's to upscale hotels. Still, some conflicts are inevitable. As more lines of work incorporate aesthetic aspects, claims of expressive freedom and disputes over "creative differences" will spread into new areas.

Choosing employees may itself be partly a design decision, often a subliminal one: Who seems to match the place? Who will appeal to customers? The most important considerations are, of course, qualities of personality and character. But like casting a play, "casting" a work role may mean considering appearance as well — not just how employees dress or wear their hair but how they look to begin with. When such considerations are overt, they, too, can provoke controversy. Given the history of legally enforced racial and gender discrimination, we tend to condemn any hiring choices that seem to reflect similarly superficial preferences.

In Britain, it may be all right for a personnel manager to tell an interviewer that his hotel hires "young, very friendly . . . people that look the part . . . [and] fit in with the whole concept of the hotel."[17] American employers who look for a certain type, however, can find themselves in trouble with the law, which rarely recognizes design as a valid reason for favoring one job applicant over another. After celebrity hotelier Ian Schrager took over the Mondrian Hotel in Los Angeles, his new management fired the bell staff and hired a new "cool-looking" crew.[18] All of the new staff was white, compared to only one of the fired employees. The EEOC filed a suit, which the hotel settled, paying each former bellman $120,000.

"Cool" comes in all colors, of course, which casts doubt on the Mondrian's rationale. But what if the hotel had fired its old bellmen and hired a cool-looking multiethnic staff? That probably wouldn't fly either. A jury made up of uncool regular folks would sympathize with the dismissed workers, says a plaintiff's lawyer.[19] To avoid discrimination charges, warns an attorney who represents employers, the new staff "would also have to be multiage. If you think 'cool' means young folks, you've got a problem."[20] The EEOC's lawyer in the Mondrian case goes further, arguing that hiring only "lithe" or "athletic-looking" people would violate the Americans With Disabilities Act, which would also protect anyone with "a limb impairment, or a facial impairment, or a disfigurement."[21]

"It's one thing to have to have somebody who's slender and athletic and young-looking playing Tinkerbell in a Broadway production of *Peter Pan*," she says. "It's something entirely different if the job is to wait on tables, or if the essence of the job is to carry bags, or to check people in and make sure to get the correct information and assign the correct room."

Looks and personal style, which vary with the individual, are more like personality, strength, or initiative than they are like the status categories of race and gender. If a charming or intelligent person can have an edge in the job market, why not a handsome or stylish one? Neither charm nor intelligence is distributed any more equally than good looks. But in the lawyer's view, personal appearance is simply not a legitimate source of value outside a few conventionally artistic fields like theater. The "essence of the job" in a hotel, she insists, must have nothing to do with look and feel, which are extraneous considerations. A hotel shouldn't use its staff to create an aesthetically pleasing environment or send signals about what sort of place it is. Form is not part of function, goes this reasoning, so the law should not recognize an aesthetic imperative.

Fitness clubs feature beautiful bodies in their advertising and in their hiring. These businesses sell aesthetic aspiration; the boom in gym memberships reflects not just health concerns but heightened competition to look good. So it's not surprising that Jazzercise Inc. declined to certify a 240-pound woman as an aerobics instructor, telling her that "a Jazzercise applicant must have a higher muscle-to-fat ratio and look leaner than the public."[22] At five feet eight inches tall, Jennifer Portnick was about one hundred pounds overweight. If she wanted to lead Jazzercise classes, the company said, she would have to develop a "more fit appearance."

Portnick filed a complaint with the San Francisco Human Rights Commission. Her argument was the same as the EEOC lawyer's: An aerobic instructor's form isn't part of her function. The "essence of the job" is to lead exercise classes, not to look trim doing so, and the essence is all that counts. Jazzercise, Portnick charged, had illegally discriminated against her. Under San Francisco's "fat and short ordinance" she had a strong case. The ordinance

> **Jazzercise Inc. declined to certify a 240-pound woman as an aerobics instructor.**

puts the burden on employers to prove that weight is a "bona fide occupational qualification" and declares that "weight may not be used as a measure of health [or] fitness." It flatly prohibits considering whether obese employees might turn off customers: "The wishes, tastes, or preferences of other employees or customers may not be asserted to justify discrimination." Under legal pressure, Jazzercise revised its rules.

More interesting than the legal result was the media's almost entirely sympathetic treatment of Portnick's cause. Beautiful bodies create anxiety as well as pleasure and aspiration, and the commentary on the case reflected that anxiety. What a relief it was to think that looks might be irrelevant even to leading aerobics classes! To argue that Portnick's obesity really made no difference at all to the job, however, commentators couldn't justify San Francisco's regulation on humanitarian grounds. They couldn't just say Jazzercise was cruel or unfair. They had to declare the law cost-free, even beneficial to the employer. So they insisted that Jazzercise's aesthetic strategy made no business sense—that, contrary to its understanding of its market, the company would actually be better off with fat instructors. Again and again, outside observers second-guessed the company's judgment and identity, declaring that obese fitness teachers would attract customers.

"Don't tell me her 'appearance' is a turnoff.[23] The large, muscular, and graceful woman was the first fitness teacher I ever had who didn't embody some impossible physical dream," wrote syndicated columnist Ellen Goodman after attending a Portnick class. The hosts of ABC's daytime talk show *The View* took the same line.[24] "A skinny broad is going to annoy me," said the show's famously hefty Star Jones. "Surely, there must be room for all types of fitness teachers," editorialized the *San Francisco Chronicle*, concluding, "We hope Portnick gets her wish."[25]

Behind these arguments is a testable business hypothesis: that Jazzercise is leaving money on the table by not providing fat-friendly aerobics classes. Nothing stops these commentators, or those who agree with them, from pitting their aesthetic theory against Jazzercise's. The business is fairly easy to enter, and many nonprofit groups also offer potential venues. Portnick herself teaches at a local YMCA. A chain of Star Jones aerobics centers would even have celebrity selling power.

Experience, however, suggests that the commentators are wrong. Despite an easy-to-enter marketplace and intense competition for new clients, the world is not full of fat aerobics instructors (although some niche classes do exist). Apparently most potential customers really do prefer teachers with trim bodies, whether because thin instructors inspire greater effort, because they're simply more enjoyable to look at, or because people who identify with fat instructors won't actually take aerobics classes.

The commentary also ignores the crucial issue of design boundaries, seeking to impose the commentators' aesthetic preferences—a range of body types—on every exercise studio. If "there must be room for all types of fitness teachers," that room does not have to be under the same roof. Jazzercise is one operator among many. Its rules do not dictate a uniform aesthetic to the entire marketplace any more than Star Jones's straightened hair means all women must wear their hair straight. In a diverse exercise marketplace, some chains might want to establish their identities around slim instructors, others might prefer fit but fat role models, and some might hire both. Just as master-planned communities can offer competing ideals that attract different sorts of home buyers—Highlands Ranch conservatism versus Prospect New Town avant-garde—so not all health clubs need to be the same. Forcing every organization into a single design strategy because that identity suits some potential customers is both intolerant and unnecessary.

But the temptation to second-guess other people's aesthetic choices is nearly irresistible. Everyone, after all, has opinions about what looks good (or bad) and when aesthetics is, or is not, a legitimate concern. Those convictions determine how we make our own world special and how we use look and feel to signal who we are. We enjoy having—and sharing—our opinions of other people's aesthetic choices, a habit that can, of course, be quite unpleasant when we're subject to those judgments ourselves: *Can you believe that hideous tie? . . . What a beautiful garden. . . . He obviously spends way too much time on his hair. . . . That's a cool car. . . . I like that house, but the green trim is too bright. . . . Bell-bottoms were ugly in the 1970s, and they're still ugly. . . . She'd look better if she colored her gray hair. . . .* Even without professional critics, the world would buzz with aesthetic judgments. They are a normal part of human social interaction, a sign of the importance we "visual, tactile creatures" place on look and feel.

Our eagerness to make aesthetic judgments can blind us, however, to the differing aesthetic values of other people. Rather than trust the trial and error of
experimentation and experience, we presume we can deduce in advance what's
best, dismissing or ignoring contrary theories and opposing tastes. If our aesthetic
preferences are good for us, we often assume they're good for everyone. Although
we live in an age of aesthetic plenitude, we sometimes forget that our tastes may
not be universal. The right house or neighborhood layout for me is not necessarily
the right house or neighborhood layout for you; our identities, as well as our lifestyles, are different. Myopic aesthetic judgments become particularly problematic
when the judges have the political power to enforce their tastes, all the more so
when the law establishes no clear stopping point for that interference.

Consider these passages from the minutes of the design review board in
Mount Pleasant, South Carolina, a suburb of Charleston.[26] An architect is presenting plans for a restaurant to be built in the Towne Centre shopping center.
Among other details, he explains: "The restaurant has a very nice back bar of
custom designed mahogany and glass shelves. They have incorporated a nice
area of glass block there instead of storefront windows to give texture and light
and visual interest." After the planning staff comments on the design, board
members weigh in:

> [The first board member said] they may have to get rid of the ceramic tile
> band, but brick detailing could be just as nice. The brick color should be
> uniform to allow the detail to be read rather than the brick texture. . . .
> He asked about the glass block. [The architect] said it is incorporated
> into the design of the bar itself to allow light through the bar. [The
> board member] said he cannot recall if any glass block was used in
> Towne Centre at all; but, he feels it is out of place. Glass block at a door
> tends to be uninviting. [Another board member] said it looks good. . . .
> [A third board member said] his three concerns are the glass block on
> either side of the door, the left elevation has no detail from the back of
> the window on, and the rear elevation is a big green box. . . . Green is
> probably better than silver, but it would not be his choice.

These criticisms, expressing board members' personal feelings about tile,
brick, glass block, and green paint, are a long way from straightforward rules
like "plant trees and hide the garbage cans" meant to avoid imposing a nui-
sance on the neighbors.

Mount Pleasant does have lots of explicit design rules—no neon, for
instance—but the board's critique is open-ended. If members don't like glass
block or ceramic tile, they say so, even if the city has no law against either material. An architect who wants his plans approved will bend his client's budget,
tastes, and aesthetic identity to suit the board, all the more so if he expects to
submit future plans to the same board.

"Design review turns architectural designers into legal strategists and
political conspirators; it suppresses artistry and innovation; and like other
forms of absolute power, it corrupts those who wield it and compromises the
processes they preside over," writes architect Denise Scott Brown.[27] In the

40

process, the goals of the original design are likely to be lost, overridden by out-siders' aesthetic judgments. Instead of glass block to "give texture and light and visual interest," you wind up with a standard plate-glass window, inoffensive but uninteresting. "In short," says Scott Brown, "design review is a lawyer's, not an artist's, solution to the problem of obtaining quality in design."

Such forced homogenization is what made Brenda Scheer begin to doubt the wisdom of many design review laws. As a planner in Boston, she and her staff used their regulatory power to reward developers who matched their idea of good design, sending back for revisions the plans they disliked. Over time, local architects got the message. "Projects submitted were more and more ac-ceptable and similar, responding to the developing sense of what my staff would accept," she writes.[28] "After several years, I was pleased: My view of the urban landscape became solidified and official."

But Scheer began to wonder whether a city of "acceptable and similar" buildings was such a good thing after all. Planners were implicitly turning the city into a single design project, reflecting a uniform vision. Intended to avoid bad architecture, design review had become an open-ended invitation to demand revisions, substituting the reviewer's judgments and priorities for the builder's. The process was stamping out variety and squelching architectural creativity. "One day," writes Scheer,

> I sat in on a review of a simple housing project. One of the staff reviewers, a recent architecture-school grad, was marking up a set of drawings—drawings that in the early days of mediocrity would have been greeted with pleasure because of their sense of context and originality. He didn't like the porch or the roof detail. The size of the brick was "wrong." A bulb clicked in my head, and the long process of questioning began.

When aesthetic experiments require official permission, even slightly un-usual ideas tend to get screened out. (Hence the objection to glass block.) Innovations may offend conventional sensibilities or, just as likely, simply be hard to explain in advance. The result, writes Scheer, is that "all over the country, in every state and most cities, adventurous design is being smoothed out or blocked outright.[29] At issue here is not the freedom of the 'prima donna' architects, but the potential of the city, of any designed environment, to be a sharp and stimulating place."

Even when planning authorities don't enjoy limitless power to revise and fiddle, they tend to overreach the boundaries of their knowledge. They don't have the building owner's understanding of or concern for the structure's organizational context and purposes. They haven't gone through the thinking to figure out how to solve specific problems of site, use, and budget. They may not share the owner's tastes or tacit understanding of what effects the design is trying to achieve. And, of course, they don't bear the costs, financial or oth-erwise, of the changes they dictate. The result can be absurd, as in the strange case of the Frist Campus Center at Princeton University.

When the school decided to establish a full-service student center in the late 1990s, it hired Venturi, Scott Brown and Associates, who had already designed 45 four new buildings for the campus and renovated many others. Robert Venturi, a Princeton graduate, and Denise Scott Brown had won plaudits for integrating the forms, colors, and decorative enthusiasm of the campus's traditional Gothic styles with the starker, machine-made geometries of contemporary architecture. Their buildings, concludes a critic, "demonstrated that a modern architect did not have to turn his back on history."[30]

The campus center demanded that ability to integrate past and present. It would begin with a three-story Tudor Gothic building opened in 1909 to house the physics department. The old Palmer Hall had the modest doors and leaded windows typical of Princeton's older classroom buildings. It was substantial but essentially private. Along with extensive remodeling inside, the architects sought to turn the building into a campus focal point and obviously public place, giving new meaning to the old structure without doing violence to the original design. An extension at the rear would be transparent, with a two-story graphic of the Princeton shield etched in the rectangular wall of paned glass. Along the path in front of the building, a freestanding arcade—a row of rectangular columns topped by a horizontal beam—would invite entry through ten different openings. Across the 215-foot-long arcade's top, FRIST CAMPUS CENTER would be carved in letters two to three feet square. Each letter would project about a foot above the lintel.

"It is the outer layer which is saying, 'This building is very open,'" explains Venturi.[31] "It does not have one single door in the center for four hundred students and physicists a day. You go through the arcade, and there are several openings that you slide into. That makes it a civic building, a community building in the campus, open and inviting."

For all the architect's thoughtful design, even his fans admit the arcade looked weird in models, "a little Potemkin façade," says one.[32] But the university trusted Venturi's judgment. "We have a long experience with Bob that is extremely reassuring," says an official. "He knows what he's doing. He's good at this." A student activist wasn't so trusting, though. When the local planning board invited comment, he made a passionate argument against "that big ugly thing." Although board members can't regulate aesthetics directly, they found another tool. What Venturi saw as an inviting outer building layer, an "iconographic frieze" integral to the overall design, the board declared an illegally large "accessory sign." Local regulations limit signs to 16 square feet and, by the planning department's calculations, the Frist carving was a 334-square-foot sign.

With a typical combination of anger and humor, Venturi vented his protests in a memo to the university titled "Why the Tasteful Frieze on the Front of the Frist Campus Center Is Not a Vulgar Sign but a Tasteful Frieze—Designed Also by a Highfalutin' Architect."[33] He cited historical precedents, from Elizabethan manor houses to Princeton's own campus architecture "teeming" with symbolic decoration. His arguments failed. The board refused to grant a sign variance. Rather than abandon the arcade altogether, as opponents hoped, the university came up with a novel solution. It erected the structure without any carving, but with room to add the letters later. The shapes of the absent words' tops still rise above the lintel. Like the partly finished Lady Liberty in Los Angeles, the odd humps serve as a monument to the ongoing conflict over look and feel.

Even without the offending sign (or frieze), the design worked. The arcade, which matches the old building's brick and limestone exterior, does create an attractive and inviting entrance that marks Frist as an important, if less clearly labeled, campus gathering place. The space between the arcade and the building forms an implicit outdoor vestibule. Campus visitors who see the mysterious humps and hear their story tend to think the town's rules absurd. These visitors aren't quibbling over the meaning of *sign*. They're wondering why off-campus authorities got to decide anything at all about a structure that is barely visible from the road. If design review can reach inside a university campus, where does it stop? 50

As Princeton's primary physics building, Palmer Hall was long ago obsolete. But it took a novel architectural solution to adapt the building to its new use, a solution no one had thought of before. The campus center's unfamiliar arcade challenged the imaginations of people looking at models, and it fit uneasily into existing planning categories. Only because the university and the architects were stubborn and wily did the arcade survive.

Without the right design boundaries, we risk turning the aesthetic imperative into a justification for homogeneity and stasis, blocking experimentation and crushing the sources of new pleasure and meaning. The aesthetic discovery process is too unpredictable for fixed, uniform standards. Even individuals with settled tastes and identities want some variety over time, as the enduring power of fashion demonstrates. New technologies, from air-conditioning to computer-assisted design, make new styles possible, while cultural and ideological changes generate new identities demanding new aesthetic expressions. There is no one best way, and a static model of "good design" threatens the process through which aesthetic meaning and pleasure evolve. Trying to avoid all aesthetic mistakes can be as damaging as mistakes themselves.

"If you go to Germany or you go to Switzerland and you go through the countryside, there are all these houses that are exactly the same, [only] a little variation.[34] Sometimes they even have coordinated geranium flowers. It looks beautiful—a great place for a vacation," says Logitech founder Pierluigi Zappacosta. The landscape is tightly regulated in these countries, curbing individuality and experimentation in the name of good design.

Things are different in Italy, which also happens to be famous for its wildly creative design industries. "If you go to the Italian countryside where people really live and work, you cannot find two houses that look the same. It's continuous experimentation. And 99 percent of them are *ugly*, but ugly—ugly, ugly, ugly," says Zappacosta. But, he suggests, the culture that allows that experimentation, tolerating failures, is the same culture that produces aesthetic breakthroughs. He quotes a design professor friend: "It is tolerance for the ugliness that is the basis for the greatness of Italian design."

Of course, somebody enjoys those coordinated geraniums, and German design is famous for qualities of its own. No single standard, *even the standard* 55 *that allows maximum variety and experimentation,* can please everyone. Again, the challenge is not to eliminate design but to get the boundaries right. We don't want to force everyone into the world of "anything goes" (itself a particular design choice) but to match design with audience, to align coherent aesthetic with shared purpose. Overstretching the bounds of design implies two unappealing alternatives: too *little* design, offering "something for 'everyone' but nothing specifically for anyone," like the department stores young people shun for their lack of identity, or too *narrow* design, imposing a single well-defined aesthetic on people it doesn't suit.[35]

When legal authorities seek to avoid conflict by eliminating distinctive aesthetic identities—whether that means banning glass block or requiring aerobics instructors who represent all body types—we find ourselves in the homogeneous world of too little design. No one is offended, but no one is pleased. Narrow design, by contrast, excludes all but a limited range of styles, imposing a single clear identity. Thus Portland's ordinance essentially dictates a New Urbanist ideal adapted from early-twentieth-century neighborhoods, excluding many modern designs.

Such sweeping bans spring from the belief that "ugly and stupid houses" are an offense against the community, a form of visual pollution. Invoking pollution is a way of taking aesthetics out of the realm of expression, where liberal societies generally err on the side of freedom, and prescribing a single design for a large territory. But fighting aesthetic "pollution" isn't as straightforward as reducing air or water pollution, because the harms are entirely subjective. While air or water pollution may also have some subjective effects, at least in theory we can base regulatory standards on objective risks to health and safety.[36]

There are no epidemiological standards for good design. As a result, regulation tends to rely on assertions of raw power, reflecting personal quirks rather than predictable rules.[37] While design review boards made up of lay citizens drive architects crazy with their "offend no one" blandness dictates (too little design), expert reviewers can just as easily use their power to enforce their favorite professional dogmas (too narrow design). The Washington Fine Arts Commission even vetoed a headquarters proposed by the American Institute of Architects, apparently because its postmodern style offended the commission's modernist views.[38]

This problem does not mean that aesthetic spillovers cause no harms. If look and feel can be subjectively valuable, they can also be subjectively detrimental. Economists talk about pollution in terms of "externalities," which impose involuntary costs on third parties who don't reap the benefits; to the person bearing them, those costs are real regardless of whether some expert can measure an objective harm.

When Bard College proposed a performing arts center designed by Frank Gehry, neighbors in its Hudson Valley community protested.[39] Glimpses of the flashy stainless-steel building, they argued, would spoil the views from hiking trails and from an 1804 mansion preserved as a historic site. To avoid lengthy court battles, the college moved the building site farther inside campus, raising construction costs by about $10 million. When I mentioned the case in a column on aesthetic conflicts, my editor responded with a note excoriating Gehry's design: "The Bard development was a modernist monstrosity that would have damaged property values in a fifteen-mile radius.[40] Isn't there an externality here that has to be addressed? And if [Bard president and symphony conductor Leon] Botstein can force me to look at something like this, the next thing you know he will force me to listen to Schoenberg in the Grand Central waiting room."

The fifteen-mile radius is hyperbole—it's hard to imagine any building whose architecture alone could affect such a wide area—but the general point is legitimate: Aesthetic choices create spillovers. They impose costs on people with different sensibilities. Not surprisingly, most aesthetic conflicts arise from externalities.[41] We don't care that much about aesthetic choices we never experience. Your ugly house bothers your neighbors; your ugly sofa does not.

But just about everything people do in society—from the way they raise their children to the way they worship God—creates spillovers, many of them subjectively harmful. Only an isolated hermit has no effect on other people. And to some onlookers, negative aesthetic externalities would include not only peeling paint, cluttered billboards, or strange architecture but bad skin, thunderous thighs, or a penchant for plaid. Taste is subjective, and aesthetic identity is often personal. Are spillovers really a sort of criminal assault, or are they something more ambiguous? Should we really ban, tax, or otherwise deter any activity that has unpleasant effects on third parties?

Economist Ronald Coase asked that provocative question in a famous 1960 article, "The Problem of Social Cost," which helped win him the 1991 Nobel Prize.[42] He began with an important but counterintuitive point: Pollution is not a simple matter of physical invasion or evildoing. It is a by-product of valuable actions. Simply eliminating the pollution at its source would require harms of its own, by eliminating or reducing that value. The self-professed pollution victim is asking to reap benefits by inflicting harms, to create a mirror image of the original problem. Seeing the Gehry building may damage observers who find it a monstrosity, but denying Bard its stainless-steel building would damage the college.

The policy issue is one of trade-offs—costs and benefits, not good and evil. "The problem which we face in dealing with actions which have harmful effects is not simply one of restraining those responsible for them," observes Coase. "What has to be decided is whether the gain from preventing the harm is greater than the loss which would be suffered elsewhere as a result of stopping the action which produced the harm."

If a Portland resident builds a house with a big garage door facing the street, people who find that façade unfriendly are harmed. But if the city forbids that design, making two-car garages impossible to fit on many lots or forcing builders to design homes with less living space, home buyers who want garages are harmed. The question from a Coasean perspective is, Which is the greater harm, and how should we avoid it? It's incorrect simply to assert that intruding on someone's line of sight is the action that should be prevented. We have to consider the costs and benefits for both sides.

Thinking of the problem as one of reciprocal harms and benefits, Coase realized that if making deals in the marketplace costs nothing, the final level of pollution will be the same regardless of how the law assigns liability. If a factory has the right to operate even if it pollutes, then people who don't want to breathe stinky air can pay the owner not to pollute. If, on the other hand, the neighbors have the legal right not to suffer pollution, the factory can pay them to waive that right. In either case, the pollution will be set at the level that makes everyone as happy as possible.[43] This insight came to be known as the Coase Theorem.

In the Bard case, chances are good that the offended neighbors would have been satisfied with less than $10 million in exchange for letting the building stay put. But an enforceable agreement would have been hard to put together, perhaps impossible. As Coase would be the first to point out, we don't live in a world where deals are free. Gathering information, rounding up all the affected parties, negotiating contracts, monitoring compliance, and so on are all costly. Transaction costs can make agreements difficult, especially when a lot of people are involved.[44] That's why air pollution that harms many dispersed people can't be controlled through simple bargaining. In the real world, the way rights are assigned does matter. We want to mitigate significant harms, but we don't want to deter activities that create more value than they subtract.

The couple won the case in court.

In that cause, Coase argued that it's essential not only to consider both the offense and the personal and social value of the activity that gives rise to it but also to look at all the options, on both sides, for ameliorating the harms. Imagine, he proposed, that a factory spews smoke that causes $100 in damage. Traditional economics might suggest that the government put a $100 tax on the factory to compensate for the pollution. That gives the company an incentive to eliminate the pollution by, for instance, installing a $90 device.

But, noted Coase, the $90 device may not be the only way to avoid $100 in damage, or the most efficient. Again, you have to consider both sides. The harm exists not only because the factory creates smoke but because neighbors are there to be damaged. Suppose instead of eliminating the pollution at the source, the neighbors could avoid it for just $40, by either installing some other technology or perhaps even moving. (Coase obviously chose these figures to illustrate the mathematics of the choice, not as realistic cost estimates.) That would be an even better approach, because it would keep the overall harms to a minimum. If the neighbors had the right not to breathe smoke, the factory would presumably pay them the $40. But the government would have to recognize that the harm had disappeared, even though the smoke had not.

In many cases, if we consider all costs, all benefits, and all possible remedies, it turns out that the least costly way to deal with aesthetic conflicts is what we might call the Italian solution—to look away from the stuff we don't like. The small cost to us is dwarfed by the large benefit to the owner and, in some cases, to other people as well. This is particularly true since the costs of aesthetic tolerance tend to decline over time, another difference from more objective types of pollution. Our senses detect changes in our surroundings more keenly than the ongoing levels of stimuli; we unconsciously adjust our expectations to the background. That's why we don't notice bad smells after a while and why we come out of loud concerts to find ordinary speech seemingly muffled. In the built environment, once-discordant elements tend to become part of the background, going largely unnoticed. And there is a systemic advantage. By tolerating minor negative spillovers from other people's aesthetic choices, we, too, enjoy the advantages of personal expression and aesthetic innovation.

These sorts of calculations, done less explicitly, help explain why home owners generally have had broad freedom to decorate their yards and home exteriors to their own taste — a large benefit to them, at a small cost to neighbors who disagree but can look away. Even when harms are too substantial for the "look away" approach to work, it's often less costly to ameliorate spillovers than to abolish otherwise valuable activities. Because the social value of mobile phone service is so high, for instance, U.S. law prohibits communities from completely banning cell-phone towers.[45] Phone companies don't have the right to build a tower anywhere they want, but the towers can't be kept out altogether. Towns have to find less costly ways to deal with spillovers, requiring disguises on towers, locating them in less intrusive places, or demanding reasonable compensation to nearby residents.

For the cell-phone towers or the Portland garage regulation, the conflict is between aesthetic considerations and other values. If the towers didn't provide a nonaesthetic benefit, no one would want them. Similarly, hardly anybody thinks houses look better with big garage doors facing the street; that design is simply an efficient way to fit a house on a lot. Like smoke from a factory, we can generally agree that a cell-phone tower or a "snout house" does create a negative spillover. That assessment is subjective, but widely shared. In a world without technical or financial constraints, pretty much everyone would agree on what to do. The dispute is about relative costs and benefits, not about what's ideal.

Because of that underlying agreement, it's often possible to find a compromise solution, incrementally improving aesthetics while preserving most nonaesthetic benefits. A big-box store whose architecture is cheap but plain can assuage the neighbors' concerns by spending somewhat more for landscaping or architectural detail, as Wal-Mart has begun to do as it moves into urban locations where neighbors are closer by.[46] Like the cell-tower solutions, these approaches generally work only if the store has a right to operate, subject to reasonable accommodations to the neighbors' sensibilities (the political version of a Coasean bargain). If offended neighbors can block the store altogether, or if a single objector can tie up the issue in court, the store may not be built, even at the cost of making the public at large worse off. Where there's enough flexibility, however, both sides can often find an agreeable solution when aesthetics conflicts with other values.

In other cases, the dispute is more fundamental. There is no agreement on what would be ideal in a world without financial or technical constraints. Tastes simply clash, making trade-offs difficult, if not impossible. When Portland bans houses without many front windows, it's outlawing modern architecture that some people like very much. Critics of the Portland rule usually cite Frank Lloyd Wright's work as something that would be illegal, but the same is true of many midcentury styles, including the Eichler tract homes that today enjoy cultlike devotion and command a price premium. By contrast to the garage rule, this taste conflict wouldn't go away if resources were unlimited. When aesthetics oppose aesthetics, one design regime or another has to win.

In an older neighborhood in Louisville, Kentucky, an art therapist and a graphic designer shocked traditionalist neighbors by building a high-style contemporary house with a façade of plastic, corrugated metal, and concrete tiling. Trying to address neighbors' concerns, the home owners changed some exterior colors, but tastes differed so radically that a satisfactory compromise wasn't possible. Neighbors sued, charging that the house violated deed restrictions. "They want us essentially to tear the house down or dramatically change the exterior," said the couple's lawyer.[47] "I don't see there's a middle ground." The couple won the case in court. The judge ruled that the neighbors couldn't pick and choose when to apply design rules that had been flouted for decades. That the house "is not in keeping with their neighborhood's traditional aesthetics cannot be a basis to selectively enforce the deed restrictions," he said.

When aesthetic preferences are diametrically opposed, the spillovers are not entirely negative. To the contrary, some third parties reap benefits. Some people in Louisville are thrilled with the unusual home; local architects have included it in special tours, and one neighbor calls it "a beautiful addition to the neighborhood."[48] The conflict isn't just between the owner and third parties but between different groups of third parties. Toting up the costs and benefits of an aesthetic spillover, we have to include not only the benefits to the owner, which are generally high, but the dispersed benefits to bystanders who share the same tastes.

Ultimately, the only way to mitigate aesthetic conflicts is to establish design boundaries that recognize the wide variety of people and the impossibility of deducing from aesthetic principles what individuals will, or should, value. We have to return to Adam Smith: to accept the importance of specialization and to understand that a *large market* of many people need not be a *mass market* of homogeneous goods. Good design boundaries won't try to find the one best way to dress, to run an aerobics class, to design a restaurant, or to build a neighborhood. They'll embrace pluralism. They'll allow competition and discovery, including discovery of how big the boundaries should be. A niche design that pleases many people will expand over time. A niche that loses popularity will shrink.

Design boundaries can surround an organization (a restaurant chain's signage and interior design, a company's dress code, a religious order's habit), an informal group (friends' costume echoes a subculture's adornment, a fan group's team logos), or a geographic area (a neighborhood, a shopping district, an office park). Boundaries work best when the rules are clear and members have voluntarily accepted them, when the units are small enough for members to exit without extraordinary cost, and when different design regimes compete.

In the built environment, the need for small units means thinking of an area not as a single design but as a collection of small, self-governing districts with their own design rules—whether prescriptive details, generic structures, or no restrictions at all. If you don't like the rules, you can move without disrupting the rest of your life.[49] The area's overall order emerges from the decentralized decisions of those competing units and the individuals who choose them. Over time, new sets of design rules develop to satisfy previously unmet demands.

In liberal societies, we take such pluralism and competition for granted in most aesthetic realms. Only repressive societies try to dictate dress by law. Only centrally planned economies try to decide without competition what furniture or dishes people should want. If you don't like the green-dominated Starbucks, you can go to the blue-dominated Starbucks two blocks away—or to the bright-green-and-orange tea bar or the Populuxe diner down the street. You can decorate your living room with distressed furniture and folk art, antiques and Persian rugs, or subdued modern couches and chocolate-and-oatmeal walls. Unless you've enlisted in a cable TV makeover show, you don't have to accept what a design czar decrees, and you can change or mix styles at will. Despite some well-publicized disputes, employee dress codes are mostly no big deal, because there are many employers and professions, with many different views of dress; one of the dreadlocked cops quickly got a job in a neighboring police department, while the other became a schoolteacher.

It's hard, however, to fully embrace the idea that there are many good ways to make a neighborhood. In Louisville, some of the most eloquent advocates of architectural freedom sneered at the neighbors' "German 'cave-style'" houses and mocked their affection for brick.[50] While the legal dispute hinged on technical questions, the public debate was between those who declared that the iconoclastic home owners "have no sense of place" and those who said they "should be applauded for trying to be different"—between those who believe continuity is good and those, including the home owners, who believe in "questioning tradition." Like the question of what dreadlocks "really" mean, this dispute can't be settled on the facts. It's a clash of values.

Such ideologically charged disputes are typical. Critiques of the built environment commonly seek not to make incremental improvements, or to offer another choice among many, but to redesign the world into someone's vision of the single right way to live. Designers often believe that the right environment will make people better, with "better" defined by the designer's vision of the good society. If we build suburbs with yards and cul de sacs, away from the smoke and crowds of the city, as the twentieth-century Garden City movement advocated, labor and capital will live in peace. If we build new houses with porches, goes today's New Urbanist reasoning, we'll be neighborly like in the good old days. (Never mind that air-conditioning makes hanging out on the porch less necessary or desirable.) If we outlaw big garages, people will abandon their automobiles. If we build unusual houses, people will be tolerant. If we make a city exactly the way I want to live, everyone will be like me.

When it comes to the built environment, a genuine design pluralist is hard to find. Certainly, the last place I expected to meet one was in an urban-planning firm in Irvine, California. The Orange County town is the epitome of tightly controlled design, a squeaky-clean Edge City of office parks and master-planned neighborhoods, a place without billboards or whirligigs. It's so tidy that when my husband started teaching at the University of California campus there he couldn't find a gas station.

On a bright April day, I've come to Irvine to talk with Steve Kellenberg, who creates master plans for large-scale developments that sell more than a thousand homes a year. These "high-production, high-velocity" businesses represent the present and future of American home construction, supplying homes for the booming suburbs of the Sunbelt.[51] I'd heard Kellenberg tell an audience of developers about survey data showing that 63 percent of buyers in master-planned communities want more diversity, while only 32 percent want their neighborhood to look consistent.

That was what I wanted to hear. Like many variety-loving city dwellers, I'm leery of master-planned communities, even though I know they're extremely popular. It's bad enough that even my little eighteen-unit town-house complex has ridiculously conformist rules—no plants by the front door, no non-neutral window coverings, no door decorations except around Christmas—but at least our homes are literally connected to each other, making the cost of spillovers high. I can't imagine wanting to live in a whole neighborhood of similar uniformity.

But people really are different.

Over and over again, Kellenberg comes back to that message, expressing a tolerance that arises as much from relentless pragmatism as from liberal idealism. If you're in the business of designing environments people will pay money to live in, you can't kid yourself about what they value. You can't design your idea of utopia and force everyone to conform to it; if you try, everyone who isn't just like you will go elsewhere to find a home.

Unlike me, some people really do prefer uniformity to variety, regardless of cost. Not everybody thinks it's bad if every house on the street looks pretty much like every other one, or if people can't change their houses much over time. Some people *like* that sort of predictability. It makes them feel secure, at home in their neighborhood. Even if cost were no object, not everybody would want the same thing I'd pick.

"We have this incredible tendency to overgeneralize about the population and to say, 'Everybody wants this—everybody wants to live in a community where you can't paint your house unless it's the right color and you have to close your garage door,'" says Kellenberg. "Well, the fact is that there really are a lot of people who want that kind of controlled, predictable environment," often because they've had bad experiences in deteriorating neighborhoods. "And there are others that find that an incredibly repressive regime and wouldn't live there if you *gave* them a house, because they believe there should be an organic, fluid, self-expressive environment."

People are different.   90

"You have people in Irvine that love living in Irvine," he says. "And you have people that moved to Irvine and leave after five years because they hate it, and they move to Seal Beach or Santa Ana," nearby towns with few design restrictions. In a diverse society, some people will indeed want a lot of rules, "but it clearly isn't something that *is the right way* of doing it for everybody." Neither is the alternative.

People are different.

Even those survey statistics are misleading aggregates. Some people care a lot about diversity; others really, really want consistency. A lot are in the middle. Some people want to be sure to run into their neighbors. Others just want to stay in with their big-screen TVs or to socialize with the friends they already have. Some people want to be able to walk to the store without seeing a car. Others want to be able to drive in and out easily. The difference isn't one of demographics—age, income, education, and so on—but of identity and attitude. In the same price range, for the same size families, you can find people who want all sorts of different neighborhood designs.

What the survey numbers actually say is that part of the housing market has been underserved. For years, large-scale developers have focused so much on those home buyers who want a predictable environment and the most house for the money that they've ignored other groups. Offer the long-ignored groups a different sort of design, and they'll reward you handsomely. This pragmatic, trial-and-error process of discovering new sources of aesthetic value is less grandiose, and perhaps less inspiring, than the ideological search for the one best way to live. But it is also less divisive and venomous.

You can see its latest products in the spanking-new streets of Ladera Ranch,   95
a huge new development about a half-hour drive southeast of Irvine. A blue-gray Cape Cod home, with the deeply sloping roof of its saltbox ancestors, sits next to an updated beige and brown Craftsman with a low-pitched roof. Down the street is a Spanish Colonial with a red-tile roof and around the corner a stuccoed house whose turret recalls the fantasy homes of 1920s Los Angeles. Although many garages face the street, violating the Portland prescription, most are recessed so they don't dominate the landscape. You see porches and yards and sidewalks—social space. And between the sidewalk and street is something no new Southern California community has gotten in a generation: a small parkway planted with trees, spindly today but promising charm and shade as the neighborhood ages.

These are mass-produced homes, with metal windows and Hardiboard concrete siding rather than wood. They'd never pass purists' tests of authenticity. But they offer something genuine and rare—variation in more than façade, rooflines and massing that match their styles, a street of different colors and different forms. Built on the empty hillsides of what once really was a ranch, Ladera Ranch is turning the previously unfulfilled desire for varied and sociable neighborhoods into extraordinary profits. The development sells twelve hundred houses a year for prices 10 percent to 14 percent higher per square foot than in the more conventional community right next door. The landscaping and construction quality cost more, acknowledges Kellenberg, but even accounting for those costs, "it still appears that there's a 7 to 10 percent lift in the base values that can only be explained by people being willing to pay more to live there."

People are different.

Specialization pays. "There really is a lot of the market that doesn't want everything to look the same, that does want to have individuality in their home, that does want a diversity of neighborhoods, that wants [the design] to feel like it grew out of the heritage of the place, that are interested in meeting their neighbors, that would enjoy having the street designed as a social space, that would like to have other social spaces and social opportunities that they could participate in," he says.

Ladera Ranch's design owes much to the New Urbanism, with its emphasis on community and its understanding of streets as social spaces. But Kellenberg dismisses the New Urbanism's one-size-fits-all doctrines, its "singular mission" that "rejects everything other than New Urbanism." Lots of beloved neighborhoods, he notes, don't conform to New Urbanist prescriptions. The design for Ladera Ranch isn't New Urbanism. It's specialization—specialization within specialization, in fact. The development includes four different neighborhood styles, each crafted to suit a different personality and lifestyle. And if you want something different, you don't have to buy a place in Ladera Ranch. You can go next door. There's something for everyone and, if there isn't, a smart developer will figure out how to fill in the gaps.

The seeming homogeneity of master-planned communities—the planning that gives them a bad name among intellectuals—turns out to be real-world pluralism once you realize that everyone doesn't have to live within the same design boundaries. Community designs and governance structures are continuously evolving, offering new models to compete with the old. This pluralist approach may overturn technocratic notions of how city planning should work, but it's the way towns are in fact developing in the United States, suggesting that these institutions offer real benefits to residents. From 1970 to 2002, the number of American housing units in home-owner associations, including condominiums and cooperatives, rose from 1 percent to 17 percent, with more than half of all new units in some areas in these associations.[52]

As an alternative or supplement to large-scale local government, some economists and legal scholars have begun debating ways to let home owners who aren't in private associations form them, whether for whole neighborhoods or just a few blocks. Some proposals envision the privatization of former city services like garbage collection and of zoning-style regulations.[53] Others want only a specialized complement to city governance, with special fees to cover services that people in that small area particularly value. For instance, suggests a legal scholar, "if artists were to concentrate their studios on a particular city block, their [Block Improvement District] could make unusually heavy expenditures on street sculptures.[54] Indeed, the prospect of forming a Block Improvement District might encourage artists to cluster together in the first place."

Some of these plans would require unanimous agreement, others a supermajority. The question of whether new boundaries can be drawn around residents without their individual consent is a difficult one. If unanimous agreement is necessary, a single holdout can make everyone worse off. But retroactively limiting what property owners can do with their homes raises the same problems of pluralism that allowing small districts is supposed to avoid.

This problem is especially great when the new district isn't truly self-governing. Many cities, for instance, allow a supermajority of home owners to petition to make their neighborhood a historic district subject to special aesthetic controls—potentially a good model of specialized design boundaries. Unfortunately, historic districts usually have to conform to procedures established by a higher level of government. They can't create processes and rules tailored to the wishes of those they govern. In Los Angeles, for instance, a Historic Preservation Overlay Zone is regulated by a five-member board.[55] Unlike a home-owner association board, members are appointed by city officials and other board members, and only three of the five must be residents of the area they govern. Since residents don't have a direct vote, they can't easily predict, or check, the board's actions.

Even some preservation activists admit to concerns. A San Fernando Valley resident who's campaigning to make her neighborhood a historic zone says she isn't looking to crush individual home owners' self-expression, only to raise awareness of the history and value of the neighborhood's midcentury Eichler homes.[56] But some local preservationists are sticklers for architectural authenticity, narrowly defined. If the board is captured by purists, she admits, it might even outlaw the pistachio-green siding she and her husband chose to match their vintage car. "I don't think we'd like that too much ourselves," she says.

Even in the best of circumstances, small, self-governing districts wouldn't eliminate aesthetic conflict. Neither do master-planned communities. As anyone who's lived in a small condo complex knows, even small groups of people disagree. Governance rules simply provide processes for resolving disputes. And they help people know what to expect, avoiding the nasty surprises and bitter conflicts that result when aesthetic rules are imposed after the fact. The best we can hope for isn't perfection but fairness, predictability, and a reasonable chance of finding rules that suit our individual preferences. The advantage of narrow boundaries is that if all else fails, we can vote with our feet, not only improving our own situation but sending a signal that the competition is offering a better design package.

The more difficult it is for people to enter and exit—to find design rules to their liking—the more general the rules need to be. A four-block special district can have very prescriptive rules that would be inappropriate for an entire city. A metropolitan area like Orange County that is made up of many smaller cities can offer a range of city-level design regimes.

In larger areas, one way to accommodate different tastes within an overall sense of structure is to make the rules fairly generic. Consider the difference between a work uniform, a requirement to wear black, and a general prescription for "business casual." All three establish an organizational identity, but each allows more individual choice and flexibility than the previous one, accommodating a wider range of appearance and personality. To attract a diverse group of employees, to avoid turning off independent or creative individuals, or simply to stay up-to-date as fashions change, it may be better to keep the dress code as general as possible.

Along similar lines, Brenda Scheer suggests that urban-design regulations should pay more attention to the urban forms that are hard to change and concentrate less on the stylistic details that are easily altered. It's easy enough to ignore a single building you don't like, especially once it's been around awhile. But street widths, setbacks, and lot sizes affect the whole experience of being in a particular neighborhood. They establish the underlying structure that creates the sense of place. "If you get the lots right and the blocks right and the street right and the setbacks right, somebody can build a crummy house and it will sit there for thirty years, and somebody will tear it down and build a nice one," she says.[57] "There's a kind of self-healing process that's available if the structure is fine."

This model allows for flexibility, personal expression, and change, while still preserving a coherent underlying design. It echoes the pattern identified by Stewart Brand in *How Buildings Learn*, which examines how buildings are adapted to new uses over time.[58] Brand explores what makes architecture resilient and capable of "learning" as its purposes change. A building, he notes, contains six nested systems: Site, Structure (the foundation and load-bearing elements), Skin (the exterior), Services (wiring, plumbing, heating, etc.), Space plan (the interior layout), and Stuff. The further out the nested system, the more permanent. Moving around furniture (Stuff) is easy; altering a foundation (Structure) is difficult. In a building:

> the lethargic slow parts are in charge, not the dazzling rapid ones. Site dominates Structure, which dominates the Skin, which dominates the Services, which dominate the Space plan, which dominates the Stuff. How a room is heated depends on how it relates to the heating and cooling Services, which depend on the energy efficiency of the Skin, which depends on the constraints of the Structure. . . . The quick processes provide originality and challenge, the slow provide continuity and constraint.

A well-designed, adaptable building, Brand argues, respects the different speeds and different functions of these nested layers. It keeps them separate, allowing "slippage" so that the quick inner layers can change without disrupting the more permanent systems. (You don't have to tear up the foundation to fix the plumbing.)

Scheer's proposal applies a similar model to the surrounding environment. She essentially adds a seventh layer we can call the Street. By limiting design restrictions to the Street, Site, and possibly Structure, rather than the usual obsession with Skin, she makes room for evolution and learning. Like Brand, she emphasizes the effects of time. Given enough slippage between outer and inner layers, we can correct flaws and adapt to changing circumstances while preserving some underlying sense of order. A city, she says, is "a living thing, it's a changing thing, and it has to adapt or it dies. A city that is not having a continuous renewal is a dying place."

A dynamic model of city life recognizes that not just purposes or technologies change over time. So do tastes. Like Capri pants and stiletto heels, aesthetic spillovers go in and out of fashion, flipping from positive to negative and back again. Hard as it is to believe today, from the end of World War II until the 1980s, the Art Deco hotels of Miami Beach were considered "tacky, in bad taste, and old fashioned."[59] When the Miami Design Preservation League was formed in 1976, recalled one of its founders a decade later, South Beach "was considered a disgrace to the city, because of its cheap neon lights, 'funny-shaped' buildings, and the signs along Ocean Drive blaring 'rooms $5 a week.'"

Similarly, American tastemakers have for decades condemned neon signs as the epitome of commercial tackiness, and many cities continue to ban neon. Others, however, have rediscovered the lively pleasures of the lights. While some neighboring cities such as Santa Monica have been forcing businesses to take down their neon signs, Los Angeles has spent about half a million dollars helping building owners restore and relight historic neon signs.[60] The city's Museum of Neon Art not only preserves vintage signs but lends them to the popular Universal CityWalk outdoor shopping area. Commercial neon has slowly regained its 1920s status as a source of public pleasure.

The built environment is filled with examples of once-scorned designs that have become architectural touchstones or popular icons. When it was new, a critic called the Golden Gate Bridge an "eye-sore to those living and a betrayal of future generations."[61] *Architectural Record* critic Suzanne Stephens provides a wide-ranging tour of similar examples:

> Because of his idiosyncratic Baroque architecture, Francesco Borromini was criticized by his [seventeenth-century] contemporary, the writer Giovanni Bellori, as "a complete ignoramus, the corrupter of architecture, the shame of our century."[62] John Vanbrugh's early-18th-century Blenheim Palace was panned for its unclassical Elizabethan corner towers, and his work reviled by his influential client, the Duchess of Marlborough.
>
> Other buildings were judged harshly in their time as well. The works of Frank Furness and his followers in Philadelphia were too contrived and too awkward for critics in [*Architectural*] RECORD a hundred or so years ago. In 1889 artists, architects, and writers, including Charles Garnier and Guy de Maupassant, called the Eiffel Tower "useless and monstrous." Frank Lloyd Wright's Larkin Building in Buffalo was deemed "ugly" by eminent critic Russell Sturgis in [*Architectural*] RECORD in 1908, and in 1959 his Guggenheim Museum was dismissed by visionary architect Frederick Kiesler.
>
> In 1931 Lewis Mumford charged that New York's Chrysler Building by William Van Alen was full of "inane romanticism" and

"void symbolism," while Douglas Haskell felt Howe and Lescaze's International Style PSFS Building of 1932 was just a "filing cabinet." . . . Will Michael Graves' 1983 Portland Building—along with recent work by Eric Moss, Bernard Tschumi, Michael Hopkins, and Frank Gehry, which have received criticism (even in these pages)—be subject to a revised perspective as time goes by? We will have to wait.

Tolerating strange styles can create significant value over time, as the un- familiar becomes familiar, leading to aesthetic appreciation. As Stephens also suggests, however, the test of time works both ways. Sometimes, we indeed come to love, or at least to ignore, once-controversial artifacts. In other cases, we look back and wonder, "What were we thinking?" Did people really believe architecture called Brutalist could be *good*? Acclaimed twenty years earlier, the Portland Building made a 2002 *Metropolis* magazine list of "The Twentieth Century's Worst Design Ideas," an assessment that itself may be subject to future revision.[63] A generation from now, we may regard Frank Gehry's buildings as beautiful art or hideous folly. Or we may find them something altogether different: nostalgic reminders of turn-of-the-century enthusiasms, regardless of their formal merits.

Time adds meaning to form. After the Twin Towers were destroyed, many news reports revisited the critical revulsion that had greeted the World Trade Center.[64] *New York Times* critic Paul Goldberger had called the buildings "blandness blown up to a gigantic size," opining in 1979:

> By now the twin towers are icons, as familiar in souvenir shops as those little miniatures of the Empire State Building. We have all come to some sort of accommodation with the towers, God help us, and there have even been moments when I have seen them from afar and ad- mitted to some small pleasure in the way the two huge forms, when approached from a distance, play off against each other like minimal sculpture. But the buildings remain an occasion to mourn: They never should have happened, they were never really needed, and if they say anything at all about our city, it is that we retreat into banality when the opportunity comes for greatness.

Shortly after September 11, I heard a radio interview in which Goldberger recalled his harsh words somewhat sheepishly. He acknowledged that the build- ings had grown on New Yorkers over time and, of course, that their destruction had given their memory a permanent emotional resonance.

As the now-lost towers testify, personally and communally we come to cherish landmarks we associate with significant places and experiences. This value itself often creates conflict, because those special places are often owned by other people. "Let's face it," says a Los Angeles activist trying to preserve the exuberant Populuxe-era architecture called Googlie.[65] "Our public spaces in Los Angeles are *private* public spaces—Ships coffee shop affected more people than any city building or the Los Angeles Museum of Art." That's true not only of L.A. but of most of the United States, a nation whose most notable landmarks include office buildings, hotels, theaters, churches, mansions, and university halls with private, often commercial, owners. Even Mount Vernon remained a private home belonging to the Washington family until 1858, when a woman appalled by its disrepair organized the Mount Vernon Ladies' Association to buy and restore the estate.[66] (The private association continues to own and support the property, which receives no government funding.)

In an influential examination of aesthetic regulation, legal scholar John J. Costonis argues that emotional attachment, not formal beauty, properly drives public efforts to preserve iconic buildings. Aesthetic regulations, he writes, "respond to our perception of the environment as a stage, rich in icons that infuse our lives with constancy, self-confirmation, eroticism, nostalgia, and fantasy."[67] Costonis's psychological insight seems sound, but his analysis offers little reassurance to building owners, for whom time often has just the opposite effect, reducing value and increasing costs. Third parties enjoy the heightened emotional benefits of continuity without bearing the escalating maintenance expense or forgoing the profits of alternative uses.

Consider Oklahoma City's Gold Dome, a 1958 bank building featuring a gold-plated geodesic dome.[68] After Bank One acquired the dome in a merger with another bank, it estimated that the building needed about $2 million in renovations, including new air-conditioning, roof repairs, and asbestos removal. With twenty-seven thousand square feet, the building was nearly six times too big for Bank One's purposes. In the era of ATMs and branches in supermarkets, banks no longer want giant showcases.[69] But locals were horrified when Bank One announced plans to demolish the dome and replace it with a small branch and a chain drugstore. Like San Francisco's Transamerica pyramid or Seattle's Space Needle, the Gold Dome had come to represent Oklahoma City. As a symbol, the dome's communal value was large, even though its private benefits had dwindled and its private costs increased.

> **Like Capri pants and stiletto heels, aesthetic spillovers go in and out of fashion.**

"It may be financial folly to restore the dome, but it would be a great gesture to Oklahoma City if Bank One could find a way to do so," wrote a local columnist, acknowledging the uneven distribution of costs and benefits.[70] "The dome is a community focal point, a serendipitous little inner-city oddity. Look at it and you're momentarily transported back to 'The Jetsons.' . . . The dome—along with the elegant, modern tower that's paired with it—is a rarity in Oklahoma City. It is an architectural landmark."

The columnist got his wish, minus the financial folly. The uproar delayed the demolition, encouraging the company to put the building on the market. At the last minute, the bank found a buyer. A local optometrist plans to convert the dome to professional offices, retail space, and an Asian cultural center. The bank will build a small building next door. The $1.1 million sales price wasn't as high as the company wanted but, said a bank official, "All things being equal, we'd rather not tear the dome down."[71]

It's easy to say something is precious if you can enjoy it at someone else's expense. Talk is cheap. Like review boards redrawing building plans, preservation authorities sometimes exercise almost unlimited power to require property owners to maintain old buildings without compensation for their troubles. One result is that the buildings don't have to be widely valued for either their pleasures or their meaning. They just have to appeal to somebody with more political influence than the owner.

Over the past decade, the Charleston, South Carolina, Board of Architectural Review has expanded its jurisdiction from a relatively small area of antebellum mansions into some of the poorest parts of town. At particular issue are four-room "freedman's cottages," believed to have been built by emancipated slaves.[72] The freedman's cottages are often in terrible shape and, even if restored, would be too small to command rents high enough to recoup the expense. One owner who was denied permission to tear down four freedman's cottages estimated they'd cost $100,000 each to repair and would still rent for only $200 to $300 a month. In another case, a man unfortunate enough to inherit a freedman's cottage spent four years fighting for permission to tear it down after Hurricane Hugo damaged the place beyond habitability. The city offered a mere $4,000 for the dilapidated structure, a ninth of its assessed value for tax purposes. Officials frequently fined the owner for not maintaining the property before finally giving him permission to demolish it.

The tiny homes do reveal something about Charleston's history, but as useful houses they're obsolete. Black Charlestonians fortunately have better housing options in the twenty-first century than they had in the nineteenth; they don't want to live in tiny, run-down houses, however historic. That makes the review board's preservationist zeal quite costly to the people who happen to own the cottages. If a freedman's cottage is of interest to historians but not to potential residents, then historians should buy and preserve it as a research site, demonstrating its value by paying the owner. Otherwise, their cheap talk just encourages neglect and, in this case, perpetuates a history of injustice.

Oklahoma City, by contrast, had to put its money where its mouth was, demonstrating that the Gold Dome really was a cherished icon. Activists couldn't force Bank One to maintain the building as a free architectural museum for their pleasure. Saving the dome required finding someone to buy it, compensating the bank. Given the value locals attach to the Gold Dome, preservationists conceivably could have put together $1.1 million from private sources, or the city could have used tax funds to buy the building. Fortunately, neither step was necessary, since the structure captured a commercial buyer's imagination, and no authenticity-oriented law hampered its conversion to new uses.

Giving the public a voice, making time for counteroffers (or, in predesignated cases, giving a city or preservation group the right of first refusal), and providing funds to buy or maintain particularly meaningful structures, while leaving the ultimate decision to the building owner, seems to strike the best long-term balance of rights in dealing with icons.[73] In Oklahoma City, the delay was crucial, because it gave the public a chance to let Bank One know how much people cared about the dome. A commercial establishment that draws its customers from the local area has a strong business motive to honor their aesthetic values, whether by improving the landscaping of a parking lot or preserving a beloved building. (An individual owner with eccentric tastes may be less susceptible to public pressure, since eccentric tastes and caring what the neighbors think don't tend to go together.)

There's no perfect solution to such conflicts, of course. If owners have to be compensated to preserve icons, there's always the danger that they'll pretend to threaten their buildings in order to extract payment. And sometimes icons will fall to the wrecking ball, lacking adequate support to save them. Even so, the greater danger lies in fostering what Scheer calls "the culture of aesthetic poverty," depriving the urban landscape of beauty, inventiveness, and meaning.[74] If building or preserving a potential icon makes it subject to de facto confiscation, property owners will erect and maintain only boring buildings. Or they'll be sure to tear down their buildings before public sentiment can interfere with their freedom of action. Or builders will limit the aesthetic details to the inside, with no free benefits to the general public.

Even without such perverse incentives, cost-conscious building owners often avoid investing in positive spillovers. "All the beauty, all the marble, all the stuff is put on the inside," laments Scheer, angry about the "fabulous internal environments" of malls and hotels that look like giant boxes from the outside. "An old hotel from the nineteenth century would die before they would do that. It would have been considered rude." Nineteenth-century hotel owners could count on controlling their building's fate, however. If they erected a showcase only to find it no longer useful, they could sell it for new purposes or raze it without punishment. Putting up a building that the public could enjoy didn't invite the public to assume control of that building's design or destiny. And those nineteenth-century hotels were special places, catering to a wealthy elite that expected aesthetic quality inside and out. When the general public began to stay in hotels more often, plain function — "the best surprise is no surprise" — was good enough.

Now, however, the quality-demanding elite is no longer so elite. It includes most of us. That means Scheer's lament about the culture of aesthetic poverty need not continue indefinitely. In the postwar era of function and convenience, the general public was relatively insensitive to aesthetics, tolerating an ugly environment in exchange for other benefits. Aesthetic regulation might have improved the landscape, but it was politically unpopular, because on the margin most people preferred low-cost function.

Now that people increasingly care about look and feel in their private choices, aesthetic regulation is less necessary to control blatant public ugliness. The same taste shift that has made the spread of design review politically viable is slowly but surely changing the definition of what's commercially necessary. If owners have the freedom to create, alter, and destroy them if necessary, fabulous external environments are sure to follow their interior counterparts. Our greatest fears of the aesthetic future are not of too little design but of too much.

NOTES

1. The building has continuously displayed patriotic murals since February 1999. McNeilly eventually won his case in a state appellate court, and the original charges were dropped. He continued to illegally erect patriotic murals on the spot, including one honoring firefighters and rescue workers after September 11. When the city charged him with new offenses for the September 11 mural, the American Civil Liberties Union filed a federal lawsuit on his behalf, citing his First Amendment right to engage in noncommercial political speech. The building's owner, who gave McNeilly permission to erect the murals, has also sued the city. Mike McNeilly, interviews with the author, July 1999 and June 13, 2002. Gary Mobley, attorney for Mike McNeilly, interviews with the author, July 1999 and October 6, 1999. Daniel Hienerfeld, interview with the author, July 1999. Virginia Postrel, "The Esthetics Police," *Forbes*, November 1, 1999, p. 174. Bob Pool, "Yearning to Paint Freely, Artist Battles the City," *Los Angeles Times*, May 17, 2000, p. B1. Bob Pool, "Ruling Will Allow Trial of Artist over Building Mural," *Los Angeles Times*, May 18, 2000, p. B5. Lawrence Ferchaw, "Painter Places Canvas over Mural for Holiday," *Daily Bruin*, May 30, 2000, p. 1. *Michael McNeilly v. City of Los Angeles*, complaint for injunctive and declaratory relief, U.S. District Court for the Central District of California, October 23, 2001.

2. Kathryn Shattuck, "Beware the Cry of 'Niyby': Not in Your Backyard!" *New York Times*, May 11, 2000, p. F1. The official quoted is Adolph M. Orlando, a building inspector in Scarsdale, New York.

3. Ron Lieber, "Is This *Your* Beautiful House?" *Fast Company*, July 2001, pp. 124–40.

4. Brenda Case Scheer, "The Debate on Design Review," in *Design Review: Challenging Urban Aesthetic Control*, ed. Brenda Case Scheer and Wolfgang F. E. Preiser (New York: Chapman & Hall, 1994), p. 1. Brenda Scheer, e-mail to the author, February 7, 2001. The survey includes only laws, not private covenants. Note that 83 percent of all cities and towns does not mean 83 percent of all people, since many municipalities are fairly small and some of the largest cities don't have design review.

5. Brenda Scheer, interview with the author, July 18, 2002.

6. Gladstone, Missouri, City Council meeting minutes, March 27, 2000. Roswell, Georgia, Design Review Board minutes, February 1, 2000.

7. Chuck Haga, "Do Palm Trees Distort the 'Image' of Eden Prairie?" *Star Tribune*, July 8, 2001, p. 1A. After a spate of bad publicity, the city reached a compromise with the restaurant, allowing it to keep the palm trees for the summer, provided they were replaced with more traditional shade trees in the fall. James Lileks, "Eden Prairie's Parrot Is in a Pickle over Palms," *Star Tribune*, July 13, 2001, p. 3B. Stuart Sudak, "Restaurant's Palm Trees Get Reprieve from City," *Eden Prairie News*, July 11, 2001, http://www.edenprairienews.com/main.asp?Search=1&ArticleID=2021&SectionID=18&SubSectionID=79&S=l.

8. Vernon Mays, "Historic Savannah Says No to Fake Bricks," *Architecture*, December 2000, p. 25.

9. Mike Johnson, "McDonald's Retro Colors Have Some Seeing Red," *Milwaukee Journal Sentinel*, July 23, 2000, http://www.jsonline.com/news/wauk/jul00/mcdon24072300a.asp.

10. Tom Jackman, "Freedom Has Its Price in Fairfax," *Washington Post*, May 25, 2001, p. B1. Leef Smith, "Landscapers Storm Driving Range Early," *Washington Post*, May 26, 2001, p. B1.

11. City of Portland, "Base Zone Design Standards: City Council Adopted Report," July 27, 1999.
12. Charlie Hales, commissioner, City of Portland, letter to Jane M. Leo, governmental affairs director, Portland Metro Association of Realtors, January 11, 1998.
13. Brenda Case Scheer, "When Design Is Against the Law," *Harvard Design Magazine*, Winter/Spring 1999, p. 47.
14. Mary Jo Feldstein, "Piercing, Tattoos Create Workplace Issues," Reuters, June 22, 2001.
15. Rhina Guidos, "Fashion Checklist: No Blush, No Lipstick . . . No Job," *Christian Science Monitor*, July 17, 2001, p. 1. Martin Griffith, "Nevada Bartender Sues Harrah's over Makeup Policy," Associated Press, July 7, 2001.
16. Drake Witham and Connie Piloto, "Dreadlocks Policy Prompts Complaint," *Dallas Morning News*, May 30, 2001, p. A16. Connie Piloto, "Officer Fired for Not Cutting Dreadlocks," *Dallas Morning News*, June 2, 2001, p. A31. Teresa Gubbins, "Identity Crisis: Police Hairstyle Restrictions Forced Soul-Searching Decisions," *Dallas Morning News*, January 29, 2002, p. C1.
17. Chris Warhurst and Dennis Nickson, *Looking Good, Sounding Right: Style Counselling in the New Economy* (London: The Industrial Society, 2001), p. 15.
18. *U.S. Equal Opportunity Commission v. Ian Schrager Hotels Inc.*, Second Amended Complaint, U.S. District Court, Central District of California, July 20, 2000. U.S. Equal Employment Opportunity Commission, "EEOC and Mondrian Hotel Settle Title VII Lawsuit," press release, August 9, 2000, http://www.eeoc.gov/press/8-9-00.html. The EEOC's suit charged that the hotel discriminated in its recruitment practices, which included "hiring talent agencies to locate prospective hotel employees, searching for prospective employees at a shopping mall, and placing advertisements in entertainment trade publications seeking individuals who are 'high energy, upbeat, handsome/pretty with cool looking individual style.'" Virginia Postrel, "When the 'Cool' Look Is Illegal," *Forbes*, November 27, 2000, p. 90.
19. Eric Steele, interview with the author, September 7, 2000.
20. Michael S. Mitchell, interview with the author, August 16, 2000.
21. Donna Harper, the EEOC's acting assistant general counsel in Mondrian case, interview with the author, September 6, 2000.
22. Elizabeth Fernandez, " 'Teacher Says Fat, Fitness Can Mix; S.F. Mediates Complaint Jazzercise Showed Bias," *San Francisco Chronicle*, February 24, 2002, p. A21. Patricia Leigh Brown, "240 Pounds, Persistent and Jazzercise's Equal," *New York Times*, May 8, 2002, p. A20. City and County of San Francisco Human Rights Commission, "Compliance Guidelines To Prohibit Weight and Height Discrimination," July 26, 2001, http://www.ci.sf.ca.us/sfhumanrights/guidelines_final.htm. Portnick declined Jazzercise's eventual offer of employment.
23. Ellen Goodman, " 'Fat Chance' to Fat Chic," *Boston Globe*, March 31, 2002, p. E7.
24. Elizabeth Fernandez, "Size-16 Aerobics Teacher Gets National Attention," *San Francisco Chronicle*, March 18, 2002, p. A11.
25. "Battle over Fitness," *San Francisco Chronicle*, March 1, 2002, p. A34.
26. Mount Pleasant, South Carolina, Commercial Development Design Review Board minutes, April 24, 2002.
27. Denise Scott Brown, "With the Best of Intentions," *Harvard Design Magazine*, Winter/Spring 1999, pp. 37–42.

28. Brenda Case Scheer, "The Debate on Design Review," p. 2. Despite all the limitations on architects' designs, Scheer also says she found the process "lame," unable to affect the larger-scale features of urban life. Brenda Scheer, interview with the author, July 18, 2002.

29. Brenda Case Scheer, "When Design Is Against the Law," p. 47.

30. Raymond P. Rhinehart, *Princeton University: The Campus Guide* (New York: Princeton University Architectural Press, 2000), p. 123.

31. Robert Venturi, interview with the author, June 9, 2002.

32. Thomas Wright, interview with the author, July 24, 2002.

33. Robert Venturi, "Frist Campus Frieze—Definition and Justification: The Polite (Sort of) Version," memo, March 24, 1998, and "Why the Tasteful Frieze on the Front of the Frist Campus Center Is Not a Vulgar Sign but a Tasteful Frieze—Designed Also by a Highfalutin' Architect," memo, March 23, 1998. Jennifer Potash, "Campus Center Approval Expected," *Princeton Packet*, July 7, 1998, http://www.pacpubserver.com/new/news/7-7-98/center.html. Jonathan Goldberg, "University Receives Approval for Building of Frist Loggia," *Daily Princetonian*, October 14, 1998, http://www.dailyprincetonian.com/Content/1998/10/14/news/goldberg.html. Jim Wallace, Venturi, Scott Brown and Associates, e-mail to the author, June 10, 2002.

34. Pierluigi Zappacosta, interview with the author, September 27, 2000.

35. Zandl Group, "Shopping Attitudes," press release, July 22, 2002.

36. I do not mean to minimize the difficulty of setting environmental standards or the controversies that often swirl around them. The point is that it is not possible *even in theory* to establish objective standards of aesthetic pollution levels. At best, we might be able to measure an effect on real estate prices, which themselves reflect subjective tastes and can thus fluctuate with the fashion cycle or the makeup of the community.

37. Robert Venturi notes that the death or retirement of a design review board member often changes what architectural plans a board will approve. Review boards are not generally elected, and members often hold office indefinitely. Robert Venturi, interview with the author, June 9, 2002.

38. Richard Tseng-yu Lai, "Can the Process of Architectural Design Review Withstand Constitutional Scrutiny?" in Brenda Case Scheer and Wolfgang F. E. Preiser, eds., *Design Review: Challenging Urban Aesthetic Control* (New York: Chapman & Hall, 1994), pp. 31–41. "Given the human nature of all professionals," writes Lai, "expertness can just as easily be a cloak for dogma and subjectivity as a basis for disinterested objectivity."

39. Tracie Rozhon, "From Gehry, a Bilbao on the Hudson," *New York Times*, August 20, 1998, p. F1. Tracie Rozhon, "Bard College Bends on Arts Center," *New York Times*, February 19, 1999, p. B5. The added cost was because the relocated center could no longer share dressing rooms and other facilities with existing buildings.

40. William Baldwin, note to the author, October 6, 1999.

41. The aesthetic ratchet effect may itself be considered an externality—though whether it's positive (because it raises standards) or negative (because it raises costs) depends on who's doing the evaluating. In *Luxury Fever*, Robert Frank treats the effect as a negative externality, ignoring the positive spillovers of a more appealing world.

42. R. H. Coase, "The Problem of Social Cost," in *The Firm, the Market, and the Law* (Chicago: University of Chicago Press, 1988), pp. 95–156. (Reprinted from *The Journal of Law and Economics*, October 1960, pp. 1–44.)

43. Obviously, the final allocation of money does depend on who starts out with the rights and gets paid to transfer them. But to a third party observing only the pollution level, the world looks the same in either case.

44. Even when there are no transaction costs, there can still be problems if the group involved is large enough. Avinash Dixit and Mancur Olson, "Does Voluntary Participation Undermine the Coase Theorem?" *Journal of Public Economics*, June 2000, pp. 309–35.

45. Christine Woodside, "Cell Phone Towers Are Sprouting in Unlikely Places," *New York Times*, January 9, 2000, sec. 14CN (Connecticut Weekly), p. 1.

46. Peter Glen, "Here Comes the Neighborhood," *VM+SD Magazine*, November 1999, http://www.visualstore.com/people/glen/pglen1199.html, "A New Wal-Mart. Custom Fit for Your Neighborhood," Wal-Mart brochure.

47. David Kiser, quoted in Martha Elson, "Family's Dream Home, Neighbors' Nightmare," *Courier-Journal*, April 25, 2002, http://www.courier-journal.com/localnews/2002/04/25/ke042502s194117.htm. Deed restrictions dating to 1925 specified that house exteriors must be of brick, brick veneer, stucco, or stone, but the restrictions hadn't been enforced for decades; many homes in the neighborhood had façades of wood, vinyl, or aluminum siding. Martha Elson, "Judge to Decide Fate of Lakeside House," *Courier-Journal*, April 27, 2002, p. 8-B. Martha Elson, "Contemporary House's Owners Win Court Case," *Courier-Journal*, July 24, 2002, http://www.courier-journal.com/localnews/2002/07/24/ke072402s247377.htm.

48. John Gilderbloom, quoted in Martha Elson, "Family's Dream Home, Neighbors' Nightmare."

49. National boundaries, like the difference between Switzerland and Italy, are obviously drawn way too expansively for this approach. The switching costs are too high.

50. Allison Arieff, "Slugging It Out in Louisville," *Dwell*, April 2002, pp. 42–51. Martha Elson, "Family's Dream Home, Neighbors' Nightmare."

51. Steve Kellenberg, interview with the author, April 19, 2002.

52. Robert H. Nelson, "Local Government as Private Property," mimeo., May 2002.

53. Robert H. Nelson, "Privatizing the Neighborhood: A Proposal to Replace Zoning with Private Collective Property Rights to Existing Neighborhoods," *George Mason Law Review*, Summer 1999, pp. 827–80. William A. Fischel, "Voting, Risk Aversion, and the NIMBY Syndrome: A Comment on Robert Nelson's 'Privatizing the Neighborhood,'" *George Mason Law Review*, Summer 1999, pp. 881–903. Steven J. Eagle, "Privatizing Urban Land Use Regulation: The Problem of Consent," *George Mason Law Review*, Summer 1999, pp. 905–21. These scholars don't seem to have substantially addressed the model provided by existing preservation districts, which tend to be at a similar scale and usually require a supermajority of local residents to petition for district status.

54. Robert Ellickson, "New Institutions for Old Neighborhoods," *Duke Law Journal*, October 1998, pp. 75–110.

55. Los Angeles Municipal Code, Ordinance 174422, effective March 11, 2002.

56. Adriene Biondo, interview with the author, February 20, 2002.

57. Brenda Scheer, interview with the author, July 18, 2002.

58. Stewart Brand, *How Buildings Learn: What Happens After They're Built* (New York: Penguin Books, 1994), pp. 12–23.

59. Barbara Baer Capitman, *Deco Delights: Preserving the Beauty and Joy of Miami Beach Architecture* (New York: Dutton, 1988), pp. 42, 16. Also, see Denise Scott Brown, "My Miami Beach," *Interview*, September 1986, pp. 156–58.
60. Kevin Starr, "Landscape Electric," *Los Angeles Times*, July 4, 1999, pp. M1, M6. Nathan Marsak and Nigel Cox, *Los Angeles Neon* (Atglen, Penn.: Schiffer, 2002).
61. Cited in John J. Costonis, *Icons and Aliens: Law, Aesthetics, and Environmental Change* (Urbana: University of Illinois Press, 1989), frontispiece.
62. Suzanne Stephens, "The Difficulty of Beauty," *Architectural Record*, November 2000, pp. 96–97.
63. "The Twentieth Century's Worst Design Ideas," *Metropolis*, August/September 2002, p. 154. The list is labeled "humor," but is at least partly serious.
64. David Dillon, "Building Debate: Should Towers Go Up Again," *Dallas Morning News*, September 16, 2001, p. 23A. Kari Haskell, "Before & After: Talking of the Towers," *New York Times*, September 16, 2001, sec. 4, p. 4. Michael Fainelli, "Twin Giants: What Will Fill Their Shoes?" *Christian Science Monitor*, October 4, 2001, p. 17.
65. John English, quoted in Scott Timberg, "Modern Love," *New Times Los Angeles*, July 11–17, 2002, p. 13.
66. "Mount Vernon Fact Sheet," http://www.mountvernon.org/press/mv_fact.asp.
67. John J. Costonis, *Icons and Aliens*, p. 37.
68. Gregory Potts, "Protesters Stage Rally To Save Golden Dome," *Daily Oklahoman*, July 24, 2001, p. 1A. Gregory Potts, "Dome Support Spreads; Bank One Plan Meets Protests," *Sunday Oklahoman*, July 29, 2001, sec. 3, p. 1. Gregory Potts, "Bank One To Try Selling Gold Dome; Decision Encourages Preservationists," *Daily Oklahoman*, August 2, 2001, p. 1A. Arnold Hamilton, "Raising the Gold Standard," *Dallas Morning News*, August 16, 2001, p. 23A. Jody Noerdlinger, "Economics, History Weigh in Dome's Fate; Bank One's Bottom Line May Seal Building's Future," *Daily Oklahoman*, December 27, 2001, p. 1C. Arnold Hamilton, "Optometrist's Bid May Save Landmark," *Dallas Morning News*, May 20, 2002, p. 17A.
69. Because of federal and state regulations, the era of convenience came late to banking, while banks in the 1950s and 1960s lavished spending on their buildings, making the industry a notable exception to today's aesthetic imperative. Virginia Postrel, "The New Republic," *D Magazine*, December 2001, pp. 48–52.
70. Charles Crumpley, "Dome Creates Dilemma," *Sunday Oklahoman*, July 22, 2001, p. 1C.
71. Bill Scheihing, president of Bank One Oklahoma, quoted in "Contract Delivered in Bid To Save Landmark Building," Associated Press, May 18, 2002.
72. Jason Hardin, "Row of Houses Spared, But Owner Says Restoration Too Costly," *Post and Courier*, May 23, 2002, p. 3B. Herb Frazier, "Owner of Freedmen's Cottage Receives Demolition Approval," *Post and Courier*, September 22, 1998, p. 1B.
73. A similar approach is to give building owners tax breaks or other compensation, in exchange for agreeing to maintain iconic structures. Unfortunately, in practice such incentives tend to emphasize authenticity-as-purity rather than icons-as-communal-meaning, often selecting buildings for historical details or "living museum" purposes and paying undue attention to aesthetic minutiae.
74. Brenda Case Scheer, "Sympathy with the Devil: Design Review and the Culture of Aesthetic Poverty," *Loeb Fellowship Forum*, Spring/Summer 1996, http://www.scheerandscheer.com/aesthetic.pdf.

Questions for Critical Reading

1. What are aesthetic boundaries, and how does Postrel claim that they can be both positive *and* negative design influences? Define the term using her text and then read her essay critically to determine the ramifications of these boundaries.

2. What role should legislation play in aesthetics? Using Postrel's examples and ideas, suggest the proper function of law in design. Does that function change when the design in question is a matter of personal appearance rather than architecture?

3. According to Postrel, what are "spillovers"? Are they inevitable? Should they help determine aesthetic boundaries? Support your answers with quotations from Postrel's essay.

Exploring Context

1. Postrel discusses the controversy around Princeton University's Frist Campus Center. Visit the Web site for the center at princeton.edu/~frist. How is the center now viewed? Does its Web presence reflect aesthetic boundaries? Are there any remnants of the dispute?

2. Local ordinances play a significant role in Postrel's analysis. Use the Web to research design ordinances for your local community. How is aesthetics regulated where you live? Compare this information to your response on the role of legislation in aesthetics from Question 2 of Questions for Critical Reading.

3. What aesthetic boundaries exist on the Web? Explore MySpace (myspace.com) until you find a page that you think is particularly lacking in aesthetic value. How can you explain this page and its presence in the MySpace community through Postrel's analysis? Relate your answer to your work on aesthetic boundaries from Question 1 of Questions for Critical Reading.

Questions for Connecting

1. What is art? Synthesize Postrel's arguments about aesthetics with Michael Kimmelman's analysis in "The Art of Collecting Lightbulbs" (p. 216). Can we create a definition of art that has a specific boundary? Relate your response to your work with aesthetic boundaries in Question 1 of Questions for Critical Reading.

2. One way to think about Julia Serano's arguments in "Before and After: Class and Body Transformations" (p. 392) is that they are concerned with the boundaries of personal aesthetics. Use Postrel's ideas about design to reconsider Serano's analysis. How can you synthesize their positions?

3. Postrel stresses the fact that people are different. How does that pluralism function in design? Use Kwame Anthony Appiah's ideas in "Making Conversation" (p. 57) and "The Primacy of Practice" (p. 63) to consider aesthetic boundaries. How does the primacy of practice influence the tensions among homogeneity, conformity, and pluralism in design?

Language Matters

1. There is a certain class of grammatical errors often called "sentence bound-ary" errors, including comma splices, sentence fragments, and run-on or fused sentences. What does *boundary* mean in this context? Are these boundaries at all like the aesthetic boundaries Postrel discusses? How might her essay help us understand the importance of these linguistic boundaries?

2. Editors often use correction symbols; your instructor might use them as well. Design new symbols to represent some common errors you make. How are design and meaning related? Would your symbols make immediate sense to someone else?

3. Narrowing one's topic can be a challenge, even for writers like Postrel. Imagine a "research pyramid" for this essay, with the broadest category at bottom and the most ridiculously specific one at the top point of the pyramid. How many different levels can you find for this essay? Would the essay have been as strong if it were less or more specific? Why did Postrel choose this level of the pyramid for her work?

Assignments for Writing

1. According to Postrel, boundaries work best when the rules are clear and have been voluntarily accepted. Write an essay in which you explore the tension be-tween expressing individual creativity and having others impose their creativity on you. Can a single standard please everyone? Can a design be subjectively harmful? Should we allow trade-offs? Do we have the right to express ourselves if we tell others that they cannot? You might want to consider your work in Questions for Critical Reading, particularly on the issue of spillovers.

2. Postrel states that individuals may expect freedom of expression, but they often feel affronted and victimized by the aesthetic choices of others. Write an essay in which you explore the conflicts between aesthetic expression and aesthetic control. If we accept what others impose on us, are we effec-tively killing creativity? If we allow others to tell us what they want, are we conforming? In making your argument, consider drawing from your work in Questions for Connecting.

3. Postrel addresses the issues facing a society in which others—from community organizations to government agencies—impose taste on individuals, asking us to consider the proper boundaries of design. Write an essay in which you explore the ethics of allowing government institutions to regulate aesthetics. In making your argument, you may want to draw on your work with legislation concerning aesthetics in Question 2 of Questions for Critical Reading. Also consider: What is design tyranny? Is environmental policy trying to legislate taste? What is the role of lawyers in design?

RICHARD RESTAK

Richard Restak received his M.D. from Georgetown University School of Medicine. He is a clinical professor of neurology at George Washington Hospital University School of Medicine and Health Sciences and president of the American Neuropsychiatric Association. Known internationally as an expert on the brain, he has written close to twenty books on the human brain and appeared on *Good Morning America, The Today Show,* and *All Things Considered.* Restak's expertise has led to multiple awards, articles in numerous national newspapers, and invitations to write entries for *Encyclopaedia Britannica, Compton's Encyclopedia,* and *World Book Encyclopedia.*

Restak's book *The New Brain: How the Modern Age Is Rewiring Your Mind* (2003) details recent research and technological advances that have provided new insights into the human brain. For example, technologies such as CAT and MRA scans can now prove such things as the harmful effects of television violence, and research on the brain can be leveraged to maximize our capabilities in areas ranging from academics to athletics. Restak suggests that research on the brain has yielded practical applications that we can use every day, from matching drugs to the disorders they can treat to identifying potentially violent individuals before they act out.

"Attention Deficit: The Brain Syndrome of Our Era," a chapter from *The New Brain,* deals with the effects of modern technology on "the plasticity of our brains." Here Restak examines the brain's ability to multitask and the consequences of multitasking—for example, the risks of talking on a cell phone while driving. Our tendency to juggle tasks, Restak warns, may be both unproductive and damaging to our brains. Diagnoses of disorders such as Attention Deficit Disorder (ADD) and Attention Deficit Hyperactivity Disorder (ADHD) have become common in recent years, and Restak suggests that one of the reasons for this might be technology's effect on our evolution.

Multitasking forces our brains to process ever-increasing amounts of information at ever-increasing rates, which raises a question: Is the recent social and cultural trend toward multitasking actually rewiring our brains and causing such problems as ADD and ADHD?

▶ TAGS: *education, feedback, technology, creativity, multitasking*

Attention Deficit: The Brain Syndrome of Our Era

The plasticity of our brains, besides responding to the people and training to which we expose it, also responds, for good or for bad, to the technology all around us: television, movies, cell phones, e-mail, laptop computers, and the Internet. And by responding, I mean that our brain literally changes its organization and functioning to accommodate the abundance of stimulation forced on it by the modern world.

This technologically driven change in the brain is the biggest modification in the last 200,000 years (when the brain volume of *Homo sapiens* reached the modern level). But while biological and social factors, such as tool use, group hunting, and language, drove earlier brain changes, exposure to technology seems to be spurring the current alteration. One consequence of this change is that we face constant challenges to our ability to focus our attention.

For example, I was recently watching a televised interview with Laura Bush. While the interview progressed, the bottom of the screen was active with a "crawler" composed of a line of moving type that provided information on other news items.

Until recently, crawlers were used to provide early warning signs for hurricanes, tornados, and other impending threats. Because of their rarity and implied seriousness, crawlers grabbed our immediate attention no matter how engrossed we were in the television program playing out before our eyes. Crawlers, in short, were intended to capture our attention and forewarn us of the possible need for prompt action. But now, the crawler has become ubiquitous, forcing an ongoing split in our attention, a constant state of distraction and divided focus.

During the First Lady's interview I found my attention shifting back and forth from her remarks to the active stream of short phrases running below. From the crawler I learned that National Airport was expected to be opened in two days since its closure in the wake of the September 11 terrorist attacks; that this season's Super Bowl would be played in New Orleans one week later than usual; and that a home run record was about to be broken by Barry Bonds.

Despite my best efforts to concentrate on Laura Bush's words, I kept looking down at the crawler to find out what else might be happening that was perhaps even more interesting. As a result, at several points I lost the thread of the conversation between the First Lady and the interviewer. Usually, I missed the question and was therefore forced to remain in the dark during the first sentence or so of her response.

On other occasions I've watched split-screen interviews, with each half of the screen displaying images or text of the topic under discussion while the crawler continues with short snippets about subjects totally divorced from the interview and accompanying video or text. In these instances I am being asked to split my visual attention into three components.

One can readily imagine future developments when attention must be divided into four or more components—perhaps an interview done entirely in the form of a voice-over, with the split-screen video illustrating two subjects unrelated to the subject of the interview and accompanied all the while by a crawler at the bottom of the screen dealing with a fourth topic.

Yet we shouldn't think of such developments as unanticipated or surprising. In 1916, prophets of the Futurist Cinema lauded "cinematic simultaneity and interpenetrations of different times and places" and predicted "we shall project two or three different visual episodes at the same time, one next to the other." Yesterday's predictions have become today's reality. And in the course of that makeover we have become more frenetic, more distracted, more fragmented—in a word, more *hyperactive.*

How Many Ways Can Our Attention Be Divided?

Divisions of attention aren't new, of course. People have always been required to do more than one thing at a time or think of more than one thing at a time. But even when engaged in what we now call multitasking, most people maintained a strong sense of unity: They remained fully grounded in terms of what they were doing. Today the sense of unity has been replaced, I believe, by feelings of distraction and difficulty maintaining focus and attention. On a daily basis I encounter otherwise normal people in my neuropsychiatric practice who experience difficulty concentrating. "I no sooner begin thinking of one thing than my mind starts to wander off to another subject and before I know it I'm thinking of yet a third subject," is a typical complaint.

Certainly part of this shift from focus to distraction arises from the many and varied roles we all must now fulfill. But I think the process of personal *dis*-integration is also furthered by our constant exposure to the media, principally television. When watching TV, many of us now routinely flit from one program to another as quickly as our thumb can strike the remote control button. We watch a story for a few minutes and then switch over to a basketball game until we become bored with that, and then move on to Animal Planet. Feeling restless, we may then pick up the phone and talk to a co-worker about topics likely to come up at tomorrow's meeting while simultaneously directing our attention to a weather report on TV or flipping through our mail.

"The demands upon the human brain right now are increasing," according to Todd E. Feinberg, a neurologist at Beth Israel Medical Center in New York City. "For all we know, we're selecting for the capacity to multitask."

Feinberg's comment about "selecting" gets to the meat of the issue. At any given time evolution selects for adaptation and fitness to prevailing environmental conditions. And today the environment demands the capacity to do more than one thing at a time, divide one's attention, and juggle competing, often conflicting, interests. Adolescents have grown up in just such an environment. As a result, some of them can function reasonably efficiently under conditions of distraction. But this ability to multitask often comes at a price—Attention Deficit Disorder (ADD) or Attention Deficit Hyperactivity Disorder (ADHD).

Perhaps the best intuitive understanding of ADD/ADHD comes from the French philosopher Blaise Pascal who said, "Most of the evils in life arise from a man's being unable to sit still in a room." The fourth edition of the *Diagnostic and Statistical Manual of Mental Disorders* (DSM-IV) provides a more contemporary definition. Although ADD/ADHD affects adults as well as children, the DSM-IV describes symptoms as they affect three categories in children: motor control, impulsivity, and difficulties with organization and focus.

The motor patterns include: 15

(a) often fidgets with hands or feet or squirms in seat

(b) often leaves seat in classroom or in other situations in which remaining seated is expected

(c) is often "on the go" or often acts as if driven by a motor

(d) often runs about or expresses a subjective feeling of restlessness

(e) often has difficulty playing or engaging in leisure activities quietly

(f) often talks excessively

The impulsive difficulties include:

(a) often experiences difficulty awaiting turn

(b) interrupts or intrudes on others (e.g., butts into conversation or games)

(c) often blurts out answers before questions have been completed

To earn the diagnosis of the "inattentive subtype" of ADD/ADHD, the child or adolescent shows any six of the following symptoms:

(a) often does not follow through on instructions and fails to finish school-work, chores, or duties in the workplace

(b) often fails to give close attention to details or makes careless mistakes in schoolwork, work, or other activities

(c) often has difficulty sustaining attention in tasks or play activities

(d) often does not seem to listen when spoken to directly

(e) often avoids, dislikes, or is reluctant to engage in tasks that require sustained mental effort (such as schoolwork or homework)

(f) often loses things necessary for tasks or activities

(g) is often easily distracted by extraneous stimuli

(h) is often forgetful in daily activities

For years doctors assured the parents of an ADD/ADHD child that the condition would disappear as their child grew older. But such reassurances have turned out to be overly optimistic. In the majority of cases, ADD/ADHD continues into adulthood, although the symptoms change.

In their best-selling book, *Driven to Distraction*, psychiatrists Edward Hallowell and John Ratey developed a list of criteria for the diagnosis of Adult Attention Deficit Disorder. Among the most common manifestations are:

1. A sense of underachievement, of not meeting one's goals

2. Difficulty getting organized

3. Chronic procrastination or trouble getting started

4. Many projects going simultaneously; trouble with follow-through

5. A tendency to say whatever comes to mind without necessarily considering the timing or appropriateness of the remark

6. A frequent search for high stimulation

7. Intolerance of boredom

8. Easy distractibility, trouble in focusing attention, a tendency to tune out or drift away in the middle of a page or conversation

9. Impatient; low frustration tolerance

10. A sense of insecurity

Other experts on adult attention disorder would add:

11. Low self-esteem and

12. Emotional lability: sudden and sometimes dramatic mood shifts

A Distinctive Type of Brain Organization

In many instances childhood and adult ADD/ADHD is inherited. Typically, the parents of a child diagnosed with the disorder will be found upon interview to exhibit many of the criteria for adult ADD/ADHD. But many cases of ADD/ADHD in both children and adults occur without any hereditary disposition, suggesting the probability of culturally induced ADD/ADHD.

As a result of increasing demands on our attention and focus, our brains try to adapt by rapidly shifting attention from one activity to another—a strategy that is now almost a requirement for survival. As a consequence, attention deficit disorder is becoming epidemic in both children and adults. This is unlikely to turn out to be a temporary condition. Indeed, some forms of ADD/ADHD have entered the mainstream of acceptable behavior. Many personality characteristics we formerly labeled as dysfunctional, such as hyperactivity, impulsiveness, and easy distractibility, are now almost the norm.

"With so many distracted people running around, we could be becoming the first society with Attention Deficit Disorder," writes Evan Schartz, a cyberspace critic in *Wired* magazine. In Schartz's opinion, ADHD may be "the official brain syndrome of the information age."

"Civilization is revving itself into a pathologically short attention span. The [20] trend might be coming from the acceleration of technology, the short-horizon perspective of market-driven economies, the next-election perspective of democracies, or the distractions of personal multitasking. All are on the increase," according to Stewart Brand, a noted commentator on technology and social change.

As ADD expert Paul Wender puts it: "The attention span of the average adult is greatly exaggerated."

"It's important to note that neuroscientists and experts within the field are increasingly dissatisfied with ADHD being called a disorder," according to Sam Horn, author of *Conzentrate: Get Focused and Pay Attention — When Life Is Filled with Pressures, Distractions, and Multiple Priorities*, which lists forces in the modern world that "induce" ADD/ADHD. "They prefer to see ADHD as a distinctive type of brain organization."

Such an attitude change toward ADD/ADHD carries practical implications. When creating an optimum environment for learning, for instance, Horn suggests, "blocking out sounds can hurt. Today's younger generation has become accustomed to cacophony. Street sounds, the screeching of brakes, trucks changing gears, and the wails of ambulances are their norm. For these people silence can actually be disconcerting because it's so unusual."

To Horn's list of ADD/ADHD-inducing influences I would add time-compressed speech, which is now routinely used on radio and TV to inject the maximum amount of information per unit of time. As a result we have all become accustomed to rapid-fire motormouth commercials spoken at truly incomprehensible speeds. Think of the last car commercial you saw where all the "fine print" of the latest deal was read with lightning speed, or the pharmaceutical pitch that names a dozen possible side effects in less than five seconds.

> **The attention span of the average adult is greatly exaggerated.**

"The attitude seems to be one of pushing the limits on the listener as far as [25] 'the market will bear' in terms of degrading the auditory signal and increasing the presentation rate of the spoken programming," according to Brandeis University psychologists Patricia A. Tun and Arthur Wingfield in their paper, "Slow but Sure in an Age of 'Make it Quick.'"

As these psychologists point out, laptop computers, cell phones, e-mail, and fax machines keep us in constant touch with the world while simultaneously exerting tremendous pressures on us to respond quickly and accurately. But speed and accuracy often operate at cross-purposes in the human brain.

In study after study both young and older listeners recall less from materials told to them at a rapid rate. A similar situation exists in the visual sphere. A television viewer's memory for information about the weather is actually poorer after viewing weather segments featuring colored charts and moving graphics than after viewing straight-forward versions of the same information in which the weather is simply described.

As Tun and Wingfield put it: "The clutter, noise, and constant barrage of information that surround us daily contribute to the hectic pace of our modern lives, in which it is often difficult simply to remain mindful in the moment."

No Time to Listen

As the result of our "make it quick" culture, attention deficit is becoming the paradigmatic disorder of our times. Indeed, ADD/ADHD isn't so much a disorder as it is a cognitive style. In order to be successful in today's workplace you have to incorporate some elements of ADD/ADHD.

You must learn to rapidly process information, function amidst surroundings your parents would have described as "chaotic," always remain prepared to rapidly shift from one activity to another, and redirect your attention among competing tasks without becoming bogged down or losing time. Such facility in rapid information processing requires profound alterations in our brain. And such alterations come at a cost—a devaluation of the depth and quality of our relationships.

For example, a patient of mine who works as a subway driver was once unfortunate enough to witness a man commit suicide by throwing himself in front of her train. Her ensuing anguish and distress convinced her employers that she needed help, and they sent her to me. The hardest part of her ordeal, as she expressed it, was that no one would give her more than a few minutes to tell her story. They either interrupted her or, in her words, "gradually zoned out."

"I can't seem to talk fast enough about what happened to me," she told me. "Nobody has time to listen anymore."

The absence of the "time to listen" isn't simply the result of increased workloads (although this certainly plays a role) but from a reorganization of our brains. Sensory overload is the psychological term for the process, but you don't have to be a psychologist to understand it. Our brain is being forced to manage increasing amounts of information within shorter and shorter time intervals. Since not everyone is capable of making that transition, experiences like my patient's are becoming increasingly common.

"Don't tell me anything that is going to take more than 30 seconds for you to get out," as one of my adult friends with ADD/ADHD told his wife in response to what he considered her rambling. In fact, she was only taking the time required to explain a complicated matter in appropriate detail.

"The blistering pace of life today, driven by technology and the business imperative to improve efficiency, is something to behold," writes David Shenk in his influential book *Data Smog*. "We often feel life going by much, much faster than we wish, as we are carried forward from meeting to meeting, call to call, errand to errand. We have less time to ourselves, and we are expected to improve our performance and output year after year."

Regarding technology's influence on us, Jacques Barzun, in his bestseller, *From Dawn to Decadence*, comments, "The machine makes us its captive servants—by its rhythm, by its convenience, by the cost of stopping it or the drawbacks of not using it. As captives *we come to resemble it in its pace, rigidity, and uniform expectations*" [emphasis added].

Whether you agree that we're beginning to resemble machines, I'm certain you can readily bring to mind examples of the effect of communication technology on identity and behavior. For instance, cinematography provides us with many of our reference points and a vocabulary for describing and even experiencing our personal reality.

While driving to work in the morning we "fast-forward" a half-hour in our mind to the upcoming office meeting. We reenact in our imagination a series of "scenarios" that could potentially take place. A few minutes later, while entering the garage, we experience a "flashback" of the awkward "scene" that took place during last week's meeting and "dub in" a more pleasing "take."

Of course using the vocabulary of the latest technology in conversation isn't new. Soon after their introduction, railways, telegraphs, and telephone switchboards provided useful metaphors for describing everyday experiences: People spoke of someone "telegraphing" their intentions, or of a person being "plugged in" to the latest fashions.

Modern Nerves

In 1891 the Viennese critic Hermann Bahr predicted the arrival of what he called "new human beings," marked by an increased nervous energy. A person with "modern nerves" was "quick-witted, briskly efficient, rigorously scheduled, doing everything on the double," writes social critic Peter Conrad in *Modern Times, Modern Places.*

In the 1920s, indications of modern nerves were illustrated by both the silent films of the age, with their accelerated movement, and the change in drug use at the time, from sedating agents like opium to the newly synthesized cocaine—a shift that replaced languid immobility with frenetic hyperactivity and "mobility mania."

Josef Breuer, who coauthored *Studies on Hysteria* with Sigmund Freud, compared the modern nervous system to a telephone line made up of nerves in "tonic excitation." If the nerves were overburdened with too much "current," he claimed, the result would be sparks, frazzled insulation, scorched filaments, short circuits—in essence, a model for hysteria. The mind was thus a machine and could best be understood through the employment of machine metaphors. Athletes picked up on this theme and aimed at transforming their bodies into fine-tuned organisms capable, like machines, of instant responsiveness. "The neural pathways by which will is translated into physical movement are trained until they react to the slightest impulse," wrote a commentator in the 1920s on the "cult" of sports.

The Changing Rhythm of Life

In 1931 the historian James Truslow Adams commented, "As the number of sensations increase, the time which we have for reacting to and digesting them becomes less . . . the rhythm of our life becomes quicker, the wave lengths . . . of our mental life grow shorter. Such a life tends to become a mere search for more and more exciting sensations, undermining yet more our power of concentration in thought. Relief from fatigue and ennui is sought in mere excitation of our nerves, as in speeding cars or emotional movies."

In the 60 years since Adams's observation, speed has become an integral component of our lives. According to media critic Todd Gitlin, writing in *Media Unlimited*, "Speed is not incidental to the modern world—speed of production, speed of innovation, speed of investment, speed in the pace of life and the movement of images—but its essence. . . . Is speed a means or an end? If a means, it is so pervasive as to *become* an end."

In our contemporary society speed is the standard applied to almost everything that we do. Media, especially television, is the most striking example of this acceleration. "It is the limitless media torrent that sharpens the sense that all of life is jetting forward—or through—some ultimate speed barrier," according to Gitlin. "The most widespread, most consequential speed-up of our time is the onrush in images—the speed at which they zip through the world, the speed at which they give way to more of the same, the tempo at which they move." 45

In response to this media torrent, the brain has had to make fundamental adjustments. The demarcation between here and elsewhere has become blurred. Thanks to technology, each of us exists simultaneously in not just one *here* but in several. While talking with a friend over coffee we're scanning e-mail on our Palm Pilot. At such times where are we *really*? In such instances no less is involved than a fundamental change in our concept of time and place.

Where Is Where?

"Modernity is about the acceleration of time and the dispersal of places. The past is available for instant recall in the present," according to Peter Conrad. For example, I was recently sitting in a restaurant in Washington, D.C., while watching a soccer match take place several time zones away. During an interruption in play, the screen displayed action from another match played more than a decade ago. The commentator made a brief point about similarities and differences in the two matches and then returned to the action of the ongoing match. During all of this I was participating in a "present" comprised of two different time zones along with a "past" drawn from an event that occurred twelve years earlier. Such an experience is no longer unusual. Technology routinely places us in ambiguous time and place relationships.

As another example, while recently sitting on the beach at South Beach in Miami I was amazed at the number of people talking on cell phones while ostensibly spending the afternoon with the person who accompanied them to the beach. In this situation the *here* is at least partly influenced by the technology of the cell phone that both links (the caller and the unseen person on the other end of the cell phone) and isolates (the caller and the temporarily neglected person lying beside him or her on the beach blanket). Such technologies are forcing our brains to restructure themselves and accommodate to a world of multiple identity and presence.

Intellectually we have always known that the "reality" of the here and now before our eyes is only one among many. But we never directly experienced this multilevel reality until technology made it possible to reach from one end of the world to another and wipe out differences in time, space, and place. Starting with telephones we became able to experience the "reality" of people in widely dispersed areas of the world. With the cell phone, that process has become even more intimate. Time, distance, night, and day—the rules of the natural and physical world—cease to be limiting factors.

And while some of us may celebrate such experiences and thrive on con- 50
stantly being connected, others feel the sensation of a giant electronic tentacle that will ensnare us at any moment.

My point here isn't to criticize technology but to emphasize the revolution that technology is causing in our brain's functioning. If, for example, through technology, anyone at any given moment is immediately available, "here" and "there" lose their distinctive meanings. We achieve that "acceleration of time and dispersal of places" referred to by Peter Conrad.

And yet there is an ironic paradox in all this: As a result of technological advances we participate in many different and disparate "realities," yet as a re-sult of our attention and focus problems we can't fully participate in them. We can shift back and forth from a phone conversation with someone in Hong Kong and someone directly in front of our eyes. Yet thanks to our sense of distraction we're not fully focused on either of them. What to do?

The Plastic on the Cheese

"If I can only learn to efficiently carry out several things simultaneously then my time pressures will disappear," we tell ourselves. And at first sight multi-tasking seems a sensible response to our compressed, overly committed sched-ules. Instead of limiting ourselves to only one activity, why not do several simultaneously? If you owe your mother a phone call, why not make that call while in the kitchen waiting for the spaghetti to come to a boil? And if Mom should call you first, why not talk to her while glancing down at today's cross-word puzzle?

Actually, multitasking is not nearly as efficient as most of us have been led to believe. In fact, doing more than one thing at once or switching back and forth from one task to another involves time-consuming alterations in brain processing that reduce our effectiveness at accomplishing either one.

Whenever you attempt to do "two things at once," your attention at any 55
given moment is directed to one or the other activity rather than to both at once. And, most important, these shifts decrease rather than increase your ef-ficiency; they are time and energy depleting.

With each switch in attention, your frontal lobes—the executive control centers toward the front of your brain—must shift goals and activate new rules of operation. Talking on the phone and doing a crossword puzzle activate dif-ferent parts of the brain, engage different muscles, and induce different sensory experiences.

In addition, the shift from one activity to another can take up to seven-tenths of a second. We know this because of the research of Joshua Rubinstein, a psychologist at the Federal Aviation Administration's William J. Hughes Technical Center in Atlantic City.

Rubinstein and his colleagues studied patterns of time loss that resulted when volunteers switched from activities of varying complexity and familiarity. Measurements showed that the volunteers lost time during these switches, especially when going from something familiar to something unfamiliar. Further, the time losses increased in direct proportion to the complexity of the tasks. To explain this finding the researchers postulate a "rule-activation" stage, when the prefrontal cortex "disables" or deactivates the rules used for the first activity and then "enables" the rules for the new activity. It's this process of rule deactivation followed by reactivation that takes more than half a second. Under certain circumstances this loss of time due to multitasking can prove not only inefficient but also dangerous.

For example, remember the speculation that cell phone–associated automobile accidents could be eliminated if drivers used hands-free devices? Well, that speculation isn't supported by brain research. The use of cell phones—hands-free or otherwise—divides a driver's attention and increases his or her sense of distraction.

In an important study carried out by psychologist Peter A. Hancock at the University of Central Florida in Orlando and two researchers from the Liberty Mutual Insurance Company, volunteers simulated using a hands-free cell phone while driving. The volunteers were instructed to respond to the ringing of a phone installed on the dashboard of their car. At the instant they heard the ring they had to compare whether the first digit of a number displayed on a computer screen on the dashboard corresponded to the first digit of a number they had previously memorized. If that first digit was the same, the driver was supposed to push a button. In the meantime, they were to obey all traffic rules and, in the test situation, bring the car to a full stop.

While the distracting ring had only a slight effect on the stopping distance of younger drivers (0.61 seconds rather than 0.5 seconds), it had a profound effect on the stopping distance of drivers between 55 and 65 years of age: 0.82 seconds rather than 0.61 seconds, according to the researchers. Distraction, in other words, reduces efficiency.

In another test of the cost of multitasking, volunteers at the Center for Cognitive Brain Imaging at Carnegie Mellon University in Pittsburgh underwent PET scans while simultaneously listening to sentences and mentally rotating pairs of three-dimensional figures. The researchers found a 29 percent reduction in brain activity generated by mental rotation if the subjects were also listening to the test sentences. This decrease in brain activity was linked to an overall decrease in efficiency: It took them longer to do each task.

A reduction in efficiency was also found when the researchers looked at the effect of mental rotation on reading. They discovered that brain activity generated when reading the sentences decreased by 53 percent if the subjects were also trying to mentally rotate the objects.

A similar loss of efficiency occurs when activities are alternated. For instance, David E. Meyer, a professor of mathematical psychology at the University of Michigan in Ann Arbor, recruited young adults to engage in an experiment where they would rapidly switch between working out math problems and identifying shapes. The volunteers took longer for both tasks, and their accuracy took a nosedive compared to their performance when they focused on each task separately.

"Not only the speed of performance, the accuracy of performance, but what I call the fluency of performance, the gracefulness of their performance, was negatively influenced by the overload of multitasking," according to Meyer.

All of which leads to this simple rule: Despite our subjective feelings to the contrary, actually our brain can work on only one thing at a time. Rather than allowing us to efficiently do two things at the same time, multitasking actually results in inefficient shifts in our attention. In short, the brain is designed to work most efficiently when it works on a single task and for sustained rather than intermittent and alternating periods of time. This doesn't mean that we can't perform a certain amount of multitasking. But we do so at decreased efficiency and accuracy.

Thanks to technology, each of us exists simultaneously in not just one *here* but in several.

But despite neuroscientific evidence to the contrary, we are being made to feel that we *must* multitask in order to keep our head above the rising flood of daily demands. Instead of "Be Here Now," we're encouraged to split our attention into several fragments and convinced that multitasking improves mental efficiency.

Instead, multitasking comes at a cost. And it's true that sometimes the cost is trivial, or even amusing, as with the following experience of a young mother: "I had to get dressed for my daughter's middle school choral program, get another child started on homework, and feed another who had to be ready to be driven to soccer practice. Of course, the phone kept ringing, too. I thought I had everything under control when the complaints about the grilled cheese started. Without getting too angry, I growled for her to just eat it so that I could finish getting dressed. What else could I do in such a rush? My daughter then said, 'I can't eat it, Mom. You left the plastic on the cheese.'"

Other times, the cost of multitasking can be much less amusing. Imagine yourself driving in light traffic on a clear day while chatting on a cell phone with a friend. You're having no problem handling your vehicle and also keeping up your end of the conversation. But over the next five minutes you encounter heavier traffic and the onset of a torrential rainstorm. Your impulse is to end the conversation and pay more attention to the road, but your friend on the other end of the line keeps talking. After all, he isn't encountering the same hazardous conditions from the comfort of his office or home. You continue to talk a bit longer, shifting your attention between your friend's patter and the rapidly deteriorating road conditions. As a result, you fail to notice that the tractor-trailer to your right is starting to slide in your direction. . . . Your survivors will never know that your divided attention, with its accompanying decrease in brain efficiency, set you up for that fatal accident.

65

In essence, the brain has certain limits that we must accept. While it's true that we can train our brain to multitask, our overall performance on each of the tasks is going to be less efficient than if we performed one thing at a time.

Cerebral Geography

Despite the inefficiency of multitasking, the brain is able to deal with more than one thing at a time. If that weren't true, we wouldn't be able to "walk and chew gum at the same time," as a critic once uncharitably described a former U.S. president. The trick is to avoid activities that interrupt the flow of the main activity.

For example, listening to music can actually enhance the efficiency among those who work with their hands. I first learned of this a year or so ago when a draftsman casually mentioned to me that he felt more relaxed and did better work while listening to background music. Many surgeons make similar claims. In a study aimed at testing such claims, researchers hooked up 50 male surgeons between the ages of 31 and 61 to machines that measured blood pressure and pulse. The surgeons then performed mental arithmetic exercises designed to mimic the stress a surgeon would be expected to experience in the operating room. They then repeated the exercise while the surgeons listened to musical selections of their own choosing. The performances improved when the surgeons were listening to the music.

In another study, listening to music enhanced the surgeons' alertness and concentration. What kind of music worked best? Of 50 instrumental tracks selected, 46 were concertos, with Vivaldi's *Four Seasons* as the top pick, followed by Beethoven's Violin Concerto op. 61, Bach's Brandenburg Concertos, and Wagner's "Ride of the Valkyries"—not exactly your standard "easy listening" repertoire.

But easy listening isn't the purpose, according to one of the surgeons interviewed. "In the O.R. it's very busy with lots of things going on, but if you have the music on you can operate. The music isn't a distraction but a way of blocking out all of the other distractions."

Music undoubtedly exerts its positive effects on surgical performance at least partially through its kinesthetic effects, an observation made by Socrates in Plato's *Republic*: "More than anything else rhythm and harmony find their way to the inmost soul and take strongest hold upon it." Thanks to music, the surgeon is more concentrated, alert, technically efficient, and—most important—in the frame of mind most conducive to healing. "Take Puccini's *La Bohème*," says Blake Papsin, an ear, nose, and throat surgeon in Toronto. "It's an absolutely beautiful piece of music that compels the human spirit to perform, to care, to love—and that's what surgery is."

Music and skilled manual activities activate different parts of the brain, so interference and competition are avoided. If the surgeon listened to an audiobook instead of a musical composition, however, there would likely be interference. Imagining a scene described by the narrator would interfere with the surgeon's spatial imaging. Listening to the audiobook would activate similar areas of the brain and cause competition between the attention needed to efficiently and accurately operate and to comprehend the images and story in the audiobook. We encounter here an example of the principle of *cerebral geography*: The brain works at its best with the activation of different, rather than identical, brain areas. That's why doodling while talking on the telephone isn't a problem for most people, since speaking and drawing use different brain areas. But writing a thank you note while on the phone results in mental strain because speaking and writing share some of the same brain circuitry.

Thanks to new technology, especially procedures like functional MRI scans, neuroscientists will soon be able to compile lists of activities that can be done simultaneously with a minimal lapse in efficiency or accuracy. But, in general, it's wise to keep this in mind: A penalty is almost always paid when two activities are carried out simultaneously rather than separately.

Questions for Critical Reading

1. According to Restak, what are the problems with multitasking? Locate passages where he discusses the impact of this practice. Do you think multitasking is possible? How does it function in your own life?

2. How does culture affect biology? Perform a critical reading of Restak's text in order to describe the ways in which what we do can change what we are.

3. What are "modern nerves"? Define the term through Restak's essay and then provide examples from both his text and your own life.

Exploring Context

1. Take the ADD/ADHD test at psychcentral.com/addquiz.htm. How does your score reflect Restak's argument? Connect your response to your work on multitasking from Question 1 of Questions for Critical Reading.

2. Explore the Web site for Twitter at twitter.com. Is this abbreviated style of blogging a reflection of the problems that Restak explores? Or is staying hyperconnected to your friends a way of combating the demands on attention? Consider the relation between Twitter and your definition of "modern nerves" from Question 3 of Questions for Critical Reading.

3. Play the Multitasking game at itch.com/games/multitasking. How does your performance in the game confirm or complicate Restak's argument? Connect your response to your work on multitasking from Question 1 of Questions for Critical Reading.

Questions for Connecting

1. Kwame Anthony Appiah, in "Making Conversation" (p. 57) and "The Primacy of Practice" (p. 63), explores the persistence of social practices and the possibilities of change. Can we use his ideas to address the problem that Restak

describes? Does multitasking, as a practice, have a kind of primacy? Draw from your work in Questions for Critical Reading in making your argument.

2. In "Ethics and the New Genetics" (p. 76), the Dalai Lama asks us to consider the ethical implications of new technologies. But what are the ethical implications of existing technologies? Is multitasking an ethical issue? Synthesize these two texts to make a larger argument about the ethics of technology.

3. How does culture shape bodies? Consider not only Restak's argument but also Julia Serano's ideas in "Before and After: Class and Body Transformations" (p. 392). You may want to draw from your work in Exploring Context in making your argument.

Language Matters

1. Create a series of presentation slides about this essay using PowerPoint or other software. Since such slides are most effective when they contain only a few key points per slide, you will have to locate the most important elements of Restak's argument; in designing the slides you should also consider how visual elements like color, font, and alignment can enhance an argument.

2. Punctuation marks control the speed of speech: Commas ask us to pause and periods ask us to stop. Given Restak's argument, how can you use punctuation in your writing to guide your reader's attention and combat ADD/ADHD? Which marks might be most helpful, and which might you want to avoid?

3. What's the difference between editing, proofreading, and revising? What would you do to this essay if you were editing it? Revising it? How can you use these different skills in your own writing?

Assignments for Writing

1. Restak examines the way the human brain responds to modern technology, claiming that the changes made in the brain by technology are the biggest changes to that organ in thousands of years. Write an essay that examines the potential benefits of this change at the end of the first decade of the twenty-first century. What is the role of television in the rewiring of the brain? What other technologies have similar effects? Is this change in brain function for the better? Is it possible that technological advances can move faster than is good for humankind? Consider using your work with Restak's concepts from Questions for Connecting in making your argument.

2. Restak looks closely at the role of modern media and communication devices in our daily lives. Write an essay in which you use Restak and your own experience to assess the ways in which current media has created a culture that demands a high-speed, high-efficiency lifestyle. Does media shape our attention? In what ways are we expected to speed up, and in what ways are we urged to slow down? Restak writes about the "crawler" on TV news. What other media features divide our attention?

3. Write an essay that examines the effectiveness of multitasking in the face of modern technologies, synthesizing Restak's text with your own experience. How does the brain multitask? What impedes our ability to multitask? Why is multitasking not as efficient as we may think? What role does modern technology play in our ability to multitask? Do we multitask more than we think? What demands do we place on ourselves when it comes to multitasking? Draw from your experience with Exploring Context in making your argument.

MARY ROACH

Mary Roach, who holds a B.S. in psychology from Wesleyan University, is a contributing editor for the science magazine *Discover*. She also has contributed to *Vogue*, Salon.com, *Wired*, *Outside*, *GQ*, and the *New York Times Magazine*. Roach is known for her entertaining writing style and unusual subject matter, as illustrated by her best-selling books *Stiff: The Curious Lives of Human Cadavers* (2003) and *Spook: Science Tackles the Afterlife* (2005). Her latest book, *Bonk: The Curious Coupling of Science and Sex*, was published in early 2008.

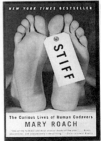

In *Stiff*, Roach explores the role of the human body once its owner dies. In her research on the uses of human cadavers Roach discovers plastic surgeons who practice new techniques on them, an expert in human decomposition, and real-life human crash test dummies. With these examinations Roach argues that our remains can be a lot more valuable above ground than below.

In "The Cadaver Who Joined the Army," from *Stiff*, Roach focuses on military-related research on corpses. Experiments range from firing bullets into corpses for ballistics research to outfitting severed legs with different types of footwear to see which is most effective in protecting its wearer from a landmine blast. Subjecting cadavers to gunshots and explosions is ethically difficult, though, and Roach explores the complicated moral and ethical questions involved. Particularly tricky is the question of "informed consent" and whether or not families know—or should know—what will be done to the cadavers after they are donated.

Ethics normally provides a set of rules for living, but Roach asks us to extend these considerations to our bodies once we are gone. What role should human bodies play in scientific research, and how do we calculate the trade-off between knowledge and ethics?

▶ TAGS: *research*, *surrogates*, *death*, *ethics*, *morality*

The Cadaver Who Joined the Army

For three days in January of 1893 and again for four days in March, Captain Louis La Garde of the U.S. Army Medical Corps took up arms against a group of extraordinary foes. It was an unprecedented military undertaking, and one for which he would forever after be remembered. Though La Garde served as a surgeon, he was no stranger to armed combat. In the Powder River Expedition of 1876, he had been decorated for gallantry in confronting tribes of hostile Sioux. La Garde had led the charge against Chief Dull Knife, whose name, we can only assume, was no reflection on his intellectual and military acumen or the quality and upkeep of his armaments.

La Garde received his strange and fateful orders in July of 1892. He would be receiving, the letter said, a new, experimental .30-caliber Springfield rifle. He was to take this rifle, along with his standard-issue .45-caliber Springfield, and report to Frankford Arsenal, Pennsylvania, the following winter. Taking shape in the rifles' sights would be men, a series of them, naked and unarmed. That they were naked and unarmed was the less distinctive thing about them. More distinctive was that they were already dead. They had died of natural causes and had been collected—from where is not revealed—as subjects in an Army Ordnance Department experiment. They were to be suspended from a tackle in the ceiling of the firing range, shot at in a dozen places and with a dozen different charges (to simulate different distances), and autopsied. La Garde's mission was to compare the physiological effects of the two different weapons upon the human body's bones and innards.

The United States Army was by no means the first to sanction the experimental plugging of civilian cadavers. The French army, wrote La Garde in his book *Gunshot Injuries*, had been "firing into dead bodies for the purpose of teaching the effects of gunshots in war" since around 1800. Ditto the Germans, who went to the exquisite trouble of propping up their mock victims al fresco, at distances approximating those of an actual battlefield. Even the famously neutral Swiss sanctioned a series of military wound ballistics studies on cadavers in the late 1800s. Theodore Kocher, a Swiss professor of surgery and a member of the Swiss army militia (the Swiss prefer not to fight, but they are armed, and with more than little red pocket knife/can openers), spent a year firing Swiss Vetterli rifles into all manner of targets—bottles, books, water-filled pig intestines, oxen bones, human skulls, and, ultimately, a pair of whole human cadavers—with the aim of understanding the mechanisms of wounding from bullets.

Kocher—and to a certain extent La Garde—expressed a desire that their ballistics work with cadavers would lead to a more humanitarian form of gun battle. Kocher urged that the goal of warfare be to render the enemy not dead, but simply unable to fight. To this end, he advised limiting the size of the bullets and making them from a material of a higher melting point than lead, so that they would deform less and thus destroy less tissue.

Incapacitation—or stopping power, as it is known in munitions circles— 5
became the Holy Grail of ballistics research. How to stop a man in his tracks, preferably without maiming or killing him, but definitely before he maimed or killed you first. Indeed, the next time Captain La Garde and his swinging cadavers took the stage, in 1904, it was in the name of improved stopping power. The topic had been high on the generals' to-do lists following the army's involvement in the Philippines, during the final stage of the Spanish-American War, where its Colt .38s had failed, on numerous occasions, to stop the enemy cold. While the Colt .38 was considered sufficient for "civilized" warfare—"even the stoical Japanese soldier," wrote La Garde in *Gunshot Injuries*, "fell back as a rule when he was hit the first time"—such was apparently not the case with "savage tribes or a fanatical enemy." The Moro tribesman of the Philippines was considered a bit of both: "A fanatic like a Moro, wielding a bolo in each hand

who advances with leaps and bounds . . . must be hit with a projectile having a maximum amount of stopping power," wrote La Garde. He related the tale of one battle-enlivened tribesman who charged a U.S. Army guard unit. "When he was within 100 yards, the entire guard opened fire on him." Nonetheless, he managed to advance some ninety-five yards toward them before finally crashing to the ground.

La Garde, at the War Department's urging, undertook an investigation of the army's various guns and bullets and their relative efficacy at putting a rapid halt to enemies. He decided that one way to do this would be to fire at suspended cadavers and take note of the "shock," as estimated by "the disturbance which appeared." In other words, how far back does the hanging torso or arm or leg swing when you shoot it? "It was based on the assumption that the momentum of hanging bodies of various weights could somehow be correlated and measured, and that it actually meant something with regard to stopping power," says Evan Marshall, who wrote the book on handgun stopping power (it's called *Handgun Stopping Power*). "What it actually did was extrapolate questionable data from questionable tests."

Even Captain La Garde came to realize that if you want to find out how likely a gun is to stop someone, you are best off trying it on an entity that isn't already quite permanently stopped. In other words, a live entity. "The animals selected were beeves about to undergo slaughter in the Chicago stock-yards," wrote La Garde, deeply perplexing the ten or fifteen people who would be reading his book later than the 1930s, when the word "beeves," meaning cattle, dropped from everyday discourse. Sixteen beeves later, La Garde had his answer: Whereas the larger-caliber (.45) Colt revolver bullets caused the cattle to drop to the ground after three or four shots, the animals shot with smaller-caliber .38 bullets failed even after ten shots to drop to the ground. And ever since, the U.S. Army has gone confidently into battle, knowing that when cows attack, their men will be ready.

For the most part, it has been the lowly swine that has borne the brunt of munitions trauma research in the United States and Europe. In China—at the No. 3 Military Medical College and the China Ordnance Society, among others—it has been mongrel dogs that get shot at. In Australia, as reported in the Proceedings of the 5th Symposium on Wound Ballistics, the researchers took aim at rabbits. It is tempting to surmise that a culture chooses its most reviled species for ballistics research. China occasionally eats its dogs, but doesn't otherwise have much use or affection for them; in Australia, rabbits are considered a scourge—imported by the British for hunting, they multiplied (like rabbits) and, in a span of twenty years, wiped out two million acres of south Australian brush.

In the case of the U.S. and European research, the theory doesn't hold. Pigs don't get shot at because our culture reviles them as filthy and disgusting. Pigs get shot at because their organs are a lot like ours. The heart of the pig is a particularly close match. Goats were another favorite, because their lungs are like ours. I was told this by Commander Marlene DeMaio, who studies body armor at the Armed Forces Institute of Pathology (AFIP). Talking to DeMaio,

I got the impression that it would be possible to construct an entire functioning nonhuman human from pieces of other species. "The human knee most resembles the brown bear's," she said at one point, following up with a surprising or not so surprising statement: "The human brain most resembles that of Jersey cows at about six months."* I learned elsewhere that emu hips are dead ringers for human hips, a situation that has worked out better for humans than for emus, who, over at Iowa State University, have been lamed in a manner that mimics osteonecrosis and then shuttled in and out of CT scanners by researchers seeking to understand the disease.

Had I been calling the shots back at the War Department, I would have sanctioned a study not on why men sometimes fail to drop to the ground after being shot, but on why they so often *do*. If it takes ten or twelve seconds to lose consciousness from blood loss (and consequent oxygen deprivation to the brain), why, then, do people who have been shot so often collapse on the spot? It doesn't happen just on TV.

I posed this question to Duncan MacPherson, a respected ballistics expert and consultant to the Los Angeles Police Department. MacPherson insists the effect is purely psychological. Whether or not you collapse depends on your state of mind. Animals don't know what it means to be shot, and, accordingly, rarely exhibit the instant stop-and-drop. MacPherson points **And ever since, the U.S. Army has gone confidently into battle, knowing that when cows attack, their men will be ready.** out that deer shot through the heart often run off for forty or fifty yards before collapsing. "The deer doesn't know anything about what's going on, so he just does his deer thing for ten seconds or so and then he can't do it anymore. An animal with a meaner disposition will use that ten seconds to come at you." On the flip side, there are people who are shot at but not hit — or hit with nonlethal bullets, which don't penetrate, but just smart a lot — who will drop immediately to the ground. "There was an officer I know who took a shot at a guy and the guy just went flat, totally splat, facedown," MacPherson told me. "He said to himself, 'God, I was aiming for center mass like I'm supposed to, but I must have gotten a head shot by mistake. I'd better go back to the shooting range.' Then he went to the guy and there wasn't a mark on him. If there isn't a central nervous system hit, anything that happens fast is all psychological."

MacPherson's theory would explain the difficulties the army had in La Garde's day with the Moro tribesmen, who presumably weren't familiar with the effects of rifles and kept on doing their Moro tribesman thing until they couldn't — owing to blood loss and consequent loss of consciousness — do it anymore. Sometimes it isn't just ignorance as to what bullets do that renders a foe temporarily impervious. It can also be viciousness and sheer determination.

---

*I did not ask DeMaio about sheep and the purported similarity of portions of their reproductive anatomy to that of the human female, lest she be forced to draw conclusions about the similarity of my intellect and manners to that of the, I don't know, boll weevil.

"A lot of guys take pride in their imperviousness to pain," MacPherson said. "They can get a lot of holes in them before they go down. I know an LAPD detective who got shot through the heart with a .357 Magnum and he killed the guy that shot him before he collapsed."

Not everyone agrees with the psychological theory. There are those who feel that some sort of neural overload takes place when a bullet hits. I communicated with a neurologist/avid handgunner/reserve deputy sheriff in Victoria, Texas, named Dennis Tobin, who has a theory about this. Tobin, who wrote the chapter "A Neurologist's View of 'Stopping Power'" in the book *Handgun Stopping Power*, posits that an area of the brain stem called the reticular activating system (RAS) is responsible for the sudden collapse. The RAS can be affected by impulses arising from massive pain sensations in the viscera.* Upon receiving these impulses, the RAS sends out a signal that weakens certain leg muscles, with the result that the person drops to the ground.

Somewhat shaky support for Tobin's neurological theory can be found in animal studies. Deer may keep going, but dogs and pigs seem to react as humans do. The phenomenon was remarked upon in military medical circles as far back as 1893. A wound ballistics experimenter by the name of Griffith, while going about his business documenting the effects of a Krag-Jorgensen rifle upon the viscera of live dogs at two hundred yards, noted that the animals, when shot in the abdomen, "died as promptly as though they had been electrocuted." Griffith found this odd, given that, as he pointed out in the *Transactions of the First Pan-American Medical Congress*, "no vital part was hit which might account for the instantaneous death of the animals." (In fact, the dogs were probably not as promptly dead as Griffith believed. More likely, they had simply collapsed and looked, from two hundred yards, like dead dogs. And by the time Griffith had walked the two hundred yards to get to them, they were in fact dead dogs, having expired from blood loss.)

In 1988, a Swedish neurophysiologist named A. M. Göransson, then of Lund University, took it upon himself to investigate the conundrum. Like Tobin, Göransson figured that something about the bullet's impact was causing a massive overload to the central nervous system. And so, perhaps unaware of the similarities between the human brain and that of Jersey cows at six months, he wired the brains of nine anesthetized pigs to an EEG machine, one at a time, and shot them in the hindquarters. Göransson reports having used a "high-energy missile" for the task, which is less drastic than it suggests. What it suggests is

---

*MacPherson counters that bullet wounds are rarely, at the outset, painful. Research by eighteenth-century scientist/philosopher Albrecht von Haller suggests that it depends on what the bullet hits. Experimenting on live dogs, cats, rabbits, and other small unfortunates, Haller systematically catalogued the viscera according to whether or not they register pain. By his reckoning, the stomach, intestines, bladder, ureter, vagina, womb, and heart do, whereas the lungs, liver, spleen, and kidneys "have very little sensation, seeing I have irritated them, thrust a knife into them, and cut them to pieces without the animals' seeming to feel any pain." Haller admitted that the work suffered certain methodological shortcomings, most notably that, as he put it, "an animal whose thorax is opened is in such violent torture that it is hard to distinguish the effect of an additional slight irritation."

that Dr. Göransson got into his car, drove some distance from his laboratory, and launched the Swedish equivalent of Tomahawk missiles at the hapless swine, but in fact, I am told, the term simply means a small, fast-moving bullet.

Instantly upon being hit, all but three of the pigs showed significantly flattened EEGs, the amplitude in some cases having dropped by as much as 50 percent. As the pigs had already been stopped in their tracks by the anesthesia, it is impossible to say whether they would have been rendered so by the shots, and Göransson opted not to speculate. And if they had lost consciousness, Göransson had no way of knowing what the mechanism was. To the deep chagrin of pigs the world over, he encouraged further study.

Proponents of the neural overload theory point to the "temporary stretch cavity" as the source of the effect. All bullets, upon entry into the human form, blow open a cavity in the tissue around them. This cavity shuts back up almost immediately, but in that fraction of a second that it is agape, the nervous system, they believe, issues a Mayday blast—enough of one, it seems, to overload the circuits and cause the whole system to hang a Gone Fishing sign on the door.

These same proponents believe that bullets that create sizable stretch cavities are thus more likely to deliver the necessary shock to achieve the vaunted ballistics goal of "good stopping power." If this is true, then in order to gauge a bullet's stopping power, one needs to be able to view the stretch cavity as it opens up. That is why the good Lord, working in tandem with the Kind & Knox gelatin company, invented human tissue simulant.

I am about to fire a bullet into the closest approximation of a human thigh outside of a human thigh: a six-by-six-by-eighteen-inch block of ballistic gelatin. Ballistic gelatin is essentially a tweaked version of Knox dessert gelatin. It is denser than dessert gelatin, having been formulated to match the average density of human tissue, is less colorful, and, lacking sugar, is even less likely to please dinner guests. Its advantage over a cadaver thigh is that it affords a stop-action view of the temporary stretch cavity. Unlike real tissue, human tissue simulant doesn't snap back: The cavity remains, allowing ballistics types to judge, and preserve a record of, a bullet's performance. Plus, you don't need to autopsy a block of human tissue simulant; because it's clear, you just walk up to it after you've shot it and take a look at the damage. Following which, you can take it home, eat it, and enjoy stronger, healthier nails in thirty days.

Like other gelatin products, ballistic gelatin is made from processed cow bone chips and "freshly chopped" pig hide.* The Kind & Knox Web site does not include human tissue simulant on its list of technical gelatin applications, which rather surprised me, as did the failure of a Knox public relations woman to return my calls. You would think that a company that felt comfortable extolling

20

---

* According to the Kind & Knox Web site, other products made with cow-bone-and-pigskin-based gelatin include marshmallows, nougat-type candy bar fillings, liquorice, Gummi Bears, caramels, sports drinks, butter, ice cream, vitamin gel caps, suppositories, and that distasteful whitish peel on the outside of salamis. What I am getting at here is that if you're going to worry about mad cow disease, you probably have more to worry about than you thought. And that if there's any danger, which I like to think there isn't, we're all doomed, so relax and have another Snickers.

the virtues of Number 1 Pigskin Grease on its Web site ("It is a very clean material"; "Available in tanker trucks or railcars") would be okay with talking about ballistic gelatin, but apparently I've got truckloads or railcars to learn about gelatin PR.

Our replicant human thigh was cooked up by Rick Lowden, a freewheeling materials engineer whose area of expertise is bullets. Lowden works at the Department of Energy's Oak Ridge National Laboratory in Oak Ridge, Tennessee. The lab is best known for its plutonium work in the Manhattan (atomic bomb development) Project and now covers a far broader and generally less unpopular range of projects. Lowden, for instance, has lately been involved in the design of an environmentally friendly no-lead bullet that doesn't cost the military an arm and a leg to clean up after. Lowden loves guns, loves to talk about them. Right now he's trying to talk about them with me, a distinctly trying experience, for I keep shepherding the conversation back to dead bodies, which Lowden clearly doesn't enjoy very much. You would think that a man who felt comfortable extolling the virtues of hollow-point bullets ("expands to twice its size and just thumps that person") would be okay talking about dead bodies, but apparently not. "You just cringe," he said, when I mentioned the prospect of shooting into human cadaver tissue. Then he made a noise that I transcribed in my notes as "Olggh."

We are standing under a canopy at the Oak Ridge shooting range, about to set up the first stopping-power test. The "thighs" sit in an open plastic cooler at our feet, sweating mildly. They are consommé-colored and, owing to the cinnamon added to mask the material's mild rendering-plant effluvium, smell like Big Red chewing gum. Rick carries the cooler out to the target table, thirty feet away, and settles an ersatz thigh into the gel cradle. I make conversation with Scottie Dowdell, who is supervising the shooting range today. He is telling me about the pine beetle epidemic in the area. I point to a stand of dead conifers in the woods a quarter mile back behind the target. "Like over there?" Scottie says no. He says they died of bullet wounds, something I never knew pine trees could do.

Rick returns and sets up the gun, which isn't really a gun but a "universal receiver," a tabletop gun housing that can be outfitted with barrels of different calibers. Once it's aimed, you pull a wire to release the bullet. We're testing a couple of new bullets that claim to be frangible, meaning they break apart on impact. The frangible bullet was designed to solve the "overpenetration," or ricochet, problem, i.e., bullets passing through victims, bouncing off walls, and harming bystanders or the police or soldiers who fired them. The side effect of the bullet's breaking apart on impact is that it tends to do this inside your body if you're hit. In other words, it tends to have really, really good stopping power. It basically functions like a tiny bomb inside the victim and is therefore, to date, mainly reserved for "special response" SWAT-type activities, such as hostage rescue.

Rick hands me the trigger string and counts down from three. The gelatin sits on the table, soaking up the sunshine, basking beneath the calm, blue Tennessee skies—*tra la la, life is gay, it's good to be a gelatin block, I* . . . BLAM!

The block flips up into the air, off the table, and onto the grass. As John   25
Wayne said, or would have, had he had the opportunity, this block of gelatin
won't be bothering anyone anytime soon. Rick picks up the block and places it
back in its cradle. You can see the bullet's journey through the "thigh." Rather
than overpenetrating and exiting the back side, the bullet has stopped short
several inches into the block. Rick points to the stretch cavity. "Look at that. A
total dump of energy. Total incapacitation."

I had asked Lowden whether munitions professionals ever concern themselves, as did Kocher and La Garde, with trying to design bullets that will inca-
pacitate without maiming or killing. Lowden's face displayed the sort of look
it displayed earlier when I'd said that armor-piercing bullets were "cute." He
answered that the military chooses weapons more or less by how much damage
they can inflict on a target, "whether the target be a human or a vehicle." This is
another reason ballistic gelatin tends to get used in stopping-power tests, rather
than cadavers. We're not talking about research that will help mankind save
lives; we're talking about research that will help mankind take lives. I suppose
you could argue that policemen's and soldiers' lives may be saved, but only by
taking someone else's life first. Anyway, it's not a use of human tissue for which
you're likely to get broad public support.

Of course, the other big reason munitions people shoot ballistic gelatin is
reproducibility: Provided you follow the recipe, it's always the same. Cadaver
thighs vary in density and thickness, according to the age, gender, and physical condition of their owners when they stopped using them. Still another
reason: Cleanup's a breeze. The remains of this morning's thighs have been
picked up and repacked in the cooler, a tidy, bloodless mass grave of low-calorie
dessert.

Not that a ballistic gelatin shootout is completely devoid of gore. Lowden
points to the toe of my sneaker, at a *Pulp Fiction* fleck of spatter. "You got some
simulant on your shoe."

Rick Lowden never shot a dead man, though he had his chance. He was working on a project, in cooperation with the University of Tennessee's human decay
facility, aimed at developing bullets that would resist corrosion from the acid
breakdown products inside a dead body and help forensics types solve crimes
long after they happen.

Rather than shooting the experimental bullets into his cadavers, Lowden   30
got down on his hands and knees with a scalpel and a pair of tweezers and sur-
gically placed them. He explained that he did this because he wanted the bullets
to end up in specific places: muscle, fatty tissue, the head and chest cavities, the
abdomen. If he'd shot them into the tissue, they might have overpenetrated, as
they say, and wound up in the dirt.

He also did it that way because he felt he had to. "It was always my impression that we couldn't shoot a body." He recalls another project, one in
which he was developing a simulated human bone that could be put inside
blocks of ballistic gelatin, much as banana and pineapple chunks are floated
inside Jell-O. To calibrate the simulated bone, he needed to shoot some actual

bone and compare the two. "I was offered sixteen cadaver legs to shoot at. DOE told me they would terminate my project if I did that. We had to shoot pig femurs instead."

Lowden told me that military munitions professionals even worry about the politics of shooting into freshly killed livestock. "A lot of guys won't do that. They'll go get a ham from the store or a leg from the slaughterhouse. Even then, a lot of them don't openly publish what they do. There's still a stigma."

Ten feet behind us, sniffing the air, is a groundhog who has made unfortunate real estate choices in his life. The animal is half the size of a human thigh. If you shot that groundhog with one of these bullets, I say to Rick, what would happen? Would it completely vaporize? Rick and Scottie exchange a look. I get the feeling that the stigma attached to shooting groundhogs is fairly minimal.

Scottie shuts the ammo case. "Create a lot of paperwork, is what would happen."

Only recently has the military dipped its toes back into the roiling waters of publicly funded cadaveric ballistics research. As one would imagine, the goals are strictly humanitarian. At the Armed Forces Institute of Pathology's Ballistic Missile Trauma Research Lab last year, Commander Marlene DeMaio dressed cadavers in a newly developed body armor vest and fired a range of modern-day munitions at their chests. The idea was to test the manufacturer's claims before outfitting the troops. Apparently body armor manufacturers' effectiveness claims aren't always to be trusted. According to Lester Roane, chief engineer at the independent ballistics and body armor test facility H. P. White Labs, the companies don't do cadaver tests. H. P. White doesn't either. "Anybody looking at it coldly and logically shouldn't have any problem with it," said Roane. "It's dead meat. But for some reason, it's just something that has been politically incorrect from before there was a term for politically correct."

DeMaio's cadaver tests represent a distinct improvement over how vests were originally tested by the military: In Operation Boar, during the Korean War, the Doron vest was tested simply by giving it to six thousand soldiers and seeing how they fared compared to soldiers wearing standard vests. Roane says he once watched a video made by a Central American police department that tested their vests by having officers put them on and then shooting at them.

The trick to designing body armor is to make it thick and unyielding enough to stop bullets without making it so heavy and hot and uncomfortable that officers won't wear it. What you don't want is what the Gilbertese Islanders used to have. While I was in D.C. to see DeMaio, I stopped at the Smithsonian's Museum of Natural History, where I saw a display of body armor from the Gilbert Islands. Battles in Micronesia were so pitched and bloody that Gilbertese warriors would outfit themselves head to foot with doormat-thick armor fashioned from the twisted fibers of coconut hulls. On top of the significant humiliation of making one's entrance onto the battlefield looking like an enormous macramé planter was the fact that the armor was so bulky it required the assistance of several squires to help maneuver you.

As with automotive cadavers, DeMaio's body-armor bodies were instrumented with accelerometers and load cells, in this case on the sternum, to record the impact forces and give researchers a detailed medical rendering of what was happening to the chest inside the armor. With some of the nastier-caliber weapons, the cadavers sustained lung lacerations and rib fractures, but nothing that translated into an injury that—if you weren't already a cadaver—could kill you. More tests are planned, with the goal of making a test dummy along the lines of those used by the automotive industry—so that one day cadavers won't be needed.

Because she had proposed to use human cadavers, DeMaio was advised to proceed with extreme caution. She gathered the blessings of three institutional review boards, a military legal counsel, and a card-carrying ethicist. The project was ultimately approved, with one stipulation: no penetration. The bullets had to stop short of the cadavers' skin.

Did DeMaio roll her eyes in exasperation? She says not. "When I was in   40 medical school I used to think, 'Come on, don't be irrational. They've expired, they've donated their bodies, you know?' When I got into this project I realized that we are part of the public trust, and even if it doesn't make scientific sense, we have to be responsive to people's emotional concerns."

On an institutional level, the caution comes from fear of liability and of unpleasant media reports and withdrawal of funding. I spoke with Colonel John Baker, the legal counsel from one of the institutions that sponsored DeMaio's research. The head of this institution preferred that I refrain from naming it and instead refer to it as simply "a federal institution in Washington." He told me that over the past twenty-some years, Democratic congressmen and budget-minded legislators have tried to close the place down, as have Jimmy Carter, Bill Clinton, and People for the Ethical Treatment of Animals. I got the feeling that my request for an interview had brought this man's day crashing down like so many pine trees behind a DOE shooting range.

"The concern is that some survivor will be so taken aback that they'll bring suit," said Colonel Baker from his desk at a federal institution in Washington. "And there is no body of law in this area, nothing you can look to other than good judgment." He pointed out that although cadavers don't have rights, their family members do. "I could imagine some sort of lawsuit that is based upon emotional distress. . . . You get some of those [cases] in a cemetery situation, where the proprietor has allowed the coffins to rot away and the corpses pop up." I replied that as long as you have informed consent—a signed agreement from the donor stating that he has willed his body to medical research—it would seem that the survivors wouldn't have much of a case.

The sticking point is the word "informed." It's fair to say that when people donate remains, either their own or those of a family member, they usually don't care to know the grisly details of what might be done with them. And that if you did tell them the details, they might change their minds and withdraw consent. Then again, if you're planning to shoot guns at them, it might be good to run that up the flagpole and get the a-okay. "Part of respecting persons is telling them the information that they might have an emotional response to," says Edmund Howe, editor of the *Journal of Clinical Ethics*, who reviewed Marlene DeMaio's research proposal. "Though one could go the other way and spare them that response and therefore ethically not commit that harm. But the downside to withholding information that might be significant to them is that it would violate their dignity to an extent." Howe suggests a third possibility, that of letting the families make the choice: Would they prefer to hear the specifics of what is being done with the donated body—specifics that may be upsetting—or would they prefer not to know?

It's a delicate balance that, in the end, comes down to wording. Observes Baker, "You don't really want to be telling somebody, 'Well, what we'll be doing is dissecting their eyeballs. We take them out and put them on a table and then we dissect them into finer and finer parts and then once we're finished we scrape all that stuff up and put it into a biohazard bag and try to keep it together so we can return whatever's left to you.' That sounds horrible." On the other hand, "medical research" is a tad vague. "Instead, you say, 'One of our principal concerns here at the university is ophthalmology. So we do a lot here with ophthalmological materials.'" If someone cares to think it through, it isn't hard to come to the conclusion that someone in a lab coat will, at the very least, be cutting your eyeball out of your head. But most people don't care to think it through. They focus on the end, rather than the means: Someone's vision may one day be saved.

Ballistics studies are especially problematic. How do you decide it's okay to cut off someone's grandfather's head and shoot it in the face? Even when the reason you are doing that is to gather data to ensure that innocent civilians who are hit in the face with nonlethal bullets won't suffer disfiguring fractures? Moreover, how do you bring yourself to carry out the cutting off and shooting of someone's grandfather's head?

I posed these questions to Cindy Bir, who brought herself to do exactly that, and whom I met while I was at Wayne State. Bir is accustomed to firing projectiles at the dead. In 1993, the National Institute of Justice (NIJ) commissioned her to document the impact effects of various nonlethal munitions: plastic bullets, rubber ones, beanbags, the lot. Police began using nonlethal bullets in the late 1980s, in situations where they need to subdue civilians—mostly rioters and violent psychotics—without putting their lives in danger. In nine instances since that time, "nonlethal" bullets have proved lethal, prompting the NIJ to have Bir look into what was going on with these different bullets, with the aim of its not going on ever again.

As to the question "How do you bring yourself to cut off someone's grandfather's head?" Bir replied, "Thankfully, Ruhan does that for us." (The very same Ruhan who preps the cadavers for automotive impacts.) She added that the nonlethal munitions were not shot from guns but fired from air cannons, because doing so is both more precise and less disturbing. "Still," concedes Bir, "I was glad when that one finished up."

Bir copes like most other cadaver researchers do, with a mix of compassion and emotional remove. "You treat them with dignity, and you kind of separate the fact that . . . I don't want to say that they're not a person, but . . . you think of them as a specimen." Bir was trained as a nurse, and in some ways finds the dead easier to work with. "I know they can't feel it, and I know that I'm not going to hurt them." Even the most practiced cadaver researcher has days when the task at hand presents itself as something other than scientific method. For Bir, it had little to do with the fact that she was directing bullets at her subjects. It is the moments when the specimen steps out of his anonymity, his object-hood, and into his past existence as a human being.

"We received a specimen and I went down to help Ruhan, and this gentle-man must have come directly from the nursing home or hospital," she recalls. "He had on a T-shirt and flannel PJ pants. It hit me like . . . this could be my dad. Then there was one that I went to look at—a lot of times you like to take a look at the specimen to make sure it's not too big [to lift]—and this person was wearing a hospital gown from my hometown."

If you really want to stay up late worrying about lawsuits and bad publicity, explode a bomb near the body of someone who has willed his remains to science. This is perhaps the most firmly entrenched taboo of the cadaveric research world. Indeed, live, anes-thetized animals have generally been considered preferable, as targets of explosions, to dead human beings.

> A Central American police department . . . tested their vests by having officers put them on and then shooting at them.

In a 1968 Defense Atomic Support Agency paper entitled *Estimates of Man's Tolerance to the Direct Effects of Air Blast*—i.e., from bombs—researchers discussed the effects of experimental explosions upon mice, hamsters, rats, guinea pigs, rabbits, cats, dogs, goats, sheep, steers, pigs, burros, and stump-tailed macaques, but not upon the actual subject of inquiry. No one had ever strapped a cadaver up against the shock tube to see what might happen.

I called up a man named Aris Makris, who works for a company in Canada called Med-Eng Systems, which engineers protective gear for people who clear land mines. I told him about the DASA paper. Dr. Makris explained that dead people weren't always the best models for gauging living people's tolerance to explosive blasts because of their lungs, which are deflated and not doing the things that lungs normally do. The shock wave from a bomb wreaks the most havoc on the body's most easily compressed tissue, and that is found in the lungs: specifically, the tiny, delicate air sacs where the blood picks up oxygen and drops off carbon dioxide. An explosive shock wave compresses and ruptures these sacs. Blood then seeps into the lungs and drowns their owner, sometimes quickly, in ten or twenty minutes, sometimes over a span of hours.

Makris conceded that, biomedical issues aside, the blast tolerance chaps were probably not highly motivated to work with cadavers. "There are enor-mous ethical or PR challenges with that," he said. "It just hasn't been the habit of blasting cadavers: Please give your body to science so we can blow it up?"

One group recently braved the storm. Lieutenant Colonel Robert Harris and a team of other doctors from the Extremity Trauma Study Branch of the U.S. Army Institute of Surgical Research at Fort Sam Houston, Texas, recruited cadavers to test five types of footwear either commonly used by or being newly marketed for land mine clearance teams. Ever since the Vietnam War, a rumor had persisted that sandals were the safest footwear for land mine clearance, for they minimized injuries caused by fragments of the footwear itself being driven into the foot like shrapnel, compounding the damage and the risk of infection. Yet no one had ever tested the sandal claim on a real foot, nor had anyone done cadaver tests of any of the equipment being touted by manufacturers as offering greater safety than the standard combat boot.

Enter the fearless men of the Lower Extremity Assessment Program. Starting in 1999, twenty cadavers from a Dallas medical school willed body program were strapped, one by one, into a harness hanging from the ceiling of a portable blast shelter. Each cadaver was outfitted with strain gauges and load cells in its heel and ankle, and clad in one of six types of footwear. Some boots claimed to protect by raising the foot up away from the blast, whose forces attenuate quickly; others claimed to protect by absorbing or deflecting the blast's energy. The bodies were posed in standard walking position, heel to the ground, as though striding confidently to their doom. As an added note of verisimilitude, each cadaver was outfitted head to toe in a regulation battle dress uniform. In addition to the added realism, the uniforms conferred a measure of respect, the sort of respect that a powder-blue leotard might not, in the eyes of the U.S. Army anyway, supply.

Harris felt confident that the study's humanitarian benefits outweighed any potential breach of dignity. Nonetheless, he consulted the willed body program administrators about the possibility of informing family members about the specifics of the test. They advised against it, both because of what they called the "revisiting of grief" among families who had made peace with the decision to donate and because, when you get down to the nitty-gritty details of an experiment, virtually any use of a cadaver is potentially upsetting. If willed body program coordinators contacted the families of LEAP cadavers, would they then have to contact the families of the leg-drop-test cadavers down the hall, or, for that matter, the anatomy lab cadavers across campus? As Harris points out, the difference between a blast test and an anatomy class dissection is essentially the time span. One lasts a fraction of a second; the other lasts a year. "In the end," he says, "they look pretty much the same." I asked Harris if he plans to donate his body to research. He sounded downright keen on the prospect. "I'm always saying, 'After I die, just put me out there and blow me up.'"

If Harris could have done his research using surrogate "dummy" legs instead of cadavers, he would have done so. Today there are a couple good ones in the works, developed by the Australian Defence Science & Technology Organisation. (In Australia, as in other Commonwealth nations, ballistics and blast testing on human cadavers is not allowed. And certain words are spelled funny.) The Frangible Surrogate Leg (FSL) is made of materials that react to blast similarly to the way human leg materials do; it has mineralized plastic for bones, for example, and ballistic gelatin for muscle. In March of 2001, Harris exposed the Australian leg to the same land mine blasts that his cadavers had weathered, to see if the results correlated. Disappointingly, the bone fracture patterns were somewhat off. The main problem, at the moment, is cost. Each FSL—they aren't reusable—costs around $5,000; the cost of a cadaver (to cover shipping, HIV and hepatitis C testing, cremation, etc.) is typically under $500.

Harris imagines it's only a matter of time before the kinks are worked out and the price comes down. He looks forward to that time. Surrogates are preferable not only because tests involving land mines and cadavers are ethically (and probably literally) sticky, but because cadavers aren't uniform. The older they are, the thinner their bones and the less elastic their tissue. In the case of land mine work, the ages are an especially poor match, with the average land mine clearer in his twenties and the average donated cadaver in its sixties. It's like market-testing Kid Rock singles on a roomful of Perry Como fans.

Until that time, it'll be rough going for Commonwealth land mine types, who cannot use whole cadavers. Researchers in the UK have resorted to testing boots on amputated legs, a much-criticized practice, owing to the fact that these limbs have typically had gangrene or diabetic complications that render them poor mimics of healthy limbs. Another group tried putting a new type of protective boot onto the hind leg of a mule deer for testing. Given that deer lack toes and heels and people lack hooves, and that no country I know of employs mule deer in land mine clearance, it is hard—though mildly entertaining—to try to imagine what the value of such a study could have been.

LEAP, for its part, turned out to be a valuable study. The sandal myth was mildly vindicated (the injuries were about as severe as they were with a combat boot), and one boot—Med-Eng's Spider Boot—showed itself to be a solid improvement over standard-issue footwear (though a larger sample is needed to be sure). Harris considers the project a success, because with land mines, even a small gain in protection can mean a huge difference in a victim's medical outcome. "If I can save a foot or keep an amputation below the knee," he says, "that's a win."

It is an unfortunate given of human trauma research that the things most likely to accidentally maim or kill people—things we most need to study and understand—are also the things most likely to mutilate research cadavers: car crashes, gunshots, explosions, sporting accidents. There is no need to use cadavers to study stapler injuries or human tolerance to ill-fitting footwear. "In order to be able to protect against a threat, whether it is automotive or a bomb," observes Makris, "you have to put the human to its limits. You've got to get destructive."

I agree with Dr. Makris. Does that mean I would let someone blow up my dead foot to help save the feet of NATO land mine clearers? It does. And would I let someone shoot my dead face with a nonlethal projectile to help prevent accidental fatalities? I suppose I would. . . .

Questions for Critical Reading

1. Should there be publicly funded ballistics research using cadavers? Support your answer using quotations from Roach's text, reading it critically to synthesize her position with your own.

2. What is "informed consent"? Define the term using Roach's text. What are the necessary conditions for it?

3. What are the proper limits for scientific research? Develop an answer through Roach's text. You will need to read her text critically in order to develop an analysis, since she never explicitly states what limits there should be.

Exploring Context

1. Visit the Web site for Bodies . . . The Exhibition (bodiestheexhibition.com), a traveling show of anatomy that uses actual human bodies. You might also use the Web to research the controversy over the cadavers used in this exhibit. How does Bodies . . . The Exhibition complicate Roach's exploration of ethics? What role does ethics—or bodies—have to play in art?

2. Roach discusses work done at the Armed Forces Institute of Pathology (AFIP). Visit the AFIP's Web site at afip.org. Does it convey the kind of work they do? What information can you find about ballistics trauma research? Connect your response to your answers about such research from Questions 1 and 3 of Questions for Critical Reading.

3. According to Roach, the Web site for Kind & Knox minimizes the company's role in the production of ballistics gel. Use the Web to research ballistics gel and gelatin. What information can you find? Is the use of gelatin in ballistics research generally minimized? Why?

Questions for Connecting

1. Is the use of human cadavers in ballistics research consistent with the notion of human dignity as it is explained by Francis Fukuyama (p. 142)? Draw from your work in Questions for Critical Reading in making your argument.

2. What roles can the body play in culture after death? Compare Roach's analysis with Diana Taylor's exploration of death and mourning in "False Identifications: Minority Populations Mourn Diana" (p. 454). How can you synthesize their positions?

3. Daniel Gilbert, in "Reporting Live from Tomorrow" (p. 169), suggests that the best way to determine our future happiness is to ask someone now living our possible future. How can Gilbert's ideas be applied to decisions about donating your body to science? Relate your response to informed consent, as you defined it in Question 2 of Questions for Critical Reading.

Language Matters

1. Imagine you could invite Roach into the discussion in your classroom. What questions would you want to ask her about this essay? What are the limits of written discourse? How might you anticipate your audience's questions when you write?

2. Listen to the latest podcast from Grammar Girl at grammar.quickanddirtytips
.com. How might you apply what she's talking about in the podcast to this essay?

3. Sometimes you can get the best feedback from peers by asking them to review
a key section of your writing—something you know isn't quite there yet. If you
were going to do a target peer revision session for Roach, which section of her
essay would you choose, and what feedback would you give?

Assignments for Writing

1. Roach discusses the use of human cadavers for military testing, suggesting
that the researchers who conduct these tests must approach the cadaver as an
object rather than a human. Find an example in which the body is objectified
and then write a paper using your example as a tool to extend or complicate
Roach's argument about the human body as object. Your work on Bodies . . .
The Exhibition from Question 1 of Exploring Context might serve as a good
starting point in making your argument. Consider: Why does Roach suggest
that body objectification is a necessary step in the experiments she discusses?
Is it possible to conduct scientific experiments on bodies without viewing them
as objects? Is body objectification limited to scientific experimentation? Is
body objectification limited to the dead? What are some of the possible steps
required in order to view a body as an object?

2. Roach explores the complicated ethical, moral, and societal issues that accompany the use of human bodies for research. Using Roach's essay as a framework
for your own, write a paper in which you evaluate the relationship between
scientific experiments and our ethical beliefs. You may want to use your work
on the limits of research from Question 3 of Questions for Critical Reading
in making your argument. Also consider: Must scientific experimentation be
conducted within a system of ethics? What happens when science and ethics
conflict? What are our ethical responsibilities with regard to scientific experimentation? What happens when our personal system of ethics contradicts the
perceived "greater good"?

3. While discussing the ethical questions involved with using human bodies for
research, Roach seems to suggest that the "greater good" of such experiments
should take precedence over ethical concerns. Write a paper in which you extend or complicate Roach's argument in the context of a current conflict or war.
Does such a conflict amplify the ethical issues associated with the use of human
bodies in military testing? What are the needs of a society that is at war? What
happens when the needs or rights of an individual conflict with the needs of
society? How much should we sacrifice in the name of war?

LESLIE SAVAN

Leslie Savan is a former columnist for the *Village Voice* and a three-time Pulitzer Prize finalist. She has written for *Time,* the *New Yorker,* the *New York Times,* the *Los Angeles Times,* and Salon.com. In 1994, she published *The Sponsored Life: Ads, TV, and American Culture.* The following selection, "What's Black, Then White, and Said All Over?" appeared in her book *Slam Dunks and No-Brainers: Language in Your Life, the Media, Business, Politics, and, Like, Whatever* (2005).

In *Slam Dunks and No-Brainers* Savan examines our everyday language to find out how it originated, what it means, and what it says about our culture. The book explores how a hot new phrase is created and spreads, how media takes advantage of trends in speech, and why we're not sure what pop catchphrases were popular in ancient Rome.

In "What's Black, Then White, and Said All Over?" Savan traces common "pop talk" that has its origins in African American vernacular. "White people," Savan writes, "draw from a black lexicon every day," and in this essay she examines the reasons for and the results of this kind of borrowing. Savan is interested in issues of media appropriation, the "wannabe" phenomenon, the impact of "black talk" on written language, and the idea of "covert prestige" being gained in the process of crossover talk. Ultimately, Savan presents a society that has accepted black vernacular as cool and worthy of imitation yet finds it unacceptable when black students speak it in the classroom.

Language has always been coupled with power. In this piece, Savan helps us to see how language circulates in culture and how its power is used by the media and in advertising.

▶ TAGS: *conversation, diversity, race, media, culture, language, collaboration, creativity*

What's Black, Then White, and Said All Over?

African American vernacular, black English, black talk, Ebonics, hip-hop slang — whatever you want to call it, black-inspired language is all over mainstream pop talk like white on rice.

The talk may be everywhere, but, oddly enough, even during the rabid debate over Ebonics in the late 1990s rarely was there any mention of black English's deep imprint on American English. Yet linguists and other language experts know that America's language wouldn't be what it is—and certainly wouldn't pop as much—without black English.

"In the past, White society has resisted the idea," wrote Robert McCrum, William Cran, and Robert MacNeil in *The Story of English*, "but there is now no escaping the fact that [Blacks' influence] has been one of the most profound contributions to the English language."

"First, one cannot help but be struck by the powerful influence of African American vernacular on the slang of all 20th-century American youth," Tom Dalzell wrote in *Flappers 2 Rappers*. "There were other influences, to be sure, on the slang of America's young, but none as powerful as that of the streets of Harlem and Chicago."

The linguist Connie Eble, author of *Slang and Sociability* and a college and youth slang expert at the University of North Carolina, Chapel Hill, calls the black influence on the American language "overwhelming."

White people (and not just the young) draw from a black lexicon every day, sometimes unaware of the words' origins, sometimes using them because of their origins. Here are just some of the words and phrases—born in different decades and now residing at various levels of popdom—that African Americans either coined or popularized, and, in either case, that they created the catchiest meaning of: *all that, back in the day, bling bling, blues, bogus, boogie, bootie, bro, chick, chill, come again, cook, cool, dawg, dig, dis, do your own thing, don't go there, freak, funky, get-go, get it on, get over, gig, give it up, groovy, heavy, hip, homeboy, hot, in your face, kick back, lame, living large, man, my bad, Micky D's, old school, nitty gritty, player, riff, righteous, rip off, rock 'n' roll, soul, tell it like it is, 24/7, up-tight, wannabe, whack, Whassup?/sup?, Whassup with that?, when the shit hits the fan, you know what I'm saying?*

You know what I'm saying. Most of us talk, and all of us hear in the media some of that talk every day. Some phrases are said with an implicit nod to their source (*street cred, chill, You the man*, as well as a fist pound or high five), while others have been so widely adopted that they're beginning to feel sourceless (*24/7, lame, in your face*). *It's a black thang* has become everybody's thing, from *It's a dick thing* to (most offensively, considering who pushed it) "Virginia Slims: It's a Woman Thing."

But black vernacular didn't just add more lively, "colorful" words to the pop vocabulary. Much as marketing has influenced pop language, so black English has changed the American language in more fundamental ways. And that's what we're talking here—not about black talk per se, but about what happens when black talk meets, and transforms, the wider, whiter pop.

First and foremost, this language of outsiders has given us *cool*: the word itself—the preeminent pop word of all time—and quite a sizable chunk of the cool stance that underlies pop culture itself. Pop culture's desire for cool is second only to its desire for money—the two, in fact, are inextricably linked. (Cool may be first and foremost, but more on why it rules later.)

A second way African American vernacular has affected the broader pop is that black talk has operated as a template for what it means to talk pop in the first place. As an often playful, ironic alternative to the official tongue, black slang has prefigured pop language in much the same way that black music has prefigured, and has often become, pop music. While there are important differences, some of the dynamics underlying black talk and pop talk are similar: Like black English, pop language sparks with wordplays and code games; it assumes that certain, often previously unacknowledged experiences deserve their own verbal expression; and it broadcasts the sense that only those who share the experiences can really get the words. For instance, black talk's running commentary on social exclusion is a model for pop talk's running commentary on media experiences.

Why do I say that pop is modeled on black and not the other way around? It's not just because black talk did these things earlier and still does them more intensely than pop, but as the original flipside to the voice of the Man, as the official unofficial speech of America, black talk is the object of pop talk's crush on everything "alternative" and "outsider."

There's an attitude in pop language that it is somehow undermining the stale old ways and sending a wake-up call to anyone who just doesn't get it. You can feel the attitude in everything from advertising's furious but phony rebelliousness to the faintly up-yours, tough-talking phrases

> **This language of outsiders has given us *cool*.**

like *Get a life* and *Don't even* think *about it*. It's not that these particular phrases are black or black-inspired, or that white people aren't perfectly capable of rebelliousness, anger at authority, and clever put-downs on their own. But the black experience, publicized more widely than ever now through hip-hop and its celebrities, has encouraged everyone else to more vigorously adopt the style of fighting the power—at least with the occasional catchphrase.

It may seem twisted, given American history, that general pop language draws from the experience of black exclusion at all. But white attempts to *yo* here and *dis* there are an important piece of identity-and-image building for individuals and corporations alike. Today, the language of an excluded people is repeated by the nonexcluded in order to make themselves sound more included. As the mainstream plays the titillating notes of marginalization, we are collectively creating that ideal mass personality mentioned earlier: We can be part black (the part presumed to be cool and soulful, real and down, jazzy or hip-hop, choose your sound) and be part white (the privileged part, the part that has the luxury to easily reference other parts).

Related to all this imitation and referencing is the most noticeable way that pop talk is affected by black talk: Black talk has openly joined the sales force. At white society's major intersection with black language—that is, in entertainment—white society has gone from mocking black talk, as in minstrel shows, to marketing it, as in hip-hop. In the more than a hundred years between these two forms of entertainment, black language has by and large entered white usage as if it were a sourceless slang or perhaps the latest lingo of some particularly hep white cats, like the fast-talking disc jockeys of the 1950s and 1960s who purveyed black jive to white teenagers. Black language may have been the single most important factor in shaping generations of American slang, primarily through blues, jazz, and rock 'n' roll. But only relatively recently has black talk been used openly, knowingly, and not mockingly to sell products.

This would have been unthinkable once. Even fifteen or twenty years ago, car makers were loath to show black people in commercials for fear that their product would be tainted as inferior or, worse, as "a black car." Although many car companies are still skittish, by 2001 Buick was actually ending its commercials with the rap-popularized phrase "It's all good." (And by 2004, a BMW ad was featuring an interracial couple.) The phrase went from M. C. Hammer's 1994 song "It's All Good" to replacing "I love this game" as the official slogan of the National Basketball Association in 2001. Both Buick and the NBA have since dropped *It's all good*, but with their help the phrase massified, at least for a while. "It's huge" among white "sorority sisters and stoners alike," a twenty-seven-year-old white friend in Chicago told me in 2003.

So it's not all bad, this commercialization of black talk, especially if it can get the auto industry to move from shunning to quoting African Americans. But it comes laden with price tags. To read them, look at MTV, which has to be *the* major force in the sea change from whites-only to black's-da-bomb.

It may be difficult to believe now, but for years MTV wouldn't touch black music videos. The channel relented only under pressure, with videos by Prince and Michael Jackson. Black just wouldn't appeal to its white suburban teen audience, MTV explained. In 1989 with the appearance of the successful *Yo! MTV Raps*, that rationale was turned inside out, and—ka-ching!—black videos began to appear regularly. Since so much of MTV is advertising posing as entertainment (the videos are record company promotions, the parties and other bashes that appear are often visibly sponsored events), MTV has contributed significantly to two marketing trends: To the young, advertising has become an acceptable—nay, desirable—part of the cool life they aspire to; and a black, hip-hop-ish vernacular has become a crucial cog in the youth market machinery.

The outsider style is not solely black or hip-hop, but, at least in the marketing mind, a black package can be the most efficient buy to achieve that style. For corporate purposes, hip-hop in particular is a lucrative formula. Not only does the hip-hop black man represent the ultimate outsider who simultaneously stands at the nexus of cool, but much of hip-hop, created by the kind of people gated communities were meant to exclude, sings the praises of acquiring capitalism's toys. These paradoxes of racism are commercial-ready.

As the critic Greg Tate wrote on the thirtieth anniversary of hip-hop, "globally speaking, hip-hop is money at this point, a valued form of currency where brothers are offered stock options in exchange for letting some corporate entity stand next to their fire. . . . Oh, the selling power of the Black vernacular."

When Sprite realized that teenagers no longer believed its TV commercials telling them that "Image Is Nothing" and that they shouldn't trust commercials or celebrity endorsements (said only half tongue-in-cheek by celebrities like NBA star Grant Hill), the soft drink's marketing department decided to up the ante. So, when you need outsider verisimilitude, who ya gonna call? Why, black rappers, of course, preferably on the hardcore side. Get *them* to testify to the soft drink's beyond-the-bounds, can't-be-bought spirit at Sprite.com launch parties (to be run later on MTV). Or get real kids, looking and sounding ghetto, to rap their own lyrics in TV spots about, say, "a situation that is not too sweet, which is an attribute of Sprite," as a Sprite publicist said. How else to get kids, usually white kids, to understand that you understand that they're sick of commercials telling them what's cool?

And so, while Sprite had long used rappers in its overall "Obey Your Thirst" campaign, now it pumped up the volume. Only by obeying the first command-ment that image is everything can you become, as Sprite did by the late nineties, the fastest-growing soft-drink brand in the world. "Sprite has really become an icon," Pina Sciarra, then director of youth brands for Sprite, said on the 2001 PBS documentary *Merchants of Cool*. "It's not just associated with hip-hop, it's really a part of it, as much as baggy jeans and sneakers." Sprite, by the way, is owned by the Coca-Cola Company, the same company that agreed (around the time of the Sprite.com launch in late 2000) to pay $192.5 million to settle a racial discrimination suit by black employees, who accused the company of paying blacks less than whites for the same jobs and of discriminating in pro-motions and evaluations. (The company denied the allegations, but the settle-ment was one of the largest of its kind at the time.)

When whites talk black—or, just as commonly, when major corporations do it for them—it makes you wanna shout, *Whassup with that?!*

Terms and Props

Before I address wannabe black talk and other points where black language crosses over into pop, a few words about what "black language" and "black words" are.

I've been using the terms "black English," "black slang," "black talk," and "African American vernacular" rather interchangeably, which, in plain Eng-lish, seems OK. Yet, at the same time, each term is a bit off the mark.

No one phrase is the perfect vehicle to explain how a people speak, because   25 "a people" don't all speak (or do anything) one way. That's one of the problems with the terms "black English" and "black dialect." "Black English" was more or less booted out of formal linguistic circles, because, as linguist Peter Trudgill wrote in the 1995 revised edition of his book *Sociolinguistics*, "it suggested that all Blacks speak this one variety of English—which is not the case." The newer scholarly term, African American Vernacular English (AAVE), has pros and cons: It "distinguishes those Blacks who do not speak standard American Eng-lish from those who do," wrote Trudgill, "although it still suggests that only one nonstandard variety, homogeneous through the whole of the USA, is in-volved, which is hardly likely." The word *Ebonics* was created in 1973 by African American scholars to "define black language from a black perspective," writes Geneva Smitherman, director of the African American Language and Literacy Program at Michigan State University. But the 1997 Ebonics controversy loaded the word with so much baggage (which we'll rummage through later) that, out-side of some hip-hop use, it has become nearly immobile.

"Black slang" can't describe black language, because clearly most black language is composed of standard English. However, when referring to actual slang that blacks created (*my bad, dis*), "black slang" is the right term. Personally, I like "black talk" (which is also the title of one of Smitherman's books). Although, like any phrase starting with the adjective "black," it might suggest that all black people talk this way all the time, "black talk" (like "pop talk") is colloquial and flexible, encompassing vocabulary and then some.

In mixing up these terms, I take my cue in part from the Stanford University linguistics professor John Russell Rickford. Rickford's not hung up over what black language is called, though he favors "spoken soul," the title of his book (subtitled *The Story of Black English* and written with his son, Russell John Rickford) and a term coined by Claude Brown, the author of *Manchild in the Promised Land.*

In *Spoken Soul*, the Rickfords spell out the dimensions of the language:

> In homes, schools, and churches, on streets, stages, and the airwaves, you can hear soul spoken every day. Most African Americans— including millions who . . . are fluent speakers of Standard English—still invoke Spoken Soul as we have for hundreds of years, to laugh or cry, to preach and praise, to shuck and jive, to sing, to rap, to shout, to style, to express our individual personas and our ethnic identities . . . to create authentic characters and voices in novels, poems, and plays. . . . The fact is that most African Americans *do* talk differently from whites and Americans of other ethnic groups, or at least most of us can when we want to.

If that approximates a definition of black language, what are "black words"? Word origins in general are difficult to trace, but the origins of black words are particularly so. In the dictionary-style *Black Talk: Words and Phrases from the Hood to the Amen Corner*, Smitherman writes that she did not include etymologies because "these are risky propositions at best when dealing with an oral language such as African American Language." Hampton University professor Margaret Lee, who published "Out of the Hood and into the News: Borrowed Black Verbal Expressions in a Mainstream Newspaper" in the linguistic journal *American Speech* and verified the black origins of each phrase with at least two sources, adds, "The approach Smitherman takes and I take is that these expressions and words were created by African Americans or were circulated in the black community before they went mainstream." In order to define black words that have gone pop, I would only add that a pop word is "black" simply if its most popular meaning or nuance was created by black people—for example, *bad* and *girlfriend* are pop when used with black nuance, but not pop when used conventionally.

Origins tend to get lost in the roaring mainstream. Some words that seem white are black, and vice versa. For instance, until I looked into *24/7*, I would have guessed its roots were cyber or maybe something out of the convenience-store industry. But *24/7* arose from a hip-hop fondness for number phrases. Rapdict.org lists some sixty number phrases, many of which are too obscure or 30 gangsta to cross over; *411* is one of the few others that has gone pop. (A recent Mercedes-Benz magazine ad advised, "Get the 411.")

Bogus, which sounds so surfer, dude, dates back at least as far as 1798, when a glossary defined it as a "spurious coin," write David Barnhart and Allan Metcalf in *America in So Many Words*. "Its origins are obscure, but one guess that is as good as any is that it is from *boko*, meaning 'deceit' or 'fake' in the Hausa language of west central Africa. The word then would have been brought over by Africans sold into slavery here." In addition, some nuances that no one doubts are African American may run deeper in black history than most people, black or white, imagine. When *bad* is used to mean good, the meaning (though obviously not the word itself) is derived, Smitherman writes, from a phrase in the Mandinka language in West Africa, "*a ka nyi ko-jugu*, which means, literally, 'it is good badly,' that is, it is very good, or it is so good that it's bad!"

Meanwhile, some words that most people would identify as black, and that black people did indeed popularize, originated among others. Southern phrases in particular jumped races, "from black to white in the case of *bubba* and *big daddy*, from white to black in the case of *grits* and *chitlins*," write the Rickfords. *Cat*, meaning a hip guy, is a dated piece of slang (though often on the verge of a comeback) that most people attribute to black jazz musicians; Ken Burns's television series *Jazz* states that Louis Armstrong was the first person to have said it. But, as Tom Dalzell writes, in "the late 19th century and early 20th century, *cat* in the slang and jargon of hobos meant an itinerant worker . . . possibly because the migratory worker slunk about like a 'homeless cat.'" However, it did take Armstrong, and then other jazz musicians in the 1920s, to introduce the word into broader usage. That old rap word *fly* (stylish, good-looking, smooth) was flying long before rap. "The most well-established slang meaning of *fly* was in the argot of thieves, where *fly* meant sly, cunning, wide-awake, knowing, or smart," writes Dalzell, who notes those uses of *fly* as early as 1724 and in *Bleak House* by Dickens in 1853. But again, *fly* didn't really buzz until black musicians picked up on it, beginning around 1900, well before *Superfly* in the 1970s and rap in the 1980s.

Wannabe Nation

Whether black-born or black-raised, black words are the ones that many white people are wearing like backwards baseball caps. That brings us to a particularly telling term that went from black to pop. *Wannabe* originally referred to people who wanted to be something they weren't; it was often said of a black person who wanted to be white. In Spike Lee's 1988 film *School Daze*, the conflict was between the dark-skinned, activist "Jigaboos" and the light-skinned sorority sister "Wannabes." Beginning around the time of that movie, *wannabe* was used by just about everybody to mean anybody who wanted to be somebody he or she wasn't—there have been surfer wannabes, Madonna wannabes, and dot.com start-up wannabes. But *wannabe* is not just a blast from decades past. More recently, "podcaster wannabes" have developed, and in just one week on

TV and radio in late 2004, I heard of "artist wannabes," "geek wannabes," and "wannabe homeland security chief" Bernard Kerik.

Racially speaking, *wannabe* has reversed field. Since at least the early nineties, with hip-hop an entrenched, virtually mainstream hit, *wannabe* has been far more likely to refer to whites, especially teenagers, who want to be black or do the style. Sometimes called *wiggers* or *wiggas* (*white* plus *nigger/nigga*), black wannabes try to dance the dance and talk the talk. Even whites who would hate to be black will maintain the right to add the occasional black flourish. Some whites flash a black word or gesture like an honorary badge of cool, to show they're down with black people on certain occasions, usually involving sports or entertainment. Or maybe they do it because some of their best friends and some of the best commercials are flashing it, too. Or maybe they just need to know that black people like them. Take "Johnny and Sally," the fictitious white couple on the very funny Web site BlackPeopleLoveUs.com, which is full of "testimonials" to their racial bigheartedness. As one unnamed black man attested, "Johnny always alters his given name and refers to himself in the third person—for example, 'J-Dog don't play that' or 'J-Dog wants to know wusssaappp.' It comforts me to know that my parlance has such broad appeal."

African Americans aren't the only people whose parlance has broad appeal. Non-Latino blacks dabble in Spanish, Catholics in Yiddish, adults in teenage talk. Cultural skin is always permeable, absorbing any word that has reached a critical mass of usefulness or fun. The human species can't help but borrow—after all, that's how languages develop.

But whether we call it wannabe talk or the less derogatory crossover talk, something about white society's sampling of black speech is more loaded than the usual borrowing. Black vernacular's contributions to English are larger in number and run deeper linguistically and psychologically than do any other ethnic group's. And black English, born in slavery, resounds with our society's senses of guilt, fear, identity, and style.

Black-to-white crossover talk, which also began during slavery, is hardly new. But, like most pop talk today, it radiates a new gloss, a veneer in which you can catch the reflection of its increased market value. Black talk comes from something real—"serious as a heart attack," Smitherman says—but, whoop, there it is, sparking out of TV commercials, out of white politicians, out of anyone who has something to promote, spin, or get over.

"Chill, Orrin," the Democratic senator Patrick Leahy told the Republican senator Orrin Hatch when things got a little testy during a Judiciary Committee hearing in 1998. Behind the *chill* was something more than "relax." One white guy was momentarily able to harness and aim some soulful black power at the other white guy. Saying the black word says, I stake myself closer to black people and their righteous anger than you do. You're more afraid of them and their language than I am—so I win this moment.

"Go on, give it up!" the signs throughout Virgin Records implored. *Give it up*'s "it" referred only obliquely to applause. (Used to introduce about every other musical act these days, the black phrase has long been a verbal welcome mat. "Everybody give it up for my very good friend Marion Barry," someone said on the old comedy series *In Living Color* in 1990.) "It" referred even more obliquely to sex. (*Give it up* originally meant "to agree to engage in copulation," according to the *Random House Historical Dictionary of American Slang* [*RHHDAS*].) No, this "it" meant your money—for "The Sacrifice Sale. Hundreds of titles: 3 for $26."

As recently as 2005, McDonald's, like many a corporation trying to sound more "urban," was getting it all wrong. "DOUBLE CHEESEBURGER? I'D HIT IT," read a McDonald's banner ad on ESPN.com. As mocking bloggers pointed out, the hip-hop slang actually meant, "I'd have sex with that cheeseburger." 40

It's not as if there hasn't been enough time to hit it right. Again, black style's market value jumped around the time *Yo! MTV Raps* debuted in 1989. In a TV spot that same year, the pasty white Pillsbury Doughboy performed a mean rap number. By 1994, Dan Rather (a magnet for every catchy, and uncatchy, turn of phrase that comes along) reported that political candidates were "dissing" each other. In 1999, a hip black guy insisted, for Wendy's, "This sandwich is da bomb."

Three years later, *CNN Headline News* asked the writers responsible for the crawl and other graphics that crowd its screen to inject some hip-hop. "In an effort to be sure we are as cutting-edge as possible with our on-screen persona, please refer to this slang dictionary when looking for just the right phrase," read a *Headline News* memo, according to the New York *Daily News.* "Please use this guide to help all you homeys and honeys add a new flava to your tickers and dekos." Among the phrases mentioned were *fly, ill,* and *jimmy hat,* for a condom. (A *Headline News* spokeswoman at the time said a mid-level producer sent the memo without top executives knowing about it.)

"You Go, Girl!" ran a 2004 headline in *Today's Christian Woman* for a story about finding supportive friends.

"She said she'd have more gay people in the White House. I'm like, 'You go, Teresa,'" a gay doctor said of Teresa Heinz Kerry at an Ohio campaign rally. "Women to Heinz Kerry: You Go, Girl," an Associated Press headline read. For a brief moment there, Teresa was the nation's "You go, girl" girl.

You go, girl! is democratic and process-oriented—every girl is presumed to have the strength that can propel her forward. But what's a guy to do? When a man needs an equally exciting, gender-saluting pop phrase that expresses personal recognition, he's almost sure to receive the hierarchical, goal-oriented *You da* (or *the*) *man!* Both black and white men scramble to the top of the heap with this winner-take-all phrase. But in the media and off, it's increasingly white men who adorn one another with this verbal king's crown. 45

In the 1998 animated movie *Antz,* the ant voiced-over by Sylvester Stallone says to the Woody Allen ant, who has just saved his species' civilization, "You da ant!" And they exchange high-fives.

"You're the man!" Karl ("Bush's Brain") Rove "bellowed back into his cell phone" to Lloyd Smith, who managed Jim Talent's Missouri Senate campaign in the 2002 midterm elections, *Time* magazine reported. Smith had just told Rove that it looked as if Talent was going to beat Democratic senator Jean Carnahan, thereby guaranteeing the Senate to Republicans.

You da man! is now so common that when the sports columnist Frank Deford compiled his 2004 Thanksgiving Day list of things "I wish we still had," he included "golf tournaments that were played without idiots screaming 'you da man.'"

But white men still scream *You da man!* because the words (especially *da*, though it's not required) still suggest a wistful tableau of black folks testifying for white folks. Beyond giving a white man props for smiting a foe, *You da man* gives him authenticity clearance, momentary proof that, at the least, he's not the Man, an oppressive white authority figure.

It's better yet if a white guy can get a real black guy to testify for him (just like in all the movies that star a somehow emotionally stunted white hero who's made to see one light or another by a more soulful black sidekick). An ad campaign a while back made this embarrassingly evident. "The Colonel?" asked what intentionally sounded like a black male voice. "He da man!" The man, of course, was Colonel Sanders of KFC. He's dead, but in the late nineties the Colonel was not only revived as a cartoon character for TV spots, but he also became black (minus a pigment change). "Go, Colonel! Go, Colonel!" the voiceover jived. "The Colonel still has a pink face and white suit," Mark Schone noted on the radio show *This American Life*, "but these days the erstwhile Southern gentleman twirls his cane to . . . old school seventies funk. . . . In an ad campaign that began on his 108th birthday, the Colonel has cabbage patched, tap danced, rapped, and played basketball. . . . What's it mean when a redneck who dressed like a slaveowner comes back from the dead and gets funky?" 50

And what's it mean when right-wingers take a catchy phrase that points out racism to express their own sense of victimization? "But to you," "Aaron" wrote to "fazz" on rightwingnews.com in 2003, "facts don't matter because Abrams committed the greatest crime of all, he was guilty of BWC (Breathing While Conservative)." (That's Elliott Abrams, who was indicted for giving false testimony to Congress during the Iran-Contra affair, pardoned by Bush I, and recently made Bush II's top White House adviser on global democracy.) "Liberals and their Libertine fellow-travelers accuse Callahan of the one inexcusable crime in America: BWR ('Breathing While Republican')," "Illbay" posted on Freerepublic.com in 2002 about a pork barrel project involving Congressman Sonny Callahan of Alabama.

Breathing while Republican (or *conservative*) is based on the phrase *breathing while black*, the more prominent *voting while black* (which resurfaced during the 2000 and 2004 elections regarding attempts to suppress black votes), and the original *X while black* pop construction, *driving while black* (police using racial profiling to pull black people over on the road or to arrest them chiefly because of their race).

Spelling B

Driving while black, itself twisted from *driving while intoxicated*, is simple, classic wordplay. And DWI to DWB to BWR is classic letterplay and codeplay. Coiled in most pop phrases—and especially in anything compressed further into initials (or numbers, like *24/7* and *411*)—is a Jack-in-the-box meaning that's just waiting to spring out. That is, the energy putting the pop in pop language comes from the power of codes. All language is codes, codes 'R' us and all that, but coded language is an African American art form. The often double meaning of black phrases, the way some words may mean their opposite (*bad, dope, stoopid/ stupid*) developed among slaves who needed to talk to each other in front of the massa without him knowing Jack.

To carry the weight of a twisted meaning not on a word but on a single letter is to pack the code tighter. Altering a letter in an otherwise ordinary word can alter the world outlook. When *boys* went to *boyz*, so went Boyz II Men. The title of the 1991 movie *Boyz N the Hood* declared it was no suburban frolic. Young black musicians and hip-hop-influenced culture in general wear wayward words like visual rap. Hip-hop and R&B singers and groups have long been seizing the Z (Jay-Z, Outlawz, Limp Bizkit), crossing an X (Xscape, Xzibit), or otherwise kurupting the language (Kurupt, OutKast, Fabolous, Ludacris, Shyne, Mystikal).

Hip-hop didn't invent deliberate misspellings as a mild social subversion [55] (remember the left's *Amerika*, the hippies' *freek?*) or as an attention-getting device (way before hip-hop, marketers were messing with the ABCs, from *Beanz Meanz Heinz* and Kool cigarettes to Kwik Save Foodstores and EZLern driving school). Wacky spelling may in fact serve the status quo quite well. In the late 1800s, a loose group of humorists called the Phunny Phellows "fed their Victorian audiences a bland diet of simple gags, sprinkled liberally with malapropisms, terrible puns, comic misspellings, blatant racism, stock characters, and shopworn topical jokes," wrote Kevin MacDonnell in *Firsts* magazine.

But deliberate misspellings have long been used to declare some form of independence, however deep or shallow it might run. In the 1920s, young people "spelled 'rats' as 'rhatz!' and shortened 'that's too bad' to 'stoo bad,'" Dalzell writes, adding that even the famous *phat*, which seems the epitome of hip-hop spelling, has a surprisingly long history. *Fat* meant "rich" back in the seventeenth century, and examples of *fat* meaning "good," "cool," or "living well" have occurred ever since. As for the "ph," in a list of "Negro argot," *Time* magazine listed *phat* "as one of several 'adjectives of approval'" in 1963. But *phat* predated that. Dalzell found that around the turn of the last century "typesetters referred to type that was easily set as being *phat*. . . . Indeed, in 1885, the Post Express Printing Company in Rochester, New York, published the 'Phat Boy's Birds-Eye Map of the Saint Lawrence River' with a drawing of a corpulent boy."

Despite their varied history, creative misspellings today are mostly associated with hip-hop culture. So much so that in his 2000 movie *Bamboozled*, Spike Lee hilariously spoofed the trend. "I respectfully submit," one rapper tells his gangsta crew, "that we from now on, henceforth and whatnot spell black B-L-A-K, not B-L-A-C-K."

Hip-hop misspellings don't just reject select bits of standard white written style; they also reflect a history, beginning in the 1800s, in which standard writers ridiculed Negro speech with exaggerated misspelling. I'm not referring to the sympathetic, if imperfect, attempts at dialect writing in literature, as in *Uncle Tom's Cabin* and *Huckleberry Finn*, but rather to another, contemporary "trend in comic writing where southern speakers, especially blacks, were portrayed as uneducated or as figures of fun," as David Crystal writes in *The Cambridge Encyclopedia of the English Language.* "Dialect vocabulary and grammar (*hain't, saw* for *seen,* etc.) were used as well as misspelling, though it was the spelling which created the impact." Some of the impact of hip-hop's mangled orthography reflects that dis: Do the disapproved thing first; do it aggressively and obviously intentionally, b4 itz dunn 2 U.

And it's that unorthodox, defiant style that larger, nonblack marketing forces are now sucking image off of. If a company abuses the alphabet today, it's usually doing so to look hip-hop fresh, sometimes to look, dare we say . . . outlaw. Customized spellings that developed in part to subvert the Man's words

: **Coded language is an African**
: **American art form.**

are now copied by the Man's corporations almost as fast as they'll funnel benjamins to Congress to make them mo' money. (Hey, just like real gangstas!)

In 1999, when Rupert Murdoch's Fox Family Channel launched two new cable channels, it fought the power by naming them the Boyz Channel and the Girlz Channel. (Both were soon zapped.) When it was still running, *Lizzie McGuire* was the most successful show on the Disney Channel lineup called "Zoog Weekendz." The STARZ!, BLACK STARZ!, STARZ! Kids, STARZ! Family digital movie channels add all caps and exclamation marks to convey their over-the-top Zness. Z bumped the old-skool S in DreamWorks' *Antz* (the name of Woody's "You da man!" ant, by the way, was "Z"). One of my favorite stupid attempts of someone to get down is the name of a spammer (apparently now deceased), "BestLoanz.com."

A quick trick to convince children that they're cool and that you, if you're a seller of stuff, are rad, is to call them "kidz" and otherwise buzz their brains with Zs; hence, the glitzoid Trollz dolls and cartoons (based on the 1960s cute-ugly Trolls); Bratz dolls (a massive seller); Nitro Battlerz (cars racing in battle domes and such); Kellogg's Gripz crackers and cookies; Hershey's Koolerz chewing gum, SnackBarz, and Twizzlers Sourz. On the health food side of the aisle, Hain's line of children's products is called Kidz, while EnviroKidz says it makes "The World's First 100% Certified Organic Cereals for Kidz."

Z—the purple of the alphabet, the last in line shall be first, the snap at the tip of the whip (Zorro's?)—is the letter that marketing relies on most to represent childlike fun, diversity, and all things hip-hop.

Z is unconventional, jazzy, but not really dangerous. Like Snoop Dogg's izzle, fo'shizzle ("for sure") pig-Latin-like lingo, Zs can be damn cuddly. (Snoop Dogg has dropped his "shizzolating." "I overdosed on it," he told *MTV News* in 2004. "I'm seeing it everywhere, you know what I'm saying?") For danger, citizens, you gotta get X.

X is pornography, the drug ecstasy, a former spouse, the signature of illiteracy, X out, cross out, the cross, an equation's unknown solution, off the charts, extra, extreme, and (in the exception exposing the rule) kisses. Generation X is the somehow canceled-out generation. *The X-Files* were stories of the paranormal too threatening for normals. *X Creatures* was a Discovery Channel show about Loch Ness monsters, giant squids, and other excessive animals. The *X-Men*—whether the original sixties comic book or its later incarnations as animated TV shows and live-action movies—is a parable about "the Other," ethnic hatred, and race relations. (The X-Men have a mutant gene that gives them great powers, but human society reviles them because they're different.)

But now outsiders are in (Outsider Art, by non-art-world, non-art-schooled, often black, and occasionally psychotic artists, draws big bucks). Exy is sexy—it's hardcore, outlaw, a black man, Malcolm X, Brand X. And today brands, rather than running from Xness, practically cut it into their foreheads with razors, probably Schick Xtreme III blades. X is death, like the Slug-X Trap for gardening. In a world of *Survivor, The Sopranos,* and Swift Boat Veterans for Truth, X or be Xed. When NBC and the World Wrestling Federation (now World Wrestling Entertainment) needed a name for their newborn, self-designated "outlaw" (and quickly Xed-out) football league, the choice was obvious: the XFL (and X marked the spot for its teams the Maniax and Xtremes). When Right Guard decided it needed another market for another deodorant, it created Right Guard Xtreme Sport. When Kraft's Jell-O sales declined, the company put the gelatin in push-up packages, named it X-TREME Jell-O Sticks, and took aim at kids: "They're extreme—yeah!" exclaimed the commercial. And when that foxy Fox needed a name for another cable channel, it chose FX. Yes, the name plays nicely on Fox, and if you happen to know that FX is Hollywood for special effects, you might get a goose bump. But more important, *F* looks cooler slapped up against a bad-ass X, the naive, open-mouthed *O* squeezed out all together. "Perpleed?" an ad for FX on a commuter train read. "What would life be like without the X?"

Well, it might not be quite so easy to sell in. In video games, X marks the spot for Microsoft's Xbox. On TV, the letter has done duty for *The X Show* (about relationships, guy talk, and big breasts), *Maximum EXposure* (about extreme activities—man eats live snakes, ex-wife attacks new wife), and, on the relatively staid History Channel, *Extreme History with Roger Daltrey.* "Beyond AM. Beyond FM. XM" went a slogan for XM Satellite Radio. *XXL* is the name of the hip-hop magazine as well as the extra extra large size. X is a ride on the wild side that yet another XXL SUV swears it will deliver: A huge sign over Times Square read, "AS NOT SEEN IN THE HAMPTONS—NISSAN XTERRA."

For pure purchased *X*, look at the Jaguar X-Type, Infiniti's QX or FX45, or any vehicular X. X crosses the chrome on cars, says the automotive writer Phil Patton, because of "its connotations of 'experimental' and 'luxury.'" Or, in the case of XTerra, "Gen X and cross-country," he says. "The S in SE or SX is supposed to suggest 'sport,' but the SX also suggests sex."

OK, so *X* brands products. Earth to me: That's what popular symbols *do.* I guess I shouldn't be surprised to see *X* infiltrate newslike missives from media conglomerates, but when I saw the following, I almost had to slip on some Nike Shox to absorb the blow: A CNBC headline for a segment about international reaction to the U.S. invasion of Iraq was succinct, if not right out of the funnies: "World Reax."

So common is *X*, especially when referring to anything "extreme," that *X* has gone from out there to dead center—or, to restate that in pop, *X* is the new *edge.* Back in 2001, when ESPN's X Games (*X* stands for "extreme sports") were beginning to go global, even ESPN execs paid to propagate X were dissing the full *extreme*. "'Extreme' is the old term," Ron Semiao, then in charge of ESPN's Global X division, told *Advertising Age* at the time. "These types of action sports have gone from being an activity of fringe groups to an ingrained part of a generation that influences its fashion, music, entertainment." He helped push for the rather uncatchy term "action sports." (Are there any other kind?) When Heinz's Bagel Bites, which was originally marketed to mothers, revamped to target X-attracted "tweens" (kids between childhood and teenhood), a Heinz executive said, "Action sports is a sport that embodies the lifestyle and personality of the Bagel Bites consumer." If true, this proves, finally: Edge is dead, long live the hole in the center.

Obviously, not everything X or Z is black or black-influenced. Extreme sports, in fact, are pretty darn white. Pornography appears in all colors. Z and X are mysterious and primal human qualities. But black, according to still-thriving stereotypes, is so often mysterious and primal, so often Z and X, that the corporate addition of those letters is black pepper for the white sauce. 70

Encouraged by the hip X and Z hopping around, other letter replacements have gained favor among wannabe companies—that is, they wanna B. I'm convinced the whole *B to B* nomenclature (meaning "business to business," the tag of telephone directories and other enterprises in which businesses deal directly with one another rather than with consumers) is a hit because it resonates with the black Bs: B-boy, B-ball, and B as a form of address, as in "Yo, B, whassup?" (This last B was probably reduced from *blood*, "a positive term, noting the genetic kinship and shared bloodlines of African people," Smitherman writes.) Sure, it makes sense in this abbreviation-loving era that *business to business* would be punched down to B2B, as in B2BMarketingTrends.com ("to help marketing professionals stay abreast of B2B marketing trends," according to a press release). But B2B has become too popular for brevity to be the only explanation. B2B has spawned B2C, B2B2C, B2G, B2E, and P2P—"business to consumer," "business to business to consumer," "business to government," "business to employee," and "peer to peer" (as in electronic file sharing), respectively. All this B-bop can make any business sound less like it consists of a bunch of suits who bore one another at meetings and more like a crew of B-boys doing some def transactions.

B as short for *be* (along with *U* for *you* and *4* for *for*) has been around for ages (even pre-Prince). But this shading of B has been bumped up lately because of its increased use in text messaging as well as in hip-hop. "Now we can b alone," a man writes to a woman on a pager in a noisy concert crowd for a Verizon Wireless spot. A Burger King TV commercial had it both ways, with nods to hip-hop and electronics: "B Real. B Good," voice-overs sang as the lyrics were spelled out on-screen to make sure we C the Bs. "2 Go. BK4U." Bouncy and at the beginning of the alphabet, B is on the mild side of businesses that want their bit of blood.

When corporations misspell, they're trying to spell it out: We refuse to put letters together the way the authorities tell us to!

Covert Operations

Wannabe or crossover talk didn't begin with hip-hop, nor is lingo-lending from one group to another confined to blacks and whites in America. Whites talking some black is part of an apparently universal phenomenon that sociolinguists call covert prestige. This means that speakers of a "standard" language (whatever the language) "have favorable attitudes toward lower-class, nonstandard speech forms," explains the linguist Margaret Lee. "However, these attitudes are not always overtly expressed, and they may be subconscious, because they stray from mainstream—or overt—values about the perceived superior status of the standard forms." This occurs, she adds, "for the most part throughout the world—when new forms enter the mainstream, in fact, they usually come from nonstandard speech."

Males are more prone than females to imbibing some of that covert prestige. Perhaps that's because, as some studies indicate, males associate standard speech with femininity. "Females tend to use more 'correct' speech forms," Lee says. On the basis of a study in Norwich, England, Peter Trudgill wrote in *Sociolinguistics*, "A large number of male speakers, it seems, are more concerned with acquiring *covert prestige* than with obtaining social status (as this is more usually defined)." This may be, he wrote, "because working-class speech is associated with the 'toughness' traditionally supposed to be characteristic of working-class life—and 'toughness' is quite widely considered to be a desirable masculine characteristic."

Covert or otherwise, black-to-white (and white-to-black) crossover talk in America began during slavery, especially when slave children and white children played together. Most of that language was never recorded, of course, and we have to wait for the development of various media to see how black speech influenced the broader English. "Slavery made its own traditions of speech and vocabulary," McCrum and his coauthors write in *The Story of English*. The entry of black English—an amalgam of Africanisms, the trade English used on slave ships, and plantation English—"into the mainstream of American life began with the Brer Rabbit stories. Later it was to sustain its place there through minstrel shows, vaudeville, music hall, radio, and finally the movies."

By the 1840s, minstrel shows had brought black language to large audiences and in the most overtly covert way possible. White men in blackface sang and told jokes using some variety of black language, often insulting imitations of it, to entertain whites. They were horror shows, "but minstrel shows were also the beginning of influence of African American style on all America," writes Allan Metcalf in *How We Talk: American Regional English Today*.

Black musical forms—spirituals, ragtime, the blues—went on to spread black language to the larger public, but by far the most influential music, until hip-hop, was jazz. Jazz fed generations of slang. Jive, the jokey, mint-cool language that arrived with the swing jazz of the thirties and forties, was slang that went on to become the pop of its time, even spawning a number of dictionaries. Cab Calloway's *Hepster's Dictionary: Language of Jive* (first edition published in 1938) listed jive words like *beat* (exhausted), *chick* (girl), *hip, hype, groovy, in the groove, jam* (improvised swing music), *joint is jumping, mellow, pad, riff, sharp, solid, square, too much,* and *yeah, man.* In *The Original Handbook of Harlem Jive* (1944), Dan Burley wrote: "in the sense that [jive] came into use among Negroes in Chicago about the year 1921, it meant to taunt, scoff, to sneer—an expression of sarcastic comment," and he relates it to the "linguistic procedure which came to be known as 'putting you in the dozens.'"

The whites ("flappers" if they were women) who jammed the Harlem clubs in the 1920s, the jitterbug craze of the 1930s, and influential disc jockeys in the 1940s all contributed to making jive the lingo for black and white youth in the know. Listen, for instance, to this forties DJ: "Hiya cat, wipe ya feet on the mat, let's slap on the fat and dish out some scat. You're a prisoner of wov. W-O-V, 1280 on the dial, New York, and you're picking up the hard spiel and good deal of Fred Robbins, dispensing seven score and ten ticks of ecstatic static and spectacular vernacular from 6:30 to 9."

"A new language has been born," Lou Shelly wrote in 1945 in another jive dictionary, *Hepcats Jive Talk Dictionary,* "and with its usual lustiness youth has made jive talk heard from one end of the land to the other." This meant, as always, that corporate interests were moving in—a process then more likely to signal a phenomenon's demise than it does today. "The end of the jive generation," writes Dalzell, "could be measured by the fact that in 1946 Hallmark cards issued a set of 'Solid Sender' cards, 'groovy as the movie MAKE MINE MUSIC,' based on the 'Disney hepcat scene.'" 80

Though jive began to dive, it kept resurfacing in the slang of later groups. In describing the beat speech of the late-forties hipster, Jack Kerouac called it "a new language, actually spade (Negro) jargon, but you soon learned it." By the 1950s, Kerouac noticed that "even college kids went around hep and cool and using terms I'd heard on Times Square in the early Forties."

Jive, writes Dalzell, "would lay an important foundation for the slang of the hipster/beat movement of the late 1950s, the hippie movement of the 1960s and early 1970s, and to some extent the hip-hop/rap phenomenon of the 1980s and 1990s." "*Cap, fly chick, groovy, homey, hung up, icy, mellow, righteous, sharp, solid,* and *square* all endured quite nicely, playing major roles in the slang of the 1960s and the 1990s."

If the 1960s were the turning point in creating pop language of a different order, that was to a great degree because, simultaneously, black language was undergoing a renaissance and was developing an increased ability to cross over. This black force met up with the big two powers, mass media and marketing, and all three have played with and against one another ever since. Smitherman describes this blossoming of black language:

> . . . perhaps the richest period of linguistic innovation was the last half of the twentieth century, particularly the 1960s and beyond. The emergence of the Black Freedom Struggle marked a fundamental shift in linguistic consciousness as Black intellectuals, scholar-activists, and writer-artists deliberately and consciously engaged in an unprecedented search for a language to express Black identity and the Black condition. This era was in fact the first period in the history of U.S. slave descendants when there was a critical mass of highly educated Blacks.

White people couldn't help but hear the newly invigorated black talk, she continues. "The 1960s was a defining moment in this cultural diffusion process with Motown, on the one hand, crossing racial boundaries with its music, and the Civil Rights Movement, on the other, crossing racial boundaries with its language and rhetoric of protest and moral confrontation, all broadcast live on the eleven o'clock news."

By the 1970s, black was beautiful enough to be in demand in the more liberal circles. As Gerald Boyd, the former managing editor of the *New York Times* and a black man, said in a round-table discussion about race, "When I started out in the early seventies, it was very popular to be black. Every white had to have one." 85

Media Bond

Now, more than a generation later, does every white—or at least every white kid—have to be one?

In the late eighties, the hip-hop movement began to bring black style—music, dance, fashion, language—back harder than anything since the introduction of jive. However, as Dalzell writes, "Unlike the hippie movement where anyone could don a tie-dye shirt and become a weekend hippie, the hip-hop culture did not provide a lifestyle that most American young people could completely embrace. Simply put, white teenagers could not, as much as they might wish to, become black. They could and did, however, listen to the music, dress the dress . . . mirror the hair cuts, adopt the rap vocabulary suitable for their daily lives, mimic the cadence of street speech, and admire from a safe distance the lives of prominent black rappers and athletes."

What made both the mimicking and the distance possible were massive media and marketing, both of which have mushroomed since forties jive. Hip-hop is, for now, the leading culture (followed by various skateboard, drug, and online cultures) that white kids can draw upon to fight the power, be that their parents, their schools, the system, injustice, or the general whateverness of life. Which is why commercial powers want so badly to be associated, however tenuously, with hip-hop. (The truism about "brand loyalty" is, Hook 'em while they're young and you got 'em for life.) For the most part, that rented association is working. If hip-hop weren't commercialized and hadn't hit the pop stage (*stage* in both senses), most of these white kids wouldn't hear or see it enough to wanna be black in the first place.

How easily a word can hop from hep or hippie or hip-hop to shopping pop. In the year 2000, few pop words could compete with *Whassup?!* Perhaps that's because *Whassup?!* (the official Budweiser spelling) was the one phenomenon that most successfully put black style through the marketing processor and coated every particle of implied transgression with a safety seal.

It was advertising, of course, that catapulted the sound into our faces. A 90
Chicago copywriter caught a short movie by filmmaker Charles Stone III in which Stone and some friends, cool black guys all, lay out deep, highly exaggerated *Whassup?!*s for every possible greeting. The ad guy, finding himself mouthing it too, figured, This is exploitable! and signed Stone to transfer his magic word to a client, Budweiser.

Said with tongue hanging out of mouth, the commercial *Whassup?!* was guttural and gross and funny. (Budweiser's spelling was wrong, Stone insisted; since the proper pronunciation is P-less, it should be spelled *Whaazzzaahhh?!* "If you make the P sound, your tongue can't be out," he told me.) After a climactic series of the guys growling *Whaazzzaahhh?!* to one another over phones and intercoms while watching a game on TV, the original spot ended with a sudden calm-down: "What's up, B?" Stone asked one friend over the cordless. "Watching the game. Having a Bud." "True. True," Stone replied. With the spots starring Stone's real-life pals, what emerged through this literally *lingua* franca was a lot of easygoing male bonding among some brotha buds.

(A note on origins: *What's up?* was not originally black. It goes back at least to 1838, Jonathan Lighter, editor of the *RHHDAS*, wrote in a post to the American Dialect Society online discussion group. Nearly a hundred years later, the phrase went mass-pop when Bugs Bunny first uttered a crisp "Eh, what's up, Doc?" in *A Wild Hare* in 1940. But somewhere along the way, African Americans began to unroll *What's up?* into a more all-purpose greeting. By the seventies and eighties, Dalzell writes, long-haired white dudes were saying the blackened *whassup, s'up,* and *z'up.* Stone said he and his pals had been doing the mega *Whaazzzaahhh?!* for sixteen years before selling their shtick to Budweiser. But he feels strongly that it's more of a black thing than Bud's or his own. "Someone suggested to me that I should trademark it," he said. "If it ever came to that, I would hope that someone in the African American community would sue me.")

Whaazzzaahhh?! was just what the nation apparently needed on the eve of a new millennium. The sound instantly became an NBA refrain, a greeting on radio sports shows, the theme of an *SNL* skit (with Brokaw, Koppel, and Shaw *Whaazzzaahhh?!* ing each other), part of another easy question on *Who Wants to Be a Millionaire?*, and the basis of numerous Web site parodies.

Largely because of *Whaazzzaahhh?!*, sales for all Anheuser-Busch beers rose by 2.4 million barrels in 2000. Just as important, *Whaazzzaahhh?!* generated at least $20 million worth of free publicity, according to Bud's ad agency, DDB Worldwide in Chicago. (DDB calls this desirable state "talk value"—it means saturation buzz, a phrase that people use almost involuntarily. But since DDB wanted to reap benefits in case *talk value* acquired talk value, it did what Stone said he wouldn't with *Whaazzzaahhh?!*—it trademarked the term.)

Whaazzzaahhh?! clearly filled a catchphrase/catchgesture void. The Arsenio whoop and the high-five, pop as they still are, had already faded into background pop. The chest bump and the victory dance required actually getting physical. Men, especially sedentary sports-fan men, were ripe for a word that could reinvigorate their manliness, update them multiculturally, and refresh their irony.

And the very sound of the earthy, vomity *Whaazzzaahhh?!* was a perfect counterpoint to the entire high-pitched, beeping wired world. *Whaazzzaahhh?!* was disgusting, low-down, and as analogue as it gets—something to make primal *Fight Club* men out of digital midgets (the 1999 Edward Norton/Brad Pitt movie about wimpy white guys fleeing office cubicles and regaining testosterone by slapping each other around in abandoned buildings came out shortly before Bud's campaign), something to add thick yang to the whiny yin of cell phones and chirping virtuosity and everything eeeeeeeeeeeeeEEEEEEEE. *Whaazzzaahhh?!* was grit thrown onto the computer screen, onto the very TV screen the ads ran on. That is—as racial myths still go—*Whaazzzaahhh?!* could make cool black men out of repressed white males.

But it took another spot of the many in Budweiser's campaign to make that perfectly clear. A bunch of preppie white guys—a sweater is draped over one's shoulders as he watches the "market recap" instead of "the game"—duplicate the plot of the original spot but instead of gutting out *Whaazzzaahhh?!*, they eke out a clunky *What are you doooo-ing?!* By the end, their war cry is very loud but very uncool, and the camera pulls back to show two of Stone's black pals watching these graceless wannabes on TV and looking at each other in disbelief. The spot, which debuted on the 2001 Super Bowl, was really funny. But think about what Budweiser was doooo-ing. It was telling its predominantly white customers that they could better identify with these loose, creative black men than they could with those ghosts-of-men honkies. Pouring on the covert prestige, it flattered white guys by telling them they shared the cool attitude of the black men—though, whew, they didn't have to *live* as black men. Drink Bud and get in touch with your inner black guy.

But not necessarily with an outer one. Because *Whaazzzaahhh?!* was yet another way for white men, and women, to bond with black people without having to actually know any. Knowing *media* black people—actors, athletes, any celebrity will do—is so much easier. If white people can bond with media black people through a phrase or a gesture, we can all "celebrate" an idyllic racial harmony while ignoring real racial politics—assaults on voting rights, racial profiling, income disparities, leaving no African American child behind.

But, hey, this ad's for Bud. Budweiser needed a hit of *Whaazzzaahhh?!* as much as many white people did. Never a big seller to blacks and without an indie bone in its image, the world's largest-selling beer, made by the world's largest brewer, could now say: These hops hip hop. Even though it's not true, true.

The Paying Dues Blues

After just a year or so, *Whaazzzaahhh?!* became mere hall-of-fame pop—no longer "top of mind," as ad people say, but hauled out now and then to fill certain mental slots (like another Budweiser hall-of-famer, "I love you, man"). But within the *Whaazzzaahhh?!* campaign, particularly the preppie spot, lie the seeds of what's wrong with media-enabled crossover talk.

Yes, merging languages is great, and we're better off when "standard" English gets goosed firmly and frequently. Anyway, it simply wouldn't be possible for white people not to use black talk—it's part and parcel of American talk. But whether our national experiments in covert prestige are enriching or exploitative depends on the attitude that insiders bring to outsiders' speech. When white people are too tickled with their ability to reference black talk, when they treat it like exotica, when it's too trendy, too knee-jerk, too associated with the selling of something (including oneself) and dissociated from the politics and

100

history that forged it, then you have to ask, What are the hidden costs, and who reaps the profits?

In his show *You Are All Diseased*, George Carlin started in on theme restaurants like the House of Blues: "Burn down the House of Blues!" he said—it has too many white people playing the blues. "White people ought to understand they *give* people the blues. . . . A couple of terms used by lame white people: 'happens to be black,' 'openly gay.' When did 'urban' become synonymous with the word black? I don't think white women should be calling each other girl-friend. . . . 'You go, girl' should probably go along with 'You the man.' "

White people crowing "You the man" does not necessarily flatter black people. "Most black people are not delighted to have aspects of the language borrowed," the linguist John Rickford says. "They think of it as appropriated."

This isn't to say that all imitation of black or hip-hop talk is simply appropriation. Spreading words can spread the word—knowledge, empathy, and certainly the broader hip-hop culture. "It's something to see videos connect white kids in Utah to black kids in South Chicago to Croats and Brazilians," the hip-hop pioneer and former Public Enemy frontman Chuck D. wrote in *Time* magazine's cover story on hip-hop's twentieth anniversary. "This is the sound and style of our young world, the vernacular used in today's speak from scholastics to sports. . . . It's difficult to stop a cultural revolution that bridges people together." Those words began to sound prescient when, five years later, a rousing rap song, "Razom Nas Bahato" ("Together We Are Many"), became the theme music of Ukraine's pro-Yushchenko "Orange revolution."

Hip-hop truly is the young world's vernacular. But borrowing black language alone doesn't bridge people together. The bridges are often not so much between people as they are between people and the media. The college slang expert Connie Eble puts into perspective, for instance, the white use of the black term of address *girl*. "Well, *girl* is just used and that's all there is to it," she says. "It's one black phrase that has been taken over by white females, middle-aged secretaries around campus," as well as students. Eble once believed that the white use of *girl* and other black slang was a sign of hope. "At first I thought, maybe race relations are improving after all. But I have absolutely no evidence that there is more mixing among the races than there ever has been. After researching it, I found that hardly any black slang entered the white vocabulary because a white student has encountered a black student. They've learned it from MTV, the movies, and rap songs."

What's wrong with whites gaining covert prestige through black talk isn't that it fails to bring the races together (that's too much to ask from any one trend or proclivity). What's wrong is that it usually allows whites to feel good about themselves without having to do anything particularly worthwhile. Such easily picked-up prestige encourages the belief that high-fiving or giving it up are the extent of political commitment that an enlightened person needs nowadays. Whites get to blacken up their act "at bargain-basement prices," as Smitherman writes. "They don't have to PAY NO DUES, but reap the psychological, social, and economic benefits of a language and culture born out of enslavement, neo-enslavement, Jim Crow, U.S. apartheid, and twentieth-century hard times."

Dearth of the Cool

The matter of whites reaping benefits from black history brings us to the black-nurtured word and concept that has risen to a status above all others: cool, or rather a dues-free knockoff of it.

Cool is the tent pole of pop culture. Without it, desire flops around; money doesn't know where to put itself. Uttered by folks from two (I've heard it) to seventy, cool is both one of the most expressive concepts of our time and one of the emptiest.

Cool is not just a black thing, by any means. Garbo, Brando, and Eastwood, to name a few obvious cool white symbols, have projected it. Other languages have long had their equivalents—the French royalty displayed *sang-froid*, for instance, on the way to the guillotine. And *cool*, meaning warmer than cold, has been around since the Norman invasion. *Cold, cool, chill, glacier, gelato,* and *Jell-O* all go back to the Latin root *gelare*, meaning to freeze, congeal; by extension, to make rigid, unmoving, with the implication of restraint and control.

Exactly when *cool* jelled into the word we know today is difficult to say. But *cool* as an elixir of composure, detachment, and style is generally thought to have come of age during the era of Count Basie and Duke Ellington. In 1947, Charlie Parker came out with a track called "Cool Blues"; in 1950, Miles Davis, perhaps *the* icon of cool, brought out the album *Birth of the Cool*. 110

But the cool—the stance, the feeling, the vibe—that early jazz musicians exemplified goes back much further. "Cool is all about trying to make a dollar out of 15 cents. It's about living on the cusp, on the periphery, diving for scraps. Essential to cool is being outside looking in," Donnell Alexander writes in the essay "Are Black People Cooler Than White People?" "So in the days when [slaves] were still literally on the plantation they devised a coping strategy called cool, an elusive mellowing strategy designed to master time and space. Cool, the basic reason blacks remain in the American cultural mix, is an industry of style that everyone in the world can use. It's finding the essential soul while being essentially lost."

To pull off such a strategy, you'd have to at times appear unmoving; you'd have to chill. "A wooden-faced model is aristocratic in its roots," says the classicist Margaret Visser, author of *The Way We Are* and *The Geometry of Love*. "Kings and queens perfected an impassive public face as the look of power. If you have no expression on your face, other people interpret *you*—you are all things to all people." While the keeping of a cool public face by nonroyals is a relatively "modern phenomenon," Visser says, it was "adopted by black culture, people who were the opposite of aristocrats, though they knew how to use that to make themselves powerful."

Sometimes that impassive look can be gotten cheaply, by wearing sunglasses. Or by using other symbols—catchphrases, designer labels, a little something to entice other people to interpret you. The more that millions of people have chased the elusive cool, the more the word's meaning has been diluted. Perhaps the seeds of change were there in the sixties, when cool began to shift from a thing to admire to a thing to idolize. But somewhere along the way, *cool* ceased to be primarily a word denoting composure or detachment and became more an all-purpose murmur of approval (where it's sometimes written and pronounced *kewl*—a blend of *cool* and *cute?*). "That's cool," one might say when a cabby suggests taking Thirteenth Street across town instead of Fourteenth. "Cool," I say instead of listening when my son tells me an amazing fact about his Yu-Gi-Oh! cards.

Perhaps, too, *cool*'s cool dissipated as people used it, as they will any fashion, not to cope with life as an outsider, but to enforce a popular-kids-in-class caste system. I used to say *neat*—until 1991, when I saw Madonna's tour movie, *Truth or Dare*. In it, Kevin Costner visited Madonna backstage and told her that her show was "neat." She acidly repeated the word, withering him on the spot for being an outdated creep and a disingenuous suckup. This was not Madonna at her coolest. Cool, as Alexander further defines it, is "about completing the task of living with enough spontaneity to splurge some of it on bystanders." Ten years after *Truth or Dare*, the caste system *cool* got a comeuppance, of sorts, in another movie, *Save the Last Dance*. In this interracial teenage romance, the white heroine compliments a black friend on her clothes: "Cool outfit." "Slammin'," the friend corrects her, "*slammin'* outfit." I'm not sure, but I doubt that *slammin'* still rules. Such words of praise come and go, but in the grand mall of franchised pop, *cool* has outlasted them all.

As *cool* rose in popularity, it needed a chump. "*Square*, a vital word of the 1950s counterculture," Dalzell writes, "became by the dialectic process of slang a vital word of the 1960s predominant youth culture; it is richly paradoxical that kids whom Beats would have found quite square used the word to vilify those who were out of touch with the latest mainstream fashions, styles, and trends." [115]

Today *cool* has everything to do with mainstream fashions, styles, and trends and very little to do with originality or art, much less with "trying to make a dollar out of 15 cents." And yet repeating the word's sound—its coo, its ooh, its refreshing pool—still gives the faint impression that the speaker is grooving to something the majority just doesn't get, that maybe he's even slyly artistic or, to veer toward another black-cultivated word of complexity, hip. John Leland, author of *Hip: The History*, says hip "refers to an awareness or enlightenment. It's the intelligence behind the mask [of cool's composure]." To that I would just add that cool and hip, as words and as forces, intertwine, overlap, and at times are indistinguishable, but that on the whole cool is central to pop culture, while hip influences it more from the sidelines.

Cool's opposite number among the pop superlatives is not *hip*, but *hot*. *Hot* and *cool* both convey the utmost in mass desirability, but *hot* doesn't know from detachment; it's all sex, passion, and hubba hubba. Magazine cover lines have hissed *hot* so often that a women's magazine editor once told me his publication had nixed *hot* as being tepid. "Hot is unusable," he said flatly. The moratorium must have lasted all of three months, because the heavy-breathing *hot* is baaack. "What's Hot?" asks a 2005 print ad for (the co-owned) *In Touch* and *Life & Style* magazines. Citing each mag's sales stats, the ad answers: "That's hot!" The lucre-and-loin-driven *hot* is simpleminded, and has none of the paradoxes of *cool* (much less of the way more subtle *hip*).

No rich concept is without paradoxes, real and apparent. Cool is rife with them. Paradox number one is that beneath the frozen face of real cool, you're actually going with the flow (no paradox at all for Buddhist cool). Paradox number two, touched on earlier, is that borrowing from the excluded can make you feel more included. This is less a paradox than a pragmatic tactic for a market that needs outsiders (and even more so, paradox itself) to sex up its merchandise. Even a few years ago, who'd have imagined that GM and Ford would "trick out" their autos with loads of bling to look like the car makeovers on the MTV show *Pimp My Ride*? ("If you had big chrome rims a few years ago, people thought you were a drug dealer or a pimp," Myles Kovacs, the publisher of the hip-hop car magazine *Dub*, told *Newsweek*. "Now you could be a CEO.") Exuding excluded cool can protect a seller from appearing, God help them, boring. So market researchers, like those featured in Malcolm Gladwell's now classic piece "The Coolhunt," stalk the ghetto for music, garb, and slang to process into product.

If white people have made a fetish out of black cool, that too goes back further than the jazz era, as Greg Tate reminds us. In the introduction to the anthology *Everything But the Burden*, he writes: "Capitalism's original commodity fetish was the Africans auctioned here as slaves, whose reduction from subjects to abstracted objects has made them seem larger than life and less than human at the same time." That paradox reverberates today "in a market-driven world where we continue to find ourselves being sold as hunted outsiders and privileged insiders in the same breath."

Anyone who tries to resist the fruit of the coolhunts is bound to fail frequently. There's almost no way not to respond positively, at least momentarily, to marketed cool, whether in the form of a hip-hop Sprite spot or Nike's latest spectacle. We are really responding to presentations of grace—paid, staged, and third-hand though they may be. But in buying the product, we're not honoring cool, we're merely possessing its congealed representation—while the real thing evaporates from our credit-card-bearing hands. 120

"Most think cool is something you can put on and take off at will (like a strap-on goatee)," writes Alexander (ESPN once hired him to help hip-hopify its language). "They think it's some shit you go shopping for. And that taints cool, giving the mutant thing it becomes a deservedly bad name." Found in "advertising agencies, record company artist-development departments, and over-art-directed bars," this "ersatz cool," he adds, "fights real cool at every turn."

When Black Talk Goes to School

White society's fetishization of black cool and black talk might go down easier if that society did not react so virulently when black vernacular left the neighborhood of entertainment and moved to more serious areas, like education. I'm talking, of course, about Ebonics.

In December 1996, the Oakland, California, school board approved a resolution to change how it taught African American students who, the board said, spoke not a dialect of English but a separate, African-based language, Ebonics. On the face of it, which was as far as most of the press went, the resolution sounded like identity politics gone mad: calling a bunch of slang a separate language and proposing to teach it. Indeed, at first many blacks, most notably Jesse Jackson, in addition to most of the media and the larger public, trashed the plan.

Ebonics suddenly became the target of a rash of nasty cartoons, Internet jokes, and fuming commentary. Since the controversy arrived during the holiday season, several "Ebonics translations" of "The Night Before Christmas" began to circulate on the Net, like this one:

I looked out thru de bars;
What covered my doe;
'spectin' de sheriff;
Wif a warrent fo sho.

And what did I see;
I said, "Lawd, look at dat!"
Ther' wuz a huge watermellon;
Pulled by giant warf rats!!

The "Ebonics Lectric Library of Classical Literature" Web site (no longer active) introduced itself thus: "Since the recent decision to make Ebonics (Ebony-Phonics) a second language in our schools it has become obvious that e-bliterations of the classics will be required. We will cover here the greater works of world Literature (Litershure) in the hopes of bridging the gap between English and the new Slanguage." 125

With the general consensus that Ebonics was broken English and teaching it meant the triumph of black special interests, the mockery and stereotypes were suddenly viewed as a healthy dose of politically incorrect humor. "The nationwide roar of laughter over Ebonics is a very good sign," John Leo wrote in *U.S. News Online.*

But most of the outrage against Ebonics was based on the erroneous notion that the Oakland schools had proposed to teach Ebonics and to ignore standard English. Although the resolution was ambiguously and poorly written—a clearer, amended version appeared a few weeks later, partly at the urging of Jackson, who subsequently supported the plan—the idea was never simply to teach Ebonics. Rather it was to compare and contrast the "home language" (Ebonics) of academically failing students with "school English"—that is, to draw on their vernacular to help them master standard English. If teachers ignored the children's home language—or, worse, ridiculed it—the thinking went, the students were less likely to be open to learning the English skills they so desperately needed. The strategy was endorsed by the Linguist Society of America as "linguistically and pedagogically sound."

"The Ebonics controversy confirmed that linguists—whether or not they describe themselves as 'Afrocentric'—are generally united in their respect for the legitimacy and complexity of the language spoken by many African American children," write the Rickfords, who are generally supporters of Ebonics in the classroom. "This perspective clashed with the more widely held public opinion that Ebonics was simply slang and gutter talk, or the product of laziness and carelessness."

Like all languages and dialects, black English follows consistent rules and a system of grammar, most linguists agree. Even vocal opponents of using Ebonics to teach English, like the linguist John McWhorter, say that black English is not simply "bad," "broken," or "inferior" English. Standard English, or the standard version of any language, is but one of many dialects itself. "One of those dialects is chosen as the standard one not because it is somehow 'better' or 'more correct' in the eyes of God, but because it happens to be the one spoken where the center of power coalesces," McWhorter writes in his book *Losing the Race: Self-Sabotage in Black America*. "We have no trouble understanding that a tiger is not a 'degraded version' of a leopard but simply another variation on 'cat'; we do not see house cats' lack of a mane as meaning that they are 'broken' versions of lions. In the same way, Black English is not 'bad standard English' but just another kind of English."

The reason for discussing the Ebonics battle here (in a book that's not about specific dialects themselves) is to look at how conflicts over language and race surface in pop language and the politics that pop can't help but speak of. For whatever you think of Ebonics as an educational tool—and you can find arguments and studies that support or derail it—you have to ask, Why the heat? Why the ridicule at the very mention of Ebonics?

Some of the contempt stemmed from ignorance (augmented by the vast majority of the news media, which seemed to willfully ignore the facts, a story the Rickfords detail in *Spoken Soul*). But some of the vehemence was due to a frustrated racism, to prejudices whose outlets of expression had been closing off for years. Condemning Ebonics was a safe way to finally voice anger at and fear of black people and their increasingly confident presence in American culture. Over the last couple of decades, most white people, unless they were outright white supremacists, had been feeling that if they were uncomfortable with black individuals or music or style, they could voice their criticism only gingerly or had to cloak it in disagreements about policies and programs, like affirmative action, welfare, or classroom Ebonics. While I really do believe that you don't have to be racist to oppose any of these programs, if you *are* racist, occasionally have such inclinations, or are just afraid of black people, then mockery of Ebonics can supply convenient cover. (The Ebonics controversy also came, McWhorter reminds us, a few months after the O. J. Simpson verdict in his criminal trial, when white anger at black support for Simpson was at a peak.)

For black opponents of Ebonics, the situation was more complex. For many African Americans the squabble over Ebonics replayed a long-held ambivalence toward their language. The other side of black pride is black shame, something that being treated as subhuman for centuries can engender. "The variously named vernacular of African Americans does have a remarkable capacity to elicit denial and shame from blacks (not to mention others)," write the Rickfords. Arguments among blacks about "talking proper" rise up regularly, they add. "During the Harlem Renaissance of the 1920s," for instance, "debate raged among the black intelligentsia, with Langston Hughes endorsing and exemplifying the use of vernacular, and Alain Locke and others suggesting that African Americans ought to put the quaintness of the idiom behind them and offer the world a more 'refined' view of their culture. These enduring attitudes reflect the attraction-repulsion dynamic, the oscillation between black and white (or mainstream) poles that W. E. B. Du Bois defined a century ago as 'double-consciousness.' "

(If one response to speaking a laughed-at language is to make it bolder and tougher, as hip-hop does, an opposite response might be to brood silently. After the Supreme Court decision against letting Florida recount votes in the 2000 election, during which the Garbo-like Clarence Thomas asked nary a question, the Court's sole black justice discussed his previously unexplained shyness on the bench with a group of high school students. He said his reticence came from fear of being made fun of for speaking his native Gullah, the Creole of the coastal Carolinas, in his otherwise all-white seminary class.)

The attraction-repulsion among blacks toward black English has its parallels among the public at large. "Americans of all types tend to bad-talk soul talk, even though it is the guts of the black music they so relish," write the Rickfords. "Appreciating sung soul is one thing, but appreciating soul as it is spoken is something else entirely. . . . In fact, middle America has quite often jeered those who speak 'jive' in the same breath and with the same enthusiasm that it has grooved to black sounds a la Bessie Smith and Mahalia Jackson and Ray Charles and Lauryn Hill."

There is, however, one other form of black speech as widely grooved to as 135 black song lyrics: individual words and phrases that have evolved from black-only slang into everyone-owns-a-piece-of-it pop. Even middle America holds on to these words as if they were talismans of the soul of a people.

None of this is to say that Ebonics itself is pop. The black talk that turns into pop, whether through the avenues of jive, civil rights, or hip-hop, did indeed begin as Ebonics (or whatever you want to call it), but the pop process has stripped that talk of its other dimensions. "The part of black language that is used by the general public is vocabulary," John Rickford says. "But the core elements of Ebonics or black language, which are the distinct grammar, phonology, and pronunciation patterns—that's not being borrowed to any significant extent, because you have to be living it." Since white people gravitate primarily to the vocabulary—with very occasional pronunciation exceptions as in *You da man* and *gangsta*—Rickford doesn't believe that popularization will be the death knell for black talk: "I don't think it has a powerful effect, at least not on black language itself. Anyway, people are always creating new terms—there's a premium on that in black English."

New terms, dwelling on the periphery, tend to have authenticity cred, and some of them, too, will eventually undergo the media glamour treatment that makes them pop. It might be a drag in real life, but marginalization can be marketable—if it's packaged right. Or, as the writer Khephra Burns put it in 1997, speaking of the students who were supposed to be at the center of the Ebonics brawl: "It can't help our children to be told at every utterance that their mode of expression—which is intimately linked to their identity—is wrong, wrong, wrong, when others who plagiarize them are getting paid."

Questions for Critical Reading

1. What is "covert prestige"? Define the term using Savan's text and provide an additional example from your own experience.

2. Savan discusses "paying the dues." What does that mean? Use Savan's text to develop a definition of the phrase, reading the text critically in order to build your understanding of the term.

3. Savan's primary concern is black talk. Using her text, suggest why other minority or foreign linguistic styles aren't used as prevalently in advertising. You will need to reread her text closely and critically to develop your answer, since she never explicitly addresses this issue.

Exploring Context

1. Savan's argument centers on the use of slang in advertising. Visit some Web sites oriented toward young adults (such as MTV.com, MySpace, Vibe.com). What sort of language is used in the online ads? Does it support or complicate Savan's argument?

2. Savan mentions the Web site Black People Love Us. Visit that Web site at blackpeopleloveus.com and expand her analysis of the site. You might want to use your work on covert prestige and "paying the dues" from Questions for Critical Reading to build your analysis.

3. Savan discusses Ebonics at the end of this selection. Use the Web to locate any initiatives concerning Ebonics in your area. Has it been an issue locally? In what ways? Why or why not?

Questions for Connecting

1. One way to think of Helen Epstein's essay "AIDS, Inc." (p. 106) is that it's about the triumph of language over advertising. How can we apply Epstein's insights about the fight against HIV infection in Africa to the appropriation of black talk by commercial culture? How might conversation defeat lifestyle branding? Synthesize these two essays to make your argument.

2. Julia Alvarez's exploration of the quinceañera in "Selections from *Once Upon a Quinceañera*" (p. 35) includes a discussion of retroculturation. How might this phenomenon influence covert prestige? Is retroculturation a form of paying the dues? Use the definition of *paying the dues* that you developed in Questions for Critical Reading in making your response.

3. In "The Dell Theory of Conflict Prevention" (p. 121), Thomas Friedman seems to focus primarily on the economic benefits of global supply chains. How does Savan's essay complicate this picture of globalization? What's the price of commercialism in terms of culture?

Language Matters

1. Locate a key sentence from Savan's text and then identify the subject, verb, and object of the sentence. How does the structure of the sentence contribute to Savan's argument? How does it make meaning, and what meaning does it make?

2. How do the headings in Savan's essay contribute to your understanding of it? Devise new headings for this essay. Where would you make the divisions?

3. Select a section of at least four paragraphs in Savan's essay. Find the topic sentence of each paragraph and then copy those sentences together to form a new paragraph. Does the paragraph made out of topic sentences make any sense? Does it reflect the flow of Savan's argument? How can you apply this exercise to your own writing?

Assignments for Writing

1. Savan focuses on the appropriation of black language into pop culture: On the one hand, black talk is fine and acceptable in commercials and ads, but on the other hand, it's seen as unacceptable in education. With this in mind, write a paper in which you evaluate the value of accepted norms for language in education. Should everyone be expected to speak "standard" English? What is the role of education in creating a national identity? How can we balance cultural uniqueness with such norms? You might want to draw from your work on Ebonics from Question 3 of Exploring Context.

2. Write a paper in which you extend Savan's argument using other specific cultural practices or traits that have been appropriated by American society. To help you complete your essay successfully, you may consider pulling from your own life experiences. You may also want to think about the different kinds of cultural practices and traits that have been appropriated in American culture, including art, language, and ceremonies. Is "paying the dues" an issue? Can you find evidence of covert prestige? Use your work on these terms from Questions for Critical Reading to help you make your argument.

3. Using Savan's essay, write a paper in which you determine the possibility of the "melting pot" ideal in America. Is it possible, or will there always be some sort of exploitation of cultures in the process? What gets lost in the melting pot? What do we gain? Can we achieve the goals of such a society without sacrificing the uniqueness of various cultures? How?

Julia Serano

Julia Serano lives in Oakland, California, where she works as a researcher in evolutionary and developmental biology at the University of California, Berkeley. She earned her Ph.D. from Columbia University in biochemistry and molecular biophysics. Aside from her scientific research, Serano is also a writer, musician, and spoken word performer as well as a transsexual activist. Serano's writings have appeared in numerous print and online magazines, journals, and anthologies. These published works include excerpts from her book, *Whipping Girl: A Transsexual Woman on Sexism and the Scapegoating of Femininity* (2007), and other works concerning gender and transexual issues. She has also self-published four chapbooks of poetry.

In *Whipping Girl*, Serano takes on issues surrounding transsexualism, sexuality, gender, and feminism. Serano pushes beyond the traditional concepts of gender relations and issues by extending them to the social view and treatment of the transgender community. Drawing on her personal experience with gender reassignment, her professional experience in science, and her knowledge of feminist theories, Serano provides critical arguments surrounding cultural and biological views of transsexuals.

"Before and After: Class and Body Transformations" looks closely at the cultural obsession with human transformation depicted throughout many aspects of culture—most noticeably pop culture. With countless makeover shows and documentaries that focus on bodily alterations airing regularly on television, human transformations have become a popular form of entertainment. Serano approaches the subject from a personal point of view; as a transsexual woman she has experienced people's curiosity about her reassignment surgery and pictures of her as a male. Serano is curious herself and wonders what drives the human interest in transformation. Class, as she points out, factors largely into this interest, for body transformations allow otherwise impenetrable class boundaries to be crossed.

What "classes" exist in our culture? Other than in pop culture, where else are human transformations seen? In what other ways are class boundaries crossed?

▶ TAGS: *technology, gender, objectification, research, class, human dignity*

Before and After: Class and Body Transformations

Transsexual lives are full of obstacles—childhood isolation, denial, depression, coming out, and managing our gender difference in a less than hospitable world. We have to navigate the legal limbo that surrounds what "sex" appears on our driver's licenses and passports, which restrooms we can safely use, and who we are allowed to marry. Many of us face workplace discrimination, police harassment, and the constant threat of violence. Yet the media focuses very little on any of this. Instead, TV shows and documentaries about transsexuals tend to focus rather exclusively on one particular aspect of our lives: our physical transitions.

Such transition-focused programs always seem to follow the same format, which includes rigorous discussions of all of the medical procedures involved (hormones, surgeries, electrolysis, etc.) and plenty of the requisite before-and-after shots. Before I transitioned, I found these programs predictable and formulaic, but I also found them helpful to a certain extent. As someone who had often thought about changing my sex, they gave me a certain understanding of what I might be able to expect if I were to pursue such a path myself. But of course, I was a demographic anomaly. Clearly these shows were being made by and for people who did not identify with the trans person in the program and who were not contemplating sex reassignment themselves. Back then, I never really questioned why a non-trans audience might be so interested in the minutiae of the transitioning process and trans-related medical procedures.

Now, after five years of living as an out transsexual, I have come to realize that these documentaries and TV programs reveal an even deeper underlying compulsion on the part of many cissexual people, one that goes way beyond natural curiosity, to dwell almost exclusively on the physical aspects of the transition process when contemplating transsexuality. Like most transsexuals, I have scores of anecdotes that highlight this tendency: During the question and answer session at a literary event, after reading a piece about the murder of trans woman Gwen Araujo, I was asked by an audience member if I had any electrolysis done on my face; after I did a workshop for college students on binary gender norms and the way we project our ideals about gender onto other people, a young woman asked me several questions about whether or not I'd had a "sex change operation"; after creating switchhitter.net, my coming-out-as-trans website, I received an angry email from a stranger complaining that I did not put any before-and-after pictures up on the site, as if the 3,700-word question and answer section and the 4,500-word mini-autobiography describing my experiences being trans wasn't sufficient for that person to fully grasp my transsexuality—he needed to see the changes firsthand.

Of course, it's not just strangers who ask to see before-and-after shots of me. When friends, colleagues, or acquaintances find out that I am trans, it is not uncommon for them to ask if I have any "before" pictures they can see, as if I just so happen to keep a boy photo of myself handy, you know, just in case.

I usually respond by telling them that before I transitioned I looked exactly like I do now, except that I was a boy. They never seem particularly satisfied with that answer.

The thing that strikes me the most about the desire to see before-and-after pictures, or to hear all of the gory details about sex reassignment procedures, is how bold people often are about it. After all, these people have to know that I felt uncomfortable as male, that it was a difficult and often miserable part of my life. So why on earth would they ask to see pictures of me from that time period? From my perspective, it is as thoughtless as if I had told someone that I was suffering from depression a few years ago and for them to have responded, "Oh, do you have any pictures of yourself from back then?" And really, is there anything more disrespectful and inappropriate than asking someone (in public, no less!) whether they have had any medical procedures performed on their genitals? So what drives these otherwise well-meaning people to want to know about the physical aspects of my transition so badly that they are willing to disregard common courtesy and discretion?

Well, I wasn't quite sure myself until about two years ago, during the height of the reality TV plastic surgery craze, when shows like *Extreme Makeover, The Swan,* and *I Want a Famous Face* filled the airwaves. These shows seemed to be catering to a very similar audience desire: to witness a dramatic physical transformation process replete with before-and-after photos of the subject. Also around that time, gastric bypass surgery began receiving a lot of media attention, and there were numerous programs dedicated to following people who were described as being "morbidly obese" through their surgery and recovery, ending of course with the mandatory before-and-after shots punctuating just how much weight the subjects had lost. On Discovery Health Channel, there is even a series that's called *Plastic Surgery: Before & After,* which often combines conventional plastic surgeries and gastric bypasses in the same episode.

Before I transitioned I looked exactly like I do now, except that I was a boy.

What really impressed me about these shows was how similar they are in format to many of the transsexual documentaries I have seen: They feature subjects who are unhappy with their bodies in some way, sympathetic and able doctors who describe the forthcoming procedures in great detail, hospital shots on the day of surgery and immediately afterward, a final scene after full recovery where the subject talks about how happy they are with the results, and side-by-side before-and-after photos that demonstrate the remarkable transformation in its entirety. Sometimes these shows are even set to slightly disturbing music that, when combined with the narrator's dramatic voice-over, impresses upon the viewer that they are watching something that is simultaneously wondrous and taboo. The only significant difference between many transsexual documentaries and these plastic surgery shows is that the former require a little more background and explanation as to why the subject wants to change their sex in the first place (presumably, the desire to become thinner or more conventionally attractive needs no explanation).

So why do plastic surgeries, gastric bypasses, and sex reassignment procedures receive such similar treatment in these programs? It is not simply because they all portray cutting-edge medical procedures. After all, there are plenty of shows that feature various medical techniques and surgeries, but they are generally far more serious and less sensationalistic in tone. Nor can it be said that the rarity of these procedures leads to the public's fascination with them. While sex reassignment is still fairly rare, 9.2 million cosmetic plastic surgery procedures and an estimated 140,000 gastric bypass surgeries were performed in 2004.¹ It also can't simply be that these shows depict transformations of some kind. After all, one occasionally sees behind-the-scenes programs about Hollywood makeup artists and costume designers who can drastically change an actor's appearance, yet they are never given the sensationalistic spin that these other types of transformations receive. There are also plenty of programs that feature nonsurgical makeovers (for example, *Queer Eye for the Straight Guy* and *What Not to Wear*), but they tend to have a more laid-back and informative feel, seducing the audience with their you-can-do-this-yourself attitude, in contrast to plastic surgery and sex reassignment shows, which have a far more cold and voyeuristic feel to them. And while a woman who changes her hair color and style, or a man who shaves off his beard, undergoes a significant transformation, one that often leaves them looking like a completely different person, the audience is not encouraged to gawk over their before-and-after pictures in the same way they do with the subjects of plastic surgery and sex reassignment programs.

I would argue that the major reason that plastic surgeries, gastric bypasses, and sex reassignments are all given similar sensationalistic treatments is because the subjects cross what is normally considered an impenetrable class boundary: from unattractive to beautiful, from fat to thin, and in the case of transsexuals, from male to female, or from female to male.

Of course, attractiveness as a class issue permeates much of what we see   10
on TV—it determines who gets to be the protagonist or love interest and who ends up being the nerdy next-door neighbor or comic relief. And while TV advertisements may encourage us to buy various beauty products that are supposed to make us look incrementally more attractive, or dieting and exercising programs that are supposed to help us lose that extra ten, twenty, even forty pounds, it is commonly accepted that we each have certain physical limits that we are unable to overcome, limits that generally determine our social status regarding attractiveness. In fact, the large amount of effort that many of us put into attaining the relatively small improvements in our appearance that are achievable by exercising, dieting, and purchasing beauty products is a testament to how much we are judged (and how we judge others) based on conventional standards of beauty and size. So when somebody does cross those supposedly impassable boundaries, essentially changing their social class from not-so-attractive to stunning, or from "morbidly obese" to thin, it can change our thinking about beauty and attraction.

As a transsexual, I find myself dealing with this same phenomenon all the time, only with gender. Whether people realize it or not, most of us value, treat, and relate to women and men very differently, although not necessarily in a conscious or malicious way. Rather, like our attitudes about beauty and attraction, these prejudices are practically invisible to us, as they are woven into our social fabric. So when I tell someone that I used to be male, they are often dumbfounded at first, as if they have difficulty reconciling that someone who seems so naturally female to them could have once been something they consider to be so completely different. The fact that a single individual can be both female and male, or ugly and beautiful, at different points in their life challenges the commonly held belief that these classes are mutually exclusive and naturally distinct from one another.

Coming face-to-face with an individual who has crossed class barriers of gender or attractiveness can help us recognize the extent to which our own biases, assumptions, and stereotypes create those class systems in the first place. But rather than question our own value judgments or notice the ways that we treat people differently based on their size, beauty, or gender, most of us reflexively react to these situations in a way that reinforces class boundaries: We focus on the presumed "artificiality" of the transformation the subject has undergone. Playing up the "artificial" aspects of the transformation process gives one the impression that the class barrier itself is "natural," one that could not have been crossed if it were not for modern medical technology. Of course, it is true that plastic surgeries and sex reassignments are "artificial," but then again so are the exercise bikes we work out on, the antiwrinkle moisturizers we smear on our faces, the dyes we use to color our hair, the clothes we buy to complement our figures, and the TV shows, movies, magazines, and billboards that bombard us with "ideal" images of gender, size, and beauty that set the standards that we try to live up to in the first place. The class systems based on attractiveness and gender are extraordinarily "artificial"—yet only those practices that seem to subvert those classes (rather than reaffirm them) are ever characterized as such.

Plastic surgery shows rarely depict people who are conventionally attractive from the outset.

Shows depicting plastic surgery, gastric bypasses, and sex reassignments are designed (whether consciously or unconsciously) to single out and exaggerate the supposed "artificial" nature of these procedures, thus giving the audience the opportunity to enjoy the spectacle of these dramatic transformations without ever bringing into question the authenticity of the class barrier that is being crossed. The more dramatic the change, the more "artificial" the whole process will inevitably seem. This is why plastic surgery shows rarely depict people who are conventionally attractive from the outset, even though such people certainly represent a significant portion of those who seek out plastic surgery. Nor do they follow subjects who merely want a nose job or a tummy tuck. Rather, these programs almost always depict people of either average or less-than-average attractiveness, and who undergo multiple procedures at once, thus creating the most dramatic and extensive physical change possible.

Similarly, the subjects of sex reassignment programs rarely ever begin the process as very feminine males or as very masculine females, even though many pre-transition trans people fall into these categories. Showing such people transitioning to become trans women and trans men, respectively, would not only make their transformation seem less dramatic; it would give the impression that sex reassignment merely confirms the subject's "natural" gender identity, as opposed to "artificially" altering that person's biological sex.

Perhaps for this reason, the most commonly depicted subject on these programs is a trans woman who starts out as a seemingly masculine male. In addition to the reasons for the media's focus on trans women rather than trans men . . . , there are additional physical reasons to account for this phenomenon. Trans women often have more difficulties "passing" as their identified sex than trans men do, not only because of limitations of the MTF* transition process in reversing some of the irreparable effects of prolonged exposure to testosterone, but because people in our culture predominantly rely on male (rather than female) cues when determining the sex of other people.[2] Therefore, some trans women require more procedures if they wish to be taken seriously as their identified sex. Sex reassignment TV programs I have seen have followed trans women not only through electrolysis, hormone replacement therapy, and bottom surgery (which are all fairly common), but also somewhat less common procedures, such as top surgery to increase the size of their breasts, tracheal shaves to reduce the size of their Adam's apples, and voice lessons to overcome their deep voices. Such shows also frequently depict trans women working with movement coaches and fashion consultants, even though it is safe to say that the overwhelming majority of trans women never engage in such a step.

These programs' concentration on trans people who undergo multiple medical procedures, or who take lessons to help them "pass" as their identified sex, tends to make invisible the many trans men and women who "pass" rather easily after hormone replacement therapy alone, or who choose not to undergo all of the procedures commonly associated with transsexuality. Focusing primarily on those trans people who undergo the most procedures during their transitions not only shows a more dramatic change—one that reinforces the idea that sex reassignment is "artificial"—but also fosters the audience's assumption that trans people are merely mimicking or impersonating the other sex rather than expressing their natural gender identity or subconscious sex.

Perhaps no element in these sex reassignment and plastic surgery shows helps confirm the audience's assumptions about gender and attractiveness more than the before-and-after photos. These pictures are designed to overemphasize stereotypes. In the programs that feature plastic surgery and gastric bypass surgery, the subject is almost always wearing frumpy clothes and frowning in the "before" picture, and dressed smart and smiling in the "after" picture, adding to the perception that they have become more attractive. In the transsexual documentaries, "before" photos of trans women almost always depict them in the most

15

---

*MTF: Male-to-female.

masculine of ways: playing sports as a young boy, with facial hair and wearing a wedding tuxedo or military uniform as a young man. Similarly, "before" shots of trans men often include pictures of them wearing birthday dresses as a child, or high school yearbook photos of them with long hair. The purpose for choosing these more stereotypically female and male images over other potential "before" pictures (for instance, ones where the subject looks more gender-variant or gender-neutral) is to emphasize the "naturalness" of the trans person's assigned sex, thereby exaggerating the "artificiality" of their identified sex.

In real life, before-and-after photos don't always depict such clear-cut gender differences. One time, a friend who has only known me as a woman visited our apartment and saw wedding photos of me and my wife, Dani, for the first time. Despite the fact that I am physically male and wearing a tuxedo in the pictures (as we were married before I physically transitioned), I do not look very masculine; instead, I look like the small, long-haired, androgynous boy that I used to be. My friend seemed a little let down by the photos. She muttered, "It's weird, because it looks just like you in the pictures, except that you're a guy." Similarly, whenever old friends meet up with me for the first time since my transition, they almost invariably comment on how strange it is that I seem like the exact same person to them, except that now I am female. It's as if our compulsion to place women and men into different categories of our brain, to see them as "opposite" sexes, is so intense that we have trouble imagining that it is possible for a person to change their sex without somehow becoming an entirely different person.

These days, whenever people ask me lots of questions about my previous male life and the medical procedures that helped facilitate my transition to female, I realize that they are making a desperate and concerted effort to preserve their own assumptions and stereotypes about gender, rather than opening their minds up to the possibility that women and men do not represent mutually exclusive categories. When they request to see my "before" photos or ask me what my former name was, it is because they are trying to visualize me as male in order to anchor my existence in my assigned sex. And when they focus on my physical transition, it is so they can imagine my femaleness as a product of medical science rather than something that is authentic, that comes from inside me.

I know that many in the trans community believe that these TV shows and 20 documentaries following transsexuals through the transition process serve a purpose, offering us a bit of visibility and the rare chance to be depicted on TV as something other than a joke. But in actuality, they accomplish little more than reducing us to our physical transitions and our anatomically "altered" bodies. In other words, these programs objectify us. And while it has become somewhat customary for trans people to allow the media to use our "before" pictures whenever we appear on TV, this only enables the cissexual public to continue privileging our assigned sex over our subconscious sex and gender identity. If we truly want to be taken seriously in our identified sex, then we must not only refuse to indulge cissexual people's compulsion to pigeonhole us in our assigned sex, but call them out on the way that they continuously objectify our bodies while refusing to take our minds, our persons, and our identities seriously.

NOTES

1. American Society of Plastic Surgeons, "9.2 Million Cosmetic Plastic Surgery Procedures in 2004 — Up 5% Growth Paces U.S. Economy Despite Reality TV Fad," press release, March 16, 2005; Nancy Hellmich, "Gastric Bypass Surgery Seeing Big Increase," *USA Today*, December 19, 2005.
2. Suzanne J. Kessler and Wendy McKenna, *Gender: An Ethnomethodological Approach* (Chicago: University of Chicago Press, 1978), 142–53.

Questions for Critical Reading

1. Serano claims that radical body transformations enable people to cross class boundaries, suggesting that physical appearance reflects class. Engage her argument through a critical reading by searching for specific passages where she makes this claim and then responding to them by providing your own examples.

2. What is natural about gender? Using Serano's text, describe those aspects of gender you believe are natural. Does Serano think gender is natural? Why or why not? What does it mean to be "natural"? You will need to read critically to form your response, since you will be drawing from many parts of Serano's text.

3. Why are people fascinated with before-and-after photos of physical transformations? Locate passages that illustrate Serano's answer and then provide your own examples that either confirm or complicate Serano's argument.

Exploring Context

1. Visit Julia Serano's Web site at juliaserano.com. How do the design and content of the site reflect her argument in this essay?

2. According to Serano, people are fascinated by before-and-after pictures of any sort of extreme makeover. Use the Web to locate sites with before-and-after pictures from plastic and cosmetic surgery. Do they reflect the kind of fascination Serano claims? Do class boundaries seem to be involved? Use your responses to Questions 1 and 3 of Questions for Critical Reading in making your argument.

3. Recently the "pregnant man" caused quite a bit of controversy. Research this case on the Web, using Serano's ideas to explore people's interest in this news item. How does this incident reflect what you had to say about gender in Question 2 of Questions for Critical Reading?

Questions for Connecting

1. In "Faith and Diplomacy" (p. 23), Madeleine Albright argues for the importance of taking religion into account when considering diplomacy. In doing so she underscores the vital importance of faith to many people and many political processes around the world while also illustrating the potential of diplomacy to bridge differences and foster peace. What role might faith and diplomacy each play in the controversial issue of transsexualism? Should faith determine policy when it comes to this matter? Can diplomacy mediate potential conflicts between religious tradition and individual sexual identity?

2. Class is also an issue in the elaborate quinceañeras explored by Julia Alvarez in "Selections from *Once Upon a Quinceañera*" (p. 35). How are class boundaries represented in these two essays? What is the cost of crossing those boundaries? Incorporate your response about class from Question 1 of Questions for Critical Reading.

3. What role might the primacy of practice play in the acceptance of radical body transformations? Apply Kwame Anthony Appiahs's ideas in "Making Conversation" (p. 57) and "The Primacy of Practice" (p. 63) to Serano's analysis, synthesizing their positions.

Language Matters

1. Gender is a primary concern in this essay, and it is also an issue in writing. Writers use a variety of techniques to avoid sexist language, including alternating their use of *he* and *she* or employing the awkward construction *s/he*. Frequently, people use a plural pronoun with a singular antecedent to accomplish this goal — for example, "Someone who wants to avoid sexist language should watch their pronouns." Which method is best, leaving aside the rules of grammar? How might or must language change to accommodate a nonsexist language?

2. What is a hyphen? How is it used? Select a passage of this essay and revise it by adding hyphens. When would you use them in your own writing?

3. Serano claims bodily transformations cross class boundaries. What class boundaries exist in writing? Is slang an issue of class? Can you determine Serano's class from her writing? What class is reflected in academic writing?

Assignments for Writing

1. Serano points out that before-and-after images of physical transformations may be so captivating because they challenge our perception of conventional class boundaries. These images of transformation have been seen in media for years. Think about a television show, documentary, or movie that portrays a transformation. What class boundaries are being crossed? What does this transformation tell us about class values in our culture? Write an essay in which you explore the connection between class and transformation, using Serano and an example of your own. You may want to draw on your work on class from Question 1 of Questions for Critical Reading in making your response.

2. In her essay, Serano points out the many obstacles transsexuals must navigate as well as the threats they face because of conventional ideas concerning gender

and class. Visit the Web site of a national transgender advocacy organization (such as gender.org, nctequality.org, ifge.org, or transgenderlawcenter .org). What issues are being dealt with in the transgender community, and how do these issues illustrate the perception of gender rights in our country? Use Serano's essay and information from your selected site to write a paper in which you examine gender rights in our country today. What rights do such organizations advocate? Are gender rights the same as civil rights?

3. Write a paper in which you use Serano to explore the complex systems through which traditional sex and gender identities are upheld. Using your insights about gender from Question 2 of Questions for Critical Reading, consider what makes gender (and class) natural and what happens when people cross either or both types of boundaries. How are these systems perpetuated, and with what consequences? Why might they be disrupted, and what actions might be taken to do so?

DEBORA L. SPAR

Debora L. Spar is president of Barnard College, a liberal arts college for women in New York City. Previous to her position at Barnard, Spar was the Spangler Family Professor at Harvard Business School. She has consulted for both nongovernmental and governmental organizations as well as for multinational corporations, and she also chairs Making Markets Work, an organization dedicated to leadership development in Africa. Her books include *Cooperative Edge: The Internal Politics of International Cartels* (1994); *Ruling the Waves: Cycles of Discovery, Chaos, and Wealth from the Compass to the Internet* (2001); and *The Baby Business: How Money, Science, and Politics Drive the Commerce of Conception* (2006).

In *The Baby Business,* Spar examines multiple facets of the baby market, ranging from prices and regulations to issues of morality. Reproduction, Spar argues, is a burgeoning industry whose consequences must immediately be considered and whose practices must be governed. The book focuses on the relationships between the economics and technologies of the baby business and the laws of our society.

In "Trading Places: The Practice and Politics of Adoption," a chapter from *The Baby Business*, Spar deals with the concept of "buying" children. As in the other sections of her book, Spar focuses on the ethics of adoption and the role of money in the practice, but she also explains that adoption presents unique differences from other aspects of the baby business, including a thriving black market and contractual agreements between birth and adoptive parents. She details the debates over adoption (particularly international adoption) and the tension between commercial and familial interests.

Globalized economies trouble us little when they lower the prices on goods such as computers, but how should we proceed when the commodity at stake is a human life? At the same time, with children around the world needing parents, how can we ethically meet their needs?

▶ TAGS: *community,* **family***, culture, supply chains,* **human dignity***,* **ethics***, morality*

Trading Places: The Practice and Politics of Adoption

> Do not be afraid, for I am with you; I will bring your
> children from the east and gather you from the west.
>
> —ISAIAH 43:4–6

The home page for Rainbow Kids is designed to rip your heart out. When you log on to the site—www.rainbowkids.com—you instantly see color photographs of beautiful, usually somber-looking children. There are some babies, some older kids. Most are toddlers, clasping toys or sporting huge bows in their hair. All these children are available—waiting, you quickly learn, for their "forever families."

As you scroll farther, you learn how to search: by country, gender, age. The toughest one is "date added," which shows, in reverse order, how long some children have been waiting. On a recent visit, for example, you could find six-year-old Bulat, who had been on the list for three and a half years. "He is described as quiet and gentle," the site reports, "and really enjoys playing sports." Ten-year-old Yamile "likes to write and draw . . . and dreams of being a doctor when she grows up." At precious.org, another adoption photo listing, you can learn about Sofia—"sweet and smart, sparkly and fun, polite and inquisitive"—or Rafael, an "A+ student" who "is dreaming to have a family." All these children, like all the Rainbow Kids, are orphans. And essentially, they are all for sale.

Officially, of course, baby-selling is illegal. The parents who visit Rainbow Kids aren't looking to *buy* their children; they're hoping to adopt them. In practice, though, adoption is indeed a market, particularly in its international dimension. There is a huge and unsatiated demand for children, the same demand that propels would-be parents to seek out fertility clinics and surrogacy brokers. There is a tragically large supply of "waiting" children and a panoply of intermediaries—adoption agencies, social workers, lawyers—that work to match the two sides.

There are prices, too, in the adoption trade, differentiated "fees" that clearly distinguish one child from another. Little Anita from Eastern Europe, for example, is a "sweet, affectionate girl" who suffers from fetal alcohol syndrome. Her adoption fees are reduced. Yi-Wei of Korea, an eleven-year-old boy found abandoned on the street, comes with a $7,500 private grant.

In purely economic terms, Anita and Yi-Wei are only tiny bits of the global baby trade, substitutes for the genetic offspring that would-be parents can't produce through other means. Although some parents choose adoption instead of (or in addition to) old-fashioned reproduction, many wander onto the Rainbow Kids site after they've exhausted all other channels of child production—after, as one mother wrote, "it felt . . . that we could not succeed at becoming parents."[1] In these cases the market for existing children functions as a nearly perfect substitute for the nonexistent ones, for the children who weren't born as a result of AI, IVF,* or sex. As with the more mechanical forms of reproduction, adoption carries an often hefty price tag, ranging from virtually nothing—the cost of adopting a teenager from the U.S. foster system—to more than $35,000, the fully loaded cost for a healthy white Russian infant.

What separates adoption from other aspects of the baby trade, however, is the obvious difference in "product." In assisted reproduction, the parent is purchasing the *potential* of a child, the hope that technological intervention will lead to the live birth of a baby. The producers, meanwhile, are selling eggs and sperm, services and promises, along with the probability that their high-tech tinkering will create a child. In adoption, by contrast, the child already exists. He or she is a little person, shorn of parents but fully equipped with the rights, dreams, and memories of a human being. Accordingly, the politics and practices of adoption are even more complex than those that surround the more mechanical forms of reproduction. It's one thing (and bad enough, some would say) to sell a sperm or an egg. It's quite another to sell a child.

As a result of this distinction, normative views on adoption split sharply into two camps. On one side are those who see adoption as a purely social interaction: It is about building families and rescuing children and assuaging the pain of missing people. In this view, there is no overlap at all

Officially, of course, baby-selling is illegal.

between adoption and commerce, and no notion of putting prices on children. As Adam Pertman, a well-known adoption advocate, puts it, "Any time we put money and human beings in the same sentence, it is a problem: We denigrate the children and we denigrate the process."[2]

From the other side, however, adoption is not only a market but indeed a market of the worst possible sort. It is a market that sells innocent children, putting a price on their heads without any concern for their well-being or for the toll imposed by being treated as trade. Moreover, opponents also charge that the very possibility of adoption, and particularly of international adoption, raises the stakes for poor, pregnant women. If these women know that they can place their children for adoption, and if they can perhaps receive some payment for their labors, they will be tempted or tricked into choosing adoption—to sell their babies for profit, in the harshest version of this critique, and expand an inherently illicit market.[3] Less dramatically, critics of international adoption also argue that it compromises the human rights of the children involved by thrusting them into a cultural context different from their own.[4]

The debates in this field are passionate, with adoptive families and adoption agencies pitted against those who condemn the process. In the United States, the proponents of adoption have tended to win: U.S. families adopt more than a hundred thousand children each year, roughly 15 percent from abroad and nearly all under the confines of a wide-ranging, state-sanctioned system.[5]

---

* AI, IVF: Artificial insemination, in vitro fertilization.

Most adoptive families are screened by licensed social workers, the FBI (Federal Bureau of Investigation), and a local court. Their homes are evaluated; their finances are reviewed; their friends are enlisted to write letters of recommendation. Indeed, adoption in the United States is regulated far more heavily than any other branch of the baby trade. In Europe, where roughly sixteen thousand children were adopted internationally in 2003, adoption is also subject to a plethora of regulatory controls.[6]

   In some respects, the debate over adoption is both small and highly personal. 10
Those who paint adoption as an intimate, admirable, noncommercial activity tend to be either adoptive parents or adoption agencies. Those who scorn it as illicit trade are neither. There is little public attention paid to the world of adoption (aside from the occasional fluff piece or horror story) and little policy overlap with other aspects of the baby business. Yet the questions that surround adoption are both fundamental and far-reaching. Because in adoption, as in surrogacy, IVF, and fertility treatments in general, there is an awkward imbalance between market forces and public perception, between what is happening on the ground and how we choose to describe it.

   One look at Rainbow Kids, for example, suggests that something close to commerce is indeed taking place. The same can be said of the seminars that adoption agencies regularly hold to describe their trade, and the stories of "available children" profiled in glossy magazines. Yet such hints of trade need not imply that adoption is illicit or immoral, or that children are being treated as commodities. Instead, market forces could be exactly what makes adoption work in many cases, what allows a vast supply of children to be matched with the equally vast demand for them. And if a little more commerce were injected into this field, more of the waiting Yamiles and Bulats might leave the world of Rainbow Kids and finally head for home.

Finding Families: The Evolution of Adoption

As a method of acquiring children, adoption has a long and fairly reputable past.[7] Historically, it was the only means by which infertile couples could obtain children, the way for them to salve unmet desires and preserve social goals. Childless couples in ancient Greece, for example, often adopted heirs; in Rome, even couples with children frequently adopted, sometimes selecting more attractive children to displace their genetic offspring. In both of these cases, the underlying motivation was largely economic: Parents needed the right kind of descendant to protect their fortunes and preserve their family name. And if they could not produce these descendants on their own, they simply acquired them elsewhere.

   During the Middle Ages, this economic relationship assumed a slightly different hue. Because European authorities gave greater sway to bloodlines than the Romans had, families moved away from a formal process of adoption, choosing instead to "take in" children from unrelated families. These children — poor, illegitimate, or simply more numerous than their parents could handle — were frequently installed, or "put out," with wealthier folk as apprentices or servants.

Although some of these wards were treated as children, most assumed a considerably lowlier station, toiling in the stables, workshops, or kitchens of their newfound families. They typically remained in these positions until they reached the age of eighteen or twenty-one, when common law returned them to independence.[8] In some parts of Europe, the putting-out system was vibrant enough to encompass most of society's "surplus" children. Putting out didn't work, however, for some of the toughest cases: the infant children of unwed mothers, the bastards of illicit love, or the orphans of famine or war. Many of these children were quietly killed or abandoned.

Across the Atlantic, meanwhile, economic necessity meant that orphans and other "excess" children were regularly assigned either to their extended families or to unrelated families that could use their labor. As early as 1627, for example, fourteen hundred poor or orphaned children were apprenticed directly to the Virginia Company; in 1740, one wealthy Georgia planter took in sixty-one orphans to join his "family" and work his fields.[9] On a smaller scale, individual families simply assumed the care of their orphaned relatives, sometimes using them as economic assets, sometimes treating them as sons or daughters of their own.[10]

This situation—a haphazard combination of economic necessity and informal family ties—prevailed until the middle decades of the nineteenth century, when adoption slowly became more of an arm's-length transaction. The early signs of this transition were subtle. First, adoption cases began cropping up in state courts, usually involving issues of contested inheritance. In 1858, for example, the nieces and nephews of a recently deceased Louisiana man sued to inherit his property, arguing that his adopted daughter had no legal rights to his estate. The state court disagreed, however, and turned to *Webster's Dictionary* to define adoption as "tak[ing] one who is not a child and treat[ing] him as one, giving him a title to the privileges and rights of a child."[11] Accordingly, the court ruled in favor of the adopted daughter and turned her cousins away. Similar language was used in Pennsylvania statutes at around this same time, clarifying the status of an adopted child as a full and lawful heir.[12]

Second, as adoption became an issue of legal concern, state governments began quietly to envelop it in more explicit legislation. Massachusetts passed the first comprehensive adoption statute in 1851, followed in rapid succession by twenty-four other states. Although there was some variation among the adoption acts, they all shared a common and unprecedented characteristic: They made adoption a legal act and subjected the adoption process to the scrutiny of the state. In Massachusetts, for example, the state retained the right to determine whether the proposed parents were "of sufficient ability to bring up the child."[13] In Washington, D.C., congressional statute laid out the means by which adopted children gained the right of inheritance and gave local judges the authority to transfer custody.[14]

As a result of these laws, adoption in the United States became increasingly accepted. Families took orphaned children into their homes and raised them as their own. Children assumed new sets of parents, and the state put contractual relationships—a couple's commitment to raise a particular child—alongside genetic ones. Yet in most cases, adoption was still occurring within the boundaries of the extended family: Parents were adopting children they already knew and orphans with whom they already felt a familial link.

At the same time, though, social changes rippling across the United States were creating a new class of orphans: children who frequently had no family to support them. These were children born to the immigrants flooding into growing cities like Boston, New York, and Chicago. They were children born into urban poverty, children born out of wedlock or to married parents who succumbed to disease or accident or simply the stress of having too many mouths to feed. In earlier eras, these children had been put out by local authorities or collected into public almshouses. By mid-century, however, the increased concentration of poor urban children had overwhelmed the public houses: Most of their charges received minimal care, and many died alone.[15] As word of their plight spread, these public orphans became an obvious focus for mid-century social reformers, a heart-rending example of the ills wrought by immigration, industrialization, and the era's roller-coaster economy.[16]

Early Experiments

Against this dismal backdrop, one might have expected the reformers to embrace adoption as a nearly perfect solution. Thousands of infertile couples, after all, were aching for children and thousands of children were living without homes. Yet the early reformers did not see this match as feasible, because the available children, they felt, were not the "type" who could ever flourish in typical middle-class homes. And so instead of finding homes, they began to construct private children's agencies, philanthropic institutions that would care for orphaned or abandoned children and offer them what the state did not. All the groups that formed these institutions were passionately devoted to the cause of orphaned children. Few, though, saw formal adoption as a viable option.[17]

The most famous of these early advocates was the Children's Aid Society of New York, founded in 1853 by a Protestant minister named Charles Loring Brace. Like others in the reform movement, Brace was appalled by the squalor and poverty he saw expanding from the nation's urban core. He was particularly aghast at New York City's ranks of homeless children—a "society," he wrote, of "irreclaimable little vagabonds"—and firmly convinced that these children could be saved only by removing them from the streets and sending them instead to "God's Reformatory."[18]

To aid in this transformation, Brace established an unprecedented program of orphan trains. For more than fifty years, he and his associates physically took children (orphaned, abandoned, or simply poor) from New York's roughest neighborhoods and loaded them onto trains bound for the Midwest.[19] Upon arrival, the children were doled out to "healthy" Protestant farm families, destined to spend the rest of their childhoods in a status that hovered between adoption and bound servitude.[20]

Brace's trains made very big news. His Children's Aid Society placed an estimated one hundred thousand children and pioneered the practice of long-distance placement.[21] Brace publicized the dire status of many American orphans and turned reform into a large-scale, well-funded activity. To a large extent, Brace's trains proved that children born to "undesirable" parents could grow and even prosper in newfound homes. He proved, in other words, that adoption by strangers could work. And yet his trains also had an unseemly side, one that would haunt American adoption for years to come. Brace, after all, had done little to check the matches that occurred when his charges disembarked. He never embraced the formal side of adoption, or its potential to make families in any way that wasn't purely functional.[22] Critics have also charged that some of Brace's "orphans" weren't orphans at all, but simply poor children, mostly Roman Catholic, who were taken from their homes without consideration of the parents left behind.[23]

Meanwhile, other agencies were clambering after Brace, trying either to emulate his success or to build a better model. Roman Catholic agencies, for example, tried to provide a religious alternative to Brace's devout Protestantism, and Jewish agencies looked after the growing floods of Jewish immigrants. There were agencies devoted to newsboys and "street arabs" and to the steady stream of infants born to unwed mothers.[24] Most of these agencies, however, conformed to the reformers' underlying suspicions about their charges, and thus to the two core solutions that they offered. Either they provided in-house care for the youngest of children, or, like Brace, they strove to rescue older children by putting them out or assigning them to homes in the Midwest.

Few of these children were ever adopted. In fact, during this period most agencies remained opposed to formal adoption, seeing it as an unnatural intrusion into a family built on blood. Adopting one's relatives, they maintained, was perfectly acceptable. So was taking in an extra farmhand or providing temporary foster care to an orphaned toddler. But unrelated children were dangerous baggage, rightful objects of pity, perhaps, but not the stuff of which families were made.[25]

Over time, however, a handful of well-placed intermediaries began to consider more direct options. In large urban centers like New York and Boston, for example, a small circle of upper-class women took it upon themselves to "save" the babies born to unwed mothers.[26] Quietly, they took these children and delivered them to friends or acquaintances looking for a child. These newborns would subsequently be adopted under state law, joining families as if, in common parlance, "they were their own."

Other brokers soon joined the trade as well: hospital nurses, private maternity homes, local court officials. These brokers operated out of commercial interest and beyond the reach of the law.[27] In 1907, a popular women's magazine took this trade one step further, launching a "child rescue campaign" that featured profiles of dependent children and offered them to interested readers. After its very first installment, the magazine received three hundred requests for the two children profiled; it subsequently found homes for nearly two thousand others—"rescued" as one adoptive mother opined, "from miserable lives and disgrace."[28]

The larger agencies, of course, disdained such matches. They fretted about the dangers of hasty or sentimental placements and warned that children born to poor or unmarried women were likely to be scarred for life. As the director of Boston's Bureau of Illegitimacy noted in 1920, "The children of unmarried parents, who doubtless make up a large number of adoptions, may turn out to show an undue proportion of abnormal mentality."[29] The best hope for such children, most agencies insisted, was to educate them outside the family environment and prepare them for a life of labor. But despite the agencies' pleas to this effect, and despite a growing chorus of experts who insisted that heredity did indeed shape destiny, childless couples besieged the few agencies willing to place infants. By 1919 a judge from the Boston probate court publicly announced that "the woods are full of people eager to adopt children—the number appearing to be in the increase."[30]

At this point, therefore, the major child welfare agencies found themselves in a quandary. On the one hand, the agencies truly believed that many of their charges were unsuitable for adoption. They believed that these children needed institutional care and the kind of treatment only professionals were suited to provide. The market, on the other hand, was revealing something very different. Comfortable families wanted these "unadoptable" children so much that they were running to less professional agencies or to shady intermediaries with no standing in the world of child reform. By standing on the sidelines, therefore, the professional agencies were losing ground.

In retrospect, it's difficult to tell whether the agencies' eventual change in attitude was due to shifting mores, better science, or fear of competition from unsavory upstarts. In any case, between roughly 1920 and 1935, most of the country's largest child service organizations began to offer and eventually promote adoption.[31] Although many of the most prominent reformers continued to insist that "bad heredity" put an adopted child at risk, they now reversed this logic, arguing that because adoption was such a risky business, it was best handled by competent professionals—namely, by the social workers who ran and managed the country's child welfare agencies. Accordingly, as these professionals moved into the adoption business, they endorsed, and then helped to enforce, an ostensibly sharp distinction between "licensed" agencies and "independent" providers, between those that were recognized by the state and those that operated apart from its control.

The Evolution of Adoption

Over the next several decades, adoption in the United States became both more regulated and more regular.[32] The U.S. Children's Bureau began to collect and publish statistics regarding adoption practices in the United States, and many states passed adoption statutes of their own, typically focusing on the procedures involved in matching available children with suitable homes. State governments also began to regulate adoption more formally, issuing licenses to approved child-placing agencies and instituting procedures for examining both agencies and parents.[33]

Under Minnesota's 1917 law, for example, prospective parents had to undergo a "social investigation" before being granted custody of a minor child. In Delaware, the law also provided for a two-year probationary period before an adoption could be finalized, and allowed for social workers or other experts to make recommendations to the finalizing court.[34] Note that in both instances—and indeed in nearly all adoption legislation passed during this period—social workers and state-licensed agencies were knit integrally into the adoption process, serving as ostensible guardians for both the child and the state.[35] By contrast, independent practitioners were excluded, relegated to a shadowy area that was generally regarded as baby-selling rather than adoption.

Yet the market, it appears, did not care. Instead, by the 1930s, the soaring demand for babies had bestowed a newfound prominence on independent adoption agencies. Unlike their state-linked peers, these agencies now openly recruited birth mothers, advertised their services to prospective parents, and charged handsomely for their work. They also guaranteed birth mothers that their identities would remain secret, and they often took—and placed—babies who were only weeks old. This relaxed attitude stood in sharp contrast with the rules of most licensed agencies.[36] But it made the private "homes" exceedingly attractive to birth mothers, many of whom wanted to relinquish their infants as quickly and as quietly as they could, and to prospective parents, who wanted children "as young as possible" and generally preferred not to know the mother's identity.[37] By offering something to both sides of the equation, therefore, independent providers could charge for their services and turn adoption into a profitable venture. At the upper end, the going price for a privately placed baby—a little girl, ideally, with blonde hair and blue eyes—was an estimated $1,000 in the 1930s, rising to $5,000 by the 1940s.[38]

Repeatedly, the licensed adoption agencies railed against this trade, arguing that "baby farms" and baby-selling rings harmed the children they served and exploited the parents involved. This they almost certainly did. At one Montreal home, for example, the proprietor regularly took in pregnant women, kept them in squalor, and then transferred their babies—filthy and unfed—to wealthy Americans who were willing to pay.[39] In New York, an attorney named Marcus Siegel placed more than ninety infants for adoption, paying the birth mothers in each case between $1,500 and $2,500 to relinquish their children.[40] Even public reports of such scandals, however, did little to stanch the demand. Instead, as one contemporary article exclaimed, "The baby market is booming. . . . We behold an amazing phenomenon: a country-wide scramble on the part of childless couples to adopt a child."[41] Estimates compiled by the Children's Bureau suggested that roughly half of American adoptions in the 1940s occurred outside the purview of licensed adoption agencies.[42]

So again the agencies were caught. They didn't want to replicate such explicitly commercial practices, because their stated purpose was to serve the child. At the same time, though, they realized that their model was under attack. As a 1937 report by the Children's Welfare League of America woefully put it, "The fact that such a large amount of adoption work is going on beyond the reach of the organized social agencies seems to indicate that in some way we have failed to meet the community's need—why has the stream passed us by?"[43]

It took some time for the agencies to respond to this query, but within a decade they had worked through a compromise of sorts, responding to the market without actually joining it.   35

Publicly, the agencies and their political allies maintained a drumbeat of criticism against the abuses of independent adoption.[44] There were stories in the mainstream media, angry denunciations when scandals broke, and even an eventual congressional investigation. Quietly, however, the agencies also began to change the way they did business. First, they essentially reversed their deep-seated distrust of heredity. Rather than suspect abandoned or illegitimate children of bearing inherently "bad genes," and rather than subject even the tiniest of children to batteries of emotional and intelligence tests, adoption agencies started assuming, for the most part, that their charges were perfectly normal. To

> **But for adoption, the combination of contraception and abortion was disastrous.**

some extent, this change in attitude was part of a larger intellectual shift, a movement away from the rigid view of genetic determinism (or "nature") in favor of environment (or "nurture").[45] But it was also deeply strategic. Because if most children were destined to fare well in their adoptive homes, then agencies no longer had to worry about finding the perfect child for a given couple; they didn't need to place "average" or "inferior" babies only in "average" or "inferior" homes. In other words, by changing their own theories of adoption, agencies were able to expand the pool of potential matches.[46]

A second change focused on the agencies' relationship with young and unmarried mothers. In earlier decades, most licensed agencies had disdained unwed mothers as criminal, feebleminded, or simply bad. Insofar as they concerned themselves with the mothers' welfare, it was typically to urge these young women to keep the children they bore, either because motherhood would redeem the fallen woman or because the bond between mother and child was considered too precious to sunder.

In the aftermath of World War II, however, out-of-wedlock births soared from 88,000 in 1938 to 201,000 by 1958.[47] Illegitimacy no longer carried quite the stigma it once had, and the development of infant formula meant that women could relinquish even tiny babies without necessarily fearing for their health.[48] As a result, mainstream agencies began to deal more directly with pregnant women, in many instances offering them care and counseling as well as a safe place in which to relinquish their child. Arguably, this change in attitude offered unwed mothers a more compassionate alternative.* It also, though, allowed the agencies to expand their rosters of available children, competing head-on with the baby farms that had long sold their services to "women in need."

Finally, during the postwar period the adoption community began to redefine its notion of the adoptable child. No longer obsessed with genetics,

---

*To woo these mothers, increasing numbers of whom came from "good" families, the agencies also began to promise that their identities would be kept secret. It was this move that led, by the 1950s, to the "closing" of most adoption records.

agencies became considerably more open-minded about placing children across religious or cultural lines. They started to place older and handicapped children, and then—slowly and controversially—to encourage adoption across racial lines.[49] As with the agencies' embrace of "bad" genes and unwed mothers, the move to interracial adoption reflected in large part the changing mores of the postwar period: Scientists were debunking eugenic theories, middle-class teens were having sex, and racial divisions were finally starting to soften. But they also allowed the licensed adoption agencies to address the threat of independent adoption. For by expanding their definition of adoptable children, by sheltering unwed mothers, and by placing babies across a broader racial spectrum, the agencies were also engaging in a sensible market realignment, expanding the supply of children to meet the soaring demand.[50] Between 1938 and 1965, the number of adoptions in the United States skyrocketed, from 16,000 a year to 142,000.[51]

Supply-Side Shocks and the Global Search

In retrospect, this period soon proved to be the heyday of domestic adoption 40 in the United States. The postwar years brought a new prosperity to the country and a renewed focus on domestic life. As soldiers returned from war and women left the factories they had staffed during the wartime years, Americans embraced a domestic ideal that nearly always included a working husband, a stay-at-home wife, and a couple of kids running through the suburban yard. Because children were an inherent part of this ideal, childless couples turned to infertility treatments with unprecedented fervor. And when these treatments proved futile or too expensive, they moved rapidly on to adoption.[52] Meanwhile, extramarital relations were also on the rise during this period, leading to more unplanned births and more young women willing to place their children for adoption. For the first time, supply and demand reached a fragile balance, and most infertile couples were eventually able to find children of their own.[53]

In 1955, the U.S. Congress launched its first investigation into the illicit baby trade, eventually finding evidence of an interstate market generating as much as $15 million a year. Aghast, Senator Estes Kefauver (D-TN), who led the investigation, wrote legislation that would make it illegal for any commercial entity to place children across state lines.[54] Only licensed agencies were exempt. But the bill never passed the House of Representatives, in part because several influential representatives knew that their constituents preferred independent adoption.[55]

As a result, U.S. adoption law remained deliberately vague. There were no federal statutes regarding adoption, and no legal distinctions between legitimate and illegitimate practice. Instead, adoption remained almost entirely under the jurisdiction of individual states, most of which maintained a relatively laissez-faire attitude. Adoption was legal in all fifty states; adoptions were finalized before local courts; and prospective parents were generally required to undergo the social investigations imposed in the 1920s. Only a handful of states, however, drew a distinction between licensed adoption agencies and independent practitioners.[56] Elsewhere, a range of intermediaries—lawyers, doctors, brokers—were free to arrange adoptive matches. Baby-selling was explicitly illegal in most states, but few of them bothered to define the limits of associated fees, consulting services, or reimbursement for a mother's pregnancy.[57]

Between roughly 1946 and 1970, therefore, the adoption market in the United States worked relatively well. More than two million children were adopted during this time, through a combination of licensed agencies and independent providers.[58] Although adoption records were increasingly shrouded in secrecy, adoption itself was a fairly public phenomenon, widely accepted as the ideal way of matching children with homes.

Abortion, the Pill, and Adoption

Very quickly, however, this situation dissolved. In 1960, the birth control pill became widely available. Then in 1973, the landmark case of *Roe v. Wade* legalized abortion across the United States. The impact of these events was complicated and sweeping: the liberation of women, the freeing of traditional mores, the separation between procreation and its recreational forms.

But for adoption, the combination of contraception and abortion was disas- 45 trous. First, the mechanics of contraception, along with the sexual freedom they entailed, appear to have contributed to a higher incidence of infertility. Women were waiting longer to bear children, and they were increasing their number of sexual partners, a practice that could lead over time to pelvic inflammatory disease and resulting difficulties with conception. More directly, the availability of safe and legal abortion meant a sharp decline in the number of unplanned births, and thus in the number of infants relinquished for adoption.

Between 1970 and 1975, the number of unrelated adoptions in the United States fell precipitously, from more than 89,000 a year to only 50,000.[59] Young women were having abortions in record numbers and relying increasingly on birth control.[60] Women who did choose to give birth were also deciding more frequently to keep their babies, in part because the ease of abortion meant that proceeding with an unwanted pregnancy had become a conscious, public choice. As one manual explained, "If the girl has decided to have the baby rather than having an abortion, there is a sense that she is obligated to care for the child."[61] Before 1973, 20 percent of white unwed mothers relinquished their infants for adoption; by 1982, only 12 percent of these women made the same choice.[62]

For the first time in the postwar period the supply of available children —particularly healthy white infants—was no longer even close to satisfying the persistent demand. And parents, emboldened now by a generation of relatively easy adoption, were incensed. By 1975, many licensed agencies had stopped accepting applications for healthy white babies, and others informed applicants that the likely waiting time for such a child was three to five years.[63]

As the adoptive market evaporated, frustrated parents began to search for new sources of supply. Some white families pushed to adopt black or biracial children, reigniting a vicious debate about the merits of adoption across racial lines.[64] Some fought for changes in the foster care system, arguing that it kept too many adoptable children in a state of nearly permanent limbo. Most, though, began to look toward the developing world, where the supply of excess children stood sadly undiminished.

Adoptions from Abroad

By this point, a small number of overseas adoptions were already taking place. In the immediate aftermath of World War II, for example, Americans had adopted some of the orphans created by war: some German children, some Greek children, and about fifteen hundred orphaned survivors of Hiroshima and Nagasaki. After these countries stabilized, prospective adopters turned to Korea, where the ravages of civil war had created thousands of orphaned and homeless children.

Between 1953 and 1962, Americans adopted an estimated fifteen thousand children from abroad, creating, for the first time, a considerable population of foreign-born adoptees.[65] They also pushed for subtle changes in the legal structure of adoption, changes that permitted these foreign-born children to enter the United States and eventually become citizens.[66] By 1984, Americans were adopting roughly ninety-five hundred foreign children a year. [67]

The next great wave of international adoptions began in the early 1990s, when the fall of communism opened a vast new supply of available children. In Romania, for example, nearly one hundred thousand babies and toddlers were languishing in horrific orphanages. In China, thousands of infant girls were abandoned each year, left by mothers struggling to comply with their nation's one-child policy.[68] And in Russia, thousands of children were living in state-run baby hospitals or aging children's homes. To their local governments, these children were a political embarrassment, evidence of what communism had not been able to provide. To Western parents, though, they were an odd source of hope—and a new supply of potential adoptees.

The first country to open fully was Romania. In December 1989, the country's brutal dictator, Nicolae Ceauçescu, was executed along with his wife. As camera crews streamed in to film the aftermath, they broadcast haunting pictures of tiny children tied to beds or neglected by their ostensible caregivers.[69] Shocked by these images, international aid agencies rushed into Romania in 1990, followed in short order by parents eager to whisk these children away. Initially, many of these parents were connected to the aid agencies or church groups that had come to volunteer in the country. They hadn't necessarily considered adoption before and were simply responding to the tragedy they saw around them.

As word of their adoptions spread, however, the broader adoption community saw the attractions of Romania: thousands of children in need of homes, fees of only around $2,000, and a legal system that was essentially collapsing. By 1991, a legion of facilitators, brokers, and adoption agencies had descended upon Romania, placing 2,594 children with American families and pushing the cost of a Romanian adoption in some cases to more than $11,000.[70]

At around this time, China and Russia also began to open their orphanages to potential foreign parents. In 1991, China modified laws that had previously forbidden foreigners from adopting; in 1992, Russia established a separate division in its Ministry of Education for foreign adoption and created a database of all potentially adoptable children. With these systems in place, adoption agencies streamed into both countries and children started flowing out. By 1996, Americans alone were adopting more than 2,400 Russian and 3,300 Chinese children each year.[71]

Meanwhile, the agencies that served this global marketplace had also begun to multiply, morphing from the handful of charitable groups that once dominated the field to include a much wider and more diverse set of agencies. By 1999, about eighty U.S. agencies devoted themselves to Russian adoptions, and one hundred fifty had programs in China.[72] Others worked in Vietnam, Guatemala, or Peru; many offered a range of countries from which prospective parents could choose.

All these agencies existed under the hybrid regulatory structure that had grown around international adoption, a structure that essentially vetted parents at both ends of an international transaction. All of them also worked with counterparts in their home countries who handled local regulations and identified available children. Together, these two tiers had come to constitute a vast and growing business in international adoption: In 2003, more than 42,000 children were adopted internationally, 21,616 in the United States alone.[73]

Structure of a Trade

In purely economic terms, adoption is the most rational aspect of the baby trade. There is a vast unmet demand for children and a ready supply of them scattered across the world. By matching demand with supply, adoption would appear to be the ideal solution to infertility, a match of immeasurable value on both sides of the transaction.

Yet the problems with this market are clear. The "buyers" don't *really* want to purchase their babies. The "suppliers" don't want to sell. And governments around the world consistently condemn baby-selling as a crime akin to slavery. But still there are surplus children in the world, and would-be parents who want to adopt them. And so adoption has generated an ersatz market of sorts, a system of structured trades in which the supply of children is channeled to the waiting demand. In this trading system, regulation replaces commerce and prices morph into fees, facilitations, and charity.

Money changes hands in this market-without-a-name, but the money is rarely buying children per se and the system is subject to a labyrinth of formal controls—far more, in fact, than exist in nearly any other sector of the baby business. The system is global and marked by significant national variation, and it sports both a (large) legal sector and a (small) illegal sector. In the United States alone, the adoption system places more than 120,000 children a year, for a cost that typically ranges between zero and $35,000.[74]

These children fall generally into one of three categories: they are older or have special needs, they are healthy newborns, or they are foreign.[75] Although some agencies deal with all three types of adoption, most are increasingly focused on a particular niche.

Domestic Trade

The first of these niches, for older or special-needs kids, resembles most closely the original model of U.S. adoption. The children here are almost entirely the product of the U.S. foster care system; they have been abandoned by their parents or taken from them by law. Sadly, this is the one area of adoption that does not suffer from a lack of supply: On the contrary, there were 534,000 children in the U.S. foster care system as of 2002, roughly 126,000 of whom were formally eligible for adoption.[76] Because these children are legally wards of the state, only state agencies can handle their adoptive placements. And the process typically is exasperating: Parental rights must be legally terminated, extended relatives contacted, and, frequently, racial considerations weighed. In the meantime, the children get older and their needs often increase.[77]

Financially, the market for foster adoption is quite different from that for either newborns or foreign children. First, because the children are wards of the state and are placed by the state, adoptive parents pay nothing. Instead, the state pays foster parents a minimal fee to care for these children until they are adopted or reunited with their birth families. In some cases, the foster parents subsequently decide to adopt their charges, getting, in effect, a free adoption. In economic terms, then, foster adoption is both a purely nonprofit venture for the agencies involved and a relative bargain for adoptive parents.

The second distinction, though, is a much harsher one, a distinction that points unambiguously to the variable price of children. Because the children who come out of foster care are simply not deemed as desirable as others: They are older, often scarred by difficult pasts, and frequently children of color. In 2002, 73 percent of the children in U.S. foster care were over the age of five, and 37 percent were African American.[78] Historically, the demand for these children has been stunted, squeezed initially by social workers who refused to place black children with white parents, and then by parents wary of adopting kids whom most would describe as having special needs.[79]

Between the mid-1980s and the mid-1990s, the number of children adopted each year from the U.S. foster system stayed stubbornly in the range of 17,000 to 21,000, accounting for only about 10 percent of the number available in any given year.[80] In 1997, however, Congress passed the Adoption and Safe Families Act, a legislative package designed to move children more quickly from foster care to adoption.[81] As the act's provisions worked their way through the foster system, adoption rates began to rise: Roughly 46,000 children were placed in adoptive homes in 2000, 47,000 in 2001, and 53,000 in 2002. These numbers suggest that the demand for foster kids is substantially higher than placement figures once indicated and that the market in this area could well increase over time. For now, however, the placement of older and special-needs kids remains quiet and noncommercial, the province of public agencies that tend only to wards of the state.

The market for newborns, by contrast, is more vigorous and commercial. Currently, an estimated twenty thousand to forty thousand U.S.-born infants are placed each year for adoption; the figures vary widely because there is no central reporting mechanism.[82] Nearly all these adoptions are handled privately, with an estimated two-thirds managed by independent (that is, unlicensed) intermediaries.[83] In a typical domestic adoption, the prospective parents pay an up-front adoption fee (usually between $100 and $500) to the agency of their choice. They then pay between $700 and $3,000 to cover the cost of a home study, the social investigation that determines whether the would-be parents are suitable adopters. If a child is found, the parents then pay a placement fee that varies widely—from $6,500, as indicated in Table 1, to more than $50,000. They also generally cover the birth mother's medical expenses and her costs of living during the pregnancy.[84]

What complicates the financial picture of infant adoption is the basic calculus of supply: the understandable fear that the dearth of (healthy white) babies means that a given couple will wait months, or even years, before finding their child. For some people—particularly singles, older couples, or homosexuals—the wait could well prove infinite, because many agencies impose criteria that explicitly work against them. As a result, prospective adopters are increasingly trying to beat the odds, usually through procedures with a decidedly commercial cast.

Some parents, for example, place ads directly in newspapers or college magazines, offering upbeat descriptions of their desire to adopt. "Devoted happily married couple wishes very much to adopt white newborn," states one typical ad. "We will give your baby a warm, loving home with strong family values and financial security." Others troll online, visiting sites such as

TABLE 1 Typical domestic adoption placement fees, 2004

Agency	Adoption fee
Children's Home and Aid Society of Illinois www.chasi.org	15% of income (minimum of $10,000 and maximum of $25,000)
Beacon House Adoption Service (Florida) www.beaconhouseadoption.com	$10,000 placement fee, $2,500 advertising fee
Adoptions from the Heart (New Jersey) www.adoptionsfromtheheart.org	$18,000
Christian Child Placement Services (New Mexico) www.nmcch.org	$12,000
Jewish Family Service, Inc. (Tennessee) www.jewishfamilyservicememphis.org	$15,000
American Adoptions (Kansas) www.americanadoptions.com	$12,000–$19,000 (African American or biracial) $20,000–$25,000 (traditional, Caucasian) $27,000–$35,000 (traditional, expedited)
Family Service Agency (Arizona) www.fsaphoenix.org	20% of gross income; minimum $6,500
Adoption Services (Pennsylvania) www.adoptionservices.org	$40,000–$52,000

Source: Agency Web sites.

www.adoptionnetwork.com or www.parentprofiles.com, where they join lists of waiting families and broadcast their credentials to potential birth mothers. "We have visions of a life that includes late nights reading books," writes one earnest couple, "eating ice cream on hot summer days, finger painting at the kitchen table and snowball fights."

Many couples also work with adoption attorneys or independent brokers, who endeavor to link them directly with birth parents.[85] In a typical case, the couple provides the broker with a file of materials about themselves and their desired child. The broker then presents these materials to a birth mother, allowing her to choose from several prospective families. In the interim, the broker frequently coaches families through the art of presentation, advising them, for example, about what color of paper to use or what kinds of photos to select.[86] Most brokers charge separately for these services, applying an hourly rate of $200 to $350.[87]

Open Adoption

Recently, some brokers and independent adoption agencies have also begun to offer a more radical version of adoption, one that arguably takes the matching of unrelated families to its logical extreme. In "open adoption," the birth mother (and occasionally the birth father) chooses the child's parents in person. Birth parents submit their personal information to a broker who specializes in open services; they review the binders and photographs of potential parents that the broker provides for them; and then they typically meet with the couples they've selected, ensuring that the fit is right. In this process, the historical veil of secrecy is almost completely removed: The adoptive parents know the birth parents, the birth parents actually choose the adoptive parents, and the child is fully informed about the details of his or her origins.

This level of transparency, according to the proponents of open adoption, ensures that the old stigmas of adoption are forever discarded. In theory, the child never has to search for his or her identity, and the birth mother is spared the lifelong burden of wondering what became of her child.[88]

All this may well be true. At a commercial level, however, open adoption also rearranges the fundamental patterns of business. In standard adoption, the adoptive parents are always the "buyers." They are the ones who historically have searched for available children, the ones who pay intermediaries to find and acquire a child. In open adoption, the adoptive parents still pay for the process, but only after the birth parents have found and selected them. It is the birth parents, then, who engage in the initial round of "buying," assuming most of the functions that once belonged solely to the agencies themselves.

In open adoption, in other words, it is the birth parents who select from the dozens of couples clamoring for their child. As a result, the agencies are thrust into a very different role: mediating transactions rather than making them. Not surprisingly, then, the largest players in open adoption are not traditional agencies, but rather a growing hodgepodge of lawyers and well-connected brokers, people who have begun to specialize in the niche of matching, not babies and parents, but birth parents and their adoptive successors.

As of 2004, the typical cost of an infant adoption in the United States ranged between $10,000 and $40,000.[89] In a handful of cases, prices as high as $100,000 were reported.[90]

International Trade

The third major segment of the adoption industry consists of cross-border trans-actions, the placement of children from one country into families in another. Once a tiny sliver of the baby business, international adoption has rapidly be-come a major enterprise, accounting for roughly 15 percent of total nonrelative adoptions in the United States.[91]

Three aspects of international adoption differentiate it from its domestic counterpart. First, because the children are moved across international bor-ders, the legal regime is proportionately more complex. International adoptions effectively happen twice: once in the country of the child's origin, and again in his or her new home.

Second, internationally adopted children are by definition more diverse than their counterparts in any single country. They come in many colors, from many cultures, speaking a range of languages. Accordingly, they raise a host of social issues that rarely occur with domestic adoption and create a more dif-ferentiated market.

Finally, because these children almost always come from poorer countries, their adoption raises a heightened concern about exploitation and human trade. Some see the flow of foreign-born children as a combination of humanitarian-ism and family-building. But for others, it is simply trafficking in lives.

Legally, the regime for cross-border adoption is vast and sophisticated. It encompasses the major child-importing and -exporting nations and is embed-ded in a formal international treaty known as the Hague Convention.[92] Under the convention's terms, both sending and receiving countries are required to establish a central authority governing adoption, an authority that provides protection for the children involved, tracks and reviews prospective parents, and ensures that no baby-selling occurs.[93]

In commercial terms, compliance with the Hague makes international adoption a fairly cumbersome procedure. Would-be parents need to undergo a home study (as they would with domestic adoption), an immigration clearance and FBI background check, and whatever requirements are imposed by author-ities in the child's home country. They typically must provide police reports and medical records and then have all the documents notarized and translated. The paperwork is mammoth, as are the opportunities for error.

As a result, the incentives for independent adoption are considerably reduced. Most would-be parents in the United States rely on licensed agencies to handle overseas adoptions, and agencies have considerable leeway in pricing their for-eign packages. Typically, they charge an application fee, a home study fee, and a program fee. Overseas charges are figured separately and generally include a set "donation" to the child's orphanage or baby home in addition to fees to the agency's local facilitator, driver, and interpreters. In exchange for these fees, most agencies can provide prospective parents with a child of their choice, usually within a year.

In international adoption, however, the notion of choice is complicated by the variety available. In domestic adoption, after all, supply essentially controls demand: There are so few (healthy white) babies that parents almost never choose among them. In assisted reproduction, choice is a factor of the components available: the egg, sperm, womb, and embryo that will mix together in an unpredictable way. Parents can choose the basic physical characteristics their child is likely to inherit, but they cannot pick a particular kid. With international adoption, however, choice is simultaneously multiplied and made concrete. When parents adopt abroad, they are almost always choosing to adopt a child who is already born.* They are adopting a particular child, in other words, and one who usually is old enough to have displayed both physical characteristics and a certain personality type. In international adoption, therefore, much more so than in domestic infant adoption or assisted reproduction, parents are literally choosing their child.

This process of selection is deeply embedded in the structure of international adoption. To begin with, parents choose the country from which they would like to adopt. For U.S. adopters, this means choosing from thirty-nine possible nations, ranging, as of 2005, from Belarus to Vietnam. All these countries have available children, but the options they offer are different. In China, for example, nearly all the available children are girls, typically between the ages of ten months and seventeen months. In Russia, there are boys and girls, with some infants and a huge supply of older, institutionalized children. In Guatemala, most of the children are very young, subtly classified as either "Latino" or "Mayan."

When parents choose a country, then, they are also choosing a particular type of child. In many cases, they are also choosing a particular price structure, one that implicitly reveals preferences as well. For example, white children are almost always more expensive than black ones; as Table 2 indicates, the typical cost of adopting a (white) Russian child in 2004 (in addition to travel costs and agency fees) was about $15,000, whereas the cost of a (black) child from Ethiopia was between $6,700 and $8,000. Children of other colors fall somewhere in the middle, ranging from about $6,000 for a Filipino child to about $7,000 for a Chinese and $8,900 for a Colombian.[94] Guatemala stands as a bit of a pricey exception, because children in this heavily Roman Catholic country are frequently placed directly after birth and birth mothers are commonly assumed to be "good girls" forced by cultural constraints to relinquish any child born out of wedlock. Costs also vary sharply by age and degree of handicap. In Russia, for example, the cost of adopting an infant through one prominent agency is $7,000 more than the cost of adopting a school-age child. Handicapped children are frequently offered with some kind of "scholarship" or financial assistance.

At the level of the individual child, meanwhile, international adoption also offers a sometimes shocking array of choices. When parents begin the adoptive

---

*There are some exceptions. In Guatemala, for example, parents occasionally identify a pregnant woman and agree to adopt her child.

TABLE 2 Sample foreign adoption fees, 2004

Agency	Application and agency fees	Program fee: Russia	Program fee: Guatemala	Program fee: China	Program fee: India	Program fee: Ethiopia
Wide Horizons for Children	$5,700	$15,000	$18,240	$7,165	$5,000	$6,700
Holt International	$2,995	NA	$8,690	$9,360	$8,190 (healthy) $5,325 (with health needs)	NA
Angels' Haven	$4,500	$11,000	$17,500	$6,000	NA	$8,000
MAPS International	$2,000	$15,650	$19,000	$12,250	$14,500	NA
Families Thru International Adoption	$4,800	$13,978	$19,000	$3,000	$12,000	NA
Commonwealth Adoptions	$200	$17,000	$26,900	$12,000	$12,000	NA

Sources: Agency Web sites (www.whfc.org; www.holtintl.org; www.angelshaven.org; www.mapsadopt.org, www.ftia.org; www.commonwealthadoption.org) and conversations with author.

process, they usually inform their selected agency of their preferences: whether they want an infant or a younger child, a girl or a boy. They describe the kind of child they feel competent to parent and the kind of family they are hoping to build. Sometimes, the selection ends there. The agency works with its counterpart in the chosen country, identifies a child, and presents him to the prospective parents, usually in the form of a photograph or short video. The parents can choose to accept the child (most do) or wait for a second referral. In other cases, however, parents play a much more active role in the selection process. They actually choose a particular child—from photos or in person—and then begin the process of adopting her.

The most extreme examples of such selection are the online photo listings mentioned earlier. On Web sites like Rainbow Kids or precious.org, agencies regularly list their available charges, organized by country, gender, or age. At any given time, the lists may contain as many as five hundred kids, all of whom are officially eligible for adoption. Many agencies also have their own online lists of waiting children, complete with photos and brief, often heart-wrenching descriptions. Interested parents are urged to contact the agency for more information and to begin the process that will "bring their child home." Although precise numbers are not available, the director of Rainbow Kids estimates that more than six thousand children have been adopted since 1997 from her site alone.[95] Hundreds more are adopted each year through various summer camps or hosting programs that bring older children to the United States to meet prospective families.

There are several ways of viewing these selective arrangements. On the one hand, photo listings and summer camps provide a crucial matching function. They relay information about some of the world's hardest-to-place children: older kids, sibling groups, and babies born with handicaps. They get this information to a wide group of prospective parents, enabling them to find—or pick—their particular child.[96] On the other hand, critics note that such arrangements operate uncomfortably like global bazaars, with well-heeled customers choosing merchandise from a glossy and sentimental catalog.

This brings us to the third distinguishing facet of cross-border adoption. In families that are forged between the first and third worlds it is consistently the parents who come from the wealthier states and the children who migrate out of poverty. It is the poor states that produce children, and the rich that consume them. In the process, poor parents are left behind, serving only as the initial fabricators of other people's children.

This essential equation has caused critics to cast international adoption in a particularly evil light: as a commercial process that both thrives off global poverty and perpetuates it. As Twila Perry, an American legal scholar, argues, "The imbalance in the circumstances . . . involved in international adoption presents a troubling dilemma: In a sense, the access of affluent white Western women to children of color for adoption is often dependent upon the continued desperate circumstances of women in third world nations."[97] Similarly, feminist critics like Janice Raymond assert that international adoption involves trafficking in *both* women and children; like surrogacy, she writes, adoption "encourages *throw-away women* who are discarded after fulfilling their breeding role."[98]

Such criticism, of course, rankles adoption proponents, who insist that international adoption has nothing to do with exploitation or global inequities.[99] Instead it is humanitarianism of the most intimate sort, humanitarianism that literally transplants some of the world's poorest and most vulnerable inhabitants into the homes and hearts of the most privileged. Through international adoption, supporters insist, surplus children are delivered to parents who want them, and surplus capital (via local fees and donations) flows to impoverished states.[100]

And so they do. Yet the claim that international adoption is a virtuous market does not negate the fact that it is nevertheless a market. Adoption agencies hold regular seminars to describe their trade. They list their children online (in some cases) and profile them in glossy magazines. They also charge clearly differentiated prices. It's hard to argue that this isn't commerce, because it is.

The Black Market

It is in the final tier of the baby market, however, that commerce becomes most explicit and extreme. This is the part of the market in which adoption agencies are replaced by baby brokers and money unabashedly changes hands. This is the unsavory but persistent realm of black market babies, a realm populated by infamous intermediaries like Georgia Tann of the Tennessee Children's Home Society, who placed more than one thousand children between 1930 and 1950 and personally reaped more than $1 million in profit. Or Ron Silverton, a California attorney indicted in 1974 for arranging unauthorized adoptions and attempting to sell a person.[101]

It is a world that has recently gone global, too, as evidenced by well-publicized stories of brokers who place attractive children with eager parents and profit handsomely from the exchange.[102] It is difficult to estimate how large this illicit market is or how deeply it affects the broader flow of adoption. In 1975, a congressional hearing estimated that more than five thousand babies were sold each year in the United States, for prices that ranged between $10,000 and $15,000.[103] Today, industry experts estimate that less than 1 percent of domestic adoptions go through implicitly illegal channels, as do perhaps 5 percent of international adoptions.[104] Accusations vary widely across exporting countries, with a handful—Cambodia, Vietnam, India, Guatemala—accounting for the bulk of alleged illegal activity.

Defining this black market, though, is tricky, because nearly all adoptions (aside from those in the foster care system) involve some transfer of money. Indeed, it is this very transfer of money that makes adoption's critics quick to deride it. But black market adoptions have a distinctive set of characteristics, a pattern of trade and behavior that sets them sharply, if subtly, apart.

First, black market adoptions occur by definition outside the boundaries of licensed trade. They are conducted by independent brokers or unlicensed intermediaries who cater exclusively to parents' demands and don't perform the home studies required by state law. The prices involved are often secretive, and key documents are frequently forged. Legitimate adoption is a hugely transparent procedure, involving social workers, judges, and local recording clerks. Black market adoption, by contrast, is quiet and covert, which helps to explain its persistent appeal.

Second, in black market adoption, the prohibition on payment breaks down. Instead of covering only the birth mother's costs for pregnancy and childbirth, baby brokers pay extra, "reimbursing" the mother for relinquishing her child. The monies involved here may be minimal—$180 for a Cambodian infant, according to a 2002 scandal, $20 for an Indian girl—but the principle is key.[105] Under legitimate circumstances, mothers relinquish their children because they cannot, or choose not to, raise them by themselves. These mothers either place their newborns through a court-sanctioned process (the norm in U.S. domestic adoption) or leave them quietly in a baby hospital or public marketplace (the typical route in China). Sometimes, mothers are also judged incapable of parenting and are forced to cede their children to the state. This is a common pattern for children placed in the U.S. foster care system and for many so-called

95

Russian "orphans." Note, however, that none of the relinquishing mothers in these cases was *paid* to place her children. In black market adoption, by contrast, the transaction is explicitly commercial: A mother (or occasionally a father) receives money in exchange for the child.

A third characteristic of black market adoption takes this phenomenon to its logical and egregious extreme. Once children are explicitly purchased and their sale occurs outside formal and transparent channels, it is only a small step toward the outright theft and subsequent resale of children. Thankfully, such cases are rare.[106] But they do occur. In 2001, for example, the United States suspended adoptions from Cambodia, citing allegations of both baby-selling and baby-stealing.[107]

These horrific examples constitute only a tiny fraction of the overall adoptive market. Yet because the extreme end of adoption is so sinister and because even legitimate adoption entails a fair measure of commerce, it is easy to conflate adoption with theft, and for critics to paint all adoptions as thinly veiled versions of baby-selling. As one critic writes, "Adoption in America today is a lucrative industry operating on greed and exploitation, with white babies its precious commodity and prices determined by desperation. Those in the white-baby business are no longer philanthropic individuals . . . but a small group of private entrepreneurs, dealers, and middlemen who have turned a placement into a deal."[108]

What complicates matters even further is that the legal distinction between legitimate and illegitimate adoption is not clear. Following state law, for example, any birth mother can legally arrange for her own child's adoption. In theory, this provision simply allows mothers to decide what is best for their children. In practice, though, it creates a massive loophole: As long as the birth mother agrees, any adoption is technically legal. And any intermediary who "helped" the birth mother or the adoptive parents can reasonably claim to have provided counseling services, legal advice, or any other innocuous service that is difficult to define as illegal. As a result, very few Americans have ever been convicted of baby-selling.[109] Laws are somewhat tighter in Europe, where all the major countries have ratified the Hague Convention and many have laws that explicitly ban baby-selling or child trafficking. Still, even with the toughest legal regime, it remains difficult to determine the provenance of an adopted child or the circumstances that surrounded his or her adoption.[110]

Black market adoption *is* different from legitimate adoption. It occurs furtively and often with forged documents; it involves payment for the child herself; and it occasionally descends into the realm of either kidnapping or theft. But these distinctions are not always obvious, and wily brokers can squeeze rather easily through the loopholes of the law. Moreover, even though legitimate adoption providers despise the black market and the shadow it casts upon all adoption, the legitimate market is itself sharply divided: between public agencies and private, between faith-based nonprofits and independent attorneys. These entities do not like to admit that they are competing among themselves, but they are.

And the terms of competition make it even more difficult to establish any lines. Because if all payment were banished from the world of adoption—a policy often espoused by adoption's foes—then all adoptions would revert to state-run agencies, putting even licensed providers out of business. Similarly, if it were illegal to transport any adopted child across state or national boundaries (another frequent proposal), then scores of intermediaries would lose their commercial niche. In the process, market efficiencies would also vanish, because state-run agencies cannot provide the speed and service of their private counterparts, and state-specific adoption would mean segregating thousands of children far from the parents most likely to adopt them.

This brings us to the central question posed by black market adoption, and indeed by adoption in general. Most people agree that it is inherently wrong to sell a child, that we can never treat babies or the parents who produced them as marketplace commodities.[111] But does this moral prohibition imply that we can never transfer children from one set of parents to another? That we can never allow any form of payment to enter into such a transfer? Does our revulsion for the black market in babies mean that parents can never pay an intermediary to get Yamile or Bulat off the Rainbow Kids list and into their homes? In the contemporary world, adoption undeniably operates as a market. The question is whether this market is necessarily bad.

Selling Souls or Saving Lives? Prospects for the Adoption Market

If one looks at adoption by itself, it's tempting to say yes across the board, to say that money should never enter the relationship between parent and child.[112] It is certainly plausible to suggest that adoption be taken out of private hands and returned fully to governments. It is possible to express deep sympathy for Yamile's and Bulat's plight while still arguing against their adoption. Indeed, on moral grounds, one can argue that the prohibition against selling children is so deep and so crucial that nothing—not even the fate of these children themselves—can violate it.[113]

If one sees adoption as part of a broader baby trade, however, such sweeping pronouncements are more difficult to make. Clearly, profits are being made in other parts of the trade: in infertility treatments, in sperm sales, in surrogacy. By what logic can we argue that the Fertility Institute of Las Vegas can charge its clients $44,800 for a gestational surrogate cycle, but Angels' Haven can't charge $8,000 to place a war orphan from Ethiopia?

Perhaps one can draw a hard and fast line at the child himself, distinguishing between the components of conception and the *product* of that conception. In other words, one can say that from the moment the child is born, he or she can no longer be traded or treated as part of a market transaction. This is a legitimate position. It also, however, often runs contrary to the interests of the child at hand. Because it takes money to bring a little boy from Sierra Leone to Milwaukee; it takes money to care for that little boy in a local orphanage and to ensure that his prospective parents can raise him in an appropriate manner. If this money does not change hands—if, in other words, the market for international adoption were to disappear—that little boy would almost certainly spend his childhood in an institution and without a family.[114] And only a tiny handful of sociologists and child welfare advocates would still maintain that any child is better served by institutional life.[115]

Alternatively, one could allow the transaction to occur but insist that it remain apart from any market influence. Practically, such a position would mean ceding adoption entirely to the state. It would mean expending state resources and replacing market structures with government bureaucracies. This kind of system is eminently possible; indeed, government agencies control the adoption process in most exporting countries (China, Russia, Guatemala, Peru) and several importing ones (the Netherlands, Australia).

In the United States, however, state-based adoption would clash head-on with a deeply seated preference for choice. It would thrust family-making into bureaucratic hands and would likely engender the kinds of delays and inefficiencies that currently cloud the foster system. In the United States, moreover, a state-based adoption system would stand in even sharper contrast with other elements of the baby market. In Australia, after all, adoption sits closer to the state, but so do IVF, egg donation, and surrogacy. If the United States were somehow to bring adoption out of the market entirely, it would mean creating a sharp dichotomy between reproductive options that can be purchased (eggs, embryos, PGD,* IVF) and those that cannot. It would mean, in practical terms, allowing the rich to purchase procreation while pushing the poor to adopt.

Such a system is indeed possible, and if we take the moment of conception as a clear dividing line then it may be the best we can do. But taking adoption out of the market would lessen the efficiencies that now exist. It would reduce the number of children available for adoption and increase the amount of time involved. It would also impose older-era guidelines on parenting, leaving government agencies to determine who is suitable to form a family, and how.

Once again, the trade-offs of such a system become most evident when compared to other means of baby-making. At a societal level, adoption almost certainly provides a better option than assisted reproduction. It draws upon the existing supply of children rather than creates new ones. It conserves financial resources that would otherwise be spent on foster care or institutional arrangements, and it avoids the cost of new, higher-tech children.

Admittedly, one wouldn't want childless couples to bear sole responsibility — or indeed any real responsibility — for solving the problem of parentless children.[116] By the same token, though, it also seems foolhardy to put adoption at a relative *disadvantage* to assisted reproduction. If we let people donate eggs and sperm and embryos, how can we insist that infants be handed to the state? If we let an unmarried fifty-two-year-old woman pay $100,000 for the IVF treatment that will provide her with newborn twins, why should we prevent that same woman from paying, say, $25,000 to adopt Sofia or Rafael?[117]

The funny thing about the adoption market is that it works. It doesn't work in every case, of course, and it works better for some kids and parents than

---

*PGD: Preimplantation Genetic Diagnosis.

others. Yet the history of adoption provides a surprisingly consistent picture of success. Whether they adopt through public agencies or private, through friends or foreign lawyers, and whether they adopt infants who look "just like them" or distant toddlers of a different race, most adoptive parents subsequently assess their experiences in rather glowing terms.[118] They embrace their adopted children as theirs and don't seem to harbor any lingering doubts about the nature of the original transaction. The only prevalent complaints revolve around shortages and bureaucratic delays: too few children, too much red tape.

For adopted children and birth parents, the picture is murkier, but not for reasons that relate directly to commerce. Some limited evidence suggests, for example, that adult adoptees resent the transactions that surrounded their placement.[119] Some studies argue that adoptees bear the lingering pain of their birth mother's "rejection" or that they face a lifelong quest to discover their genetic origins.[120] Most adoption experts currently argue that open adoption is better than closed and that adoptees have a right to know the circumstances of their birth.[121] None of these complaints, however, has anything to do with the *business* of adoption. On the contrary, critics reserve their sharpest bile for the old model of state-based or licensed agency adoption, where all transactions were secret and power rested with a handful of social workers.

Similar complaints are voiced by, or on behalf of, birth mothers, now commonly regarded as the most vulnerable element in the adoption triad. During adoption's heyday in the middle of the twentieth century, birth mothers were routinely denied any say in their child's destiny, or even their own. They were routed into unsavory maternity homes by parents or boyfriends, where their children were frequently taken before they even awoke after the birth. For many birth mothers, placing their child for adoption remains a harrowing memory, a loss from which they never fully recover.[122]

Yet again, the tragedy of adoption in these cases has little or nothing to do with the market. Women didn't relinquish their children in the 1950s and 1960s because they had a financial incentive to do so; they relinquished them because they didn't have the means or social standing to raise them on their own. Circumstances changed somewhat after the advent of birth control and abortion, because the sudden dearth of adoptable infants made brokers more willing to offer enticements, and birth mothers more ready to accept them. A far more important change, though, was that birth mothers began to exercise choice and discretion, deciding whether to place their children and, increasingly, with whom.

Again, therefore, the introduction of market forces actually enhanced the options that birth mothers faced. At the extreme, as noted earlier, market forces have put birth mothers into the buyer's position, enabling them, literally, to select from a catalog of potential parents. Such options do not imply that the decision to relinquish a child has become easy, or that birth mothers see their choices as representing some kind of pleasant parental supermarket. By the same token, though, it is difficult to argue that market forces have worsened the plight of birth parents.

Those who do advance accusations along these lines generally focus on 115
the less-developed world, where, they contend, women are coerced by their
own poverty to relinquish children they would prefer to raise.[123] But again, it
is hard to blame the market for *causing* these women's undeniable pain, or to
believe that halting cross-border adoption would do anything to alleviate their
situation. Instead, the adoption market sends capital flowing in precisely the
direction that adoption's opponents desire: from rich countries to poor, from
wealthy parents to abandoned, neglected, or relinquished kids.

The market for adoption isn't always pretty. There are children who come
from abusive backgrounds and never recover. There are children who yearn
for their genetic origins or cultural roots, children who ache for an identity
that eludes them. There are children who go to bad homes, and children, like
Anita and Yi-Wei, who may never find homes. It is tempting in this market to
focus on the nasty underside and on the abusive practices that will always scar
adoption's edges.

But setting adoption within the larger baby business presents a starkly different view. For there are children created by IVF who will also grow up to be
abused, children born by sperm or egg donation who will also eventually yearn
for their own genetic roots. All these children are also created through market
transactions, none of which operate under the regulatory apparatus that has
long hovered over adoption.

In fact, the U.S. adoption market—clunky and cumbersome as it may
be—could even offer a model of how a modified baby business might function.
It is a model where money undeniably changes hands, and where some intermediaries profit from transacting in children. Yet it is also a market that combines a relatively small for-profit segment with a much larger nonprofit one. It
is a market where government agencies provide oversight and regulation, and
private entities compete to provide service. It is a market where parents have to
prove that they are suited to parent, but also where most parents—be they gay
or straight, single or married, rich or working class—can hope to find "their"
child. And it is a market that essentially works.

In September 2005, just before this book went to press, I returned to the Rainbow
Kids and precious.org sites to check on the children I had chosen at random some
nine months before. Bulat had found his forever family. Yamile, Sofia, and Rafael
were still waiting.

NOTES

1. From a post at www.frua.org, a chat room for parents interested in adopting
   from Russia and Ukraine.
2. Quoted on "Internet Adoptions," *CNN: The Point with Greta Van Susteren,*
   January 22, 2001.
3. For critiques along these lines, see, for example, Jacqueline Bhabha, "Moving
   Babies: Globalization, Markets, and Transnational Adoption," *Fletcher Forum
   of World Affairs* 28 (Summer 2004): 181–96; Anne L. Babb, *Ethics in American
   Adoption* (Westport, CT: Bergin & Garvey, 1999); and Christine Gailey, "Seeking

'Baby Right': Race, Class, and Gender in US International Adoption," in *Yours, Mine, Ours . . . and Theirs: International Adoption*, eds. Anne-Lise Rygvold et al. (Oslo: University of Oslo, 2000).

4. See Drucilla Cornell, *At the Heart of Freedom: Feminism, Sex and Equality* (Princeton, NJ: Princeton University Press, 1998); and Emma Nicholson, "Red Light on Human Traffic," *Guardian Unlimited*, July 1, 2004, available at www.guardian.co.uk/child/story/0,7369,1250908,00.html. For a critical response, see Carra E. Greenberg and Diane B. Kunz, "Enemies of Intercountry Adoption," mimeo, Center for Adoption Policy, 2005.

5. Adoption data are surprisingly difficult to find, since they are no longer collected in the United States by a single organization. For recent statistics, see National Adoption Information Clearinghouse, "How Many Children Were Adopted in 2000 and 2001?" (Washington, DC: National Adoption Information Clearinghouse, August 2004).

6. Peter Selman, "Trends in Intercountry Adoption 1998–2003: A Review of Recent Statistics for Receiving States," Adoption Working Paper 1, School of Geography, Politics and Sociology, University of Newcastle upon Tyne, work in progress, March 22, 2005.

7. For descriptions of adoption's long history, see E. Wayne Carp, *Family Matters: Secrecy and Disclosure in the History of Adoption* (Cambridge, MA: Harvard University Press, 1998); Leo Albert Huard, "The Law of Adoption: Ancient and Modern," *Vanderbilt Law Review* 9 (1956): 743–63; and Stephen B. Presser, "The Historical Background of the American Law of Adoption," *Journal of Family Law* 11 (1971): 443–516.

8. For more on the apprentice system, see Philippe Ariès, *Centuries of Childhood*, trans. Robert Baldick (London: Pimlico, 1996).

9. Arthur Wallace Calhoun, *A Social History of the American Family from Colonial Times to the Present* (New York: Arno Press, 1973), 306–7, 232.

10. See the description in John Demos, *A Little Commonwealth: Family Life in Plymouth County* (New York: Oxford University Press, 1970), 73–75; see also Margaret Marsh and Wanda Ronner, *The Empty Cradle: Infertility in America from Colonial Times to the Present* (Baltimore: Johns Hopkins University Press, 1996), 17–20.

11. *Vidal v. Commagere*, 13 La. Ann. 516 (1858). Cited in Presser, "Historical Background of the American Law of Adoption," 461.

12. See the discussion in Presser, "Historical Background of the American Law of Adoption," 463–64.

13. "An Act to Provide for the Adoption of Children," Acts and Resolves passed by the General Court of Massachusetts, Chapter 324 (1851).

14. Julie Berebitsky, *Like Our Very Own: Adoption and the Changing Culture of Motherhood, 1851–1950* (Lawrence: University Press of Kansas, 2000), 23. For other state laws during this period, see William H. Whitmore, *The Law of Adoption in the United States and Especially Massachusetts* (Albany, NY: Joel Munsell, 1876), 79–83; and Jamil S. Zainaldin, "The Emergence of a Modern American Family Law: Child Custody, Adoption, and the Courts, 1796–1851," *Northwestern University Law Review* 73, no. 6 (1979): 1038–89.

15. In 1849, for example, Folks reports the following statistics for one New York public almshouse: "514 children were cared for . . . 280 died." See Homer Folks, *The Care of Destitute, Neglected and Delinquent Children* (New York: Macmillan Co., 1902), 21; see also Peter C. English, "Pediatrics and the Unwanted Child in History: Foundling Homes, Disease and the Origins of Foster Care in New York City, 1860–1920," *Pediatrics* 73 (1984): 699–711.

16. For more on the movement to reform orphanages and the care of abandoned children, see David M. Rothman, *The Discovery of the Asylum: Social Order and Disorder in the New Republic* (Boston: Little, Brown, 1971), especially 206–36; and William I. Trattner, *From Poor Law to Welfare State: A History of Social Welfare in America*, 5th ed. (New York: Free Press, 1994), 112–27.

17. For example, in the first forty-five years of operation, the Boston Female Asylum, an orphanage in Boston, placed only 4.9 percent of its charges for adoption. See Susan Lynne Porter, "The Benevolent Asylum—Image and Reality: The Care and Training of Female Orphans in Boston, 1800–1840" (Ph.D. diss., Boston University, 1984). See also E. Wayne Carp, "Orphanages vs. Adoption: The Triumph of Biological Kinship, 1800–1933," in *With Us Always: A History of Private Charity and Public Welfare*, eds. Donald T. Chritchlow and Charles H. Parker (New York: Rowman & Littlefield Publishers, Inc., 1998), 123–44; and Peter Romanofsky, "The Early History of Adoption Practices, 1870–1930" (Ph.D. diss., University of Missouri at Columbia, 1969). Some charitable institutions did rely on adoption, but they were few in number and generally under attack. See Marsh and Ronner, *The Empty Cradle*, 106–7.

18. From Charles Loring Brace, *The Dangerous Classes of New York*, quoted in Miriam Z. Langsam, *Children West: A History of the Placing-Out System of the New York Children's Aid Society, 1853–1890* (Madison: State Historical Society of Wisconsin, 1964), v.

19. The bulk of the orphan trains ran from 1854 to 1904, although a handful traveled as late as 1929. See Burton Z. Sokoloff, "Antecedents of American Adoption," *Adoption* 3, no. 1 (Spring 1993): 20.

20. For more on Brace and the orphan trains, see also Marilyn Irvin Holt, *The Orphan Trains: Placing Out in America* (Lincoln: University of Nebraska Press, 1992); Langsam, *Children West*; and Henry Thurston, *The Dependent Child: A Story of Changing Aims and Methods in the Care of Dependent Children* (New York: Columbia University Press, 1930).

21. Sokoloff, "Antecedents of American Adoption," 20.

22. Brace himself argued that "very many" of his charges were adopted. Yet the historical record strongly suggests otherwise. See Joan Heifetz Hollinger, "Introduction to Adoption Law and Practice," in *Adoption Law and Practice*, ed. Hollinger (New York: Matthew Bender & Co., Inc., 1991), 1–32. For Brace's account, see Charles L. Brace, "The 'Placing Out' Plan for Homeless and Vagrant Children," *Proceedings of the Conference of Charities and Correction* (Albany, NY: Joel Munsell, 1876), 140.

23. See the discussion in Carp, *Family Matters*, 10–11; Bruce Bellingham, "Institution and Family: An Alternative View of Nineteenth-Century Child Saving," *Social Problems* 33 (December 1986): S33–S57; and Langsam, *Children West*, 45–67.

24. For a description of this proliferation, see Folks, *The Care of Destitute, Neglected, and Delinquent Children*, 64–71, 179–97; LeRoy Ashby, *Saving the Waifs: Reformers and Dependent Children, 1890–1917* (Philadelphia: Temple University Press, 1984); and Holt, *The Orphan Trains*, 106–17.

25. See, for example, Katherine P. Hewins and L. Josephine Webster, "The Work of Child-Placing Agencies," Children's Bureau publication 171 (Washington, DC: Government Printing Office, 1927); W. H. Slingerland, *Child-Placing in Families: A Manual for Students and Social Workers* (New York: Russell Sage Foundation, 1919); and Romanofsky, "The Early History of Adoption Practices," 66–104. For a description of the growing role of sentiment in child placement and the

eventual embrace of foster care, see Viviana Zelizer, *Pricing the Priceless Child: The Changing Social Value of Children* (Princeton, NJ: Princeton University Press, 1985), 177–84; and Susan Tiffin, *In Whose Best Interest? Child Welfare Reform in the Progressive Era* (Westport, CT: Greenwood Press, 1982), 61–109.

26. See Berebitsky, *Like Our Very Own*, 130; and Romanofsky, "The Early History of Adoption Practices," 117–23.

27. See the description in Carp, "Orphanages vs. Adoption," 134.

28. From *Delineator*, May 1908, 808, quoted in Berebitsky, *Like Our Very Own*, 62.

29. Ada Elliot Sheffield, quoted in Carp, *Family Matters*, 18.

30. Robert Grant, "Domestic Relations and the Child," *Scribner's Magazine* 65, May 1919, 527; cited in Zelizer, *Pricing the Priceless Child*, 190.

31. For a description of this shift, see Elizabeth S. Cole and Kathryn S. Donley, "History, Values, and Placement Policy Issues in Adoption," in *The Psychology of Adoption*, eds. David M. Brodzinsky and Marshall D. Schecter (New York: Oxford University Press, 1990), 276–78; and E. Wayne Carp, ed., *Adoption in America: Historical Perspectives* (Ann Arbor: University of Michigan Press, 2002), 199.

32. A similar process occurred in Great Britain, where adoption was legalized in 1926. See Margaret Kornitzer, *Child Adoption in the Modern World* (New York: Philosophical Library, 1952), xi–xiii.

33. See Tiffin, *In Whose Best Interest?* 207–8.

34. Barbara Melosh, *Strangers and Kin: The American Way of Adoption* (Cambridge, MA: Harvard University Press, 2002), 26.

35. For more on the more general embrace of professional social work during this period, see Tiffin, *In Whose Best Interest?* 253–80.

36. During most of this period, professional social workers were adamant about not separating infants from their mothers for at least several months. See E. Wayne Carp, "Professional Social Workers, Adoption, and the Problem of Illegitimacy, 1915–1945," *Journal of Policy History* 6, no. 3 (1994): 161–84. For an alternative view, see Regina Kunzel, "The Professionalization of Benevolence: Evangelicals and Social Workers in the Florence Crittenton Homes, 1915 to 1945," *Journal of Social History* 22 (1988): 21–43.

37. See Melosh, *Strangers and Kin*, 36–38; and Zelizer, *Pricing the Priceless Child*, 169–207.

38. Zelizer, *Pricing the Priceless Child*, 199. For a related picture but lower estimated prices, see Frederick G. Brownell, "Why You Can't Adopt a Baby," *Reader's Digest*, September 1948, 55–59.

39. See *Hearings Before the Subcommittee to Investigate Juvenile Delinquency of the Committee on the Judiciary*, United States Senate, 84th Congress, 1st session, July 15 and 16, 1955 (hereafter cited as Kefauver Commission), 50–71.

40. Kefauver Commission, 10, 110; and "Adoption Tale Told by Unwed Mother," *New York Times*, July 17, 1955, 32.

41. Vera Connolly, "Bargain-Counter Babies," *Pictorial Review* 38 (March 1937), quoted in Zelizer, *Pricing the Priceless Child*, 192–93.

42. Cited in Carp, *Family Matters*, 26. For similar estimates in the late 1940s and early 1950s, see Huard, "The Law of Adoption," 761; and Richard Perlman and Jack Wiener, "Adoption of Children, 1953: A Statistical Analysis," *Iowa Law Review* 40 (1955): 339–40.

43. "Regarding Adoptions," Children's Welfare League of America, Special Bulletin (March 1937), 8, cited in Carp, *Family Matters*, 31.

44. See, for example, "Moppets on the Market: The Problem of Unregulated Adoption," *Yale Law Review* 59 (1950), 715–36. Although not written by a social worker, this article lays out the standard argument that many social workers and licensed agencies put forth.

45. Much of this shift was driven by postwar embarrassment over Nazi atrocities committed under the banner of eugenics. . . .

46. They also began charging for their services. See Zelizer, *Pricing the Priceless Child*, 201–7.

47. Clark Vincent, "Illegitimacy in the Next Decade: Trends and Implications," *Child Welfare* 43 (December 1964): 515.

48. In the days before infant formula, removing a baby from her mother also often meant condemning the child to death.

49. See, for example, Alice Lake, "Babies for the Brave," *Saturday Evening Post*, July 31, 1954, 26–27, 65; and Michael Schapiro, *A Study of Adoption Practice: Adoption of Children with Special Needs* (New York: Child Welfare League of America, 1957).

50. Because out-of-wedlock births have historically been higher among African Americans, and because African American couples have tended to be less interested than whites in adoption, adoption agencies in the United States typically have had trouble finding a sufficient number of black families to adopt all the available black children.

51. Carp, *Family Matters*, 28.

52. For more on changing views toward childlessness during this period, see Elaine Tyler May, *Barren in the Promised Land: Childless Americans and the Pursuit of Happiness* (Cambridge, MA: Harvard University Press, 1997), 127–79.

53. See Arthur D. Sorosky, Annette Baran, and Reuben Pannor, *The Adoption Triangle: The Effects of the Sealed Record on Adoptees, Birth Parents and Adoptive Parents* (Garden City, NY: Anchor Books, 1979), 35.

54. See Kefauver Commission; and Linda Tollett Austin, *Babies for Sale: The Tennessee Children's Home Adoption Scandal* (Westport, CT: Praeger, 1993), 109–27.

55. Lincoln Caplan, *An Open Adoption* (New York: Farrar, Straus & Giroux, 1990), 87; and Austin, *Babies for Sale*, 152–53.

56. By 1976, only four states—Connecticut, Delaware, Massachusetts, and Minnesota—explicitly prohibited private placement. See Margaret V. Turano, "Black-Market Adoptions," *Catholic Lawyer* 22 (Winter 1976): 54.

57. Generally, statutes against baby-selling are expressed as prohibitions against receiving compensation for relinquishing maternal legal rights. For an overview of the relevant statutes, see Avi Katz, "Surrogate Motherhood and the Baby-Selling Laws," *Columbia Journal of Law and Social Problems* 20, no. 1 (1986): 1–53; Turano, "Black-Market Adoptions"; and Daniel G. Grove, "Independent Adoption: The Case for the Gray Market," *Villanova Law Review* 13 (Fall 1967): 116–36.

58. These are very rough estimates based on voluntary disclosure. No data exists for 1945–1950, 1952–1954, or 1956. See Penelope L. Manza, "Adoption Trends: 1944–1975," *Child Welfare Research Notes* #9 (U.S. Children's Bureau, August 1984), 1–4.

59. Berebitsky, *Like Our Very Own*, 173. Kathy S. Stolley, "Statistics on Adoption in the United States," *Future of Children* 3 (Spring 1993): 30–33.

60. Between 1973 and 1983, the number of abortions performed on teenaged girls rose from 244,000 to 412,000. See Alfred Kadushin and Judith A. Martin, *Child Welfare Services* (New York: Macmillan Publishing Co., 1988), 471.

61. Kadushin and Martin, *Child Welfare Services*, 495.
62. Christine Bachrach, "Adoption Plans, Adopted Children and Adoptive Mothers," *Journal of Marriage and the Family* 48 (May 1986): 243–53.
63. Kadushin and Martin, *Child Welfare Services*, 539.
64. This debate became one of the most contested issues in the history of U.S. adoption. For a discussion, see Andrew Billingsly and Jeanne M. Giovannoni, *Children of the Storm: Black Children and American Child Welfare* (New York: Harcourt Brace Jovanovich, 1972); Elizabeth Bartholet, *Nobody's Children: Abuse and Neglect, Foster Drift, and the Adoption Alternative* (Boston: Beacon, 1999); Randall Kennedy, "Orphans of Separatism: The Painful Politics of Transracial Adoption," *American Prospect* 17 (Spring 1994): 38–45; and Lucille J. Grow and Deborah Shapiro, *Black Children—White Parents: A Study of Transracial Adoption* (New York: Child Welfare League of America, 1974).
65. Carp, *Family Matters*, 34; Howard Altstein and Rita J. Simon, *Intercountry Adoption: A Multinational Perspective* (New York: Praeger, 1990), 3.
66. The process was not necessarily simple, because adoptive parents had to document, first, that they satisfied federal criteria for parental fitness; second, that they had fulfilled all requirements of their child's home country; and third, that their child fit a narrow definition of "orphan." For a review and critique of these requirements, see Elizabeth Bartholet, "International Adoption: Current Status and Future Prospects," *The Future of Children: Adoption* 3, no. 1 (Spring 1993): 89–103.
67. INS data, as reported in Adam Pertman, *Adoption Nation: How the Adoption Revolution Is Transforming America* (New York: Basic Books, 2000), 23.
68. In 1979, China instituted a draconian "one child" policy that prohibited couples from bearing more than a single child. Although there were some exceptions, couples were generally required to receive birth permits prior to attempting to conceive, and women either had to be sterilized or use an IUD after the birth of their child. For a discussion of how this policy has affected both adoption and China's own demographics, see Valerie M. Hudson and Andrea M. den Boer, *Bare Branches: Security Implications of Asia's Surplus Male Population* (Cambridge, MA: MIT Press, 2004); and Karin Evans, *The Lost Daughters of China: Abandoned Girls, Their Journey to America and the Search for a Missing Past* (New York: J.P. Tarcher/Putnam, 2000).
69. See Carol Sisco, "Strict Romanian Birth Rules Bred Orphanages, Says Expert," *Salt Lake City Tribune*, November 14, 1991, B1; and Bill Snead, "The Abandoned Children of Romania's Orphanages," *Washington Post*, September 17, 1991, 6.
70. Pertman, *Adoption Nation*, 73; and John Taylor, "Romania's Lost Children . . . Omahans Challenge System, Bring Home Maria," *Omaha World-Herald*, July 2, 1991, 29.
71. *Immigrant Visas Issued to Orphans Coming to the U.S.*, available at http://travel.state.gov/family/adoption/stat/stats_451.html.
72. W. Tyree, "The Business of International Adoption," *Japan Times*, June 9, 1999, 1–2; and Madelyn Freundlich, *The Market Forces in Adoption* (New York: Child Welfare League of America, 2000), 43.
73. Statistics on intercountry adoption are notoriously difficult to find. No international institution collects them, and researchers have thus been forced to cobble together estimates from sending and receiving countries, many of which also have no central collection mechanism. For a discussion of this problem, see R. H. Weil, "International Adoptions: The Quiet Migration," *International Migration*

Review 18, no. 2 (1984): 276–93; and S. Kane, "The Movement of Children for International Adoption: An Epidemiological Perspective," *Social Science Journal* 30, no. 4 (1993): 323–39. For the best recent estimates, see Peter Selman, "The Movement of Children for Intercountry Adoption: A Demographic Perspective," Poster Presentation P275, at XXIVth IUSSP General Population Conference, Salvador, Bahia, Brazil, August 18–24, 2001. Figures for 2003 come directly from Selman, personal conversation with author, February 9, 2005. See also Selman, "Trends in Intercountry Adoption 1998–2003."

74. Precise data are unavailable, because no U.S. agency collects adoption statistics regularly. See *How Many Children Were Adopted in 2000 and 2001?* (Washington, DC: National Adoption Information Clearinghouse, 2004).

75. A fourth category—adoption by a relative or stepparent—is not considered here.

76. Susan Freivalds, "What's New in Adoption?" in "2005 Adoption Guide," special issue, *Adoptive Families* (2005): 11.

77. Complaints about the U.S. foster care system are voluminous. See, for example, Carole A. McKelvey and JoEllen Stevens, *Adoption Crisis: The Truth behind Adoption and Foster Care* (Golden, CO: Fulcrum Publishing, 1994); and "Health Care of Young Children in Foster Care," *Pediatrics* 109, no. 3 (March 2002): 536–41.

78. The Adoption and Foster Care Analysis and Reporting System (AFCARS), estimated as of August 2004, available at http://www.acf.hhs.gov/programs/cb/publications/afcars/report9.htm.

79. For more on parental preferences, see Mark E. Courtney, "The Politics and Realities of Transracial Adoption," *Child Welfare* 76, no. 6 (1997): 749–80.

80. Freundlich, *Market Forces in Adoption,* 68–73.

81. Adoption and Safe Families Act (ASFA) of 1997, P.L. 105–89, November 19, 1997.

82. See Hollinger, "Introduction to Adoption Law and Practice," 1–56; and *How Many Children Were Adopted in 2000 and 2001?* (Washington, DC: National Adoption Information Clearinghouse, 2004).

83. Hollinger, "Introduction to Adoption Law and Practice," 1–68.

84. These costs vary widely. For estimates, see http://costs.adoption.com.

85. For the growth of independent adoption and an argument for its merits, see Mark T. McDermott, "Agency Versus Independent Adoption: The Case for Independent Adoption, *Adoption* 3, no. 1 (Spring 1993): 146–51.

86. See the description in Caplan, *An Open Adoption,* 14–15; and Laura Mansnerus, "Market Puts Price Tags on the Priceless," *New York Times,* October 26, 1998, A1.

87. Interview with Mark T. McDermott, Washington, DC, January 7, 2005. The rate of $350 is at the very high end of the market.

88. See Annette Baran and Reuben Pannor, "Open Adoption," in *The Psychology of Adoption,* eds. Brodzinsky and Schecter, 316–31; and Annette Baran, Reuben Pannor, and Arthur D. Sorosky, "Open Adoption," *Social Work* 21 (1976): 97–105.

89. *2005 Adoption Guide,* 40; *Costs of Adopting: A Factsheet for Families* (Washington, DC: National Adoption Information Clearinghouse, June 2004).

90. Mansnerus, "Market Puts Price Tags on the Priceless," A1.

91. See William L. Pierce, "Accreditation of Those Who Arrange Adoptions Under the Hague Convention on Intercountry Adoption as a Means of Protecting,

Through Private International Law, the Rights of Children," *Journal of Contemporary Health Law and Policy* 12 (1996): 535–59.

92. Formally, the Hague Convention on the Protection of Children and Cooperation in Respect of Intercountry Adoption. See Ethan B. Kapstein, "The Baby Trade," *Foreign Affairs*, November 1, 2003, 115–25; and Peter Selman, "Intercountry Adoption in Europe after the Hague Convention," in *Developments in European Social Policy: Convergence and Diversity*, eds. Rob Sykes and Pete Alcock (Bristol: The Policy Press, 1998), 147–69.

93. The United States has approved the treaty but has yet to formally ratify it.

94. These particular fees are from Wide Horizons for Children, available at www.whfc.org. Other agencies' fees vary but follow a similar pattern.

95. Conversation with author, April 2005.

96. In economic terms, they reduce the information asymmetries that would otherwise exist. For a critical examination of this process, see Lisa Cartwright, "Photographs of 'Waiting Children': The Transnational Adoption Market," *Social Text* 74, vol. 21, no. 1 (Spring 2003): 83–109.

97. Twila L. Perry, "Transracial and International Adoption: Mothers, Hierarchy, Race and Feminist Legal Theory," *Yale Journal of Law and Feminism* 10 (1998): 105.

98. Janice G. Raymond, "The International Traffic in Women: Women Used in Systems of Surrogacy and Reproduction," in *Reconstructing Babylon: Essays on Women and Technology*, ed. H. Patricia Hynes (Bloomington: Indiana University Press, 1991), 97. Italics in original. For similar arguments, see Raymond, *Women as Wombs* (North Melbourne, Australia: Spinifex Press, 1995), 144–54; and Kenneth J. Herrmann Jr. and Barbara Kasper, "International Adoption: The Exploitation of Women and Children," *Affilia* 7, no. 1 (Spring 1992): 45–58.

99. For a balanced argument along these lines, see Madelyn Freundlich, "Families without Borders—I," *UN Chronicle* no. 2 (1999): 88.

100. See, for example, Bartholet, "International Adoption."

101. For Tann, see Zelizer, *Pricing the Priceless Child*, 199; and Austin, *Babies for Sale*. For Silverton and similar cases, see Lynne McTaggart, *The Baby Brokers: The Marketing of White Babies in America* (New York: The Dial Press, 1980); and Nancy C. Baker, *Babyselling: The Scandal of Black Market Adoption* (New York: Vanguard Press, 1978).

102. See, for example, Holly C. Kennard, "Curtailing the Sale and Trafficking of Children: A Discussion of the Hague Conference Convention in Respect of Intercountry Adoptions," *University of Pennsylvania Journal of International Business Law* 14, no. 4 (1994): 623–49.

103. Hearings before the Subcommittee on Children and Youth of the Committee on Labor and Public Welfare, 94th Congress, 1st session (1975), 141–45.

104. Author interviews with Mark T. McDermott, past president of American Academy of Adoption Attorneys; and Thomas C. Atwood, president and CEO, National Council for Adoption, Washington, DC, January 7, 2005.

105. For Cambodia, see Sara Corbett, "Where Do Babies Come From?" *New York Times Sunday Magazine*, June 16, 2002, 42; for India, see Raymond Bonner, "For Poor Families, Selling Baby Girls was Economic Boon," *New York Times*, June 23, 2003, A3; and Gregory Katz, "The £18 Babies," *FT Magazine*, June 19, 2004, 20–23.

106. Even groups critical of international adoption tend to agree that cases of outright kidnapping are extremely rare. See, for example, Marie-Françoise

Lucker-Bubel, "Inter-Country Adoption and Trafficking in Children: An Initial Assessment of the Adequacy of the International Protection of Children and Their Rights" (Geneva: Defense for Children International, 1990), 2. For a discussion of how trafficking allegations skew the debate over international adoption, see Elizabeth Bartholet, *Family Bonds: Adoption and the Politics of Parenting* (Boston: Houghton Mifflin Company, 1993), 150–60.

107. See Corbett, "Where Do Babies Come From?" and Thomas Fields-Meyer et al., "Whose Kids Are They?" *People*, January 19, 2004, 74–78. For earlier allegations, see Marlise Simons, "Abductions in Salvador Fill a Demand: Adoption," *New York Times*, December 17, 1985; and *International Children's Rights Monitor* 5, no. 4 (1988).

108. McTaggart, *The Baby Brokers*, 1. See also the discussion in Daniel G. Grove, "Independent Adoption: The Case for the Gray Market," *Villanova Law Review* 13 (Fall 1967): 116–36.

109. For individual cases, see McTaggart, *The Baby Brokers*; and Robert D. McFadden, "Adoption Lawyer Throws a Party," *New York Times*, March 3, 1979, 26.

110. For a legal discussion of these ambiguities, see James B. Boskey and Joan Heifetz Hollinger, "Placing Children for Adoption," in *Adoption Law and Practice*, ed. Hollinger, 3–26, 3–39.

111. For a classic argument along these lines, see Margaret Jane Radin, "Market Inalienability," *Harvard Law Review* 100 (June 1987): 1849–1937. For a rare and extremely controversial argument in favor of the marketplace, see Elisabeth M. Landes and Richard A. Posner, "The Economics of the Baby Shortage," *Journal of Legal Studies* 7, no. 2 (June 1978): 323–48.

112. For arguments that baby markets are inherently bad, see J. Robert S. Prichard, "A Market for Babies?" *University of Toronto Law Journal* 34 (1984): 341–57; Robin West, "Submission, Choice and Ethics: A Rejoinder to Judge Posner," *Harvard Law Review* 99 (1986): 1449–56; and Tamar Frankel and Francis H. Miller, "The Inapplicability of Market Theory to Adoptions," *Boston University Law Review* 67 (1987): 99–103.

113. See, for example, Perry, "Transracial and International Adoption," 147.

114. Of course, theoretically it is possible that funds and efforts could be devoted to helping the child's relatives or neighbors care for him. This is the option offered by many critics of international adoption. Under current circumstances, however, it seems highly improbable that sufficient monies will flow in this direction.

115. For a discussion, see E. Wayne Carp, "Two Cheers for Orphanages," *Reviews in American History* 24, no. 2 (1996); and Deborah A. Frank et al., "Infants and Young Children in Orphanages: One View from Pediatrics and Child Psychiatry," *Pediatrics* 97 (April 1996): 569–78.

116. As Posner asks rhetorically, "Are the infertile to be blamed for a glut of unwanted children?" See Richard A. Posner, "The Ethics and Economics of Enforcing Contracts of Surrogate Motherhood," *Journal of Contemporary Health Law and Policy* 21 (April 1989): 21–31.

117. For a compelling argument along these lines, see Bartholet, *Family Bonds*.

118. There is a voluminous literature evaluating the success of adoptive placements. See, for example, Rita J. Simon and Howard Altstein, *Transracial Adoptees and Their Families: A Study of Identity and Commitment* (New York: Praeger, 1987); Barbara Tizard, "Intercountry Adoption: A Review of the Evidence," *Journal of Child Psychology and Psychiatry* 32, no. 5 (1991): 743–56; William

Feigelman and Arnold R. Silverman, *Chosen Children* (Westport, CT: Praeger Publishers, 1983); Janet L. Hoopes, "Adoption and Identity Formation," in *The Psychology of Adoption,* eds. Brodzinsky and Schecter, 144–66; and James A. Rosenthal, "Outcomes of Adoption of Children with Special Needs," *The Future of Children: Adoption* 3, no. 1 (Spring 1993): 77–88.

119. For one argument along these lines, see Hearings before the Subcommittee on Children and Youth (1975), 579–81.

120. See Betty Jean Lifton, *Lost and Found: The Adoption Experience* (New York: Dial Press, 1979); and Arthur D. Sorosky, Annette Baran, and Reuben Pannor, "Identity Conflicts in Adoptees," *American Journal of Orthopsychiatry* 45, no. 1 (1975): 18–27.

121. For the classic argument in favor of open adoption, see Annette Baran and Reuben Pannor, "Open Adoption," in *The Psychology of Adoption,* eds. Brodzinsky and Schecter, 316–31; and Annette Baran, Reuben Pannor, and Arthur D. Sorosky, "Open Adoption," *Social Work* 21 (1976): 97–105. For a discussion of the politics behind the open adoption movement, see E. Wayne Carp, *Adoption Politics: Bastard Nation and Ballot Initiative* 58 (Lawrence: University Press of Kansas, 2004).

122. See Anne B. Brodzinsky, "Surrendering an Infant for Adoption: The Birthmother Experience," in *The Psychology of Adoption,* eds. Brodzinsky and Schecter, 295–315.

123. See, for example, the arguments made in Bhabha, "Moving Babies"; and Perry, "Transracial and International Adoption," 101–64.

Questions for Critical Reading

1. Is adoption a compassionate social practice, a troubling economic market, or both? Analyze Spar's essay and select quotations that support your position.

2. Spar spends a great deal of time detailing the history and evolution of adoption. Why do you think she provides this information? In what ways does it support her argument? Perform a critical reading of the structure of her argument using that section of her essay.

3. According to Spar, what role does race play in adoption? Does this reflect the economic function of race in general?

Exploring Context

1. Spar opens this essay talking about the Rainbow Kids Web site at rainbowkids.com. Explore the site. Is her description of it accurate? What can you find on the site to further support or complicate Spar's argument? Are Yamile, Sofia, and Rafael still waiting to be adopted? How does your exploration relate to your response to Question 3 of Questions for Critical Reading about the role of race in adoption?

2. Visit Adoption.com (adoption.com). Does the site suggest that adoption is a humanitarian endeavor or an economic one? What evidence can you find for each perspective? Use your response on these issues from Question 1 of Questions for Critical Reading in your answer.

3. Spar is currently president of Barnard College. Visit her page on Barnard's site at barnard.edu/president. How does this essay reflect Spar's body of work as an academic and as a leader?

Questions for Connecting

1. Is there a global baby supply chain? Apply Thomas Friedman's ideas about global economics in "The Dell Theory of Conflict Prevention" (p. 121) to Spar's discussion of international adoption, connecting your response to your work on adoptions and economics from Question 1 of Questions for Critical Reading.

2. The Dalai Lama calls for a new ethics for biotechnology in "Ethics and the New Genetics" (p. 76). How do his insights apply to the practice of adoption? Can we use those insights to separate the social and economic aspects of adoption? What ethical guidelines should we follow in this practice?

3. Is adoption consistent with human dignity? Use Francis Fukuyama's understanding of the concept in his essay of that name (p. 142) to explore Spar's analysis. How might Factor X enable us to draw a line between ethical and unethical adoptions?

Language Matters

1. Apostrophes indicate possession. Go through Spar's text and locate some examples of the apostrophe, which is perhaps one of the most frequently misunderstood marks of punctuation. Can you use Spar's ideas about the complexities of adoption to think about why people don't use the apostrophe when they should? What are the complexities of "possession" in today's world, in writing and in reality?

2. Locate the strongest transition in Spar's essay. What makes it strong or effective? How can you use this strategy in your own writing?

3. What are higher and lower order concerns in writing? Apply these concepts to Spar's writing. What are the higher order concerns of the essay? Are there any?

Assignments for Writing

1. Spar states that what separates adoption from the rest of the baby trade is the difference in product: purchasing an existing child through adoption rather than a potential one through assisted reproduction. Write an essay in which you explore the risks, costs, and benefits of assisted reproduction versus adoption. You might want to use your response about the ethics of adoption from Question 2 of Questions for Connecting. Also consider: In which situations is one option better than the other? Why do adoption agencies put potential parents through rigorous testing before they are allowed to adopt? Why, in assisted reproduction, are potential parents not put through the same kind of testing? What are the dangers of adoption or of assisted reproduction?

2. Spar explains that adoption presents unique differences from other aspects of the baby business, including a thriving international black market and contractual agreements between birth and adoptive parents. Write an essay in which you evaluate the ethics of international adoption. You may want to begin with the work you did in Question 1 of Exploring Context and Question 2 of Questions for Connecting. How can we differentiate between children in need and children being sold? Is international adoption a humanitarian or an economic industry?

3. Much of Spar's essay lays out the complications of domestic and international adoptions. Write an essay in which you propose the best means of regulating adoption. Consider: Should governments oversee adoptions, or are they best handled by private agencies? Should domestic adoption be a free market? How can we best regulate international adoptions?

JAMES SUROWIECKI

James Surowiecki writes the business column "The Financial Page" for the *New Yorker* and has contributed to publications such as *Slate*, the *Wall Street Journal*, and *Wired*. Surowiecki was also a writer for the Motley Fool Web site and editor-in-chief for the Fool's "Rogue" column. Surowiecki edited the anthology *Best Business Crime Fighting of the Year* (2002) before publishing his book *The Wisdom of Crowds: Why the Many Are Smarter than the Few and How Collective Wisdom Shapes Business, Economies, Societies, and Nations* (2004).

Surowiecki's argument in *The Wisdom of Crowds* is that even when the few are elite, brilliant, or successful, the many are generally smarter. Whether guessing the weight of an ox at a country fair or the answer to a question on *Who Wants to Be a Millionaire?* the crowd tends to be remarkably correct. Though the thought is counterintuitive, a large and largely inexpert group can come up with answers that are often more accurate than those of any of the smartest individuals in the group. Surowiecki shows how group wisdom can predict everything from elections to the location of a lost submarine more accurately than individual experts. This technique, Surowiecki argues, can be as effective in the worlds of business, economics, and science as it is in our daily life.

In "Committees, Juries, and Teams: The *Columbia* Disaster and How Small Groups Can Be Made to Work," from *The Wisdom of Crowds*, Surowiecki acknowledges that sometimes collective knowledge can fail—with disastrous consequences. However, these exceptions, including "verdict-based" juries and the Mission Management Team of the space shuttle *Columbia* during its final mission, prove the rule while underscoring that it's not sufficient simply to seek the advice of the crowd. Surowiecki suggests that groups are correct only under specific circumstances. Understanding how to foster those circumstances is part of Surowiecki's goal in this excerpt.

Group work is frequently a requirement of college, and it is also a common working practice across an array of professions and careers. Knowing how small groups can fail and, more important, knowing how to make them succeed can offer you valuable insights for your future.

▶ TAGS: *collaboration, education, diversity, knowledge, groups*

Committees, Juries, and Teams: The *Columbia* Disaster and How Small Groups Can Be Made to Work

On the morning of January 21, 2003, the Mission Management Team (MMT) for NASA mission STS-107—the twenty-eighth flight of the space shuttle *Columbia*—held a teleconference, its second since the *Columbia*'s launch on January 16. An hour before the meeting, Don McCormack had been briefed by members of the Debris Assessment Team (DAT), a group of engineers from NASA, Boeing, and Lockheed Martin, who had spent much of the previous five days evaluating the possible consequences of a large-debris strike on the *Columbia*. During the shuttle's ascent into the atmosphere, a large piece of foam had broken off the left bipod area of the shuttle's external fuel tank and had smashed into the ship's left wing. None of the cameras that were tracking the shuttle's launch had provided a clear picture of the impact, so it was difficult to tell how much damage the foam might have caused. And although by January 21 a request had been made for on-orbit pictures of the *Columbia*, they had not been approved. So the DAT had done what it could with the information it had, first estimating the size of the foam and the speed at which it had struck the *Columbia*, and then using an algorithm called Crater to predict how deep a piece of debris that size and traveling at that speed would penetrate into the thermal-protection tiles that covered the shuttle's wings.

The DAT had reached no conclusions, but they made it clear to McCormack that there was reason to be concerned. McCormack did not transmit that sense of concern to the MMT during its teleconference. The foam strike was not mentioned until two-thirds of the way through the meeting, and was brought up only after discussions of, among other things, a jammed camera, the scientific experiments on the shuttle, and a leaky water separator. Then Linda Ham, who was the MMT leader, asked McCormack for an update. He simply said that people were investigating the possible damage and what could potentially be done to fix it, and added that when the *Columbia* had been hit by a similar strike during mission STS-87, five years earlier, it had suffered "fairly significant damage." This is how Ham answered: "And I really don't think there is much we can do so it's not really a factor during the flight because there is not much we can do about it."

Ham, in other words, had already decided that the foam strike was inconsequential. More important, she decided for everyone else in the meeting that it was inconsequential, too. This was the first time the MMT had heard any details about the foam strike. It would have been logical for McCormack to outline the possible consequences and talk about what the evidence from past shuttles that had been struck with debris showed. But instead the meeting moved on.

Hindsight is, of course, twenty-twenty, and just as with the critiques of the U.S. intelligence community after September 11, it's perhaps too easy to fault the MMT at NASA for its failure to see what would happen to the *Columbia* when it reentered the Earth's atmosphere on February 1. Even those who have been exceptionally critical of NASA have suggested that focusing on this one team is a mistake because it obscures the deep institutional and cultural problems that plague the agency (which happen to be many of the same problems that plagued the agency in 1986, when the *Challenger* exploded). But while NASA clearly is an object lesson in organizational dysfunction, that doesn't fully explain just why the MMT handled the *Columbia* crisis so badly. Sifting through the evidence collected by the Columbia Accident Investigation Board (CAIB), there is no way to evade the conclusion that the team had an opportunity to make different choices that could have dramatically improved the chances of the crew surviving. The team members were urged on many different occasions to collect the information they needed to make a reasonable estimate of the shuttle's safety. They were advised that the foam might, in fact, have inflicted enough damage to cause "burn-through" — heat burning through the protective tiles and into the shuttle's fuselage — when the shuttle reentered the Earth's atmosphere. The team's leaders themselves raised the possibility that the debris damage might have been severe. And yet the MMT as a whole never came close to making the right decision on what to do about the *Columbia.*

In fact, the performance of the MMT is an object lesson in how not to run a small group, and a powerful demonstration of the way in which, instead of making people wiser, being in a group can actually make them dumber. This is important for two reasons. First, small groups are ubiquitous in American life, and their decisions are consequential. Juries decide whether or not people will go to prison. Boards of directors shape, at least in theory, corporate strategy. And more and more of our work lives are spent on teams or, at the very least, in meetings. Whether small groups can do a good job of solving complex problems is hardly an academic question.

Second, small groups are different in important ways from groups such as markets or betting pools or television audiences. Those groups are as much statistical realities as experiential ones. Bettors do get feedback from each other in the form of the point spread, and investors get feedback from each other in the stock market, but the nature of the relationship between people in a small group is qualitatively different. Investors do not think of themselves as members of the market. People on the MMT thought of themselves as members of that team. And the collective wisdom that something like the Iowa Electronic Markets produces is, at least when it's working well, the result of many different independent judgments, rather than something that the group as a whole has consciously come up with. In a small group, by contrast, the group — even if it is an ad hoc group formed for the sake of a single project or experiment — has an identity of its own. And the influence of the people in the group on each other's judgment is inescapable.

What we'll see is that this has two consequences. On the one hand, it means small groups can make very bad decisions, because influence is more direct and immediate and small-group judgments tend to be more volatile and extreme. On the other hand, it also means that small groups have the opportunity to be more than just the sum of their parts. A successful face-to-face group is more than just collectively intelligent. It makes everyone work harder, think smarter, and reach better conclusions than they would have on their own. In his 1985 book about Olympic rowing, *The Amateurs*, David Halberstam writes: "When most oarsmen talked about their perfect moments in a boat, they referred not so much to winning a race but to the feel of the boat, all eight oars in the water together, the synchronization almost perfect. In moments like that, the boat seemed to lift right out of the water. Oarsmen called that the moment of *swing*." When a boat has swing, its motion seems almost effortless. Although there are eight oarsmen in the boat, it's as if there's only one person — with perfect timing and perfect strength — rowing. So you might say that a small group which works well has intellectual swing.

Swing, though, is hard to come by. In fact, few organizations have figured out how to make groups work consistently well. For all the lip service paid, particularly in corporate America, to the importance of teams and the need to make meetings more productive, it's still unusual for a small group to be more than just the sum of its parts. Much of the time, far from adding value to their members, groups seem to subtract it. Too often, it's easy to agree with Ralph Cordiner, the former chairman of General Electric, who once said, "If you can name for me one great discovery or decision that was made by a committee, I will find you the one man in that committee who had the lonely insight — while he was shaving or on his way to work, or maybe while the rest of the committee was chattering away — the lonely insight that solved the problem and was the basis for the decision." On this account, groups are nothing but obstacles, cluttering the way of people whose time would be better spent alone.

> **Instead of making people wiser, being in a group can actually make them dumber.**

The performance of the MMT helps explain why. First, the team started not with an open mind but from the assumption that the question of whether a foam strike could seriously damage the shuttle had already been answered. This was, to be fair, partly a matter of bad luck, since one of the team's technical advisers was convinced from the beginning that foam simply could do no serious damage, and kept saying so to anyone who would listen. But there was plenty of evidence to suggest otherwise. Rather than begin with the evidence and work toward a conclusion, the team members worked in the opposite direction. More egregiously, their skepticism about the possibility that something might really be wrong made them dismiss the need to gather more information, especially in the form of pictures, leading to the DAT's requests for on-orbit images being rejected. Even when MMT members dealt with the possibility that there might be a real problem with *Columbia*, their conviction that nothing was wrong limited discussion and made them discount evidence to the contrary. In that sense, the team succumbed to what psychologists call "confirmation bias," which causes decision makers to unconsciously seek those bits of information that confirm their underlying intuitions.

These problems were also exacerbated by the team's belief that it knew more than it did. For instance, when the shuttle managers turned down the request for pictures, one of the justifications they offered was that the resolution of the images would not be good enough to detect the small area where the foam struck. In fact, as the CAIB noted, none of the managers had the necessary security clearances to know how good the resolution of the photos would be, nor did any of them ask the Department of Defense—which would have taken the pictures—about picture quality. In other words, they were "making critical decisions about imagery capabilities based on little or no knowledge," and doing so with an air of complete assurance.

Social scientists who study juries often differentiate between two approaches juries take. Evidence-based juries usually don't even take a vote until after they've spent some time talking over the case, sifting through the evidence, and explicitly contemplating alternative explanations. Verdict-based juries, by contrast, see their mission as reaching a decision as quickly and decisively as possible. They take a vote before any discussion, and the debate after that tends to concentrate on getting those who don't agree to agree. The MMT's approach was practically, though not intentionally, verdict-based. You can see this especially clearly in the way Linda Ham asked questions. On January 22, for instance, the day after the meeting where the foam was first mentioned, Ham e-mailed two members of the team about whether the foam strike might, in fact, pose a threat to the shuttle's safety. "Can we say that for any ET [external tank] foam lost," she wrote, "no 'safety of flight' damage can occur to the Orbiter because of the density?" The answer that Ham wanted was built into the question. It was a way of deflecting genuine inquiry even while seeming to pursue it. As it happens, one of the members of the team did not give Ham the answer she was looking for. Lambert Austin answered her question by writing, "NO," in capital letters, and then went on to explain that there was no way at that point to "PRECLUDE" the possibility that the foam might have seriously damaged the tiles. Yet Austin's cautionary note garnered little attention.

One reason for the team's lack of follow-through may have been its implicit assumption that if something was wrong, there was no possibility of fixing it. At that January 21 meeting, you'll remember, Ham said, "And I really don't think there is much we can do so it's not really a factor during the flight because there is not much we can do about it." Two days later, Calvin Schomburg, the technical expert who insisted throughout that the foam could not seriously damage the tiles, met with Rodney Rocha, a NASA engineer who had become the unofficial representative of the DAT. By this point, the DAT was increasingly concerned that the damage inflicted by the foam could potentially lead to burnthrough on reentry, and Rocha and Schomburg argued over the question. At the end of the discussion, Schomburg said that if the tiles had been severely damaged, "Nothing could be done."

The idea that nothing could have been done if the damage to the tiles had been uncovered in time was wrong. In fact, as part of the CAIB investigation, NASA engineers came up with two different strategies that might have brought the *Columbia* crew back to Earth safely (though the shuttle itself was doomed from the moment the foam struck). There was no reason for the MMT to know what those strategies were, of course. But here again, the team had made a decision before looking at the evidence. And that decision—which roughly

amounted to saying, "If there is a problem, we won't be able to find a solution" —
undoubtedly shaped the team's approach to figuring out whether there was a
problem at all. In fact, the CAIB report includes personal notes from an unnamed
NASA source that say that when Ham canceled the DAT's request for pictures
of the *Columbia*'s wing, "[she] said it was no longer being pursued since even if
we saw something, we couldn't do anything about it." This was not exactly the
ethos that brought *Apollo 13* safely back to Earth.

One of the real dangers that small groups face is emphasizing consensus over dissent. The extreme version of this, . . . is the kind of groupthink
that Irving Janis described in his account of the planning of the Bay of Pigs,
where the members of the group become so identified with the group that the
possibility of dissent seems practically unthinkable. But in a more subtle way
small groups can exacerbate our tendency to prefer the illusion of certainty to
the reality of doubt. On January 24, the DAT engineers met again with Don
McCormack, who had become their unofficial liaison to the MMT, to present the
findings of their foam-strike study. The briefing room where the presentation
took place was so crowded that engineers ended up out in the hallway, which
said a lot about how worried people were. In any case, the DAT offered five different scenarios of what might have happened. The team's conclusion was that
it was likely that the shuttle was safe. But they qualified their conclusion by
saying that their analysis was profoundly limited by their tools and their lack of
good information. Because the MMT had refused to authorize on-orbit images,
the engineers did not know where exactly the foam had struck. And the Crater
algorithm they were using had been designed to measure the impact of pieces
of debris hundreds of times smaller than the one that hit *Columbia*, so there was
no way to be sure that its results were accurate. The engineers stressed, in other
words, how uncertain their analysis was. But NASA management focused instead on their conclusion.

An hour after the briefing, the MMT met, and McCormack summarized
what the DAT had said. "They do show obviously there's potential for significant damage here, but thermal analysis does not indicate that there is potential
for a burn-through," he said. "Obviously there is a lot of uncertainty in all this
in terms of the size of the debris and where it hit and the angle of incidence and
it's difficult." This was a relatively obscure way of explaining that the engineers' analysis was built on a lot of untested assumptions, but it was at least an
attempt at caution. Ham responded by again asking a question that answered
itself: "No burn-through, means no catastrophic damage and the localized
heating damage would mean a tile replacement?" McCormack said, "We do
not see any kind of safety of flight issue here yet in anything that we've looked
at." Ham came back with another nothing-is-wrong question: "No safety of
flight and no issue for this mission nothing that we're going to do different,
there may be a turnaround?" Then, after a short interchange between Ham
and McCormack and Calvin Schomburg, one of the other team members on
the conference call said that they hadn't been able to hear what McCormack
had said. Ham summarized neatly: "He was just reiterating with Calvin that
he doesn't believe that there is any burn-through so no safety of flight kind of

issue, it's more of a turnaround issue similar to what we've had on other flights. That's it? Alright, any questions on that?" For all intents and purposes, when that meeting ended, the *Columbia*'s fate had been sealed.

What's most striking about that January 24 meeting is the utter absence of debate and minority opinions. As the CAIB noted, when McCormack summarized the DAT's findings, he included none of its supporting analysis nor any discussion of whether there was a division of opinion on the team about its conclusions. More strikingly, not one member of the MMT asked a question. Not one member expressed any interest in seeing the DAT study. One would have thought that when McCormack mentioned the uncertainties in the analysis, someone would have asked him to explain and perhaps even quantify those uncertainties. But no one did. In part, that may have been because Ham was so obviously anxious for the problem to be resolved, and so convinced that there was nothing to talk about. Her attempts to briskly summarize McCormack's conclusions — "No burn-through, means no catastrophic damage" — effectively shut off discussion. And anyone who's ever been in a business meeting knows that "Alright, any questions on that?" really means "There are no questions on that, right?"

The MMT failed to make the right decision in part because of problems that are specific to the culture of NASA. Although we think of NASA as a fundamentally meritocratic, bottom-up culture, it is in fact deeply hierarchical. This meant that even though the DAT engineers had serious qualms from the beginning about the foam strike, their concerns — and, in particular, their insistence that they needed images of the Orbiter's wing before they could make a truly informed analysis — never received a serious hearing from the MMT. At the same time, the MMT violated nearly every rule of good group decision making. To begin with, the team's discussions were simultaneously too structured and not structured enough. They were too structured because most of the discussions — not just about the debris strike, but about everything — consisted of Ham asking a question and someone else answering it. They were not structured enough because no effort was made to ask other team members to comment on particular questions. This is almost always a mistake, because it means that decisions are made based on a very limited supply of analysis and information. One of the consistent findings from decades of small-group research is that group deliberations are more successful when they have a clear agenda and when leaders take an active role in making sure that everyone gets a chance to speak.

The team also, as I've mentioned, started with its conclusion. As a result, every new piece of information that came in was reinterpreted to fit that conclusion. This is a recurring problem with small groups that have a hard time incorporating new information. Social psychologist Garold Stasser, for instance, ran an experiment in which a group of eight people was asked to rate the performance of thirty-two psychology students. Each member of the group was given two relevant pieces of information about the students (say, their grades and their test scores), while two members of the group were given two extra pieces of information (say, their performance in class, etc.), and one member of the group received another two. Although the group as a whole therefore had six pieces of useful information, their ratings were based almost entirely on the two pieces of information that they all shared. The new information was discounted as either unimportant or unreliable. Stasser has also shown that in unstructured, free-flowing discussions, the information that tends to be talked about the most is, paradoxically, the information that everyone already knows. More curiously, information can be presented and listened to and still make little difference, because its contents are misinterpreted. New messages are often modified so that they fit old messages, which is especially dangerous since unusual messages often add the most value. (If people are just saying what you expect them to say, they're hardly likely to change your thinking.) Or they are modified to suit a preexisting picture of the situation.

What was missing most from the MMT, of course, was diversity, by which I mean not sociological diversity but rather cognitive diversity. James Oberg, a former Mission Control operator and now NBC News correspondent, has made the counterintuitive point that the NASA teams that presided over the *Apollo* missions were actually more diverse than the MMT. This seems hard to believe, since every engineer at Mission Control in the late 1960s had the same crew cut and wore the same short-sleeved white shirt. But as Oberg points out, most of those men had worked outside of NASA in many different industries before coming to the agency.

> **When that meeting ended, the** *Columbia*'s **fate had been sealed.**

NASA employees today are far more likely to have come to the agency directly out of graduate school, which means they are also far less likely to have divergent opinions. That matters because, in small groups, diversity of opinion is the single best guarantee that the group will reap benefits from face-to-face discussion. Berkeley political scientist Chandra Nemeth has shown in a host of studies of mock juries that the presence of a minority viewpoint, all by itself, makes a group's decisions more nuanced and its decision-making process more rigorous. This is true even when the minority viewpoint turns out to be ill conceived. The confrontation with a dissenting view, logically enough, forces the majority to interrogate its own positions more seriously. This doesn't mean that the ideal jury will follow the plot of *Twelve Angry Men,* where a single holdout convinces eleven men who are ready to convict that they're all wrong. But it does mean that having even a single different opinion can make a group wiser. One suspects that, had there been a single devil's advocate pushing the idea that the foam strike might have seriously damaged the wing, the MMT's conclusion would have been very different.

Without the devil's advocate, though, it's likely that the group's meetings actually made its judgment about the possible problem worse. That's because of a phenomenon called "group polarization." Usually, when we think of deliberation, we imagine that it's a kind of recipe for rationality and moderation, and assume that the more people talk about an issue, the less likely they will be to adopt extreme positions. But evidence from juries and three decades of experimental studies suggests that much of the time, the opposite is true.

Group polarization is still a phenomenon that is not well understood, and there are clearly cases where it has little or no effect. But since the 1960s, sociologists have documented how, under certain circumstances, deliberation does not moderate but rather radicalizes people's point of view. The first studies of the phenomenon tried to elicit people's attitudes toward risk, by asking them what they would do in specific situations. For instance, they were asked, "If a man with a severe heart illness is told that he must either change his way of life completely or have an operation that will either cure him or kill him, what should he do?" Or, "If an electrical engineer who has a safe job at a small salary is given the chance to take a new job that pays much better but is also less secure, should he move?" Individuals answered these questions privately at first, then gathered into groups to reach collective decisions. At first, researchers thought that group discussions made people more likely to advocate risky positions, and they termed this the "risky shift." But as time went on, it became clear that the shift could be in either direction. If a group was made up of people who were generally risk averse, discussion would make the group even more cautious, while groups of risk takers found themselves advocating riskier positions. Other studies showed that people who had a pessimistic view of the future became even more pessimistic after deliberations. Similarly, civil juries that are inclined to give large awards to plaintiffs generally give even larger awards after talking it over.

More recently, University of Chicago law professor Cass Sunstein has devoted a great deal of attention to polarization, and in his book *Why Societies Need Dissent*, he shows both that the phenomenon is more ubiquitous than was once thought and that it can have major consequences. As a general rule, discussions tend to move both the group as a whole and the individuals within it toward more extreme positions than the ones they entered the discussion with.

Why does polarization occur? One reason is because of people's reliance on "social comparison." This means more than that people are constantly comparing themselves to everyone else (which, of course, they are). It means that people are constantly comparing themselves to everyone else with an eye toward maintaining their relative position within the group. In other words, if you start out in the middle of the group and you believe the group has moved, as it were, to the right, you're inclined to shift your position to the right as well, so that relative to everyone else you're standing still. Of course, by moving to the right you're moving the group to the right, making social comparison something of a self-fulfilling prophecy. What's assumed to be real eventually becomes real.

It's important to see, though, that polarization isn't just the result of people trying to stay in tune with the group. It also results, strangely, from people doing their best to figure out what the right answer is. As we saw in our discussion of social proof—remember the passersby who ended up staring into an empty sky—people who are uncertain about what they believe will look to other members of the group for help. That's the point of deliberating, after all. But if a majority of the group already supports one position, then most of the arguments that will be made will be in support of that position. So the uncertain people are likely to be swayed in that direction, in part simply because that's more of what they'll hear. Similarly, people who have more extreme positions are more likely to have strong, coherent arguments in favor of their positions and are also more likely to voice them.

This matters because all the evidence suggests that the order in which people speak has a profound effect on the course of a discussion. Earlier comments are more influential, and they tend to provide a framework within which the discussion occurs. As in an information cascade, once that framework is in place, it's difficult for a dissenter to break it down. This wouldn't be a problem if the people who spoke earliest were also more likely to know what they were talking about. But the truth is that, especially when it comes to problems where there is no obvious right answer, there's no guarantee that the most-informed speaker will also be the most influential. On juries, for instance, two-thirds of all foremen—who lead and structure deliberations—are men, and during deliberations men talk far more than women do, even though no one has ever suggested that men as a gender have better insight into questions of guilt and innocence. In groups where the members know each other, status tends to shape speaking patterns, with higher-status people talking more and more often than lower-status people. Again, this wouldn't matter as much if the authority of higher-status people was derived from their greater knowledge. But oftentimes it doesn't. Even when higher-status people don't really know what they're talking about, they're more likely to speak. A series of experiments with military fliers who were asked to solve a logic problem, for instance, found that pilots were far more likely to speak convincingly in defense of their solution than navigators were, even when the pilots were wrong and the navigators were right. The navigators deferred to the pilots—even when they had never met the pilots before—because they assumed that their rank meant they were more likely to be right.

That kind of deference is important, because in small groups ideas often do not succeed simply on their own merits. Even when its virtues may seem self-evident, an idea needs a champion in order to be adopted by the group as a whole. That's another reason why a popular position tends to become more popular in the course of deliberations: It has more potential champions to begin with. In a market or even a democracy, champions are far less important because of the sheer number of potential decision makers. But in a small group, having a strong advocate for an idea, no matter how good it is, is essential. And when advocates are chosen, as it were, on the basis of status or talkativeness, rather than perceptiveness or keenness of insight, then the group's chance of making a smart decision shrinks.

Talkativeness may seem like a curious thing to worry about, but in fact talkativeness has a major impact on the kinds of decisions small groups reach. If you talk a lot in a group, people will tend to think of you as influential almost by default. Talkative people are not necessarily well liked by other members of the group, but they are listened to. And talkativeness feeds on itself. Studies of group dynamics almost always show that the more someone talks, the more he is talked to by others in the group. So people at the center of the group tend to become more important over the course of a discussion.

This might be okay if people only spoke when they had expertise in a particular matter. And in many cases, if someone's talking a lot, it's a good sign that they have something valuable to add. But the truth is that there is no clear correlation between talkativeness and expertise. In fact, as the military-flier studies suggest, people who imagine themselves as leaders will often overestimate their own knowledge and project an air of confidence and expertise that is unjustified. And since, as political scientists Brock Blomberg and Joseph Harrington suggest, extremists tend to be more rigid and more convinced of their own rightness than moderates, discussion tends to pull groups away from the middle. Of course, sometimes truth lies at the extreme. And if the people who spoke first and most often were consistently the people with the best information or the keenest analysis, then polarization might not be much of a problem. But it is.

The obvious temptation is to do away with or at least minimize the role that small groups play in shaping policy or making decisions. Better to entrust one reliable person—who at least we know will not become more extreme in his views—with responsibility than trust a group of ten or twelve people who at any moment, it seems, may suddenly decide to run off a cliff. It would be a mistake to succumb to that temptation. First of all, groups can be, as it were, depolarized. In a study that divided people into groups of six while making sure that each group composed two smaller groups of three who had strongly opposed views, it was found that discussion moved the groups from the extremes and toward each other. That same study found that as groups became less polarized, they also became more accurate when they were tested on matters of fact.

More important, as solid as the evidence demonstrating group polarization is, so too is the evidence demonstrating that nonpolarized groups consistently make better decisions and come up with better answers than most of their members, and surprisingly often the group outperforms even its best member. What makes this surprising is that one would think that in a small group, one or two confused people could skew the group's collective verdict in the wrong direction. (The small group can't, in that sense, rely on errors canceling themselves out.) But there's little evidence of that happening.

One of the more impressive studies of small-group performance was done in 2000 by Princeton economists Alan S. Blinder and John Morgan. Blinder had been vice chairman of the Federal Reserve Board during the mid-1990s, and the experience had made him deeply skeptical of decision making by committee. (Interest-rate changes are set by the Federal Open Market Committee, which consists of twelve members, including the seven members of the Federal Reserve Board and five presidents of regional Federal Reserve banks.) So he and Morgan designed a study that was meant to find out if groups could make intelligent decisions and if they make decisions as a group quickly, since one of the familiar complaints about committees is that they are inefficient.

The study consisted of two experiments that were meant to mimic, crudely, the challenges faced by the Fed. In the first experiment, students were given urns that held equal numbers of blue balls and red balls. They started to draw the balls from the urns, having been told that sometime after the first ten draws, the proportions in the urn would shift, so that 70 percent of the balls would be red and 30 percent blue (or vice versa). The goal was to identify, as soon as possible, which color had become more prevalent. This was roughly analogous to the Fed's job of recognizing when economic conditions have changed and whether a shift in monetary policy is needed. To place a premium on making the right decision quickly, students were penalized for every draw they made after the changeover had happened. The students played the game by themselves first, then played together as a group with free discussion, played as individuals again, and finally once more as a group. (This was to control for the effect of learning.) The group's decisions were both faster and more accurate (the group got the direction right 89 percent of the time, versus 84 percent for individuals), and outperformed even the best individual.

The second experiment demanded more of the students. Essentially, they were asked to play the role of central bankers, and to set interest rates in response to changes in inflation and unemployment. What the experiment was really asking was whether they could detect when the economy had started to slow or was picking up steam, and whether they would move interest rates in the right direction in response. Once again, the group made better decisions than the individuals, who moved interest rates in the wrong direction far more often, and made them as quickly as the individuals. Most strikingly, there was no correlation between the performance of the smartest person in a group and the performance of that group. In other words, the groups were not just piggybacking on really smart individuals. They genuinely were smarter than the smartest people within them. A Bank of England study modeled on Blinder and Morgan's experiment reached identical conclusions: Groups could make intelligent decisions quickly, and could do better than their smartest members.

Given what we've already seen, this is not shocking news. But there are two important things about these studies. The first is that group decisions are not inherently inefficient. This suggests that deliberation can be valuable when done well, even if after a certain point its marginal benefits are outweighed by the costs. The second point is probably obvious, although a surprising number of groups ignore it, and that is that there is no point in making small groups part of a leadership structure if you do not give the group a method of aggregating the opinions of its members. If small groups are included in the decision-making process, then they should be allowed to make decisions. If an organization sets up teams and then uses them for purely advisory purposes, it loses the true advantage that a team has: namely, collective wisdom. One of the more frustrating aspects of the *Columbia* story is the fact that the MMT never voted on anything. The different members of the team would report on different aspects of the mission, but their real opinions were never aggregated. This was a mistake, and it would have been a mistake even had the *Columbia* made it home safely.

Questions for Critical Reading

1. Much of Surowiecki's essay is about the many ways in which small groups can fail. Working from his argument, what are some elements essential to the success of small groups? Use quotations from the text to develop your answer. You will need to read his text critically to compose your response, since it will depend on abstracting those factors essential to the success rather than the failure of small groups.

2. What is "group polarization"? Define the concept using Surowiecki's text and then provide an example from your own experience.

3. Are the benefits of small groups worth the risk? What does Surowiecki think? Begin by critically rereading Surowiecki's text and then support your position by using quotations from the text.

Exploring Context

1. At the center of Surowiecki's analysis is the *Columbia* disaster. Visit NASA's Web site at nasa.gov. Can you find any evidence of change in NASA's culture that might prevent such a disaster from happening again? How are missions handled? Who seems to work there?

2. Visit the Web site for the Advocates, a jury consulting firm, at theadvocates.com. How might such a service influence the small group dynamics of a jury? How do they represent themselves in terms of Surowiecki's argument? You may want to draw from your work on group polarization in Question 2 of Questions for Critical Reading.

3. How do small groups work together online? Explore an online collaboration tool such as Google Docs (docs.google.com). How does the interface promote collaboration? How does it open that collaboration to the pitfalls of small groups documented by Surowiecki? You may want to draw from your work on small groups from Question 1 of Questions for Critical Reading.

Questions for Connecting

1. Can the failure of small groups help explain the challenges of cultivating community and diversity on college campuses? Synthesize Surowiecki's ideas and Rebekah Nathan's analysis in "Community and Diversity" (p. 228).

2. Michael Pollan discusses a different kind of small group in "The Animals: Practicing Complexity" (p. 281). In what ways are organic farming ecosystems like the small groups that Surowiecki discusses? How does the success of organic farming point to strategies for small group success? Relate your response to your answer to Question 1 of Questions for Critical Reading.

3. What is the economical potential—and risk—of small groups? Synthesize Surowiecki's ideas and Thomas Friedman's discussion of global supply chains in "The Dell Theory of Conflict Prevention" (p. 121).

Language Matters

1. Indexes help you locate important information quickly. Create a simple index for Surowiecki's essay. What terms or entries would you include? How often do they appear in the text?

2. Surowiecki ultimately believes in the power of small groups. Working in small groups in class, debate a common grammatical issue or error, such as the run-on sentence. Should it be an error? How important is it? How does your discussion reflect Surowiecki's ideas?

3. Why is *"Columbia"* italicized in this essay? What are the rules for using italics? Develop a system to help you remember when to use them.

Assignments for Writing

1. Surowiecki discusses ways in which group dynamics contributed to the failure of the *Columbia*'s Mission Management Team. Using Surowiecki's observations, write a paper that determines the best practices for organizing and running a small group. In composing your response, consider these questions: What makes a small group more than just the sum of its parts? How can group identity be made to serve the purpose of the group? What is the ideal structure for a group? How important is cognitive diversity, and why? How can "group polarization" be avoided? In what ways could "talkativeness" be regulated to ensure equal participation?

2. Although the Mission Management Team's decisions were made as a group, Surowiecki pays particular attention to the actions of a few individual members. Using Surowiecki's observations, write a paper that evaluates the influence of an individual person in a group setting. To what extent can an individual voice influence a group? Is a small group more than just the sum of its parts? How does individual identity exist in the larger group identity? How is dissent productive to a group decision? In what ways could an individual voice dissolve group polarization? How do the studies Surowiecki mentions support your evaluation? You may want to use your work from Questions for Critical Reading and from Question 2 of Questions for Connecting.

3. Surowiecki describes the pitfalls of logic that await a small group, paying particular attention to the effects of flawed reasoning on group decisions. Using Surowiecki's observations, write an analysis of the error in reasoning that played the biggest role in the Mission Management Team's failure: Describe all instances of the error, identify its origin in flawed reasoning, and trace its consequences for the group's decision-making process. Consider these questions: Could the Mission Management Team's errors be seen only in hindsight? In what way did the Mission Management Team's small group dynamics affect its decisions? Does the fundamental error belong to one person, several people, or the group as a whole? Why? Whose influence was most powerful within the group? Whose influence should have been the most powerful within the group?

Diana Taylor

Diana Taylor holds a B.A. in creative writing from the University of the Americas, a Certificat d'Études Supérieures from the Université Aix-Marseille, an M.A. in comparative literature from the National University of Mexico, and a Ph.D. in comparative literature from the University of Washington. As a professor of performance studies and Spanish at New York University, her areas of research are varied, ranging from Latin American performance to trauma studies. Taylor is also the founding director of the Hemispheric Institute of Performance and Politics. She is the editor of several collections and has won multiple awards for three books of her own: *Theatre of Crisis: Drama and Politics in Latin America* (1991), *Disappearing Acts: Spectacles of Gender and Nationalism in Argentina's Dirty War* (1997), and *The Archive and the Repertoire: Performing Cultural Memory in the Americas* (2003). In 2005, she was awarded the John Simon Guggenheim Fellowship.

Taylor's *The Archive and the Repertoire* deals with performances in the Western hemisphere, particularly in response to tragedies such as the terrorist attacks of September 11, 2001. The book examines cultural performances and the part they play in making political statements, memorializing tragic events, and creating cultural identities.

In "False Identifications: Minority Populations Mourn Diana," from *The Archive and the Repertoire,* Taylor addresses various performances in response to the death of Princess Diana. It is curious that minority populations in New York City would design murals in memory of a former member of the British Royal Family, and the effect is made even more perplexing when murals of Diana share space with depictions of Mother Teresa and Mike Tyson. Taylor tracks these performances, the gradual alterations made to them, and the worldwide responses to this "universal" tragedy. Taylor also tracks the parallels between the responses to Diana's death and those of more "local" figures, such as Selena and Evita, to examine the "virtual act of identification" and individuals' "need for active participation" in such situations.

We usually think of responses to death as intensely personal, but in an age of global celebrity, how do we collectively mourn the famous? And what do those performances of grief tell us about ourselves and our emerging global culture?

▶ TAGS: *mourning, community, diversity, religion, identity, aesthetic boundaries, culture*

False Identifications: Minority Populations Mourn Diana

We sat on the sofa—my young daughter, Marina, on my lap—lamenting the death of a woman we didn't know. As the coffin slowly made its way toward Westminster Abbey, the commentators reverentially droned on about the silence, the mood, the dramatic demonstration of public emotion. But there were so many publics, it seemed, participating in what looked like one and the same theatre of mourning. The exclusive, well-behaved public of dignitaries and movie stars inside the Abbey, the charged "popular" audience on the meadows outside, the two billion people watching each other watching around the world. Everywhere the camera rested, people were sobbing silently. The emotion was contagious: the pity for Diana and her boys, the terror of sudden death, the rage at the ungiving queen, the contempt for the unloving husband. As in theatre, emotion gave way to applause. It erupted outside the Abbey following the Earl Spencer's eulogy and pushed its way inside, back to front, uninvited, disrupting the solemnity and reminding the high and mighty that this was, after all, the public's command performance. Then, as the hearse carrying the remains made its way out of London, the public threw its last bouquets at the departing diva. The incessant repeats of the coverage assured us we were watching "live." What does live mean, I wondered out loud, watching as we were across the Atlantic? "It means we're live and she's dead," Marina explains. Then, "You won't die, will you, Mummy?" punctuated by crying. "No, darling, no, I promise," suddenly crying too, but embarrassed. Our tears were of a different kind—hers about pity and fear; mine complicated by my determination to resist this kind of identification which I found coercive and humiliating.

What's Diana to me, that I should weep for her? This was an odd mirroring effect—one Diana crying for another.

Once again, I was that awkward, chubby child in Parral, Chihuahua—my hair pulled back in pigtails so tight that my eyes wouldn't shut, my skirt pinned together because I'd popped my button, wearing my cowgirl boots, my fringed suede jacket, and my beloved little gold scissors earrings that opened and closed. My Anglo-Canadian grandmother said I looked like a savage. Princess Anne, she reminded me, didn't wear suede jackets, to say nothing of the scissors earrings. I certainly was not her "little princess" and I would never grow up and marry the Prince if I didn't shape up and act like a good girl. Every holiday brought a new corrective for my savage condition: a royal calendar, a commemorative teacup. Now, there she was, the other Diana, the one who had been tall and blonde and beautiful, the one who would never be caught dead without a button, the one who would sooner have died than be chubby; the one who had married the Prince. And look what happened to her. Here, once more, I was caught in a drama that had unexpectedly become my own. I felt a shudder, sensed the ghost.

Downloading Grief

Whose fantasy was this, I kept wondering during the weeks following the death and funeral of Diana, Princess of Wales? Or, rather, how did so many disparate fantasies come to converge on this rather ordinary human being? The disparity between the accident-as-incident and the spectacularity of the worldwide reaction demanded reflection. Diana's ghost, I suspected, had more to tell us about international relations than did Madeleine Albright. What was the basis of such seemingly widespread identification? Were we watching a hodge-podge of funerary traditions, or was this really a case of multicultural mourning styles coalescing before our eyes? What were the politics of such memorializing energy and the mimetic performances of grief being enacted simultaneously in various parts of the world, the synchronized moments of silence, the condolence book signings, the floral shrines? In Argentina, a magazine ran a drawing of Santa Evita and Santa Diana sitting side by side in heaven. There she was, "the most beloved lady of our time," gracing the stamps of the Togolese Republic. The Trinidadian carnival featured a number, "Paparazzi Is Hell," as a "Tribute to the Queen of Hearts." Memorial walls on the Lower East Side of Manhattan were painted by U.S. artists of color. One mural, by Chico, places her next to other female Latina victims: Selena and Elisa (Figures 1–3), both murdered by people close to them. Was this a conspiracy mural? On another, Diana is a savior, along with Mother Teresa, in "royalty and holiness" (Figure 4). And here, in an admonishing mural by A. Charles that covers a synagogue on Houston Street, Diana's death is depicted as media overkill (Figures 5–7). She's placed next to fallen African American icons Tupac Shakur and Mike Tyson. "Live by the gun, die by the gun." The murals made visible the versions of the saint, victim, and media object circulating in the public sphere. How did these global images get downloaded onto these neighborhood walls? Why would minority populations care about her, when their own icons—from Evita to Selena to Tupac—had fared so poorly in the media? By what mechanism did Diana's popularity get construed as "the popular"? The world willingly suspended its disbelief as this most aristocratic of women, married to a prince and future king, the mother of princes and future kings, who socialized with billionaires and celebrities, was transformed before our eyes into the "people's princess" and "queen of people's hearts."

Diana's life, death, funeral, and afterlife as quasi-sacred relic on display illu-   5
minates the way multiple, intersecting social dramas play both globally and locally. All sorts of issues, ranging from eating disorders, to unhappy marriages, to AIDS, to the workings of the media, to neocolonialism, to globalization, seem magically incarnated in her image. The tragic emplotment of the events surrounding Diana and the theatricality of the staging, transmitted internationally, create the illusion of a cohesive, "universal" audience. But is this not perhaps an international spectacle, in the Debordian sense, that "presents itself simultaneously as all of society, as part of society and as an instrument of unification" as it "concentrates all gazing and all consciousness"?[1] There is a difference between playing to a global audience and claiming that the drama has a

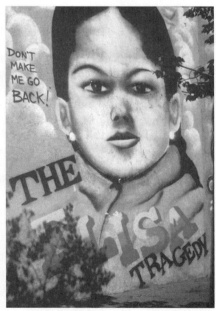

Figures 1, 2, 3   Murals by Chico on East Houston Street in New York City: Diana, Selena, Elisa.

Photos by Diana Taylor, 1997.

Figures 4, 5 *(top)* Mural by Chico, "In Memory of Royalty and Holiness," on 11th Street and Avenue A, New York City. *(bottom)* Murals by A. Charles on Houston Street and First Avenue, New York City.

Photos by Diana Taylor, 1997.

Figures 6, 7   Murals by A. Charles on Houston Street and First Avenue, New York City: Overkill, Diana, Tupac Shakur.

Photos by Diana Taylor, 1997.

universal appeal. By looking at the nature and staging of these social dramas, I explore how globalization gets cast as "universality" and how this "universality" gets downloaded strategically and reconfigured on the local level.

Social Drama

If we follow Victor Turner's model of the "social drama" for a minute, a model he claims to be universally valid, we can easily recognize the four phases he identifies: (1) the breach, or social rupture and flouting of the norm; (2) crisis, in which the breach widens and escalates; (3) redressive action, which seeks to contain the spread of the crisis; and (4) the reintegration, the reordering of social norms.[2] Each of the four stages unfolds in a different dramatic mode, each rivaling the last in pushing the limits of theatricality.

The breach—her divorce from Charles and her estrangement from the Royal family—was pure melodrama. Played in the shrill key of interrogatives, declaratives, and denunciations, the drama unfolded in explosive, sporadic cries and whispers. Almost everyone could (and apparently did) tune in to the latest episodes featuring the insensitive husband, the other woman, the disapproving mother-in-law. The boundaries of the "appropriate" were repeatedly emphasized

She's placed next to fallen African American icons Tupac Shakur and Mike Tyson.

and transgressed. This private drama so publicly enacted situated protagonists and spectators alike on, and often over, the very brink of the admissible. I, like millions of others, lived the traumas of the infidelities and the self-destructive behaviors, eavesdropped on conversations, and shared the thrill of revelations and denials. When she wasn't struggling to hold back the tears, the captions pointed at the evidence of vulnerability. Her pain became the spectacle, played out in a hide-and-seek mode of strategic self-exposure on her part and unrepentant voyeurism on mine. What made it all so thrilling, of course, was not its originality but its predictability: Her story, played out so glamorously in the here and now, was basically the same old story. I, like many, many others, had lived it or seen it all before.

Her death—the crisis—was tragic drama. The fateful crash, which I (like those before me) will replay at length later, moved Diana out of the "same-old" and cast her as the "one." We're alive and she's dead—she's left the anonymity of the "we" to inhabit the singularity of the "she." She crystallized into the original, quintessential, tragic lover, beautiful princess, angel of mercy, and doting mother. Her sudden uniqueness, her tragic magnitude, allowed us to forget for a moment that she was also very much the product of a long history of collective imaginings that have normalized heterosexuality, glorified maternity, fetishized youth and femininity, glamorized whiteness, eroticized imperialism, and promoted a discourse of volunteerism. Live? Or one more repeat of the live?

The redressive action—the funeral—was a theatrical performance. Following in the tradition of other state funerals, this event was one more repetition, only the latest but never the first or the last of such spectacles. Eleanor of Castile, apparently, had a sumptuous send-off in 1290. Evita's funeral in 1952 was a magnificent spectacle, as massive and stately as Diana's. It was a performance, orchestrated with a beginning, middle, and end. The theatricality emanated from the careful choreographing of color, movement, sound, space, and regalia. Theatricality, commonly thought to be an attribute of theatre, clearly precedes and extends beyond it. Communities without theatre (such as non-Western cultures like the Mexica) understood, and were ruled by, theatricality. And issues concerning theatricality lay at the center of many of the tensions between the Queen and the British population. How much or how little theatricality should the country demand in honoring the passing of their Princess?

The theatricality of the event, as state spectacle, claimed visual power 10
through layering, the addition and augmentation of traditional and nontraditional elements. Diana's funeral, weighed down in splendor, outdid those that had come before. But repetition was not simply a mimetic return to former displays of pomp and circumstance. Rather, the pomp associated with the past served to monumentalize the present. Each *re*incarnation gains power through accumulation. Citationality thus was put to the service of originality, enhancing the "new," nontraditional touches, such as Elton John singing his pop hit "Candle in the Wind," in itself recalling an earlier death. Yet, the prescribed, twice-behaved nature of funerals also has another, ritual function. The formal handling of painful or dangerous transitions, or passings, helps regulate the expenditure of emotion. Funerals have long served to channel and control grief. But this televised funeral, with its insistence on participation, seemed to provoke the very emotions it was designed to channel. The spectators, as much as the casket and the visible Royals, became the spectacle for a global audience brought together, perhaps by grief but most certainly by television, newspapers, journals, and the Web. Unlike these earlier events, the media and communications systems performed the identification they claimed to report, assuring us that the loss, like the Princess, was ours.

The phase of reintegration, the period of reordering social norms, played itself out in multiple, less cohesive, less centralized dramas. After the initial phase of virtual participation through frantic memorialization, Diana's ghost became a site of intense renegotiating among various communities. Would the status quo ruptured by the breach be restored? Would the monarchy be reinvigorated, or permanently outmoded? Was Diana the new face of Tony Blair's kinder, gentler, more modern England? Did the burial site constructed by her brother emblematize England's "image in the world [as] a low tech 'theme park of royal pageantry'"?[3] Or had she been transformed into a thoroughly non-British relic in a pay-per-view shrine out of Disney? Are the ruptures and divides made visible by her death overcome in this moment of reintegration, or are the divides more starkly visible than before?

The Hauntology of Performance

Various modalities of expressive culture are made visible through the social drama paradigm outlined by Turner. And he is probably correct in affirming that this four-stage model illuminates all types of social conflict, ranging from office disputes to national conflicts. However, I am less convinced that these dramas play internationally and cross-culturally in any clear-cut way. The "drama" of Diana's death and the "theatricality" of her funeral elide rather than clarify the "trauma" of border crossings as specters traverse ethnic or national boundaries. What counts as a drama in one context gets demoted to a mere incident elsewhere. The Diana specter becomes visible and meaningful as it dances within various scopic, political, and economic repertoires—and vice versa. England's rose occludes Norma Jean as the new candle dancing in the wind. The dance performs more plays of substitution or, in Joseph Roach's term, surrogation: England's rose crowds out Selena, the Rose of Texas; her funeral outdoes Evita's as the most overproduced funeral of the century for a woman.[4] The specter, the spectacle, and the spectator are all dancing at this funeral. Maybe because it's so hard to get a handle on, *spec-ere* (to see) that phantoms, fantasy, and performance have traditionally been placed on the opposite side of the "real" and "historical." The fantasies in play may be linked to so-called universal and eternal anxieties about a glorious life, an unexpected death, and the fall of the great. The iterative and highly stylized nature of this stately display should not suggest that it is not, at the same time, deeply political and historically specific. What conditions allow these fantasies to become visibly incarnated in a woman no one cares much about? Though the specter may come in and out of time, and though performances make visible the conflicts that otherwise remain diffuse, both specters and performances are very live. "Haunting," Derrida notes, "is historical . . . but not dated."[5] The fantasies converging around the figure of Diana, I suggest, require certain conditions of visibility and bring various histories, ontologies, and hauntologies of performance into focus.

In *Unmarked*, Peggy Phelan outlines the "ontology of performance," stressing the liveness of the performative event, the *now* in which that performance takes place: "Performance's only life is in the present. Performance cannot be saved, recorded, documented, or otherwise participate in the circulation of representations of representation."[6] An event such as Diana's death and funeral, however, also begs us to look at the flip side of performance's ontology, at what Derrida has called its "hauntology." Many cultures are grounded on the notion of a second coming: the Mexica, the Christian, the Jewish, the Marxist, to name a few. The ghost is, by definition, a repetition, Derrida's *revenant*. This is the moment of postdisappearance, rather than the moment preceding it that Phelan points to. The sumptuousness of the ceremony performs the sacralization of the *remains*, theoretically antithetical to performance. The remains, in this spectacle, take on a life of their own—so much so that one tabloid photo montage has Di looking on at her own funeral from the corner with a bittersweet smile, one more witness to an event that has overtaken her. The body we assume lies in the coffin is all that we have to assure us that Diana was real. It provides the authenticating materiality that sustains the performance of resuscitation. In spirit, she was present at her funeral, as perhaps, inversely, we could argue that she was absent from her life. The shrine housing her remains will continue to guarantee the materiality of the global phenomenon that is Diana, the massive reappearance of the revenant. Politically and symbolically, we haven't seen the end of her. The caption of a recent photograph of a London newsstand states that "one might be forgiven for imagining that Diana never died last August. The Princess of Wales still keeps the presses roaring."[7] The February 2, 1998, cover of *People* depicts Diana as active in death as she was in life: "In death as in life, she has raised millions for charity."

My view of performance rests on the notion of ghosting, that visualization that continues to act politically even as it exceeds the live. Like Phelan's definition, it hinges on the relationship between visibility and invisibility, or appearance and disappearance, but comes at it from a different angle. For Phelan, the defining feature of performance—that which separates it from all other phenomena—is that it is live and disappears without a trace. The way I see it, performance makes visible (for an instant, live, now) that which is always already there: the ghosts, the tropes, the scenarios that structure our individual and collective life. These specters, made manifest through performance, alter future phantoms, future fantasies. Diana may have been the product of one way of envisioning royalty, but she has changed the look, style, and scope in which royalty will be performed, and desired, in the future. Her enactment left a trace. Every woman running for political office in Argentina today wears the obligatory dyed blonde bun and Dior suit associated with Evita. In one sense, of course, the live performance eludes the "economy of reproduction," as Phelan puts it.[8] But I would argue that its efficacy, whether as art or as politics, stems from the way performances tap into public fantasies and leave a trace, reproducing and at times altering cultural repertoires. Performance, then, involves more than an object (as in performance art), more than an accomplishment or a carrying through. It constitutes a (quasi-magical) invocational practice. It provokes emotions it claims only to represent, evokes memories and grief that belong to some other body. It conjures up and makes visible not just the live but the powerful army of the always already living. The power of seeing through performance is the recognition that we've seen it all before—the fantasies that shape our sense of self, of community, that organize our scenarios of interaction, conflict, and resolution.

What conditions of visibility are needed to conjure up the ghost? Of all the many potential specters, why do certain ones gain such power? Why Diana and not somebody else? Why, as Michael Taussig asks in *Mimesis and Alterity*, does the spirit (and, I would add, the ghost) need embodiment at all?[9] Evita's corpse, perhaps, can shed some light on the need to give material shape to a political force. The most politically powerful woman in the world in the early 1950s, Evita has the world's most expensive corpse. It cost $200,000 to embalm her and three wax copies were produced to trick all the would-be body snatchers. The copies were so authentic that Dr. Ara removed the tip of her little finger to distinguish her real body from its replications. The original, here as elsewhere, is never as whole as its representation. Her body, the most politically charged fetish of the twentieth century, is key because it anchors the "other Eva," the more powerful one, the one whose ghost continues to dominate Argentine politics. *Spec-ere*, to see, is possible only through a history of spectacles and ghosts. Performance, be it artistic or political, accomplishes a moment of revisualization. It

Figure 8   Dr. Ara and Evita's corpse. From *Página 12*, September 22, 1996.
Photo courtesy of Diana Taylor.

disappears only to hover; it promises or threatens to reappear, albeit in another shape or form.

Performance becomes visible, meaningful, within the context of a phantasmagoric repertoire of repeats. But there is a double mechanism at work. On the one hand, we see only what we have been conditioned to see: that which we have seen before. So part of the grief we feel surrounding Diana's death is that she is so familiar to us. She represents the most general, undifferentiated version of the death of the beautiful woman, a scenario so powerful, so naturalized that it underwrites the Western imaginary and seems always to have been there.[10] On the other hand, the spectacle presents itself as a universal and unifying event. But spectacle, to conjure up Debord for a minute, "is not a collection of images, but a social relation among people, mediated by images."[11] The spectacle, then, is that which we do *not* see, the invisible that "appears" only through mediation. Diana's specter unites the spectators in the fantasy of loving and losing a woman no one really knows even as it hides the social relations among the very people who, theoretically, participate in the fantasy. Diana's death looks more like one more repetition of the same. Her death (singular and sudden) represents both the instant of her passing ("real," not-performatic) *and* the reappearance of another death: Evita, Selena, Marilyn Monroe, Mother Teresa. As Elisabeth Bronfen argues, "The death of a beautiful woman emerges as the requirement for a preservation of existing cultural norms and values. . . .

Figure 9   "La Otra Eva," *Página 12,* **Radar section, September 22, 1996.**
Photo courtesy of Diana Taylor.

Over her dead body, cultural norms are reconfigured or secured, whether because the sacrifice of the virtuous, innocent woman serves a social critique and transformation or because a sacrifice of the dangerous woman reestablishes an order that was momentarily suspended due to her presence."[12] This seemingly universal scenario elides the politics of cultural transmission. What we don't see, as the world mourns Diana, is that these women (judged innocent or dangerous, and usually both) form part of profoundly different imaginaries, and the borders of these imaginaries are policed. The specter hides the spectacle. The mourning rituals may be similar; they may even encourage fantasies that they are communicable to different populations. But the politics are untranslatable.

Policing the Imaginary

Chicanas and Chicanos, as well as other Latinos, mourned Selena en masse, covered her coffin with thousands of roses, gathered tens of thousands of signatures in commemorative books, declared an official Selena Day, and attempted to inscribe her name and face on everything from Web sites to memorial walls to Coca-Cola bottles. The similarity of the rituals highlights the lack of empathetic reciprocity; theatricality blinds even as it makes visible. The redressive moment of one social drama (Selena's funeral) signals the moment of breach in another. A few hours before her funeral, Howard Stern had already shipped her back to Mexico: "Selena? Her music is awful. I don't know what Mexicans are into. If you're going to sing about what's going on in Mexico, what can you say? . . . You can't grow crops, you got a cardboard house, your eleven-year-old daughter is a prostitute. . . . This is music to perform abortions to!"[13] According to Stern, this death proves too lowly to constitute a drama. It's reduced to an incident— no drama, no breach. These nondramas don't travel. How, then, do some ghosts dance over cultural boundaries while others are stopped, strip-searched, and denied entry?

The specter is as visible and powerful as the cultural scenarios surrounding it. Stern's "What can you say?" relegates Selena to the ignominy of particularism: poverty, deviance, genocide. Stern sets himself up as the *migra* of the imaginary, the border police who ensure that certain identifications don't sneak into dominant culture. There are no fictions of the reciprocity that Walter Benjamin ascribes to translation here, no lip service to communication, no invitation to make meaning in this puzzling affair—we don't understand you, what are Mexicans into?[14] Punto. The performance of explicit noncaring performs the breach even as it denies the drama. By refusing to acknowledge a loss, it forecloses the possibility of redressive action and reintegration. The contempt of mourning rite denies the ghost its afterlife: This is about aborting. Diana, on the other hand, is invoked in hushed, reverential terms. She is assured an afterlife either as saint, as mother of the future king, or as a fund-raiser for charities. Guaranteed a visa, her face crosses borders on stamps, calendars, magazines. Her image serves as the occasion for bringing artists together in the service of disenfranchised communities, even as members of those communities are denied the stage. Yet everyone, it seems, is invited to participate and conjecture—to participate by conjecturing. The staging of her death ricochets between twin poles of singularity and universality; Diana's life and death, though utterly unique and one of a kind, nonetheless sheds light on misery, suffering, and stoicism everywhere. The coverage relished each detail, including what she ate for dinner on that fateful night! Yet it shunned particularism, stressing that this death was also about everything and everyone. Immediately, the death was aestheticized as drama and cast in the most powerful and universalizing paradigm available to meaning-making culture: tragedy.

Tragedy

Diana's death and funeral is the clearest example I have ever witnessed of an Aristotelian tragedy of international magnitude, "made sensuously attractive . . . enacted by the persons themselves," provoking pity and fear in millions of spectators. True, Aristotle insists that tragedy is the "imitation" of an action, rather than the real action itself.[15] And in a sense, of course, the distinction between art and life is a vital one. But there is also a way in which life imitates or is constructed through art, and not the other way around, that allows us to think of life as performative in the early Butlerian usage of the term as "a stylized repetition of acts."[16] The "Diana" we knew was a performative construct, the product of stylized acts—royal protocol, fairy tales, designer styles, and Hollywood fantasy—a real princess, a royal model as well as a new model for royalty. Her wedding provided the role and inserted her into a script shaped by tradition. She temporarily fit the bill (a young, aristocratic, malleable, good-looking virgin), the way an actor might be typecast for a role. What, one wonders, is real about this live performance?

Diana's death seemed similarly scripted, not by royal protocol this time but by "fate" and the media. Everything about it was "impossibly tragic." It was sig-nificant and of Aristotelian "magnitude" due to the nobility and beauty (heroic stature) of the woman, the struggle to shape her own destiny, the tricks to ward off fate (the real driver leaving the Ritz as decoy). Diana's *hamartia* (tragic flaw) was so simple, so human according to the media/chorus: She merely wanted to be happy. The *peripeteia,* or reversal of fortune, was abrupt. The inevitabil-ity of the *catastrophe* was almost a given, considering the persistent mad chase by the paparazzi and the equally mad attempts at flight. The identification, as always in tragedy, was written into the performance. We don't have to know these great figures in order to weep for them.

And the timing couldn't be more tragically ironic. Just as she was start-ing her new life, which she had attained against all odds, she died on the very night he gave her "the ring." Not only that, she died with her lover—the latest version of the "star-crossed lovers," as one tabloid called them. Even the names played into the tragedy as Dodi, meaning "my beloved," and Di raced off to their "destiny" (as the accident is repeatedly alluded to by the tabloids). It was already written—not just in Aristotle but in the *Song of Songs*: "Dodí li va-aní lo" (My beloved is mine and I am his). Others find her death already coded in Genesis. The spectacle of the death elicits the specters of the already there. We're moved because we already know the story: the dark tunnel, the frantic chase, Diana the huntress hunted down. The paparazzi, who dedicated their lives to "doing Di," to banging, blitzing, hosing, ripping, smudging, and whacking her (all words, we learn, for taking pictures rapidly), finally got their prey.[17] The pace of the drama was fast, the tunnel tomblike in its dark enclosure; the plot revolved around sex and love; the reversal from supreme happiness to sudden death was precipi-tous; the end unexpected, shocking. And there was even a whiff of conspiracy about this end to a life that was otherwise so transparent, so devoid of mystery. Was the thought of Diana marrying an Egyptian playboy with a purportedly mafioso background too much for the royal family? The innocent woman had little by little become the dangerous woman—the woman whose bulimia, sui-cide attempts, and infidelities threatened the image of the royal body, and now, its ethnic purity and exclusivity. Or was her accident contrived by the royal fam-ily to elicit popular support for itself? Project Interflora, an online site warning of royal conspiracy, had also seen it all before and warned its audience, "REMEMBER! Awaken!!!!" It reads the "Di thing" as a way of assuring the "continuance of the Monarchy." The floral tributes are an example of "Flower Power . . . an MI5 mind control program aimed at mass manipulation of the hearts and minds of the people of Britain. . . . These floral tributes are NOT spontaneous!" Even

Aristotle could not have envisioned a more perfectly crafted plot. While one tabloid headline screams out "She didn't have to die!" the way that the media "made sense" of her death stressed the tragic inevitability of "the love she died for."[18] Anyone who has grown up with *Romeo and Juliet* or *West Side Story*, not to mention Agatha Christie and the Old Testament, might find something to relate to in this drama.

Diana's death precipitated a process of transformation and resolution on multiple levels. Diana, the dangerous and transgressive woman, "died a lover."[19] However, she was buried a mother, an innocent victim, a model of humanitarianism, a quasi-saintly do-gooder, and a member of the royal family. Once again, her image was transposed from one economy to another: The fairy tale princess in the heavy gown of the wedding photos and the formally attired, motherly wife of the early years had already given way to the casual, lightly clad, jet-setting image of her final years. Her death weighted her down again with the heavy brocade of the royal colors. She was back in the fold, center stage in the state's (polyvalent) self-imaging. After her wedding to Dodi, a sumptuous state funeral would have been unthinkable. Even as it was, the Queen initially demanded that "Diana's body should not be placed in any of the royal palaces and should be taken to a private mortuary."[20] The body, now saturated with the sacred/abject power of the transgressor, had to be kept away from the royal. It was "private" now, exiled to the mundane sphere of the ordinary. But the non-Royals wouldn't have it, not for "their" Princess. It was the Queen's turn to undergo public shaming. The "people" forced her to perform her emotions, whether she felt them or not. "Show Us You Care," demanded the *Express;* "Your People are Suffering: SPEAK TO US MA'AM," the *Mirror* shouted from the stands. "Where is Our Queen? Where is Her Flag?" the *Sun* wanted to know. "Let the Flag Fly at Half Mast," the *Daily Mail* insisted, giving the Queen her own little lesson in protocol.

> **The coverage relished each detail, including what she ate for dinner on that fateful night!**

The funeral was equally dramatic, though in a different way. This was imperial theatre, theoretically brokered by the "people" and elaborately negotiated by all parties. The behind-the-scenes bickering of how much or how little (whether in terms of spectacle, emotion, or viewers) was suspended by the splendor of the affair. The lavishness of the funeral made visible that the feuding, like the body, could be laid to rest; now that Diana was dead, rivalries and contentions could be forgotten. The country was once more united in tragedy, and the overwhelming sensual experience (the smell of the flowers, the echoing sound of the horses' hooves, the trembling bodies of sobbing spectators) rekindled the erotic, though ambivalent, attraction to the state. So the funeral was an act of national conflict and resolution, an act of remembering one Diana by forgetting the others, of celebrating a life and transcending (obscuring) it with claims to a higher purpose and a sanctity it never had. The transgressive, casual Diana was now thoroughly snuffed out, in part, by the very people who claimed to love her.

The funeral as imperial theatre was the opposite of the death as drama. As in theatre, a word that refers both to the physical, institutional frame and the intentional action that takes place within its limits, the theatricality of the funeral elided issues of Diana's relationship to the monarchy by normalizing the rite of passage within the demarcations of historical tradition. Tensions disappeared behind the sensuousness, the ceremony of it all. The route, the lines of spectators, the choreography of the funeral party: This was a deliberate staging of the restoration of order, carefully modeled on previous, orderly funerals. It was about the "again," "now," and "as always" of royal self-representation. It disappears only to reappear. The achingly slow procession signaled the seemingly eternal and stable quality of a royal order now so openly up for grabs. The monarchy on show was very different from the one that waved at the world during the wedding. But the physical staging was also an act of restoration; it bracketed and emplotted the event, the first and last act of the Princess of Wales. After the abrupt crisis caused by the crash, the funeral provided aesthetic closure and emotional resolution. As in ritual, this final stage promised to be deeply conservative. The restitution of the social order, disrupted but probably not profoundly altered by the crisis, meant that Diana once more returned to the official body she tried so hard to elude. As Charles, the two young Princes, Prince Philip, and Earl Spencer followed the coffin on foot, it was clear that the procession was as much about possession and control as about emotion and empathy.

What do "the people" have to do with this imperial theatre, with the struggles between the Queen and the Prince, the Windsors and the Spencers, the Tories and Tony Blair's Labour Party? Que vela tenemos nosotros en este entierro? How do "the people" get constructed? The "staging of the popular," as Néstor García Canclini argues in *Hybrid Cultures*, "has been a mix of participation and simulacrum."[21] Newspapers around the world ran the same article, extending the reach of the we as it extended its audience. The same picture of Diana would appear, often with the same text, reporting on our reaction to the devastating turn of events. One Web site instructed the user to "send your feelings, condolences, or memorial regarding Princess Diana by *clicking here*." The "Princess Diana fax poll" (set up by the *Post*) asked people to define what she meant to them.[22]

In England, the event was interpreted as a "revolution" (of sorts) because it showed "the people" their new power. The *New York Times* reported the "remarkable confrontation between the British people and Buckingham Palace and . . . an even more remarkable royal retreat."[23] "The people" won their show-down with the Queen. They had demanded the pomp and ceremony of empire self-fashioning. The ritual, traditional to the extreme, could be read as a subversive reversal, for it was the public, not the Crown, who ordered it. Now, Tony Blair would have us believe, the old aristocratic ways vanished in one more act of surrogation: The Queen is dead, Long live Diana, the Queen of the people's hearts. Diana was the new face of the new England: stylish, youthful, and compassionate. Hegemony now enjoyed a more casual, photogenic look. Diana, like England, was coming out of a depression. She would be the goodwill ambassador, the kinder, gentler, post-Thatcher face of England. Instead of politics, style. Instead of bitter ideological divides, consensus and national unity. "The people" were featured as actors, rather than spectators, in the national drama.

The drama, then, is not just about Diana's tragic death, her regal funeral, or the current political situation in England. The event, commentators insist, is performative; it is about changing structures of feeling. It changed the way the English performed their emotions: Out with stiff upper lips and mean-spirited politics; in with touching, smiling, and generous public displays of spontaneity. Diana touching AIDS patients, or dying children, signaled a new mode of being (British).

Loss

Loss. A ghost is about loss, loss made manifest, the vision of that which is no longer there. But what, I wonder, has been lost? Diana's candles, like Evita's and Mother Teresa's, provided the thousand points of light that corporate governments no longer feel compelled to provide. Lost, too, were both a working-class and a feminist agenda. Unlike Evita, who came from a working-class background and wielded unprecedented political power in Argentina, Diana and Mother Teresa had no political aspirations. Evita's popularity, channeled into a formidable populism, exceeded her death to the point that her ghost is still the most politically powerful player in Argentine politics today. This world is not ready for another Evita. The female powerhouse of the 1940s and early 1950s becomes the apolitical, unthreatening sophisticate of the 1990s. Evita too is denied a visa. When she was resuscitated in the movie *Evita*, Madonna was a style, a "look." The passionate public of political actors who maintained Evita in power melted into teary-eyed spectators and consumers. Evita's prophecy of her revenance, "I will return, and I will be millions," seemed ironically fulfilled. For here she was, incarnated by Madonna, of all people. Even the walls cried out in protest: "Out Madonna, Evita lives." Evita lives, but only in Argentina. In the United States, she is a lipstick, a fascist, a whore, and an oddity. What next, Frank Rich asks? Maybe "Barbie-like Evita dolls laid out in little clear plastic caskets."[24] The conjuring act accomplishes one more disappearance by repetition—one face for another, one name for another, Evita dissolves in Madonna, while Madonna gains visibility through Evita.

So the choices were not, and never could be, between Diana and Evita, but about Diana and Mother Teresa. A 1998 *New Yorker* cartoon by Frank Cotham showed winged inhabitants of heaven moving along Princess Di Way and Mother Teresa Blvd. The way of the Empire and the way of the Church each take their ambassadors on the clearly one-way journey across borders, unsolicited yet living proof that the First World cares. In the language of love rather than power, these women claim to relinquish their enormous political, economic, and symbolic capital to the have-nots. As with all overloaded icons, these women looked so transparent. It's all so simple, this love talk. One could love Diana and love Mother Teresa and still hate politics, as if the naturalized act of charitable

Figure 10. Evita fades into Madonna on the cover of *La Maga*, January 31, 1996.
Photo courtesy of Diana Taylor.

giving had nothing to do with the expansionism of imperialism, Catholicism, and late capitalism.

Lost too, perhaps, is the colonial nostalgia for the Royal Love. For viewers in the former colonies, Diana also embodied a love-hate relationship with empire and imperialism, which she simultaneously represented and transcended. Her estrangement from the Royals allowed for the ambiguous positioning, the nepantla of Latin American postcolonialism, or the "ambivalence" stemming from what Homi Bhabha refers to as the "double articulation" (the like, but not quite) of the colonial predicament.[25] What options do colonials have but to juggle the complicated play of identification/disidentification? She was living proof that the Royal Love had failed. Yet the love of the Royal could continue through our love of her. And our love for her led us to the possibility of transcending the racism at the heart of colonialism through her new romantic attachment to Dodi. This dark, sexy, playboy Other, the ultimate consumer, was the antithesis of Charles, the ultimate, old fashioned, nerdy "one of them." It made her, supposedly, "one of us"—one of those left out or betrayed by an atrociously uptight establishment. Okay, Dodi was a billionaire jet-setter, maybe not quite one of us, and in our heart of hearts we wonder if they would have been happy, but the beauty of fairy tales depends precisely on the suddenness and untimeliness of their endings.

In another way, of course, Diana's death was about the loss of another form of materiality. Her image gave a "universal" face to the disembodied globalism facilitated by satellites and the World Wide Web. A product of intercommunication systems, the Diana we saw was never and always live. Never live because, as one publication put it, "No Pix, No Di."[26] Her liveness was a product of mediation. Susan Stewart, in *TV Guide*, writes, "I know for a fact that Diana existed apart from television: I once shook her hand. It was exciting—she was already an international icon—but almost meaningless. All I remember is a blur of blond hair, a purr of a greeting. There are at least a dozen film clips of Diana more vivid in my mind than our actual off-screen meeting."[27] Her physical existence, redundant even in life, served merely to authenticate her more complete, real, and ubiquitous image that continues to defy the limits of space and time.

Thus, she was never (but is always) live and here everywhere, haunting our present. A Virtual Di, her image outlives her death; the signifier has no need of the signified, except as authenticating remains. She existed; that's enough to hang our dramas on. The Web asks us to light a candle for her, expanding the simulacrum of participation. She is a fetish, a sacred image whose meaning emanates not from within but is assigned to it from without. As a fetish (whether in psychoanalytic terms or as commodity fetishism), her success stems both from the facility with which anxieties and fears are displaced onto her and the process of disavowal whereby the public can admire the image while ignoring the violence that contributed to its making. Her vulnerability, unhappiness, and physical distress only contributed to her popularity, for as someone noted, the unhappier she was, the better she looked. After her death, a new (and improved) generation of commodities circulate with her image on them: commemorative stamps, plates, and dolls. The music and books she inspired reached the top of the charts and grossed millions of dollars. Her name is invoked in the war against drunken driving, land mines, AIDS, bulimia, and other assorted social ills. A new army of designers will take charge of dressing and tutoring the ghost. Sightings have been reported. New performances, political, artistic, or entrepreneurial, rise out of these archival remains. Other women will dance in that space of impossibility made visible by her performance.

Negotiating the Local

After the orgy of promiscuous identification has passed, do communities feel the abandonment and exploitation of the one-night stand? When we look in that colonial mirror, does her reflection look back at us, or do we see ourselves, complete with pigtails and popped buttons? The murals in Figures 1–7, as spaces of communal, public mourning, show signs of ongoing debate. Rather than simply reiterate the universal show of love and loss, the murals make the events local, bringing them right into the heart of the community. "Why do we care about Diana?" they seem to ask. By honoring her untimely death, the memorial walls situate her squarely in the long, unacknowledged history of untimely deaths in these neighborhoods. They call attention to the gang and police violence in New York City that people prefer to overlook. But the walls also manifest the anger of the unrequited, the "why should we care about her when no one cares about us?" The Latino murals to Princess Di now have "Die" written all over them. Someone has written "NO MORE SPECTACLES AT ALL LADY DIE" in yellow paint on the admonishing mural that had warned about media overkill (Figure 11). The mural that had declared its love for Diana, announcing that she would be missed worldwide, now has a consciously postcolonial message on it: "We spent years of toil to break from the tyranny of British rule. NO SAINTS, NO SINNERS" (Figure 12). The Holiness and Royalty mural featuring Diana and Mother Teresa not only screams "DIE! DIE! DIE!" but participates in another form of circulation (Figure 13). This mural shows more than the displaced images of transnational globalization. It captures, too, the flip side of that same economy that leaves people out in the cold: the displaced people, poverty, and homelessness that volunteerism does not dissipate on the Lower East Side. The homeless man places himself, like an offering, at this "altar" to holiness.

Diana's ghost keeps dancing, tracing the convergence of preexisting phantoms and the latest crisis — always a rewriting, an updating, a making actual, of something that is already. Because we are all caught in transnational

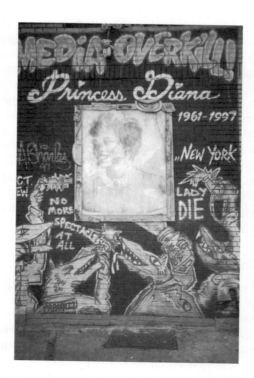

Figure 11 **"No More Spectacles," graffiti-altered mural by A. Charles, on Houston Street and First Avenue, New York City.**
Photo by Diana Taylor, 1997.

Figures 12, 13 (*top*) "No Saints, No Sinners," graffiti on the Diana mural by Chico, on East Houston Street, New York City. (*bottom*) "Die, Die, Die," graffiti on "In Memory of Royalty and Holiness" mural by Chico.

Photos by Diana Taylor, 1997.

economic and iconographic systems, we have no choice, it seems, but to participate in the circulation of capital, symbolic as well as economic. How we download these images and engage with them, however, reflects the power of the
local community in framing the terms of the debates. On one level, of course,
Diana's death and funeral constitute a global drama of mass appeal. Here are
all the ingredients of a successful tearjerker: the death of a noble, beautiful,
and misunderstood princess. Thus, it is both a first and a repetition, a ghosting, a performative reappearance. In this particular staging, "the people" are
not only the consumers but also the constructed of this death. The spectacle
of the specter makes the spectator. Instead of mourning, the undifferentiated
multitudes consume grief—the recipients, not the agents, of an emotion that
is not their own. "The people" light imaginary candles for Diana on the Web in
a virtual act of identification. But, on another level, the event has also staged
the need for active participation. Is it so strange that we may want to act in
a drama we know full well is not our own? If we must engage, as it seems we
must, these muralists show that people will establish the terms of conversation. Rather than constitute one more space for a downloading of the global,
it opens one more strategic site for the negotiation of the local. Maybe it's not
so odd that we, like the artists of the memorial walls, may wish to insert our
own version of events by placing her next to our victims, next to other icons
of caring, knowing full well that the gesture will never be reciprocated. But as
always, there is the ambivalent push-pull of the imperial fantasy. The DI erupts
in DIE. These rituals of passing insist that we forget that we don't belong, even
as we remember.

We walk around the streets of the Lower East Side, Marina and I, taking photo-   35
graphs. The walls change constantly, reflecting new social interests and concerns. The synagogue, later converted into a Yiddish musical theatre venue,
on which A. Charles painted Tupac, Tyson, and Diana, was boarded up for
a year. It recently opened as a posh movie theatre, showing excellent alternative films (Figure 14). After September 11, Chico used the wall on which
he painted "In Memory of Royalty and Holiness" to commemorate those lost
in the attack. I had forgotten that he had long since painted over the faces of
Diana and Mother Teresa. He had clearly wanted to blot out his bout with false
identification. "What was here before?" I asked Marina. She too has forgotten. Later we remember: a huge, banal "Wouldn't it be beautiful?" had been
written on an equally banal image of the sun setting over the peaceful sea. It
had nothing to do with anything—very unusual for mural art. No wonder
we didn't recall. On Houston, the three large walls dedicated to Diana, Elisa,
and Selena had also undergone change. Chico had repainted Selena and Elisa,
whose faces are still up today. Diana was gone, surrogated by the image of a
cat and a dog against the New York skyscape. "Overpopulation is killing us:
Please spay or neuter," and below it the name of a clinic. Even Selena had an
arrow over her head, pointing to a pharmacy around the corner (Figure 15).
Lots of disappearances, lots of forms of forgetting. Soon, we will forget that we
have forgotten.

Figure 14   The facade that A. Charles painted on Houston Street undergoes gentrification.
Photo by Diana Taylor, 2000.

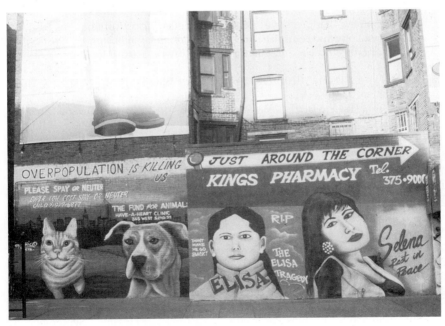

Figure 15   "Overpopulation Is Killing Us," mural by Chico on East Houston Street.
Photo by Diana Taylor, 2000.

NOTES

1. Guy Debord, *Society of the Spectacle* (Detroit: Black and Red, 1983), 3.
2. Victor Turner, *Dramas, Fields, and Metaphors: Symbolic Action in Human Society* (Ithaca: Cornell UP, 1974), 37–42.
3. Winston S. Churchill, "Modernizing Britain, the Tony Blair Way," *New York Times,* January 2, 1998, A17.
4. Joseph Roach, *Cities of the Dead: Circum-Atlantic Performance* (New York: Columbia UP, 1996), 2.
5. Jacques Derrida, *Specters of Marx* (London: Routledge, 1994), 4.
6. Peggy Phelan, *Unmarked: The Politics of Performance* (London: Routledge, 1993), 146.
7. Warren Hoge, "Diana's Hereafter, an Eternity of Newsstand Life," *New York Times,* February 9, 1998, A4.
8. Phelan, *Unmarked,* 146.
9. Michael Taussig, *Mimesis and Alterity* (New York: Routledge, 1993), 10.
10. See Elisabeth Bronfen, *Over Her Dead Body: Death, Femininity and the Aesthetic* (New York: Routledge, 1992), 181.
11. Debord, *Society of the Spectacle,* 4.
12. Bronfen, *Over Her Dead Body,* 181.
13. Quoted in Maria Celeste Arraras, *Selena's Secret* (New York: Simon and Schuster, 1997), 24.
14. Walter Benjamin, *Illuminations: Essays and Reflections* (New York: Harcourt, Brace and World, 1955), 72.
15. Aristotle, *Poetics,* trans. Gerald F. Else (Ann Arbor: U of Michigan P, 1973), 25.
16. Judith Butler, "Performative Acts and Gender Constitution: An Essay in Phenomenology and Feminist Theory," in *Performing Feminisms: Feminist Critical Theory and Theatre,* ed. Sue-Ellen Case (Baltimore: Johns Hopkins UP, 1990), 270.
17. Sarah Lyall, "Diana's Hunters: How Quarry Was Stalked," *New York Times,* September 10, 1997, A1.
18. "She Didn't Have to Die!" *Globe,* September 16, 1997, cover; "The Love She Died For," *Globe,* September 16, 1997, 22.
19. Barbara Kirshenblatt-Gimblett, "Issues and Methods" class, Performance Studies, New York University, September 1997.
20. Kamal Ahmed, "Charles and the Queen at War over Diana," *Guardian,* International ed., September 9, 1997, 1.
21. Néstor García Canclini, *Hybrid Cultures: Strategies for Entering and Leaving Modernity,* trans. Christopher L. Chiappari and Silvia L. López (Minneapolis: U of Minnesota P, 1995), 11, n. 1.
22. "Princess Diana Fax Poll," *New York Post,* September 4, 1997, 5.
23. Warren Hoge, "Flower Power," *New York Times,* September 9, 1997, A1.
24. Frank Rich, "101 Evitas," *New York Times,* December 11, 1996, A27.
25. Homi Bhabha, *The Location of Culture* (New York: Routledge, 1994), 86.
26. Max Frankel, "No Pix, No Di," *New York Times Magazine,* September 21, 1997, 53.
27. Susan Stewart, "TV Bids Farewell to Its Princess," *TV Guide,* September 20, 1997, 24.

Questions for Critical Reading

1. What is "social drama"? Define the term using Taylor's text and then provide your own example.

2. Taylor uses the term *ghosting*. What does she mean by this term? How does she use it in this essay? Define the term using her text and then perform a critical reading of the role it plays in her overall argument.

3. Why do minority populations mourn figures like Princess Diana? What's the social function of mourning? Perform a critical reading of the essay to formulate your response, and support your position with quotations from Taylor's essay.

Exploring Context

1. Visit princess-diana.com. How does this tribute site reflect Taylor's argument? What other populations continue to mourn Princess Diana? Connect your response to your work on mourning from Question 3 of Questions for Critical Reading.

2. Using the Web, research another celebrity or political figure who has recently died. How are they mourned? Who mourns them? How does mourning take place online? Is there any social drama or ghosting involved? Draw from the definitions of these terms you created for Questions 1 and 2 of Questions for Critical Reading.

3. Google Fight (googlefight.com) lets you compare the results from two different search terms. Stage a Google fight between Selena and Princess Diana or between two other objects of mourning such as Evita and Mother Teresa. How do the results confirm or complicate Taylor's argument?

Questions for Connecting

1. Taylor is interested in the social function of mourning and the identifications of racialized and colonial subjects. Use her ideas to further explain the appropriation of black talk as explored by Leslie Savan in "What's Black, Then White, and Said All Over?" (p. 363). Does slang partake in social drama? Does black talk work as a form of ghosting? Use your definitions of Taylor's terms from Questions for Critical Reading to compose your response.

2. What role might the primacy of practice play in mourning? Apply Kwame Anthony Appiah's ideas in "Making Conversation" (p. 57) and "The Primacy of Practice" (p. 63) to Taylor's argument. Is cosmopolitanism evident in the identifications that Taylor examines? How can you synthesize their positions?

3. Taylor's essay focuses on the end of life. In contrast, Debora L. Spar's "Trading Places: The Practice and Politics of Adoption" (p. 402) focuses on the beginning of life. Use Taylor's ideas about hauntology and social drama—drawing from

your work in Questions for Critical Reading—to examine Spar's essay. Is the baby market a kind of social drama? Do international adoptions represent a kind of false identification?

Language Matters

1. How do foreign languages affect our understanding of language in general? Use your experience with a foreign language, learned at school or at home, to think about your own writing. Does understanding the grammar of another language help you in your writing?

2. Wikipedia is an increasingly popular resource, though one that usually plays little role in academic writing. Start by reading Wikipedia's entry for Diana Taylor. Then write a short piece that could serve as the entry for this essay. What information would you include? Before writing, you might want to check out Wikipedia's style manual at en.wikipedia.org/wiki/wikipedia:Manual_of_Style. What grammatical issues seem most important in a Wikipedia entry, and why? How does writing for this online encyclopedia differ from academic writing? Why might that influence the usefulness of this source in research?

3. What's the social function of grammar? Why do we even have grammar? Connect your answers to Taylor's concepts.

Assignments for Writing

1. Engage Taylor's text by assessing the relationship between culture and politics, and then write an essay in which you examine the role of popular culture in political discourse. How do societies construe their politicians? Does "popularity" matter in political discourse? Why or why not? What is the appeal of foreign political figures to other cultures? What is the role of performance in culture and politics? You might want to begin your response with your work from Question 2 of Exploring Context.

2. Taylor examines the reactions of people around the world to the death of Princess Diana. Analyze the role of celebrity in today's society, and then write an essay in which you examine the power of celebrity in our society. What effect does the cult of celebrity have on society? Is the mirroring of style, appearance, and actions positive or negative? Do things like location, religion, nationality, gender, or race factor into an individual's or a society's reaction to celebrity?

3. Explore the specific reactions people have to universal tragedy throughout Taylor's essay, and then write an essay in which you evaluate the function of individual tragedy for groups. What function does the press have in the shaping of universal tragedy? How does the concept of social drama interact with this widespread identification? What is the role of collective imagining?

KENJI YOSHINO

Kenji Yoshino is the Chief Justice Earl Warren Professor of Constitutional Law at New York University. Previously, Yoshino was a professor of law and the deputy dean of intellectual life at Yale Law School, where he earned a J.D. after graduating from Harvard and Oxford universities. His articles have appeared in various law journals as well as the *New York Times,* the *Village Voice,* the *Boston Globe,* and the *Nation.* His book *Covering: The Hidden Assault on Our Civil Rights* was published in 2006.

Covering offers a unique perspective on the familiar concepts of assimilation and passing, utilizing Yoshino's background experience as both a law scholar and a gay Asian American. Yoshino combines personal narrative and legal argument to lay out a new definition of civil rights. The term *covering,* as Yoshino uses it, means "to tone down a disfavored identity to fit into the mainstream," and Yoshino argues that though Americans value the idea of the melting pot as a model for our culture, that ideal can have unintended negative consequences. Despite our avowed appreciation for multiculturalism, the unstated public expectation is still for people of all genders, sexual orientations, and races to conform to rigid expectations.

The selections here, "Preface" and "The New Civil Rights," form something close to a set of bookends for Yoshino's argument in *Covering.* After defining the concept of covering and the problems caused by it in the "Preface" and investigating the issue of a distinct "True Self" and "False Self" in the second excerpt, Yoshino moves on to propose a new paradigm for civil rights. Questioning the idea of legislating civil rights, Yoshino suggests that the next step may have to occur in bars, restaurants, and Internet chat rooms; he also suggests that in order to accommodate an increasingly diverse population, the model of civil rights itself must change. Yoshino points the way by helping us to rethink our model of civil rights and the mechanisms used to bring those rights into existence.

The United States is more diverse than ever. How can we balance the rights of diverse groups with the demands of individuals and the nation?

▶ TAGS: *community,* *identity,* *social change,* *diversity,* *civil rights,* *human dignity*

Preface

Everyone covers. To cover is to tone down a disfavored identity to fit into the mainstream. In our increasingly diverse society, all of us are outside the mainstream in some way. Nonetheless, being deemed mainstream is still often a necessity of social life. For this reason, every reader of this book has covered, whether consciously or not, and sometimes at significant personal cost.

Famous examples of covering abound. Ramón Estévez covered his ethnicity when he changed his name to Martin Sheen, as did Krishna Bhanji when he changed his name to Ben Kingsley. Margaret Thatcher covered her status as a woman when she trained with a voice coach to lower the timbre of her voice. Long after they came out as lesbians, Rosie O'Donnell and Mary Cheney still covered, keeping their same-sex partners out of the public eye. Issur Danielovitch Demsky covered his Judaism when he became Kirk Douglas, as did Joseph Levitch when he became Jerry Lewis. Franklin Delano Roosevelt covered his disability by ensuring his wheelchair was always hidden behind a desk before his Cabinet entered.

I doubt any of these people covered willingly. I suspect they were all bowing to an unjust reality that required them to tone down their stigmatized identities to get along in life. Sheen says he needed to "get a name people could pronounce and connect with" if he "wanted to work commercially." Yet he now regrets having done so, and has exhorted his sons—Emilio and Charlie—to use the family name. One of them has not done so, signaling the enduring force of the covering demand.

In a supposedly enlightened age, the persistence of the covering demand presents a puzzle. Today, race, national origin, sex, religion, and disability are all protected by federal civil rights laws. An increasing number of states and localities include sexual orientation in civil rights laws as well. Albeit with varying degrees of conviction, Americans have come to a consensus that people should not be penalized for being different along these dimensions. That consensus, however, does not protect individuals against demands that they mute those differences. We need an explanation for why the civil rights revolution has stalled on covering.

Covering has enjoyed such a robust and stubborn life because it is a form of assimilation. At least since Hector St. John de Crèvecoeur's 1782 *Letters from an American Farmer,* this country has touted assimilation as the way Americans of different backgrounds would be "melted into a new race of men." By the time Israel Zangwill's play of that name was performed in 1908, the "melting pot" had acquired the burnish of an American ideal. Only with the civil rights movement of the 1960s was this ideal challenged in any systematic way, with calls to move "beyond the melting pot" and to "celebrate diversity." And notwithstanding that challenge, assimilation has never lost its hold on the American imagination. Indeed, as our country grows more pluralistic, we have seen a renaissance of the melting pot ideal. Fearful that we are spinning apart into balkanized groups, even liberals like Arthur Schlesinger have called for a recommitment to that ethic. In the United States, as in other industrialized democracies, we are seeing the "return of assimilation."

I recognize the value of assimilation, which is often necessary to fluid social interaction, to peaceful coexistence, and even to the dialogue through which difference is valued. For that reason, this is no simple screed against conformity. What I urge here is that we approach the renaissance of assimilation in this country critically. We must be willing to see the dark side of assimilation, and specifically of covering, which is the most widespread form of assimilation required of us today.

Covering is a hidden assault on our civil rights. We have not been able to see it as such because it has swaddled itself in the benign language of assimilation.

But if we look closely, we will see that covering is the way many groups are being held back today. The reason racial minorities are pressured to "act white" is because of white supremacy. The reason women are told to downplay their childcare responsibilities in the workplace is because of patriarchy. And the reason gays are asked not to "flaunt" is because of homophobia. So long as such covering demands persist, American civil rights will not have completed its work.

Unfortunately, the law has yet to perceive covering as a threat. Contemporary civil rights law generally only protects traits that individuals cannot change, like their skin color, chromosomes, or innate sexual orientations. This means that current law will not protect us against most covering demands, because such demands direct themselves at the behavioral aspects of our personhood. This is so despite the fact that covering imposes costs on us all.

The universality of the covering demand, however, is also a potential boon for civil rights advocates. I, too, worry about our current practice of fracturing into groups, each clamoring for state and social solicitude. For this reason, I do not think we can move forward by focusing on old-fashioned group-based identity politics. We must instead build a new civil rights paradigm on what draws us together rather than on what drives us apart. Because covering applies to us all, it provides an issue around which we can make common cause. This is the desire for authenticity, our common human wish to express ourselves without being impeded by unreasoning demands for conformity.

> **We must instead build a new civil rights paradigm on what draws us together rather than on what drives us apart.**

I thought I would make this argument in purely political terms. As a law professor, I have become accustomed to the tones of legal impersonality. But I came to see that I could not compose an argument about the importance of human authenticity without risking such authenticity myself. So I have written this . . . in a more intimate voice, blending memoir with argument. In trying to make the stakes of assimilation vivid, I draw on my attempts to elaborate my identity as a gay man, and, to a lesser extent, my identity as an Asian-American.

Yet this is not a standard "coming out" narrative or racial memoir. I follow the Romantics here in their belief that if a human life is described with enough particularity, the universal will begin to speak through it. What interests me about my story, and the stories of others, is how similar they are in revealing the bones of our common human endeavor, the yearning for human emancipation that stirs within us all.

The New Civil Rights

To describe the new civil rights, I return to the source of my argument. What most excited me about gay civil rights was its universal resonance. Unlike other civil rights groups, gays must articulate invisible selves without the initial support of our immediate communities. That makes the gay project of self-elaboration emblematic of the search for authenticity all of us engage in as human beings. It is work each of us must do for ourselves, and it is the most important work we can do.

In looking for a vocabulary for this quest for authenticity, I found psychoanalysts more helpful than lawyers. The object-relations theorist D. W. Winnicott makes a distinction between a True Self and a False Self that usefully tracks the distinction between the uncovered and covered selves. The True Self is the self that gives an individual the feeling of being real, which is "more than existing; it is finding a way to exist as oneself, and to relate to objects as oneself, and to have a self into which to retreat for relaxation." The True Self is associated with human spontaneity and authenticity: "Only the True Self can be creative and only the True Self can feel real." The False Self, in contrast, gives an individual a sense of being unreal, a sense of futility. It mediates the relationship between the True Self and the world.

What I love about Winnicott is that he does not demonize the False Self. To the contrary, Winnicott believes the False Self protects the True Self: "The False Self has one positive and very important function: to hide the True Self, which it does by compliance with environmental demands." Like a king castling behind a rook in chess, the more valuable but less powerful piece retreats behind the less valuable but more powerful one. Because the relationship between the True Self and the False Self is symbiotic, Winnicott believes both selves will exist even in the healthy individual.

Nonetheless, Winnicott defines health according to the degree of ascendancy the True Self gains over the False one. At the negative extreme, the False Self completely obscures the True Self, perhaps even from the individual herself. In a less extreme case, the False Self permits the True Self "a secret life." The individual approaches health only when the False Self has "as its main concern a search for conditions which will make it possible for the True Self to come into its own." Finally, in the healthy individual, the False Self is reduced to a "polite and mannered social attitude," a tool available to the fully realized True Self.

This paradigm captures my coming-out experience. My gay self, the True Self, was hidden behind an ostensibly straight False Self. Yet it would be wrong to cast the closeted self as purely inimical to the gay one. In my adolescence, this False Self protected the True Self until its survival was assured. Only at this point did the False Self switch from being a help to being a hindrance. And even after I came out, the False Self never disappeared. It was reduced to the minimum necessary to regulate relations between the True Self and the world.

I could slot other civil rights identities into Winnicott's paradigm. The importance of the paradigm, however, lies in its self-conscious universality. Winnicott posits that each of us has a True Self that must be expressed for us to have the feeling of being switched on, of being alive. And if the True Self embodies the importance of authenticity, the False Self embodies our ambivalence about assimilation, which is both necessary to survival and obstructive of life. The goal is not to eliminate assimilation altogether, but to reduce it to the necessary minimum. This is what the reason-forcing conversation seeks to do.

When I describe the uncovered self in Winnicott's terms, many people respond immediately with stories that attest to the concept's universality. Most of these have little to do with conventional civil rights categories. They often pertain to choices about people's careers or personal lives, like the woman who left a career in law to write plays, or the man who left his fiancée at the altar to pursue his first childhood love. I nonetheless hear the same themes threading through these stories as I do through the traditional civil rights cases. These individuals cannot articulate what authenticity is, but know an existence lived outside its imperative would be a substitute for life.

Parents often respond to the concept of the True Self by speaking of their children. Based on extensive clinical research, psychologist Carol Gilligan argues that children have an authentic voice they lose as they mature, with girls retaining it longer than boys. (The breaking of this emotional voice mirrors the breaking of the physical voice, as the voices of boys break earlier and more dramatically than those of girls.) Gilligan's work is replete with instances of parents awed by the directness and realness of their children. These parents suggest that one of the most agonizing dilemmas of parenting is how much they should require their children to cover in the world.

This psychological discourse about authentic selves sounds distant from current civil rights discourse. We must close that gap. The new civil rights must harness this universal impulse toward authenticity. That impulse should press us toward thinking of civil rights less in terms of groups than in terms of our common humanity.   20

Two recent cases show that the Supreme Court is sympathetic to that shift. In the 2003 case of *Lawrence v. Texas* . . . the Supreme Court struck down a Texas statute that criminalized same-sex sodomy. Many assumed the Court would use this case to decide whether to give gays the judicial protections currently accorded to racial minorities and women. But while the Court struck down the statute (and overruled *Bowers v. Hardwick* in the process), it did not do so based on the equality rights of gays. Rather, it held that the statute violated the fundamental right of all persons — straight, gay, or otherwise — to control our intimate sexual relations.

Similarly, in the 2004 case of *Tennessee v. Lane*, the Supreme Court considered the question of whether two paraplegic individuals could sue Tennessee for failing to make its courthouses wheelchair accessible. (One plaintiff was forced to crawl up the courthouse steps to answer criminal charges against him; the other, a certified court reporter, alleged she had lost job opportunities because some county courthouses were inaccessible.) Again, the Court ruled in favor of the minority group without framing its ruling in group-based equality rhetoric. Rather, it held that all persons — disabled or otherwise — have a "right of access to the courts," which had been denied in this case.

In an era when the Supreme Court has closed many civil rights doors, it has left this one wide open. It is much more sympathetic to "liberty" claims about freedoms we all hold than to "equality" claims asserted by a subset of the population. It is easy to see why. Equality claims — such as group-based accommodation claims — inevitably involve the Court in picking favorites among groups.

In an increasingly pluralistic society, the Court understandably wishes to steer clear of that enterprise. Liberty claims, on the other hand, emphasize what all Americans (or more precisely, all persons within the jurisdiction of the United States) have in common. The claim that we all have a right to sexual intimacy, or that we all have a right to access the courts, will hold no matter how many new groups proliferate in this country.

The Supreme Court's shift toward a more universal register can also be seen in its nascent acceptance of human rights. I worked on a friend-of-the-court brief in the *Lawrence* case produced by a team centered at Yale Law School. With the former President of Ireland and U.N. High Commissioner Mary Robinson as our client, we argued that decisions by international tribunals and courts in other Western democracies had recognized the fundamentality of the right to adult consensual sexual intimacy. We knew this argument would be resisted by some justices on the Court, who do not take kindly to arguments that decisions outside the United States should guide their jurisprudence. But to our surprise, the majority opinion cited our brief for the proposition that *Bowers* violated "values we share with a wider civilization."

At the end of their lives, both Martin Luther King Jr. and Malcolm X argued for this transition from civil rights to human rights. Both believed that civil rights unduly focused on what distinguished individuals from one another, rather than emphasizing what they had in common. As Stewart Burns, one of the editors of the King papers at Stanford, observes, King "grasped that 'civil rights' carried too much baggage of the dominant tradition of American individualism and not enough counterweight from a tradition of communitarian impulses, collective striving, and common good." Similarly, Malcolm X exhorted Americans to "expand the civil-rights struggle to the level of human rights," so that the "jurisdiction of Uncle Sam" would not prevent us from allying with our "brothers" of other nations.

The universal rights of persons will probably be the way the Court will protect difference in the future. I predict that if the Court ever recognizes language rights, it will protect them as a liberty to which we are all entitled, rather than as an equality right attached to a particular national-origin group. And if the Court recognizes rights to grooming, such as the right to wear cornrows or not to wear makeup, I believe it will do so under something more akin to the German Constitution's right to personality rather than as a right attached to groups like racial minorities or women.

One of the great benefits of analyzing civil rights in terms of universal liberty rather than in terms of group-based equality is that it avoids making assumptions about group cultures. I've touched on the problem that the covering concept might assume too quickly that individuals behaving in "mainstream" ways are hiding some true identity, when in fact they might just be "being themselves." A female colleague of mine gave me a powerful version of this critique: "Here is what I dislike about your project. When I do something stereotypically masculine—like fixing my bike—your project makes it more likely people will think I'm putting on a gender performance rather than accepting the most straightforward explanation for what I'm doing. I don't fix my bike because I'm trying to downplay the fact that I'm a woman. I fix it because it's broken."

She gave another example: "When I was in graduate school, there was an African-American man who studied German Romantic poetry. Under your model, I could easily see someone saying he was 'covering' his African-American identity by studying something so esoteric and highbrow. But it was clear to me he was studying Romantic poetry because he was seized by it. And if someone had assumed he was studying it to 'act white,' they would have diminished him as a human being."

The coup de grâce: "Your commitment is to help people 'be themselves' — to resist demands to conform that take away their ability to be the individuals they are. But the covering idea could perpetuate the stereotypes you want to eliminate. One way minorities break stereotypes is by acting against them. If every time they do so, people assume they are 'covering' some essential stereotypical identity, the stereotypes will never go away."

I have literally lost sleep over this criticism. But in my waking hours, I take it more as a caution than as a wholesale indictment. I agree that we must not assume that individuals behaving in "mainstream" ways are necessarily covering. My ultimate commitment is to autonomy as a means of achieving authenticity, rather than to a fixed conception of what authenticity might be. (Here I follow Winnicott, who observes the True Self is not susceptible to specific definition, as its nature differs for each of us.) In talking about classic civil rights groups, I have focused on the demand to conform to the mainstream because I think that for most groups (except women) these are the demands that most threaten our authenticity. But I am equally opposed to demands that individuals reverse cover, because such demands are also impingements on our autonomy, and therefore on our authenticity.

I have literally lost sleep over this criticism.

In practice, I expect the liberty paradigm to protect the authentic self better than the equality paradigm. While it need not do so, the equality paradigm is prone to essentializing the identities it protects. Under an equality paradigm, if a woman who wore a lot of makeup were protected by a court because makeup is an "essential" part of being a woman, this could reinforce the stereotype that women wear makeup. But if the same woman were given the liberty right to elaborate her own gender identity in ways that did not impinge on her job performance, she would be protected from demands to be either more "masculine" or more "feminine." Marsha Wislocki-Goin would be protected for wearing "too much makeup" and Darlene Jespersen would be protected for not wearing it at all. Each woman would then have the full panoply of options from which she could fashion her gender identity. And in protecting that range, the law would not articulate any presupposition about what an "authentic" or "essential" woman would look like. Authenticity would be something these women, and not the state or employer, would find for themselves.

Group-based identity politics is not dead. As I have argued, I still believe in a group-based accommodation model for existing civil rights groups. This is in part because I believe we have made a commitment to those groups to protect them from such covering demands. The statutory language of the Civil Rights Act and the Americans with Disabilities Act already protects racial minorities, religious minorities, women, and individuals with disabilities *as groups* against covering demands. It has been the courts that have erroneously limited the ambit of those protections. Such a group-based equality paradigm is completely consistent with the individual liberty paradigm. In fact, the equality and liberty strands of antidiscrimination law are inextricably intertwined.

Moreover, even if we shift the focus of civil rights law away from equality to liberty, identity politics will still be crucial. If it weren't for the gay rights movement, or the disability rights movement, cases like *Lawrence* or *Lane* would never have made it to the Court. But I'm sympathetic to the Court's desire to frame these cases not as "gay" or "disability" cases, but as cases touching on rights that, like a rising tide, will lift the boat of every person in America. Ironically, it may be the explosion of diversity in this country that will finally make us realize what we have in common. Multiculturalism has forced us to vary and vary the human being in the imagination until we discover what is invariable about her.

While I have great hopes for this new legal paradigm, I also believe law will be a relatively trivial part of the new civil rights. A doctor friend told me that in his first year of medical school, his dean described how doctors were powerless to cure the vast majority of human ills. People would get better, or they would not, but it would not be doctors who would cure them. Part of becoming a doctor, the dean said, was to surrender a layperson's awe for medical authority. I wished then that someone would give an analogous lecture to law students, and to Americans at large. My education in law has been in part an education in its limitations.

For starters, many covering demands are made by actors the law does not—and in my view should not—hold accountable, such as friends, family, neighbors, or people themselves. When I hesitate before engaging in a public display of same-sex affection, I am not thinking of the state or my employer, but of the strangers around me and my own internal censor. And while I am often tempted to sue myself, this is not my healthiest impulse.

Law is also an incomplete solution to coerced assimilation because it has yet to recognize the myriad groups subjected to covering demands outside traditional civil rights classifications like race, sex, orientation, religion, and disability. Whenever I speak about covering, I receive new instances of identities that can be covered. This is Winnicott's point—each one of us has a False Self that hides a True one. The law may someday move to protect some of these identities. But it will never protect them all.

Most important, law is incomplete in the qualitative remedies it provides. I confronted this recently when I became a plaintiff in a lawsuit against the Department of Defense. Under a congressional statute called the Solomon Amendment, the department threatened to cut off $350 million of federal funding from Yale University if the law school did not exempt the military from the law school's policy of protecting gays against discrimination by employers. Our suit argues that the statute is unconstitutional. I believe in this lawsuit, and was heartened that the vast majority of my law school colleagues signed on as plaintiffs. I was also elated when the district court judge, Judge Janet Hall, granted summary judgment in our favor. (As the government has taken an appeal, the case is still pending.) But there is nothing like being a plaintiff to realize that lawsuits occur between people who have no better way of talking to each other.

When I think about the elaboration of my gay identity, I am grateful to see litigation has had little to do with it. The department is the only entity I have ever wanted to sue. Even when I encountered demands for assimilation, my best response was to draw my interlocutor into a conversation. Just as important, framing the project of self-elaboration in purely legal—and therefore adversarial—terms would fail to honor all those who were not adversaries. I have described in these pages many individuals who helped me toward myself. But there were many more. I think here of my law professor Charles Reich, who wrote a memoir about coming out in 1976, when it was an act of real courage to do so, and who let me write the essay that begins this book in his class, though its relationship to the law was then entirely unclear. I think of the chair of my midtenure review committee, who sat me down when I was the only untenured member of the faculty and, unsurprisingly, a mass of nerves, to give me the verdict of the committee. He told me his only advice for the coming years was that I should be more myself, that instead of reasoning within the law as it existed, I should speak my truth and make the law shape itself around me. And I think of my parents, whose response to this manuscript was to say, with calm and conviction, that they were proud of the man I have become.

For these reasons, I am troubled that Americans seem increasingly to turn toward the law to do the work of civil rights precisely when they should be turning away from it. The real solution lies in all of us as citizens, not in the tiny subset of us who are lawyers. People who are not lawyers should have reason-forcing conversations outside the law. They should pull Goffman's term "covering" out of academic obscurity and press it into the popular lexicon, so that it has the same currency as terms like "passing" or "the closet." People confronted with demands to cover should feel emboldened to seek a reason for that demand, even if the law does not reach the actors making the demand, or recognize the group burdened by it. These reason-forcing conversations should happen outside courtrooms—in workplaces and restaurants, schools and playgrounds, chat rooms and living rooms, public squares and bars. They should occur informally and intimately, where tolerance is made and unmade.

What will constitute a good enough reason to justify assimilation will   40
obviously be controversial. But I want to underscore that we have come to some consensus that certain reasons are illegitimate—like white supremacy, patriarchy, homophobia, religious intolerance, and animus toward the disabled. I ask us to be true to the commitments we have made by never accepting such biases as legitimate grounds for covering demands. Beyond that, I have sought

to engender a series of conversations, rather than a series of results—what reasons count, and for what purposes, will be for us to decide by facing one another as individuals. My personal inclination is always to privilege the claims of the individual against countervailing interests like "neatness" or "workplace harmony." But we should have that conversation.

Such conversations are the best—and perhaps the only—way to give both assimilation and authenticity their proper due. These conversations will help us chart and stay the course between the monocultural America suggested by conservative alarmists and the balkanized America suggested by the radical multiculturalists. They will reveal the true dimension of civil rights. The aspiration of civil rights has always been to permit people to pursue their human flourishing without limitations based on bias. Focusing on law prevents us from seeing the revolutionary breadth of that aspiration, as law has limited civil rights to particular groups. I am not faulting that limitation, as I think prioritization is necessary, and that the law's priorities are correct. But civil rights, which has always extended far beyond the law, may now need to do so more than ever. It is only when we leave the law that civil rights suddenly stops being about particular groups and starts to become a project of human flourishing in which we all have a stake.

We must use the relative freedom of adulthood to integrate the many selves we hold. This includes uncovering the selves we buried long ago because they were inconvenient, impractical, or even hated. Because they must pass the test of survival, most of the selves we hold, like most of our lives, are ordinary. Yet sometimes, what is consequential in us begins to shine.

Questions for Critical Reading

1. What does Yoshino mean by the "new" civil rights? Define the term by locating passages from his text. What makes it new? How does it differ from "old" civil rights? Use Yoshino's text to define liberty and equality paradigms as part of your response.

2. What is "covering"? Define the concept using Yoshino's text and then offer your own example.

3. How does Yoshino think we can achieve the new civil rights? Provide passages that show his position and then respond to it. Do you think his vision is possible? Is it something we should strive for? In making your response, reread Yoshino's text critically to locate points of connection between his position and yours.

Exploring Context

1. Explore the Web site for the U.S. Commission on Civil Rights (usccr.gov). Which paradigm does it reflect, liberty or equality? Use your definition of these terms from Question 1 of Questions for Critical Reading.

2. Yoshino uses recent Supreme Court decisions to make his argument. Visit the Web site for the Supreme Court at supremecourtus.gov. What recent cases have concerned civil rights? What impact do these cases (or the lack of such cases) have on Yoshino's argument?

3. According to Yoshino, changes in civil rights should come not from legislation but through conversation. Visit BlogPulse's trend tool (blogpulse.com/trend) and search for *civil rights* and related terms. Are people talking about these is-sues online? What does this say about Yoshino's argument? Connect your explo-ration to your response to Question 3 of Questions for Critical Reading.

Questions for Connecting

1. Kwame Anthony Appiah also extols the power of conversation in "Making Conversation" (p. 57) and "The Primacy of Practice" (p. 63). Place his ideas in conversation with Yoshino's essay, synthesizing their ideas about the power of conversation. Is Yoshino also calling for cosmopolitanism? How do civil rights function like other social practices?

2. Though explicitly concerned with aesthetics, Virginia Postrel's "The Boundaries of Design" (p. 296) might also be considered as an essay on civil rights and indi-vidual liberties. How do Postrel's arguments affect Yoshino's? How are the chal-lenges of locating aesthetic boundaries similar to the challenges of civil rights? Can Postrel's insights help us achieve a new civil rights, or do they point to the difficulty of such a project? Use your understanding of the new civil rights from Question 1 of Questions for Critical Reading in your response.

3. Francis Fukuyama argues for the necessity of a concept of human dignity in his essay of the same name (p. 142). What role might human dignity play in civil rights? Is Factor X an essential component of a new civil rights? Synthesize the ideas of Fukuyama and Yoshino into an argument about human rights.

Language Matters

1. Every part of speech and every punctuation mark has certain "rights"; for exam-ple, the period has the right to end a sentence and the comma does not. How can we describe the rules of grammar using Yoshino's ideas of liberty and equal-ity paradigms?

2. Defining terms is an important part of academic writing. Locate a passage where Yoshino defines a term. What strategies does he use? Does he offer a dic-tionary definition? An example? An authority? How should you define terms in your own text?

3. Is there a form of covering that takes place in peer revision? Are people tempted to tone down unfavorable comments? How does Yoshino's discussion of cover-ing offer advice for more effective peer revision?

Assignments for Writing

1. Yoshino discusses the concept of groups and individuals covering in order to conform to the mainstream. Locate your own example of covering and then write an essay that extends or complicates Yoshino's argument through your example. Does your example reinforce or refute Yoshino's ideas about covering? Are any civil rights at stake in your example? What relation is there between covering and civil rights? You will want to use your definition of the term *covering* from Question 2 of Questions for Critical Reading.

2. Yoshino discusses the challenges to civil rights posed by the proliferation of groups engendered by a diverse society; he offers his own vision of how to transform civil rights to account for these groups. Write a paper in which you suggest what changes we should make to civil rights and how we might achieve those changes. Draw from your work in Questions for Critical Reading and Questions for Connecting in making your argument. Consider, too: Should we use a liberty paradigm or an equality paradigm? Would you propose a different paradigm of your own? Is legislation the best way to achieve your vision for civil rights? Is conversation?

3. In Question 3 of Exploring Context you examined current online conversations about civil rights. Yoshino suggests that such conversations are the best means of achieving a new civil rights. Write a paper in which you argue for the role of conversation in social change. Is talking about an issue enough to engender change? Does it matter who is doing the talking? How does change happen in society?

SEQUENCE 1

Rites/Rights of Passage: Identifying the Self

JULIA ALVAREZ

MADELEINE ALBRIGHT

JOAN DIDION

DEBORA L. SPAR

In this sequence, you will examine the connection between rites that help us form our identities and the larger rights of our communities. You'll begin by using Julia Alvarez to consider the role of quinceañeras in the development of self-identity. Building on that analysis, you will use Madeleine Albright to explore the ways in which national as well as personal identities can be shaped by forces such as religion. Then you'll turn to a difficult and very personal rite of passage—the death of a loved one—using Joan Didion to consider the ways in which death changes those who are left behind. The final assignments of this sequence turn to the family, first by synthesizing Didion's and Alvarez's ideas and then by using Debora L. Spar to determine what rights should be allowed in the creation of families through international adoption.

▶ TAGS: *kinship*, *family*, *change*, *tradition*, *loss*, *religion*, *community*, *mourning*, *culture*, *death*, *identity*

Assignment 1. ALVAREZ

How do quinceañeras help to define self-identity in the Hispanic community? Write a paper in which you define the relationship between these rituals and self-identity. In making your argument you may want to use the other rituals you explored in Question 3 of Exploring Context (p. 53) or some of the concepts you synthesized in Questions for Connecting, such as super-replicators or cultural performance.

To help you begin your critical thinking on this assignment, consider these questions: How do traditions, both native and acquired, contribute to the development of identity? How does gender determine self-identity in the Hispanic community? Why do only girls receive quinceañeras? What part does retroculturation play in the establishing of self-identity? Is this rite of passage similar to or different from rites of passage in other cultures? Does the commercialization of the quinceañera affect its overall value in establishing a girl's self-worth and self-identity? If so, how?

Assignment 2. ALVAREZ AND ALBRIGHT

Quinceañeras often have a religious component. And, as Albright's essay makes clear, religion is often a significant force in shaping identities, both personal and national. Write a paper in which you explore the ways in which personal and national identities are shaped by faith. You might begin by revisiting your work on the relationship between religion and diplomacy in Question 1 of Questions for Critical Reading for Albright (p. 31).

To help you begin your critical thinking on this assignment, reflect on these questions: What role does religion play in shaping personal and national identities? Can retroculturation assist in creating a faith-based diplomacy? How do quinceañeras transcend national borders? In what sense are they a kind of international diplomacy? Do girls have a right to a quinceañera or to other rites of passage?

Assignment 3. DIDION

One of the more difficult rites of passage we must face is dealing with the loss of a loved one. Write a paper in which you analyze the effect death has on an individual. You might want to start by using the definition of *grief* you created in Questions for Critical Reading (p. 102) as well as your arguments on the ways in which Didion's essay is concerned with creating meaning in life.

To help you begin your critical thinking on this assignment, consider these questions: How does grief inform self-identity? How does Didion change as a person because of this experience? How does an unexpected death have a greater effect on an individual? Is a distant encounter with death, such as knowledge of a national disaster, as much a rite of passage as an intimate encounter is? How so?

Assignment 4. ALVAREZ AND DIDION

Both Alvarez's and Didion's essays are centrally concerned with families. Both, too, consider the ways in which families, whether immediate or extended, influence who and what we are. Using both Alvarez and Didion to support your argument, write a paper in which you examine the role that family plays in shaping self-identity.

To help you begin your critical thinking on this assignment, ask yourself these questions: Does a sense of cultural identity come from the home or the culture as a whole? How do families change when a loved one is lost? Do rites of passage such as quinces or mourning make families grow closer? Where is the boundary between an individual and the family? Do we find that boundary in the ordinary instant?

Assignment 5. SPAR AND ONE OTHER

Write a paper in which you identify and analyze the challenges that emerge when children are raised outside of their native culture. Utilize the ideas of Spar and one other author in this sequence to assist. Consider starting with your analysis of the role race plays in adoption in Question 3 of Questions for Critical Reading for Spar (p. 436). You might also want to use the Rainbow Kids or Adoption.com Web sites in supporting your argument.

Also think about these questions: Do parents have a responsibility to educate an adopted child in the culture of his or her heritage? Should race or ethnicity play a role in the adoption process? How might retroculturation help in adoption? What role should faith or religion play in adoption? Does adoption involve a kind of mourning?

Surviving Alone, Surviving Together: Ethical Conflict in a Global Economy

KWAME ANTHONY APPIAH

HELEN EPSTEIN

THOMAS FRIEDMAN

DEBORA L. SPAR

This sequence asks you to examine how we can survive and indeed thrive in an interconnected and diverse world. The first assignment, with Kwame Anthony Appiah, asks you to develop a set of conceptual tools for creating social change. You will extend these tools using the work of Helen Epstein, considering how they can be used to create change on a global scale. The third assignment more specifically asks you to apply that work to the global fight against terrorism, drawing additionally from Thomas Friedman's work on mutant supply chains. In the final assignment, you will use Debora L. Spar to consider the limits of global cooperation and the boundaries between surviving together and surviving alone.

▶ TAGS: *international policy*, *globalization*, *ethics*, *terrorism*, *community*, *social change*

Assignment 1. APPIAH

Appiah discusses his choice of cosmopolitanism as a rubric for moving forward. At the same time, he also discusses the problems of realizing social change. Based on his discussion of the primacy of practice, how can we advocate for change in social practices? Write a paper in which you identify the best tools for achieving social change. You may wish to build on the cultural practice you explored in Question 2 of Exploring Context (p. 73) in constructing and supporting your argument.

Assignment 2. APPIAH AND EPSTEIN

Epstein describes two very different approaches to HIV/AIDS prevention in Africa. She points out that in South Africa, where open discussion of the epidemic is taboo, prevention programs that avoid the harsh realities of the AIDS epidemic are popular but less successful than their counterparts in Uganda, where the realities of the disease are openly acknowledged. To what extent can Appiah's primacy of practice be applied to AIDS prevention in countries with stringent social taboos? Drawing on Epstein's and Appiah's ideas, write a paper in which you determine how individuals acting locally can create global change. You may want to draw from your definition of *social cohesion* from Question 2 of Questions for Critical Reading for Epstein (p. 117).

Ask yourself these questions: How can we overcome the primacy of practice when such practices put lives at risk from disease? What role does conversation have in creating change locally or globally? How can we take action to solve problems like HIV/AIDS even when we hold different values? Is social cohesion an effect of cosmopolitanism, or do these two concepts work against each other? What role might global companies and advertising play in social change?

Assignment 3. EPSTEIN AND FRIEDMAN

Friedman argues that countries participating in global supply chains become economically interdependent and are thus less likely to be involved in political conflicts. At the same time he warns that terrorists are using similar supply chains to spread violence around the world. Given that both terrorism and HIV/AIDS threaten lives without respect for borders, how can we mitigate terrorist supply chains? Write an essay in which you use Epstein's insights about HIV/AIDS prevention in Africa to propose strategies for fighting terrorism globally. Use your work on the role of collaboration as well as your analysis of mutant supply chains from Questions for Critical Reading for Friedman (p. 138).

Also think about: How can we promote collaboration while minimizing its destructive potential? How can social cohesion play a role in the fight against terrorism? What about lifestyle brands? What role do supply chains play in the transmission of and fight against HIV/AIDS in Africa?

Assignment 4. SPAR AND ONE OTHER

Spar focuses on the ethical questions concerning international adoption, a practice that can be seen as either a humanitarian endeavor or as a global black market in babies. Using Spar and one of the other authors in this sequence, write a paper in which you determine the limits of international policy on individuals.

Should international adoptions be more closely regulated? Are babies part of a global supply chain? Should governments mandate individual behavior? When health is at stake, as in HIV/AIDS, does that make a difference? How do we work together while retaining our rights as individuals?

SEQUENCE 3

Yes We Can, But Should We?
The Politics of Science

THE DALAI LAMA

KENJI YOSHINO

FRANCIS FUKUYAMA

MADELEINE ALBRIGHT

How can we develop an ethical system to guide us in scientific and technological progress? In this sequence of assignments, you will begin to answer that question first by working with the Dalai Lama's examination of genetic technologies, considering the ramifications of these technologies for economic and political stability. Then you will turn to Kenji Yoshino's discussion of civil rights, synthesizing his ideas with the Dalai Lama's to argue for the best balance between progress and rights. In the third assignment, you will discuss all of these issues specifically in the context of stem cell research, folding Francis Fukuyama's ideas about biotechnology and human dignity into your analysis. Finally, you will use Madeleine Albright to look at the role of religion in science. If our ethics are not based in faith, then what system can we develop to guide us in the search for new knowledge?

▶ TAGS: *diplomacy*, *morality*, *biotechnology*, *knowledge and responsibility*, *human dignity*, *ethics*, *civil rights*

Assignment 1. THE DALAI LAMA

The possible consequences of genetic manipulation reach far beyond the sphere of science. Consider, for example, the role of national and global politics in relation to scientific breakthroughs that have the potential to literally change the face of humanity but will almost certainly not be available to everyone. Write a paper in which you examine the consequences of technology in terms of social and economic stability. How does the Dalai Lama characterize the relationship between knowledge and responsibility? In what ways does genetic engineering have the potential to perpetuate our disparities on social, political, and ethical levels? Should new technologies be available to everyone?

Assignment 2. THE DALAI LAMA AND YOSHINO

According to the Dalai Lama, rapid advances in technology demand new ethical standards. Yoshino makes a similar argument in claiming that the proliferation of groups in a diverse society necessitates a new civil rights. Synthesizing the positions of these two authors, write an essay in which you determine the best means of balancing political rights and technological progress. You might want to use the understanding of Yoshino's concept of civil rights that you developed in Questions for Critical Reading (p. 488) in making your argument.

And consider: Are scientists just another group demanding rights? Should we use a liberty paradigm or an equality paradigm in considering the ethical quandaries raised by biotechnology? Are reason-forcing conversations the best means of achieving the Dalai Lama's vision for ethics, or is legislation? What role does a moral compass play in both science and civil rights?

Assignment 3. THE DALAI LAMA, YOSHINO, AND FUKUYAMA

In the first two assignments of this sequence you were asked to consider the impact of science and technology on social and economic stability as well as on political rights. Fukuyama addresses some of these same concerns in his discussion of biotechnology and human dignity. Synthesize the ideas of these three authors to write a paper in which you determine the ethics of stem cell research. Your goal in writing this paper is not to argue for or against this particular field of scientific inquiry. Instead, you will want to propose how we can make decisions about such difficult matters.

Reflect on the Dalai Lama's moral compass. Does human dignity help us find that moral compass? Is human dignity part of the True Self or the False Self? How do the needs for both a moral compass and human dignity limit any claims to a liberty paradigm for civil rights?

Assignment 4. ALBRIGHT AND ONE OTHER

The authors you've examined so far have largely separated ethics from the question of religion, even though faith serves as the foundation for many people's ethical systems. Albright suggests that we should take faith into consideration when it comes to foreign policy. Should we do the same for science? Working with Albright and one of the authors from this sequence, write an essay in which you determine the role faith should play in science. You might want to begin by revisiting your response to Question 1 of Questions for Critical Reading for Albright (p. 31), in which you explored whether faith was ultimately a help or a hindrance to diplomacy.

Also ponder: How can we create an ethical system apart from religion? Should faith play a role in determining research agendas? How can we accommodate religious concerns while still pursuing technological and scientific progress?

SEQUENCE 4

The Talking Cure: Conversation as Social Medicine

DANIEL GILBERT

HELEN EPSTEIN

JAMES SUROWIECKI

STEVEN JOHNSON

In this sequence you will analyze the role conversations can play in creating social change. To start, you will explore Daniel Gilbert's concept of a surrogate, a way of predicting your own future happiness through conversations with someone experiencing the future you would like to have. Then you will extend Gilbert's idea using Helen Epstein's analysis of HIV/AIDS prevention in Africa in order to consider the potential for conversation to create social and not just personal change. Yet conversation is not without its risks, and so you will turn to James Surowiecki's analysis of the failure of small groups in order to determine the limits of conversation as a social medicine. Finally, with Steven Johnson, you will synthesize these positions to consider technologies that can harness conversation as social medicine.

▶ TAGS: *conversation*, *social change*, *technology*, *surrogates*

Assignment 1. GILBERT

According to Gilbert, surrogates can offer us an accurate sense of our future happiness. Write a paper in which you assess the potential of the kind of surrogates that Gilbert describes. You will want to extend, complicate, or refute Gilbert's argument for surrogates and their reliability in predicting the future. Consider these questions: What role does individuality have in determining our future happiness? Is Gilbert correct in claiming that we are not as unique as we believe? Can surrogates be used to examine all future events? How can surrogates be used to control social processes? If we are not unique, why do we see ourselves as individuals? Use your definition of *surrogate* from Question 2 of Questions for Critical Reading (p. 187) as well as your work with Yahoo! Answers from Questions 3 of Exploring Context (p. 188).

Assignment 2. GILBERT AND EPSTEIN

In the last assignment you considered the power of conversation—specifically conversations with surrogates—to help people shape their futures. Epstein, however, is concerned with the future of more than just individuals. Her analysis of HIV/AIDS prevention programs concerns the future of that disease on the African continent. Using Gilbert's and Epstein's ideas, write a paper in which you determine the power of conversation to change people's behavior. Consider drawing from your work with Epstein, particularly your analysis of how social networking sites like Facebook can facilitate conversations around HIV/AIDS, from Question 3 of Exploring Context (p. 118).

Contemplate these questions to help you in formulating your argument: Could surrogates play a role in the fight against HIV/AIDS? What role does imagination play in social cohesion? How might Gilbert explain the failure of the loveLife campaign? Can conversation about the disease function as a kind of super-replicator?

Assignment 3. SUROWIECKI AND ONE OTHER

To some extent, Surowiecki's essay is centrally concerned with the failure of conversations—for example, the conversation of the Mission Management Team concerning *Columbia*. You've already explored the potential of conversation to create change, but what are the risks of conversation in group or social settings? Write a paper in which you explore the failures of conversation using the work of Surowiecki and one or more of the other authors you've read. Recall your determination of whether or not small groups are worth the risk from Question 3 of Questions for Critical Reading for Surowiecki (p. 451).

Consider, too: What are the risks involved when conversation fails? Given those risks, is conversation a good choice as social medicine? Given Surowiecki's analysis, how might surrogates fail to predict your future? Does group polarization threaten social cohesion?

Assignment 4. JOHNSON AND TWO OTHERS

Johnson explains that by altering the type of feedback given to a system, the public can alter the response of that system. Specifically, he demonstrates this power through his analysis of Slashdot. Using the work of Johnson and two of the other authors you've read in this sequence, write a paper in which you determine how technology can harness the power of conversation in creating social change. Draw from your own analysis of Slashdot in Question 3 of Questions for Critical Reading (p. 214) as well as Question 1 of Exploring Context (p. 214). What other technologies can enable this transformative power of conversation?

Ask yourself: How does technology enable the spread of super-replicators? How does it enable greater access to surrogates? What role might technology play in the prevention of HIV/AIDS? How can it be used to expand Uganda's success at that task? Can technology mitigate the factors that cause small groups to fail?

Wonderful Displays: Revelations of Art and Culture

MICHAEL KIMMELMAN

DIANA TAYLOR

VIRGINIA POSTREL

RICHARD RESTAK

In this sequence you will evaluate the role that art plays in shaping culture as well as the boundaries for creative expression. First you will explore Michael Kimmelman's argument by locating your own example of a "wonder cabinet." Then you will read more generally about the role that performance plays in culture by examining Diana Taylor's argument. With that base of understanding, you will then turn to the limits of artistic expression by exploring the rights of individuals and of communities using the work of Virginia Postrel and by exploring, more abstractly, the roles of chaos and order in both art and society. In the next assignment of the sequence, you will apply your ideas to the question of censorship as a way of making your understandings of the boundaries of art concrete. In the final assignment of the sequence, you will use Richard Restak to think about the future of art and aesthetics in a technological culture.

▶ TAGS: *culture*, *art*, *performance*, *aesthetic boundaries*, *censorship*, *creativity*, *technology*

Assignment 1. KIMMELMAN

Kimmelman states that the great collector is touched to the core by the confusion and the dispersal in which things are found in this world. Locate your own example of a wonder cabinet and write an essay in which you extend or complicate Kimmelman's argument through this example. Does your example participate in finding order out of chaos? Can a collection of dissimilar objects in itself be considered ordered? What is the purpose of collecting? Does collecting make sense of a senseless world? In making your argument, consider using your exploration of eBay in Question 1 of Exploring Context (p. 226).

Assignment 2. TAYLOR

Taylor examines cultural performances and the part they play in making political statements, memorializing tragic events, and creating cultural identities. In suggesting that Princess Diana's funeral was a performance, she asks us to consider what *performance* means as well as the relevance of performances to culture. Using Taylor's argument, write an essay in which you determine the effect of performance on a culture. Can performances create social change, or are they just "play"? You might want to begin with your analysis of the social function of mourning from Question 3 of Questions for Critical Reading as well as your definitions of *social drama* and *ghosting* (p. 477).

Consider these questions too: Did Princess Diana's funeral unite cultures? Why or why not? How does art bring cultures together? Can the expression of art help to form a cultural identity? What makes the funeral of a celebrity or political figure a "performance" and not just a funeral?

Assignment 3. TAYLOR AND POSTREL

Taylor and Postrel are both concerned with the role of aesthetics and performance within a culture. Postrel, however, specifically considers the boundaries of individual aesthetic expression within a community. Drawing from Postrel's analysis and Taylor's ideas, write a paper in which you argue how best to balance the rights of the community and those of the individual in terms of art and aesthetics. You might want to begin with your answers to the Questions for Critical Reading for Postrel (p. 329), particularly your response to spillovers and legislation in relation to aesthetics.

What role should artistic creativity have in a community? What is expressive freedom? What is visual pollution? Are murals a form of visual pollution? Why or why not? Does social drama play a role in aesthetic boundaries? What spillovers are caused by community expressions of mourning? What is the hauntology of aesthetics?

Assignment 4. KIMMELMAN AND POSTREL

Art and aesthetics, Kimmelman and Postrel seem to suggest, have in part to do with organizing the world as a means of both creative expression and community formation. Write a paper in which you examine the functions of order and chaos in art, aesthetics, and community. Your examination of local design ordinances from Question 2 of Exploring Context for Postrel (p. 329) might serve as a specific foundation for your analysis.

But also think about: Is art simply the ordering of chaos? How do we determine the best balance of order and chaos? Do aesthetic boundaries represent that balance? Does a wonder cabinet constrain disorder? Are wonder cabinets a kind of aesthetic boundary? Is chaos a spillover of art or collecting? Is order?

Do communities need art? How do communities negotiate order and chaos, and what role does art play in that negotiation?

Assignment 5. KIMMELMAN, TAYLOR, AND POSTREL

All of the authors you've read so far are centrally concerned with the impact of art and aesthetics on culture. Examine the intersection of aesthetics and culture more closely by writing a paper in which you use all three of these authors to make an argument about the ethics of censorship.

Weigh these questions: Does a community have the right to regulate artistic expression? What about when that expression threatens to cause disorder? What role does censorship play in social drama? Are collections a kind of ghosting? How does the reaction of minority communities to Princess Diana's death suggest the limits of any form of censorship?

Assignment 6. RESTAK AND ONE OTHER

Restak asks us how technology affects the way we perform everyday tasks. On the one hand, technology enables us to perform many tasks at once; on the other hand, none of the tasks is done well because of the competing demands on our brains. Using Restak and one of the other authors from this sequence, write a paper in which you determine the impact of technology on creative expression. Draw from your discussion of the relation between culture and biology from Question 2 of Questions for Critical Reading for Restak (p. 344).

Also ask yourself these questions: Is multitasking a form of performance? Can multitasking be tragic? Are we moving so fast that we are unable to appreciate art? Are we moving into a future that will make the arts unnecessary in culture? How might the rewiring of our brains change our understanding of art and aesthetics?

Trouble with a Capital "C": Communities and Integration

REBEKAH NATHAN

KWAME ANTHONY APPIAH

THOMAS FRIEDMAN

MARSHALL POE

In this sequence you will explore the role of diversity in forming successful communities. You'll begin by using Rebekah Nathan's work to consider the possibility of a fully integrated community. You will then expand that analysis using Kwame Anthony Appiah's, suggesting the tools we can use to form successful and diverse communities. Such communities are not without risk, and so you will turn to an analysis of Thomas Friedman to examine the dangers of community both in general and, more specifically, through an analysis of ethnic conflicts in the world today. Finally, you will use Marshall Poe's examination of Wikipedia's success to imagine an open, collaborative world. In completing these assignments, you will gain an understanding of the challenges facing community formation, the risks of diversity, and the possibilities of integration in the world today.

▶ TAGS: *community*, *globalization*, *diversity*, *education*, supply chains, *ethnic conflict*, *integration*, cosmopolitanism

Assignment 1. NATHAN

Nathan notes that despite AnyU's best efforts to unite the university's population, students who make up the different communities within the school would rather bond within their own social groups than venture outside of them. Assess the situation Nathan talks about in her essay. Thinking beyond Nathan's findings, write a paper in which you examine the possibilities of communities becoming fully integrated. Is such integration even possible in a world made up of so many diverse and differing communities? The purpose of this essay is for you to apply the concepts in Nathan's essay to your own specific observations and experiences. Rather than simply writing a story about your own opinions, you should instead use your experiences among and observations of diverse communities, on an academic campus or elsewhere, to explore the possibilities of a truly integrated community. You may also want to use your responses to Questions for Critical Reading and Exploring Context (pp. 246–247) in supporting your argument.

Assignment 2. NATHAN AND APPIAH

In the last assignment you considered the possibility of integrating communities and the challenges inherent in such a task. Appiah's ideas about cosmopolitanism and the processes of changes in practice offer additional insight on this topic. Using both Appiah and Nathan, write a paper in which you determine the key tools necessary for successfully forming diverse communities. You might build your argument from the work you did in Question 2 of Questions for Critical Reading for Appiah (p. 73), in which you explored the tools needed to enact cosmopolitanism.

Also consider: Can we form diverse communities in practice without agreeing on the values behind such communities? How does the challenge of accomplishing diversity on college campuses reflect the challenge of embracing community on a global scale? Can conversation overcome ego-centered networks?

Assignment 3. FRIEDMAN AND APPIAH

Appiah argues for the need for cosmopolitanism among world citizens; in Friedman's essay we see how companies and nations also benefit from "world citizen" attitudes. Yet Friedman also illustrates how such networks can have undesirable effects and consequences. Use Friedman's examination of global networks and mutant supply chains to complicate Appiah's discussion about the importance of interconnected social networks, writing a paper in which you explore the dangers of a connected, flattened world. In the end, is a completely interconnected world really the ideal world? You might begin your critical thinking by revisiting your discussion of collaboration and mutant supply chains from Questions for Critical Reading for Friedman (p. 138).

Also contemplate: Can cosmopolitanism mitigate mutant supply chains? Is terrorism a consequence of the lack of diversity? How can we agree on practices for global peace while holding different values? Can businesses contribute to cosmopolitanism?

Assignment 4. FRIEDMAN, NATHAN, AND APPIAH

All three authors you've read so far discuss collaboration in one form or another, extolling its virtues while also warning of its dangers. Write a paper in which you use all three of these authors to propose strategies for minimizing ethnic conflicts in the world today. You might consider choosing a specific contemporary ethnic war, such as the one in Darfur.

Ask yourself: How does the experience of community and diversity on college campuses play out in the larger world? What are the limits of cosmopolitanism? Though the Dell Theory of Conflict Prevention seems to promote peace between nations, what tools are there for promoting peace *within* nations?

Assignment 5. POE AND ONE OTHER

Poe explores how the collaborative construction of knowledge plays out on the Internet, but the ideas and problems he touches on have much wider implications. Using Poe's work and at least one other reading from this sequence, consider the possibility of a world that is completely "open," without any rules aside from those agreed upon by a majority. Examine the lessons that could be learned from entities like Wikipedia and use these lessons to write a paper in which you argue how our world would differ if it were left completely "open."

In making your argument, respond to these questions: What would happen to minority groups in such a society? Would groups form more diverse connections between each other, or would there be greater segregation? What chance would cosmopolitanism have in such a world? Would global supply chains be possible? Would they be necessary? Is such a world possible or even desirable?

Deep Impact: Technology and Our World

MARSHALL POE

THOMAS FRIEDMAN

RICHARD RESTAK

FRANCIS FUKUYAMA

In this sequence you will explore the impact of technology on ourselves, on our world, and on what it means to be human. You'll begin by looking at the ways in which technology has changed our understanding of "experts," specifically using Marshall Poe's analysis of Wikipedia and the collaborative creation of knowledge. In the next assignment you will turn to Thomas Friedman's examination of the globalized, "flattened" world to determine the economic and political effects of technology. In the final assignments of this sequence, you will use first Richard Restak's work and then Francis Fukuyama's to assess technology's impact on biology and our concepts of the human race. In performing these analyses, you will gain a new understanding of the ways in which technology permeates our lives. You will also gain conceptual tools for assessing and perhaps mitigating technology's impact on humanity.

▶ TAGS: *politics*, *technology*, *knowledge*, *human dignity*, *multitasking*, *collaboration*, *economics*

Assignment 1. POE

What is the power of experts? Does a consensus determine the truth? Poe's essay asks us to consider these questions, since the collaborative authorship of Wikipedia suggests that experts are not vital in the creation of knowledge. Write a paper in which you suggest the proper boundaries between experts and nonexperts in relation to knowledge.

Also think about: What role does technology play in this process? Should experts be granted special status in relation to knowledge? What makes an expert "expert" anyway?

Assignment 2. FRIEDMAN

In the first assignment of this sequence you were asked to consider the impact technology has had on our concept of what an "expert" is. Friedman is also concerned with how technology has changed our world, addressing this topic both directly, through his opening narrative about the construction of his laptop, and more generally, through a discussion of the complex networks of supply chains around the world. Write a paper in which you consider the ways in which technology has influenced both economics and politics.

Consider: How did social networking sites affect the 2008 presidential election? How did television determine the outcome of the 1960 election? How do supply chains determine international or domestic politics? How did the economic crisis or "financiapocalypse" of 2008 reflect the dangers of a technologically interconnected world? In what specific ways has technology connected economics and politics?

Assignment 3. RESTAK AND ONE OTHER

Through your analyses of Poe and Friedman you've considered the impact of technology on knowledge, economics, and politics. But Restak raises a far more fundamental question: How is technology rewiring our brains? How can the strategies described by Poe or Friedman mitigate these effects? Write a paper in which you use the work of Restak and one of the other authors from this sequence to explore the ways in which collaboration can counteract the detrimental effects of multitasking. You might want to begin with your examination of multitasking from Question 1 of Questions for Critical Reading for Restak (p. 344).

In thinking critically about this assignment, ask: How does Wikipedia represent the benefits of collaborative attention to a subject? Does it represent a kind of antidote to "modern nerves"? Do mutant supply chains represent the potential for a kind of hyperfocus? Does global interconnection through supply chains minimize the effects of ADD?

Assignment 4. FUKUYAMA AND ONE OTHER

Fukuyama is centrally concerned with what it means to be human, particularly in relation to emerging genetic technologies. Throughout this sequence you've considered the impact of technology on ourselves and on our world. Now, using the work of Fukuyama and one of the other authors from this sequence, write a paper in which you determine the point at which science, financial wealth, and access to technology will be, or is already, intrinsic to the development of the human race. Your definition of Factor X from Question 1 of Questions for Critical Reading (p. 166) will be a critical starting point for thinking about your argument.

Ask yourself: What makes us human? Are we overreaching the ethical boundaries of science? What are the benefits of genetic manipulation to our development, and what are the possible pitfalls? Will genetic engineering level the playing field between people, or will it merely reinforce the economic stratification present today?

SEQUENCE 8

Every Body's Right: Buying Bodies

MARY ROACH

DANIEL GILBERT

DEBORA L. SPAR

JULIA SERANO

In this sequence you will explore the implications of the human body as object and commodity. That exploration will begin with Mary Roach, as you locate your own example of the human body as object in order to extend or complicate her discussion of human cadaver research. Then, by using Daniel Gilbert's ideas about predicting future happiness, you will consider how to best make decisions about the use of our bodies after death. The next assignment turns from the end of life to its beginning, as you use Debora L. Spar's analysis of the global adoption market to determine the role that economics should play in adoption. Finally, with Julia Serano, you will examine the function of the media in objectifying the body. As you complete this sequence you will have a better understanding of the complex issues at play when the body is treated as a commodity, to be given, bought, sold, or transformed.

▶ TAGS: *research*, **body**, *economics*, *media*, *adoption*, *objectification*, *makeovers*

Assignment 1. ROACH

Roach discusses the use of human cadavers for military testing, suggesting that the researchers who conduct these tests must approach the cadaver as an object rather than a human. Find an example in which the body is objectified and then write a paper using your example as a tool to extend or complicate Roach's argument about the human body as object. Your work on the Bodies . . . The Exhibition from Question 1 of Exploring Context (p. 361) might serve as a good starting point in making your argument.

Reflect on: Why does Roach consider body objectification a necessary step in the experiments she discusses? Is it possible to conduct scientific experiments on bodies without viewing them as objects? Is body objectification limited to scientific experimentation? Is body objectification limited to the dead? What are some of the possible steps required in order to view a body as an object?

Assignment 2. ROACH AND GILBERT

Gilbert suggests that our imaginations cannot reliably predict our future happiness. Given that argument, the question of informed consent regarding the donation of our bodies to research becomes somewhat problematic. How can we know if we're making the right decision about our future? Write a paper in which you propose the key factors in making the best decisions about the use of our bodies after death. Begin with your discussion of informed consent from Question 2 of Questions for Critical Reading for Roach (p. 361); also consider the definitions of *surrogate* and *happiness* that you created in the Questions for Critical Reading for Gilbert's essay (p. 187).

In formulating your argument, think about these questions as well: Does informed consent represent the limit of surrogates' usefulness? What role might super-replicators play in the process of body donation? Does such a decision have more to do with our future happiness or our current happiness?

Assignment 3. SPAR AND ONE OTHER

In the previous assignments in this sequence you've explored the idea of the human body as an object after death, but Spar raises questions about newborn bodies as commodities. Using Spar and one of the other authors you've read for this sequence, write a paper in which you determine the role that economics should play in international adoption. You may wish to begin with your discussion of adoption from Question 1 of Questions for Critical Reading for Spar (p. 436).

Also think about these questions: Do ethical standards in the area of human commerce shift when the bodies in question are living instead of dead? What processes of informed consent might be used in international adoptions? Do the benefits of adoption outweigh any concerns about a black market? How might Gilbert's understanding of surrogates aid in limiting the role of economics in adoption? How could a super-replicator transform the economics of adoption?

Assignment 4. SERANO AND ONE OTHER

So far in this sequence you've viewed the human body as an object in research and in adoption and considered the questions of ethics and economics involved. Serano's essay also discusses the objectification of the body, in this case through a media-driven public fascination with extreme transformations of the body. Using the work of Serano and at least one other author from this sequence, write a paper in which you explore the consequences of the body's objectification in the media. Start with your work in Questions for Critical Reading and Exploring Context for Serano (p. 398), particularly your examinations of before-and-after photos and their effects.

Give consideration to: What role do adoption Web sites play in fueling the black market for babies? How do they promote a kind of fascination? Are class boundaries also at issue in adoption? How does the media's treatment of transsexuals act as a kind of super-replicator? Can media representations of extreme body makeovers serve as a kind of surrogate?

SEQUENCE 9

The Melting Not: One American Culture?

LESLIE SAVAN

STEVE OLSON

REBEKAH NATHAN

MADELEINE ALBRIGHT

In this sequence you will explore the problems and potential of community and diversity. You will begin by using Leslie Savan's analysis of the appropriation of black talk by pop talk to consider the possibility of achieving a melting pot ideal in America. Then you will turn to Steve Olson's argument about genetics and race to further explore why ethnicity persists in society, despite the lack of any genetic basis for conceptions of race. Rebekah Nathan's exploration of these issues on college campuses will provide you with an opportunity to ground them in very specific and very local examples. Finally, with Madeleine Albright's essay, you will explore the role that faith might have in achieving the goal of a melting pot society. At the end of this sequence, you will have a greater understanding of the challenges of community and diversity. But you will also have a set of conceptual tools for describing and perhaps solving this challenge.

▶ TAGS: *melting pot,* **diversity**, *religion, faith, diplomacy, community of descent, ethnicity,* **race**, *education*

Assignment 1. SAVAN

Using Savan's essay, write a paper in which you determine the possibility of actualizing the melting pot ideal in America. Is it possible to achieve that ideal, or will there always be some sort of exploitation of cultures in the process? What gets lost in the melting pot? What do we gain? Can we achieve the goals of such a society without sacrificing the uniqueness of various cultures? How?

Assignment 2. OLSON AND SAVAN

According to Olson, there is no longer any genetic basis for race, yet he also makes it clear that concepts of race and ethnicity in Hawaii and elsewhere continue to persist. Synthesizing Olson's and Savan's arguments, write a paper in which you explain the reasons for the persistence of ethnic divisions in America and in which you consider the possibility of a solution to these divisions. Begin with your response to Question 3 of Questions for Critical Reading for Olson (p. 277), in which you located reasons for the persistence of race. Incorporate Savan's ideas in making your argument.

Ask yourself: What role do the media and advertising play in the persistence of race and ethnicity? Does covert prestige promote the end of race, or does it further entrench racial divisions? Does one need to "pay the dues" in order to join a community of descent? What role does education play in the persistence of race and ethnicity, according to both authors?

Assignment 3. NATHAN AND ONE OTHER

Nathan examines the challenges to achieving community and diversity on college campuses, bringing issues from the essays you've read so far down to a specific and local level. Using the work of Nathan and one other author from this sequence, write a paper in which you propose strategies for achieving community on college campuses. You might want to use your experience at your school as an example to support your argument. You could also draw from your work in Question 3 of Questions for Critical Reading for Nathan (p. 246), in which you identified the tools needed to reach this goal; synthesize these tools with the concepts from the second author you've chosen to work with.

To further help you think critically about your argument, ponder these questions: How does Savan's discussion of the controversy over Ebonics suggest the challenges of forming community on college campuses? How might paying the dues suggest a solution? Does covert prestige contribute to the problem? How might communities of descent function on campus? How does Olson's discussion of schools in Hawaii also emphasize the challenges of such a project?

Assignment 4. ALBRIGHT AND ONE OTHER

So far in this sequence you've examined some of the challenges of achieving an integrated community. And though Albright's explicit concern is the role of faith in diplomacy, she does have a lot to say about the role of religion in integrating communities. For this last assignment, use ideas from Albright and one other author from this sequence to write a paper in which you propose what role religion and faith might play in achieving the vision of a melting pot in the United States. You might decide that such a vision is impossible, in which case your argument should work with Albright and another author in order to argue that point.

In crafting your argument, reflect: Could faith play a role in mediating appropriations of ethnic languages? Could religion provide a neutral language through which groups might communicate? Does faith function as a community of descent? Can it transcend race? What role might religion play on college campuses? Could it enhance community, or would it be divisive?

SEQUENCE 10

Putting the "I" in Team: The Practices of Collaboration

JAMES SUROWIECKI

MARSHALL POE

THOMAS FRIEDMAN

MICHAEL POLLAN

In this sequence you will explore the practices of collaboration. You will begin by using James Surowiecki's exploration of the failure of small groups in order to deduce the best practices for making such groups successful. Then you will extend those ideas by using Marshall Poe's analysis of Wikipedia to determine what role the size of a group has in its success. In the third assignment of this sequence you will use your understanding of collaborative practices to propose strategies for minimizing their dangers, as represented in the mutant supply chains examined by Thomas Friedman. In the last assignment of this sequence, you will use Michael Pollan's idea of the holon to argue for the role of the individual in collaboration. At the end of this sequence you will have an understanding of what makes groups succeed or fail. You will also understand the dangers of collaborative processes and the strategies you can use to avoid those dangers, all the while preserving the individual within the group.

▶ TAGS: *holons, technology, groups, Wikipedia, knowledge, collaboration, supply chains*

Assignment 1. SUROWIECKI

Surowiecki discusses ways in which group dynamics contributed to the failure of the *Columbia*'s Mission Management Team. Using Surowiecki's observations, write a paper that determines the best practices for organizing and running a small group. In composing your response, consider these questions: What makes a small group more than just the sum of its parts? How can group identity be made to serve the purpose of the group? What is the ideal structure for a group? How important is cognitive diversity, and why? How can group polarization be avoided? In what ways could "talkativeness" be regulated to ensure equal participation by all members of the group?

Assignment 2. POE AND SUROWIECKI

While Surowiecki explores the failure of groups, Poe focuses on the success of the group effort behind Wikipedia. One way to account for the vastly different results of the collaborative efforts in these two essays is to consider the size of each group. Write a paper in which you use both Surowiecki and Poe to explore how the dangers, advantages, and strategies change as the size of a group collaboration increases.

In composing your response, ask yourself these questions: Would the small group practices you identified in the first assignment of this sequence work for Wikipedia? Would a bottom-up organization work for a small group? Does the cathedral model or the bazaar model have an optimal size? Could the "Cunctator" have succeeded as a member of the Mission Management Team? Could group polarization and talkativeness plague Wikipedia? How is the sense of community altered by the size of the community?

Assignment 3. FRIEDMAN AND POE

Friedman's essay is largely concerned with the benefits of collaboration represented by global supply chains. But in turning to mutant supply chains, he reveals the dangers that collaboration can pose as well. Using Friedman and Poe, write a paper in which you propose a solution to mitigate these dangers that incorporates Wikipedia's strategies of collaborative knowledge. You might want to begin with your discussion of collaboration in Question 1 of Questions for Critical Reading for Friedman (p. 138).

In formulating your argument you might also think about these questions: How could Nupedia's neutral point of view work for the Internet at large? How could it mitigate terrorist propaganda? What significance does the aphorism "given enough eyeballs, all bugs are shallow" have for this situation? How can your solution avoid the fear of centralized authority that the Cunctator worried about?

Assignment 4. POLLAN AND ONE OTHER

So far in this sequence you've considered practices of collaboration, practices which are also at work on Polyface farm, as Pollan makes clear. Yet in introducing the concept of the holon, Pollan also suggests the role that individuals play in group processes. For this final assignment, use the work of Pollan and one other author from this sequence to write a paper in which you determine the importance of the individual in collaboration. You might draw on the definition of *holon* that you developed for Question 2 of Questions for Critical Reading for Pollan (p. 292).

Also consider: Does the individual hurt or hinder the small group processes that Surowiecki describes? Could an individual have made a difference on the Mission Management Team? Are Wikipedia's contributors holons? How are supply chains similar to Polyface?

Acknowledgments (continued from page iv)

Richard Restak, "Attention Deficit: The Brain Syndrome of Our Era." From *The New Brain: How the Modern Age Is Rewiring Your Mind* by Richard Restak. Copyright © 2003 by Richard M. Restak. Permission granted by Rodale, Inc., Emmaus, PA 18098.

Mary Roach, "The Cadaver Who Joined the Army." From *Stiff: The Curious Lives of Human Cadavers* by Mary Roach. Copyright © 2003 by Mary Roach. Used by permission of W. W. Norton & Company, Inc.

Leslie Savan, "What's Black, Then White, and Said All Over?" From *Slam Dunks and No-Brainers* by Leslie Savan. Copyright © 2005 by Leslie Savan. Used by permission of Alfred A. Knopf, a division of Random House, Inc.

Julia Serano, "Before and After: Class and Body Transformations." From *Whipping Girl: A Transsexual Woman on Sexism and the Scapegoating of Femininity* by Julia Serano. Copyright © 2007 by Julia Serano. Reprinted by permission of Seal Press, a member of Perseus Books Group.

Debora L. Spar, "Trading Places: The Practice and Politics of Adoption." From *The Baby Business: How Money, Science, and Politics Drive the Commerce of Conception* by Debora L. Spar. Copyright © 2006 by Harvard Business School Publishing Corporation. Reprinted by permission of Harvard Business School Publishing Corporation.

James Surowiecki, "Committees, Juries, and Teams: The *Columbia* Disaster and How Small Groups Can Be Made to Work." From *The Wisdom of Crowds: Why the Many Are Smarter Than the Few and How Collective Wisdom Shapes Business, Economies, Societies, and Nations* by James Surowiecki. Copyright © 2004 by James Surowiecki. Used by permission of Doubleday, a division of Random House, Inc.

Diana Taylor, "False Identifications: Minority Populations Mourn Diana." From *The Archive and the Repertoire* by Diana Taylor. Copyright © 2003 by Duke University Press. All rights reserved. Used by permission of the publisher.

Kenji Yoshino, "Preface" and "The New Civil Rights." From *Covering* by Kenji Yoshino. Copyright © 2006 by Kenji Yoshino. Used by permission of Random House, Inc.

Art Credits

Author Photos

Alvarez: Ramon Espinosa/AP Photo.
Appiah: Corbis News/Corbis.
Didion: Corbis Entertainment/Corbis.
Epstein: Peter Peter.
Fukuyama: Eric Feferberg/Getty Images.
Gilbert: Corbis News/Corbis.
Johnson: Neilson Barnard/Getty Images.
Kimmelman: Fred R. Conrad/*The New York Times*/Redux.
Olson: Haraz N. Ghanbari/AP Photo.
Pollan: Corbis News/Corbis.
Roach: David Paul Morris.
Savan: Jerry Bauer.
Serano: David Huang.
Surowiecki: David Surowiecki/Getty Images.
Taylor: Corbis News/Corbis.

Book Covers

Albright: Book cover from *The Mighty and the Almighty: Reflections on America, God, and World Affairs* by Madeleine Albright. Copyright © 2006 by Madeleine Albright.

Alvarez: Cover design by Roseanne J. Serra; cover photo by Trujillo-Paumier/Getty Images. Courtesy of Penguin Group.

Appiah: From *Cosmopolitanism: Ethics in a World of Strangers* by Kwame Anthony Appiah. Used by permission of W. W. Norton and Company, Inc.

The Dalai Lama: Jacket cover from *The Universe in a Single Atom: The Convergence of Science and Spirituality* by His Holiness The Dalai Lama. Used by permission of Morgan Road Books, an imprint of the Doubleday Broadway Publishing Group, a division of Random House, Inc.

Didion: Book cover copyright © 2005 by Alfred A. Knopf, from *The Year of Magical Thinking* by Joan Didion. Used by permission of Alfred A. Knopf, a division of Random House, Inc.

Epstein: Courtesy of Picador Press.

Friedman: Courtesy of Picador Press.

Fukuyama: Courtesy of Picador Press.

Gilbert: Book cover copyright © 2006 by Alfred A. Knopf, from *Stumbling on Happiness* by Daniel Gilbert. Used by permission of Alfred A. Knopf, a division of Random House, Inc.

Johnson: Reproduced with the permission of Scribner, a division of Simon and Schuster, Inc., from *Emergence: The Connected Lives of Ants, Brains, Cities, and Software* by Steven Johnson. All rights reserved.

Kimmelman: Courtesy of Penguin Group.

Nathan: Courtesy of Penguin Group.

Olson: Cover of *Mapping Human History* by Steve Olson (Boston: Mariner Books, 2003).

Poe: Courtesy of the *Atlantic Monthly*.

Pollan: Courtesy of Penguin Group.

Postrel: Book cover from *The Substance of Style* by Virginia Postrel. Reprinted by permission of HarperCollins Publishers.

Restak: Courtesy of Rodale Press.

Roach: From *Stiff: The Curious Lives of Human Cadavers* by Mary Roach. Used by permission of W. W. Norton and Company, Inc.

Savan: Book cover copyright © 2005 by Alfred A. Knopf, from *Slam Dunks and No-Brainers* by Leslie Savan. Used by permission of Alfred A. Knopf, a division of Random House, Inc.

Serano: Courtesy of Perseus Books Group.

Spar: Courtesy of Harvard Business School Publishing.

Surowiecki: Jacket cover from *The Wisdom of Crowds: Why the Many Are Smarter Than the Few and How Collective Wisdom Shapes Business, Economies, Societies, and Nations* by James Surowiecki. Used by permission of Doubleday, a division of Random House, Inc.

Taylor: Diana Taylor, "cover image," *The Archive and the Repertoire*. Copyright 2003, Duke University Press. All rights reserved. Used by permission of the publisher.

Yoshino: Book cover, copyright © 2006 by Random House, Inc., from *Covering* by Kenji Yoshino. Used by permission of Random House, Inc.

Interior Images

Kimmelman: *Charles Willson Peale*, courtesy of the Pennsylvania Academy of the Fine Arts, Philadelphia. Gift of Sarah Harrison (The Joseph Harrison Jr. Collection). *J. Dennis Welsch*, courtesy of the Mütter Museum/The College of Physicians of Philadelphia.

Olson: Map of Hawaii, *Mapping Human History* by Steve Olson (Boston, Mariner Books, 2003).

Taylor: All photos by Diana Taylor.